QUINCY HARKER, DEMON HUNTER VOLUME 1-3

JOHN G. HARTNESS

Charlotte, NC

FALSTAFF
BOOKS
WWW.FALSTAFFBOOKS.COM

YEAR ONE

PART I
RAISING HELL

CHAPTER ONE

I *fuckin' hate demons.* That's what ran through my head as I got out of the car and walked up the sidewalk to the Garda home. It was a nice place, for the suburbs. There was a two-car garage off to one side, a neatly manicured lawn leading up to flowerbeds in front of a nice little porch, and an SUV in the driveway because I'm sure the garage was full of bicycles, tools, lawnmowers and other shit that I only see when I get a call out here in the 'burbs. I live in a condo in the middle of downtown Charlotte, so the only time I see lawn equipment is when I get lost in a home improvement store looking for a new mallet or maybe a new wheel for my grinder.

I walked up to the pale yellow siding nightmare of a home and stepped up on the front porch. The welcome mat was a little askew, the only imperfect thing in an otherwise totally *Good Housekeeping* image. I took a deep breath and closed my eyes, opening my Second Sight and taking a look around. My third eye saw nothing out of the ordinary on the porch, no roiling black evil miasma ready to consume my soul and suck me down into the depths of Hell. It looked just as Martha Stewart in the supernatural spectrum as it did in the visible one. *Good,* I thought, *maybe the little darlin's just on the rag and I can get the fuck out of here and back uptown before the game lets out and traffic gets stupid.*

I opened my eyes and snapped back to the mundane world. After a second to adjust back to seeing the world with my eyes instead of my soul, I rang the bell. A dog immediately went apeshit on the other side of the door, as if the real trouble wasn't already in the house. A couple of shouted "shut up"s later, the door opened and a flushed forty-something man opened the door. The top of his balding head stopped at about my nose, but I'm tall, so I was used to that. His polo shirt had sweat stains under his man boobs, and it stretched tight across his spectacular belly. He looked up at me, close-set brown eyes set deep in a florid face, capped off with a red nose that only happens when you've hit the bottle pretty hard for a pretty long time.

"You Harker?" he asked, glaring up at me.

"Yep," I said.

"You got ID?" he asked.

No. I just randomly wander up to houses in suburbia and pretend to be an exorcist, hoping to arrive at the exact time their appointment was set for. I bit my tongue before that one could escape and just handed him my card.

"You got any photo ID?" He had that belligerent tone of a middle manager, the kind of guy that shits on all his employees' good ideas until somebody smarter than him hears them, then takes credit for the good one.

I didn't bother to hold back this time. "You want my badge number, too? This shit doesn't exactly come with a union card, pal. You called me, remember? I'm here, the right time, the right address, now let's see if I'm in the right place. I'm Quincy Harker. You got something needs banishing, or should I just go back to my sofa and NFL network?"

"Sorry, sorry. No need to be a—" he cut himself off, but I didn't.

"Dick? Yeah, I'm a dick. You're the stupid bastard who lets a demon into his teenage daughter, yanking me off the couch in the middle of the first Panthers playoff run in living memory, but of course *I'm* a dick because I didn't immediately take off my hat and wipe my shoes before entering your fucking Ikea palace here. Now point me towards your daughter's room and get out of my way before I do something really dickish, like turn you into a toad."

I pushed past the stammering jackoff and stomped towards the stairs, registering him mumbling something about the bedroom at the end of the hall. I didn't need his instructions; as soon as I stepped onto the second floor, I could feel what I was there for. This time the sense of evil, of just *wrongness* was so strong I didn't need my Sight to find it. It almost knocked me over the second I turned toward the door.

The hallway was just like a normal two-story house, scene for slaughter in so many slasher flicks. There was a small bathroom to the right of the stairs, and three bedrooms arranged around the left-hand hallway. One of these would be the master bedroom, with its own bath, and the other two would be the kids' rooms. The one on the left had pictures of motorcycles and rock bands with more makeup than KISS, but the one at the end of the hall was unadorned. Just a simple brass nameplate announcing it as Kayleigh's room.

I could tell from thirty feet away that Kayleigh's room had some seriously evil shit in it. I rolled my head and cracked my knuckles, then opened up my Second Sight to get a good look at the evil in the magical spectrum.

I slammed my Sight shut almost as quickly as it came into focus, shaking my head to clear the images from my mind. But there is no Visine for the mind's eye, and I was stuck with that shit forever. Whatever was on the other side of that door wasn't human, was powerful as shit, and was really hungry. It was also in a really good mood, which disturbed the fuck out of me. There's nothing worse than a happy demon, at least as far as the humans around it are concerned.

"Mr. Garda?" I yelled down the stairs.

"Yes?" his voice came back. I might have heard ice cubes jingle in a glass. Good—if this was as bad as I thought it was, he was going to need to get seriously drunk.

"Who else is home?"

"What do you mean?"

"I mean, who else is in the building? Is your wife here? Your son?" I left off the "jackass," but it was pretty well implied.

"No, they're gone. My wife is out of town on business for two weeks, and my son has been staying at a friend's house since Kayleigh got sick. It's just you, me and Kayleigh." *And whatever has got its claws wrapped around Kayleigh's soul.*

"That's good. You might want to make yourself scarce for a little while." *Please don't ask a lot of fucking questions.*

"Why?"

Shit. "Because what I'm dealing with up here is pretty dangerous, and I don't want you to get hurt." *And I don't want this fucker to have another vessel to jump to if your daughter suddenly becomes uninhabitable.*

"I don't think I can—"

"Would you please just get the fuck out so I can quit worrying about your fat ass and save your daughter?" I yelled. Maybe a little direct, but I really didn't want to have to fight this thing more than once. I heard a clatter of footsteps and then the front door slammed shut. Nice. I didn't believe he'd actually leave. Maybe that panicked edge in my voice was useful after all.

I turned back to the door. "Just you and me, now, buddy. So why don't you come out of the girl and let's handle this like men?"

The voice that answered rang through my head like a dentist's drill, piercing and ululating. "I can't come out. Not yet. But when I do you'll see that I'm nothing like a man."

7

Then it laughed, and in that laugh were the screams of millennia of tormented souls, all shrieking together to make one terrible sound.

"Then I guess I have to come in," I said, and strode to the door. I lifted a size 11 Doc Marten and kicked the door just beside the lock. The jamb splintered, the door flew in, and my worst nightmares were realized.

"Oh fuck me," were the only words that came to mind as I looked at the picture before me. Geiger couldn't have imagined a sense of greater torment. Hieronymus Bosch had nothing on the cruel artist that created the image before me. I didn't throw up, but only because I learned years ago never to have breakfast before an exorcism. You puke on a couple of nuns and that gets drilled into you pretty fast.

The thing in the bed used to be a pretty little girl. I knew this because I'd seen enough pictures of her around the living room and on the walls going up the stairs to figure it out. There wasn't anything pretty about what was in front of me. It still kinda looked like a little girl, if that little girl's face was stretched into new positions from screaming for the last two days, if that little girl's pajamas were covered in piss, shit, sweat, blood and pus, if that little girl's matted hair was stringy with vomit and other bodily fluids. If that little girl, who probably stood around five-two and weighed maybe a hundred ten pounds last week looked like she was about to give birth to a goddamn baby elephant.

The demon hadn't possessed Kayleigh Garda. It had *impregnated* her. And it was about to deliver Hell on earth.

I staggered back from the shock and the stench and raised my Bible in front of my face. The thing laughed. I realized that I wasn't talking to Kayleigh, or the demon that possessed her—I'd been talking to her soon-to-be-born half-demon child this whole time. Kayleigh was gone, dead from the inside as the demon consumed her body and soul. And in a couple of hours, it was going to burst free of Mommy and move on to eating anything and anyone it could find. I backed slowly out of the room, then turned and ran down the stairs, almost tripping over an Xbox controller in my mad dash to the front door. I took several deep breaths, then stepped out onto the porch where Kayleigh's dad stood chain-smoking Camels. I guess he hadn't really left after all.

I walked over to him and leaned on the porch rail.

"Well?" he said after a moment's silence.

"It's worse than I thought."

"How bad is that?" His voice went up a little on the end, like he was fighting off panic. I didn't blame him. I was a little, too, and it wasn't my little girl up there. Of course, I did have to live in this dimension, so demons running loose sounded like a terrible idea to me.

"Your daughter is dead. I'm very sorry."

"But I heard her, she was talking just a minute ago!" He spun around to rush back inside, but I grabbed his arm right above the elbow.

"That wasn't her. That was the demon. It was using her vocal chords." *Please don't make me explain.*

"What? That's stupid. It was Kayleigh. She's up there, and she's in trouble, and you're too chickenshit to help." He pulled against my grip, but got nowhere. I'm a lot stronger than I should be for my size.

"Demons don't have voices like you and I do. If they're possessing someone, they can control their body completely, use their voice perfectly. You'd never know it wasn't Kayleigh if it didn't want you to. But this thing, it won't have to use Kayleigh's voice for long."

"You mean it's going to let her go?" I hate it when they hope for the best.

"I mean it's almost through with her. It's killed her and has devoured almost everything it can. When it's finished, it will leave Kayleigh and come out here looking for another meal. If that happens, it will be almost unstoppable, because it will have one foot in our world and one foot in Hell. Usually demons can't stay in this world past sunrise, but not this one. It won't be bound by normal demonic rules, and it will be very, very hungry. I need to destroy it while it's still in your daughter."

I watched him process as much of that as he could, and thought he got pretty far for a mundane, but I could almost see the moment when hope made him go stupid again. "But you can save her, right?"

Yep, every friggin' time. Sometimes I think we should have left Hope locked in Pandora's box. It causes as much trouble as it fixes. "No. She's dead. Her heart is still beating, but Kayleigh is dead. The demon inside her has eaten her soul. All that's left up there is a meat suit that a demon is wearing with a face that kind of looks like Kayleigh's, but not really very much. And if I don't get up there, and send this thing back to Hell before it delivers, we're going to all be in a lot of deep shit."

I saw the realization cross his face a second or two after I said the word "deliver." "Deliver? You mean my Kayleigh is pregnant with a demon? But, she's only fifteen! She wears a promise ring! This can't happen! We had the talk, we agreed that she should wait... She doesn't even date." He collapsed into a chair on the porch and I just stood there, staring at him. The man wasn't the least bit surprised that his daughter was possessed by a soul-eating demon from Hell, but the mere thought of his precious little girl bumping uglies with some senior in the back of daddy's Lexus reduced him to tears. People and their fucking priorities.

I went back inside, but not before popping out to the trunk of my Honda for a few extra goodies. I sealed the door behind me both mystically and physically. Mystically with a spell of warding designed to provide a non-lethal shock to humans trying to get in, but a lethal shot of balefire to anything from any of the lower realms. Angels could come and go with no problem, although I wasn't expecting anyone from the upper reaches to come join my party. Physically I wedged a chair under the door.

A few strides and a lot more deep breaths found me outside the bedroom again. I so did not want to do this. But it's my job. This was why they paid me the little bucks.

I raised my foot to kick the door in again when a soft voice called from within. "Come in, John Abraham Quincy Holmwood Harker. We've been waiting for you."

CHAPTER TWO

I fucking hate demons. I hate them even more when they know who I am. There's power in names. That's one of the things you learn early in my family, and I understood it before I could read. Names identify things, and people, and if you can find out the true name of someone or something, you have a great deal of power over it. Fortunately, the names our parents give us only very rarely match up with our true names, so knowing my full name only gave the demon the tiniest hold on me. But it did give the monster a pretty good idea of what I could do, which was information I was trying to keep quiet until it became important.

I opened the door. The Atrocity Formerly Known As Kayleigh sat up in bed and grinned at me.

"Hello, Mr. Harker. Are you here to celebrate my birthday? Are you my cake? Because childbirth always leaves me hungry." Kayleigh's once-lustrous hair was dark with sweat and matted all around her face. I knew what it meant. Demons aren't born the normal way, the anatomy doesn't work. They consume their host from the inside out, starting with the soul and moving on to the mind and then the flesh. They feed on pain and fear, and once they've taken all a host has to give, they burst out of the body and go looking for more places to cause pain and fear. It leaves the host body looking a little like the soldiers from *Alien*, only tenfold. From the look of things, this demon was going to burst out of Kayleigh any minute and go cause trouble all over Charlotte, and all over the world if left unchecked.

That's where I came in—the checking. I began the Catholic rites for exorcism, speaking slowly and under my breath, more to distract the demon than to actually try to pull it out of the girl.

"And what are you trying to do, Harker? Exorcise me? You know that takes faith, and a direct line to something higher than yourself. Do you even believe there's a higher power, Harker? What do you pray to when you get down on your knees every night? Tell you what. I'll be outside this little womby-womb in a few minutes and then you can get down on your knees in front of me." The demon's voice was shrill, piercing, a dentist's drill to my brain.

I closed my eyes to focus on my ritual. I mumbled my way through the litany, the part that's supposed to be performed with an audience chanting along either in unison with me or call-and-response style, depending on the line. I've never been one for the litany. I'd rather keep the innocent bystanders out of the room, bystanding where they can't get their souls munched on like canapés.

"I command you, unclean spirit, whoever you are, along with all your minions now attacking this servant of God, by the mysteries of the incarnation, passion, resurrection, and ascension of our Lord Jesus Christ, by the descent of the Holy Spirit, by the coming of our Lord for judgment, that you tell me by some sign your name, and the day and hour of your departure. I command you, moreover, to obey me to the letter, I who am a minister of God despite my unworthiness; nor shall you be emboldened to harm in any way this creature of God, or the bystanders, or any of their possessions."

The body on the bed writhed and screamed at me, shouting profanity in about seven human languages and three demon variants that I recognized, then it flopped to the bed and lay still. I watched it for a few seconds then shook my head. It's always the same thing. I walked over to the bed, well within arm's reach, and leaned down, far too close to a monster who had a thing for biting.

All demons have a thing for biting. And fucking, and killing, and desecrating holy places, and raping, and pillaging, and burning. Burning is one of their favorites. But this one liked to bite, I could tell from the way it had morphed Kayleigh's teeth to sharp points as it had taken over her body. So I did what any reasonable human being would do—I put my face right next to its ear and whispered, "I know you're faking, you son of a bitch."

It reacted about like I expected. It was fast, the body of a coltish preteen with years of community league soccer behind her meshed with the unholy might of a hellspawn enabled her to lunge from the bed faster than any human could react. A normal priest would have been lying on the floor with his throat ripped out.

I'm not a priest, and I'm sure as hell not normal. I'm Quincy motherfuckin'

Harker, and the blood of Dracula himself runs through my veins. I dodged the demon's bite, yanked the silver cross from my belt and brought it around and down through the back of What Used to Be Kayleigh's skull. I put the tip of the cross right on the little ball in the back of her head where the skull meets the spine, the soft spot that just barely protects the medulla. It didn't protect it enough. The three-pound crucifix, blessed in holy waters from the font of St. Peter's Church, crunched through the thin bone walls and severed the brain stem, shutting down all neurological activity instantly. She died so fast her body didn't know it was dead until a couple of seconds later, when it stopped getting signals from the brain. She collapsed face-first on the hardwood floor, limp, dead.

I knelt beside her. I turned her over and pulled her the rest of the way out of the bed so she was lying on the floor looking up at the ceiling. I sat down, cross-legged, and pulled her head into my lap as the last light of Kayleigh fled her eyes, and then I closed them. I closed my own eyes and felt a tear slide down my nose. I took a deep breath, looked up at the ceiling and said, "If you're up there, you son of a bitch, and if for once in your worthless existence you're paying attention—take care of her."

God and I have an interesting relationship, to say the very least.

I closed my eyes again, took another deep breath, and then opened them to look down at the dead girl in my lap. "You can open the eyes now, asshole. I know you're still in there."

The demon opened his eyes and smiled at me. "Why Harker, I must thank you for this gift. This body is young, strong…" The demon trailed off as it realized there was something wrong.

"Paralyzed?" I offered.

"What did you do? How did you do that? Why can't I get out? Why can't I make it work? What's going on?" The demon's eyes were darting side to side, looking for a clue, but it had no mobility from the neck down.

"Oh, sorry about that. You see, I knew you'd just about finished eating Kayleigh's soul, so I only had a few seconds to get her out of there before you were done with her, and then her soul would be gone, with no chance of Heaven. That didn't seem very nice to me, so I decided to fuck with your plan. And while I was fucking with your plan, I decided to just fuck with you at the same time. You see, when I crushed Kayleigh's brain stem, I didn't just kill her body and free her soul. I left her body a quadriplegic, and that gives you a whole lot of fuck-all to work with." My mom always told me I swear too much. I told her she was provincial and old-fashioned. She told me that both statements were true. She was right. I swear too much. But almost always only at demons. Except when I swear at people. And angels. And minor elder Gods. And traffic lights. And a lot at elevators. Fuck it, I swear too much.

"But why—"

"Why can't you just jump out, like you always do? Yeah, that's the necklace I slipped on little Kayleigh while I was praying. It's got these twelve little charms on it, all around the cross. One for each apostle."

"You put me in a Saints' Chain? You son of a—"

I punched him in the face. It wasn't terribly effective, since his body was dead and he didn't feel pain, but he was surprised, and it did shut him up before he said anything bad about my mother. I don't abide anyone saying anything bad about my mother.

I leaned in so my face was uncomfortably close to the demon's. "Here's the deal. You can stay trapped inside that dead body by the Saints' Chain and hope that in a few hundred years the body will decay enough for the chain to fall off the neck and let you loose, or you can tell me what I want to know and I'll banish you right here and now. So what's it going to be, a couple centuries in a lead-lined box, or scurry on home like a good insect?"

He glared at me for a long moment, which would have been unbearable for most people. I've had what some people would call an interesting life, and what sane people would call an absolute fucking nightmare existence, so being glared at by a demon didn't even register.

"Fine, what do you want to know?" it asked.

"Who summoned you?"

"Like I have any idea. I don't know, and I don't care. All I cared about was getting out of Hell and up here on furlough for a couple weeks until some self-righteous prick like you found me and sent me home. You know, it's not too late—we could still party." I felt the demon's essence pressing on my mind, trying to worm into the cracks in my consciousness and take hold. I blinked twice, then focused my eyes on the demon's and *pushed* with my own being, flooding the demon's mind with the essence of me. And the essence of me isn't very pretty. You know you're an asshole when a glimpse inside your head makes a demon draw back, and that's exactly what happened.

"Wanna play some more?" I asked.

"Hell no! I'll tell you the whole thing, just let me go after that. It was a frat party, Saturday night, Omega Sigma Iota. Some horny fucktards called me up to persuade the girls at the party to be just as horny as they were. It didn't work out quite like they had planned. They all got laid, just like they instructed. But maybe they didn't all get laid by who—"

"Or what?" I interrupted. I'd had a few conversations about human sexuality with demons in my past, and they had pretty flexible views on inter-special relations.

The thing inside Kayleigh grinned at me, and my stomach did a couple of flip-flops and a barrel roll or two. Thinking about what the demon made those boys have sex with made me really happy I'd skipped breakfast.

"Or what," it confirmed. "They expected a fucking. They got one. I held up my end of the deal, and I got this barely-used meat suit all to myself. Until you came along and fucked it all up. So send me home, shitheel. I'm going to have a world of trouble with the boss when I get home."

"You mean Lucifer?" I asked.

"No, fuckwit. I mean my wife. The last time I got a chance to run off after some young live bait, she did macramé with my intestines for a millennia. And that was her idea of a warning." Good to know even demons had women troubles. Not that I had enough time to chase women to give me troubles.

"I'm going to have to have your name to banish you." True Names have power, and someone who holds a demon's True Name can call or banish it from anywhere. I could see his reluctance in giving me his real Name. I didn't blame him. I wouldn't trust me with it, either. But he didn't have a choice. He whispered his Name to me, and I repeated it until I got all the syllables right. Demon language is kinda like all the nastiest-sounding parts of Latin and German thrown in a blender with a bunch of apostrophes and just a little bit of Klingon sprinkled in for garnish. I finally got it right, and was ready to proceed.

I reached into a pocket of my leather jacket, pulled out a vial of holy water, and sprinkled it on Kayleigh's forehead. "Begone from this vessel, Krag'tharis-man'teak, in the name of the Father, and of the Son, and of the Holy Ghost, I banish thee." I opened myself up to the Source, closed my eyes, and *pushed*. I felt the demon leave Kayleigh's body and opened my Sight.

Before me stood a humanoid figure, shimmering from within with a reddish light. The demon's spirit manifested as a nearly seven-foot tall winged human with goat hooves and clawed hands. It looked at me, eyes wide in, I don't know what, surprise that a human could actually banish it? Shock that someone without any real faith could perform the ritual? I couldn't tell, and the demon's soul didn't stick around long enough for me to ask. I watched closely as a small hole opened up in the aether behind the demon, and the soul was sucked back to Hell where it belonged.

I stood up, Kayleigh's limp body in my arms, my knees protesting from sitting on the floor too long. I put her in the bed, pulling the covers up tight around her neck and taking the Saints' Chain off her body. If you ignored the blood seeping from her neck wound, it looked almost like she was sleeping. I knelt beside the bed and put one hand on her forehead.

"All right, God. I know you're up there, probably watching something stupid like soccer or *The Dick Van Dyke Show* reruns, but this one needs a little help. She didn't deserve what happened to her, so she doesn't deserve to deal with your usual Purgatory bullshit, or some stupid line at the Pearly Gates, or whatever crap you've cooked up this year to keep the humans cooling their heels outside of heaven while you and your band of merry fuckwits sit on clouds and play harps or whatever it is you bastards do. So let her in, and take care of her like you didn't do while she was alive."

"You know, Q, one day he's going to actually listen to one of your 'prayers,' and I'm pretty sure he's gonna be pissed." The voice from behind me was cultivated and slightly British. It was also female, which made it all the worse.

"Hello, Glory." I stood and turned to the angel in the corner. "Was she one of yours?"

"No. She wasn't mine to watch. Sorry, you'll have to blame someone else this time." Glory leaned against the wall, casually gorgeous like a woman who is beautiful the minute she rolls out of bed, all Heidi Klum class and Sandra Bullock girl-next-door sexy rolled into one stunning package that stood about five and a half feet tall and had blonde curls falling down her back like a waterfall of gold. She was dressed for work, not business, which meant jeans, boots and a silky-looking tank top that made me want to run my hands all over her torso. I thought better of it quickly. Copping a feel on a celestial body is a good way to get disintegrated.

"Who was her angel?" I asked. Yes, guardian angels are real. Yes, everybody has one. No, they're not really worth a shit, as was evidenced by the dead girl in the bed I was standing beside.

"I'm not going to tell you, Q. It's not your day to die." Glory was my angel. As such, it was her job to keep me from dying before my appointed time. I didn't make it easy on her. Picking fights with angels is a good way to get dead, and I've done it more than once.

"So it's Michael? Gabriel? One of the big boys?" I pushed, trying to see if I could get something out of her. I needed to punish someone, some*thing* for this girl's death, and sending the demon back to Hell just didn't feel like enough. I have a thing about supernatural beings fucking around in the heads of innocent young women. Call it a family issue.

"I'm not telling you. I will tell you that it was her time. She was dead by tomorrow no matter what. If she didn't go to that party and get possessed, then she would have wrapped her car around a tree on her way to school in the morning. Or maybe she would have had a massive aneurism. Or just tripped going down the stairs and broken her neck. I don't know the how, I just know the when, and this was all part of The Plan."

"Fuck the Plan."

"You seem to do everything in your power to do just that every single day. But not today. Now what are you going to do about her?"

"I'm going to find the frat boys who thought it was a good idea to summon a demon just to get a little underage pussy on a Saturday night, and I'm going to emasculate them with a blender and a bottle of Tabasco sauce."

"That's not what I meant. You have a dead teenage girl in her bedroom and the murder weapon with your fingerprints all over it. How are you going to deal with the whole not going to jail thing?" I hate it when she talks like a Joss Whedon character. It's bad enough my guardian angel ripped off her name from a *Buffy* character, I really can't deal with it when she starts talking like the show, too.

"I've got a plan."

"Is it better than your last plan?"

"I don't remember my last plan." I totally remembered my last plan. This one wasn't all that much better.

CHAPTER THREE

I t took a little mojo, three fairly complicated spells, a minor summoning that wasn't exactly on the white side of magic and a whole lot of arguing with Glory, but by the time I left the Garda residence, Kayleigh's body was exorcised and sanctified, Mr. Garda was on his way to the drugstore to buy some Nyquil for his sick daughter, and the toaster was rigged to blow the gas oven sky-high about ninety seconds after I got into my car. I hated to do that to the poor guy, he'd really lost enough for one day, but most people's minds aren't built to deal with the kind of shit I spend my life dealing with. So a little suggestion mixed with some fairy dust I keep in my toolbox for situations best forgotten, and Mr. Garda would never remember that his daughter died in her bed a couple of hours before delivering literal Hell on earth.

He'd feel guilt, of course. He was a parent who'd lost a child, and I could only imagine what that felt like. Fortunately, given my line of work, it looked pretty unlikely that I'd ever have to find out. Which meant I also wouldn't spawn any demon-summoning, high-school-girl-raping, overprivileged doucherockets like the ones I was about to visit some seriously unholy vengeance upon. Although, thinking about it, my plans for the fucktards that got Kayleigh knocked up with a demon baby pretty closely mirrored some of the smiting the Almighty did back in the Old Testament days, back when he actually paid attention to what happened down here, before we got to too much begetting for him to keep track of.

I pulled up in front of the frat house at about two in the morning, but you'd never know it was late from the music blaring and the drunk kids hanging out of the windows and lounging on the porch and front yard. I walked up the sidewalk, my boots making a solid *thunk-thunk* rhythm that sounded a lot like the beat of fists on flesh. That thought almost cheered me up a little as I bounded up the steps and flung open the door.

"If you're not a member of this frat, get the fuck out." I didn't say it very loudly. I didn't have to. I *pushed* my voice to make sure everyone in the building heard it, and put just enough suggestion behind it laced with imagery of fire and bloodshed that a veritable flood of bimbos and hangers-on cascaded down the stairs and out of the house like rats following the Pied Piper.

"What the fuck, dude? Who the fuck are you? Where the fuck is everybody going? We still got a party goin' on here!" A shirtless, blonde college-age Justin Bieber lookalike with a square jaw and more abs than an Olympic sit-up team walked up to me and bumped chests with me.

I stared at him. He actually *bumped his chest into mine*, like we were fucking gorillas in a mating ritual or something. I backhanded the little fuck to the ground and stepped on his balls. "I'm the motherfucker that just ended your party, shitbird. Now get the rest of your brothers into the living room. I've got questions. You've got answers." He scurried backward until he could reach the stairs, then scrambled to his feet and started rounding up members.

Another one came up to me, all full of bluster and righteous indignation. "What is this about? I'll have you know, my father is Jacob Marlack; he's a very important attorney in this city and I know my rights—"

I cut him off by grabbing his throat in my left hand and marching him backward into the living room where most of his fraternity had gathered. I steered him to the couch and shoved, forcing him to sit. "I'm going to say this once, and I get irritable when I have to repeat myself, so pay attention. I don't give a fuck who your daddies are, how much money they have, or what they do for a living. I don't give a flying shit if you can buy Rhode Island. I'm here for information and the faster I get it, the fewer of you bleed. Are we clear?"

I looked around the room. A couple of the boys looked like they wanted to say something, but the ones next to them either smacked them or just shut them up. And they were boys, for fuck's sake. Most of them had three chest hairs between them and they'd already summoned a demon. They were so fucked and they had no idea. I felt bad for them for about a second and a half, then I remembered what Kayleigh looked like, lying in her bed, dead at my hand because these assholes wanted to bang an underage girl. These stupid fucks that could have had their choice of college tail but wanted something different. And I had to clean up the goddamn mess.

"Last Saturday night you boys had a little party."

I started, only to be immediately interrupted by the drunkest of the Overindulged Ones. "We have a fuckin' party every fuckin' night, asshole. You're going to have to be more spefi . . . scepifi . . . specific." He grinned and high-fived the brother sitting on the couch next to him.

I gathered my will and murmured, "*Sobrietate.*" Then I pushed my will at him. He went from happy drunk to a little green, then pale, then sweating, then miserable and holding his head as he went from tanked to stone-cold sober in about three seconds. I was impressed that he didn't puke.

"May I continue?" I asked. There were nods all around. The boys were looking from me to their now-sober friend with what I thought were appropriately frightened glances, so I thought I might make some headway this time. "Now, at this party was a cute girl named Kayleigh. She looked a lot like the girl in this picture." I produced a snapshot I'd pulled down off the wall in Kayleigh's house. You know, before I burned it to the ground with her demon-violated corpse inside.

"Anybody recognize Kayleigh?" Lots of shaking heads. "Really? You guys are absolutely certain you've never seen her before?" A lot more shaking of heads, but several sideways glances, too. Most of them landing on Mr. My Daddy's a Lawyer. Big surprise.

I walked over to young Mr. Entitled. "What's your name, kid?" He was exactly the kind of kid I would have hated in college, if I'd gone to college. Tall, thin but with a layer of muscle that said he'd spent his time on the lacrosse field or cross-country team. The kind of confidence and good looks that come from decades of breeding and successful parents. He had perfect teeth, brown hair that curled artfully down just over his eyes in a tousle that looked like it took at least an hour to perfect. I wanted to punch him in his perfectly straight Roman nose.

"I don't have to answer any of your questions, fucktard. I know my rights." He seemed determined to tempt me to violence.

I took a deep breath, let the mental roulette wheel land on "fuck it," and gave in to temptation. I punched him in the nose. "You have the right to tell me what I want to know, or you have the right to bleed. Your call." I leaned in close, where his buddies couldn't hear what I was saying, and whispered "I'm not a cop, you little shitball. I'm your worst fucking nightmare. I'm somebody who actually gives a shit about that little girl, and really wants to do bad things to the people that hurt her. And your name is on top of my list. So tell me what went down, and I might decide that you're not worth the time and effort to destroy." I pulled in a little of my will and lit up my eyes with soul-fire. It's a cheap parlor trick, but it scares the shit out of the mundanes. It did the job this time, too.

"Fine, fine, I'll talk, but not here. Let's go to the library." He stood up, and I backed off enough to give him a little room. He turned to the rest of his brothers and said "This is nothing, just a protective big brother who needs to look at some security tapes to make sure we didn't take advantage of his precious little darling. Eric, can you come help run the computer for me?" He walked off, obviously expecting everyone to just go back to normal now that he'd made his proclamation. Must be nice to have minions. A big kid with close-cropped red hair and sprinkling of freckles that would keep him getting carded well into his forties got up and walked close behind. I shrugged and followed them.

My idea of a fraternity house library was a room with a couple of ratty desks and a huge stack of *Penthouse*. These guys had different ideas. They led me through the house, every room looking pretty much like I expected, decorated in video games, beer signs and posters of half-naked women. Until they led me through a pair of heavy wooden double doors that opened into the kind of library that would make a dedicated bibliophile fall to their knees weeping. The room was lined with ceiling-height bookcases, and leather spines stared out at me from every angle. No paperback bestsellers here—I spied a complete set of legal manuals from three different countries, about fifteen different Bibles and holy books, and one entire corner shelf unit glowed in my Sight so brightly that the magical aura bled over into the real world, casting pale purple light on everything within four feet of it.

The lead kid noticed my squint and chuckled. "Impressive, isn't it? We have one of the largest occult libraries in the South, and no one suspects it. After all, what kind of idiot would trust a bunch of drunken frat boys with some of the most powerful magical texts in history?"

"An amoral idiot that doesn't care what happens to anyone who wanders by the front door would be my guess." I sat on the arm of an overstuffed leather chair, making myself the apex of a triangle that let me keep one eye on the door and the other on the shelf of spell books.

"Careful, Mr. Harker, that's my father you're talking about."

I opened my mouth to speak, but he held up a hand. "Yes, I know who you are. You don't dabble in the occult circles in this town without learning who the other players are, so to speak. I knew you the second you walked in, all billowing duster and self-righteousness. How is little Kayleigh? Has she delivered yet? Is it a boy?" The smile on his face made me want to punch him again, and keep punching until my hand got tired, but I thought better of it. This kid was way more than he seemed, and I needed to know where he learned his tricks before I killed him, so I could go and kill his teacher, too.

Just for the record, I don't kill every bad guy I come across. I don't believe that killing is the best solution to every problem. I'm not one of those "every problem is a nail" guys. I just kill the monsters that are so far removed from human that they'll never feel or show a shred of remorse no matter what they do or who they do it to. And frat boys. Apparently, I kill frat boys, too, because this little bastard was in dire need of defenestration.

I took a deep breath and shoved all my murderous thoughts way down deep inside. "You seem to have me at a disadvantage, Mr...." I let the name trail off as I made my way over to the shelf of magical goodies. The texts there were pretty typical, if incongruous by their setting. There was a *Necronomicon*, a *Satanic Bible*, the collected writings of Aleister Crowley, a treatise on the Marquise de Sade, an entire shelf of introductory spell books, and several volumes of Martston's *Creatures of the Otherworlde*, an encyclopedia of things that go bump in the night. I had about four volumes myself, but had never seen a complete set. The shelf before me was missing only *Volume Seven - Sasquatch to Vampire.*

"Alexander Marlack," the kid said, extending a hand. "And this is Eric Brown, our chapter President." I shook his hand, managing to keep from wiping it on my jacket when he let go. Marlack gestured to a pair of sofas that faced each other across a coffee table. I sat in the center of the one facing the door. I watched *Deadwood*; I know what happens when you sit with your back to a door.

"So you knew you were putting a demon inside that little girl," I said as I sat down. I tried to keep my voice even, but it was pretty hard since most of my concentration was focused on not burning the two little bastards to ash where they sat.

"We did." Marlack's face was expressionless, like we were talking about the weather.

"Why the hell would you do something like that?" I asked. I suppose I hoped somewhere deep down that there was a piece of these little shits worth saving.

"I wanted to see if we could actually summon a demon. And when we did, we needed somewhere to put it. Kayleigh wasn't someone we'd miss, so I stashed the demon there." The smug prick could have been talking about a tech stock split, the level of emotion he was showing.

"And you knew that it would eat her from the inside out and then go on to wreak indescribable havoc until it was banished, right?"

"That fit with what I'd read, but as I had never summoned a demon, I had no proof." He leaned back and crossed one ankle over the other knee. "But what is that to you? Why are you here?"

"Why am I—you soulless piece of trash—I'm here because less than four hours ago I put a cross through the back of that girl's head to keep her from destroying the entire neighborhood."

"Oh, so you murdered a little girl and you're here to make yourself feel better because we're the monsters that put a demon in her?" His friend hadn't spoken, but at least had the good grace to look ashamed at what he'd done. Marlack just grinned, stood up and started pacing the room like he was making a closing argument. "You killed that girl, Mr. Harker, not us. And don't tell us that there was nothing you could have done—there are dozens of exorcism rituals available if you're willing to look for them. You just didn't look. You did what you do—you rushed in there, guns blazing, coat swirling in the mist at your feet and killed that child. Admit it, you're worse than the demons you claim to hunt!" He timed himself perfectly, finishing his little spiel right in front of me, bent over with his finger in my face.

The only problem for him was that I was a few years past being intimidated by rich college kids in expensive libraries. I stood up, grabbing his extended finger in my fist and bending it back sharply. As I stood, he dropped to one knee and started pawing at my hand, trying to get me to cut loose. Wasn't happening.

"Listen to me, you entitled little fuckbag. I came here hoping there was a better answer for what happened that night than statutory rape and demon summoning, but now I find out that it was worse. You weren't just an ignorant pawn; you knew exactly what the fuck you were doing. And instead of trying to find some way to make it right, or even show a scintilla of remorse about the little girl that died because of you, you rabid fuckmonkeys sit there and try to turn this around on me! Well, Mr. Marlack, I guarantee you one fucking thing. You've hurt your last little girl." With that, I reached out into the world around me and drew in my will. I focused my eyes full of soulfire on little Alex Marlack and shut out everything but the screams.

CHAPTER FOUR

I walked out of the room about ten minutes later feeling pretty good about myself. That feeling lasted all the way to the front door, where I first caught sight of the flashing blue lights and the three cop cars surrounding my beat up Honda. There was a woman in a dark pantsuit leaning on the front fender of my car, and my heart sank through my kneecaps when I saw her.

Detective Rebecca Gail Flynn, rising star of the Charlotte Mecklenburg Police Department, fervent non-believer in anything supernatural and spectacular pain in my ass. She'd decided a couple of years ago that I was a fraud, and that it was her sworn duty to bring me in. Since then I'd had a ridiculous number of jaywalking tickets, broken taillights, random license checks a block from my house and a couple of anonymous tips called in about my arsenal of automatic weapons. None of her best efforts had ever turned up anything incriminating, but they certainly made it harder to do business with a certain level of my clientele who are uncomfortable with their business dealings being observed by a mortal, much less a mortal police detective.

Of course, I'd never killed a teenage girl in her bed and burned down her house three hours before running into her, either. Detective Flynn looked positively radiant illuminated in flashing blue LEDs as she walked toward me flanked by two gigantic officers with biceps the size of my thighs and no necks. *Good thing I didn't inflict any* physical *damage on the assholes* here, I thought.

"Mr. Harker, how are you this fine evening?" she asked.

"Well, Detective Flynn, I'll have to admit that I was having a glorious night until you showed up. Blue isn't exactly my favorite color, you know," I replied. I stood on the sidewalk in front of the frat house, arms folded. Flynn and her gorillas had me blocked from my car, and they knew where I lived anyway, so there was no point trying to get away from them. I decided to hang tight and see what her game plan was.

"Let's see if you prefer orange. I hear it's the new black, you know." She smiled at her pop culture reference. I didn't. If she was talking orange jumpsuits, she must have thought she actually had something on me for a change. "Would you like to come down to the station and answer a few questions for me, Mr. Harker?" It was phrased like a question, but it had all the earmarks of an order. Too bad I've never been the obedient type.

"Nah, I think I'll just go home and catch up on *Downton Abbey* if it's all the same to you." I stepped forward, reaching out as though I'd open the door to my car, but one of the no-necks moved into my path.

"It's not. All the same to me, that is. Come with us, Mr. Harker." She gestured to one of the waiting cruisers.

"I'll follow you in my car." I reached again, and the no-neck put his hand on my chest. I looked up at him, judging whether or not I could take him. I could, but he'd slow me down enough for his friend to Taser me.

"You'll ride with me," Flynn said, and walked past me to the most obvious unmarked car in the world. The dark blue Chevy sat a few yards in front of my car, engine running. I shrugged and followed her, since I wasn't going to get to go home until I dealt with her questions. I slid into the passenger seat and pulled out my cell phone.

"Who are you calling?" Flynn asked.

"I thought I'd give my lawyer a call. Since I'm being held by the police and all."

"You're not being held, Mr. Harker. You're just being casually questioned about an assault that was reported by one of the fraternity brothers here."

"I've never seen you do anything casually, Detective Flynn. I might like to watch that sometime."

"Don't hold your breath. And give me your phone. You don't need to call anyone."

"I don't think you get to make that determination," I said, but handed my phone over. It didn't matter; I'd already sent the text to Uncle Luke telling him that I was getting arrested again. It happened so often since Flynn put me in her sights that I had a shortcut programmed into the phone.

We rode without speaking to the police station, Flynn tapping the steering wheel in time with the radio. It was never good for me when cops were in a good mood. I followed her into the station and down the hall to Interview Room #3. This wasn't my favorite of the interview rooms, but I didn't complain. They were all pretty much the same. Room #1 was a little bigger, but was often disgusting from previous interrogations. Room #2 was the same size as #3, but the chairs wobbled, and Room #4 was small, almost as though it were for juvenile offenders only.

I took a seat on one side of the table and Detective Flynn sat across from me. There was a tape recorder in the center of the table, with a small microphone next to it. A pair of security cameras monitored the room from the corners of the wall near the ceiling, and the obligatory two-way mirror covered one wall. I murmured a quick disruption spell under my breath as Flynn closed the door, gathered my will and pushed out at the cameras and the recorder. I smiled a little as the red lights on the cameras winked out. I was pretty sure there didn't need to be a record of anything we said tonight.

Flynn sat down and pressed the button on the tape recorder. "Just to make sure we don't have any misunderstandings, right, Mr. Harker?" Flynn said with a fake smile.

I returned her smile with one of my own, equally fake. "Absolutely, Detective. I certainly want to cooperate to the fullest with the lawful authorities."

Her smile flickered momentarily when she noticed the tape recorder wasn't working. She turned to the mirror and said, "The recorder in this room is out; can someone bring me a spare?"

A few seconds later one of her no-necks came in carrying a fresh tape recorder. She set it on the table beside the one I'd already cooked and reached down to the floor to plug it in. As soon as her eyes were off me, I murmured, "*Adflicto Affligo,*" under my breath and pushed my will at the new device.

Detective Flynn successfully plugged the recorder in and smiled as the red light winked on when she pressed the Record button. I smiled just as widely as it flickered out a couple of seconds later. She turned back to the mirror, but before she could speak, I said, "I'll just break the next one, too, Detective." I pitched my voice low, so the people on the other side of the glass couldn't hear me, but there was no mistaking my words.

Flynn whirled around and glared at me. "You did this?" She gestured at the recorders. "How?"

"Magic. I've explained before that there are stranger things on heaven and earth than are dreamt of in your philosophy, Detective. But I'd suggest you keep your voice down or your compatriots on the other side of the mirror will think you've lost your mind. Again." My last little barb was a reference to some department-mandated therapy the good Detective had undergone after being first on the scene to a school shooting several years back.

26

Her eyes narrowed, and I could almost see her calculating the best place to start cutting to keep me alive the longest and still inflict the most pain, but all she did was turn back to the mirror. "This recorder's on the fritz, too. I'm going to take my notes manually."

She turned back to me. "What do you know about a fire in Midwood this evening? The Garda residence, to be specific."

"I know nothing."

"Bullshit. You were seen leaving the house moments before the first 911 call was made. A girl died in that fire, Harker, and I know you had something to do with it."

"Let me guess. An anonymous tip placed me at the scene, right?"

"And then we pulled the Garda's phone records and saw that someone in that house called your cell phone this afternoon and spoke to you for four minutes. That's a lot longer than leaving a message, but not a casual chat. That was you, booking an appointment at the Garda's for tonight, wasn't it?"

I tried my best to look chagrined, but I'm very bad at it, so I'm sure I failed. "Yes, Detective, I did have an appointment at the Garda's house tonight, to discuss the possible possession of their daughter. But she was fine when I left her, and the house was intact." Technically true, since in comparison to having a demon in her womb, dead was certainly further along the scale to "fine."

"And then what were you doing at the Omega Sigma Iota house?" Flynn asked.

"I was working on a case."

"The same case?"

"I'm not at liberty to discuss it."

"Get liberated." Detective Flynn probably had a finely tuned sense of humor, with a rapier sharp wit and an appreciation for Jerry Lewis movies. It just never showed its face when I was around.

"Yes, it was the same case. It seems a couple of frat brothers summoned the demon which possessed Kayleigh Garda." I was never terribly cautious discussing the details of my cases with Detective Flynn, since she didn't believe in what I did anyway. I've found that bland honesty goes a long way into making people ignore the truth, particularly when the truth is hard to believe.

"What was Kayleigh Garda doing in a frat house?" Flynn asked.

I felt my neck start to get a little red. "Well, Detective, I bet she was being stupid, which is the inalienable birthright of the high school student, which is why there are things like laws and police departments to protect them. But good job, Flynn. I bet you passed 'Blaming the Victim 101' with flying colors."

"Don't give me that shit, Harker. I'm just wondering how anyone that young even finds out about a party at a frat house."

"Good lord, woman, did you even go *near* a college? You don't have to know about a party at a frat house, there's *always* a party at a frat house. All Kayleigh Garda had to do was walk past the house on the sidewalk wearing a little bit of makeup and her slutty best friend's shoes and they would have thrown open every door and poured her first drink for her!" I've found my tolerance for police stupidity has decreased as I've grown older, and I'm older than almost everyone I know, dashing good looks aside.

"Can the attitude, Harker. I don't need it. I've got a suspicious fire with your fingerprints all over it, a prominent citizen's kid getting harassed, again with you neck-deep in it, and a dead teenager in her house with injuries that don't look like they came from a fire, and once again the evidence points straight at you, so maybe, just maybe, you want to cooperate with me for once instead of giving me a bunch of bullshit about demons and witches and things that only exist in fairy tales. What do you think of that?"

"I think I want my lawyer." I leaned back in the chair and crossed my arms. There was obviously no way I was getting her to see sense, so I may as well move along to the "spend the night in jail" portion of my evening.

"Fuck your lawyer. You tell me what I want to hear or I'll put you under the fucking jail." Flynn leaned over the table and got right in my face.

I leaned in, getting uncomfortably close to her, but she couldn't back down or she'd lose face in front of everybody watching through the glass. Then I whispered, so low that she had to get even closer to hear me, "You want to know what happened tonight? Well here's the real fucking deal, Detective. I've shit all over your cameras and recorders so nobody can hear this but you, so here you go. Those overindulged fucktards at the frat house summoned a demon and let it play with Kayleigh Garda. It fucked her fifteen-year-old body and destroyed her mind. Then it impregnated her, with a demon. Not a baby, not a human, but a fucking demon that ate her from the inside out, starting with her soul.

"By the time I got there tonight, Kayleigh's soul wouldn't fill a thimble, much less her body. I stopped the demon from completely destroying her soul, and sent it back to Hell where it belonged, but it killed Kayleigh in the process. Then I went to the frat house and found a couple of junior sociopaths who don't give a fuck who they destroy so long as they don't miss their tee time. I had just finished bringing down a fuckton of fiery vengeance on the little bastard who called up a demon to rape and destroy Kayleigh Garda when you showed up. I know the drill from here, so why not just call one of your pet apes to take me down to holding for the night until my Uncle Luke shows up to pay my inflated bail in the morning?"

She leaned back, shook her head briefly, then leaned in and slapped the shit out of me. "Fuck you, Harker. And fuck your bullshit stories. One of these days you're going to fuck up and leave some evidence we can use, and then you're done. Game fucking over." She reached into a pocket and pulled out a handcuff key. She dropped it on the table and said, "You know your way out by now. Don't make me waste the time walking you out."

"Keep your key, Detective," I said, shaking my wrists and letting the loosened handcuffs drop to the table. "I was out of those things before you ever stepped into the room." I stood up, brushed some imaginary dust off the front of my jacket, and headed for the door.

I bumped shoulders with the no-neck partially blocking the door in the hallway, and forgot to check my strength until I'd almost knocked him flat. I flicked out a hand and caught the front of his uniform shirt before he hit the ground and pulled him back to his feet. No point in completely pissing off every cop in the building.

CHAPTER FIVE

Uncle Luke was waiting for me outside the station, his Mercedes convertible purring in a No Parking zone and roundly ignored by all the dozens of cops walking past. Uncle Luke looked the same as ever—short, high cheekbones, wavy dark hair, skin the white of a fresh notebook paper and piercing eyes that took in everything around him. Uncle Luke didn't miss anything, and didn't mind people knowing it. I walked around the car and slid into the passenger seat, flipping the radio to a classic 90s station. Luke immediately flipped it back to show tunes and we battled over that for a while before Luke finally snapped the radio to OFF and reached over and cuffed me on the back of the head.

"What the hell were you thinking, setting fire to the house?" he asked me, his sibilants getting that extra little hiss that told me his fangs were out and he was really pissed at me.

"Seemed like a good idea at the time," I muttered, rubbing the back of my head. Uncle Luke, as he had decided to be called this generation, packed quite a punch for an old dude.

"Much to my chagrin, your mother said the same thing about conceiving you."

"And look how awesome that turned out, Unc. Her and pops both rotted away to dust, but you and I are still kicking! Ain't immortality grand!"

"Oh, fuck off." He drove in silence for a couple of minutes, but it didn't take long for his curiosity to get the better of him. "What was it?"

"Demonic possession. A bad one. It had a little girl. I had to take pretty drastic measures."

"You couldn't exorcise her?"

"Possession isn't the right word, I guess. It was more like demon impregnation. And she was about to give birth to it."

"Fuck me."

"Fuck us all. If that thing had gotten out…"

"You couldn't banish it." For a converted bad guy, Uncle Luke had a pretty good handle on right and wrong.

"Nope. It would be native to this plane. An immortal, amoral, incredibly powerful monster that could never be sent home. Just what I want hanging around the suburbs."

"Yeah, that would send property values straight into the shitter." When you live as long as Luke, real estate speculation is a long-tail game.

His cell phone rang as we were turning into his driveway. He pressed a button on the steering wheel and spoke into the air. "Card here."

A reedy voice came over the car's speakers. "Master, sunrise approaches. Will you be home in time?"

"I'm almost home now, Renny."

"Very good, Master. I will prepare your rooms."

"Renny? I've told you not to call me Master. It's a new century. We need to change with the times."

"Yes, Master, I'll try to remember." Renfield clicked off and Uncle Luke just shook his head.

He looked over at me. "They never change, do they?"

"At least as often as you do, Mr. Luke Card. Or Mr. Alucard. Isn't that the name you used when you hired Dad? Why not just own it? Be fucking Dracula. I bet nobody would believe you."

"I'm sure they wouldn't, but I don't want to take the chance. Besides, if I have to invent new identities every few decades, what of it? It just gives me opportunity to see the world."

"At night," I reminded him.

"Yes, at night." Luke let out a little sigh as we pulled into his four-car, light-tight garage. His entire house, all eight thousand square feet of it, was outfitted with lightproof shades and light locks for all the doors. Luke slept most days, but if he needed to be up, he could go anywhere in his home safely. And since those shades were all bulletproof and the walls reinforced with plate steel, pretty much anyone inside was safe, too.

We walked through the garage into the kitchen where Renfield waited for us. He'd been a college student in the sixties, studying hotel management. Uncle Luke was looking for a replacement for his last Renfield and offered this one a live-in position as housekeeper, butler, personal assistant and chef. He didn't mention the blood-drinking thing until the contract was signed. But Renfield VI took it all in stride and deposited the paychecks. He was getting close to retirement age now, and had begun looking over recent Johnson & Wales hospitality majors for a replacement. I wasn't sure what Luke had planned for Renfield when he retired, but I'm pretty sure it involved memory wiping and white sand beaches. I'd been with Uncle for four Renfields counting this one, and he always provided for their well-being after they left his employ.

"Master, you didn't tell me you were bringing Mr. Quincy," Renfield chided. Only the Renfields got to scold my uncle; it was a perk of the job. I guess if you're going to be Dracula's manservant, you're going to grow nuts of steel pretty quick.

"My apologies, Renny. My... nephew wasn't planning on visiting today, but he ran into some difficulties last night that required my services."

"Oh dear. Mr. Quincy, are you injured? Should I fetch my sewing kit?"

"No, Ren. I'm good. I just got arrested for burning down a house, that's all."

"Oh. Well, if that's all, then. I shall fix you some breakfast. Eggs and bacon?"

"Kippers?" I asked. Some things you never outgrow, and I'm a turn of the century boy at heart. Turn of the twentieth, that is.

"No, sir. I'm sorry, but North Carolina seems to be lacking in good kippers."

"You can only expect so much from the Colonials, Ren. No matter how far they've come, they still drink shit beer and don't understand proper football. I'll take the bacon and eggs, though. Poached, please."

Renfield laughed at my soccer joke and went off to the kitchen, happy to have someone to cook for. I knew that Uncle sometimes sat with him and smelled the food just to make Ren feel better, but it wasn't the same. I made my way into the den, where Luke sat waiting for me. I took a chair across from him and waited for it.

He didn't make me wait long. "So you burned down the house to hide the evidence of demon infestation?"

"Yep."

"How did you get caught?"

"I went after the assholes who started the whole mess. They summoned the demon, raped the girl, then let the demon play with her. I think I convinced them that was a bad idea. One of them had a rich daddy. He made up some bullshit about seeing me leave the house right before the fire broke out and called the cops. There's no evidence. I can't be convicted."

"It may be inconvenient enough for you to merely be charged. Your identity cannot become known."

"I have good documents."

"I know. I had them forged for you."

"So what's the worry?"

"Who was this rich daddy you speak of?"

"Some asshole lawyer."

"Good god, child, talking with you is like pulling teeth. Does the asshole lawyer have a name?"

"Have you ever thought, *Uncle*, that maybe the reason I don't always give you much information is because it's something I want to handle on my own, without you drinking the bad guys. Maybe every once in a while I don't want you to get involved."

"I am involved, Quincy. I just got you out of jail."

"Fair enough. His name is Jacob Marlack, and he's got a serious collection of black magic texts that he lets his idiot son play with."

Uncle Luke didn't respond for a long time. I hate it when he does that; he gets all super-still and just sits there, like a statue covered in clown white makeup. After a couple of interminable moments, he looked at me and said, "Fuck."

Uncle Luke doesn't swear much. And when he does, it's usually pretty old-school stuff. For him to drop an F-bomb was a big deal. "What's the deal with Jacob Marlack?"

"I know him. He's a powerful witch. I met him many years ago when he was just beginning his study of the dark arts. I thought I had persuaded him to stop. Apparently I was wrong."

"Why don't I know this guy?" I've worked with Uncle Luke almost since we moved to the States, right after my parents died.

"I met him before I met your father. He tried to kill me in Romania."

"Wait, what? You knew him before—"

"Yes, before all that. Before your mother, before your father, before that fat shite Van Helsing, before any of them."

Yeah, all that happened, apparently. All I know outside what's in the book (which Uncle Luke wrote, by the way) is that as far you'd know from Luke, Van Helsing's first name was "fat shite."

Uncle Luke went on. "Marlack was a young wizard then. This must have been shortly after your President Lincoln was shot by that actor."

"John Wilkes Booth," I added.

"Yes, him. Well, a few years after that, I was in my home in Romania when I heard a pounding at the door. It was rather uncommon for me to receive visitors at my home during those years—"

"On account of the whole 'eating the villagers' thing, and the fact that everyone for fifty miles was terrified of you."

"I could do with a little healthy fear on your behalf, young man." He smiled when he said it, so I was pretty sure he didn't want to rip my throat out, but it was good to keep in mind that Uncle Luke was really Dracula every once in a while. This was shaping up to be one of those nights that I didn't want to lose track of the fact that one of history's greatest monsters was sitting ten feet from me.

He continued. "I answered the door, hoping it was just a lost traveler. It was late, and I felt the need for a snack. But when I opened the door, I faced a man holding a massive silver crucifix and brandishing it in my face. I instinctively flinched, but there was no power in the talisman other than the native pain I feel in the presence of silver. I felt nothing of the repulsion I had often felt when in the presence of holy symbols and holy men. That's when I realized two things: that holy objects only held sway over me when wielded by true believers, and that this man had no more faith in God than I do."

"I'm pretty sure he believes God exists, but I don't think they're friends on Facebook," I quipped. Renny brought my eggs with a large glass of orange juice and a Coke. He set the whole meal up on a little folding tray complete with silverware and tiny solid gold salt and pepper shakers. It was just like room service, but I didn't have to tip. I started to eat as Uncle Luke went on.

"I smacked the fool's hand away and pulled him inside. I looked into his eyes, wondering what kind of fool comes to a supposedly haunted castle in the middle of the night, and saw no fear there. That gave me pause, and as I hesitated, the fool pulled a clove of garlic out of a coat pocket and shoved it in my face."

I snorted back a laugh and orange juice almost came out my nose. Luke continued. "Exactly. I pushed the garlic away;, not because it harms me in some way, but because the smell was so strong it made me gag. My senses are very heightened, so strong smells are unpleasant, and I never liked garlic even when I was alive. The Gypsies cooked with garlic. It makes me think of them. And I hate Gypsies. So I looked at the man and asked him if he had anything else he wanted to try. He pulled out a vial of holy water, but I stopped him before he could throw it on me. I think I broke his arm at that point. I dragged him into my den and put him in a chair, then demanded an explanation as to why he had sought me out."

"He told me his name, Jacob Marlack, that he was from the United States, and that he was looking for books of magic. I told him I had none, and that for humans to meddle with forces beyond their reckoning was folly. I then offered to feed him to my wives so that he could gain a greater understanding of the powers of which I spoke. He declined my offer, and demanded to be given my magical texts. I repeated that I had no such things, and he grew angry with me. I have long since lost any fear of a mortal's anger, but this was something more. This Marlack was no longer just a man, and as his rage grew, his scent changed. He no longer smelled human, but began to reek of sulfur. I wanted him out of my home, so I called upon my servant to dispatch him."

"Was this the first Renfield?" I'll own it—he had me wrapped up in the story. Luke doesn't often talk about the old days, so any time I get a chance to see behind the curtain into his past, I'm all over it.

"No, this was Curtis. He was my valet and my guard. Curtis had spent time with the English Army in India or some other sweltering place, and he was a man of some size and great strength. But when he laid hands upon Marlack, the American flung him aside as though he were a child. Curtis' skull smashed against the stone walls and he died instantly. I was quite annoyed at this point, for good servants are difficult to find, and discreet ones even more so. I rose and advanced upon Marlack, determined to drink from the fool and perhaps bespell him into a few decades of servitude for his insolence, but when he spoke, the voice was not his own, or anything belonging to this world.

"It spoke of power, and hunger, and ageless times before men walked the earth. It spoke of destruction like I had never witnessed, even I, who had walked the earth for half a millennium, and I was afraid."

Luke looked at me, and I'd never seen that expression on his face before. "I was afraid of that creature then, and I am afraid of it now. I forbid you to pursue this investigation further. I will speak no more of this."

"The hell you say," I said. "You don't forbid me shit, *Uncle*, because I'm not your kid, I'm not your blood, and I'm not your goddamn servant. I'm going after this motherfucker, and I'm going to bring him down. Now you can either finish the story, and maybe I can get some good info out of it on how to bring him down, or not. But either way, there will be justice for Kayleigh Garda, and I'm going to bring that justice down around Jacob Marlack's old demon-possessed ears. I've fought demons before. They don't scare me."

"A fact I understand all too well. But this is more than just a demon, and it's more than a sorcerer. It is some evil blend of the two, and you should be scared."

"I'm not."

"Then you're a fool."

"Not the first time that charge has been levied, Unc. Now what happened with you and Marlack?"

He took a deep breath and looked to the sky as if for help. Both were oddly human gestures for a vampire as old as Uncle Luke, and they made him seem more vulnerable somehow.

"He spoke to me for a long time, Marlack did. He tried to persuade me to work alongside him, using my natural abilities and his magic to enslave entire countries. I was not interested. I was still a feudal lord at heart; I had my keep, I had my villagers paying tribute, I had my servants—I had no need for globalization. I was perfectly happy with a virgin to eat once a month and plenty of donors for the between times. Once Marlack understood this, he ransacked my library looking for magical texts that simply weren't there, then left, muttering about 'provincial fools' and 'bumpkins' under his breath the entire time. I stood atop my battlements and watched him go, hoping that my path would never cross his again. I know that humans consider me to be a monster, and perhaps I am a creature of my appetites, but that man is more than a monster—he is pure evil."

CHAPTER SIX

I leaned back and digested both my eggs and Uncle Luke's story. After a while, I spoke. "So he didn't do anything but change his voice and that made you think he was carrying a demon around in his head?"

"The fact that his eyes glowed purple may have had something to do with it as well," Luke replied.

"Okay, that's something to go on. Purple fire may be his demonic signature," I said.

"Like always saying the wrong thing at the wrong time is yours."

"Kiss my ass, Unc. I'm going to go upstairs and get some sleep."

"Then what?"

"Then tonight I'm going to pay Mr. Marlack a visit, and we're going to discuss the etiquette of statutory rape, demon impregnation and having me arrested. I expect the conversation to turn violent. It may even start there. Thank Renny for breakfast for me. And Uncle," I said, standing up and heading for the door.

"Yes?"

"Thanks for bailing me out. I really didn't want to have to deal with this bullshit while I was awaiting trial for murder."

"You're welcome. After all, what is family for?" He laughed, one of those old-school super villain laughs, then flashed into smoke and disappeared.

I looked around the study. "I hate when you do that!" I yelled to the empty air, then headed upstairs to my room to catch a few hours' shuteye.

I live in an apartment near Uptown, but I've kept a room at Uncle Luke's for as long as I can remember. We all did—my brother, my sister and me. I walked into my room and looked at their picture on the dresser. It's the only thing I've got from the old days. I'm not Luke, I don't drape my walls in velvet tapestries and bitch and moan about days gone by and gripe about all the "horseless carriages" and the general decline of civility. I just keep one photo, taken when we were all in our twenties, of me, James and Orly. That was before we realized how different I was, how much of mother's blood was changed and passed down to her firstborn. That was back when we thought vampires were just stories that mother told us at night to make us keep our windows locked from the inside.

I looked at the picture, yellowed and brittle and framed for its own protection, and thought about how much I felt like that paper some days. Old past my time, frayed around the edges and getting brittle with age. Then I shook my head, tried to derail my self-pity train, and poured myself a stiff drink. None of that OJ and Coke shit, either. A proper drink, Scotch with no ice and one lone drop of water to release the flavor. I knocked back the first one, and used the second to chase a couple of Vicodin down the old windpipe. It promised to be one of those days—the kind where my dreams are way more real than I want to deal with—so anything I could do to hold them at bay would be welcome. I checked email and surfed the web for a little while looking for information on Jacob Marlack, then when my eyes got heavy and the whiskey and painkillers started to take effect, I kicked off my shoes and sprawled, face-down and fully clothed, on the duvet and nearly drowned myself in goose down and opulence.

I awoke some five hours later, undrowned in feathers and with a taste in my mouth like the sewers of Riyadh City. I looked around the room and saw a fresh can of Coke sweating on the night stand where by all rights my Scotch should have been, but Renfield is an industrious and slightly morally superior fellow, so I chose discretion over drugs and whiskey and chugged the soda. I stripped down and walked into my bathroom, finding the customary towels and washcloth laid out for me.

I don't know if Renny just comes in and does these things when I'm here, or if there's some little magical spell he casts each day to freshen up the linens in the room, but everything is always sparkling and dust-free, no matter what ridiculous hour of the day or night I happen to wander in. Sometimes I wonder exactly who is thrall for whom in my uncle's relationship with this Renfield, then I decided I don't really give a shit, as long as he doesn't get in the way. And he never gets in the way.

A quick shower later, and I dressed in a change of clothes from my armoire. In any other place I'd call it a closet, or if I were feeling particularly genteel, a wardrobe. But in Uncle Luke's place, it was an armoire. And I offered up another silent prayer of thanks to Saint Renfield for the clothing in there, because it all fit and had been mended since the last time I dressed there. That had involved a werewolf and a misunderstanding about a gambling debt. Actually, he'd understood the amount of my debt perfectly, just not my complete and utter disinterest in paying. That led to an unpleasant discussion and little bits of fur and brain matter becoming rather embedded in the fabric of my jeans. Renfield had either replaced those jeans, or done an amazing job of getting wolf brain out of the knees, because they felt like brand new. I only knew they were my old pants when I found a spare fang in the right front pocket.

I got dressed and headed downstairs, groaning a little when I remembered that my car was still at the frat house. Gods only knew what those little fuck-wits had done to it by now. Renfield met me at the bottom of the stairs, a little smile on his lips.

"Mr. Quincy, good evening. I trust you feel better after your nap?"

"I do, thank you for the Coke. I would join you for dinner, but I have to get going. There's some pressing business I need to attend to with a man who calls demons for fun. Could you call me a cab?"

"Of course, Mr. Quincy. You are a cab."

"You know, just because a joke never gets old, doesn't mean it was ever funny in the first place. Now how about arranging some transportation for me?"

"Certainly, sir. Your keys are in your duster, on the hook by the front door. Right front pocket." Of course. Renfield was a manservant, an old-school, get-shit-done kind of manservant who didn't need to be told to go get his boss's nephew's car from out front of the house where he'd been arrested the night before, he just did it. And we won't talk about how he got those keys from the pocket of the pants I was sleeping in, but it explained the dream I had about Salma Hayek in the movie theatre watching *E.T.* Well, it explained part of the dream, anyway.

"Thanks as always, Ren. You're the best."

"I know."

I chuckled a little as I walked past him and out the front door. The sun had set, but that didn't give me a good gauge on time. It was fall, so that could be anywhere from six to eight in the evening. Either way, it was about the right time to go pay Mr. Marlack a visit. A visit I sincerely hoped he was not going to enjoy.

CHAPTER SEVEN

I wasn't surprised when I found out that Marlack's office was on the top floor of one of the massive monuments to small penises and corporate dickheads downtown. I also wasn't surprised to find that he was still at work at 8:15 PM on a Thursday. I was surprised to find magical wards poured into the concrete on the building's cornerstone and etched into the windows in the lobby. The wards on the windows flared briefly as I pulled the heavy glass door open and stepped into the atrium. My boots thunked across the marble floor, and I watched as the wage-slave security guard struggled awake behind his huge circular desk.

"Don't worry, Frank, it's just me." I waved my library card at him as I walked past the desk to the bank of half a dozen elevators.

"Huh? My name's Dennis. Who's Frank? And who are you?" The guard was almost fully coherent by the time the express elevator dinged open and I stepped inside. I gave him a little wave as the doors slid closed, then pressed the button for the sixty-fourth floor.

Nothing happened. The button lit up for a second, then went dark. I looked around, then noticed the card reader set above the bank of buttons. Obviously Mr. Marlack didn't want any unexpected or unauthorized visitors.

Since the next time I willingly walk up sixty-plus flights of stairs will be the first, I pressed my fingertips lightly to the card reader, focused my will on the device, and whispered, *"Laborious pro merda,"* which loosely translated into, "Work you piece of shit." I pressed the button for the top floor again, and this time the elevator jerked into motion. I leaned against the back wall of the elevator car, arms crossed, feeling pretty darn satisfied in myself. After all, I'd saved the girl's soul from Hell, figured out who was responsible, and was about to go do some serious smiting. That was a pretty good couple of days for me, even with an arrest thrown in for good measure. All I had to do was bludgeon Marlack into losing interest in the occult, and then finish showing his son the error of his ways. No problem.

Until the doors opened on the sixty-fourth floor and I stepped out into the biggest damn casting circle I'd ever seen. The elevators sat in the center of the floor, and the second I stepped out, I felt myself cross a magical barrier that had every hair on my body standing at end. And you have no idea how uncomfortable that is while wearing pants. I turned in a slow circle, trying to take in all the unnatural details I could before I opened up my Sight. As bad as this place looked in normal light, I really didn't want to know what it looked like in the magical spectrum, but I was pretty sure I wasn't going to have that choice.

The floor was black marble with gold inlays. To a normal observer, the gold was in random patterns, but if you turned your head just a little and squinted just right you could see the runes set into the floor. That kind of precise gold work must have taken months, and cost millions, but given the kind of critters Marlack's kid played with, Daddy obviously knew enough to set his defenses. I was standing inside one edge of a ten-foot circle, and I couldn't break it if I tried. The second I stepped into it, the circle invoked, bringing up a mystical barrier between me and the rest of the known universe. Nothing was getting into that circle unless I, or someone else, summoned it. That wasn't the part that worried me. I was much more concerned with the fact that I couldn't get *out*.

The rest of the floor, as much as I could see through the shimmer of the magical wall, was decorated in early twenty-first century office dickhead. Lots of exposed chrome and uncomfortable seating, a lot of track lighting and no plants or magazines anywhere. The whole place was designed to make you think the man in the office was very important, and that you aren't. As soon as my eyes lit on the doors to the office, some dark wood double doors that were probably brought back personally from an expedition down the darkest reaches of the Amazon, the golden knob turned and the doors flung outward. Following in their wake was a tall man, thin but not gaunt, wearing a very sober pin-striped suit and a classy red striped tie. He looked every inch the captain of industry, and appeared to have no more magic than poor old Dennis down in the lobby.

Until I closed my eyes and *looked* at him. That's when I saw the power swirling around him like a heavy green fog. That's when I could read the sigils carved onto his soul from twenty feet away and knew I was in the presence of a man who lusted for power like I lusted for Angelina Jolie, and would do absolutely anything to get it. He walked across the floor, his perfectly polished loafers making a thin *click-click*, the brisk click of his steps counting down the remainder of my time on earth, I'm sure.

"Mr. Harker, I presume?" He stopped just in front of me and held out a hand.

I looked at the hand like it was something disgusting, which it was. After a few seconds, he pulled it back. Marlack looked up at me with a rueful grin. "I suppose civility was too much to ask for. So be it. What do you want?"

"I'm here to tell you to stop."

"Stop what?"

"Playing around with things you don't understand. You're messing with stuff humans have no business getting involved in, Marlack."

"I've been involved with those things, things like your Uncle Luke, since long before you were born, Mr. Harker. I don't think I'm going to stop now just because you don't approve of my son's recreational activities."

"Recreational?" I spluttered. I couldn't even get the word out right. "You call summoning a demon and letting it rape a little girl recreational?"

"No." Marlack's smile disappeared and his eyes went cold. "No, I call it stupid. And I appreciate you dealing with the situation before it got out of hand. But it has been dealt with, and now your services are no longer needed. So, thank you for sending the demon back to Hell. Now, please leave my office."

"I don't think so, pal. You've got a lot to answer for, not the least of which is giving that douchecanoe you call a son the books to raise demons with in the first place. What the hell were you thinking?"

"I was thinking that he needed to start learning to use his gifts, the gifts I worked very hard to bestow upon him. And if he decided to use those gifts on some whore at a party, then the world loses one whore, and nobody notices. Even you only care because he happened to pick an underage whore. If she'd been eighteen and white you wouldn't give a damn. But Laws a'mercy, we gots to help the little brown girl! We gots to take our liberal guilt and uncle's money and help the poor little wetback!"

"Fuck you, pal. Your kid raised a demon, and you taught him how. There's a price for that, and now it's time to pay up."

"And who appointed you the Morality Police, Mr. Harker? Who gave you the badge and the gun and told you to clean up Dodge City?" He was right in front of me now, less than five feet away, inches from the edge of the circle, which he could obviously pass through without any trouble.

"I did. When I promised that little girl's father I'd try to save his daughter." An image popped into my mind, one I'd worked very hard to keep buried for the past several days. It was a little girl looking at me through the back window of a car as it drove away. I blinked a few times to shove the image back down inside and focus on the asshole at hand.

"Well, Sheriff, I suppose we are at an impasse," Marlack said.

"I don't think so," I said, and stepped back, crossing into another circle as I did so. The barrier that had surrounded the two of us flicked out of existence as the new circle invoked. His power flickered to life in the material plane, and a solid barrier of will sprang into existence along the edges of the circle he stood in, freeing me but separating the two of us. I reached out and touched the surface of the circle, watching the vibrant green magic swirl and pool around my fingertips. I pushed against the magic, and it turned hot to the touch. I snatched my fingers back.

Marlack laughed. "You can't think my circle is so weak, can you, Harker?"

"I don't know," I replied honestly. "I haven't tested it yet." With that I drew a silver dagger from the small of my back and jabbed it into the barrier. The blade penetrated about an inch into the circle, then stopped, slowed as if I had stabbed some almost solid mass. The green magic swirled faster, focusing on the blade, and the silver dagger turned red, then white-hot, and melted, falling into two puddles separated by the circle's scribing.

"You're going to have to do better than that," Marlack said with a smile.

"I can." I didn't boast. I didn't yell. I just pulled out a 9mm Glock pistol and fired fifteen rounds into the magical barrier. I angled the shots off to the side, away from Marlack's face and more importantly angled the ricochets away from my own. Green lights flared up with each impact, and I saw Marlack's brow furrow, but his circle held.

"Now are you beginning to understand what you're dealing with, boy?" Marlack asked after the ringing in my ears subsided a little.

"I'm getting a pretty good picture," I said. I stepped into the office and began pulling thick law books off the shelves. I took my time building a nice little two-foot wall around the outer edge of the circle, all the time ignoring Marlack's queries. Once I had the circle completely ringed in bound paper, I pulled out my Zippo, drizzled a little lighter fluid across the tops of the books, and lit them on fire. The books with lighter fluid on them blazed to life, and the fire quickly spread to the entire ring of books. Marlack was perfectly safe from the flames within his circle, but unfortunately for him there was still plenty of air traveling through his magical barrier.

I walked across the office and looked for a way to open his floor-to-ceiling windows, but apparently they don't allow that sort of thing in high-rises. So I put my fist through the glass, shattering it and letting some fresh air in. At least for me. The added oxygen just made the book fire blaze up even higher, and Marlack began to cough. I pulled a chair over from Marlack's desk and sat by the window, keeping the worst of the smoke from my eyes.

A fire alarm blared to life, but a whispered, "*Silencio,*" shut the fire alarm system down before the sprinklers kicked in. Marlack coughed inside his precious circle for a couple more moments, then with a wave of his arms and flash of green light, he dispelled his protective barrier. Another wave of his hands and my circle of burning books broke apart and flew into all corners of the room. Some of them even hurtled through the air and out the open window I was sitting next to. I would have been concerned, but there was too much smoke for Marlack to see me, much less throw a book at me.

I got up and walked over to the coughing wizard. Tears streamed down his face, and soot stained his forehead. I grabbed him by the throat and pulled him upright. "Now we're going to talk about your book collection, and then we're going to talk about what kind of punishment your son gets to face."

Marlack glared at me, then coughed up a mouthful of sooty air in my face. I blinked and wiped my face to clear my vision, and when I could see straight again, Marlack was standing several feet away, perfectly composed. There was nothing in my hand but his necktie. I hate illusionists.

"That was a good trick, Mr. Harker, but not quite good enough."

"I think it did alright. It got my hands around your throat." I stepped forward, shoving myself forward with my enhanced strength and speed, but Marlack vanished as my hands went right through his neck. I really, really hate illusionists.

I spun around, looking for the annoying magician. Marlack stood in the center of the room, in a circle surrounded by more circles and sigils than my eye could trace. I looked down, making sure that I wasn't trapped in any of the room's many inlaid circles myself, and started toward him.

"*Debilitatio.*" Marlack pointed at me, and a bolt of green energy flew from his fingers. I leapt into the air, but the spell was cast on me, not just hurled in my general direction, so the magical arrow bent like a guided missile and followed my every move. It struck me square in the chest as I came down from my leap, and all my limbs turned to jelly. I landed on the inscribed marble in a heap, unable to move or feel any of my extremities.

I listened to those goddamn dress shoes *click* across the floor again, thinking about what kind of pansy wears hard-soled shoes to a fight as Marlack stepped over me. He reached down and rolled me onto my back before kneeling beside me. "Now I think it's time for this charade to end, Mr.

Harker. Let's stop pretending that you are any threat to me, and I'll stop pretending that you're going to live through the night. *Vis vires.*"

With the murmured Latin, his hands glowed a deep purple, almost black against his pale skin. He reached out with his long fingers and wrapped one hand in the collar of my shirt and the other around my belt. Marlack stood, and hefted me over his head as he did so, like a professional wrestler hoisting a child. My two hundred and forty pounds bounced in his grip like it was nothing, and Marlack strode to a window, hefted me once more, then chucked me through like so much battered garbage.

I felt my skin tear as the glass shattered across my face, then the cold wind rush by as I made my rapid descent. I had just enough time to think that maybe Marlack was more than I had expected when I spun over in midair and saw what was rushing up to meet me.

I had just enough muscle control to mutter, "Oh fuck," before I landed face-first on the roof of a parked Suburban.

CHAPTER EIGHT

I lay there, face full of broken glass and Chevrolet factory paint, thinking about the poor choices I'd made in life.

That's total bullshit. I lay there thinking, *Fuck that hurt,* until the first flashing red and blue lights showed. Then I shifted my internal monologue to just, *Fuck.* I still couldn't move, although I wasn't sure if it was due to Marlack's spell or the grievous injuries I'd just sustained, and I could tell by the sirens that there were ambulances and police arriving on the scene. The last thing I wanted to do was explain to some overzealous public servant exactly how I was still alive after a sixty-plus story fall onto several tons of Detroit steel.

That's more bullshit. The last thing I wanted to do was fight Marlack again, but the next to last thing I wanted to do was deal with the cops or the EMTs. So I made myself move. I peeled my broken body off the roof of the broken car like the coyote in a Road Runner cartoon, leaving a fair amount of blood, skin and a couple of teeth behind. I knew from experience that the blood and skin would replace itself in a few hours, but the missing teeth were going to be a problem for the next couple of days.

I had just rolled to the ground and pulled myself up to my knees when I heard one of the last voices I wanted to hear right in that moment, the usually welcome tones of Detective Rebecca Gail Flynn.

"Mr. Harker. This is where I would typically say something witty like 'fancy meeting you here,' except that I am totally and completely unsurprised at seeing you here. After hearing reports of strange flashing lights, explosions and a man falling to his doom from the upper offices of the Pantheon Building, it brings me no surprise at all to see you here in the middle of an explosion of blood, broken glass and property damage. I'm not even surprised to see you alive, no matter how bizarre that may be." She reached down, helped me to my feet, then continued helping me right into a spin that ended with me face-down on the hood of the destroyed Suburban with handcuffs clicking shut around my wrists.

Flynn hustled me into a nearby squad car and gave the uniform behind the wheel strict instructions to take me to jail, directly to jail, and not to allow me to pass "Go" or collect my two hundred dollars. After a quick thump on the roof of the car, Flynn receded in the back mirror and I turned to face the driver.

"I don't suppose you'd consider a detour through the emergency room, would you? I think my everything might be broken," I said through the Plexiglas divider.

"Detective Flynn said straight to the station. So you go straight to the station." He never turned, not even flicking his eyes up to the mirror.

"But do you want to be the one that 'just follows orders' or do you want to be the guy that takes compassion on a fellow human being that's suffering?" I tried to make myself look suffering. It didn't take much, since I was still bleeding from a dozen cuts and my left eye was swollen almost completely shut, but my escort still wasn't looking.

"I want to be the one that's not playing crossing guard outside all through the winter. So you're the one that's going straight to the station." He kept his eyes firmly focused on the road, leaving me to bleed and throb at my own pace.

The drive to the station took a solid twenty minutes, during which the worst of the bleeding stopped and a couple of small shards of glass expelled themselves from my face as the cuts there started to heal. I decided that I had lost three teeth in the fall, and hoped I hadn't swallowed them. That always made for an unpleasant morning after. Officer Silence held a hand on the back of my head to keep me from further injury as I got out of the car, a nice touch I thought. He perp-walked me in through the back door and up to Central Booking, where I was fingerprinted (again), had my mug shot taken (again), and was escorted to the drunk tank for holding (again). I settled in on my bench and rubbed my chafed wrists while taking stock of my situation.

I'd failed horribly in my attempt to beat Marlack into submission, or even understanding of his wrongdoings. He wasn't just unapologetic; he was gleeful about his depravity. I'd ended up in jail, where I was somewhat less than effective in both avenging Kayleigh Garda and protecting any other girls from Marlack's brat and his fraternity brothers. All in all, I had to admit it was a pretty godawful night. I was sitting there, minding my own business and listening to my blood clot, when a voice jarred me from my moping.

"That's my seat." I looked up at a lump of a head atop a mountain of flesh sitting somewhere near seven feet off the ground.

I stared at him, not moving. My mind flashed back to everything I'd ever learned about predators, both human and not. Then I thought *fuck it*, and stood up. "If this seat means enough to you to die for, then have it. I'll go sit over there. But if you start some bullshit about that being your seat too right after I get comfortable, then we're going to have a problem. The kind of problem that involves somebody washing a lot of your blood down the drain in the center of the floor and me quite possibly causing serious injury to my hand while beating your fucking face in. Got it?"

The mountain held up both hands and backed up a couple of quick steps. "Hey man, I don't want no trouble. You can sit wherever you like. I was just gonna say that I'd been sitting there before I had to go pee, and could you scoot over a little. Okay? But I'll go sit somewhere else. Just don't beat me up, please?" His voice was a lot higher when he was scared shitless, and on second look he was just a fat lush spending his weekend in the drunk tank, not some hardened criminal trying to establish jailyard supremacy.

I stood up. "Never mind, buddy. Total misunderstanding. I'll go sit over here. You have a nice sleep." I crossed the room to the other bunk, all of eight feet away, and sat down facing the now-terrified drunk.

A dreadlocked head popped over the bunk, looking down at me. "You are not a nice man." The head said, then broke into a grin. "I'm Jake."

"I'm not interested."

"I'm not trying to pick up a date, bro, just making conversation. What happened to you? You look like you got run over by a steamroller."

"I fell down."

"Shit, man, how far?"

"About sixty stories."

"Bullshit!"

"Fuck off then." I lay down on the bunk and put my hands behind my head. Jake's head disappeared for a minute, then the rest of him spun into view as he dropped down off the top bunk and sat at my feet. He was a skinny black dude with long dreads, a pierced nose, the bloodshot eyes of the cosmically stoned, and a Bob Marley *Legend* t-shirt. I shook my head. I tend to immediately discount the musical opinions of people wearing shirts with records that were released before they were born. Of course, before I was born they were making music on wax cylinders, so I suppose I'm only a poseur if I wear a Mozart shirt. Which I never will.

"Hey man, I'm just trying to be friendly. How did you fall that far and live? Did you go, like, super-limp or something? Are you like a superhero? Or are you just really, really fucked up? I mean, I read once that if you're fucked up enough, you don't get tense at the moment of impact, and you can like live through almost any fucking thing. Like getting hit by a bus or whatever. Is that what happened to you?"

It took me a minute to parse the sentence, but when I did I just shook my head. "Go away, kid. I've had a really shitty night and I just want to sleep this off, get up in the morning, post my bail, and go home. I don't want to deal with fighting for turf, I don't want to deal with making friends, and I don't want to talk about my night. You got all that? Good. Now get your ass off my bunk and leave me alone."

"Nah, I don't think so." He leaned back and grinned at me.

I sat up, looking around for a weapon. That's when I noticed that no one else in the cell was moving. At all. Not like they were asleep, like they were frozen in time. Or like I was suddenly *outside* of time. I jumped out of the bunk and stomped across the cell, trying to find something to kick that wouldn't hurt too much in the jail slippers I was wearing.

After a minute of fruitlessly looking for something to use as a weapon, I turned back to my bunk, where "Jake" was now sitting cross-legged in the center of the bed, smiling at me like a cat with a bellyful of canary. Then I realized what was happening. "Goddammit, Glory, what the fuck are you doing here?"

"Guardian stuff. You know, making sure you don't become somebody's prison bitch while you sleep, that sort of thing." My angel's voice sounded strange coming through Jake's weed-scarred vocal chords, but it was probably doing all sorts of good things for him being inhabited by one of the Host.

"Yeah, like that was going to happen." I looked around the cell and waved at the others in my little twelve by twenty room. There was Tubbo, the innocuous fatty that I'd given up the first bunk to. He was probably three hundred fifty pounds of Jell-O and milquetoast, not exactly the stuff my nightmares were made of. Then there was skinny Jake, too high to tie his own shoes, much less subdue me. That only left one little guy stretched out on the top bunk across the room, a banker-looking dude about five-eight with wire-rimmed glasses and a receding hairline. He looked too timid to take eleven items through the express lane at the grocery store, much less attack anyone.

"It was. The guy whose body I'm inhabiting? He killed three people last night in a psychotic break. In the movie in his mind, you're his high school girlfriend and this whole conversation has been taking place after prom. You two had been waiting months for this perfect moment, and he was about to seal the deal with you."

"Not while I'm still breathing," I said, looking back over at Jake. He looked harmless, if high. "Are you sure he's delusional?"

"He thinks Fox News really is fair and balanced," Glory replied.

"Yup, batshit crazy," I agreed. "What about these two dweebs? Weren't they going to help?" I pointed at Tiny and Tubbo on the other bunk.

"They aren't the 'get involved' type. The fat one is so scared he pees a little every time anybody speaks to him, and the other one is a complete blank to me." Her brow furrowed as she said that.

"What do you mean?" I asked.

Glory stood up, in Jake's body, and walked over to the side of the bunk where the little guy was frozen. She stared at him for a few seconds, then turned back to me. "Run."

"What? Where?" I asked. Glory/Jake had this look of pure terror on his/her face, like nothing I'd seen before. What the hell could scare an angel? I found out as the little nebbishy guy, who looked like a less butch Les Nessman off the old TV show *WKRP in Cincinatti*, sat bolt upright in bed, bounded across the room, and wrapped his legs around Jake/Glory's neck. The second he touched the angel, time started moving at its normal pace again, which is to say way too fast for my comfort.

Nebbish had his legs locked around Jake's neck, and I could tell from the look on Jake's face that he had no idea how he'd gotten there. Apparently whatever was in the other prisoner bounced Glory out of Jake on contact. Then Nebbish straightened his legs out and twisted at the hips, crossing his ankles and pushing himself upwards on his hands in a sitting position. The twist he put on Jake's neck resulted in a very unhealthy-sounding *POP*, and the dreadlocked head lolled to one side, eyes going blank in death.

Tubbo saw the body drop to the floor in front of his bunk and curled up the fetal position. I could smell the urine flowing from across the cell. *No help coming there.* Nebbish dropped from the top bunk, straightening his shirt as he stepped up to me.

"Mr. Harker, what a pleasure to meet you. I was instructed to tell you that Jacob Marlack sends his warmest regards. And by 'warmest,' he is referring to the Hell he has hired me to send you to. Have a nice trip." Nebbish threw a punch at my midsection that probably would have sent his fist out through my spleen if it connected. I decided that it shouldn't connect, so I sidestepped the punch and grabbed Nebbish's wrist. I pulled, and he flew past me to crash face-first into the bars of our cell.

He turned around, and the look on his face made me take an involuntary step back. The little bastard was *smiling*. Blood was streaming down his forehead from where his head impacted the bars, and he was grinning at me through the red drops. He came at me again, keeping his hands low and outside to prevent me from going around him this time. I saw what he was doing, so I didn't go around him. I went straight at him instead, diving headfirst across the floor, rolling over onto my back as I slid between his spread legs, and kicking upward with a front snap kick from the floor. My slipper caught him square in the nuts, and he toppled forward. He recovered fast enough to turn his tumble into a forward roll, and was back on his feet facing me by the time I scrambled to my feet.

"What the fuck are you?" I asked.

"What am I?" Nebbish repeated. "You ask the wrong question, mortal. I am not a what, but a who. I am the Grand Marquis Fornas, leader of twenty-nine of Hell's legions, corrupter of the sciences, defiler of the experiments, and despoiler of the philosophies. I am a warrior, a poet, a scholar, and your doom." He lunged at me again, but I'd used his monologue to maneuver us around so that Tubbo was right behind me, and when Fornas leapt, I dropped flat, leaving the Grand Marquis to fly face-first into a great big pile of terrified, gibbering drunken pee. He shrieked with rage and turned to fling himself at me again, but with enough time to think for once, I caught him in midair and pressed my right hand to his forehead.

"*Exorcizo te, omnis spiritus immunde, in nomine Dei Patris omnipotentis, et in noimine Jesu Christi Filii ejus, Domini et Judicis nostri, et in virtute Spiritus Sancti, ut descedas ab hoc plasmate Dei, quod Dominus noster ad templum sanctum suum vocare dignatus est, ut fiat templum Dei vivi, et Spiritus Sanctus habitet in eo. Per eumdem Christum Dominum nostrum, qui venturus est judicare vivos et mortuos, et saeculum per ignem.*"

I wasn't sure if it would work with me not knowing Nebbish's True Name to cast out the demon, but I poured my will into my right hand and felt the tattoos flare to life along my arm and my palm. They burned as the power of The Word coursed through me, and Nebbish dropped to his knees screaming. I screamed right along with him, because having holy magic run through your arm feels an awful lot like sticking your middle finger in a light socket while being struck by lightning and peeing on an electric fence all at the same time.

The air around us went dark as noxious purple-grey smoke billowed from Nebbish's mouth, nose, ears and eyes, and all I heard over the sound of screaming was more screaming and a faint fire alarm in the distance. Finally, after what felt like a year but was probably all of thirty seconds, Nebbish's eyes went back to normal human hazel eyes, all the smoke in the room cleared in an instant, and I fell to the floor with a diminutive accountant on top of me.

I lay there trying to catch my breath and wondering exactly how I was going to explain this to the nice man lying on top of me when suddenly Nebbish's weight was lifted off me and I was hauled roughly to my feet. My eyes were still trying to focus, but I got a good look at Detective Flynn as the two uniforms dragged me out of the cell and down the hall.

"I warned you, Detective, I'm the reason we can't have nice things," I said, giving her my best saucy smile. Then I passed out.

CHAPTER NINE

I came to in Interview #1, appreciating the upgrade to the bigger room this time. I wasn't handcuffed to anything, and there was a bottle of water in front of me, so I drank it to try and get the taste of demon smoke out of my mouth. Even three-day-old grocery store sushi can't hold a candle to the nasty that is demon funk.

I downed the water in a long pull, squeezing the sides flat as I went. I held it up and shook it at the camera in the corner of the room, then turned it upside down in the universal sign for "more?" No dice. I set the empty bottle on the table, turned to the big two-way mirror in one wall that served as an observation window and waved, then pointed at the empty bottle again.

"Service in this restaurant sucks. I'll have you know that my review will reflect as much," I said, pushing my chair away from the table. I'd just put my feet up and leaned back when the door opened and Detective Flynn stomped in. She strode across the room, knocked my feet off the table, and sat down across from me. I sat up and scooted my chair forward, putting my elbows on the table and situating myself directly in front of the microphone. I fully intended to blow it up, but I wanted to make it look good for the observers.

"What the fuck happened in there, Harker?" Flynn asked.

I raised an eyebrow. "Why Detective, such language is unbecoming a professional like yourself. I don't know that I will ever be able to repair my image of you."

"Go fuck yourself. Now what happened in that cell?"

"Why should I bother telling you? You won't believe me."

"Try me."

"I've been trying you for three years now. Every time you haul me in, I start off with the truth and have to go further and further afield of it to find something you'll believe. Why don't you just tell me what you want to think happened in there and I'll agree to it?"

"I don't know how you did it, but somehow you managed to goad a man in custody for shoplifting into fighting with you in a holding cell, and then you set off some kind of smoke bomb, filling the jail with smoke and obscuring exactly what was going on in there, while for some reason the shoplifter and a low-level pot and Adderall dealer got into an altercation, leaving the dealer dead, and the shoplifter attacking you, of all ridiculous people. Those are things that I know happened. Now I want to know *why*."

"I told you, I can't explain it in any way that you will believe."

"And I told you to try me."

"I'm tired of wasting my breath, Detective. And I'm tired of being here. So why don't you either put me back in holding, or show me to the door?"

"Why don't I just fast-track an arraignment on murder charges, hold you here until that happens, and then throw away the key? I'm tired of this, Harker. I'm tired of all the weird shit happening when you're around, I'm tired of not being able to explain anything to anyone, and I'm tired of the goddamn mess you leave behind!" Flynn was standing with her hands on the table, sweat staining the neck of her dark purple blouse, and her hair falling from the usually neat ponytail. Her jaw was clenching and unclenching rapidly, and a vein had popped out a little on her forehead. My expert analysis revealed that she was *pissed*.

Unfortunately for Detective Flynn, any electronics in the room, and my own chances of getting out of jail that night, I was in pretty shite mood myself. I stood up slowly, doing that twitchy thing I know I do with my fingers when I'm about to lose my shit, where I tap each finger in succession off my thumbs, faster and faster until I just make a fist and really get the shit-show started. It goes back to when I was younger and tried to keep my temper by counting to ten. Usually I lost interest in counting along about the fifth language, and just hit whatever was pissing me off. I was really hoping I could keep my shit together enough not to punch Detective Flynn. I kinda liked her, and really didn't need the drama that punching cops brings in America.

"Detective Flynn," I began slowly. "If you think it's tough being around me, having to occasionally clean up some of the mess when I leave, being thrust into the middle of pieces of my strange and cursedly interesting life, please take a second and think how it must feel to *fucking live it*. I don't get to go home after filling out paperwork about the man who died in the cell tonight, I get to go home and see his face in my dreams. I don't get to put a neat little label on the fire and smoke that billowed through your precinct tonight, I have to live with the fucking scars." I rolled up my sleeves and showed my tattoos.

Usually they aren't visible, being applied with a magically enhanced UV ink. But when I call upon the power stored there, they burn out the ink, the hard way, by setting the ink on fire while it's still in my skin. That leaves a nasty set of burns that takes weeks to heal. Then I have to go back in to a mystical tattoo artist and have the work redone. In UV ink again. With spells entwined into the design. Spells that take a piece of my soul to fuse to my body and my being. It takes about three weeks to be healed enough to get the tattoos done, then about another four weeks to heal from the tattooing. So I don't burn those up lightly. Also, having second-degree burns running the length of both arms and down each finger hurts like a son of a bitch.

I went on. "Now I'm going to tell you what happened in that cell. And I'm going to make sure that everyone behind that glass can hear it this time. But there will be no recording. Are we clear?"

"What do you intend to do about that, Mr. Harker?" A voice came through the grill under the window.

"This." I replied. I held my arms out toward the ceiling, spread out from my shoulders in a "Y." "*Futue te ipsum!*" I said at the top of my lungs and pushed my power out through my fingertips. The camera on the wall exploded in a shower of sparks, the table recorder in the center of the table flew six inches into the air and landed on its back, smoking. The two-way mirror shattered, and three very surprised men in suits stood staring at me from the other side. One man sitting at a computer suddenly jerked a set of headphones off his head and threw them to the ground, cursing as sparks flew from his laptop. A high-pitched squeal came from Detective Flynn's pocket, and she jumped up, reached into her pants, and threw her smoldering cell phone onto the ground. I smirked as all the men in the observation room did the same.

"Now that we can chat undisturbed by all these electronic toys, let me give you all the lowdown on what happened here tonight. If there's anyone in that room that you don't think is high enough in the food chain to hear what I'm about to tell you, now's your chance to send them home." The suits looked at each other, then at the technician, who was still rubbing his scorched ear. After a couple of seconds of silent consultation, one of the suits with a square jaw and air of authority tapped the tech on the shoulder and pointed at the door. The skinny tech pouted for a second, but then looked at me and apparently decided that he wasn't that interested in finding out the truth if I had anything to do with it.

"Good," I said. "Now let's be clear about this—there are things in this world that men and women aren't meant to understand. We aren't supposed to know these things exist, much less how to fight them. The things that go bump in the night, the monsters in the closet, the shadow out of the corner of your eye—that's where I live. These are the things I deal with every fucking day, and neither your gun, nor your badge, nor that little medal of St. Jude you wear on a silver chain around your neck will protect you from the shit that is going down in our fair city these days. Nice choice, by the way, St. Jude. I've always tossed an extra coin his way when I make an offering. I figure if anybody's gonna look after me, it'll be him."

"Why don't you tell us exactly what it is that's got you so scared, Harker?" Flynn asked. She was back in her chair, burning pants forgotten as she pretended to be having just another normal day at the office. Her left hand trailed up to trace the medal under her shirt, but she caught herself and with a visible effort pulled it back to the table.

"Jacob Marlack," I said.

"Yeah, he's the one who filed the most recent complaint against you," Flynn replied.

"Like I give a fuck about his complaint. I'm much more concerned about the fact that he's summoning demons. Actually, it's worse than that. He's letting his fratboy son summon demons and use them to seduce and rape underage girls."

Flynn looked at me for a long moment and then sat back down, leaning on the table. "Why is it never just drugs? Other detectives get meth heads flipping out and shooting their wives and children over a fucked up batch of bastardized cold medicine. I get an overgrown Harry fucking Potter and his evil wizards."

"I guess you're just lucky, Detective," I said.

"That's not exactly what I'd call it." She turned to where the mirror used to be and spoke to the three men standing there. "I assume since you haven't called for the men in white suits with the jacket that buckles in the back that you're taking this seriously?"

The men looked at each other, then the one with the square jaw walked out of the room. A few seconds later the door to the interview room opened and he stepped in. He walked like twenty years of military, and had a "don't fuck with me" set to his jaw. He pulled a chair from the wall over to the table and sat down, sliding a badge holder over to me. I opened it, and staring back at me was a picture of Crew Cut with the name "John A. Smith" under it in blue block letters. Written over the picture were the words "US Department of Homeland Security" and on a line right below that, in much smaller print, "Paranormal Division." A gold badge on the facing side displayed the Homeland Security logo with an assortment of the world's major religions' holy symbols arranged in a circle on the shield the eagle was holding.

"Pleased to meet you, Mr. Smith," I said, sliding the badge back over to him. "Looks like we're in the same line of work."

"And what do you call your line of work, Mr. Harker?" Smith asked. He didn't return my smile. I decided not to feel hurt.

"I call myself a security specialist."

"You lying sack of shit, you call yourself a demon hunter." Flynn leaned back in her chair, arms crossed across her chest.

"Same thing, Detective. Same thing."

"What can you tell us about Marlack?" Smith asked.

"What else do you want to know? He summons demons, lets them screw little girls, and then casts them aside like so much garbage," I said. "Now are you going to help me kill this motherfucker, or what?"

CHAPTER TEN

I gave Crew Cut my most charming smile, which I've been told reminds people of Anthony Hopkins from *Silence of the Lambs*, but he didn't even blink. In fact, he stared at me so long without blinking I started to wonder if he had eyelids. Finally, he nodded a little and waved to the other two men.

One came into the room and Smith said, "Bring us some more water. I think we're going to be able to work with Mr. Harker here."

"Are you fucking insane?" Flynn asked. "Because he is. You heard what he was babbling about, right? Demons, monsters, things that go bump in the night? What the fuck, Smith? You can't possibly believe in this shit." Flynn stood up and started pacing around the interview room muttering to herself.

"Detective, you're still in this room as a courtesy," Smith said. Flynn froze in her pacing and turned slowly to stare at the back of the agent's head. "Now if you'd like to sit down and contribute to the discussion, that's fine. If you'd like to sit down and keep your goddamn mouth shut, that's also fine. But you will sit the fuck down, right the fuck now, or you will leave this room. Do you understand me?"

Smith never raised his voice. He never changed the cadence of his speech one bit, and didn't even turn to look at the stunned detective. But there was no question in my mind that he was not a man to fuck with. And I am not widely regarded as someone who knows many boundaries. Flynn stood there gaping for several seconds until the door opened and the other suit came back with three bottles of water. He set the water on the table and stood there, awaiting further instruction. Smith waved a hand, and the suit in the room with us and the suit still in the room behind what used to be the two-way mirror both left and made themselves scarce.

"They'll take up positions outside the doors to make sure we aren't disturbed. Now, Detective, we have a problem to deal with. Are you part of the solution?" He motioned toward Flynn's chair, and she sat.

I unscrewed the cap on a bottle of water and sucked it down, still trying to get the taste of exorcism out of my mouth. "So what can I do for you, Agent Smith?" I asked.

"Just exactly what you intended to do before meeting me—kill Jacob Marlack."

Flynn's head whipped back and forth between Smith and me. "What? Are you serious? We can't just—" Smith held up a hand, and Flynn cut her words off like a spigot.

"He kicked my ass the last time I tried. You got something to help even the odds?" I asked.

"Information," Smith replied.

"You want to elaborate on that, pal, or are we going to play cat and mouse all night?" I downed the last of my water and reached out for another. Smith gave me a little "go ahead" with his hand, and I took another drink. Rate I was going, I supposed I could drown Marlack in piss if nothing else came to mind.

"We think Marlack has been at this game for quite a while, and may have some enemies that could come in handy." He pushed a piece of paper across the table at me. I took it, and looked at the names written there. My eyes widened at the third name on the list.

"These are some of Hell's heaviest hitters. You're telling me that Marlack double-crossed these guys and lived to tell the tale?" I asked.

"Somehow that's exactly what he's done. And along the way he's done a lot worse than just giving a few teenaged girls over to be demon meat. He's engineered mass killings all over the world, with his fingers in pies from Cambodia to Haiti. For about the last century and a half, if there's been incredible bloodshed and suffering, he's been involved.

"But never the front-page stuff, only the stuff where the 'civilized' world won't pay attention," Smith continued.

"You mean he only kills brown and yellow people," I translated.

"Pretty much. That keeps him off the radar of the people with the resources to root him out and take care of him once and for all."

"Until now. What's different now?" I leaned back and put my feet up on the table and sipped my water while studying Smith. He was a white guy, late forties but still looked like he could kick a normal human's ass pretty well. He probably ran, did calisthenics, took target practice three or four times a week, that kind of thing. He wasn't a golf course and gym kind of lean, he was the walk into the woods for a week with a bandana and pocketknife kind of whipcord muscle. But there was something in his eyes that held me. This was a man that had seen some serious shit, and walked away from it, but not without leaving some pieces of himself behind.

"I'm different now. We have a very small department, but we have the full force and authority of the Department of Homeland Security at our disposal."

"Like the boys in those *Mission:Impossible* movies. All the toys, but none of the backup. If we fuck up, we're on our own. Right, Agent 'Smith?'" I put a little extra emphasis on the name to let him know that I knew it was fake. He smiled a little half-smile that was as close as I'd seen him come to a grin.

"That pretty much sums it up. Now I've given you some valuable information about our friend Jacob Marlack. Do you know what to do with it?"

Then it clicked. "You can't do it yourself. That's why you want me. You don't have enough magic to light a fucking candle, do you?"

"Not even the tiniest bit," Smith confirmed.

"So I get to be the sword."

"And I'm the arm. Exactly."

"Well loosen your grip on my johnson. I've got this."

"And where do I fit into this little magical Justice League?" Flynn asked.

"Do you want in, Detective?" Smith asked her, and something in his tone told me he was asking a lot bigger question that his words would indicate.

Flynn must have heard the same thing, because she didn't answer right away. She looked at Smith, then at me, then at the shards of glass on the floor. "This is one of those moments that no matter what I say, I'm probably going to look back on it in twenty years and regret my decision, isn't it? If I say yes, I go down the rabbit hole with you lunatics and my career stalls at Detective. I'm done with any kind of real career advancement, and any good things that happen to me in my job, I don't get to tell anyone about. If I say no, I spend the rest of my life working cases and saying, 'What if?'"

"If it makes you feel any better, the odds of you living twenty years in this line of work are pretty slim," I said. That's my idea of being helpful. I kinda liked Flynn. She was a pain in my ass, but she was a constant, something steady that I could count on. I wasn't sure I wanted her involved in my world, not really.

"I'm in." I was afraid of that. No detective worth a damn could turn down something like this, and Flynn was one of the best I'd ever met.

"Fine, then. Let's get Mr. Harker out of here and see what can be done about our friend Marlack. Mr. Harker—"

"Call me Q. Looks like I'm stuck with you for a little while, no need to stand on formalities. Right, Smitty?"

"Sure," the agent replied. I'm sure he gave not a single shit what I called him, as long as I killed what he wanted killed and didn't rack up too big a civilian body count in the process.

"And what would you like me to call you, darlin'?" I looked at Detective Flynn. "Becky? Gail?"

"Flynn will do just fine. And if you don't mind horribly, I'll keep calling you fucknuts. At least in my head." She stepped to the door and opened it. "Let's go. I'll have to do some fast talking to get your release paperwork processed, but—"

"I've got it covered, Detective," Smith said. "I might not be able to light a candle magically, but when it comes to paperwork, I'm the greatest wizard you've ever seen."

I stood up and followed Flynn out the door. "Why Agent Smitty, did you just make a joke? Was that an honest-to-Jebus federal agent sense of humor? I thought they removed those when you stepped in the front door of Langley."

"They reissue them when you're assigned to smartass wizards with vampire DNA." Smith shouldered past me through the door as I stood there gaping. *Shit. He knows about Luke. I'm so fucked.*

61

CHAPTER ELEVEN

The ride from the police station to Marlack's office building was a circular exercise in me trying to get information out of Smith and him deflecting my questions into questions about what we knew about Marlack. Which resulted in a whole lot of him not learning fuck-all new, and me not learning fuck-all, period. We pulled up in front of Marlack's high-rise and I was impressed to see that the ruined Suburban was gone and the glass in the front of the building had already been replaced.

"It's an illusion," Smith said as we got out of the car. "No way he could have spun glass out of the air that fast."

"It's not an illusion, Smitty. It's called a fuckton of money. He didn't have to spin glass out of the air. He just called an emergency glass repair place and paid them triple their daytime rate," I said. "There's not a hint of magic anywhere on the outside of the building."

"I assume that changes as we move inside?" Flynn asked.

"Yeah, if you had a magical Geiger counter that thing would blow your eardrums the second we stepped off the elevator. Speaking of which, is there a plan? Because I can speak personally to the fact that just going in and punching him in the face isn't very effective. And there are no SUVs out front to break our fall this time," I said.

"Marlack's not here. We're just searching the place," Smith said.

"With what warrant?" Flynn asked.

"With this one." Smith drew his pistol and rapped on the front door with the butt of it. When the guard came to the door, Smith pointed the gun at his forehead, and the door opened.

"Key card," Smith said to the wide-eyed guard. It was Dennis, the same guard I'd bespelled earlier in the evening.

I reached out, touched his forehead with one finger and whispered, "*Somnus.*" His eyes rolled back in his head and he collapsed in a heap on the floor. "Take a nap, Dennis," I said.

Flynn knelt down and felt around for a pulse. "What did you do to him?" She asked.

"Would you believe a sleep spell?" I asked.

"Why not?" she asked. "How long will he be out?"

"A couple hours. He'll wake up feeling refreshed," I lied. He'd wake up feeling like the worst hangover in the free world, but I was pressed for time.

We rode the elevator up in silence, by the thirtieth floor everyone was humming along to "The Girl from Ipanema." The doors dinged open on Marlack's penthouse office, and again I marveled at how quickly things could get cleaned up if you had more money than God.

"What are we looking for, Smith?" Flynn asked. I wandered the office studying the characters scribed in the protective circles on the floor. If I could get a sense of the origin of Marlack's magic, maybe I could get a hint on how to stop him. I found a few symbols I recognized, then came across a set that looked familiar, but I couldn't quite place them. I pulled out my cell phone and dialed a number.

"Hey, why didn't your cell phone blow up?" Flynn asked.

"Because mine was confiscated, remember? We had to stop by and get my personal effects out of hock before we left the station?" There was no way I was going to fight a badass wizard in the jail slippers they'd put me in after they confiscated my Doc Martens. I listened to the phone ring several times, then a familiar voice came on the line.

"What do you want, Quincy, I am getting ready for bed," Uncle Luke said. He sounded grumpy. I must have interrupted his bedtime snack. I just hoped whoever he was munching on didn't bleed out.

"I was calling for Renny, Uncle Luke. That's why I called his phone."

"You call my Renfield, I decide if he can answer." I knew I should have waited another ten minutes for sunrise, but I decided time was of the essence. Put another check mark on Quincy's List of Bad Decisions.

"Sorry about that, Uncle. But I need to talk to Renny. I need him to research some symbols for me."

"Get your own Renfield. Mine's busy."

"No he's not. He's probably just standing there waiting for you to hang up the phone and go to sleep so he can take your nightcap away and give her a cookie and glass of orange juice." I could almost hear Luke look around the room, realize I was right, and hand the phone to Renny.

"Mr. Quincy, what can I do for you?" Renny's voice was crisp, not at all like someone who was a thrall to a vampire and got kept up to all hours of the night dealing with my uncle and then run ragged all day cleaning up my messes and managing Luke's business interests. I decided to continue to ignore the exhaustion he must be dealing with and just keep being the inconsiderate ass my uncle raised me to be.

"I need some help, Ren. I've got some symbols here that I know are mystical, but I don't know where they're from. If I could find their origin, I might be able to inflict serious carnage upon a very bad man. Do you have time to help a brother out?"

"Does this have anything to do with the unpleasant situation the other night that left a young girl dead and her family's home burned to the ground?"

"If I had anything to do with anything like that, which I'm not saying I did, then this would directly lead to me beating the ever-loving shit out of the man responsible," I said, keeping an eye on both Detective Flynn and Agent Smith as I fenced with Renny. Normally I would have dispensed with all the bullshit, but I still saw a greater than zero chance of one or both of them trying to put me in jail for a very long time.

"Send me the images. I'll commence to research the moment I have dispensed with my duties here," Renny promised.

"Thanks, Ren." I hung up the phone and texted the pictures to Renny, then walked over to where Smith and Flynn were poking around a large desk and bookcase at one end of the room. I walked over to join them and sat on the edge of the desk.

"What did your uncle's man have to say?" Smith asked.

"That's a little annoying, you know?" I shot back.

"What, the whole bit where I know who you're talking to and everything about you and you know nothing about me?"

"Yeah, that."

"Too bad. Now what did Renfield know?"

"Nothing yet. He'll do some research and let us know. You find anything in his files?"

"Nothing," Flynn said. "It's way too clean for any legit businessman. There's not even a receipt for a strip club or any record of his pulling even a minor tax dodge. It's perfect. That's how you know he's dirty."

"So where do we go from here?" I looked at Smith.

"Until we hear back from your guy, we're done. We knew this wasn't a case we'd make in the material plane. It's on you to find something on Marlack."

"Why do I need anything on him? He admitted to me that he summons demons. He admitted that he lets the demons have their way with innocent girls. What more do I need?" I might have raised my voice. I might also have stood up and waved my arms a little. There might have been a little glow around my fingers that made Smith pull back a little.

"What else do you need? You need a way to beat him. Or did you forget the bit about being thrown out a window the last time you tried to go toe-to-toe with this guy? I don't give a shit about evidence. I haven't been looking for proof, because this motherfucker's never going to trial. I've been looking for a way to kill him, or at least send him to Hell where he belongs."

"What the actual fuck are you saying, Smith? We're not arresting Marlack?" Flynn put herself right between me and Smith, and she was tall enough to get right up in his face. Not so much me, I'm pretty tall.

"Arrest him? Where have you been, Detective? Do you think that your jail could hold Harker here for a second longer than he wanted to let you? Then what good do you think it's going to do against the guy that kicked his ass?" Smith didn't back down an inch. I'm not sure he knew how.

"Could we just stop going on about him kicking my ass? Just for a minute. Because, you know, I'm going to have to go do it again. And I'd like to have one tiny shred of confidence left, if it's quite all right with you two," I said.

"So due process is out the window?" Flynn asked, still nose to nose with Smith.

"Due process isn't even in the same zip code, sweetheart."

That's when it happened. I'd been waiting for the tragic slip for a couple hours. It's the same mistake men over fifty with crew cuts always make with really smart women in their early thirties. They can hold it in for a while, but eventually there's a misplaced "sweetheart" or "darling" or, when it gets really good, a "cupcake."

Flynn decked him. Smith was a solid-looking man, a good two hundred pounds and a hair under six feet tall, and it looked from the bulges in his cheap government suit that had some muscles under that jacket. It didn't help. Flynn uncorked a right hook that came from her knees, and she's a tall chick. At five-ten or so and probably one-eighty, she was no wilting lily. Flynn looked like she worked out, and from the way Smith's head rocked back, she had a hell of a punch. She caught him on the point of the jaw and he dropped to one knee, reaching out for the edge of the desk to keep from going all the way down.

"Let's be crystal fucking clear about one thing, Smith. This might be your show, and we might play by your rules, but I'm nobody's fucking sweetheart. I am a gold-shield detective, a veteran of the US Marine Corps, a marathon runner, a sharpshooter, a certified pilot and a black belt in three different martial arts. If you need backup, I'm your girl. If you need somebody to patronize, look elsewhere."

"Sorry about that, sunshine." Smith shot her a sideways grin from his knee. "Sometimes my prejudices slip out. I'll try to keep my chauvinism in check if you promise not to hit me every time I mess up." He reached up, and Flynn grabbed his hand and pulled him to his feet.

I cleared my throat. "If you two have decided who has the bigger dick, and my money's on Rebecca Gail, I've got news from Renfield." I waggled my phone at them.

"What have you got?" Smith asked.

"Renfield says that the symbols on the floor indicate an alliance with Gressil, a prince of Thrones, sort of a colonel in the army of Hell," I said.

"Does that help us?" Flynn asked.

"Yeah, it tells us who Marlack is working with, and I know how to use that. But it's not going to be pretty, and it's going to be really dangerous. You two might not want to be around for the next part."

"I'm not letting you out of my sight, Harker, so you can get that idea out of your head." Flynn turned the same look on me she'd just used on Smith. The biggest difference was, I didn't care.

"Fine. Suit yourself. But I'm not going to have time to look out for you two, so I'd suggest when we get there I draw you a circle and you stay in it, no matter what."

Flynn opened her mouth to argue, but Smith touched her on the arm. He gave her a little shoulder shrug, and she let it go.

"Great," I said. "Now let's go. We've got to get to Marlack's house before sunrise, and I still have a stop to make."

"What's the stop?" Smith asked as we walked toward the elevator.

"24-hour grocery. I need a late-night butcher who has plenty of pig's blood around."

"Why does he even bother asking?" Flynn muttered under her breath as she stomped off toward the elevator. I don't think she'd gotten the memo on the enhanced vampirish senses yet.

CHAPTER TWELVE

We pulled up in front of Marlack's house in Smith's Government Issue black sedan with blackwall tires. He wouldn't let me get out at paint "FED" on the hood in Day-Glo yellow, no matter how obvious he was being with his choice of vehicle. I know, I asked several times. Smith rolled down his window at the squawk box by the gate, but I leaned forward between the front seats, pointed at the closed wrought iron gate and said, "*Lane patescit.*"

A few sparks sputtered out from the control box to the left of the squawk box, but I wasn't planning on Marlack being around long enough to care. We drove through and up the long circular drive to the front steps. I got out of the car and walked around to the trunk. Smith popped the latch and I dug out two pints of pig's blood, four wax pillar candles, a stack of porno mags big enough to keep a varsity football team occupied for a month, and a small box of sidewalk chalk.

"Keep the dogs from fucking up my circle, will you?" I asked Detective Flynn as she got out of the car.

"What dogs—" She started, then drew her sidearm as four SWAT team rejects with MP-5s and Dobermans came out of the house and leveled their weapons at the three of us. I ignored them and went about my business drawing a circle on the driveway and reinforcing it with pig's blood. Smith had his badge in one hand and a Smith & Wesson pistol in the other, so I decided the security goons were pretty unlikely to interfere.

At the cardinal points of the circle I took out my pocketknife and blended a little of my blood with the pig's and placed a candle to lock the circle in this dimension. I lit the candles walking widdershins while murmuring an incantation I learned from a voodoo priestess in Charleston. She taught me a lot of things about magic, and the different ways to use bodily fluids in conjuring, and my left hamstring still twinges a little when I think of her. But I always smile.

Once I had the candles lit and the circle invoked, I stepped out and placed the porno mags in the center of the circle. Then I raised both hands to the sky and said, "Glory, if you've still got any juice with the Big Guy, I'm gonna need a fuckton of forgiveness after this one." Then I focused my will and shouted, *"Asmodeus, conjure te!"*

Nothing happened.

I did it again, this time adding a few drops of my blood splattered into the circle as I summoned Asmodeus.

Still nothing.

The third time I shouted the invocation I didn't stop with Latin. I moved into French, German, Italian, Spanish and finally finished by slicing another gash across my palm, flinging a good tablespoon of my blood into the circle and shouting "Asmodeus, you horny motherfucker, get your three-peckered ass up here and take my goddamned offering, you putrid bucket of herpes!"

"That's my boy." A sibilant voice issued from a cloud of crimson smoke that billowed into existence in the center of the circle. "Hello, Quincy."

"Hello, Asmodeus."

"It's always so good to see you. You're looking well."

"You look like someone lit a bloody fart."

He laughed. That was a good sign. I tried to keep the demonkind amused, or at least off-kilter. If you let them get their feet under themselves, you're fucked. "Quincy Harker, you know I love the women of your plane, but why are these only photographs? What kind of weak-assed shit is this?"

"This isn't a social call, Az. You've got a problem."

"I'm a Prince of the Seraphim condemned to Hell for all eternity, never to see the face of my Lord again and to spend the rest of my days licking the ass of that fuckup Lucifer. I've got more problems than you've got blood cells, vampling. What is it this time?"

"Gressil," I said simply.

"That idiot? He could fuck up a wet dream, I'll give you that, but he's more of an annoyance than anything."

"He's building an army. He wants your spot." I watched the smoke carefully. If it stayed red, Az was interested. If it turned black, he was pissed. Any other color, and he already knew about Gressil's treachery and I'd wasted two pints of pig blood and four perfectly good candles.

The red darkened slightly. "Talk," Asmodeus said.

"He's been working with a human sorcerer, Jacob Marlack, to send little demons through and breed here on earth. Only one reason he'd be making more demons where you couldn't see them. He's coming after you." There was another reason, but Asmodeus was too proud to realize it. You see, most demons are pretty stupid. They like to eat, fuck and kill, not necessarily in that order. Marlack was giving these baby demons a chance to do all three, and they got to stick around our plane for a little while afterwards and kill a lot of brown people. A bonus for any demon that didn't think too far down the "What's in it for this guy?" path.

"That fucking asshole. I knew he'd been spending a lot of time with his pet human the past hundred years or so, but I didn't think there was anything more to it than some death and debauchery. I should have known he was working another angle. Motherfucker!" The smoke was black now, so I made my play.

"Well, Az, tonight's your lucky night. Guess whose front stoop I summoned you onto?" I waved my hand at the mansion in front of me.

"What's your piece of this, Harker? You don't do shit out of the goodness of your heart, especially not for my kind."

"He hurt a little girl. I don't like that. I want to see him suffer, and he kicked my ass when I tried to take him out."

"So you want me to be your enforcer?"

"I want you to put your lieutenant in his place. Best way to do that is to take out his pet wizard. Solve my problem, solve yours."

"What do I get out of the deal?" Az asked. The smoke was back to red now, but there were enough flashes of black throughout his form that I knew I still had him. Asmodeus didn't get to be a Prince of Hell by being forgiving of treachery.

"You get to kill the wizard and anybody left inside the building two minutes from now." I sent a raised eyebrow at the security guards, who had frozen in place as soon as the demon summoning started. Smart guys, they didn't need to end up dead. One turned around and ran inside while the other three bolted around the right side of the house, taking the Dobermans with him. They were less concerned with their guns than the dogs, because their rifles clattered to the porch in their wake.

"And what's to keep me from just breaking your little circle and eating your soul right now?" Az asked.

"This," I said. I opened my shirt and showed him the medallion hanging around my neck. He saw it, and a flash of blue shot through the red smoke.

"Where the fuck did you get one of those?" the demon asked.

"Not on the list of shit I feel like sharing with you, Az. Now do we have a deal?"

"I will enter the house and kill Jacob Marlack. I will also kill anyone still inside the house after I enter."

"Then?" I prodded.

"Then I will return to Hell." He would be pulled back to Hell at sunrise anyway, because the transition between day and night broke all summonings, but I wanted to make sure he didn't linger a second longer than it took him to finish his mayhem inside the house.

"And you will harm no one that is not within the walls of the main house."

"And I will harm no one not inside the main house."

"Then you are free to hunt, demon." I reached out with a toe and scrubbed a break in the circle, setting the Prince of Hell loose on the earth. Asmodeus took on what I've always thought of as his fighting form when he stepped out of the circle. He had long legs that ended in hooves, red skin, arms that hung almost to his knees and ended in wicked claws, and a narrow mouth full of long pointed teeth. He turned his black, pupilless eyes on me and smiled.

"One day we're going to dance like this and I'm going to decide that it will be worth the punishment of Lucifer to break our covenant, Harker. That will be the day I wear your intestines for a necklace as I face my judgment."

"That will be the day I give you an enema with holy water and fuck you in the ass with a dildo made from the true cross, you nasty bastard. Now go kill that motherfucker."

Asmodeus gave me a grin that made my blood freeze and said, "We'll see, Harker. One day we'll see." Then he turned and strode into the house, kicking the double doors in with one huge hoof.

As soon as he was out of sight, I slumped against the car and reached in my pocket for a bottle of Wild Turkey from one of my other stops. I knocked off about a third of it in one slug, then held it out to Smith, who took a long pull and passed it over to Flynn. She shook her head and handed it back to me. I screwed the cap back on and put it away, still leaning against the car.

"Was that a real demon?" Flynn asked. She was staring at me, but hadn't come any closer.

"As real as your..." I let it go. I know I'm tired and terrified when I can't even make a smartass remark about a cop's boobs.

"Yeah, it was real," I said.

"That's fucked up," she said, staring into the house. We kept hearing random crashing from the house, but I could tell that Az hadn't found Marlack yet. Then the light show started, and I knew it was just a matter of time.

"Fucked up is my life, sweetheart." I took another pull off my bottle and offered it to her again. This time she took a slash.

"Like I told him, I'm nobody's goddamn sweetheart." She held the bottle out to me, then the first scream rang out from inside the house. It was a high-pitched thing, like an animal being tortured, and it went on far too long. Flynn took another drink of whiskey and handed the bottle back to me. I finished it off, then tossed the empty into the bushes by the porch.

"Aren't you worried about fingerprints?" Flynn asked.

"Mine aren't on record anywhere," I said.

"Bullshit. As many times as I've booked you, your prints are—"

"Mysteriously missing from your system, Detective," Smith said.

"I think I hate you both," Flynn replied.

"That's the safer sentiment," I said. Smith nodded. The screams from inside the house stopped, and a couple of minutes later Asmodeus walked out, picking his teeth with a claw.

"My work here is done, Harker. Are you sure you don't have anyone else you want me to kill?" the demon asked.

"That's a long list, Az. And I don't think all the Unholy Host could get to my whole list by sunrise. Good night, and good luck with Gressil."

"That fuckwit needs the luck. He's going to be spinning coals in the lowest level of the pit for the next five thousand years." Az stepped into the circle, shifted back to smoke, then billowed out of existence. I blew out the candle and scuffed another few bits of the circle out of existence, just for good measure.

"You got this?" I asked Smith. "I'm fucking beat."

"What, you're just going to leave? I thought you wanted justice for that little girl," Flynn asked.

"I got it. Marlack's dead. And just like I expected, it didn't bring Kayleigh back. At best it erased a little of the dark from my soul, but I probably put as much black on it by consorting with Asmodeus as I took off by bringing that cocksucker to justice."

"And what about his kid? I thought that was important to you?" Flynn kept poking.

"Tomorrow morning your cyber division is going to get an anonymous link in their email pointing them to a backdoor onto the Omega Sig server. That server will have video files on it of several high-ranking fraternity members, including young Master Marlack, forcing themselves on young women. Some will be students at the university, some will still be in high school. That should take care of his ass."

"When did you set that up?" Flynn asked.

"When I talked to Renny on the phone tonight."

"Your uncle's butler is a hacker?" Smith asked. It had taken me all night, but I'd finally managed to surprise the fed.

"A Renfield is a lot more than a butler. He's my uncle's daytime eyes and ears and business partner. And yeah, this one's a CIA-level hacker. Now can I do like the book says and go the fuck to sleep?"

"Get in, I'll drive you home," Smith said.

I was snoring in the back seat before we pulled out of the driveway, dreams of little girls walking through the gates of Heaven dancing in my head.

PART II
STRAIGHT TO HELL

CHAPTER ONE

"I don't get why I'm stuck with the babysitting detail. I'm a fucking gold shield, for God's sake, I don't do babysitting!" The gold shield in question was Detective Rebecca Gail Flynn, currently sitting on my couch bitching about a new assignment from her boss, Agent John Smith of the Department of Homeland Security. Flynn had shown up on my doorstep unannounced about half an hour before bearing a twelve-pack of OMB Copper and a bad attitude. Since then she'd been sitting on my couch consuming one of those things and sharing the other pretty much nonstop.

"You understand that we're not friends, right, Detective?" I asked from my chair. It's not that I had anything going on, I just wanted to make sure any change in our relationship was approved by all the appropriate higher powers and that I was notified beforehand. Rebecca Flynn spent most of the last three years trying to throw me under the Mecklenburg County jail, and I hadn't quite gotten to the "forget" part of "forgive and forget." Frankly, I wasn't laying too heavy odds on forgiveness, either.

Flynn stopped mid-tirade and looked over at me. "Wait, what?"

"You come in here like we're middle-school girlfriends and start pouring your heart out to me. I'm not interested in decorating our Trapper Keepers, I'm not letting you paint my toenails, and I'm sure as fuck not going to braid your hair. You've tried to throw me in jail at least a dozen times in the past dozen months, and now we're supposed to be BFFs just because we work for the same anonymous dickhead? I don't think so, Detective. But thanks for the beer. You can bring that by anytime."

She stood up and stomped to the door. "Well, excuse the ever-loving fuck out of me, Harker. I just wanted to vent for a minute to one of the few people who I can talk to about this shit. I mean, I can't even tell my boyfriend what I'm doing because it's so goddamn classified."

"Why not just tell him?" I asked.

"What?" Flynn looked confused by the question.

"Why not tell him anyway? Who gives a fuck about their security clearances? Jesus, Flynn, don't you ever do anything you're not supposed to do? You want to tell the guy you're banging about our work, tell him about it. Especially if it means you don't interrupt *Monday Night RAW* to bitch to me."

She stomped back to loom over my chair. "You'd like that, wouldn't you? I tell him some classified shit and get him and me both fucking disappeared to Gitmo or Area 51 or some other place that doesn't even officially exist. Then you wouldn't have to deal with me anymore."

"I don't mind dealing with you."

"You just said..."

"I said we aren't friends. We're not. Friends hang out. Friends check up on each other. Friends give a little more of a fuck than I'm really capable of giving, and certainly more than you give about me. But that doesn't mean I don't like you. I just want you to know where we stand. You know, so when you eventually succumb to the inevitable sexual tension and decide to jump me." I took a long pull off my beer and waited for the explosion.

I didn't have to wait long. "What the actual fuck are you talking about? The inevitable sexual tension? Are you that fucking high on yourself?"

"I'm a pretty good-looking guy. You're a very attractive woman. We face intense situations full of adrenaline and endorphins and emotion. That's the kind of shit that gets all fraught and stuff. So, you know, if you ever just want to tear your clothes off and throw yourself at me, I want you to know that I'm here for you." I finished off my beer and pulled another from the box on the coffee table.

Flynn stood there for a minute, just staring down at me. Her mouth opened, then closed, then opened, then closed. I was just about to make a remark about fish when she finally looked me straight in the eyes and fell onto the couch laughing. "Holy shit, Harker, I thought you were serious there for a minute."

"I meant every word," I said, deadpan.

Flynn froze in mid-guffaw, stared at me, then collapsed into laughter again. "You asshole," she said when she finally got her breath back. She sat up on the couch wiping tears from her eyes and took another beer. We clinked bottles together and she sat back. "Oh fuck, I needed a good laugh."

"And I needed you to quit bitching, so let's call this a win-win. Now about that boyfriend?"

"What about him?" Flynn asked.

"Tell me about him. You never mentioned a boyfriend before."

"I never mentioned anything before, Harker. I was always arresting you," she reminded me.

"And doing a terrible job of it, by the way. What was your record, twenty arrests and nothing ever even made it to trial?" It helps when all the crimes you commit are against monsters that usually turn to ash or slime when they're killed. And all those breaking and entering charges were really hard to prove when the perpetrator always wears gloves. Good thing for me they were in fashion when I was coming up.

"Fuck you." But she grinned when she said it this time. Used to be she would draw a weapon when she told me to fuck off. I considered this an improvement.

"So?" I asked.

"So what?"

"So what about your boyfriend?"

"Why do you want to know?" Flynn grinned at me and I knew we'd moved from hanging out to flirting. I was okay with that. Flynn was a good-looking woman, and as long as she had someone to go home to, I could probably keep my baser instincts at bay.

"I want to know what kind of competition I'm facing." I gave her my best rakish grin. Since I learned about rakish grins when rakes were still a thing, my rakish grin is pretty good.

"He's an EMT. His name is Roger. He's tall, dark and handsome, and he's absolutely crazy about me."

"So he's a good person, good-looking, and probably has a solid, working-class, pull himself up by his bootstraps attitude. I think I hate him already. Show me a picture."

"Why? If you hate him, why should I show you a picture?"

"So I can see if he really is better looking than me, then I'll know I hate him."

She pulled out her phone and pressed a couple of places on the screen, then swiped at a couple of other things and handed it to me. He was a very good-looking man, milk chocolate skin, short cropped hair, big smile full of perfect teeth, lots of muscles and his arm around Flynn in that relaxed manner that only the exceptionally handsome have, when they know they have nothing to fear from mere mortals.

"You're right, he's better looking than me. I definitely hate him."

"Are we friends now, Harker? You hate my boyfriend, I brought you beer, and you listened to me bitch about work. I think that makes us friends." Her dark eyes told me she was enjoying the game, but I knew better than to push my luck. That way lay madness.

"Nope, still just adversaries thrown together by the heat of battle. That makes the sexual tension better. That way, when we eventually succumb to the inevitable and screw each other's brains out in a night of torrid passion, probably right after surviving some completely implausible terrorist attack or serial killer kidnapping, we can wake up not only to our personal recriminations but to millions of angry emails to our producers about how everyone in the universe feels cheated by our rushing through the bumping of uglies instead of falling slowly like that cheesy movie *Once*."

"I liked that movie!" Flynn protested.

"Proving, without any physical exploration whatsoever, that you do indeed, have a vagina."

"You're fucking incorrigible."

"And you're fucking Chocolate Superman."

"I'm telling him you called him that. He'll probably kick your ass."

"He'll probably love it and want to give me a half-assed bro hug when we finally meet. Then we can talk about the Panthers draft and how they always need another receiver or a better o-line, and I'll pretend that I don't hate him."

"You don't hate him." She turned suddenly serious in that way women have when you know you're tap-dancing drunk through a minefield. Fortunately for me, I ran out of fucks to give long before Detective Flynn was born. But I let her off easy this time.

"I don't hate him, Becks. I don't even fucking know the guy."

"What did you call me?" She'd gone from casually flirting, to defending her man, to strangely concerned in a span of seconds.

"I called you Becks. I figured since we're just one step away from sharing mani/pedis, I could come off the formality a little and maybe not always refer to you as Detective Flynn." I looked at her, and she just stared back for a long minute before she replied.

"No, it's fine, it's just...my father used to call me Becks. Nobody's called me that since he died. It just...took me by surprise, I guess."

Fuck. I knew that. Well, I guess my subconscious knew that. I knew Flynn's father. Sergeant Paul Flynn, CMPD, the reason little Rebecca Gail put away her dolls at the age of eight and instead picked up a set of toy guns and a plastic nightstick and proceeded to beat the shit out of every boy in the neighborhood that dared play Cops & Robbers with her. Flynn the elder was shot and killed while pursuing a mugger. At least that was the official story.

In reality, Paul Flynn stumbled on a young vampire having a snack in one of the few alleys downtown Charlotte had to offer, and when he stepped into the alley to confront what he thought was a sexual assault in progress, the newborn turned on him. Baby vamps are dangerous—they haven't yet developed much in the way of impulse control, and this one had been a crack addict before she was turned, so it wasn't exactly of sound mind in the first place. She never should have been turned, and I'd been splitting my time between hunting down *les enfant terrible* and its maker, and I stumbled into the alley just a few seconds too late for Officer Flynn.

Killing the newborn vamp was child's play for me. I took its head with a katana I carried everywhere at the time, due to a ridiculous fascination with the *Highlander* TV show and a desire to have hair like Adrian Paul. But Flynn was down, his chest torn open by the vamp. I didn't have to worry about him coming back turned—there's more to it than just being ripped apart by a vampire, but I felt responsible for his death. If I had focused on the fledgling first, then the maker, I probably could have saved him.

I sat by him in the alley as the life fled his eyes and listened to him talk about his little girl, his pride and joy. He told me to tell his daughter he loved her, to tell "Becks" that he was proud of her, then he asked me to watch out for her. If I'd know what a pain in the ass she was going to grow up to be, I never would have agreed to it. But I did, and as her father bled out in my arms in an alley, Rebecca Gail Flynn and I were tied together for the rest of her life. And all that led in a convoluted way to her sitting on my couch talking about her boyfriend and me pretending I had no interest in seducing a woman a century or more my junior.

I shook my head and tried to focus on the present. *Her dad—go with that.* "Oh yeah, and he died, right? Sorry, I won't call you that again."

CHAPTER TWO

The drive to the college took about twenty minutes, and then almost that long looking for someplace to park where Flynn's cop car wouldn't stand out like a neon sign screaming "PO-PO HERE." We finally just stuck the blackwalled cockblock on wheels in a garage and took up a position on a bench outside the kid's apartment.

"You know us sitting out here means that at some point you're going to have to make out with me," I said, leaning back and lacing my fingers behind my head.

"You remember what the world was like before my grandfather was born. I don't think so," Flynn shot back, pulling out her phone. She pressed a few buttons and I heard Smith answer. "We're here," Flynn said.

"How did you get him to come with you?" I heard Smith ask.

"I mentioned coeds and he jumped at the chance."

"Good one. All right, I'm leaving now. You two have this 'til dawn?"

"No problem." Flynn slipped her phone into her pocket and leaned back on the bench, mimicking my posture and letting out a contented sigh.

"Nobody likes a smartass, Detective," I said.

"But you're a smartass, Harker."

"And nobody likes me, do they?"

"Oh don't be such a baby. So I played you a little, what's the big deal? At least we got a couple beers before we had to go on stakeout."

"Yeah, about that. I gotta piss. I'll be back in a minute." I walked around behind a tree and relieved myself, opening up my Sight in the process.

Through my third eye, the whole area surrounding the apartment complex lit up like a magical Christmas tree. I stepped back, almost splashing my shoes, and quickly closed down my Sight.

I walked back to the bench and sat down. "Somebody has laid some serious wards around this place. Whoever is looking out for this kid has some heavy juice at their disposal."

"Anything look out of place?" Flynn asked.

"No, everything looks hunky-dory. Wake me up if that changes." I turned sideways on the bench and laid my head down in her lap, preparing to go to sleep. She gave my shoulder a shove and dumped me onto the grass.

"Get up, dipshit. We're on duty."

"Correction, *you're* on duty. I'm helping out a friend. I'm not getting paid for this shit, and while there are plenty of things I'm happy to do in the company of a beautiful woman at this hour of night that don't include sleeping, watching some over-privileged African prince sleep is not on the list. Besides, I'll hear anything out of the ordinary and wake up faster than you can say 'what the fuck is that?'"

"I don't know. I can...what the fuck is that?"

"That wasn't very fast," I replied.

"No, really. What the fuck *is* that?" She pointed to the roof of the complex. I followed her arm with my gaze and saw what looked like a man running the roof beam of the apartment complex. I opened my Sight and saw nothing out of the ordinary. Whatever his intentions, he was human.

"That's a dude. He's nimble as fuck, but he's human. That makes him your department." I try not to fight humans any more than is absolutely necessary. I tend to break them. Permanently.

Flynn was already on her feet and headed to the central stairwell in the apartment building. It was one of those twisting jobs with a pair of apartments separated by the staircase on each floor, so she had a bunch of little flights of stairs to get to the kid's third-floor doorway. She made it just about the same time as the ninja-garbed attacker swung down off the roof and onto the landing. I sat on the bench watching.

"You gonna help her?" came a voice from beside me.

"If she needs it. You bring popcorn?" I turned to see Glory, my guardian angel, sitting beside me.

"You're terrible. I thank the Father every day that you're not my partner."

"I'm worse, sweetcheeks. I'm your responsibility."

"That's the truth," the angel muttered. I could tell that I had an effect on the angel's spiritual well-being because I'm pretty sure I have the only guardian angel in history that mutters, grumbles and bitches this much.

"What's up, Glory? You didn't just come down here to admire the form of Detective Flynn's posterior as she kicks that ninja dude's ass. Or did you? I've always wondered about the sexual preferences of angels."

"We're neuter, Q, we don't have sexual preferences."

"No wonder you're so fucking boring."

"Thanks, Q. Love you, too. Now are you going to help her, or what?" Glory pointed up at the landing, where Flynn had the first ninja down and handcuffed but didn't see the second one sneaking up behind her with a drawn knife.

"Hey, Flynn!" I yelled. "Watch your six!" She didn't look, just lashed out with a mule kick that caught the second ninja in the gut and dropped him like a sack of potatoes. I was pretty sure I heard the *thunk* of his head hitting concrete even from fifty yards away.

"That wasn't exactly what I had in mind, Q," Glory said.

"Yeah, but you're a better person than me."

"I'm not even a person."

"But I set the bar pretty goddamn low. So what brings you down here slumming? It's not just to bust my balls about not helping Flynn win a fight she can win on her own, so spill it."

I looked at Glory, and she looked away from me. A lot of people won't meet my eyes, either because I make them uncomfortable or because they've heard stories about Uncle Luke bespelling people and are afraid I'll put the whammy on them. Glory never looks me in the eye because she says they really are windows to the soul, and she's a little scared of what she sees there.

"Spill it, Glory," I prodded.

"This kid? The one you've been assigned to protect?"

"Yeah? What about him?"

"He's the real thing."

"What real thing?" I asked. Glory just sat there. "Wait, you mean he's really the Lion of Judah? Like, descended directly from David and everything? Like, can open the seals that bring about the end of the world?"

"Yeah, like all that. He's the real deal, Q, so you might want to pay attention to your partner." I looked over to Flynn, who was now tangling with a third ninja, and this one looked like he might have the edge on her in one-on-one combat. I turned back to Glory, but the angel was gone.

"Fuck," I muttered under my breath and started to the apartment at a dead run. The first ninja was up again and had gotten loose from Flynn's handcuffs somehow. I figured I had about six seconds before she was overwhelmed. Good for her I'm a little faster than most people. I made it to the front of the building in three, turning the last dozen yards into big bounding leaps, sending me higher each time. I landed right in front of the building and sprang straight up, easily clearing the railing on the third-floor landing and scaring the shit out of the new ninja, who was about to close with Flynn.

He had a black-bladed tango knife in one hand and wicked curved thing in the other. I didn't waste time sparring with him, just grabbed both wrists and jerked him forward, simultaneously planting my right foot on the ground and sticking my left into his sternum. He came to crashing halt, both shoulders dislocated with an audible *pop*, and I let go of his wrists and kicked him back-ward to fall on top of the second ninja, who was just starting to rise.

I turned to the first ninja, who was advancing barehanded on Flynn, flicking out kicks and punches as he eased in toward her. I drew my Sig from under my arm and put three in his chest over Flynn's shoulder, dropping him instantly. I turned back to the broken ninja and put two in his forehead, then pointed my pistol at the third ninja's face.

"You want to die?" I asked.

He shook his head.

"You gonna talk?" I asked.

He shook his head again.

"That's not the right answer," I said, then shot him in the left thigh. He writhed around on the porch but didn't scream. I had to give him a little credit, he was a dedicated son of a bitch.

"Now you gonna talk?" I asked.

He shook his head again.

"I think you see how this is going to go, don't you?" I asked. He nodded, but I shot him in the left thigh this time. More writhing and flopping, but still no screaming.

This time I pointed the gun at his crotch. "Would you like to reconsider?" I asked.

"Harker, stop!" Flynn said from behind me.

"We need to know who sent these fuckers, Flynn, and I don't know if we have time to ask nicely."

"That's fine, but he's not going to tell you anything."

"I'm pretty sure if I start shooting inches off Mr. Winky here, he's going to get persuaded pretty fucking quick."

"As much as I appreciate the save, Captain Fuckwit, their vocal chords have been severed." She held up the head of the first ninja so I could see the jagged scar across his throat.

"Oh, shit." I remembered hearing something about assassins that would have their tongues or voice boxes removed so they couldn't reveal details about who hired them. "Well, that sucks," I said and shot the third ninja in the forehead.

"What the fuck, Harker?" Flynn asked. "You can't just go around shooting people."

"I didn't. I shot the bad guys. All of them. Now we don't have to shoot anybody else."

"But you can't just kill everyone we run across," Flynn protested.

"Yeah, I kinda can. As a matter of fact, I'm pretty sure that's exactly my job. You see, these guys weren't just bad Jackie Chan movie rejects. They were real ninjas. Assassins. Hired killers. You get the picture? They weren't here to dance, they weren't here to chat, and they sure as fuck weren't here to be reformed. They were here to kill us and take the kid. By the way, have you maybe checked on him since the whole attempted kidnapping thing?"

"I was going to do that as soon as I called for backup," she said. "I thought it might be good to get the dead bodies off his doorstep before we knocked."

"Good call. But call Smith, not the cops. This needs to disappear, not turn into an all-day lovefest downtown." I leaned down and picked up one of the bodies, then tossed it over the rail onto the ground. The dead ninja flopped over onto his face and lay there, looking not much different than me on more than one Friday night. I deposited his friends beside him and motioned to the door.

"You want to do the talking? I ended up with all this new blood on my clothes, so I thought I should disappear for a second." As she stepped to the door, I summoned my will and murmured "*cameleon.*" The air swirled around me, and my vision went a little blurry at the edges as the spell bent light around me and caused me to blend in perfectly with my surroundings. No point scaring the kid, and a blood-covered goon with a pistol on his doorstep at three in the morning is usually cause for alarm.

Flynn rang the bell, then tried the knocker, then the bell again, then the knocker. After a solid couple of minutes, a trembling voice came from inside the apartment. "Fuck off! I've got a gun and a dog! And I've called the cops!"

"Charlotte-Mecklenburg Police, is everything all right in there?" Flynn held her badge up to the peephole. Peepholes are the worst inventions in the modern world for security. It's way too easy just to shoot somebody through one. But Flynn wouldn't do that. Hell, she didn't want me to kill the ninjas, which is kinda like not wanting to step on a cockroach.

"Yeah, we're fine. What happened out there?" The voice seemed a little less shit-scared now, and more curious. And maybe a little stoned.

"Firecrackers," Flynn said. "Can I come in? I have a few questions for you."

"Umm...sure," the voice came, then the sound of several locks being undone. The door opened, and I followed Flynn in right on her heels. My spell kept bending the light around me, but the brightness of the apartment made it a lot harder to stay unnoticed. I took up a position by the door and hoped nobody else came in.

"Are you Wallace Gubegna?" Flynn asked, looking around the apartment. It was your basic college place, decorated in early Spencer's Gifts and stoner chic. A poster of Bob Marley dominated one wall, and the other was taken up by a huge television with an expensive game console and surround sound system. A Salvation Army couch lined one wall, with a montage of landscape photos above the sofa. They were the usual kind of things, sunsets, beach scenes, all blown up and taken from interesting perspectives. I looked at the art, then chuckled as I caught sight of a three-foot high bong sitting on the floor next to the couch. Some things are universal for young men—experimenting with wine, women and drugs was definitely on the menu here. My college experience had been a little different, focusing more on the absinthe and necromancy than the marijuana and cheap sex.

"Yeah, I'm Wally. You a cop?" Wally Gubegna was a good-looking kid of about twenty with dark brown skin, long dreads and an easy smile. He stood about five-ten and weighed maybe a buck sixty soaking wet, so he was a skinny little dude. He never would have stood a chance against those ninjas, not that very many humans would have. He flopped down on the couch and put his feet up on a milk crate that served as a coffee table.

"I am. I'm Detective Flynn with the Charlotte-Mecklenburg Police Department on assignment to Homeland Security. We believe that some people are trying to abduct you. Do you have any idea why?"

"Because I'm the Lion of Judah and can open the seven seals that bring about the apocalypse?" He said it so matter-of-fact, like "it's cold outside" or "I smoke a ridiculous amount of weed," that I almost didn't catch it, but when I did, it was all I could do to hold onto my concealment spell.

"Well…that's certainly one theory," Flynn said. She was rattled but trying to hold it together.

"Oh come on, Agent. Or Detective, or whatever. You take out three assassins on my porch and come in here with a wizard under a masking spell and I'm supposed to think this has something to do with the fact that my second cousin is the President? I'm not in any kind of line of succession, have nothing to do with politics, and frankly have only the slightest interest in ever returning to Ethiopia. So you must be here to either start or stop the end of the world."

CHAPTER THREE

I dropped my spell, since the kid already knew I was there. "Good call, Junior. We're here to make sure you don't go around breaking any seals. Been to the circus lately?" I asked as I stepped into the apartment's kitchen. Silence came from the living room for several seconds, then Wally laughed as he got my "seals" pun. I opened the refrigerator and took out a beer. I popped the top open on the edge of the scarred countertop, the scratches in the Formica evidence that I wasn't the first person to forget a bottle opener in that kitchen. As kitchens go, it was definitely one, and one that belonged to multiple college-aged boys. There was beer in the fridge, along with mustard, a jar of pickles and two pizza boxes of indeterminate age. The dishes in the sink weren't yet sentient, but I'd have to consult Glory on the souls of fungus before I could wash anything with a clear conscience.

I walked back into the den and sat down in what must have been the primo gaming chair. I knew that because I immediately felt a sharp pain in my ass and pulled a PlayStation controller out of the seat. "So yeah, we're here to save the world. Got any idea who wants to wreck it this week?"

"Man, I have no idea, but that shit is getting tired, you know? I thought when I got here, all this Revelation shit would be over, and I could just be me, be Wally for a while. I guess that was too much to ask, huh?"

"It was when you went around throwing out the Lion of Judah line to get laid, you dumb fuck." I turned the chair to face him and got the satisfaction of seeing him blush through his dark complexion when I called him on it.

"Who told you that, man?"

"I was twenty years old once, Wally. I know what it's like."

"Yeah, in 1895," Flynn muttered so low that Wally couldn't hear her. I gave her a look that very clearly told her I could.

"It was just this one chick, man. She seemed cool. We were hanging out over at Boardwalks," he said, naming a local oyster bar that turned into a meat market on the weekends. "We were hanging out and talking philosophy, and that turned into talking religion, and I'm like an agnostic, you know, but I might have mentioned…well, you know."

"I know that your dick might have brought about the end of the world, you little jackass," Flynn grumbled.

"Oh come off it, Flynn. Most of the worst ideas in the world were because of a guy trying to impress a girl. I mean come on, look at the Cuban Missile Crisis. That was all to get Marilyn in the sack again. And let's not even talk about Pearl Harbor. Wally just wanted to get laid. Everybody wants to get laid. It's the fact that he's such a fucking stoner that he can't keep his mouth shut that pisses me off."

Wally stood up and puffed himself up with the righteous indignation that can only be mustered by those under thirty. He stuck one arm out towards the door and said, "I think the two of you should leave. I appreciate your assistance tonight, but I can handle anything that comes to visit by myself. I have a handgun by the bed and a shotgun in the closet."

"That's good, Wally. That's excellent defense against human attackers. *Debilitato*." I reached out and touched him lightly on the forehead and pushed my will at him. He instantly fell to the floor, writhing in pain. "What good is your gun now, jackass? The people coming after you are bad fucking news, and since we took out their Plan A, they're going to have to improvise. That never goes well for the target. *Libertado*." With a word, the spell released and Wally sat up, staying on the floor and putting his back to the sofa.

"Okay, okay, I get it. What do we do?" he asked, once he could speak again.

"We split up and cover the apartment the best we can, hoping that the reinforcements for the bad guys don't arrive before the reinforcements we called in. Agent Flynn stays in here with you and tries to keep you from doing something else stupid, while I wait outside and hope that I don't have to clean up any more of your messes."

"Why are you going out there? Aren't you better off facing them in here?" the kid asked.

"That depends. You got sprinklers in your apartment?"

"I don't think so."

"Then I'd better wait outside. We took out the ninjas without blowing anything up, but I don't have a whole lot of faith in my ability to do that twice in one night."

I stepped close to Flynn and whispered, "Don't let him out of your sight, not even to piss. He's scared enough to go full-on stupid." Then I moved past her and opened the door. "Try not to get anybody killed while I'm out there," I said, then stepped out onto the landing. Smith hadn't shown up with his cleaners yet, so I pulled out my phone to send him a text message. Nothing like trying to get your boss killed texting while driving to liven up a night.

I didn't get a response, so I walked back to the car, wrapped myself in a concealment spell again, and sat down on the hood. It was cold, but not too bad, and I don't suffer from hot or cold nearly as much as normal humans. Nothing stirred in the still night, so I waited patiently for about twenty minutes until Smith drove up in another car that screamed "cop" at the top of its lungs. The only thing more government agent than his car was the man's suit—navy with pinstripes, cheap dress shoes that looked like shit to run in, and a red tie with little blue diamonds on it. With his stick-up-my-ass posture and high and tight haircut, Smith screamed "ex-military government hired thug" louder than Wally's dreadlocks and tie-dye screamed "college stoner." Part of me just wanted to lock the two of them in a padded room for three days with a plate of hash brownies and a bottle of Jose Cuervo, but the rest of me figured that probably would bring about the apocalypse.

Just to make sure I had my quota of stereotypes for the evening, a black SUV pulled up behind Smith's car and a pair of neckless giants got out wearing tactical pants, combat boots and turtlenecks. I slid down the hood of the car and intercepted Smith at the bottom of the stairs.

"Harker," he said as I got close.

"*Aperio*," I said as I fell into step behind Smith. "How did you do that?"

"I heard you."

"Bullshit. Nobody hears me unless I want them to."

"Then I smelled you."

"Also bullshit. I don't wear cologne, I don't use hair products with scent, and even my deodorant is fragrance-free. I'm a stealthy motherfucker, but you just called me out without even trying. What are you, Smith?"

He turned and looked me in the eye from one step up. Smith was a solid man, six foot and slightly north of two hundred pounds, but I'm tall, so he didn't gain much height advantage being a step up on me. "I knew you were there because it is my job to know where you are. It is my job to never be surprised, and to never, ever let anyone or thing get the drop on me. And I am very goddamn good at my job. You want to know what I am, Harker? I'm a grumpy fucking civil servant that got called out of bed to clean up the mess left by a pair of very junior agents who had one job—"

"Watch the junior shit, Smith. Let's not forget that I'm old enough to be your grandfather. And as far as our one job, we did it. Wally's alive. That was the job, right? Not let the kid get killed or kidnapped? Well, we covered that one. There might have been a few more bodies than you like, but at least I piled 'em up nice and neat for your zombies to get rid of. Yeah, recognized them. Gonna take a little more than a turtleneck to hide the death-funk from me.

"So what's the problem, Smith? We kept the kid alive, killed the bad guys, and didn't even get the local constabulary involved. What more did you want out of us?"

Smith actually took a second before he answered, and when he did, it was like talking to a human being instead of a federal agent. "I'm sorry. You're right, you did exactly what I asked you to do, and the Lion is still safe. What does he think is going on?"

"He thinks somebody wants to use him to open the seven seals and bring about the end of the world." I couldn't help myself. I needed the chuckle I got when Smith's jaw dropped open. "Yeah, he knows. He's known since before he came here. And in the 'big fucking surprise' category, he told a girl about his destiny to get laid."

"Fuck me. You're joking." Smith actually face palmed himself right there on the steps.

"I wish. Not the fucking you part, but the joking part. Have you actually met this kid?" I asked. Smith turned and started back up the stairs. I followed. I had more questions, and while stubborn, Smith was still a better option for info than the zombies.

"No. I've read his file, but that's it."

I reached out and grabbed Smith's elbow before he reached for the door. "Does his file say he's a big stoner?"

"No, but who really cares? Everybody in college smokes a little weed."

"I'm not talking a little weed, I'm talking a bong the size of a bazooka. This kid is a major pothead."

"Well, that wasn't in the file, but I don't see how it's going to affect our protection detail."

"Then you've never spent any time with serious stoners. Getting him to take this shit seriously might be an issue."

"He can't be that bad," Smith said, then turned to knock on the door.

"Famous last words," I muttered as the door opened and a cloud of marijuana smoke billowed out.

CHAPTER FOUR

"Nice," I said, walking into the apartment. "You're a cop, Flynn. You couldn't keep this little shithead from blazing up for ten minutes?"

"It's been like half an hour, bro," Wally said from the couch where he sat cross-legged with his bong between his legs and a lighter in his hand. He had the relaxed grin of somebody who's smoking some really good shit. I took a deep breath. It was some really good shit.

I sat down next to Wally and said, "Let me hit that shit." I held out my hand and he put the bong in it. I took the lighter and lit the weed, sucking in a good lungful of smoke. I leaned back, holding the marijuana smoke in my lungs for most of a minute before I let it out in a long breath. Then I reached over and smacked Wally in the back of the head.

"Now stop being a fucking idiot," I said. I stood up and walked to the small kitchen, dumping the last of the weed in the sink and giving the bong a quick rinse.

"What the fuck, man!" Wally was on his feet after me like a deranged spider monkey, and when I turned around to put the bong in the dish strainer, he bumped chests with me.

"What the fuck? You wanna know what the fuck, you fucking little douche?" I slapped him across the face, not hard enough to break the skin, but hard enough to get his attention. "What the fuck is a yard full of dead guys who were trying to kidnap your dumb ass and you're in here burning one like it's a goddamn Dave Matthews concert. What the fuck is a team of highly trained fucking professionals working to save your worthless ass and you not having any more respect than to tell some cheap coed slut that you're the motherfucking Lion of goddamn Judah just to tear off a piece of college tail!"

"But you smoked my weed," he whined.

"I'm the fucking adult in the room, I get to smoke all the fucking weed I want. When you're as old as I am, you can smoke all the weed you want." I didn't mention that he'd have to get to a century and a quarter to be as old as me or that I metabolized marijuana quicker than humans, just like I did all drugs.

"But it was my weed."

"Shut the fuck up."

"Are you children finished?" Smith asked from the door. "Because I have a few questions for Mr. Gubegna, and I'd like to get them answered before we leave."

"Leave?" Wally asked. "I'm not going anywhere. I live here. You assholes can leave anytime."

"Mr. Gubegna, I'm Agent John Smith with the Department of Homeland Security, Paranormal Division. I don't officially exist, nor does the division I'm a part of. Do you understand what that means for you?" Wally shook his head.

"That means that as soon as I stepped out of my car, *you* ceased to exist. With one phone call from me, you're gone. Erased from this world. All records of your birth, education, immunization, junior soccer league, high school prom—all gone. Everyone who ever knew you will forget about you, or they'll disappear too. Now do you understand me?"

Wally nodded, then walked back to the couch and sat down. I felt so bad for him I almost gave him back his bong. I looked at Smith, who had no more expression on his face than ever. That was a seriously scary dude, even to me.

"Now what do you know about being the Lion of Judah?" Smith said.

"It's all bullshit, man. It's some religious shit that my grandma believes in. Something about Cousin Morrie being President, and my uncle David being a true descendant of *that* David, I'm the crossroads for a whole bunch of hereditary lines and stuff. According to Grandma, that makes me the Lion of Judah, and I have the power to bring about the end of the world by opening the seven seals. I can't do any of that shit man, I'm just trying to study architecture and get a job in like New York or San Francisco, yeah, San Francisco, where I can get my medical marijuana card and draw awesome buildings and shit, man."

"That might not be in the cards, Mr. Gubegna. There are some very bad men who very much believe that you really can bring about the end of the world, and they plan on using you to do just that," Smith said. "So you need to come with us until we can make sure there is no threat."

"How you gonna do that, man? You gonna kill me? Because from what I see, that's all your boy here knows how to do." He pointed at me.

"Not true," I protested. "I also bake. I make a molten chocolate soufflé that is out of this world. But I do kill a lot things," I admitted.

"We aren't going to kill you, Mr. Gubegna, but we need to make sure no one can use your abilities, either," Smith said.

I stood up. "This is bullshit, Smith. Are we taking him with us or not?"

"We are. I would like it to be voluntary if possible."

"But you only kinda give a fuck, right?" I asked.

"Pretty much," Smith agreed.

I turned to Wally. "You have sixty seconds. Pack a bag. Don't forget underwear and deodorant. Leave the weed. If you're not back out here in one minute, I'm going to come into your bedroom, knock you unconscious and carry you to Agent Smith's car. If you try to climb out the window, the agent on the ground out back will knock you unconscious and carry you to Agent Smith's car. So within the next three minutes, you will be in that car and you will be leaving this apartment. Your decision is whether or not you're awake to see it, and if you remember clean underwear. Do I make myself absolutely clear?"

"I'm not going." He got right up in my face and glared at me with a faceful of twenty-something bravado.

I raised one eyebrow and said, "Forty-five seconds."

"I said I'm not fucking going, you fucking pig!" A little drop of spit flew from his lips and landed on my cheek just below my right eye.

I reached up, wiped the spittle from my face and said, "Thirty seconds."

Wally stood there for about another ten seconds, then he turned and stomped into his room. I heard a closet door open and close, then listened to drawers open and close for a minute or so. After a little over a minute, Wally came back out, tennis shoes on and a windbreaker on over his Grateful Dead t-shirt.

"Did you remember deodorant?" I asked.

"Yes, asshole."

"Underpants?"

"Fuck you."

I slapped him again. Still not hard by my standards, but my patience was wearing thin, so it probably came across a little harder than I expected. Either way, it spun Wally around and dropped him to the floor.

"The fuck, man!" He bounced back up, fists clenched at his sides.

"Bad idea, son. I'm the one that kills things, remember? Now get your fucking bag and get in the car. And if you decide to open your goddamn mouth to me again, try not say anything that's going to make me want to knock your punk ass out, okay?"

"Whatever," Wally grumbled as he pushed his way past me to the door.

I turned to follow, but Flynn put a hand on my arm. I held back and let Smith leave first. "What was all that about?" she asked.

"I was getting bored. This is where we were going to end up anyway, with the little shit going with us and being all pissed off about it. I just moved up our timetable by about half an hour."

"What aren't you telling me?"

"Lots of things, Detective, some of which I'll never divulge except under torture. Feel free to tie me up sometime and find out." I grinned at her, and Flynn rolled her eyes.

"I mean what aren't you telling me right now?"

"That whoever sent those ninjas has had plenty of time to realize they aren't coming back and move on to Plan B. And I'd like to have the kid secured long before Plan B gets here."

That's when the first explosion came from the apartment's parking lot. I pushed past Flynn to the door, where I saw the SUV that carried Smith's zombie goons burning merrily away in the parking lot.

"Fuck. Plan B's here," I said.

CHAPTER FIVE

I vaulted the balcony railing, landing in a crouch just past a puddle of blood left behind from the zombie cleanup crew. That's a problem with certain flavors of undead—their vision goes to shit quick, so they don't always pick up on all the little details that make the difference between a place really being cleaned up and just having all the corpses and major organs swept under the rug.

I didn't have much time to worry about the mess the zombies left behind because Smith's car slid to a stop right behind the burning mass of metal and glass that used to be a Suburban. Both back doors flew open and Smith and Wally scrambled out. Wally stood stock-still beside the car, making a prime target of himself in the firelight, but Smith hit the ground running, sprinting around the car and grabbing the stunned stoner around the waist. Smith's driver got out of the car and moved to the trunk, which opened at the push of a button. Never wasting a movement, the agent reached into the trunk and slipped on a bulletproof vest, then slapped a Velcro holster with a pistol onto his chest and came back up with an AR-15 in hand. He walked backward toward the apartment, sweeping the rifle right to left in a classic cover pattern.

I sprinted past him, using my enhanced strength to up my speed way past human levels, and shouted, "More guns in the trunk?" as I passed him.

"Yeah, another AR and a shotgun," he yelled back, then squeezed off a short burst of automatic fire down the driveway. I got to the car and hung the rifle over one shoulder on its sling, then grabbed the shotgun. I grabbed a black case that looked to be full of spare AR mags and turned to make my way back to the apartment before whatever blew up the SUV made its debut.

I wasn't fast enough. Not by half. I got about two steps from the car when a red dragon the size of a city bus dropped out of the sky and wreathed the driver in a stream of fire. He was engulfed in seconds and dead on the ground heartbeats later. I ran past the dragon, scooped Wally up over a shoulder, and jumped from the ground to the balcony.

"Take cover!" I shouted back to Smith, then I flung the door open to Wally's apartment and shoved him inside. "If you come out before I come get you, you fucking deserve every bad thing that happens to you." I slammed the door in his face and hopped back to the ground.

I found Smith taking cover under the lowest stairwell, rifle poking through the space between steps, and plinking at the dragon. "That's not going to do anything," I said.

"I can see that, smartass. Any suggestions?" Smith growled.

"Yeah, I just need you to get his attention so I can find the little bastard," I replied.

"What little bastard? That thing is huge!"

"That's an illusion. There's no such thing as dragons," I said.

"And you know this how, exactly? If there's anything I've learned, it's that there's some weird shit in this world."

"Oh there's plenty of weird shit, Smitty, but if there were dragons, I'd know."

"Oh?"

"For fuck's sake, do we have to do this now? Uncle Luke wanted one for a pet, so we spent forty fucking years combing Europe and Asia for a goddamn dragon, okay? There's no such thing as a motherfucking dragon! But there are fucking illusionists, and I hate fucking illusionists."

I cast a camouflage glamour on myself and stepped out from under the steps. Smith ran out, firing at the dragon with every step. The beast turned its attention toward him, and it belched out a huge fireball that Smith managed to avoid but took out all the bushes in front of the apartment building. Just before the fireball, I saw a little shimmer of light off to one side of the driveway and opened my Sight.

"Gotcha, fuckwad," I murmured as the streams of magic forming the fireball and illusory dragon jumped into view, all streaming back to a point about four feet off the ground and about a hundred yards in front of me. I unslung the AR from my shoulder and knelt down, putting my eye to the scope. There was still nothing visible to my naked eye, so I started with a short burst, sweeping side-to-side and hoping to hit something I didn't like.

There's something to be said for shooting things—even if you don't hit what you're aiming at, usually just getting close will annoy or distract somebody enough that they can't cast delicate magic, like, say, maintaining the illusion of giant red dragon floating through North Carolina. I spun off the last of my magazine in the general direction of the spellcaster, and the dragon flickered out of existence. So did the fireball, and suddenly I was looking through the scope at my illusionist.

"I fucking hate illusionists," I muttered, and squeezed the trigger. Nothing happened. I pressed the button to eject the magazine, then saw that I had dropped the ammo bag halfway across the front lawn. "Fuck me sideways," I said as I stood up. I pointed at him and yelled "*Sagitta,*" conjuring a bolt of mystical energy and sending it across the distance between us.

"Eat my Magic Missile, motherfucker." I watched the wizard fall and grinned as he hit the ground clutching his shoulder. He wouldn't die from that shot, but a blast of magic to the shoulder would keep him down until we got Wally someplace safe.

Which the gunfire from behind me told me would not be his apartment. I turned and saw Smith drop a pair of black-clad military types, obviously mercenaries, with two quick three-shot bursts from his AR.

"You okay up there?" I yelled. Smith gave me a thumbs-up over the balcony rail, and I started off in a quick jog to his car, hoping that his driver left the keys in the ignition and I wasn't going to have to dig through his Kentucky Fried Bodyguard for them. I was lucky for once—the keys were there. I slid into the driver's seat and drove the sedan right up under the balcony in front of Wally's apartment, ignoring the grass and curbs in the way.

I got out and shouted up to Smith, "Get Wally!" He stood up, kicked in the door, and disappeared into the apartment. He appeared back in the doorway seconds later, motioning for me. I hopped onto the roof of the car, then up onto the landing.

"Where's Wally?" I asked.

"Gone. Flynn's hurt. I need you to help her."

"What can I do?"

Smith just looked at me.

"Oh no. I don't do that. Ever. That's totally not my thing." I held up both hands and stepped back.

Smith grabbed one arm and pulled me into the apartment. Flynn was lying on the floor of the living room, three dead mercs around her. She'd given as good as she got, but the numbers game eventually got to her. She was bleeding from bullet wounds in her thigh and shoulder where her vest didn't cover, and there was a cut over her left eye that looked pretty nasty.

"You've done it before. I've seen the records," Smith said.

"Yeah, then you know how well that fucking ended," I spat.

"She'll die before an ambulance can get here and you know it."

"She's a cop. She knew the risks when she put on the badge."

"She's your friend, dammit."

"I don't have friends, Smith. I have people that I kill, and people I watch die. Guess which fucking category Flynn falls into."

"We need her, Harker. She may be the only person that knows where they took Wally. And without him, it's all over. Everything."

"Do it, Q." The new voice came from behind me, and it could only belong to one person. Well, not even a person, really. I looked around and time had stopped. Smith was frozen in mid-berate, the dust and debris raining from the ceiling was hanging in mid-air, even the noise of the burning bushes below was silent. I turned and faced my guardian angel, who was leaning in the doorway holding a bottle of wine.

"Glory," I said, trying not to fall too much in love with the angel. She was five-six or so and the kind of beautiful that you think might melt your eyeballs if you stare at her too long. She wasn't rocking the wings tonight, just a leather jacket, tattered Guns n' Roses tour shirt and ripped jeans. Her blonde hair was tied back in a ponytail, and she had a pair of sunglasses perched on her head.

"Did I tear you away from a hot date at a Scorpion concert?" I asked.

"I was watching over a nineties metal guitarist. He has more trouble staying alive than you do. Now would you save the girl so we can move on?"

"You know I can't do that, Glory. And you know why."

"No, I don't." Her voice lost the usual lilt and turned to steel. "I know that you're being a fucking child while the fate of the world hangs in the balance."

"I don't think I've ever heard you swear before, Glory."

"You're a bad influence. Now do it."

"No."

"You know you're eventually going to do what I want, so why fight me?"

"I'm not fucking healing her, Glory, I can't take it. It almost killed me last time."

"The last time you didn't know what would happen. Now you do, and you'll be able to control it better."

"There's no guarantee of that."

"I can help." That was new. Usually Glory wouldn't interfere personally on our plane, so she was taking this Wally shit seriously.

"How? You know what this takes from me."

"I know, Q. I know the bond is deep, and I know it's hard for you to deal with, but I think I can help make it easier on you this time. And Q?'

"Yeah?"

"We need her. *You* need her. She's important to the work we have to do."

"So you're telling me to suck it up and heal the cop?"

"Suck it up and heal the cop, Q."

"Fine." I turned back to the apartment and the world blurred into motion again. I turned sideways past Smith and knelt beside Flynn in the middle of the floor.

"Hey, Flynn, nice pincushion impersonation. Are there any bullets you didn't decide to stop with your body?" I asked, taking her wrist in my hand.

"Yeah, the ones I put in those three motherfuckers." Her voice was thready, but her attitude was intact. That was good because this was about to be a wild ride.

"Flynn, you're bleeding out. The bullet in your leg nicked your femoral artery and you'll be dead in minutes if I don't take some pretty drastic measures. I can save you, but it's not going to be easy on either of us."

"Do it. I've been shot twice and caught four in the vest tonight, I think I can handle anything you can dish out."

That's what you think, I thought. I looked down at her and said, "All right, do exactly as I say."

I pulled my pocketknife out and made a slash across her wrist, then made one just like it across my own. "Drink," I said, pressing my wrist to her lips. She struggled, but she was too weak to resist much, and as my blood flowed across her lips, the magic in my body kicked in and she started to drink. I pulled her arm to my mouth and drank from her as she sucked on my wrist. We locked eyes and I pushed my will out, diving into her consciousness with my own.

I felt my hold on my own body grow faint as I dove past Flynn's mental defenses, opening my mind and soul to her completely. I watched her first steps, her first bike ride, her first kiss, the first sloppy fumblings in the back of her tenth-grade boyfriend's Prelude, her first real love, her first real heartbreak. I lived every moment of her life in the seconds our souls entwined, and I felt her footsteps through my memories as she relived all the decades of my life—my loves, my triumphs, my many, many failures, the people I'd lost, the loved ones I'd watched grow old and fade away to time, the monsters I'd fought, the monsters I'd called friend, and all the pain of the last woman I'd shared myself with this completely.

"Come back, Q." The voice was faint, and I tried to ignore it. It would be easier to just stay here, hide inside Flynn's life for a while and then fade away quietly. But that's not how I'm going out, I know. I'll never go quietly into that good night, so I turned and reached back to myself, finding Glory's hand reaching back for me. She clasped hands with me, then wrapped her arms around my soul and drew me back into myself. I felt her leave my body, leaving behind just enough of herself to dull the pain of the memories the healing dredged up, and came back to myself staring into Flynn's eyes.

Flynn stared into my eyes, her eyes locked on mine by my will. I blinked, and the spell was broken, the world snapped back into motion. Glory was gone, Smith was yelling, and I felt fear like I hadn't felt in decades. Flynn pulled her wrist from my lips and jerked her whole body away from me, curling up into a retching ball on the carpet. I fell back onto my ass, feet splayed out in front of me and my head swimming with memories, sensations and the taste of fresh blood, a taste I hadn't had cross my lips in more than fifty years. Flynn shook and retched again, convulsed once in sharp pain as her body expelled the bullets forcefully from her healing wounds, then pulled herself up onto Wally's blood-spattered sofa and covered herself with a throw blanket.

She took a corner of the blanket and wiped my blood from her mouth, looked over at me and said in a shaky voice, "What the bleeding fuck was that?"

I opened my mouth a couple of times, but nothing came out. I wiped my face with the back of my hand and rolled over onto my knees. I pulled myself to my feet using a chair and staggered into the kitchen. I pulled three beers out of the fridge and popped them all open on the edge of the counter. I drained one, then went back into the fridge for another. I walked back into the den a little steadier, collapsed into a chair and held out a beer for Smith, who was sitting on the arm of the couch alternating concerned looks at Flynn and me.

I handed the other beer to Flynn and said, "That was a blood bond. It's a way that I can heal someone who is mortally wounded, but the cost is high."

"Define high," Flynn said, trying to calm her shaking hands enough to get the beer to her lips.

We're bonded now. I thought, and saw her eyes widen at my presence in her head.

"What the fuck was that?" Flynn asked.

"Exactly," I said. "We're linked together now, you and I. Closer than you'll ever be with anyone in the world."

"For how long?" The words came out almost in a whisper.

"You already know the answer to that," I said.

I watched her eyes as she searched through my memories, then saw the color drain from her face as the realization hit her. "Fuck me."

"Yup," I said. "Forever."

CHAPTER SIX

"Am I a vampire now?" Flynn asked, looking around. "Everything looks different, sharper somehow. And I can hear—fuck, I can hear everything! Is this what the world is always like to you? So loud, with so much...everything going on?"

"Yeah, kinda, but I've had a century or so to get used to it. It'll fade into background noise eventually."

"But what about..." *This?* she asked inside my head. *Is this forever?*

"Yeah, but it's affected by a lot of things. Like distance, for one, and how tired one of us is. It takes more out of you than you think, touching somebody's mind like that. So I try not to do it often."

Flynn was only half-listening, standing up under new legs and moving through the apartment slowly, looking at everything. She was like a giant newborn, or a college kid on a really good shroom trip, exploring everything, wanting to touch everything. I decided to step in when it looked like she was going to lick the wall.

"Flynn," I said. She ignored me. "Flynn." I called her louder. "Goddammit," I muttered, then focused my will on her. *FLYNN!* I mentally shouted, and she whirled around, clutching her temples.

"What the fucking fuck, Harker! That hurt!" She sat back on the couch and sucked down the last of her beer.

"We still have a stoned Lion of Judah to save and an apocalypse to avert, remember?"

"Yeah, okay, I remember. What's the play?"

Smith came out of his shocked silence at the same time Flynn did, so he took over. Good thing, too. I only had so much "leader" bullshit in me, and I was about to run out. "What did they look like? The men that came in here?"

"They looked like the first guys, like low-rent ninjas, but these were more like a tactical squad than the cliché black outfits. They had guns and flash-bangs and came in fast-roping off the roof. They were definitely pros. They sacrificed the first guy, but once he was in and had me engaged, they threw in two flash-bangs to disorient me, then swung in with smoke grenades going. They were in and out in seconds. I saw them go back out the way they came in, but I was too busy dying to see where they went from there. What was going on outside?" Flynn asked.

"An illusionist made a fake dragon and threw some fireballs at us. Once I convinced him to drop the smoke screen, we took him out pretty easy. But he was enough of a distraction to make it easy on these guys up here," I said.

"How did you know the dragon was an illusion?" Flynn asked.

"Holy shit, did you two go to the same cop school for dumbass questions, or what?" I threw up my hands. "There was a while in the thirties when the Nazis were looking for objects of power. My uncle wanted to make sure as much powerful magic as he could lay his hands on stayed the fuck out of Hitler's grubby little paws. So we spent a lot of time traipsing through Europe looking for magical shit. One of the things we were looking for was dragons. Not only did we never find one, we never found any indication there had ever been any. Ergo, there are no dragons."

"That logic sucks," Flynn said. "How do you know there aren't dragons in South America?"

"I don't care if there are dragons in South America. I've only ever cared if there were dragons in Europe and if there was a dragon on the front lawn fifteen minutes ago. Fortunately for me, there were no dragons in either place. Because there are no fucking dragons! Now can we get back to Wally, the dope-smoking, tail-chasing end of the goddamn world?"

"Good idea," Smith said. "We need to find him. That's probably going to be your job," he said, pointing at me.

"Motherfucker," I sighed. "Can't you people do *anything* without me? How did you ever make the goddamn dryads go extinct with this kind of work ethic?" I knelt by a blood spatter at the shattered sliding glass door, dabbed my fingers in it, and brought it to my nose. Different type than Flynn or any of the corpses she generated, so it must belong to one of our escaped baddies, or Wally. Either one would be just fine.

I walked to the dinette and sat down at the table, sweeping aside a pile of homework or D&D character sheets, I couldn't really tell which. "I need a bowl of water, a needle, a tongue depressor and a stick of chewing gum," I said to Flynn.

"And I want a pony," she shot right back. "Come the fuck on, Harker, where do you think I'm going to get that shit in a dope fiend's apartment at two in the morning?"

"Get me stuff that looks close. But start with the bowl of water." She brought me a cereal bowl that was mostly clean and filled with water, then went off in search of supplies.

"Is she going to be okay?" Smith asked.

"You know she can hear you, right?" I asked.

"Yeah, but I want to pretend like things are normal, for a little while longer, anyway."

"You got a weird definition of normal, Smitty. But yeah. She'll be fine. She's already healed physically, and the more we work together, the easier it'll be for her to learn to shut me out."

"What about you?" he asked.

"I have a lot more trouble shutting me out, but I'm a persistent bastard with myself." I dipped my bloody finger in the water and swirled it around widdershins, or counterclockwise. The blood diffused off my hand and turned the water a very pale pink, and I took my finger out.

"I mean, will you be okay?"

"First off, you don't really give a shit, so let's not pretend that you do. Secondly, I've got a pretty fucked up definition of okay myself, so yeah, I'll be fine."

Smith opened his mouth to press, but Flynn walked back in just then. I heard enough to know she'd been waiting for a break in the conversation to come back in, and she knew I knew. *Thanks.*

No problem. Are you okay?

As okay as I get. Now get outta my head. I mentally closed the door between us and said, "Let's see what you found."

She handed me a wooden pencil, a sewing needle and a pack of Juicy Fruit. I opened the gum and took a piece, starting to chew as they both watched me. "What? Magic is thirsty work, my mouth gets dry," I protested.

I dipped the needle in the pink water, pushed it through the eraser on the pencil, and then dipped the whole end of the pencil, needle and all, back into the mixture of water and blood. I focused on bindings, on the forces that hold things together, the connections that make us who we are, and pushed my will into the needle. "*Corpus ad corpus, sanguinem sanguini. Corpus ad corpus, sanguinem sanguini. Corpus ad corpus, sanguinem sanguini.*" I repeated the incantation three times stirring the needle through the blood/water mix counterclockwise the entire time. After the third repetition, I held the pencil aloft and twirled it slowly between my fingers. When the needle pointed to the broken sliding glass door, the tip began to glow a bright white.

"They went out that way," I said.

"We knew they went out that way, jackass. We were out the other way," Smith said.

Flynn stared at the glowing tip of the needle. "What did you do?" she asked in a whisper.

"It's called sympathetic magic. I mixed the blood with something unlike itself, but it remembers what it was like to be whole, with the rest of itself. So it'll point the way to the rest of it."

"So it'll lead us to more of whoever's blood that was." She pointed to the floor.

"Yeah, so we're hoping that guy didn't bleed out in the woods a hundred yards away. Then we're screwed."

"But for now we can follow the needle?"

"Just like a compass," I said, doing just that. I walked to the sliding glass door, stepped through onto the balcony, and when the shine of the needle didn't waver, I jumped down and started toward the woods behind the apartments.

"Hey, wait for us!" Flynn yelled, then jumped over the balcony rail to land right behind me. "Whoa," she said. "I didn't know I could do that."

"You won't be able to for long. Once your body metabolizes my blood, the strength and speed will fade. The senses, too, but not as much."

And this?

This you're stuck with. There was more magic to the bonding than physical, and this is part of it. I jammed part of my life force into you so you wouldn't die, so now you and I are magically linked until we die. Sorry about that.

So far it's not so bad.

I haven't made my weekly pilgrimage to the Uptown Cabaret yet. I flooded my mind with images of nubile girls writhing on top of me and felt Flynn withdraw from my head with the sensation of a slamming door.

"Slow down, you inhuman bastards," Smith panted as he caught up to us. We were walking at a good clip, but Smith was only human, and he was jogging to keep up.

"Humans say the sweetest things," I said, but slowed down to a comfortable human pace.

"Do you have any plans for what we're going to do when we catch up to them?" I asked Smith.

"I have a couple of ideas," Flynn growled. I looked over at her and she shrugged. "The fuckers shot me. That's not on the list of stuff I forgive easily. Cut a girl some slack, will ya?"

Not to mention that she just got a blood transfusion from a pseudo-vampire, I thought, working to keep my thoughts my own. We picked our way through a couple hundred yards of woods, led by my enhanced vision and a glowing sewing needle. After one particularly dense patch of kudzu, we broke through into a little tuft of grass bordering the parking lot of a local strip mall.

"Well, shit," I said, turning and trying to get my spell to pick back up.

"What's wrong?" Smith asked, leaning over with his hands on his knees.

"They're out of range."

"How were you able to follow them this far?"

"They must have had a car waiting here. If the guy was still bleeding, then that—yup, there it is!" I pointed to a couple of drops on the pavement. "He was still bleeding, so the magic was able to find more blood from the same guy, but this is as far as we go."

"Fuck. Now what?" Flynn asked.

"You're the detective, sweetcheeks. I just make magic and cast out demons."

"You'll need magic just to walk if you ever call me sweetcheeks again, asshat."

"Fair enough," I said. "But seriously, without something closely tied to Wally, I'm not going to be able to track him with magic. And I mean something that meant a lot to him, not hairbrush samples and the shit you dredge up out of the bottom of the shower."

"So let's get to detecting," Smith had caught his breath and took back control of the situation. "Let's take this party back to police headquarters and start looking up internet chatter and poking through airport security camera footage."

"Not me," I said. "I'm heading to Luke's to get some rest, some decent food, and some research. I hate to admit it, but Christian mythology is one of my weaker spots, so I'm gonna need to study up on Revelation if I'm to have any shot at getting us through this. Plus, Renfield's there."

"What's that got to do with anything?"

"The man is a hacker with backdoors into every system in the country. If our kidnappers came in by air or rail, and they have any record anywhere in the world, Ren will find them. Besides, he makes the best Western omelet in North Carolina, and I'm starving."

CHAPTER SEVEN

I called Luke while Flynn and Smith were waiting on their ride back to the apartment complex, and he pulled up in his newest ride, a jet black Mercedes S-class with leather everything. Smith raised and eyebrow at me when he saw it, and I could feel Flynn's motor rev higher just looking at it.

"Not my ride, kids, but Uncle Luke has always had a taste for the finer things in life," I said, walking around to the passenger door.

"That I have," Luke said as he stepped out of the car. "Quincy, my boy, aren't you going to introduce me to your—" the "friends" or whatever froze on his lips as he locked eyes with Flynn. I saw the subtle signs of challenge, watched his pupils dilate, his nostrils flare and his back arch, almost like he was a cat ready to defend his territory. For her part, I saw Flynn instinctively clench her fists and shift her body weight to her back foot, ready to react if Luke pounced.

"Ahem." I cleared my throat and they both gave themselves a little shake and looked away from the other quickly, neither wanting to meet the other's eyes, but neither wanting to give ground either. "Thanks for picking me up, Uncle Luke, but hadn't we better get going before the sun comes up?" We were half an hour from his house with less than an hour before sunrise, a lot closer than he usually liked to cut things.

"Yes, of course. A pleasure to finally meet you, Detective." He slid back into the car, smooth as butter even though the introductions had certainly *not* gone as planned. I got into the car and Luke pulled out into traffic, weaving the performance sedan through the light traffic on our way to his place.

"You did it again," Luke said almost before we were out of the parking lot. He shifted gears and sped through a yellow light, then cut left across several lanes of traffic taking a winding back road at a good bit more than the posted speed limit. I wasn't worried about Luke's driving, but I was a little worried about deer running across the road suddenly.

"She was dying," I said. I looked over at Luke. He gripped the steering wheel so tight he was making indentations in the plastic, and you could carve granite with the line of his jaw. "I had no choice, Uncle."

"There is always a choice. You should have let her die." The words were hard, flat, emotionless, and probably right. Luke sighed, and I watched the set of his jaw relax a little. "You didn't have to watch what it did to you last time, Quincy."

"I had to live through it," I reminded him.

"But you couldn't see the full effect it had on you. When she died, it almost took you with her. I don't want to, I mean, I don't want *you* to have to go through that again."

"This is different, Luke." I reached out and patted him awkwardly on his shoulder. We weren't a touchy family, so those kinds of things never came easy to me. "I had to do it. Glory told me so."

The car actually wobbled as Luke turned to stare at me. "The angel told you to meld with this human to save her?"

"Umm, Luke, could you maybe—Look out!"

His attention snapped back to the road long enough to whip the car around a stopped city bus and thread the needle between two semis passing through a traffic light in opposite directions. We blew through the red light leaving screaming tires, blaring horns and heart palpitations in our wake.

Luke pulled over into an abandoned parking lot and turned to me. "Tell me everything. Leave nothing out." He didn't compel me to tell him, his mental powers don't work on me, but he used a tone I'd only heard a few times in my very long life. I told him the whole story, from finding Flynn on the floor bleeding out, to sharing blood with her, to bonding souls with her, to the connection I felt to her even now, half a city away.

"And this is different, Uncle. When I bonded with Anna, that was one thing. That was love, she was the woman I wanted to share my life with. This...partnership with Flynn isn't like that. The bonding is different, like we can go deeper in some ways, but it's also easier to lock her out of my thoughts than it ever was with Anna. It's strange, but...I think it's going to be okay."

"I don't know about okay, but I agree that it sounds different. But I worry, Quincy. What happened with Anna was devastating for you, and I'd hate for you to suffer that way again."

Join the club. I remembered little about the aftermath of Anna's death, just images and flashes more than a coherent thread. I remembered holding her body, a Nazi officer's bullet lodged in her brain. I remembered holding that officer's heart in my bare hand, his body lying in the snow at my feet with a fist-shaped hole in his chest. I had a flash of me attacking a squad of German infantry, and then an image seared into my brain of dozens of dead soldiers around me. There was nothing after that, just a period of blackness where my grief and loss totally overwhelmed me. The next thing I remember is being in France with Luke and his Renfield of the time and killing a lot of Nazis with the French Resistance. I remembered a lot of wine in France, a lot of Scotch across the British Isles, and not much else for a few years. My memory kicks back in somewhere around 1946 in the Arizona desert, with no Luke or Renfield anywhere around. I reconnected with them in New Jersey after a few years wandering the desert and annoying the various shamans I found there. We never spoke of Anna again, until tonight.

"I need to borrow Ren when we get back to your place," I said, desperate to change the subject.

"Of course," Luke said, his shoulders relaxing as we got on safer ground. I'm pretty sure Luke's never been scared of me, what with the whole being Count Dracula thing, but I do think that I sometimes make him nervous, and I know he likes me enough to miss me if he had to kill me, so it was better to stick to the shallow end of our conversation for a few days, at least until he was more comfortable with the idea of me bonding to Flynn. Hell, until *I* was more comfortable with the idea, not to mention Flynn. I could still feel her, just behind my eyes, no matter how far she and Smith drove. I could feel her right now, the uncomfortable way the seat belt dug in between her boobs... *whoa, definitely don't need to be thinking about Flynn's boobs. Not now, and sure as* fuck *not when she's around. She hears that...*images of what a Sig .40 could do to even my superhuman healing ability flashed through my head.

"Naturally, Renfield will be at your disposal once he finishes his morning duties," Luke's voice snapped me back into the car and safely away from Flynn's chest.

"Unc, this is a little more important than him making sure you've had your warm milk and cookies before beddie-bye," I said.

Luke glared at me. "Making the house light-tight and securing all entrances is more than 'warm milk,' you insolent whelp. It is the peace of mind that allows me to garner any rest at all. Not that I shall find an easy time of it today, with the news you sprang on me weighing so heavily on my mind."

Oh. My. God. Luke was laying it on thick today. He knew as well as I did that the second the sun was above the horizon, he would sleep the sleep of the dead, only waking in situations of extreme danger or pain. I'd spent a decent part of my adolescence testing the limits of Luke's sleep, often with hilarious results. My favorite was the time I put makeup on him to look like my mother. I took a photo with an old flash camera, which was enough to wake Luke and send him into a double fury—one for waking him up, and the other for making him up to look like a very ugly woman.

"Fine, I'll be in your study reading the Bible. Send me Renfield when you're done with him."

"The Bible? You? We must truly be at the end times if you're reading the Bible."

"Uncle, that is exactly what I am trying to prevent." On that brilliant note, Luke pulled the car back out onto the road and headed toward his house, double-time.

CHAPTER EIGHT

"What can I do for you, Master Quincy?" Renfield asked as he stepped into the library. I really was reading the Bible, brushing up on my Book of Revelation in preparation for dealing with the upcoming Apocalypse.

"I need to stop the end of the world, Ren. Got any ideas?" I closed the New International Version Bible I was reading and put it on the stack beside me. I'd already worked my way through a couple of King James versions, the English Standard, The New Jubilee edition, the American Standard Version, the Concordant Literal Version and two different Illustrated Bibles trying to cull as much information about the end of the world, the seven seals, and The Lion of Judah as I could. It all started to blur together after about three versions. I never claimed to be much of a scholar. That was Uncle Luke's deal. And Orly's, but he was long gone.

Orly was my youngest brother, the only one of us born long enough after "the book" came out to reap the benefits of our family's fame. By the time he came along, my parents had become the darlings of the university lecture circuit, so Orly tagged along and got the chance to spend his childhood in great libraries and reading rooms all around New England. His favorite smell was bookbinder's glue, and his favorite pastime was looking up obscure facts. James and I were more robust, not to mention older, so our bookish little brother traveled with Mother and Father while we bounced around boarding schools playing cricket and rugby.

"Well, Master Quincy, I suppose if we're to stop the end of the world, we should first make sure we can keep the seven seals intact, shouldn't we?"

"That makes sense. All of the versions I've seen say if all the seals are broken, then we're fucked. Is that about it?"

"Indelicately phrased, but accurate," Renfield agreed.

"So if I'm reading these stories right," I waved my hand at the stack of Bibles, "the first four seals release the Four Horsemen of the Apocalypse."

"They are commonly considered to be metaphorical, and many scholars consider those seals to have been broken long ago, with each Horseman being symbolic of a period of great tribulation experienced by the Jewish people, the Chosen Ones."

"Yeah, I'm pretty sure Jerry Falwell has something to say about that Chosen people thing. But what if they're more literal? What if these seals unleash some kind of physical threat into the world that has to be taken care of or the world ends?"

"You mean like actual men on horses?" Renfield asked. "That's a bit literal for most religions, isn't it?"

"Yeah, but if the Four Horsemen aren't Ric, Tully, Arn and Barry, then we have a problem." Of course, that's when my phone rang. I looked down and saw "Flynn" on the display. I opened myself to our link and felt her worry. "Looks like we have a problem, Renny old pal."

I slid my finger across the screen to answer the phone. "Yeah, what is it?"

Flynn's voice came on the line, and I would have heard the fear in her voice even if I didn't feel it in my heart. *This is going to be a pain in the ass*, I thought. *What happens when she gets laid?* I shoved those thoughts aside, figuring if we didn't stop the Apocalypse, that wouldn't be an issue. "What's up, buttercup?" I asked.

"We're so fucked," she said.

"You want to be a little more specific, Detective?"

"There's been a break-in at the CDC in Atlanta. White male, late twenties, six foot, one-eighty busted in the front door shouting about the end times and shot up a bunch of doctors and security guys on his way to the Hot Labs. He shot his way in there and took aerosolized botulin toxin, anthrax and smallpox samples."

"Well, that sucks for Atlanta, and probably the world in general, but I think we're going for more of a 'think global, act local' approach right now, Becky."

"Don't call me Becky, asshole. The break-in was five hours ago. The car was last spotted getting off I-85 north at Brookshire."

"Heading right for downtown," I said.

"Local enough for you?" Flynn asked.

"What's the play? The sun's up, so Luke's out of commission. I'm pretty well exhausted, so anything we do is going to have to be fast and mostly non-magical."

"I'm at headquarters. Come pick me up and we'll move out from here."

"Smith with you?"

"Yeah, I'm here. What do you need?" Smith's voice came on the line. She must have had me on speakerphone.

"Intel. We need to know where he's going."

"We need to know what he wants first."

"I got that covered, Smitty. He's the first Horseman, and he's on a pale horse. He's Pestilence, and he wants to infect as many people as possible. So you figure out where the biggest impact of a biological attack downtown would be, and Becky and I will try to stop him without getting dead."

"I told you not to call me—" I hung up on her.

"Ren, I'm gonna need a fast car."

"Gear up, Master Quincy. I'll be out front with our ride in two minutes." The stocky middle-aged manservant sprang out of his chair and hightailed it to the door, his short little legs almost a blur. I chuckled a little to myself.

I went upstairs and threw on a black leather jacket and my Doc Martens. I slipped a Sig 9mm into a shoulder holster under my left arm and tucked a Ruger LC9 into my right jacket pocket. A couple of knives got tucked into my belt and a wrist sheath, and I was ready to go. I hustled down the stairs and out the door, to find Renfield parked in front of the house with Uncle Luke's H3 Hummer rumbling by the curb.

"Didn't want to draw attention to yourself, Ren?" I asked as I opened the door and climbed in. The Hummer was high enough that even I needed the running boards, and I strapped my seatbelt on tight as Ren pulled away from the house.

"If the end of the world is nigh, Master Quincy, I do not intend to be a spectator." He reached down beside his leg and patted the stock of a shotgun.

"Damn, Renfield," I said. "I didn't know you even knew how to shoot one of those things."

"When your uncle found me, I was little more than gator bait down in the Louisiana swamps. I learned how to shoot before I learned how to read."

"I never knew that." This Renfield had been with Luke for the last twenty years, and I'd been in the American Southwest studying Coyote magic when the last one retired. When I reconnected with Luke, he was established in North Carolina with a new Renny.

"Yup, that's why my gumbo be so good, donchaknowboy?" he said in a bayou patois the likes of which I hadn't heard in decades. We both laughed until he pulled up to the curb in front of Police Headquarters.

I pulled out my phone to text Flynn but put it away when I saw her walk out of the station. She looked up and down the street, shielding her eyes from the morning sun, then hustled toward the idling behemoth when I rolled down the window. "You could have tooted the horn," I said to Renfield.

"Your uncle replaced it with an air horn. I really don't think you wanted me to 'toot' that, did you?"

"Point taken," I said. "What's the story, morning glory?" I asked as Flynn slid into the back seat.

"Morning glory, buttercup, fuck a duck Harker, you'd think I was a goddamn florist or something. Take a left on Davidson," she said. "Renfield, I presume?" she asked.

"Indeed, Detective. The pleasure is all mine."

"I'd be a lot more pleasurable if there wasn't a psycho with a shit-ton of aerosolized death heading to the convention center," Flynn replied. She fiddled with the straps on her bulletproof vest and checked the magazine in her sidearm.

"Are we sure that's where he's going?" I asked.

"You're sure he thinks he's one of the Four Horsemen of the Apocalypse?"

"I'm pretty sure he *is* one of the Four Horsemen. Pestilence, to be more specific."

"Then I'd bet all our lives on him going to the convention center. The Southern Baptist Convention National Meeting kicked off with a prayer meeting twenty minutes ago, and delegates from all across the country will be there for the next four days," Flynn explained.

"That would be pretty much perfect, then. He crop-dusts the place this morning, they have the sniffles when they go to the airport Friday, and the disease is spread throughout the country by the time they change planes, go out to dinner Saturday night and go to church feeling like crap Sunday."

"But they can't miss church because they were the delegate..." Flynn chimed in.

"And probably have some kind of show and tell or report or some such shit," I agreed.

"So Monday morning our pandemic begins."

"And the first seal is broken all to fuck," I finished.

Renfield pulled the Hummer up onto the sidewalk in front of the Convention Center and got out, grabbing his shotgun. "Then we'd better make sure none of that happens. Shall we?" he said, then slammed the door.

A startled security guard came out the front doors at us, but Flynn badged him into silence. "Have you seen this man?" She held up a grainy surveillance photo that could have been any white guy with a baseball cap.

The cop stared at the photo, then shook his head. "He's not going to know anything," I said. "I'm going to have to do this my way."

"What's your way?" Flynn asked. "Magic?"

"No," I replied. "Noise and firepower." I stepped through the main doors of the convention center and fired one shot into the ceiling. All the men and women within a hundred feet ducked, screamed, and started running in the opposite direction. I looked up, actually aimed this time, and fired again. This time I hit something instead of just randomly firing, and when I shot the top off the sprinkler, it triggered the failsafe in the system that douses everything in that wing if the system is damaged. So the fire alarm started blaring, the sprinklers showered the hallways in water, and people started to stream out of meeting rooms, heading for the exits in droves.

"Follow me!" I shouted and ran down the length of the hall. I stopped at the top of a set of escalators and pointed down. "Our guy is in one of two places—the main ballroom or the exhibit hall. You two go clear the exhibit hall. If you make enough ruckus by the front doors, everybody will haul ass for the loading dock doors. That's what you want. Get everybody clear, and the guy who doesn't want to leave, that's your bad guy."

"What are you going to do?" Flynn asked.

"I'm going to the only other place where he has a ton of targets at eight in the morning, which also happens to be the only other place where they shut off the smoke detectors because of the fog machines used in the performance. I'm going to church."

CHAPTER NINE

I got to the main ballroom only to find my path blocked by a smiling young volunteer with perfect teeth, perfect hair and sparkling blue eyes. He had creases in his dress shirt, creases in his blue jeans, and I wouldn't have been surprised to find creases in his underpants. He held up one hand as if that was going to slow me down, then got in front of me when I didn't look like I was stopping.

"I'm sorry, brother, but we can't interrupt Pastor Steve's message." He pointed to a monitor, which showed a twenty something kid with a lot of hair product and skinny jeans exhorting the crowd to do something.

"Junior, I'm going in that room, and I'm going in there right now. Your only decision is how much of your blood ends up on the floor," I said, giving him my best *Don't Fuck with Me* look.

He smiled right back up at me and said, "I'm sorry brother, but I can't let you—" His words cut off as my fist smashed his perfect lips into his perfect teeth and sent his perfect head careening into the perfectly solid door behind him. He slumped to the floor and I yanked the door open.

I immediately felt like I'd walked into a rock concert, or maybe a political rally. Hell, maybe it was both. The stage was a good fifty feet wide with more lights and sound gear than I saw on the Grammys. There were three or four guys stationed around the room on camera platforms, plus a huge boom and a couple more dudes wandering the stage with cameras on their shoulders. The room was packed with believers, at least five thousand strong. Finding my nutbar in the middle of this crowd of nutbars was going to be worse than finding one specific stripper in Las Vegas.

I looked around, trying to decide where I'd be if I wanted to disperse a lot of germs into the crowd all at once. The guitar player hit a power chord, the crowd leapt to their feet, and the lights started flashing and moving around in time with the music. It all looked a lot more like a KISS concert than a prayer breakfast, but I'd spent a lot of time with Buddhists in my life, so I was used to a quieter style of praying, with less kick drum. All the concert trappings made something in my head click, and I started for the backstage area at a run.

"Backstage" was really behind some portable curtains set up across the hotel ballroom, but they still had security guys with lanyards guarding the area, just like at a concert. I didn't waste any time explaining myself, I just laid out the security guy with a punch to the jaw and kept running. I scouted backstage quickly—sound guy, no; wardrobe lady, no; guy messing with the foggers, no—then I froze and backed up. Kneeling with a silver canister in front of a huge fogger was a white guy, about six foot, and a bit under two hundred pounds, wearing a baseball cap and a black jacket. It was the jacket that gave him away. All the other crew guys wore khakis and black polos, but this guy had on a jacket and ball cap. Sitting on the floor next to him was a small aluminum canister, like the kind they used for chemicals in all those disaster movies.

I moved up behind him, my Docs not making a sound on the carpet, and pressed the barrel of my Ruger to the back of his head. "You twitch and I'll aerosolize your brain."

"You can't stop what's coming, heathen. The signs are clear. The end times are upon us, when the earth shall open up and disgorge the faithful and we shall ascend!" He stood up, his arms spread wide. I looked down at the canister, but it still looked intact. I couldn't read the writing on it from the distance, but the markings on it were unmistakable—Bad Shit Inside, Do Not Fuck With.

"What the hell is wrong with you, man?" I asked. "Why would you want to destroy the world?"

"I'm not destroying it, my child," said the idiot in front of me who was at least seventy years my junior. "I am helping to cleanse it! And we are beginning right here, with these false prophets!" He turned to face me and I saw vials strapped all over his chest, wired together with what looked like det cord.

"Fuck me," I whispered as I stepped back from the psycho wired to blow disease all over the room. He held a trigger in his left hand and another length of det cord in his right. I'd interrupted him before he could wire the canister to blow, but there was still enough biological agent on him to kill everyone in the room three times over. Not to mention what all that det cord would do to my complexion.

He raised a hand, and I mimicked his movement, focusing my will on the trigger. "*Cataracta*," I said just before he squeezed the trigger, and suddenly all the water vapor in the immediate vicinity coalesced into a waterfall pouring over his hand and through the trigger, preventing the det cord from doing any det-ing. He looked at his hand, brows knit, then turned to me.

"No matter, I can—" I didn't care what he thought he could do, all I wanted him to do was die. I raised the Ruger to his face and squeezed the trigger twice, putting two 9mm rounds into his forehead. I stepped forward and caught his sagging body, lowering him to the ground with the greatest of care. I rolled him over onto his back and cut away his explosive germ-dispensing vest, carrying it and the canister several feet away.

A stagehand walked over to see what the noise was, but I pulled the badge out of my back pocket and whispered, "Homeland Security. We're investigating some irregularities with gun permits at the church headquarters." I figured it was probably true for at least one church there, and this guy didn't look like he cared one way or the other. He just held up his hands and backed slowly away from the man with the gun and the corpse.

I pulled out my phone and pressed the speed dial for Flynn. "Did you find him?" she asked. "It's a nuthouse down here, but no sign of our guy."

"Yeah, I got him. I'm backstage in the main ballroom. We're going to need a way out of here that doesn't involve carrying several samples of the world's most infectious disease out the front door through thousands of Bible-thumpers, though."

"Don't worry about that, Master Quincy. I have that well in hand," Renfield said into the phone. He sounded like he was in a tunnel, so I figured Flynn had me on speaker.

"Fine, but get up here quick before I have to do too much explaining. I have a dead guy surrounded by a bunch of megalomaniac preachers. Leave me here too long and they'll try to resurrect his ass."

"We'll be there in ten," Flynn said, then hung up on me.

They made it in five, with a flatbed cart and a stack of black tablecloths to cover the body in, too. I loaded the metal canister and the vials of disease into a big road case, padded the vials with more tablecloths, and followed Flynn and Renny out through the service hallway. I left the empty road case on the sidewalk, and we loaded the dead psycho and his cargo into the Hummer.

"Where to now?" I asked as I slid into the passenger seat.

"Smith is still at Headquarters. We should meet up with him there and then try to figure out what the next seal is going to be."

"Oh, we already know that, Miss Flynn," Renfield chimed in.

"It's Detective, Ren. And what do you mean?"

"Well, the next Horseman, of course. We already know what he will be. The next Horseman is War."

"War?" I asked, more out of a sense of *Fuck, my days sucks* than *What did you say?*

"Yes, Master Quincy. The second Horseman rides a red horse, and he is typically thought to represent the aspect of War." Renfield pulled into the underground parking garage for Police Headquarters, ignoring the frantically waving uniform in his little guard hut.

We parked and Ren got out to talk to the agitated patrolman while I sat there for a second, trying to process.

"What's wrong?" Flynn asked from the back seat. "We stopped Pestilence, now we just need to stop War. Then we find Wally before these psychos get any further along the Apocalypse checklist, and we save the world. Come on, let's do this."

I still didn't move. I'd seen war up close and personal. Germany in 1917, then again in 1944. I had no desire to see what the physical embodiment of war looked like. *Suck it up, Q. You've lived through a lot of things you didn't like, so put on your big boy pants and go kick some ass.* I took a deep breath and opened the door.

"Let's go, Princess, we've got a war to stop." I got out of the Hummer and headed to the elevator, only to meet Smith coming out of it.

"Turn it around, kids, we've got our next target."

"Already?" I asked, reversing course for the SUV. "Can't we at least get the germ warfare out of the back seat before we go off into the war zone?"

Smith froze in his tracks. "You've got all that shit in the back of the car?" he asked, grabbing for his cell phone.

"I wouldn't call that baby tank a *car* necessarily," I said, waving at the Hummer, "but yeah. We couldn't exactly leave the dead guy in the ballroom with the anthrax, could we?"

"Are those douchebags from the CDC still fucking around in the break room? Well send them down to the garage. Tell them we've got a corpse and all their stolen germs for them to take back to Atlanta," Smith said into his phone. "No, I don't give a fuck what they do with the body. We did our job, we made it dead. They can make Soylent Green out of it for all I care. Now get them moving, we've got another situation to deal with."

Renfield walked back up from his conversation with the gate guard. "Everything all right?" I asked.

"Master Quincy, as you move along through this life you will come to understand that very few disagreements cannot be smoothed over with judicious application of twenty-dollar bills."

"You bribed a cop to let us park here?" I grinned at Ren.

"Of course not." He stiffened. "I would never do such a thing. I simply mentioned that both our superiors had a vested interest in the cargo of our vehicle, and that it might be in his best interest if he let me alert the interested parties to our presence. Then I borrowed his mobile phone, which, being the clumsy sod that I am, I dropped into a grate in the floor. Then I offered him a small token of my apology in the form of seven hundred dollars. He was so preoccupied with counting his money that he forgot all about calling his supervisor."

"Nicely done, Ren, if a little unnecessary. You are actually allowed to be here, so you could have saved your money," Smith said.

"Fear not, Agent Smith, I shall be turning in a receipt for reimbursement. My employer has not reached his current state of fiscal comfort by simply passing around cash at the drop of a hat."

"He's saying my uncle is a cheap bastard," I translated for Smith.

"I got that."

"And that you just bought that beat cop a new iPhone," I continued.

"I got that, too."

"Then what are we waiting for? I thought we had a war to stop? We should probably take your car. Mine's full of dead guy." Smith shook his head and led the way to a row of identical black Suburbans parked along the wall.

CHAPTER TEN

I sat in the back with Ren, going over ammunition and weapons. I had six rounds left in my Ruger, plus two spare magazines. My Sig P226 MK25 was still holstered, with one in the pipe for 16 rounds in the pistol, plus two 15-round magazines in the holder under my opposite arm. I drew the pistol and checked the laser sight, making a bright red dot on the back of Flynn's seat.

"Don't point that thing at me, dickhead," she said without turning around.

"Oh quit your whining, the safety's on," I said, then checked to make sure I was right. It was going to take some getting used to, being around a woman who could see through my eyes if she tried hard enough. I holstered the Sig and checked my knives to make sure they were all accessible and sharp.

"You look like you're ready to take on a giant," Ren said.

"I don't know what we're getting into, but I have a feeling it won't be pretty," I replied.

"It won't. It seems that our friendly neighborhood Apocalypse cult has broken the second seal, and War is taking the form of a pissed-off motorcycle gang," Smith said from the front seat.

"Huh?" I asked.

"The local gang task force has been keeping an eye on the local Renegades MC for a while now, suspecting them of heading up a major meth distribution ring. Today they shot the surveillance detail and rode across town to burn down the clubhouse of a rival gang, the Devil's Rejects. None of the Rejects survived, but one of our surveillance team made it out of the initial attack. She said they all followed a tall man driving a red Mustang convertible."

"The red horse," I said.

"Slightly updated," Smith agreed.

"So where are they now?" Flynn asked from the passenger seat.

"They went back to their clubhouse where they sealed themselves in tight and commenced to shooting anyone who walked within fifty yards of the place. Which is a problem because there's a daycare right across the street."

"I assume it's been evacuated?" I asked.

"Can't. We tried to get a van in there, but the Renegades are better armed than we expected. They hit our van with an RPG. We lost four officers."

"So we have a bunch of psycho bikers with rocket launchers led by a mystical embodiment of the spirit of War, and if we don't stop them, they'll burn the city to the ground and usher in the end of the world, is that it?" I summed it up, as much for myself as anyone else.

"Yeah, that's pretty much got it in a nutshell," Smith agreed.

"Face impossible odds and save the world from certain destruction? Must be Tuesday," I sighed, leaning back and resting my head against the SUV's soft interior.

We pulled into a grocery store parking lot a couple football fields away from the clubhouse and got out of the Suburban. A uniform walked up to us and said, "I assume you're the government assholes the captain said would be coming."

"You got a problem, Officer?" Smith asked.

"My friend was in the van those fuckers blew up. So yeah, I got a problem with a bunch of feds coming in here and giving these bastards some kind of get out of jail free card just to get them to roll over on their supplier or whatever other bullshit you come up with."

I could see Smith take in a deep breath to unload on the kid, so I stepped forward. "You know what, Officer, you're right. Those sonsabitches shouldn't get away with this shit. And I'm here to make sure they don't. You see," I put my arm around his shoulder and walked him a little bit away from Smith and Flynn. "I'm not really *with* them. They're suits, they don't understand that sometimes you have to do bad things to bad people. And those guys," I pointed down the street at the clubhouse. "Are definitely bad people. I'm the guy that comes in to do the bad things. But we have to make the suits think all the shit we do is their idea, you know?" He nodded. "So how about you go give the asshat with the bad haircut enough of a half-assed apology to get his panties unbunched and take us inside that rolling command center where we can piss off your captain by taking over this little shit-show?"

"He's still a dick," the patrolman grumbled.

"Who, Crew-cut?" I jerked a thumb back at Smith. "Yeah, he's a total dick. But he's a dick with some authority, and that lets me get shit done."

"Whatever," the young cop said, shrugging off my arm. He turned and walked back to Smith, sticking out his hand before Smith could unload on him. "Sorry, man. Sean Nash, one of the officers killed in the van, was my training officer. He was like a big brother to me, so I'm a little on edge. I was out of line. It won't happen again."

"See that it doesn't," Smith said, and I all but heard him add the world "soldier" to the end of his sentence. *You could take the soldier out of the military, but you can't make him a spy*, I thought.

"Can we get started?" I asked. "Or do you guys actually need to whip 'em out?"

The patrolman led the way to the Mobile Command Center, and we went up the folding stairs into the high-tech RV. It was kinda like a tour bus, if you were looking to take over a small country instead of put on a rock show. One whole wall was taken up with monitors, all showing different scenes around the area, including one long-range infrared scan of the clubhouse that showed a *lot* of activity.

"Who's in charge here?" Smith asked.

A forty-ish woman with glasses and a black tactical uniform turned from the monitor she was studying. "I'm Lieutenant Ferguson. What can I do for you?"

"I'm Agent Smith, Homeland Security. I believe you got a call that we were coming?" Smith held out his hand.

Ferguson didn't take it. I admired her a little for leaving Smitty hanging. Showed serious stones. "I did, and I have to say I don't understand what jurisdiction Homeland has here. This is obviously a local law enforcement issue."

"Really? And the rocket-propelled grenades? You have a lot of those in the Charlotte metro area?" Smith asked, letting his hand drop. "This gang has obviously escalated their activities, stepped up their game so to speak. That means somebody's backing them. We want to know who."

I admired his facility for bullshit but was worried we were running short on time. "How long since you've seen any movement outside the club?" I asked a nearby tech. The skinny little guy was sitting there, his eyes glued to the monitor in front of him, trying very hard to be invisible while the people above his pay grade fought right by his shoulder.

He looked up at me and I gave him a "move it along" gesture with one hand. "It's been at least an hour since anyone's gone in or out," he said.

"We gotta get eyes in there," I said to Smith.

"What's your hurry?" Smith asked.

"The last guy was trying to infect thousands of people at one shot with a virus fierce enough to create a worldwide pandemic. I don't think the embodiment of War is going to be content with just blowing up a few local cops. Something bigger is going on here."

"Something that involves RPGs and a lot of guns," Flynn added.

"This would be a real bad time to tell me the President was scheduled to be in town today," I said.

"No, we've got no alerts like that," the lieutenant said. I heaved a sigh of relief, which quickly cut off as her eyes went wide.

"What is it?" Flynn asked.

"The First Lady is giving a speech at J.C. Smith tonight," Lieutenant Ferguson said. "We've provided some extra security, but the college was keeping her visit low-key. It's a speech to some big-time alumni and donors about HBCs."

"HBCs?" I asked.

"Historically Black Colleges," Ferguson explained. "I went to JCSU, I sometimes forget that not everybody knows all the code words."

"I studied abroad," I explained. "So I don't understand a lot about American college life."

"Yeah, he doesn't even understand March Madness," Flynn added.

"Well, Mrs. Obama will be speaking at a luncheon in about…two hours, so if you think she's the target—" I didn't hear the rest, on account of already being down the steel steps and on my way across the parking lot.

Where are you going? Flynn's voice came through my head.

Things to do, people to kill, I replied, keeping a tight lid on my thoughts.

You think you're going to just waltz in there and take out an entire motorcycle gang and one of the Four Horsemen all by yourself?

Well, I wasn't actually thinking waltz, more like a samba, or a quickstep. I pictured a heavy steel door closing and cut off the connection.

I walked back to the Suburban and Renfield. "Ren, were going at this the wrong way," I said.

"What do you mean, Master Quincy?" Renfield was screwing down a scope onto a Remington 700 rifle, getting ready to back me up, I supposed.

"We're reacting, but we need to get ahead of these fuckers. We can't keep chasing the puppets, we've got to get to the puppeteer."

"I understand the metaphor, but not exactly the plan," Renfield said.

"I need you and Flynn to find Wally. He's the key to this whole thing. If we can't get him away from the bastards that nabbed him, we have zero chance of stopping this shit."

"There is a certain logic to that, Master Quincy," Renfield agreed.

"Glad you approve," I said with a barely-restrained eye roll. It was easy for Renfield to forget that despite his fifty years of age, he wasn't really the two decades older than me he looked, but more like less than half my age. "So go back to the source and figure out where they would have taken Wally." *Flynn, meet me and Ren out by the car. Tell Smitty to stay there.*

On my way.

"And what would be the source in this situation, Master Quincy?"

"Pretty sure that's going to be Revelation, Ren. There's gotta be something in there that's symbolic. Think like a psychopath that wants to end the world and figure out where he's taken Wally to open the Seven Seals." I kept my connection to Flynn open, so everything I said to Renfield, she got simultaneously.

"And what shall we do when we locate our missing Lion?" Ren asked.

"Then we call in the big guns," Flynn said, walking quickly up to the Suburban. "What will you be doing while we're playing Giles and Willow in the library?"

"I'll be putting on my blonde wig and doing what I do best, kicking ass," I said, turning back to the Command Center as Ren and Flynn got into the SUV and pulled out of the parking lot. I met Smith walking in my direction halfway there. "Good, I didn't want to have this conversation in there." I jerked my head toward the van.

"What's up?" Smith asked.

"Somebody in there is in on this whole mess. I don't know who, but someone is tipping the bikers off to police movements."

"How do you know?" Smith asked.

"It's the only answer. How else did they know the van pulling up outside the daycare was full of cops? The video was rolling while you were pissing on fire hydrants with Lieutenant Ferguson and there were no markings on the van. Also, no hesitation on the bikers' part. They didn't wait five seconds from the time the van pulled up outside the daycare before they opened the door and blew those cops to pieces."

"Sounds suspicious," Smith agreed.

"And something smelled wrong," I added. "You know that stinky fear-sweat that people get when they're guilty of something? That smell was all over that Command Center like the smell of Axe body spray in a frat house."

"What are you, a werewolf now?" Smith asked with a half smile.

"That's not funny." I scowled at him. "Don't ever joke about that. Were-wolves are gross, man." Then I let a grin slip through to let him know I was joking. Kinda. Werewolves *are* gross.

"So what's the play? If we can't count on the police for backup, I don't know if the two of us can get in there on our own."

"Well whatever we do, we have to do it now. If the First Lady is going to be going on in less than two hours, my bet is that's the attack," I said.

"Still doesn't tell me the plan," Smith pointed out.

"I don't have much of one right now, but I'll figure it out between here and there," I said, pointing to the clubhouse.

"So your plan is you're going to walk down the sidewalk, kick down the door and shoot everybody? That's fucking insane," Smith said.

"It's also not my plan," I corrected. "I'm only going to kick the door down if it's locked, and I won't shoot anybody that doesn't try to kill me. Sound better?" I asked.

"Much," Smith said. "I'm going to go back in here and make sure that nobody accidentally shoots a missile up your ass."

"Thanks," I said. "I'm going to go knock on the door and try to kill my second Horseman. This keeps up, I'm totally getting a codename."

CHAPTER ELEVEN

I t was a long couple of blocks to the clubhouse, and it felt like there were eyeballs on me the entire time. Probably because there were. I knew the cameras from the Command Center were aimed my way, and even before I got reasonably close I could see the glint of a rifle on the roof of the biker's hangout. I focused my will and muttered *"inflecto"* under my breath, pushing my energy toward the barrel of the gun. I couldn't tell if it did enough damage to the barrel to make it misfire and blow up in the sniper's face, or just bent it enough to miss. That's the trouble with magic at a distance, you can't really tell when the subtle things work. You can almost always tell when things go wrong, but you don't often get a second chance.

I was about twenty yards away from the front door when I saw a flash from the roof and heard a muffled scream. *I guess I broke it. Well, that's one I don't have to kill inside,* I thought as I continued to the front of the building.

"That's far enough," came a booming voice from inside.

I focused myself for a second and said, *"amplifico."* "I just want to talk," I lied. My spell made it so that anyone within fifty yards heard me just as clear as if I held a megaphone.

"I got nothing to say, now fuck off!" the voice replied.

By then I was at the building, but I stopped behind a solid section of cinderblock. There are plenty of handguns and assault rifles that can punch through block walls, but almost everything can punch through a window or a door, even a steel one. I decided to pause where I had a little better cover and armor up. I took a pair of titanium knuckle dusters from my back jeans pocket and focused my will on the metal. I poured my energy into the knucks, muttered, "*imitantes*," and felt the texture of my skin begin to change. To say it was painful would be an understatement, kinda like saying Hitler was a bit of an Anti-Semite or that Mount Everest had a little snow on top. I bit back a scream as my skin tightened and became solid, shedding all the moisture and dead cells and turning into a gleaming sheath of flexible titanium. Have you ever wondered what like would be like if your scrotum ever became made of metal? Me neither, but it hurts like a motherfucker. All of a sudden your family jewels are rattling around inside a completely non-permeable tin can, and that is not a comfortable feeling.

With my new bulletproof skin on, I finished my long walk to the front door and knocked gently. Yeah, what the fuck ever, I kicked the fucking door in like the steel-plated badass I suddenly was. The door flew off the hinges and crashed to the floor several feet from the frame, taking two bikers to the ground with it.

"Avon calling, motherfuckers," I said as I drew my Sig and swept the room. It was crammed with bikers, all suddenly gone still at my apparently unexpected entry. The bartender brought his sawed-off shotgun above the level of the bar and swung in my direction, but I put two in his chest and he went down, shotgun clattering to the concrete beside him. One of the bikers shoved the door off himself and jumped up to run at me, but I put two in his forehead within half a second of his hand touching the butt of his gun.

"I'm not a cop, bitches. I don't have rules of engagement. As far as I'm concerned, every fucking one of you is already guilty, and I'm just here to execute. Now where the motherfucker called War?"

"I prefer Ares, Tin Man." I turned to see a giant leaning against a pool table. He was all of seven feet tall and well over three hundred pounds, with a shaved head and goatee. Tattoos sleeved both arms and peeked out of the collar of his black t-shirt. He wore engineer boots, a black leather vest, dirty jeans and I could see a chain dangling from one belt loop back to his wallet. In other words, he looked like every shaven-headed biker I'd ever seen, only super-sized. He had a sword in one hand and a pistol in the other. He laid the pistol on the pool table and lifted the sword over his head, charging at me like some kind of white trash William Wallace or something.

I stepped to the side and emptied my Sig into his side and back as he passed. He stumbled, but didn't fall, and I watched as the wounds sealed and the bullets popped out, eleven in all *plinking* to the floor in quick succession. *Fuck. Well, that's going to make things a little more difficult.*

He spun around and charged me again, this time with his sword out to the side for a lateral cut. I picked up a round table and used it for a shield, dropping my shoulder into Ares' midsection. He slammed into me like a freight train, but I had myself balanced and my back leg braced, so I didn't budge. He didn't budge much either, just bounced off me with a *whoof!*

He laid into me with his sword, each blow taking huge chunks out of my improvised shield. I tried to strike back with the base of the table, but kept needing to bring it around to block. *Wait a goddamn minute,* I thought, *I'm made of fucking* metal. After his next strike, I dropped the table and landed a solid uppercut right to his chin. Ares wobbled a little, then shook his head as if to clear it, and came back with another sword cut for my head. I threw a titanium arm up and quickly realized why that was a bad idea. My skin was hardened, but the bones under it were not, and every bit of the force of the blow transferred. I felt both bones in my left arm snap, and I dropped to my knees with a scream.

"How'd you like that, Tin Man?" Ares asked.

I knelt on the floor, my left wrist in my right hand. I pulled hard on my wrist, feeling the bones of my arm slide across each other then *snap* into place. I fell forward, my forehead pressed to the floor as stars danced in my field of vision. But the arm was set and I could feel the bones begin to knit back together. In a couple of days, that arm would be good as new. I could only hope the same would be true about the rest of me.

Ares reached down and grabbed a fistful of my metallic hair, yanking me up onto my knees again. "You thought you could waltz in here with your puny little magic and fight me? I am the god of War, you ignorant mortal puke!"

"And I'm the prince of cheating, you arrogant douchebag," I said I reached over my head and poked him in the eye. He dropped my hair with a roar, and I spun around on my ass and head butted the god of War right in the balls. Time seemed to slow around me as his eyes went wide and his face bled to white, then shifted to red, then finally to purple. His sword fell from his hands and clattered to the floor, followed by the giant Horseman himself.

He dropped to his knees right in front of me, and I stood up. I reached down to him, grabbed his chin and turned it up to face me, then released his face and smashed my metallic fist into his nose, spraying blood and snot all over the floor. Ares spun on his knees, pushing himself up onto his feet and giving me a shove to create some distance. He swung wildly a few times, but it was obvious he couldn't see what he was swinging at.

I ducked his punches with ease, peppering his face and nose with stinging jabs. I kept the blood flowing from his nose and the tears flowing from his eyes while I slowly regained some use of my left arm. I couldn't make a fist, but at least I could stretch the arm out for balance, so I was less likely to topple over randomly. After half a minute of this, Ares let out a bellow and just charged me, lowering his head for a bullrush. I sidestepped him and stuck out one foot, sending the huge man sprawling through tables and chairs. He fetched up against the base of a pool table, and I almost went sprawling when I stepped on something hard and round. I looked down to find the hilt of Ares' sword under my foot.

I picked it up and felt the big claymore humming with power, obviously the focal instrument of the Horseman's magic. I felt the magic of the sword warring with my own powers, but I'd spent decades handling unruly magical toys and wrestled the sword under control in a matter of seconds.

"Put that down, Tin Man. Humans aren't meant to wield that kind of power," Ares said, circling around me slowly. I pivoted, keeping the sword between me and the temporary god of War, but this exposed my back to the rest of the bikers.

"Tell your boys that the first one to get within six feet of me gets a sword in his gut," I said.

I heard the whisper of something cutting through the air and dropped to one knee as I spun. The claymore was sharp enough to cut through flesh and bone with no trouble, and it cut one biker off at the thighs before he got close enough to hit me with the tire iron he was swinging. I didn't have time to decide whether or not the tire iron would have actually done anything to my metal head when I felt the floor vibrate with Ares' charge.

"Some guys never learn," I muttered under my breath as I straightened my legs and leapt straight up. I transferred the sword to my left hand, barely managing to hold onto the heavy blade with my busted arm as I gripped one of the building's bar joists with my right.

I looked down at Ares, tangled once again in a pile of furniture, and swung myself over to land on a pool table. "Anybody who doesn't want to die should leave right now," I announced. "This dickhead cares even less for your well-being than I do, if that's possible, and the cops outside want vengeance for their dead buddies. If you walk out the front door right now with your hands up, you'll probably not get shot."

One of the bikers, an older guy with a long gray beard stepped forward. "And what if we decide to throw in with Ares here and kill you?"

"Well, for one thing, I'm a lot harder to kill that it looks. And for another," I spun to my left and threw a knife, splitting the old biker's Adam's apple. He dropped like a stone, dead before he hit the ground. "I think I said it was time to go if you don't want to get dead. Clock's ticking, bitches." I didn't expect more than one or two to take me up on my offer to leave, but I certainly didn't expect the whole bunch to come at me all at once. Then I saw Ares, his eyes glowing red as he leaned against the bar and grinned.

"Have fun, boys, but be careful of the sword. It's sharp," Ares called over the sound of a dozen bikers drawing knives and brass knuckles and charging me. I leapt from one pool table to another, taking a bald head off at the shoulders as I jumped. *One down.* I hopped over a pool cue swung at my ankles and threw myself flat to the table as another one stabbed where he expected me to be. I wasn't there, and Ares' sword slid between his ribs like his lungs were butter. He collapsed, taking the sword to the floor with him, and I rolled off the other side of the table onto the floor. I felt a hammer blow to my shoulder and looked down, but there was just a small ding in my armored skin. A stunned biker stood ten feet away, holding a smoking 9mm and staring at me.

"Yeah, that's my skin, jackass," I said as I stepped over to him and buried one of my remaining knives in his gut. I angled the blade upward to pierce his heart, then spun around, using his body as a shield until I could get my back to a wall. Then I shoved the dead biker away from me and drew my Sig. I fired three rounds, and three bikers dropped. Then my head snapped back as a bullet ricocheted off my forehead, slamming the back of my head into the wall. I sagged to the floor and looked around for the shooter. I spotted him standing twenty feet away with a smoking pistol in his hand. I sighted down the barrel of the Sig but couldn't decide which one of the guys I should shoot, so I fired four times, two rounds for each of him. The guy on the left was the real one, and he dropped. I had a moment to shake my head and try to clear my vision, but it wasn't happening.

I struggled to my feet, one arm broken and throbbing, concussed and seeing double, but still titanium-skinned and getting more pissed off by the moment. Four more bikers advanced on me from the left and I lifted my left hand with a wince and shouted, *"Incendere!"*

A ball of fire the size of my fist flew from my fingertips, growing in size as the air in the bar and my rage fueled it. I continued to pour my will into the fireball until it was the size of a beach ball, then released my control of it as it hit the nearest biker square in the chest. Flames exploded from him, dousing all four thugs in a bath of flaming death and pain. They went down, rolling around like we were all taught in kindergarten. Problem is, magical fire is harder to extinguish than phosphorous. It'll burn until its target is destroyed, or I tell it to stop. And I didn't want it to stop. One biker managed to keep his feet, and he was running around like a chicken with its head cut off, spreading the fire to all corners of the bar. After a solid two minutes of running around screaming, he collapsed in a corner under a Confederate flag and died. I knelt to the floor in the smoke and confusion and etched some symbols on the floor with a knife from my belt.

The fires didn't die with the bikers, who were all gone within a minute except the one running around panicked. The fire spread to the pool tables, the bar tables, the walls, the bar itself, and before long the room was engulfed in flames. I concentrated as best I could and muttered "*purgo*." A sphere of clean air formed around my face, and I looked for Ares. He was still leaning against the bar with his arms crossed, watching me.

He pushed off the bar and walked toward me slowly. "I liked this bar. The body I inhabited caused a lot of mayhem in this bar, and I was going to use those idiots to cause even more. Now I'll just have to do it by myself. That's not as much fun. You'll have to die, of course. Not only are you fucking with my plans, but you killed all my toys. Can't have that. Say goodnight, now, wizard."

"Goodnight, fuckwit," I said, then poured my energy into the circle I'd carved into the floor. The binding circle sprang to life, trapping Ares in the center of my magical energy, which I had, in turn, tied to the earth beneath the building. There are a couple of pretty major fault lines running under Charlotte, and fault lines mean ley lines. I tapped into the magical river of power that was Charlotte's main line, and linked the spell to it. As long as the city wasn't wiped from the Earth, that circle wasn't going anywhere.

I watched Ares pound on the walls of his invisible prison for a few more seconds before I realized that I only had enough energy to keep my spells active for a few more seconds. The circle would hold forever now that it was tied to the ley lines, but my titanium skin and clean air were both about to run out. Neither of those were anything I was interested in happening while I was in a burning building.

"Gotta run, Ares. You have fun in there. Maybe, learn a trade, or a foreign language," I said, backing away toward the door. Trapped or no, I wasn't turning my back on one of the Four Horsemen of the goddamn Apocalypse. I felt the doorknob hit me in the ass, literally, and I flung the door open just as the liquor bottles behind the bar started to explode.

I got halfway across the parking lot and let my air bubble down. The smoke was still a nuisance out here, but the air was breathable. I took a few more steps and reversed the spell turning my skin to metal. Then there was a huge explosion from behind me, and the world went black.

CHAPTER TWELVE

I woke up staring into Agent Smith's gray eyes and his grayer crew cut. "If I'm dreaming, kill me. Because you're the ugliest fucking Florence Nightingale I've ever seen."

Smith leaned back onto his heels. He was kneeling beside my head on the floor of the Mobile Command Center. "He's alive. I told you he was hard to kill." There was a strange look on Smith's face, one of the corners of his mouth was bent upward and a few of his teeth were showing. It looked involuntary, and a little bit painful. Then I realized it.

"You're smiling!" I said. "I didn't know you knew how."

"Fuck you, Harker," he said, his normal scowl returning.

"That's my Smitty," I said, heaving myself up to a sitting position. Three Smiths swum in front of me for half a second, then they snapped into focus. "Fuck, that hurt."

"What part?" Smith asked.

"The broken arm was a bitch, and the concussion sucked, but I wasn't expecting to get blown up," I replied. "So that part was pretty much no fun."

"Yeah, apparently there was a van load of fertilizer bomb behind the bar, which caught fire and blew the whole building to hell. You were under most of a wall for an hour. We figure the plan was to take his band of merry men over to the Johnson C. Smith campus where the First Lady was speaking and blow themselves up, Al Qaeda style," Smith said.

"Shifting all the attention to the Middle East, who we're already inclined to shoot at..." I said.

"Yeah, and you kill the President's wife and kids with a Quran anywhere on your person and we'll have a shooting war within the hour," Smith finished.

"Pretty good plan, frankly. It's exactly the kind of attack a terror cell would try on U.S. soil, and exactly the kind of ruse that would work. Where's Ares?" I asked.

"He's still standing out there, pissed off and stuck in that magic circle you left him in. We tried to secure him, but couldn't break the lines." Smith looked grumpy at that.

"Don't even think of recruiting that asshole. He's the embodiment of War, he lives for nothing but combat. You stick him in one peaceful little village and you'll have civil war in three hours and a nuclear incident in six."

"Sounds like my kind of guy." The corner of Smith's mouth twitched again, and I looked away. Watching that guy try to crack a joke was more painful than my last confession, which took seven hours and made three priests retire.

"Where's the sword?" I asked.

"Still laying where we found you. I wouldn't let anyone touch it."

"Good call," I said. "It does funny things to humans."

"You're human, Harker," Smith said, and I looked at him with one corner of my own mouth twitching.

"Mostly. Today's a good day to be a little something different, though." I got to my feet, checking the various hurt parts, and decided nothing was permanently damaged. My concussion was gone except for a splitting headache, and my left arm was back to at least half strength. I was covered in bruises from having a building fall on me, but I learned how to ignore bruises a long time ago, so I did. I opened the door and walked down the metal steps, looking around. The Command Center was in the middle of the street right outside where the biker bar had been. Debris was scattered everywhere, like a bomb had gone off or a building exploded. Which it had, so I figured it made sense.

The only thing still standing from the bar was a pissed-off god of War, still locked into my circle. He was a clear spot in a football-field sized blast zone littered with body parts, bricks, shattered pool tables, motorcycle pieces, and glass.

I walked over to a pile a cinderblocks and pulled Ares' sword out of the rubble. It still thrummed with power, and I felt it reaching out to me. I allowed the power to touch me, to explore who I was and what I was. I felt the power draw back at the part of me that came from Uncle Luke, and embrace the rage that ran through my human side, all the feelings of rage and loss that came from more than a century of living. I felt the magical essence of War search through my soul, and eventually decide that I was lacking. I wasn't the avatar War wanted.

"Good," I said quietly. Didn't need the local constabulary to see me talking to a sword, even a magical one. Maybe especially a magical one. "Now that we've got that settled, I need you to do something."

I walked up to the shimmering circle and stood facing Ares. "What's your name?"

"I told you, pitiful human, my name is Ares, and I am the god of War!" The giant in the circle roared, then beat on my metaphysical boundary with both fists. I felt the barrier give a little, then felt it snap back to full strength. *Shit. He's stronger than I thought.* I didn't anticipate him being able to do anything to that circle, especially not once it was tied into the city's ley lines.

"I mean what was your name before War manifested in you?" I pushed at him a little with my will, just enough for him to know I could probably pull it out of him, but that wouldn't be comfortable for either of us.

"Josh. Josh Monroe," he said, looking at me through narrowed eyes.

"Josh Monroe, I'm sorry for this. You got caught up in forces you couldn't possibly understand. Most humans can't. You became a pawn in a bigger game, and your side lost. So I'm sorry." With that I reached out with a toe and broke the circle. The second my aura touched the circle I'd cast, all the energy I poured into the circle rushed back into me, and all the energy I'd trapped from the city's main ley line poured back into the line, triggering a small earthquake. Most people wouldn't feel it, but I was at the epicenter of the quake, so it rocked me and Ares a lot harder. I knew it was coming, so I recovered my balance faster, and before Ares had a chance to gather his wits, I plunged his sword into his chest, shoving the six-foot blade through to the hilt. His eyes went wide and he looked down at the sword sticking out between his ribs.

Ares opened his mouth, but no sound came out. He just let out a small wheeze, and blood poured from his mouth as the light left his eyes. I watched as the god of War dropped to his knees and fell sideways, taking the sword from my grasp as he did. I turned around and motioned for a couple of the cops to come forward.

"Pack his body up and get it back to police headquarters. Take the sword in a separate car. Put it in a rifle case, or something, but whatever you do, *don't touch it* with your bare hands. There's a biological contaminant on the metal connected with the attack we foiled this morning. Do you understand?" They nodded, and I walked back to where Smith stood outside the Mobile Command Center.

"Let's roll. By my figuring, we've got one more Horseman to stop before we have to deal with Death himself."

"Actually, Flynn just called. They took out Famine at the North Mecklenburg Water Treatment Facility. He was going to poison the water supply for half the county."

"Nice. How did they figure it out?"

"I asked, she said something about being a detective and leaving that kind of work to her. She sounded a little smug."

"If she took out a Horseman with nothing but her wits and Renfield, then she's got plenty to feel smug about," I said. *Flynn?* I sent down our link.

Her mind came back weakly, as if she was a long way from me. *Yeah? I'm having trouble connecting. I'm on 77 heading back into town. Where are you?*

At the biker joint. Just meet us at headquarters.

Will do. You okay? You sound funny, if that makes sense.

It does. I got my egg scrambled a little, makes it hard to concentrate. I'll see you in a bit. And Flynn?

Yeah?

Nice work. Not many humans could take out a Horseman on their own.

I wasn't on my own. Renfield was with me. He's pretty impressive for a butler.

Don't let him hear you call him that. I chuckled and cut off our connection.

"She okay?" Smith asked.

"How could you tell?" I asked.

"You both get kind of a dazed look on your face when you're talking in your head. It's pretty easy to figure out after a while."

"Fair enough. But what won't be easy to figure out is where is Death going to manifest. Let's get back to HQ. I need a big map."

CHAPTER THIRTEEN

I had a huge map of Charlotte tacked to the wall of the conference room and was scribbling on it with magic markers when Flynn and Renfield walked in.

"Is it Arts & Crafts time, Harker?" Flynn asked. "Because I have this awesome elbow macaroni and yarn necklace I've been dying to make."

"I'm trying to figure out where Death will manifest," I said, circling one last point on my map.

"What do you have so far?" she asked, stepping in to look at the map.

"A whole lot of fuck-all," I replied. "The last three Horsemen popped up in different places, attempted to attack more different places, and there's no pattern to any of it." I pointed to the map. I'd put pushpins in where the Horsemen appeared and attacked, or tried to. It all looked random.

"What are all these pins?" Flynn asked.

"Known supernatural actives in Charlotte. Green pins for friendly, red pins for hostile, and blue pins for the ones that just want to be left alone, like the ghost of Queen Charlotte."

"The ghost of Queen Charlotte is here?" Flynn asked.

"Part-time. Poor girl gets bounced around between Charlotte and Kew Palace just outside London. She doesn't really do anything, just hangs out wherever there are statues to her."

"Oooh, so she's stuck at the airport?" Flynn asked. "That doesn't seem very restful."

"It's not. And she doesn't know why she can't move on. Might have something to do with her jewels not being laid to rest with her, but I haven't really cared enough to go look for them," I replied.

"That's awful, Harker. You should help her," Flynn said.

"No profit in it," I said. "And since she's not hurting anybody, I figure let her haunt the airport, and the palace, and Queen Square in Blumbury until she figures out how to move on or she goes apeshit and becomes a problem. For now, there are enough red pins in my map to keep me busy for the rest of even my life."

"Good point. There seem to be a lot of things in town that don't like you," Flynn pointed out.

"Those aren't the ones that don't like *me*. That list is way longer. These are creatures or magic-users that don't like anybody, and will kill humans on sight."

"Oh."

"Yeah, so any bright ideas?" I waved at the map.

"Have you tried to cast a spell?" she asked.

"A spell to do what?"

"Find Wally. Isn't he still the point of all this? If we find him before he breaks the fourth seal, won't it all be over?"

Fuck, she's right, I thought as I swept all the notes and crap off the conference table. "Renfield, bring me Wally's overnight bag from his apartment."

"What are you going to do with that?" Smith asked.

"Well, since you two went off the reservation and killed the third Horseman instead of finding Wally, I'm going to have to break out more mojo. Watch and see," I said, putting on my inscrutable face.

Renfield hurried back in a few minutes later with a blue and white duffle with ASICs on the side and put it on the table. I started digging around in the bag, then just turned it upside down and dumped everything out onto the table. T-shirts, crumpled jeans, socks and underwear all spilled across the table. I swept all the clothes onto the floor. I opened his toiletries bag and spilled a razor, deodorant and a couple different tubes of toothpaste out. I turned the little bag inside out, then tossed it aside. I grabbed the duffel and opened the side pocket, reaching all the way down into the corners.

"Gotcha!" I said, pulling my hand out with a plain wooden box about two inches by four inches. I flipped a tiny latch on one side and the top slid open, revealing a fake cigarette. "I knew that little bastard wouldn't go anywhere without his favorite one-hitter."

"What are you going to do with that?" Smith asked.

"The same kind of sympathetic magic I cast using his blood back at the apartment. Because this is something he carried with him a lot, it will have a lot of his energy soaked into it. It's even better because it's wooden. Natural materials absorb energy better than metal or plastics. Hopefully I can get a rudimentary tracking spell off this thing. If I cast it right, maybe I can make it light up and gimme a puff whenever we're going in the right direction."

Nobody laughed. *Tough room. One little apocalypse and they get all serious on you.* I closed my eyes, focused my will on the little pipe and murmured "*Corpus ad corpus, sanguinem sanguini. Corpus ad corpus, sanguinem sanguini. Corpus ad corpus, sanguinem sanguini.*" With the third incantation, I felt a tug along my magical senses pulling me off to the left. I opened my eyes and saw Flynn staring at me, her eyes wide.

"What the fuck was that?" she asked.

"You felt that, huh?" I wasn't surprised. Our bond was unusually strong, and with me throwing magic around this close to her, if she had any sensitivity at all, she was bound to feel it.

"Yeah, like something wants us to go east," she said.

"That's the tracking spell. The pipe wants to go to its owner now."

"Why didn't I feel anything when you cast the spell in the apartment?" she asked.

"I don't know for sure, but it might have something to do with the newness of the bond, or the weakness of your body. You were just recently brought back from the dead, you know."

"I wasn't that bad," Flynn scoffed. I just looked at her, one eyebrow in the air. "Was I?" she asked. I still didn't say anything. Exactly how close she was to dead was not something I wanted to discuss in a building full of mundane cops. I wasn't sure I ever wanted to discuss it, but I figured I probably wasn't going to be given a choice.

"Well, now that the spell works, let's get after this kid," Smith said. "I want four units rolling with us. Two snipers, a full insertion team—"

"No," I said. "Just us."

"What the fuck, Harker? You think you're still a solo operator? You're a goddamn government agent now, and you have the full weight and power of the United States Government behind you. You don't have to do this lone wolf bullshit anymore," Smith growled in my face.

"It's not so much lone wolf bullshit, Smitty, as it is a desire to limit the body count. How many men did you lose going after Ares?"

"Six in the botched vac of the daycare, a couple more across the op. I'd say we lost nine altogether."

"How about we handle this next one my way and we don't lose anybody?" I crossed my arms over my chest and waited.

"What's your way?" Smith asked, crossing his own arms.

I thought about making some crack about whipping them out and measuring but did the uncharacteristic thing and kept my smartass comment to myself. "Flynn drives and waits outside with your team of heavies. You, me, and Renfield go in quiet, see if we can get to the kid before the fourth seal is broken. If we can get to him, we kill the bad guys, get Wally out, and it's all sunbeams and unicorns."

"If we can't?" Smith asked.

"Then Flynn comes in with the heavies and avenges us."

"Whoa," Flynn said. "Avenge?"

"There's only two ways this thing goes down, Becks, and that's with all the bad guys dead, or everybody dead. Sorry, but them's just the facts of it."

"I told you, don't call me—"

Fuck. I saw her eyes go wide just before she finished the sentence. She was about to say, "Don't call me Becks, only my father called me Becks," and I knew it. So my mind unconsciously went back to that night in the alley and looking in her father's eyes as the last light went out of them, and right there, tied me with a bond tighter than blood or love, was Detective Rebecca Gail Flynn. I felt all her pain come rushing up through the years in one half-second. All the milestones missed, all the father-daughter dances that never happened, all the prom dates her cop dad never scared the shit out of, all the graduations missed—high school, college, Police Academy. I felt all that loss pour through our connection as she saw through my eyes the last moments of the father she'd idolized.

She looked up at me, eyes suddenly full of tears and recriminations, and I felt the door in my mind slam shut, cutting off our connection like a light switch. "We need to talk," Flynn said.

"Not now," I replied.

"No, not now. But you better not get dead, motherfucker, because you have some serious explaining to do."

"I'll try to survive. You know, for your sake." I turned back to Smith. "Sound like a plan?"

"What the fuck just happened?" the agent asked. I looked over at Renfield, who gave me the tiniest shake of his head. He was right, Smith didn't need to know anything about Paul Flynn's death and my promise to him.

"Remember that connection you made me forge to Flynn's soul?" I asked. Smith nodded. "We just had a whole argument, without ever having to yell at one another. It's not really satisfying, but it's better for the crockery. Now, the plan?"

"It's fine, but why is he coming with us instead of Flynn?" Smith pointed at Renfield. "I don't like involving civilians in my operations."

"And ordinarily I would applaud that effort and go home straightway, but this endeavor requires certain skills which I possess that I daresay would escape most, if not all, of your men," said the dapper little manservant.

"He means he can pick any lock ever made and move like smoke," I said.

"I do have certain skills in that regard." Ren tipped an imaginary hat.

"So whattaya say, Smitty? We rollin' or not?"

"Might as well try it your way, since it worked so fucking swimmingly with Ares," Smith said, then turned and started walking to the front door, where Ren had left the Hummer parked. We climbed in, Flynn behind the wheel, and headed down Elizabeth toward Kings. Following the marijuana-beacon, we turned left on Central and followed it down past Eastway toward Albemarle. The beacon started shifting right after we crossed Eastway, and pulled hard right onto Norland. I motioned for Flynn to park in a school parking lot, and we got out.

"Of course," I said, staring across the street at the cemetery. "If you're going to raise Death, why not start with a bunch of dead people?"

CHAPTER FOURTEEN

The cemetery was pristine, with rolling hills of freshly-mown grass and not a soul in sight. There was a green tent still standing from a recent interment, but all the holes were filled and all the heavy equipment was gone. Fresh flowers dotted some of the nearest graves, and a few tiny plastic flags fluttered in the light breeze. I didn't really need the one-hitter in my pocket pulling me toward the small chapel in the center of the graveyard; the fact that the only two cars that weren't government-issued in the entire place were parked outside of it was clue enough.

Smith and I walked side-by-side to the front of the building, with Renfield hanging back a little and keeping an eye open for trouble coming up behind. I saw the goon standing by the door before he saw us, and I drew my pistol, keeping it down by my leg and dropping a step behind Smith as we approached.

The goon saw us and stepped forward, holding up a silver shield. "Sorry, folks, this is an active crime scene. You can't go in there."

We were still a good ten yards away, so I pretended not to hear him. "What was that, Officer?" I yelled, putting one hand up to my ear.

The goon took a few more steps forward and we closed to about fifteen feet before he repeated, "You can't be here right now, there's been a murder. You'll have to come back later."

"A murder?" I asked, then raised my gun and shot him in the left eye. He dropped like a stone, the back of his head turning to a mess that resembled nothing more than a raspberry cobbler.

Smith stopped in his tracks and spun to face me. "What the actual fuck was that about, Harker? That was a human, not a monster! You can't just go around shooting people for no reason!"

I didn't stop walking. "No reason, Smitty? He's helping to open the *seven fucking seals*. I think that takes him right off the Dalai Lama's Christmas card list." I was at the door and tried the handle. It was every bit as locked as I expected it to be. "Renfield, take care of this before I blow it up." I gestured at the door.

"I don't believe the Dalai Lama sends Christmas cards," the slight man said as he knelt before the chapel doors.

"That explains why I've never gotten one. And here I thought he didn't like vampires. I feel better now. Thank you, Ren."

"Happy to help, sir." He pulled a small leather case out of his pocket and slid a couple of thin metal rods out of it. He manipulated the rods within the lock for a few seconds before I heard a tiny *click* and the cylinder rotated. Renfield stood up, put away his tools, and motioned at the door. "After you, sir."

I turned to see Smith standing on the bottom step fuming. "You wanna bitch at me some more or you wanna go save the world?"

"I'm thinking," he growled.

"Well, you think about it, and I'm going to go in here and see what else needs killing."

"Master Harker?" Renfield tapped me on the shoulder.

"Yeah, Ren?"

"There seems to be a certain odor emanating from the building."

"Yeah, you'll have that where they bury lots of people, Ren." Then I smelled it. "Shit," I said under my breath.

"No, Master Harker, I don't believe that's the smell," Renfield said.

"Stay here, Ren. No matter what, you stay here," I said and turned to the door. Then I thought for half a second and turned back. "Scratch that. If it all goes to shit, you get Detective Flynn out of here. It won't do any good long-term, but it might give her a few extra hours."

"I don't think I understand, sir."

"Yeah, and I'm sorry about that, Ren, but I don't have time to explain. And we won't be going in stealthy anymore, so you should stay up here where it's safer. Smith, come with me. We've got a lot of bad things to kill."

"I don't think I can trust your judgment on what needs killing, Harker. That man back there—"

"That man allied himself with creatures that are working on opening a portal to Hell right under this church, right fucking now. So that put him on the 'Bad Guys' list. And I don't believe in rehabilitation, Smith. I see big nasties, I put them down. And there's some serious big nasty going on here today, I can smell the brimstone all the way up here. So can we please haul ass before they break the fourth seal and unleash Hell on Earth?"

I pushed through the door and went into the chapel without looking to see if Smith was following me. I opened up my Sight as I crossed the threshold and almost went mind-blind with the force of the magic hammering against me. The inside of the little church looked about like those places do, with half a dozen rows of pews split by two aisles leading to a small pulpit with a clear space in front for a casket. There was an electric organ off to the right of the pulpit, and a font of holy water off to the left. Light from a dozen or more stained glass windows depicting events in the life of Christ sent a crazy-quilt of colors dancing around the room, and a rose window in the small choir loft shone white light through a huge dove onto the communion table down front.

And laid out on the communion table was a man I assumed was the priest. At least that was my guess based on the robes. I couldn't have identified him by anything more than his teeth or DNA because his face was missing. So were his hands and a fair amount of the flesh from his torso. His organs were laid out on the table in front of him, like some kind of twisted sacrament, and a goblet full of a thick red liquid sat beside his head.

The body glowed red to my Sight, and the smell of brimstone became so thick I could almost taste it as I drew near. I holstered my gun and knelt by the body. Something gold glittered from within his abdominal cavity, and I looked closer. I took a deep breath and reached into the priest's body, wrapping my hand around the object and pulling it free with a squelching sound. I reached down and used his robes to wipe the crucifix free, then wiped my hands. I set the crucifix on the table by his head and stepped over to the font. I dipped my hand into the holy water and leaned over the priest's body. I dabbed a little holy water on his forehead and closed my eyes.

"*Per istam sanctan unctionem et suam piissimam misericordiam, indulgeat tibi Dominus quidquid,*" I whispered.

"You know it's supposed to be olive oil, right?" Glory's voice came from behind me as I knelt by the body.

"Yeah, and it's supposed to happen before he's dead, too. But I figured it couldn't hurt."

"And you're not opposed to covering your fists in holy water before you try to find the steps down to wherever the ritual is taking place, either."

"That thought had crossed my mind." I turned and looked at Glory. She was wearing Smith's body, and it was really disconcerting to hear the angel's voice coming from Smith's grizzled face. "Glory, I need you to do something for me."

"I'll try."

"If this all goes to shit, get Flynn out of here. Get her to her mother's, or church, or somewhere. But get her as far from here as possible."

"Why Harker, I'd almost think you care about this girl," Glory said, and I saw a little smile on her face.

"I made a promise to her father. And I keep my promises." I leaned over the font of holy water, preparing myself for the coming battle.

"That you do, my reckless ward. That you do indeed." I watched Smith's eyes go blank, then watched his consciousness take control again as Glory left him.

"What the fucking fuck was *that?*" the agent asked, turning around looking for whatever had just been in his head.

"You, my dear Smitty, have just been touched by an angel. Now let's go downstairs and kick some ass," I said, pointing to a thin door behind the organ.

CHAPTER FIFTEEN

The first thing I noticed when I opened the door to the stairwell was the stink. Brimstone—real, unfiltered, straight-from-the-bowels-of-Hell brimstone—is way stronger than sulfur. It's like sulfur on steroids, with a dash of blood and rot mixed in. And it was brimstone I smelled. Even without my Sight, I could tell there was some serious mojo being thrown around downstairs, and it wasn't anything good for anyone. The chanting in Enochian was another dead giveaway. The language of angels wasn't something to be thrown around lightly, and anyone willing to play with that shit under a slaughtered priest was definitely working against the common good.

Smith and I crept down a narrow stone staircase, pressing our backs to the wall opposite a row of flickering torches that cast long shadows ahead of us. The chanting grew louder as we moved closer, and I began to be able to pick out a few words here and there. None of them were words that I wanted to hear in an occult ritual—things like "devourer," "ravager," "destruction," that kind of light-hearted little ditty.

I held up a finger to Smith and he froze. I opened my Sight and pushed my will outward from myself, using my Sight to peek around the corners and get a sense of what was ahead. I got a feeling of rage, pain, and fear and pulled my Sight back in as a dark consciousness locked onto mine.

"We've been made," I whispered to Smith as I stepped off the wall and strode openly into the room. What had once been a storage room for communion candles and decor for the multiple denominations the chapel served had been turned into a collage out of a haunted house or a horror movie. It was so over the top it would have been funny if there hadn't been a terrified black kid bent backward over an altar stripped to the waist with Enochian symbols drawn on his chest in blood.

The pulpit had been a pair of file cabinets in a former life, covered with red velvet and with Wally tied to it. There were black candles scattered all around the room, probably fifty or more of them. Black fabric draped every wall, and half a dozen men and women in black robes and golden goat masks surrounded the altar. They all looked up when I walked in, and their chanting trailed off to silence.

"Hi kids, how's it hanging? Gonna raise a little hell?" I asked, stepping up to the altar and putting a hand on Wally's chest. I also made it a point to step across the huge circle drawn on the floor around the altar and drag my foot through the lines, breaking the circle and disrupting any protection it may have offered the idiots outside of it.

"You cannot stop the Acolytes of Armageddon, fool! Leave now before we smite you down!" the goat-head nearest Wally's right shoulder bellowed at me.

"You know I'm standing right here, pal. No need to yell. Or do these things make it hard to hear?" I reached out and yanked his goat mask off and threw it over my shoulder. A Rick Moranis look-alike, horn-rims and all, goggled at me from inside his cavernous black hood and robe. "Is that better? Can you hear me now?"

"You can't interrupt the ritual!" Moranis bleated at me. "We've already begun summoning Death incarnate! He whose arrival will signal the oncoming Apocalypse! The sacrifice must be completed!" The little dude stretched out his right arm and jabbed a curved dagger downward toward Wally's chest. I gave the kid a shove and he toppled over, homemade altar and all. The nerd with the knife staggered forward and I stuck out a leg, sending him sprawling. He tumbled into a heap at Smith's feet and his knife slid across the floor.

"Where did you guys find each other, Henchmen-R-Us?" I asked. "'Cause I was way more worried about the thug you left guarding the door. *This* is your fearless leader? He couldn't summon a cheeseburger at McDonald's, much less bring about the end of the world."

"You're right, Mr. Harker. Eric was simply a cog in my machine. He was never intended to be the leader of anything, merely a distraction for meddling do-gooders."

"You mean like *moi*?" I pointed at my chest.

"I mean exactly like you. I thought if you decided Eric wasn't a threat, then you would probably do something brash and stupid, like break the containment circle and free our Dark Lord."

"What do mean...oh fucksticks." I turned to see Wally getting up from where I'd toppled the altar. There was no hint of the enthusiastic but addled stoner I'd met the night before. Standing in front of me with his eyes gone completely black was Death himself. Power rolled off him in waves, and I felt it even without using my Sight.

"Mr. Harker, I must say that I am pleased to finally make your acquaintance. You have sent so many to my realm, I feel as though we are old friends." Wally/Death raised his hand and the two goat-heads nearest him dropped to the floor. "Ahhh, they were full of life. Delicious, but you know that, don't you, Mr. Harker?"

"It's been a while since I ate my meals *tartare*. Trying to live in civilized company nowadays. You know how it is."

"No, I don't. And I suggest that if you wish to continue breathing, you stop moving toward your gun, Agent Smith. Or whatever they are calling you now." I turned my head a little and saw Smith put his hands up.

"That's nice. Just stay there for now. I'll let you know when it's time to die."

"So what's the plan?" I asked. "You gonna go up out of here and kill everybody, is that it? Gonna wipe the Earth clean as a baby's butt? Bring about the end of the world? Without Wally, you can't open any more of the seals, can you?"

"With Death at my command, I won't need to open any more—" The lead goat-head cut off in mid-soliloquy, dropping to one knee, then falling face-first to the concrete. He pressed one hand into the floor and flopped himself over, ripping at his mask. I watched his face turn red, then purple, then move right on to black as the life poured out of him into Death's upraised left hand.

"Let me guess, you have altered the deal, and I should pray that you don't alter it further," I said, frantically scrambling around in my brain for anything that would get me out of this mess. Wally was gone, as far as I could tell, possessed by the spirit of Death, just like the other Horsemen.

"Exactly. Now, Mr. Harker, are you going to get out of my way and let me pass, or are we going to do this the hard way?" Death asked.

"I only really know the hard way, sorry." *Flynn, you there?*

On the stairs. He hasn't seen us yet.

Us?

Renfield wouldn't let me come alone.

That's probably good. You're going to have about half a second if I do this right, a lot less if I screw it up.

I got this. All you need to do is piss off the most badass of the Four Horsemen enough to drop his guard for a second.

That's kind of my specialty. I wasn't one hundred percent on exactly what Flynn had in mind, but from the images in her mind it involved Renfield, a sniper rifle, and me maybe dying. I was good with two out of three.

Death hadn't moved, just cocked his head a little to the side. "What are you plotting, parasite?"

"Now that's just rude," I said. "Stuff like that really hurts, and it makes me want to poke holes in your meat suit." I drew my Sig and leveled it at his chest.

"You won't shoot. You like this mortal and think there's some chance of saving him. You'd never—" Death's character assessment was cut off and proven wrong as the 9mm round slammed into his chest, followed by two more in a tight grouping. He staggered back, then smiled at me. I hate it when the bad guys smile; it always means things are about to get painful for me.

Death waved a hand, and three misshapen chunks of lead and copper slowly wiggled their way out of his chest and *clinked* to the floor. "That was anti-climactic. My turn." He stretched out a hand, and I felt my life force begin to drain away. I started to go weak, then my vision started to dim, then feeling started to fade in my extremities. I fought to stay on my feet as the blackness crept over me, clinging to consciousness by a thread.

Drop, jackass! I heard in my head. I fought harder, struggling against the weight of Death's life-draining power.

Fall down, you moron! Flynn's mental "voice" hit me like a slap across the face and I realized what was happening—she was feeding me her life force to keep me alive, but she was running out, and I was screwing up the plan. For the first time, I saw the whole thing unfold in front of me and dropped to my hands and knees.

A loud *crack* split the air inside the room and Death's head snapped back. His hold on me vanished as his attention was diverted, and I felt my energy rush back along our severed connection. I fed some back down the line to Flynn and stood up, pulling a flask out of my back pocket. I unscrewed the lid of the flask and threw the whole thing at Death. It hit him in the chest and toppled over, covering him in holy water.

"*Ego te demonium in inferni profundos abyssos expello,*" I said, pushing my will outwards and enveloping Death in my will and the power of the holy water. I could feel the Horseman fighting me, struggling against the incantation as I repeated the words again and again, increasing volume until I was yelling at the top of my lungs. I felt him begin to break free when out of the corner of my eye I felt more than saw a slight figure dash past me and tackle the avatar to the ground.

Renfield reached beneath his shirt and pulled out something shining on a golden chain. He pressed the necklace to Death's forehead and bellowed, "In the Name of God, the God of Yisrale: may Michael be at my right hand, Gabriel at my left, Uriel before me, Raphael behind me, and above my head, the presence of God. I command you to *begone!*" With a crack of thunder that almost split my eardrums in the confined space, a blinding light flared out from Renfield's hand, then all was still.

I stepped forward, my gun trained on the bodies on the floor, but everything looked moderately normal. Renfield was on his knees, hunched forward and either sobbing or retching, or maybe both. I couldn't really tell. Beside him lay Wally, all hint of Death's possession gone and the happy-go-lucky dreadlocked college kid restored to his very mortal glory. Wally lay there with his eyes closed and a tiny smile on his face. For a second I waited for him to wake up, then I saw the round hole in the center of his forehead, and I dropped to one knee.

I put an arm around Renfield's shoulders. "I'm sorry, buddy. The first one is always the hardest. But you did good, Ren. You saved a lot of lives today."

"That doesn't help," the kind-hearted little man said, sniffling. "We were supposed to save this one."

"No," I said. "We were supposed to stop the end of the world. And that's bigger than any of us. Bigger than all of us. And that's what you did. You saved us all. What was that, anyway?" I pointed to the necklace he was white-knuckling.

He opened his hand to show me the Star of David lying in the palm of his hand. "It was an ancient Jewish ritual of banishment."

"I didn't know you were Jewish, Renfield."

"There's more to me than meets the eye as well, Master Harker," Renfield said, struggling to his feet. "Now, should we being cleaning this...?"

"No, I've got that covered," Smith said. "Harker, you never told me your butler was a wizard."

"I'm not," Renfield said, clearing his throat. "I am neither a butler nor a wizard. I am an executive assistant, and I have many skills in many areas. Some of them I choose not to disclose until they become needed."

"Well, Ren, I'm damn glad you decided to disclose this one today. Let's get out of here before the press shows up and I have to mojo a dozen asshole reporters," I said, walking to the stairs. Flynn sat on the stairs and I held out a hand to help her up.

You okay?

I'm not sure yet. You have a lot of explaining to do.

True, but I'm not going to do it in front of Smith, and I'm not going to do it without alcohol. So if you want answers about your dad, you'll have to come with me.

Fucker.

True enough.

She reached up and took my hand, and we walked up the stairs into the daylight.

EPILOGUE

The sunset painted the sky with broad strokes of red, orange, and purple, with a single white contrail slicing over the city as I stepped out into Uncle Luke's backyard. The scene looked like something out of a twisted Normal Rockwell painting—Renfield in a fresh suit identical to the tattered one he'd left the cemetery in, a crisp white "Kiss the Chef" apron wrapped around his middle as he turned steaks and potatoes on Luke's thousand-dollar extravagance of a grill, the most frivolous purchase in the history of cooking devices. Smith stood beside him, offering advice on how and when to flip the steaks, which Renfield promptly ignored. Smith's own steak was already steaming on a plate, one half step past *tartare* in prep and stewing in a plate full of juices.

Luke stood on the porch glaring at the last rays of sunshine as they retreated across the yard from him, their poisonous golden light fading into a more welcome blue and lavender-hued evening. I stood next to him for a moment, looking out across the yard at more activity than the home had seen since Luke and I moved to Charlotte decades ago.

"Looks like a strange family picture, Uncle," I said, passing him a bottle of dark red liquid I brought out from a cabinet in the kitchen. Luke liked his dinner room temperature, but that made storage a bitch. But after a while we'd determined the right mix of anticoagulants to keep blood fresh for at least a week, so he could hunt less frequently and stay in one place longer.

"Well, we have always been a strange family, Quincy," the king of the vampires replied with a sigh. "I wish your parents were here to see this. They always worried that you would grow up twisted by my influence."

"Luke, I can't say that I'm well adjusted, but I'm pretty sure it's not your fault. I've done plenty of twisting all on my own." I patted him on the shoulder and walked across the yard to where Flynn sat on a two-seater swing.

I put the plastic grocery bag on the seat beside her and sat down. I pulled an Olde Mecklenburg Dunkel out of the bottle and pried the top off with my pinky finger. Flynn reached in and took out a bottle of Olde Meck Copper and tilted the neck towards me.

"These aren't twist-tops," she pointed out.

"I'm a super-hero, it comes with some perks," I replied as I used my finger to pop open her beer. We sat there in silence for a few moments, drinking and watching the Ren and Luke cooking show. I finished off my beer and opened another.

"You know that's a winter brew, right?" Flynn asked.

"I spent a lot of time in Germany, where they invented Dunkel. I get to drink it whenever I damn well please."

"How did my father die?"

"That's all the small talk we're going to do? You're drinking beer out of season, then right into the heavy shit?"

"I'm not looking for foreplay, Harker, I want information."

"Are you sure you want *this* information, Rebecca?"

"I need to know."

"Let's start with what you remember, what you were told."

She took a deep breath and I could see her focus, put herself back in the moment. "I was ten. It was late, past my bedtime, but I stayed up late to wait for Daddy. Mom and Dad let me do that on Fridays because it wasn't a school night. Mom was asleep on the couch, so I had turned down the TV really low so she wouldn't wake up. I was watching Nickelodeon because grown-up TV was boring. I knew something was bad when the doorbell rang. Nobody had ever rang our doorbell that late before. I opened the door and two policemen were standing there. One of them I knew; it was Uncle Robert. He wasn't really my uncle, but he was my dad's partner. His face was all red, like he'd been crying, and when he looked down at me, two big tears rolled down his cheeks. The other man was older, skinny, with a lot of medals and things on his uniform. I didn't know him then, but he was Chief McFrayn, the Chief of Police. Once he saw me, he knelt down in front of me and asked to see my mom.

"'Is my daddy dead?' I asked him.

"The skinny man knelt there staring into my eyes for a long time, then he said 'Yes, darling, he is. A bad man killed your daddy, but your daddy killed the bad man, too. Your daddy is a hero.'"

I sat next to Flynn while she told the pieces of the night that she remembered. It was standard disjointed little-kid memory stuff, pieces here and there. When she finished, she knocked off the last of her beer and handed me another one to open. "Your turn, Harker. What happened to my father? They wouldn't let us have an open casket, said it would be too hard for me to handle. Why wouldn't they let me see my father's body?"

"Because there wasn't enough left to see," I said simply. "The initial vampire attack drained most of his blood and his essence with it. But the vamp that attacked your father was a newborn, and insane to boot. So after she was full, she took a few minutes to play with her food. By the time I got there, your father was just barely hanging on."

I remembered it like it was yesterday. The light mist making everything slick, the newborn vamp running out of her master's lair, flush with new power and starving from her rebirth. Her maker laughing at his insane progeny and daring me to do something about it. I'd been hunting him for weeks, following a trail of bodies across the South as he bounced from Atlanta to Charlotte to Knoxville to Memphis back to Atlanta, then to Charleston and back up to Charlotte. I finally cornered him on the top of the Bank of America parking garage, catching him as he snacked on a violinist for the symphony who was just a little too slow getting her car unlocked. He drained her in front of me, then opened his wrist and dribbled just enough of his blood down her dying throat to turn her, but not enough to satisfy the new urges she didn't understand. She sprang back to life, desperate for blood, and ran at me.

I fought her off and put her through the windshield of a parked truck. I hoped that would keep her out of the way until I dealt with her maker, but no such luck. I turned to face him and heard the truck door open behind me, then listened to her feet dash away through the garage.

"What's it going to be, Hunter? You going to fight me, or chase down the murderer I just turned loose on the city? You know she's going to go kill someone. She can't help it. But you can. You can stop her. All you have to do is let me go."

I couldn't. I'd chased this maniac for a month and a half up and down the East Coast. There was no way I was going to let him go. The city would just have to fend for itself for half an hour.

"And in that half hour..." Flynn said.

"Yeah. In that half hour, there was an altercation at Mythos, a dance club that used to run downtown, and your dad and his partner were called. When they arrived on the scene, your father noticed a severely intoxicated woman in the neighboring parking garage. He sent his partner, your Uncle Robert, into the club to see what the call was about while he tried to help the woman. She turned out to be the newborn vampire, and she attacked him with a savagery that you can only imagine. He was not only killed, he was horribly mutilated. There was no way a child's last memory of her father should be that."

"Where were you?"

"Two blocks away. If took me less than fifteen minutes to destroy the vampire and track down the newborn. But it was too long. She was kneeling over your father's body when I got there, and she came at me again. This time I decapitated her with one swipe of my katana. I mentioned this was the 90s, right? Long coats and katanas seemed somehow in keeping with the decade. Anyway, I killed it and checked on your dad. He was almost gone, but with his dying breath he made me promise to look after Becks for him. So I have."

"You have what?" Flynn asked. Her eyebrows were crawling high into her hairline at this point.

"I've been around every major event in your life, Detective." I opened my mind and let her see the memories I carried—her high school graduation, college commencement, Police Academy graduation, her first collar, more bad first dates than she even remembered having, and a couple of embarrassing karaoke moments with other cops in her precinct.

"You've been..."

"Keeping a promise."

"Spying on me!"

"It was never like that, and you know it." And she did, we could feel each other through our link and she knew that I was telling the truth. There was never anything prurient in my skulking. I was just keeping a promise to her father.

"When were you going to tell me?"

"When I had to. It was going to come out eventually, with us working this closely." I sat there, watching her out of the side of my eye. We rocked back and forth on the swing for several minutes, her not speaking a word to me.

"Thank you," she said at last.

"For what?"

"For being with him at the end. All these years, all I knew was that a bad person killed my daddy, and his partner was okay. I assumed he died alone, and I didn't want that."

"I was right there, his hand in mine."

"Good. Thank you."

I didn't say anything else, just sat rocking beside Flynn as the smell of cooking drifted over the darkening lawn.

PART III
HELL ON HEELS

CHAPTER ONE

I was headed home after a particularly disgusting exorcism when my cell phone rang. I took a minute to find a dry spot on my jeans (the back of the knee is good for this, no matter what you do, unless you're absolutely submerged, you usually stay dry there) and wipe off my hands before I answered.

"I'm tired, dirty, sober, and pissed off, so what do you want?" I growled into the phone.

"You have the sweetest phone voice," said Detective Rebecca Gail Flynn of the Charlotte-Mecklenburg Police Department, currently on special assignment to the Department of Homeland Security's Paranormal Division, a division that didn't officially exist. "How quickly can you get over here?"

"Where is here?" I asked. "Because if it's your apartment and you've got the jacuzzi running, the answer is fifteen minutes. If it's police headquarters, the answer is at least two hours."

"Let's try putting those two together and getting you to HQ in fifteen minutes. We've got a bad one," Flynn replied.

"You *think* you've got a bad one. I've still got most of a bad one splattered all over my clothes. I'm going to have to bill these people for a new pair of shoes, at the very least. Do you have any idea how much food a person can eat when they've been possessed by a gluttony demon for a week? And do you have any idea what happens to that food when the demon is exorcised?"

"That's a no on all counts, Harker, and I don't give a shit. Just get your ass over here. You can shower in the locker room, and I'll get you something to wear."

"No dice," I replied. "Meet me at my apartment in twenty. I'll leave the door open." I hung up on her protests and slid the phone into my pocket as I walked to my car. I tossed my exorcism bag into the trunk of my old burgundy Accord and shrugged out of my leather duster. It was a little ostentatious, but it looked the part of a wizard a lot more than I did, and it kept me from getting completely covered in puke on gigs like this. I emptied the pockets, then left the duster laying on top of a bush for the next homeless guy to find. Then I grabbed a towel from the trunk and wiped myself down as best as I could. I put another towel on the seat of the car and headed home to clean up, mentally tallying up the cost of the new wardrobe so I could add it to the client's bill.

I was lathering up for a second scrub-down when I heard someone enter my apartment. "If that's Detective Flynn, I'm in the shower. If it's my order from Playmates R' Us, I'm in the shower. If it's anyone else, fuck off!" I called from the open door of my bathroom.

"Playmates R' Us?" Flynn asked as she came in and leaned against the counter.

"A man can dream," I replied, rinsing off and reaching down to turn off the water. I pulled the curtain back and grabbed a towel from the rack, a little disappointed that Detective Flynn had decided to give me my privacy. I wrapped a towel around my waist and stepped out into the bedroom. Flynn was sitting on the end of my bed, looking impatient.

"Where were you, Harker? Your clothes smell like shit," she said, kicking the pile of puke-covered clothes even farther away. I had them all piled up on a towel to be taken out and burned. Days like this it was a damn good thing I have a rich uncle.

"Puke, actually. That's the remnants of about thirteen pizzas and a gallon or two of ice cream, by my best guess."

"What were you doing, teaching Ouija lessons to sorority girls?"

"That's not a bad idea, and probably a fuckload cleaner than this gig. No, I was exorcising a fifteen-year-old bulimic who had suddenly started eating her family out of house and home. Seems Little Miss Size Six wanted to be Little Miss Size Two and found a spell on the internet that promised to help her lose twenty pounds in a weekend. It was really a spell to summon a gluttony demon into the caster's body, so she was well on her way to eating herself to death by the time her parents called me in."

"That's disgusting."

"That's not even the disgusting part," I said.

"No, I mean a fifteen-year-old girl who's a size six thinking she's fat. What the hell is this world coming to? I'm a size twelve and I think I look pretty good."

I dropped my towel and opened the dresser for some boxers. "I'd have to agree, Detective. Looks like everything's in the right places to me."

"Oh for God's sake, Harker!" Flynn exclaimed, covering her eyes.

"What?" I asked, then looked down. "Sorry," I said. "Raised in Europe, remember? All your American hang-ups about being naked kinda missed me."

"I thought you grew up in Victorian England?"

"Edwardian, to be precise," I called out. "I was born in London in November 1896, but by the time I could remember anything, what you call the Victorian period was over and we were much more Continental."

"But you still didn't run around flashing people!"

"Meh, it was more of 'do what you like, just don't scare the horses.' We did whatever we liked in private and with close friends, but we were much more reserved in public."

"Well, as far as you being naked is concerned, let's keep it a little reserved. We're not that close friends."

"What's wrong, Detective? See something you like?" I turned to her and flexed a little, showing off my abs. It would probably have been more impressive if I had abs, but exercise was never a strong point of mine. When you come by your superhuman strength the old-fashioned way, by having a vampire bite both your parents and muck about with your DNA before you're even conceived, you don't sweat the gym membership too much.

Flynn ignored me, so after a few seconds I pulled on a pair of black jeans and a black t-shirt. I sat next to her on the bed, pulled on a pair of socks and started lacing up my Doc Martens. The all-black ensemble was a little pretentious, but since I only owned black jeans, black t-shirts, and black boots, it certainly made dressing for work easier.

"So what's the deal? I'm pretty sure you didn't come here just to ogle me as I scrubbed chunks of puke out of my hair," I asked.

"I think there's a vampire on the loose in Charlotte," Flynn said.

"Yeah, his name's Dracula, but he'd really rather you just call him Luke. Or even Mr. Card."

"I'm not talking about your uncle, asshole. There's another one."

"Impossible," I said, standing up. I dug my phone and wallet out of my pants and tied the towel around the bundle of disgusting clothes. I dropped it onto the tile of the bathroom, figuring at least then it wouldn't soak into the carpet.

"Why is it impossible?"

161

"Because my uncle lives here, and he doesn't like other vampires. He barely tolerates me, and I'm his fault, for Christ's sake. No way would he let another real vampire run free in Charlotte." I held up a hand. "And before you even say it, there is also no way a vampire could operate within a hundred miles of here without his knowledge. He knows these things. It's kinda creepy, but he does."

"Then either he's gotten sloppy, or we've got something else feeding on humans that looks an awful lot like a vampire."

"And how do you know what a vampire attack looks like, Detective? If I recall correctly, the veil was lifted for you just a few months ago, and before that you had no idea that the monster under your bed was real."

"What do you mean, the monster under my bed was real?"

"There are monsters under children's beds. Or at least, there are a lot of times. They're little guys, almost completely harmless unless they eat too much. They're called gurties, and they feed on dreams and imagination. And what better place to find that than in a kid's bedroom? So they live under the bed, and usually there's no problem."

"Usually?"

"Yeah," I said. "Every once in a while they eat too much, and the kid turns nuts. Did you know having your dreams taken away from you could make you crazy? Well it can, and when it does, I go kill the gurty and the kid goes into therapy."

"What happens to the kid?" Flynn asked.

"Nothing. I can't rebuild devoured dreams; once they're gone, they're gone. All I can do is make sure the gluttonous little bastard doesn't do it to anybody else. But you were saying something about a vampire?"

"Yeah, there have been three bodies discovered in the past three nights, all with similar wounds, and all of them completely drained of blood."

"In populated areas?"

"Nearby. One in the alley between the library and Spirit Square, one in the parking deck across from the Blumenthal Center, and one behind the pizza joint in NoDa." She named two Uptown locations and one spot in the trendy arts district just north of Uptown.

"Those are way outside Luke's typical hunting grounds, and besides, he doesn't drain his victims completely. That's how..." My voice trailed off. "You said three bodies in three nights?"

"Yeah? Why?"

I was already out of my bedroom and into the living room. I slid my Glock holster onto my belt and grabbed two silver stakes from a wood block in the center of the dining room table. Leave me alone. They're pretty and when arranged right, look like some kind of funky centerpiece instead of a home defense system. I stopped at the door. "You coming?"

"Where are we going? And what's got you in such a rush?"

"It takes anywhere from one to three days for a vampire to rise. Vampires are made by completely draining a living victim. If these people really were attacked by a vampire, and if the first victim was found three days ago, then your coroner is in for a surprise right about—"I never finished my sentence. Both our cell phones rang at the same time, with the same Caller ID—Smith.

"You drive," I said to Flynn as we left my apartment and ran down the stairs. I pulled out my phone and pushed the green button. "Go ahead, Johnny." John Smith was no more our supervisory agent's real name than mine was Santa Claus, but I let him have his little illusions.

"Get down here right away, there's—"

I cut him off for a change. "A vampire outbreak at the morgue. You've got three, maybe more, baby vamps that just woke up and are hungry as hell. Have they killed anyone yet?"

"No, the Assistant M.E. saw the bag moving, opened it, and freaked out. He slammed down the quarantine shields quicker than you can say 'ebola.'"

"Good thinking on his part," I said. "We're on our way, be there in five." I could have run from my place to the Medical Examiner's office in less than five minutes, but this exercise wasn't about me, it was about Flynn, so I slid into the passenger seat of her Homeland Security-issued Suburban and buckled my seatbelt.

"How did you know these were vampire attacks, Flynn?" I asked as she put the SUV in drive and screeched out of my parking garage. I was hoping for something easy like pinpricks in the neck, or pale skin, or something that I could rationalize away.

"I don't. Not really, but what else drains the blood from its victims and leaves the bodies perfectly posed?"

"What do you mean, posed?" I felt a chill run down my spine at her choice of words. I really didn't want to hear the next few words out of Flynn's mouth, but I had to.

"All three bodies were left out in the open, where they would be found quickly. And each body was fully dressed, eyes held closed with silver dollars, and their hands folded across their chests."

"Holding a single red rose?" I asked. My voice was very quiet, but Flynn's head snapped around to stare at me anyway.

"How did you know that? I didn't tell you that. Are you doing that see through my eyes thing again?" Her words came out in an angry tumble, and I held up a hand to stop her.

"No, it's nothing like that. I knew there was a rose because I've seen these kills before, and there's always a rose."

"Wait, you've seen these before? Are you telling me these people were killed by someone you know?"

"Yeah," I said. "I know who killed those people. And I know what he wants."

"Who?" Flynn asked. "What does he want?"

"His name is Augustus James Renfield, and he's here to kill Dracula."

CHAPTER TWO

"What?" Flynn asked.

"Gus was the first Renfield. He was a good manservant for a long time, and Uncle Luke promised to turn him after his term of service was over. Unfortunately, as the years went by, Luke realized that most people aren't meant to live forever, so when the time came to turn Gus, Luke refused to do it.

"Gus was batshit crazy, you see. Not the cute kind of crazy they show in the movies where he eats flies, but the fucking scary kind of crazy, where he eats eyeballs. He worked for Uncle Luke for twenty years until he finally went completely around the bend. When Luke fired him, he came calling demanding to be turned. Uncle Luke refused, and Gus stormed off, promising to be back.

"He kept his promise. He came back the very next day, when the sun was up, with stakes. But he didn't know that I was around, so when he went down to the basement to add a little oak to Luke's diet, I beat his ass and sent him packing. We thought he died of natural causes until a couple decades later when we ran into him in Vienna. He was snacking on a tenor out back of an opera house when we found him.

"I don't know where or when he found someone to turn him, but he did. He was a full-on vampire and strong as hell. He beat me to a pulp and went toe to toe with Luke for a couple minutes before he bolted. The next morning we found the tenor on the doorstep of the apartment we were renting, his eyes closed with silver dollars and rose in his hands, folded neatly on his chest."

"Holy shit" was all Flynn said as she turned into the coroner's office parking deck. She straddled two compact parking spaces with the Suburban and got out.

I slid out after her. "You just gonna park like a dick?" I asked.

"I'm the government. Anybody doesn't like it, I'll send them to Gitmo." She never broke stride, just walked straight to the elevator and pushed the button.

I got there just as the doors slid open, and I pressed "G."

"How crazy is this guy?" Flynn asked.

"Makes me look well-adjusted," I said.

"Fuck. Okay, so super-crazy."

I laughed a little. A very little.

"How strong?"

"I can't get close to his raw strength. He's got nothing on Luke, but if he gets me in close quarters and I don't have anything ready for him, it's going to be a bad day for me. That reminds me." I pulled out my cell phone. One bar. I stared at the screen until the elevator doors slid open and I stepped out into the Coroner's Office lobby. The morgue shared a lobby with about half a dozen other esoteric and often messy government offices, like the pistol permit office, the place where folks buy their garage sale licenses, and the office where they process protests to tax valuation. But the lobby was nice, and I had perfect cell reception.

I pushed one of my speed dials and held the phone to my ear. After three rings, a cultured male voice answered. "Card residence. How many I help you?"

"Ren, it's me," I said into the phone.

"Master Quincy, how good to hear from you. Will you be joining us for dinner this Friday? You know your uncle loves to —"

I cut him off. "Ren, I need you to wake Uncle Luke. Follow emergency protocol Pitchforks and get him out of the house. Right now."

"Master Quincy?" Renfield sounded confused, and I didn't blame him. We hadn't used the Pitchfork protocol, named after the final scene in *Frankenstein*, in years.

"This is not a drill, Ren. My uncle's safety is in your hands. Execute Pitchfork, right the fuck now."

"What do I tell him when he asks what the threat is?"

"Tell him it's your granddad," I said.

"I'm sorry, Master Quincy, I don't understand. My grandfather is long deceased and had no quarrel with…" I could almost hear Ren's eyes go wide as the realization dawned on him.

"Exactly. The first Renfield is in town, he's killed three people already, and I'd bet dollars to doughnuts that Uncle Luke is the top of his hit list. Now get Luke somewhere safe and gear up for a fight. I've got some leads to follow up downtown, then we'll come collect you and send this rat bastard to Hell where he belongs!"

I hung up on Ren's assurances that he would handle everything, and looked over to where Rebecca was waiting for a main elevator going down. I took a couple of steps in her direction, then started to run. I passed her at a full sprint heading for the stairs.

"Come on!" I yelled at her.

She didn't hesitate, just drew her sidearm and ran after me. "Why are we taking the stairs?" she shouted at my back.

"Remember that whole super-hearing thing?" I asked over my shoulder. I got to the fire stairs and almost ripped the door off the hinges.

"Yeah, I remember. You hear something?"

I nodded, starting down the stairs. "Yeah, the screaming's already started."

The screaming was going on in earnest by the time I made it to the morgue, having left Flynn a couple of floors above me on the stairs. I kicked in the Plexiglas quarantine doors, silver stake in hand, and froze. Instead of there being one newborn, starving vampire in the room, there were at least two, and from the looks of the shaking bag on the exam table to my right, about to be more.

I didn't waste time, just jammed the silver stake through the bag and in the rough area of the heart of the creature trying to get out of the bag. Silver covers a lot of sins when dealing with supernatural creatures. With vampires in particular, it lets you miss the heart by a couple of inches and still kill the thing. The bag went still, and I pulled the other stake from my belt. One vampire was stalking a human across the room, who I assumed was the coroner. He wasn't moving, and the vampire wasn't in a hurry, so obviously this one had already learned how to mesmerize its prey.

Fast learners. That's never good. The other vampire was standing in the center of the room, smiling at me. It had none of the hallmarks of a newborn. No red eyes, no confusion on its features, no blood running down its mouth from the first time the fangs break through the skin. Apparently that's painful and involved some pretty significant restructuring of the jawline. I don't have fangs, and I've never spent enough time close to a vampire's mouth to notice.

Flynn burst into the room just about the time realization dawned on me. "Becks, get out of here!"

"Oh fuck, Harker, I just got here," she panted. I forget that normal humans, even slightly magically enhanced humans, get a little winded after four flights of stairs at a dead run. "Can't I just shoot one of these bastards before I go?"

The answer was obviously "no" since as soon as she got the words out, the vamp in the center of the room flew into action. Not quite literally, but almost. He moved with inhuman speed, vaulting over the exam table and sprinting at Flynn. This put him headed right past me, and he apparently hadn't heard of me, or what I can do.

Like match him almost speed-for-speed. He was headed past me for Flynn at a dead run, faster than a human eye could follow. Lucky for Rebecca Gail Flynn, I'm a little more than human. I stuck my right arm out and delivered a clothesline that would have made Nikita Koloff proud. The vampire turned completely over in midair before landing on his belly in the middle of the morgue. I jabbed down with my other stake, but he rolled out of the way and sprang to his feet before I could strike. This put my face at the unfortunate level of his knees, and he took a second to introduce me to his right knee with extreme prejudice.

I flopped flat onto my back, then nipped up onto my feet in a move I'd perfected watching Sunday afternoon Kung-Fu Theatre as a child. Okay, as a seventy-year-old, but a very spry septuagenarian. Vamp threw a punch that was intended to cave in my face, but I sidestepped and swung an elbow that would have crushed his throat if it had connected. He grabbed my arm and flipped me. I used my superhuman agility to land on my feet and kick at his balls. He slipped out of the way and slammed down on my knee with both fists. There was no way I could ever beat him fair and square, so it was probably good for me my moral compass broke in the 1920s.

Becks, you got silver in your pistol? I asked over the mental link that Flynn and I shared. I tried to stay out of her head as much as possible to give her privacy. She tried to stay out of my head even more because my head is a very disturbing place. But this time I needed backup, and she was all I had. Well, her, her marksmanship medals, and sixteen rounds of silver-tipped ammunition.

Yeah, I swapped out mags on the stairs.

Good. Wait for the opening.

The vamp and I exchanged punches, blocks, parries, and kicks for what felt like at least half an hour, which probably meant a minute and a half, then I overextended with one punch. It was an error of a millimeter or less, but it was all he needed. He leaned back out of the way of a devastating right cross, then grabbed my arm and pulled me past him onto a nearby exam table.

Now! I shouted to Flynn mentally as I switched targets for a second and turned my dive into a roll, flipping over the table onto my feet and throwing my second and last silver stake across the room at the third vamp. The foot-long hunk of sharpened silver went into the vampire's head right behind and below the right ear, *crunching* through the skull and burying itself into the monster's brain and severing the spinal cord. It dropped like a stone at the coroner's feet, who took a good look at the critter before him, threw up, and fainted dead away.

With two less vampires and one less human to worry about, I spun around and saw Flynn locked in a contest of wills with the last vampire. He had her gaze; you could almost feel the force of her will struggling not to be overcome by the powerful vampire's suggestion. I decided that while Flynn had a hella-cious amount of willpower, this wasn't the night to make her go toe-to-toe with the varsity squad of monsters. I picked up a metal bowl from a nearby table and smashed it into the side of the vampire's head with a loud *bong*.

The vampire turned to me and smiled. "Is that the best you could do, human?"

"Boy, do you have the wrong city," I said with a grin. "All I needed to do was distract you. She's gonna—"

I never got a chance to tell him what Flynn was going to do because she commenced to doing it the second the vamp's eyes swung back in her direc-tion. She put three in the creature's chest, dropping it to the ground instantly. Then she took a few steps forward, lowered her weapon to the ground, and put two more in the vampire's head.

She looked up at me with a shaky smile. "Thanks for the save."

"No problem. You know I got your back."

"Yeah, but what was all this?" She gestured around the room at the three dead vampires.

"I don't know. They shouldn't have turned this quickly. Not all of them, anyway. Something weird is going on here, and I think we might have a bigger problem than just a pissed-off Renfield on our hands."

CHAPTER THREE

"I'll have to give you an A-Plus for understatement on that one, Harker." Agent John Smith's voice came from the doorway to the morgue. He looked like every federal agent in every cop movie, except his suit had razor-sharp creases, and his salute was snappy and tight. His salt-and-pepper hair was buzzed close to his scalp, and the wrinkles around his eyes would have been called smile lines on anyone else, but on Smith you could tell those were lines caused by a man who's stood on many a hill surveying the forces arrayed against him.

"You know something I don't know, Agent Johnny?" I asked. I kept playing with different variations on his fake name, but he never cracked, no matter what I called him.

"I know a great many things you don't know, Harker, but I don't know shit about these guys. As far as I knew, they were human a couple of days ago. Obviously, that wasn't the case."

"Obviously," I agreed. I turned to the coroner, who was just getting to his feet. "Are you okay to be in here? Because a lot the things we deal with can seriously fuck with your worldview."

The white-haired man just laughed at me. "Son, I've been dealing with the aftermath of man's ill treatment of other men for thirty years. If there's anything left under heaven that can shock me, I can't wait to see it."

"I'm afraid that will have to wait another day or two, sir," Smith said. He flashed his badge at the coroner, who gave it a once-over and nodded. "I'm John Smith with Homeland Security, and this is my scene now."

"It can be your scene all you like, Agent Smith," the doc said, wiping his wire-rimmed glasses on his lab coat. "But this is my morgue, and these are my dead bodies." He gestured at the vampires, who were now scattered all over his morgue. Unlike on television, real vampires don't turn to dust when they're killed, unless they're really, really old. Or burned by the sun. Massive sunlight exposure will cause them to burn up and turn to dust, but it's not instant, and it's very smelly. Not something you want to be around.

"Fair enough, Doctor...?" Smith raised an eyebrow.

"Strunin. Doctor Jacob Strunin, Chief Medical Examiner." He extended a hand, and Smith shook it.

"Okay, Doctor Strunin. You are hereby deputized into the Department of Homeland Security, Paranormal Division, under my direct supervision. Please understand that revealing any information that we uncover as part of our work here will result in your immediate arrest for treason, which I will prose-cute to the fullest extent of the law. Do you understand me?"

I watched the little doctor's face pale, then he stood up straight, nodded his head and said, "I understand. Now can we get down to the business of figuring out why these dead people just tried to kill me?"

I laughed and walked over to clap the little doctor on the shoulder. "That's the spirit, doc. But these aren't dead people. Hell, they're not even people!"

"What are you trying to say, Mr.- um, I'm sorry, I didn't catch your name."

"Harker. Quincy Harker, Demon Hunter, at your service." I gave him my most florid bow, but my courtly manners left something to be desired, and I had to grab onto an exam table to keep from falling on my ass in the middle of the morgue.

"Well, Mr. Harker," the doctor said, obviously holding back a laugh at my expense. "What are these bodies if not people?"

"Doc, these are vampires." I waited for the inevitable, but it didn't come. He just knelt by the nearest corpse and peeled back the top lip.

"Hmmm... There are definitely extended canines. That seems to validate your theory." He pried open an eyelid and poked at the eyeball. "The vitreous fluid seems thick, almost viscous. I can't prove that they are vampires without a more complete workup, but there's also nothing proving they are not vampires. So, we have vampires in North Carolina. Who knew?"

I raised my hand, but that's as much because I'm a huge smartass than as anything else. "I was pretty much aware of it."

The doc shot me a dirty look. I ignored it because that's what I do. He knelt down again and started poking at the vampire corpses. "What are the odds that these guys are going to get up and come after me again?" he asked, not moving back at all.

"Zero," I assured the man. "We staked them with silver. Destroying the heart gets rid of the blood reservoir, and silver is supremely poisonous to vamps, so it's kind of a double-whammy."

"Hmmm..." Strunin murmured. "So that old wives' tale is true, what about the others?" He looked at Smith, who jerked a thumb at me as if to say I was the resident expert. Which I suppose I was, living most of my life with a vampire.

"Running water, not a thing. Scattering rice in front of one, not a thing. Garlic—there's actually an interesting story there, but let's just say that Bram Stoker had a thing against Italian cooking and we'll leave it at that. Garlic does nothing. Holy Symbols can burn, but it's because they're usually made of silver. They don't reflect in old mirrors because mirrors used silver backing. New mirrors aren't a problem. What else? Oh yeah, sunlight is definitely a thing; it'll crisp a vamp in seconds. They can get drunk off drinking blood from a drunk person, but most drugs don't affect them, oddly enough. They don't eat or drink, and they can't really turn into a bat or fog. But as you saw, they can bespell you, so don't look one in the eyes unless it's a vampire you know and trust. And let's face it, unless you're me, there probably aren't very many vampires you know and trust."

"And this rule doesn't apply to you because?" It was almost funny, watching him put two and two together and get five. I saw him think back to the introduction, then back to the first time he read *Dracula*, either in Classic Comics or the whole novel. Or worse, saw one of the movies. But I saw him recognize the Harker name, try to rationalize it with the age of the man in front of him, and eventually give up.

"Jonathan Harker is a character in *Dracula*," the stunned doctor said.

"I called him Dad," I said. "My parents were fairly important to that book."

"But...how *old* are you?"

"Older than I look, and let's leave it at that. I'm not immortal, like Uncle Lu-, like Dracula. But I age very slowly. And I know a few things about vampires, and one of those things is that these vampires are real-dead. Like forever dead. Almost like human dead, except without all that annoying bleeding."

"So we know what killed them, which is to say you," Strunin said. "And we know that they were vampires, so what am I looking for in my examination."

"Nothing," I said. "You're not doing the examination. I am."

"Excuse me?" The doctor took off his glasses and polished them furiously on his lab coat. If he polished those lenses any more, he'd wear a hole in them.

"We aren't doing a medical examination, Doc. We're looking for other clues. Like you said, we know what killed them. Silver poisoning. Now we need to learn as much about them as possible." I reached down and hefted the nearest vamp onto a nearby exam table.

"Like this guy," I said. "We know he's European from his hair gel. I can smell it, and it's a kind only found in France. They don't even ship to the US because they're French, and 'fuck you' is the motto of France. His nails are done, so he comes from money or is old enough to have learned to appreciate a good manicure. His shoes are recently shined, so I would guess he flew in within the past week."

"And you know this because?" Flynn asked.

"I've lived in this town a long time, and the only place I've found to get a good shoeshine is the airport. And this shine is just a few days old." I pried open the dead vampire's mouth and peered inside. I pulled a tiny flashlight out of my pocket and shined it inside the mouth.

"Well, we know he's old," I said, closing the mouth.

"How do we know that?" Doc Strunin asked.

"He's got most of his teeth, which means that he lived probably no earlier than the eighteenth century, but his dental work is friggin' terrible, so he was turned no later than 1850."

"So you're saying that my twenty-first century murder victim is actually an eighteenth century vampire?" Flynn asked.

"That's what it looks like, detective," I replied. "Seems that these were decoys Gus sent in to lure Uncle Luke out into the open by making him think there was a new vampire in town. Now, where would we find a bunch of eighteenth-century relics in Charlotte?"

"I have no idea," Flynn replied. "I thought we bulldozed anything over thirty years old."

Just then Flynn's cell rang. She answered it at the same time that Smith reached into his jacket and pulled out a vibrating phone. The phone on the coroner's desk lit up, and I felt left out because nobody was calling me. I had the mental connection between Flynn and me locked down as much as I could, but I still felt the spike of anxiety, excitement, and fear at whatever she was hearing. Everyone hung up at about the same time, and I looked at each one in turn. Flynn looked a little flushed, and I could feel the blood rushing in her veins. Smith looked like a rock with salt-and-pepper five o'clock shadow, and Strunin was pale, with a couple of little beads of sweat popping out on his forehead.

"Let me guess, another corpse?" I asked.

"Looks like a vampire attack," Smith confirmed. "Parking deck at The Green downtown."

"The one under the hot dog place? I know it. What level?" I asked. I checked the magazine in my Glock and made sure I'd returned my silver stakes to my sheaths.

"Bottom floor," Flynn said. "I'll drive." She started for the door, keys in hand.

"No way," I said, not moving.

She froze in mid-stride and spun back to me on one heel. "What?"

"You're not going," I said. I watched the red start at her neck and creep upwards and knew there was an explosion coming.

"Why in the ever-loving fuck would you think I'd let you go by yourself?" She bit off each word with an almost audible click of her teeth.

"If this is Gus, you can't hang with him. You do pretty well against regular vamps, and if it's a fledgling, I'm not worried at all unless you come down with a terminal case of the stupid. But Gus is a badass. He's shared blood with every old vampire he can find for over a century, and he gets a little bit stronger each time. He's faster than me, smarter than me, and so much stronger than me it's not even funny."

"So what makes you think you can beat him?"

I held out my right hand, palm up, a little over waist high, and focused my will. "*Solis Ortus!*" I shouted, and a ball of light coalesced in the air above my hand, growing brighter and brighter until we all had to look away.

"*Eclipsis!*" I said, and the light dispersed. "I have a few other tricks at my disposal that might make vampires uncomfortable," I said. "But I can only focus on two or three things at a time. I can fight Gus and cast spells at the same time, but I can't pay attention to keeping you alive while I do it, and Gus will know it. So please, just stay here and let me do the heavy lifting."

"Can I at least go to the safe house and wait with Ren and Luke?" Flynn asked.

"You can. He can't." I gestured at Smith. "No offense, but Uncle Luke still kinda thinks he's a sovereign government. He doesn't like being reminded that there are people who outrank him in this country."

"Fair enough. I'll stay here and run point on the investigation into these dead vamps' clothes. I'll find out everything I can about who they were and what brought them here. If it's your friend Augustus, maybe they can give us some insight into his plans."

"Sounds like a deal. Now I'm gonna jog over to Matt's Chicago Dog and take care of a little vermin problem in their parking garage."

CHAPTER FOUR

A s always, *The Girl from Ipanema* was playing in the elevator as I rode down to the bottom of the parking garage. I don't think I've ever noticed a different song in an elevator. I don't know if it's just the song that elevator people use, or if I notice that song because it's so annoying, and other songs don't bug me, so I ignore them. Either way, I stepped out into the garage humming *Ooh...but I watch her so sadly*, and almost missed the sound of shoe leather on concrete that told me my target was somewhere off to my left.

I took a handful of marbles out of my jacket pocket and gripped them tightly in my right hand. I brought my fist up to my mouth and whispered *"Lumos"* into my closed hand. I cracked my grip just enough to let the light stream through my fingers for a second, then closed my fist again.

I walked down the ramp, trying to look innocuous and vapid, like any other yuppie trying to find his SUV or mini-van, or crossover, or whatever it is yuppies drive. I'm not a car guy. I have a shitty Honda Accord and an old Harley that I keep at Luke's. I heard the scuff of shoes poised for a leap as I turned the corner into the lowest level of the garage. I tensed, then dove forward into a roll as my attacker sprung for me.

I was rewarded with a surprised gasp, then a heavy *thud* as the vampire crashed into the side of a parked car. I spun around and flung my fistful of glowing marbles out in front of me. Immediately half a dozen little balls of sunlight flew into the air and hovered a little over head height, banishing all the shadows in the garage and leveling the playing field pretty quickly. I saw the vampire, a man turned in his thirties or forties, dressed in contemporary clothes, spin back toward me and launch himself at me again.

He was fast, but I was expecting his leap. I dove under him, staying low to the ground to avoid his claws and fangs, then popped up to my feet five yards away from the pissed-off vampire.

"I'm going to drink you dry and burn your carcass, human," the vampire hissed.

I grinned at him and said, "Human? Somebody's been feeding you bad information, friend." He came at me again, staying on his feet this time, just using his speed to close the distance between us in half a second. He slashed at my throat with his razor-sharp claws, but my throat wasn't there. I dropped straight down to one knee and let his hand pass harmlessly over my head. Then I stood up, throwing my entire body weight behind an uppercut that should have taken his head off and ended our little encounter right then.

Except it didn't. I heard a loud *crack* as his jaw broke, and he staggered back a few steps, but then he cracked his head from side to side and grinned at me. He grinned and my blood ran cold because that was the smile of a man who knew he had the upper hand and was just there to toy with me.

"This is going to be fun," he said, and while I disagreed pretty vehemently, I didn't argue because I was too busy drawing my Glock and emptying the magazine into the vampire's center mass. I put sixteen silver-tipped rounds through that bastard and he didn't go down.

"Silver?" he asked. "I like silver. He ripped open the top three buttons on his shirt to show me the silver crucifix hanging around his neck.

Fuck. I'd seen vampires that weren't bothered by holy symbols. Hell, Luke kept crucifixes hanging all around his place, but I'd never seen one able to touch silver with his bare hands. Either this guy was super old, or somebody'd figured out how to build a better bloodsucker. Either way, I was not a fan.

I barely got my nose out of the way of his next punch, and I snapped out of my reverie pretty damn quickly. He came at me with punches, kicks, round-houses, jabs, and some wild-ass chops that I couldn't tell came from watching too much Kung-Fu Theatre or too much Ric Flair. Either way, I knew he'd cave my ribcage in if I let him connect.

I tossed my gun at his face and used the momentary distraction to draw my silver stakes. Even if silver didn't hurt him, getting a pointy thing in the chest will ruin pretty much anything's day. He batted my pistol out of the air, and I slashed out at him with one stake. He blocked my cut, and it felt like I'd just wrapped my arm around a lamppost, backward. The stake clattered out of my now-numb left hand, and he grabbed the front of my shirt.

The vampire drew me to him, his fangs extending as he leaned in to bite me and drain my life force. I flailed a little, battering uselessly at his face and shoulders, then I slumped in his grasp, awaiting my fate. His face got to within inches of mine, and I could smell the stench of the grave on his breath.

Just before his fangs broke my skin, I held up my last marble and whispered through my abused vocal chords, "*Solis Ortus!*"

Several things happened at once. The grip on my throat loosened as the vampire gave me a strange look. The marble floated between us and burst into light like a miniature sun, and the UV rays burned part of my assailant's face off. He jerked back, smoking like the crowd at a Dave Matthews concert, and turned to run. I left the marble-sized sun floating and took off after him. He was fast, but he ran like I'd melted an eye, which I found out was true when I caught up with him.

I yanked him around, and he used his momentum to follow through with a punch that knocked me back a good ten feet. If I hadn't let myself roll with it, he probably would have broken my jaw. As it was, he just turned to run again. I stood halfway up the ramp and watched his feet as he turned the corner and started up the next level. I focused myself, drew in my will and murmured, "*Constringo.*" I sent my will out with a gesture, and the fleeing vampire's ankles snapped together as if tied by a rope. I found him struggling to stand halfway up the Level 2 parking ramp, one eye turned to black goop, half his face a charred mass of smoking flesh, and part of his mouth burned away revealing one fang.

"What are you?" he asked as I stepped up beside him.

"I'm your worst fucking nightmare, asshole," I said, dropping to one knee with all my weight on the stake in my hand. I *crunched* through his ribcage and pulverized his heart with the silver point. Then I reached behind my back and drew a silver-plated kukri. I used the big curved knife to decapitate the vampire, then I dragged his corpse out of sight. I put his head on his stomach and turned to find his victim, hopefully before it was too late.

I quickly scanned the area where we fought and found nothing. So I started the laborious car-to-car search, walking every inch of the parking garage. As I walked, my mind flashed back to another parking garage and another search that ended a lot worse than I hoped this one would. I was chasing a newborn vamp through downtown and it had just been spotted in the Seventh Street Station garage near a nightclub called Mythos. It was the hottest thing downtown at the time with people lined up out the front entrance trying to get in and lined up around the back entrance grabbing a quick smoke, ducking out to puke when the night got too heavy, or slipping off into the shadows for a little illicit activity.

I remembered the thump of the music driving my footsteps as I heard the gurgle of a life passing through a shredded throat. I turned a corner and the vamp looked up from its meal. That blood-smeared face has stayed with me for years—the blank, animal look, all humanity gone, nothing inhabiting the creature but hunger like a living thing. The beast dropped its prey and came at me, but a baby vamp hasn't been a match for me in decades. I dropped it with two silver throwing knives then took its head with a ridiculously long sword I carried because it was the 90s and I wanted to be the third MacLeod on *Highlander*.

I was too late for the victim, though. I remember running to him, but his throat was nothing more than a mess of flesh and blood. He pressed something into my hand, and I saw it was a school picture of a little girl, a little brown-haired girl who would end up a central character in my own story. I knelt beside him, then turned myself around and sat with his head in my lap. He stared up at me, brown eyes full of fear. Not for himself, but for his daughter, left alone in a world that didn't take care of little girls without fathers. I promised him that I'd look after her, wiped the sweat and blood from his face, and held him while he died.

When the light had left his eyes, I reached down into my lap and snapped his neck to make sure he wouldn't come back. The last thing that little girl needed was her father knocking on her door in a few days asking to come in for a snack.

All these things rolled through my mind as I searched the parking garage for this vampire's victim. I felt Flynn behind my eyes as I peered into cars, trucks, vans, stairwells and elevators.

"No comment, Detective?" I asked the air. I knew she could hear me if I just thought my questions, but this felt better to me somehow.

I don't know what to say. You told me you were there when he died. You told me he asked about me right before he went, but the whole thing about breaking his neck... I never knew that.

"I didn't think it important until now, but I figured it might come up, so I decided to go ahead and tell you."

I'm glad of that, and I'm glad you did what you did, it's just...I don't know, Harker, what am I supposed to feel?

"Love, if I had any idea what a woman was supposed to feel about anything, I'd have a fucking lot more second dates!" I laughed and then froze. Something wasn't right about the echo. Something else was—*there!* "Found you!"

I ran over to a dark blue Prius with its driver door open. A young woman was lying in a pool of blood by the car's front wheel, her neck shredded and her purse and keys lying on the ground next to her. She was trying to breathe, but there wasn't enough of her throat left to hold the air in.

"Goddammit," I muttered, flashing back again to that other parking garage so many years ago. I knelt beside the woman and pulled her into my lap. She didn't have the strength to resist; she just lay there staring up at me with terrified eyes.

"Don't worry, miss, it'll be fine. I'm with the police, and help is on the way." I said all the reassuring things, all the lies that I hoped would make her feel a little better, but she just stared at me, a frightened woman who no longer had the vocal chords to speak with while she drew her last few breaths.

Her purse caught my eye, and I reached into it, pulling out her wallet. "I'm not going to rob you, darling, I just want—there it is, here we go." I opened her wallet and pulled out her driver's license. "Alright, Suzanne Jonas, you can relax. We'll be able to get in touch with your parents and tell them what happened." She relaxed visibly at my words.

"Do you have a husband?" She shook her head. "A boyfriend?" Another head shake. "A dog?" A weak nod. She was fading faster. "I'll take care of the puppy, Suzanne Jonas. I'll make sure it's cared for and that your parents know that you loved them very much." A tear rolled down her face, then she let out one long, ragged breath, and was still.

I knelt there, holding her body as it slowly went cold, thinking about all the people I'd watched die over the years, and the ones that I'd killed myself. The count was a lot higher than I liked in both categories, and every face flickered across my memory as I knelt in Suzanne Jonas' blood in the parking garage. Then I took a deep breath, squared my shoulders, and snapped her neck to make sure she stayed dead.

Do you just do that to everybody you watch die? Flynn's voice was snotty inside my head, but I let it go. I knew where she was coming from, and I didn't have the energy to fight anyway.

"She was drained. I had to make sure she didn't come back. She was a nice lady. I didn't want to have to kill her tomorrow."

"Don't worry, monster," came a woman's voice behind me. "You won't be around tomorrow to kill anything."

CHAPTER FIVE

I turned to see a petite woman in her twenties pointing a crossbow at me. A crossbow, of all things? I had just about enough time to wonder if this was an *Arrow* rerun before she pulled the trigger, and the bolt leapt at my chest. I dropped the corpse and sprang out of the way, letting the broadhead bolt sink into the Prius's tire instead of my ribcage.

"What the hell, lady? Didn't your parents teach you not to shoot at strangers?" I said. My mystery assailant was nowhere to be seen. I guessed she was off somewhere reloading. That's the worst thing about crossbows—nobody's made a semi-auto version of them yet.

"They taught me not to take candy from strangers and not to let vampires live to see another sunset." The girl's voice came from near where she'd been standing. I hopped over the roof of the BMW she was hiding behind and tapped her on the shoulder. She spun around and nearly buried a knife in my leg, but I was a little too quick for her. Which meant she was ridiculously fast for a human. I'd better watch out for this one.

She darted away again, but I got a little better look at her this time. Black tights with leather chaps, good for flexibility and protecting the knees. Black hoodie with what looked like a bulletproof vest under it, and if she really knew anything about hunting vampires, I'd bet she had a chainmail choker or something of the like under that hoodie, too.

I revised my earlier guess at her age downward after I looked at her for more than half a second, deciding she was probably in her early twenties. Auburn hair snaked out from under the hood, and her features were Western

European, speaking to maybe Germanic or French heritage. She had a big damn knife and a crossbow, and I wasn't in too much of a hurry to see what else she was packing, weapons-wise, but I also wasn't just going to run away and let a psycho with a fetish for pointy things run around my city.

I stopped at the end of the car, focusing to hear her movements. She was smart enough to stay still when I was trying to track her, but she wasn't enough of a pro to control her breathing. I could hear the little panting of her breath a couple of cars over, so I crept backward the length of the car and then crab-walked sideways. She was kneeling behind the tire of an SUV, listening hard for me. *Hate to disappoint you, kid, but I've been skulking around places I wasn't welcome since long before there was such a thing as a parking garage.*

"You want to tell me why you want to shoot me, or should I just go ahead and get that paternity test?" I said. The girl whirled around, but her reflexes were far better than I expected. She fired a new bolt dead at my chest, forcing me to throw myself backwards to keep from getting skewered. Then instead of running again, she leapt *at* me, knife drawn. I scurried backward to keep her from slicing off anything I really value with the knife, but she just kept on coming.

I finally landed a solid kick to her face that left her on hands and knees for a moment, shaking her head like a bulldog that finally caught a car. I took the opportunity to scramble to my feet and draw my ASP extendable baton. I left my Glock holstered. I didn't want to kill the kid; I just wanted her to stop trying to kill *me*.

"Hey honey, can we talk?" I asked, keeping the baton low in front of me.

The girl tossed her crossbow away behind her and slid her knife into a sheath on her hip. I stood up a little straighter, relaxing as the hostilities seemed to be lessening. Until she reached behind her back and pulled out a pair of escrima sticks and came at me in a whirling dervish of metal-tipped wooden pain and suffering.

Escrima sticks are those two-foot long wooden sticks that you see Filipinos use in martial arts movies. They're used in arnis, the national martial at of the Philippines, and they're absolutely lethal in the hands of an expert. This girl was an expert because once she got moving, nothing in the world was getting through the spinning barricade of pain she was wielding. I blocked a couple of strikes with my ASP, took a couple of brutal shots to the forearm and thighs, and managed not to collapse whens she scored a solid hit on my left knee.

"Ow, goddammit!" I yelled. "Would you fucking *quit* that?"

To my complete shock, she did. She froze for a minute and stared at me, then came at me again. I backed away, blocking and parrying as well as I could with one bum knee, but finally got frustrated and flung my ASP at her head to try and gain a little space. She ducked, and I hopped over the back of a Mercedes, setting off the car alarm and adding even more noise to our little scrap.

I took advantage of the momentary confusion to focus my will and draw a deep breath. When my attacker came around the end of the car and started at me again, I flung a handful of dust at her and said, "*Somnos*." She took in a face full of dust, sneezed once, and fell face-first onto the concrete floor, dead asleep. Her escrima sticks clattered to the floor beside her and rolled under a nearby pickup.

"Nighty-night," I said under my breath. A face full of sleep spell was enough to keep a full-grown man out for eight hours. It should have been enough to keep this little slip of a girl knocked cold for twelve or so. So imagine my surprise when I rolled her over and she kicked me square in the family jewels. I toppled over, pinning her beneath me, and just wrapped my arms around her thrashing form. I'm not the biggest guy, but I had at least a hundred pounds on her, and even with my agonized balls, I had enough presence of mind to bear hug the little assassin and not let her go.

She fought like a wildcat, kicking and flailing and biting at me, until I head-butted her in the nose one good time. I heard a wet *crunch*, and blood started to pour from her nose. Then she shifted gears from trying to get loose to kill me, to just trying to get away.

"Hold still, dammit, I don't want to hurt you!" I said once I got my breath back a little.

"Go fuck yourself, vampire!"

"I'm not a vampire, jackass! I killed the vampire. It's the next floor down."

She froze at that, then pulled back a little from me. She looked at my face and said, "Show me your teeth."

I gave her my best disarming smile, which admittedly looks like I'm going to murder someone, especially when I make it a point to show off my not-exceptionally-pointy incisors. "Satisfied?"

"Not even close, but I guess you're not a vampire. You wanna get off me so we can talk about this, or you just gonna dry-hump me in the middle of the garage?"

I let her go but drew my Glock and aimed it at her leg. "You touch those fucking sticks again and I'm going to shoot you in the kneecap. I am not in the mood to fight you any more tonight, so I'm just going to end this shit right here and now. You understand?"

"I got you," she said. I watched as she reached up and with a quick jerk to the right and gout of bright red blood she set her nose back in place. "Fuck! That really hurts." She glared at me.

I didn't bother with sympathy because I typically don't have any. "It's not nice to kick people in the balls. Bad things happen to people who aren't nice, like broken noses."

"Sorry about that. I thought you were a vampire."

"Yeah, about that," I started.

She held up a hand. "Not here. Or at least not yet. We need to deal with these bodies before the police get here. Then we need to be someplace else, *fast*. I don't know why nobody's called it in, with all the noise we were making, but I'm not going to look a gift horse in the mouth. Can you get the vampire up here? If we put both bodies in the trunk of her car, then it'll be easier to get rid of everything."

She started to stand up and I grabbed her arm. "Hold up there, speedy. First off, a Prius does not have a two-corpse trunk. They don't even make cars anymore with two-body trunks. We'd need to steal an SUV at least. But it's not a thing. The cops aren't coming. They've got the elevators and the automobile entrances blocked off, and men on all the stairwells waiting for me to give them the all clear. So we don't have to worry about the authorities showing up because I am the authorities." And boy, did that ever feel weird to say out loud.

She looked at me with a raised eyebrow and I sighed. "I'm going to reach into my back pocket. Don't try anything stupid or I will shoot you, okay?"

She glared at me, a sullen scowl that made her look even younger. "Okay."

I pulled out my wallet and flipped it open to the badge and photo ID Smith insisted I carry. It listed me as a Special Consultant, Department of Homeland Security. It also listed my name as Quince Goddamn Harper because that's what I told the woman at the ID office when she asked me for the fourth time. My photo was accurate, but unflattering, as I was giving the finger to the camera and rolling my eyes when it was taken. Smith kept pestering me to get a new one, but I was putting it off until the mostly deaf and completely illiterate woman responsible for typing my name incorrectly three times in a row retired.

"This looks like you printed it at home on your inkjet," she said, tossing the leather bi-fold back to me.

I snatched it out of the air and tucked it back in my pocket. "That right there should be proof enough that it's real. If I were going to try and fake a government document, I'd likely do a better job than they could manage."

"Good point. Now what? We leave her here and do what with the vampire?"

"There's nothing else to be done with the vampire, he's forever-dead."

"So what, we just leave?" She asked.

"No, now we go find a place with really, really cold beer and you answer a few questions for me, starting with who you are."

"I'm all for a beer, but you might need something stronger when I tell you the truth about myself. It's a little hard to believe, even for somebody who hunts vampires."

"Why not try me, then we'll head to this little joint called Valhalla. It's just a couple blocks from here and they have fish and chips that are almost good enough to deserve the name."

"Sold," she said, holding out a hand. I shook it and she looked me straight in the eye as she continued. "My name is Gabriella Van Helsing, and I'm the great-granddaughter of the man who killed Dracula."

Well, fuck. I heard echo through my thoughts as this news registered with Flynn.

My thoughts exactly, I thought, then went rapidly in search of that beer.

CHAPTER SIX

I walked a couple of steps behind Gabby, as she told me to call her, and pulled out my phone. I sent a quick text to Ren saying nothing more than "911 - Van Helsing in CLT. 911!" Then I sped up to catch the trim woman, noting briefly how nice the view was from the back. For a cold-blooded killer sworn to destroy part of my family, she had a really fantastic ass.

"So you're a descendant of the Van Helsing from the movie, huh?" It was all I could do to not append "that fat shite" in front of "Van Helsing." That's the only way I've ever heard the name, after all.

"Yeah, he was my great-grandfather. I never knew him—he died long before I was born." I knew that was true, since she didn't look to be any older than her early thirties, and besides, I'd been in the room with her grandparents when old Abraham died in 1906. Old Abraham had always been kind to me, with his thick beard and funny accent, even if he did always ask me questions about Uncle Luke. Mother and Father made me promise to never tell Abraham about Uncle Luke, so it was in complete ignorance of his old nemesis standing right outside the window in the snow that Abraham Van Helsing, legendary vampire hunter, passed in the wee hours of the morning. He was surrounded by his son and daughter-in-law, my parents, the other survivors of the hunt on Dracula, and me.

I watched raptly as the old man's breathing became labored, then rattled to a stop sometime in the darkest hours of the night. I watched Abraham, I

185

watched my parents for clues on how to act, I watched his family, and every once in a while I went to the window and stared out at Uncle Luke.

Luke stood on a small hill almost a hundred yards away from the window, unmoving. It's in the stillness when vampires look least human and more like the dead things they really are. Luke stood for hours, never moving so much as an eyelid as his old adversary railed against the dying of the light. I looked out the window one last time after they pulled the sheet up over the old man's face, and Luke raised his hand, as if in tribute, then disappeared. I didn't see him for months after Van Helsing's death, and when he returned, there was a new shadow in his eyes, a new tone of melancholy in his voice.

"Hey, you okay?" Gabby's voice snapped me back to the present. "Is this the place?" she asked, gesturing to a heavy wooden door with antique hardware. The wooden sign above the heavy door read, "Valhalla."

"Yeah, this is it," I said, pulling the door open for her. We entered a low-ceilinged pub with dark wood and about a dozen beer taps. The place was almost full, but the noise level was surprisingly low. We took a booth in the back, and I ordered a double shot of Johnny Walker Black and a beer back.

"Jesus, Harper, go easy on that stuff. I don't want to have to pour you into a cab," Gabby said.

"I've got a quick metabolism," I said. Our drinks showed up almost immediately, and I slammed my scotch and motioned the waitress to bring me another. I knocked back half my beer in one long pull and waved a few fingers at the vampire huntress. "Okay, tell me a story, Miss Van Helsing, if that's even your real name." I knew it was her real name long before she pulled out her own wallet and slapped her ID down on the table. There was no mistaking her grandmother's eyes, and her great-grandfather's cheekbones, and the fire in her eyes that was all hunter. She was going to be a serious problem.

"This might sound a little far-fetched, but you handled yourself back there like somebody who's seen a thing or two outside the ordinary, so maybe you'll be able to handle it." I managed not to snort my beer at the understatement, which I considered an enormous accomplishment, especially with Flynn laughing her ass off inside my head.

You're so fucked, Harker. It's like she's you, only with boobs!

I hadn't noticed her boobs until that point, so I took a moment to rectify that oversight. Not bad. Pert, like her ass, and her smile, which fell off her face as she caught me staring at her chest.

"My eyes are up here, asshole."

"That's not what I'm looking at, love. I mean, they're nice and all, but they're not exactly what's holding my attention right now. That amulet, where did you get it?" She pulled a gold chain and the rest of the piece of jewelry came into view.

"My father gave it to me when it became obvious I wasn't going to follow his footsteps and stay the hell away from the family business. It belonged to—"

"Van Helsing," I said, the words soft. I remembered it dangling from the old man's hands as he spun it in front of the firelight to entertain a chubby-cheeked little boy. I could almost hear his accented voice talking to my mother. *Now, Mina, I know he seems like just an ordinary little boy, but ve must take every precaution to make sure he grows up and remains ordinary. Mein Gott, child, just think what changes that monster may have wrought upon you and Jonathan in your time under his thrall!*

It wasn't until much later that I realized he was using the amulet to see if I felt its power, to see if I was attracted to magical things. I wasn't, not then. It wasn't until much later, long after old Abraham was dead and buried, that my talents manifested.

"Yes, how did you know?" Gabby asked, her face suddenly a mask. I could feel the tension rolling off her in waves. Every nerve tight as a bowstring, she was ready to bolt at a moment's notice.

"I...I saw it in a book, I think. A photograph, or maybe an illustration. It's how he warded himself from Dracula's mental powers, right?" I put on a face of an enthusiastic fan, burying the level of my interest.

"Yes, exactly!" she said, clapping her hands a little. "It allows the wearer to resist magical spells and abilities. I'm not sure why it worked on your knockout dust, though. It shouldn't have any effect on biological or chemical agents."

"Maybe it's because I bought it at a Chinese herb shop. The lady at the counter insisted it was ground up unicorn horn and was good for helping others sleep, or for keeping part of me awake, if you know what I mean."

"Oh great, so I got knocked out by a dose of Viagra? Brilliant." Yeah, but that was a lot easier than telling her she got knocked out by a spell cast by the nephew of the man her entire family was dedicated to destroying.

"So what brings you to Charlotte?" I asked. "I'm guessing it's not a gig at one of the banks, like most people."

"I'm hunting a master vampire. I picked up his trail outside Boston, and I've been chasing him down the east coast for the past nine months. He never stays more than a couple of weeks in any city, and he's usually fastidious about his kills. This is the first time he's used lackeys and the first time he's turned anyone. I don't know what caused the change in MO."

"Power," I said simply.

"Excuse me?" Van Helsing asked.

"He's been building a power base. He started in Boston because that's where the seat of vampire government in the US is. Or was. My guess would be that he killed all the members of the council and just installed vamps loyal to him in their seats. Or he just killed people until they all started agreeing with him."

"You talk like you know this guy." She looked at me over her beer, some local brew called a Jam Session. I hate cute beer names, but it's a decent brew.

"I know vampires. Consensus-building isn't exactly on their resumes."

"And how do you come to know so much about vampires, Mr. Harper?" She was still using the misspelling typed on my badge, and as long as it kept her a couple steps away from Uncle Luke, I was happy to keep her a little confused as to my real identity.

"I don't know if you noticed the small print on my badge or not, but I'm a part of Homeland Security's Paranormal Division. We're kinda like *The X-Files*, but without the skeptics. I hunt down things that go bump in the night, and I make them stop bumping. Vampires are one of the most common supernatural creatures, and unlike witches and most weres, they don't just want to be left alone to dance naked under a full moon. They eat people to stay alive, and that's also how they make more vampires, so I have a professional interest in vampires."

"But what's your story, Harper? Nobody graduates from college and wants to be a vampire hunter. It's personal. It's always personal. My family has been in this business for over a hundred years, why are you doing it?"

"A vampire attacked my mother. My father rescued her, with some help, but he lost a good friend and got a little chewed in the process. So I grew up knowing that there were bad things out there and that sometimes good people have to stand up against them." More half-truths. If I get much better at this, I might rethink my personal ban on marriage.

"So now what, Mr. Secret Agent Man?" Gabby asked.

"Now I think the best solution is for you to let us handle this. We've got plenty of resources and plenty of experience. We can take care of one vampire, even if he is powerful."

"But it's not just one vampire," she protested. "You saw that tonight. This guy's got minions, and that means he's organized and might be making a move on the local vamp boss. Do you have any idea who that is?"

"We do. We've actually got a relationship with him and have used him as a resource from time to time."

"God, the government really will get in bed with anybody. But I guess the devil you know, and all that. But if you think I'm leaving just because you pat me on the head and send me on my merry way, you've got another think coming. I've been chasing this bastard for months now, and the only way I'm leaving Charlotte is with his heart in a box. Figuratively speaking, of course. I don't actually carry vampire hearts around in a box. Oh, hi!" She turned to the waitress, who was standing by my elbow looking both shocked and a little queasy at the talk of vampire hearts.

"Do...you two know what you'd like to eat?" the poor pale woman asked.

"I'll do the fish and chips, please," I said.

"I can do the same. You have malt vinegar?" Gabby asked. The waitress pointed to a bottle on the table and turned to beat a hasty retreat.

"You guys order enough for three?" asked Detective Flynn as she passed the waitress en route to our table. "Detective Rebecca Flynn, Charlotte-Mecklenburg PD." She held out a hand to Gabby, who took it. Gabby looked back and forth between the two of us, eyebrows crawling to the ceiling.

"I'm on temporary assignment to Homeland Security as Q's partner," Flynn explained. She turned to me. "Cleanup is done with the garage, and Smith wants to debrief you back at HQ as soon as you're done with your date night. His words, not mine."

"Oh good lord, Becks, it's not a date! She's cute enough, but for Christ's sake, I'm old enough to be her father!" And that was just how I looked. I was really old enough to be her great-grandfather. "But I'd better go ahead and boogie. You can fill Miss Van Helsing here on everything we do at Homeland Security, and she can give you all the information she had on the new fangboy in town. I'll go make nice with the boss, and y'all have a nice kibbutz."

I left the two women waiting on their fish and chips, something I truly regretted missing out on, and hauled ass back to my car, parked on the curb out front of The Green garage. I hopped into the Honda and smoked the tires pulling out into traffic. I had to get to Uncle Luke and find a way to get him out of town. There was a new Van Helsing in town, and the last thing in the world I needed was a rematch of Stoker's novel in the streets of Charlotte.

CHAPTER SEVEN

"I'm not leaving" was Luke's response to the news of Gabriella Van Helsing's appearance. "I won't let that fat shite's granddaughter run me out of the city I love, especially when that ungrateful bastard Augustus is in town."

"I'm not saying she should run you out of town, Uncle Luke. I'm just saying that this would be a great time for that New York vacation you've been talking about for the past decade or so. You haven't even seen Times Square since it went all Disney! You'd barely recognize the place. And Broadway! You love the theatre."

"Oh yes, Quincy, I'll jet off to New York and watch some has-been television 'actor' in a stage version of a mediocre movie because that's what passes for original art these days. No, these fools think they can just waltz in here and take over my city? Well, they've got another think coming!"

"I think only one of them wants to take over the city. I think the other wants to kill the one who wants to take over the city. And every vampire, like, ever. So, by extension…you," I said. "Ren, would you help me out here?"

"I'm sorry, Master Quincy, I must agree with the Count's assessment of these circumstances. The only acceptable response to a threat from an outside force is to destroy the threat. Abandoning our city and our responsibilities to it simply is not an option."

"What responsibilities?" I asked. "You drink people, and every once in a while you bail my ass out of jail or something else stupid that I've done. And I have the whole federal government to do that now! So I'm good. And we can find people for you to drink in Atlanta, or Nashville—"

"I hate country music," Luke cut in.

"Then Memphis! Whatever. Please, Uncle Luke, just take a couple weeks and vanish while I deal with Gus and little miss Helsing. I'll get everything straightened out and you can come home, I promise." I reached into my pocket and grabbed my vibrating phone. The screen read "Flynn," so I swiped my finger across it.

"You've been talking to me inside my head all night and *now* you decide to call? What's up?"

"The whole head-to-head thing was giving me a headache. Where are you?"

"I'm at Luke's, trying to get him to leave town for a little while. You?" Our bond allowed me to see through her eyes so I didn't really need to ask, but I was trying to respect her boundaries. It was hard, something about old dogs and new tricks, but I was getting there.

"I'm on my way home for a little sack time. I left your girl at the Hyatt House downtown. She's registered under the name Mary Jane Watson."

"Like in *Spiderman?*"

"Apparently she's a comic book nerd and a vampire hunter. Who would have guessed?"

"I suppose the two go hand in hand. What's the plan?" I asked.

"Like I said, I'm going to sleep for a while, then get back at it in the morning. By then forensics will have everything from your dead vampires and we can try to figure out where this guy is operating out of. Then if we're lucky, we can stage a daytime raid."

"You know that doesn't really matter, right? Vampires don't really sleep all day. Luke sleeps because he prefers it to the reminder of being stuck indoors, but he can function in daytime just fine if he has to. And I bet a SWAT team breaking down the door qualifies as 'has to.'"

"Well, shit, then. I guess I'll just let you go first, then. Meet me at the station at 10. We'll see what we can dig up on Augustus' location and make a plan from there."

"Deal. I'll see you there." I pressed a button on the screen and slid the phone back into my jeans.

"So you and your little human think you're going after Augustus Renfield on your own? Are you delusional or just stupid?" Luke asked.

"Not the first time you've asked me that question, Uncle. And not the first time I've ignored it. Can I crash here for the night? Between fighting vampires in the morgue, fighting vampires in the car park, and fighting a vampire hunter, I'm beat."

"You must be tired, Master Quincy," Ren remarked.

"Why's that?"

"You called it a car park. You never let your British show unless you're extremely tired, or around a bunch of Englishmen."

I chuckled. "Or drunk, Renfield. I get very British when I drink, too." I went upstairs to my room and stripped down for a shower. After a long shower under steaming water, I lay awake on top of my sheets thinking for a long time.

Seeing Gabby Van Helsing brought back a lot of memories and sent my thoughts spinning down corridors in my mind that had long been deserted. I flashed back to that night watching old Abraham pass on; I remembered birthdays and Christmases with his family, then more birthdays and Christmases with just my family, then the one Christmas we had between my mother's death and my father's passing. I remembered burying my parents, my brothers, every friend I ever had. It was a melancholy parade of funerals that marched across my memory until the sun rose and I got up to take another shower and meet Flynn.

I had just pulled on my black jeans when there was a knock at my door. "Come in."

Renfield opened the door and stepped in with a glass of orange juice. "Good morning, Master Quincy. I brought you some juice."

"Thanks, Ren, but I could have gotten it myself. I'm heading down in a few minutes anyway."

"I understand that, sir, but I wanted to ask you something first. Something...of a personal nature."

"Something you didn't want my uncle to hear you ask me," I clarified.

"I don't want you to think I'm keeping secrets from him, sir, it's just that..."

"Go ahead, Ren. I'm something of an expert on keeping secrets from Uncle Luke. I know you'd never do anything to endanger him."

"Of course not, it's nothing like that. It's this new vampire, sir. I'm worried."

I looked at Ren. He didn't look worried, but he never did. Renfield was the most unflappable human being I'd ever met, and I'm really old, so I've met a lot of people. "What are you worried about, Ren?"

"He's scared, sir."

"Luke?"

"Yes, sir. It took me a little while to recognize it because I've never seen the symptoms, but he's honestly frightened of this vampire and his challenge."

I sat down on my bed and started lacing up my Doc Martens, noticing that Ren had not only shined my boots in the few hours I'd been asleep, he'd also replaced the worn lace in my right boot, emptied the pockets of the jeans I'd been wearing, put all that crap on my dresser, and either bought me a new duster or just pulled one from a magical leather duster supply he has somewhere in Luke's house.

I thought about what he said for a minute, then looked up at him. "I don't think he's afraid that Gus will hurt him, or kill him, or somehow win. I think he's afraid that he's actually going to have to do something about Gus once and for all. That he's too far gone to save, and there's no more last chances. I think that's the thing he's most afraid of—that he's going to have to destroy someone he once cared about quite a bit."

"He really is a soft touch, isn't he?"

"For an undead monster who lives by consuming the life force of others, yeah, he's a real teddy bear."

"I don't find that funny, Master Quincy," Ren sniffed.

"I wasn't joking, Ren," I let my voice get hard. "I know you think you know Luke. I know that right now you do know him better than all but two or three people in the world. You know what he likes for breakfast, how he likes his blood mixed with a little cabernet so he can pretend to be human, what TV shows he prefers, even what period of art he really cares for. But you've got to understand, underneath all of that is a hard-core motherfucker who did not become the thing mother warned their children about in Eastern Europe for decades by handing out candy canes at the Christmas parade.

"When he wants to be, when he *needs* to be, he can drop all that 'Uncle Luke' bullshit in a hot second and turn into Count Motherfucking Dracula, Vlad the Goddamn Impaler, Lord of the Undead and One Hundred Per Cent Baddest Son of a Bitch on the Planet. If you forget, ever, for even a second, that your employer can rip your heart out of your chest with his bare hands and drink the blood from it while it still beats hot in his palm, it may be the last mistake you make."

"You don't think he'd hurt me, do you? I've been nothing but loyal and faithful."

"And as long as that's the case, you'll never have a problem. But Gus? He turned on my uncle. He felt betrayed, and betrayed Luke in turn. So no matter how much it pains Uncle Luke to do it, he will bring down hell upon the head of Augustus Renfield, and God help anyone who gets in his way. Because this ain't no movie BS. This is the real deal, and Dracula is gonna get biblical on a motherfucker. That's what you've been noticing. It's not fear. It's regret moving into resignation at the knowledge that after all the time and all the second chances, he's going to have to solve Gus for good."

CHAPTER EIGHT

I first met Augustus in Paris after the war. World War II, that is, which is the only war Paris has known in my lifetime. I had spent some time in the end of the war working with the French Resistance, and I was making my way back to my apartment late one night when I heard a muffled scream from an alley.

I ran into the alley, which might have been more of a stumble given the amount of good French wine I'd consumed, and saw a gaunt man holding a woman against a wall. To most normal people, I'm sure it looked like they were making out. But I knew the difference between two people kissing and one person drinking blood from another's neck.

"Merde," I muttered, and ran down the alley. I picked up a piece of lumber lying on the ground by a wall undergoing repairs and swung it hard across the vampire's shoulders. The board broke into two pieces with a resounding *crack*, and I shook my hands at the sting.

The vampire slowly drew himself up to his full height and turned to face me. "That was very rude," it said. "I don't abide rudeness during my meals." The face he turned to me was an almost normal face, except for the pallor. He had mousy brown hair that parted on one side and hung down a little too long in the front. He wore a brown tweed suit and a striped shirt, and there was just a hint of blood on his brown bowtie. His features were preternaturally narrow, with cheekbones reaching almost to his hairline and the sunken cheeks of a man who hadn't fed in months. But there was no shortage of food in Paris after the blitz, what with the orphans and widows and homeless.

He reached out and took my shirtfront in his hand, and I marveled at his fingers, the longest and boniest appendages I'd ever seen. He pulled me to him and locked gazes with me. "I think you shall become my meal since you interrupted this one. She'll never taste the same."

He turned his attention to the young woman he'd been drinking from when I happened by. "Goodbye, my dear." He then flicked out his other hand and ripped her throat out, without ever losing his bemused, slightly surprised expression. Her eyes went wide, and she opened her mouth to scream, but it's hard to do more than gurgle with your vocal chords ripped out. She collapsed against a wall, crimson pouring down her bodice and covering her body as she died.

"You bastard," I growled. "You could have fed from her without killing her."

"I could have," he agreed, "but why? She was food. I was finished with her. Wasteful, I admit, but I don't believe she would remain fresh in this heat."

He still had a grip on my shirtfront, but it was loose in his fingers. I reached up to knock his hand away, but he caught my wrist in those skeletal fingers and shook me, hard. My head whipsawed back and forth, and my wine threatened to make a surprise appearance all over this vampire's dandy bowtie.

"What are you doing here, human? Do you blindly rush into death often? I would expect that to be a poor choice."

"Human is only part of the picture, vampire. I'm a little more than you're accustomed to," I said, pulling my wrist free and lifting him off his feet with a short uppercut. Gus staggered back a few steps, giving me all the room I needed. Or so I thought. I charged him, my shoulder low to catch him under the ribs and smear his accent all over the opposite wall.

Except he wasn't there. He spun out of the way faster than anyone I'd ever seen, and I learned to fight dirty from friggin' Dracula. He landed four quick shots to my midsection, and I heard a sharp *crack* as each punch landed, signaling a cavalcade of broken ribs and pain for me.

I dropped to one knee, the pain in my ribs making breathing all but impossible. I felt the whistle of a fist through the air and rolled to one side, barely avoiding the double-fisted blow that would have broken my neck. I looked up into the mad face of my attacker, and there was something strangely familiar there. He stomped down, and I caught his foot with both hands and shoved him backward. He toppled over onto his back, and we both leapt to our feet. We threw punch after punch, faster than any human could ever punch or block, but it took less than a minute for the pain in my ribs to sap the strength from my blows and the speed from my blocks.

I was just a hair too late getting my arm up, and he flicked out a jab that caught me flush on the point of the chin. I saw stars, birds whirling around me head, the whole bit as I sank to my butt in the alley. He stood over me, droplets of blood-sweat beading his brow.

"What are you?" he asked. "You're right, you're not human. Or at least not completely. But you're not a vampire, nor a were of any type I've encountered."

"What he is, Augustus, is my nephew. And thus off-limits for your appetites." Uncle Luke's voice came from the mouth of the alley. I have never before and rarely since been so happy that my uncle, the blood-sucking Lord of the Undead, has an overprotective streak. I peered past Gus to watch Luke stride down the alley, his raincoat billowing out behind him like the long cloaks he favored in the movies. He stopped about ten feet from us, just out of leaping range for his psychotic former manservant.

I caught a flicker of movement out of the corner of one eye and turned my attention back to Gus. I drew in a sharp and extremely painful breath at what I saw. Where he used to look like a harmless, if a little lecherous, skinny man in a boring suit, now his eyes were wild and rolling in his head like a dog caught in a bear trap. More bloody sweat poured from his brow, the crimson staining his shirt collar. Something, I couldn't tell what—fear, rage, excitement—vibrated through him like electricity.

"You!" the gaunt man hissed at Uncle Luke.

"Me," Luke replied calmly. "I see you found some measure of control over your abilities and have made something of a life for yourself. I am glad. I never wished you ill, Augustus. I just didn't think this life was the best for you."

"You didn't want the competition, *Sire*. You didn't want anyone else to taste the power, the sweet, sweet power that comes with the blood. But I did, yes, I have drank from the spring of eternal life and I have felt the power run through my veins! And now you can't stop me, *Sire*. No one can stop me!"

He sprang at Uncle Luke, all gangly arms and claw-like fingers, like some crazed spider flying through the alley. Luke simply swung a hand up and slapped him out of the air. Gus bounced off one brick wall and then crashed to the broken cobblestones, writhing. Luke reached down and helped me up, then opened his wrist with a thumbnail.

"Drink," he said, thrusting his arm at me.

I gaped at him. I'd drank from Luke before, but only when mortally wounded. This was painful, but nothing life threatening, so I didn't understand why he was so insistent.

"Drink, Quincy," he repeated, his voice an urgent hiss. "Drink, then *run*.

Augustus is powerful and completely insane. He will have no restraint, and now that he knows we are close, he will destroy you if given the opportunity. You must heal, and then you must return to our quarters and pack our things. If I do not return by sunrise, flee. I will find you."

I drank, taking in the stolen life force of Dracula himself. Drinking blood is gross, let's start there. It's coppery, thick, and nasty shit. And I only know this because of some ill-conceived experimentation Uncle Luke and I did in 1918, after both my brothers died in the influenza epidemic that killed a good portion of, well, the world. We wondered why I could visit them and not even get sick, and then it occurred to Luke that I hadn't really aged much in the past few years. I was twenty-two and still looked fifteen, a useful trait with the ladies, less so when drinking in bars. They weren't all that strict, but the more I looked like a little kid, the less likely I was to get served from the top shelf.

Anyway, drinking human or animal blood is nasty, but drinking vampire blood? Let's just say I understand how people fall under the thrall of unscrupulous vamps. It's like the very best red wine, but sweeter, and the rush you get is like no drug I've ever tried. And I've tried pretty much every drug that can be created without a chemistry set, and some that can't.

I let the warm liquid flow across my teeth and down my throat, feeling my ribs knit back together, all my bruises fade, and even feel a little indigestion clear up. The cut on my chin from shaving that morning even healed in seconds. I tore myself free from Luke's arm with a profound sadness and feeling of loss. I licked my thumb and ran it over his wrist, using the magic in my spit and his blood to heal the wound.

"Now go," he said, wiping his arm dry against his cloak.

I turned to do just that, but it was too late, Gus was on us again, and this time he was equally intent on killing me as he was destroying Luke. But he couldn't handle both of us at top form—not many things can, honestly. He charged me, rightly considering me to be the weaker of the two threats, but I was well into my magical studies by that point, so I focused my will and said "*Ventos!*" I flung my hand in his direction, and a whirlwind picked up every piece of debris in the alley and pelted him with it.

It was a petty distraction, of course, but I just need to get him to close his eyes for an instant. He did, and I dropped the spell. Luke didn't run by me, he didn't leap past me, he jumped *over* me in a flying kick and took Gus square in the chest.

"Run!" Luke shouted at me, but I didn't. Why bother, right? We had this guy dead to rights now that we were healthy and working together, didn't we?

Well, no. Luke's kick caught the off-balance Augustus square and knocked him flat, with Luke rolling through to come up on his feet at the other end of the alley, but Gus popped right back up with not so much as a scratch on him and dove for me, his fangs out and aiming for my throat.

I flung up a hasty shield spell, just enough to slow him down for a second or two, but that's all Luke needed. He grabbed Gus from behind and smashed his face into the cobblestones at my feet.

"Run, damn you, or I'll never be able to concentrate!" Luke yelled at me. This time I did as I was told—I ran. I hauled ass back to the small apartment house where we had three rooms, and I woke up the current (and brand-new) Renfield.

The poor guy hadn't yet gotten used to being up all night and sleeping a few hours here and there during the day, so he was in his nightshirt when he answered the pounding on his door.

"Master Quincy? What is wrong?" he asked through bleary eyes.

I said one word, the one word that ever since Luke and I belly-laughed our way through *Frankenstein* had meant "pack all our shit and be ready to move." I looked at Renfield, and I said, "Pitchfork."

He goggled at me for a moment, then he drug up "Pitchfork" in his memory, and his eyes got wide. I reached out and caught the lamp he nearly dropped as he turned to go back into the room.

"Renfield, are we clear? We are Pitchfork."

Renfield turned to me, all signs of sleepiness gone from his face. "Indeed, Master Quincy. We are Pitchfork." Then he turned back to his room and started packing. Luke made it to the apartment just before sunup, and Renfield and I loaded him into the limousine we had specially prepared for just such an occurrence. It had a separate passenger compartment for Luke that was completely light tight, as well as a regular compartment that was big enough for two other passengers. Renfield drove, and I started the journey back in Luke's compartment with him.

"You look like me after that five-day bender in Berlin back in 1926," I said.

"Yes, that was quite a time you had. Who knew that you would celebrate your thirtieth birthday by getting in a fight with six Germans, three Austrians, and one random Italian woman who just happened to be walking by at the wrong moment?"

"In my defense, I was drunk at the time," I replied.

"If I recall correctly, nephew, you were drunk for the entirety of 1926," Luke replied, smiling. He winced, putting a hand to his split lip.

"It was an experiment. I wanted to see what would happen if I got drunk every day for a whole year."

"And what were your findings?"

"I found that it takes a lot of money to get me drunk, and I don't get fat like normal people. So I got drunk a lot, and I got very poor very quickly. I don't recommend it as a lifestyle. Nor do I recommend doing battle with incredibly strong vampires in alleyways. Who was that beast?"

"That was my old manservant, Augustus Renfield."

"The one who...?"

"Yes, the one from the book. There were a few things incorrect in the story, of course."

"Of course. It mentions the fact that you're dead, after all," I agreed.

"Well, I am dead, but not forever dead as Stoker implied. And Renfield was not always a madman, but he certainly became one after many years in my service. I believe your aunts may have had something to do with that."

"You never talk about them," I observed.

"They were a mistake. I do not enjoy discussing my mistakes."

"A mistake you made three times." I might have taken a little too much joy in twisting the knife, but Luke so rarely showed any self-doubt or vulnerability, I couldn't resist.

"Well, it takes a certain amount of experimentation to prove a theorem. I had to know that all three of them were mistakes, you see." He gave a little half-smile, and it made me feel better that he was still capable of laughing at himself.

"So this Renfield, the original. What's his problem?" I knew by the twitch under his eye that I had hit on a sensitive subject, but I wasn't about to let go. "Go on, Uncle. He almost killed us both tonight, I deserve to know about him."

"I promised him eternal life in exchange for three decades of service. The same offer I make to all my valets. Most of them realize after only a few years that they are not cut out for service to one such as myself and do not last the term, or they realize that there is a great deal more "forever" than "living" in living forever, and they choose a generous mortal severance instead. Augustus came to neither of those conclusions. He fixated on becoming like me, becoming one with the night, until it drove him quite mad.

"He was mad long before his term was up and could not fulfill his terms of the bargain, so I was under no obligation to turn him. He did not see things quite that way and escaped from the asylum, insisting that I give him The Gift. I refused, and he ran away."

"Until today?" I asked.

"Oh, but I wish it were so," Luke replied. "He returned to England some years hence, already one of the undead. And the power he had! He was the strongest of us I had ever seen! I know not how he grew so strong, but I believe it is from drinking the blood of many elder vampires. As you know, there is power in the blood, and the older the vampire, the more power there is to be found. Augustus found that power and returned to England to destroy me. I could not vanquish him and keep those I cared about safe, so I returned to Transylvania, in part to escape, but mainly to do battle on familiar ground. Van Helsing went with me, as did Holmwood, and your father, leaving you the man of the house to look after your brothers and mother."

"I remember that trip," I said. "I was eight or nine. I never knew where Father went, only that we had to get dressed up when he came home and that Mother cried a lot that summer."

"She wept for Arthur Holmwood, who Augustus killed with his bare hands. It was likely to his funeral that you went upon your father's return. She wept in fear of repercussions from our visit, for although we thrashed Augustus soundly, he escaped before we were able to mete out a final, killing blow. But we did defeat him, and we imprisoned him within my old castle there, hopefully until such a time that he either died of hunger or found himself somehow and became less of a danger to others."

"Apparently neither of those things happened," Luke said, staring out the black windows at a history only he could see.

"Apparently not," I agreed. "Now what?" I asked.

"Now we find out where he sleeps and we kill him at high noon, when his power is at its lowest point."

"That's a plan I can get behind," I said. "You get some rest, we'll be at the safe house in an hour." I slid between compartments and directed Renfield to one of our many boltholes around the French countryside.

CHAPTER NINE

"Obviously, we didn't kill Gus. We couldn't find his lair, so after several days of searching, we left Paris and worked very hard to forget about him." I finished my little tale and stood up, ready to go out and face the day. Or at least face police headquarters, where I was overdue to meet Flynn and Smith.

"Until last night," Ren said.

"Until last night," I agreed. "Look, Ren, I don't know what to tell you about Gus. He's the only Renfield my uncle's ever had that went cuckoo, and maybe he was a little nutso before Luke took him on. But it's not like it's a thing, people that work for Luke going crazy and getting turned into über-vamps. So if you're worried about that..."

"That's not it at all, Master Quincy. I merely wanted some background on the man so that I might better understand the monster he's become. If I understand him, I'll be better prepared to fight him should he attack us here."

"No!" I said, a little more vehemently than I intended. "Gus is bad juju. If he comes after you here, do not engage, just get the hell out. Luke can take him if he's rested and Gus doesn't get the drop on him, and if he doesn't have to worry about anyone he cares about becoming collateral damage. That's one thing that kept him from going full out against him back in Paris—he was worried I'd get caught in the crossfire somehow. So if he comes here, get to safety, and call me as fast as you can."

"What will you do?" Renfield asked. "You've already said you can't beat him."

"In a fair fight, I can't. I don't stand a chance. He's faster, stronger, and can withstand way more punishment. Good thing for me, I don't fight fair." I patted Ren on the shoulder and stood up. "I gotta roll. Becks and Smith are waiting for me at headquarters. I'll be back at dusk to put my head together with Luke and plan tonight's hunt."

"I'll take care of him while you're away," Ren said.

I looked at the sincere little man, all creases and quiet competence. "I know you will, buddy."

B y the time I grabbed a nasty fast food biscuit and kickstarted my system with a jumbo soda, it was 10:30, so I was almost an hour late when I strolled into the conference room we'd appropriated from the Charlotte-Mecklenburg Police Department. I stopped dead in my tracks at the sight of Gabriella Van Helsing standing next to Flynn, both in pant suits and sensible shoes that screamed, "I'm a government agent and I have at least one firearm hidden under this suit jacket."

"What the flying green fuck is she doing here?" I asked as I sat at one end of the table. It wasn't a power thing, it was just closer to the outlets and I needed to charge my phone. I plugged the electronic everything into the wall and put my keys next to it. I left more phones in stupid places until I started putting my keys next to them. That way I can't leave without getting my keys, and I see my phone under them.

"Ms. Van Helsing is on detachment from the Federal Bureau of Investigation, here to explore the possibility that the deaths we've experienced are part of a larger pattern, a serial killer that has been working the United States for nearly sixty years." I couldn't see enough in Smith's eyes to see if he knew her cover was bullshit or not, so I went along with it.

"That's nuts," I said. "How could one killer operate for so long without drawing attention to himself? I'm sure what we've got here in Charlotte is an isolated incident. You can stay if you like, and help us with our investigation, but let's not be thinking that this a great time to push the yokels aside and make a name for yourself, because it's not."

"I assure you, Mr. Harper, that is the last thing I intend to do. As a matter of fact, as a gesture of goodwill, I brought in all the data from the Bureau's geographic profile. It shows the most likely location for this bloodsucker's safe house to be somewhere between Fifth Street and Eighth Street on College. Do any of you know of any abandoned building in that area?"

"Not really," Smith said. "That's right in the heart of Uptown. I mean, I suppose there are some hidey-holes around Discovery Place where he could build a nest, but I can't imagine anything would really be private enough."

"The Carolina Theatre," I said. Everybody turned to look at me. "Oh come on, folks. It's right there in the center of the profile zone, and it's been abandoned forever. It's perfect. It even has the vampire-ready architecture. If he's anywhere downtown, that's where he'll be."

"Abandoned theatres do tend to make excellent hideouts," Van Helsing agreed. "Particularly if there are any Deco or Gothic features, many older vampires will feel very much at home there."

"I've never been inside the place," I said. "But from the pictures I've seen, it's currently decorated in Early Decay. But it was big-deal Vaudeville-style theatre back in the day."

"Then that's our most likely spot," Van Helsing said. "We should launch our assault soon. Vampires are perfectly capable of functioning during daylight hours, but they are weaker, and exposure to sunlight is fatal to their kind."

"So if you find yourself in a pinch, break a window," I said. "What's the team?" I asked Smith.

"Just the four of us," he replied. I raised an eyebrow. "We don't have enough men trained in dealing with supernatural threats. We learned that the hard way dealing with War a few months ago. And since I'm in no hurry to throw perfectly good men away, I thought we'd skip the suicide mission today."

"Makes sense," I said. My scrap with the incarnation of War itself wiped out two street gangs, one biker gang, and a dozen very brave and very unprepared police officers.

"Let's load up. We should be able to do this in one Suburban," Smith said.

"There are four of us, Smitty. We could do this in a Hyundai." I followed him down the hall and we boarded an elevator. A couple floors later, the doors opened up into a parking garage full of all-black SUVs and sedans. We piled into a Suburban and rolled out of the underground garage, blue lights flashing. It was a little anticlimactic that there was no traffic in the middle of the day and that our ride in the urban assault vehicle was only about six blocks, but sometimes when you work with the government, you've got to do things the government way.

I strapped into the passenger seat and sent a little mental "knock knock" back to Flynn, who was sharing the backseat with Van Helsing.

Yeah, what's up, Harker?

Harper, I corrected. *At least for today. The chick next to you isn't FBI, she's—*

Flynn cut me off. *I was there, remember? At least part of the time. I know who she is. But why hide your name? It's not like the connection is that obvious.*

It would be to her. I knew her family growing up. There's a chance there might be old pictures of me around. I'd like to keep my ID hidden unless it's absolutely necessary. And the how? My badge printed wrong, remember? The stupid woman down in HR who can't do anything right except file enough discrimination complaints every year that everyone's terrified to fire her? She strikes again. But this time she may be useful.

That would be a first. Fine, I won't do anything to blow your cover, but you're on your own with Smith.

Yeah, that was a whole different issue. But before I got a chance to communicate anything to our boss, we were at the theatre. The only thing to indicate there had ever been a Carolina Theatre was a blue neon sign running up one wall. Every other indication that the building we were looking was anything other than the backside of a bank or warehouse was gone. I walked up to a side entrance, but it was locked.

"Anything?" I called to Smith, who had gone over to the small door in the front of the facade.

"No. Locked up tight."

"The alley it is, then," I said. I motioned for him to head my way and turned to see Flynn and Van Helsing walking toward me. Flynn tossed a pile of metal at me, and I snatched it out of the air. I turned it over in my hands a couple of times, then looked at her.

"Ummm, thanks, but I'm not into the whole bondage thing," I said.

She took the thing out of my hands, shook it once, undid a clasp, and tossed it around my neck. Once it settled into place, she tightened one strap around my throat until I croaked and yanked down on it, hard, then she relaxed her grip and fastened it into place. I reached up and patted my neck, now protected by a chain mail neck guard that ran from just under my ears to my collarbone.

"Good thinking," I said.

"Kevlar's great, but this is definitely a job where being wrapped in sheets of metal is preferable," she replied.

"Yeah, I don't know many vampires that pack pistols, but a mouthful of metal is a good way to ruin a vamp's day," I agreed.

"Especially since it's been doused in holy water and brushed with silver oxide."

"Holy water, huh?" I asked. "No wonder it burns a little." I grinned at her and started down the alley. Flynn was right behind me, with Van Helsing following her. Smith had rear guard, covering the alley behind us with his Mossberg full of silver shot.

I put an ear to the door but heard nothing through the reinforced steel. I turned to Smith. "Who brought the key?"

He moved past me to the door and pulled a spool of det cord out of his backpack. In less than a minute, he had a line of explosive running the length of the door's hinge and wires connected to a handheld detonator.

"Let me try something before we completely give up on the element of surprise," I said. I knelt in front of the door and pretended to fiddle with a set of lock picks. All I really did was put my head close to the lock and whisper, "*Aperio.*" The lock clicked open and I pushed the door inward. Blackness yawned before us as I peered into the abandoned theatre.

I stepped through the doorway first, flicked on my red-lensed flashlight, and all hell broke loose.

CHAPTER TEN

The second I clicked on the light, I heard a creak on the wooden floor off to my right. I swung the light in the direction of the sound and almost dropped the flash at what I saw. There must have been two dozen vampires on the stage, all rising from a sleeping position and turning their attention to the door.

"Guys, we have a situation here," I said. I drew half a dozen glow sticks from my back pocket, cracked them all at once, and threw them as far around the room as I could. "Get as much light in here as you can, and go back-to-back. There's a fuckton of fangs in this room, and none of them look happy to see us."

Flynn, Van Helsing, and Smith all charged the room at that point, Smith firing a white phosphorous flare out into the gutted auditorium. A section of rotted flooring immediately caught fire from the sparks, adding to the illumination, but also pouring smoke into the sealed room and starting a bonfire in one of Charlotte's last standing historic landmarks.

I glared at him. "Was that really a good idea? Flares? Indoors? Didn't your mom ever tell you not to set off fireworks in the house?"

"Seemed like a good idea at the time," he replied. "Isn't that what you always say when you do something stupid?"

"Shut up, Smitty," I growled and leveled my pistol at his head. He dropped to one knee, and I put two in the head of the vampire that was coming up behind him. Smith, in turn, pulled the trigger on his shotgun and literally cut the legs off a vampire charging in from my left. I stomped on the monster's neck with my boot, breaking its neck and rendering it forever dead.

I heard pistol fire from behind me, but I couldn't spare a thought for Flynn and Van Helsing because three vampires converged on me at once. Or at least they tried to, but since they had obviously never fought together, it didn't go well for them. The one that got the closest fastest ended up in my grasp, and I spun him around to block a huge punch from an overgrown vamp coming at me head on. He hit the first vampire so hard in the head that the creature's skull exploded. I dropped my undead shield and put four in the big beast's chest, but that was only enough to bring it to its knees.

Then the third beast had me. It caught me from the right in a flying tackle, which is always a bad idea. Any time you leave your feet in a fight, bad things can happen. In this case, the bad things happened to me, as the vamp drove me into the stage floor and then stood up to stomp my ribcage in. But just as it lifted up its foot, the pain kicked in and the vampire looked down at its chest. The chest with a silver stake poking out of it. When it tackled me, I managed to roll around and draw one of my stakes before we landed, then staked the bastard when he landed on top of me.

I yanked the stake from his chest, he dropped, and I turned to jab the stake through the eye of the giant vamp I'd left on his knees in front of where I'd once stood. Except he wasn't there, he was stomping across the stage at the girls, who were shooting everything in sight but not killing nearly enough. They had four or five vampires around them, plus the big boy. Smith wasn't doing much better. He'd dropped his Mossberg and drawn a katana, which I'd never seen before. But the numbers game was getting to all of us. Even with my few seconds' reprieve, I still had half a dozen bloodsuckers all converging on my position and very little idea what to do about them.

"He's mine," came a voice from the balcony, and I looked up to see Gus swooping down from fifty feet away. That bastard always knew how to make an entrance. He glided down to the stage, an honest-to-God *cape* billowing out behind him, landing on one knee about ten feet in front of me. His vampire minions backed away, leaving an alley for him to approach me. He stood and swept his cape back off his shoulders, letting it flutter behind him like a black velvet banner. He walked toward me, almost stalking, his polished black riding boots echoing across the stage.

Everything stopped in that surreal moment. All the other fighting stopped as his henchmen watched our confrontation. He was playing the role of the Master Vampire to the hilt, and I knew exactly where he learned it, He had Uncle Luke's shtick down cold, from the cold glare, to the shoes polished to a mirror gloss, all the way to his hair plastered tight to his skull with more product than a Lady Gaga concert. He stopped in front of me and looked at me, a little smirk curling up one corner of his mouth.

"Did you actually think you could beard the lion in its den, little man? In what world are you strong enough or smart enough to best me?"

I kept my voice low but looked him straight in his cold gray eyes. I wasn't afraid of his mind control powers; I'd been training with the OG boss vampire for a hundred years. I locked gazes with him and said, "If you leave Charlotte right now, I won't hunt you and you can keep your pitiful little pseudo-life for as long as you like. But if we throw down, I'm not going to stop until you're true dead and I've scattered your remains at sunrise over Freedom Park. You got me?"

He snarled and reached out with his left hand, grabbing me around the throat and picking me up one-handed. "You insolent fool, you dare to threaten me? I should snap your neck right now!" His face grew mottled with rage and his grip tightened. Just like I'd planned.

The problem with picking someone up by the throat is that you have to lock your elbow to do it with any touch of aplomb. And with your elbows locked and held straight out in front of you, your elbows become vulnerable to all sorts of nasty things. Like people smashing you in the elbows and dislocating both of them in one sharp blow.

So that's exactly what I did to Gus. I reached up and punched him on the back sides of his fully extended elbows. There were two loud *snap* sounds, and he dropped me, screeching in pain. I hit the floor and rolled, coming up with my pistol back in my hand and putting silver-tipped hollowpoints in the chest of the three nearest vampires. My gun clicked empty, so I drew a pair of silver stakes from the back of my belt and went to work.

I was a whirlwind of silver and smartass comments, taking out half a dozen vampires in half a minute. The vampires covering Flynn, Van Helsing, and Smith all turned to look at the carnage I was creating, and all became part of carnage. Flynn and Van Helsing took out two vampires each, and when I turned to see how Smith was doing, I watched him pull his hand back through a gaping hole in a vampire's chest. I gaped at him, but he just held a single bloody finger to his lips. He spun on his heels and grappled at another vampire, and my attention returned to the undead murderer at hand.

I looked down at Gus, who was still working on getting his elbows back into alignment. I stepped forward and put a foot on one of Gus' ankles. "Stay still, asshole," I growled down at him.

He looked up at me and said, "I'll have your soul for breakfast for this insult, H—"

I cut him off, still trying to avoid Van Helsing figuring out my name. "You won't do shit, Gus. You'll either run now with your tail tucked between your legs like the good little butler you really are, or I'll rip those useless arms off your body and beat you to death with them."

He glared at me. "You don't have the stones, boy." His voice was low and dangerous, and I could feel the hate rolling off him like steam. He bent over, stomped on the fingers of one hand, then pulled until his elbow popped back into place. He swapped arms, repeated the process, then stood up, flexing his newly-restored arms. I could see the pain in the beads of sweat dotting his forehead, but he never let it touch his face.

"I believe the question is, is that the best you've got?" he asked as he charged me. I dove to my left, landing in a roll and coming up with my hands already spinning a warding spell. "*Murus!*" I said, pouring my will into the words.

Gus slammed into my hastily drawn circle, then pounded on it as he howled in rage. "You cannot defeat me, Quincy Harker! I will never let you leave this place alive!"

He was looking more and more correct as Smith's flare continued to burn and catch more segments of the audience seating on fire. I looked out to see most of the audience chamber engulfed in flames and smoke roiling across the entire building. The vampires didn't care, of course, but my human companions and I were starting to have a rough time breathing.

I looked up at the ceiling and the fly grid, some eighty feet above the stage. All old wood, it was ripe to catch fire and come down on all of us in a heap of burning wood and death. I focused my will, opened a tiny hole in the top of my dome, thrust out my hand and yelled, "*Foenestra!*" I unleashed my magic in a tight beam, focused down to a two-foot circle, and blasted a hole through the grid, all the rigging, and the roof of the theatre. All the debris flew up, and so did the smoke.

The air cleared almost instantly, but what goes up, must come down, in this case in the form of chunks of four by four and nails.

"Heads up!" I yelled, running full tilt for the side of the stage out of the drop zone. I watched Smith reach up and bat a chunk of wood out of the air, then turn right back to beating a vampire's face in, and saw a two-foot length of lumber pin one vampire to the floor, coming down straight through its neck and knocking him flat. The wood missed his heart, brain, and spine, so he just lay there writhing like a bug in a kid's science project.

I heard a scream and turned to see Van Helsing lose her footing and go down in the center of a circle of vamps. Flynn tried to get to the fallen slayer but found herself surrounded. I turned to run across the stage to help the women, but Gus was on me in an instant. He grabbed the back of my coat and

pulled me back to him, wrapping me up in a full nelson and effectively immobilizing me.

"Watch, Harker," he hissed into my ear. "Watch as my minions tear your
friends limb from limb. Watch as we destroy even the faerie, with all his
strength and magic." He turned me to look at Smith, who was hard-pressed by
a cluster of four vampires.

Faerie? Smith? It made a certain amount of sense, but I couldn't think about
that just then. I had to come up with something, and fast, or all my friends,
and Van Helsing, were going to be a vampire buffet. I struggled against Gus's
grip, but he held me tight. I thrashed and heard a sharp hiss as a beam of
sunlight from the hole in the ceiling danced across the back of his hand. A
thin tendril of smoke climbed from the back of Gus's hand, and I saw my out.

I looked up, focused my will, and shouted, *"FOENESTRA!"* at the top of my
lungs. Power flew from me, scattered without the focus of a gesture, and
blasted through the wooden grid and the rest of the ceiling. Wood, brick, and
steel flew upward from the roof, falling outward onto the surrounding streets
and alleys, but that couldn't be helped. As the dust cleared, sunlight streamed
into the theatre from the new twenty-foot skylight I'd created, and vampires
burst into flames all around the stage. Gus dropped me like a hot potato and
ran for the shadows, but most of his minions weren't so lucky. The four
around Van Helsing died almost instantly, and three of the ones surrounding
Flynn met the same fate. The few survivors scattered to the shadows and the
dark places under the theatre, but we were in no shape to pursue.

Gus stopped in front of a stairwell leading down into the bowels of the
building, glared at me across the stage and shouted, "This isn't over, Quincy
Harker! I'm not done with you, or your 'Uncle' Vlad, either!" Then he turned
and ran down into the safety of the theatre's catacombs.

I turned to see Gabriella Van Helsing standing less than ten feet away from
me, a nickel-plated Colt 1911 pistol leveled at my head and a scowl on her
face. "Just what did he call you?"

CHAPTER ELEVEN

"**G**o ahead, Agent *Harper*," Van Helsing said. "Tell me your name again." The Colt didn't waver, not even a little. Pretty impressive for a slight woman who had been getting the shit beat out of her by vampires less than two minutes before.

I sighed and took the gun from her. It was a lot harder than it should have been because she's really strong and fast. For a human. But since I'm not exactly human, it still wasn't that hard. I ejected the magazine, cleared the chamber, and handed it back to her.

"Point that thing at me again and I'll slap the taste out of your mouth," I said. "I usually don't hit women, but you're better armed and a better fighter than most men, so I'll make an exception if I have to." I took a deep breath. "My name is Quincy Holmwood Harker. Yes, I am that Quincy, born from that Jonathan Harker and Mina Murray. I am the apparently immortal or at least stupidly long-lived son of two parents that Dracula fed on, shared blood with, but didn't turn. That does something to your DNA, we're not exactly sure what."

"How old are you?" she asked.

"About a hundred-twenty," I said. "And yes, I knew your great-grandfather. He was very nice to me when I was a little boy. He let me pull on his beard and gave me sweets when my parents weren't looking. Visiting with him was one of the bright spots of my childhood."

"What kind of monster are you?" she asked. At least she put the gun away.

"I don't think I am a monster," I said. "I'm not a vampire, a were of any flavor, or a demon. I guess you could call me a wizard if you felt the need, but I guess I'd prefer the term magic-user."

"You lied to me," she said, and the betrayal in her eyes hurt more than the bruises Gus had left.

I tried to weasel out of it, but I knew it was useless. "Technically, I didn't lie to you. My ID badge was misprinted, and I just didn't correct you."

"You're an asshole," she hissed.

"No arguments there," Flynn chimed in.

"Not helping," I said.

"Not trying to," Flynn said, and I could feel her grin through our mental connection. Having a hitchhiker in your head pretty much always sucks, but it sucks worse when the hitchhiker is an insufferable smartass.

"You're a monster," Van Helsing growled, and I could feel the situation slipping away from me.

"I'm not a monster, I'm a guy. We're all assholes, and we all lie, but that doesn't mean you have to do something stupid." I held out my hands, palms out, trying to calm her down. I had my usual level of success in calming down angry women, which is to say none.

"You lied to me to keep me from know what you were, and now I find out that not only are you part vampire, but the bloodsucker that my great-grand-father thought he'd killed all those years ago is alive? What am I supposed to do about that?"

"That's really two questions," I stalled, trying to come up with one, much less two, valid answers. "About the me lying to you thing, I've always been a big fan of forgiving and forgetting, personally."

Flynn barked out a laugh. "You're still mad at your uncle for bespelling the 1919 White Sox into throwing the World Series, and that was almost a hundred years ago!"

"Not helping," I said. "Besides, there are forgivable sins, and then there's baseball. You don't mess with baseball. Anyway, you can forgive me or not; that's your call. But about the other thing—about Count Vlad Dracula still being alive regardless of what Stoker put in his little bedtime story? That's nobody's fault but Stoker's. Not even your grandfather."

"Great-grandfather," she corrected.

"I know, but I feel old enough already, so we're going to skip that part if it's quite all right with you. Look, Abraham knew that Luke wasn't dead. He even knew that Luke was there when he died."

Her eyes widened briefly at that, then narrowed in suspicion. "How would you know that?"

"Because I was standing at the foot of his bed when he waved out the window at him. Your grandfather, Abraham's son this time, would never invite Luke in, so he stood out in the snow and watched through the night as we kept vigil. They were never friends, but there was an understanding at the end between hunter and vampire."

"And what if I think you're full of shit? What if I decide to go after your uncle anyway?"

"That would be a very bad choice," I said.

"What, you think he'd turn me? I'm not afraid of living forever."

"Says everyone who's never tried it," I said. "Get back to me in seventy years or so and let me know how it's going. But that's not the point. I'm not the least bit afraid of Luke turning you. He hasn't turned anyone since my mom's best friend Lucy. Nowadays he'd just kill you."

"Others have tried," she shot back.

"Fine, then. Don't forgive me and work with us to take down the vampire that's an actual threat to the people of this city. Stay pissed and go after Luke, you know, the vampire that the whole genre is based off of. He's taken down more vampire hunters than I've gotten lap dances, and let me tell you, that's a pretty big number."

"Fuck this, I'm going after him." Van Helsing started to storm out the door, but Flynn got in front of her.

"Look, Gabriella, let's all just take a minute to dial it down…" Flynn took her by the arm, and the vampire hunter shook free and gave Flynn a hard shove.

"Bitch, don't you put your monster-loving hands on me!"

"You'd better think twice about calling a police officer a bitch in this town, or you'll find yourself brought up on charges for impersonating an FBI agent, *bitch*. I checked your backstory, and it's thinner than Harker's last excuse for being late."

"Hey! Whose side are you on?" I asked.

"Shut your pie hole, Harker," Flynn snapped. "And you, miss high-and-mighty vampire hunter, I'm telling you as the local law enforcement that any harassment of our citizens, including Mr. Lucas Card, major donor to the Policeman's Charity Ball and the funds for families of fallen officers, will be handled with extreme prejudice."

"I'm feeling pretty damned prejudiced right now, why don't we just settle this shit? I kick your ass, I'm free to do whatever I like to Dracula. You kick my ass, I leave town and forget I ever heard about Lucas Card." She assumed a fighting stance.

Flynn mirrored her and nodded. In a matter of seconds, the whole mess had escalated from me pissing off another pretty girl to a pair of badass women about to throw down in the middle of a theatre full of recently-ashed vampires. I was looking around for the popcorn vendor when Smith stepped between them.

"Cut this shit out, NOW," he said, in a voice that was a cross between a drill sergeant and middle school principal. He held out one arm to each woman, muscles bulging beneath his tactical uniform. But nobody was looking at his arms. We were all focused on his eyes, which had flashed to a deep yellow, like a big cat's. His pupils were vertical and oval, and his eyes seemed to glow with an inner light. Flynn took a step back, as did Van Helsing.

"What the fuck are you?" Van Helsing asked the question that was hanging in the air.

"Pissed off is what I am," Smith replied. "I'm pissed off that my squad can't get along for the time it takes to clear one building and make sure that there are no more vampires running around. I'm pissed off that there was a vampire nest in the middle of my city, and I'm pissed that the so-called Master of the Vampires either didn't know about it or didn't care enough to do anything about it. You got any other questions?" He turned his full attention to Van Helsing, but she didn't flinch.

"Yeah," she said, right up in Smith's face. "What. The. Fuck. Are. You? Did I say it slow enough for you that time?"

"I heard you the first time. I just ignored you because it's none of your fucking business. Is that clear enough?"

"Yeah, it's clear that this whole team has been infiltrated by monsters, so you won't be any fucking good at stopping them. I'm better off on my own." She turned to go. I cut her off at the door.

"Don't do this," I said. "Hang with us. We're not monsters. Okay, I'm not. I don't know what the hell Smith is, but whatever it is he turns into, it can't be much worse than mid-level government functionary, can it?"

She laughed at that, and I reached out and touched her arm. "Look, I'm sorry we lied to you about some stuff, but I've got some people to protect, so I can't go telling all their secrets, you know?"

"I get it," she said. "I understand why you did what you did. I've just gotta go process. I mean, it's not every day that you find out a whole branch of the government is run by monsters." She pushed past me to the door and walked out into the daylight.

Smith stepped up beside me. "Wait 'til she finds out about the Supreme Court." I gaped at him, but he just gave me a smile.

CHAPTER TWELVE

Despite blowing most of the roof off of the old theatre and letting the sunshine in, as the song goes, there were still a *lot* of places for vampires to hide in the Carolina Theatre. And after hearing the ruckus we caused upstairs, none of them were very eager to come out and tangle with us. Which is usually fine, because I'm a live-and-let-unlive kinda guy most of the time, but in this case, we spent the rest of the day combing the theatre for stragglers and clues as to where Gus would go to hide or what he had planned next.

It was early evening when Smith, Flynn, and I reconvened on the stage to go over what we'd learned. We sent all the other agents home and gathered around a table I dragged out from some backstage office. I dropped the few clues I'd picked up throughout the day onto the table, but it didn't amount to much. I had a couple of takeout menus, a listing of upcoming Broadway and Symphony shows coming to town, and a course catalog for Central Piedmont Community College. I was pretty sure most of that stuff had been left by the last people to rent the theatre, since I didn't see Gus as the type to take night classes in Japanese or try the best new place for Pad Thai, especially since vampires can't process normal food.

Smith hadn't fared any better, picking up a few parking stubs and collecting wallets from the vampires we staked and beheaded. If their IDs weren't lying, none of the vampires from Gus's crew were local, which meant he was traveling in something big and with a light-tight cargo compartment. That narrowed down his parking solutions pretty dramatically, so Smith got on the phone and started calling long-term lots that were big enough to handle that type of vehicle, and Flynn opened her laptop and started looking up parking citations for oversized vehicles in the past couple of weeks.

I had nothing, so I sifted through papers aimlessly for a few minutes, then started scouring the floor for clues from our earlier fight. I don't know what I thought I was looking for, but I found a whole lot of nothing.

A few minutes after the last rays of sunlight stopped flickering through my impromptu skylight, my cell rang. I looked at the display and swiped my finger across the screen. "What's up, Luke? Met up with an old friend of yours today. Boy, that Augustus, he's got more issues than Reader's Digest."

"Quincy, while I often do not mind you borrowing my manservant for your little forays into mortal law enforcement, I must ask that if you are not going to have him home in time to prepare my breakfast, please leave a note. It is only common courtesy, after all," my uncle's cultured voice came through the tinny speaker crystal clear, pissiness and all.

"What are you talking about, Unc?" I looked around the stage just to make sure, but nope, no Renfield. Just like there hadn't been a Renfield there all day.

"Where is Renfield, boy? I just woke up, I want my breakfast, and I am without my manservant! Are you being deliberately obtuse, or is it a natural state?"

"Don't get bitchy, Uncle, I don't have your butler. I haven't seen Ren since I left the house this morning, and I haven't heard anything out of him all day. Did he go out grocery shopping or something? I know it's low on your priority list, but he has to eat, and he keeps a few things around the house for me, so maybe he went shopping."

"He did. Much earlier. There is a new six-pack of that beer you like in the refrigerator and a receipt on the counter from before noon. No, he's not out shopping. And he never stays out past dark without a very good reason."

I started to feel a sick feeling in my stomach. "What reason would be good enough?"

"What are you talking about, boy?" Luke tended to call me "boy" when he was upset. Some things you just learn to live with when dealing with monsters that are hundreds of years old. "Boy" was one of those things.

"I'm saying has he *ever* been gone when you woke up before? For any reason?"

Luke paused and took a deep breath. After what felt like forever, he answered. "No. He hasn't. Quincy, do you think something is wrong? Had something happened to him?" I gotta give him credit, Luke sounded legitimately worried. In that moment, he sounded more human than I'd heard him sound in years.

217

"I don't think something happened, Uncle. I think *someone* happened," I replied.

"Augustus," Luke said.

"Augustus," I agreed. "After we thumped him here, I bet he went to your place and decided to hit you where it would hurt the most—threatening the people who rely on you for protection."

"That son of a bitch!" Luke exploded, and I pulled the phone away from my ear. Smith's head whirled around, and I dialed in my suspicions about him a little further. "I'll destroy him once and for all. If he's harmed a single hair on that man's head, I will tear him apart with my bare hands!" I held the phone further away from my head as Luke ranted. Super-hearing comes in handy a lot of the time, but when people are yelling into a cell phone, it turns every conversation into an argument.

"Luke," I said, but he ignored me. "Luke!" I shouted, and he fell silent.

"Don't do anything crazy," I said. "We're on our way."

I turned to Flynn. "You get that?" I asked.

"Yeah."

"Explain it to Smith while I pull the car around front. Grab all our weapons and be ready for some superior cover-up work in tomorrow's paper if we find the bastard," I said, turning to the door.

Two minutes later we were speeding down Seventh Street headed toward Luke's house. We turned right off the main road into Luke's neighborhood, then left into a housing development.

"I still can't get over Dracula living in a housing development," Flynn said as a cavalcade of nearly identical split-level houses circa 1964 rolled by outside the windows.

"It wasn't a housing development when he built here. It wasn't even Charlotte when he built here. I'm sure if he'd known the city would actually grow into something, he would have stayed far away. But he likes it here, so we stick around."

"What about you, Harker?" Flynn asked. "Do you like it here?"

I looked over at her, but there was none of the normal mocking in her eyes. I thought for a moment, then said, "Yeah, I like it here. I've lived here longer than I've lived anywhere as an adult, so it feels as much like home as anywhere that's not London. And even London doesn't feel much like my London anymore. There have been a few changes in the last hundred years or so. Charlotte's a good place to live, and there's enough turnover in the population that I can change apartments and names every ten years or so, and as long as I don't go back to my old hangouts, I don't get outed too often."

"How long have you been here?" Flynn asked.

"Well, Luke's been here in one name or another for a lot longer than me, but I got here in the seventies. If I had to live in America during those years, I was at least going to live in the South where bell bottoms weren't quite as big as some places." I chuckled, then grew focused. "We're here. Smith, I need you to take the back entrance. Can you handle it solo?"

"Kid, I was breaching doors when you were still trying to figure out how tie your shoes."

"I rather doubt that since I learned to tie my shoes at the turn of the century. The twentieth century." I parked the Suburban in the driveway and headed for the door. I took the front steps two at a time and hit the door at a run. Good thing for everyone Luke had it unlocked.

He was waiting for us in the living room. Smith joined us a couple of minutes later, shaking his head.

"No sign of anything out back," he said.

"Luke, what do we know?" I asked.

"We know that rat bastard Augustus had kidnapped my Renfield and is using him for bait to lure me out. We know that I'm going to find him and do largely unpronounceable things to him that wouldn't be possible if he weren't an undead monster. We know that you're standing between me and the front door, thereby impeding my ability to kill Augustus and get my manservant back."

"We know that you have voicemail," Flynn cut in.

"What?" Luke whirled around. "I have voicemail?"

"That wasn't Luke asking if anyone left him a message," I translated. "That was Luke admitting he had no idea there was an answering machine."

"True enough," my somewhat technophobic undead monster uncle agreed.

Flynn pressed a button on the console beside the phone and a tinny voice informed us that we had one message.

"Hello, Count." Augustus' voice came through, a little scratchy for the recording, but there was no question who it was. "I have something of yours. I believe you'll want it back. Did you actually believe this simpleton could replace *me*? This human fool doesn't have the power to light a candle, much less destroy the Lord of the Undead. But that's what I'm going to do, Count. Or should I call you Vlad, now that you're landless?

Regardless, meet me at the bandshell behind SouthPark Mall at midnight. That will be a lovely place to settle our differences. Oh, and bring the Harker brat. I might have something for him, too." The recording clicked off and we all looked at each other.

"How does a European vampire from the nineteenth century even know there's a bandshell behind SouthPark? How does he even know there's a SouthPark?" I asked the room.

"It means nothing to Augustus, but the location is significant to my current Renfield. He was an oboe player in the symphony before I brought him into my employ," Luke said. "But that matters little at this point. All that matters is rescuing Renfield and destroying that psychopath Augustus once and for all."

"Hold your horses, Luke," I cautioned. "You know I'm usually the last one to argue for discretion as any part of valor, but I've got an idea."

"I know that look," Luke said. "Ever since you were a child, you got that look on your face whenever you were about to do something you thought was clever. It usually ended up with you crying and blood streaming down your face."

"That's kinda the plan here, too, Uncle, except I don't plan on doing the bleeding and crying this time," I said with a grin.

CHAPTER THIRTEEN

We pulled up to the rear of SouthPark Mall in two cars. Me and Luke in his Mercedes coupe, and Flynn and Smith coming in from the opposite direction in a black Suburban. We had little chance of fooling anyone who was paying even a little attention, but it was worth a try. Luke and I started the long walk across the grass down to the bandshell while Smith and Flynn walked in from the side.

The bandshell at SouthPark Mall was built when the Symphony and mall management got tired of building temporary staging for the Summer Pops series. So they got together and built a little stage with a curved roof out on a little island behind the mall. In the summer, yuppies and music lovers of all stripes bring lawn chairs and sip wine while listening to the Symphony. It's a nice little gig, and now every time I tried to pick up a chick at a concert, I'd think of Gus. One more thing for the asshole to answer for.

I saw the scrawny rat bastard from a hundred yards away, and judging by the low growl he let out, I knew Luke saw him too. He was standing near the front edge of the stage, right smack in the middle. A few feet away, he had Renfield tied to a chair, and even from a distance, I could tell the man had been beaten, and badly.

We stopped just on the mall side of the moat in front of the stage. Twenty feet of water separated us from our prey, but he either thought it was too far for me to jump, or counted on his ability to kill Renfield before Luke could run the bridges at the side of the stage.

"So glad you could join us, gentlemen," Gus said when we came to a halt.

"Augustus, I command you to release my manservant at once!" Luke commanded, and suddenly I saw the vampire that kept an entire countryside cowed before his power. Every inch of cultured businessman was gone, and left standing beside me was a man who expected his every whim to be obeyed, and woe betide the fool who crossed him.

Gus laughed. He actually had to step away from the edge of the stage to keep his balance, he was laughing so hard. "You impotent old fool," he sneered. "You actually think you can still command me? I, who have not only grown greater than I ever was as a human, but I have evolved into the pinnacle of the Nosferatu!"

"Vampires who refer to our kinds as Nosferatu are invariably assholes," Luke muttered to me. I turned to him in shock. "What?" he asked. "You don't expect me to *listen* to this douchebag, do you?"

"No, but I didn't expect you to know the proper use of the term douchebag, either." I drew my Glock from a shoulder holster and shot Gus in the throat. The report echoed across the expansive lawn, and blood spattered all over the stage. Gus dropped but sprang to his feet almost immediately.

Bad news for him was that twenty feet was less than my standing broad jump, and that Luke was faster than he expected, so when he hopped back to his feet, we were standing directly in front of him. He made a few gasping noises, spraying bloody mist across the stage.

"What?" I asked. "I'm sorry, Gus, I can't hear you." I broke up laughing at my own joke, which just served to further enrage the pissed off and newly perforated vampire before me. I holstered my largely useless pistol and got ready for a fight. Luke slid over to the side to position himself between Gus and Renfield, then when Gus charged me, Luke set to work untying Renfield. Everything was going according to plan.

The only problem was that the plan consisted of me going toe to toe with a powerful vampire for long enough to get Ren to safety, preferably without getting dead. Gus dove at me first, so I caught him by his lapels and rolled backward, placing two feet into his gut and flinging him over my head into the moat.

He leapt back onto the stage with a little splash, and I hopped to my feet to meet him. He sprang at me again, not giving me enough time to get a spell ready, so I sidestepped his charge and punched him in the back of the head as he went by. He sprawled on the stage but was back up in an instant. This time he was more cautious, stalking me, feinting a jab here and there. He was consciously ignoring Luke and Ren, which set off alarm bells to me. Then I heard a rustle from above, and it clicked into place. I put everything I had into one massive punch, which took him right on the cheekbone. Gus's head snapped to the side, his whole body spun with it, and he dropped once again to the deck.

"Luke!" I shouted. "Look up!" He paused in walking Renfield across the bridge to the lawn and looked up. The entire roof structure was covered with vampires, staring down at us, just waiting for the right moment to strike.

Apparently, when I noticed them was the right moment because a good three dozen vampires dropped to the stage around me. The nearest half dozen or so vampires to me got a rude awakening when they landed because decking Gus gave me just enough time to focus my will on the Zippo lighter I carried, shout "FRAGOR!" at the top of my lungs, and jump straight up into the rafters the vampires just fell from.

A fireball ten feet in diameter erupted from the Zippo, engulfing the nearest vampires and turning several of the older ones to dust instantly. The fresher vampires, the ones turned more recently, burned more like humans, except they turned completely to ash when they died. I dropped from the ceiling onto the back of another vamp, snapping its neck like a rotten branch.

That only left thirty vampires plus Gus to go. I glanced over to where Luke almost had Ren over the bridge to the relative safety of the lawn, then turned my attention back to the horde of angry and slightly singed vampires surrounding me. I drew my Glock and put rounds in the chests of the four nearest vampires on my right side, and they dropped like stones. A silver-tipped bullet in the throat won't do much more to Gus than piss him off for a while, with an added side of shutting him the hell up. But to a new vampire, a silver bullet through the heart turns them to real dead real fast.

Four bullets wasn't doing much to get me out of harm's way, so I breathed a sigh of relief when rifle shots rang out from the left side of the stage.

We're in position, Flynn's voice came across the mental link we shared, and for a second I had the weird double vision where I saw through my eyes and hers as well, but I shook my head and dialed it back a little. Flynn and I usually keep enough of a conduit open to each other that we know when one of us, usually me, is in trouble, but sometimes you just don't want to see life through the other person's eyes. On the other hand, I learned the hard way that my nicknaming her EMT boyfriend Black Superman was pretty damned accurate.

Flynn and Smith were set up in mini-sniper perches on the lawn behind a little grassy knoll with Remington 700 rifles just casually blowing the heads off vampires. Stoker never mentioned that a high-powered rifle round is better than a stake, but I guess he also never fired a really powerful, accurate weapon before. Some of the vampires turned to run up the hill at Flynn and

Smith, but they barely made it onto grass before they were taken out with headshots.

I emptied my Glock and pitched it onto the grass behind me, flung one more fireball that took out four vamps, then went hand to hand with the last few vampires until the platform was littered with bodies. I stood in the center of the stage, panting, with blood dripping from my hands, staring upstage at Gus. His throat had healed, but I knew what repairing that damage took out of him. He stepped down toward me, then looked me up and down from ten feet away.

"There's more to you than I expected, Quincy Harker," Gus said with a sneer.

"That's what your mom said when I left her this morning," I replied. I don't care if I live to be a thousand, which is unlikely given my mouth, but I will never get tired of "your mom" jokes.

Gus looked perplexed for a moment, then his eyes narrowed and he bared his fangs in a terrifying grimace. Terrifying, I'm sure, if you don't get to see Dracula in his old man boxers far more often than anyone would like. After that, I'm hard to scare.

Just before he charged me, Gus's eyes went wide and a crimson stain bloomed on his shirt. A slender piece of wood ripped through the front of his clothes, and Gus dropped to his knees, revealing a smiling Gabriella Van Helsing standing behind him with a second stake in her left hand to match the one buried in Gus's back. I stepped forward, then looked at Gus again, wondering why he wasn't toppling over like a good dead vampire.

That's when I got a better look at the angle of the stake, and my blood froze. "Move!" I shouted to Gabby, but she just looked at me. "You missed the heart! He's playing possum!" I yelled, and Gabby went white.

Gus hopped to feet, reached behind his back, and wiggled the stake free. "Ouch," he said. "That got stuck on some ribs. For that, I'm going to make this hurt. A lot." He flung the stake at Gabby, who knocked it out of the air, but left herself open to Gus's first punch, which would have been Gabby's last if it had landed. I poured on the speed and caught the vampire's arm before he could crush Gabby's face, then found myself far closer to Gus than I really wanted to be.

He had my throat in one hand, then his left hand flashed out, moving faster than anything I'd ever seen before, and he pulled Gabby in close to both of us.

"There are some three-person scenarios I've considered with Miss Van Helsing," I admitted, "but sorry to say, Gus old boy, you weren't in any of them."

"It's long past time someone silenced your insolent tongue once and for all," Gus hissed, spit and a little bit of blood from his nearly-healed throat splattering across my face.

"While I often agree with that sentiment, Augustus, the time for that is not now, and the place for that is not yours." Uncle Luke's cultured voice rolled across the bandshell and everything stopped. Gus and his minions froze, Flynn and Smith stopped shooting things, and even the urgent alert from my bladder stepped it down a notch.

Luke continued, stepping to the center of the stage. "Release my nephew, Augustus. Release my nephew and let us settle this like we should have many decades ago, like men."

"We are not men any longer, Vlad! That's what you've never accepted! We're not men and never will be again. And while you long for more time as a human, I revel in my greatness! I accept my superiority and thrive in it, like you never have! And when I destroy you, I shall rule over all the world!"

"You shall die, Augustus," Luke said, and I could hear the disappointment in his voice. "You shall die, and I shall be the one to do it."

And then, it was *on.*

CHAPTER FOURTEEN

The last time I saw my uncle really throw down was in Tibet in the 1920s. We were wandering the Himalayas looking for enlightenment or some such crap, when we came across a band of particularly territorial yeti. Their clan leader challenged Luke to single combat, one of those "win and I won't rip your arms off" kind of challenges. It was very ceremonial, and when Luke drew first blood, we were welcomed among the clan with drinks and roast moose.

This was nothing like that. This was like a ballet set to Rob Zombie where all the dancers are psychotic mass murderers tweaking on crystal meth. It was easily the most terrifying thing I've ever seen, and I've summoned Japanese sex demons for kicks. Luke and Gus flew at each other, and I mean that literally. They each took about two steps, launched themselves into the air, and crashed together a good twelve feet in the air. They spun around and around in midair, grappling for an advantage and tearing into each other's biceps with their nails. Neither one would release their grip, so they spun around a couple of times, then crashed to the stage and rolled over and over, each man trying to gain purchase on the other.

After a few seconds of struggle, Gus pushed off backward to get some space. His black shirt hung in rags from his arms, and blood streamed from a dozen little cuts on his upper arms. He ripped the rest of his shirt off and threw it behind him, and I saw more ribbons of blood running from little cuts all over his torso.

Luke was in about the same shape, and he shrugged out of his suit jacket and tore his white dress shirt away from his body, reveling dozens of little holes in his arms where the other vampire's claws had scrabbled for purchase. Luke shot Gus a nasty grin and leapt for him, covering the twenty feet that separated the two vampires in a single leap. Gus braced for impact, and caught Luke with a solid punch to the chest. A *crack* echoed across the stage as Luke's impact broke ribs, and he grimaced in pain.

Luke hung in there, though, with the increased pain tolerance that comes from living through the Industrial Revolution. And being a vampire. He wrapped his hands around Gus's neck and started to squeeze, the muscles of his arms standing out in ropes. Gus hammered on my uncle's arms, but Luke was too strong. I knew there wasn't much to be gained from choking Gus, but crushing his throat looked like a good start. Gus got his hands in between Luke's arms and broke the hold, but Luke ripped a chunk of newly regrown throat out when he let go.

Gus kicked Luke off him and clambered to his feet. Luke did some wild vampire ninja flip thing and landed on his feet, then spun around to kick Gus in the jaw. Gus responded with several quick punches to Luke's face, then landed a huge roundhouse on Luke's jaw. Luke spun around, and Gus hit him several more times, staggering Luke. Luke ducked the next punch and lashed out with a kick to Gus's knee, toppling the other vampire. Luke stood, then stalked over to where Gus lay writhing on the floor, holding his leg.

He reached down, pulling Gus to his feet by his hair, then drew back his hand for a killing strike. His hand was different, transformed into something I'd never seen on Luke. It was more claw than hand, with elongated fingers and nails that curved into claws. His hand flashed down, but Luke wasn't as hurt as he seemed, because he got his own claws up to block, and broke free of Luke's grasp. Gus took a step back, measuring Luke, and I got my first good look at them both in their *Nosferatu* form.

When vampires are injured, or starving, or hurt badly, all vestiges of humanity fall away and their monstrous nature is revealed. Luke's face became very bat-like, his fangs were extended, and his hands were crooked into claws. Gus looked more cat-like, but similar, with arms elongated and his fangs very pronounced, Gus sprang at Luke, but instead of trying any funny moves this time, Luke just stood tall and snatched the oncoming vampire out of the air, then slammed him onto the stage floor.

He slammed Gus into the floor, then picked him up and smashed him into the floor again. He repeated the process a third time, and this time when he picked Gus up, the other vampire hung limp in his grasp. He bashed him face-first into the wooden stage a fourth time, then he lifted Gus over his head, brought the thrashed vampire down across one knee, and snapped his spine like a rotten twig. The *crack* sounded across the bandshell, and Luke let the body fall to the floor. He stood over his old adversary, then with a long sigh, he reached down and ripped Gus's head from his shoulders.

Luke stood, holding Gus's head by the hair, and stretched his arm high over his head. "Does any other dare challenge the Dracula?" he shouted, and his voice rang through the night. All Gus's minions looked from one to the other, and I knew in my heart of hearts that it was over, that we were done with Gus, that Luke could switch back into this über-civilized form, and we could all go home.

Gus's minions weren't that smart. They rushed Luke. Eight young and brutally stupid vampires against one old vamp who had just been through the fight of his life. They probably thought it would be a cakewalk, that they'd knock off a legend and be the hot new stuff on the bloodsucker scene. They didn't have a fucking chance.

Luke ripped the first one's arm off and literally knocked him out with it. No shit, he caught the punch the vamp was throwing, put one hand on the creature's shoulder, and gave a hard yank. He pulled the vampire's right arm off, gripped the wrist like Babe Ruth, and hit the stupid bloodsucker across the face with his own arm. The vampire toppled back and laid flat on the stage, his unseeing eyes staring up at the lighting rig. Two more descended on Luke immediately after, and they fared no better. A single hard punch from Luke pulverized the heart of the first vampire, and the next fledgling died when Luke knocked him down and smashed his skull flat with one stomp.

Two of the five remaining vampires chose discretion as the better part of valor, but Smith put a .308 round in each of their heads from fifty yards. That wouldn't kill them, but it would keep them down long enough to decapitate.

One turned to me and smiled, obviously thinking that a human would be a better option. I smiled back at him, put a hand on his chest, and whispered, "*Fuego.*" He looked puzzled for a moment until his clothes burst into flames. He almost made it to the moat before he was completely consumed. The last two vampires went at Luke together, and it went about like everyone, including the two idiots, expected. Luke twisted one of them around until he could look at his own ass and punched the other guy so hard in the chest his heart exploded out the back of his ribcage.

I looked around the bandshell, silent except for the sound of blood dripping from the rafters and a few cicadas chirping in the distance. "Well, I'm glad that's over. It is over, right, Luke?"

I turned to see Luke and Van Helsing standing toe to toe. Gabby had a pistol in her right hand and a silver stake in the other. Luke had nothing in his clawed hands except blood and bits of dead monster. Gabby gave up half a foot in size and wasn't fueled by magical mystery fighting mojo, but she also hadn't had the shit beat out of her by a super-vamp in the last five minutes, so the scrap was looking pretty even.

"This is not how my night ends, people," I said, walking to the two of them. I stopped a couple of feet away, then glared at Luke.

"Uncle, it's time to look human again. You're making the company nervous."

"The company wants to kill me, Quincy." The fangs made everything Luke said extra-sibilant and menacing. There were times that was a good thing. This wasn't one of them.

"A lot of people want to kill me, Luke. Hell, half the time my own partner wants to kill me! You can't hold that shit against people, or you'll just spend all your time worrying about who wants to kill you today."

I don't want to kill you nearly as much anymore, Flynn's voice came from inside my head.

But admit it, you spent years wishing I'd just drop dead.

Oh yeah, like the first several years I knew you,

"Don't worry, vampire, after tonight we won't have anything to worry about because you'll be dead, and I will have finally honored my great-grandfather's legacy."

At Gabby's words, something snapped in Luke's eyes, and for once in my life, it snapped in a good way. In the matter of thirty seconds, his hands returned to normal, his face returned to normal, and his fangs withdrew, cleaning up his speech a lot. It's hard to speak clearly with spikes hanging out of your mouth.

"You really are Abraham's granddaughter?" Luke looked at Gabby, really *looked* at her for the first time. He reached out with one hand and touched her face. Gabby froze, her eyes wide as the leading figure in her childhood nightmares stroked her cheek with the back of his knuckles.

"Great-granddaughter," she whispered.

"No matter," Luke said. "I see it. I see it in your eyes. The fire, he had that same fire you have. Whenever Abraham saw something he wanted, he got that fire in his eyes. He looked at me the same way you look at me now. Not like something to fight, like something to overcome. I am not your challenge, young Van Helsing. You are your own challenge. You must win your own battle before you can ever hope to vanquish me."

Gabby's hands twitched, her finger tightened on the trigger, then relaxed. Tightened, then relaxed. I gathered my will, readied a spell that would throw up a barrier between the two of them, then let out a breath I didn't know I was holding when Gabby stepped back and holstered her pistol.

She turned to me and tossed me the silver stake. "I think this is yours, Harker."

I caught it on the fly and stuck it through my belt. "Thanks. We all gonna be cool now?"

"Once your uncle tells me why he let my great-grandfather go to his deathbed thinking he'd won."

"Because he had won, young Van Helsing. He had cost me my latest minion, my latest two brides, and my home. The only thing he hadn't managed to do was kill me."

My blood ran a little cold at Luke's admissions. He was talking about my parents as his bride and minion, which freaked me out more than a little.

Luke kept talking, and I kept shutting up. Gabby was getting more ancient history out of Luke in minutes than I'd gotten in a century and change.

"I became a different man after my encounter with Abraham and Quincy's parents. They showed me that I could no longer behave as a feudal lord, as I had for centuries. From watching them and learning from them, I realized that the world was changing quickly, and I would no longer be able to stand apart from it as an overlord, but must drift outside the world, in its shadowy places. I believe your grandfather was unwittingly responsible for my survival all these years. For if it were not for him pointing me in the direction that the world was moving, the twentieth century certainly would have destroyed me."

Gabby laughed, a short ironic bark. "So by trying to destroy you, he helped save the thing he most hated."

"I don't believe he hated me, not at the end. I believe he wanted to study me and wanted to render me harmless, neither of which I would ever allow," Luke said with a slight smile. "But I believe we achieved some level of mutual respect. At least I did."

I remembered that night in the old man's cold bedroom. I remembered the tears of Gabby's grandfather, the stony expressionless mask on my father's face, and most of all I remembered the tiny upturn of his lips as Abraham waved to the window and the old adversary standing out in the snow, always on the outside looking in. I remembered that night and felt a kinship with my uncle that I'd never felt even in all our travels and battles together. We were both destined to stand outside the window, looking in on a warm and normal life we could never truly know.

Luke turned to me almost like he felt me staring at him and nodded to me. I nodded back, then let the moment pass like a shadow in the night. I turned to Smith. "This would be a really good time to tell me you have a cleanup crew on retainer. Or at least a budget for this." I waved my hand at the entrails and puddles of blood and body parts strewn all over the bandshell.

"Yeah, lemme make a couple calls. I'll get the cleaners out here and get the movie shoot excuse planted with the security guards." He pulled out his cell phone and pushed a few buttons.

Flynn walked up to me and leaned on me, her arm on my shoulder. "Not a bad night, Harker. We got the bad guys and didn't lose any of the good guys."

"True enough, but where's Renfield? That was kind of the point of all this in the first place, wasn't it?"

"He's in the Suburban, out like a light. Augustus had him drugged to the gills, so your uncle stashed him in the car while we took out the vamps. What's so funny?"

I chuckled again. "Sorry, it's just ironic that after all this time tending to all of us, this whole mess was about us taking care of Renfield, and then he ends up sleeping through it all in the car."

So, of course, that's the moment the dapper little manservant decides to reappear. "I assume by the fact that you're upright that we won?" Renfield set a small red cooler down on the edge of the stage and passed me a beer.

"How in the world did you find a cooler full of beer?" I asked, twisting the top off and knocking down half the beer in one long pull.

"I put it in the back of the Suburban," Smith said. "I figured if we lived through this shit, we'd need one." He reached down and passed a longneck to Flynn, then popped the top on a bottle of his own. The four of us sat on the edge of the stage looking out over the lawn while Luke and Gabby talked about her great-grandfather.

"You're right, Flynn," Smith said. "This was a pretty good night."

"Yeah," I agreed. "We beat the big bad, and Gabby learned that not everything with fangs is a monster."

"Too often the monsters are the ones in suits, not a fang or claw in sight," Flynn said.

"That's what the police are for," Flynn said. "They take care of the things that walk in the daylight."

I raised my bottle to the others sitting with me. "And we handle the things that go bump in the night."

PART IV
HELL FREEZES OVER

CHAPTER ONE

I smelled the blood from the front steps. For a murder that happened upstairs in the master bedroom at the back of the house, that's pretty bad. The smell of blood is visceral for me, probably because it's at the core of everything I am. From my dad's dalliances with Uncle Luke's "wives" back in Transylvania, to Luke drinking from both my parents and meddling around in my DNA, to everything I deal with on the job, blood is kinda my gig. But not like this. Not the cloying, nose-clogging, overwhelming stench of it that boiled out of the Standish house like fog rolling in off the ocean.

The coppery-hot scent of it crept into every nook and cranny and wrapped itself around me like a moist blanket, promising to flavor every meal I touched for the next three days. I hadn't smelled blood like that since the Somme, when the mud ran red for two years after over a million men lost their lives in 1916. Luke and I spent most of that year running all over the front rallying British and French troops and pushing back vampires and werewolves recruited by the Germans to attack in the night and demoralize the Brits. The Kaiser's boys had never encountered sheer British pigheadedness on that scale before. They died by the thousands, but nothing the Germans threw at them, military or magical, could make those stiff upper lips waver.

But the smell of blood pouring from the Standish house in waves took me back to France, and I could almost hear the screams of young men dying in the distance again. I snapped back to the present when I caught a young uniform staring at me. I walked up to him, flashed my Homeland Security badge, and said, "Where's Detective Flynn?"

He stiffened at the sight of my fed creds. "Upstairs, sir. I think she's still in the bedroom." I took a step for the door, then moved aside as a forty-something sergeant came hustling down the steps, turned left away from the cops gathered in the driveway, and threw up in the bushes. The cop on door duty took a small notebook out of his pocket, opened it, and made a tick mark on a sheet of paper.

"Running the pool?" I asked.

"Yeah," he said. "Sarge over there makes five."

"Mostly rooks?" I asked. Rookie cops were famous for puking at messy crime scenes.

"Not really," the officer, whose nameplate identified him as Vasquez, replied. "Two rooks, but everybody else has had some years on them. We even got one of the techs."

"Shit," I said. "Now I really don't want to go in there." I wasn't lying, either. The chances that this was something right in my wheelhouse were pretty high, and if it made veteran cops lose their cookies, it was going to be a bad night. Oh well, when you're the demon-hunting part-vampire magic-wielding nephew of Dracula, there aren't really that many uneventful evenings at home in front of the TV.

I squared my shoulders and went inside, keeping my Sight locked down tight while I observed the room with my mundane eyes. Small foyer, large family room off to the right dominated by a massive TV over a fireplace with a game system and controllers on a shelf. To the left was what looked like a formal dining room, with a table for six set with holiday dishes. There was a light layer of dust on everything there, so I figured it wasn't used much. I saw a door through the dining room open into a bright kitchen with nice tile floors.

I didn't pay too much attention to the downstairs, just enough to notice that there wasn't a drop of blood anywhere. If the scene had been as messy as everybody was saying, how had the killer gotten out without leaving a drop down here? I climbed the stairs to the second floor, regretting leaving my jar of Vicks VapoRub in the glove box.

I took a pair of booties from a box at the top of the stairs and slipped them on over my shoes. *You'll want to double-bag unless you're tired of those shoes,* came a voice in my head.

Thanks, I thought back, reaching for a second pair of shoe covers. Most of the time the voices in my head are either bad memories or delusions, but ever since I saved Detective Rebecca Gail Flynn from bleeding out by sharing blood with her, we were linked more closely than any two people ever should be. Unless we were both very careful about shielding, we were in each other's head all day, every day, which made for some truly awkward moments.

The stairs ended in a hallway that led left to a small bathroom and linen closet, then right to three bedrooms. Two of the bedroom doors were closed, with kids' names on the doors in bright wooden cutout letters. The door to the master bedroom stood open, with a uniform standing in the hall just outside.

"Flynn inside?" I asked, holding up my creds.

"Yes, sir, but I can't let you in there." He moved to block my path, and I managed to keep myself from laughing. Not only could I break every bone he ever cared about, but I could magically heal him, then kick his ass some more. But he was taking his doorman duties seriously, so I gave him a little credit there.

"You see that badge says Homeland Security, right? You know Flynn is on the same task force with me, right?"

"I do know that, sir, but this is our crime scene, and until somebody tells me different, nobody gets in without a CMPD badge or clearance from somebody over my head."

Somehow I still managed to keep from laughing. *Flynn, get out here*, I sent through the mental link we shared. *Your puppy is showing his teeth.*

"Let him through, Birk," Flynn's voice came from around the corner. "He's almost harmless, so he can come in."

"Good job, Junior," I said as I passed the uniform. "Now she's pissed at both of us."

Leave him alone, Harker. Flynn's voice rang in my head as I stepped across the threshold.

"I didn't start it," I protested as I stepped into the room. I froze as I caught sight of the scene. I took an involuntary step back and this time heard the *squish* of soaked carpet beneath my feet. I looked down, and my blue-bootied shoes were islands in a sea of crimson, two of the few things in the room that didn't look like they'd been painted with reddish-brown drying blood.

The mother and two children were in the bed, on top of the blankets, lying peacefully as if sleeping, or posed. She was a trim woman who looked like she did Pilates three times a week without ever breaking a sweat. Her blonde hair was pulled off to one side with care, like her husband didn't want it to get bloody when he murdered her. The irony of it was almost enough to make me scream.

Lying on either side of her were her kids, maybe eight and ten, maybe younger. I've gotten worse at guessing ages since nutrition had gotten so much better. All kids look like giants to me now. These two were as different as night and day—the boy dark with curly brown hair spilling over his face, and the girl slight and blonde, looking almost ethereal lying there.

Their eyes were closed, thank God, but their slit throats made a huge grin across their necks like some demented comic book villain. All three of them had their necks slashed from ear to ear, then long slashes up the inside of each arm and slices across the wrists, just to be thorough. Looking at the blood-stains on the woman's nightgown and the kids' pajamas, I guessed that the femoral arteries would be opened up as well.

I wish you were wrong, came Flynn's voice in my head. *But the doc confirms it—the major arteries in the neck and the veins in the arms were opened. They bled out in a minute. Two tops.*

The walls were a study in arterial spray-painting, with arcs of blood droplets reaching to within a few feet of the ceiling. The mattress was soaked, with blood dripping from the comforter onto the floor and pooling all over.

Sitting in one corner beside the bed, a butcher knife in his hand and a puddle of blood spreading out from his ass, was the man of the house, Darin Standish. Fortyish, Latino, trim, dressed in silk pajama bottoms and nothing else but blood. To put the icing on the cake, in his left hand, almost impossible to see clutched in his fist, was a rosary. *He was praying before he did this.* That thought ran through my head, and I almost lost my own lunch. If I'd eaten anything in the past six hours, it would have been gone that second. As it was, I had to take a few deep breaths through my mouth to keep my gorge down. I got myself together, gave myself a mental shake, and got back to the body.

From the position of the body, I was guessing that he killed his family, then sat down and cut the arteries in his own legs, slashed open one wrist, and made it halfway through his own neck before succumbing to blood loss. I was staring at a seriously dedicated suicide. I reached out to the body, stretching my senses just to edge of the mundane world, but sensed nothing malevolent in the room.

"You getting anything?" Flynn asked in a low voice. Our link was more secure, but she didn't like the idea of letting me inside her head on a regular basis. I didn't blame her; I wouldn't trust me with my deepest and darkest secrets, either.

"Nothing except nauseated," I replied. "This is as bad as anything I've ever seen, and I've been around the block once or twice."

"Yeah, it's awful. Look at that little girl, such an angel..." She was right, of course. The little girl was the place everyone immediately looked in a tragedy. And this one was more cherubic than normal, with apple cheeks even in death, a halo of blonde hair spread out on the pillow beneath her, and a tiny gold cross around her neck.

I mentally wrote off my pants as a total loss and dropped to one knee in front of the father, opening my Sight. The "real" world swam out of focus, becoming less immediate as my senses shifted into the magical spectrum. Nothing changed in the magical spectrum—no demonic taint, no dark magic sigils carved on the dad's aura, nothing to explain why this apparently happy man would murder his family in the most brutal way imaginable.

I stood up, turning my attention to the daughter. Sometimes nasty things from other dimensions can break free using a child's belief in monsters as the anchor point. But not here. It was like this child had never known fear a day in her life. The girl looked exactly the same through my Sight, just as innocent and beautiful, with her cross glowing in my Sight like a beacon, a ray of light in a murky Otherworld. I looked all around the room with my magical senses, then dropped my Sight and turned to Flynn.

"There's no magic here," I said, turning for the door. I squelched my way to the stairway and was about head down when Flynn caught me.

"What are you doing? Where are you going?" she hissed at me.

"Well, I was going to eat ice cream and binge-watch *Justified* on TV, but if you've got a better idea, I'm not married to that one."

"There is a dead family up there, and we don't have any idea who or what killed them. You can't just *leave.*"

"Oh, I can. I promise I can. You're welcome to watch me just leave. Look, Detective, I'm the supernatural guy. I'm the one that believes in all the weird shit. You're Scully. You're the one that thinks the world is a normal place that operates under normal laws. So you should be ecstatic when I tell you this was a normal murder/suicide. So now, dear skeptic, I take my leave." I made my most florid bow, which was pretty good given the amount of time I spent in Europe, and once again tried for the door.

"Stop."

I stopped and turned back to Flynn. "I need your help. Even if this isn't anything more than a human nutball, it's as deranged a rat bastard as I've ever encountered. And that puts it right in your wheelhouse."

"I wish that were a little less true, but go on."

"So there's absolutely no evidence of magic here?"

"Let me look again," I said, and opened my Sight again. Using my Second Sight is like laying a filter over the world in front of me. Everything goes a little fuzzy, and I can see bright spots of color where magic was used, or where supernatural creatures touched this plane of existence.

The Standish's bedroom looked as mundane as any house I'd ever been in.

There were the normal minor cold spots where ghosts passed through from time to time, but that could just have been grandparents looking in from the Other Side on the kids, or a curious spirit here and there. The little girl's cross glowed with a white halo of purity, like it was recently blessed, and the rosary in the father's hand radiated the same kind of minor blessing. But there was no hint of dark magic or demonic presence anywhere. I let my Sight drop and the room returned to ugly reality.

"Sorry, Flynn, there's nothing. It looks like they went to church recently, but that's all I've got. There was absolutely nothing supernatural about this murder. I know that's hard to take, but most of the nastiest things humanity has ever done have been like that—completely without supernatural help."

"I know. People are the nastiest creatures in the world."

"In a couple of worlds, Detective."

CHAPTER TWO

I left a very disappointed Detective Flynn at the house going over details with the crime scene techs and working on recreating the events of the previous night. I had less than no interest in reliving someone's murder, so I went home. Even with the sun high in the sky, I was exhausted. Flynn's call had come in around eight in the morning, and I'd been fleecing an all-night poker game until after seven, so once I finally got home, I was asleep almost before my head hit the pillow. That's when I got my first hint that this case wasn't as mundane as it seemed.

I came awake seconds after I fell asleep. At least it felt that way. It was dark as the devil's own asshole in my room, which was odd since I distinctly remembered it being almost noon by the time I got showered and into bed. I looked around for a clock, but couldn't see one, then pawed the nightstand for my cell phone, with equal lack of success. With my eyes useless, I focused on listening to the room, but I heard no sounds of life, not even my air conditioner or the fan on my computer. Complete silence is so rare in today's world that I noticed it more acutely than I had in previous decades. But this silence was pervasive, like a blanket covering everything around me.

Finally, out of the edge of my peripheral vision, I caught a glimpse of some kind of low light, a glimmer or shine off in the distance. Distance? I was in my bedroom, which is barely fifteen by twenty. A decent room, certainly, but there was nothing in my whole condo that could be measured in anything resembling "distance."

Fuck, another dream.

I don't dream. At least, on a good night I don't remember them. On a bad night, I wake up right in the middle of them, thrashing about in my bed, sheets a sweat-sodden rope twisted around my middle tight enough to cut off blood flow to my feet, a scream caught in my throat, fighting with everything I've eaten for the past twenty-four hours to get up and out past my teeth. If I'm lucky I manage to get control of myself before I puke or piss myself. If I'm unlucky, it's another 3AM run to the all-night laundromat reeking like a homeless man on a two-week bender. They know me there.

I've seen some shit. I suppose it's impossible to get a century under your belt without seeing some shit, but my family tree, particular "gifts," and undeniable talent for sticking my nose in where it doesn't belong have put me in situations to see more shit than a sewer rat. And when I sleep is when all the barriers between the nasties in my mind and my memories crumble, and the worst things I've seen across over a hundred years and six continents come out to play.

Antarctica. It's what you were wondering. There's nothing fucking scary in Antarctica because there aren't enough people there. The whole fucking continent has about five thousand people on it in the summer, such as it is, and less than two in the winter. And they all chose to be there, and they all have enough shit to do just to stay alive and do their jobs to not fuck around with anything supernatural. Not enough time on their hands to get really stupid.

The other six continents? Full of assholes. Assholes who fuck with things that should be left alone and call up shit that people like me have to put down. And make me do shit that I have to live with forever, especially when I'm alone in the middle of the night without any whiskey to dull the screams that echo through the dark hallways of my soul.

I stood in the dark long enough for the glimmer of light in the distance to take shape, and I couldn't tell if I was moving toward it or it was moving toward me, in that weird *Pan's Labyrinth* way that things move in dreams without actually moving, but I realized the the light was the outline of a door, and I've known enough about lucid dreaming for long enough to know that I was meant to open it. So I did. I reached out my hand and opened the door.

And was immediately back in the middle of the Standish family's bedroom. The only difference was there was no blood and no dead people. It looked like the bedroom of a happily married middle class couple from Whitebread, USA. There were no signs of death or destruction, just a patterned white and mint green comforter that I had seen at Target a couple weeks ago and now was under no circumstances ever going to purchase, no matter how well Renfield said it matched my curtains.

I felt something warm in my hand, and I looked down to see the little Standish girl standing beside me, throat mercifully intact, looking up at me with blue eyes the size of saucers. She opened her mouth, but no words came out.

"What is it, honey?" I asked. She moved her lips, but again nothing.

I got down on one knee in front of her. "It's okay, sweetheart, nothing can hurt you here. Nothing can ever hurt you again," I said. I reached out a hand and stroked her hair. She opened her mouth, and blood poured out. Not arterial spray, but a waterfall of crimson down her face, painting the front of her nightgown and cascading to the floor. I skittered back, trying to stay out of the blood, but my hands squished in red-soaked carpet.

I scrambled to my feet, and the room looked like it did that morning when I'd first walked in. The eggshell walls were painted in some bastardized Jackson Pollack spatter, but only red. Red everywhere, all the way up to the ceiling and spattered across the blades of the white wicker ceiling fan centered over the bed. The little girl came toward me again, holding out both her hands, and now blood was flowing from her wrists down to her fingers, out of her eyes like tears turning her cheeks crimson, and blood streaked her legs from her cut arteries, puddling around her feet with every step.

I kept backing away, and she kept coming, an inexorable vision of death in red and angel-blonde hair. She stretched out her arms to me, silent supplication like a toddler begging to be held. I shook my head and backed away, away from the abattoir of the bedroom, away from the hemorrhaging little girl, away from the memories of blood coating every surface.

I felt something solid behind me and turned to see a giant door in dark oak, a wooden engraved surface stretching up high above my head, with a knob just barely within reach. I realized that somehow I was seeing this door through the little girl's eyes, and if I wanted to get through, I was going to have to get back to my normal size.

Let's be clear—I did not want to go through that door. As a matter of fact, if going back through the Industrial Revolution was one of the choices other than going through that door, I'd be lighting gaslights and heating my house with coal again in a matter of seconds. But I knew it wasn't an option. I had to go through the door before whatever piece of my subconscious dragged me into this shitshow would let me find the exit.

So I willed myself taller, and the door shrank to a more normal size. It was still a pretty massive door, all carved oak and antique brass hardware with crosses and fleur-de-lis carved and embossed into anything that stood still long enough. I gripped the knob and turned, and once again was transported. This time I was someplace cleaner, if no less uncomfortable for me. I was in a church. A huge sanctuary with dark stone floors, cushy benches for pews, and hundreds upon hundreds of people all kneeling.

I felt that warm little hand in mine again and looked down at the thankfully blood-free Standish girl gazing up at me in something akin to adoration. She beamed a smile up at me that made me forget at least a decade of the nastiest parts of humanity, and I couldn't help but smile back. That smile faded as I saw my shoes—nice loafers unlike anything I've worn since an unfortunate investigation into a Wall Street broker in 1983 who literally sold his soul to a demon for hot stock tips. Even back then I could have told him just buy Apple, but I've met the guardian angel that sat on Steve Jobs' shoulder, and that dude had some serious mystical horsepower behind him.

I walked down the main aisle of the sanctuary, kneeling and crossing myself in the middle before my diminutive guide led me down an aisle to sit next to a good-looking woman of almost forty. Thirty-eight, to be precise, because I'd read Annie Standish's brief bio in Flynn's head while I stood over her cooling body. That meant the khaki- and polo-clad body I currently inhabited must be Darin Standish, the late Mrs. Standish's apparently loving husband right up until the time he severed every major artery in her body and bled her like the first deer of the season, then sliced himself up like Christmas ham before bleeding out in the floor of his bedroom. A head of curly hair atop a shy smiling face leaned forward and waved excitedly at me—Clay Standish, excited to see his dad in a way only preteen boys can still be.

I turned to the front of the church and felt the world *shift* like it only ever does in dreams. Everything blurred, and suddenly we were all somewhere else. Or more correctly, we were nowhere. Or I was, because I was alone. The church and all the people—gone. The Standish family—gone. Even my little girl guide was gone. It was just me, standing in a foggy, featureless plain surrounded as far as the eye could see with nothing.

"Now what?" I asked, and found that I'd spoken aloud for the first time since the dream started.

A voice from above started to speak, and for a few seconds I just listened, trying to make out the words. I knew them, something about them resonated with me like something I'd heard all my life, just in a slightly different dialect or accent. Then the voice rose in volume, then rose again, then climbed to a scream, then a shrill shriek that bored into my brain like a dentist's drill and drove me to my knees. I clapped my hands to my ears and screamed in pain, but the din of the chanting was so loud I couldn't even hear myself scream. I rocked back and forth on my knees, screaming in time with the chanting, then collapsed sobbing into a ball, rolling on my side and shrieking.

Then something hit my face like a slap and I was awake, curled up in a fetal position in the floor of my bedroom, my sheets tangled about me so tightly they cut off circulation to my legs. I was soaking wet from sweat, but also freezing cold, like…

That's when I noticed Flynn lying sprawled on the floor on the opposite side of my bed, completely unconscious. I got up, fell to the floor again, my feet on pins and needles, disentangled myself from the sheets and crawled over to the unconscious detective.

"Flynn?" I asked, shaking her arm. Nothing. "Flynn!" I shook harder, probing her mind through our link. She was alive, but stunned almost to insensibility. Her eyes rolled back in her head and she started to shake uncontrollably. I didn't know what the hell was going on, but I knew shock was a real possibility, so I sat back against the bed, pulled her into my lap, and wrapped my arms around her. Her shivering continued unabated, so I reached behind me and pulled a blanket off my bed to cover us up. I used a corner of the blanket to wipe the sweat and water from my face, then I held Flynn tight to my chest, trying to let my warmth soak into her.

I focused my will and whispered *"Fiero,"* concentrating just on pulling up heat, not setting my entire bedroom on fire.

After what seemed like half an hour of sitting on the floor holding her to my chest, Flynn woke up.

Her eyes fluttered open, and I felt her consciousness twine into mine, like an old couple holding hands, comfortably connected. She looked up at me, gave me a warm smile, and said, barely audible, "This is nice, Harker, but you're not just wet, you're naked, too. And that means it's definitely not a roll of quarters poking me in the butt right now."

CHAPTER THREE

A few minutes later we were both sitting on the couch in my den after I'd thrown on a pair of sweats and a *Preacher* t-shirt. I poured a healthy slug of bourbon in both coffee cups, ignoring Flynn's protests.

"You're off duty, have a drink. You are off-duty, right? What time is it? Hell, what *day* is it?" I asked.

"It's about seven at night, and it's Monday. Or Monday night, anyway. You slept the whole day away."

"It happens," I replied. "While I'm not strictly nocturnal, like Uncle Luke, I usually do my best work at night." I thought about that for a second, then decided there wasn't anything going to save that statement, and just let it die. "What else did you find out at the Standish place?"

"Nothing," Flynn put her coffee cup down and leaned back on the sofa. "It appears to be exactly what you said it was—a perfectly mundane murder-suicide. Sad but ordinary."

"It's not," I said, remembering that little girl's face looking up at me.

"What do you mean?"

"Well, it wasn't monsters in the closet that had me screaming on my bedroom floor," I said.

"Yeah, I was gonna ask about that, but I was waiting for the right time. Like a month or so past never seemed like a good call."

"Ordinarily that would be perfect. With the shit I've seen in my life, the last place you want to go running around is the dark alleys of my mind. But this time we kinda have to pay attention to the signals I'm getting because this wasn't a dream. This was a visitation."

"A visitation?" Flynn asked. "From who?"

"The little Standish girl."

"Emily?"

"Yup, in the flesh. Well, more like in the ether, but you get the idea."

"Why would the ghost of a murdered little girl come to you in a dream, Harker?"

"Fuck if I know," I said honestly. "Maybe her ghost sensed something out of the ordinary about me at the crime scene and followed me home, despite my wards."

"Wards?" Flynn looked around the room at the door, ceiling, trying to see what I was talking about.

"You can't see them without the Sight," I explained. "And the really nasty ones you can't even see with talent. The first layer just tells nasty and uninvited things to leave, that they aren't welcome here. The next layer backs that up with a little spell of banishment that sends most things short of an archdemon or major seraphim back to wherever it came from. The next—"

Flynn held up a hand. "Wait a second, Speedy. You're telling me you warded your apartment against *angels*? Why? Aren't they the good guys?"

"Technically, yes. I mean, they still carry out the will of God and all that shit, but ever since the Great War, they've had free will, so when they're not doing what the big guy wants, they come up with ideas of their own. Most of those ideas are really stupid, like New Coke and Jar-Jar Binks, but every once in a while they decide to do something truly dangerous, like try surfing. That's where we get tsunamis. So I warded my place against the Host from both zip codes, north and south. If I can go through my life without speaking to another angel, I'll be thrilled."

"Present company excepted, I hope," came a voice from the door to my bedroom. I turned to see a vision of loveliness in a white v-neck t-shirt and white yoga pants standing there. Glory's hair was tied into a long, loose blonde braid that spilled down and around one shoulder. Her blue eyes looked worried, and her normally Revlon-commercial lips were drawn tight.

"Morning, Glory," I quipped. Not even a hint of a smile. I must be in bigger trouble than normal. "What's up?"

"I should ask you the same thing," Glory said.

"Harker?" Flynn said from beside me. I looked over and saw her standing by the couch, gun in hand and trained on the angel in my doorway. "Who is that, and how did she get in here?"

The stunned look on Glory's face was almost certainly mirrored by my own. "You can see her?" I asked.

"Of course I can, she's standing twenty feet away from me. By the way, sister, there's about a zero percent chance of me missing from this distance, so let's keep all hands where I can see them, okay?"

"Put the gun down, Rebecca," Glory said.

"Not a chance, cutie."

"I wasn't asking," Glory said, then something in her voice changed. "Put the gun down, *now.*" She put a little extra emphasis on the last word, the kind of emphasis that made her eyes flash blue lightning.

Flynn holstered her weapon, staring at her hands the whole time like they weren't under her control. Which they weren't, not completely. She looked at me for help, but I could only shrug.

"Rebecca Gail Flynn," I said, "meet Glory. She's my guardian angel. And I don't think she likes having guns pointed at her."

"It's rude," Glory said.

"So is popping into the middle of a conversation uninvited," Flynn shot back.

"Touché," Glory admitted. "Now that we're done fencing, may I sit?"

"I was hoping that this whole thing would degenerate into Jell-O wrestling, but if that's not going to happen, come on over." I waved Glory to a seat on the couch and I moved over to an armchair where I could keep an eye on both of them. "So what are you doing here, Glory?"

"I could ask you the same question, Q," the angel said.

"I live here."

"That's not what I meant and you know it. Why did you lock this little girl's soul to the Earth? What are you planning?"

"What are you talking about?" I asked. "I haven't done anything with anybody's soul, at least not lately."

Glory pointed to the corner of my living room, by the TV that usually just sat gathering dust unless the Panthers were playing and I happened to be awake in my condo. "I'm talking about the soul of a little girl sitting in the floor of your den playing with her dolls."

"What the actual fuck are you..." I opened my Sight and shut my mouth, deciding to see for myself what Glory was talking about. I immediately regretted it. Glory was telling the truth. I didn't know if she was even capable of lying, being an angel and all, but that was irrelevant in the face of the ghost playing dolls in my living room. Little Emily Standish looked just as angelic as she had in death, just as peaceful as she had in my dream, and just as goddamn creepy as you'd expect from a ghost in a bachelor pad.

"Glory, why is there an eight-year-old ghost in my den?" I asked.

"That's what I wanted to ask you, Q. And how can your little friend here see me? I'm supposed to be invisible to humans unless I decide otherwise."

"Flynn might not be exactly one hundred percent normal human anymore, remember?"

"Oh, shit, that's right. But she can see me? I didn't think the last one could."

"First, her name was Anna. Second, you weren't around nearly as much back then. Something about leaving me to live my own life, et cetera, et cetera, blah blah blah."

"That was before I had a century's worth of proof of exactly how dangerous you are to yourself and the rest of the universe when left alone for more than five minutes."

"I'm going to let that one go and say that I don't know if Anna could see you or not, because she never mentioned it. But apparently Flynn can see you, so maybe you two should shake hands, or go for coffee, or whatever. But can you please for the love of fuck do it after we figure out why I'm being haunted by a preteen murder victim?"

"Maybe she wants your help," Flynn said. Glory and I both turned to look at Flynn, who just shrugged. "It's kinda the logical answer, right? You wander into her murder scene, throwing magic around like some kind of scruffy superhero, and she notices you. You don't pick up on whatever she wants you to see, so she follows you home and shows you something in your dream that gives you a clue. Then you help me catch her killer, she goes to Heaven, and everybody's happy. Right?"

I looked at Glory, then back at Flynn. It made sense, in the perverse way things happen in my life. "Fine," I said. "Then we're going to need all your case files, photos, and everything you've got on the Standish family. If something from the dark side of the tracks killed these people, there's a good reason for it. I hope."

"You hope?" Flynn asked, going to a briefcase on my dining room table.

"Look, sometimes things are just nasty. There's no real reason for what they do, they're just assholes. The same holds true for monsters and people. There might not be a reason for what happened to the Standishes. Could be they just ran into a monster with too much time on its hands."

"That covered up every single trace of any evidence? Come on, Harker, you don't believe that any more than I do," Flynn demanded.

"That's just it, Becks," I protested. "I don't know what I believe. Nothing about this crap makes any sense, least of all why there was a little girl walking around in my head last night."

"Well, here's what we have on the family. Annie Standish, thirty-eight, civil engineer at McFarland & Greene. Steady employee, nothing out of the ordinary. She had three days of PTO left this year, had already scheduled them for Christmas week. Married thirteen years to college boyfriend Darin. Two children, Emily and Clay, ages eight and ten. Studied at NC State, got her Master's at Clemson, where she met Standish. They both graduated, got married immediately, and went to work. Married almost ten years before Clay comes along. Easy delivery, no complications, she goes back to work a month later. Couple years later along comes little Emily. Same story, textbook delivery. These people have a friggin' storybook life, Harker. They're so nice and easy that they're totally boring. There's no reason for anyone to target them."

"Okay," I mused. "The wife was a civil engineer. Not exactly a high-risk profession. Pretty unlikely she pissed off any supernatural agencies with a bridge design. What about hubby? What did he do?"

"He was a compliance manager for an investment bank," Flynn replied.

"I don't even know what that means," I said. Flynn looked at me, unbelieving. "Seriously, I have no idea what those words mean. Look at me, Becks, I was born when people still lit their houses with hurricane lamps, and most of my ridiculously long adult life has been spent either battling the forces of darkness all over the world, or studying arcane texts in dead languages. I'm an expert in a lot of shit, but modern banking is beyond me."

"He was the guy who made sure that the stock brokers weren't breaking any laws," Flynn explained. "He was almost a lawyer for the bank, making sure that no SEC rules were broken."

"So he wasn't boring enough to just be a banker or a lawyer, he was a half-banker, half-lawyer, all Yawnsville."

"Unless he caught somebody moving money illegally and shut them down?" Flynn theorized.

"The kind of people who launder money and murder people over it aren't often the same people who can mojo a husband into murdering his whole family. No, this wasn't a work thing. There's something supernatural here, or there wouldn't be a ghost playing tea party in my den. Did they go to church?"

"Our Lady of Holy Comfort, right here in town." I saw Glory start a little at the mention of the church.

"What is it, Glory?" I asked.

"I...I can't say, Q. Sorry, above my pay grade."

"What do you mean, you can't say? Is there something going on at that church? Do the angels know something?"

Glory stood up from the arm of the couch, where she'd perched through Flynn's recitation of the Standish family's boring life story. She paced my living room, shaking off sparkles of light with every step. Her wings rustled and she toyed with her braid just like a nervous human until I finally stood up and grabbed her by the shoulders.

"Glory, stop it." I gave her a shake, and she looked up into my eyes. If you've never locked gazes with an angel, I don't recommend it. There are things humans aren't meant to see, even humans with supernatural abilities. Maybe *especially* humans with a supernatural streak and really long lives. The purity of the soul staring back at me from Glory's eyes was like a mirror, reflecting every nasty thing I'd ever done, every impure thought, every vindictive moment and every commandment I'd shattered. I let go of her and turned away, dropping to one knee and trying valiantly to keep my dinner where it was supposed to be.

"You shouldn't do that, Q," Glory said from behind me.

"No shit, angel-face," I said when I was ninety percent certain I wasn't going to paint my carpet in day-old fast food. I coughed a little, wiped my mouth with the back of my hand, and got to my feet. "What's the deal with the church?" I asked.

"I really can't tell you. I would if I could, but I have orders I can't break," Glory said, looking miserable.

"Of course you can break them, G-money. You just open your mouth and tell me what I need to know."

"It doesn't work that way for us, Q. If we're given an order by one of the Host that outranks us, we can't disobey. Remember what separates humans from the Host? What caused the War in Heaven?"

"Free will," I whispered.

Glory nodded. "We've gotten a modicum of freedom in the last few millennia, but not much. I still couldn't tell you if I wanted to. Which I don't, because I don't want you to die."

CHAPTER FOUR

I f I've learned anything from the past century of wandering the Earth, and the jury is certainly out on that question, it's not to bother arguing with supernatural beings. Angels, demons, faeries, and all those other kinds of magical creatures just see the world differently, probably because they aren't of this world in the first place. So when Glory told me she couldn't clue me in as to what was going on at the kid's church, I decided to go ask the folks on the other team if they knew what was up.

"Where are you going?" Glory asked as I went to my closet and pulled out a long black leather coat. Cliché, I know, but when dealing with demons and black wizards, it's best not to be too subtle. Not that I've ever been accused of being subtle.

"You can't give me the information I need, so I have to go follow up with other sources," I said. "No harm, no foul on your part, darling, but I *have* to know what's up with this kid and why she's suddenly decided to go tiptoeing through the tulips of my nightmares. Because, let's be honest, the inside of *my* head is the last place a sweet little girl like that needs to be walking, no matter how dead she is."

"He's got a point," Flynn said. "I've been inside his head, and it's ugly in there. But what are these other sources you're talking about? Sounds like something I'm not going to approve of."

"Which falls directly under the category of things I give zero fucks about. Sorry, Flynn, but you don't get a vote in this one," I said, checking the pockets of my coat for all the usual accoutrements. Salt, check. Silver stakes, check.

Holy water, check. Flask of Macallan 18, check. Snub-nosed thirty-eight hammerless revolver, check.

"I don't think that's quite correct, pal," Flynn said, putting herself between me and the door. "You see, when you started hitchhiking in my head, we became partners. And this looks a lot like the kind of thing a partner needs to know about, unless she wants to suddenly find herself on her knees with a migraine in the middle of the police station, or grocery store, or wherever I happen to be when you start getting your ass kicked again. Which I do feel every bit of, by the way."

"Yeah, sorry about that," I said. "We should work on getting some better shielding set up. I've kinda developed a bit of a high tolerance to pain over the years. Knowing that you'll eventually get over it takes a lot of the sting out of even the most vicious beatings."

"Be that as it may, until we get that set up, let's work on you getting your ass kicked less, shall we? And the way we start working on that is by you *not* going stupid places without backup. So where are we going?"

I looked at her, then looked at Glory. My guardian angel was studiously being no help whatsoever, sitting on my sofa reading *The Way of Kings*. I didn't own the book, so I knew she brought it with her. That's angelic power, right there—strong enough to carry a Brandon Sanderson novel and still fly.

"I'm going to Mort's," I said. I squeezed my eyes shut and stood there, waiting for the explosion, but nothing came. I slowly opened one eye, then the other until I was looking at a very confused Rebecca Flynn.

"Mort's, the dive bar on Wilkinson?" she asked. So she did know it, but apparently she only knew the cover.

"Yeah, that's it," I confirmed. "Gotta go meet a guy about some informa-tion. I'll call you tonight. Or you call me if anybody else bites it."

"Hold it." Flynn pressed her back to the door. "Obviously Mort's is more than just a dive bar, so why don't you clue me in?"

"Mort is a demon who lives in the back room of the bar. He's a leech, feeding off the sadness and pain of the humans that come into his bar," Glory said with a snarl.

"His place is also a kind of informal safe haven and meeting ground for a lot of the things that go bump in the night around town. It's where people in the know go to sell a little extra piece of their soul for a few more years in the corner office, or a few extra points of profit on a business deal, or just to look better in a bikini for a few more years."

"So what are you going to do there? Won't most of the customers want to kill you on sight?" Flynn asked.

"Yeah, but Christy, Mort's manager, has a strict no murder policy, so I'll be fine."

"How does she enforce that if the clientele is as nasty as you say? With a demon in the basement and who knows what in the bar, I think one little bar manager might have more than she can handle," Flynn said. "I'm going with you."

"No, you're not," I said. "Don't worry about what Christy can or can't enforce. She's one of the most powerful witches I've ever met, so nobody messes with her."

"So you're going to a demon's bar run by a black witch to get information on a ghost? This doesn't sound crazy to you?" Flynn said.

"I'm over a hundred years old, super-strong, super-fast, know more spells than most D&D rulebooks, and Dracula is the first number on my speed dial. My definition of 'crazy' might be a little broader than most people. Besides, I never said Christy was a black witch."

"But she works for a demon."

"And my uncle is the most famous bloodsucking villain in literary history," I pointed out. "That doesn't mean much. I've never seen Christy do anything evil. To the contrary, most of what I've seen her use magic for has been protection of the innocent, or keeping the peace in general, both pretty white-magicky type things. Who knows? Maybe she just took the job there to keep an eye on Mort."

"You don't believe that," Flynn said.

"Nah, but there is a slim possibility. Look, you wanna come with me, fine. Just don't interfere unless I'm in real trouble, and don't eat or drink anything unless it comes from me or Christy. Even from a sealed bottle. A twist-off top will not keep out magic."

"Is there really anybody in there that's dumb enough to mess with your partner?" Flynn asked with a smirk.

I stopped and turned to her, working really hard not to grab her by the shoulders and give her a shake. "Rebecca, let me be real clear. I'm a badass as far as humans are concerned. Or mostly human, or whatever I am. But when it comes to the things that sit in the dark corners of places like Mort's bar looking for prey, I'm like a high school quarterback going up against Brett Favre. I'm not even in the same league as these things, so watch your step. Seriously. There are guys sitting at the bar eating peanuts and watching football that can turn your skin inside out without blinking an eye. And I don't have near enough mojo to throw down with them."

"So why are we going in there, if you know you might not be able to walk out?" The look in her eyes said she got the message, at least as much as anyone really can without seeing what a manifested demon can do.

"One, it's the only place in town where I can get the information I need. And two, they have excellent fried pickles. And you know how I love some fried pickles. But seriously, it's a Sanctuary. No one is allowed to raise a finger to another creature on the premises."

"And these monsters abide by that?" Her eyebrows were crawling up around the middle of her scalp at that.

"They need a safe place to drink and watch the game, too. Plus, remember the whole thing about being run by a demon and managed by the most powerful witch in three time zones? They keep a tight rein on the clientele."

"Then why are you so worried about me? If it's a Sanctuary, then nothing is going to hurt me while I'm there."

"Yeah, but unless you plan on staying there forever, which has been done, eventually you'll leave, and Sanctuary will no longer apply. So try not to draw attention to yourself. Any more than you will just by walking in."

"Not used to women?"

"Not used to delivery. You walking through the door is the demonic equivalent of Domino's knocking on the front door of a frat house."

"Oh," she said, and her voice was small and decidedly less enthusiastic. I hated to scare her because usually that's not conducive to shooting the bad things, but in this case, I wanted her afraid. Because if she was afraid, she wouldn't unwittingly violate any of the hundreds of little social mores that exist between predators like humans and demons.

We took Flynn's car because rolling up to a bar in my shitty little Toyota just never did anything to impress anybody. At least her confiscated Escalade made us look like thugs, and the long coat and hat pulled down over my face did nothing to dispel the illusion.

I knocked on the door, and an old-school peephole slid open in the steel-reinforced door.

"Password," a pair of red-rimmed eyes appeared in the hole.

"Open the fucking door, you dimwitted twat," I replied.

"Close enough. Come on in, Harker. Try not to break anyone this time." The door opened and a half-shifted werebear stood beside a small podium with a ledger on top. "Sign in," the bear said, motioning to the ledger.

"Are you fucking high?" I asked. "I'm not fucking signing anything, especially not here, of all fucking places."

"I never said you had to sign your real name. Nobody does. You'd be amazed at how many Donald Trumps and Mickey Mouses we have in the bar tonight."

"Fair enough," I said, picking up the pen and writing "Jimi Hendrix." I passed the pen to Flynn, who signed "Lucille Ball."

Mort's place looked like any stereotypical dive bar, only darker. Beer signs along the walls provided most of the illumination, along with a rectangular light fixture over the room's lone pool table and the glow of the jukebox in the corner. Mort's one nod to contemporary decor was a color-changing bar top, but I knew it was magic and not LEDs that made the colors shift with the mood of the inhabitants. I know because I cast the spell in exchange for a rather extravagant bar tab I'd run up on one of Luke's birthdays a decade or so earlier.

The bar was a deep blue when we walked in, tinged with green at the edges. Calm, with a hint of horny and depressed. That's about what I wanted to see when I walked into a demon bar. A couple spots of purple appeared at the corners of the twelve-foot expanse of blue as the inhabitants got a good look at me. Plenty of the denizens of Charlotte's underworld hate me on sight, so I wasn't surprised that I made enough impact to shift the bar's color. As long as most of it stayed purple, lavender, or blue I was okay. If more than a third of the surface went red, I needed to think about getting out of Dodge. Mort loved the early warning system, and it did provide a lovely up-light for the highball and martini glasses scattered all along its length.

I stepped up to the bar and Christy slid me a Newcastle and flashed me a smile. "Where you been keeping yourself, handsome?" she asked as she eyed Flynn.

Christy was a plump Asian woman in her forties with an easy smile and a slow temper, as long as you followed her rules. And her rules were simple: don't start shit in her bar. That was it. Follow that one, and you'd never see her dark eyes flash pupil-less black.

"Who's your friend?" Christy asked me.

"Detective Rebecca Flynn, Charlotte-Mecklenburg Police," Flynn replied, flashing her badge with as much subtlety as anyone can have flashing a badge in a demon bar.

"You do know you can lie about that shit every once in a while, right?" I asked. She looked at me like I was nuts. "You do understand that you don't have to tell every single bad guy in the city that you're a cop, don't you?"

"It makes it easier if I have to shoot anyone later. Identifying myself right off the bat means that if I have to blow somebody's face off, I have to fill out less paperwork."

"I can understand that," Christy said. "You should see the paperwork we have to run for the Alcoholic Beverage Commission."

"What the hell kind of crime lord's joint is this? Cops welcome, paperwork in order, what the shit? Am I on an episode of *Punk'd?*" I asked.

"I don't think that show's still on the air," Flynn said.

"Besides, Harker, I already knew Detective Flynn," Christy said, and both women shared a laugh, probably at my expense.

"Huh?" I said, confused. That was starting to be my natural state around Flynn, and I didn't like it.

"I worked vice a few years ago when I was new to the force. I did a couple of undercover cases here. There was something hinky going on with one of the regulars, but we never could pin anything on him. This was before I knew anything about the supernatural, so that's probably how he kept us from nailing him."

"Don't worry, we took care of him," Christy said. She turned to me. "You remember that incubus with a thing for little boys?"

"Yeah," I said, a glower on my face. "I remember that as soon as I was ready to chase him down and do lots of unpleasant things to him, he disappeared. I always figured you had something to do with it, but couldn't come up with a good way to ask."

"He's buried behind the sand trap leading up to the green on the fourteenth hole at the Country Club. And under the sand trap on the twelfth. And in the water hazard on eight. And—"

"We get it. He's in a lot of pieces scattered in a lot of places. Good job," I said.

Christy looked at me. "We don't shit where we eat, Harker. That's the first rule. This stupid fuck couldn't control his impulses, so we controlled them for him. Now, what can I do for you?"

"I need to know what's going on at Our Lady of Holy Comfort," I said, leaning on the bar.

Christy's face did something I thought impossible—she turned white as a sheet. The bartender's eyes got big, and she looked around as if to make sure no one overheard me. Useless since there were three vampires sitting at various tables around the room, and they could hear a fly fart in a hurricane a mile away. If any of those guys wanted to hear what Christy was saying, all they had to do was listen.

"You're gonna have to talk to Mort about that," Christy said, and my blood ran a little cold. I'd been going into Mort's for more than a decade and had never laid eyes on the big boss. I'd hoped to maintain that status quo for a little while longer, but it seemed like my luck was running like normal —shitty.

"What's the big boss got to do with this?" I asked, keeping my tone light but casting my eyes around the room using the mirror behind the liquor bottles to see if anyone was paying undue attention to us. All the other customers seemed to be firmly ensconced in whatever they were up to, be it pool, drinking or just not looking anywhere near me.

"All I know is I have directions that if anyone asks about that particular church, they go straight to the boss's office." Some of the color had returned to Christy's face, but I could see by the green in the bar top nearest her that she was still pretty nervous.

"Well, lead on, then," I said.

"It's the door between the two restrooms. He knows you're coming," Christy said. "She has to stay out here, though." She nodded at Flynn.

"Oh, hell no." The detective responded about as well as I expected her to. "No way am I letting this idiot go in there alone while I sit out here sipping piña coladas and fending off the unwanted advances of denizens of the underworld."

"Don't worry, sweetie, most of the guys in here wouldn't be caught dead with a human. A live one, that is," Christy said. "And it's not like it's negotiable. Harker *is* going to go back and talk to the boss, and you're *not* going with him. It's up to you two how much furniture and how much you get broken before we all come to that conclusion, but that's how this debate ends. So you want that piña colada now, or after I start throwing magic missiles around in here?"

Flynn looked an awful lot like she wanted to take her chances throwing down with Christy, and in a normal fight I'd give Flynn the edge every time. Christy tops out at about five-three and carries a few extra pounds on her, almost all of them in exactly the right places, while Flynn is tall, at least five-eight, and all lean muscle and Krav Maga classes. But all it would take is one well-placed spell, and Flynn's sleeping it off for the next day and a half, while Christy wouldn't even break a sweat.

Don't even try it, I sent to Flynn through our mental link. *You have no shot. I don't know if I could take her in a spell duel, and I know I can't take out her and the three bouncers watching us right now.*

"Fine," Flynn said after a long second, and I let out a breath. She turned to me, and I was surprised to see genuine concern in her eyes. "Please don't do anything too stupid. I'm actually starting to like having you around. A little. A very little."

"I'll try to refrain from abject stupidity for at least the next ten minutes," I said, turning to go through a secret entrance between the restrooms at a dive bar to have a chat with a demon about a Catholic church that my personal guardian angel was afraid to talk about. I apparently need a new barometer for "abject stupidity."

CHAPTER FIVE

After all these years, the monsters still find ways to surprise me. The last thing I expected when I stepped through the door Christy opened into the back room of Mort's was a magic show, but that's exactly what I walked in on. There was a small stage set up in one corner of the room, and on it a man in a tuxedo, top hat, and black cape with red satin lining. He was tall, thin almost to the point of gaunt, with a long face, the kind of face that always looks sad. His eyes were sunk in his face, and his cheeks were hollowed out, all of which gave his face a kind of beetle-browed skeleton look that would have been creepy even in the most innocuous of settings.

He was performing magic tricks for an audience of three—a little boy perched on a stool watching avidly, his feet tapping the rungs of the stool beneath him and his hair bouncing as the boy's head bobbed to the rhythm of the magician's background music. The boy was flanked by two bodyguards, both minotaurs in tailored double-breasted suits. They had huge double-headed axes strapped across their shoulders and Uzis in their hands. I didn't want to think about what was tough enough that they would have to unstrap those big axes. Usually a couple seven-foot bullmen with submachine guns was enough to deter trouble. Of course, it hadn't kept me out, so I guess they did have a point.

The magician juggled balls, then blew on each ball as it reached the apex of its arc, causing the balls to burst into multicolored flame, which he continued to juggle. He spun the balls of fire faster and faster until they blended into one long circle of fire, which the magician stuck his arm through, then another arm, then his entire torso, never letting the ring stop spinning until it settled on its hips and morphed again into a circle of solid multicolored light, flashing a rainbow hula hoop around his waist. He reached down once again, grabbed one end of the color loop, and flipped the stream of colors from around his waist into the audience, grabbing the tail of the rope at the last second when it dropped to the floor, a harmless length of connected handkerchiefs in all the colors of the rainbow.

The little boy on the stool clapped and laughed, then shot a pointed look at his bodyguards, who clapped politely. The magician bowed grandly from the waist, doffing his top hat as he did so. He came up with the hat held in front of him, top pointing toward the stage.

"For my next trick, I will pull a human out of this hat," he said, then began to wave his hand above the top hat's brim.

"Why don't you try something new and pull a living human out, Clive?" I called from the back of the room.

The magician's head snapped up and his eyes locked onto me like a missile guidance system. "Harker." His tone implied that he was slightly less than thrilled to see me.

"In the flesh, no thanks to our last meeting." I gave a little half bow, never taking my eyes off the man in the cape. It had been thirty years or more since I last saw Clive Hardwick, also known at the time as Zoltan the Spectacular, star of stages all over California. He was the real deal as far as magicians went; he had power in spades. It all emanated from the demon that lived in his top hat, of course, but Clive was allowed enough of a leash to use the demon's magic for card tricks and sawing the occasional woman in half.

Not as part of his show, you understand. Clive and his demon just liked cutting people into little bits. I heard of some strange disappearances in the days after his show left town, and I followed Clive around from town to town for a couple months. I finally put an end to his private butcher's practice behind a magic and comedy club in Fresno, when I banished his demon and beat Clive to within an inch of his life. Clive got in a few shots, too, including one that left me with second-degree burns over more than half my body. He burned most of my hair off and a fair chunk of my face. It took six months and more than a dozen donations from Uncle Luke to put me back together. But when I walked out of the alley that night, I was damn sure the only one capable of walking.

Honestly, I thought he'd died. He was well into his sixties in 1983, and he hadn't exactly been the poster boy for clean living (not that I'm one to talk). So I was a little surprised to see him in Charlotte in the back of a bar where I was supposed to meet with a big-deal demon. And I was even more surprised to open my Sight and see that he had another demon living in his hat. That thing must have been the penthouse of pocket dimensions.

Clive didn't waste time. I always admired that just a little bit in a "you're an evil bastard and I'm probably going to kill you, but this one aspect of your personality is kinda cool" way. He didn't launch into a monologue about what he was going to do to me, he just summoned up a glowing purple ball of energy and threw it at me.

In the second and a half before the sphere hit me, I didn't have enough time to analyze it. I didn't know if it was eldritch energy, demonfire, angelfire, distilled dragonfire, regular fire-fire, or some other kind of energy. I couldn't tell, and frankly I didn't give a shit. I just dropped flat to my stomach and let the ball of bad intentions fly over me and burn a hole in the brick wall behind me.

"That's new," I said, dusting myself off. "Did you get an upgrade when your new hitchhiker moved in upstairs?" I motioned at his hat.

"My Lord Duke Dantalion granted me one his finest spell crafters for my service," Clive grinned as he stroked the hat. It was a little creepy, like he actually cared for the thing in there. I guarantee whatever demonlet Dantalion had sent up from the fifth circle didn't feel the same way about Clive.

"Nice to hear you and Dandelion are getting along so well," I said. My fingers were quickly twining together a piece of string I found on the floor with a couple of pop tops from beer cans.

"What are you doing there? I can't quite…oh, I don't care what you're doing, Harker. It will all end the same way, with you burned to cinders in this room. *Infernos!*" He thrust both his hands out at me, and a stream of fire shot out like water from a fire hose.

I finished with my makeshift bracelet and tied it to my wrist. I held up the representation of a shield and focused my will. "*Inverso!*" A blue-white half-sphere appeared in front of me, centered on my wrist. The fire-stream hit my shield and split, bending around my shield and spewing off harmlessly to the sides.

Unfortunately, the heat didn't go with it, so after less than a second of Clive's fireboats, my wrist started to smoke and blister.

This brought back unpleasant memories of our last meeting, so I tried something I didn't think of decades back in California. I drew my Glock and shot him three times. Or shot at him, rather. Clive flicked up a hand, and with a quick "*Dispersos!*" sucked all the kinetic energy from my bullets. The spent slugs dropped to the floor, harmless, but Clive had to stop his fire assault to save himself, so I got what I needed—breathing room.

"Come on, Clive," I called out, flipping a couple of tables and taking cover behind them. "You couldn't beat me decades ago, don't you think I've learned new tricks in all that time?"

"Ahhh, that's where you're wrong, Quincy," Clive called back from the DJ booth, where he was hiding. "I've not only learned a few new tricks of my own, I've got backup to help me make them more spectacular than ever!" With that, he pulled his hat off, waved his hand over the opening, and shouted "*Sica!*"

Daggers flew from the opening of his top hat. Dozens of them, all streaking across the room right at me. I ducked, and most *thunked* into the overturned bar table, some flew over the top, and a couple skittered along the floor.

I quickly stripped off my makeshift bracelet, added a couple of knots of my hair into the weave, focused my will on the scruffy little band of aluminum and copper, and whispered "*redirectus.*" I wrapped the bracelet around my fist, brass knuckles style, and stood up, throwing my hand at the stage like a punch as I came up. A wave of force pulsed out from my arm, catching the stream of deadly blades and reversing their course.

As usual, things didn't go exactly as planned. Not all of the knives reversed perfectly along their axis, so some went careening off in random directions. None of them headed in my direction, which was the good news. It wasn't great news for the kid sitting in front of the stage, though. While several dozen knives whipped toward Clive at ridiculous speed, a good six or so whirled and tumbled toward the boy, who sat watching our little magical duel with unrestrained glee.

I didn't think about who the kid was, or what kind of parent lets a cherubic, tow-headed little boy with glasses taking up half his face sit in the back of a demon's bar watching an evil wizard do parlor tricks. I didn't wonder about the obvious control he had of the goons surrounding him, goons who were already moving to intercept the missiles streaking toward their young charge. Missiles that were going to be way faster than any human's reactions. I didn't think about anything, other than *Oh shit, I kill this kid and Glory is going to have my balls for earrings.* My guardian angel likes kids, and getting one killed would put me on her shit list for most of an eternity, at least.

So I didn't think, I just acted. Describes a lot of decades for me, especially the 60s and those years in San Francisco and St. Maarten. I flung a hand out toward the kid and shouted "*Inertius!*" Immediately, all the forward momentum of the knives halted, and they dropped to the floor with a thunderous clatter. But since energy can't be destroyed, it had to be redirected somewhere, so I redirected it to Clive. Actually, Clive's shoes.

All the forward energy of dozens of knives flying through the air at blinding speed suddenly transferred itself to Clive's shoes, yanking his feet right out from under him and dropping him flat on his back and sending his hat spinning across the stage beside him.

The biggest problem was that Clive never cancelled his spell, so his hat was still firing knives at the rate of several blades per second. As it spun around the room, knives bounced and clanged around the bar, thunked into the table I ducked behind, and one buried itself into the shoulder of a bodyguard who finally wrapped himself around the little boy, who still sat clapping on his stool, laughing and shrieking with joy at the chaos and bloodshed around him.

The hat spun, spitting knives in every direction, until it came to rest on its side right next to Clive. That pointed the mouth of the hat right at the old magician's side and neck, which were promptly filled with razor-sharp four-inch daggers. The skeletal old magician tried to roll out of the way, but the hat just kept spewing sharpened death at him until he finally collapsed. When Clive died, his spell was broken, and after one last hiccup of blades, the hat fell still. I stood up from my cover behind the table, looking at the carnage Clive and I had wrought upon Mort's private room. There were knives poking out of almost every vertical surface and more than one horizontal one. Shattered glassware littered the bar and every tabletop, not to mention the spilled drinks and the utter destruction wrought upon the front of the jukebox. It must have gotten some spray from a fireball, too, because it was *wrecked*.

I stepped over to the hat, sprinkled a little holy water from a vial in my coat pocket into the depths of it, and murmured a quick exorcism. Clive's little buddy shrieked a number of rather unpleasant names at me, then let out one final shriek as my magic banished him back to hell. I tossed the hat over Clive's dead face and looked around. The little boy had scrambled out from under the body of a pincushioned guard and was now back on his stool, looking over the wreckage.

"You okay, kid?" I called out.

"I'm fine, Mr. Harker. But I seem to be in need of a new magician. This one has sprung a few leaks. Do you know anyone who would like a job?" The voice coming from the kid was way older than anything that should come from that body and I started to have a bad feeling about this little boy.

"No, I don't know of anyone right offhand. Let me guess, that's you in the little ankle-biter, isn't it, Mort?"

"Mortimer Jacobus Venesta, at your service, but I prefer Mort. My parents called me Jake, but that was so long ago that I'm the only who remembers those days. Well, maybe your uncle."

"How old are you?" I asked before I could remember never to ask a monster anything more than was absolutely necessary. You give away information just by the act of asking, so it's always better to keep your mouth shut when dealing with ridiculously powerful creatures from the lowest circles of Hell. Which I was pretty sure is exactly what I was dealing with.

"I came into this world somewhere along 1790, so I suppose your uncle has been here longer. And we won't mention my time before I came over."

No, we wouldn't. The last thing I wanted was to chitchat with a demon about his millennia in Hell. And that's what this kid was—the earthly vessel for Mort, the demon.

CHAPTER SIX

"So, Mr. Harker, what can I do for you this evening? I assume you want something since it's been more than a few years since our last conversation, and that ended with a certain amount of broken architecture." Mort and I weren't exactly strangers, even though I'd never been to his place of business, and I'd certainly never seen him in this current body. We'd had a disagreement some years ago about the acceptable uses of fresh corpses that resulted in the death of a lot of ghouls and the destruction of a few automobiles and one small warehouse. I had almost forgotten about it, but obviously Mort hadn't. I decide just to breeze along like we'd never tried to kill each other and hope I could outrun him if it came to that.

"Yeah, I need some information," I said. I walked over to the seating area in front of the stage, picked up a toppled stool, and sat down across from the little demon host.

"What kind of information?" Mort asked.

"What's going on at Our Lady of Holy Comfort?" I asked. I figured no point in beating around the bush. He'd either tell me or not, and the fewer opportunities I gave the centuries-old demon to trap me into something with my words, the better.

The demon got a thoughtful look on his face, then he broke into a grin. "Oh yes, the Church of the Holy Blankie! I know that one, some big goings-on going on down there. Didn't your little guardian angel fill you in? Oh, I guess she wouldn't, would she?"

Her word was "can't" not "won't," but I'm not here to parse grammar with him, I thought, trying not to let anything show on my face.

"Not talking? Afraid I'm going to twist your words into some binding agreement that binds your soul to my service and traps you into wearing women's underpants for a century? Don't worry, Mr. Harker, I have plenty of people entering into agreements with me willingly—I don't need to trick people. And as far as underpants, I'm not interested in what type, if any, you wear."

"So what's the deal at the church, then?" I asked.

"Well, it's not that simple."

"Why not? You just went through this whole spiel about how you weren't going to make me do anything ridiculous to get the information, now you're telling me the exact opposite."

"I didn't actually say any of that." The demon kid folded his arms across his chest.

"And people wonder why demons have a terrible reputation as welshers."

"I'll have you know that I have never reneged on an agreement in five millennia of dealing with you hairless apes!" I'd struck a nerve, and decided to push my edge. Not the safest course of action, I'll admit, but if you're looking for someone to tweak a demon's nose in its own lair, I'm your guy.

"But you certainly took advantage of the ignorance and purposeful misunderstanding of your temporary business partners, didn't you?" I swear, dealing with demons is worse than faeries. Faeries can't lie, it's a genetic thing. So they've learned to obfuscate and evade with the best of them. Actually, they are the best of them. Demons are a lot like that, with more negotiations ending in eviscerations, and less arbitration.

"There might be a few souls currently serving thousand-year sentences as fulfillment on contracts they didn't read thoroughly," Mort admitted.

"So what do you want me to do?" I asked.

"You're not going to refuse to work for me on principle?"

"I don't have that many principles, Mort, and the ones I have are pretty flexible. So what's the gig?"

"I need someone killed," Mort said.

"What do you need me for?" I asked. "You've got to have dozens of killers wandering through the doors every hour on the hour."

"I do, but they can't take this guy out. He's got some real juice, magically speaking."

"Like Clive?" I asked.

"Yeah," the boy snorted out a laugh. "If Clive were actually talented, and ever had more power in his whole body than you have stored in your pinky finger."

"I typically don't just kill random people as favors for demons. That's a good way to really irritate a guardian angel, you know," I said. Since he already knew about Glory, I could use her as the "bad cop" to try and spin this negotiation to something I wouldn't hate doing.

"Oh, I don't think you'll mind killing this one. I've heard you have developed quite the soft spot for innocent young women? Well, this is right up your alley, Mr. White Knight. This magician, let's call him Danvar the Magnificent, goes through lovely assistants like some guys go through underwear."

"Not seeing the problem, Morty. So the guy has issues with women, and he fires a lot of assistants. What's the big deal?"

"I never said he fired the girls. I said he goes through them. He hires them, brainwashes them into mindless pleasure drones, uses them up, and when he's tired of them, he wipes their minds and leaves them in whatever city he happens to be in when he gets tired of them." Mort watched my face as his story unfolded, and the glee in his eyes told me that I wasn't nearly as good at hiding my emotions as I wanted to be, particularly when dealing with a demon. *Lock it down, Harker, or you're gonna get yourself killed. Or worse.*

"Okay, that's pretty bad. And it's definitely on the list of things I don't approve of. But why do you care? This guy sounds like the kind of guy I'd expect you to invite over for milk and cookies instead of hiring somebody to take him out."

"Pretty good, Harker. I never thought you'd be able to hold out that long without making a joke about the new body," Mort gestured at his chest. "The last one ran out of steam, so I had to go take over a new one. It was that or go back downtown, and I've gotten accustomed to the weather up here, if you catch my drift."

I did. I was a little nauseated by it, but I did. Mort's old body died, which happens eventually to bodies inhabited by demons, and he went to get a newer model. I could only hope that the kid who used to walk around in that body died before Mort took it over. Otherwise he was still trapped in there, his consciousness shoved off to the side while Mort used his body. Yeah, that's the guy I was working for. A real prince.

"So where do I find this magician, Mort? And how do I verify your story? I'm not just going to murder this guy on your say-so."

"Ri-ight," Mort drawled. "You've grown a pair of morals since coming to Charlotte. Or is it since you started running with that delectable little policewoman you left out in my bar to entertain the boys. Tell me, Harker, does she wear the handcuffs, or does she put them on you?" He leered at me, a disconcerting image coming from a kid who should be entranced by cartoons and comics, not sitting in the back of a bar hiring a hitman to take out an evil magician.

"You probably want to leave Flynn out of this, Mort, she can more than take care of herself." Just to be sure, I sent a thought her way. *You okay out there?*

Fine, but bored. Nobody out here is stupid enough to start anything with me. I thought I'd at least get to arrest somebody. I could tell from the tone of her thoughts that she really was bored, so that was reassuring.

"I'll look into him, Mort. I'm not making any promises, but if he's as bad as you say, he deserves anything I can do to him. One question, though. What did he do to cross you?"

"Why Quincy, old pal, can't I just want to help clean up my community?"

"One, we're not pals. And two, no, you can't. You've never cared anything about a community as long as you can make a profit and wreak some havoc. So since this guy is just doing exactly what you usually want people to do, I want to know what he did to piss you off."

"He killed my mom," the boy's voice came through for the first time, and all the hair on my arms stood up. "She went to see a magic show, and she didn't come home all night. A couple days later the police came to my house and told me my mom was dead. I'm not stupid, so I went on the web and looked it up. She was…raped a bunch of times, then she walked out in front of a bus and killed herself. So I called Mort to help me get the man that did that to her."

This was bad. This was more than bad, this was some epic awful. The boy wasn't just still alive inside his body with Mort wearing his skin suit, he'd invited the demon in to get back at the man who killed his mother. The worst part was, I couldn't blame him. I thought about some of the things I'd done in the past driven by grief, and summoning a demon wasn't anywhere near the worst of them.

"So, you gonna help us? Me and little Bobby here, I mean." Mort's voice returned, and it was easy to look in his eyes and tell that the demon was back in control. I shuddered a little, knowing now that the boy was a willing passenger to everything Mort was going to do with his life.

"Like I said, I'll check it out. If this is for real, I'll make sure Danvar the Molester's show has a shortened run."

"Bring me proof, and I'll tell you everything I know about Our Lady of Holy Comfort and what's going on there." He held out a hand, and I shook it.

I looked into the demon/boy's eyes, and they went human for just a second. He had blue eyes, the boy did.

"Please get the man that killed my mom, Mr. Harker. I don't want to be stuck in here forever for nothing."

Before I could say anything in response, its eyes went black again and Mort smiled up at me. "Happy hunting, Reaper."

I took my hand back and turned for the door. I stopped with my hand on the knob and turned back to Mort. "Mort, you know I'm not just a stupid human, right?"

"I know what you are, Harker. Maybe even better than you do."

"Then you know you do not want to jerk me around on this. Because if I come back here and I find out you've played me…"

"Spare me the threats, Harker. I stopped being afraid of humans somewhere around the Crusades. Now go be a good Reaper and kill something, won't you?"

I walked out, feeling not for the first time in my career like I'd made a deal with the devil. And that *always* ends well.

Flynn was sitting at the bar sipping on a Stella when I walked out. Christy was polishing a section of bar top as far away from where Flynn sat as possible while still being behind the bar. The wood and Plexiglas surface was glowing a deep maroon all around Christy, but faded to a cool blue-green at Flynn's seat. Whatever had Christy riled up, Flynn gave not a single fuck about it.

"What did you do?" I asked in a low voice as I stepped up beside her.

"Nothing much, just played a game of pool or two," she replied. I looked around, but the lone pool table was abandoned, and the green felt showed no new bloodstains.

"What happened?" I pressed.

"There was a disagreement about the break, so I did."

"You broke?" I asked. "What exactly did you break?"

"That guy's nose, and his brother's jaw. But they're fine. They're weres, so they heal fast, and I think they're jackals or something like that, so it was the only way to keep from killing them." Her voice stayed low and calm, but we were collecting some looks. A lot of people wouldn't mess with Flynn if they thought she was under Christy's protection, but everyone in town knew I was fair game.

"What about Sanctuary?" I asked.

"They touched me first, so I was clear. Christy's not happy about it, but she's a woman, so she's letting it slide."

"What do you mean, they touched you?" I was a little surprised at the anger I heard in my own voice, and I zeroed in on the lycanthropes drowning their pain in a couple pitchers of beer over in one corner.

"It's not a thing, Harker. And don't start trying on the shining armor. I don't need one, and the suit won't fit you anyway." She was right, of course. Rescuing damsels in distress never ended well for me. They always ended up inside my head.

"What do I owe you, Christy?" I asked.

"Six months of staying the hell out of my bar and a promise that I never see her again at all," the fiery manager shot back.

"Can't promise anything, so here's some cash for the beer you had to comp the dogs." I jerked a thumb over my shoulder at the weres. "But tell them to be more careful who they're sniffing around next time. All humans aren't created equal anymore." I dropped a couple of twenties on the bar and we walked out onto the street.

"Where to now, boss?" Flynn asked with enough snark in her voice that you could cut it with a knife.

"I need information, and Glory can't or won't give it to me," I replied.

"I thought that's what you went in there to find? Don't tell me I got felt up by two shapeshifters with dog breath for nothing."

My vision blurred a little red at the mention of the were-jackals mauling Flynn, but I blinked a couple times before she noticed. I hoped. "I got some information, but I need to confirm it. So I've got to go get help from the last person in the world I want to ask."

"Smith?" Flynn asked.

"Smith," I confirmed, and slid into the passenger seat. Flynn put the car into gear and we headed off to admit to my boss that he might know more than me about something magical.

CHAPTER SEVEN

We pulled into the garage underneath police headquarters and headed to the elevator. "What's your plan?" Flynn asked.

"What kind of plan?"

"To get the information you need out of Smith?"

"Well, I thought I'd ask," I said, honestly confused.

Flynn looked at me like I'd grown another head. "Yeah, when has that ever worked?"

I stepped into the elevator and turned to her. "What are you talking about, Becks?"

"Look, Smith is the single most tight-lipped human being I've ever met—"

"The jury's still out about that whole human thing," I reminded her. "I, for one, am not a hundred percent sure what Smith is, but I don't think he's human. Not totally, at any rate." There was definitely something magical about Agent John Smith. He looked human from the outside, but there was something in the eyes that spoke of too many years for a normal lifetime. And he was definitely stronger and faster than a typical human.

The doors dinged open, and we stepped off into the second-floor offices of the Charlotte-Mecklenburg Police Department. I followed Flynn as we meandered through cubicles and hallways until we came to the small block of offices "temporarily" assigned to Agent John Smith and his Department of Homeland Security Domestic Terrorism Task Force. At least, that's what it said on our badges and business cards. In reality, we were one team of the government's Paranormal Division. Basically, if something went bump in the night, we bumped back. Harder.

Flynn went to her office and I stepped up to Smith's door. I raised my hand to knock and the door swung open on its own.

"Come on in, Quincy," Smith said from his seat behind his desk. He was dressed like he always was, in a pinstriped charcoal suit with a muted burgundy tie and an American flag lapel pin. He looked up at me over a pair of reading glasses that I suspected were just for show, and his gray-blue eyes locked onto mine.

"What can I do for you, Harker? How are things at Mort's?" He motioned to a chair, and I sat in front of his desk. I noticed immediately that the chair was low to the ground, giving Smith an uncommon height advantage. He's not a small man, but I top out several inches over six feet, so I usually look down on him a little. This time he was the tall man in the room. *Oh well, his room, his playing field.*

"Mort's fine," I replied. "Christy sends her best. I need to know about a magician by the stage name of Danavar."

Smith leaned back in his chair and looked at me. "Why?"

"Because Mort wants me to kill him. Says he's basically a serial rapist , and he's operating without Mort's permission. So he wants him dead."

"And you're now playing hitman for demons?" Smith asked, one eyebrow climbing toward his brush-cut gray hair.

"Mort has information I need," I said.

"Information on what?" Smith asked.

"Our Lady of Holy Comfort Catholic Church," I replied.

"What do you need to know?" Smith's eyes were flat, revealing nothing, but that was no different from every other day. Still, I felt like there was something underneath this conversation, something he was either waiting for me to ask, or something he didn't want to tell me.

"I need to know everything. Hell, at this point I'd settle for knowing *anything*. Something serious is happening there, something so big that Glory won't talk to me about it. No, scratch that. She's not allowed to talk to me about it."

"Which makes it completely irresistible to you," Smith observed.

"You're not wrong," I admitted. "So what's the deal?"

"I don't know. I've heard some rumblings, and I know Flynn's homicides yesterday morning were members there, but there's been nothing from my sources about the place."

"And who are your sources, Smith? Where is your thumb on the pulse of the dark underbelly of the Carolinas?"

"Let me tell you one thing, Harker. You don't ever want to know how I get my information. I promise you that."

For some reason, I believed him. Smith had the eyes of a man who's seen some shit in his lifetime. And since I've seen more than my fair share of shit myself, I didn't push. "Yeah, I didn't figure you'd know. That's why I went to see Mort." I let that one just lay out there, the assumption that a demon knew more than him was exactly the kind of thing that would grate at Smith.

"How's Christy?" he asked, not batting an eye. I hate inscrutable mother-fuckers like Smith. They make me work twice as hard for every scrap of information.

"She's fine. Buxom. Badass. Still taking zero shit and giving zero fucks."

"Good to hear. I like that girl. Hate she got mixed up with a dick like Mort, but I can understand it, given the circumstances." He said that like I was supposed to know how Christy got tangled up working for Mort, but I had no idea. And of course, phrasing it like it was common knowledge meant that I couldn't ask what the deal was without revealing my ignorance, which would give Smith insight into another hole in my knowledge. If he really knew at all and wasn't just playing me. Which I would never figure out without asking him about it, the one thing he'd just insured I'd never do. Bastard played the game better than me, even in his off-the-rack suits.

"So, how old is Mort this time?" Smith asked, taking a file out of his desk drawer and opening it.

"Looks like he's hopped into an eight-year-old," I said, trying but not quite managing to keep the disgust out of my voice.

"That's not cool," Smith said.

"No, it's fucking disgusting," I replied, the bile I felt making its way into my voice.

"That's not what I meant," Smith interrupted me with a hand. "I have an arrangement with Mort about his continued existence on this plane. 'No deals with kids' is very much a part of that arrangement. He and I are going to have a conversation about this." I had a distinct feeling that conversation wasn't going to be a whole lotto fun for Mort and would probably result in a fair amount of broken furniture. Or people.

"So why Danvar? And why you?" Smith asked.

"No idea," I replied. "I just know the magician is mind-slaving his assis-tants, raping them into oblivion, and then casting them aside. I don't think any of that would be a problem, except he picked up a woman in Mort's terri-tory, and now Mort wants a message sent."

"And he wants you to send the message," Smith said.

"I think me killing Danvar is only part of the message. If the local monsters think I'm under Mort's control, they'll fall in line pretty quick. Between Mort and me, we pack some pretty serious punch. I wouldn't mess with the two of us."

"I wouldn't either," Smith agreed, more out of politeness than any sincerity, I thought. I've watched Smith open fire on a dragon with a handgun and not back down a single step. It was an illusionary dragon, but he didn't know that at the time.

"But you can't kill Danvar," he continued.

I started a little. Smith was generally pretty hands-off on my life outside the cases we worked together. This kind of directness was a little unprecedented.

"Why not?" I asked. "Is he not really a child molester? I wouldn't put it past Mort to lie about that kind of thing."

"No, he's everything Mort described to you, and more. He drains the life force from women, abuses them inside and out, bleeds them of their happiness and their life force, then sets them loose on the world as husks—lifeless, soulless walking shadows that torment their loved one by their mere presence until a few months later they commit suicide."

"And eventually you'll get to the part that says why I *shouldn't* kill this asshole."

"Yeah, I will. He's my informant. I'm working on turning him to give me inside information about Mort and his operation. That's why Mort wants him dead. Not some suddenly rediscovered noble purpose bullshit about not wanting the poor kids to be victimized."

"Still seems like a pretty good guy to come down with a terminal case of dead," I said, reeling at the idea of Smith using somebody like that as a source.

"And most of the time, I'd agree with you. But I'm pretty close to bringing this douchebag over to the side of the angels, and part of that is him agreeing to cease his less savory activities."

"Smitty," I said, knowing full well he hated that nickname, "purse-snatching is a less savory activity. Fixing a horse race is a less savory activity. Sucking out somebody's life force and personality so you can live forever is just fucking disgusting, and this guy needs to be put down."

"No." Smith didn't bother meeting my gaze this time. He knew he was wrong, and he didn't care. When he finally looked at me across his desk, his eyes were cold, just gray chips in his stony face. "This isn't negotiable, Harker. Stay away from Danvar. I'm not asking."

"I didn't come here to ask permission, Smitty. I came here to see if this guy was as much of a threat as Mort claimed, and if you had information about the church. Since the answer question one is yes, and question two is no, I guess I'm gonna have to go kill the rat bastard."

Smith stood up. "Don't do this, Quincy. I'd hate for us to end up on opposite sides of this thing."

"Yeah, so would I. So stay out of my way," I said.

"That's not how this works," Smith said, leaning forward onto his fists.

He opened his mouth to continue, but Flynn flung the door open. "We've got another one," she said, gesturing to me.

"Another what?" I asked, standing.

"Another family slaughtered in their home. Let's go."

I turned back to Smith. "We'll continue this later." I followed Flynn out the door and down the hallway. "How long were you standing out there?" I asked as we stepped into the parking garage elevator.

Flynn gave me her best "innocent" look, which sucked. "I just heard the last few minutes. I felt the tension rising in you and wanted to be able to interrupt if things got stupid. I felt them moving toward stupid, so I interrupted. But we do have a case."

"Same M.O.?"

"Oh yeah. Bring a spare pair of shoes. This one's even worse."

CHAPTER EIGHT

t was a good twenty-minute ride from downtown to the University area where the Nettles family home stood in a nice suburban neighborhood named Whispering Falls, or Rambling Brook, or Fallen Spruce, or whatever stupid collection of nouns the developed pulled out of the hat this time. Flynn parked in the driveway, right behind the crime scene van. I pulled my car in beside hers, then got out and jerked my head toward the CSI van. Those guys have been known to do nasty science-type things to people who get in their way.

"Don't worry," Flynn said as she opened the door and slid out of the car. "If this is anything like the Standish place, they won't be leaving anytime soon." Good point. When there's twenty liters of blood scattered around a house, it takes a while to process a crime scene.

I got out of the car and took a look around, first with my eyes, then with my Sight. In the normal spectrum, it looked like any other house on the street. Brick two-story, white shutters, white siding for the eaves, small front porch, large back deck that extended far enough out to be seen a little from the front of the house. An attached two-car garage sat off to the left with the doors closed, a sidewalk leading up to the front door, where half a dozen cops milled around. The perimeter was set for two houses back on each side, but that did nothing to stop the crowd of lookie-loos from gathering, phones at the ready, trying to get a gruesome or sad photo for their internet profile.

I walked up to a uniform taking photos of the outside of the house. He was noting placement of the kids' bicycles, tire tracks, things like that. "Hey, Officer..." I let the pause drag on so he'd hopefully take the bait and supply his name.

No such luck. I had to read his nametag. "Officer Aguirre, could you make sure you get photos of everyone along the tape as well?"

"Sure..." he trailed off as he took in my long coat, black t-shirt, no visible badge.

"He's with me, Aguirre. Just do as he asks," Flynn said, shooting me a look. I opened my Sight and scanned the crowd. Nobody stood out as a bad guy, but I wondered if the homeowner's association knew that one of their neighbors was an elf.

I followed Flynn into the house, and my nose was immediately assaulted by the coppery smell of blood, the salty tang of fear-sweat and other, less savory smells of death. I wandered through the downstairs, poking around the kitchen, checking the channels on the television, doing all the things I could think of to keep me out of the upstairs. Finally, out of excuses, I put on two pair of booties over my shoes and climbed to the second floor.

Flynn was right, it was worse than the Standish place. She was waiting for me at the top of the stairs. A pair of crime scene techs were visible in the master bedroom off to the left, so I turned right to look at the children's rooms. Just going from the decoration on the doors, they had a boy and a girl, just like the Standishes.

"Are we seeing a pattern, here, Flynn? Two kids, boy and a girl? Is that significant?" I asked, my hand on the door to the little boy's room.

"It could be," Flynn replied. "It's honestly too early to tell. We can't build a dependable pattern off just two crime scenes. To get a real pattern we need more data points, which means either—"

"This fucker has to kill again," I supplied.

"That," Flynn agreed, "or we find cold cases with the same M.O., either locally or nationwide. I contacted the FBI and sent them the details of the case. They're running everything we have through their database, so hopefully today we'll hear if there are any other cases like this in the U.S."

"Let's hope the answer is no," I said.

"Why is that?" Flynn asked. "I mean, I understand it on a human level. We don't want anyone else to have gone through this, ever. But that's not what you meant, was it?"

"No, it wasn't. If this is local, then it's probably something I can deal with. If this is a demon that's been traveling for years, with no significant weaknesses and a long history of getting away with this shit, there's a good possibility that it's either too strong or too smart for me to handle, which is not only bad for yours truly, but severely reduces our chances of stopping this thing before it's eaten its fill."

I turned the knob and stepped into the Nettles boy's room. If ever there was a stereotypical American boy's room, I was standing in it. A Cam Newton poster hung in place of pride over his bed, Cam in his "Superman" pose after scoring a touchdown. A huge Carolina Panthers head hung over a small desk with a stack of *Chronicles of Narnia* and Harry Potter books on it. Framed on the desk was a picture of the kid, Carey, I remembered his name finally, with a smiling Luke Kuechly in the picture with him. A single bed sat under a window, a military-style footlocker at the end of the bed. In the middle of the bed, tangled in the covers like he was sleeping with it, was a football. This was a kid who loved his Panthers.

I knelt to open the footlocker and felt a rush of cold across my arms. I looked around and drew back as Carey Nettles appeared, sitting on the footlocker with a somber expression on his face. I reached for the footlocker again, and Ghost Carey shook his head at me, putting his hands over mine. I felt the grave-chill again and drew my hands back.

"Hi Carey," I said, looking right at the boy. He started a little, obviously used to being ignored. I went on. "Most people can't see you, can they?"

He shook his head.

"Well, most people don't know how to look. My name is Quincy, and I'm one of the good guys. I know how to talk to people like you, and a lot of times I can help them move along on their journey. Do you know what I mean?"

He looked at me, sadness filling his deep eyes. He nodded slowly, then looked around the room.

"I know, it's a little scary, leaving behind everything we're familiar with. But it can be exciting, too, getting to see new things, right?"

He nodded again, a little less pain in his eyes.

"Carey?" I asked. "Can you answer a few questions for me before you go?"

He nodded.

"I know you can't speak to me, but I'll ask yes or no questions, and you can just nod, okay?"

He nodded again.

I took a deep breath. "Did someone hurt your family, Carey?"

The ghost sat on the edge of the bed, just looking up at me. After a long moment, he nodded.

"Was it someone you know?"

Nod.

"Was it someone who lives here?"

Nod.

"Carey, did your daddy hurt you and your mommy?"

Long pause, then nodded. A single shiny tear streaked down his face. I reached out without thinking to wipe it away, but my hand passed right into his face, startling us both.

"I'm sorry, Carey. I didn't mean to scare you." The irony of my words was not lost on me, as I apologized to a ghost for me scaring him, but this wasn't a haunting in the real sense, this was a lost little boy who didn't know how to find his mommy and daddy. "I just have one more question, then I'll help you find your mom and dad." *Or at least your mom,* I thought. I only had a little bit of faith in his mother and father sharing an afterlife, but this wasn't the time or place to discuss that.

Carey looked up at me, trust shining on his ethereal face. He nodded once, telling me that he could be brave a little while longer.

I took a deep breath. "Carey, when your daddy hurt your mommy and you, was it really your daddy, or was there something else with him?"

I saw the boy try to say something and shook my head. I hadn't asked a yes or no question, and the mute spirit couldn't answer anything. I held up a hand.

"Hold on, buddy, I've got it. Let's try this—was it really your daddy who hurt you?"

Carey shook his head.

"So somebody else was with him?"

Another head shake. Well, that didn't make any sense. If he wasn't being controlled by something...wait a minute.

"Carey, was somebody else *in* your daddy?"

A vigorous nod. He grinned and gave me a "thumbs up." So it was as I suspected—his father wasn't evil, he was possessed. That gave me some direction, at least. Now to send this kid on his merry way.

"Carey, are you ready to go find your mom and dad?" The little ghost boy nodded.

I sketched a quick circle on the floor with a piece of chalk I found in the kid's desk. It wouldn't hold much, but I didn't expect Carey to try and jump into my skin suit, either.

"Step inside the circle, Carey." He hopped down off the bed and stepped into the circle. I spun out a little of my energy to invoke the circle, and a glowing white light snapped into being all around the edge of the circle.

Carey drew back, frightened.

"Don't worry buddy. I won't let anything hurt you anymore." I focused my mind and called, "Glory! Get your yoga-firm ass down here. I need your help."

"You know I can't get involved in this fight, Q. And stop checking out my ass, it's perverted."

"It's a nice ass, and what do you mean you can't help me?"

"We've talked about this. I can't help you on this case."

"This is different. All I need you to do is open a door to Heaven and let this kid in to find his parents. And I kinda need to know if they're in there." I talked fast, but it's really hard to confuse an angel. They're otherworldly smart and can tell when I'm lying. I didn't really expect Glory to do it, but when she sighed, I knew I had her.

A fair number of my most successful interactions with women over the decades have been preceded by a resigned sigh on their part. I'll take it. Glory waved her hands in the air, spoke some Latin phrases, and the fabric of reality split wide open. Searing white light spilled into the room, and I had to avert my eyes. I also had to cover them with both hands, and a second later I pulled a pillow off Carey's bed and pressed it to my face to save my sight. Heaven isn't something mortals get to peek into and keep their Earthly vision.

I heard Glory speaking more Enochian, then the light around me dimmed considerably. I put the pillow down and looked past Glory to see a couple in their early thirties standing in a pool of light. Carey's face lit up when he saw his parents, and I looked over at Glory.

"We all good?" I asked. She nodded, and I dropped the circle around Carey. He ran to his parents, who looked up at me with a smile. The mom held a preteen girl by the hand, presumably Carey's sister, and his father looked at me with a grateful smile. Whatever this man had done, it wasn't by his hand, and left no stain on his soul, or he'd never be allowed near the soul of an innocent child. Carey and his family vanished, leaving more questions behind than they answered.

"That was bold, Q," Glory said, waving a hand and sealing her portal. I reached out with a toe and scrubbed out the edge of the circle, dispersing the magical energy into the world and erasing any trace of me from the room.

"Didn't have to be, Glory. If you'd give me the info I need."

"I can't, Q. I really, really want to, but I can't. It's not my decision, and I don't get to contradict my bosses. You know that."

"Yeah, I know. That whole war in Heaven thing. Whatever, thanks for helping with that. I couldn't send him on myself because if I just banished him, there's no guarantee where he would have ended up."

"Thanks for doing that. I couldn't stand the thought of that little boy just wandering the Earth forever."

"Don't tell anybody about it, Glory. I've got a reputation to uphold. Which

I will ruin forever if I stay in this room talking to nobody any longer. Get out of here, I've got a crime scene to investigate."

"Later, Q. I hope you figure it out. I really do." I could see in her eyes that she wasn't lying. Well, that and the fact that angels can't lie. They can't. Neither can demons. Both of them can obfuscate like motherfuckers, but they can't *lie*. The trick is getting either bunch to give you a straight answer, so you know what they really mean. This time I felt like Glory was being straight with me. She couldn't tell me what was going on, but that didn't mean she didn't want me to put a stop to it.

CHAPTER NINE

The rest of the house was spirit-free, thank God. I spent a little time checking out the daughter's room, but there was nothing there. Just a preteen girl's room with posters of musicians I'd never heard of and actors that I couldn't tell apart. A stack of *Ms. Marvel* comics spoke to a budding love of geekdom and good writing, and my heart pulled a little at the pictures of Elizabeth Nettles riding a horse at some kind of camp, her kayaking with a huge grin, accepting some award at a school function. I couldn't find anything to indicate she was anything other than a well-adjusted twelve-year-old girl. Still no computer in the kids' rooms, so I'd have to check the family PC down in the dining room for anything dangerous, but I was pretty sure I felt a strikeout coming there, too.

I pulled the door closed to the daughter's room and turned to go into the parents' room and murder scene. The blood had soaked all the way across the threshold into the hallway, making me grateful for double-bagging the booties. The room looked almost like someone had rollered the walls in reddish brown paint, there was so much blood splatter. Where the Standish scene had been contained mostly to the bed area, this room showed signs of a struggle with overturned furniture and bodies scattered all over the floor and bed.

Carey and Elizabeth were in the bed, and that's where most of the blood on those walls came from. It looked like the kids were stood up on the bed, their throats slit, and the spray directed around the room for maximum coverage. Sandy Nettles was lying on the floor at the foot of the bed, barefoot and bare-legged. Dressed in an oversized t-shirt and panties for bed, she'd obviously come awake when her husband brought the kids into the room.

She put up a fight, too. She was away from the bed, and there was a shattered lamp and alarm clock lying on the floor against one wall. Looked like she threw things at her husband to try and get him to stop. My guess was, she could have thrown a tank at him and nothing would have stopped what was going to happen here. Whatever was doing this shit had more power than almost anything I'd ever run across, and that had me plenty worried.

Sandy lay in a pool of blood so deep the carpet couldn't hold it all, so there were literal puddles of her blood on either side of her head. Her throat was slit deep enough I could see her spine through her throat, and every other major artery had been opened, too. It wasn't overkill in the classic sense—it was too clinical, too cold. There was no rage here, just the need for a huge volume of blood. That was reminiscent of blood magic, but there was no other hint of magic anywhere in the room, not even on the husband's body.

Jim Nettles lay facedown on the carpet, most of his body's blood streaking out from his legs and wrists. I felt a second's relief that I didn't have to see his empty eyes staring up at me, accusing, demanding answers, screaming for justice that I couldn't provide. I gave myself a shake and snapped out of my pity party, remembering that I wasn't the dead one in the room, so I had it pretty good.

I opened my Sight and scanned the room quickly. It had the same clean energy as the Standish scene, an almost sterile feeling in the magical spectrum, which was really odd for a place where so much blood had been shed. I filed that away on my list of things to poke Glory about and kept looking around the room. I turned slowly in place, scanning the walls, ceiling and floor with my Sight, but nothing leapt out at me as demonic or even supernatural in nature. For all I could tell with my third eye, this was committed by a completely unassisted human.

If there hadn't been an identical murder/suicide less than a day ago, and if I hadn't been haunted by the ghost of a cherubic second-grader ever since, I would have walked away from this one, too. But I was being haunted by sweet little Emily Standish, who stared at me from the Nettles' closet door with her big, blue, accusing eyes. So I kept looking. There had to be something here, something I missed at the Standish home...*there*. There was just a glimmer of light coming from the dresser. I dropped my Sight and walked across the room. A jewelry box, a stack of folded clothes waiting to be put away, a wallet and change dish, and a couple of framed photos sat on the polished wood surface. *Here we go*, I thought. I opened the jewelry box and pawed through it, dumping the contents onto the dresser.

"Hey, you can't do that!" One of the crime scene techs rushed toward me all in a tizzy.

"Calm down, Chow Yun Fat, I'm working here." The Asian man stopped in his tracks, his jaw agape.

"Who the fuck are you? I'm totally reporting you. You can't just come in here while I'm working and make racist comments. I'll have your fucking badge, you asshole. I'll make sure you—"

I held up a hand. "*Obliviscor*," I whispered, then blew the irate man a kiss. His eyes glazed for a moment, then refocused on me.

"What are you doing?" he asked again for the first time.

"I'm checking for surveillance," I replied. "Detective Flynn asked me to. Told me to turn the room over to you once I was done." I gave him one of those "what can you do" shrugs and turned back to the jewelry. My fingers brushed against a silver medal, and I felt a tingle through my fingers, like a tiny electric shock. I brushed aside more rings and brooches until I felt it again, then drew out a silver medal on a string of glass beads, with a small silver crucifix dangling from the end.

Whoever this fucker is, he's a nasty piece of work, I thought to Flynn.

Why? What did you find?

The Focus for his spell on the Nettles family. Bastard enchanted a rosary to lock them under his influence. I'm coming down.

I stomped through the assembled cops and crime scene techs on my way to the front door. Flynn stood in the foyer talking to a neighbor but broke away when I came down.

"Aguirre, finish taking her statement. I'm sorry, Mrs. Ravin, I need to speak with my consultant." She followed me out into the yard and across the grass to my car. I opened the trunk and sat on the bumper, pulling off the blood-soaked booties and stripping off my shoes and socks.

"I wondered about the sneakers," Flynn asked as she caught up to me.

"Stopped at Walmart on the way over," I said. I put the booties, sneakers and socks all in a big plastic bag, then scrounged around in the trunk for an old towel I kept back there for emergencies. I wiped the last of the blood off my feet and threw the towel in the bag with the bloody shoes. I grabbed my Doc Martens out of the trunk and pulled on a pair of thick boot socks to go with them. Flynn stood there silent for several minutes while I laced up my boots, then finally she broke.

"Well?" she asked.

"Deep subject," I replied, keeping my petty little grin to myself somehow.

"Don't fuck with me, Harker. I need to know what's going on."

I held out the medal. "This is a big deal," I said. "It takes a lot of power to corrupt a truly holy object, and saint's medals and crucifixes are inherently holy. Put them on a rosary, and one that's seen some use, and they are significant objects of faith, at least to the owner. This might not mean shit to the Buddhist guy across the street, but to Jim Nettles, this is probably the focal point of all his prayers. I'm guessing his mother died of cancer, probably sometime when he was newly married, or around thirty. He prayed with this rosary through that whole time and carried it for a long time after. Then his wife had a scare, and he started carrying it again recently."

"How did you get all that? Some kind of psychokinesis?" Flynn asked. "A spell?"

"Nah, more like old-school Sherlock Holmes shit," I replied. "Most of that psychokinesis bullshit is just that—bullshit. There are a few PKs out in the world, but most folks do it with magic. Strong emotions leave impressions on objects, and magic can bring those to the front. But this was all detective work. There were pics of a woman bearing a slight resemblance to Nettles in the house holding both kids as infants, but nothing more recent of her. And this necklace is about ten or fifteen years old and shows signs of a lot of handling. So he prayed with this thing a lot, but there aren't enough religious items in the house to make me think he did that recently. They did the church thing, but it didn't drive them. And St. Peregrine is the patron saint of cancer patients, so all that makes sense."

"But what about the wife? What makes you think she had cancer?"

"No, she was a survivor. It was the bras. There was a mastectomy bra on the dresser with a prosthetic built in, and she wore a bra to sleep in. Speaks to a woman with confidence issues centered around her breasts, and some cancer patients have trouble letting their partners see the scars, so they wear their prostheses to bed. But her cancer would have been enough to get him to pull that old rosary out and pray with it again. I'd bet we find out that they started going to church again about two, two and a half years ago. Probably right about the time she was diagnosed."

"So what killed them?" Flynn asked.

"It's not the what. We know the what, or the who. Jim Nettles killed his family and then opened every artery and vein in his body that he could reach. What we don't know is the why, and we don't know what needs an offering of that much blood to break through the Veil. And we really, really hope it's still locked on the other side."

"How are we supposed to find out those things? Especially the bit about whether or not this big bad is still locked away?" Flynn asked, keeping her voice low to not attract attention from the surrounding cops. Most of them knew she was on some oddball assignment with Homeland Security. Most of them didn't know she was working for the real-world equivalent of the *X-Files*.

"Nothing came through here, it would have left a mark," I said with more confidence than I felt.

"You're full of shit." The problem with trying to lie, or even fudge the truth, with someone who is literally inside your head is that they are *literally inside your head*. Flynn felt every nuance of every word I said, so she knew I was lying.

"Of course I'm full of shit, Becks. I can't tell what kind of magic is causing this because *I can't feel any magic at all*. Do you know how fucked up that is? It's like walking into a room where you know people died, but you can't see what killed them. They're just dead. No bullet holes, no stab wounds, no ligature marks, nothing. That's what I've got—a fucking conundrum that's hiding in an enigma. And not only do I have nothing, but my best resource has been ordered not to help me. So we're fucked. So I'm going home, and I'm going to do what I do when I don't have any other options."

"Get drunk?"

"That too. No, I'm going to call Luke. Maybe he's seen something like this, or read about it. The bastard's been alive long enough to remember when Gutenberg first played with movable type. If it's in print, he's probably read it."

"Don't forget Renfield. He's a smart little dude," Flynn added.

"Good call. You sticking around here?"

"Yeah, I need to talk with the officer that found the bodies, get the okay from up top to take over the case from the local detective, smooth it over with those guys, all those political things that you don't have to deal with."

"Beauty of being freelance, Detective," I said, walking to the front of my car. "On the other hand, nobody's gonna reimburse me for the shoes I just ruined."

"Take it up with your rich uncle, Harker. I'll swing by later and see what you've figured out."

CHAPTER TEN

"I can't say that I've ever heard of anything quite like that, Quincy, but that also stands to reason, doesn't it? I mean, if there was something forcing people to commit horrific murder-suicides, but it went to such amazing lengths to hide its supernatural origins, then we wouldn't know it was supernatural at all. The only way we would discover these crimes is if, as happened to you, someone were to become haunted by a victim, or by sheer process of elimination." Uncle Luke sat on my couch, a snifter of brandy in his hand, lecturing to the room. I've always thought that his talents were wasted on being one of the most famous monsters in history. If it weren't for the whole sucking human blood to live thing, he'd be a hell of a college professor. He even looked the part, with leather patches on the elbows of his corduroy jacket, his dark hair curled just a touch longer than his collar, and his refined features that spoke of good breeding and blazing intellect.

"What do you mean, process of elimination?" I asked, sipping my third scotch. After the second one, the smell of blood started to ever so slowly fade from my nostrils, supplanted by the peaty oakness of a good Dalmore single malt. By the third, the sharp edges on my memories were starting to soften, and I could close my eyes without seeing every detail of the Minnie Mouse nightshirt Sandy Nettles died in, the pink fabric bunched up high on one leg, showing an expanse of toned thigh streaked with blood where she died fighting for her life and her children.

"Well, I suppose we'd have to go through every single homicide in the country and filter them out based on similar patterns in victimology, crime scene details, information about the perpetrators, and any other data points we can find," Luke said. "If we could access that kind of information, we could, theoretically, see if anything like this has every happened before. But we would need basically all the world's police departments to be networked, with the same type of cross-referencing and recording the same details. I'm afraid the task is so daunting as to be impossible."

"Eight," Renfield said from my desk across the room. Renfield took up residence at my computer almost as soon as we started talking about the murders and buried himself in the internet and the darknet. For a guy who knew about the deepest, darkest recesses of the web, he looked like a stockbroker. His light brown hair was a little disheveled, and there was an excited look behind his wire-rimmed glasses, but otherwise Renfield looked perfectly put-together in khakis, a v-neck sweater over a nice Oxford dress shirt, and loafers that I was pretty sure cost more than my car. This was a confluence of several things. First, Luke took very good care of his Renfields financially. Second, this Renfield had a bit of a shoe fetish, and lastly, I had a really shitty car.

Luke looked over at his manservant, the most recent to bear the name of "Renfield," now as much a title as an ode to my uncle's inability to remember his minion's names. "Exactly what are you talking about, dear boy? This recent trend toward *non sequitur* does not bode well for your continued employment. I understand that you humans decline at a rapid rate, but I cannot keep someone in my service once their faculties begin to fail, I'm sure you understand."

Renfield shot my uncle a withering look. "Just as I'm sure you understand that your inability to keep track of the conversation at hand has more to do with your personal deficiencies than any imagined failings on my part. There have been eight similar cases in the United States since the end of the Civil War, where nine fathers murdered their families in their beds over a period of weeks. Each instance culminated in a city-wide or regional tragedy resulting in massive loss of life. For instance, the Great Chicago Fire in 1871 came right on the end of a streak of horrific murders among the city's businessmen. Nine families were slaughtered, with the fire bringing an end to the streak. A similar streak of murders was documented in San Francisco—"

"Let me guess," I interrupted. "In 1906, right before the great quake?"

"Exactly," Renfield confirmed. "There were also similar catastrophes ending strings of mysterious family slayings in Boston in 1942 when the Coconut Grove nightclub burned; in 1913 in Dayton, Ohio, when the Great Dayton Flood killed over three hundred fifty people; and tracking through the last century and a half to the most recent, when Hurricane Katrina touched down in New Orleans, devastating the French Quarter and bringing to an end the activities of the Crescent City Ripper, as he was being called by the press."

"I never heard of that," I said.

"Neither did I, and I read the newspapers religiously," said Luke.

"But neither of you read the newspapers specifically published and targeted to the African-American community, I assume," Renfield said. Luke and I shrugged and nodded. Renfield nodded back and said, "I thought so. The Ripper never received any mainstream press coverage because he was killing African-Americans in a city with a high crime rate, so he remained largely unnoticed until Katrina hit, then he vanished."

"Let me guess," I said, "after eight families were slaughtered."

"Nine," Luke said. I looked at Renfield, who nodded. I turned a raised eyebrow back to Luke. "Nine is a holy number," he said. "It has power. Whatever is doing this is working to bring about something nasty, and it's getting better at it."

"You think it harnessed the power from the nine murders to cause these disasters? Including Katrina?"

"I don't know if there's enough blood magic in North America to create a Category 4 hurricane out of whole cloth, but there's probably enough power in a couple dozen deaths to steer one," Luke said.

"So you think whatever this is building to could be bigger than Katrina?" I asked.

"It would seem to follow," Renfield replied.

"But we're not near any oceans, and most buildings of any size have enough fire suppression to keep Mrs. O'Leary's cow out of business," I said.

"But there are fault lines running all through the Carolinas, and there is some precedent for magical events triggering seismic tremors," Luke said.

"What fault lines? Why haven't I heard about this?" I asked.

"They haven't been active in decades, but most seismologists agree the Charlotte area is long overdue for some seismic activity," Luke went on, ignoring me.

"So now we think that these murders are just building up what, psychic energy to trigger a giant earthquake?" I looked around to see if anyone was laughing. No one was. "Seriously?"

"Seriously," Renfield said. "Take a look here." He brought my laptop over to the couch where I sat across from Luke. He showed me some pictures with red and yellow circles on them, then overlaid those pictures onto a map of the Carolinas. One of the red circles was directly over Charlotte.

"I have no fucking idea what any of that means, except that it's gotta be bad," I admitted.

"Well, nephew, at the root of it, that's all you need to know. Something is killing people and is planning to use the energy from those violent and tragic deaths to trigger a giant earthquake that will wipe out the whole city and kill thousands of people."

"Fuck," I said, leaning back on the couch.

"My sentiments exactly," said Luke.

"So what do we do about it?" I asked.

"Well, you stop it, of course," Luke replied.

"Why me? Why don't you stop it?" I asked. Every once in a while I like to beat my head against the walls of the universe and rail against my destiny a bit. It never gets me anywhere, but sometimes makes me feel better for a few seconds.

This was not one of those days. Luke, of course, had an answer.

"Quincy, my dear boy, I am a legendary creature of the night, with a centuries-long tradition of striking fear into the hearts of humans everywhere. I do not save the world, I terrify it. You, on the other hand, are a white hat of almost mythic proportions. There are demon mothers in the sixth circle of Hell who use tales of your exploits to scare their children into obedience. You have saved more lives than Jonas Salk and Marie Curie combined. You are the greatest advancement of humanity since the pasteurization of milk. This, clearly, is your department."

We kept hashing around ideas, I kept hammering scotch, until finally I waved my uncle and his assistant off so I could crash for a few hours of drunken slumber. I dropped into my bed, only taking enough time to strip off my shoes and pants, and was asleep almost before my head hit the pillow. Of course, that's where the real shit started.

E mily Standish was standing at the foot of my bed when my eyes cracked open. She wasn't doing anything, just standing there with the preternatural stillness that only the dead can achieve. That's the one thing you eventually notice about dead people, how they don't move much. Even the animated ones, or the undead, like Uncle Luke. They don't have the constant motion of the living. There's no chest rising and falling with each breath. There are no twitching fingers, or tapping feet, or shifting of weight from one foot to another. There's no constant blinking, swallowing, eyes flitting from one thing to another. There's just...stillness.

I looked down at little Emily standing there, staring up at me with innocent, still eyes.

"What?" I asked, my voice soft, tongue thick with sleep.

Nothing.

"What do you want?" I sat up in bed, shaking the sleep off.

Nothing.

"Why won't you leave me alone?" My voice was louder now, sharper, echoing off the mirror above my dresser.

Nothing.

"Goddammit, what do you want?!? I'm trying, dammit, can't you see that? I don't know where to go! I don't know what to do! If you want me to do something, just fucking tell me!" I threw off the covers, surprised to find myself fully dressed.

"Help me," she said, stretching out a hand to me.

I couldn't resist, I stepped forward and took her hand. The room spun around us, twirled into a vortex of streaks and dashes of light twisting, whirling and spinning us until it stopped so abruptly that I almost fell over.

We were back in the church, but this time I was wearing Darin Standish's body. I remembered the polo shirt, remembered thinking how much I hate polo shirts and most people that wear them. But here I was, kneeling beside Annie Standish at the communion rail, bowing my head, then lifting it and opening my mouth as the priest put the wafer on my tongue.

The wafer dissolved as the priest spoke over my head, but instead of the normal Latin or English blessing, the priest began to chant in Ancient Enochian, the language of the angels. I've heard it before, most recently from Glory, but something about this was different. There was a power to these verses that was like nothing I'd ever heard or felt. Each word battered my eardrums and made the room spin. It was like Enochian, but as spoken by God himself, and nothing my mortal mind was capable of processing.

"OLSON FVORSGGO HOIAD BALTON SHCALZON PHOSOBRA
ZOLRORITAN AZPSAD GRAATAMAL
HOLQ NOTHO AZIMZOD COMMAHT ANOBLO ZIENSO
THILGNON GEALD IDSBOBOLEH GRAMCASARM"

I clapped my hands over my ears and clenching my teeth to keep the screams in. My stomach did a couple of rolling flips while my eyes teared up from the sensory overload. As quickly as it began, it was over, and I looked back up at the face of the priest. Except there was no face, just a cowled form standing over me with a brilliant white glow from where his face should have been.

The cowled not-priest reached down for me and pulled me up by my shoulders until I was at eye level. The glow coming from within his/its cowl grew until I had to shut my eyes against the brightness, but still the light hammered my lids with a relentless pounding. The priest leaned in close and put his not-face next to my ear, then whispered to me in Enochian, only this time I could understand it perfectly.

"Prepare thyself and thy world for the coming of my children,
For they come to usher in a new dawn.
They shall bring the light to the darkness,
They shall bring the fire to the water,
They shall bring salvation to the defiled,
They shall bring law to the evildoer,
They shall bring order to the chaos.
Prepare thyself, for the door is opening,
And there shall be no return to that which was before."

The priest-thing released my shoulders and I dropped back to my knees at the communion rail. I lifted my head, and I was back in the Standish house, kneeling on the blood-soaked carpet in an empty room. I turned, and little Emily stood in the door staring at the bed where she died.

"I know, sweetie, it can't be easy coming back here. I'm trying to figure out what happened to you, so I can make it right."

She shook her head.

"What, you don't want me to figure it out?"

She shook her head again.

"You do want me to figure it out?

She nodded.

Realization hit me. "You don't want me to try to make it right."

She nodded. "You just want me to stop whatever's coming?"

Another nod.

"Is it going to be an earthquake?"

Nothing.

"A fire?"

Nothing.

"You don't know?"

Nod.

"If we don't know what it is, how am I supposed to stop it?" I asked, feeling my frustration grow.

Nothing. I was never good with kids. Dead or alive. "Is there something here?" I asked.

She nodded, so I turned my attention to the room. It looked just like it had when I was first there, peaceful except for the incredible amount of blood.

There were still little evidence markers lying around the floor where my subconscious had logged every piece of evidence, but my dream-brain had cleaned them up.

But wait, if I was dreaming, then I could bring all that evidence back, *in situ* as it were. I closed my eyes and focused my mind on restoring the crime scene to *exactly* how it had been in real life.

There it was. Lying under the bed, mostly hidden by the puddle of gore and the frilly dust ruffle. I dropped to floor level, ignoring the blood soaking through my pants, and reached out for it. I pulled it back into the light, then sat back on my haunches to examine it. It was identical to the one I'd found on James Nettles' dresser, except this medallion was dedicated to Saint Christopher, patron saint of travelers. But everything else was the same—the same glass beads, identical crucifix, and the same nasty spells bound to it.

"This is what I was supposed find, isn't it?" I turned on one knee to look back at little Emily Standish, but my perspective did that *shift* thing again, and I wasn't looking at Emily from the foot of the bed, I was standing in the doorway of the bedroom, and her father was standing by her bed, a huge kitchen knife in hand.

"No!" I shouted, and charged the room, but ran into a wall of invisible force. Darin Standish looked up at me, and his eyes were bright with glee. He knew what was coming, and he knew exactly how much he was going to enjoy it. I pounded on the barrier, but couldn't break through. A tiny part of me still knew I was dreaming, but the rest of me didn't care as Standish pulled his daughter up into a sitting position in bed, then nestled in behind her like he was giving her a hug. His glittering eyes never left mine as he dragged the blade across her throat, cutting almost all the way to the spine. I drew back all my strength to attack the barrier, focused my will to level it with a spell centered on my fist—

And woke up on the floor of my bedroom, with my fist encased in Glory's right hand.

"Quincy, STOP!" the angel bellowed, and she put the power of The Word behind it. I froze, hand in mid-punch, and felt all the power, rage and terror drain out of me as my eyes caught sight of the crumpled Rebecca Flynn lying against the far wall, knocked out cold with a trickle of blood coming from one ear.

CHAPTER ELEVEN

"**B**ecks!" I yelled, and ran across the room to her side. Well, in the movie in my mind, that's what happened. What really happened was, I yelled her name and tried to run to her side and I sprawled across the carpet in my bedroom because I was lying on the floor tangled in my sheet. Then I realized that I was butt-naked, again, so I pulled the sheet around my midsection and eventually made it to Flynn's side.

"Becks," I said, shaking her shoulder, trying to rouse her without doing any further damage. I turned back to Glory. "Is she all right?"

Glory closed her eyes for a second, then opened them again. "She's fine. Not even concussed, which is surprising given how hard you threw her against the wall."

I gaped at her. "Wait, what? I did this?"

"Do you see anyone else here, Q? I'm an angel, I don't kick human's asses unless they really deserve it. Like murderers, televangelists, or you, almost every day."

I shook Flynn's shoulder again, then sent a tendril of thought out to her. *Flynn, you in there?*

Fuck, my head hurts. What did you hit me with?

Yeah, sorry about that. I was having a nightmare.

I know.

"You know?" I was so surprised I spoke out loud.

"No screaming," Flynn groaned. Her eyes fluttered open, and she immediately raised a hand to cover them from the light.

"*Obscures*," I said, and gestured toward the ceiling light. It popped and the room fell into darkness. I heard broken glass tinkle against the inside of the light fixture.

"Oops," I said. "I'll get that later. Rebecca, are you okay?" I turned back to my partner/police liaison, who was trying to pull herself into more of a sitting position against the wall, with little effect.

"You wanna sit up?" I asked. She nodded and I got up on my knees. I leaned forward, put my hands under her armpits, and lifted her into a sitting position.

"Better?" I asked.

Flynn nodded, then giggled a little.

"What?" I asked.

She pointedly looked down, then raised her eyebrows. "We've got to stop meeting like this. People will talk," she said with a little laugh.

"Don't worry, the secret of your torrid affair is safe with me," Glory said. "But really, Q, put that thing away before you put someone's eye out."

"Leave me alone, angel. I've gotta piss. Something you wouldn't know anything about, existing on rainbows and good wishes like you do." I stood up, holding the sheet around my waist, and walked back to my dresser. I pulled out clean underwear and picked up the jeans I wore the day before off the floor.

"You okay for a second, Becks?" I asked.

"Yeah, do what you gotta do." She waved me off from the floor.

. I nodded and walked into he bathroom, leaving the sheet at the door. I took care of business, then washed my hands and face. I stared into the mirror for a long moment, looking deep into my own eyes.

What the fuck are you doing, Harker? I asked myself. I worked hard to keep my thoughts on lockdown, what with my connection to Flynn being enhanced by proximity. *You know you can't touch her. She's human, and that never ends well for anyone. Luke would kill you just so you wouldn't go through it again. And God himself only knows what Glory would have to say about it.* I stood there a minute longer, until I felt like I had control of my emotions, then I pulled on my boxers and jeans and stepped out into my bedroom.

Glory and Flynn were sitting on the end of the bed, Glory holding a glass of water and patting Flynn on the back. I walked into the room and leaned against my dresser.

"Good morning, Detective Flynn, so nice of you to stop by," I said. "Again."

She looked up at me and gave me a little wave. "Hi."

"We've got to stop meeting like this," I said.

"No shit, Sherlock," Flynn replied.

"No, Rebecca, I'm serious," I said. "This is twice you've come into my apartment uninvited, and twice that it's almost gotten you killed. I don't know how you missed it, but I have the ability to toss around pretty heavy amounts of magic, and all my dreams are awful, especially lately, since this little brat won't stay out of my goddamn head!" I pointed to the corner of the room, where Emily Standish stood watching the proceedings in silence.

"Harker, I'm sorry." Flynn looked up at me and I could see her eyes were rimmed with red. "But I know exactly how bad your dreams are, because *they keep waking me up*. Every fucking night, I've got to meander through my own dreams, never knowing when I'm going to get plucked out of my subconscious and dropped into the middle of yours. And you're right—your head is a fucked up place that I would avoid walking through if I could. But I can't. I have no more control over this shit than I do the weather. So you might as well give me a key because if I wake up one more time from that goddamn Standish house, I'm coming straight over here and yanking you out of your dream. And start sleeping in boxers, for Christ's sake. I'm tired of looking at your johnson."

I stood there staring for a minute, then turned, pulled open the top drawer of my dresser, and grabbed a key ring. I tossed the ring to Flynn, who caught it on the fly, then just stared at it.

"What is this?"

"I'll never understand women," I said. "You asked for keys. Here's a set of keys. But pay attention to the key ring."

"What's the deal?" Flynn asked, holding up the key ring. It looked for all the world like just a ring with a pink stone hanging from a chain. Which technically, it was. It was also a little more.

"That's rose quartz," I said. "That particular crystal is tuned to my magic. When you go to unlock the door, touch the crystal to the knob first. It'll disarm any wards I might have in place, and give you a sense if I'm in the middle of a casting or a summoning. The crystal will take on different colors depending on what's going on in here. White, blue, green, pink, yellow, purple —those are all fine. You can come in and nothing will blow up. If the stone glows red, be very careful. There's something going on that could be dangerous. If the stone turns black, then you have a decision to make."

"What's that?" Flynn asked.

"Whether or not what's outside with you will kill you, or destroy a significant portion of the free world. Because whatever's going on behind the door certainly might," I said.

"This is not the kind of romantic passing over of the key that I've had with guys before," Flynn quipped.

"I'm still half-naked. If you'd feel more comfortable doing this after wild monkey sex, I'm sure I could oblige," I said, probably a lot less than half-joking.

Flynn blushed to the roots of her hair, and Glory covered her mouth to hide her laughter, albeit poorly. "I think I'll pass," Flynn said, then reached for the water Glory was holding and downed the rest of the glass.

"So now what?" Flynn asked after she had her more prurient instincts under control. Or maybe they were instincts toward uncontrolled laughter. I sometimes have a hard time with modern humans.

"Now I need Darin Standish's rosary. It was found under the foot of his bed." Flynn's eyes widened, then she nodded as she remembered the dream.

"I can get it. What do we need it for?"

"I want to confirm that it's the same magic that's on the one I took from the Nettles house."

"Sounds like a—wait, you took evidence from a crime scene?" Flynn's voice went up a full octave as she realized what I said.

"That's my cue," Glory said, then vanished.

"It's not like there will ever be a trial, Becks," I said. "Remember, the killer was also the last victim? And whatever we find out about who killed these people, we'll never go after it in a court of law. So yeah, I grabbed Jim Nettles' rosary. Now I need to compare it to Darin Standish's so I can confirm the two murders are connected. Then I need to go see a man about saving a soul."

"Whose soul are you saving, Q?

"My own, maybe," I said. "Now go get me the rosary while I take a shower and get cleaned up."

"You have no idea what time it is, do you?" Flynn asked.

"Remember, Becky-lass, we old farts need lot less sleep than you young whippersnappers."

"Well this young whippersnapper isn't going into the office at four in the morning just so you can hocus pocus over a dead man's rosary. It's going to have to wait until morning. I'm going home, and I'm going to get a few more hours sleep. Then I'll bring you the rosary."

"Wanna crash here?" I asked, pointing toward the bed. "I know, it looks like a bomb went off in here, but I changed the sheets like two days ago."

"All that talk, and now you're trying to get me into bed," Flynn said with a tease in her voice.

"Don't worry, Becks, your virtue will be intact. I'm not sleeping. I've got some translating to do from this dream. But if you want to grab couple hours without driving home—"

Flynn was already barefoot, having kicked off her shoes the second I made the suggestion. "Done, Q. And thanks," she said, pulling her sweater off over her head and moving her hands to the waistband of her pants.

"Now shoo," she made waving motions at me, so I grabbed a clean shirt, socks and boots, and went into the living room. I fired up the computer, started searching out Enochian texts, and tried very hard not to think about the gorgeous police detective lying in my bed not thirty feet away.

CHAPTER TWELVE

I waited about forty-five minutes to make sure Flynn was completely out, then I put on my boots and grabbed my car keys off the table by the door. I closed the door silently behind me and pressed my thumb to the center of the knob, activating my "away" spells. Anything with even a touch of ill intent would get a nasty surprise if it tried to get through that door.

"Where do you think you're going?" the voice behind me asked.

I turned and saw Glory in my hallway, leaning against a wall.

"You should do your cone of silence thing," I said. "Unless, of course, you want all my neighbors to hear us fight."

"What are we going to fight about, Q?" Glory asked.

"About me going to wake up the priest at Our Lady and ask some difficult questions about his recently deceased parishioners," I replied.

"We're not going to fight about that," Glory said.

"Oh, why not?"

"Because you're not going," the angel said flatly.

"Remember that whole thing about going where angels fear to tread?" I asked. "Well, that's kind of my life's motto, Glory. Whenever there's something too dirty or scary or morally ambiguous for you and your lot to figure out, Harker takes care of it. Demon summoned to Earth got loose and now threatens all of creation? We can't touch it, because a human summoned it, and humans have free will. But Harker can take care of it. Lion of Judah smoked too much ganja and let it slip that he's the key to bringing about the Apocalypse? There's that pesky free will again, better call Harker.

"You see, Glory, I know exactly the limitations of what you and yours can do, because I've been the one pushing your boundaries for almost a century. And I know that you and your harp-playing bosses don't want me to talk to the priest at Our Lady, so that's exactly what I'm going to do.

"Because no matter how much your pals upstairs might want this all swept under some supernatural rug, I made a promise. I made a promise to a little girl who died wondering why her daddy hurt her. And I'm going to keep that promise, no matter what. So you can lead, follow, or get out of the way because I'm going to go see a man about a murder."

"You know I could stop you," Glory said, the sadness writ large on her face.

"I know you can try," I shot back.

"Q, please stop this before it goes too far."

"Too far? Eight people are *dead*, Glory. How much further do you want it to go? Do you want me to wait until whoever's sucking up the magical energy of human agony and death releases it into a giant earthquake or fire or whatever? You want me to wait until the body count gets high enough for you? No dice, Glory. I'm going to go talk to this priest. And I'm either going to get some answers, or I'm going to figure out the rest of the questions."

"And there's nothing I can do change your mind?" Glory asked.

"Outside of actually fight me, no," I said.

"Fine," she said, and stepped aside to leave me a clear path to the elevator. "Just be careful. I almost like you, Harker. I'd hate to have to watch you go to Hell." Nice, my guardian angel thinks I'm going to Hell if I die. That's reassuring.

H alf an hour later, I pulled into the parking lot of Our Lady of Eternal Comfort Catholic Church. It was still pitch dark, so I was more than a little surprised when the first door I tugged on was open. I walked through the side door right into the sanctuary, just before the altar. There were a few lights on, but not many. A silence hung heavy over the church, almost anticipatory in nature, like something I felt in London right before a bombing run was coming during the blitz. The energy was anything but peaceful, and I rubbed my arms in a vain attempt to lay the hairs down.

I caught a flicker of movement out of the corner of my eye and turned to see a man's back duck into a small room at the back of the church. I saw a small green light come on over the door and realized the priest had entered the confessional. *Perfect.*

I made my way to the back of the room, stopping before the priest's compartment. I touched the wooden door, making contact with the door and frame at the same time. I gathered my will and whispered "*combino.*" The wood blended together along the crack, effectively sealing the door. I was pretty sure I could let him out when I was finished.

I opened the door and let myself into the other compartment of the confessional and sat down. I looked at the low, padded rail, then thought better of it. Kneeling has never been one of my things, and I didn't feel like I was starting today.

"Welcome, my son. What is troubling you tonight?" The priest's voice through the grille was soothing, warm and compassionate. It didn't sound anything like the bellowed Enochian from my dream, but who knew what evil lurks in the hearts of men, right?

"How did you know I came for confession?" I asked.

"It's 5AM, son. There are only three reasons someone comes into a church before dawn. They're looking for a place to sleep, they're looking for something to steal, or they've got something to confess. You're too well-dressed to be homeless, so I'm choosing to err on the side of virtue over larceny."

I gave a little chuckle. "Well, you're right, padre. I'm not here to crash, and I'm not here to steal. I'm here looking for answers."

"Many come through our doors seeking answers. I have hope that I can provide you with what you seek."

Man, this guy was good. He had the whole sincerity thing down cold. "I hope so too, Father."

"What can I do for you, my son?" He asked.

I focused my attention on the face past the grate and said "I need to know what happened the Standish and Nettles families." The priest's head snapped up and I saw his eyes go wide through the mesh screen.

"I'm sorry?" he said, as though he were having trouble hearing me.

"I said, I need to know what happened to the Standishes and the Nettles. You remember them, right?" I growled through the screen. "Parishioners here, brutally murdered this week, father killed his wife and children then opened up every vein he could reach? Am I ringing any bells here?"

The priest turned and jiggled the handle a little, ready to leave. Unfortunately for him, there wasn't really a door anymore.

"Yeah, that's not gonna work," I said.

"What did you do?" he asked.

"I might have fused the wood together at the doorjamb. I'll let you out when I'm done with my questions. Now, what do you know about what killed these families?" I asked.

"Nothing," the priest replied. "I just heard about Annie and her family this morning, and then for the same thing to happen to Jim and Sandy...well, it's terrible. I can't understand why anyone would want to hurt them. They are both lovely families, well-liked within the church, and…" He looked up at me, and his eyes narrowed. "Are you with the media? I will not have these families turned into some kind of spectacle just for your ratings or sales numbers."

I liked this guy. If my dreams weren't pointing toward him as a mass murderer and perhaps the vessel for the destruction of my entire city, he seemed like somebody I could drink a beer with. But everything I'd seen showed him up to his eyeballs in this shitpile, so I had to stay on him.

"I'm not with the media. I'm with the police." Not exactly true, but I've been lying to priests since my first confession somewhere along about the time electric light bulbs were starting to catch on. I pressed my badge to screen, then took it down before he got a good look at it. *No need to waste time explaining exactly what the Department of Homeland Security's Paranormal Division was*, I thought. "I know you knew the families. I know they were members here. What else can you tell me about them?"

"Nothing," he said, and his voice shook with emotion. "They were all members, yes. The children were active in Sunday School and Vacation Bible School in the summer. Jim Nettles played on the church softball team. Annie Standish volunteered with our annual coat drive in the winter. Darin Standish, I didn't know him as well, but he came to services once or twice a month, and was always friendly. There's no reason for anyone to want to harm these people."

Except you, or whatever's living in your skin, I thought. "Padre," I said, letting a little menace creep into my eyes. "I know there's something going on with you and these families. The only point of convergence is right here at your pulpit. So think about it. What is it that got these people killed? What happened here last Sunday?" I opened my Sight to watch his aura while he replied. It glowed with a steady yellow light, purity tinged with blue for a protector. This was a man who genuinely cared about his flock. So why did he cast a spell in an ancient magical language to make Darin Standish and Jim Nettles murder their families?

"Nothing happened, I swear it! Sunday was a perfectly normal Mass. The Nettles family were all at the morning Mass, and the Standishes attended the later service. Carey was very excited; he was going to see his first Panthers game with his father that afternoon. I told him I hoped he got a football." He did, too. The ball I found in his bed was an official NFL ball, one of the ones Cam Newton, the Panthers quarterback, gave to kids in the stands after he scored a touchdown.

I heard a choked sob from the screen. "Why would someone do this, Detective? Who *does* this to a family? To children?" The only change in his aura was a tinge of red with his anger. No black, no gray, no nasty greens and browns that indicated guilt, or possession, or lies. He was the real deal, a pastor genuinely upset at losing members of his flock.

"I don't know, Father," I said, reaching up and touching the screen where his hand was pressed. I felt nothing, not even a tingle of malicious magic. This man was as holy and God-touched as anything I'd ever encountered. It didn't make any sense.

"I don't know," I repeated, "but I'm damn sure going to find out." I opened the door and stepped out, touched the other door and released my spell, then scanned the sanctuary, reaching deep with my Sight to find something, anything that could point me in the direction of whatever was turning God-fearing, football-loving Catholics into some of the worst butchers of humanity I'd ever seen.

I walked the sanctuary for several minutes while the priest cried and prayed in the confessional. The whole time I paced the room, I scanned it for some demonic taint, some evidence of dark magic. There was nothing. Not even a mischievous pixie or a disgruntled brownie upset by the cleaning crew. It was the most blessed building I'd seen in years, and that made it all the more perplexing. Because something in this church was turning men's hands against their own families, and I couldn't for the life of me figure out what it was.

Then my phone rang, and I was forcibly reminded that it wasn't my life at risk.

CHAPTER THIRTEEN

"This better be a real emergency," I said into the phone. "Like the Krispy Kreme on Sharon Amity is out of glazed doughnuts, or something equally important."

"Where are you?" Flynn's voice was heavy with sleep.

"I went to church," I replied.

"Did anything burst into flames?" Even sleepy, she was still a smartass.

"Both my ass and the building are still intact. As a matter of fact, as holy places go, it might be the most sanctified place I've ever set foot. I'm pretty certain that I'm the most unholy thing to set foot in the church in weeks."

"Well, something there has been doing a number on people, because we have another dead family, this one right off Wendover, not three miles from the church."

"Goddammit," I muttered. "I was literally *just* inside the place, for the last hour and change. There is no way anyone there did anything magical, black or otherwise, within the last month. It's cleaner than the friggin' Vatican," I said. Admittedly, there's a *lot* of magic thrown around the Vatican on any given Sunday, so maybe that wasn't the best analogy, but Flynn understood where I was coming from.

"I'm on my way to the new crime scene. I'll text you the address."

"I'll see you there," I said, then slid my finger across the screen, ending the call. The text from Flynn came in moments later. I dropped the address into my GPS app and found the house, less than five minutes away. I opened my car door and slid behind the wheel, preparing to go walk through my third incredibly violent crime scene in as many days.

After a few seconds, I put my head against the steering wheel and closed my eyes. Visions of the Standish and Nettles homes flashed before my eyes: pictures of abandoned kids' rooms, mothers with their throats cut so deeply they were almost decapitated, dead fathers sitting on their bedroom floors staring at the carnage they had wrought.

"Fuck that noise," I said to myself, and cranked the car. I pulled out into traffic away from the crime scene. It was time to start getting to the bottom of this shit, one way or another. And it looked like it was definitely going to be "another."

A quick Google search on my phone showed me that Danvar the Magnificent was playing at The Laugh Laboratory, a comedy club styled after a mad scientist's lab located in the NC Music Factory, a renovated mill turned into a set of nightclubs, restaurants, and party zones. I expected the place to be pretty much deserted at dawn, and I wasn't disappointed. The parking lot was empty except for a couple of pickup trucks with Super Clean Party Clean-Up logos on the side, and a green Mini Cooper with a scruffy looking dude asleep behind the wheel. I thought about rousing the sleeping beauty and sending him home, but if he was drunk enough that he shouldn't drive, but smart enough to actually *not* drive, I figured I was doing the world a favor by letting him sleep it off.

I looked around, saw no sign of the cleaning crew, and walked around to the back door of the Laugh Lab. It was locked, of course, but that didn't matter to me. I thought about picking the lock, just to make sure I still could, then decided that kneeling in front of a doorknob in broad daylight was exactly how I never wanted to start a conversation with a nervous cop or security doofus.

I pressed my hand to the deadbolt and whispered *"recludo."* I felt the tumblers click into place through my fingertips and turned the knob easily. The door whispered open, and I ducked through into the (hopefully) deserted club.

For once, things went my way and the club was empty. I navigated a maze of tables and chairs, meandering through to the dressing room off the side of the stage. Behind a thin black curtain was a short hallway with two doors on one side and one at the end. The first door had a simple piece of white tape on the door reading "Opener." The second door said "Employees Only," and the door at the end of the hall had an honest to God gold glittery star on the door above a small printed piece of paper that read DANVAR THE MAGNIF. I guess they ran out of room on the page to make truly magnificent.

I tried the dressing room door, but it was also locked. A quick spell, and I was inside. The dressing room was spacious, way more room than one assistant-raping magician needed. A makeup counter with lights surrounding the mirrors dominated one wall, covered in flowers in vases and bouquets just lying around. A long couch sat under a series of photos of famous comedians and magicians on the opposite wall, and a small fridge with a microwave on top sat next to the door. A small door marked "restroom" stood closed at the back of the room, but it was on the makeup counter where I found what I needed.

"Here we go," I said, opening the makeup kit. I pawed though the various concealers, blushes, and creams until I found what I was looking for—a small black plastic comb. I plucked a few hairs from the comb and sat down cross-legged in the floor.

From my pockets I pulled out a selection of spell components and set them on the floor in front of me. Four candles for the four points of the compass, check. Knife, check. Chalk, check. Matches, check. String, check. I drew a hasty circle around myself, then placed the candles at the cardinal compass points. I lit each candle in turn—North, East, South, West—for positive spell casting. If I were casting a spell intended to harm, I would have drawn the circle widdershins and invoked the candles backwards, but this was a simple finding spell, nothing dark about it, except my intentions for Danvar once I found him.

I plucked a few hairs from the comb and set them on the floor in front of me. I drew my knife and cut my thumb, squeezing a few drops of my blood onto the hairs, then placed the blade of the knife across the hairs. I focused my will on the blade, blood and hairs, muttered "*contineo*," and released my will onto the knife. It blazed with white light, then flickered to darkness. I picked the knife up and stood up, slowly turning inside my circle. As the point of the knife neared the northern compass point, it began to glow, brightening as it zeroed in on a direction. I continued to turn, slowly rotating past the direction the knife indicated I should go. As I got further away from pointing north, the glow faded more and more until it was dark. I turned in the other direction, reversing course, and as I neared north, the blade shone once again, confirming the spell worked.

I reached out with a foot and scrubbed out the edge of my circle, feeling an inrush of energy as the protections dissipated. I flicked my fingers, and the candles went out, snuffed by my will. North. Danvar was somewhere to the north of me. Didn't make sense, all the decent hotels were to the southeast, in downtown. Unless Danvar purposefully didn't stay in decent hotels.

Decent hotels mean decent security, and means that people aren't used to hearing screams from the rooms next door. But north, north led to the University, which was also pretty clean-cut. Then it came to me—Sugar Creek. There were a lot of cheap hotels near the intersection of Sugar Creek Road and I-85, and a lot of them weren't the type of place to report the occasional loud noise in the middle of the night.

I left the Laugh Lab the way I came, equally unnoticed, and got back in my car. The guy sleeping in his Mini was gone, and I pulled out of the Music Factory without seeing another soul. I turned left onto Tyron, heading north to Sugar Creek with a dagger blazing merrily away on the passenger seat.

My gut was right. The dagger kept glowing like a firebrand as I turned left onto Sugar Creek, then cruised into the parking lot of the Imperial Extended Stay Motel right beside the interstate. The parking lot was mostly deserted, with the construction workers that took up most of the rooms in the hotel out on job sites. I pulled into a parking spot beside a banana yellow Cadillac with New Jersey vanity plates that read MAGICMN.

The dagger kept glowing as I pointed it toward the door, so I figured my intuition and magic had led me to the right place. I dispelled the location charm with a wave of my hand and a pinch of salt from a McDonald's bag crumpled up in the floorboards behind my passenger seat. The spell was effective, but there aren't very many times when you really want to be carrying around a knife that glows like a roman candle.

I stepped out of the car and leaned on the bumper of the Cadillac. A moment's concentration and I whispered *"aqua,"* sending my energy into the gas tank of the car. With no other magical changes to the car, it wasn't going to run very well with a tankful of clean water. Danvar's getaway handled, I stepped up to what I thought was his door and kicked it in.

Sometimes I forget my own strength and the shoddy nature of modern construction. The door didn't just open, it flew off the hinges and slammed into the TV sitting on the end of the dresser. The TV toppled forward and shattered on the floor, and I heard another thump and a muffled shriek as a body hit the floor.

I stepped through the door and looked around. Danvar the Magnificent was lying on his back on the floor between the bed and the wall. In front of him was the ubiquitous cheap hotel round table covered with playing cards, an empty Wild Turkey bottle, a single overturned yellow plastic cup, and a huge glass bong with a naked mermaid on the front with the carburetor protruding from her legs.

Danvar was a remarkable sight, the finest example of not wanting to see behind the curtain that I'd ever encountered without demonic involvement. He lay flat on his back, turtled in a cheap hotel chair that had apparently gone over with him in it when I kicked the door in. His skinny legs stuck out of his white striped boxers, and his arms flailed the air unconstrained by anything more than a yellowed wife beater. He looks to be at least seventy, gaunt to the point of being skeletal, with a lush white goatee his only visible hair anywhere.

"What the fuck?" Danvar bellowed from the floor.

A skinny woman in nothing but black lace panties stood up from the floor on the far side of the room. I quickly surmised that she was the cause of the thump and squeal I heard when I "opened" the door. She looked to be about twenty-five, with brown hair and a birthmark just to the left of her bellybutton. I figured she was the new "assistant."

"You want to leave," I said to her.

"I can't leave my master," she replied, casting a loving glance in Danvar's direction.

"Can you at least go lock yourself in the bathroom until the crashing and cursing stops?" I asked. She nodded and did just that.

"Who the fuck do you think you are, shitbait?" Danvar asked me, coming to his feet and getting untangled from the chair and table.

"You're Danvar the Magnificent, right?" I asked, focusing my will around my right hand.

"Yeah, I'm Danvar. And I believe I asked you who the fuck you are."

"I'm Quincy Harker, motherfucker, and this is my town. Maybe you've heard of me?"

"Nope," he said, diving onto the bed, his hand darting under the pillows and coming out with a small black revolver.

He squeezed the trigger, but I was ready. I held up my hand and shouted, "*Perfringo!*" The magic enveloped the handgun, and it blew up. That did a number of bad things to Danvar, including blowing his fingers off. One whizzed by my ear, splattering bloody mist all over the right side of my face. One blew backward and smacked Danvar in the forehead, and I think the rest were reduced to tiny pieces by the explosion.

Danvar collapsed onto the bed, howling and clutching his wrist. He held up the damaged stump and shrieked at me. "What the fuck? What the fucking fuck?"

While I admired his devotion to the f-word, I quickly grew tired of hearing him scream, so I stepped forward and punched him in the jaw, really hard. His eyes rolled back in his head and he flopped back onto the bed, out cold. I looked around the room, and it was pretty well destroyed. The door was bent at almost forty-five degrees and was laying in the closet. The table and chairs were overturned, and they were the least damaged things in the room. The TV was crushed into the carpet, and the room's occupant was bleeding all over the comforter. All in all, a good start to my visit.

CHAPTER FOURTEEN

Danvar the Magnificent woke up in his boxers and wife beater, tied to a chair in a cheap motel with his own belt and neckties, with a towel duct-taped to this wrist to staunch the bleeding from his missing right hand. It was not his best morning ever. Then there was the matter of the wizard sitting on one of the beds in his motel room juggling balls of fire.

Danvar's eyelids fluttered open, and he shook his head to clear it. He let out a groan, then tried to move his right hand. His eyes flashed wide open then, and his mouth opened to let out a scream.

"Don't do it," I said, flicking a fireball at his face. It stopped three inches from his nose and exploded, showering the scrawny magician with little licks of flame. He let out a little shriek and tried to move away, but his ankles and wrist were secured, so he was going a whole lot of nowhere, and fast.

He looked over at his latest victim, who sat on the bed filing her nails and watching the whole proceeding with the kind of detached disinterest that is only found in the deeply unconcerned or the tragically damaged. I'd looked in her eyes, and she definitely fell into the second category.

"Amelia, untie me," Danvar demanded.

I laughed, and the little bastard's attention locked back onto me. "What's funny, you little illusionist? She is my assistant, and she will never sit by and let you torment me so."

"First off, jackass, I'm about as real as it gets, so don't even think that any of this is illusion. Secondly, her name is Amanda, you rotted prick. And third, she's totally saved you already. Who do you think cauterized your stump so you wouldn't bleed to death?" Danvar's eyes went back to his right arm, so I flicked out my fingers and severed the rope holding that hand down.

He held up his handless arm and gaped at me. "What kind of monster are you?" he asked.

"I don't really know. I might even be human. But here's what I do know. You're a magic-wielding assclown who kidnaps women and brainwashes them into being your sex slaves and assistants, then when you get tired of them, you wipe their brains and dump them wherever it's convenient. Somewhere along the way you pissed off a demon named Mort, who hired me to kill you in exchange for information I need."

Most of the time when someone's lost a lot of blood, like a hand, they get a little pale. The level of pale Danvar hit when I mentioned Mort was far beyond blood loss. I'd blown off his hand, tied him to a chair, and as much as told him I was going to torture and kill him. But one mention of the little demon club owner, and the Magnificent One was shitting in his boxers.

"I don't know what you're talking about," Danvar stammered.

"Don't bother lying to me, Danvar. What's your real name, by the way? I feel stupid calling you by your lame-ass stage name."

"Rupert," Amanda said from the bed. "I looked in his wallet once while he was sleeping. He never told me, just made me call him Master, or Magnificent, or SuperCock." Every word out of her mouth was just tossed out there with no inflection, like she was reading from a teleprompter, or like the computer voice in a cell phone.

"SuperCock?" I looked at Danvar. "Everything I learn about you makes me hate you a little more. Look, I'm not an assassin. I've killed plenty of people in my time, but I don't make a habit of doing favors for demons, and I usually only kill people who are actively trying to kill me. So let's make a deal—you tell me everything you know about what's happening at Our Lady of Comfort Catholic Church, and I won't kill you."

"You'll let me go?" SuperCock asked, and by the light in his eyes, I knew he didn't understand exactly what that would entail.

"Oh sure," I said. "I'll let you go. I'll cut off all access to magic, and I'll probably make you impotent just out of some twisted sense of justice, but I'll let you go."

"Fuck yourself," he grumbled.

"Biologically impossible," I replied. "I'm gifted, but not in that level of either endowment or flexibility. So do want to tell me about the church, or do you want me to just shoot you?" I drew my Glock and leveled it at his forehead.

"Wait! Stop! Don't shoot! There are people who will miss me. Powerful people." His eyes narrowed. "I can put you in touch with them. Maybe they know something about your church."

I looked at him. Really looked him over. He was giving off all the normal signs of being terrified, but none of the standard tells people give off when they lie. "How do I get in touch with these people?"

"In my phone," Rupert said. I grabbed the phone and opened up the contacts browser.

"You really should lock your phone. I mean, anybody can access your personal information this way," I said. "Who am I looking for?"

"I don't know his real name, but he's in there under Smith. That's the name he goes by here."

My stomach sinking, I scrolled through the numbers until I got to the name Smith. Sure enough, the number was familiar. *Fuck.* I pressed SEND and then switched the phone to speaker.

Smith's gruff voice filled the room after the first ring. "What do you want, Rupert? I told you that we'd contact you when we needed you to move again. For now, just work on getting back in Mort's good graces and stay the fuck out of sight. The guy that's looking for you is the real deal, and he will kill your worthless ass if he catches up to you. I'm trying to talk him down, but he's a stubborn fuck. So what do you want?"

"Hi Smitty, stubborn fuck here," I said.

"Goddammit, Harker," Smith said. "Do not do anything stupid. I need that fucker to get close to—"

"I don't care, Smitty. He doesn't know shit that can help me, you don't know shit that can help me, my fucking *angel* can't tell me anything that will help me, so the only thing I can do is go to Mort, tell him I killed this sorry motherfucker, and see what he knows."

"Harker, I am *ordering* you—"

"The fuck you are," I said. "The list of people I've taken orders from in this lifetime is pretty short, and your name is nowhere on it. But don't worry, I'm not going to kill your precious rapist informant, Smitty. I'm gonna take the pieces of his hand I blew off back to Mort and hope he buys that as proof that I killed SuperCock here."

"SuperCock?" Smith said, and I shook my head.

"Long story involving his latest victim, who's at this location and is going to need a lot of fucking therapy before she can—Goddammit! Fuck!" I swore loudly at the gout of blood that squirted across the phone's screen. I looked up and Amanda was kneeling on the bed, right behind Danvar, with her nail file buried to the hilt in his eyeball.

"Never mind, Smitty," I said. "You traced this call, right?"

"Yeah, I'm about three minutes away. I've got a breach team and an ambulance with me."

"You'd better call a meat wagon, too. Our victim just opened Danvar's carotid artery with a nail file, then stabbed him in the dick a couple times before burying her cosmetic implement in the magician's eyeball."

"Fuck," Smith's voice was a little awed.

"Yeah," I said. "Impressed me, too. But look on the bright side, I don't have to lie to Mort about Danvar being dead." I turned my attention back to Amanda. "No, sweetie, you probably should just leave the nail file in his eye now."

She looked back at me, confusion all over her face. "But I broke a nail when I stabbed him. How am I supposed to take care of that?"

I turned back to the phone. "Drive faster, Smitty."

T wo minutes later the parking lot was full of black SUVs and flashing lights. Smith stormed into the room, his flat-top quivering with rage.

I stood up as he walked in. "Smitty, I'm sorry," I said. "I really had decided not to kill him, but I guess hearing that set Amanda off, and she—"

Smith nailed me right under my jaw on the left side of my face with a right cross that landed hard enough to slam my mouth shut and drop me straight backward on my ass. I sat there for a second looking up at my assailant, who was also kinda my boss, then I got to my feet.

Smith stood there breathing hard, his nostrils flared and his heart beating fast enough for me to hear it without enhanced senses. He didn't speak, just clenched his jaw and fists and squared up for a fight. I took a deep breath and looked down into his face. I could almost see the lightning in his storm-gray eyes.

"That's your one," I said. "I figure every friendship, or business relationship, or partnership, or whatever we are, gets one shot at the other. One punch, with good reason, and you've got one get out of an ass-kicking free card. You just used yours. I deserved that for fucking up your operation."

I stepped forward, until we were almost touching. I felt more than saw the agents behind Smith move their weapons to the ready position, or thumb the safeties off, or if they were really smart, twitch a little closer to the door in case they had to run.

When I spoke, my voice was low, and had all the sincerity of my century on Earth behind it. "But let me be very fucking clear. If you ever lay hands on me in anger again, we will throw down. And I will not hold back. And only one of us will walk away from that fight."

Smith looked up at me, his five-ten and stocky frame bulked up to my six-four lean form. Our eyes locked, and before either of us spoke again, volumes were said and received.

"That day's coming, Harker. But you're right. Today ain't that day. Now get the fuck out of my crime scene before I change my mind."

Of course I didn't move. I'm not smart enough to walk away from trouble, or an armed government special ops team with a leader that wants to beat my head in. Instead, I pointed to Amanda. "She needs help. Serious help. The kind that takes years, costs serious money, and keeps people in rooms with soft walls until it works. You gonna make sure she gets that?"

"She'll be well taken care of, Mr. Harker. That's why Agent Smith brought me into this case." I looked past Smith and saw a heavyset woman in a business suit standing in the doorway. She carried a briefcase instead of a gun and wore pumps instead of combat boots, but this woman exuded the same type of confidence that the special operators around her did. She was either one of the best in the world, or thought she was.

"And you are?" I asked.

"Dr. McColl," she replied, stepping forward and holding out her hand.

"Don't look like any Irishwomen I've ever known," I said, shaking her hand.

A grin split her face, and a broad white smile stood out in stark contrast to her ebony skin. She laughed, and said, "I married an Irishman. Sergeant Sean McColl, 82nd Airborne. We met in Iraq."

"He on the team, too?" I asked, only to see her face fall.

"He didn't make it home from Iraq."

"Sorry to hear that," I said. I sensed something more to her story and remembered something I'd heard about from Luke a few years back. "Djinn?" I asked.

"Yeah," she replied. "His unit stumbled upon a Djinn ruling a small village like a king. Sean objected, and the Djinn wiped them out. The Army called it a 'training accident.' Even crashed a pair of helicopters to cover it up."

"But you didn't buy it, poked around into too many rabbit holes, and ended in the Freak Squad," I finished her story.

"Pretty much covers it," she agreed.

"Doctor McColl helps civilians and our personnel alike deal with the after-effects of encountering the supernatural for the first time," Smith said.

I chuckled a little.

"Something funny about that?" McColl asked. I could tell she was sensitive about her work.

"No, not at all," I said. Might have been useful for me, if my first encounter with the supernatural hadn't been *in utero*. "I guess when you've walked the walk as long as I have, the supernatural isn't so super anymore. Anyway, I'll leave you to the cleanup. I've got a crime scene to walk, a demon to interrogate, and a ghost to lay to rest. Good to meet you, Doctor. And Smith, we'll finish this later."

"Count on it, Harker."

CHAPTER FIFTEEN

I was in a foul mood when I walked into Mort's, which is exactly the wrong mindset to be in when you walk into a room where most of the inhabitants want to eat you, kill you, maim you, or some combination of three. The second I stepped through the door, the room fell silent, except for a pair of twenty-something weres, maybe foxes, making out in a back corner. The anger was rolling off me in waves, and I'm sure every sensitive being in the room felt it. I stepped up to the bar as a couple of humans scurried for the door, their eyes never leaving me.

Christy came over to me, a Stella in hand. "Here, take the edge off," she said, sliding the bottle to me.

"Why, whatever do you mean?" I asked.

"Harker, I like you, for no good reason, I might add. But understand that my rules apply to you, too, and if you break Sanctuary out here, your safe passage will be revoked, you will be banned, and you will be removed from my bar. With extreme prejudice. Everyone in here will get a shot at you, and I don't care how good you are, I don't think you're walking out of that. So please, before you start something, understand that I *will* finish it, no matter how unpleasant that becomes."

I thought about it for a minute, then decided that if two people usually on my side think I'm far enough gone that they have to threaten me with epic ass-kickings unless I get my shit together, then maybe the problem isn't with the rest of the world, maybe it's with me. I sat down on a stool, drank my beer, and brought my emotions under control.

"Sorry, Christy. This case is a motherfucker, you know?"

She leaned on the bar. This had the dual effect of bringing her close enough to talk without the whole bar overhearing and pushing up into my eyesight some of the most expansive and impressive cleavage this side of the Mississippi. "They're all motherfuckers, Harker. That's why motherfuckers like you have to deal with them. If this shit were easy, the mundanes could handle their own problems. But it's not, and they can't. So come on, Ethel. Put on your big girl panties and do the job."

I gave her a little half-smile and said, "Is that supposed to be motivational? Because if so, I think that job at Hallmark is out of the question."

"Nah, the look down my shirt was motivational. The talking was just cover." She reached under the bar and buzzed open the door into the back room. "Go on back. And remember, there's no Sanctuary back there, that's only for the public part of the bar. So be careful."

I drained the last of my beer and set it on the bar. "Thanks, Christy," I said.

"You're welcome, Quincy. Good luck."

I'll need it, I thought as I walked back into Mort's lair. My mind as racing as I stepped into the room that not twenty-four hours before had looked like nothing so much as a theatre, but now was a nicely-appointed office, with a full wet bar, dark hardwood floors, a pair of leather couches in a seating area, an oak desk the size of a small car, and floor-to-ceiling bookshelves, all filled with leather-bound volumes with gold lettering on the spine.

Mort sat on one of the couches, a can of Coke in his hand. A pair of minotaurs stood behind him. I couldn't tell if they were the same minotaurs from earlier or not, but they didn't have any obvios perforations, so I assumed not. I'll admit to being a touch speciesist, but I've never cared enough to learn to recognize individual minotaurs.

"Harker," Mort nodded, and raised his Coke can to me.

"You know that's creepy as fuck, right?" I said, sitting down. I turned to the nearest minotaur. "Get me a Coke, would ya?" He glared at me, then looked over at Mort.

"It's fine, David. Just get one from my mini-fridge." The minotaur turned and walked over to a section of wood paneling that wasn't covered in bookshelves. He pressed a piece of moulding, and the panel slid out of the way to reveal a small refrigerator. He opened the fridge, grabbed a Coke, and closed everything back up. He brought me the soda and handed it to me without comment.

"Thanks," I said. The minotaur grunted.

"Now that you've peed on the hydrant by being an ass to my security, can we get on to business?" Mort asked.

"Sure," I said. "Danvar's dead." I didn't elaborate because I wanted to get my information and get out. "Now what's going on at the church?"

"Hold on, Harker," Mort held up a hand. "Our deal was that you kill Danvar. Did that happen?"

I didn't say anything.

"Did you kill Danvar, Harker?" Mort's voice got low. "And know that I can tell if you're lying." Of course he could.

"No, I didn't kill him. But he is dead."

"What happened, Harker? How did he get all dead if you weren't the one one doing the killing?"

"His latest assistant," I said. "She opened his carotid with a fingernail file then jabbed it through his eyeball into his brain. All I did was blow his hand off. And beat him up a little. She did the rest. Sorry," I said. I was about as unsorry as I could possibly be, but maybe with enough contrition, I could get Mort to tell me what was going on at the church anyway.

No such luck. "Oh, that's too bad, then, Mr. Harker. Our agreement was very clear—you kill Danvar, you get information. You didn't hold up your end of the deal, so I am understandably disappointed, and unfortunately for you, under no obligation to tell you anything about the happenings at Our Lady of the Holy Comfort."

"You're not," I agreed. "But I was hoping that since you got the end result you desired..."

"Oh, but I didn't," Mort protested. "I didn't care a whit about Danvar living or dying. I had a rather sizable wager on whether or not you would murder a man in cold blood. I counted on your single-mindedness and general misan-thropy to carry the day, but apparently I was mistaken."

Great. I was the subject of a supernatural bet. And I was the cause of Mort *losing* said bet. Pretty much guaranteed I wasn't getting the information I needed easily.

"All right, Mort, what's it going to take?" I asked, sipping my Coke in what I hoped looked like an "I don't give a shit what the answer is" pose.

"What is *what* going to take, Mr. Harker?" Mort grinned at me.

"What's it going to take for you to tell me what you know about what's going on at the church?" I asked, wondering what my chances were against two minotaurs and a demon. I figured I was 50/50 against either one, but both was going to stretch the limits of my creativity.

"Oh, that?" Mort asked. "That one's so easy I'll do it for free. Nothing." Mort finished his soda and tossed the empty can back over his shoulder. The minotaur, obviously used to such behavior, caught the can on the fly. Mort just sat there, grinning at me like the cat that ate the canary.

"What do you mean, nothing?" I asked.

"I mean nothing, Quincy. I know absolutely nothing about that church. I've never been nearer to it that passing by on the road, and no one has mentioned anything about it in the bar. Not just recently, but ever. That's what I know, Harker—not a goddamn thing." He leaned back in the couch and crossed one leg over the other and put his hands behind his head. He was grinning to beat the band, and it all started to sink in.

"You played me," I said. After all these years, all the warnings to other people about dealing with demons, and I make a rookie mistake like that. I felt my face flush as it all sank in.

"About time you figured that out," Mort replied.

"You fucking played me, Mort."

"You are absolutely correct, Q."

"You just wanted to use me to kill Danvar, didn't you?"

"Finally! He gets it!" Mort threw his arms wide, as if to give the world a big hug. "I'm so proud of you, pumpkin!" He stood and walked over to me. "Come on, Q. Let's hug it out."

That was it. My vision went red, and every bit of restraint I had went out the window. I threw a straight right that flattened Mort's nose and knocked the demon six feet backward to land on the couch again. He shook his head, ran a hand over his bloody nose, and glared up at me.

"That was a mistake, Harker. Your last one. I never promised you information about the church. I just told you I'd tell you everything I know. Well, I held up my end of the bargain. If you don't like the outcome, well, that's what you get when you make a deal with the devil. But to lay hands on me? In my house? I don't give a good goddamn who your uncle is. That. Doesn't. Happen."

Mort was on his feet, and I watched with my mouth open as his form shifted, stretched, and grew from a harmless-looking little boy to an almost seven foot tall behemoth with muscles on top of muscles and a bloodthirsty grin stretching from ear to ear.

"You like this version? It's Bobby 2.0, the upgraded version. This is what Bobby could grow into with proper diet, exercise, a steady diet of protein and anabolic steroids, and a decade or two of mixed martial arts training. Or he could just let a demon live inside him and he gets to look like this whenever I need him to beat up an annoying business associate. Like right now. Hold him, boys."

The minotaurs charged me, but I wasn't going to make it that easy on them. I ducked under the grasp of the one on my right and stepped inside his reach. I kicked his knee sideways, and the big man-bull dropped to the floor. I grabbed him by the horns and steered him around between me and his buddy, then planted a foot in the middle of his back and gave him a shove.

In the move in my mind, this resulted in the minotaurs going to the ground in a tangled ton of bullman-flesh, leaving Mort for me to deal with one-on-one. In reality, the second minotaur vaulted the first one like an Olympic hurdler and charged me, horns-first.

I sprang straight up, grabbed a ceiling joist, and swung out into the seating area, landing on Mort's coffee table. This put me within striking distance of Super-Mort, and he caught me in the ribs with a sweeping sideways blow that took me off the table and flipped me backwards over one of the leather couches onto the expensive-looking rug. I took a minute to make sure I bled on the rug, then came to my feet, flipping the couch at Mort as I did so. He caught it without even a grunt, and it was a seriously heavy wood-and-leather sofa.

Mort swung the sofa around like a baseball bat, and I dropped to my stomach. He quickly reversed grip and swung the huge piece of furniture down at me. I rolled onto my back and got my hands up in time to keep from getting crushed, but still was faced with a giant pissed-off demon swinging hundreds of pounds of decor at my head.

I gripped the sofa with both hands, focused my will and shouted *"Infiernus!"* The wood frame and leather burst into flames, and I let go of the couch and rolled to my right. I came up on one knee in front of a minotaur, and I pulled my Glock as I came to my feet. I pressed the pistol to the underside of the monster's jaw and squeezed the trigger four times. The pistol spat 9mm slugs into the bellman's jaw, and they rattled around in his brainpan, generally making a mess of things. I stepped back to let the dead minotaur drop to the ground and turned to Mort.

The 'roided out demon-child was holding the flaming sofa, looking at it like it was a new toy. That's when I realized the error of my ways. If you're going to use something as a weapon against a denizen of Hell, fire probably isn't the best choice. Mort was born in fire, so setting stuff on fire around him just made him comfy.

It didn't do much for me, though, so when Mort chucked the couch at my head, I dropped my gun, rolled forward under it, spun around, and shouted *"Aquas!"* at the flying sofa. A stream of water sped from my hands like a fire hose and soaked the couch, putting out the fire and filling the room with noxious smoke. With a moment's concealment, I drew a knife from my boot and opened my Sight to find the other minotaur. He stood out against the smoke, limping around trying to find me to rip me limb from limb. He wasn't moving very quickly. I'd obviously done some damage with my kick, so I circled around him and sliced through his hamstring.

He dropped to one knee and I stepped up behind him, pressing my knife to his ear. "You can live or you can die tonight, Bessie. You want to live?"

He nodded.

"Then you drag your busted-up leg the hell out of this room and you never raise a finger to me again, you understand?"

"Mort will kill me," the minotaur whispered.

"Only if he makes it out of here, which I do not intend to let happen. So who are you more afraid of, the guy with the knife in your ear, or the guy that might kill you someday."

"Y-you," the big monster stammered, and started limping towards the door. That left me Mort, who was throwing more furniture around trying to find me in the smoke. The air cleared a bit, and Mort found me sitting atop his desk, legs crossed, wearing my best unconcerned with the world look.

"There you are, Harker. Time to die!" He charged me, and I sat there cross-legged as he ran right through me.

I dispelled my illusion and gave Mort a little whistle. He turned and charged me again. This time I went to the rafters again, using the bar joists in the room as my own personal jungle gym. Mort followed me swing for swing, until I got to the wall and jumped off, jumping ahead to the wall and bouncing off. Mort tried, but he was a little heavier than me, so he ended up with both feet buried in the drywall. His upper body flipped backward, and Mort was hanging upside down by his feet. Still buried to the knees in the drywall and concrete.

That was the opening I'd been looking for. I grabbed a hunk of sidewalk chalk and sketched a hasty circle on the wall, trapping Mort within. I called up my will, focused it on Mort, and said, "*Vade in domum tuam.*"

Mort looked at me and said, "Go home? That's the best banishment you could come up with?"

"Fuck off, Mort. I'm tired," I said, then grinned as the circle began to glow with an infernal red light. "Besides, it worked, you sonofabitch."

The circle glowed faintly, with a bright blue-white light, then it shifted to a blinding yellow flash, then the circle was empty, and all that was left of our encounter was a smoldering sofa, a thousand pounds of dead minotaur and a circle burned into the wall with a pair of footholes in it. I looked around the destroyed office, then walked back out into the main bar.

Every eye in the place turned to me as I stepped out of the private office. "So, Mort's dead," I announced. "And I'm in a shit mood. If anybody's feeling suicidal, this is the time to step up. Otherwise, I'll be leaving."

I stopped at the end of the bar where Christy stood, bar rag in hand, polishing the same square foot of bar she'd been polishing when I walked out.

"Is he really dead?" Christy asked.

"No," I said. "You can't kill a demon on this plane. But he is banished, so he'll either have to be summoned back here, or find a hole to crawl out of on his own. There aren't very many of those left, I've seen to that over the years."

"Then I'd better get the summoning circle ready," she said.

"Wait, what?" I stammered. "You're going to call him back? Why? You have a chance to run this place on your own, or at the very least get out of here and live free of Mort."

She gave me a sad little smile, like I was the slow child in first grade who couldn't understand why Dick ran after Jane. "Q, it doesn't work that way. This bar isn't on Earth. We're in a pocket dimension just outside of Hell's sixth circle. Mort is a mid-level seventh-circle demon, which makes him stronger than all but the very toughest sixth-circle demons. He was the one enforcing the Sanctuary here, not me. All my power comes through me, from Mort."

"Why? Why in all the hells would a demon run a bar for Earthbound monsters?"

"It's different. Nobody else was doing it, and it was a diversion. Torturing souls gets boring after a millennium or two, so he wanted something to change it up. And by moving in on the sixth circle, he insured—"

"That no one would challenge him because anyone strong enough to take this place from him would be too busy trying to move up in Hell's hierarchy to care about this little dive bar," I interrupted.

"So Mort got to play in the mortal world a little, got to wreak havoc on Earth and the sixth circle, and stayed pretty invisible to his seventh circle kin," Christy finished.

"That's a lot smarter than I gave him credit for."

"Not smart enough to leave you alone, no matter how often I warned him," Christy said.

"You warned him about me? Why?" I was thoroughly confused.

"You're one of a kind, Harker. There's never been another being like you in the history of the universe. Part human, part vampire, with a moral compass that changes directions like humans change socks and enough magical knowledge and power to be truly dangerous. You're a singularity, and those are either extremely valuable or extremely powerful. But they are always extremely dangerous. That's you, Q, in a nutshell."

I thought about it for a second, then opened my mouth to speak. But nothing came out. A singularity? That was gonna take a while to wrap my head around. I closed my mouth and nodded.

"I'm gonna go summon my boss back from Hell. You should probably be gone when I'm finished."

I nodded again and headed to the door. I never looked back, because you never know what might be behind you, but nothing jumped me before I opened the door and walked back out into the deserted parking lot. I call that a win.

CHAPTER SIXTEEN

"How bad is this one?" I asked Officer Aguirre when I stepped up to the door.

"Those boots might survive," he said, looking down at my Doc Martens. "Detective Flynn is upstairs. She's been waiting for you a while."

"Yeah, I had some stuff to do," I said.

"Whatever it was, I hope it included getting your affairs in order, because she is *pissed*."

I chuckled and said, "Aguirre, a woman may some day be the death of me, and it might be Detective Flynn, but it won't be today. I'm good to go in?"

"Yeah, go ahead."

I'm here, I sent to Flynn.

About damn time, she replied. Aguirre was right, she was pretty grumpy. *Anything new?*

No, same shit, different beautiful dead babies. Get back here and do your mojo thing so you can tell me you don't know shit.

I bit off a smartass reply, put my head down, and headed up the stairs. No matter how much fun winding Flynn up is on a normal day, this wasn't it. There were dead children upstairs, again, and I didn't know what was killing them. And if I didn't figure it out by tonight, we'd wake up to four more bodies tomorrow morning, and the morning after, until either our killer changed his plans, or Our Lady of Holy Comfort ran out of four-person families.

That wasn't a comforting thought.

The Lemore house was a little different from the other two crime scenes. It was a sprawling Dilworth ranch, with all the bedrooms arranged on the left side of the house, with an entryway into a formal living room front and center. The garage, mud room, and kitchen were at the end of the house on the right, and that looked like how most people entered and left the house. Dinner dishes were loaded into the dishwasher, but it had never been run. Maybe the mother was waiting for a full load and died with a dishwasher half-full of unwashed dishes. That struck me as sad, somehow, that those dishes would never get clean.

Through the kitchen was a smallish dining room with a bedroom off it that was converted into an office. Then we had the den, or great room, or whatever the real estate agents call them nowadays. It sat right behind the formal living room and was dominated by a fireplace with a huge TV hanging above it. A couple of discarded game controllers lay on the floor in front of the fireplace, and I could just hear the dad's voice telling the kids that he wasn't buying another one when theirs got broke because someone stepped on it. The whole place was just like the other two—a Donna Reed slice of heaven dropped into the middle of the twenty-first century.

I turned left and made my way down the hall past the guest bathroom to the bedrooms. The door to the master bedroom was open, but I wasn't ready for that yet. I knew what was waiting for me in there: a pile of cops and crime scene techs all trying to be professional while holding back tears and nausea, dead children looking like little sleeping angels, a mother who died knowing she couldn't save her babies, and a father who somewhere in his consciousness must have been raging against whatever force made him destroy everything he'd ever built, and no clues. Never any clues, no hint who was behind this unnecessary, spiteful suffering, no arrow pointing the way for me to direct my rage. Just more goddamn questions.

I opened the door on the right instead and stepped into the little girl's room. Her name was Jeannie, judging by the sparkly blue letters on the door, and she loved *Frozen* and all things having to do with that movie. I stepped into a suburban winter wonderland, with walls painted pale blue and covered in snowflakes, to a white plush rug and ceiling painted with white and glitter to look like stars sparkling through a snowfall. Emily Standish sat on the bed, looking up at me with her big, sad eyes, holding the hand of a gorgeous little girl I assumed was Jeannie Lemore. Jeannie wore a *Frozen* nightshirt that hung almost to her feet. She was around ten, forever trapped on the verge of transitioning from a little girl to a teen heartbreaker. Her black hair was done up in cornrows adorned with pink, white, and blue beads that I could almost hear click against each other as she played.

"Hello, Emily," I said. "You must be Jeannie," I said to the other little girl. She nodded.

"Can you tell me what happened?" I asked, kneeling down to be on eye level with the girls. Jeannie's brown eyes were big and round, almost too big for her face, the kind of eyes you knew would show all the secrets of her soul when she got older. Except for the obvious, of course.

She shook her head. I looked to Emily, who just looked back at me. Emily raised a hand, held it out to me, and I touched fingers with her. Nothing happened, and I looked back at Emily, who just sat on the bed, ethereal and inscrutable.

"What is it, honey? I can't touch you here. I can barely even see you..." I closed my eyes at my own stupidity.

I opened my Sight and reached out to Jeannie, pressing my fingers to the sides of her head. In the physical world, my hands passed through the space where Jeannie sat and my fingertips touched, but in the world outside, my fingers pressed to the girl's temple, and her eyes flickered up to lock onto mine.

I felt myself falling backward and almost broke contact with Jeannie's head to catch myself, but remembered what I was doing and let myself fall into the contact. I tumbled head over heels, closing my eyes to keep from losing my breakfast, which shouldn't have been much of a concern since I hadn't eaten in a day and a half.

When I stopped moving, I opened my eyes and saw that I was back at the communion rail in Our Lady, kneeling between a lovely woman in a pretty green dress and a little boy in a short-sleeved dress shirt and khakis. The part of me that was Jeannie Lemore instantly labeled these two "Mommy" and "Dwan." I didn't even know they made khakis for eight-year-olds, but I'm not exactly part of the khaki-wearing set. I watched as the priest stopped at the family next to us, said a few words, placed the communion wafer on the man's tongue, and moved on to the man with us, who Jeannie-me identified as "Daddy."

The priest pressed his hand to Daddy's forehead and began to speak, not the normal rhythmic Latin that always lulled Jeannie to sleep, but a harsher tongue, more sharp edges and guttural sounds than Latin. I knew it to be Enochian, the ancient language of angels and demons. That's how I knew there was something wrong with the church, because the priest was speaking the tongue of demons. But when I went to investigate, there was no hint of demonic activity anywhere, much less in the priest. Everything about him screamed "holy" to the high heavens. But where would a legit holy man in modern North Carolina learn a magical language that has never been widely spoken on Earth and hasn't been spoken at all in the US since the 60s? Where could he learn a language that died thousands of years ago if not by the very creatures that spoke it?

My eyes snapped open and I came back to myself, kneeling in Jeannie Lemore's bedroom and staring into the eyes of her ghost. "You did it!" I said to the little girls. "I understand now, and I know how to stop it. I hope."

The two little girl ghosts looked at each other, then they stood up from the bed, joined hands, and walked through the wall of the house. When they reached the wall, a portal opened up, and they vanished in a flash of purest white light. I fell backwards on my ass in the middle of the floor, then scrambled up and bolted toward the master bedroom.

"Flynn!" I yelled as I hit the hallway. "Flynn, where the fuck are you?!?"

She turned from her examination of the parents' dresser drawers. "What is it, Harker? What do you want?"

I pulled her aside and said in as much of a whisper as I could manage, "I figured it out. You've got to come with me. Right now. We're finishing this. Today."

"What the fuck are you talking about, Harker? What did you find? Who's doing this? Where are we going?" She fired questions at my back as I dragged her down the hall and out the front of the house.

"You drive, my car sucks," I said, yanking open the door to her unmarked car and reaching out to slap the magnetic bubble light onto the top of the car. "Haul ass, Flynn."

We sat there.

"Well?" I said. "Let's go!"

"Where, jackass?" Flynn asked. "You haven't even thought it at me yet."

"Fuck. Sorry. The church. We've got to go the church. The fathers are all being possessed, and I know how to stop it now."

She put the car into gear and pulled out onto Queens Road, lights flashing. She turned right toward Third Street and then looked at me sideways. "I thought you'd checked the place for bad mojo and there was nothing there."

"I did. There is no demonic possession at the church. It's as sanctified a place as I've ever known."

"Then what's making these men murder their families? What are we going there to kill, Harker?"

"We're going to church to kill an angel, Flynn. What else?"

CHAPTER SEVENTEEN

This time we walked into the church through the front doors. I stepped into the sanctuary and spotted a couple of little old ladies kneeling in prayer, the sweet kind of women who probably went in to pray for the souls of their dead husbands every day before volunteering in the daycare until it was time for cutthroat bingo in the fellowship hall in the afternoon, then dinner at Golden Corral before watching Pat & Vanna and going to bed at eight o'clock because there wasn't anything worth staying up to watch on television since they took *Dallas* off the air.

"Get them out of here," I said to Flynn. She peeled off and started hustling the ladies down to the church Family Life Center for cookies and milk or whatever. The priest I spoke to in the confessional was now standing at the communion railing, and he turned as I walked down the center aisle. He spun around, a wide smile on his face, resplendent in his black robe.

He was a young priest, almost certainly under forty. His hair was longer than I was used to on priests, long and wavy, curling just a little bit over his collar. His blue eyes and crisp jawline were guaranteed to make him a hit with the young women of the congregation, and the couple days' stubble he sported made him approachable enough for the men not to hate on sight.

"Quincy Harker, so good to see you again," he said, throwing his arms wide and giving me a huge smile.

"Padre," I nodded. "Or is there another name I should use?"

"We don't really do the whole 'name' thing," he said. "But if you need to call me something, how about Dominus? I could live with that, I suppose." He waved his hands and his entire body was enveloped in an otherworldly glow, and his eyes became orbs of pure lightning. Other than that, you couldn't really tell him from a normal person.

"Not really in the mood for pizza right now, Domino's. But if it's an ass-whooping you're looking for, just let me know. I've got one right here with your name on it."

"Oh, Quincy, let's not fight," the angel/priest said. "I'm not here to destroy you. I'm here to recruit you."

"Recruit me?" I said, honestly baffled. "For what?"

"There's a purge coming, and I need a stronger vessel. My ethereal energy will burn this body out in a matter of days, weeks at the most. But your body is different." Dom walked through the gap in the communion railing and sat down on the polished oak.

"Thanks for noticing, I've been working out." I ran a hand over my abs, but the angel didn't laugh or give me any indication that he was anything other than batshit crazy.

I decided on a different tactic. "What was that about a purge?" I slid sideways into a pew, as much for cover as support. "Like some kind of war? Don't you remember what happened the last time there was a war in Heaven?" I didn't, of course, since it happened a couple bajillion years ago.

"But this will not be a war in Heaven, nor anywhere. I have no interest in overthrowing the Father, or in taking over His domain. I just want to be rid of you cockroaches down here, and I want you to help me."

"What cockroaches? Humans? And did you miss the part where I *am* a human?" I asked.

At least mostly human, Flynn's thoughts echoed in my mind.

All the parts that matter, I sent back an image of me in my towel. Flynn blushed.

Quit flirting, we've got serious trouble, Flynn replied.

Yeah, no shit. A psychotic angel wants to recruit me to be a general in his war on humanity. You gotta get out of here. If he catches sight of you, he'll either send you to Hell or just will you out of existence.

Flynn's thoughts froze for a second, the psychic equivalent of her mouth dropping open. *He can do that?*

And worse. He's a seraph, one of the Host. The big deal of angels. I can't hope to beat him, just maybe get lucky and send him back to Heaven where he can do less harm. So get out of here.

I'm not leaving you to fight him alone.

You're just going to get me killed if I have to watch out for you. Now get the fuck out of here!

Fine.

Flynn?

Yeah.

Pray for me.

I cut off the mental connection between me and Flynn and turned my attention back to Dominos.

"Girl problems?" the angel asked.

"I got 99 problems, dickhead, but she ain't one," I replied. He looked confused. I don't know that I expected a seraph to be a Jay-Z fan, but I was reaching for any common ground here.

"Why do you want to destroy humanity?" I asked.

"You breed too fast, make too much noise, and have captured too much of the Father's attention for too long," he replied.

"Oh, so this is like a jealous big brother kind of thing. I get that. I had siblings. You hate them a lot of the time. They make Mom and Dad give them all the love, and you feel all ignored. But then one day, they're gone, and you're all alone, and you don't want anything more than to be able to sit down with your shitty little brother and have a beer with him. So if humanity is your little brother, you could probably wipe them out, but you'd miss them eventually. I mean, the cosmos would be just way too quiet without them, right?"

He looked pensive for a moment, and I wondered if that bullshit spiel had actually worked. He lowered his head, as if overcome by emotions. I even saw his shoulders shake once, twice, then he looked back up at me.

"That was the stupidest thing I've ever heard. And I was here when your kind first learned to use fire."

We're clear. Take this motherfucker down. Flynn sent an image of her and the old ladies sampling the communion wine in the church kitchen.

I'll try. If I don't make it out of here, feed my cat.

You don't have a cat.

Well, if I get out of this, remind me to get a cat.

"Yeah, but I distracted you long enough for the civilians to get clear," I said. I focused my will and said *"clavum,"* throwing my hand in his direction. A stream of spikes shot from my palm, streaking straight at the angel's face.

He laughed and floated into the air, my spikes flashing under his feet to shatter against the pulpit. "You'll have to do better than that, Harker," he said. He held out both hands wide from his sides and cast bolts of white energy in my direction.

I dove behind the pew and covered my face in my hands as the wooden bench turned to splinters that cascaded down over me. I kept my face covered and scurried along the floor to the end of the row. I hopped up and shouted *"Infierno!"* at the angel, pointing my hands at him like I was throwing a basketball. A globe of fire materialized between my fingertips and streaked toward Dominus.

He laughed and took to the air, easily dodging my fireball, which struck the pulpit and spread fire across the front of the church. The carpet started to burn, and the communion rail was engulfed in seconds.

I jumped a couple of pews and dropped to the floor again as Dom threw another bolt of force at me. Another pew blew to splinters as I rolled forward along the stone floor. I hopped up and flung my hands at him again. I shouted *"Ningor!"* and the air over the angel coalesced into a roiling mass of white clouds, which immediately began to dump ice and snow upon the pissed-off seraph. It didn't do much more than annoy the angel, but at least the sanctuary wasn't on fire anymore.

Dom flew left, right, and sideways, but my little storm cloud followed his every move. Finally, after trying to dodge the blizzard I dropped on his head, Dom landed at the front of the church and directed his attention upward. As he focused his attention on dispelling the storm, I sprang over the pew in front of me and charged the distracted angel.

I've had worse ideas. I'm sure of it given the number of times I've ended up in hospitals in my life. So running straight at a demented angel who wants me to join his army might not be the stupidest thing I've ever done, but it definitely makes the top ten. He flicked out a hand, and I ran into a brick wall. An invisible brick wall made completely from the angel's willpower, but nonetheless, I dropped straight back and flopped to the floor like a fish out of water.

"That's your best shot, Harker? Just charging at me like a bull? Maybe I didn't make it clear—I just need your body, and I don't really need it to be alive when I'm in there. Frankly, it would be easier if I just killed you and took over right now." He raised both hands over his head, and that white energy enveloped his fists, growing to a sparkling orb the size of a beach ball. Then he brought both hands down over his head like he was chopping wood and I was a reluctant hunk of oak. The ball of energy flew at me, promising to blow me to bits the second it hit. My life flashed before my eyes, and in my considered opinion, I hadn't slept with nearly enough redheads. I closed my eyes, waiting for the bolt of angelic fire to hit me right between the eyes.

CHAPTER EIGHTEEN

Except it never hit. A streak of white flashed in from the ceiling of the church and hurled itself between me and the white-hot fireball half an eye blink before I was incinerated.

"Cutting it a little close, aren't we?" I asked my guardian angel.

"Can we hold off the smartass comments until I'm maybe not on fire?" Glory replied as Dom's power crackled along the shield of wings she surrounded me with. I smelled burning feathers and shouted "*Aquos!*" A thick cloud of steam erupted from Glory's back as a hundred gallons of water materialized around the angel.

"Thanks," she said.

"No problem," I replied. "I assume you have a plan for how to deal with our flying friend up there?" I pointed to Dom, who had taken off and was now floating above the sanctuary.

"I do, but I don't wand to spoil the surprise," Glory said, then unfolded the cocoon of wings she'd saved me with, and flew up to face the psycho seraph.

"Hey, Domino's, why don't you pick on someone your own species!" Glory called.

"If there were anyone here with even an iota of my power, I would happily do battle with them. As it is, I have to settle for you." He threw bolts of power at Glory, which she avoided without breaking a sweat.

"That the best you got? You're gonna have to go back through Gabriel's boot camp if you can't take out one little guardian," Glory taunted.

Dom threw more bolts of energy, and now Glory had to expend a little energy avoiding them. The whole time, I watched her left hand. When she dodged one particularly close blast, I stood up and shouted "*Tempestus!*"

Hurricane-force winds shot from my hands, buffeting Dom around the ceiling and providing the opening Glory needed. She charged the distracted seraph, landing a punch on his chin that knocked him into a midair flip, then she reversed course and hit him from above with both feet, driving Dom to the floor.

I charged the pulpit again, this time with no intention of tackling the angel. Instead, I veered to the right and the last minute and grabbed a hunk of sidewalk chalk from one jacket pocket. I knelt on the floor of the church and drew a shaky circle around the downed angel, then focused my will into the chalk and invoked the circle. A flash of blue-white energy pulsed along the lines, and the circle snapped to life around the shaken angel.

"What the heaven do you think you're doing, mortal?" Dom asked, reaching out with a finger to touch the circle. The magical boundary crackled on his outstretched finger, and he snatched back the scorched appendage, sticking it into his mouth and sucking on it in a very human gesture.

"I think I'm locking you away until I figure out what to do with you," I said.

"And I think I know exactly what to do with him," Glory's voice came from above me. She floated to the ground right beside me and glared at the imprisoned angel.

"Release me, Glory," Dom said with a smile.

"Kiss my ass, Dom," Glory replied, extending the middle finger of her right hand.

"Sorry about that, Dom," I said. "I'm a bad influence on angels."

"That's the damn truth," Glory said, and held up a fist. I bumped it, and we stared at Dom, who fumed inside the circle, then turned to Glory with rage in his eyes.

"Guardian, I order you to release me. As one of The Host, I command you." He flared his wings out as far as he could in the circle and put enough of his power into the words to make his eyes glow white.

"There's a problem with that, Dom," Glory replied. "You're no longer one of The Host."

"What?" the imprisoned angel said.

"Huh?" I added, equally eloquent.

"I just came from Gabriel, you poor misguided bastard. He sent me down with a message, and Uriel loaned me something to deliver it with." Glory stretched her arm into the air, and suddenly there was a flaming longsword in it. She swung the sword down, then up, then down again, slicing through my circle like it was nothing. She raised her arm again, opened her hand, and the sword vanished.

Dom's eyes flickered, then the fire went out and his mouth opened wide in a howl of pain and rage that shook the windows in their frames. His wings, the pride of every angel, lay on the floor of the pulpit, trapped inside the circle with Dom, just a pile of useless feathers now. The suddenly former angel dropped to his knees, gathering the feathers to his body, but at his touch, they turned gray and melted into a fine dust that drifted away on the currents of air.

"What have you done to me?" Dom shrieked.

"I just carried out the sentence, Dominus," Glory said, and her voice was heavy with sadness. "You did this to yourself the second you took the Father's work onto yourself. We carry out the will of God, not the will of The Host. We don't make decisions of life and death, Dominus. The second you did that, you abandoned The Host and all we stand for."

"We? Who the heaven do you think you are, *Guardian*? You've no right to call yourself one of The Host."

"I don't?" Glory asked. "Do you not recognize me, Dominus? I know it's been a few centuries, but have I changed all that much?" She spread her wings, and Glory was surrounded by a yellow-white light so bright I had to turn away and cover my face with my hands.

When the glow faded enough for me to turn back to her, she had folded her wings and was back to being Glory, my everyday, run-of-the-mill guardian angel. Dom, however, was on his knees in the circle staring up at her in adoration like she had just cured cancer or invented pizza.

"You," he said, and the love in his voice was like the sum of every mother speaking to every newborn throughout history.

"Me," Glory replied, and the sadness in her tone made me think of every single Tom Waits song ever, all being played at the same time. Glory raised her right hand, looked down at the kneeling former angel, and said, "I'm sorry, Dom. I don't know where we failed you, but perhaps the Morningstar can heal you and make you fit for service again."

Her hand flashed a blinding white, and Dom disappeared in an explosion of sulfur and red-tinged smoke. My pitiful little circle vanished from the wood in a blaze of burnt chalk, and there was no trace of our fight except for a lot of splintered pews and the stench of brimstone on the pulpit. Lying on the floor where Dom had been, blissfully unconscious, was the priest I had met the day before.

I picked up the priest and laid him on a padded pew, smoothing down his robes and putting a hymnal under his head for a pillow. Then I turned to Glory.

"What the ever-loving fuck was all that?" I asked, crossing my arms and staring at her.

"Here's what I can tell you, which isn't much. Dominus was insane. He acted alone, without knowledge of The Host or anyone else."

"Anyone?" I asked, eyebrows climbing.

"I don't get into what The Father does and doesn't know. I always assume that He knows everything and sometimes just waits for us to figure things out for ourselves. He does like His children to be independent, you know."

"Then he must fucking *love* me," I muttered.

Glory took hold of my chin and turned my eyes to hers. I looked deep into them, really *looked* for the first time, and behind the blue I saw more than I could process. I *saw* the love, the compassion, the forgiveness for every stupid, hard-hearted and small-minded thing I'd ever done. I stared into her eyes until I felt like my heart would burst, and then I tore myself away, tears rolling down my face.

"That's just how I feel about you, Quincy Harker, and I have nothing like the capacity for love that Father has. So yeah, he fucking loves you. And don't you forget it."

I stood there for a moment, trying to pull myself together. When I could speak again, I looked back at her. Fortunately, she had de-magicked her eyes, so I could look at her without being overwhelmed.

"So it's over? The murders? The magically-induced unnatural catastrophes? All done?"

"All done. No more murders, and no more using the death of innocents to manipulate the Earth's energies. And hopefully Dominus can be rehabilitated."

"In Hell?" I raised an eyebrow.

Glory looked at me like I was a particularly slow first-grader. It was a look she'd used before. I've given her plenty of opportunities to perfect it over the years. She said, "Hell isn't for punishment, Quincy. The punishment is being away from the presence of the Almighty. The redemption comes in the hope to some day earn the right to be in His presence again. If Dominus truly repents and learns from his mistakes, he may one day become part of The Host again. That is our most sincere hope."

"Our? I thought being part of The Host was like a rank thing, and Guardians were a step below."

"Usually that's true." Glory gave me a little smile. "But you're a special case.

You get into a little more trouble than most humans, so you require a higher level of guardian. So you get me." She gave me a dazzling smile, the kind that's supposed to distract me from asking any questions she doesn't feel like answering. I knew she was playing me, but I let her. She wasn't going to tell me anything more about her status among the angels, or about the attention I was receiving from Heaven, so I figured I'd just chalk it up to a win and move along.

"Yeah, I got you. Ain't you the lucky one?"

"I am, Harker. I truly am. Peace be with you, my friend." Glory gave me a quick hug, then vanished in a stream of sparkles.

"Kid definitely knows how to make an exit." I grinned and turned to the door.

Let's get out of here, I sent to Flynn.

Did we win?

We're still alive, so yeah, we wo,. I replied.

Meet you at the car. You're driving, she thought at me.

Drunk on communion wine?

Fuck off, Harker, that shit's stronger than I thought.

I've never heard anybody slur their thoughts before, Becks.

Just open the car door, asshole.

I looked back at the church, and as the sun flickered behind a cloud for a second, I thought I saw the figure of little Emily Standish standing in the doorway. She gave me a little wave, then turned and walked through a patch of sunbeam, and was gone.

"Peace be unto you, little one," I murmured, then walked to the car and rode away.

The End

THE CAMBION CYCLE

PART I
HEAVEN SENT

CHAPTER ONE

I guess most people don't meet their guardian angel at a murder scene. I guess most people don't meet their guardian angel at all, but I've never been most people. So while it didn't surprise me too much to see an angel hanging around the newly deceased body of Lincoln Baxter, Esquire, prosecuting attorney extraordinaire, it surprised me quite a bit to find out that she was there for me, not for the soul of Mr. Baxter. But I'm getting ahead of myself. I do that.

It was about seven years ago. The sky dumped rain in buckets, and there was no blood to speak of, so either Dead Lincoln had been lying there getting rained on for a while, or he'd been shot somewhere else and dropped in the parking lot of the Harris Teeter on Randolph Road. Since that strip mall was fairly high-rent, even seven years ago, I figured he hadn't been there that long. That left a body dump, and that meant trace evidence, although most of it was currently getting washed into storm drains thanks to the mid-June thunderstorm. This was before every house had streaming video, so I hadn't yet binge-watched every episode of every *CSI* franchise, but I still understood a little about fibers and transfer from a couple of cases I spent working with Scotland Yard back in the 1960s. Admittedly, the culprit in those cases had eventually turned out to be a pair of ghouls resurrected by an Oxford medical student with a talent for the occult and a moral compass that only pointed south, but the theories were sound.

I had a few advantages that Scotland Yard didn't have. I could use my Sight to take note of the fact that there was no magical trace around the body, but that didn't really mean much. Magical energy and running water don't get along very well, and it was pouring rain. What meant a lot more, although I had no friggin' idea exactly what it meant, was the pair of ethereal wings the deceased was sporting. I could only see them in the supernatural spectrum, but they glowed a pale golden yellow in my Sight, and I'd never seen them before, which made this murder pretty unique.

The blonde standing just outside the police cordon was also pretty damned unique, and the presence of a beauty like that at a murder scene at three in the morning should have been conspicuous as hell, except that no one seemed to see her but me. So I turned my Sight on her, and quickly dropped back into the normal spectrum, rubbing my temples from the glare. I'd never seen anything like her either, and that was two more new things than I typically liked in one night.

I shook my head and looked up just in time to see the rotund form of Detective Rich Sponholz lumbering toward me. Sponholz was a decent enough detective, if he wasn't winning any marathons. He was a big man, thick through the shoulders and arms, obviously an athlete who lost the drive to work out after years of paperwork and stakeouts. He didn't like me much, so it was no surprise that his face was turning red and his finger was waving wildly at me long before he covered the twenty feet between us.

"Goddammit, Harker, I told you to stay the fuck away from my crime scenes," he started in on me when he was still almost ten feet away. "I've got enough bullshit to deal with, this being that prissy fuck from the DA's office, without you coming down here talking about ghosts and devils and your hocus-pocus bullshit."

Okay, so Sponholz might have had a few blind spots in his worldview, but I usually didn't hold that against him, or anyone else for that matter. Most humans don't go through life calling the most famous vampire in history "Uncle" or throwing around magical spells from the age of sixteen. Me? Well, let's just say that when your parents are Jonathan Harker and Mina Murray, you don't come from exactly "normal" stock. So I didn't begrudge the good detective his prejudices, but I did turn to see how my ethereal visitor reacted to his diatribe. She seemed unfazed, like she either didn't hear what he was saying (yelling, really) or like she was so focused on what else was going on that she didn't notice him.

"And good morning to you, too, Detective," I said when he came near enough to converse normally. I'm not opposed to a good shouting match but only when I think it might get me something. And I've been around long enough to know that yelling at cops never gets me anything good. "What can I do to help you this fine morning?"

"You can fuck right off, that's what you can do, Harker," Sponholz replied. "It's the middle of the night, it's raining like pouring piss out of a boot, and I've got a dead city attorney lying in the grocery store parking lot. The last goddamn thing I need is you."

"Well, in that case, I'll just leave," I said, turning to go.

"Wait a minute," the detective said, grabbing my elbow. I expected him to do something like that, which is how I kept my reflexes in check. I *really* don't like people grabbing me, and it usually ends up in broken or missing body parts for the grabber. But I kinda liked Sponholz, despite his insistence that I was a fraud, and I didn't like jail, so I chose not to break his arm.

I turned back to him instead. "Yes, Detective?"

"What are you doing here?" he asked.

"What do you mean, Detective?"

"I mean, why are you in the parking lot of a closed shopping center in the middle of the night where a city attorney just happens to be lying in a pool of his own blood?"

"Actually, I think you'll find he's likely lying in a pool of rainwater, motor oil, and leaked engine coolant. I saw very little blood. But I was only able to examine things from behind the police line. You see, I arrived after your boys and girls in blue called in the body. I have a police scanner, and I like to stay abreast of what goes on in my city."

Sponholz's face turned three different shades of red as he spluttered at me. "Y-y-your city? *Your* city? You nut bar, what in the hell...oh never mind, just go home."

"Take a look at the amount of blood by the body, Detective. He wasn't killed here. Have a nice day!" I called after Sponholz as he stomped away.

"That attitude is going to get you in trouble someday, Quincy Harker," my mysterious lady said.

"It's already done that," I replied. "More times than I can count. But that's not the important thing."

"What's the important thing?" she asked, a little smile playing around the corner of her mouth.

"The important thing is what in the hell is an angel doing hanging around a dead lawyer in North Carolina? Don't you have somebody to save or a plague to call down on Egypt or something?"

"We don't do much plaguing nowadays. Just a lot less call for that kind of thing. And as for the saving thing, well, that's what I'm doing. Kinda. I'm Glory, your guardian angel."

"My guardian angel is named after a villain from *Buffy the Vampire Slayer*?"

343

"What can I say? Joss Whedon's a genius. Now, how did you know I wasn't just another onlooker?"

"Well, partly because you wouldn't have been 'another' onlooker, you would have been the only onlooker. It's three in the morning. There's nobody here but you, me, and the cops. Speaking of whom, let's move this conversation somewhere a little more private."

"What's wrong, Harker? Don't want to be seen talking to an angel?"

"Sweetheart, with a body like yours, talking isn't the only thing I wouldn't mind being seen doing. But since you don't seem to be visible to anybody but me, I'd rather not look like I'm completely out of my mind."

She at least had the good grace to look chagrined when she looked around and realized I was right. "Shit," she muttered under her breath. "I'm still not used to this whole walking among the mortals stuff. Let's go." Then she vanished. Because that's what angels do. They just appear and disappear whenever they feel like it, with no regard for the laws of physics or polite conversation.

Because I can't just teleport to wherever I want to be, I trudged through the rain to my battered navy Toyota Camry. Not the flashiest of cars, but almost impossible to spot on a crowded street if I needed to stake something out, and not nearly interesting enough to steal, which is probably good for the thieves given the assortment of mundane and magical weapons and accessories I keep in the trunk. I got in the car and gave myself a shake, rummaged around in the floorboards behind the passenger seat for napkins from a couple of McDonald's takeout bags, and dried off my face and hands enough to hold onto the steering wheel.

"That seems like quite a nuisance," said a voice beside me. I whipped my head around, gathering my will for a spell as I did, then relaxed and let the power flow out of me when I saw it was Glory.

"Jesus Christ, angel! You could give a guy a heart attack doing shit like that," I grumbled.

"That doesn't seem like a term of endearment when you say it like that," she said, chewing on her bottom lip in an absolutely human, and adorable, fashion. Now that water wasn't pouring into my eyes, I took a good look at my visitor from the ethereal realms. She didn't look all *that* much like Clare Kramer, the actress that played her namesake on *Buffy the Vampire Slayer*, but she did have curly blond hair, kewpie-doll cheeks, and brilliant blue eyes. She looked to be about five-eight or so, and I learned a long time ago not to guess at a woman's age or weight, and I was betting that translated into angels, too. But she was trim, and fit, and no matter how I tried to get a peek at her back, I couldn't see even a hint of wing. No halo, either. I was starting to get disappointed at the shortcomings of my guardian angel when I realized that she had just materialized in my passenger seat out of thin air, completely dry, as thought raindrops didn't touch her. *Yep, she's plenty magic, halo or no.*

"They're spiritual," she said, pointing at the area over her shoulder. "The wings. I don't need them for anything while I'm here. They just help me ride the currents as I navigate the planes."

"Navigate the planes?" I repeated, having no idea what she was talking about.

"You know, Heaven, Hell, Earth, Purgatory, Valhalla...all of those." Her voice was bright and cheerful, like she talked about Valhalla like it was a real place every day. Hell, maybe she did.

"You...fly between the planes?" I asked.

"That's how we get there," she said. "You would have to use a spell, or have a spell go wrong. Or die, of course. But that shouldn't happen any time soon. Not if I have anything to say about it." With that, her expression became stern and her eyes flickered, like there was lightning behind them. Apparently she took the "guardian" part of her job description seriously.

I shook my head, then asked her the question that had been on the tip of my tongue ever since I first saw her. "What are you doing here?"

"You mean Earth, or here specifically?"

"Let's start with here specifically. If we need to broaden the scope of our conversation to include the whole planet, I'm going to need a drink. You know, now that I mention it..." I leaned over, reached across the startled angel's lap, and popped open the glove compartment. I reached in and pulled out a flask, twisted off the top, and let eighteen years of oak-barrel-aged Macallan pour down my throat. I turned the flask up and let the flavor of the Scottish moors wash over my tongue and teeth, swallowing what felt like centuries of fine craftsmanship with every drop.

After I shook the last drops from my flask, with a warm fire burning in my belly and throat from the whiskey and the slightest fuzziness at the edges of my vision, I tossed the empty flask back in the glove box, closed the door, and leaned back in my seat. "Now we can talk," I said to the angel. "I am now sufficiently fortified to hold a conversation with an angel in my economy car."

"Well, like I said, I'm Glory, and I've been assigned as your guardian angel. Not everyone gets one, but you seem to find yourself in more trouble than most, so you get me." She smiled brightly at me, and I found myself wishing desperately for more whiskey.

"And if I say no?" I asked.

"What?"

"What if I say 'thanks but no thanks'?"

"You mean refuse my protection?"

"Yup."

"I don't know if you *can*. As far as I know, no one has ever tried. Besides, why would you want to? It's not like I'm going to be watching your every move and tattling to Father whenever you sin. Trust me, the last thing I want to do is watch you and some of the women you go out with."

"Those are all perfectly nice girls, thank you very much."

"Regardless, that's not what my job is about. I'm here to take care of you, not anyone you might be sleeping with."

"And I say no thanks." I laughed a little bit, one of those short, barking laughs that almost sounds like a cough. "Sweetie, I'm pushing a hundred years old at this point. If something out there was going to kill me, it would have done it long ago."

CHAPTER TWO

So there I was, sitting in my car with a stunned angel sitting next to me. I chuckled again and started the car. I pulled out of the parking lot and headed up Randolph into Uptown. I had a new condo, and the bed was calling me pretty loudly.

"Why were you there?" Glory asked.

"What do you mean?"

"What were you doing at the crime scene?"

"I could ask you the same thing, I suppose."

"You could, but I'd answer instead of ducking the question. I was there looking for you. I felt like it was time we met, so I followed your aura."

"You followed my aura?" I asked.

"Of course. I'm your guardian angel. Quincy, I can sense you no matter where you are."

"Don't call me Quincy."

"Why not? Your name is Quincy."

"Only my family calls me Quincy. And nowadays that list only has one name on it."

"Of course. Your 'Uncle Luke,' as you call him. But what do your friends call you, Quincy?"

"All my friends are dead, Glory."

"What about that nice policeman you spoke to back at the crime scene?"

"He hates me, in case you missed it. He threatens to put me in jail on a regular basis."

"I'm sure you deserve it. There have been some less-than-savory activities in your past, if you'll recall."

"Pretty sure I can't forget 1944. Wait a minute. Exactly how long have you been spying on me?"

"You're a fairly new assignment. I've only watched over you for the past twenty years or so. But that's plenty of time for me to understand that you have only the loosest understanding of the term 'law' as it applied to you."

"Twenty years, huh? And you decided that we need to meet tonight? What the fuck is going on?" I'd never met an angel before, so I wasn't one hundred percent sure she wasn't going to smite me for cursing, but she wasn't carrying a flaming sword, so I thought I might get away with it. Besides, I was starting to feel seriously creeped out knowing there was an angel watching my every move.

"Nothing is going on," the angel replied. "I just felt it was time we began to interact more directly, that's all."

"So angels are terrible liars. That's good to know. Now, you want to stop bullshitting me and tell me what you want with me?"

"You want to tell me why you were in that parking lot in the middle of the night?" I could feel her eyes boring into me from the passenger seat, but I kept my gaze locked on the wet street unrolling in my headlights. I passed the Mint Museum, didn't say anything. I passed Presbyterian Hospital, didn't say anything. I crossed under I-277, didn't say anything. Finally, I got caught by a red light just before my right turn onto College. I took a deep breath and let it out slow.

"I felt something." I felt something putting those words out there. Stupid. Yeah, my life hasn't exactly been a Norman Rockwell picture of normalcy, but it hasn't been all that weird, either. The occasional monster, a rogue wizard every once in a while, but nothing really heavy-duty on the psychic or mystical front. Until tonight. Tonight I'd been jolted stone sober by a sudden need to get to the parking lot of the Cotswold Mall. Whatever happened, it killed a good buzz and cost me well over two hundred bucks in top-shelf liquor.

"I was on my way home from my book club," I continued.

"They read at The Men's Club?" Glory asked, naming the strip club I'd spent most of the evening in.

"Usually the young ladies there are more interested in pictures. Pictures of Andrew Jackson, pictures of Ulysses S. Grant, you get the idea. They have a particular fondness for pictures of Benjamin Franklin."

"Not the point, Q."

"Q?" I looked at her. A playful little smile curled up one corner of her mouth, and she gave me a saucy look right back.

"Yeah, Q. You don't want me to call you Quincy, and calling you Harker all the time sounds like I'm angry with you—"

"Which you probably will be," I added.

"I will be if you interrupt me," she fired back. "But Q was the best I could come up with on short notice. Unless you'd like me to use one of your other names. Like Holmwood, maybe?"

"No thanks," I said, finally noticing my green light and turning onto College. I drove for a couple blocks and pulled left into my building's parking garage. The condo boom in the 80s and 90s had hit Charlotte with a vengeance, but the recession in the early 2000s put a lot of luxury places on the market for ridiculously low prices. With a little financial backing from Uncle Luke, I bought my condo for well under market value. Not to mention the deal I got for the rest of the building. I had the top floor to myself; was just a couple blocks from good restaurants, the library, and Spirit Square—a great place to see a play or a concert; and I had a view of the city in all directions from twenty-five floors up. As far as lairs went, I'd had worse. Northern California in the early sixties was particularly unfortunate.

I pulled my car into my reserved spot and got out. I walked around to the trunk and pulled out a black backpack, slung it over one shoulder, and walked toward the elevator. I clicked the lock button on my remote twice and got the chirp of my alarm engaging, then pulled open the door to the elevator lobby to find Glory standing there.

"That's really annoying," I said.

"So is leaving me in the car without a word."

"Fair enough." I slid my keys into the pocket of my jeans and pulled out my wallet. I withdrew a plastic key card and inserted it into a slot on the elevator panel just above the buttons. Then I pushed the "up" button and pulled out my card.

"What does that do?" Glory asked.

"It tells the elevator to ignore all other call buttons and come straight down to the garage without stopping. It does the same thing on the inside of the elevator, too."

"Isn't that kind of rude to the people waiting for the elevator?"

"There are four elevators, so only a little. And if they don't like it, they can buy their own building." I gave her my best "devil-may-care" grin and stepped through the opening elevator doors. She didn't grin back. I guess "devil-may-care" might be the wrong attitude to wear around angels. The doors slid shut with her on the other side, but I managed not to jump when her voice came from right beside me.

"Tell me more about this feeling that dragged you from the presumably warm embrace of a half-dressed twenty-something young lady out into the pouring rain in the middle of the night."

"I can't really describe it, if we're being honest."

"I'm an angel, Q. We are incapable of telling a lie. So please, feel free to be honest."

Well, that's an interesting little tidbit. Angels can't lie. But earlier she was definitely hiding something, so they don't have to tell the whole *truth.* "I just suddenly felt like something was *wrong*, like something in my world had shifted somehow, like there was..."

"A disturbance in the Force?" the angel supplied, somewhat less than helpfully.

"Yeah, frankly, that's pretty much exactly what it was like. There was something fucked up in the universe, and I had to go try to deal with it. And that's what got me out of the Champagne Room with Olivia and Lili and out into the cold-ass rain. Speaking of which, I should have done this a long time ago." I focused my will and muttered *"inflammo"* in a low voice. I slowly released my will into the spell, and my clothes began to steam. A few seconds and I was completely dry. I released the energy I'd taken in and looked at Glory. "That's better."

"Why didn't you do that before now?" she asked.

"Well, I probably would have, except somebody materialized out of friggin' thin air into my car and scared the shit out me!"

I stared at her for a moment, and eventually Glory blushed and said, "Oh, you mean me? I really am sorry about that. But tell me more about this compulsion. How did you know where to go?"

"Why are you so interested in how I got to the crime scene? If you're supposed to be my guardian angel, what does it matter? You just need to keep me from getting killed, right?"

"I suppose so, but it would be easier if I understood you a little more, knew why you were drawn to trouble in the first place. Maybe I could be more useful."

"It's not that I'm drawn to trouble, gorgeous, trouble sometimes finds me," I said, peeling off my t-shirt and tossing it on the floor of my bedroom. I raised my voice to yell to Glory in the living room, but I didn't need to. When I turned around, she was right in front of me, standing in the entrance to my bathroom. I pushed past her, then turned and shoved her gently out the door and closed it. I relieved myself, then opened the door.

She was sitting on my bed now. I don't care if you're some kind of monk, and I'm pretty much the furthest thing from one, but the sight of a gorgeous blonde sitting on your bed in the middle of the night is going to stir some pretty unholy thoughts, angel or not. I stood there staring at her for a few seconds, then shook my head like a disturbed Labrador or something.

"That's a little disgusting, you know. I'm an *angel*, Q."

"Yeah, but I'm not," I replied, then paused. "Wait a minute, how did you know what I was thinking?"

"I've dealt with human males for centuries. You're always thinking the same thing. Why should tonight be any different?"

"Good point," I conceded. "Now what? Are you just going to sit on my bed like some *Playboy* centerfold while I take a shower, then watch over me while I sleep?"

She thought for a moment, then nodded. "Yep, that's exactly what I'm going to do. Why are you showering, anyway? You just stood in the rain for half an hour looking at a corpse."

"Yeah, but that got me wet, it didn't get me clean. Besides I need to wash off the stripper perfume and glitter. I can't go to bed smelling like lilacs and regret. I'll never get to sleep."

CHAPTER THREE

G lory was gone when I woke up, but I have to admit, I slept like a baby. I don't know if it was having an angel watching over me, or if it was getting home barely two hours before sunrise, but I woke up feeling refreshed and ready to take on the world. Or at least ready to take on whatever killed Lincoln Baxter. I made myself some coffee, grabbed a yogurt out of the fridge, and fired up the laptop. Turns out Mr. Baxter was a well-loved member of the community, which I knew, who left behind a teenage daughter from his first marriage and twin sons from his second. I wrote down "teenage daughter" and "two wives" on a legal pad by the computer.

An hour of internet searching gave me a list longer than my arm of people who wanted Baxter dead. As an assistant DA, Baxter prosecuted a lot of bad guys. Some of them, like the Mexican gang MS-13, still had friends on the outside. Some, like David Patton, aka The Park Road Strangler, managed to get their cases overturned on a technicality and got loose. And then there were the white collar guys like Bill Montgomery, who watched his net worth turn to net worthless when Baxter indicted him on a host of charges related to a Ponzi scheme he was running on North Carolina's elderly. So there were a few people who wanted our boy dead. My job was to find out who made it happen and what they did that was so powerful it jacked up the whole city's energy. There were a couple of places to find that kind of information, but only one open during mundane business hours. Good thing for me Christy made the best Bloody Marys in town.

My Camry stood out in the parking lot of Mort's Bar not because it was the best car in the lot, or the worst, but because it was the *only* car in the lot. I looked around a barren expanse of cracked asphalt, crushed beer cans, discarded cigarettes, and used fast food wrappers, but the only sign of life at the place was the tattered "OPEN" sign stuck in one window. I walked across the parking lot past the two Harley-Davidson Fatboys pulled right up to the front of the building. I banged on the door, and a panel slid open revealing a pair of yellow eyes rimmed in red.

"Password?" a gravelly voice asked. I could smell the brimstone on his breath from several feet away.

"Fuck off right back to the sixth circle, you repugnant cockweasel," I replied.

"Good to see you again, too, Harker. You know, one of these days I'm going to take offense at that and—" Doug the Door Demon started to say, but the second I heard the lock click open, I shoved the door into his face and cut him off.

"Owwww! What was that for?" The four-foot demon whined as he jumped backward off his stool and tried to keep the heavy metal-clad door from squishing him like a bug against the wall. "Come on, Harker, I thought were pals?"

"Pals?" I turned toward Doug. He was a spite demon, a prankster type that got his rocks off flattening tires and tying people's shoelaces together, but he was far from harmless. In the past he'd been known to cut brake lines, switch medications, jam up traffic signals, and otherwise do those nasty little things that can result in someone getting annoyed, or getting dead. I didn't like Doug, and never had. "You thought we were pals, you bottom-feeding little sulfur-sniffer? You're not fit to lick the dogshit off my boots, you worthless little fucktard.

"The only reason I haven't boiled your blood from the inside is that you haven't crossed the line from being an irritating little fuck to being a real threat. But if you ever do decide to move up in weight class, you worthless pile of Satan's jizz-drippings, just call me. I'll send you back to Hell so fast Lucifer himself will wonder if he installed an express elevator. Now fuck off, I'm going to see Christy."

I pushed through the inner door into Mort's, the only agreed-upon Sanctuary in the city of Charlotte. There are some places where humans are safe, and there are some places where monsters are safe, but Mort's is the only place where the two can mingle without anyone trying to eat the other. On premises, at least. What happens outside the parking lot is not something Christy is worried about.

Christy is the bartender/manager/peacekeeper/den mother of Mort's. As far as anyone can tell from a glance, she's human. She's a cute little Asian woman about five-two, curvy, with a ready smile and an ear to listen with. She's provided bartender services for me ever since I landed in Charlotte back in the 80s. Come to think of it, she hadn't changed any more than I had in the past couple decades, which spoke to something a little more than human in her DNA, too. She was pouring a scotch when I barged through the door, and as I watched her, she took one ice cube from behind the bar, deposited it into the drink, then set it on the bar in front of her.

I walked over, picked up the glass, and drained the scotch in one long swallow, then set the glass down on the bar. I waved at it in the universal sign for "Please, by all that is holy, give me more booze." Christy repeated her pour, then deposited that in my hand.

"Not much holy here, Harker," Christy said with a smile. "Now what do you want?"

"Can't I just want some company and a drink?" I put on my best "innocent" face. My innocent face looks kinda like a cross between Hannibal Lecter at a wine tasting and Uncle Luke at a Red Cross fundraiser. But it did get a chuckle out of Christy, which was all I wanted anyway.

"Sure you can. Just not at one in the afternoon. In case you missed it, we're barely open."

"Yeah, but you're never closed. Which is a little odd, if you think about it. Do you sleep, Christy?"

"You know I don't answer personal questions, Harker. It's one of the rules." She pointed to a sheet taped up behind the bar. It had a list of rules, most of them boiling down to "Don't start shit in here, or I'll fuck you up." But right there at number eight was "Bartender doesn't answer personal questions. Ever."

"Yeah, but I've gotten a lot of people to break a lot of rules in my day," I said with a grin.

"Who ever said I was a person?" She grinned right back. Dammit, she got me again. One day I'd trip her up into admitting something about herself. Or maybe I'd just actually investigate. But as long as she stayed neutral, I didn't need to go digging around in Christy's secrets.

"So, you here to meet your buddy?" Christy asked. Something in my expression must have told her I had no idea who she was talking about. Maybe it was the way my hand dropped to the butt of my Glock, riding on my hip mostly masked by my long coat. Maybe it was the way I snapped open my Sight and gathered my will, making the ring on my left middle finger glow a little. Or maybe it was the way I looked at her with one eyebrow climbing for the sky.

Her face turned sober. "There's a guy here looking for you. He's been here since early last night. He asked a few people what you looked like, then he took the corner booth by the bathroom and just waited. He orders a beer every half hour or so to keep me from throwing him out, but no food, no guests, and no interest in the girls." Christy motioned at two succubi meandering through the empty tables cleaning ashtrays and bussing drinks. In busier times, they were cocktail waitresses. With only two customers, though, they were just ambulatory furniture. Or collateral damage, if this next conversation went sideways.

I thought for a second, then held up two fingers to Christy. She stared at me for a minute, then nodded slowly. I held up one finger and pointed to the back. She nodded again.

"Well, I guess I shouldn't keep my old buddy waiting any longer, should I?" I asked. I held up one finger and pointed straight down at the bar. She nodded. So the owner of the other motorcycle wasn't waiting with his buddy in the back corner; he was crouching under the bar waiting to take a shot at my exposed back.

I pressed a hand to the front of the bar, gathered my will, and muttered "*debilitato.*" I released my will, and I heard a strangled gasp from under the bar, then a soft *thump* as my would-be assassin toppled over, paralyzed.

"*Now* I think I'll go have a conversation with my friend at the back table," I said. "Christy, is Sanctuary revoked for these guys?"

"Oh yeah," she replied. "Hide under my bar and point a gun at my belly? Fuck yeah, their Sanctuary is revoked. Paint the ceiling with their brains if you want. I've got cleaners on speed dial."

I walked back toward the restrooms, then slid into a booth just between the bathrooms and the emergency exit. I had it on good authority that emergency exit did not lead out on Wilkinson Blvd., but someplace much farther away.

"I understand you're looking for me," I said to the man in the booth. He was tall, taller than me, even, and lean to the point of being gaunt. He had deep-set eyes that looked blue, then gray, then purple, depending on how the light struck, and a trim beard along his jawline. He was dressed in biker chic, but the elbows of his leather jacket showed no signs of him ever laying a bike down. His hands were folded in front of him on the table, and they were huge. He had preternaturally long fingers, with clipped nails and no dirt or grease ground into his knuckles. This man was no biker, and we both knew it.

"Yes, Mr. Harker. I am indeed." Even without the sibilant letters, I got the impression that he was much more comfortable speaking in a hiss.

"Well, you found me. And I found your little friend up front, so let's have a private conversation, shall we?"

"Very well, I will be...succinct. You have no reason to care about Lincoln Baxter, or his death. This affair has no bearing on you, unless you wish it to. And trust me, Mr. Harker, you do not wish it to." He leaned forward, and those shifting eyes turned the color of thunderclouds. He reached out and grabbed my wrist with his right hand, and his fingers wrapped all the way around my wrist almost twice, and I'm not a little guy. "Do you understand me?"

He gave me a hard glare, and I felt a *presence* pushing on my mind, like someone trying to control me. I tried to behave, I really did. But behaving myself has never been my strong suit, and I only respond in two ways when I'm threatened: I either break whoever is threatening me into many small pieces, or I laugh like a jackass. This time my lizard brain decided that "laugh like a jackass" was the proper response to being threatened by some mystical whatchamacallit in a dive bar barely after lunchtime. So I did. I laughed in his face. Brayed, really, just like a donkey.

He jerked back and let go of my wrist, and then my lizard brain let the switch flip to "fight." I reached out and grabbed him by the hair and pulled, slamming his face into the table. Then I shoved the table into him, effectively pinning him into the booth by his skinny midsection. I slid out of the booth and nailed him with a right cross to the jaw that spun his head around, then I put both hands on the back of his skull and slammed it into the table again.

Now that I had him disoriented, I yanked him out of the booth by the back of his collar, grabbed his belt in my other hand, and bum-rushed him out into the middle of the bar. I needed a little more room than the back hallway provided for the biblical ass-kicking I planned to unleash on this fuckwit.

"Not my affair, huh?" I punctuated that by throwing him to the floor. I'm pretty sure I heard something crack when he hit the hardwood.

"I don't wish it to, huh?" This time I capped my sentence with a kick to the ribs, and I *know* I heard something crack under the toe of my Doc Martens.

"No reason to—" I didn't get to finish that sentence because as I reached down to pick his assclown up and continue beating him bloody, he reached up with a hand and swatted me away. Yeah, he didn't punch me. He didn't throw me, toss me, or fling me. He kinda flicked one hand out, and when that hand hit me in the chest, I flew fifteen feet straight back and crashed through a table before collapsing in a pile of splinters and former restaurant furniture.

CHAPTER FOUR

Once I decided that I hurt too much to be dead, I shook my head, which was a bad idea because the room didn't stop wobbling when my head did, but I managed to clear enough cobwebs to stagger to my feet. The skinny man was standing right where I'd tossed him, perfectly still. He didn't look like I'd bounced his head off a table a couple of times, then kicked the shit out of him wearing my heaviest ass-kicking boots. He looked more like he was waiting for something.

I was that something. As soon as I locked eyes with him, a smile stretched across his face from ear to ear. Then it kept going, all the way across his face until his grin literally split his face open. He reached up with one hand, grabbed his nose, and pulled it backward over his head. He grabbed his lower jaw with the other hand and pulled down, ripping his skin-suit all the way down and revealing his true form.

"Oh, fuck," I said as I looked my first Archduke of Hell in the face. I'd fought lots of demons, everything from imps and annoying little fucks like that, all the way up to reaver demons with foot-long claws instead of fingers. But I'd never met one of the real big deal demons before. I'd never even heard of one coming anywhere close to Charlotte, and I liked it that way. But standing in front of me on cloven hooves was a legit fiend, bat wings and all. He was every bit of seven feet tall, and if his meat suit was gaunt, it was camouflaging some serious muscle because this guy was built like Hulk Hogan, only bigger. He looked mostly human, except for the cat-slit yellow eyes, the red skin, the fangs, the horns curling out of his forehead, and the hairy goat legs. Okay, so he looked pretty much nothing like a human, except for walking on two legs.

"That was a mistake, Mr. Harker," the demon grumbled. "We were content to live and let live, as it were. But no man lays hands on Duke Orobas and lives!"

Shit. Orobas was a legit badass, an archduke with twenty legions of hellspawn at his disposal. He had been through some wars in the land Way Down Under and was still standing, which didn't bode well for yours truly. He started my way, and I ran down my personal inventory looking for anything that would help. I drew my Glock and put ten rounds in the demon's chest, but he didn't even flinch. Even the fact that my bullets were blessed and dipped in holy water didn't help. I dodged right under one of his big slicing blows and looked up when I heard Christy whistle.

"Harker, use this!" she shouted, and pitched me her shotgun. I spun around and planted the barrel right into Orobas' midsection. I pulled the trigger, and the demon actually staggered back. He looked down and seemed every bit as surprised as I was when he found a bloody hole there. I racked another shell and fired again. Orobas staggered, so I ran the slide and fired again. And again, and again. I put five shells into that bastard, and he never went down. After the slide clicked empty, the demon looked down at me and did the worst possible thing I could imagine. He smiled.

"Ouch," he said, very slowly and very distinctly. "I actually *felt* that. I haven't felt pain since Michael came at me with that Satan-damned flaming sword. Good for you, little wizard. You actually put up a fight. More than I can say for—"

"Get out," came a voice from behind Orobas. I couldn't see who was speaking, but I knew. I looked over at Christy for confirmation and she nodded.

Orobas turned, and I moved over to one side so I could see Mort. Mort was the proprietor of this fine establishment, and a being of some power besides. I say "being" because up until this day, I had no idea what Mort really was. Given that what was standing at the end of the bar looked for all intents and purposes like a twelve-year-old human girl holding a very large housecat, I was pretty sure I still had no idea what Mort was.

"Mortivoid?" Orobas' voice rose, and it was obvious these two knew each other. My attacker grinned down at me, then turned to face Mort. "How many millennia has it been, old friend? You're looking well. I'm sorry, I had no idea this human was your snack. Here, have it." He gestured back at me. I scrambled to one knee and pulled a piece of chalk from a pocket. I sketched a rough circle around myself on the floor, focused my will, and with a whispered "*protego*," invoked the circle. A shimmering blue-white wall of energy sprang up around me, giving me enough protection to survive at least two, maybe three, direct hits from a demon of Orobas' power.

But Orobas seemed to have lost all interest in me. He circled Mort, or at least the girl I assumed was Mort, turning his head this way and that, checking her/him/it out from all angles. After a good minute of this, Orobas stood in front of Mort and looked down on her(?).

"Why that form, Mort? It can't be very powerful on this plane, and it's not terribly attractive," the big demon said.

"I disagree, Oro. I have a thick, glossy coat in many variations of color, and I have *very* sharp claws. Would you like me to show you?" Mort replied, and now I was even more confused because the *cat* was talking. "I've ridden many forms, Oro, you know that. This one amuses me, and it keeps the humans guessing. You wouldn't believe the things I hear from my customers while they give me lovely ear scratches. And every once in a while I let them pet my belly, and they let me scratch them in return. It's lovely, Oro! I get to shed blood in the center of a Sanctuary, and no one even thinks anything of it!"

"You always had a flair for the ironic," Orobas said.

"And you always had a flair for the overly ambitious. It's time to go home now, Oro. Or at least time to leave my bar. The human is under my protection as long as he remains here, and even you aren't brazen enough to attack him outside in broad daylight. So give him whatever warning you feel you need to give, and then leave."

"Are you throwing me out, Mortivoid? Are *you* actually daring to give *me* orders?" The big demon's voice rose with every word, until he was practically bellowing in Mort's face. Which made him look spectacularly silly, since he was basically screaming at an overweight housecat. He got right down in Mort's face, spraying hot demon spittle all over the cat's thick fur.

Mort did what cats do—he reached up and clawed Orobas right on the tender tip of his nose. The demon reared back, howling in anger and shock, and it was all I could do not to fall over laughing and break my protective circle. I somehow managed to stay upright, but my eyes went wide when Orobas struck a huge downward hammering blow with both hands at the head of the little girl holding Mort. Orobas' fists slammed into some type of force barrier just inches from the child's forehead. She never even blinked, but something told me that there was a lot more to that little girl than met the eye, too.

I gathered my will and began to open my Sight, but a whistle from Christy cut me off short. She pointed to her forehead, where the mystical third eye is usually located in art and drawings, and shook her head. I raised an eyebrow and gathered more of my will, and she shook her all the more vehemently.

"I really wish you wouldn't do that, Mr. Harker. Particularly since I am currently doing pitched battle with my cousin on your behalf." Mort's idea of pitched battle and mine obviously differed pretty wildly, since all he was doing was walking toward Orobas slowly, carried by a prepubescent girl in a pinafore dress with an honest to God bow in her hair. Orobas twirled his hands in midair, called up a ball of fire the size of a basketball, and hurled it right at Mort and the girl. Mort didn't blink, didn't try to dodge, didn't waver on his path an inch. He just walked his carrier into the ball of fire, and out the other side, none the worse for wear. The lace trim on her dress wasn't even scorched.

The cat-bearer walked right up to Orobas, who stood staring at Mort. Mort meowed at his handler, and she lifted him up to her shoulder. By standing with his front paws on the girl's head and back paws on her shoulder, Mort was able to look the larger demon more or less in the eye.

"I told you to leave, Oro," the cat said.

"I don't take orders from hijackers, Mort. Wear your own skin, or at least something properly combative. You look ridiculous in that thing."

"You know I've never cared for fashion. What I care about is peace and quiet. And you are, as they say on the television, beginning to damage my calm." Huh. Mort's a *Firefly* fan. Who knew?

"I will damage more than that if you don't scurry back into your little hidey-hole and let me at Harker. He has insulted my person, and he must suffer the consequences."

Mort turned to me. "Mr. Harker?"

"Yeah, Mort, what's up?" I asked.

"I think you should apologize to Orobas, don't you?"

"What the fuck?" I raised an eyebrow.

"His feelings were hurt, Mr. Harker. I think you should apologize. Otherwise, as his host, my feelings will be hurt. And you don't want to hurt *my* feelings, do you, Mr. Harker?" His voice never changed. There was never a hint of threat in his posture. He never even raised an eyebrow at me. But I knew that he was really saying, "Take what I'm offering you and shut the fuck up, human." So I did.

"I'm sorry, Orobas. It was not my intent to show you any disrespect, and I sincerely apologize for any distress I may have caused you." I poured on a little of the flowery language I remembered from my youth and tried to keep every hint of "go fuck yourself" out of my tone. It must have worked, at least enough to satisfy the most basic requirements of demonic courtesy, because Orobas waved his hands in the air again and was suddenly back in his human-ish form, crazy-long fingers and all.

"This isn't over, Harker. When I see you again, and I *will* see you again, you won't have Mort to hide behind." Orobas turned and swept out the front door, his long coat billowing out behind him. He paused for only the briefest of seconds to reach behind the bar and pick up his flunky, then he tossed the unconscious biker over his shoulder and continued on his merry way.

"I can never get my coat to billow," I bemoaned. "Why is that?"

"Too much Kevlar," Christy replied from the bar. "Now come over here and get some liquor in you before you fall over."

I couldn't argue, and I'd made it a policy long ago never to argue with an armed woman, especially one who hid a shotgun behind a bar. No telling what else she had back there. I collapsed my circle, scrubbed through the line in a couple of places with my toe so nobody could come after me and invoke it without at least a little bit of effort.

I sat down at the bar, and the little girl came and stood next to me. Mort climbed off her shoulder onto the bar and paced back and forth in front of me, his tail twitching. I picked my whiskey up off the bar. No need to add cat hair to my diet. Mort was currently walking around as a huge orange and white short-haired housecat, with bright green eyes and a little paunch that let me know that Mort was taking good care of this current body. He walked up and sat down right in front of me, those emerald chips locking onto my own eyes.

"What the sweet evergreen fuck were you thinking, Harker?" the cat asked, and I'll admit, it was pretty disconcerting, being cussed at by a cat sitting on a bar at barely two in the afternoon.

"Which time?" I asked. "When I sucker-punched the demon? When I decided to stand up and fight the demon fair? When I hid like a mouse in my little circle while you people, donor body and all, stared him down and ran him out of Dodge?"

"Let's start with the beginning, shall we? Why did you think it was a good idea to come in here, shit on my bar, wipe your ass with my Sanctuary, *and* put yourself in a position to get not only yourself, but any other human in a three-block radius, killed?"

"Well, it sounds bad when you say it like that," I said, knocking back the last of my drink and putting the glass down on the bar. Mort reached out with one paw and knocked it to the floor, where it shattered.

"Sorry, Christy," he said to the bartender, who wore a scowl that said it wasn't the first time he'd done something like that. "Feline instincts, I can't help it."

"God, Mort. Cats really *are* assholes," I said.

"Cats possessed by demons are even worse. I can't tell whether it's Mort being a dick, or his host. I'll be glad when this episode of 'Stupid Pet Tricks' is over," Christy said, walking over with a broom and a dustpan.

I turned back to the cat, who looked a great deal like he wanted to claw my eyes out. "I don't know, Mort. There's something strange going on, and this is the place in town to go if you want to find out about strange."

"Well, that's true enough, I guess." He licked his paw and started cleaning his head with it. "I suppose a run-in with Oro was inevitable once he started asking about you and glowering at everyone."

"It does kinda happen that way," I agreed. "People ask questions about me, and eventually I show up with answers. It's not often that I show up with answers they like, but I do bring answers."

"But you said you came here to ask about something, not looking for the guy who was asking about you. Coincidence?"

"You don't believe in that shit any more than I do. Lincoln Baxter was found dead last night. Somebody cut his throat from ear to ear, then drained his blood and dumped the body in a mall parking lot."

"What does that have to do with anything? Stupid humans kill everything anyway. Not like he was going to live very long in the first place," Mort said.

"Then why was my guardian angel at the dump site?"

I saw Mort's hackles actually raise. "What?" he asked, scouting back a little on the counter.

"What's wrong, Mort? Not a fan of the angelic host?"

"De-mon, you jackoff. Look it up. No, I am not a fan of those prissy fucks. But if one was hanging around a crime scene, then you're right, something's fucked up. And since when are you important enough to have a guardian angel?"

"I asked her the same thing," I replied.

"It," Mort corrected me absently.

"Huh?"

"Angels are neuter. They have no genitalia, thus they are neither he nor she, but properly referred to as 'it'." Mort gave me a look that was suspiciously like a cat grin.

"Whatever, dude. She looks like a chick, talks like a chick, and I'm pretty sure I'm not ever going to get a chance to inspect any closer than that."

"Yeah, Harker, if there's ever been a babe that's out of your league, I'd say anything with wings and a halo qualifies. But what was she doing at the murder scene of some human lawyer?"

"How did you know he was a lawyer?" I asked.

"The same way he knew full well that Lincoln Baxter was less human than you are, Harker. He was a regular here," Christy chimed in.

"You're speaking out of turn, Christy," Mort said, and there was a warning tone to his voice.

"Oh, like I give a fuck, Garfield." She glared at him. "Why don't you just tell him, so he can get the hell out of here and start causing a ruckus in somebody else's place of business. Then I can get started cleaning up his mess."

"Hey!" I protested. "It wasn't just me. Orobas threw me through the table, so that wasn't my fault."

"And the face-shaped dents in the back table?" Christy gave me the eyebrow. I wilted.

"Yeah, that was me. Sorry." I turned back to Mort. "So what were you going to tell me?"

He didn't meet my eye, just became very interested in licking the back of his paw. "Come on Mort, spill it," I prodded.

"Lincoln Baxter wasn't exactly human," Mort grumbled under his breath.

"Yeah, I got that. What was he? And why would anybody want to kill him?"

"Pretty sure those answers are one and the same," Christy said.

"You gonna tell him, or you gonna let me do it?" Mort snapped.

"If you'd get on with it," Christy shot back. "We don't have anyone to do a drumroll for you, so spit it out."

"Fine," Mort said. "Baxter was Nephilim." He shrank back within himself just saying the word, but it meant nothing to me.

"What's a Nephilim?" I asked. Mort looked even more uncomfortable, if that were possible for a cat. His tail was thrashing around, and his gaze kept flitting around the room.

"Abominations. Some of the nastiest beings in all the planes," Mort said.

"Not answering the question, Mort. What are Nephilim?"

"They half-human, half-angel bastards with no allegiance to anything and none of the limitations of the Host."

"So Lincoln Baxter was an angel…" I mused.

"Half angel," Mort corrected. "Half-human, half-angel, all asshole."

CHAPTER FIVE

"I thought angels couldn't...I thought they didn't have...fuck, how do angels make babies?" Renaissance and rococo art aside, everything I'd ever learned about angels said that they were neuter. Genderless. Made it easy to refer to them as nutless wonders when they didn't help out down here as much as I wanted them to, because they really were. Nutless, that is. Except apparently not.

"Look," I started again. "I admit I've done a lot more studying of the denizens of the lower planes, mostly because angels don't usually go around killing humans, so I don't have to fight them."

"Looking at how you handled Oro, I'd say that's probably a good call on your part," Mort said.

"Look, Meow Mix, that was a friggin' Archduke of Hell. I think it's safe to say I was punching up a little in weight class."

"Whatever, meat sack," the cat demon replied. "You don't have to understand how it happens, just understand that sometimes angels and humans make babies. These babies are called Nephilim, and they live on Earth, just like you humans. Well, just like those humans you hang out with."

"Hey!" I protested. "I'm human."

"At least eighty percent," Mort agreed with a piercing look. I didn't know what kind of demon Mort was, but as cats go, he was a dick. "So most Nephilim don't have any idea that they're part divine. They just go through life, usually doing really good shit all the time, never harming a living soul, that kind of boring horseshit. Sometimes they figure out what they are, either through dreams, or noticing that they're really hard to kill, or some kind of near-death experience. These are the ones that cause trouble. They either get hyper-holy, in which case they're assholes, or they get all kinds of nihilistic, in which case they're violent assholes."

"Or they turn out like Baxter, a fucking psychopath," Christy chimed in. She was wiping down the bar and doing something with liquor bottles that looked a lot like adding water to vodka, but I decided not to ask.

"Or that," Mort agreed. "Baxter was a piece of work. He was Nephilim, all right, but he acted more like a Cambion than a lot of half-demons I've known."

"Hold up," I said. "You're saying that the Cambion are real?" I asked. I'd heard of these mythical half-human, half-succubus demonspawn, but in almost a century of traipsing all over the world and peeking in all of civilization's dark corners, I hadn't found any real proof of their existence.

"Of course they do, idiot boy." Mort actually managed to make a cat's mouth sneer at me. I never knew you could sneer without lips, but he managed. "The universe relies on balance. If there's a yin, there's gotta be a yang. If there are Nephilim, there have to be Cambion. Angels...demons. Pizza...asparagus. Beer...Zima. You get what I'm saying."

"All but that last one. You know as well as I do that Zima is not of this universe," I said.

He nodded. "Yeah, it was a sixth-circle idea that never really panned out. Like New Coke, just not quite evil enough to catch on."

"So what's the point? Baxter was a Nephilim, and he was a psycho Nephilim, and somebody punched his ticket. Sounds like the suspect list is about half a mile long at this point, but really, what's the big deal? Some asshole angel got killed, so what?" I asked.

The cat looked at Christy, who shrugged. Mort turned back to me. "Are all humans this fucking stupid, or are you just a shining example? Look, fuckwit, you're missing the point. The point is not that something killed *Baxter*; the point is that something *killed* Baxter. Killed. Made dead. Took the part-angel son of a bitch and made him not be here anymore. That takes a lot of juice. And this ain't the first time it's happened, either."

Now I was really interested. "There are more?"

"More what?" Mort asked.

"Goddammit, I can't tell which part of you is a bigger douche, the demon or the cat!" I exploded. "More dead Nephilim, you fuzzy prick!"

"There's no need for name-calling," Mort said, suddenly all prim and proper licking one paw and washing behind his ears.

"I'm pretty sure I can't kill you, but I could have you spayed," I growled.

365

Mort looked at me, eyes wide. "You are an asshole, Harker."

"We call these our given circumstances, Mort," I replied. "Now, about those other Nephilim?"

"Baxter is the third in the past few weeks, which is really odd. Usually the Nephilim don't hang around each other, mostly because they hate each other, and usually they don't die, like ever. So three dead Nephilim in one city in one month is way outside the realm of chance."

"Do you think it might have something to do with Big Ugly back there?" I pointed in the general direction of the booth where my mild disagreement with Orobas began.

"Oro?" Mort asked, his voice dripping with the disdain that you always knew cats would sound like if they could talk. Well, this one could, and he sounded every bit as obnoxious as I always thought a talking cat would. "Oro has way more important things on his mind than a couple of dead angels. He's one of Hell's top dogs, and he doesn't mess around with small fish."

"So why was he here waving me off the case?"

"I don't know," Mort admitted, and the cat at least had the courtesy to look embarrassed.

"So we've got something killing supposedly un-killable half-angels, a high-ranking demon telling me not to poke around in a case, and you don't think they're connected? I'm no Sherlock Holmes, but I think you might be missing the boat there, Morty."

"And what do you propose to do about it, Harker?" the cat asked.

"Now that I know there are two more dead Nephilim, I want to see if their bodies are still in the morgue. I have a couple of connections in the police department that may be useful, too."

"The bodies are long gone, but you can probably get the autopsy reports," Christy said. "Here." She slid a piece of paper across the bar with two names written on it.

"These are the other two Nephilim?"

"Those are the names you'll find their corpses under," Christy confirmed. I nodded and turned to go. "Harker?" she called.

I stopped and turned back to her. "Yeah?"

"Be careful. These things are way outside your usual weight class, and they think they're right about everything. That makes them way more dangerous."

————

The autopsy reports were a dead end, since they don't tend to give those out to people without some official rank or, you know, job, and I had nothing like that. All my trip to the morgue got me was a distaste for the smell of formaldehyde and a lot of blank stares from paper-pushers who weren't buying any of my lies about "Freedom of Information Act" or the public having a right to know. Smart bureaucrats are something I have no super-power against.

I was just walking out the front door when my old buddy Detective Sponholz walked in. He took one look at me, scowled, and turned to leave again. I put on a little extra gas and pressed the door closed before he could pull it open.

"Where you headed, Detective?" I asked.

"Anywhere you aren't, Harker," the portly investigator replied.

"What's wrong, Detective? Scared that if you share information with a civilian, I'll show you up?"

"More like scared anything I say to you will end up on the internet," Sponholz replied. "What are you doing here? I got a call that some reporter's down here digging around in my case files, and when I show up, it's everybody's least favorite asshole—Quincy Harker."

"That's not fair, Detective. I must be *somebody's* favorite asshole," I replied.

"Nope, I checked. Called everybody on Earth. You're the winner. Asshole of the year. Now what do you want?" Sponholz suddenly turned serious.

"I want the autopsy reports for these two cases." I handed Sponholz a scrap of paper with their names on it.

He immediately looked suspicious, kinda like he did when I spoke, or show up unannounced at crime scenes. "Why do you want autopsy reports?" he asked. "Do you think these two might be somehow connected to Baxter?"

"I don't know," I replied. "But these bodies were both found in similar circumstances, rainy parking lots, early morning, not very much blood at the scene...it's not much of a stretch to think they might be connected. Have you found anything?"

"I'll be honest with you, Harker, and I don't know why I'm even giving you this much, I've just started looking myself. I wasn't on the first one of these cases, but I remembered the Brecker scene once we got everything buttoned up this morning, so I came down to get the files and check it out myself."

He didn't know why he was telling me that, but I did. It had a lot to do with a very minor truth incantation I was murmuring under my breath and the piece of quartz crystal I was channeling my will through while he spoke. The spell didn't *force* him to do anything, just made him more likely to respond to suggestions or answer questions honestly.

"How about I help you?" I offered, and focused my will on the crystal.

He started to shake his head, and I could almost feel his resistance, then his eyes glazed for a second and he said, "Alright, sure. I mean, two heads are better than one, and it's better to keep you where I can see you." He walked over to the officious woman behind the desk and filled out two forms, one for each report. He handed them in, paced around in front of the Plexiglas window for a few minutes, then reached into a slot cut under the window and pulled out two thin manila envelopes.

"Come with me," Sponholz grumbled, and I followed him down a short hallway to a small room with no windows.

"This looks like the kind of place where you guys bring out the rubber hoses," I joked.

"Not for years, Harker. Not for years," Sponholz said, and I chuckled at what I thought was his little joke. Until I saw the drain in the floor and decided he might not have been joking. Regardless of the room's former uses, it now held a small table and four chairs, with one weak fluorescent light overhead. Sponholz dropped the two envelopes on the table and sat down in one chair. I sat opposite him and reached for a file. He slapped the back of my hand, and I was impressed with myself as I didn't break any of the bones in his hand. I was hardly even tempted.

"Here's how this is going to go," Sponholz said. "I'm going to look through these autopsy reports. I'm not going to tell you shit about them. Then, when I'm done, you're going to look through these autopsy reports. You're going to tell me anything out of the ordinary that you notice. Do you understand me?"

"Sounds like this partnership is kind of a one-way street, Detective," I said, looking him in the eye.

"That's because it's not a partnership. We're not buddies, partners, pals, or friends of any sort. You are a consultant to the Charlotte-Mecklenburg Police Department, and I am the officer overseeing you. You are here because you always seem to pop up where the weird shit happens, and this case qualifies. So anything you see that's weird, you flag. Anything that you see that's unusual, you flag. Anything you see that's abnormal in any way, you—"

"Flag. I get it," I grumbled. Oh well, I got half of what I wanted. I got into the room with the files, and I was going to get access to them, even if I wasn't getting the benefit of Sponholz's expertise. I leaned back and waved at the envelopes. "You first, *partner.*"

A couple hours later, I had a clearer view of the method of the murders, even if I had no idea what I all meant. I closed the last folder and slid it back into the second envelope. "Let's recap," I said.

"All three victims were killed between 10 p.m. and 4 a.m., the quietest time of night in those areas. Their bodies were dumped in areas where they would be found quickly, but where the dump itself was unlikely to be seen. Cotswold

Mall, the Eastland Mall parking garage lower level, the parking lot behind Independence Arena are all public places, but also places that are unlikely to be patrolled around the clock. So our killer knows the city and knows which places are just deserted enough to make great dumping grounds," Sponholz said, his manner cool, but professional. At some point over the last two hours, he seemed to have resigned himself to working with me, at least for today.

"What else do we know?" I asked.

"Your turn, smartass." Sponholz pointed at me. "You've got my quid, now for a little pro quo."

"Fair enough," I said. "All the bodies show signs of extreme exsanguination, and not the kind that is consistent with the trauma they experienced. Each man was struck a sharp blow behind the ear, which would have rendered him unconscious, but all three men died from excessive blood loss."

"An easy call, since all their throats were slit," Sponholz said. "What have you got that's new?"

"I have agreement from the coroner that they weren't killed where the bodies were found. Like Baxter, the first two men were not found with nearly enough blood around them to explain the level to which they were drained. So they were killed elsewhere and then dumped."

"What else?"

"When is it your turn to detect, Detective? Regardless, there are ligature marks on each man's hands and feet that show he was bound, and judging by the directional marks on the ankles and the angle of the cuts on the throat, these men were hung upside down, their throats cut, and their blood drained, just like hunters do with deer."

"They weren't murdered," Sponholz said, his eyes big.

"They were butchered," I said.

CHAPTER SIX

I left Sponholz at the morgue and headed over to Luke's place, after a detour down Monroe to get a bowl of Lupe's chili and a little alone time to process everything I'd learned today. And hammer down a six-pack of Foster's to help my bruises fade. By the time I left the restaurant, it was close to full dark, and he'd be waking up soon. Renfield met me at the door with a smile. This Renfield was tall, thin almost to the point of gaunt, and getting way on in years. He'd been with Uncle Luke for a long time, even given the extra years hanging with the King of Vampires grants humans, and I could tell his time was coming to an end. But he still had a sparkle in his eyes and the key to the liquor cabinet on his ring, so I was always happy to see him.

"Master Quincy," he said, pulling the door open wide.

"Renfield," I replied with a nod.

"Your uncle has begun to stir. I expect him to be down for breakfast within the half hour, after he finishes his daily ablutions and newspaper." Luke is still the only person I know who reads the entire newspaper before he begins his day. He claims it's a habit he picked up from Mark Twain, but I've never found any proof he ever met the famous writer, riverboat captain, and newspaperman. Like myself, Uncle Luke has sometimes been known to embellish his proximity to some historical events and downplay his participation in others. For example, he's all too quick to bring up my poor decision-making in helping Pol Pot into power in Cambodia, a mistake I've long regretted and which set in stone my policy of never again interfering with the politics of Asia. They really are fucking inscrutable, and I hate getting bluffed. But you'll never hear him mention the St. Valentine's Day Massacre, where he got hungry and pissed off with a bunch of mobsters and ate them all. Capone took credit for the murders, shot up a bunch of corpses, and rose to power in Chicago, but if investigators ever looked around, they would see the same thing I'd seen this morning—not enough blood for all the deadness.

But anyway, Luke also had the best mystical library of anyone I had contact with. Anyone who didn't want to kill me, that is. Pesky thing about people who collect mystical texts—they either do it for nefarious reasons, or to destroy those with nefarious motives. Since my motives often are way more gray-tinged than some practitioners would like, I'm *persona non grata* in a lot of the magical circles. And let's not even mention Luke.

"Let him know I'm in the library whenever he's feeling ready for company," I said to Renfield, taking a left under the grand staircase in the foyer and heading to the large, wood-paneled room where I hoped to find more information on Nephilim and the things that killed them.

"I will do so, Master Quincy. Would you like something to eat brought in?" Renfield had a hell of a mommy instinct, always making sure I ate. I'm blessed with a hellacious metabolism, so even though I just knocked off a meal at Lupe's, my stomach rumbled at Renfield's mention of food.

"Yeah, send in a sandwich or something. Don't go to any trouble." I felt like I had to say it, no matter how useless. I know Renfield would whip up something worthy of a five-star restaurant and deny there was any trouble to it.

I was barely into my second tome when Renfield came in with a tray bearing a cold Sam Adams beer, a roast beef sandwich, chips, and a pickle spear. It looked like it had just come from a New York deli with crisp lettuce, fresh tomato, and rare roast beef almost dripping. I pushed away the book I was leafing through and dove in.

"Hey, Renfield," I said before the thin man reached the door. "What do you know about Nephilim?"

He froze and turned around very slowly. The look on his face told me I'd hit a nerve, but I didn't understand why at first. "Master Quincy, why in the world would you wish to know about those abominations?"

"Abominations? Isn't that a little strong?" I asked.

"I don't think so," he replied. "They are a mix of the earthly and the divine, creatures that were never meant to exist. I feel that abomination is a perfectly acceptable way to refer to them."

"There are those who would call me the same thing, Renfield. What would you say to them?" My uncle's voice was low, but dangerous. I could tell Renfield was choosing his next few words carefully. Uncle Luke wasn't a terribly vindictive man, but he had been known to eat employees in a fit of pique.

"I should hope that I am not put into a position to converse with such close-minded people, sir, but if I am, I am certain that you need no help from me in defending your honor or emotional well-being." The stiff-necked man then turned and continued his trek out of the room and vanished into the kitchen area.

I looked over at Luke, who stood with one eyebrow raised, his gaze locked onto the hallway where Renfield had disappeared. "What's up with Renfield, Uncle?" I asked.

"He has recently been reminded of his mortality, Quincy. I am afraid his time with us grows short."

That rang a little odd. Uncle Luke had gone through several Renfields by this point, the name becoming more of a title than anything else. But all of them had died of natural causes, as far as I was aware, and all after extremely long lives. This Renfield looked no more than sixty, but being around Luke made people's lifespans blurry, and I didn't remember how old he was when he came to the position.

"What's up with him?" I asked.

"Cancer," Uncle Luke replied. "It seems he knew about it when he took the position, but was hoping the exposure to my magic and his duties would either cure him or hold the tumor at bay indefinitely. That has not been the case."

"Bummer," I said. "Sorry about that. How long does he have? And have you started looking for a replacement?"

"As I understand it, his time can be measured in weeks, and I have not yet begun the search for his successor. That task is usually undertaken by the current Renfield, but..." His voice trailed off, and he raised a wine glass full of a rich red liquid to his lips.

"Yeah, I get it." I walked over to an antique sideboard. "Which bottle is the unleaded cabernet?" I pointed to two decanters. One held wine, I was fairly certain. The other, well, it was always better to ask before you drank anything in Uncle Luke's house. I poured myself a glass from the crystal decanter Luke indicated.

I followed my "uncle" into the parlor, where we sat opposite each other in armchairs that Luke had bought over in Europe. He said they reminded him of Louis XIV. I couldn't see anything particularly Louis XIV about the chairs, but I'd never met the man, so I just kept my mouth shut.

"What do you know about Nephilim, Uncle?" I asked as soon as we were both seated.

"I'm fine, Quincy, how are you? Yes, it has been a few weeks, but I hardly noticed, what with my own social obligations taking up all my attention lately. I hope you've been well. You look pale. Are you getting enough sun? Vitamin D is very important for those of you who still walk among the living," Luke answered breezily.

"I get it," I said. "It's been a couple weeks since I dropped by. Sorry about that, but I've been busy."

"Doing what?"

"Excuse me?"

"You've been busy doing what, exactly? I'm interested to hear what you've been doing in the five weeks since I've last seen you, Quincy. Because that's what it's been, hasn't it? Five weeks. Over a month and not a peep from my favorite nephew. I was really starting to worry about you."

"If you were worried, you have all my numbers," I replied.

"What's wrong, son? Are you still following around that human girl like some type of dark guardian? What happened now?"

"Her college graduation was a couple days ago. I watched her walk across the stage. Because her father can't. So now she's my responsibility," I said. Luke had heard it before. He'd been hearing it for about a dozen years or more, and he bought it about as much this time as he ever did.

"Oh, good god, Quincy, sometimes you behave like that fat shite Van Helsing, with his rigid moral code and his crusading for good. He was a *human*. You made a promise to a human. We break those all the time. We have to because they die so damned fast."

"Yeah, but he was a human who didn't have to die quite so fast," I replied, and then I was back there. It was the late 90s and I was back in an alley off Seventh Street, chasing a baby vampire through the rainy streets of a deserted Uptown Charlotte. I'd spent the last six weeks hunting down a rogue, a vampire who owed allegiance to no one and followed no one's laws, not those of man or of the Shadow Council, the ruling body of the supernatural world. I took down the rogue, but not before his progeny gutted a Charlotte cop in a parking garage. He laid a promise on me as he died—to look after his daughter. I spent the next month doing just that, sitting in a tree outside a fifth-grade girl's window listening to her cry herself to sleep.

"You could have saved him, but how many more would the rogue have slaughtered while you were off saving one human? Where was he when you finally caught up to him?"

Luke was right, of course. "He was walking into the lobby of the Omni hotel. It took some quick spell-slinging, but I got him through the hotel and into the attached mall before he hurt anyone else, then convinced the witnesses that we were filming a movie after I bounced the rogue off several marble columns *en route* to crushing its skull with a giant planter."

"How many of those witnesses would be dead if you had gone off after the infant?" Luke prodded as I fell silent.

"At least a dozen," I replied.

"And do you think any of them might have a sad little girl at home crying into her pillow had you made a different decision?"

"Yeah," I admitted, albeit reluctantly. "I *know* all this, it's just…"

"It's hard. I understand."

"You do?" I raised an eyebrow.

"Of course I do," Luke said. "You're a very talented man, Quincy Harker, and you hate to lose. You feel like there should have been some way you could save both the girl's father and all the people in the hotel. But there wasn't. You made a choice. It was for the greater good. It will hurt as you fulfill your promise to the girl's father and watch her grow up half-orphaned, but you can take comfort in knowing that you did the right thing."

"Is that really going to make me feel any better?" I asked.

"Not a bit," Luke said, leaning back in his chair and crossing his legs. We sat there in silence, me studying the dregs in the bottom of my wine glass while Luke looked at me. I sat there for several minutes before I finally looked up at him and asked the question I really wanted an answer to.

"Are we, Uncle?" I asked, surprised to find my eyes moist. "Are we more than this? Are we more than anything? What's the point, Luke? Why are we doing this, year after year, decade after decade? We get a message from the Council, 'Something needs to be killed.' And we kill it.

"But for what? Why are we doing this? There's just another thing, right? I killed the rogue, he made a baby. I killed the baby, but not before it killed a cop. And now there's a new something out there, and it's killing *angels*? What the hell am I supposed to do against something that can kill an angel? I'm only human." I held up a hand as Luke cleared his throat.

"Okay, I'm mostly human. But we have no idea what that means. We know I don't get old. At least, not at any reasonable human rate. We know that I'm faster and stronger than humans, and we know that I have a predilection for magical talent. But what does that matter? Anything that can kill an angel could swat me down like a fly without even breaking a sweat. I'm supposed to hunt down something that powerful and take it out when I couldn't even hold my own against one lousy demon this morning?"

Luke raised an eyebrow at me.

"There was a demon, at Mort's—"

"I know."

My mouth snapped shut. I thought for a few seconds, couldn't remember talking to Luke earlier, then asked. "You know?"

"Mort called me. Christy, actually, since Mort doesn't have fingers right now, but let's not split hairs. He told me of your fight with Orobas, and the murder of the Nephilim."

"Why?"

"Mort and I have a long history, and he knows that it would upset me if you, as he put it, got dead. So he called me, hoping I would tell you to drop the case."

"And are you?"

"Am I what?"

"Telling me to drop the case?"

"Would you?"

"Of course not."

"Then I won't bother. Now, let's retire to the library and see what we can find about Nephilim."

CHAPTER SEVEN

When someone's been collecting books for as long as Luke, their library is bound to be impressive, and his was about exactly what you'd expect for someone raised in European nobility. The room, easily the largest on the main floor of the house, was lined with floor-to-ceiling bookcases. There wasn't a single window, and a light-tight vestibule leading in guaranteed that Luke could spend days on end in the library without any stray sunbeams making their way inside. Comfortable reading chairs with ottomans were arranged in several loose sitting areas, and a six-foot long cherry wood table with sturdy legs and a surface scarred from decades of leather tomes marking it dominated one wall. Floor lamps dotted the room, but most of the illumination came from a giant chandelier in the center of the room. It cast a warm yellow glow all around, brightening to a brilliant white as Luke turned a dimmer on the wall.

"I'll start here with the religious texts; you work over there in the crypto-zoology section." Luke waved a hand at the far right corner of the room and strode over to the left wall. He hopped up on a ladder, one of two that ringed the room on tracks mounted in the ceiling, and pushed off, gliding almost soundlessly along the room until he came to the section he wanted. I walked to the corner, passing on the ladder for the moment. Luke's bookshelves had their own organizational system, one that would baffle Dewey and the Library of Congress librarians, but made perfect sense to him. I didn't understand the genesis of it, but since I'd worked with Luke for seven or eight decades, and lived with him off and on for at least half that time, I knew where almost everything was. And if worst came to worst, I still had a map tucked into the copy of the Bible that Luke kept on a lectern at the front of the room. There was something special about that Bible although he wouldn't tell me what it was. It wasn't an expensive book, not leather-bound, or rare, or anything special really, just a battered old King James Bible. But Luke treated it like a holy relic, carrying it from home to home over the years, so I knew that anything I hid in its pages would be safe.

I spent the next six hours scouring dusty tomes for information on the Nephilim, digging through everything from an unexpurgated copy of Bullfinch's *Mythology*, still bearing the original title "Mythology and the Fantastical Creatures that Walk the Earth." Bullfinch changed the title and carved out all mention of vampires, werewolves, and magic as a real thing after a brief visit from Uncle Luke and several of his mystical pals that he never deigned to mention to me. No matter how obscure or rare the text, all I found about Nephilim was that they were half-divine, half-human, and not to be trusted. Most texts didn't mention them at all, and the ones that did treated them like fairy tales. Which was ironic because the writers were the same guys who knew fairies were real.

Finally, with Renfield asleep on a couch and even Luke starting to yawn, I hit pay-dirt with Fortner's *Zoological Fantastical*, a semi-serious tome of children's poems, cartoonish drawings, legends, and folktales written in eighteenth-century England. Fortner was a giant in the field of arcane animals, but he masqueraded as a feckless author of children's fantasy novels. That kept the more human-appearing monsters from hunting him and provided a healthy living besides. Luke had apparently visited the man late in his life, fulfilling one of the writer's lifelong dreams of actually meeting a creature generally assumed to be mythical. *Zoological Fantastical* provided a comical illustration of a Nephilim, a skeletal man with elongated arms and a narrow head with overlarge eyes set just a hair too far apart to be normal. In general, all the features of the Nephilim were just a little bit *too much.*

But what grabbed my attention was the next entry in the book. I turned the page and saw a drawing of a normal man. Just a human, a little short, maybe a little portly, holding a knife and smiling a wicked smile. The caption under the drawing read "Cambion." I scanned the description, then pulled the book closer as the words grabbed my attention.

"The Cambion," the entry read, "is the very antithesis of the Nephilim, despite the similarities in their origin. The Nephilim, while divine in origin, is completely remorseless and lacking in conscience, a feature in its personal composition that shall, over time, distance it from close relationships and may spare unwitting humans damage from proximity to the being. The Cambion, to contrast, seems perfectly human, sometimes almost alarmingly so. The Cambion moves through human society without anyone, sometimes including the creature itself, being any the wiser. Born of the unholy union of a demon and a human woman, the Cambion possesses exceptional physical prowess, beyond that of any human. The Cambion is as much a minion of chaos as the Nephilim are slaves to order, and a Cambion will thrive in positions of extreme busyness and excitement. The Cambion and Nephilim are blood enemies and will instantly hate each other violently upon introduction of the two."

I closed the book. "Hey Luke," I called.

"Yes, Quincy?" he said from my elbow. I hate when he does that, and he really only does it when he's excited about something. Whatever was going on with these dead half-angels, it had Luke ready to rumble.

"What do you know about Cambion?"

His brow knit for a moment, then he looked up and me and nodded. "It makes sense that they would be involved in this somehow. Cambion and Nephilim have a hatred for one another that goes deeper than anything we can fathom. They are internally wired to despise and destroy the other."

"So they're real?" I figured I'd start with the easy questions.

Luke chuckled. "Yes, they are real. In fact, you have encountered several although you were unaware of it at the time."

"Yeah?" I raised an eyebrow. I thought I'd know it if I'd been dealing with a demon, even half-demon. And then there was the part of me that hoped that Luke would give me a little warning if I was dealing with a demon, even a half-demon.

"Of course," Luke replied, oblivious to the concern in my voice. "There was Hans, in France in the latter stages of the Second World War. You remember Hans?"

Of course I remembered Hans. He was a nebbishy little German guy living in Paris when the Nazis invaded. Because he was German, and as white as my pillowcases, the Nazis left him and his little pub alone. They never knew that he had a little radio room built onto his wine cellar and spent his early morning hours, after last call, relaying signal intelligence for the French Resistance.

"But Hans was one of the good guys," I said. "How could he be a demon?"

"Half-demon," Luke replied. "And he never had any inkling of his heritage. He only knew that he liked being where things were exciting, and that things were very exciting in Paris."

"But you knew?"

"I knew the second I laid eyes on him. Once you know what to look for in a hellspawn, you can't miss them."

"And what exactly are we looking for?" I asked the obvious question.

"The Cambion are usually smaller than normal, short and slender, with close-set eyes and a prominent brow ridge. Narrow features, typically, they do not tend to be attractive people. Long, thin fingers, almost preternaturally long and slender. The kind of hands you'd expect on a concert pianist, or a safecracker, which they are equally likely to be. But it's the eyes that give them away," Luke said, his own eyes closing as if looking back on the demons he'd known. "Their eyes are never still, no matter how deeply they may concentrate on something. The slightest noise and they will flit around like a hummingbird."

I thought about it, and the things he was saying did describe Hans. He was perpetually nervous, with eyes always scanning the room. I chalked it up at the time to the fact that he had a radio rig in his basement that guaranteed execution if the SS found it, but it all fit.

"So if we have dead Nephilim, we probably have a Cambion involved somewhere," I suggested.

"At least one," Luke agreed.

"And the best place to find out about demonic activity is Mort's," I said.

"Where you are specifically not allowed to set foot until this business is settled," Luke replied.

"Says who?"

"Says me, as your guardian."

"Luke, you haven't needed to be my guardian for six decades."

"That notwithstanding, it is my duty to keep you safe. That is the task your mother saddled me with on her deathbed, and I intend to fulfill it. No matter how much more difficult it is since I can't bespell you."

"Yeah, well, you should have thought about the consequences before you bit my mom and threw my dad to your psycho wives. Being born of two parents who were both bitten by vampires does weird things to your DNA."

Luke actually looked a little embarrassed. "I will admit that when I first, ahem, met your mother, that I was not exactly thinking long-term." I really think that he would have blushed if his blood actually still flowed.

"Don't sweat it, Luke. I've seen the pictures. Mom was hot when she was a kid. I can't blame you for wanting to take a bite."

"You are amazingly crass, Quincy."

"I live but to amaze, Uncle." I shot him a grin, then waved at the books I had scattered across the table. "But back to the matter at hand. If going to Mort's is out, and I'm pretty sure we're going to revisit the whole 'you giving me ultimatums' thing, then we need another way to track down a Cambion that we've never seen. So what do we have as far as evidence?"

"It seems the answer is precious little," Luke said, pacing the huge rug in the center of the library. "We know that three Nephilim have been killed, their blood drained, and their bodies left for the human authorities to find. We know nothing about a murder weapon or any connection between the victims."

"Yeah, the cops were turning over every stone in those people's personal and professional lives, and so far *nada*. So let's look at the blood. Why would someone drain the bodies? Are Cambion vampiric?"

"You mean, do they feed on human blood?" Luke shot me a look. "No. As far as I know, vampires are the only sanguivores that currently exist."

"How long have you been waiting to just casually drop the word 'sanguivores' into conversation?" I asked.

I got him again. This time I swear the tips of his ears turned just a tiny bit pink. "Quite a long time, actually. Be that as it may, vampires are the only creatures I am aware of that feed on human blood. So there must be some other quality in the blood of a Nephilim that makes it desirable."

"Or maybe a bunch of qualities," I said, reaching for a book I'd discarded several hours before.

"What have you found, my boy?" There he was, at my elbow in a blink again, all hint of muddled pacing long gone.

"Bevan's treatise on demonic possessions and exorcisms has an appendix on types of demons, and he includes Nephilim in there." I pointed. "Isn't that odd? I mean, demons are demons, and Nephilim are half-angel, so why would he put them in the same category?"

"Remember your theology, Quincy. If Lucifer was the first to fall, then all the existing demons are his progeny."

"So demons are just angels with a public relations problem?"

"A little more than that," Luke replied. "But Bevan does raise an interesting point about the basic similarities between their origins. Regardless, what does he say about the blood?"

I flipped pages to the back of the book and found the appendix I was looking for. "Apparently it has all kinds of powerful effects, depending on what species the drinker is."

"That makes sense. Inherently magical substances affect different magical beings in very unique ways. For example, the mushrooms that make up a faerie ring are completely harmless to humans, if slightly hallucinogenic, but they are very poisonous to dwarves and duergar and the like. Even brownies won't go near them."

"Right," I said, pointing back to the book. "But paying a little more attention to the possible motive for our murders—Nephilim blood is like Viagra, cocaine, and ecstasy all rolled into one for demons. It heightens all physical sensations, the more extreme the better, apparently. It allows them to 'perform as though they were human men in their early twenties,' so I guess it causes huge demon boners, and...oh fuck."

"Oh fuck what?" Luke asked. "I find the concept of demon erections as distasteful as you do, I'm sure, but that hardly accounts—"

"It opens gates," I said, pointing at a drawing on the next page of a human-looking wizard opening a portal, obviously to somewhere Very Not Nice because a huge demon was pulling himself through. I was able to specific with the gender because I recognized the demon's manifestation—Orobas, the same demon that had kicked my ass at Mort's. "Nephilim blood is blended with Cambion and human blood to create a gate into this world. Somebody has used Nephilim blood to bring Orobas back into this world. And now it looks like our old buddy Oro is planning to create the daddy of all gates."

"Well," Uncle Luke said, pulling out a chair and sitting at the table across from me. "Oh fuck, indeed."

CHAPTER EIGHT

"That's not all," I said.

"That's enough, don't you think?" Luke said from his chair.

"Not quite. Aside from its effects on humans, which is to induce psychosis, hallucinations, paranoia, and violent tendencies, Nephilim blood has one more effect on a Cambion. Well, any extraplanar creatures, it seems."

"And what might that be?" Luke asked.

"A touch of Nephilim blood to the third eye masks the demon from Sight." The Sight was what I used to see through the illusions mystical creatures cast to hide their appearance. The third eye was a *chakra*, or focal point for energy in the body. It wasn't really a physical point, more like an energy node floating just outside the body. I'm not sure how you smear blood on a *chakra*, but probably dabbing a little on your forehead and focusing your energy on it would be close enough to get you there.

"Are you certain?"

"Well, it's one of those things that I can't really be sure of until it's way too late, so I guess I should just assume that I won't be able to use my Sight to pick out our bad guy in a crowd." Unless I found some Nephilim blood myself and figured out a way to use it to level the playing field. Probably not happening since I've never spent much time working on *chakras* or any of that deep-thinking magical stuff. I was always much more the "lob fireballs at bad guys" kind of magic-user.

"Well, that's too bad, since we're likely headed to a crowded scene," came a voice from the door of the library. I stood and spun to the door, drawing my

Glock, but Luke was already on his feet and at the door, fangs out and in full vamp mode, something I hadn't seen in decades.

Not that it mattered. The leggy blonde in the doorway just stuck out her arm and stopped Luke cold. He ran into her outstretched hand and crumpled to the floor like he'd just run headlong into a Mike Tyson uppercut. She looked down at him with a cold look on her face, and I came to the quick realization that, guardian or not, this angel had a badass side to her.

"I will apologize for entering your lair uninvited, vampire, and as you are important to Quincy, who is my charge, I will ask for your forgiveness. But understand this: I am an angel of the Lord, and if you attack me again, even in misunderstanding, I will wipe you from the face of the Earth and leave not even a pile of ash behind."

Luke lay on the floor looking up at the angel, then very slowly got to his feet. "Your apology is accepted, my dear. But you should understand this: you are not the first angel I have met, and I'm still here. I make no promises about the seraph."

"If you two are done measuring things that I want to know absolutely nothing about, would you like to tell me why you're here?" I asked Glory.

"There has been another murder. Another Nephilim was found this morning, and this one was not dumped in a mall parking lot in the middle of the night. This body was found on the front steps of Trinity Presbyterian Church. The police are already on the scene, and your friend Detective Sponholz seems to be in charge."

"Great," I grumbled. "That'll make everything peaches and ice cream. Let's go." I started for the door, but Luke's voice stopped me.

"Quincy, wait."

I stopped. He sounded worried. Dracula, lord of the friggin' vampires, sounded *worried?* Now I was a little nervous. I looked at him, one eyebrow climbing.

"Be careful."

"Not a chance." I grinned and walked past Glory and out the door.

———

Trinity Presbyterian Church is a huge Gothic church in one of Charlotte's ritziest neighborhoods. There's a lot of stained glass and stone involved in anything that goes down there, including murder. Our Nephilim this time was a woman, sitting on the top step leaning over like she was just resting her head against the wall. Except for all the blood pooling around her. This was obviously not just a body dump; she was killed right there on the steps, or very nearby.

I walked up to the police line and a tall, thick-necked cop with flinty eyes and a scowl on his face stepped up to meet me. "Move along," he said in a voice that sounded a lot like someone rubbing two boulders together.

"I'm working with Detective Sponholz on this case. If you could call him over, he'll badge me through."

"No can do," said the cop, who looked a lot like a linebacker run a little bit toto fat. "Detective didn't tell me anything about a CI."

"CI? Do I look like a friggin' CI to you?" I asked. "Don't answer that. Just go get Sponholz. Tell him his consultant is here." Somedays I wish I had gone a little more legit with my life choices. It doesn't happen often, but sometimes. The uniform gave me a suspicious glare, but turned and walked off. I watched him go over to Sponholz, make a few dismissive gestures in my direction, then stiffen as he got a response he wasn't expecting. He turned and walked back to where I waited, as patiently as I could fake.

"Detective says you're clear," he mumbled.

I opened my mouth to say something, but a sharp pain in my ankle reminded me that I was traveling with an angel on my shoulder these days. Or at least with an angel close enough to kick me when I was about to say something smartass. I closed my mouth and ducked under the tape.

"Don't touch nothing," the gorilla muttered at me as I walked past. I bit my tongue and walked over to where Sponholz knelt by the body.

"How'd you hear about this?" Sponholz asked, not looking up.

"A little bird told me," I replied. "What do we know?"

"Why don't you give me the benefit of your expert eye and tell me what you see, then I'll think about telling you what we know."

I cocked an eyebrow at the rotund detective, who just stared back at me, blank-faced. If there was anything nefarious behind his continued testing of me, I couldn't find it. I shook my head at him and knelt on the stone steps beside the body.

The woman was fit, in her mid-thirties at the most, with auburn hair worn in a low ponytail. Her eyebrows and nails told me she took pride in her appearance, and that regular salon visits were a part of her routine. She wore an expensive-looking blouse and jacket with heels and slacks, but there wasn't much in the way of jewelry. Not an ostentatious woman, but she didn't hide her femininity, either. There was a slight smell of animal around her, and a few stray hairs on her pants, so I knew she owned a cat, and there was neither a ring nor a line where it had been removed, so she was likely single.

"No purse?" I asked. Sponholz shook his head. "Wallet?" Shake. "Any ID?" Another shake.

My physical exam finished, I closed my eyes and opened my Sight. When I looked at her again, I could see the faint outline of wings floating from her shoulders, and a rapidly dimming golden aura around her.

"She's definitely Nephilim," I muttered.

"What's that?" Sponholz asked, snapping my attention back to the mundane world.

"Nothing, just making some mental notes. Who found her?"

"Lady over there." He gestured to a woman sitting in the open back of an ambulance with two EMTs tending to her. "She's the church administrator. Showed up for work early this morning to get some laps in over at the gym and saw her sitting on the steps. She thought the victim was a new member wanting to use the workout facilities, or maybe a neighborhood jogger. The victim was non-responsive, so she gave her a little shake. That's when she realized that she was standing in a puddle of blood."

"And that explains the blanket, and the shivering, and the thousand-yard stare," I said, looking over at the witness. She was a trim fifty-something woman with a few gray roots showing among her dark brown hair, the very picture of a someone who got up early to work out. Standing next to her was a well-dressed young man with a lot of hair gel and a mostly respectable hair-cut, who I assumed to be the one of the pastors, or ministers, or whatever name the church had come up with for them nowadays.

"Yeah, the youth pastor found her about twenty minutes ago. She hasn't been able to pull herself together enough to make a statement, but it doesn't matter. The guy confirmed the victim wasn't a member of the choir, or the church for that matter. He doesn't know who she was." I didn't either, but I was a lot more concerned with *what* she was then *who* she was.

"Have you searched the car?" I asked.

"What car?"

I pointed off to the side of the church. "It's half past seven. Choir practice is cancelled. There aren't really many onlookers, and I assume you've got somebody photographing the crowd in case the killer come back to gloat."

"Yeah, but that doesn't—"

I pointed to the lot again. "There are ten cars in that parking lot for two churchgoers. The Camry's mine, and the shitty Ford with blackballs is prob-ably yours. That leaves half a dozen cars to search. One of them probably has a purse in it, and that'll have the victim's ID."

Sponholz glared at me. "I don't like it when you say things I can't argue with."

"Here's another one," I said with a smile. "You're fat."

I ignored his upraised middle finger and turned back to the corpse. I opened my Sight once more and gave the dead Nephilim another look. Her aura was even thinner, but that wasn't what I was looking for. I searched the area, scanning the surroundings with my third eye, then I found it.

"Gotcha!" I said, hopefully under my breath. There, under the corpse, was the slightest trace of another aura. Human auras are strange enough, but half-angel auras were even tougher to decipher. One thing I did know was that our Cambion left a little tiny trace smeared on the steps behind our Jane Doe. I couldn't tell if that's where he stood as he killed her or what, but I knew that there was enough aura transferred that I'd know it if I saw it again.

"Got what?" Sponholz said from my elbow.

"Nothing," I replied, trying to sound depressed. "I thought I saw a piece of paper in the blood, but it was nothing." I stood up, both knees popping like rifle shots. I turned and looked at the crowd, my third eye still open to the metaphysical world. Nothing. Not a hint of demon anywhere, and I had to keep Glory in my peripheral vision or she blinded me. I'd have to talk with her about that. I did get a faint golden glow off a car in the lot, a snazzy BMW M-class convertible in cherry red. I pointed to it.

"I bet that's her car," I said.

"The Beamer? Why?" Sponholz asked.

"How many church choir directors do you know that can afford a BMW sports car? And how dumb would they have to be to drive it if they could?" I replied.

"Good point. I'll go check it out. Stay here." He lumbered off to the car, waving a uniform over as he went. I watched in the distance as the uniform roped off the area around the car with crime scene tape, then Sponholz tried the doors. Locked. I could almost *feel* the glee roll off him as he realized he was going to get to cause havoc, then I saw him reach into his pocket, pull out his fist with something I couldn't see clenched in it, then shatter the driver's side window.

"I really hope that's the right car," I said to myself, watching him work. Moments later, Sponholz had the door open and was waving me over. I was at his side in seconds, peering into the car. There were no signs of a disturbance, just a Starbucks cup in the holder and an iPhone plugged into a car charger. I reached for the phone, but the rotund detective elbowed me out of the way and reached into the car himself. He pressed a button on the phone, and the screen came to life. A picture of the victim hugging a gigantic golden retriever filled the screen.

"Well, I guess we found the right car," I said. Sponholz just grunted. I pushed the unlock button and walked around to the passenger door. I opened the door, leaned in, and popped open the glove compartment, then jerked back and hit my head on the doorframe in surprise.

"Whoa!" I said, rubbing my head. I stared at the black pistol that had fallen to the seat. "Hey Sponholz, our victim was packing."

"Yeah," he said, looking at the gun. "Glock 19. Good gun. Dependable, lightweight...good glovebox gun."

"Who brings a gun to a church?" I asked myself, reaching back into the car and fumbling around in the glove compartment. Inspection receipts, a couple maps (who carries actual paper maps anymore?), a GPS charger, and finally, buried under a roadside flare and a spare set of keys to something, I found what I was looking for—the registration.

"Terese Dover," I said.

"What's that?" Sponholz looked up at me, and it was his turn to crack his head on the doorframe.

"Our vic is very likely Terese Dover of Matthews, North Carolina," I said, passing the vehicle registration across to the grumpy detective.

"Who the hell is Terese Dover, and why did someone want her dead?" Sponholz asked.

I had no idea, but this was the second dead half-angel in as many days, and if experience was any teacher, that meant something bad was brewing, and it was going to be up to me to deal with it.

CHAPTER NINE

"Who the hell is Terese Dover?" Dennis asked, looking up from the slip of paper I handed him.

"A dead woman, and I need to know everything about her," I said, sitting down in the armless chair beside Dennis' desk. Dennis Bolton was an informant I hired from time to time, a college kid I'd pulled out of a bad scene on New Year's Eve at the turn of the millennium when what he thought was a LARP turned into a dark magician's plan for ritual sacrifice. Dennis survived, but he saw a few things that made him never want to watch a horror movie again. His GM-slash-necromancer didn't survive to see the dawning of the year 2000, and after a few fire spells and an hour or two of nasty shotgun work, all the zombies were returned to their appropriate level of dead. Ever since that night, Dennis was my go-to guy for all things buried on the internet and the dark web. It's good to keep a few nerds on call for the tough ones.

"What killed her?"

"In the medical sense, a cut throat. In the perpetrator sense, I don't know yet. But I think there's something ugly brewing, and this is almost certainly tied to it."

"Makes sense, given the date," Dennis said, typing and clicking away on his souped-up Powerbook.

"What's the date?" I've never been the best in the world at keeping track of crap like dates. One of the many reasons I've never had a girlfriend of more than a few weeks. Chicks always want you to remember things like anniversaries, birthdays, and when you promised to meet them for expensive dinners. Or any dinners. Or at all. Monsters aren't real considerate of personal plans, so I've missed a lot of second dates. That means I haven't had a whole lot of third and fourth dates.

"Tomorrow is the Equinox, Harker. Isn't that something you wizard-types keep track of? Like Easter, or Christmas?"

"Nah, that's for the Wiccans. I don't really do the whole prayer thing. Now Christmas, I can keep track of. I'm oblivious, not dead. Even I can't miss all the crap in every store. But there aren't a whole lot of Vernal Equinox displays in the front of Walmart, ya know?"

"Wizards shop at Walmart?"

"One, I don't like being called a wizard. It sounds like a douche in a pointy hat and a robe, and I don't do hats. And two, everybody shops at Walmart. You can't really help it. Now what about Terese Dover?"

"She works, er…worked for AmeriBank. She was an investment banker, mostly working on financing construction projects. Office buildings, developments, that kind of thing."

"Construction, huh? Doesn't sound like the kind of thing that gets somebody killed. See if there's anything in her personal life that's out of the ordinary."

"You mean like fetish club membership, donations to the Church of Satan, subscriptions to freaky S&M magazines?" Dennis had a little bit too much of a gleam in his eyes for my comfort.

"Yeah…sure, pal. All of that, too. But I was thinking more like a relative in prison, some family or school connection to anything shady, too much money or not enough, repeated deposits or withdrawals in the same amount that don't correspond to a normal payment, that kind of thing."

His face fell beneath his close-cropped curly hair, and for a moment he looked like a really depressed Bobby Hill, from a *King of the Hill* cartoon. "Oh. Okay. I'll look into all that stuff, too. But I wouldn't ignore the work stuff, Harker. There's a lot of big money in these developments, and that's a lot of motive."

"Fair enough," I said. "I'm gonna head over to her office and talk to her co-workers. You let me know if you find anything. And keep an ear to the ground on the BlackNet about anything big going down on the Equinox. I don't think demons are much for email, but maybe some of their human pawns are using the web to communicate." I stood up and walked to the door. "And Dennis?"

"Yeah, Harker?"

"Be careful."

"Don't worry," he said, pushing his wheelchair back from the keyboard. "It's not like I'm gonna go run around in the sewers in a cape anymore."

"Yeah, well...even so, don't get dead."

"You too."

I let myself out through the front of the VCR repair shop Dennis ran as a front for his real job, which was selling information. I knew I wasn't his only client, but I'd never seen anyone else entering or leaving the shop. I didn't ask too many questions. I just took the information he gave me, paid the tab, and hoped someday he'd forgive me for cutting his legs off with a spell to save him from the grasp of a hungry demon.

———

Terese Dover's office was on one of the top floors of the AmeriBank tower, a corner office furnished in sleek chrome, glass, and black leather. Her desk was huge and designed to intimidate, but it was a lot less imposing with its drawers hanging out and fingerprint dust all over it. I ducked under the crime scene tape and stepped inside. It looked like it had been tossed, but carefully. Sponholz and his boys had obviously taken a little care in the process, making a token effort not to piss off the city's biggest employer.

I stood in the center of the room, between the ego-boosting desk and a small sitting area set off at one end of the room, and opened my Sight. Traces of Nephilim energy glowed off every surface. This was certainly Dover's place, and she was one hundred percent definitely half-angel. I'd felt the same energy coming off Lincoln Baxter's body, and there was a hint of the same energy around Glory, only hers was cleaner, purer, like it was the source and Dover's energy was a diluted version. Which I guess it probably was.

I turned to the stone-faced security guard behind me. "Are any of Ms. Dover's co-workers available for me to speak to?"

"No, sir." Amazing. I never even saw his lips move. The block of granite in a rent-a-cop suit just stood in the doorway, staring at me like I was something he'd scraped off his shoe.

"What about any of her superiors?"

"No, sir."

"Her secretary?"

"Ms. Dover's assistant has taken a personal day. She was distraught at the news. We all were." He looked about as distraught as a brick wall, but since he was also built like one, I didn't challenge him. It was way too early in the day to go breaking the humans. Besides, I was on the side of the angels, literally, for once, and I was kinda liking the way it felt. I decided not to screw anything up.

"Fine, take me to HR." Sponholz had obviously beaten me to the workplace, the benefit of actually *being* the police, instead of just kinda working alongside them. But he was maybe the laziest cop I'd ever met, so I had high hopes that when he didn't find anything in her office, that he wouldn't have thought to visit Human Resources.

I followed my security golem to the elevator, and we rode down forty-something floors until the doors dinged open on the twelfth floor. I stepped out, and my shadow followed.

"I'm sure I can find it from here," I said. I pointed to the sign on the wall with an arrow pointing right and the words "Human Resources" over it.

"You are my responsibility until you leave the building," the guard replied. I took that to mean a lot more of "I'm not letting you out of my sight, jackass," than "I'm terribly concerned about your well-being."

I sighed and started down the hallway to the right. The HR office had a sizable waiting room with about ten chairs, a circular desk with a grandmotherly-looking woman seated behind it, and a wall of pamphlets with titles like "What to do if you are sexually harassed," "How to manage intra-office relationships" and "Good personal hygiene makes a happy workplace!" The last one had a cartoon figure on the cover with wavy stink lines emanating from it. I stepped up to the desk. Aunt Bea was on the phone chatting about some pound cake she had tasted at the church dinner the night before, and when I opened my mouth to ask for the personnel records on Terese Dover, she held up one finger to shush me.

I don't like being shushed. I don't know anyone who does, but there are some people who deserve it. I'm typically not the chatty type, so generally if I open my mouth to say something, it's either relevant or tied to a spell. So I don't like being shushed. And I certainly don't like being shushed, not once but *twice*, so when a glorified file clerk shushed me so she could tell Mrs. McGillicutty how many eggs to put in her pound cake, I became irritated. It's bad for technology, and sometimes people, when I become irritated.

I focused my will, flicked a finger toward the telephone, and whispered "*mortus*." I released the power, and the line indicator lights on the phone went dead. Aunt Bea looked around, puzzled, then pressed a few buttons on her phone. She looked around, puzzled, then finally seemed to notice me standing there. Directly over her desk. With a two hundred-fifty-pound security guard beside me. Because we were hard to notice.

"Huh," she said with a puzzled look up at me. "My phone's on the fritz."

"You should call tech support," I said without a hint of a smile, even when she turned and picked up the handset as if to dial. "But before you do, I need to speak with someone about Terese Dover."

"Oh, Ms. Dover? Wasn't that such a tragedy what happened to her? And right there on the steps of a church and everything. I didn't even know she went to church, do you know that? And I make it a point to know a little something about almost everybody." She beamed like being a busybody was an achievement.

"I'm sure you do," I said with what I hoped was an ingratiating smile that kept all the "I want to strangle you" off my face. "I'm working with the police investigating Ms. Dover's death. Who could I speak to about her?"

"That would be me," came a new voice from off to my right. I turned to see a trim Asian woman in her thirties standing outside the door to one of the offices. She was dressed for downtown, with a black skirt and burgundy blouse under a long jacket. She walked over to me and gave me firm handshake. "My name is Lina Flores, VP of HR. Please come this way."

She turned around and walked off in that "I know you'll follow me" way that people who are very much in charge of their environment have. I did just what she expected and followed her into a small office with a desk, two chairs, and one moderately sad-looking plant. There were a few diplomas on the walls and a couple of photos of Ms. Flores—one that looked like her college graduation, one of her with a man in ski gear in front of a snowy backdrop, one a big family photo with her face smiling in the front row. I gave her a look and a nod at the security golem.

"Gerald, please wait outside," she said. Now I knew the golem's name at least.

Gerald frowned. "I have strict instructions not to—"

She waved a hand. "Where do you think he's going to go, Gerald? I doubt he'd survive a jump from my twelfth-floor window, and you'll be right outside. Now get out. I will likely have to discuss sensitive personnel matters, and I can't do that with you here."

I didn't bother to correct the sharp little HR vice-president that a twelve-story drop would hurt like a sonofabitch, but it wouldn't even come close to killing me. I tend to leave out the "I'm not completely human" conversation until my second date. Or at least my second meeting over a murdered coworker. Tomato, to-mah-to.

Flores sat down behind her desk, so I followed her lead and took one of the armless chairs facing her. She opened a file drawer, pulled out a manila folder, and placed it on her desk.

"What can I do for you, Mr. Harker?" she asked with a little smile.

"As you know, Ms. Dover was killed this morning. While we understand the shock and grief her coworkers must be facing, time is always of the essence in these types of investigations, so we cannot allow people a typically appropriate time of mourning before we begin our investigation."

"Let me stop you right there, Mr. Harker. The police were already here, and they confiscated Ms. Dover's computer, searched her office, and interviewed several of her coworkers. And you haven't shown me a badge, or any type of official ID. You also seem to know nothing at all about the activities of the police department, and those things all add up to you not being with the police. So who are you, and why are you snooping around my dead employee?"

Fuck. I needed to think quick. *Fuck it, here goes nothing.* "Ms. Flores, do you believe in magic?" I asked, whispering *"incindare"* under my breath and sending a small gout of flame up from my palm.

The startled executive jerked back, almost toppling over in her chair. "What the hell?!?" She stood up and backed away, bumping into the bookcase behind her.

I closed my fist and the flame winked out. "Ms. Flores, there are things in the world that most people never hear of outside of children's stories. The monster under the bed, the boogeyman in the closet, the thing that goes bump in the night. They're all real, and I have spent my life fighting them. I think that Ms. Dover got mixed up in something ugly, something way outside her experience, and she paid the ultimate price for it. This is the kind of thing the local police are not very well-equipped to deal with, so I'm piggybacking on their mundane investigation with my very much not mundane one. But I need your help.

"I need to know everything about Terese Dover. Who loved her, who hated her, where she shopped, where she ate lunch, what she liked, what she disliked, where she vacationed—I need to know everything. And I need you to help me."

Now that the initial shock of seeing the world beneath her world was fading a little, Flores latched on to the only thing she still understood—rules. "I'm sorry, Mr. Harker. I can't help you. I don't know what your little magic trick was supposed to prove, but it didn't work. There are very strict regulations that cover what I can and cannot discuss with you and..."

Her words trailed off and her eyes went wide. I swept myself a clear spot about two feet in diameter on her desk, drew a quick circle with a piece of chalk I carried in a pocket, and muttered a short incantation. An imp appeared in the circle on her desk, a twelve-inch naked red man with goat hooves, bat wings, a forked tail, and short red horns curving from his skull.

You know, basically every childhood nightmare of the devil? Well, that was standing on her desk.

The imp turned around, looked up at me, then started hopping up and down, shaking his fists. "Goddammit, Harker!" the tiny demon yelled, and its voice was shrill and almost comical. "I told you to stop bringing me up here if I can't eat or fuck anything!" He turned to Flores and leered at her. "Hey baby," he said, grabbing his penis, which was large out of all proportion to his size. "You want some of this? Come on sweet cheeks, you know you want to try it. You know what they say, 'Once you go red, you fuck 'til you're dead'." The horny little demonlet cackled like he'd invented the dirty limerick and turned back to me.

"Whatever you want, the answer is go fuck yourself."

"Why you gotta be like that, 'Thew?" I asked, a small smile threatening to crack my face.

"It's gotta be like that because fuck you, that's why." He turned back to Flores. "What about it, baby girl? You decided you want to come ride the crimson pony? Just reach out with your hand and erase the circle old Fuckwit McDickhead over there called me into, and I'll make you scream in ways you've never imagined."

"He's probably right there," I said. "Demons have barbed penises, kinda like cats, only with more sulfur smell. You get hooked up with 'Thew and you'll definitely scream."

"And don't worry about size, sexy," the imp chimed in. "My thundercock isn't the only thing that grows." As if to prove his point, he swelled to twice his size, almost completely filling the circle. He jerked his tail back as it grazed the chalk line, a yellow spark of magical energy arcing out from the circle to zap him.

"Ow, Lucifer damn it!" he yelled, pulling his tail around and putting the tip in his mouth. After a few seconds, he looked back up at Flores and held out the tail. "It's pretty flexible," he said, a lascivious grin splitting his crimson features. "You should see the things I can do with it. I can tickle your—"

I cut him off with a word. "*Silencio.*" The demon's lips kept moving, but no sound came out. "Now do you believe in monsters?" I asked. "If you need a little more convincing, feel free to let the little guy out. I'm sure he'd love to show you all the things he can tickle with that tail."

Flores looked up from the imp on her desk. She was very pale, and for a moment I thought she was going to faint. Then she turned to the side and vomited very quietly into a trash can next to her desk. She stayed hunched over the black Rubbermaid receptacle for several long moments before she sat up, wiped her mouth with a tissue from a desk drawer, and looked at me, her composure completely restored.

"What can I do for you, Mr. Harker? And would you please remove your demon from my office?"

I waved a hand, and the illusion of the demon winked out of existence. I reached out with my finger and scrubbed out a tiny part of the circle, making it useless for any real spellcasting. I wouldn't want anyone to actually summon a demon into the woman's office, after all. Real demons don't come in miniature sizes. The smallest ones I've ever heard of are the size of a large dog and will reduce a human being to nothing more than scraps in less than five minutes flat. But my illusionary hornball demon was pretty useful in convincing people that the supernatural is real. After all, who wouldn't get nervous at the thought of a hellspawn with a crush on them?

CHAPTER TEN

I spent about an hour chatting with the suddenly cooperative HR guru and came away with the contact information for three people who filed complaints about Terese Dover within the past six months; a folder containing no fewer than seventeen letters of recommendation, promotion, and awards for productivity from her superiors; and Ms. Flores' phone number. You never know.

Loud music blared down the hall as I stepped off the elevator at 340 South, an upscale apartment building on the edge of Southend, a recently revitalized part of town that went from strip clubs to antique stores almost overnight. I checked numbers on doors against the piece of paper in my hand, my confusion rising every step I drew nearer to apartment 614. I stopped in front of the right door and raised my hand to knock, although with the level of Metallica that was screeching at me in the hallway, I knew no one in the apartment had any chance of hearing me knock.

But I knocked anyway, with the expected lack of result. I tried again, and the third time I switched over to pounding. After that, with my temper growing and the amount of time before the Equinox shrinking, I kicked it in. The frame splintered, the door crashed in, the chain holding it shut snapped, and my foot hurt.

A young woman in exercise gear was on a treadmill in the middle of the room screaming heavy metal along with the cable TV music station at the top of her lungs. She froze in mid-chorus when I came crashing in, her hand upraised in a stuck salute to the gods of rock. She looked to be in her mid-twenties, and judging by the six-pack she was sporting in her sports bra and her sweatpants, she spent a lot of time on that treadmill.

"What the fuck?" She hopped off the treadmill and took a couple of quick steps to a small table next to the couch. She pushed a button on a remote and turned off the TV, then picked up her cell phone with one hand and started rummaging around in her purse with the other.

I didn't move any closer, just closed the door behind me and stood a foot or so into the foyer. I was a good fifteen feet away from her, trying to stay as far away as the small apartment would let me so she didn't feel any more threatened by the big guy who just kicked her door in. Plus, if she tried to shoot me, the farther away I was, the better. I just focused my will in case I needed a quick spell and tried to look harmless.

"Are you Janet Hamilton?" I asked.

"That depends completely on who the fuck you are and what the fuck you're doing in my apartment." She turned to the phone. "Hello, 911? There's a—"

So much for harmless. I released my will with a whispered "*magnos.*" A focused little pulse of electromagnetic energy flickered out from my fingers, and her cell phone was a paperweight. Her TV and DVR were also probably fried, as well as the remote, anything else electronic in her purse, and probably the stereo. At least this time I managed not to blow out all the power in the building.

She tossed her useless cell phone and pulled her other hand out of her purse. She held a small canister with a red button on top of it. "Don't come any closer. I've got pepper spray."

"Calm down, Ms. Hamilton. My name is Quincy Harker, and I'm working with the police." I held up the wallet containing my PI credentials, including what might or might not have been a fake badge I picked up at Morris Costumes a couple years ago. She lowered the pepper spray and her shoulders immediately relaxed. It was amazing how effective that line was. I might have to consider actually working with the cops if this kept up.

"I'm a private investigator consulting with the Homicide Division. We're looking into the death of your employer, Ms. Dover."

A sneer crossed her previously gorgeous face. Nobody's attractive when they sneer. "That bitch? Who cares? Everybody I know is glad she's dead."

This wasn't exactly what I expected to hear. "I met a woman at your office who told me you were so upset over Ms. Dover's death that you were unable to come in to work."

"That's HR-speak for 'she called in and told us to fuck off.' I figured if Satanna wasn't coming in, I'd take a little vacation, have some 'me' time, and generally chill. That keeps me from having to pretend that everybody in the world didn't hate her when people call in to give their bullshit fake condolences all day."

"So you didn't like her? But we found a ton of commendations in her personnel file."

"Yeah? And how many of them were from the bosses, and how many were from normal people?" She tossed the pepper spray back into her purse.

I thought for a moment. All of the complaints were from so-called "normal people" while all the commendations were from superiors. "So she liked to punch down, as they say?"

"Yeah, that's a good word for it." She pulled her hair back into a messy auburn ponytail and walked into the kitchen, pulling open the refrigerator and grabbing a water bottle. "I'd offer you something, but I don't want you to stay."

I barked out a short laugh. "I get it. I just need to know if you have any idea who hated Ms. Dover enough to kill her."

She leaned on the marble-topped island in her kitchen and gave me a direct look. Her green eyes were bright, but there was no mirth there. "Look, pal. I hated that bitch. She was a horrible boss, and I'm pretty sure some of the shit she did was illegal, or at least borderline illegal. But I didn't kill her, and I don't know anybody who would. We're bankers, for God's sake. It's not like we're mobsters or anything like that. Hell, we don't even handle mortgages. And in today's market, that's something that *could* get you killed. If she was a normal person, I'd say you should talk to a boyfriend or girlfriend, but as far as I know, she never dated. So I've got nothing. Except a busted door."

"Yeah, sorry about that. You couldn't hear me knock, I guess."

"Not a chance. I was rocking out, getting a good sweat on, and yelling every nasty thing I ever wanted to call Satanna and wouldn't get the chance. So now I've got to take a shower, and there's nothing to secure my door with." She leaned further over the island, giving me a pretty clear view down the front of her sports bra. A drop of sweat ran down her collarbone and into her cleavage. I watched its journey, thinking about following it all the way down that very, very flat stomach to its natural destination, then gave myself a little mental shake and looked back up at her eyes.

She was watching me watch her with a little smirk on her face. "You gonna repair my door, Mr. Detective, or you just going to stand guard outside my shower and make sure I stay safe and sound?"

Nobody's very attractive when they smirk, either, and after all my time on this planet, I'm not immune to feminine wiles, but I am pretty damned resistant. So it didn't take me too much effort to slap on a rueful expression and shake my head.

"As much as I'd love to wash, I mean watch, your back, Ms.—"

"Miss," she said, wiggling her left hand at me to show the distinct lack of rings there.

"Miss Hamilton," I continued. "I have to get back to the station and keep going on our investigation. So if there's nothing else you can think of about why someone might want to harm your boss, I'll have to be on my way."

"Your loss, Detective. I don't know any reason somebody would take out Satanna, any more than you guys know why somebody killed her two buddies."

I had been digging through my pocket for a business card, but at her mention of buddies, my head snapped around.

"What buddies?" I asked.

"Mr. Baxter and Mr. Lacey." She stared a little, like she expected me to know more of what was going on than I did.

"Ms. Dover knew them both?"

"Yeah, they were in on some big development deal a couple years ago. It was right before she came to AmeriBank. I think it was that mixed-use place out in Belmont, maybe."

I kinda knew the place she was talking about. It took a fifty-acre piece of worthless property off I-85 about half an hour outside of Charlotte and turned it into a live/work/play development with homes, condos, and apartments at multiple price points, with the condos and apartments built over street-level shops and restaurants. There was a movie theater, skate park, and small water park attached, all fronting a gated neighborhood of million-dollar homes. The lots sold quickly, thanks to the privacy and the half-acre of woods surrounding each one. The condos and apartments did pretty well, too, and the shops were some of the most high-end in the area. If Dover had anything to do with that, she should have made out pretty well.

"Where did she work before AmeriBank?" I asked.

"I don't know," she said. "Some other bank. And she was a big deal there, so AB had to really lay out some coin to get her to jump ship."

"Huh," I mumbled. That was something to think about. "Thanks, I'll look into that." Why hadn't Sponholz mentioned the connection to the earlier victims? That raised an eyebrow, at least.

"You see anything else you want to look into, Detective?" she asked, batting her eyelashes at me. That would work better if her eyelashes didn't still have treadmill sweat on them. I love getting sweaty with a woman, but I'd rather if I'm the reason she's hot and bothered, not her exercise routine. With this one, I think all I could take credit for was the "bothered" part.

"I'm sorry, Miss Hamilton, I have to get back to the investigation. But if you think of anything else...regarding the case...feel free to give me a call." I finally found a business card crumpled in the back pocket of my jeans and slid it across the countertop to her. I gave one last, slightly regretful, look at her cleavage, then turned and walked to her door.

I put my hand on the door jamb, focused my will, and whispered. "*Restoratus.*" I've found through long practice that it doesn't always matter if the words you say are really Latin, or really anything, as long as the intent is clear. The words are mostly a way to focus the mind and thus focus the magic. That's not the case with summonings or more complex spells, like healings. Those are more about asking the universe to do something for you, and you have to ask nicely and in the right languages. The universe, or God, or Allah, or Gaea, or however you want to frame it, does not respond to current Standard American English. Or maybe the complexity of carving passages between dimensions is just so complicated that you have to focus completely on the words to distract yourself from not believing that you can do what you're about to do. One of those if probably close to how it really works. I don't pretend to understand it. It's fucking magic, you're not supposed to understand.

But however it works, it worked, and Janet Hamilton's door frame, lock, and door were as good as new when I took my hand off the jamb. I turned around, gave her a wave, and headed off to figure out what else Sponholz wasn't telling me about Terese Dover, Lincoln Baxter, and the other dead half-angels.

CHAPTER ELEVEN

I got back to my car and grabbed my phone from the charger. It was a new smartphone, and the battery life was for shit, but it played music and had a camera built in, so I splurged on it. Besides, it was Luke's money, and he had plenty. When you start life as a rich-ass fifteenth century mildly psychotic Count and invest wisely, or at least kill a lot of rich people over the course of a few centuries, you're never short on cash.

"Yeah?" Dennis answered on the third ring.

"Boltron, what's up?" I tried to put a cheerful tone in my voice, not an "I only call you when I want something" tone.

"What do you want?" Apparently I failed.

"What makes you think I want anything?" I tried again.

"Because you only ever call me Boltron when you want something.

Shit. Busted.

"Besides, I hate being called Boltron. You know why?"

I didn't want to ask. I didn't care why, honestly, but I had to ask or he'd never help me out. "No, why?"

"Because I know when you call me Boltron, you're not thinking of the cool lion Voltron, you're thinking of the lame as shit vehicle Voltron. And nobody wants to be the vehicle Voltron, Harker. Everybody wants to be the fucking lion Voltron. But I don't get to be the lion Voltron, do I, *Quincy?*" He said my name like it was French for "shithead."

"I guess not, bro. Sorry."

"Sorry? *Sorry?* I'm stuck in a wheelchair with no fucking legs and all I get is sorry? I have to be the fucking vehicle Voltron forever, and you're *sorry*? Well—"

"Well next time you decide to be a fucking idiot and dress up like Gandalf to try and get into some coed's pants, I'll just let the fucking demon eat you, okay? Does that sound like a plan, shitweasel? Now shake off your goddamn pity party, pull your shit together, and get to fucking work. We've got four dead people with only the thinnest legit connection, a high holy day of magical buggery coming up in thirty-six hours, and no fucking clue what to do about it. So get your fucking hands off your dick and let's figure this shit out so nobody else dies. Okay?"

There was silence on the line for long enough that I thought I had maybe gotten a little too verbally medieval on his ass. After a solid two minutes of nothing but background noise coming through the phone, Dennis spoke again.

"Okay."

"Okay?"

"Yeah, okay. I'm back. Now what did you find out?"

So I filled him in on everything I had learned, and after about a minute of me talking, I heard keys clicking in the background. A few seconds later, Dennis spoke. "Okay, I've got Terese Dover's employment history and banking records, as well as Lincoln Baxter's. Brecker was even easier, but this Lacey guy has his shit locked down."

"Well, what can you tell me about the others?"

"They definitely all worked on the Pinehaven development. It was one of the first multi-use developments on Lake Wylie. The most expensive houses fronted the lake, another pricing tier overlooked the golf course, and the cheapest houses, the ones that started at only a half-million, those were closer to the retail and entertainment area. And all the shops either had apartments or condos over them. It was worth a ton of money and became the model for development in the area."

"Yeah, I've been there."

"How'd you get in?"

"Part of the golf course was built over a small family cemetery, the kind people used to have in the 18th century. They called me in when a poltergeist visited one of the homes near the sand trap on the 12th hole. I showed up and noticed that the teenage daughter's bedroom window overlooked the green. I had a brief conversation with her about playing around with spells she read online, dumped a full container of salt into the sand trap, and laid the spirit to rest. They haven't had any problems since then."

"Not supernatural problems, at any rate," Dennis replied.

"What's that mean?"

"It means that there have been a lot of complaints about the building quality, and more than one lawsuit filed against the developer since the place opened up. But it turns out the developer, one Kevin Lacey, had a good lawyer. The contracts on the homes are airtight and protect the builder against any liability past three years. The problems didn't start appearing until year five, so all those people are on the hook for their sinking foundations, substandard shingles, cracked driveway pavement, and undersized electrical wiring."

"Sounds like our dearly departed Mister Lacey had himself a hell of a lawyer."

"He did indeed," Dennis said. "A hell of a lawyer who left private practice two years after Pinehaven sold its first house and moved into public service as an assistant district attorney."

"A very tall district attorney named Lincoln Baxter?" I asked.

"One and the same."

"So how does Terese Dover tie into all this? I suppose she moved money around for the project?"

"A little, but not much. It looks a lot more like she was responsible for the cash on the back end, moving money around through shell corporations and holding companies, bouncing it to and from offshore accounts until it came back, clean and virtually untraceable, into the accounts of our 'unconnected' victims."

"And what about Brecker?" I asked.

"He was the contractor for the development. I can't find anything specific that he did that was shady, but it does look like there have been a ton of small things going wrong with the buildings ever since the project was completed."

"So Lacey sells a huge project to a bunch of rich whales, Brecker the contractor cuts corners to pad everyone's pockets, Baxter writes the contracts that protect them from lawsuits in the long term, Dover moves their money around to hide it from the tax man, and they get away with this how, exactly? Don't buildings get inspected? Isn't there some kind of oversight into all of this?"

More clicking of keys, then Bolton comes back on the line. "You called it, Q. The entire project was overseen by the same city inspector, from plan review to final certificate of occupancy. A guy by the name of Kevin Gilbert, who, as of this conversation, is still alive. And according to the records at the Government Center, is at work right now."

"That's only about a block and a half from Police Headquarters. I'll call

Sponholz and get him to put a uniform on Gilbert. If he's tied into this some-how, he's either our killer, or the next target."

"Good call. I'll keep digging and see if I can figure out anything else about Gilbert."

"Like whether or not his mom was touched by an angel?"

"Something like that." Dennis chuckled and hung up the phone.

"That wasn't funny," came a voice from beside me in the car.

I jumped so high my head literally hit the ceiling and turned to Glory, pistol in hand. She looked at it and smiled a little.

"You don't think that will actually do any good, do you?" she asked.

"No, but it's the natural response when someone scares the shit out of me," I replied.

"You're very profane," my guardian angel said, her lips pursed in disap-proval. I'd seen people purse their lips before, but not since the Prohibition-ists. Those people were always pursing something. Serious pains in the ass.

"You're very fucking observant," I replied, emphasizing the "fucking." It was a dick move, and I knew it, but I didn't respond well to fright, especially when I wasn't allowed to kill the thing that frightened me. I didn't particularly *want* to kill my guardian angel because that seemed like a bad idea on so many levels. That's not even considering the fact that I wasn't sure I *could* kill her, even if I wanted to.

"There's no need to be childish."

"I try to stick to what I'm good at."

"Well, let's focus on something else you're good at—stirring up trouble. You're sticking your nose into some powerful matters, the kind of thing that can get even a powerful wizard destroyed. Are you sure you want to follow this road to the end?"

"Do I have a choice? It looks like whoever is killing these half-angels wants to use them to open a portal and bring a bunch of big nasties through. They've already brought Orobas through, and God only knows who or what else. I don't know if I can handle this, but I know that I probably won't survive whatever they want to bring through."

"Good point. Anyone with any magical talent will be the first ones killed if there is a demonic invasion of this plane. They wouldn't want anyone to stand against them."

"I hate it when I'm right."

"So what's the plan?"

"You are assuming I have one. I suppose I head over to Kevin Gilbert's office and make sure the cops have an eye on him. Then I kill who- or what-ever comes after him, and *voila*, the day is saved."

"Because it's always that easy." I'm obviously a bad influence, even on the divine. Now my guardian angel was a smartass, and we'd only been on speaking terms for a couple of days.

"Exactly," I said. "Now let's go protect a city drone from any demonic ramifications of his being on the take ten years ago. Because this time, the angels aren't necessarily the good guys, but they're the ones I have to save."

"Probably not the last time in your life you'll say that," Glory replied, and I'll admit that I was a little frightened to see there was no humor in her eyes.

CHAPTER TWELVE

The dozens of people running from the Charlotte-Mecklenburg Government Center when I pulled up was a dead giveaway that everything was fucked. I pulled the Camry up onto the curb and hopped out, leaving the engine running and a startled angel in the passenger seat. If she was really going to keep me alive, she was going to have to work on her reaction time.

I burst into the lobby, fighting like a salmon swimming upstream against a tide of terrified people, and stopped cold at the thing causing all the commotion. It was a demon, and by the size of it, a powerful one. It was at least ten feet tall with bat-like wings that must have been twenty feet from tip to tip. Long, curving horns stuck out from its forehead, giant black swirls slicing through the air as it whipped its crimson head from side to side, looking for more tasty morsels.

Muscles rippled across its broad chest, and thick black hair covered its torso and limbs. Its preternaturally long arms ended in three clawed fingers and a thumb, and it had cloven hooves instead of toes. A prehensile tail lashed out, piercing the chest, leg, or neck of anyone unfortunate enough to be too close. Its eyes glowed a sulfuric yellow, and scraps of fabric dangled from its mouth full of a triple row of razor-sharp teeth.

The second I burst into the room, the demon froze. It sniffed the air, its tail coming to a point, then twirling around to point its metal-clad tip directly at me. The demon turned, looked at me, and *smiled*. I've never been so frightened in my near century on this planet as I was when that monster grinned at me. I knew in that moment that I was about to die, I was going out in the most painful way imaginable, and that monster planned to laugh the whole time it devoured my soul.

Then Glory broke through the throng behind me, and I learned what a guardian angel can really do when the shit hits the fan. The gorgeous blonde in dressy casual clothes was gone, and in her place was a nearly six-foot angel of fucking righteousness in chain and plate armor with a sword made entirely of light. And not some janky red or blue lightsaber, I mean a four-foot bastard sword with a blade so bright it seared itself into your vision if you looked too closely at it. Her blond curls were tied back into a tight ponytail, and a golden helmet covered most of her face. She ran across the marble floor and launched herself into the air with enough force to crack the tile she leapt from.

Her blade flashed down as she vaulted over the demon, leaving a broad line of black blood spewing from the monster's shoulder. It whirled on her, and I pulled my will together in a hurried attack. "Separatus!" I shouted, thrusting both arms forward, fingers out straight and palms pointed to the floor, making a knife-edge with my hands. A glowing disc of force flew from my fingertips, slicing through one of the demon's legs just above the ankle. It began to turn back to me, but that's the moment the upper leg fell off the now-severed lower leg, and the beast crashed forward in a face-first sprawl. It crushed the information desk to splinters and plastic shrapnel, then clambered to its knees and reached for me.

I jumped back, my augmented strength helping me cover a good ten feet, and the demon's claws whistled harmlessly several feet in front of me. I looked past the creature and saw Glory charge in, sword raised high over her head. I raised my hands to cast another spell, but caught Glory's eye as she shook her head. *Fair enough*, I thought. If she wanted to handle the demon, I'd be happy to let her. I wasn't really sure I had anything stronger to call up, anyway. She slashed down with the blinding blade, then back up in a continuous loop, and both of the demon's wings flapped to the ground like giant ebon kites. Gouts of blood spurted from the monster's shoulders, and it whirled on Glory once more, but she was already on the move.

She was a ballet of holy magic and death, always striking at just the point where the demon couldn't reach her. She wove in and out and under its flailing claws like she was boneless, made of water. The thing couldn't touch her, and as it became more and more frustrated, it also grew weaker and weaker, as every stroke of her blade opened another cut, carved out another chunk of flesh, severed another limb. Finally, after long minutes of ducking and weaving, the demon stretched just a little too far and lost its balance. The gargantuan beast flopped forward, catching itself on its bloody elbows, and Glory spun around, raised her sword high overhead, and brought it flashing down in a final blow.

The demon's body collapsed, the head fell to the floor a few feet away, and the severed pieces immediately started to smoke and dissolve into extradimensional goop. Within seconds, the monster was well on its way to being nothing more than a stinky black mess all over the cracked marble floor of the Government Center. I turned around and took in the carnage that surrounded us. At least a dozen people lay dead and dismembered around the lobby, and that many more were cowering around columns or benches, clutching wounds or simply too terrified to run. The glass doors were shattered, some from people trying to get out, and one from me and Glory charging in like the Light Brigade. Literally, in her case.

I turned to Glory, shielding my eyes from the glow of her sword. Her brow knit briefly, then she seemed to realize what was blinding me, and the sword winked out of existence. So did her armor, leaving her standing in the middle of the wreckage in jeans, tennis shoes, and a Sunnydale High t-shirt.

"What the everloving fuck was that?" I asked after I took a long pull from the flask I often carry in my back pocket.

"That was a demon, Q. I thought you'd seen them before," Glory replied.

"Not that," I said. "What the hell happened to you?"

"Oh, that. Well, you don't expect a guardian angel to be defenseless, do you? The job isn't all about making sure you don't drown in Farmer Dante's pond while running away from the hayloft he caught you in with his daughter."

I'd forgotten about that. I wondered exactly how it was that I found all those stepping stones, and why there were stepping stones in a pond in the first place. "That was you?"

"No, but I've heard stories about you. There's an entire class on you in Angel Academy."

"There's an Angel Academy?"

"No, but if there were, there would be a class on Protecting Idiot Humans Who Really Try To Get Themselves Killed. And you could fill an entire syllabus."

"Why was there a huge-ass demon in the lobby of the Government Center?" I asked. "Do you think it was here after Gilbert?"

"I doubt it. I don't think that thing could fit in the stairwell, much less an elevator. I think it was probably here as a distraction."

"Well, it was a pretty good one," I said. "Oh shit." I looked at Glory, and the look on her face mirrored what I was feeling in my gut. If the distraction was so good, what were we going to find when we located Kevin Gilbert?

CHAPTER THIRTEEN

The answer was a drained husk hanging in the men's room on the fifth floor. Kevin Gilbert was deader than your average doornail, and paler than Uncle Luke.

"Fuck, we're too late," I said. "Can you sense anything about the killer?"

"I'm not allowed to intervene except in matters of life and death," Glory said. "While this certainly concerns death, your life is not in immediate danger, so I can't actively help you."

"Great," I muttered. "What's the point of having an angel if you can't use them to break the rules of nature?" I didn't wait for a response, just opened my Sight and looked around the bathroom.

That's not the best idea, by the way. The Second Sight utilizes all sorts of odd spectra, and there's some creepy shit in public restrooms. This one was pretty clean, mystically speaking, just a couple of smears of bad soul on the mirrors where some amazingly narcissistic executive spent too much time fixing his hair and gloating about the bad things he was going to do to his employees. And yes, people do leave that kind of psychometric fingerprint on things, if they have strong enough feelings. The strongest feeling I found in that bathroom was the abject terror centered on Kevin Gilbert's rapidly cooling body. His Nephilim nature was evident in the wing-shaped nimbus of gold that still sparkled around him, but his last moments were obviously filled with fear and knowledge of what was coming.

"That's a little odd," I said.

"What's that, Q?" I was starting to get used to Glory calling me "Q," not that I was willing to let her know that yet.

"There's no glee, or mirth, or even arousal in the room," I said. "Usually someone who kills in such a specific way, with such obvious intent, has some real hatred behind it. But I'm not picking up any emotion at all from our killer. It's almost like it was just a job for him, or he was just following orders."

"Are you sure the killer is a man?"

"As long as it's a human, it's a man. The number of women who can subdue a grown man then lift his body to be drained like a deer ready to be dressed is pretty small. Especially when you factor in that it had to be done between the time the demon first appeared and the moment we got here. Yeah, it's either a guy or some supernatural creature, so it's just easier to refer to it as male."

"That makes sense. I just wanted to make sure you weren't missing something."

"I probably am, Glory. I'm just pretty sure it isn't the gender of our killer."

"So whoever it is has Gilbert's blood—what's next?"

"Well, the Solstice is tomorrow, so maybe it has something to do with that," I said.

"Oh shit," Glory said, then clapped both hands over her mouth.

I laughed out loud. I couldn't help it. She'd known me less than two days and I already had my guardian angel swearing. A couple more weeks on the job and she'd be rolling blunts and listening to Dr. Dre.

"That's not funny," Glory said. "The solstice is a period of weakening the barriers between the realms. It's much easier to bring across much stronger beings than would normally be able to pass between dimensions."

"How big?" I asked, thinking back to Orobas and the ten-foot monstrosity that she just sliced and diced.

"Big enough to make that thing in the lobby look like an ant."

"Fuck," I said. "I guess we should probably figure out who's running this party, get ourselves invited, shit in the punchbowl, and send everybody home early before things really get rolling, huh?"

"Sometimes I don't understand human metaphor. You don't actually want to defecate in a punchbowl, do you?" the very perplexed angel asked.

"No, Glory, I just want to wipe my ass with this guy's very carefully drawn-out plans."

"Is that another metaphor? Or do you have a strange fixation with rather unpleasant bodily functions?"

"Is both an option?" I asked, opening the door and stepping out of the restroom, almost running into a rotund government functionary with a bad toupee. "You *really* don't want to go in there, bub. I just blew chunks across all three sinks after what I saw in the lobby. I'd go down a floor if I was you."

He turned away and bolted for the elevator, and I grinned at Glory. "Come on, angel. Let's go stop an apocalypse."

"How do you know where we're going?" Glory asked from my passenger seat. I got back to the Camry just in time to sweet-talk the tow truck driver into not hooking her up and hauling her away, so I still had wheels.

"I don't, but I know someone who will. Dennis is one of the most tech-savvy people I know, and he's got more than a little experience with things that go bump in the night. If anybody can whip up a high-tech solution for finding a low-tech beastie, it's him."

We pulled into Dennis' driveway about fifteen minutes later, a modest split-level on the east side of town. I parked behind his van and hopped out.

"Shit," I said as soon as I took a good look at the house. The front door was hanging open, and the storm door was lying in the bushes beside the front stoop.

"What's wrong?" Glory asked. It was still a little creepy that she never had to use the car doors.

"Somebody's been here, and it looks like they either killed or took Dennis."

"How do you know?"

I pointed to the front stoop and the three brick steps leading up to it. "Dennis never uses the front door. He's got motorized lifts to get from floor to floor, and a wheelchair on each floor, but he can't navigate those steps. The back door has a small ramp. Dennis uses that entrance. He says it's safer if burglars don't know the owner of the house can't run after them."

"Smart," the angel remarked.

"He's a smart dude," I replied. I hopped up the steps and looked at the door. It didn't look that out of the ordinary. It wasn't destroyed, or burned through or anything, just kicked in, like I'd done to Janet Hamilton's door that afternoon. That was only about hours before, but it felt like a lifetime.

I pushed the door open wider and drew my Glock. I slipped through the opening and swept the room with the barrel of my pistol. The front parlor was empty, as were the small dining room and kitchen. I motioned behind me to Glory, pointing her upstairs, and I went down the steps to the basement. Dennis went long days without ever leaving the bottom floor of his house, and he didn't really need to. It had a full bath, his office with all his computers, a den with a TV and every gaming system imaginable, and a small mini fridge full of sandwich meat, mayo, and sodas. A freelance web designer didn't need a whole lot more.

The stairs spilled out into a small foyer, and I passed through that quickly on the way to the den. I swept the room, then moved on to the bathroom and the office. Nothing. If Dennis was in the house, he was upstairs.

"He's not upstairs," Glory said beside me, shattering that inkling of hope.

"Whatever we're after must have taken him to slow me down."

"How? Do you think the killer came here after killing Gilbert?" Glory asked.

"No, there wasn't time. He must have subdued Dennis, then gone to the Government Center and cut the demon loose in the lobby while he murdered Gilbert."

"So Dennis was what, in the trunk of his car?"

"Or the back of his van. Dennis is brilliant, but he's not exactly a fighter. And he only lost his legs a few years ago, so he's not all that nimble moving around without his chair. All the killer would need to do is gag him and bind his hands, and Dennis would be largely helpless."

"Do we know that he's still alive?"

"No," I replied. "But I have to assume he is." Because if he wasn't, it would mean I'd failed him. Twice.

"Now what?" Glory asked.

"I don't know. Maybe there's a clue in whatever he was last working on. I know he was looking at possible locations for the ceremony." I sat down at Dennis' computer and clicked the mouse. The machine sprang to life, asking for a password.

"You know his password?" Glory asked.

"We were close," I replied. "That, and it's written on a sticky note stuck to his monitor. Dennis left it there for me in case I ever needed to get into his computer, and he always said that no one would expect a hacker to keep a password out in the open like that."

"How very meta of him."

"That's what I thought," I agreed. I clicked on the icon for a maps program still open on the desktop. A map of Charlotte popped up, with certain areas highlighted in green, yellow, and red.

"Good man, Boltron," I said with a relieved sigh.

"What is it?"

"He color-coordinated the map. The red circles are mystical hot spots, but not relevant to our case, like Luke's house and Mort's. The yellow circles are maybes, but unlikely to be the place that our main event is going down. The green circles are big magical focal points in town, exactly the kind of place that you would want to open a highway to Hell."

"Really? A hard rock reference? Now?" Glory didn't look amused at my AC/DC pun.

I just shrugged. "Seemed appropriate. Anyway, there are four focal points large enough and secure enough or remote enough for our guy to open a big hole in the universe. The big racetrack up in Concord, but I'd gonna guess no on that one. My gut says he wants to cause as much havoc right out of the gate as possible, and the speedway is pretty deserted after dark. Then there's the bandshell out behind SouthPark Mall, and I think that one's probably out as well. Same reasons—the potential for mayhem in the middle of the night is much less than the other two options."

"Why does the ritual have to be performed in the middle of the night?"

"Well, the Solstice starts at midnight tonight, and I don't think our boy wants to keep Dennis around any longer than he has to."

"That means…"

"Yeah, that means we have about six hours to find this guy, rescue Dennis, and stop this assclown from setting loose Hell on Earth. Literally."

"What are the other two options?"

"They're both pretty reasonable choices, if you think about it. The first is the Charlotte-Douglas International Airport. Tens of thousands of people go through there every day, and they all leave a little bit of their energy behind. Couple that with the anger people feel when traveling, and most folks think a busy airport is already a kind of hell. But I think it's the last one. Spirit Square Center for Arts & Education, downtown. It's the old First Baptist Church building, so the irony would appeal to a showboating demon like this one, and since it's right in the middle of downtown, as many people pass through or by it in a day as the airport. Plus, it's a lot closer to all our dump sites and the Government Center. Our killer is comfortable in the Uptown area; I'd be very surprised if it wasn't someone who knows Charlotte like the back of his hand. A realtor maybe, or postal worker—someone whose job requires them to drive all over town…mother*fucker*." I put my elbows on Dennis' desk and dropped my head into my hands.

"He played me like a goddamned fiddle, didn't he?"

"Am I supposed to—"

"Oh cut the shit, Glory!" I snapped at the angel. "How long have you known?"

"Known what?" She was obfuscating again, but now I knew she couldn't tell me a direct lie.

I stood up and turned to face her. "How long have you known that Sponholz is the Cambion?"

"I've always known," she said, not meeting my eyes.

"And you weren't going to tell me, were you?"

"No, I wasn't. You have to understand, Quincy." No "Q" this time, I was Quincy again. That was fine. I wasn't in the mood for nicknames. "I couldn't tell you. And it's not like I didn't want to, I *couldn't*."

"The fuck you couldn't. Don't give me that shit, Glory. You could have—"

She slapped me. It was just a simple open-handed slap, but she swung my head sideways and made my ears ring.

"No, *you* don't give *me* that shit, John Abraham Quincy Holmwood Harker. I am an Angel of the Lord, and unlike all you humans walking around on Earth fighting, farting, and generally fucking everything up, I don't *have* free will. So when I tell you that I couldn't say anything about the killer's identity, it's because I *couldn't* say anything. I wanted to tell you, but when I am given an order from one of my superiors, I can't violate that directive, no matter how much I would like to."

"Oh." I didn't have anything better to say. Besides, I was a little concerned that if I said much more than that, she'd slap me again.

"So now that you've figured it out, what are you going to do about it? My ability to interfere may be limited, unless your life is in direct danger."

I gave her my best grin, which was hampered a little by the fact that I couldn't feel half my face. "Oh don't worry, darlin'. I'm going to go to an old church and try to stop a well-armed police detective who happens to be half demon from opening a portal to Hell with the blood sacrifice of one of my four friends in the world. I'm pretty sure 'life in danger' will barely scratch the surface of the shitstorm I'm about to stir up."

CHAPTER FOURTEEN

To add insult to the injuries I was almost certainly about to face, it cost me ten bucks to park downtown because of a basketball game. There were cops all over the place, so I knew if I just left the car somewhere, I'd probably never get it back before it was turned into scrap. I ran down the steps at the Seventh Street Station parking garage and hauled ass up the block to the rear entrance of Spirit Square. The thick glass doors were locked, but a side door looked to be hanging a little funny in the frame. Upon closer inspection, the lock had several suspiciously bullet-like holes in it, and the door opened freely.

I slipped into the lobby, keeping close to the walls to stay as much out of view as possible of the completely glass front of the building. Glory kept close behind me as I slid along the wall and up the short steps into the main lobby. I stepped away from the wall, less concerned about someone noticing my feet than when my full body was in view. I got through the main lobby and passed the Duke Energy Theater on my left, then opened my Sight as I started up the ramp to the main theater, once the sanctuary of the First Baptist Church, now a music and theater venue named after native musician Loonis McGlohon.

The doors to the theater stood open, and I heard screams coming from inside. Most days I would have charged right in like a kamikaze pilot, with about the same results, but since I had my third eye wide open, I saw the cat's cradle of magical threads woven across the open doors, tripwires all leading to something spectacularly unpleasant, I was sure.

Instead of running through the door and triggering whatever terrible thing Sponholz had planned for me, I turned around and walked back down the ramp.

"Where are you going?" Glory asked.

"I have a buddy who does theater around town. He was doing a couple shows in here last year, and I came over to have lunch with him. He took me all through the place, showed me how a few things work, including how the actors get to the stage from the dressing rooms downstairs."

"You don't think the Cambion has covered those entrances?"

"I think he's probably covered those, yeah. Especially since they're just open stairwells. But what I hope he hasn't covered is the door the tech staff uses to move the big cherry-picker from room to room to work on lights."

"I have no idea what you're talking about, and I'm divine in nature, Q."

"Just goes to show that there's only one omniscient being, Glory." I gave her a grin and hopped up the steps to the Duke Energy Theater. I reached the heavy glass doors, locked, of course, and drew in my will. I focused my power to needle-thin stream of force and whispered *"sesame."*

"Really? Sesame?" Glory said with a raised eyebrow.

"I just need something to focus the magic for simple stuff. If I was raising a demon, or banishing one, I'd have to actually use a spell. But just brute force bashing a lock open, I can do with 'sesame.'" I pushed the door open, and we slipped into theater's tiny airlock lobby/vestibule. I repeated the process with the door to the theater, and we slipped into the small venue.

"Where is this secret door, Q?"

I led her down the right-hand wall of the theater to the tiny "backstage" area, then pressed my ear to a door painted to match the rest of the wall. I heard movement on the other side, but it was muffled by soundproofing or distance. Either way, it sounded far enough away that Sponholz wasn't going to be standing right there when I opened it, so I pushed the crash bar and flung the door open.

I managed to avoid making any noise as I slipped onto the stage and found myself behind Sponholz and what he obviously planned as his entry point for whatever he planned on bringing through to this world. Dennis lay on a makeshift altar in the middle of a summoning circle that stretched the entire width of the stage. Sponholz had an elaborate set of symbols inscribed on the floor, some Latin, some Enochian, some in languages I didn't even recognize. A huge pentagram was perfectly drawn in the center of the circle, with a smaller circle in the center surrounding Dennis and the altar. The lines of the pentagram weren't drawn with chalk, like a normal circle, or even salt, which I use when I'm working with particularly nasty critters.

Nope, the lines of the pentagram were drawn in liquid, a thick, viscous fluid that looked black in the dim light. I recognized the smell instantly—blood. Seems like I found Sponholz's use for Nephilim blood. Candles burned at each point of the star, five black pillars illuminating Sponholz standing in the center of the circle, chanting and waving a dagger over Dennis' chest.

"You go to the other side of the stage and come at him while I distract him," I whispered to Glory.

"No can do, Q," the angel whispered back. "I can't interfere in this kind of thing, even to save your life. Orders from upstairs, sorry."

What good is a guardian angel if they can't help you cheat and can't save you from the absolute worst of your decisions? I shrugged and returned to my regularly scheduled lack of faith in anything religious. With no help coming from Glory, I had to resort to the old-fashioned methods of dealing with bad guys. I drew in my will, focused on the candles, and whispered, "*cumulonimbus.*" Then I blew out a breath magically amplified into a strong breeze, which immediately blew out three of the candles.

Sponholz looked up and smiled. "Why, Harker, so good of you to come. I was hoping you'd show up. So was your friend here." He brought the dagger down and drew a thin line of blood across Dennis' chest. Dennis stirred, but his eyes stayed closed.

"What's wrong with him? If you've hurt him, Sponholz, I swear to God I'll play jump-rope with your intestines."

"He's fine," the Cambion cop said. "I need him alive until the stroke of midnight, so normally I'd say you have about an hour and a half to say good-bye. But since I don't expect you to live past the next five minutes, that would be overstating the situation."

"What the hell are you doing, Sponholz? Summoning a bigger demon than Orobas and that monster you cut loose at the Government Center? Why would you even do that?"

"You think too small, Harker. I'm not planning to summon anything. My master's plans go much further than that. Too bad you won't be here to see them come to fruition."

"Yeah, because I believe you've got what it takes to kill me," I shot back.

"Oh, I don't. But he does." With that, Sponholz nodded to something behind me. I didn't bother to look around because I knew that trick. It was the oldest one in the book. I turn around, and Sponholz shoots me in the back. Or I don't turn around, and whatever is back there gets a free shot at my exposed backside.

I chose a mix of A and B, where I kept my eyes on Sponholz until the last moment, using my enhanced senses to listen for the creak of a footfall on the stage, then dove forward into a front roll. I came up in a crouch with my

Glock in my hand, spun around, and put four rounds in the chest of the demon standing where I had been moments before. Four rounds out of about nine that I squeezed off, but I never claimed to be a brilliant shot. Bullets ripped through the stage curtains and buried themselves into walls and floor, but the demon didn't budge. Instead, it stood there, its image flickering between demonic and that of a really pretty blonde woman.

"Glory?" I asked, confusion making forget momentarily about the Cambion behind me trying to sacrifice one of my very few friends.

"Q? You shot me," she said. "You *shot* me! Why would you do that?"

"Because I thought you were a demon!"

"Oh, that's what that tickle was," she replied. Glory closed her eyes, and the golden glow of her aura flashed into view, burning the demonic image away in an instant.

"Again with the distraction?" I said, turning back to Sponholz, who had re-lit the candles around the circle somehow. Probably magic. "What are you now, Detective? David Copperfield?" My smartass remarks froze on my tongue as I turned fully around. Apparently tired of waiting, the half-demon cop was standing in the center circle holding Dennis Bolton's bloody heart in his hand. Sponholz resumed his incantation, and as he spoke the words, the blood of the Nephilim began to glow and smoke along the lines of the penta-gram. The heart in his hand started to do the same, and Sponholz reached up with his knife and cut a long slash lengthwise along his arm. Blood flowed down his forearm to his elbow, dripping onto the floor and starting to smoke and glow like the rest of it. Sponholz began to chant in a loud voice, and a portal began to appear over the circle.

"By the mixing of the blood, Angel, Devil, and Human, I pierce the veil.

By the blood of the angels, I pierce the veil.

By the blood of this human, I pierce the veil.

By the blood of this demon, I pierce the veil.

Find the veil rent asunder, my Lord, and open the path to Glory.

Find the veil rent asunder, my Lord, and open the path to Salvation.

Find the veil rent asunder, my Lord, and—"

"Oh, for fuck's sake," I muttered under my breath. I raised my Glock and squeezed off the last six rounds. Three of them struck Sponholz in the chest, knocking him flat on his back and scrubbing out part of his inner circle with his ass. He lay there for a few seconds, then rolled over and clambered to his feet. The portal stopped growing, but it didn't close, just hung there in midair, some ten feet above the stage.

"That hurt, you asshole," he growled at me. "And I dropped my heart. I need that heart for the ritual."

"I wasn't trying to damage my friend's heart," I replied. "I was trying my best to shoot out yours."

"Well, it's a good thing the department issues us all these handy bullet-proof vests, isn't it?" he said with a smile. "Now my ritual is fucked, and I've only got a couple of hours to get everything set up, and I have to kill you before I can get things started again." He shook his right arm like his shoulder hurt, then drew his service weapon from a shoulder holster and leveled it at me.

The pissed-off Cambion got off four or five shots before he realized that I had thrown up a magical shield. He holstered his gun, lowered his good shoulder, and charged me like a balding rhinoceros. My mystical shield was tuned to protect against projectiles, not people, and he was moving faster than any normal person should, so I failed my dexterity check and caught two hundred eighty pounds of half-demon right in my gut. He bulled me backwards until we crashed into the baby grand piano parked upstage, and my ribs made ugly noises on impact.

Sponholz let me go and I dropped to my knees, all my wind gone. He threw a vicious side kick to my head, and I flopped facedown like a carp on the stage. I got myself up to hands and knees, but a stomp between my shoulder blades put me back flat on my stomach. I tried to pull my will together to cast a spell, but he kept distracting me with high-level tactics like kicking the shit out of me. I finally managed to trap one foot with my right arm and twist him around until he dropped to the stage on his ass.

I rolled away from him before dragging myself to my feet, then looked back at him. "Why, Sponholz? What's in this for you?"

"I'm a creature of chaos, Harker. It's what I do."

"But you've always been a decent cop," I said. "Maybe not great, but decent. Why betray that now?"

"Have you seen what's happening all around us, Harker? These are already the end days. I'm just helping it along. The world's going to shit fast. What does it matter if a couple million more damned souls move in and help us along?"

It clicked at the mention of "damned souls." Sponholz's wife had committed suicide back in the fall, and by his faith, she went straight to Hell the instant she died. Opening a gateway to the underworld was the only way he was ever going to see his wife again. I could understand the motive, even if I couldn't condone it.

"You know Lucifer won't let her come back, right?" I asked. Sponholz's face crumpled, but he pulled it back together quickly.

"We have a deal. I give him the portal; he gives me Rachel."

"Is it in writing? Did he promise that she'd be in her right mind? With her memories? Intact?"

"Why would he betray me?"

"Oh my fucking God, Rich, how goddamn stupid are you?!?" I yelled. "He's the fucking Father of Lies, the dude singlehandedly responsible for original sin! Why *wouldn't* he betray you? It's what he does, you idiot!" I threw my hands up, and Sponholz drew his sidearm again.

"That's a good place for those hands, Harker. You keep them there, and maybe after I'm done, I'll shoot you in the head instead of throwing you to the demons that come through."

Demons? He was planning on bringing through more than one? I really had to deal with him quickly. Then I had to figure out how to close that damn portal.

"Turn around and get down on your knees," the detective said, moving toward me with his gun leveled at my chest.

"Why, Rich, I'm not that easy," I said without moving.

His eyes narrowed, and he reached for my shoulder to spin me around. Most people wouldn't move when someone points a gun at them. For most people, that's a really good idea. But, as we've discussed, I'm a little *augmented,* shall we say? The second Sponholz reached for me, I grabbed his wrist and pulled forward, stepping to one side and bringing my knee up at the same time. He shot, but I wasn't in front of his gun anymore, so the bullet buried itself in the stage floor while my knee buried itself in his gut.

His breath *whooshed* out, and I threw a left hook that caught him right behind the ear and drove him to his knees. A right to the temple, then another left, and he sprawled on his stomach on the floor. I moved over and stomped down on his right wrist with my heel, listening to a satisfying *crunch* as a lot of those little bones in his hand and wrist turned to powder. I kicked the gun across the stage, then hauled him up by his collar.

"How do I close the portal?" I hissed in his ear.

"Go fuck yourself," he said between gasps of pain.

"Nah, I think I'd rather get you fucked instead, demon-boy. Why don't I just send you home to Daddy? You think you'd like that? I hear they have all sorts of things they can do with the living down there." I stepped around in front of Sponholz, tagged him with another left to the temple, then landed an uppercut on the point of his jaw that snapped his mouth shut and made his eyes roll so far back in his head that I expected to see his optic nerve. He dropped to his knees, unconscious.

I picked up the comatose Cambion/cop and hauled him to the altar. I laid him across Dennis' lap, then reached down to pat my friend's cheek. "Sorry, buddy. You deserved a lot better than what you got, but I hope you know that this one, at least, saved a lot of people from some very bad things." I set his bloody heart on the altar next to him, then wiped my hands on his shirt.

I pulled a piece of chalk out of my pocket and repaired the circle where Sponholz had scrubbed it out with his butt when I shot him. Then I fixed the few Enochian symbols that were scuffed or askew and drew a new inner circle. I picked up the dagger Sponholz dropped, and pricked my finger with it. I shook a drop of my blood onto the circle and poured just enough of my will into it to invoke the circle. I felt the magical barrier snap into place around me, shielding me from anything that went wrong with what I was about to do.

"Q, what are you doing?" Glory asked from the stage.

"You still aren't allowed to help me, right?"

"That's unfortunately true."

"Then I think this is my best bet for closing the portal and getting rid of the bodies." With that, I began an incantation. This spell was very precise, between contacting a specific plane of existence and needing to send only specific things through, so I wanted to focus my energy very tightly to make sure nothing happened that I wasn't expecting.

"R*egna terrae, cantata Deo, psallite Cernunnos,*
Regna terrae, cantata Dea psallite Aradia.
caeli Deus, Deus terrae,
Humiliter majestati gloriae tuae supplicamus
Ut ab omni infernalium spirituum potestate,
Laqueo, and deceptione nequitia,
Omnis fallaciae, libera nos, dominates.
Exorcizamus you omnis immundus spiritus
Omnis satanica potestas, omnis incursio,
Infernalis adversarii, omnis legio,
Omnis and congregatio secta diabolica.
Ab insidiis diaboli, libera nos, dominates,
Ut coven tuam secura tibi libertate servire facias,
Te rogamus, audi nos!
Ut inimicos sanctae circulae humiliare digneris,
Te rogamus, audi nos!
Terribilis Deus Sanctuario suo,
Cernunnos ipse truderit virtutem plebi Suae,
Aradia ipse fortitudinem plebi Suae.

Benedictus Deus, Gloria Patri,
Benedictus Dea, Matri gloria!"

I poured my will into the spell, and the portal above my head opened wide for the briefest of moments. I tried to resist the temptation to look, but couldn't quite. It was a Hieronymus Bosch landscape of horrors in there—lakes of fire, imps with whips, demons rending the flesh from men and women with their bare hands—and above it all I could feel a *presence*, a malevolent overlord taking delight in the suffering of others.

I shuddered, then took a step back, careful not to disturb the circle, as the altar with Sponholz and Dennis rose into the air, then was sucked into the portal to Hell. I released my will, and the portal winked out of existence, but not before I sensed that malevolent entity's attention focus on me for the briefest of seconds, and I felt terror like I had never felt before.

I scrubbed the circle out with my toe, and the magical barrier came crashing down. I stepped intentionally on the outer circle, smearing it into nonexistence and obscuring enough of the symbols to make it unusable to anyone who didn't read Enochian. At the time I knew of two people in Charlotte who could read Enochian, and I was pretty sure Uncle Luke wasn't planning on opening any Hell-portals anytime soon.

"What was that for?" Glory asked.

"I had to get rid of the bodies, and I figured if I threw something through the Gate, I could close it. Now no one has to figure out how to hide the bodies."

"I'm sorry about your friend's death," she said.

"Thanks," I replied. "He was a good guy." I was hopeful that Renfield could help me through some of the harder points of making someone vanish in the legal sense, not just the physical sense. I looked around the theater, the bullet holes in the walls, the giant summoning circle of blood in the floor, and knew that someone was going to come looking to me for information. But not tonight. For tonight, the world was as safe as it ever was, and I had another lost friend to mourn.

P **Epilogue**

. . .

"Not that I'm not flattered that you wanted to share something personal, Harker, but what about that story is so important that you had to drag me out of bed at three in the morning and talk 'til sunrise?" Detective Rebecca Gail Flynn asked from my sofa. I looked at the window. She was right, there was sunlight peeking in through the blinds. I'd talked nonstop for about four hours.

"I know you and Glory have been through some shit, but it's none of my business, seriously. It's not like I thought you were banging your guardian angel, and who am I to say anything if you are?"

That was a disturbing thought, but what was more disturbing was the level of emotion I felt coming through the mental link I had with Flynn. I saved her life a few months ago by letting her drink a few drops of my magical blood, and that created a bond closer than that of mother and child. I felt a flurry of things—relief, worry, confusion, jealousy, and a little...*lust*? Definitely on the list things I needed to explore later. When I had more to drink. And maybe opiates. But not now.

"A body was found last night, dumper at a strip mall in University."

"Yeah, I heard about that on the police radio."

"I went to take a look. It was a Nephilim."

"I'm sure that's just a coincidence," Flynn said, but her crinkled brow said something different.

"Yeah?" I asked, my eyebrow reaching for my hairline. "Because the story I just told you happened seven years ago. And seven is a number of power. If there was anything about that ritual that was tied to a specific time, this year is the first time that it could be attempted again."

"But you sent Sponholz to Hell. There's nobody to carry out the ritual."

"Any Cambion could do it," I said. "And I never figured out what Sponholz wanted or who put him up to it. He had a little power, but he had nowhere near the brainpower to think up something like that."

"But it could still be a coincidence, Harker. Just because a half-angel gets murdered doesn't mean..."

"Look at the calendar, Flynn." I cut her off. "The Solstice is in three days. And there was one more thing about the body that makes me sure that this is someone trying to open the portal again."

"Oh, fuck." She looked at me, eyes wide.

"Oh, fuck, indeed," I agreed. "The body's throat was cut from ear to ear, and all its blood drained. Somebody is trying to open that portal, Bex. And if we don't stop it, we're looking at Hell on Earth."

PART II
HEAVEN'S DOOR

CHAPTER ONE

"Y**ou're** trying to tell me that last night's murder is the beginning of a plot to open the gates of Hell? Real, literal, lakes of fire and little bastards with pitchforks *Hell?*" Detective Rebecca Gail Flynn sat on my couch gaping at me. I'd just spent half the night telling her the story of me and my guardian angel Glory stopping a Cambion, a half-human/half-demon/all-psychotic, from doing that exact thing seven years ago.

"Yeah, that's about it. Normally, I'd follow that up with an 'I know how crazy this sounds,' or some shit like that, but I do know how crazy this sounds, and you helped me fight the Four Horsemen of the goddamn *Apocalypse* without batting an eye, so why should a little demon mischief flip your switch?" I was tired and a little grumpy that Becks didn't seem to believe me.

"I get it, Harker, I really do. I can *feel* how much you believe this shit. And I've never seen you actually scared, so that means something, too. But...*Hell?* It's a lot, you know?" She leaned back on the couch and blew out a long breath. Without taking her eyes off my apparently very interesting ceiling, she said, "Okay, who's the new dead guy?"

"His name's Pat Dugan. He's a software engineer for Red Hat."

"What did he do?"

"I just told you, he was some kind of computer nerd."

"That's not what I meant." Now she looked at me. "I mean, how did he die? Was it like the others?"

"Kinda," I said. "His throat was cut, and his blood was partially drained, but not completely. And he was beaten before he was killed. And I mean beaten like he went five rounds with Mike Tyson, not just thumped on the head a few times."

"Tortured?" Flynn asked.

"I don't think so. There was none of the normal kinda stuff I associate with torture. His fingers weren't broken, one tooth missing, but that corresponded to a split lip, I couldn't see any electrical burns, or smell any charred flesh, no—"

"I get it," Flynn interrupted me. "There are a lot of ways to torture someone, and none of them were used on Dugan."

"Apparently not. The only reason I know he's involved in this case is because I saw the wings."

"The wings?" Becks asked.

"Yeah. When I looked at the body with my Sight, there were golden wings. He was a Nephilim, no question."

"Why were you there?"

"What?"

"Why were you at a random murder scene in the middle of the night, Harker?" Becks asked. "This is the kind of thing that I would have arrested you for two years ago. The only reason I don't suspect you now is that I know you didn't do this thing. Or if you did, you're having a psychotic break and don't know you did it. I'm not sure which of those is worse for the surrounding area."

"I'm pretty sure having a mystically enhanced wizard go batshit crazy in the middle of a city is about as 'worse' as it gets, Detective." But she was right. I didn't have anything to do with Patrick Dugan's murder, and if I did, Becks would know about it. Ever since I gave her some of my blood to save her life, we can't keep secrets from each other. It's hard enough just keeping my thoughts private, much less any impressions that come with deception. That just wasn't gonna happen with anyone as deep inside my head as Flynn was now. Truth be told, most days I didn't mind having an unbreakable mental bond with her. Kept some of the shadows at bay when the nights got real dark.

"You're avoiding the question, Harker. Why. Were. You. There?"

"I told him to go." Glory walked out of my kitchen and sat down on the couch next to Flynn. She handed her a glass of orange juice. "Good to see you, Rebecca."

"Hello, Glory," Rebecca said, accepting the glass. "We were just talking about you."

"I heard," my guardian angel replied. "He didn't even leave out any of the really bad parts. That was good, Q. A solid recounting, if uninspired."

"Oh, I was plenty inspired, Glory. Inspired by being scared out of my shorts of this shit starting up again."

"You should be. You didn't beat Orobas last time, you just beat his minion, and even that barely."

"And not without cost," I said. My friend Dennis died because I brought him into my fight. That was just one of the reasons I didn't sleep well at night.

"No battle is won without cost, Q," Glory said, then looked a little abashed at her tone. "I'm sorry. This is just scary for me, too. I don't know if we can beat Orobas. And I don't know how much I can intervene without risking..."

"Risking what, Glory?" I asked, standing up and starting to pace my living room. "What happens if you break the rules? Just this once? I mean, what's the worst thing they can do to you? You're an angel, for fuck's sake, it's not like they can—"

"They can," Glory said, her voice small. "They can, and they have before. To one of the greatest of us, one of the Father's favorites. His golden, glowing son. Remember the Lightbringer? The Morningstar?"

"Oh," I said. "Him."

"Yes, Quincy, him. So if you want to know what is the worst thing that the Heavenly Host can do to one of their own who rebels and causes problems, look no further than the case of God's favorite angel, Lucifer. And since I'd rather not end up condemned to never see the face of my Father again, I'm going to tread lightly. If you don't mind, of course." All the angels in Heaven and I get the sarcastic one. I guess that fits.

"So where do we go from here? We have a dead half-angel, we think we have a demon returned to rezone Charlotte as a suburb of Hell, and neither of us have slept all night," Flynn asked, downing her OJ and standing up.

"Keep talking, I can hear you!" she called out over her shoulder as she went to the kitchen and rinsed her glass. "I'm putting on some coffee. Glory, you want some?"

"No, thank you, Rebecca. Caffeine and divine power do not mix."

I looked at her, then shook my head. "Yeah, all we need is you to get jittery and inadvertently save somebody." I sat back down in my chair, leaning forward toward Glory. "So what's next? Where *do* we go from here?"

"Well, you have a detective, so I'd suggest you work on solving the murder of Mr. Dugan. And since this isn't your first run-in with Orobas, perhaps there are people who would know about it if the demon were back in town."

"That all sounds good, but first things first. I need breakfast and a shower," Flynn said, walking back into the room with a plate full of doughnuts and two mugs of coffee. She put the doughnuts on the coffee table, handed me the mug that read "World's Greatest Granny!" and kept a souvenir mug from Epcot Center for herself.

"Where the hell did you get these coffee cups, Harker?" Flynn asked, sitting on the couch beside Glory and grabbing a doughnut.

I took a sip of my coffee and reached for my own doughnut. "Where does every bachelor shop for kitchen supplies? I went to Goodwill."

"So what do we know?" Flynn asked after we each knocked back a couple of Krispy Kremes.

"We know that Patrick Dugan is dead, exsanguinated, and a half-angel. We know that likely means Orobas is back in town—"

"But we don't *know* that Orobas is back. One dead Nephilim isn't enough to prove that," Flynn countered.

"Are you willing to let another one die just to confirm my suspicions?" I asked.

"I'd rather not, but I am a homicide detective, Harker. I deal with dead people all the time. And sometimes, there has to be more than one person dead before I can be any good at my job. They don't do task forces for simple murders; for us to get the resources we need, someone else is going to have to die. But in the meantime, I'll go hit up Paul in the crime lab to see what he found at the scene. As soon as I take a shower and put on some fresh clothes. I might have to go to work on no sleep, but at least I can look like I'm well-rested." Flynn stood up and walked to the door of her bedroom. She stopped and turned to look back at me.

"Harker?"

"Yeah, Becks?"

"Is this really as bad as you're making it out to be?"

"If I'm right, it's nowhere near as bad."

"That's good, right?"

"No. Because if I'm right, it's way worse than we can even imagine."

CHAPTER TWO

"You know we don't do a breakfast menu, right, Harker?" Christy asked when I walked into Mort's. Mort's was a bar owned by a demon, and Christy was his bartender, bouncer, enforcer, information merchant, and the maker of the best Bloody Mary's in Charlotte.

"You lie like a rug, you beautiful succubus," I said, leaning over the bar to kiss one cheek.

"Not even close. And not terribly original, either. Why can't you believe that I'm just a normal, run-of-the-mill human, Harker?"

"Because I'm a normal, run-of-the-mill human, and you're not even close."

"Yeah, if normal humans have vampire DNA and throw spells around like a Dr. Strange comic."

"I have never once called upon the Eye of Agamatto." I grinned as I slid onto a barstool. Christy and I had a running game going—I tried to figure out what kind of supernatural creature she was, and she didn't tell me. I don't know if she would tell me even if I got it right, but it was a cute little diversion, so I kept it going.

"Where's Mort?" I asked. "Back room?"

"Yeah, but you can't go back there right now. Seriously, Harker, don't even stand up off that stool until I tell you it's okay. I don't want to have to shoot you."

"That's good because I don't want to be shot. Let him know I'm here, and I'll just sit here and have breakfast until he's ready to see me."

Christy nodded and reached for the vodka. I don't usually drink until after lunch, but since eight a.m. Charlotte time is three p.m. Moscow time, it was after lunch in Russia. Perfect time for vodka, by my logic. As Christy tossed ingredients into a glass for my Bloody Mary, I took a look around the bar at the other inhabitants.

There was a vampire in a booth in the back, passed out face down on the table. He'd be there until after sunset, but when he woke up, he'd probably be hungry. And have a hellacious crick in his neck. A couple of lycanthropes in human form shared a table by the door, but I could smell the fox on them from where I sat, and their narrow faces and long noses were dead giveaways, along with the flaming red hair.

I couldn't see the three tables down the hallway near the bathrooms and the back door but decided it wasn't worth snooping over. A huge human sat in one corner booth with a beautiful woman who looked way out of his league. I opened my Sight just a little bit, and sure enough, she really *was* a succubus. I almost got up and went after her until I remembered two things— first, the sign over the bar declaring it Sanctuary and the vehemence with which Christy enforced the rules about not hassling the other supernatural beings, and second, the fact that she almost certainly wasn't going to kill the dude, and he might be enjoying it. Shit, for all I knew, he asked her to feed off his life force in exchange for getting off. I'd seen weirder shit on the internet, so why not? As long as his kink didn't hurt anybody but himself, he could do what he wanted.

And I really didn't want to make Christy pull out the sawed-off double-barrel she had tucked away under the bar. She nodded at me as she sat my Bloody Mary on the bar, then said, "I'll go tell Mort you're here. No promises on whether or not he'll see you, but I'll tell him."

Mort and I had a love/hate relationship. I loved the information I got out of him but hated having to consort with a demon to get it. But my job very often isn't pretty, and the pesky thing about hunting demons is that they don't often show up at Mass.

Sometimes, but not often.

Christy came back about a minute later and motioned for me to follow her. I went through a small door at the end of the bar into the back room. The last time I was there, Mort had a demon magician doing tricks for his amusement. I took exception to the tricks and killed the stage show. Mort wasn't pleased. This time I stepped through the door into a bouncy castle.

A bouncy castle. One of those big inflatable rooms that kids get for their birthday parties. Except huge, tall enough for me to stand up in. Christy stood in the doorway, hand extended palm up.

"Give me your shoes," she said.

"What?"

"Your shoes." She pointed at my feet for emphasis. "Boss doesn't want any street shoes fucking up his balloon house, so give me your shoes."

"You first." I looked at her feet and saw a pair of black leather boots with three-inch stiletto heels.

"Fuck off, Harker," Christy replied, but I heard the smile in her voice. It was mirrored on her face, but she wiped it off fast. "You're cute, but I don't date humans."

"That's fine. I think we've established that I don't qualify." I was stalling until I could get my sea legs under me. It had been decades since I was on a boat, or any other floor that moved very much, and I wanted as much balance as I could muster before I dealt with Mort. He was a naturally unnerving fucker, and I didn't want to give him any more edge than that.

"You're close enough to human for me to use the easy out. Now give me your shoes. The wind in here messes up my hair, and that makes me grouchy. You wouldn't like me when I'm grouchy."

"Angry," I corrected, sitting down to unlace and pull off my Doc Martens, not the easiest thing to do when the floor keeps moving underneath you.

"Excuse me?"

"The quote is 'you wouldn't like me when I'm angry,'" I said.

"I know what the TV show said. I also know what I meant. You wouldn't like me when I'm grouchy. You'd fucking piss yourself if you ever saw me angry."

I looked in Christy's eyes and saw the truth there. I still had no idea if she was human, demon, angel, or some other kind of monster, but I knew she had power and that I didn't want to piss her off. So I shut the fuck up and handed her my shoes.

"Thank you," she said. "I'll have these behind the bar for you. If Mort kills you, I'll send them to Goodwill."

"Seems fair. You want to send them out to be shined, too?"

"They're suede, you dick." She turned and went back into the bar, laughing.

I turned and wandered farther into the bouncy castle, which was more like a bouncy maze. Imagine wandering through a giant, squishy, red and blue tunnel, where the floor has way too much give, and the noise of the fans keeping the building inflated made hearing anything more than a few feet in front of you impossible. I walked the red-tinged halls of Mort's inflatable house for a good five minutes, traveling a lot farther than I would have been if we were in normal space, and walking through seemingly endless plastic-lined corridors.

Finally, I turned a corner and stepped out into a room the size of a basket-ball court. Mort sat in a recliner in the center of the room in front of a bank of televisions. On each screen was a different room, all apparently in the bouncy castle. Some screens showed people wandering aimlessly, lost as hell trying to get out. Some showed people in a bouncy arena, either dueling or wagering on duels. And some screens showed people and monsters doing what they usually do when they don't think anyone is watching them. With some monsters, and pretty much every single type of demon, that is not something you want to see with any food on your stomach. My Bloody Mary made a run for it, but I managed to keep down breakfast.

"Hello, Quincy! So good to see you again!" Mort stood up and gave a florid bow. The last time I'd seen Mort, he was possessing the body of a little boy. The time before that he was riding along inside a low-budget porn actress. This time he was an athlete. I cocked my head sideways, trying to see if I recognized him from somewhere, but I couldn't place him. He was tall, African-American, and good-looking. He had muscles on top of his muscles, and nothing on but his boxer briefs, so I could see exactly how muscular he was. And pretty much how blessed he was in other areas, too.

"Hi Mort," I replied. "New suit?"

"Yes, someone made a poor decision in wagering on the Super Bowl, so I get to wear his body during the offseason. Too bad training camp is coming up. I promised him he could have control back by then."

"And what else is he going to have when he gets his body back?"

"Oh, nothing much. A little chlamydia, but he could have gotten that anywhere. I wasn't allowed to do any permanent harm to his body, reputa-tion, or career during my tenure in his body, but I was allowed to get laid. A lot. I missed sex, Harker. I spent *three years* wearing that kid, and you'd be amazed how few women actually want to fuck a prepubescent boy. I expected it to be a much more popular kink, but not so much."

"That's strangely encouraging, Mort. What happened to the kid?" Mort was a passenger demon, hopping from body to body pretty much whenever he felt like it. But he wasn't always very careful with his toys, and sometimes the bodies he hung out in weren't good for anything but paperweights and doorstops when he moved on to the next host.

"Coma," Mort said. "Just like when I found him. I put him back where I got him and left him hooked up to plenty of machines for breathing, feeding, shit-ting—all that garbage you mortals have to deal with. He'll be around if I ever need him again."

"I'm sure that's heartening to somebody," I said.

"Oh, who cares, Harker? You don't. You don't give any more of a shit about these humans than I do; you just fake it for some ungodly reason. Although I suppose by definition, *all* my reasons are ungodly." He let out a laugh that sounded like fingernails down a chalkboard, high-pitched and shrieky, all out of proportion to his Adonis-like body.

"Now what do you want, Quincy? I have important things to do, and only a few more days of using this body to do them."

"Then what, Mort? Gonna hop back inside a kitty cat?"

"That was more fun than you'd think, being a cat. It's a lot like being a demon, actually. You do what you want, you don't give a fuck about anything or anyone, and if you decide you don't like someone, you can take a shit in their shoe. But no, I have several options lined up for my ride. There's a businessman who wants to trade a year of carrying a demon around in his meat suit for a guaranteed ten years of wealth, a model who wants me to magically make her a size zero until she's fifty, and a housewife who just wants me to murder her entire family for her. She offered the rest of her life in exchange."

"That last one's a trap, Mort. Better go with the stockbroker."

"I never said he was a stockbroker," Mort said a little too quickly.

"You didn't say lawyer, and stockbrokers are the only other people willing to wager a year of having your slime inside their head for a decade of comfort. His morals are so fucked he probably wouldn't even notice you were there."

"True," the demon jock mused. "But why do you say the housewife is a trap?"

"Think about it, Morty. What's the one thing we know about people?" I mused. Mort gave me an arch look, and I answered my own question. "People don't change. So why would a housewife want to make a literal deal with the devil to kill her husband and kids that she loves? She wouldn't. So either she knows she's dying and wants to take you to Hell with her, or she knows they're all about to die and she's going to double-cross you somehow. Either way, it's going to be more effort than it's worth. And the model is just stupid. She's probably a really hot size six and wants to be skinnier, and if you ride along with her, you'll have to live in the head of a stupid person for a year. Nah, take the stockbroker. It'll feel just like home."

"You are a heartless fuck, aren't you, Harker?"

"Nah, I just don't like bankers. Now can we quit dicking around and get to it?"

"Ah yes, I was waiting for the threats. Are going to forego the empty threats this time?"

"Yeah, Mort, I thought I'd skip those this time. We both know I can't really hurt you, so why let my mouth write checks my ass can't cash? I need information."

"I didn't think you were here to enjoy the bouncy castle. But it is fun, isn't it?" He punctuated this by standing up and starting to do jumping jacks.

The floor roiled under his weight, and I started bouncing opposite him. I decided to nip that shit in the bud before I barfed in the bouncy house, so I drew in my will and said, "*Levitas!*" I thrust both palms at the floor and smiled as I floated six inches off the ground.

"You know that's not a real word, right?" Mort said, sitting back down in his recliner.

"Be glad I didn't say '*wingardium leviosa,*' you snide prick," I said.

"Fine, fine." Mort waved a hand and the bouncy castle disappeared. We were in a big room that mirrored the front of the bar. Then I looked around and realized we were actually *in* the front of the bar. Same werefoxes over there, same passed out vampire in the booth, same Christy behind the bar.

"That's impressive," I said.

"Of course it is, it was meant to be. Now what do you want, Harker?"

"Information."

"Would you care to be more specific? What brings you to my doorstep at this ridiculous hour?"

"There was a Nephilim killed last night in Charlotte. His throat was slit and his body partially drained of blood. I think Orobas is back, and I need to know if I'm right."

"You're partially right. Orobas can't be back, though."

"Why not?"

"Because he never left."

CHAPTER THREE

I was on my feet, one hand reaching for my gun and the other tracing sigils in the air. "What the fuck do you mean, Orobas never left?"

Mort never moved. He didn't even look like he thought about moving. Christy, on the other hand, reached under the bar and brought out her twelve-gauge. She leaned on the bar like it was a sniper perch and pointed both barrels at me.

"I know you're tough, Harker, but I don't think you're tough enough for these slugs. They've got a little hellfire sprinkled on them, and they'll light every scarred part of your soul on fire. If you're pure, they can't even touch you. But you've lived a long time in some interesting places, and I'm willing to bet you're almost as far from pure as I am. Now sit your ass down and stop scaring my customers."

The singular would have been a better way to phrase it since the succubus and her beau were nowhere to be seen and the werefoxes shifted and bolted for the door the second I stood up. The only one in the room now except for me, Mort, and Christy was the vampire, who was still face-down on his table.

But not unconscious, as I realized when he spoke. "Oh, for shit's sake, child. Please sit down before she gets any louder. My head is splitting. Christy, would you please refrain from killing the stupid human for long enough to get me some coffee, some O-positive, and a couple Vicodin?"

Christy looked at me with narrowed eyes, then put the shotgun down on the bar. "No problem, Jacob. Harker, *behave*."

Mort looked at me, a little smile playing around his lips. "Yes, Quincy, do sit down. Besides, what exactly did you think you could do to me? Kill me? I'm a passenger demon, remember? All you can do is kill my body, and then what happens? I go to Hell. Big deal. It's long past time I went to visit dear Mummy and Daddy anyway. But you'd have to deal with killing a potential future Hall of Famer. And I don't think that would go over well with the sports fans in this town, do you?"

He was right, of course. He'd be in Hell yukking it up with all the other pitchfork-toting fucktards, and I'd be so deep under the jail that not even Becks or our Homeland Security buddy, Agent John "There's No Fucking Way That's My Real Name But I'm Not Telling You Anything Different" Smith, could find me. And that's if I was lucky. If I was unlucky, rabid football fans would draw and quarter me at midfield and spread my intestines across both end zones. I sat down.

"What does he want?"

"Who? Orobas? I have no idea," Mort said, leaning back in his chair. "I suppose he wants to rip your heart out and eat it, but the list of people who want your internal organs for entrees is long and varied, I suppose."

"You could say that, but why does this particular asshole want to kill me?"

"You spoiled his fun a few years ago, remember?"

"Oh, I remember. He wanted to open a portal to Hell in the middle of my city. I objected, and he murdered one of my best friends in the attempt."

"Well, he's still pissed about that." Mort waved his hand and a glass appeared in it. I couldn't quite tell what was in it, and I didn't want to ask. Mort saw me looking and tipped the clear liquid in my direction. "Want some? It's the vitreous humor of Central America virgins. Belize, specifically."

I swallowed hard and said, "No thanks. Trying to cut back."

Mort threw his head back and cackled at me. "Harker, you are a treasure! It's a vodka martini, for Lucifer's sake! You can't drink vitreous humor, everybody knows that. Actually you can, but there's no point. It's mostly water and salt, no real flavor to it. And a little gooey, like thick broth. But this is vodka."

"I'm good. Had a Bloody Mary earlier. Now about Orobas?"

"Yes, Oro. What about him?"

"Where can I find him?"

"No idea."

"Who is working with him this time?"

"Not a clue."

"What is his endgame?"

"Haven't the foggiest."

"Goddammit, Mort!" I snapped, then pulled myself under control. "Do you know anything useful?"

"Useful, yes. I know many useful things. Germane to your current problem, no."

"Then what fucking good are you?"

"You know Orobas is on this plane. That's more than you knew when you walked in. And I didn't even charge you for the information, so as you humans say, quit your bitching." He was right. I knew that Orobas was in town, but nothing else.

"Where else does he hang out?" I asked.

"I've never asked. Probably because I don't care. Let me be clear, Quincy. There are several reasons people come here in particular. First, it is a Sanctuary. They know that no matter what happens, or how drunk they get, if they are in my establishment, or on its grounds, they are safe. Sanctuary is old magic, Harker, extending far past anything you understand. Older even than me and my kin, which is saying something indeed. That is the reason our patrons feel safe, and I will never jeopardize that.

"Second, they know that I will never ask questions. I don't have to. The laws of Sanctuary protect me as well, so I know that no one who comes in these doors will harm me. And third, they know that I know things and come here to get information. But everyone knows this, so if they have something to hide, most people don't talk to me. Orobas is not a stupid demon, Harker. He does not blab his business in public, and he certainly doesn't tell me anything that he doesn't want spread all over town like the clap."

"That's great, but if that's the case, why do you know so much?"

"Just because Oro is not stupid doesn't mean the rest of my customers aren't. Most of them are morons, and even worse when you add alcohol. So I add lots of alcohol and glean lots of information. Just not from Oro."

"That's somewhat less than helpful," I said. "And if the power of Sanctuary is so damn strong, how did your buddy Oro almost rip my head off seven years ago?"

"Some spells weaken with time, but old magic grows stronger. When you last met Orobas, we were a fairly new establishment, just a few years old. Since that time, the club has thrived and put down roots in the community. That gives this place spiritual weight, strengthens the bonds, that sort of thing."

It made sense. I didn't know a whole lot about the old magic, just that it was nothing I wanted to fuck with. "Fair enough, I guess. So you have no idea where I can find Orobas or who his new minion is?"

"I never said that," Mort replied. "I believe that Oro can be found in the emergency room of St. Matthew's. He is the head trauma surgeon there."

Sonofabitch. It made perfect sense. A demon feeds on fear and pain, and nowhere is that more evident than in the only hospital in the city not affiliated with some huge corporation. St. Matthew's was a small church-run hospital with an overflowing emergency room and an empty bank account. Kept afloat by church backing and a prayer, Saint Matt's was the last chance for the indigent, the addicted, and the people who needed medical treatment for gunshot wounds they weren't prepared to explain to the authorities. I'd been patched up there myself more than once.

I stood up. "Thanks, Mort. You've been more help than you probably realize or intended."

"That's me, Harker. I'm a giver. Where are you going?"

"I'm going to the hospital. I hear there's a demon there that needs banishing."

"Well, the only good part of that plan is that you'll be close to the morgue. If you go after Oro without serious backup, he's going to rip your arms off and beat you to death with them. He almost killed you last time until we interfered, and he's gotten nothing but stronger after feeding on human pain and suffering for most of the last decade."

I stood there for a minute, thinking. Then I took a deep breath and let it out. "Yeah, but that's the job. I pick the fights I can't possibly win, then I go win them. I always knew someday I'd run into the thing that's bigger and badder than me. Maybe today's that day."

Mort opened his mouth, but just then my cell phone rang. "I think you may have been literally saved by the bell, Quincy."

I knew it was Becks before I looked at the caller ID. Our mental bond was strong enough that I could feel whenever she was focused on me, no matter how far apart we were. I swiped my finger across the screen and held the phone to my ear. "Yeah, Becks?"

"Harker?" Her voice sounded funny.

"Yeah?"

"Are you okay?"

"I'm fine, why?"

There was a long pause on the line. "Never mind, it's nothing. You need to get out here."

"Where's here? You at the crime lab with Paul?"

"No, I'm in Matthews."

"Matthews? I thought they had their own department?" Matthews was a small city just outside Charlotte, but still inside Mecklenburg County. I frequently wasn't sure whether I was in Charlotte or Matthews, even after decades.

"They do, but they found a body that sounded a lot like the one you saw last night, and they notified us. Smith was in the building when the case came in, and he laid claim to it."

"Wow, for once the government really is on our side."

"Ours, yes. Mine, not so much. Finnick and Ramos were supposed to catch this case, and Coren and Mazer had the one from last night. Now I've got both of them. So I've got two fresh homicides and half the division pissed at me. So could you please get your ass out here and do that mojo that you do? I need to know if this chick was Nephilim or just a murder victim."

"Will do. Text me the address. I'll be there in fifteen." I ended the call and turned back to Mort. "Looks like you're stuck with me for at least a day."

"The day is young, Harker. I have no doubts you can drive someone to a murderous rage before nightfall."

I thought about it for a second and figured he was probably right. I'm just a charmer that way.

CHAPTER FOUR

The body was like the first one, in the middle of a strip mall parking lot. It was just like the first dead Nephilim I saw, all those years ago. Except it was daylight instead of pouring rain in the middle of the night. And the dead half-angel was a woman, not a gangly lawyer. And this strip mall was about three times the size of the last one.

And there was a big blue tent erected over the body and the surrounding parking lot. I pondered as I walked up to the crime scene tape exactly how bad the scene could be that they couldn't just cover it with a sheet. An enthusiastic and red-faced beat cop marched over to me with his hand held up as I approached.

"I'm sorry, sir—"

"Yeah, me too," I said as I ducked under the tape. His hand went for his taser, and mine went for my badge. I was quicker on the draw, fortunately. I've been tasered a few times. It hurts, and every once in a while you piss yourself. I tossed the rookie my badge holder and never slowed as I blew past him. I pulled back a side of the tent and stepped inside, then stopped cold at what I saw.

There was a very good reason not to let the public see the body, and an even better reason not to let the press see her. Not only was this a dead woman, this was a stark naked dead woman staked to the asphalt with big-ass nails in the center of a red pentagram. Her stomach cavity was sliced open, the sides peeled back and nailed to the ground, and my fucking name was written around the perimeter of the circle. Using her intestines for letters.

Whoever had done this shit took his time and wanted everyone to know exactly who he was after. And what he planned to do to me when we met. I decided in a split second that I was going to take this fucker out if it was the last thing I ever did. And there was a pretty good chance that was going to be exactly the case.

Flynn stood off to one side of the body, a sketch pad in her hands, with the crime scene photographer. He was snapping pictures and circling the body while Flynn took notes on her drawing. She didn't look up as I approached. "Glad you could make it, Harker."

"I would have come sooner if you'd mentioned that I got an invitation," I said, pointing to my name scrawled on the asphalt. "Please tell me that's really written in paint."

"Not even close, Detective," the crime scene guy replied. Becks shot him a nasty look, and he went back to snapping pictures like a pervert at a Victoria's Secret fashion show.

"You can call me Harker. You're Paul, right?"

"Yes, sir." He stuck out a gloved hand, and I shook it.

"What can you tell me, Paul?" He was a quick study, I'll give him that. He looked to Flynn before he opened his mouth again. She nodded, then looked at me with one of those little "yeah, it was petty, but fuck it, I'm the boss" smiles.

"It appears that the crime occurred sometime between midnight and four a.m. She was found this morning by the manager of the hardware store at the opposite end of the parking lot. He likes to come in before his shift and run laps."

"I suppose that's a thing," I said. "I suppose you'll tell me that there's no trace captured in the…material used to write my name on the ground?"

"Too soon to tell, sir."

"What about her clothes?" I asked.

"None were recovered."

"Interesting. Thanks, Paul." I waved him off, and he went back to taking pictures. "The other bodies were all fully clothed," I said to Flynn.

"You think this woman is special somehow?"

"I don't know, to be honest. If this is Orobas working through an interme-diary, he could be doing this just to fuck with me, to throw me off the scent. If the minion is going off the reservation, then she might be important. Who is she?"

Flynn looked at me, and I would have felt the sarcasm even if we weren't tied together mentally. "I don't know yet, Harker. Let me whip out my cell phone and run her through the instant worldwide facial recognition

443

program that all cops have in their back pockets, just like they do on TV. I have no goddamn idea who she is. There's no ID, and it'll take hours to run her prints. And if she's not in the system, we have to go wider. It could be days before we get a result. We'll have a better chance just sitting at the station waiting for someone to come in and fill out a missing person's report."

"Not a bad idea," I said. "I'd alert all the departments in nearby counties to the murder and make sure they know you want to be notified of any new missing adult female reports immediately."

"You think? Gee, Mr. Harker, is there anything else you think I should do in *my* murder investigation? The one *I* called *you* in on?" Some of the old fire was back in Becks' eyes, and she was obviously flashing back to the time when she didn't like me very much. Okay, not at all. And it wasn't really that long ago, either.

"Sorry." And I was, really. "I didn't mean to step on your dick."

She laughed at that. "You asshole. If I couldn't feel your emotions and know you were sincere, I'd think you were trying to make me laugh just so I wouldn't be as pissed at you anymore."

"I can be sincere and still want you to not be so pissed at me, can't I?"

She laughed again, then turned serious. "Have you looked at her yet?"

"Yeah, I'm looking at her right now."

"No, asshat. I mean *looked* at her."

"Oh. Yeah, not yet. Hang on." I closed my eyes and focused my energy. When I opened my eyes again, my Sight was overlaid on the image of the mundane world. People glowed with their personal auras, Flynn with the gold and blue mix that I had learned to associate with guardians or protectors. Paul, the crime scene guy, was surrounded by a light green aura, of a type that I usually saw with scientists or researchers. Most of the cops were surrounded by blue with varying levels of gold, but one working the perimeter had a cold blue light shining from within him, shot through with grey and black. He was dangerous, the kind of guy who shot first and kept a cheap pistol in his glove compartment to throw down beside the body later. They were rare, particularly in the Charlotte PD, but I tried to keep an eye on them whenever I saw them.

I turned my attention to the body and took a step back. The ethereal golden wings I expected to see in the woman's aura were there, but so was something else. I stared at her long enough for Flynn to notice something was wrong and touch my shoulder. I gave a violent shake and snapped my vision back to the "normal" world.

"What was it?" she asked.

I didn't respond. I couldn't speak yet. I stared off into space, still processing what I'd seen.

"Harker." Flynn shook me this time, and I focused on her at last. "What did you see?"

"Let's go get some coffee," I said, then turned and walked out of the tent. I had to put some distance between me and the dead woman in the parking lot before I threw up or destroyed something. I walked into a CupABucks coffee shop and cut in front of a soccer mom hemming and hawing over her latte choices.

"Hey!" the blonde woman in yoga pants squeaked.

I turned to her and held up my badge. "Homeland security, ma'am. We're investigating a possible terrorist attack in this parking lot. Now if your goddamn coffee is more important than the safety of every single American man, woman, or child, then you feel free to stand here with your thumb up your twat debating choices when we all know you're just fucking around until the National Drink of the White Girl, the Pumpkin Spice Latte, comes back in style. So go do some crunches and shut the fuck up or I'll ship your husband off to Gitmo."

I turned back to the stunned clerk, who probably called himself a barista, but was really a pimply-faced kid working his way through his first year of college. "Give me two large black coffees, no bullshit."

"Excuse me?" The kid, Bruce, if I was to believe his nametag, looked honestly confused.

I leaned forward. "Bruce, right?" He nodded. "Good. Let me be clear, Bruce. I need two cups of coffee. The strongest, blackest shit you can find. Blacker than my shriveled little heart. Blacker than the girl you picked up from your economics class last week. Blacker than...fuck it, I'm out of metaphors. Just take two of the biggest cups you have, fill them full of the strongest coffee you have, and fucking sell them to me. No lattes, no cappuccinos, no foam, no whip, no *bullshit*. Just give me a couple of goddamn coffees. You with me?"

"Yes, sir." A terrified Bruce turned away and started fixing my coffee.

I felt a tug on my sleeve. I turned around, and Soccer Mom had her pepper spray out and pointed at my face. In the other hand, she held a cell phone.

"I'm calling the cops. If you move, I'll spray your ass into oblivion."

I smiled at her. She turned pale at my smile, which was the intended result. I whispered "*reversari*" under my breath and released my will. The top of her sprayer glowed for an instant, then everything went back to normal. Except that, for the next three minutes, her pepper spray worked backwards. I snatched her cell phone with my right hand, then held it up in front of her face. A little squeeze, and the aluminum body crumpled, the screen shattered to dust, and the circuit board experienced what I believe the experts refer to as a "catastrophic failure." I dropped the devastated scraps of phone to the floor and just kept on smiling.

"Go for it," I said in my coldest "yes, I eat babies raw" voice. I first used that tone on a mugger in London around 1919, not long after my father died. I was walking along and he stepped out of the shadows with a knife. I used that exact inflection on the mugger, and he ran screaming back into the shadows. Shortly after that, rumors surfaced of a return of Jack the Ripper, claiming that the Ripper attacked an independent businessman who managed to escape with his life. Soccer Mom didn't assume I was the Ripper, at least I didn't think so, but she did back away until she was out of arm's reach then turned and bolted for the door.

She ran right into Becks, who had to talk to the other cops on the scene before following me. The tiny tornado in stretchy pants and a sports bra almost bowled Flynn over as she bolted, but Rebecca regained her footing just in time. Flynn walked over to the counter just as Bruce put two big-ass cups of coffee on the counter. I dropped a twenty in the tip jar and handed Flynn her coffee.

I led her to a corner of the shop where I had a clear line of sight on the entrance and everyone in the room. We sat down, and Becks leaned in to me. "Okay, Harker. Spill it."

I took a deep breath. "She was a Nephilim, but that's no surprise."

"Yeah, we expected that."

"But I didn't expect a personal message on the body," I said.

"What?" Flynn exclaimed, then lowered her voice and leaned in again. "What are you talking about?"

"The killer didn't just leave my name spelled out in her guts, although that was a nice touch."

"A nice touch? Are you fucking high?"

"God, I wish," I replied honestly. "Yeah, it made sure that I would find out about this killing even if you weren't involved with the case. It was effective. And so was the other message." I took a big sip of coffee, stalling.

"What was the other message."

"It was twofold. First was the message itself, which was written on her torso. It says, 'I'm coming for you.'"

"That's direct enough," Flynn said.

"Yeah, but that's not the part that worries me."

"Go on."

"It's what he wrote it in. He used her soul, Becks."

"I don't understand. How can you use a soul to write a message?"

"A soul is a person's essence. It's everything that makes them who they are, and when you die, it either goes to Heaven or Hell. In some rare cases, it's left to walk the earth. That's how we get ghosts."

"Okay, that makes sense so far. What about the writing?"

"In the Otherworld, the part of the universe that I peek into when I look at things with my Sight, souls are corporeal. They have mass and substance. Someone who knows how to step into that world can literally touch souls. This guy didn't just touch her soul, he ripped it to shreds and painted her corpse with it."

"So that means..."

"Yeah, that means she didn't go to Heaven. She didn't go to Hell. She isn't a ghost. When she died, instead of following the natural order of things, she was torn apart at an almost elemental level. She was destroyed, Becks. Destroyed more completely than anything I've ever seen. And now the thing that did that is coming for me."

"Fuck. I'd be scared, too."

I shook my head and drank more coffee. "That's not it. I'm not scared for me. I mean, seriously, I've seen the century flip twice. I know my warranty's up, and whenever somebody or something punches my ticket, so be it. But there are people I give a shit about, and I don't want them to get hurt. Luke can take care of himself, but..."

"If you say it, I might shoot you right here in the CupABucks," Flynn warned.

I didn't care. I said it anyway. "I want you to get off this case, Flynn. This one's too much for you. Too much for any human."

"Let me use small words and short sentences so you'll understand me. Fuck. You."

"Dammit, Becks, you don't—"

"No, motherfucker, *you* don't understand. I know you feel guilty because you didn't save my dad. I get it. I feel shitty that my dad died when I was a little kid, too. But that doesn't change the fact that I'm a *cop*, Harker. I stand between the bad things in this world and the innocent people in it. That's not just my job, it's a goddamn calling. And I'm not going to stop doing my job because things get scary any more than you would."

"But this thing is out of your league," I protested.

"Yeah, well, it's out of your league, too," Flynn countered. "And you don't see me asking you to sit on the sidelines, do you?"

I had to admit, she was right on all counts there. "No, you're right."

"Of course I'm right. I'm always right. Look, Harker, I get it. It's dangerous.

It's a big bad, and we have barely any chance of getting out of this alive. But that's the fucking job, isn't it? You said it yourself—there are things that go bump in the night. We're the ones that bump back. So put on your fucking big boy pants and let's find this thing. And when we do, we'll bump it right back to the Hell it came from."

I'm pretty sure that was the moment I realized I was in love with Rebecca Gail Flynn. Then everything got *really* fucked up.

CHAPTER FIVE

"I love you."

"What?" Not exactly the reaction a man hopes for when he professes his love for someone. But I suppose a woman doesn't usually think that a horrific demonic murder scene is the kind of thing that inspires professions of love, either.

"I said, I—"

"I heard you." Becks stared at me. I didn't look away. I looked into her brown eyes and let the walls inside me fall down. I let her feel everything I felt about her, everything I'd felt about her for years but kept bottled up and renamed and wrongly filed in the card catalog of my brain. I let it all out, let her feel the love, the joy, the abject fucking terror rolling through my every cell.

Then I felt our mental connection blink out, severed like it was cut with a machete. My eyes widened, and I stared at Flynn. "Becks..." I started, but she just stood up and stalked out of the café.

I followed her, easily keeping up with her fast walk, and grabbed her elbow. Not my best move.

She whirled around and drew her pistol in one smooth motion. She jammed the barrel of her Smith & Wesson under my chin and got almost nose-to-nose with me. "You listen to me, you sick son of a bitch. I don't know what kind of game you're playing, but you come near me again and I swear to God I will blow your fucking brains out."

"Rebecca..."

"No. You don't get to talk now. I get to talk now, and you get to listen, or I'm going to ventilate the top of your goddamn head. I don't care who your uncle is. I don't care how old you are. I don't care that you can throw magic around like we're in a fucking Dungeons & Dragons game, you don't get to fuck with me that way. You don't get to tell me to back off on a case because you *love me*. What kind of candy-ass bullshit is that? You don't love me. You barely know me. We've worked together for what, a year? A year and a half? Jesus fucking Christ, you think that gives you the right to—"

I've made a lot of bad decisions in my life. Some of them have gotten good people hurt, even killed. Many of them have caused immense property damage, and one was responsible for the extinction of an entire species of South American monkey. But I have never really expected to die from one of my bad decisions.

Until I kissed Becks right in the middle of her rant. That one I thought had a better than fifty-fifty shot of getting me killed on the spot. So I made sure it was worth every drop of blood that she was about to spill. I wrapped one arm around her waist, the other around the back of her head, and I crushed her to me. I planted my lips on hers in mid-sentence, cutting off her speech by putting my mouth on hers. I held her tight to me, tangled my fingers in her hair, and kissed her like there was no tomorrow. Because if she thought there was an ounce of deception in me right then, there wouldn't be.

She struggled for a second, and I thought I was done. Then she relaxed into it and kissed me back like we were teenagers under the bleachers at a football game. She held me tight, and I poured everything I'd ever felt about Rebecca Gail Flynn into that kiss. After well over a minute, I pulled back. She looked at me, hair coming loose a little from her ponytail and her lipstick smeared, and holstered her pistol.

"So you're not going to shoot me?" I asked.

"Not right this second." Then she hauled off and slapped the fucking taste out of my mouth. She swung from the heels and laid an open-handed slap on my face that spun my head around and made my eyes water. Not to mention made my lip bleed.

I wiped the blood off my lip with the back of my hand. "I suppose I deserve that?"

"You suppose? I could charge you with assault, you dick. Contrary to what you've seen in shitty Nicholas Sparks movies, kissing a woman is not an acceptable method to get her to stop yelling at you."

"Apparently not, since you're still yelling at me. But you did put your gun away, so I'll call that a win."

"Yeah, take 'em where you can get 'em, Harker, because you're not going to get many in the 'W' column with me around."

"So that means you're planning on sticking around?"

"Yeah, I'm not going anywhere." She gave me a lopsided little smile, shook her hair loose, then pulled it back into a neat ponytail again.

"Now do you see why I don't want you on this case?"

"Oh, I understood it before you owned up to loving me. Which was only a surprise because of the location. I mean, goddammit, Harker, you've been alive for over a hundred years. I thought you'd know something about romance by now."

"I spent at least fifty of those years traipsing all over the world with my vampire uncle who traded his humanity for the power to avenge his wife's murder. My views on romance might be a little skewed."

She thought for a moment, then nodded. "Okay, that's a valid point. But still, a CupABucks? Right beside a murder scene? You have the heart of a fucking poet."

"I do, actually. It's in a jar in my closet. He wrote a limerick in the 1930s that Luke didn't approve of." I held it for a moment, then gave her a grin. She laughed, and I felt the wall between us come down. I could *feel* her presence again, and it was like water in the desert. I didn't know how much I missed that connection until it was gone. *Shit*, this whole love thing was going to make fighting big nasties really complicated.

"So…now what?" she asked.

"You mean about the case, or about us?"

"For now, let's focus on now what about the case. At least while we're less than a hundred yards away from a murdered woman. We should talk about us later."

"Tonight? My place?"

"I'm good with that. I'll bring sushi from that place on Sardis."

"Deal. You know I love their firecracker rolls."

"Now that dinner twelve hours from now is sorted, what about the woman with her guts strewn all over the parking lot?"

"Okay, fair enough. I've already spoken to Mort this morning, and he's not being terribly forthcoming with the assistance, so probably not a ton of help coming there. How about you go back to the station and ride herd on Paul while I go talk to Renfield and maybe avail myself of his computer savvy while Uncle Luke sleeps."

We turned to head back to our cars, and of course that's when a pair of black Suburbans and a black Sprinter van pulled into the parking lot. The van backed up right to the side of the tent, and Agent John Smith hopped out of the passenger side of the lead Suburban, his coffee cup from the high-rent joint next to police HQ in one hand and his badge in the other.

Smith marched over to us. Smith marched everywhere, his military background evident in every step. Not to mention his close-cropped haircut. His steel-gray hair stuck up like bristles on a brush, and his neat goatee matched the silver atop his head. Smith walked right up to Becks, his stocky frame blocking our escape.

"Flynn. Harker." He nodded to each of us in turn. "Where are we?"

I drew a breath to respond with something like "the parking lot," but Rebecca elbowed me in the gut. The air *whooshed* out of me, and I shut up.

"We have an unidentified victim, staked to the ground inside what appears to be a pentagram, with Harker's name written in entrails around the perimeter of the circle."

"Entrails?"

"Yes, sir. The victim's intestines were used to write Harker's name on the outside of the circle."

"That's nasty, even for a demon."

"There's a reason they make lousy interior decorators, Smitty." I couldn't help it.

"Do you know her, Harker?" Smith asked, turning his blue-grey eyes on me.

"The victim? No, never seen her before. At least, not that I can remember. And there was no specific aura or signature around the circle or the body. But this is Orobas. I know it."

"How can you be sure?" Smith asked.

"I talked to Mort today. He confirmed that Orobas is still in the city, and actually never left. He's just been waiting until the right moment, with the right minion, apparently."

"You trust that hitchhiking little fuckwit?" Smith and Mort didn't get along. To the point that Mort put him on the very short list of people that the laws of Sanctuary didn't apply to. I never heard a straight answer as to why they hated each other, just that Smith didn't set foot inside Mort's, and Mort didn't step outside."

"He's never steered me wrong yet," I replied.

"So what's next?" Smith asked. I looked over his shoulder and watched as a couple of men in Tyvek suits loaded a stretcher into the back of the Sprinter van. They stepped out, closed the back doors, and pulled away.

"Well, our initial plan was for Flynn to go back and oversee the autopsy and see what the crime scene guys turned up, but since your boys just loaded the body into a van and drove off with it, I guess part of that is off the table."

"What?!?" Becks exclaimed, starting to move after the departing van.

I grabbed her arm. For the second time in one morning. At least this time, she didn't put a gun under my jaw. "Hold up, Flynn. You can't catch them on foot, and it's not like Smitty here won't tell us where he's taking the body. Right, Smith?"

"Of course I will. They're just going to the county morgue. All the ME vans were out, so I had a couple of my guys lend a hand. We grabbed a stretcher from the morgue, then came over here. The body will be waiting on you when you get downtown."

Flynn's shoulders relaxed, and she looked back to Smith. "Okay. That's fine. I just wish you would have mentioned that first."

A silence hung in the air. I figured if she was waiting for an apology from Smith, we might all be white-haired before that happened. So I stepped in. "So now what's next? I was heading over to Luke's to do some research on Orobas and see if I can come up with any other ways of identifying Cambion. Orobas has managed to stay hidden for seven years, so I bet his new half-demon lapdog is using Nephilim blood to mask its identity."

"Maybe you should come with me instead," Smith said. "We've got a pretty extensive library at my office, including a few books picked up when a certain Alexander Marlack disappeared last year. Not that you'd know anything about that, of course."

"Of course," I replied, somehow keeping the grin off my face. Marlack was an asshole lawyer whose privileged asshole son summoned a demon last fall and let it rape and impregnate a teenage girl. I had to burn down the girl's house with her in it before she gave birth to a demon that could walk both planes. Then I went after the son, which led me to the father, which led me to summoning a demon myself to deal with those assholes.

I hate demons, but sometimes when you need to pound a nail, you have to have a hammer. And sometimes you need a really big, flesh-rending, life-devouring hammer that besmirches your immortal soul just by being in the same room with it. But killing that particular dickwhistle was totally worth it.

CHAPTER SIX

We sped along Independence Boulevard in Smith's Suburban, strip malls and car dealerships whizzing by our windows. We rode in silence for a few minutes, until Smith looked over at me.

"So, you and Flynn finally got some things sorted out, huh?"

"Not even close. But what makes you say that?" I asked.

"The way you two were being very careful not to look at each other for very long, no touching, not even accidental, that kind of thing."

"You're pretty observant, Smitty. That's a little more than the typical human would pick up on." It was kind of a game by this point—I try to figure out exactly what Smith was, and he tries to hide his real identity from me. He was just a little bit *off*. He didn't quite smell right for a full human, and he didn't quite move right, either. He wasn't a were-something, I'd figured that much out, but I couldn't get him to even admit he was more than human, much less tell me what he was. So I kept poking at it, and he kept obfuscating.

I opened my mouth for another guess, but just then Smith's cell phone rang. He pressed the screen on his dash, and a voice came over the car speakers.

"Agent Smith?"

"Speaking. I have Quincy Harker with me, so nothing classified."

"You take all the fun out of espionage, Smitty," I said with a grin. He replied with the same stoic look he always wore. Sometimes I wondered if the man knew how to smile.

"Sir, this is Sergeant Jade from Dispatch. You asked me to relay any calls that came in that I thought were odd, and this one seemed to fit."

"What is it, Sergeant?"

"We just got a call about a disturbance at Freedom Park. Some folks protesting construction or widening roads or something are raising hell out there."

Smith looked exasperated, and it showed in his voice. "That's not exactly what I was thinking about when I told you to call me with anything unusual. I'd say a bunch of hippies bitching about something is pretty normal."

"So would I, sir. Except for the reports of a giant plant monster tossing huge rocks around the park and destroying the bandshell."

"What?" The bored and frustrated look was gone from Smith's face.

"The report said something about a giant tree-thing walking around and throwing shit at people. Park benches, trash cans, boulders, that kind of thing. I've got a couple squad cars on the way. I'll let you know what they say."

"Never mind, we're on our way." He tapped the screen to end the call, then turned to me. "I'm going to drop you off at the entrance to the park, then I'll head to the station and get started on our research."

"You're not going to back me up?"

"Harker, it sounds like you're going to fight an Ent. I don't even have a can of weed killer on me, and I bet bullets won't do much to something made of wood and grass, or whatever this thing is made of."

He was right, but I wasn't ready to admit it. I drew my Glock and checked the magazine, then made sure my spare mags were in my back pocket and topped off.

"You think you're going to shoot the plant monster, Harker? I didn't hire you for your marksmanship."

"Good thing since I'm not a great shot," I replied. "No, I just want to make sure I can shoot out your tires if you really do try to leave me there."

Smith didn't respond, just flipped a switch on his steering column to turn on his flashing blue and red lights, then started passing people like they were sitting still. I suppose the giant engine is another reason the feds like their Suburbans. It can't *all* be to compensate for tiny penises, right?

Ten minutes later, Smith pulled off to the side of Princeton Avenue and looked at me. "Try not to get turned into fertilizer, Harker. I need you on this serial case. If it's anything like that mess you were in seven years ago, it's going to take everything we have to stop whatever this guy has planned."

I didn't bother asking how he knew about my run-in with Orobas seven years ago. Even if the most interesting bits weren't in any official records,

Smith had good sources. Better than mine, sometimes, and one of my sources was a friggin' angel.

"Thanks, Smitty. I'm sure your only concern is for my well-being," I said as I stepped out of the SUV.

"Nah, I just don't want to deal with the paperwork if you're on one of my cases and get killed. So if you're going to die, try to do it off the clock."

I just shook my head and slammed the door, then turned to see what kind of shitstorm I was walking into. A steady stream of people cascaded out of the gates of Freedom Park, and a fair number were just hauling ass down the greenways and ungated exits, too. I didn't see any sign of a giant plant monster, so I did what every sane, well-adjusted human being does when faced with hundreds of people running in terror from something.

I ran right in.

Good thing for me I've never been accused of being sane or well-adjusted, and reports of my humanity are muddled at best. I hopped the low fence around the parking lot by the softball field with one easy bounce and ran toward the bandshell. The sergeant had mentioned destroying the bandshell, and that part of the park was popular with protestors, so it all fit. It took me a couple minutes to jog there, and when I arrived, the waterfall of escapees had slowed to a trickle.

When I crested a small hill, I got a good look at the lawn area across the small pond from the bandshell. Sure enough, what I saw fit into the category of "giant plant monster" pretty well. It was a good ten or twelve feet tall, covered in chunks of grass, flowering plants, and hunks of sod. What I could see of whatever constituted its muscles and bones looked like tree branches, roots, and thick vines. From somewhere inside its head, a reddish-orange glow emanated, like there was a pissed off fire inside the thing. Which, frankly, would piss me off, too, if I were made of sticks.

The plant-thing was chucking rocks the size of my head at a couple of Charlotte cops who were trying to take cover behind a two-wheeled ice cream cart. I guess any port in a storm, but if I were a normal human, I would have stayed right the fuck away from that thing.

As previously stated, I am far from a normal human. Step one was to get the cops to stop shooting long enough for me to get close and try to take out the beastie. It just wouldn't do to get shot in the ass trying to save the city. Or at least the park. Let's just accept the fact that I don't want to get shot in the ass and leave it at that.

I ran over to where the cops huddled behind the cart and crouched behind them. "You guys know that thing can totally see over this cart, right?" As if to prove my point, a basketball-sized rock arced high over the cart and sunk itself a foot into the ground behind us.

"We know, but we got no place else to be," one of the cops said. He was young, nowhere close to out of his twenties. A young, good-looking African-American kid who really didn't need to get his brains splattered all over the park.

"You do now. This is now officially federal government business. I'm Agent Harker from Homeland Security." I even pulled out my badge.

"We know you, dickhead. You're that moron who thinks he's a wizard that's banging Detective Flynn," the other cop, a fat guy in his forties, grumbled at me. He was white, fat, and stupid. If he wanted to put his head in the way of a falling rock, I didn't have a problem with that.

I glared at Fat Cop and said, "First, don't call me dickhead, fuckwit. Second, I don't think I'm a wizard. I do magic, that's all. No funny hat, no robes, no hobbits. And third, keep your fucking bullshit speculation about my and Detective Flynn's personal interactions to yourself, or I'll have your ass busted back down to parking lot traffic monitor at Carowinds."

"You don't have that kind of juice," Fat Cop replied.

"I have a badge that says Federal Motherfucking Government on it. You want to see how fast the department budget gets cut when I pull a few strings? Just keep annoying me, greaseball. Now if you two fine gentlemen would like to live to see tomorrow, how about you stand up, run like holy hell, and stay the fuck out of here until I get shit sorted. How does that sound?"

Black Cop nodded, then got up and ran like there was a two-for-one sale at Krispy Kreme. Fat Cop sat there glaring at me for a few more seconds, then stood up and ran to his car. Well, it was more like a fast waddle, but he still moved with some purpose at least. I stood up, then reached out and snatched the big umbrella off the top of the cart. It came free with a snap, and I folded it shut. I reared back and chunked that folded umbrella like a javelin, channeling all my former Olympian ancestors with my mighty throw.

Okay, more like I used my vampire-infused blood to hurl it like Ahab chunking a harpoon, but I'll take that, too. The umbrella expanded a little in flight, which is the excuse I'm sticking with for why I buried it into the monster's chest instead of its eye like I planned. But I hit it, which is some level of triumph. And I pissed it off, which wasn't the best idea I'd ever had.

The plant monster turned to me, the fleeing cops completely forgotten. It plucked the umbrella from its chest, snapped all the ribs and the fabric off it with a quick swipe of one hand, and hurled it back at me. The plant's aim was dead on. The spear whizzed just a little over my head and buried itself two feet into the ground. I got the distinct feeling that even if the spear went through me, it was thrown with enough force to bury itself at least a foot in the dirt.

"Okay, Plan B," I muttered, wondering to myself exactly what Plans A, C, and hopefully D were. I reached down and picked up the ice cream cart high above my head, then took a couple of running steps and chunked that at the monster.

It caught the cart in midair. It staggered back a step but didn't go down. And of course, because playing catch with a forest elemental is exactly what I want to be doing with my morning, I opened my Sight, looking for any mystical trace that meant the creature was being controlled by someone nearby, but there was nothing. No strands of magic linking it to anything around, no traces of dark magic, just the rich verdant glow of nature magic. Yup, I was about to be squished by a real-life giant flower child. My life sucks sometimes.

CHAPTER SEVEN

I couldn't see any ties between the monster and its surroundings. But I also didn't find anything tying it to another plane, either. So I was kinda at a loss about how to deal with the thing. I dodged a couple of big rocks, then hauled ass to hide in a nearby copse of trees when the giant tree came at me directly.

I hid behind a couple of small maples, and almost immediately vines crept along the ground and twined around my feet. "*Infernos!*" I shouted, pointing at the vines. A small stream of fire flew from my fingertips and burned the vines away, but more slithered toward me. I retreated to the sidewalk, but nature's assault pursued.

The giant fern-covered bastard wasn't chasing me, just sending vines, so I figured I could deal with those. I took a couple of running steps, then leapt for a nearby light pole. I scurried up the side, using speed as my leverage, then swung around so I was perched on the light fixture like a demented superhero, or a skinny gargoyle. That broke my contact with the ground and confounded the creature for a few seconds. I had to use them wisely, or I was screwed.

"*INFERNOS!*" I bellowed, pulling in power from the nearby electrical lines and converting it to magic. That hurts like a sonofabitch, by the way. A fireball bigger than my head flew from my hands and crashed into the elemental's chest, only to burst into about a bajillion pieces and scatter sparks all over the ground.

Yup. I was screwed.

By now the vines were back and climbing the pole, so I decided that moderate insanity was better than sitting there getting strangled by kudzu, so I jumped off the top of the light pole. I hit the ground rolling and was really glad for my oddball ancestry. If I were just human, I probably would have broken both legs, but since Dracula and his wives all took a bite out of my parents at different times, it left me a little more human than human, as the song goes.

I sprinted across the grass to a small concession stand and jumped up on the roof, wracking my brain for ideas. A tree-monster that was immune to fire? That was just totally unfair. A thought hit me, so I stopped, picked up one of the big-ass rocks lying around everywhere, and chunked it at the creature like a shotput. It flew true, arcing high in the air and coming down to smack into the elemental's shoulder. Kinda. Except instead of breaking off the monster's arm, like I'd expect when a basketball-sized rock hits something in the shoulder, it bounced off onto the grass. No effect. It was like I'd hit the monster with a balled-up piece of newspaper.

I opened my Sight again, this time focusing on the creature, not whether or not it was tied to another plane. Most of the creature was surrounded by green pulsating magic, the magic of life, of the earth and nature, but the core of the thing, deep in its center, glowed bright crimson red. It was like someone put a very bright light behind a pool of blood, that kind of dark, roiling red. Even for a giant tree monster, that wasn't normal. I scanned the area with my Sight, looking for anything similar, and saw a flicker of red light from the water just in front of the bandshell.

Great, I thought. *I find what I'm looking for, and of course it's underwater.* I kicked off my boots, carefully set them aside, put my pistol in one and spare ammunition in the other, and jumped off the roof. Good Doc Martens are expensive, and the last thing I wanted to do was fuck up my boots if this thing went sideways. Well, *more* sideways. My days and nights are pretty odd, but fighting an honest-to-God Ent in the middle of Charlotte is weird even for me.

About five seconds after I hit the ground running, I regretted leaving my boots on the roof. The plant-monster, obviously tired of throwing things at me, decided to take a less direct approach, this time making the entire lawn erupt in thorny root growth. I ran on because stopping would have let the razor-sharp spiked vines and roots twine around me and give me the old iron maiden treatment, but every step was excruciating. I put a foot down and brought it back bloody. I stepped again and pierced my sole on more thorns. Lather, rinse, repeat the bloody process for every step. Eventually, I sacrificed the small pains for fewer, larger agonies as I started to jump across the grass ten feet at a time, still racing for the water. I finally reached the edge of the pond, took a deep breath, and dove in headfirst.

And couldn't see shit. Not only was the water dirty and murky, but whatever I was looking for was apparently very mundane to the normal eye. I resurfaced, hung on to the lip of the artificial island where the symphony frequently performed, and focused just long enough to open my Sight. This time I could feel as well as see the flickering red whatever beneath me. And I could also see the tendrils of green magic racing across the surface of the water at me like a vanguard of pissed-off snakes. Except these snakes were vines, and they weren't there to bite me—they were there to drown me. So much better.

I gulped in air, dove again, and swam straight at the red glow. I got there in seconds, reached out, and grabbed it. As soon as I did, I let my Sight drop so I could see what the thing was in the mundane world.

It was a thermos. I'd just dashed across a field of thorns and jumped in water full of who knows what for a thermos. I surfaced and dragged myself up onto the island, then onto the concrete stage, hoping the man-made surface would give me a little barrier against the elemental's attack, at least for a few seconds. I look down at the thermos in my hand and shook my head. That's all I needed, an angry shrubbery and a magical thermos. I reared back to throw the stupid thing back into the water but felt something rattle in it and stopped.

I unscrewed the lid and held my hand under the mouth of the thermos. I gave it a little shake, and after a pint or so of pond water poured out, a small vial dropped out into my hand. I recognized the dark red substance as blood immediately since you don't drink "wine" with my uncle more than once before you learn the difference in viscosity between Cabernet and O-Positive. I blinked and focused my Sight on the object in my hand. Sure enough, the vial of blood was the source of the red glow in the thermos, and it matched exactly the shade of red emanating from the tree-dude's chest. I blinked away the Otherworld and threw the vial to the ground. I lifted my foot to grind the glass to dust under my boot heel, then remembered I wasn't wearing boots. I decided I didn't want to mix the blood coating my feet with the enchanted blood of whatever-the-hell the vial contained. That and stomping on glass with my already ripped and abused foot was just adding injury to injury. Instead, I found a nearby brick and smashed the vial to smithereens.

The tree-man let out a bellow, which was interesting since it had no visible mouth, and I watched as the red glow went out in its chest. I stood on the stage, waiting for the elemental to topple over and return to its natural state, like inanimate, but it didn't happen.

"Shit, it's always the hard way," I muttered to myself, then yelped as I felt a tickle on my leg. I looked down and hopped away, wincing with every step. The stage was covered in vines, and every one of them was reaching for me, trying to turn me into a literal hedge wizard. I took two running—well, limping—steps and dove back into the pond, swimming underwater back to the sloping hill leading to the giant tree-thing.

I pulled myself out of the water and was immediately ensnared by winding grass and weeds. It seems the elemental had decided that shoving thorns into my feet wasn't going to stop me, so it was going to mummify me in plant matter instead. Roots wrapped around my throat, cutting my air to a trickle, while super-grown grass wove itself into a blanket pinning me to the ground. I was very quickly bound up like Gulliver in Lilliput, stuck to the ground, face-down and unable to move except my lips.

Good thing my mouth is almost my deadliest weapon. I couldn't touch the life force around me, and the ley lines were all out of whack with the powerful magic used to animate a tree giant, so I reached down deep into my own soul, focused my will, and shouted, "*Incendiarus!*"

It came out more of a croak than a powerful bellow, but it had the desired, if excruciating, effect. I burst into flames. Every inch of my skin turned into living fire in an instant. I burned myself like a goddamn roman candle, but in seconds, I was free. I released the spell and got to my feet in the middle of the scorched patch of earth I was pinned to seconds before. I was buck naked, burned to a crisp, and really, really pissed off.

I wasn't exactly not on fire anymore, so when I took a step, I singed the grass beneath my feet. After a yard or so, the grass literally retreated from me, leaving me nice cool topsoil walk in. I stalked the elemental, smoke coming off my shoulders and the top of my head.

"You want to take the gloves off, motherfucker? Well, let's dance, bitch." I held up both hands and bellowed "*Infernos!*" Flames shot from my palms like water from a firehose, dousing the plant monster in fire and setting it ablaze. I let the fire die out from my hands and picked up a rock the size of a softball.

"*Infammato!*" I poured magic into the rock, and it burst into flames. The *rock* was on *fire*. I hurled the fireball at the elemental and caught it right in the head. I repeated the process with two or three other small rocks until I came to one of the boulders the thing had chucked at the cops earlier. I picked up the big stone with both hands, lofted it over my head, and screamed "*Flambeé, motherfucker!*"

I hurled the boulder, now basically just a mass of congealed lava, overhand at the now-smoldering Ent and hit it right in the center, where the old red glow used to be. Now there was a new red glow as the boulder punched a hole in the tree-beast, and it began to be consumed by flames from the inside out. The elemental teetered, then collapsed backward onto the lawn, breaking apart into just a collection of saplings, vines, twigs and leaves, all burning merrily on the grass.

I walked over to what had been the head of a ten-foot monster just seconds ago, kicked it into nothing but glowing cinders, then reached down into where its chest had been, pawing around for what I knew was in there but couldn't see anymore. After a couple seconds, I pulled free exactly what I expected to find, a glass vial just like the one I pulled out of the pond. I reached in my pocket to pull out an evidence bag and was painfully reminded of two things. One, I had burned off all my clothes when I magically set my skin on fire. Two, I had *set my skin on fire.*

Adrenaline exhausted, the searing agony of being covered in extensive burns hit me like a Mack truck. I screamed, fell to my knees, screamed again from touching the ground, and passed right the fuck out. But I didn't let go of that vial, and the goddamn plant monster was dead.

CHAPTER EIGHT

"**Y**ou're an idiot."

Those were the first words I heard when I regained consciousness. On the bright side, they were in Becks' voice, so I had that going for me. On the less bright side, she was one hundred percent right.

"But I'm a cute idiot," I croaked. It's remarkably hard to speak when you've been choked by trees and set on fire. But I had the opportunity for a smart-assed comment, and I wasn't going to waste it.

"Not right now, you're not. You look like Deadpool. Only Deadpool if he had a skin condition that made him look even more fucked up."

"So I'm like a less cute Ryan Reynolds? I'll take that."

"You look like a stunt mannequin of Ryan Reynolds that got blown up, dragged behind a truck for a mile, then dipped in acid. I don't think there's an inch of your skin that's not burned. How are you even talking?"

"I learned some badass meditation techniques from a Buddhist monk in the sixties. And I didn't set my lungs, throat, or mouth on fire. Just my skin. Have you called Luke?"

"Yes, and *what?* Did you just say *you* did this? Like on purpose?"

"Yeah. It's a long story. That goes better with morphine. And tequila. And preferably many other narcotics."

"Well, for now you'll have to make do with a nice fresh red. While it's recently decanted, I can vouch that it's aged appropriately." The new voice was deeply cultured, the dulcet tones of a man who had seen multiple centuries pass in front of his eyes. The voice of the man I referred to as "uncle," but who had been a father to me for many years. The man, the myth, the many, many legends, Vlad Tepes. My uncle Luke, Count Dracula. He stepped to my bedside, every bit the European aristocrat even after decades in the States. Luke was tall, with dark hair and the pale skin you'd expect from a man who hadn't seen the sun since a century before Shakespeare was born. He wore a tailored suit that probably cost more than my entire hospital bill, with a pocket square perfectly matching his tie. I saw Uncle Luke ruffled once, in Europe during World War II. It wasn't pretty, and I never wanted to see it again.

"Hi, Luke," I said. I gave him a little wave.

"Hello, Quincy. You do understand that when I promised your mother I would take care of you, none of us believed that it was an endeavor that would require quite these great lengths, correct?"

"We didn't expect me to celebrate my hundred-twentieth birthday, either, did we?"

"Well, if you insist on setting yourself on fire every time you face a difficult foe, you certainly won't make it one hundred twenty-one. Oral, or intravenously?" he asked, holding up a wine bottle and an IV bag.

"Let's just go for both barrels, Unc, This shit hurts a lot more than it looks like."

"I find that hard to believe," Luke said, handing me the wine bottle and hanging the bag on the IV stand beside my head. He quickly hung the bag to drip into the IV alongside the morphine, but in trying to get the blood to flow, he set off some kind of alarm that had a nurse rushing in seconds later.

"What is going on in…" She started off ready to read Luke the riot act, but he turned his gaze on her and had her under his complete control in seconds. Her face went blank, and she stopped in her tracks.

"Come over here," Luke said to the dazed nurse. She walked over to the IV contraption. "Make this work. He needs this blood as quickly as our machines can put it into him."

She pushed buttons and tweaked tubes, and the mixed blood and morphine started to flow into my veins together. Luke looked at her nametag.

"Nurse Banks," he said. "You will disable all alarms on this equipment, then go to your station and ignore anything you see or hear from this room, or the three of us. Do you understand?"

"I understand." Her voice was flat and her eyes dull, but she pushed a bunch of buttons, then walked out.

"Holy shit, you can really do that?" Flynn asked.

"Yes," Luke replied. "I find it distasteful, but it does prove useful at times."

"So you're giving Harker blood? Why couldn't they just do that here?"

"The blood from the blood banks does not have my unique qualities, Detective."

"Wait, you're giving him *your* blood?"

I decided that there was nothing to be gained from me being part of this conversation, so I lay in my bed and drank my merlot mixed with Dracula blood and kept the fuck out of it. I felt the morphine, and I felt the wine, but most of all I felt the power and healing properties of Luke's blood coursing through my veins. My skin began to heal itself, rebuilding itself on an almost cellular level underneath the sheets and the gauze that covered me. I felt better immediately, but I knew from unfortunate past experience that it would be a while before I was back to full strength.

"So you're giving him your blood to heal him, like he did with me." Flynn's face was knit in concentration. This was all new to her. A year ago, she didn't even believe in magic. Now she was kinda dating a dude that was born in the nineteenth century and still looked in his late twenties.

"Exactly."

"And you know this will work because you've done it before?"

"My dear, I am over half a millennium old. I've done almost everything before."

"Wow." She sat down in the chair and started to stare at me. "Will I be able to see it?"

"See me heal? I don't know. I assume so, but I've never been hurt in quite this way before, so I don't know exactly how it's going to...ow *fuck*!" I knew one thing, re-growing all your skin at once hurt like a bitch. I wasn't sure which hurt worse, the burning it off or the growing it back. I was pretty sure the burning it off part. And I really wasn't looking forward to the itching as all my hair grew back.

"Are you okay?" Flynn leaned forward.

"I will be," I said. I took another long swig of wine, then followed that with a long gulp that drained the bottle to the halfway point. "I'm going to need to get in the shower soon. I think all my new skin is growing back under the old, burned skin, and I'm gonna need to get that off me."

"Like a snake shedding its skin?" Becks asked. Her eyes were bright and curious, and I could only chuckle and shake my head.

"Yeah, kinda like that. Luke, did you bring me some clothes?"

"I did. These were in your rooms at my house. I hope they are adequate." He held up a small shopping bag.

"They'll be fine. I just need to be able to walk out the door without every-body seeing my junk." I lay there for a couple minutes, alternating drinking from the wine and just letting the morphine and blood infusion take effect. I started to feel better, stronger, more whole within seconds. By the time I knocked off the bottle of wine, I was loopy as hell from the booze and morphine, as well as on a rush of healing energy. I was ready to take on the world, if not so much walk a straight line.

"Help me stand up," I said, tossing back the bloodstained sheet that covered me. "I think I'm pretty good, Luke. If you want to disconnect the IV, I should be able to go shower."

"Lay there for a few more minutes. You need all the blood you can get."

"I don't have time, Uncle. I only had three days until the solstice before I lost an entire day in here. And has anybody heard from Smith? I figured he would have blown up my phone by now."

"You didn't have a phone when you got here, Harker. I think between the swimming in the pond and the setting yourself on fire, you probably lost it, destroyed it, or melted it," Flynn said.

"I think melting it counts as destroying it," I replied with a grin.

"Oh, shut up, you drunk. Anyway, I talked with Smith. Told him what happened, and that I would be here with you until we could get you moved. He said something about research and questioning suspects. Then he asked what happened, so I told him," Becks said.

"And how did you know what happened? As far as I knew, I was alone in the park with the tree-thing."

"Oh, Harker, that's so cute. Like anybody is alone anymore. One of the cops you rescued videotaped the whole encounter with his phone and his body cam. He said he didn't think anyone would believe his report without proof, so he made sure to get it all on tape, so to speak. I told him that his burden of proof didn't include YouTube, then confiscated his phone and body camera. That was a helluva fight."

"Yeah, you should see the other guy. I flattened him." I giggled, and that's how I knew I was really high. Giggling—not my thing. "Oh, I left my boots and my gun—"

"On the roof of the concession stand. Yeah, I've got them," Flynn said.

"Good. Those are my favorite boots."

"And the gun?"

"Nah, I like my Colt 1911 better. The Glock is nice and easier to conceal, but that Colt has some sentimental value."

"Which he'll be happy to tell you about later," Luke said. "Some time when he has less alcohol and narcotics in his system. But right now, the IV is finished, so you may go bathe. If you can manage to walk to the bathroom."

"I'll be fine," I said. I swung my legs onto the floor and stood up, fresh as a daisy. Then almost fell over and had to grab the handrail on the bed because I was a very drunk daisy. Under normal circumstances, one bottle of wine will give me a good buzz, but mix it with a couple doses of morphine, and I was blotto.

I looked over at Flynn. "I could probably use a hand getting to the shower," I admitted.

She looked at Luke, who shook his head. "I brought the wine and donated blood to the cause. It is your turn to suffer for your association with our dear Quincy, Detective. It happens to us all eventually."

I wasn't sure how to take that, so I kept my mouth shut. I gave Flynn my best puppy-dog eyes, and she let out a huge sigh and took my elbow.

"I am not getting any closer to you than this, Harker. You're still oozing a little, and I really like these clothes."

"They're nice clothes," I said, trying to be the good boyfriend. "They cover almost all of you, and those pants definitely do not make your butt look big." I was being sincere because I was too drunk to lie. Her butt looked great in those pants.

"I don't think that comment had the effect you were looking for, Quincy," Luke said.

"Why not? Her ass looks great," I protested.

"Can we not talk about my ass with your five-hundred-year-old uncle?" Becks asked.

"I guess, if that's what you want," I replied. "When can we talk about your ass?"

"I'm not answering that," Becks said. She got me to the bathroom door and had me sit on the toilet while she set up the flip-down chair in the small shower.

I reached out with one foot and pushed the door closed. "Alone at last," I said, in my most romantic voice. Or at least, my most very stoned romantic voice.

Becks straightened up and said, "All set." Then she reached for the door, but I kept it closed with my foot.

"What if I need you?" I asked.

"I'll be right outside."

"I'd feel a lot safer if you were in here with me."

"I'd feel a lot safer if I weren't in a bathroom with a drunk burn victim."

I made a pouty face, and she laughed. "Okay, fine. I'll sit here while you get cleaned up."

"You just wanted to see me naked, Detective," I said, standing up and peeling off the hospital gown.

"Not like that," Flynn said with a wince at my destroyed body. The gown stuck to me in places and pulled off chunks of burned flesh. I didn't mind since I had nice, new skin underneath it, and I took great glee in yanking off the bandages and the skin attached to them.

Then I hopped in the shower, and immediately almost went down. I caught myself with the grab bar and sat down on the fold-out seat. I typically shrug off the effects of drugs and alcohol quickly, but I expended a lot of energy fighting the elemental, then even more healing, so I was staying intoxicated a lot longer than normal.

I turned on the water to a medium warm and started scrubbing off my skin. I sloughed off an entire suit of charred and destroyed epidermis, then made another pass to make sure I got everything I could reach. "Hey, Becks?" I called.

"Yeah, Harker? You need me?"

"Yeah, actually, I do."

"What's up?"

"Umm…this is gonna sound like I'm putting the moves on you, and on any other day, I would be, but…there are some places I can't reach."

Her voice sounded amused. "So you want me to come in there and wash your back?"

"Yeah, exactly."

"I thought you'd never ask," she said, opening the shower curtain. Rebecca Gail Flynn stood there, already naked with her hair tied back. Her clothes were folded in a neat pile in the far corner of the bathroom, and she looked at my fresh man-suit and smiled. "Nice. The hairless look kinda suits you, Harker. Definitely shows off some muscle definition."

"Yeah," I said, looking her up and down. "Looks good on you, too."

She stepped into the shower and pulled the curtain behind her. I stood up, kicking the seat so it folded flat to the wall.

Flynn wrapped her arms around me and pressed her head into my chest. "I thought I was going to lose you."

"I'm a lot harder to get rid of than that, Becks. You're stuck with me, for a long time to come."

"I can live with that," she said, turning her face up to mine.

I bent down, kissed those lips I'd stared at for months, and we clung to each other under the pounding water. Eventually we got around to washing my back.

CHAPTER NINE

At least Luke gave us a little alone time before he got impatient and knocked on the door. We were almost dressed, or at least Flynn was, since my clothes were still in a bag on the dresser.

"Yeah, Luke, what's up?" I called through the door.

"Are you two quite finished?"

"Yeah, I suppose. I feel pretty clean." I grinned at Becks, who was even prettier when she blushed.

"Good," Luke responded through the door. "I've hypnotized three nurses into ignoring the sounds coming from the bathroom, and Detective Flynn's phone has been ringing almost constantly. It's almost as if you were in the middle of an important investigation."

"You act like it's the end of the world, Luke."

"It may well be, Quincy."

"Oh yeah. Good point." I opened the door and walked out into the main room wearing a towel and a slight grin.

"You look better," Luke said. "Refreshed."

"Growing a brand-new skin will do that to you," I replied, stepping into my underwear and jeans.

"Is that what we're calling it?"

"Oh, leave him alone, Luke," Flynn said, stepping out of the bathroom and sitting on the bed to put her shoes on. She picked up her phone. "It's Smith, checking on you. I'll text him."

"Tell him I got burned to a crisp, but I'm all better now," I said. I laced up my Docs and clipped the holster to my belt. I threw a light jacket on to hide my gun and looked over at Becks. "We ready to roll?"

"Where are we going? What's our next move?"

"You're going to call someone in the permits department and find out what eco-friendly bunch had a protest permit for today, then I'm going to go see how they're connected to the murder of a bunch of half-angels, or if they're part of some other angle Orobas is working."

"And what am I doing in this plan?" Flynn asked.

"Making sure I don't get burned up again?"

"That could be a full-time job, the way you handle investigations."

"It's kept me busy for the better part of a century," Luke said. "Since you seem to be feeling better, I shall take my leave. I have a bit of blood to replenish, and not that many hours until sunrise to find a suitable donor. Then I shall have Renfield look into the reports your crime lab has logged and see if anything leaps out at him."

"How is he going to get our crime lab reports?" Flynn asked.

"I think it is better for all involved if you know nothing about that," Luke replied, then turned and moved quickly out of the room.

I chuckled a little. "He can't help it. He hasn't worn a cape in over eighty years, but he still kinda swoops when he walks."

"Is Renfield hacking the police department computer system?" Flynn asked.

"I don't think he's currently hacking anything. By now, I think he's got his backdoors built into anything we need access to." Somehow, that didn't seem to reassure her.

We walked out into the hall and turned toward the elevators. I froze.

"What's wrong?" Flynn asked.

"The nurses aren't going to let me leave. I need a disguise or something." I started looking around for a lab coat or a baseball cap. That always worked on TV.

"You're wearing a disguise, you big idiot," Becks said with a smile.

"What are you talking about?"

"You look a little different from anything they saw in that hospital bed, remember? Hell, you look different from any time I've ever seen you, what with the whole bald look you've got going on."

Oh yeah, new skin. I forgot about that. We walked past the nurses' station like we were just ordinary visitors, turned into the lobby, and pushed the down button on the elevator. We rode in silence down to the basement parking lot, got in Flynn's car, and pulled out onto the street.

"Where to, Harker?"

"Let's start at the scene. There's something I need to check on."

Becks pointed to the car toward Freedom Park and flipped on her lights. Then she glanced sideways at me. "Are we going to talk about this?"

"What's there to talk about?" I asked. "I told you I love you, and I'm guessing that you like me a little bit, too."

"Just because I had sex in a hospital shower with you? Maybe that's just something I'm into." She didn't look at me, but I could see a little smile.

"Oh, you were into it, alright. But don't forget, Becks, I can feel what you feel. I try not to read your thoughts, but I can't shut out strong emotions. Just like you can't shut mine out. I know you can sense what I'm feeling for you, just like I sense all the confusion running around inside you. But I can feel what's underneath all that confusion, too. And that's love, or as close to it as I know anything about. So we love each other, and we can't hide from each other, and we just had amazing sex in a hospital shower. So what else do we need to know?"

A wave of sadness and fear poured over me, and I looked over to see tears streaming down her face. "I need to know you're not going to leave me. I need to know that you're not going to get yourself killed fighting some goddamn demon, or monster, or fucking *plant monster!*" She pulled the car over to the side of the road and turned to me.

"Harker, you need to understand this. When my dad died, I was crushed. I was just a little girl, and my hero was gone. But I pulled my shit together because my mom needed me. She fell apart, crawled inside a bottle of Xanax, and never crawled back out. She drank and drugged herself to death before I graduated high school. I moved in with my boyfriend and his parents to finish out the year, then he got in a car wreck the week after graduation coming home from a party I didn't go to. He wrapped his truck around a tree, and his parents couldn't stand to look at me after that, so I moved out. I lived in my car for a couple months until I went to college and moved into the dorms. I didn't have a real boyfriend after that. For fifteen years.

"So this is a little scary for me, Harker. I haven't lived for a hundred years. I haven't watched world wars and industrial revolutions. I'm just a normal girl who's watched everyone she ever loved die, no matter how young and no matter how much I loved them. So this...thing we're doing. *This* scares the fuck out of me. Not monsters, not demons, not even the fact that I just hung out with fucking *Dracula*. But you scare me, Quincy Harker. Because if you die, if you leave me, I don't know if there'll be enough left of me to put back together again."

"Then I'll just have to keep my century-long streak of staying alive in spite of myself, right?" I tried to lighten the mood, but she was having none of it. "Look, Becks, I know you've had it rough. I've been there, remember?"

"Yeah?" she said, letting a little bitter flavor creep into her voice. "Where were you when I was sleeping in my car?"

"Sitting in my own car fifty yards away pissing into a coffee cup keeping an eye on you," I replied. Her eyes went wide, but I kept going. "You were safe, and it was warm. The only time you almost had trouble was one time a couple of MS-13 'bangers wandered by looking for trouble. They saw a little hot chick curled up in the hatchback of her Geo Metro and decided they should bash in the back window and have a little fun with her. I convinced them that was a bad idea."

"I never knew."

"You weren't supposed to. Look, Becks, I know you're scared. I am, too. This isn't the first time I've done this whole sharing a mind thing, but it is the first time I've fallen for somebody this hard, this fast. And it almost killed me when I lost Anna. So I know what it's like to lose your heart and soul. I can't promise you I'm not going to be in danger, but I will promise you that I will *never* leave you."

"That's my guy, the herpes of relationships." But she smiled when she said it, so I felt like my little pep talk had served some purpose.

"There aren't even shots for me," I quipped back. "Now let's go to the park."

CHAPTER TEN

Freedom Park was lit up like Christmas when we pulled into the parking lot. Firefighters still stalked hot spots and sprayed water once in a while on a smoldering chunk of elemental, and cop cars stood sentry, their blue lights strobing through the normally quiet neighborhoods around the park. We walked through a crowd of onlookers as Flynn badged us under the cordon of crime scene tape. We walked straight to the center of the activity, a cluster of cops in cheap suits standing together near where I'd knocked off the plant monster.

"Hey look, it's Mulder and Scully," a fat detective I recognized as Emrack called out as we approached.

"What happened to your hair, Harker?" another detective, whose name I didn't know, jeered.

"I got the shampoo and your wife's Nair confused when I took a shower this morning. By the way, that's a cute birthmark on her butt," I shot back. He took a step in my direction, but Emrack put a hand on his chest, holding him in place.

"Don't let those guys bother you," Flynn whispered.

"It's been a long time since a fat fuckwit like Emrack has gotten to me," I said. I knelt by the ashes of the tree-critter, bringing handfuls of the ash to my nose and sniffing deeply. I put my nose to the ground and breathed deep. "There's something here, but I can't remember where I've smelled it before."

"Would you recognize it if you smelled it again?"

"I'm pretty sure, but it's not a hundred percent," I admitted. I opened my

Sight and scanned the area for any hints of magical energy. There was still a little green energy in the remains of the creature, but that was to be expected. I looked around and finally spotted something out of place. Just a glimmer over a hill, but the same green energy pulsed in the distance.

I stood up. "Come with me, and cover me," I said to Flynn.

"Cover you from what?"

"Anything that tries to kill me," I replied. I took off at a fast walk toward the glow, ignoring sidewalks, police tape, and anything that wasn't the pulsing verdant light in front of me. I crested the hill and had to shield my eyes from the glare. What I thought was one source was actually a circle of seven individual green lights all coming together, weaving together to make one big undulating mass of energy. I dropped to my belly at the top of the hill and motioned for Flynn to hit the deck with me.

"There's something down there calling up a shit ton of the same magic that animated the elemental," I whispered.

She got up on her elbows for a better look. "It looks like a bunch of hippies in a drum circle. Can't you hear them?"

I dropped my Sight and listened. "Yeah, I hear them. They're not very good. Enthusiastic, but not good."

"But they're calling magic with it?"

"Yeah," I said. "It doesn't take much if the area is predisposed to it, and there are a fuckton of ley lines running through this park. I can't tell what they're doing from here, but we need to stop them before they get ambitious and call up another monster. I'd really rather not burn myself half to death twice in one day. Hang back and shoot anybody that looks more threatening than me."

I stood up and walked over the hill. The drummers ignored me, and I pretended not to notice the unmistakable smell of marijuana floating my way. Great, because stoned wizards make the best decisions. Still twenty yards or more from the circle, I held my right hand out to my side, palm up, and whispered, "*Flambé.*"

A ball of fire appeared floating above my hand, and I snapped my wrist forward. The fireball shot toward the stoner magicians and exploded into sparks right in the center of their circle. The drumming stopped instantly, all but one scrawny white kid with dreadlocks and no shirt, who was wailing away on a djembe with his eyes closed. He was lost in the music, his kokopelli tattoo glistening with sweat, and he pounded on the drum.

I muttered "*infernum!*" and summoned up another fireball. This one I flung right at the kid, and he jumped as the ball of magical fire hit him right in the drumhead and exploded with an impressive *boom* for a ball the size of a grapefruit.

He quickly switched from beating on the drum to beating out the sparks, then took the drum off his neck and shouted up at me. "Hey man, what the hell do you think you're doing?"

"I think I'm giving you stupid fucktards a taste of what I went through earlier today, thanks to you and your fucking hippie bullshit magic," I yelled back, even though I was only five yards or so away from him now.

Shirtless Hippie came at me, flailing his fists before he ever got going. He looked like a psychotic Don Quixote who thought he was both knight and windmill, his skinny arms waving everywhere as he ran at me. I stood right in front of him and kicked him in the gut when he got close enough. It was more like I just held my foot up and let him run onto it, but it had the same effect. He went down like a pile of smelly, hairy straws, and I stepped on him a little on my way to interrogate the rest of the circle of dumbasses.

"Who's in charge here?" I asked when I got to the center of their circle. Against experienced magic-users, there's no way I would ever put myself in the middle of a circle, but these guys couldn't lock me down in Alcatraz, much less a half-invoked summoning circle.

"Dude, nobody's in charge, man. That's like a totally patriarchal monotheistic way of looking at the world, and we aren't about that, man." The idiot in front of me was wearing the official uniform of the southern stoner. He had on a tie-dyed music festival t-shirt, ripped khaki shorts one size too big held up with a braided belt, and flip-flops that cost more than my jeans. I did the only logical thing anyone could do when confronted with such obvious poseur douchebaggery—I slapped the piss out of him.

I didn't hit him because that really might have killed him. I drew back my right hand and laid an open-handed slap across his face that spun him around and sat him down on the grass holding his jaw. His eyes were a little crossed, and there were four lines on his face where my fingers struck.

"You don't even know what half those words mean, you ignorant little shit. Now keep your goddamned mouth shut unless you've got something worthwhile to say." I looked up at the rest of the circle of morons. "Now who had the bright idea to summon a plant elemental and have it go on a rampage through the park? Because if that's how you're protesting, I think you need to go back to hippie school."

"I brought the spell. I bought it from some guy I met at a concert," a waif girl with long honey-blonde hair in pigtails said. Good move, she probably figured I was less likely to punch her. She was mostly right. I was less likely to punch a girl, but I would if I needed to.

"So are you evil or stupid?" I asked.

She narrowed her eyes at me, a look that probably intimidated men that wanted to sleep with her. But since I had recently consummated a relationship with a woman who didn't use crystals for deodorant or smell like patchouli, I had a better standing offer. That, and I'm notoriously hard to intimidate. Something about my upbringing, probably.

"Answer the question, or I slap Dipshit again," I said, raising my hand to the cowering idiot on the ground. I didn't take my eyes off the girl, but directed my next remark to the boy directly behind me. "And if you even think of pulling that knife on me, I will take it away from you and break both your arms. Do you have anyone willing to wipe your ass for you for the next six weeks? Because that's the shit you need to think about right now."

I heard the him thump back down on the grass and looked back at the girl. "Well, which is it? Evil? Or stupid?"

She stuck her jaw out, and I could see her trying to hold her shit together. So it was stupid. That's good. I didn't really like killing pretty twenty-something girls, but I would if I had to.

"He told me it was a spell to make the trees and grass grow."

"Did he have a name?"

"He said his name was Jones."

"Of course he did. And he was a powerful wizard and knew you were a powerful witch, and you both wanted to make the grass grow and the earth bountiful, right?"

A single tear escaped, and she dashed it away with the back of her hand. "Yeah, that's all I wanted to do—make the trees and grass healthier. Is that so bad?"

"I think this is what we mean when we talk about unintended consequences, you moron. You made the shit grow, alright. But you also made it sentient and very, very pissed off. And then I had to come deal with it, and that meant I set a lot shit on fire, including me. I don't like being set on fire. It makes me grumpy."

"What are you going to do to me?" She was openly terrified now, so a large part of my job was done. The rest of the hippies collectively looked like they were about to crap their pants, too, so I doubted any of them were going to be playing around with magic in the foreseeable future. Still, I didn't have much success getting people to stop using magic once they started. It was usually a bell you couldn't un-ring.

Still, she didn't kill anyone. Not even me, despite my best efforts to get myself killed. And she did try to do things right. "Here's the deal, kid. You're an idiot. A kind-hearted idiot, but an idiot nonetheless. And that's often the most dangerous type because you see the best in everybody. So here's what we're going to do. You're going to give me your spell book, and I'm going to give you the name of someone to contact. She can hook you up with someone to teach you, and she'll give you the name of someone good, and mostly harmless. But if I hear of you stepping off the path of light once, just a little bit, I will find you, and I will wear your skin for a winter coat. Do you understand me?"

She went even paler and nodded. I wouldn't really make a coat out of her skin, of course. Human skin is way too thin for that. Doesn't even really keep the rain off all that well. But she didn't know that.

I turned in a circle, making myself glow a little for added effect. "And the rest of you, get haircuts. Get jobs. Fucking go sell weed at Phish concerts for all I care, but quick fucking around with magic. You're going to get somebody killed, and it's probably going to be you. Now get out of here." They all bolted, except for the girl.

I motioned to the ground, and we both sat. I waved Becks over. "This is Detective Rebecca Gail Flynn of the Charlotte-Mecklenburg Police Department and Homeland Security. What you did today could very easily be considered a supernatural terrorist event, and we could have you sent to a pocket dimension that is kinda like Gitmo, but with more monsters. But we're not going to do that. What we're going to do is take a statement from you where you describe the man who gave you the spell, and then we're going to go through your spell book. Anything in there that could be dangerous, I'm going to destroy. You can keep all your blessings, protection spells, and wards, but anything that could be used offensively is outta there. You good with that?"

"Do I have a choice?" Some of her old fire was back, and while I liked seeing it in young people, I preferred to see it from a distance. A great distance.

"Of course you have a choice," Flynn replied. "You can do this, or we can send you to the magical prison dimension Agent Harker just described."

"Or I can lobotomize the magic out of your brain. That's always an option. But it's your call, so you decide. But you need to decide right now."

She closed her eyes for a minute, obviously swallowed the part of her that wanted to call us fascist pigs, and handed me her backpack. I poked around in there and brought out a battered copy of Alexander Schictling's seminal work on magic for beginners, *Spells for Complete Idiots*. Never has a book been more truthfully advertised, or more a pain in my ass because of it. Too bad Schictling turned himself into a toad and got run over by an ice cream truck because I really wanted to strangle him every time some kid handed me a copy of his book.

I knew right where to go for the stuff she had no business screwing around with, so I set to ripping out pages with gusto. Each page I tore out, I tossed into the air, and it burst into flames. Ashes fluttered all around me as I tore out summoning spells, binding spells, love potion recipes, and battle magic spells. I left her the illusions, the astral projection stuff, and the harmless environmental manipulation stuff, although it was really a lot easier to grow tomatoes with water, fertilizer, and patience than with magic.

By the time I was done with the book, Becks had a solid description of the guy who gave her the spell. Unfortunately, it boiled down to "white guy between thirty-five and sixty wearing a baseball cap somewhere between five-six and six-two, and maybe around one-eighty to two-twenty." In other words, completely average white dude of middle age and unremarkable size. Everything I ever wanted in an eyewitness description.

I grabbed a pen out of the girl's backpack and scribbled a name in the inside front cover. I wrote a phone number underneath it. "This is the number to a woman named Christy. She's a bartender at a place called Mort's. It's owned by a demon, but Christy knows everyone in the city with an ounce of supernatural power, and she's good people. Tell her I sent you her way and that you need a light witch mentor. And if you fuck with her, have your affairs in order. She's a lot less forgiving than I am."

"Whatever got into your head to make you think this shitshow was a good idea today, get it out of there, and fast. A lot of people could have died because you believed the wrong dude. This magic stuff is serious business, and if you fuck it up, people die. Do you get that?" Flynn asked.

The girl nodded.

"Good," Becks continued. "Now we're going to go try to find this son of a bitch and keep him from destroying our city."

"That's going to be harder than it looks." I looked up, and Glory stood over us, her arms crossed and a really irritated look on her face.

"What's up, Glory?" I asked.

"While you two have been busy washing each other's backs and playing kindergarten teacher, our friendly neighborhood serial murderer has left another pair of bodies for us. He's almost at the number of dead Nephilim he needs to open the portal to Hell. So if you're quite finished being guidance counselors and playing house, come with me to the latest crime scene. That is, if you're still interested in saving the world."

CHAPTER ELEVEN

Flynn and I followed a pissed off angel into the church, and I wish that were the beginning of a bad joke. It looked like something out of a horror movie, with blood almost literally painting the front of the sanctuary. We were there before the crime scene techs, before the bright lights and evidence cards, before the bustle that dulls the edge of even the most horrific scenes. The metallic smell of blood almost bowled me over, with the horrible underlying miasma of death and shit and puke and sweat and pain and fear that accompanies horrific murders. I didn't need my Sight to know that the energy of this place was corrupted, and it would take a lot of work to put the church back right.

The sanctuary was a big room, all Gothic arches and rose windows. My rubber soles moved almost silently across the floor, and I could hear the occasional *drip-drip* of blood falling to the stone. The only light in the place was one chandelier over the pulpit and a rack of prayer candles on either side of the main door, with the odd streetlight peeking in through the stained glass and casting crazy-quilt colors all around the room. Every single candle in the rack blazed brightly, casting a flickering yellow glow that made long dancing shadows across the walls. It made me feel like the killer stopped on the way out the door to light fresh candles everywhere, in a mockery of prayer.

Everything about the room felt like a message, a mocking Zodiac letter to the cops, a nasty letter from Jack the Ripper to investigators, a blood-soaked "you can't touch me" from the killer to me, addressed very specifically by writing my name in blood all over the walls of the sanctuary. "HARKER" shrieked at me from every window, a crimson-turning-brown message that I couldn't miss if I were blind.

The room was dim, but I could make out the shape of a body lying on the communion table as if in state. The robes marked him as a priest, and the glimmer of golden light around him in my Sight told me he was Nephilim. He was gutted, his body ripped open and spread across the table, with a lake of blood pooling on the floor beneath the table.

The splintered light from the chandelier and the windows cast long shattered shadows all over the room as the light fixture swung. I looked up to see what was making it move, then stopped dead as I realized what I was looking at.

"Tell me that's not…"

"I wish I could," Glory said.

I pulled a small flashlight from my pocket and shone a light up at the grotesque display hanging from the ceiling. A young boy, no more than twelve, hung from the chandelier, wearing nothing but his white underpants splattered red with his own blood. His feet were bound at the ankles with a nail jammed through them for dramatic effect. His arms were spread wide and lashed to the curved arms of the light, then a huge nail jammed through each palm. A wicked slash marked one side, but the cause of death was obviously the fact that his throat was cut from ear to ear. Everything else was just window dressing, a message not just for us, but for Glory and her bosses, too. And the *piece de resistance* was on the boy's head, where a battered Atlanta Braves ball cap was tacked to his head with at least two dozen nails, hammered into the child's skull to make a modern-day crown of thorns. I lowered my light from the mockery of the crucifixion and looked back at Flynn.

"Becks, you shouldn't be in here."

"Why, because it's gross? Because it's an affront to everything anyone holds holy? I get it, Harker. I don't think I did until right this second, but I get it now. This motherfucker wants to send a message? Well it's received, loud and goddamn clear. He wants to mock God? He thinks using faith as the model for his butchery is going to what? Rattle me? Scare me? Fuck that. Fuck him, and if you think this is doing anything more than pissing me off and making me stronger in my faith, then fuck you, too." The vehemence in her voice was matched by the fire in her eyes, and I backed off.

"That's not really what I mean, but I'm glad that your faith is strong because you're going to need it to beat this bastard. I meant that you should go call this in before we step in something and fuck up the crime scene. I don't want to have to fight a Cambion, a demon, *and* Paul from the crime lab."

It didn't work. Didn't lighten the mood at all. Flynn just looked at me and nodded. "You're right," she said. "I'll go call it in. Look around quickly for anything magical, then meet me outside."

"Are we going to talk about that before you go?" Glory asked, pointing the walls.

"I was really trying to think of a way not to," I said. "I need to not be the focus of the police investigation, and I don't know how to do that without destroying evidence."

"So destroy the evidence," Glory said.

Flynn and I whipped our heads around. "Why not?" the angel asked. "You know the police can't do anything to stop these killings. You also know there will only be one more Nephilim murdered, then a human, then either the Cambion will sacrifice itself or kill one of its own ilk to open the portal for Orobas, and then your world is probably destroyed."

"Unless we stop it," Flynn said.

"We'll stop it," I said.

"I hope you're right. I like this world, and most days I like some of its inhabitants," Glory replied.

"Thanks." I gave her a wry look.

"You're welcome. But you need to remember that Orobas has learned a lot in seven years, and he didn't like you much to begin with. After you spoiled his plan last time, he's had nothing but time to study you and find a way to beat you. It won't be as easy this time."

"Last time cost me one of my best friends," I reminded her.

"That's going to feel like chump change when he's through with you this time, Harker. Do you not get it?" Glory's voice rose as she went on. "He doesn't just want to win, he doesn't just want to open a portal to Hell anymore, he wants to destroy you and everything you've ever cared about."

"Then he's going to have to come heavy because I've learned a lot in seven years, too. And this time I know what I'm up against, and I might not be ready, but I'm a lot more prepared than I was last time. Becks, get outside. Call this in, and I'll give the place a quick scan to see if there's anything mystical that can lead us to the Cambion."

"Done. You've got about five minutes before the first units get here. Be somewhere else before that happens." Flynn turned around and walked out the main entrance.

I turned to Glory. "You think Orobas is going to kill her, don't you?"

"It would be the best way to incapacitate you. Especially now that you've admitted your feelings about her."

"It's been a long time, Glory. I didn't think I could feel like this again. After what happened the last time..."

"I know. Luke told me."

"You talk to my uncle?" Every time I think I can't possibly be surprised anymore, the universe reminds me that it is very large and very fucking weird. By doing something like having my guardian angel casually mention that she had a conversation with my uncle, Dracula.

"Not often. He doesn't like to be reminded that there is an afterlife. I'm honestly not sure if it's because he doesn't want to believe, or if he's afraid of where he'll end up."

"Does it really work that way?" I asked.

"You know I'm not going to tell you that, not even if I could."

"I know, but it's worth a shot," I replied with a little grin. "But what did Luke say?"

"He said that when Anna died—"

"Was murdered," I corrected. I could still feel her in my arms. Seventy years gone, and I felt it like it was yesterday. Kneeling in the snow, the cold seeping through my damp pants, holding Anna's body as her blood and life poured out onto the ground around us. Then looking up at the Nazi who stood there with his pistol still smoking.

He grinned at me, then said, "You should thank me, friend. Now there's one less Jewess stinking up the city."

That particular son of a bitch learned what his own shit smelled like from the inside when I took his own knife and opened him up from bellybutton to backbone. I hacked him almost in half, then literally ripped his head off. All I remembered after that was a lot of red on a lot of snow, and a lot of black uniforms torn to pieces before me. I have a flash of me holding a leg in one hand and an arm in the other, and I'm pretty sure they didn't start the day on the same people. I spent the rest of the war racking up a body count rivaling that of the Black Plague and drinking my way through Europe.

"It was a bad time," I said. "I lost myself for a long time, and I don't know what I would have done if there hadn't been a ready supply of Nazis to kill. If anything happens to Flynn, you should probably find a way to teleport me to a nice quiet terrorist camp, or a pirate ship in the Pacific. Because I don't know if there are enough bad guys in America for me to work through my anger on."

"Why don't we just work on not letting anything happen to her?" Glory said. I looked at her, and for the first time in our relationship, I really understood what she was there for. She watched over me to keep me from getting killed, sure, but she was also a failsafe. A last resort in case I went off the deep end. It made sense. I wasn't exactly known for my restraint, and my temper was obviously a work in progress. Glory was there to take me out if she had to, and I had no doubt that she would be more than capable if push came to shove.

"Yeah, that would be better for everybody," I agreed.

Everything okay in there? I hear sirens coming. Becks sent me a message through our mental link. She didn't use that much, preferring to keep some part of her head private at least. I felt the concern resonate through our connection and sent her a quick reassuring pulse of feeling.

Bending to the task at hand, I opened my Sight again, this time spreading my net wide and peered around the room. The intensity of the residual emotion almost bowled me over, most of it centered on the bodies of the boy and the priest on the communion table. Their souls were gone, but without the tatters of energy that I saw at the parking lot murder.

"They moved on, at least," I said, continuing my look around.

"Even Orobas himself can't touch the soul of a priest and an innocent in the House of the Lord," Glory said. "No creature under Heaven is that powerful. This man, and the child with him, were with God before the monster that did this had a chance to even reach for them." The angel's voice was cold, as if she knew how little comfort she had to give.

"There's nothing here," I said. I dropped my Sight. "This son of a bitch is good. If we're going to catch him before he completes his ritual, either he's got to make a mistake, or we're going to have to get lucky."

"Both things that seem more and more unlikely with every body we find," Glory said. "The police are here. You need to get outside before they find you. I'm going to be out of contact for a few hours. Try not to do anything egregiously stupid."

"No promises," I said, then ran for a side door. I stopped by the door and turned back to look at the sanctuary. "She's right," I muttered. I pulled in my will and focused my attention on the walls, on my name splattered across the gray stone in crimson essence. *"Erasa,"* I said, releasing my energy and watching the blood vanish, breaking up into dust and falling to the floor.

I pushed out of the door into the night, ready to move around the front of the church and pretend to be surprised when I re-entered that House of God turned House of Horrors.

CHAPTER TWELVE

I walked to the front of the church and stood with Becks as Paul and the rest of the crime scene techs arrived.

"What do we have, Detective?" Paul asked.

"Double homicide, lots of blood. Similar MO to the Matthews case. I've called Agent Smith from Homeland; I assume he's going to want to claim jurisdiction of the case."

"You're damn right I am, Flynn," Smith's voice boomed from the street as he slid out of the Suburban, his ever-present coffee clutched in one hand. "Set up a perimeter. Get some of the locals to help you man it. Anybody but me, Harker, Flynn, or a tech tries to go into that church, shoot 'em."

The stocky ex-soldier stomped up to where we stood by the bottom of the steps. "Is the scene secure?" he asked.

"We didn't see anyone else around," I replied.

"Go ahead then," Smith said to Paul. He took a photographer and another tech into the church.

"You're gonna need a ladder," I called after them. "And a rope!"

"Bad?" Smith asked.

"The worst thing I've seen in a while," I said.

"That's pretty bad," Smith agreed. "You find anything the techs won't?"

"The killer left another message for me. My name written all over the walls in blood. I wiped it out before they got here. And both our victims were Nephilim. I saw the wings," I confirmed.

485

"So that's four that we know of. Our guy is either close to getting his freak on or he's ready," Smith observed.

"He either needs one more Nephilim, or he's killed one we don't know about, which I think is unlikely given the amount of taunting this dickhead has been doing to me. So let's assume that four is an accurate count of dead half-angels. That means he needs a human and a Cambion to complete the summoning."

"I doubt this one plans to use himself as the sacrifice," Flynn said. "Something about all the taunting just seems way more narcissistic than what you told me about the last killer. So I think he'll have a plan to find another Cambion to serve as the sacrifice. As far as a human goes, those are pretty simple."

"Yeah, only a million and a half of those running around this town. But Cambion are pretty thin on the ground," I said. "I don't know of any central repository for birth records of half-demons, though."

"And if he knows the trick of masking his true nature with Nephilim blood, then you wouldn't have any way of knowing who he was," Smith added.

"That's what we've got Paul for," I said. "At least, I hope so. Did your research turn up anything, Smitty?"

"A great big pile of fuck-all," he grunted. "There was plenty in Marlack's books about how to summon demons and how to communicate with the Lords of Hell, but not shit on demonspawn or anything useful in this case."

"Damned inconsiderate evil necromancers, not ever having useful shit in their spell books. Where's Giles and Willow when you need them?" I quipped.

Smith turned to me with a glare. "Do you take *anything* seriously, Harker? We've got people dying here, and you're making fucking *Buffy* references?"

"There's plenty I take seriously, Smitty. I'm pretty serious about catching the demonspawn son of a bitch that's writing my name in innocent people's blood all over my city. I'm serious about keeping the people I care about safe from the aforementioned demonspawn motherfucker, and if you really want to know how serious I can get, you can ask the plant elemental that I killed this afternoon by *setting myself on fire*. So yeah, there's shit I take seriously. But there's nothing so goddamn dark I can't crack a joke about it. I've fought demons hand-to-hand, beat the ever-loving fuck out of one of the Four Horsemen of the Apocalypse, and eaten Flynn's cooking. And I've come out of all that alive, if maybe a little scarred. So if you don't like me poking shit with a stick, too goddamn bad. Because even though I talk a lot of crap, when it hits the fan, I'm not just the smartass you want by your side, I'm the smartass you've got."

"That almost inspired confidence, Harker," Smith said with a grudging smile. "Especially the bit about surviving Flynn's cooking. That's some serious stamina there."

"If you two assholes are quite finished, Paul just radioed me. He's got something inside," Flynn said.

We pushed through the big doors with Smith in the lead. Paul stood at the front of the sanctuary holding an evidence bag. There was a small piece of white material in the bag stained red, presumably with blood.

"What have you got, Paul?" Smith asked.

"It appears to be a small fragment of torn wax-treated paper," the tech replied. "I found a similar piece under the body in Matthews this morning. At the time, I chalked it up to possibly being something in the parking lot under the body, but now that I have a sample to test against, I'll see if the two scraps match."

I stared at the bag, dialing in my enhanced vision to focus on any details that were apparent. The white paper was maybe a quarter inch on each side, with a hint of a deep blue on one torn corner. "What do you think it is?" I asked.

"I have no idea, Mr. Harker," Paul said. "But I will run tests to determine whether or not the two pieces match, then I will try to extrapolate the meaning of this blue design on the corner. I believe there was also a bit of blue on the piece from the parking lot."

"Good eye, Paul. Please let us all know as soon as you have something."

"Yes, ma'am."

"Anything else?"

"We have a tentative ID on the victims."

"That was fast," I said.

"I Googled the church directory. The priest is Gaines Pence. He's the senior priest here. The..."

"Child," I supplied.

Paul looked at me, stricken. "Yes. The child is Eugene Ziban. He's an altar boy here. He's...he was twelve years old. I'm sorry, Detective. I know it's not professional, but who would *do* something like this? This is...just awful."

Flynn put a hand on the young tech's shoulder. "I know, Paul. It's terrible. But sometimes people do terrible things to each other, and that's where we come in. We figure out who did these things, and we make damn sure they don't do them again."

"Ever," Smith said, his face grim.

"Did you find the kid's clothes?" I asked, changing the subject. Every head snapped to me. I didn't flinch. I needed to know.

"They're already bagged," Paul said.

"Did the kid...did Eugene have a wallet?"

"It's in the bag."

"Detective, I need you to come with me, open the bag, and get the kid's wallet. We need to maintain chain of evidence." I knew chain of evidence was useless because this killer was only ever going to face one judgement, and that wouldn't take place on Earth. But I needed Paul to think we were still working this like a mundane case.

"What do you want with his wallet, Harker?" Smith asked.

"Either in his wallet, or in his cell phone will be his emergency contact. Somebody has to tell his parents what happened." Those words hung heavy in the air for a long, silent moment before Flynn moved.

"That's for the ME to do. After the autopsy, when they can come positively identify the body," Becks said. "Not our gig, thank God."

Just then we heard a muffled *thump* from the rear of the sanctuary. Smith, Flynn, and I whirled around and drew our weapons, each pointing in a slightly different direction. There was nothing there, but when I listened harder, I could just barely pick up the sound of someone moving near the back of the church. I motioned for the others to follow me and for Paul to stay put. He nodded and crouched between two pews. His other techs looked around, then knelt behind the first row, taking what cover they could find.

Smith moved through a pew to one wall and Flynn the other while I moved silently up the center aisle, my Glock in hand and flashlight held crossways under the pistol, just like the professionals on TV all do. I didn't count on it doing shit to improve my mediocre aim, but at least I had a light. I figured if it was anything really dangerous, I wouldn't do shit with a pistol anyway, but it was good start.

We got to the back of the church and still saw nothing. I opened my Sight and scanned the area, and jackpot! I holstered my gun and pointed at the confessionals tucked into the back corner of the sanctuary. The smaller rooms looked like four freestanding closets, and my Sight told me there was someone alive in the one nearest the back wall. Someone whose daddy lounged around on clouds and played harp all day.

There's another Nephilim in the room, and it's hiding in the confessional, I sent to Flynn. *Cover me.* She nodded, and I held up a hand, palm out, for Smith to hold his position. I wanted Flynn where she could shoot the half-angel if it came at me and Smith where he could run it down if it got past me.

I didn't need to worry about either option. I yanked open the door, and the man that greeted me was the most terrified mostly human being I'd ever seen.

He was a skinny dude in his early thirties, short, with thick glasses and lank dark hair plastered to his head with sweat.

"Please don't kill me!" the man cried as he curled up even further into a little ball on the floor of the confessional. "I don't want to die, please don't kill me! I've got so much to live for!"

Personal hygiene obviously wasn't one of his motivating factors for seeing another sunrise because this dude stank to high heaven. And not just fear-sweat, either. He had that acrid stink that long-time tweakers carry like a cologne, and I knew immediately why he was in the church.

I turned to Flynn and Smith. "It's okay, just a junkie who crawled into a dark safe place to sleep it off and then heard some things he couldn't un-hear. He's still kinda fucked up, from the drugs I mean. The rest of it would fuck up anybody, no matter how well-adjusted."

Flynn walked up behind me and looked down at the twitching, babbling mass of half-angel. "What's wrong with him? Oh, never mind, I smell the meth-funk."

"BO and cat piss, that's the smell of somebody who's been on crystal a long time," I replied. I knelt down to the tweaker's side. "Hey man, be cool. Nobody's gonna hurt you. Did you see who did this?"

He looked at me, eyes wide. "What are you, man? What *are* you?"

"I'm just a guy. Just a normal guy, like you. But I work for the government, and I need to know if you saw who did this."

He shook his head, and I felt disappointment well up inside me. "Nah, man, you ain't like me. And you ain't no normal dude, either. I don't know what you are, but I ain't never seen nothing like you. Me, I'm special. I ain't normal neither, but you ain't like me. You ain't like that other dude, though. You ain't black inside. You ain't gold like me, but you ain't black neither. You ain't red like the dog-dudes, or blue like the vampires, but you ain't gold. You're like, silver. Ain't never seen silver. She's pretty. She's green, with a little pink. You got some of that pink, too. You like her, don't you? Heh. It's okay, man. She likes you, too. I can see it. You got a taste, man? I could really use a little sumpin-sumpin, if you know what I mean."

"I don't have anything on me, man. I'm sorry. But you saw the other dude, the one that was here a little while ago?" I slipped into his freaked out cadence, but couldn't quite match his lingo.

"Yeah, man, I saw him. I saw right through the walls, man. He was fucked up, that dude. All black and red inside. And I heard him, too. Heard him super-loud." *Shit.* I looked into the addict's eyes. There was nothing there. No recognition, no nothing. I waved a hand in front of his face, and he snatched his head back, but didn't track my hand with his eyes. He was blind as a bat.

I turned to Flynn and Smith. "He's blind. He sees with Sight. That's what the color bullshit is about. He reads auras. He won't be worth a fuck as a witness, but he's Nephilim, and if our guy gets anywhere near him, he's toast."

"Three Nephilim in one church? That seems like a big coincidence, Harker," Flynn said.

"It probably isn't one," I replied. "If the guy in the pulpit was half-angel, people like him would naturally be drawn to the place just because it felt right. That priest's juju was all over this sanctuary, until he died, but until that, he was probably a beacon for the partially divine all over town."

"I guess that makes sense. But what do we do with your new buddy here?"

"I'll take him," Smith said. "I know of a couple of safe houses around town. I'll take him there and sit on him while your techs process the scene. When the sun comes up, I'll put a few agents on him and we can get back to the hunt."

"How does that sound?" I turned to the blind half-angel, but he was staring up at Smith, a look of pure horror on his face. He pointed to the agent, gasped once, and passed out. But not before he pissed himself, sending a stream of urine cascading into the floor and all over my leg.

"Thanks, Smitty. I knew you were a scary fuck, but did you have to make the guy piss all over my foot?"

"Sorry," Smith said. He didn't look very sorry. Like, not at all. Asshole. "I'll get a couple of my guys to load him into the car. Call me if your techs find anything bigger than a postage stamp." He stomped out the front door.

"Smith's gonna deal with this guy, and I gotta get some dry pants," I said to Flynn.

"I'll hang here with Paul and meet up with you when they're done."

"Your car's at my place," I said in a voice low enough to keep the techs from overhearing.

"Shit, you're right. Okay, I'll come with you, but I'm not washing your back again." But she smiled when she said it, so I had a little hope. And a boot full of tweaker piss, but at least I still had hope.

CHAPTER THIRTEEN

She really didn't wash my back, but when I got out of the shower, I found hard-nosed Detective Rebecca Gail Flynn, scourge of Charlotte bad guys and badass chick, curled up on top of my bedspread, fast asleep. I looked over at the clock on my bedside table, saw the 3:45 a.m. in glowing blue numbers, and decided that a few hours of shuteye would do us both good. The rush I got off Luke's blood had long since run its course, and I was feeling the weight of all my one hundred twenty years. I grabbed a spare blanket out of the closet, lay down next to Becks, and pulled the blanket over us both.

Sunlight was streaking in the window when I felt the body beside me stir. I looked over at Flynn, auburn curls splayed out on the pillow like a waterfall, and felt something twist in my gut. I was so completely fucked. I'd fallen for this human woman, hook, line, and sinker, and if anything happened to her, I wasn't sure I'd ever be able to get myself back. So I just had to make sure nothing happened to her. She stirred, stretching like a very contented cat, then I watched her snap awake as she realized she wasn't in her own bed.

"Chill out, Becks, it's okay. You fell asleep while I took a shower, so I laid down with you and we caught a few hours of shuteye. We both needed it."

"Why are you naked?" I looked down. Yup, naked.

"I walked in here after the shower, and you looked so cute I just decided to let you sleep. Then I realized how much yesterday took out of me, so I decided to sleep a little, too."

"Still doesn't explain the naked part."

"I got out of the shower, dried off, and got into bed. None of that requires clothes. So I didn't wear any."

"You sleep naked?"

"You don't?"

She let out a sigh. "I've gotta pee. This is not the time to discuss sleepwear." She got out of bed and stretched, pulling her shirt up just enough for me to get a glimpse of her flat belly. I liked what I saw, a fact that was obvious and exacerbated by my own need to relieve myself. Which, of course, got a lot more difficult the more I saw of the gorgeous detective. She clumped off to the bathroom and closed the door. I walked out into my den, then across the room to the guest bathroom. I thought about baseball long enough to be able to pee, then gave my face a quick wash in the sink.

I wandered back into the bedroom just as Flynn opened the bathroom door. "Jesus, Harker! Put that thing away, will you?"

"Yeah, yeah," I muttered. "If you see anything you've seen before, feel free to shoot it." I grabbed a pair of underwear out of the dresser and stepped into them. "Happy now?"

"Yeah, not bad. Face it, Harker, guys are just way sexier in underwear than out of it. I mean, face it, you've got a decent body, and you're actually a pretty good-looking guy."

"Glad to hear you don't think I'm a troll," I quipped, digging around for a pair of jeans. I put on my pants and an undershirt, then walked over to the closet and pulled out a black dress shirt. All my dress shirts are black, long sleeve, and basically identical. I was doing the whole "wear the same thing every day" long before Mark Zuckerberg started bragging about it. I always just thought I was fashion ignorant and basically lazy. I never knew I was simplifying my decision tree, or whatever bullshit other lazy fashion ignora-muses came up with.

"Oh no, you're a definite hottie, but all guys look a little silly naked."

"I'll take your word for it. I've spent a lot more time examining the naked female form, personally. And I'm a fan."

"Took you a hundred years to figure that out, huh?" She grinned at me.

"Nah, I developed a pretty good theory in my first twenty years. The last century has just been additional research. But I'm finally ready to announce my findings—I like naked women."

"Yeah, better change that plural to singular, if you want to see *this* woman naked again." I knew I wasn't in trouble because she was still smiling. As long as I kept her laughing, I was okay.

"You've got a deal. I like naked *woman*."

"Good to hear. Now do you have a new toothbrush lying around? My mouth feels like death."

"Under the sink."

She went back into the bathroom, leaving the door open this time. I followed her in, assuming the open door was something of an invitation. I grabbed my own toothbrush and proceeded to chisel the remnants of the day before out of my mouth, then put a little gel in my hair to tame the bedhead and gave my stubble a quick glance and promise to tend to the thicket as soon as we caught the murderer.

"What's the plan?" Flynn asked, sitting on my bed to put her shoes on.

I grabbed a fresh pair of Doc Martens from the closet and sat next to her to put them on. If there's anything running around the world with Dracula for a mentor will teach you, it's to have spare clothes around. The bootful of tweaker piss I got in my boot the night before wasn't even on the top ten list of most disgusting things to ever happen to my wardrobe.

I looked over at Flynn. "We'll grab a quick breakfast, then call Smitty and see if the junkie we found at the church has told him anything."

"Do you think we can use that guy? He was pretty nuts, and he didn't actually see anything."

"Remember, Becks, we aren't looking at a burden of proof that will stand up in a court of law. We just need to figure this shit out beyond our reasonable doubt, and then put two in the Cambion's head."

"I don't like this vigilante shit, Harker. We're the good guys; we're supposed to be better than this."

I turned to her and put on my serious face. "No, *you're* the good guys. I'm the guy who gets shit done. Sometimes I work with the good guys, and my endgame is always tilted toward the side of the angels, but a lot of rules either don't apply to me or can't be applied to the things I hunt. This is one of those things. A Cambion with the knowledge to open a portal to Hell? Even if we had evidence to get an arrest and a conviction, we can't put that thing in the general population in prison. And we sure as hell can't send it to a psych ward where it will have all that disturbed mental energy to feed off of. No, Becks, this is one of those black and white times when it's kill this motherfucker or a lot of innocent people die."

"Doesn't mean I have to like it."

"You wouldn't be the woman I fell in love with if you did. We all need a moral compass, Becks. You're mine."

"Great, I'm Jiminy Cricket."

"Could be worse, you could be my fairy godmother. Now let's go grab some breakfast and then find this asshole. By my reckoning, the Cambion only needs one more Nephilim and then a couple other sacrifices for the ritual, which is probably scheduled for some time in the next three nights."

"Why the next three? I thought the Solstice was tomorrow?"

"Solstice is like the full moon. It's more a rough period of time than a specific date on the calendar. Astronomically, it's about when the sun and Earth are either at their nearest or farthest points. That's a very specific moment, but magically, there's a little gray area on either side of the exact moment, basically because ancient druids and wizards and witches didn't have much in the way of high-tech astronomical tools, but they could feel the strengthening of our connection either to the lands of light or the lands of shadow. The summer solstice is specifically better for casting lighter spells, but all magic is strengthened. The winter solstice, which we're fast approaching, is one of those times when the physical plane is in much greater contact with the shadow planes, so it's easier to cast darker magic."

"Like opening a portal to Hell," Flynn added.

"Exactly. So since we're more closely contacting the shadow planes right now, there's a period of about seventy-two hours that our Cambion has to work with."

"So how did you know when to catch him last time?"

"I got lucky. I read a bunch of Dark Ages bullshit about how the ceremony had to be done at midnight, and I bought it one hundred percent. Fortunately for me, Sponholz bought it, too. Otherwise I don't think we'd be having this conversation."

"So you saved the world just by getting lucky?"

"Happens more often than you'd think," I said. I stood up and held out my hand. "Come on, chickadee, let's go get some breakfast. This pile of sexy requires coffee to function. And bacon. Then we can go visit our ear-witness at the safe house. Smitty texted me the address while we were asleep."

"Hmmm, a man that runs on caffeine and bacon. That's my kind of guy." She stood, gave me a quick kiss, and swooped past me out the bedroom door. I stood there for a second, wondering if I'd ever get used to having a woman that ridiculously pretty, smart, and badass interested in me. I decided the answer was "probably not," and that I was completely fine with that.

CHAPTER FOURTEEN

I was on my second helping of bacon when he walked in. He was disheveled, looking like he hadn't slept in a couple days, and his eyes were red. I was sitting in IHOP with my chair facing the door, and I pegged him for trouble the second he pushed through the door. His shirt was untucked, and his socks didn't match, but that wasn't what gave it away. No, it was the air of frantic emptiness he carried with him like his own personal cross. This was a guy that had nothing left to lose, and that made him very dangerous, even if he was completely human.

I held up a hand to interrupt Flynn talking about a new DNA report that Paul just sent to her phone. "Becks." I kept my voice low but put enough force behind it that her head snapped up.

"What's wrong?" I don't know if she read my voice or felt the concern through our mental link, but her phone was instantly forgotten.

"The guy that just came in. He's trouble."

Flynn nodded, then said loudly, "Okay, honey. Let me just go wash my hands and we can go." She stood up and walked past me to the restrooms. That not only got her out of the line of fire if something went to shit, it also put her on her feet and mobile enough to deal with a threat if one arose.

Her movement caught the man's attention, and he called out to her. "Are you Detective Flynn?" I felt her freeze right behind me and turn. My attention was divided between the man and the inertia-dampening spell I was muttering under my breath.

"I'm Detective Flynn," Becks said, not moving any closer. That kept her out of my way if I needed to do something and still kept the guy's attention on her. "What can I do for you?"

"You can tell me why you're in here eating breakfast while my son is lying the morgue, for one thing."

The man's voice shook. So did his hands, and I could see that he was barely holding on. *Shit.* It hit me then. He was the altar boy's father. What the fuck was he doing here? And how the fuck did he know we were here?

"Sir, I assure you, the department is doing everything we can to find out what happened to your son, and as soon as we know anything—"

"Don't you lie to me, bitch! I see you in here, eating fucking pancakes with your asshole boyfriend instead of out there figuring out who killed my boy!"

"Sir, Mr. Harker is an investigator with Homeland Security. He is assisting in our investigation. We believe that your son's death may be connected to others in the area, and we are putting all our resources—"

"Goddammit, bitch, I said shut up!" He pulled a pistol out of his pocket, and I realized I probably wasn't getting that refill on my coffee.

I got up and held up both hands, palms toward him so he could see that I was unarmed, at least as far as he probably considered "armed." "Calm down, sir. We don't want anybody to get hurt here."

"Hurt? *HURT?!?*" he screeched. "You didn't see your little boy lying dead on a table in the morgue. No, you were here having breakfast with this idiot cop, chatting about the goddamn weather like nothing bad ever happened!"

No, I saw your little boy hanging from a chandelier with nails in his hands, but we spared you from that. That's what ran through my head. What came out of my mouth was some nonsense meant to be reassuring but really only intended to give Flynn enough time to get her hand on her service weapon.

Whatever I said, it didn't calm him down one bit. I suppose nothing could, and I didn't really blame him for that. He looked back to Rebecca. "What are you doing here, bitch?"

"Sir...Sir!" This time I shouted, and I covered most of the distance between us in two quick steps. Sometimes having Dracula's blood in your veins is really handy.

His head snapped to me, and he stepped backwards, just out of my reach. He trained the gun on me. "Stay back, asshole."

"I'll stay back, but you call Detective Flynn a bitch one more time, and one of us is going to shoot you. I don't make any promises about which one it will be, but watch your mouth."

"Fuck you," he spat at me. "My boy is dead, do you hear me? Dead!"

"I don't have to hear you," I said. "I saw. I saw it, and I'm sorry. No parent should ever have to go through that. But we are only human, and we have to eat. And we have to sleep. Because if we don't, we can't do our jobs, and then nobody finds the son of a bitch that killed your boy."

He looked like he was wavering, and I thought I had him. I thought I was reaching him, but then somebody pushed through the front door, and the door chime rang out, and his eyes went wide and paranoid again, and he lost it.

"You're just trying to distract me! You don't care about my boy! You don't care about anything!" He raised the pistol, and I went for him. I slapped the gun out of his hand, but not before he got a shot off. It was a little gun, maybe a .22. It sounded more like a loud handclap than a gunshot in the restaurant. I slapped his hand, the gun went to the floor, and I punched the distraught father in the jaw. He was out before he hit the ground, and I turned around to make sure the errant bullet hadn't hurt anyone.

"Is everyone okay?" I asked. A room full of people nodded back at me. "Was anyone hurt?" The same room full of people shook their heads. "Does anyone really have to pee right now?" Half the room got up *en masse* and bolted for the restrooms.

"Detective, will you get some uniforms in here to take this gentleman to the station? And they'll probably need to get statements from everyone here. As soon as they get here, we've got to go. As he so vehemently reminded us, we have a murderer to catch."

"Actually, I think you're going to the hospital," Flynn said, pulling out her cell phone. "Call 911," she said to the nice lady at the cash register.

"Why would I...*oowwwww!*" I looked down at my left arm and saw the shirt sleeve soaked with blood. "Did that son of a bitch *shoot* me?"

"If not, then you *really* need to see a doctor because you're bleeding out of your skin for no reason. Which might be even worse than getting shot," was Flynn's response. That's my girl, always helpful. I felt her concern, though, so I sent reassuring feelings to let her know I didn't think it was all that serious.

I moved my arm around. It hurt, but really not too bad. A lot less than any of the other times I'd been shot, even wearing a Kevlar vest. "I don't think he hit anything vital, but I'd like to get the bleeding stopped."

Flynn knelt to the unconscious man, checked his pulse and his pupils to make sure I hadn't accidentally killed him. Satisfied with what she found, she rolled the man over onto his stomach. When she was done, she waved me over to a nearby table.

"Come here," she said. "Sit." I sat. Flynn reached into her pocket and pulled out a small pocketknife. She cut the sleeve off my shirt and rolled up my t-shirt.

"I could have taken that off, you know."

"It was ruined anyway," she replied, not looking up from my arm. "Bullet holes and bloodstains are the end of most clothes."

"Some of my favorite shirts have bullet holes and bloodstains," I protested. She ignored me, which was probably safer for me anyway.

"This doesn't look too bad. The bullet just grazed you, but you should still have it cleaned and bandaged, so you don't get an infection."

"I don't get infections," I said, keeping my voice down.

"Can we skip the part where you're all macho and don't want to go to the hospital and go straight to the part where you do what I say?"

I took a second to think about it, then said, "Yeah, that's fine, but I'm driving myself."

"Take a cab. You're losing blood. But there is this nice ambulance right outside."

I looked out the big windows, and sure enough, a pair of EMTs were running for the front door. I let out a sigh and waited for them to fuss over me and eventually load me into the ambulance for the three-minute ride to the nearest hospital.

*****

At least they didn't make me wear a stupid gown once I got to the hospital. The nurses just sat me back in an exam room with a big bandage on my arm waiting for an ER doc to get loose and deal with me. I had run through all my emails, checked my Facebook twice (doesn't take long when you only have a dozen friends and half of them are scam accounts) and read the opening of a new Rick Gualtieri novel by the time the doc came in. He was a hefty Asian dude with a big smiling round face and a lab coat that probably never met in the middle.

"Good morning!" he proclaimed, gesturing broadly with his left hand. His right was clutching a big white-and-blue cup from WhattaBean, the snazzy coffee shop a couple blocks away. Popular with bankers, WhattaBean proudly proclaimed that it had the best coffee beans anywhere, harvested by hand from Argentina. I didn't see any real difference in their coffee and the swill at the Exxon station, except for the four-dollar price tag, but coffee nerds like Smitty swore by the stuff.

"I'm Doctor Cho. What can we do for you this morning?"

"I got a little shot. I need a few stitches, then I've got to find a murderer. So can we move this along, Doc?"

The doc seemed a little offended for a moment, then I could almost see him actually process the words that came before "hurry the fuck up." He looked at my face, then at the badge I held up with my right hand, and nodded.

"Absolutely. I can get you out of here and back on the case, as it were, in just a few minutes. Let me just clean and numb the wound, then we'll get this stitched up and you can be on your way. Do you think you'll need a prescription for pain?"

"I won't ever say no to a few Vicodin," I replied.

"Not a problem. You might feel a little pinch," he said, as he turned and set his coffee cup on the table behind him. Something tickled in the back of my head, then he stabbed me in the arm with a goddamn burning railroad spike and I almost came off the exam table.

"Jesus fucking Christ, Doc, what the fucking *fuck?*" I looked down at my arm, and he was just pulling a tiny needle out of it.

"Sorry, sometimes the Novocain gives off a slight burning sensation when it goes in," the inscrutable Asian master of understatement said. I turned my head so I didn't have to watch him sew my flesh back together and thought about all the other scars littering my body and the interesting and mundane ways I'd acquired them.

A few minutes later, he slapped some Steri-strips over the wound and pronounced me done. "Keep that clean and leave the strips on until they fall off on their own. Make an appointment with your primary care physician for a follow-up in a week to ten days, and good luck catching whoever you're after," the doc said.

I thanked him, we shook hands, and he picked up his coffee cup and tilted it up, knocking back the last swallow. Then he pitched the empty cup in the trash can and walked out. I hopped off the exam table and stepped toward the door, then froze.

I stared at the coffee cup in the trash, glaring up at me like a beacon. I reached down and picked up the cup, turning it over and over in my hands. The blue-and-white swirl pattern spun in my hands, undulating as I turned the cup this way and that.

"Son of a bitch…" I whispered.

"Excuse me?" the nurse asked.

"I gotta go." I pushed past her out the door and headed down the hall toward the Emergency Room exit.

"Sir! You have to sign this paperwork before you can leave!" the little nurse called after me.

"National security, sorry!" I yelled back to her. I was in the hall and moving fast. An overweight security guard stood up off his stool and moved like he thought he was going to intercept me but sat back down when he saw the badge clipped to my belt. He slapped the automatic door opener, and I bolted through the double doors into the waiting room.

I yanked my cell phone out and dialed Paul the second I was outside and away from a hundred prying ears and coughing sick people.

"Crime lab, Paul speaking." He answered the phone like a banker, but he was as solid a tech as I'd seen.

"Paul, it's Harker. I need to ask you about the scrap of paper you found at the parking lot murder," I said.

"I've processed it. What do you need to know?"

"Were there any substances found on it?"

"I found blood from the victim, some traces of silica from the asphalt, and coffee."

"What about wax?"

"What about it?" Paul asked.

"Was the paper coated with wax?"

"Yes."

"Was it a coffee cup?"

"It certainly could be, although I suppose there are other things it could be as well."

"Was there coffee and wax on the paper you found at the church?"

"Yes, and it was an identical blend."

"What does that mean?"

"The similarities in the coffee means that the beans were harvested from the same region, specifically near Buenos Aires."

"That's in Argentina, right?" My education focused a lot more on Europe than South America. I could find Lichtenstein blindfolded from the Black Forest, but I was a little soft on Argentina.

"Yes. Why?"

"I think it may become relevant," I said, looking down at the cup in my hand. "Thanks, Paul." I hung up and dialed Flynn.

"How's the arm?"

"Come get me. I'm outside the ER on Caswell."

"Harker, I'm a little—"

"I know who it is, and we've got to move. I can't talk over the phone. Get here, *now*."

I paced in front of the Emergency Room entrance for five minutes or so before Flynn pulled up, lights and siren rolling. I opened the door and slid in.

"Drive. We've got to get to South Boulevard."

"What's on South?"

"That godawful big pink building. The safe house that's supposed to have our witness is there. But I'm willing to bet anything it's empty." I held up the coffee cup. "Look familiar?"

"Yeah, it's from WhattaBean, that hipster coffee place Smith loves so much."

"It's also the exact piece of paper that was found underneath our parking lot victim. It was also the type of scrap of paper that was by the priest's body last night. Paul matched the analysis of the coffee to the same crop in Argentina."

"They can do that?"

"Fuck if I know, but Paul says they can, and that's good enough for me."

Flynn didn't say anything for a long moment. "What are you saying, Harker?"

"I'm saying that Agent John Smith is the Cambion, and we have to find him before he kills our Nephilim eyewitness and opens a doorway to Hell."

CHAPTER FIFTEEN

I navigated while Flynn drove like a bat out of hell. The "safe house" was actually a condo in a huge pink monstrosity of a skyscraper in Charlotte's South End, a newish neighborhood that developed from the corridor of strip clubs and local businesses. There were still a few local stalwarts, like Mr. C's diner and the Leather and Lace topless bar, but most of the place was taken over with sterile construction projects instead of cool old buildings. With the siren going, it only took us about five minutes to get there from the hospital, and we left the car in the front of the building and bolted inside.

I flashed my badge at the fat guy behind the counter and said, "Is Agent Smith here?"

The guard, whose polished name badge designated as "Marvin," hopped right up and inspected my badge. He gave it a thorough looking over before he handed it back to me and stood up. "Smith? Mean guy, crew cut going gray?"

"Yeah, that's him," I said.

"No sir, I haven't seen him in weeks. Not since we had a witness in that terrorism case in DC. They stashed one of the witnesses here for a couple days. I stood guard outside her door." I was pretty sure that his idea of "standing guard" involved a whole lot of sitting, but I didn't argue.

"Has anyone brought a witness in here today? What about last night?"

"I just came on at eight, but there's nothing in the logs about a new John or

Jane Doe. That's what we call the people that want their identities hidden." He grinned like it was his original thought or something. I didn't bother correcting him.

"Let me see your log book," Rebecca asked. He handed her a blue three-ring binder open to this morning's visitor logs. We flipped pages back an extra day, but there was no entry showing Smith or any John Doe coming into the building.

"Is there another entrance?" Flynn asked.

"Yeah, there's a back stairwell, but nobody is supposed to use it. Everybody's gotta come through here and get logged right. And I don't let anybody through without signing in, unless they got a key card." He seemed very proud of his adherence to the rules, and I started to think that he might have some slight learning disability or something. And that would make him easier for an asshole like Smith to take advantage of.

"Does Agent Smith have a key card?" I asked.

"Yeah, but only to the condo. He doesn't get one to the front door, on account of the condo not really being his and it belonging to the government. So I have to get up and let him in whenever he comes here."

"But the overnight guy might not have made Agent Smith sign the book if he came in, right?" There was no way Smith was getting past this guy without signing a book, but maybe a bribe to the other guard would keep him off the books.

"Well…maybe not. He was supposed to, but I wasn't here, so I don't know." Marvin avoided eye contact like the plague, so I thought I might be on to something.

"Does the night guy ever bend the rules for Agent Smith or other people?" I asked. I had to keep the pressure on if we were going to find Smith, and the clock was ticking.

"Sometimes he does favors for people. He says it's not really against the rules if the people are allowed to be here anyway, and Gerald is real smart, so I try to do what he says." Marvin was getting a little overwrought, so I nodded to Flynn.

She leaned her elbows onto the raised front of the desk. "It's okay, Marvin, you aren't going to get into trouble. We just need to see if Agent Smith is in the condo. But we don't have a key. Can you take us up there and show us the condo? Agent Smith or the man with him might be in trouble, and we need to get into that condo."

"I'm sorry, ma'am, I can't open the condo for anyone but Agent Smith."

I held out my badge. "Marvin, we work with Agent Smith. He may be hurt and need help. Or the man he brought here might be hurt. You need to take us to that condo, and you need to do it right now." I put on my sternest voice, and Marvin responded to the authority I pretended to have. Good thing, too. My next step was going to be knocking him right the fuck out and stealing his keys. This was easier on Marvin's head and easier on my fist.

Marvin nodded, and I led him to the elevator. We rode up six floors then followed Marvin to the door of the condo. He looked back at me, his eyes a little wide. I gave him a reassuring nod, and he swiped a keycard through the door.

I smelled it the second the door cracked. "Stay here, Marvin. Do not let anyone come into this room, no matter who, unless one of us tells you. Okay?"

Marvin stood ramrod straight and snapped off a rough salute. "Yes, sir!" I knew that nothing was getting through that door unless it killed Marvin, so I'd at least have a few seconds' warning. I motioned for Flynn to follow me, and I drew my pistol.

I slammed the door open and ran through in a crouch, sweeping the gun barrel from side to side as I went in, checking the room for threats. When the mundane world appeared secure, I opened my Sight and checked the Other-world. Nothing.

Nothing except the fading golden wings around the body of our witness, who sat tied to a chair in the middle of the den, his throat cut from ear to ear. The smell of death was heavy, but it was all blood and bodily fluids, no ripe smell of decomposition. I walked over to the body and felt his forehead.

"He's cold. Been dead a couple hours at least." It was obvious that he was our last Nephilim sacrifice, even without my Sight. His throat was cut almost to the bone, but there wasn't nearly enough blood on the carpet to match up to the severity of the crime.

"But not more than that. It's only been five hours since we left Smith at the church."

"Yeah, I figure he brought this guy here right away, made him comfortable, and then killed him."

"There was no making this guy comfortable, Harker. He knew Smith was the killer. Remember at the church? As soon as Smith opened his mouth, this poor bastard pissed himself, then passed out in fear. He knew what was up, and we were just too stupid to see it."

She was right. Too stupid, too slow, too whatever. Just never quite good enough. Not for Becks' dad, not for Bolton, not for this poor son of a bitch. Well, that shit was about to be over. Once and for all. But we had to move, and now. Smith now had all the angel blood he needed to complete the ritual, so once he found a human to murder and just a tiny bit of Cambion blood, which he could supply in spades, the entire Queen City was in deep shit.

I shook myself out of my little pity party and turned to Flynn. "Okay, how do we find him?"

"What?" She looked at me, confused.

"You're a detective. This is your part. My part comes when we find him, and I send him to Hell to meet his daddy."

Flynn stared at me for a second, then nodded. "Okay, yeah. Let me think... he was in a Homeland Security Suburban when he left the crime scene. If it's still here, we can trace it."

"Parking deck," I said, already moving for the door. "Call this in. But let's find some way to keep it locked down as much as we can. If Smith is our Cambion, he might not be the only one in Homeland."

Rebecca froze in mid-stride at that, then I saw the logic of it flicker across her face. "Fuck."

"Yeah, exactly."

We headed for the elevator, leaving Marvin behind to stand guard until Paul and his crew arrived. The parking garage was a small thing, underneath the condos. It would have been very difficult for a Suburban to navigate, so we checked the oversize vehicle area first.

My shoulders sagged when I saw the black behemoth with government plates sitting astride two parking spaces like it owned the building. "Goddammit," I swore. "We needed a break."

"Be chill, Harker. I got this," Flynn said, moving to the car. She drew her pistol as she approached. *There's somebody behind the wheel. Looks too big to be Smith,* I heard in my head.

I drew my Glock and moved to the opposite side of the SUV. *I see him. You cover him, I'll yank open the door.* I did just that, pulling the door almost off the hinges as Flynn moved into position opposite me. The man in the car didn't budge, probably because he was dead. He wasn't a sacrifice, but he was just as dead. He was a big man, about the size of one of Smith's Homeland Security driver-goons, wearing what looked like an expensive track suit. His neck was broken, and his head twisted all the way around so he was staring at the back of the vehicle.

"You better keep an eye out behind you, motherfucker," I muttered at the absent Smith. I slammed the car door. *"Fuck!"* I punched the side of the Suburban, leaving a dent.

"Feel better?" Flynn asked.

"No. Now I'm pissed off and my hand hurts."

"Well, I got nothing for the hand, but I might be able to help with the other." I walked around the car to where she stood with the driver's door open.

"What's the story?"

She held up a wallet. "Our victim is one Timothy Lang. He lived upstairs."

"And?" I asked.

"And...that means he was probably on his way to his car when Smith ran into him. I'm guessing Smith took Mr. Lang's car so we couldn't just track the Suburban, and then killed him because he's a dick."

"Yeah, no reason to kill this guy," I agreed.

"Except that Smith's a demon."

"Half-demon."

"Whatever. Anyway, now we just need a little old-fashioned police work and a little bit of luck. Okay, a lot of luck, but it's about all we've got right now." She pressed a button on her phone, then another one to turn it on speaker.

"CMPD technical operations, what can I do for you, Detective?" Nobody *ever* answers the phone that happy to hear from me. Just shows how much nicer Becks is than me, I guess.

"Mandy, I need a favor," Flynn said.

"Anything you need, Detective." Jesus, maybe I should try this whole "being nice to people shit sometime." Nah.

"I need to know vehicle registration info for a Timothy Lang. He lives in The Arlington."

"Is that the big ugly pink building?"

"Yeah, that's the one."

"Okay, I have a Cadillac Escalade registered to that name and that address."

"Perfect. Can you activate the onboard assistance on that car?"

"I need to know what it's for, Detective. We can, but we're only supposed to—"

"Timothy Lang has been murdered and stuffed in the car used by a suspect in two murders at St. Peter's last night. If we can locate Lang's vehicle, we can probably close three or more murders before lunch." That's another part of the whole "being nice" thing that just never occurred to me—explaining yourself. I would have just yelled at the poor woman on the other end of the phone until she did what I wanted. Becks' explanation took about the same amount of time, and people are easier to understand when they aren't sobbing into the telephone. I really might have to give this whole "being nice" thing a try.

"No problem, Detective. Okay, I've got it."

I opened my phone, ready to input the address. Turns out I didn't need to.

I knew how to get to that house from anywhere in the city. Flynn and I exchanged a look, then hauled ass to her car as she hung up with the tech. We slammed the doors shut and Flynn peeled out onto South Boulevard, heading for the one place Smith could go to hit me in the gut the hardest.

His GPS placed his car parked right outside my Uncle Luke's house.

CHAPTER SIXTEEN

We got there in less than fifteen minutes, but we were still running late. We pulled up in front of Luke's house to find a half dozen thugs in cheap suits standing in front of the house.

"Stay here until I clear a path," I said to Flynn.

"I'll cover you," she replied, slewing the car sideways to put the driver's door away from the house.

I got out and started moving toward the door. Two no-necks closed ranks, and I moved them, forcibly and with extreme prejudice. They landed hard on the front lawn, and four more came at me.

"*Incendiare!*" I said, and a nimbus of fire engulfed my fists. "Come get some, fucktards."

They did. Two of them drew collapsible batons from their belts and went for my legs, while one took a step back and drew a gun. The last one just tried to bull-rush me, but I braced myself and dumped him on his ass with a picture-perfect hip toss. Thirty years of judo classes and pro wrestling videos and I might have picked up a few things.

Flynn put down the guy with the gun, drilling him right between the eyes with her Smith & Wesson .40 service pistol. I caught one baton in my right hand, the other in my left, and channeled my will to send heat down the metal rods. The fire vanished from my hands as the radiant energy poured into the sticks, and the thugs screamed as their weapons suddenly burned the fuck out of their palms. Getting burned is no fun, as I recalled from recent unpleasant experience.

I dropped the baton in my left hand, flipped the right-hand baton around so I held it by the grip, and, insulated from my own heat by magic, I knocked both goons out cold with shots to the head. I didn't give a shit if they were unconscious or dead. They were between me and my uncle, and that was not where they wanted to be. I looked around, saw no more bad guys, and stepped up onto the porch.

Only to get knocked back a good ten feet onto my ass when Orobas stepped through the door. And when I say stepped through the door, I mean he put a foot into the door, kicked it to splinters, and stepped *through* the door. He almost stepped through me as well, but I wasn't as well anchored to the porch, so I just sprawled on the grass instead.

Orobas stood in the doorway grinning down at me. His demon form was pretty unnerving, since he looked like every damn picture of a demon I'd ever seen, what with the red skin, goat legs, bat wings, and big fucking fangs and all. "I've missed you, Quincy Harker. It will feel good to rend your flesh beneath my fingers and pick my teeth with your shinbones."

"I'm glad you're so concerned with oral hygiene these days, Orobas. From what I remember of our last little argument, your breath smelled like you'd been brushing with a giraffe dick and rinsing with raw sewage." I drew my Glock and squeezed off a dozen rounds. Flynn took my shooting as a sign to do the same, and she put ten bullets in the center of Orobas' chest.

It didn't do shit. He jerked back with each impact, but just barely. The distraction was all I needed, though. I got to my feet and charged Orobas. I caught him around the waist in a perfect tackle that took both of us to the ground. I pushed off with my feet and arms and flipped right through the tackle and back up onto my feet, pulling some real *Matrix* shit that normal people just can't do.

Orobas cleaned my clock and embarrassed me the last time we scrapped, but I learned a few things since then. I reached into a coat pocket and grabbed a small box, then slipped on the rings inside. One plain silver band on each middle finger, no adornment, no jewels, just a plain band of silver metal. That happened to be blessed by the Pope and the Dalai Lama. There aren't a whole lot of things those guys agree on, but the concept that demons on Earth is a bad thing is one everybody can get behind.

Then I reached behind my back and unclipped a black cylinder from my belt. I brought it around in front of me and focused my will on the tube. A brilliant white beam of light extended from the hilt with a thrumming sound.

"A lightsaber, Harker?" Orobas said with a smirk. "I don't think Obi Wan Kenobi can save you this time."

"How about a soulsaber, dickhead?" I asked, advancing on him, my blade of concentrated mystical energy weaving patterns of pure magic in the air before me.

"How did a two-bit hack like you learn to conjure a soul blade? That magic has been lost to men since...that fucking winged bitch!"

"That's Miz Winged Bitch to you, fangboy." Glory descended behind me in a shaft of light whiter and brighter than even my soulsaber. Which wasn't all that surprising when you consider that her light was a conduit to the divine, and my light was generated by my admittedly spotty soul. She was a gleaming vision of righteous fury in chain mail and swinging a sword of fire.

"Kill them!" Orobas screamed. "No one enters the house until the ritual is complete!" *Fuck.* That meant the ritual had already begun. We needed to end this shit, and now. Orobas waved a hand, and a blade of pure darkness appeared in his hand. The demon charged Glory, and they came together with a concussion like a dozen mortars all landing at once. Then the rest of Orobas' minions charged me, and it was on.

Only thing between me and the front door of Uncle Luke's house was half a dozen goons with bats and knives. No problem, right? Usually not, but these goons were also Cambion that had fully embraced their demon side and taken on exceptional strength and agility in exchange for the human half of their souls. They weren't full-on demons, but they weren't normal men, either.

I ducked under a wild swing by the first goon, only to find my jaw directly in the path of the second asshole's bat. I spun to one side, lashing out with my magical blade. I heard a scream as the first demonspawn vanished in a flash of light, then got stood up by a kick to the shoulder from the first goon.

I heard the flat *crack-crack* of a semiautomatic pistol and knew that Rebecca had joined the fight. A splash of blood across my face was the only warning I got when she shot a giant thug about to crush my head with a pool cue, but as soon as he dropped, another one took his place. I winnowed the cadre of asshole demon helpers down to a pair of the smartest ones before they managed to crack a bat down on my right wrist and disarm me. I knelt on the ground in front of the Cambion and closed my eyes against the home run I knew he was about to swing at my temple, but the blow never landed.

Instead there was a screech of brakes, then a crash of crumpling metal as a black Hummer pulled up beside Flynn and a giant black Adonis kicked the driver's side door out. The door flew almost ten feet, and a figure stepped out of the truck with a football in his hands. He hurled the football at the head of the goon nearest me, and the half-demon went down, knocked completely unconscious. In all my days, I never, ever expected to be rescued by a hitch-hiker demon riding the body of a franchise quarterback. But that's exactly what happened. He reached back into the truck and hauled out football after football, flinging each one at a Cambion and either knocking it out or killing it outright.

"*WHERE IS SHE, YOU SON OF A BITCH!*" Mort yelled, and I worried for the QB's ability to call signals in the next game.

Orobas turned to Mort and smiled. "Mortivoid, my dear boy, whoever do you mean?"

Mort in the football player's body covered the distance to Orobas in about five seconds, and he leveled the demon with an uppercut that would have killed a human. As it was, Orobas flew back several feet and crashed into the steps of Luke's porch.

"Where is she, you fire-sucking son of a spite demon!" Mort stalked over to where Orobas lay on the steps and stood over him, fists clenching and unclenching with every furious breath.

"She's inside, Mortivoid. What's left of her, that is," Orobas said, looking up at Mort with a smile. "I mentioned that you would regret siding with this piece of human excrement, didn't I? It took me almost seven years to find the relationship, but once I began to suspect, it was obvious."

"Get her out here. Now."

"Of course. Anything for such an old friend." Orobas stood, and Mort took a step back.

Glory stepped forward, her sword raised, but Mort raised a hand. "Not now, Glory. Not until he gives me my...until he gives me Christy."

"Motherfucker," I whispered. I looked at Mort. "She's your daughter. Oh, fuck. That means..."

"Yes, Quincy, it means she is a Cambion, and one of the final components for the spell," Orobas said with a smile. He waved his hands, and Christy appeared, standing in front of Mort.

"Oh, baby, I was so worried about you..." Mort's voice trailed off as he saw it. We all saw it at the same time. Christy stood there in front of us, held in place by Orobas' hand on her shoulder. But nothing held her head as it slowly tipped forward to land on the ground at Mort's feet.

The lifeless eyes of the Cambion that I almost considered a friend stared sightlessly up at me, and I tore my eyes away from her to glare at Orobas. He stood behind Christy's headless body, grinning at me over her neck like some perverted carnival cutout picture booth.

"You son of a *bitch!*" I screamed and raised my soulsaber. Orobas knocked me flat with a casual swipe of his hand, then shoved Christy's body at Mort. The demon riding inside the quarterback dropped to his knees, sobbing like a man who's lost the only thing on any plane of existence he ever cared about. Which he probably had.

Glory went at Orobas, her sword flaming again. She crashed into the demon and turned her head to me. "Harker, get in there! You have to stop Smith before he finishes the ritual, or everything we've ever done was for nothing."

I looked back at Flynn to tell her to cover the door and saw her sitting on the ground with one last Cambion goon standing over her. He held a knife in one hand, and I saw the blood drip from the blade onto the ground.

"Becca!" I screamed, and ran for her. The Cambion turned toward me, a nasty smile on his face, and I shouted *"Separato!"* without breaking stride. He kinda exploded. It looked a lot like he was drawn and quartered, only there were no horses, and he fell into a lot more parts.

I got to Flynn's side and knelt there, patting her face and sobbing. "Becks, Becca, baby, please no. I can't lose you, too. I can't. I don't know what I'll do. I swear to God if you die, I'll fucking kill everything. Oh fuck, Rebecca, please don't die…"

"Don't be such a fucking pussy, Harker, it's just a flesh wound." Flynn's voice snapped me out of my hysteria like a splash of cold water.

"But I…I couldn't feel you in my head."

"That's because he knocked me the fuck out. He slammed me into the car before he tried to stab me. My vest isn't great against knives, but it turned the blade enough that all he did was cut me. He didn't get in very deep."

"Are you sure? Let me see." I reached for her stomach, but she slapped me away.

"Harker!"

I snapped my head up. Flynn looked dead into my eyes. "I'm. Fine. Now would you please go kill that motherfucker Smith and keep him from summoning more demons?"

I kissed her on the forehead and turned to the house, charging into a heap of shit one more time, just to save the world.

CHAPTER SEVENTEEN

T here wasn't even enough door left to slow me down, so I just barreled into the foyer and whipped my head from side to side looking for Smith. I closed my eyes and strained to hear inside noises over the sounds of a shrieking Mort and the tumult of Glory and Orobas throwing down. Either Luke had some oblivious neighbors, or he had someone cast a hellacious masking spell on this place.

I heard chanting to my right, so I sprinted in that direction, taking the library doors right off the hinges. I walked into something out of a horror movie, complete with asshole bad guy in robes and a no-shit goat mask. Smith had a casting circle drawn on the floor, and he had a large pentagram scribed inside it. At the five points of the star sat five jars full of blood, and I knew exactly where those came from. Staked to the floor with the same nails he'd used on the kid at the church, naked as the day he was born with Enochian sigils drawn all over his body in blood, lay Renfield. I couldn't tell if he was unconscious or dead, the magic of the circle screwed with my vision just enough.

"Oh, you are so fucked now, Smitty," I said as I stopped just outside the circle. I couldn't get in to kill him myself; the circle protected him. I'd have to find some way to take down the circle to stop the casting. "Luke's going to rip your head off and shit down your neck when he hears about this."

"Then it's good for me that I'm planning on burning this house down to the earth when I leave, isn't it?" He gestured toward the desk, and I noticed for the first time the pair of gallon jugs with a digital clock attached to them. The readout displayed eleven fifty-seven, and somehow I just knew that the big boom was planned for noon.

"It's not nearly as good as midnight, but really, there is a lovely symmetry to it, isn't there?" Smith looked at me and grinned. "You truly are a stupid bastard, aren't you, Harker?"

"You've been working for Orobas all along, haven't you?"

"I've been working for Uncle Oro my whole life. You could say I'm just carrying on a family tradition."

"What kind of shit are you spewing, Smitty? Am I supposed to believe you're related to Sponholz?"

"I don't care what you believe, Harker. In three minutes, you'll be dead, and I'll be the new ruler of this plane. It's too bad my little brother's dead. This could be just one more thing I beat him at."

Brothers? It made a kind of sense, but I'd never heard of any woman bearing a demonspawn and living through the trauma. "Wait a second...*Uncle Oro?* He's not your father?"

"No. Little Richie thought he was, but that's just because Mom and I never bothered to tell him any different. It served her purposes for him to think she was the only human in history ever to birth a Cambion and live, and I just didn't care enough to tell him."

"Your mother was a succubus. She was the demon half, and you had a human father."

"Fathers, actually. Mating with a succubus can be a...*draining* affair for many humans. Dear old Daddy didn't have quite enough stamina to keep up with Mummy's appetite."

I was a little nauseated by the conversation, but the longer I kept him talking, the less incantationizing he was doing. He finally stopped walking his circles and looked at me. "Huh. I'm monologuing, aren't I? Isn't that what we used to laugh about when we talked about stupid things the bad guys do? I should probably stop." He stepped to Renfield's head and nudged the manservant with one foot. Ren stirred and looked around, dazed.

"Good morning, Renfield. Time to die." Smith dropped to one knee, picked up a ceremonial dagger lying in the pentagram, and stabbed Renfield in the chest.

"NO!" I screamed, drawing my soulsaber and charging the circle. I slammed the blade of pure energy into Smith's magical barrier, hard. And again, and again, and again, until the hilt tumbled from my numbed fingers. The hilt tumbled to the floor, the mystical blade winking out of existence as soon as I was no longer holding it, and I slammed into the magical barrier of the circle.

Smith just laughed from inside his safe haven. "You can't break my circle, Harker. You're not strong enough to break one demonblood circle, let alone two." I looked down and saw what he meant. Two lines of dried brown blood twined around each other like snakes, making two tangled and interwoven circles. I opened my Sight and saw the magical energy braided together, making something much stronger than the sum of its parts. There was no way I was ever going to BS my way through that thing.

Smith knelt by Renfield's body, cutting open his chest and pulling out his heart to drip blood into a bowl by the topmost point of the star. He reached to one side and picked up another bowl of blood that I assumed came from Christy. He began to chant as he poured a small amount of the Cambion blood into the bowl of Renfield's, and I felt the pressure of a great magical working taking place near me.

I studied the woven circles in front of me, tracing the paths of their power, and realized the flaw in Smith's plan. One casting circle, formed properly and invoked by a strong wizard, could probably keep me out. Two circles, one inside the other, would be an even bigger deterrent. But two circles woven together? That formed a stronger whole, a circle completely impervious to brute force.

But not to penetration.

I straightened my hands into knife edges, then focused my will on my fingers, extending my personal energy outward into a narrow tip extending out from each hand like a needle. Then I inserted the needle into the woven energy, just like splicing a rope.

Or like stabbing through a bulletproof vest. I shook my head, throwing aside all thoughts of Becks and her injuries for the moment, because if I couldn't focus right now, there was no question she was going to die. If I could get this right, then I could see if she was lying about her wound or if she was really fine. But right now, I had to *focus*.

I pushed, and the hole in the circle grew wider. Smith looked at me, and his eyes went wide, but he didn't falter in his incantation. I got both hands into the circle's barrier up to the palms, and rotated my arms until my palms faced away from each other. I flexed my shoulders and pulled the magic of the circle away from itself, spreading the woven fibers of magic apart to make a six-inch hole that could only be seen in the Otherworld.

"Hey Smitty," I said. He looked into my eyes, and I said, "That was my friend, you son of a bitch."

Then I drew my Glock, jammed the barrel through the magical circle, and put fifteen nine-millimeter bullets into that traitorous half-demon mother-fucker. I shot him full of holes from his guts to his eyeballs, and he slammed backward into the wall of his circle, shattering the casting, shattering the circle, and shattering the remains of his worthless skull when he hit the floor. I felt the magic dissipate, the casting broken, and the portal to Hell remained unopened, at the cost of one of my few friends. Again. I was really starting to want to kill Orobas.

I took one step toward Renfield, then looked again at the huge vault door that led to Luke's private sleeping chambers. It looked intact, but scarred, which was a pretty good way to describe me right about that moment. I holstered my gun and knelt by Renfield's side. I closed his eyes, pulled out my handkerchief, and wiped the worst of the blood off his face.

Then the timer on the gallon jugs of gasoline reached triple zeroes, and for the second time in as many days, I was burned to a goddamn crisp.

EPILOGUE

I stumbled into the church smelling like smoke and death. I hit my knees in the center aisle and just stayed there for a long moment, gasping for breath. I looked up, and the famous fresco that once made up the entire back wall of the sanctuary looked down on me, its scenes of love and redemption looking empty to my eyes. The last time I prayed was the night my father died, the night that unbeknownst to me, to all of us, first tied me to Quincy Harker and set in motion the string of events that led to me kneeling soot-smeared and bloodstained on the stone floors of St. Peter's.

I looked at the fresco, looked around at all the trappings of faith, and felt something well up inside me. It bubbled up from deep within me, something I didn't know I still had. I dragged myself to my feet, using the pews for support. I stood, feet spread wide and weaving in the aisle. I looked at the altar, looked at the stained glass and polished wood. I looked around at all the little reminders of God and all His glory, and I screamed. I screamed with a rage that flowed out of every atom of my being. I railed at God, cursed Him and His inattention, cursed His willingness to let good men die and monsters live, and poured out all my fury in my words.

I shrieked and cursed for a good five minutes before I ran out of words. I collapsed onto a nearby pew and sat panting, bent over with my head on the pew in front of me. I had no tears. I hadn't cried since I watched the other policemen pull my father's casket out of the hearse. All I had was rage. Rage, and pain, and more rage.

"You feel better?" I knew Glory's voice. She manifested herself to me more than once, just so I wouldn't think Harker was crazy.

"No. And fuck off."

"I don't think so."

"No really, fuck off."

"Can't. You're my problem now. I just got a new assignment, and you're it. Seems like somebody thinks you're important enough for your very own guardian angel."

"For all the good it did the last guy."

"That's cold, Rebecca. I know you're angry, but I didn't make Q go after Smith alone."

"But you didn't stop Smith, either."

"I couldn't. I can't interfere with any malevolent creatures that Harker might piss off. Same goes for you now."

"Is he dead?"

"Which one?"

"Harker. I don't give a fuck about that lying asshole Smith."

"You'd better. Because Harker's alive, and Smith isn't. And it would probably be easier for everyone involved if it were the other way around."

"He's alive?" My rage pulled back a tiny bit. Just an iota, but enough that I could look up at Glory without wanting to strangle her.

"He's alive. He's running like the hounds of Hell are on his trail, but he's alive."

It felt like my heart started beating again. I reached out through our link, and she was right. I could feel him. It was faint, like he was weak and far away, but he was alive. That was the first moment I had felt his presence since the explosion. Harker, or my own fear of what I would feel, had been keeping our connection severed until then.

I let out a sigh. "Good. If he killed Smith, he's got to get out of here. Homeland Security will come down on him like an avalanche of assholes. Even the goons Smith hired were Homeland agents."

"That's what he said. And he told me to give you this." The angel held out her hand. Dangling from it was a small black box. A jewelry box.

"Oh, hell no. If he wants to pull some shit like that, it's going to have to be in person. No way is he getting you to do his dirty work. If he's giving me a ring, he's gonna sack up, get down on one knee, and ask me like a man."

Glory laughed. "That's almost exactly what I told him."

"I bet you didn't say sack up."

"You're right, I didn't."

"Is he going to be okay?" I asked.

"I don't know, Rebecca. I don't know if any of us are going to be okay by the time this thing ends."

I stared at the angel for a second, then we stood up and turned to the door. I had just stepped into the aisle when the door exploded off its hinges. In the doorway, smoke wafting from his once-immaculate suit, stood the man Harker introduced to me as his Uncle Luke.

Except the urbane businessman I knew was nowhere to be seen. This wasn't a multi-millionaire with an extensive jazz collection, legendary wine cellar, and deep knowledge of European history. This was a pissed off vampire with half a millennium of killing under his belt, and a lust for vengeance in his eye.

He stalked down the aisle to me, stopping just out of arms' reach. "Is he alive?"

"Harker? Yeah, he's alive. He killed the Cambion, who also happened to be our boss, but then he had to get out of town."

"Smith is the one that murdered Renfield?"

My mind flashed back to the remains of Renfield's burned and tormented body, and I closed my eyes. He was one of the few good ones, and now he was gone, just so a half-demon asshole could prove a point. If Smith wasn't already dead, I'd have shot him.

"Yes. From what Smith's surviving goons told us, Ren wouldn't give him the combination to your vault door. He knew he was going to be used for the sacrifice, so he took your secret to the grave."

Dracula closed his eyes for a moment, then let out a long sigh. "He was loyal. He was a good man. Very good. And he has been avenged."

"To some degree," I said.

"What do you mean?" The full attention of the King of the Vampires was on me, and I could almost *feel* his mind pressing against me.

"I mean that there's no way Smith was working alone. Smith was a Homeland Security Supervisory Agent. He ran the entire Charlotte Field Office. Every one of the Cambion we fought tonight was an agent. This shit is not just one guy, Luke. I have no idea how high up in the government this goes, but just because Harker killed Smith doesn't mean that Orobas' plan is done. I bet that demonic motherfucker is off somewhere working on his Plan B. We need to find him, and all his fucking minions, and finish this once and for all. And we have to make it look like they were all corrupt because that's the only way Harker can ever come home."

"We're going to need help. And I'm going to need a place to stay. My house seems to have come down with a bad case of the inferno."

I tossed him my key to Harker's place. I figured he wouldn't mind. He pulled out a cell phone and started tapping at the screen. "Who are you calling?"

"Reinforcements," he said. "This is too big for just the two of us. I should have done this seven years ago, but Quincy talked me out of it. I'm calling in the Shadow Council."

PART III
HEAVEN HELP US

CHAPTER ONE

"Welcome to the Breakfast Dish, I'm Alma. What can I get you, stranger?" The hefty woman with a graying bun smiled at me and her voice cut through the chatter of the diner as the bell over the door announced my entrance.

"Two eggs, fried, bacon, toast, and enough coffee so I don't sleep for a week," I said from the door.

"Good enough," she said with a smile. "Sit anywhere you like and I'll bring it right out to you. You heard the man, Jarrod, get them eggs cracking!"

I crossed the scuffed tile floor to sit at the counter. The cracked red vinyl seat groaned under my weight and spun a little as I settled onto it. I nodded to the man sitting at the corner and pulled a folded newspaper out of my back pocket.

I spent a quiet few minutes reading the box scores, listening to the reed-thin man, who the waitress called Herman, pontificate to anyone who would listen, and anyone who wouldn't, about how miserable the Reds' pitching was this year, then turned to the classified ads. I had a fleeting thought about trying to pick up a used washer and dryer, then decided that I didn't plan on staying in Lockton that long. Just that morning I had secured a small apartment over one of the shops on Main Street on a month-to-month agreement. I flipped to the job listings and gave a quick scan, more to kill time than anything else. I hoped I wouldn't be there long enough to need the second month, and I certainly didn't plan on getting a day job at this point in my long life.

"Anything interesting in there, stranger?" Jarrod asked from the grill.

"Not so you'd notice, friend," I replied, folding the paper and putting it back in my pocket as Jarrod scooped a pair of fried eggs onto a plate, slapped a couple of strips of perfectly crispy bacon down beside them, and slid the plate under my nose. The smell of fresh breakfast cleared the last of the cobwebs from my brain and I dug in.

"So what brings you to Lockton, buddy? We don't get too many strangers around here." The man called Herman turned his attention to me.

"I'm a software developer working on a new mobile app for off-interstate travel, highlighting local eateries and points of interest off the beaten path. I'm here taking some photos and working on the graphical user interface. The first draft of the software is in beta right now. Once that gets all the testing completed, we'll work on the micro-payment side of things, then we'll get the launch site optimized and be good to go. Maybe another four months, maybe six, and we'll be out for sale." Herman's eyes glazed over after the second disconnected buzzword, and I called it a job well done. I pretty much had no idea what I'd just said, but I figured Herm didn't either, so my cover was going to survive at least through breakfast.

I finished my eggs and bacon in peace, having successfully bored Herman. The food was delicious, but the lights were a little too bright and my shoes pinched. The bright red Flash t-shirt was so not my style, but I was trying to be inconspicuous, so my usual black leather coat and Doc Martens were out of the question for now.

I dropped a ten on the counter and turned to leave, then froze as a big wall of trouble strolled in. The man was tall, broad, and thickly muscled, and he sniffed the air as he stepped into the diner. The bell over the door *dinged* his arrival, and all heads turned to him. He preened a little, enjoying the attention. I stood motionless as the newcomer paused in the doorway, looking around the room.

"Mornin' hon," Alma called out, her voice cheerful. "Just sit anywhere you like."

His eyes scanned the room, then landed on me. One eyebrows went up, and I almost *felt* the challenge in his gaze. His eyes were brown, with flecks of gold that I could see from across the room. He could look me in the eye, as tall as me, but much broader, with a thick beard trimmed close and wiry dark hair covering his arms. He rolled his shoulders and cocked his head to one side, taking me in with a glance. My t-shirt, jeans, and sneakers weren't exactly made for intimidation, but he recognized another predator as quickly as I had. Great, not forty-eight hours out of one frying pan, and here I am right back into the fire.

Werewolf. The word came into my head without any prompting, and the second I had the thought, I knew it was correct. Everything I'd ever known about werewolves fell into place at once, and it all made sense. Big, dark, hairy, arrogant as fuck—he looked every bit the alpha dog. That meant there was a pack in Lockton. No rogue wolf carried himself with that kind of confidence. They always had an air of whipped cur about them, like they were expecting somebody to come around and kick the shit of them. Which usually happened sooner rather than later.

The big wolf looked me up and down, then locked eyes with me again. He nodded, and I nodded back. A pair of predators acknowledging each other, and then moving on. I didn't feel the need to piss on my territory, and I hoped he wouldn't either. I'd been in enough fights in the last week, and I needed time to heal, recharge, and let the world forget about Quincy Harker for a little while. I was very happy hiding out in a small town in the guise of Harold Quinn for as long as I needed to, or at least until Flynn and Luke could clear my name.

I walked to the door, and the werewolf slid out of my way, allowing me to pass without ceding the appearance of dominance. I stepped out into the street, knowing that my time in Lockton just got a lot more complicated.

I walked down the sidewalk, my Sight open to overlay the Otherworld onto my view of the ordinary world. Nothing looked out of place, but that didn't mean anything. I'd made a couple of quick laps through the town before I rented my stay-by-the-month apartment and didn't see any monsters, magicians, or werewolves then. But they were there, and now I had to deal with them.

I turned right past Lucky's Pawn Shop and walked down the narrow alley. I stepped into the back parking lot, then walked up the stairs to the studio "loft" above, really just a big room with a small bathroom hastily built out in a corner. I unlocked the door, then drew a pair of runes in the air along the doorjamb at eye level. The wards I had protecting the apartment dropped, and I turned the knob.

"Be pretty damned embarrassing to get dropped by my own magic," I muttered as I closed the door behind me and re-activated the protections spells. I didn't take down the wards when I left that morning, just opened a portal in them to let me or any visitors through. Except I didn't expect to have any visitors. Not here, not in this life.

I opened the fridge, took out a Stella Artois, popped the top off with a thumb, and drained half the beer in one long draught.

"Fuck," I muttered. "That's all I need. Goddamn werewolves."

———

I slipped out into the night, muttering an incantation of cloaking then resetting the wards on the door. It wouldn't make me invisible, but it would help me blend into the shadows and disguise my features from a distance. Anyone looking at me from more than ten feet away or so would only remember a tall guy in a long coat. A little dab of vinegar behind each ear to hide my scent, and I was ready to hunt some wolves.

In my pocket I carried a folded printout of home sales within the past five years, with two houses circled. The wolf was young, so I assumed the pack had moved in fairly recently, but everyone seemed to know him when he walked in, so he wasn't a complete stranger. I didn't remember hearing a car door slam before he came in, and the engines in the parking lot were all stone-cold when I left the diner, so I assumed he lived within walking distance. That helped narrow my search. I headed east to the first house on my list, dodging the very few streetlights and keeping out of sight the best I could without looking like a burglar.

A tricycle on the lawn of the first place pretty much marked it off my list, but I walked around the side of the house and hopped the fence regardless. A backyard full of toys and little piles of dog poop confirmed that this was a were-free zone. Werewolves don't like their domesticated cousins, especially the yippy little variety, so the dachshund going apeshit through the sliding glass door at me would have been a snack if there were any bipedal furballs hanging around.

Back on the sidewalk, I revisited my poor life choices while I walked across town. It's not that big of a town, so I didn't get very far. I basically only made it through the past few days, where I landed in Lockton, Ohio, after killing a federal agent who happened to be a half-demon serial murderer trying to open a portal to Hell in North Carolina. It's not the first time I've had to stop that sort of thing, but it is the first time I had to go on the lam afterwards.

The second house on my list was at a cul-de-sac with open lots on either side of it and a patch of woods behind it. In other words, exactly the kind of place you would expect to find a pack of werewolves. Dogs aren't terribly creative, and they don't get any better just because they walk on two legs some of the time.

I didn't even have to sneak around to confirm my suspicions; there was a wolf on the front porch smoking a cigarette. He wasn't one of the guys from the diner, but his thick chest and shoulders, his posture, and the aura around him all cried "wolf!"

Sticking to the shadows, I slipped between two houses about fifty yards out from the wolf den and slipped through the woods to reach the back of the house in question. The yard dropped off in a steep incline in back, and a big wooden deck stuck out over the grass. I crept under the deck, keeping an ear out for feet or paws around me, but the place seemed silent.

I stepped out into the yard, bunched my legs, and jumped ten feet to vault over the railing and land on the deck. It's really handy sometimes to have Dracula's DNA mixed up in yours. Other times it's a huge pain in the ass, but at that particular moment, it was a bonus. I crouched on the deck and peeked into a nearby window, the shadows and my spell masking me from the occupants.

The lights from the living room blazed out onto the porch, and three werewolves sat around the screen, pointing and laughing. All the laughing stopped when I tapped on their sliding glass door. The biggest wolf, the one I'd seen in the diner that morning, walked over to the sliding glass door and opened it. He stepped out onto the deck, then slid the door closed behind him.

"I figured I'd be seeing you sometime," he drawled. "You wanna fight, or you wanna talk?"

"I guess that's your call, isn't it?" I asked. I held my hands out to my sides and summoned glowing orbs of energy to float above the palms. "Are you sure I'm somebody you want to throw down with?"

"I don't want to throw down with anybody, wizard, but I also don't like people skulking around my property in the middle of the night."

"I'm too tall to skulk. Sneak maybe, but not skulk."

"Whatever. You want to talk, come on in and grab a beer. You want to fight, throw those little glowballs at my ass and we'll throw down. But I'm going back inside. *Arrow* is on and I haven't seen this one."

CHAPTER TWO

"I don't give a shit what you have to say, Detective. Now what do you have to say for yourself?" The red-faced pudgy man bellowed in my face. Again. He'd been alternating between screaming at me and cajoling me for two hours, playing both sides of the Good Cop/Bad Cop routine, and it was starting to wear very thin.

I was tired of this shit. I'd been dealing with all goddamn night, and I was over it. My partner/maybe fiancée/wizard/demon hunter/whatever else he was, Quincy Harker, was MIA. My immediate supervisor within Homeland Security was dead at Harker's hand. I had a pissed-off Lord of the Vampires to deal with, and I was really jonesing for a decent cup of coffee. Not to mention I needed to use the bathroom. I decided to lead with the easy one.

"I have to pee."

Homeland Security Deputy Director, Southeastern Region, Peter Buprof backed up a little. That was a bonus. The look on his face was priceless, too. It was kinda like you'd expect a dog to look when it finally caught the car it had chased for years. He looked so confused it was all I could do not to giggle, which I felt would be highly inappropriate, given the circumstances. Not to mention the evening's body count.

"What the fucking fuck did you say, Flynn?"

I stood up and walked to the door. "I said, I have to pee. And I'm going to go pee. Then I'm going to go to my office, and I'm going to fire up the very nice Keurig single-cup coffee maker that my Uncle Morris gave me for Christmas last year, and I'm going to make myself some real coffee, not like

528

the shit they keep in the squad room. I'd offer you some, but you're being a dick, so drink the swill. Then I'll come back, and you can keep asking me the same questions you've been asking me for the past two hours."

Buprof moved to get between me and the door. "The fuck you will. You aren't going anywhere until I say you are."

"Am I under arrest, Deputy Director Buprof?"

His eyes got wide at my formal tone. "What?"

"I'm sorry, did I suddenly develop a stutter, or have you lost your comprehension of English since you've been yelling at me in mostly monosyllables and profanity since we got here? I asked if I was under arrest. Should I repeat the question? In Spanish? How about French? My Mandarin isn't very good, but I've got a pretty functional grasp of Farsi, if that works better for you."

He looked at the floor, his nostrils flaring as his forehead flushed an even deeper crimson. The way the vein in his left temple was throbbing, I was afraid he might stroke out right there in the interview room. Then I'd be blamed for two Homeland Security deaths in one week. And this one wouldn't be a half-demon serial murderer, so I might even feel bad about it.

After a solid fifteen seconds of staring at the floor, Buprof raised his bloodshot eyes to mine. "No, you are not under arrest, Detective. You are answering my questions completely voluntarily."

"Then I am voluntarily going to the bathroom and to get a cup of coffee. I'll be back in ten minutes or so. Why don't you take a minute to go wash your face? You're looking a little flushed." I reached past the Director and pulled the door open.

I stepped out into the hall and walked to the ladies' room, ignoring the stares from the squad room and the offices around the floor as I passed. I walked into the stall farthest from the door, sat down, and buried my head in my hands, thinking back to the events of the past few days, including being betrayed by someone I trusted, getting stabbed, and finding out a friend died at the hands of my ex-boss. This wasn't the worst week of my life, that was reserved for the time right after my dad died, but this was definitely number two with a bullet.

I felt something pull in my side, then something warm on my belly, and yanked off my jacket. I probed my black t-shirt and felt dampness under my fingers. "Fucking hell," I muttered, standing up and taking the shirt off. The small dressing I had taped over my belly wound was soaked through with blood, and now was nothing more than a sopping red square on my torso. I peeled the tape from around the gauze and stepped out of the stall.

A patrolwoman stood at the sink washing her hands. She looked up as I stepped out, starting to give me that little smile that women give one another when they find someone else working in the boys' club, kind of a solidarity thing that we can only express when no guys are around to see it and get threatened. But the smile faded as she recognized me, then her eyes widened as she saw the knife wound on my belly. The staples in my belly weren't going to do me any favors in bikini season, but that wouldn't matter much if I didn't figure out how to stop the world from ending before it got warm again.

"Detective, are you..." She was torn. I could see it on her face. Part of her wanted to shun the accused cop-killer, or girlfriend of a cop-killer, or agent-killer, or whatever Harker was supposed to be. But part of her was still a cop, and we protect and serve, and I was standing in front of her bleeding. And another part of her was a female cop, and there aren't many of us, and we try to look out for one another.

I gave her a little smile. "It's just a flesh wound, Santos. You don't need to bandage me up. I just need to wash the wound a little and dry it before I put my shirt back on and get back to my interrogation."

"I hate to...I mean, is it...I mean...Never mind, Detective. I'm sorry, I'll go."

I stepped in front of her. "Don't apologize. You're better than that. Ask me what you want to ask."

She straightened up and nodded. She looked me in the eye and asked, "Is it true? Are you dating Harker? And did he kill Agent Smith?"

"Yeah to both," I said. "But here's the other part. The part that hasn't gotten out in the whisper-mill yet. Smith was dirty. He was the serial killer we were chasing, and Harker and I knew it. But most of the evidence burned up along with Smith's body in that fire, so it's gonna be a bitch to prove it. So yeah, I'm dating Harker. And yeah, he killed Smith. But he saved a lot more lives in the process, and the real bad guy is dead, so now I have to patch up my shit and get back to proving his innocence."

Officer Santos looked me up and down, then nodded. "Detective, I don't know if I could stand in the middle of a public bathroom with no shirt on and blood running down my stomach and defend my *husband* that well, much less a boyfriend. So if you need any help, you let me know. I got you."

"Thanks, Santos. I appreciate it."

"No problem, Detective. Now get that stomach cleaned up. There's a first aid kit in the supply closet right behind the door there." I looked where she was pointing, and sure enough, there was a door I'd never paid attention to marked "Maintenance" right behind me. I nodded my thanks to Santos again and looked in the supply closet.

Fifteen minutes later, I was back in Interview Room One sitting across from Deputy Director Buprof holding a steaming cup of hazelnut blend and wearing a clean shirt I kept in my office. I felt more in control of myself with a fresh dressing on my stab wound and some caffeine coursing through my system. I was ready to take on anything that Buprof could throw at me.

He sat across the table from me with a digital recorder. He pressed a button on the recorder and pointed a remote at the two-way mirror behind him. I knew that turned on the video camera on the other side of the glass, so everything I said from here on out would be recorded in two locations. At least. God only knew how many other recording devices were set up on the other side of the mirror.

"Now, Detective, please recount for me the events of this evening, starting from the moment you arrived at Mr. Card's home."

I'd already been through this a dozen times in the hours since all the shit went down, but Buprof was a relatively new addition. He'd arrived from Washington on a Department of Homeland Security jet just a few hours ago, all hellfire and brimstone to root out the corruption in the Charlotte office and bring me and Harker to justice. I knew the drill. Get the suspect to repeat herself, hoping that she'll make a mistake, trip herself up in some way. I was telling the truth, so there was nothing to trip up. Harker and I had been investigating a series of murders similar to a set of killings he investigated seven years ago.

In both cases, Nephilim, or half-angels, were being murdered and their blood harvested to open a gate to Hell for the demon Orobas to bring a bunch of his nasty siblings and pals through to our world. Both times, the culprit was a Cambion, an offspring of a demon, in this case Orobas, and a human woman. They hid their identities from Harker by smearing Nephilim blood on themselves, which masked their supernatural nature. Both times Harker stopped the Cambion, who was a member of law enforcement. The first time, he did it by casting the bad guy into his own portal to Hell. This time he shot the bad guy, our supervisory agent with Homeland Security, in the face. A lot.

It would have been a lot cleaner for everybody involved if he'd sent Agent Smith to Hell, but that wasn't how things went down. And now Harker was on the run, and I was getting ready to repeat my story for a camera and a very upset Homeland Security middle manager.

Until the door opened into Interview One and a thirty-something man with an expensive suit, a slight limp, and a neatly trimmed dark brown beard stepped into the room.

"What the ever-loving fuck do you think you're doing?" Buprof said, standing up from the table. There went that vein again. I made a mental note to tell the good Director to go see a doctor when we were done here. If he decided against sending me to Gitmo, or Area 51, or wherever Homeland sent people they considered to be rogue members of their version of the X-Files.

"I think I'm stopping this bleeding circus right here," the newcomer said, putting a hand on my shoulder. "My client is going home. She is a sworn officer of the law, she has given her statement at least ten times already by this point, and while her incompetent excuse for a union representative may have allowed this sideshow to continue, I have no intention of doing so. I think it's time we ended this charade and all went home, don't you?" The trim man spoke with a cultured British accent, and when I gawked up at him with my confusion written all over my face, he looked down at me with deep brown eyes and gave me a conspiratorial wink.

"She's not—"

I stood up. "We've covered this already, Director. I've given a statement. I'm not under arrest. I'm going home." I spoke a little louder. "Captain, could you come in here?"

I heard a door slam, then the door into the interrogation room opened and my boss, Captain Benjamin Herr, stepped in. He didn't look happy, but he didn't look like he wanted to shoot me, either.

"Captain, am I on administrative leave pending an investigation? I need to know if I should plan to come back to work as soon as my side heals, or start looking for a new job." I figured I may as well cut straight to the chase and find out where I really stood with my department. I was pretty sure most of the Charlotte-Mecklenburg Police Department wasn't in league with a demon, but I had my doubts about Homeland Security.

Captain Herr thought about it, then shook his head. "No, Flynn. Your story matches what we saw from the dash cam of your department car, and it fits with the evidence. As far as I'm concerned, you're good. I'm going to put you on desk duty for another week or so until you heal up, and you'll have to be cleared by the department psychologist before you're back on active duty, but you're not suspended."

"I have some vacation and sick time coming, could I—" I started, but Captain Herr held up a hand.

"Take it. Get some rest, find out if your asshole boyfriend is okay, and make sure he knows that CMPD has no intention of building a case against him."

"Thank you, sir," I said, standing.

"Hold on a minute, Detective," Buprof said. "Just because your little band of blue brothers isn't going after your murdering sack of shit boyfriend doesn't mean Homeland Security won't. As of right now, you are officially suspended from the Department of Homeland Security. You are to surrender your credentials immediately."

I reached into the inside pocket of my jacket and took out my badge holder. I flipped it open to my Homeland credentials, took them out of the holder, and put the laminated ID card on the table. I held up the wallet holding my gold shield and Charlotte-Mecklenburg Police Department ID at Captain Herr. "You want this, Captain?"

"Did I stutter, Detective?" Captain Herr turned my own smartass comment back on me. "I said you're in the clear. That means you're in the clear. If Homeland doesn't want you anymore, CMPD will be glad to have you back with us full time."

"Thank you sir," I said. I slid my badge back in my pocket and stood up.

"Where the hell do you think you're going?" Buprof asked. "We're not done here."

"I believe that I clearly stated the opposite of that, Deputy Director," my newfound attorney said. He didn't raise his voice, didn't even hint at needing to raise his voice, but he spoke with such quiet assurance and carried himself with such calm strength that Buprof was forced to turn his attention to him.

"And who the fuck are you, exactly?" Buprof asked.

"Watson," the tall man replied. "Dr. Jack Watson, Esquire. I am Detective Flynn's attorney." He produced a business card from his jacket pocket and passed it over to the confused Homeland Security Director. "My contact information is on that card. All inquiries concerning my client should be addressed to me from this moment forward. Now, if you gentlemen will excuse us?" He nodded to Buprof and Herr and steered me out into the hall.

I leaned in to him. "Who are you again?"

He held out a hand. "Jack Watson. Now please let's not tarry. While I am an attorney, and I do have my J.D., I'm not what most Americans think of as a doctor, and I am not exactly licensed to practice law on this side of the pond, unless our mutual friend Mister Card has made some very effective telephone calls very quickly."

"Watson?" I asked, thinking to myself, *there's no friggin' way*. "Not...?"

"Yes, actually," he replied. "Doctor John Watson was my great-great-grand-father. So yes, *that* Watson."

It appeared the Shadow Council had arrived.

CHAPTER THREE

I stood on the porch for a minute staring after the back of the retreating Alpha, then shook my head and went inside, dissipating my balls of glowing purple energy as I went. I was a tiny bit bummed that I didn't get to throw those at anybody. I didn't design them to kill anything, but they were gonna look *really* cool.

This was a new one on me. Walking into a werewolf's den didn't usually involve IKEA furniture in my experience, but this place was furnished in early 21st century modern craptastic sofas and bookshelves. The Alpha was sprawled in a recliner sipping a Coors Light while two other werewolves sat on the sofa watching television. Sure enough, there was Oliver Queen climbing a salmon ladder, all abs and attitude.

"Beer in the fridge?" I asked, pulling the sliding glass door closed behind me. If I needed to get out of there in a hurry, a pane of glass wasn't going to slow me down very much. Hell, if the wolves decided to evict me with extreme prejudice, the walls wouldn't slow me down much, either.

"Yeah," Alpha replied. "Grab me another Coors while you're at it."

I paused for a second, wondering if it was a test or some kind of macho dominance thing. Then I decided I didn't care, and I grabbed a Coors Light for the wolf and a Heineken for myself. I popped the top off the bottle with my thumb and handed the can to the were.

"Thanks."

"No problem."

"You know we got a bottle opener, right?" He pointed to my thumb, which bled a little from the edge of the bottle-cap.

"I heal fast," I replied, then held up my thumb. The tiny cut stitched itself shut in seconds, another of the useful abilities my vampire-enhanced blood granted me.

"That's handy," said the Alpha.

"You got a name?" I asked.

"I think I get to be the one asking questions," he replied. "You know, my house and all." He didn't raise his voice, didn't even take a stern tone, but it was pretty clear from the attention the wolves on the sofa paid to every syllable that this was not the dude to fuck with.

I shrugged and stepped over to in front of his chair. "Quincy Harker." I held out a hand.

"So not Harold Quinn?" he asked, taking my hand. His grip was firm, but not overly strong. He had nothing to prove, so he didn't bother to try. We shook, and I stepped over to a chair at the end of the couch. This put a coffee table between me and all three werewolves, space that I was going to need desperately if things got noisy.

"Nope," I said. I didn't bother explaining to him about my undercover status. I figured a werewolf might understand all about keeping his identity masked. I also didn't ask how he got my name, assuming he either asked the waitress or had some way to scan recent property rentals. He was the local Alpha, after all. If he didn't have the town pretty well wired, then he wasn't much of a pack leader.

"Fair enough. I'm Drew Semper. I'm the Alpha around these parts. The one by you is Billy, and the big dumb one is Rocco." He pointed at the two couch-surfing weres in turn, and they nodded to me. I nodded back.

"How long have you guys been in town?"

"About three years, maybe four." I appreciated the fact that he didn't lie to me, either. I knew from my hour on the computer that afternoon that the house was rented on an annual lease to a Luna Holdings, LLC, out of New Jersey, and had been rented to the same company for a little over three years.

"What are y'all doing here?"

"Why do you care?" Drew shot back. The wolf called Rocco started to growl low in his throat, and Drew and I both gave him a sharp look. "Be nice, Rocco. Our guest here might be nosy, but he hasn't threatened anybody yet."

After being around a fair number of people who thought I was threatening them just by walking into a room, I found Drew's self-confidence refreshing. "I care because I'm here trying to keep a low profile, and if you guys are running some kind of small-town protection racket, or redneck meth lab, or undercover gambling ring, or anything that might bring down federal attention on this town, then we're going to have a problem."

Drew put the footrest of his recliner down and leaned forward. "Are we? Are we going to have a problem, Mr. Harker?"

"Only if you want to, Mr. Semper."

"What if I told you we already had a problem?" *Oh shit. Wolf politics.*

"I'd tell you if it was going to put more eyes on this town, then that would be an issue for me."

"What are you hiding from, Quincy?"

"I don't think that's any of your business, Drew." I followed his move into first-name territory, unwilling to yield to his Alpha games. He stood up and stepped toward me, sliding the coffee table out of the way. I stood up to meet him.

We just looked at each other for a long moment, passing a whole lot of communication between us without ever saying a word. Finally, Drew turned and walked into the kitchen.

"Another beer?" he called over one shoulder.

"I wouldn't say no." I sat back down in my chair, then leaned forward and tugged the coffee table back into place. Drew came back with three Coors Lights and an opened Heineken for me. "Thanks," I said, draining off the last of my first beer and setting it on an end table beside the sofa.

"Coaster," the wolf identified as Billy said, pointing to a rack on the table. I nodded at him and got a coaster. No point in fucking up a guy's furniture.

"Now, Mr. Harker, what brings you to Lockton?" Drew asked once he was settled back into his chair.

"Not so much being *in* Lockton as being *out* of Charlotte."

"Charlotte's a nice town. What's that in, North Carolina?"

"Yeah," I said. No real surprise that a werewolf in Ohio didn't know much about Charlotte.

"Why'd you leave Charlotte?"

"I had a disagreement with my boss at Homeland Security."

"There's a wizard working for Homeland Security?"

"Until about two nights ago, there was a half-demon called a Cambion working as a supervisor for Homeland Security."

"What happened two nights ago?"

"He and I had that disagreement I mentioned."

"And this disagreement didn't go well for him, I take it."

"And thus I am in Lockton, Ohio, home of the World's Largest Nothing. Not a tourist trap for miles, no traffic cams, and no reason for anyone to visit."

"The perfect place for a man on the run."

"I'm not on the run," I protested. "I'd just rather not deal with the consequences of my actions right now."

"Story of my life," Drew said, holding up his beer. I saluted with my bottle, and we drank deeply.

We finished our beers in a relatively comfortable silence. As comfortable as you can be when in the literal den, fireplace and all, of a bunch of werewolves who could probably tear you limb from limb quicker than you could kill more than two of them. Right now, we were operating on manners and the threat of mutually assured destruction. I knew that if I tried anything, I wouldn't make it out of the house alive, and they knew that if they jumped me, at least one of them would be dead on the floor in seconds. Nobody wanted to take the chance that they would be the lucky winner, so we were at a stalemate.

Drew stood up, flowing to his feet in that liquid movement that true predators have. He looked down at me, and I focused my will on my fists. I didn't bother with the glowing light this time. If shit was about to get real, I wasn't going to need pyrotechnics, just firepower.

"Our pack has been in this part of the world for a long time, Harker, and we can stay here and in the towns around here because we don't start shit with anybody. We know the drill. We hunt animals, not people, and we don't let anything else hunt people in our territory. If you're cool with that, you can stay. But if you've got ideas about summoning anything nasty, starting some kind of coven, or otherwise fucking with the people of Lockton, then we're going to have a problem."

I didn't so much let my will dissipate as it popped like a soap bubble. "What?"

"You heard me. We look after these people. So if that's a problem, you need to move on to greener pastures. We don't know shit about you, except for some rumors Billy picked up on the BlackNet. And that shit is too farfetched even for me to believe, and I'm a friggin' Ohio werewolf, for fuck's sake."

"Yeah, that's probably the true stuff. If it sounds just cosmically fucked up, I'd believe it." I turned to Billy, who showed me the BlackNet version of my Wikipedia page on a tablet. "Yup, all that's pretty much true. Except that thing about Zaire. Never been there."

"You're saying you're really Dracula's nephew and you're over a hundred years old?" Billy asked.

"Nephew is just how we describe it. There's no real blood relation." I didn't bother trying to explain the whole thing about him nibbling on my mom before she and Dad were married, and I sure as fuck wasn't going into Dad's time with Uncle Luke's "wives." I didn't know the whole story there, and didn't want to. If they wanted to read about that part of my origin, they could read the book. Or watch one of the countless nearly unwatchable movies.

"So he's real?" Drew asked, his voice a little hushed.

"The werewolf is asking the wizard if Dracula is real?" I raised an eyebrow.

"Fair enough." Drew walked to the fridge and grabbed another round for everyone. I wasn't finished with the last one yet, but I didn't want to be rude.

He sat down and leaned forward, looking hard at me. "So what's it going to be, wizard? Are you going to move on, are we going to throw down, or are we going to try to be good neighbors?"

I took a long pull off my beer. Whatever I said next was not just going to impact the direction my evening was to take, but was going to have a big impact on how long my life in Lockton was to be. Even if I fought these guys and won, that would bring a lot more attention down on this little town than I wanted. The Lockton police department was two guys, one receptionist, and one cell, usually reserved for a pair of drunks on Friday or Saturday night. A trio of bodies would draw attention at the state level and maybe higher, and certainly make the papers. That was attention I couldn't afford. And that was if I won the fight, which wasn't a lock by any stretch. Werewolves are tough, fast, and resistant to a lot of the magic I used against creatures like demons, by virtue of the fact that they actually *belong* on this plane of existence.

"I think that as long as you guys have all your shots and nobody tries to hump my leg, we oughta be able to get along fine. I don't have a problem with lycanthropes as a rule, I just get nervous when any supernatural critter shows up that I didn't know about," I said. I took another drink of my beer, so I wouldn't waste too much if I had to smash the bottle across somebody's head.

The big one they called Rocco growled at me again, but Drew waved a hand at him. Drew stood up and stuck out his hand. I got out of my chair and shook it, feeling the power in his grip that he wasn't even trying to impress me with. That's what was impressive about it, that he wasn't trying.

"Welcome to Lockton, Mr. Harker. I hope we don't ever have to find out the answer."

I didn't ask the question. We both knew what the other one was thinking, and I was glad I wouldn't have to find out who was the bigger badass tonight.

"Now, since you're here..."

Oh shit, here it comes. I knew it the second he opened his mouth.

"There's something we could use your help with."

Yup. Right into the shit again. I will never fucking learn.

CHAPTER FOUR

I walked through the door of Harker's condo, expecting him to pop out from behind a door and tell me that it was all some kind of joke, some magical illusion bullshit of his and we could go back to the way things were a few days ago. Before we found out that Agent Smith was a half-demon serial killer, before Smith murdered Renfield, before Harker put a bullet in Smith's face and had to go on the lam.

But no, nobody jumped out from behind a door. There were a lot of people in Harker's living room, though, and I only recognized two of them. Luke was there, which made sense since his house was currently a pile of rubble. The other one had me draw my sidearm and level the Sig Sauer .40 pistol right at her face.

"What the fuck are you doing here, Van Helsing?"

Gabby Van Helsing was good in a fight, but she wasn't one of my favorite people. The first time we met, she almost killed Harker, then drew down on Luke. Now she was sitting in Quincy's living room, drinking his beer, and chatting with Luke like they were old friends.

Gabby stood and held her hands up. "I'm unarmed, Detective. Please don't shoot me."

"I don't believe you. No way do you sit in an unfamiliar room without a weapon or three somewhere around you."

An athletic black woman laughed from the couch. "She knows you, Gabs. Might as well come clean."

Van Helsing shrugged. "There is a pistol in an ankle holster, a pair of knives in the back of my belt, and four small stakes strapped to my forearms. I'll strip down if you really want me to, but I've got to let you know, I'm not into chicks."

Luke stood up and put himself between my gun and Van Helsing. "Detective...Rebecca, please put away the gun." Luke looked like hammered shit, and that was even taking into account that he was buried alive just the night before. His eyes were sunken into his skull, his cheeks were drawn, and he was pale, even for a guy that hadn't seen the sun since well before the American Revolution. He looked around the room, took a deep breath, and continued. "Gabriella is one of us. She is here to help clear Quincy's name and bring the real perpetrator to justice."

I raised an eyebrow at the Vampire Lord. "The real perpetrator was brought to justice, Luke. Harker killed him. That's why he had to run, remember?"

Watson slipped past me into the apartment and walked over to the kitchen area. "We believe that your Agent Smith was merely one cog in the machine, Detective. He had resources significantly beyond his normal capacity either as an agent of Homeland Security or a Cambion, and we feel that the conspiracy must go higher within the government."

I looked at the trim British dude who stood at Harker's kitchen counter pouring a drink. "Are you serious? You're talking to me about some kind of Illuminati shit?"

"We are a secret organization of powerful beings hidden from society for over a hundred years. It only stands to reason that there might be another one or two out there," Watson said, his voice mild, but his eyes serious. "Drink?"

"I'll take a Coke. Harker keeps them in the door of the fridge."

"He's out," the woman on the couch called from the den. I looked at her and she raised a familiar red-and-white striped can at me with a smile.

"And who the hell are you, lady? Besides the bitch who drank the last Coke, that is."

She laughed again, a bright, tinkling sound that felt somehow out of place in this room full of grim faces and serious demeanors. I liked her in spite of myself, and in spite of her drinking the last soda.

"I'm Jo," she said, and walked over to me, her hand out. We shook, and her grip was very strong. This was a woman who'd seen hard work and wasn't afraid of it. She was short and stocky, with broad shoulders and the no-bull-shit stride of an athletic woman. Her hair was cropped short, and her brown eyes sparkled with amusement. "This is some fucked-up shit, right?"

"You can say that again," I muttered.

"Oh, please don't," Watson sighed, walking behind me to head to the living room and sit on the arm of the couch. "Let's move forward into the problem at hand. Countless rehashing of how 'fucked up' the situation is moves us no closer to a resolution."

"Well, can I at least get a handle on who everyone is before I dive right into hunting down a demon boss?" I asked, poking my head into the fridge. Empty. These fuckers had devoured the normally meager stores in Harker's refrigerator. I took a glass down from the cabinet and poured water from the tap over some ice cubes, then went into the living room with everyone else. I grabbed a chair and sat between Harker's two sofas facing the door.

I looked around the room. Luke was there, looking like ten miles of bad road. Watson sat on the couch next to him, all perfect posture, trimmed beard and piercing intellect burning behind his eyes. Gabby sat across from him, keeping one eye on me and the other on Luke. Apparently there was still a little distrust there. The black woman sat beside Gabby, looking around the gathered people and giving me the occasional small smile.

"So who the fuck are you people? Luke I know, and Gabby I've met, but this dude walks into police headquarters introducing himself as Dr. Watson's great-great-grandson, and I've got no idea who you are, lady. No offense."

"None taken," the unidentified woman said. "I'm Jo. For the purposes of this gathering, Jo Henry. It's actually Jo Marinton, but it's easier to remember why I'm involved in all this mess if I just go by Granddaddy's name."

"Your grandfather's name was Henry?" I asked, starting to put things together in my head but not sure I was going in the right direction.

"Yup," she confirmed. "John Henry. Steel-driving man, hero of the battle of the railroad man versus the steam engine, all that. That was Granddaddy. Great-great-granddaddy, technically, but I figure we can let that slide."

"I thought he died after that whole thing with the steam engine." I was pretty impressed that I managed to dredge that little bit of history up on demand.

"Nah. He had a heart attack, and he almost died, but he really was as strong as the legends say. Old man was way harder to kill than anyone should have been back then. He lived to be almost eighty, even after that whole mess with the steam engine when he was a young man."

"Impressive. So what do you do?" I asked.

"For the Council, or for a living?"

"I dunno, whichever. Does working for the Council not pay much?"

She laughed, a musical sound that made me smile. Out of all these weirdos, she seemed the most *real*, like somebody I could have a beer and talk politics with, or sports, or just hang out. The rest of them were either a little terrifying, like Luke; a little psychotic, like Gabby; or a little too *British*, like Jack. But

Jo seemed fun. I was relaxing a little around her, which was nice. There hadn't been a lot of relaxation in my life the past few days.

"Working for the Council doesn't pay shit," Jo said. "Like, literally, it's a volunteer gig. Some of us come from money, or are at least old enough to have some stashed, like Luke here." The Lord of the Vampires tipped an imaginary hat. "Or we kill things that are old and have a lot of money stashed, like Gabby."

"They don't need money after I burn them to ash." The sweet smile she gave me when she said that definitely pushed the needle on her well into "psycho" territory.

"Or they get royalty money off books written by and about their family." Jo pointed at Jack, who held up a glass of whiskey.

"I am also an attorney, and a rather good one at that," he offered up in a token protest. "But the fact that Old Doyle promised half the revenue from the Holmes character to my father doesn't hurt."

"Yeah, helped you afford that posh Oxford education, right old chap?" Gabby needled him in a terrible Cockney accent.

"Cambridge, thank you very much, and yes, it was very posh, and yes, Doyle's money definitely paid for it. Too bad I didn't go there straight out of high school, instead of spending a few years in the Army first." He reached down and knocked on his left leg, which gave off an odd metallic sound. I just looked at him, and he raised the hem of his pants to show a prosthetic leg. "Courtesy of an IED outside Kabul. I'm accustomed to it now, but it does cause certain challenges with airport security here in the States."

"So I'm one of the few members of the Council that actually has a day job. I'm a freelance editor, mostly nonfiction books. Self-help books, career guides, that kind of thing. It gives me the freedom I need to drop everything and come running whenever these guys call."

"And how many of these guys are there? Is this everybody? Or are there more Shadow People that I'll run into later?"

You know that feeling when a room gets uncomfortably quiet, like when the awkward guy from work tells a racist joke that he thinks will be funny and it's anything but funny? Yeah, that happened. Everybody kinda looked at each other, or their drinks, or the carpet, or basically anywhere but at me.

After giving the pause long enough to become truly uncomfortable, I clapped my hands. "Okay, that's fine. You can't tell me anything about the Council because I'm not on the Council. That's cool. I get operational security and partitioning information. I've done my fair share of interagency partnerships in my time. So I guess all I need to know this—are there any more

Council members here, and do I need to know anything else before we get to work?"

"No," Luke said, standing up and walking over to me. "To both of those things. We are the sum total of the Council that is currently here and working on this problem. There are more Councilors, but they are handling other issues at the moment."

"Okay, so what's the plan?" I asked, finishing up my water and walking over to the liquor cabinet. Harker always kept at least one bottle of Macallan tucked away behind the swill of a tequila selection in the bar, so I fished around behind bottles until I found the good stuff. Only a third of the bottle remained, but it was enough. I poured myself a generous slug and left the bottle out where the others could see it. I returned to my seat and looked around the room.

"What? There's no plan?" I asked.

"We just got here, Detective," Jo protested.

"Call me Flynn, or I suppose Rebecca if you have to," I replied. "Alright, since we don't have a plan, I guess that's Step One—make a plan."

"We need to figure out how high this problem goes within Homeland Security," Watson said. "Right now we aren't sure if Smith was an isolated mole, or if there's a widespread conspiracy."

"Assume he wasn't working alone," I said.

"Why's that?" Gabby asked. "You need to make some justification for your boyfriend shooting a federal agent in the face?"

"Not that one," I said. "He deserved everything he got and then some. But no way was he acting alone. He had organization, and he managed to kill four people right under our noses and get away with it. That takes help, and a ton of resources."

"So do you think his accomplice is someone inside Homeland Security?" Jo asked.

"Worse," I said. "I'm pretty sure that someone inside Homeland Security is his boss."

CHAPTER FIVE

"**T**ell me again how we're not going to jail for this? I did mention that little disagreement with Homeland Security, right?" I whispered to Drew the next night as we stepped into the deserted hallway of Lockton High School. It smelled of disinfectant layered over years of teen spirit, that miasma of body odor, gym shoes, and hormones that just rolls off teenagers like cheap perfume off a stripper's ass.

"Rocco is the strength and conditioning coach for the football team. He gave me the keys," Drew said in a normal voice.

"And that gets us out of jail how exactly?" I didn't bother hiding my "I'm not convinced" voice.

"Because Billy is a dispatcher for the county 911 service and he's on duty tonight. So nothing about this is going to get reported. So as long as Chief Clark doesn't happen to ride by the school, we're good. And Chief Clark hasn't been out of the house after ten o'clock without a good reason for at least two years."

I couldn't argue with the man. He knew his town, after all. "Fine, then what are we looking for?"

"I don't want to influence your impressions. Just tell me what you sense, or however you do that shit."

I opened my Sight and almost fell down as I was overwhelmed by the magic thrown around in that hallway. I quickly shifted back to the mundane spectrum and turned on Drew. "What the ever-loving fuck was that?"

He held up both hands and took a step back, then seemed to catch himself and stepped back up to meet me. "That's what I wanted to know. What did you see?"

"I saw so much shit I could barely sort it all out. You seriously need to warn a motherfucker before you pull something like that. It's like if I shoved smelling salts and cayenne pepper right up your super-sniffer, Lassie."

He bristled at the dog joke, but didn't push it. "Alright, sorry. I didn't know it would be that bad. But you'll agree there's something fucked up going on around here?"

"That's putting it mildly. There is serious demonic influence all over this place. It's like somebody has been...oh no."

"Oh no, what?"

"Somebody's been playing with demons here, haven't they?" I should have known. It's not like they call me Quincy Harker, driveway repairman. Anytime somebody wants me to take a good look at something, odds are there's a demon involved.

"We think so. I told you Rocco is an assistant football coach, right?" Drew started walking down the hall without bothering to turn on a light or his flashlight. Not being a werewolf, I called up a floating ball of light and set it over my shoulder so I didn't trip over anything left in the hall by a lazy janitor or asshole teenager.

"Yeah. What about it?"

"Well, the team is really good this year. They haven't lost a game."

"Good for them," I said. I didn't hear a problem yet.

"Yeah, it's great. School spirit is up, the town is behind the team, there are even talks about forming a booster club for the first time in years."

"So what's the problem?"

We turned down another hallway, this one marked "Gym." "The problem is, they shouldn't be."

"Shouldn't be what?"

"Good," Drew said. "They didn't lose very many players to graduation, so most of the players from last year are back. And they weren't very good last year. Rocco's been amazed at the gains they've made in the weight room—he says that you can't make gains like that even with steroids. He's talking about some kids packing on twenty or thirty pounds of muscle just since school started."

"That's only been a couple of months," I pointed out.

"That's what I'm saying," Drew agreed. "Rocco says that there's something funky with these kids, and they don't play like normal, either. They run their routes perfectly, make throws like Tom Brady. It's like all of a sudden they're the Green Bay Packers instead of the Lockton Lions."

"Are you sure all this is legit? I mean, no offense to Rocco, but..."

"I know, he doesn't look like the brightest bulb in the box, but he knows football, and he knows jocks. So if he says this shit ain't natural, then it ain't natural. And now you're telling me there's a demon running around the school, too."

"Yeah, there's definitely something here. Let me take another look." I opened my Sight again, this time shielding myself a little instead of throwing my supernatural vision wide open. The athletic wing was even more covered in demonic essence than the first hallway we were in, so whatever was hanging around the school, it was more active down there. I looked past the glare of the demon taint but couldn't get any real hints on what type of hellspawn we were dealing with from the trail of badness it left in its wake. But there was a door on the far left side of the hallway that radiated evil like a homing beacon.

I motioned to Drew. "If you can do that half-way change thing where you get really big and scary, this might be a good time to do it." I pointed to the door. "There's something behind that door, and it's not very nice at all."

"I can do that." Drew started stripping down in the hallway. I gaped at him. "What? You think my clothes just magically disappear? I've ruined more jeans trying to transform while wearing clothes than I care to count. And I really like these shoes." I looked at his feet. They were nice hiking boots, so I kinda understood him. He got naked, then shifted into his half-wolf form.

If you've never seen a human turn into a werewolf, then good for you. It's not pretty and usually incredibly painful. The benefit to having an Alpha wolf with you is he's way too macho to scream as his bones realign themselves and his body miraculously packs on another fifty percent of its muscle mass.

I asked Luke once where the extra matter came from, because laws of nature and all that. His response—"it's magic, you idiot." I shut up at that point. No point debating physics with a guy who lives on human blood with no working digestive system. Especially coming from a wizard who makes fireballs with his mind and throws them at people.

After a few seconds of what must have been excruciating pain, Wolf-Drew stood in front of me, seven feet of hair, muscle, and teeth that didn't really get hurt by anything but fire and silver. And magic, but I didn't plan on throwing any bolts of pure energy at my partner for the evening. He shook himself all over and nodded at me. Verbal communication was pretty much out until he shifted back since I didn't speak Wolf and his jaw was now shaped all wrong for forming words. Didn't matter. Whatever I sensed behind that door was very unlikely to be big on conversation.

Drew and I crept across the hall and I pressed my ear to the door. I heard a soft *huff-huff* of breath behind me and turned to Drew. He tapped himself on the chest and gently nudged me out of the way. He had a point. My hearing is better than a normal human's, but I've got nothing on a werewolf, even one half-transformed. He put his head to the door and held up two fingers.

"There are two of them?" I asked.

He nodded, then waved his hand in the air to indicate one was close to the door and one across the room. At least, that's what I thought it meant. I nodded back at him, and he moved to the other side of the door. I drew in my will and whispered "*Fiero*" under my breath. A six-inch sphere of flame appeared floating over my outstretched palm, and I flung open the door. I lobbed the magical fire grenade into the room and was greeted by a very satisfying *WHOOSH* as it exploded inside the room. The contained space gave the fireball a little extra oomph, a fact I learned both in the real world and playing way too much *Dungeons & Dragons* in the 80s.

I gave the fire a couple of seconds to die down, then stepped into the open doorway. I stood there for a minute, letting the smoke billow around my boots and long coat, casting what I thought should be an appropriately badass image for a demon-hunting wizard, only to find a pair of imps standing in the room grinning at me.

"Got any more of those, human? That tickled," the first imp said, then launched himself at me from twenty feet away. His wings unfurled and he flew at me like a clawed lawn dart. I dove to the right, drawing my Glock as I hit the ground on my side.

Drew stepped into the doorway as soon as I moved, no doubt chomping at the bit after my failed theatrics. He reached out one hand and swatted the imp to the ground, his reflexes and strength a match for a minor demon any day. The only problem was that speed and power were not the only weapons imps came equipped with.

"Drew, watch the tail!" I yelled, hauling myself to my feet.

Drew either heard me or he'd dealt with imps before, because he dodged to one side as the little bastard's spiked tail came up over its shoulder and jabbed at his leg. The six-inch spike buried itself in the drywall beside the door, and Drew stomped on the demon's back. I heard the monster scream in pain and turned to find the other one.

I was a little late, since it was almost on me already. I threw myself flat on my back as the imp leapt at me. It flew harmlessly over me, then snapped its wings out in a heartbeat and whirled around to dive-bomb me where I lay on the floor. I squeezed off three quick shots with my pistol, then rolled out of the way. I kept rolling after it smacked into the floor, the nasty tail jabbing into the tile beside me. The razor-sharp point penetrated into the floor easily, leaving me to think unpleasant thoughts about what it would do to my chest.

I scrambled to my feet as the imp got to its wobbly feet. I shot it twice in the face, which knocked it back onto its ass, but had no other real effect. I didn't expect it to, I just needed a little separation.

"*Frigidos!*" I shouted, holstering my Glock and thrusting both palms out at the imp. Daggers of ice materialized and flew toward the demon, tearing holes through its wings and drawing blood from its face and torso. *So my magic can hurt it. Good to know.*

I spared a glance for Drew, who was methodically stomping the head of the imp he was battling. It wasn't dying and wasn't going to from that kind of damage, but it also wasn't getting up, so he was in pretty good shape.

"Fuzzy!" I shouted. Drew's head snapped up with a snarl, and I tossed a vial from my coat underhand to him. "Catch!"

He caught it and cocked his head at me. "Pour it on the demon," I shouted. "It's holy water!"

Drew did as I said, and the demon shrieked in agony. Apparently Drew had opened enough of a cut on the imp's skin for the holy water to touch its blood, and the little bastard melted away to nothing as Drew was in mid-stomp.

I turned to the remaining imp and held up a second vial of holy water. "Plenty more where that came from, asshole. Now you can go back to Hell, or I can vaporize your ass right now, and you won't just be dead on this plane, but you'll be forever-dead. Your call." I cocked my arm back to throw, but the imp wrapped its wings around itself and popped out of existence. Seems like even demons have a sense of self-preservation.

"What the fuck did you do that for?" I turned to see a human and very naked Drew standing in the room bitching at me. "That thing can come back and hurt more people, and you'll be the reason. Everything it does from here on out is on you, Harker. We had a chance to destroy that thing, and you didn't take it."

"I try not to destroy things that are the pets of bigger and badder things if I can help it," I said. "That imp can't come back across the plane unless someone or something summons it," I explained. "And whatever summoned it is the real problem, not some shitty little pitchfork monkey from the First Circle. You killed one—that sends enough of a message. Being able to kill this one and choosing not to sends an even stronger one. It says we don't give a fuck what this guy calls up from the Pits, we can handle it."

"Why don't we just see if that's true," came a new voice from the doorway. I hate surprises. They never end up being a pony, or even a stripper. It's always a pair of socks for Christmas, or another fucking demon.

CHAPTER SIX

The room erupted in chaos as I made my pronouncement about Smith. I stood there watching the train wreck of conversation until they all ran out of steam and stared at me.

"Are y'all quite finished?" I asked.

Jack nodded at me. "Please proceed, Detective. What makes you think that Agent Smith's actions are not simply those of a deranged monster infiltrating a major governmental agency?"

"Have you ever used one word when three would do?" I asked. Watson gave me a flat stare, so I just went on, making a mental note that this dude had *zero* sense of humor. "Smith couldn't have been working alone. He did too much with little or no oversight, and there's no way some government functionary wouldn't have been looming over his shoulder every time we tried to do something. Ergo, we have at least one more Cambion to find inside Homeland Security."

"An organization that has currently suspended you," Watson pointed out.

"True enough," I said. "But now that I have the whole Justice League behind me, I'm sure one of you is a super-hacker or something."

"Or something," Jo said. "I wouldn't even call myself a mediocre hacker, but I know my way around a secure server. I'll see what I can dig up about Homeland's Paranormal Division and see if there's anything suspicious about any of their people." She pulled a laptop out of a bag and walked over to Harker's kitchen bar area. "Does this place have Wi-Fi?"

"No idea," I said. "I've never seen Harker touch a computer except to throw it out a window."

"Which he does with a frequency that is both disturbing and expensive," Luke said. He walked into Harker's bedroom and came out with a sleek MacBook. "I believe this should have all the information you need within its files. The password is 'Lucy&Mina.' Don't forget the ampersand."

"Thanks, Luke." Jo opened Harker's laptop, then her own. "You folks work on how to get into Homeland and deal with the boss. I'll message Sparkles and see what we can come up with."

"Sparkles?" I repeated.

Jo grinned at me. "Now *he's* a hacker. This guy can break into any system anywhere. And he's one hundred percent loyal to the Council. If there's a Big Bad, Sparkles will find him."

"Sure, but…Sparkles?"

"Long story." Jo smiled at me again and turned to her computers.

"So what's our play?" I asked the group.

"We wait until Jo finds the bad guy, then we deal with him," Watson replied. He had a dark look in his eyes that belied his oh-so-proper diction. This was a man that had seen some shit, and wasn't afraid to go back there.

"With extreme prejudice," Gabby added. Every word that came out of that girl's mouth reinforced my mental image of her wearing Hannibal Lecter headgear, I swear.

"Well until she's done, I'm going to go do what I do—detect things," I said, turning to go.

Luke intercepted me before I had done more than turn around. "You can't," he said, giving me a stern look. "It's not safe out there for you until we know more about what we're facing."

"Don't get in my way, Luke. I will not be fucked with on this. I don't know what Harker is to me yet, but I know he's important, and I know that whatever asshole was pulling Smith's strings won't quit just because we killed his puppet. So I'm going to go out there and do what I can to find him."

"And do what, exactly?" Luke asked. I looked at him. There was no malice there, no teasing or taunting, just an honest question. And I had to pause because I hadn't exactly given that part a whole lot of thought.

"I don't know yet, but I'll figure it out when I get there."

"That's a pretty solid symptom of Harker exposure," Jo said from behind Luke.

"Kiss my ass," I snarled. But she was right.

"Sorry," she said. Her words made it clear that she was anything but sorry, but I didn't feel like getting into a fight with her over it. "I just meant that

Harker could go off half-cocked like that, but it doesn't work that way for people like us."

People like us? Did she mean cops? Vampires? Wannabe superheroes? I gave her a quizzical look, and she laughed.

"No offense, Detective. I mean normal human beings. Harker got away without making a plan because he had magic and superpowers. We aren't wizards, and we can't shrug off knife wounds and bullets."

"Speak for yourself, mortal," Luke said.

"Fair enough," Jo ceded. "Most of us can't shrug off knife wounds and bullets. We have to plan before we go running in after the monsters."

Just then my cell phone buzzed in my pocket. I pulled it out and tapped the screen. "Fuck."

"What's wrong, Detective?" Luke asked.

"There's a disturbance call. The captain asked for me by name."

"Isn't that a little out of your normal bailiwick, Detective?" Watson asked.

"Do you really talk like that or are you just screwing with me?" I asked, completely honest.

"I'm sure I have no idea what you're talking about," was the very stiff upper lip reply.

"He really talks like that," Jo said. "But his point is valid. Why are you going to a domestic disturbance call? Especially when you're supposed to be on leave?"

"This isn't an ordinary disturbance call, and it's not a domestic disturbance. It's at a bar."

"Doesn't make it any less not your problem."

"Still true. Except my captain knows this bar is a supernatural hot spot," I clarified.

"Mortivoid's pub?" Luke asked.

"Yep, there's some kind of shitstorm going down at Mort's, and I'm the lucky one who gets to go check it out." I started for the door, only to be cut off by Luke. Again. "That's starting to get old, Luke."

"My apologies, Detective." He sounded somewhat less than completely sincere. Like not at all. "I feel that I would be remiss in my duties as your protector if I allowed you to go unescorted to this 'disturbance.'"

"Thanks, Luke, but I got this...wait a minute, my *what?*"

Luke at least had the courtesy to look embarrassed. "Quincy made it very clear on several occasions that if he was not able to, in his words, look after you, that I was to fulfill his self-appointed duties in that regard. I think this situation qualifies."

"Ignoring the absolute chauvinistic bullshit inherent in that statement and accepting that there are a lot of things running around Mort's that I probably can't handle without a little help, what exactly are you going to do about it? It's less than an hour until sunrise. We can get there in twenty minutes, but then you're stuck in Mort's place all day. And that's ignoring the whole sleeping all day thing."

"I can go without sleep if the situation warrants, but you are correct that my aversion to sunlight makes me an untenable choice for your companion. I was going to suggest Gabriella serve as your partner for this excursion. She is very capable and has experience dealing with several different types of supernatural creatures."

"I got this," I repeated, and reached for the doorknob.

"I'm afraid I insist." I looked into his eyes and saw the implacable stare of a man who has seen the absolute worst humanity has to offer and has walked through those fires for a long time. There was not a word in the dictionary that was going to make him change his mind.

"If I try to ditch her, you'll just send a car, won't you?" I felt bad almost immediately.

"I would, but I have no cars, and no one left to send in one." The bleak look on his face reminded me of everything Luke had lost in a few short hours. All of the man's possessions were now just so much ash, and so was his manservant and companion Renfield. Smith paid for that, but we needed to figure out who was pulling his strings and extract a little payment from that asshole, too.

"I'll just take an Uber if you try to escape. Let's go, cop-lady. We got bad guys to shoot and monsters to maim." Gabby breezed past me and Luke and opened the door with a grand flourish. I shook my head and walked through. Me and the psychopath, just like I liked it. Not.

———

M ort's looked quiet from the outside, which was to be expected since it was almost dawn. I was dead tired and fresh out of patience for monsters and their bullshit, so I didn't bother with any of the normal pleasantries at the door. I just banged on it until the little green door-goblin opened up, then I stuck my Sig in his face.

"Open the goddamn door," I growled.

"Regular bullets won't kill me, you know. I'm technically a member of the Fae, so only cold iron—"

"Have you ever been shot in the eyeball?"

He gulped a little. "No."

"Do you think it's likely going to feel good?"

Another gulp. "Probably not."

"Is it going to make it hurt any less that you know it won't kill you?"

"Almost certainly not."

"Then open the goddamn door and get out of my goddamn way."

He did exactly what I asked, keeping the thick metal door between us as Gabby and I walked into Mort's anteroom. I kept my gun drawn, and Gabby spun a silver stake around in her hand like it was a toy.

"That was nice," my nutjob partner said. "I almost thought you would have really shot him."

"That's because I would have," I replied.

"Really?" Her voice was light, teasing.

Mine was not. "Really."

"I don't believe you."

"I don't give a shit what you believe. You weren't the one holding the door. It only matters what I believe, and what that little snotball believed. Now I've had a really fucked up couple of days, and I don't expect it to unfuck itself anytime soon. So if you'll excuse me, let's go see what passes for a disturbance in a demon bar."

I pushed open the door into the main bar and saw...nothing. Not a single monster at any of the tables, no one behind the bar, nothing. There were no customers, no employees, and no Mort. Nothing looked out of place, no over-turned tables, no toppled chairs, no broken glasses or bottles. In short, it looked more placid than I'd ever seen it. Of course, I usually only came to Mort's with Harker, the one-man chaos vortex, so "placid" went out the window a few seconds after we arrived usually. But not this time. Everything looked calm. The only difference between this visit and every other trip I'd made to Mort's was that the wooden sign proclaiming "Sanctuary" was missing from over the bar.

Which wasn't anywhere on the list of things I'd consider a good sign.

I kept my pistol out as I made my way to the door at the end of the bar. It led to Mort's back room, where the hitchhiker demon usually stayed out of the public eye. I listened at the door for a moment, but heard nothing. I turned the knob, stepped through, and found the source of the "disturbance."

Mort sat alone in an empty bar, but it looked nothing like the 20th century dive bar Mort's was made out to be. This looked like a pub from Europe sometime between the Dark Ages and last week, all carved wooden furniture, candles, and pewter tankards. It had a weighty feeling about the room, like we were underground, or in a building set into a hill.

Even in the dim light from the wall sconces, Mort was easy enough to spot. Especially since he was the only person there. He had apparently returned the body of the NFL quarterback he'd been wearing when I saw him the day before, and now he was dressed in the skin suit of a thirtysomething white guy with a ponytail and goatee. He was big, too, with raw muscle bulging under his t-shirt.

"Hi Mort," I said, walking over to his table and pulling out a chair. I holstered my pistol and sat down. Gabby stood behind my left shoulder and a few feet back, close enough to be useful but not so close as to screw with my draw if I needed to reach my gun. She might be a psycho, but she knew her way around a fight. I looked Mort up and down. "Borrow a biker?"

Mort glanced up at me, his face solemn. "Murderer," he replied. "I thought I might want a body that deserved whatever punishment the authorities assign to it."

My hand drifted to the butt of my gun. "Punishment?" I asked. "Punishment for what?"

"I find it likely that we may break a few mortal laws in our quest, Detective. If the body I inhabit is already someone that you think should spend the rest of its life imprisoned, then I can do so with relative impunity."

"*Our* quest?" I asked, thinking there was no way he was saying what I think he was saying.

"Yes, our quest. Orobas killed someone very near and dear to me. He must pay for that. As must his master and all of his many minions. It is entirely possible that the streets of this city may run red with blood before my thirst for vengeance is slaked."

Yup, he was saying *exactly* what I thought he was saying. Mort, the demon bar proprietor, just volunteered to join the Super-Friends. Fuck me running.

"I like this guy," Gabby said from behind me. "He's got my kind of style."

Of course she likes him. He makes her look sane.

CHAPTER SEVEN

I turned to the door, and there stood the stereotypical high school football coach. About six feet tall and two-twenty, with a little bit of a gut, brown mullet going gray at the temples, and a hell of a farmer's tan. He was even wearing the tall white socks, short shorts, and polo shirt version of the uniform, complete with a whistle around his neck.

"Who the fuck are you supposed to be, Varsity Football Barbie?" I asked, drawing in my will and starting to mutter an incantation under my breath.

"My name is immaterial, mortal. All that should concern you is my displeasure, which is great. You have banished or destroyed two of my favorite minions, and that has made me wroth."

I ignored his stupid archaic language, focusing on finishing the ritual of banishment I'd begun. I shouted "Amen!" and flung a ball of energy at him, only to watch in dismay as he held up a hand and caught my spell in midair. I didn't know that could happen. It's not that I couldn't do it, I literally had never heard of anyone even attempting it.

The demon coach turned the glowing orb of light over and over in his hands, looking at it with a little smile playing across his lips. He looked up at me and clapped his hands together, dispersing the spell in a flash of light. A wave of magical backlash blew through me and dropped me on my ass, leaving me with a sore butt and ringing ears.

I shook my head to clear the sparkles from my eyes and heard a tremendous roar from the far side of the room. I pulled myself upright and saw Drew, transformed again into his giant half-wolf form, slam into the coach from the side and send him clattering through a row of desks, ending up under the blackboard in a heap of fur, flesh, and twisted metal.

My Glock was going to be no use against that thing, and the one vial of holy water I had left felt pretty inadequate as well. I took a quick inventory of what I had on me and found my arsenal very wanting in the demon-slaying equipment department. I had a couple of silver-edged daggers on my belt and a pouch full of wolfsbane, since I expected to tussle with werewolves. I even had a couple of flash-bangs loaded with powdered silver nitrate, great for immobilizing weres and completely fucking useless against a demon. All I had was my wits, my magic, and a big goddamn werewolf for a partner. Nothing about this screamed "easy" to me.

Drew and the demon were going toe to toe, throwing haymakers and generally knocking the ever-loving shit out of each other. While the bad guy was occupied, at least for a few seconds, I looked around for anything in this classroom that might be useful. My eyes landed on an overturned desk, with one leg bent at an odd angle, and I got an idea.

I ripped the leg off the desk and swung it through the air a couple of times, testing it for balance and heft. It was just a two-and-a-half-foot aluminum tube, so it wasn't going to be worth a shit as a club, but I only needed it to work for a few seconds. I focused my will on the desk leg, imagining it in my head to be the flaming sword of the archangel Uriel, who stood guard at the gates of the Garden of Eden after Adam and Eve were kicked out.

"*Apparatio*," I whispered, letting my will flow into the aluminum in a slow trickle. As the spell took hold, the makeshift club began to shimmer in my hand, transforming into a flaming three-foot blade.

I turned toward the scuffle and shouted, "Hey, dickhead!"

The demon turned to me and jerked backward at the sight of the flaming sword. "Where did you get that?" it hissed.

"I called in a favor with an archangel," I said, charging the demon with the flaming sword. "Uriel sends his regards!" I swung the flaming blade at the demon's head, and when it brought its hands up to block the strike, I popped the cap off the vial of holy water concealed in my left hand and splashed it all over the demon's face. It screamed as the sanctified liquid burned its eyes and clapped its palms over its face.

"Begone, unclean thing!" I shouted. "In the name of the Father, I banish thee! In the name of the Son, I banish thee! In the name of the Spirit, I banish thee!" I threw as much will as I could muster quickly into the incantation and ripped open a small Gate behind the demon. I dropped the chair leg and the empty vial and shoved the demon into the Gate. It plunged through the rip in dimensions, and I pulled all my power back out of the rift, sealing it shut before anything on the ugly side of the universe noticed it and came through to our side.

The illusion I cast on the desk leg vanished the second I let go of it, and it clattered to the floor, just another piece of scrap metal. I dropped to my knees, every ounce of energy gone, and pulled the teacher's wastebasket over to me. I puked into the trash can for several moments, and after the second round of revisiting breakfast, Drew padded out into the hall and came back human and dressed again.

He sat on the teacher's desk while I vomited up my last month's worth of meals and looked down at me with curiosity written all over his face. Finally empty, I just lay flat on my back on the floor, the cool tile feeling good against my sweat-soaked head.

"That seems to have sucked," he said after a minute or two, apparently deciding that I was done.

I waited a few seconds to make sure he was right before I answered. "Yeah, that wasn't the best."

"What the fuck happened? You had a sword, then it was a piece of scrap. Then we were fighting a demon, then the demon was gone. Did I miss something?"

"I cast an illusion on the leg of the desk to make it look like something a demon would be afraid of—an archangel's sword. Then I opened a portal to Hell, shoved the demon through it, and closed the door on it."

"That sounds like a really good thing."

"It's about as good an outcome as I could have hoped for."

"Then why the puking?"

"There are two ways that I know of to open a Gate. One involves a protective circle, an involved ritual, a safe space, and about four hours of spellcasting. It's extremely difficult, but if you follow all the steps and take the time to create a circle within a circle to contain whatever you summon through the Gate, then you can perform the spell without any real danger to yourself or the rest of the world."

"That's not what you did here."

"The other," I went on, "involves basically taking all of my personal stores of magical energy and a decent chunk of my physical energy, and using those to rip a hole in the universe. It's exceedingly dangerous, borderline suicidal, and frankly completely fucking stupid. It leaves you drained of all magical energy, and you feel like you've got been run over by a truck for about a week. Not to mention the fact that you have a completely unprotected doorway between Earth and Hell for the time that the Gate is open."

"And that's what you just did."

"It seemed like a good idea at the time," I said, then promptly passed out.

―――――

T he next day about noon, after half a dozen Advil and three bottles of the red Gatorade, I stepped through the doors of Lockton High. Only this time, I went in through the front door like I belonged there. Because I did. Or at least the persona I wore belonged there. I followed the signs to the main office and stepped into the barely-controlled chaos that is a high school office half an hour before school starts in the morning.

"Can I help you?" The harried woman behind the desk barely looked up from her computer as she held up a finger to the student she was talking to.

"I'm Harold Quinn. I'm the emergency substitute for Mr...." I let my words trail off like I forgot the name of who I was supposed to be subbing for. I remembered, but I remembered him more as Ashkaranoth, the demon I sent back to Hell less than twelve hours before. A couple hours of research between bouts of the chills and more vomiting turned up his name, but not really anything else about him. He was a low-level lieutenant, traded back and forth between higher level demons depending on mood and who lost at cards that week or whatever gambling games demons played. He didn't have the power or the brains to get himself to this plane, and he didn't have anywhere near the juice to corrupt the school to the degree that I felt while walking the halls.

So now I was wearing fake glasses, khaki pants, and a polo shirt, working for seventy-five bucks a day as a substitute Social Studies teacher for a bunch of middle America teenagers who cared less about Social Studies than I did, if that was possible. Rocco got me in as the sub for the banished coach/teacher, proving once again that he was more than just an empty head on top of a pile of muscles, but I had to figure out exactly what constituted "Social Studies" on my own. Education in England in the beginning of the twentieth century was a little different than Ohio in the early twenty-first, but as far as I could tell, it was kinda like world history mixed with civics.

I stepped into the room and the noise level didn't just increase, it *blossomed*.

"We got a sub!" one kid yelled.

"Fresh meat!" bellowed another.

"Where'd they find this asshole, working the express lane at Walmart?" a girl in the front row muttered to her neighbor.

I held up a hand and stood in the front of the room, waiting for silence. After a couple of minutes of shouts and muttered aspersions toward my manhood and my ability to control the horde, the class quieted down. I figured they would. I could afford to play the long game—I wasn't going to age, and they weren't going to leave unless I let them. And if it really got ugly, I'd just turn one or two of them into toads.

"My name is Mr. Quinn. I will be your substitute teacher today, and for the rest of this week. Coach Karan had an emergency and had to leave town unexpectedly." *And this plane of existence*, I didn't add. "He didn't leave any lesson plans for me to follow, so we'll be making this up as we go along. As long as you treat me and your classmates with the respect we all deserve, we'll get along fine. And who knows, you might even learn something."

"Fuck this noise, I'm going to the weight room."

I was expecting this. In any group, there's always one person that has to push the envelope, has to determine exactly who's going to be the lead dog. I know, because it's usually me. This time it was a meathead sophomore with more muscle than brains. He had a Mohawk haircut that looked like something out of a bad 80s movie, a sprinkling of zits across his cheeks, and a sneer on his face that told me he was probably a big deal jock at this school. The black and red letter jacket helped with that, too. He started for the door, and I stepped in front of him.

"Get out of my way," he snarled.

He was almost tall enough to look me in the eye and outweighed me by a good thirty or forty pounds, all of it muscle and bad attitude. If I was a normal human, he would have worried me a little. I've never been accused of being normal.

"Get back to your desk," I said. I looked down the couple of inches at him and kept my voice very even. No point in my getting angry, I was going to win this debate no matter how poorly it went.

"I don't think so, pencil-neck. I can go lift any time I want." He pulled a crinkled piece of paper out of his pocket and shoved it into my chest.

I took the piece of paper, looked at it, then folded it into neat quarters and handed it back to him. "This says you have permission to be in the weight room during lunch, before and after school, during study hall, and during any class where the teacher excuses you from class."

"Yeah, that's right. So *excuse* me." He gave me the nasty grin of a shitty kid who's used to getting his way from all the adults in his life. I never liked those kids.

"You're not excused. Go sit down."

"I don't want to."

"I don't give a shit."

"You can't cuss at me. You're a teacher!" The outrage in his eyes made it clear that he didn't expect anyone to ever turn any tables on him and treat him like he treated other people.

I reached down with one hand and grabbed his belt buckle. I held onto the lapels of his jacket with the other to steady him, and I picked him up until he was directly at my eye level. His eyes widened, and I heard a gasp or two from the other students in the class.

"Listen here, shitball. I'm not a teacher. I'm a *substitute*. I didn't go to college for this crap. I don't want to make a career out of pretending to care whether or not you ever turn into anything more than a used car salesman at your daddy's Chevy dealership on the outskirts of town. I don't even want to be in this fucking town, so if you think you can intimidate me by threatening the seventy-five dollar a day gig I've got babysitting you fuckwits, you've got another think coming. Now you have two choices. You can go sit down and pretend not to be a total goddamn douchenozzle, or you can keep pushing me and find out how close to the principal's office I can get when I throw your ass down the hallway face-first."

I set him back down on his feet and took my hands off of him. "What's it gonna be, pal? You want to sit down and pretend to learn something, or you want to dance?"

He looked around like he was waiting for a buddy to step up and back his play, but everybody else wearing a letter jacket was very conspicuously staring at their textbooks. He gave me one last glaring squint that probably intimidated a lot of freshmen and middle school kids, then stomped back to his seat and dragged a book out of his backpack.

I turned to the rest of the class. "Now, what chapter were you on?"

CHAPTER EIGHT

The parking lot of Harker's building was full of moving vans and contractor trucks when we got back there, me in my car and Mort a little wobbly on his body's Harley. I will admit that he looked pretty intimidating walking through the marble lobby with his engineer boots clumping across the polished floors. We got out of the elevator on the top floor, and I stopped dead in my tracks. The once-quiet top floor of Harker's building was bustling with activity, as his full-floor apartment was turned into a construction site. Hammering and the sounds of machinery echoed through the halls. Workmen hurried every which way, weaving around each other as they carried toolboxes and paint cans through doorways.

Mort, Gabby, and I slipped into the main living room and closed the door behind us, cutting the noise down to an almost bearable level.

"What the hell is going on out there?" I asked.

"Renovations," Watson replied from one of the sofas. "Once Luke realized exactly how many of us were likely to be working out of this space for the foreseeable future, he took a few steps to guarantee a little more space and privacy for all of us."

"In other words, he's building out some extra bedrooms so we don't all have to cuddle in Harker's bed or bunk with him in a light-tight safe room," Jo said from the table. She sat behind her laptop, hair pulled back in a ponytail. "What's with the demon?" she added.

At the word "demon" the room exploded into activity. Watson rolled off the couch and sprang to his feet, drawing a pistol from somewhere as he stood. The door to the bedroom flew open, and Luke dashed into the room, only to stop short when he saw it was Mort standing in the living room.

"Oh," the vampire said. "Hello, Mortivoid."

"Hello, Vlad," Mort replied with a nod of his head. "Would you please tell your minion to lower his weapon? I just got this suit, and I don't want to have to go search for another one."

Luke turned to Watson and motioned for him to put the gun away. Watson gave Mort a skeptical eyeball but tucked the gun into the back of his pants and sat down on the arm of the couch. "Mort, I must offer condolences on Christy's death. She was a fine woman and a very capable bartender. Her Bloody Mary was a true work of art. She shall be missed."

"Thank you, Vlad. I appreciate the sentiment."

I looked from Mort to Luke and back again. I didn't know if Luke knew that Christy was Mort's half-human daughter, and I sure as hell wasn't going to bring it up. I remembered the look on Mort's face when he rolled up on Orobas during the fracas at Luke's place, and it scared me. I didn't need to see that again anytime soon. I had a bad feeling I'd be seeing it in my dreams regardless.

"Now what are you doing here, Mortivoid? We have an arrangement. I don't eat your customers, and you don't stick your nose in my business."

"Your business became my business when Orobas killed my daughter. I want his head for a soup tureen. I want to send his soul back to Hell a torn and shredded thing, a scrap of consciousness so wisp-thin that demons will use him for toilet paper. I want to—"

"We get it. You're pissed. Moving right along." Gabby shouldered her way past Mort and I *en route* to the fridge. She opened the door and stuck her head inside. "Did nobody go grocery shopping? We're out of beer."

"Can we not freeload on all of Harker's food and drinks and instead figure out how we're going to clear his name and get him back to Charlotte?"

"Missing your half-vamp booty call, Detective?" Gabby asked as she walked past me to the liquor cabinet with a glass of soda water over ice. I watched as she poured the last of Harker's vodka into her drink and sat down on the sofa next to Watson.

"One, he's not half-vampire," I said as I walked over to where Gabby sat. I leaned over and plucked the vodka and soda from her hand. "Two, he's my fiancée, not my booty call. And three, if you think I'm going to sit here and let you insult Harker while you drink his booze in his living room and I won't slap the taste out of your mouth, you've got another think coming." I took a step back and handed the drink to Mort. "Hold this."

Gabby stood up and got in my face. "You wanna go, Miss Cop? We can go.

I don't know what your problem is with me, but we can solve it right now if you want to."

"My problem with you is that I think you're a goddamn psychopath, and I can't handle any more crazy in my life right now. So if you're determined to keep being part of the problem, then would you please get the fuck out of my city before I shoot you right between the fucking eyes? Or if you want to be part of the solution, then please stop being such a pain in my ass!"

Gabby stared up at me for a long moment, her dark eyes boring into mine. "I like you, cop. You got stones. But you ever touch my drink again, we're going to have problems." She reached around me and reclaimed her drink from Mort. "And I'm a sociopath, not a psychopath," she said, sitting back down on the sofa.

A knock on the door ended any further explorations into Gabby's twisted psyche. I looked around, but everyone had that edgy look that said they were not at all expecting a pizza, so I put a hand on my pistol as I went to the door. Mort stepped back into the kitchen, and Gabby set her drink down on the coffee table. I didn't see her or Watson's hands, so I figured they had me covered if whatever was on the other side of the door wasn't friendly.

I put my eye to peephole and instantly relaxed. I turned back to the room and motioned for them to be calm, then opened the door wide enough for Officer Santos to come in. "Santos, what brings you out here? And how did you find me, anyway?"

"I looked up Harker's address. I just figured you'd be here." She looked past me into the room. "Oh, I'm sorry. I didn't know you were having guests..."

"No, it's fine," I said, moving her into the room and closing the door. "It's fine. These are some friends of Harker's. We're working on a way to clear his name."

"Oh yeah, that's your lawyer guy from this morning." Santos pointed at Watson, who nodded.

"And I am Lucas Card; I am Quincy's uncle," Luke said, extending a hand. They shook, and I suppressed a smile as Santos rubbed her hand after. Luke's hands are *cold*.

"Pleased to meet you," Santos said. "Detective Flynn, can I speak to you for a moment?"

I motioned her into Harker's bedroom. "Sorry, there's not really anyplace else to speak without the group," I said, leaning against the dresser. I didn't bother telling her that Luke could hear us talk through the closed door, and probably through the solid floor if he wanted to.

"What's up, Santos?"

"I just wanted you to know that Director Buprof took over the search at the scene this morning and kicked all our crime scene guys off."

"The scene? You mean Mr. Card's house?"

"Yeah," Santos said. "I'm probably not supposed to say anything, but it seemed really strange to me."

"Strange doesn't even begin to describe it. How long have they been there?" I asked, moving to the door and opening it.

"Only a couple of hours. I came over here as soon as my shift ended."

"Thanks, Santos. We'll head over there now and see what's going on. I appreciate you keeping an eye out for me."

"No problem, Detective. If you need anything, just let me know." She left, and I turned to see Watson standing up and grabbing his suit coat.

"Where do you think you're going, Watson?" I asked.

"Well, since you are almost certainly going to Mr. Card's residence, and he is unable to accompany you thanks to the daytime hour, a fact that your Mr. Buprof is almost certainly aware of, you will need someone with solid legal footing to accompany you. I am that someone."

"What in the world makes you that someone?" I asked.

"I am Mr. Card's legal counsel; therefore, I am his legal proxy in all instances where Mr. Card is unable to attend to his affairs himself, especially when he is indisposed due to a medical condition, such as his extreme reaction to ultraviolet light."

"So since he can't go out in daytime, you get to ride along," I translated.

"Exactly what I said." I was almost starting to like the smug bastard. Almost.

"Fine, come on," I said, turning to the door.

"I'm going, too," Mort said. "But this time I'd like to ride in the car. I don't like motorcycles."

"Maybe you should have thought about that before you hitchhiked into a biker. And no, you're not coming."

He got in front of me. That shit was really getting old. "Yes, I am. If Orobas is there, he'll just kill you. And if this Buprof is a Cambion, he'll probably kill you. If any of the Homeland Security agents are working for Orobas, *they'll* kill you. Get the picture?"

"Why won't they kill you?" I asked.

"They could try." Mort gave me a look and my blood ran cold. I decided I didn't want to fuck with the scary-looking biker demon, especially since he was more unhinged than normal after losing someone he actually gave a shit about.

"Fine, come on. But you two ride in the car," I said, picking up the helmet and keys Mort put on the table when he walked in. "I'm borrowing your Harley."

CHAPTER NINE

T here are a lot of things that my childhood and early life provided. I had loving parents, wonderful brothers, a very bizarre surrogate grandfather who rambled a lot about monsters and killing them, and eventually a caring albeit equally bizarre uncle. I also had a certain level of celebrity and prosperity unknown to most people, thanks to the events of a certain book about my parents and Uncle Luke.

What I did not have, and had never experienced before, was Friday night high school football. Frankly, I didn't have football at all until well into adulthood and didn't start paying attention to it until I was over ninety years old. When you don't really age, you get to take your time exploring hobbies, and I had a lot going throughout most of the twentieth century.

So when I stepped out of my pickup in the Lockton High School parking lot the next night, I was completely unprepared for what I found. There were tents, vans, grills, the whole nine yards. It looked more like what I'd seen on TV of a college tailgate than a clash of high school athletes. There were banners pledging allegiance to one player or another, signs proclaiming what the Lions should do to the Ravens, the mascot of the rival du jour Warren G. Harding High School.

My head was on a swivel as I walked through the promenade of insanity, looking not just at the spectacle of teen sports, but also keeping an eye out for any sign of supernatural influence. I couldn't just wander around with my Sight active, because it blurred my normal vision and there was too much going on for me to be distracted and stay safe, so I cast a minor detection spell on myself before I entered the throng, hoping that anything hinky I encountered wouldn't be immediately malevolent.

I made my way to the concession stand without incident, grabbed a jumbo soda and a popcorn, then made my way to a seat in the home grandstand. I settled in behind an African-American family decked out in red and black with lion paws painted on their faces and a giant red foam finger on the hand of an octogenarian matriarch. I assumed they were there supporting #5, the starting quarterback, mostly because the parent-aged man and woman wore jerseys with the number on them. I figured they would be enthusiastic enough to hide my lack of jumping up and down.

The game started, and I saw what Rocco was worried about. The Lions looked like they were matched up against the other school's junior varsity team. Actually, it looked more like a college team playing against middle schoolers, the strength and speed levels were so disparate. After a perfect forty-yard pass for the third touchdown of the first quarter, I leaned down to the proud father in front of me.

"Your son?" I asked, pointed to the number on his jersey.

"Yeah, that's my boy, Javon Henderson. Remember that name, mister. You're gonna hear it on TV some Sunday."

"If he keeps playing like that, I believe it," I agreed. "How long has he been a starter here?"

"This is his first year," his dad said. "He's just a sophomore, and we've already got scouts calling from Ohio State, Miami of Ohio, Penn State, and Notre Dame. Just think about, buddy. My boy might play quarterback for Notre Dame."

I didn't bother telling him that Notre Dame was also the training ground for all the exorcists in North America. That wasn't on the list of things he needed to worry about. "That's great. He's got a ton of talent." I patted the man on the shoulder and leaned back. I wasn't joking. The kid had talent. The kind of talent that gets college graduates drafted in the first round into the NFL. Not the kind of talent that a fifteen-year-old kid from Ohio shows off in his first year of varsity ball. I didn't have to grow up with football to see that something was making these kids better than they had any right to be. Something that in all likelihood had a much darker side.

It was late in the third quarter, with the third string offense on the field and a three-touchdown lead for the Lions, when I felt it. Something was probing me. Something magical. I looked around but didn't see anything that looked out of the ordinary. The Lockton third-string running back broke loose and headed for the end zone, bringing the whole stadium to its feet. I used the confusion to mask me opening my Sight and sweeping the crowd for my magical Peeping Tom.

With the Otherworld laid over the mundane world, active or latent magic lit up like a miniature sun to me. With no surprise at all, I saw that three quarters of the football team glowed like sparklers on the Fourth of July, as did almost the entire coaching staff. As I kept looking around the stadium, there were two surprises to my magical vision. First, the quarterback didn't exhibit any signs of magical ability or tampering. He was just that damn good. And second, there was a woman in the stands giving off enough magical energy to power Cleveland. And of course, she was staring right at me.

My cover blown, I slipped out of the crush of humanity with as little fuss as possible, managing to only kick over one oversized soda on my way to the aisle. I hustled up the stands to the exit and through the gate into the parking lot without incident and thought I was at least close to home free when I felt a pulse of energy whizz by me and saw the tire of a battered Ford Focus to my left melt under the assault of a walnut-sized fireball.

"Goddamn it, just one time I want to have shit work out the way I plan," I muttered and turned around. There was nothing surprising in what I saw— the woman I saw in the stands glowing like a Christmas tree was standing in the parking lot glaring at me. She was a pretty woman, mid-twenties with long dreadlocks pulled back into a ponytail, jeans, a cream-colored sweater with a purple scarf, and hiking boots. If she didn't open conversations by hurling balls of fire at me, she looked like somebody I might enjoy talking books with. Except that all my reading lately had been on the summoning or banishing of demons, so my literary conversation game was kinda lacking.

"Can I help you?" I called out. She was still about fifty feet away, and I was okay with that. I didn't want to blow my cover and get into a big magical duel with a thousand or more townsfolk just a couple hundred yards away.

"What are you doing?" she asked. She started walking toward me, and I started walking backward, keeping the distance between us the same.

"I'm walking away so you don't blow up any of these cars if you miss again."

"I didn't miss. Consider that a warning shot." She reared back and flung another mini-fireball at me. The burning projectile zipped at me with a lot more velocity than my bigger fireballs, making me scramble to throw up a shield and deflect the burning orb into the ground. It exploded with a huge flash, and I blinked to clear the glare from my eyes.

When I could see again, the woman was right in front of me, a glowing sword of energy emanating from each fist. I pulled my shield in from a big curved tower in front of me into a more traditional buckler radiating out from my forearm and blocked her first slash easily. It turned out to be a distraction, though, and I barely avoided the stabbing thrust from her other hand.

"You're good at this," I said with a grunt, wrapping both of my arms in auras of energy and using them to slap her strikes away. I didn't want to hurt her until I knew she was evil. After all, an inappropriate body count was one of the reasons I was stuck in Lockton in the first place. I mean, Smitty definitely needed killing, but in hindsight I might have been just a little too public with the whole shooting a federal agent in the face thing. I was determined not to kill anyone in Lockton unless I knew for sure they were evil. And hopefully not well-connected.

"I've killed a lot of demons, asshole," the woman replied, shooting out a kick at my left knee. I checked the kick, but took a stinging shot to my shin as a result. She was too good for me to keep pulling my punches. If I didn't cut loose soon, she was going to get a shot through my defenses, and that would be bad. But if I did cut loose, I'd probably kill her, which might be worse.

I went very low to get under a head strike, then dropped her to her butt with a leg sweep. She went down with a *whoof*, and I had the time I needed.

"*Silencio!*" I said, dropping my shields and tossing tendrils of power out at her like Spider-Man's webbing. Strands of magical power flowed from my fingertips and wrapped around her face, tying her mouth closed.

"*Restrictus*," I said, aiming the flow of my power down her body. More tendrils of energy flowed out of me, wrapping her entire body in glowing ropes of power. Trussed up like a turkey, my mystery attacker struggled against her bonds, but spinning the bonds out of my own energy instead of the life-force of people or things around me gave me two advantages.

One, I wasn't draining anyone of the energy of their life and soul. That wasn't my thing, if I could help it. Two, if she fought against the bonds, I could just throw more power at them and keep her tied up as long as I had the reserves. Which wasn't going to be long, given my current energy levels. I still wasn't anywhere close to recovered from opening the Gate, and I could feel the toll this little duel was taking on my magical energy.

I bent over, hoisted my attacker up across my shoulders in a fireman's carry, and started walking up the hill to the school. I saw a security guard heading our way about a hundred yards away, and whispered "*inconspicuous*" under my breath. I let out a little more power into a little "ignore me" cloud around me, encouraging anyone who saw me to see exactly what they expected to see and not to take notice of anything I did. It wasn't a foolproof spell by any stretch; anyone with no real preconceived notions of what is "normal" wouldn't be affected, but I figured it would be good enough to fool a busy security guard at a distance.

I was right. The guard turned around and went back to the game, convinced that we were nothing he was interested in. I used the copy of Rocco's key I'd made just for tonight's adventures, and a couple of minutes later, I deposited my bundle of pissed-off witch onto the floor of "my" classroom.

I looked down at the scowling woman. "I'm going to let you go now, but I want to make a couple of things clear first. I am not the bad guy, so if you think I'm a demon, then you're barking up the wrong tree. I'm here to help. Also, there aren't any innocents around now, so I'm not going to pull any more punches. You try to throw another fireball at me, I'll shove it so far up your ass light will shine out of your ears. You get me?"

She nodded, and I released the magic binding her. She instantly scrambled to her feet and backed up, putting most of the classroom between us, then muttered a brief incantation and surrounded herself with a shield of power, ostensibly keeping me from putting any magical bonds on her again. She didn't have to worry about that. If this conversation didn't go well, I didn't have enough energy left to tie her up magically, I was just going to shoot her.

CHAPTER TEN

W e rolled up to Luke's house about ten minutes later, and it looked even worse after I'd had a little time away from it. The place was crawling with men and women in Homeland Security windbreakers and stupid dress shoes that should never be worn to muck around explosion sites. I put down the kickstand on Mort's motorcycle and two agents were on me like bodyguards on paparazzi.

"You can't be here, ma'am," the first no-neck agent said.

"Get back on your bike, Detective. This is a Homeland Security matter now," the second one followed.

"This is so far from a Homeland Security matter it's funny," I said. "Get me Buprof."

"The director isn't available right now, ma'am," No Neck One said.

"Get in the vehicle, Detective," No Neck Two said, putting his right hand on my shoulder. That was a bad idea. I grabbed his wrist in my right hand, ducked under his arm and twisted it around behind him in a hammerlock. I pushed down on the back of his head with my left hand and slammed his face into the roof of my car. His knees buckled and he went down.

I whipped out my handcuffs and had him bound in three more seconds, then I stood up, my Sig in my hand. "The next motherfucker that decides assaulting a police officer is a good idea is going to have a much worse day than this jackass. Are we clear?"

The three agents approaching my car immediately stopped and put their hands up. I nodded and holstered my weapon. I looked down at No Neck

Two and asked, "Are you going to behave, or do I have to leave you like that?"

He glared at me but didn't say anything. "Fine," I said. "See if you can convince one of your pals to uncuff you." I stomped off toward the wreckage with Mort and Watson in tow, only to see a highly agitated Deputy Director Buprof moving in my direction, all red-faced and blustery. I steeled myself for the inevitable confrontation, and he didn't disappoint.

"What the ever-loving fuck do you think you're doing here, Detective? You're suspended! Hell with suspended, you're fucking fired! And you sure as fuck need to get the fuck out of my crime scene. You've got no legal right to be here, so get your little friends here and go." He stood there tapping his foot, arms folded across his belly, barely holding in his dress shirt from the strain.

"While you are partially correct, Director, you are, like so many Americans, rushing to judgement. As Mr. Card's counsel and his legal proxy, I am certainly within my rights to be here, accompanied by whatever assistants I require to complete my assessment of the damages to his property as I deem necessary." Watson stepped forward, a business card in his outstretched hand. "Watson, as I'm sure you'll recall. Jack Watson. I am the solicitor on retainer for Mr. Card and his enterprises."

Buprof looked at the card in his hand, then at Watson, then at Mort. "The fuck you think this is, some kind of a joke?"

"I assure you, Director, I am deadly serious. We are here to conduct a thorough inspection of Mr. Card's property for the purposes of his insurance coverage and would appreciate it if you and your people would vacate the premises while we did so."

"Yeah, like that's going to happen. Fuck off, you gimpy little prick," Buprof said, giving Watson a shove on one shoulder. He took a step backward, his foot came down on a piece of rubble, and his lost his footing with his prosthetic leg. He went down to one knee, catching himself with one hand before he went sprawling. My hand drifted to the butt of my pistol, but I didn't draw. Yet.

"See," Buprof said, "it's not safe around here. You should go." He glared down at Watson, and I would have sworn I saw a yellow gleam in his eyes. Was *everybody* in Homeland Security a demon? I could believe it about the TSA, but this was more than I was expecting.

Watson didn't bite. He didn't lose his cool, although anger flashed across his face so fast I almost didn't believe I saw it. He simply stood up, dusted off his pants, and looked at Buprof with the disappointed gaze of someone dealing with a particularly stubborn child. I knew that look well. After all, I was dating Quincy Harker.

"I'm not leaving. In fact, you are," Watson said, stepping up to just inside the boundaries of polite distance from Buprof. "We have a right to be here, and you are outside your jurisdiction. We have clearance from Captain Herr to look over the wreckage and remove anything of value before it is stolen, so long as Detective Flynn ensures that we do not compromise the police department's evidence gathering. Here is the notice to that effect." He reached into his jacket and pulled out a folded piece of paper.

Buprof glared at him, then held out his hand. Watson handed him the paper, Buprof read it over once, then passed it back to him. "Fine, but be quick about it. I'll give my team their lunch break, but you'd better be gone by the time they get back. And I'll be watching you personally."

"So long as you watch us from the seat of your vehicle, that will be fine," Watson said, tucking the paper back into his coat.

Buprof stomped off, yelling at his team to clear out for thirty minutes. Watson turned to me. "Do you have any idea what they would be looking for?" he asked. His eyes were a little wild and there was a hint of sweat on his upper lip. He looked decidedly un-British.

"No clue. Good thing we've got some time," I replied.

"We probably don't have that much time," Watson said.

"Why not?"

"That letter was somewhat less than genuine," he said. "I might have printed it at Harker's condominium and signed your captain's name myself."

"You forged my boss's signature? On a document you gave to a Deputy Director of Homeland Security?" I shook my head. "You're all insane. Every single one of you. It's not just Gabby and Harker, you're all nuts. What does it say for your organization when the *vampire* is the least crazy one of you?"

"That we picked the right vampire?" Watson gave me a rakish grin. "Now, about that searching..."

"I'll take care of that," Mort said. "Whatever that little piece of Pit trash was looking for, I should be able to sense it as easily as he could." Mort started walking toward the rubble, but I grabbed his arm.

"Slow down, there, Speed Racer," I said. "At least keep your eyes open. Luke didn't have any real idea what Buprof was looking for, but that doesn't mean it's not hidden in some trapped chest or something."

"What do you think this is, Detective? A computer game? Most magical artifacts require activation. It's unlikely that the Count ever realized the true power of the item he possessed, since he has no magical affinity. I would expect it to be something triggered or activated by the ritual that Agent Smith was trying to complete before our dear Mr. Harker interrupted him."

"Then it would be over there." I pointed in the general direction of the front rooms of the house. I didn't know exactly where in Luke's place the ritual had happened, but I knew roughly where the explosion emanated from. I followed Mort to the piles of debris that used to make up Luke's house, picking my way through the still-smoking wreckage.

Mort motioned me back, and I stopped at the edge of what used to be the house. Mort walked farther, stopping every now and again to kick aside a chunk of rock, or to lift a section of wall and peer beneath it. He always put everything back exactly where he found it, taking a lot of photos with his phone, furthering our ruse of documenting all this rubble for insurance.

After several long minutes, Mort stopped and turned to me. "You should come over here, Detective."

I did, trying not to turn an ankle and bust my ass on the treacherous footing. "What is it, Mort?"

"I believe this to be either your friend or the former Agent Smith." He pointed to a large slab of wood that looked like the underside of Luke's gargantuan dining room table. I could just see what looked like a finger sticking out from under it. "I wished to give you the opportunity to say goodbye if that is something you desire. I understand that is something that humans do."

"Thanks, Mort." I didn't want to see Renfield's body under that table, and didn't know if I wanted to see Smith's either. I wasn't sure if I would spit on him or kick his corpse, and just thinking about poor Ren made me well up a little. "I think I probably shouldn't disturb the body, though," I said, stepping back.

Mort looked at me, momentarily puzzled, then nodded. "As you wish, Detective." His oddly formal cadence was somehow reassuring. I think it would have bothered me if he just behaved like everything was normal. This proper speech pattern, while unusual, gave me something else to focus on instead of what might be my dead friend's body beneath a few inches of oak.

He leaned over and picked up the table, swinging it up on one end with no apparent effort, even though I knew that table weighed several hundred pounds. I couldn't help myself, I looked at the body beneath it.

It was Renfield. He was face down, thankfully, but I recognized his trim form instantly. He still wore his black dress pants and the burgundy cardigan that was his favorite item of clothing for relaxing after work, protected from the worst of the fire by the heavy table, which was too thick and treated to burn easily. One bedroom slipper hung from his left foot, with only a tattered sock on his right. I had a sudden urge to find his other shoe and put it on him. It just seemed too un-Renfield to be seen with only one shoe, even in death. I blinked back tears, then started as Mort pushed the table away to crash amidst the rubble.

"What the hell, Mort?" I exclaimed, almost falling but catching myself on a jagged chunk of wall that still stood.

"I believe this is what your Director Buprof was looking for, Detective." He bent over and pulled a sword in a battered scabbard from underneath Ren's body. It looked old, and dirty as hell, with some scorch marks, but since everything I knew about swords began and ended with "put the pointy end in the bad guy," that was all I could see.

"What is it?" I asked.

"It is a sword, Detective. They are implements of war, used in combat since time immemorial."

"I know it's a sword, Mort. What I don't know is why Buprof would want it."

"And you don't need to know, Flynn. All you need to know is that you're lucky I don't have you fucking sent to Gitmo after the stunt you and your limey bastard lawyer just pulled. This letter is a fake as his leg, you traitorous bitch. How dare you come in here and interrupt my investigation into the murder of a federal agent. John Smith was my friend, he was a loyal agent, and he was—"

"He was a demon, you pitchfork slinging pit monkey," said Glory, who appeared out of nowhere at my left elbow and stepped between me and Buprof. "I know what you are, and I know you're out of your depth here. You don't have any real juice, imp. You're just making this all up as you go along. Well, you stepped in it now because the Host knows what you're trying to pull, and they aren't happy. Now why don't you crawl back into whatever burning craphole you slithered out of and leave Detective Flynn alone?"

I shrank back in horror as Buprof underwent a complete transformation before my eyes. The portly, tight-assed Deputy Director and shrieking functionary vanished as a nasty smile crept across his face. Buprof's face reddened even further, until his skin was a dark crimson, and his eyes went yellow, with vertical slits for pupils. He opened his mouth in a wide grin, and I saw a double row of pointed teeth in his now fully revealed demonic face. He held the grin and let his true face shine through for a few interminable seconds, then slammed his disguise back into place before he spoke.

"The Host? You think I'm afraid of the Host? You're more even more deluded than you are sanctimonious, you bitch. The Host aren't going to stop us, the Host..." He cut himself off short, then gave Glory a sneer promising a host of terrible things.

"Never mind the Host. They aren't a problem. You are. You're not just pissing me off, you're interfering with a federal investigation, and I want you to get the fuck out of here before I throw every last one of you under the nearest jail." Buprof was back in bureaucrat mode, and I think I liked the demon more.

"Try it." Mort's voice was cold, and my hand dropped back to the butt of my gun. I felt goosebumps crawl up my arms, and I suddenly wanted to be anywhere else in the absolute worst way.

"Mortivoid, how absolutely fucking typical," Buprof said with a wide smile, turning his attention to Mort for the first time since we arrived. "How's the family?"

Mort shoved me to the side as he went at Buprof, and it was only Glory's quick reflexes that kept me from crashing to the ground. I guess there's some value in having a guardian angel after all. Tossing the sword aside, Mort tackled the burly agent around the midsection and drove him to the ground. The two rolled around in the dirt and wreckage for a few seconds before I drew my Sig and fired a single round into the dirt beside the two wrestling demons. Mort and Buprof separated, both clambering to their feet to stare at me.

"Cut the shit, you two, unless you want the only real human Homeland agent in the state to wonder why you two are rolling around in the dirt like pissed-off kindergarteners." Buprof threw a nervous glance at one of the nearby Suburbans, confirming that not every Homeland Security agent in the state was an escaped demon.

The Deputy Director Demon got up and dusted himself off, then stepped up to Mort again. "I will give you but one warning, Mortivoid. Leave. This does not concern you. The Legions have ignored your dalliances with mortals for far too long, and they are no longer inclined to do so. Interference with our plans here will not be looked upon favorably."

"Murdering my daughter is not looked upon favorably either, Burferon. So tell your superior, whoever he is, that he has made a powerful enemy. I will see someone suffer for what happened to Christy, and I spent enough time in the Pits to know suffering. Intimately." Mort picked up the discarded sword from the rubble and wrapped his hand around the scabbard, preparing to draw it.

Buprof's face went ghost-white as his eyes locked on the weapon in Mort's hand, and his bottom lip started to quiver.

"Count yourselves fortunate. I have to go. There's...something I must attend to." He turned around and hurried off, looking for all the world like something scared the crap out of him, rather than him being scariest thing in the area. Within half a minute, he was tearing away from the house in a black

Suburban with a dozen agents loading all their gear into matching SUVs and rolling in his wake.

"What the hell was that all about?" I turned to Glory, who shrugged.

"Can't say," the angel replied.

"Can't, or won't?" I asked. I was still pissed at her for holding back information that might have wrapped up our investigation earlier, and maybe kept Renfield alive, and here she was doing it again.

"Does it matter, Detective? If I can't, I won't. And if I won't, I won't. So the two words are interchangeable in this case, aren't they?" If all angels were like this, I was beginning to understand why Harker enjoyed being a sinner so much.

"Whatever." I turned to Watson and Mort. "Judging from his hasty retreat, that might be exactly what he was looking for." I pointed at the sword in Mort's hand.

"I knew that from the moment I picked it up. Now please take this blessed thing." He held the sword out to me.

I stared at it, not terribly interested in holding something that made Mort nervous and sent Buprof running for the hills. "Why me?"

"It doesn't have to be you. It can be the angel, it can be the cripple, I don't care," Mort said, and his voice crept high with pain. "But I have to put this piece of hallowed tin down before it sets me alight like a candle!"

I took the sword. I didn't feel anything weird about it, but the way Mort sighed with relief, you would have thought he was sunburned and I just dropped him in a vat of aloe. "What's wrong with you, Mort?" I asked.

"The sword," he grumbled, rubbing one hand with the other as if to restore feeling in it. "It burns me. It must be blessed or divine in some way. It hurts to touch it."

"You didn't appear to be in any pain when you were confronting Director Buprof," Watson said, stepping up beside Mort, gingerly picking his way across the rubble.

"I was raised in the Pits, Mr. Watson. You learn at a very young age to hide pain. Or not. If you choose not, you don't get to an old age. So I didn't let on that I was being cooked from the inside out."

"Probably a good idea," I said. "Glory, you want to shed any light on the origin of this little pigsticker?"

The angel looked at me, then shook her head. "I'd love to, Rebecca, but..."

"You can't," I finished the sentence for her.

"Exactly."

"Some help you are."

"We all have rules, Detective. Even angels."

"I don't," Mort said.

"Say that in the presence of the Morningstar," Glory countered.

"If it's all the same to you, I'd rather not," Mort demurred.

I sighed. "If you two are done debating theology, can we get back to the house and see if anyone knows anything about this damn sword?"

"A lovely idea, Detective. Shall I drive?" Watson asked.

"Do what you like, I'm not riding with you," I said, striding back to Mort's Harley. "You still haven't figured out which side of the road you want to play on!"

CHAPTER ELEVEN

"**W**ho the fuck are you and what the fuck are you doing here?" spat the woman standing in "my" classroom at nine o'clock on a crisp fall Friday night. I decided that I liked her, despite her alarming tendency to throw fireballs first and ask questions later. Throw enough f-bombs around, and I'll probably get on board with what you're saying. What can I say? I appreciate a good poetic rhythm to swearing.

"I'm Quincy Harker. I hunt demons. I'm here because somebody is calling up nasty shit around here and turning it loose on kids. That's not cool." It was more the summoning demons thing and less the siccing demons on teenagers thing that had me concerned. I think most teenagers are assholes that would benefit from a little up-close time with a good old-fashioned Pit Lord or even a run of the mill Torment Demon.

"You're a demon hunter?" She looked dubious.

"Yup." I honestly didn't give a fuck if she believed me or not. I just didn't want to kill her if she turned out to be one of the good guys. My soul had enough black marks on it already.

"Prove it." She wasn't throwing fireballs anymore, which was good. She was just standing in the fourth row of desks staring at me with her arms folded across her chest.

"No." I stopped proving shit to people after World War II. If there's one thing I picked up from Luke, and frankly there are many, it's that being the oldest person in your zip code means you don't have to answer to anybody.

"Why not?"

"It's not a fucking parlor trick, lady. It's what I do. Take it or leave it, it's the truth. You don't believe it, I don't care. But you start flinging those little fireballs at me again, I'm going to blast a hole in your ass big enough to drive a truck through, and fuck the cleanup crew."

I could almost see the wheels turning behind her eyes. She looked me up and down a couple of times, then finally nodded at me. "Don't you want to know who I am and what I'm doing here?"

I cocked my head to the side. It looked like she'd come to a decision, but I wanted to confirm it before we moved into the "getting to know you" part of the evening. "Are we gonna fight some more?"

"I'm not planning on it."

"Then sure, go ahead." If I didn't have to kill her, then I didn't mind learning who she was. If I was just gonna have to hide the body, then it didn't matter.

"I'm a witch."

"No shit, Sherlock." I got to know Holmes briefly before he died. Fun guy, but he fucking *hated* that phrase. So, of course, I used it every chance I got around him. Made me almost misty-eyed thinking about it now. Nah, not really.

She held up a hand at me, so I held off on any more smartass comments. "Let me try that again. My name is Beth Kirkland. I teach English here. And I'm a witch."

"Good to meet you, Ms. Kirkland. At least while I'm here, I'm Harold Quinn. I'm filling in for Coach Karan, who is unexpectedly absent for an unspecified time."

"And I suppose you know nothing about that?" She gave me one of those looks that says "fill in the blanks."

I was feeling charitable, so I figured I'd give her a little more rope to hang me with. "I don't know anything about Coach Karan actually being a demon and getting tossed back into Hell, that's correct."

"I never liked that son of a bitch."

"Me neither." I don't like demons as a rule, and I certainly don't like the ones that try to kill me.

"But if Karan was the demon, why are you still here, Mr. Demon Hunter?"

"I said he was a demon. I never said he was *the* demon, Ms. English Teacher. He wasn't strong enough to juice up a whole football team, even if everyone on the coaching staff was a demonic minion. Which they aren't, by the way."

"I know. I cast a divining spell on them during last week's game. Only some of the coaches are demons. There are a few that are completely human, except for one latent wizard and one werewolf."

"Rocco," I said.

"Yes," she agreed. "A perfect job for a wolf, a strength coach for a high school. Lets him get his natural aggression out lifting weights all the time, and gives him another pack to be part of."

"You teach sociology, too?"

"Minored in anthropology. I spent a lot of time focusing on Xeno-Anthropology at Notre Dame."

Now it was my turn to fold my arms over my chest and raise an eyebrow. "Exorcist?"

"No, nothing like that. But I grew up in a family of witches, so I wanted to go somewhere that had some coursework in nontraditional religious topics, and I got a scholarship to Notre Dame. It was either there or Cambridge. Those were the only places I could find with any real opportunity to study demonology and spell craft."

"Yeah, Hogwarts has been closed to new students for a while now," I quipped. I knew of at least half a dozen other places someone could go to study about witchcraft and spell-slinging, but they all worked very hard to keep themselves hidden. I was glad to see their efforts were working, it made me feel like I had a shot at staying off the radar myself.

"So what's the play?" Beth asked.

"Well, I was kinda planning on hanging around the school long enough to see who the demon is, maybe figure out what it wants, and then send it home with extreme prejudice."

"You're not going to kill it?" she asked.

"I thought you said you'd fought demons before," I said, folding my arms over my chest. My bullshit detector was going off like a Geiger counter at Chernobyl. You don't kill demons. At least not easily, and certainly not demons with the kind of power this one was throwing around. A lot of times the best you can hope for is to send it back to Hell and hope it doesn't find a way out anytime soon.

"It's been a while." She didn't meet my eyes when she said it. Because of course she didn't.

"Yeah, like your whole life? Look, sweetheart, this isn't fucking playtime. This isn't a goddamn movie or some kind of bullshit academic lecture under your pretty little golden dome. This is real life, and real people are going to get real hurt. And I don't have time to waste on a fucking amateur ghostbuster who watched too many *Paranormal State* reruns and now thinks she's a goddamn expert on all things supernatural."

She looked me in the eye, then, and she was *pissed*. "Okay, Mr. Big-time Demon Hunter, here's the deal. My kid brother is missing, probably dead, and I think it's got something to do with whatever is going on here. He was a sophomore here last semester, and when I came home for fall break, he was missing. The police said he ran away, but the more I talked to his friends and poked around the school, the surer I became that something fucked up was going on. So I got a job as a perma-sub for an English teacher on maternity leave and started looking for the source of the magic."

"What made suspicious of the school? The winning football team?"

"That was part of it. The Lions have always sucked. There just aren't enough people in town to build from. The school's too small. But now they're rolling over bigger schools like they're the friggin' Steelers, and it's the same kids that got their asses kicked nine games out of ten last season. So something's definitely going on there. But that's not all."

"It never is," I grumbled.

"What?"

"Demons never just fuck with one thing. They're total shit-stirrers, so with most demons, if they're doing one thing, they're doing a bunch of things. They might all feed into the same big plan, but it might just be more opportunities to fuck with humans."

"Or kill them."

"Or kill them," I agreed.

"I think that's what's happening here. I think someone is killing any students with any magical or psychic Talent." Most normal people don't have shit for magical Talent. A little bit of *deja vú*, a tiny precognitive moment once in a blue moon, that's about all most folks get in their lives. Then there are the folks with Talent. They're rare, but not as rare as most folks think.

"What makes you think something is taking kids with Talent?"

"I checked the school records. Since the beginning of this school year, there have been a record number of transfers, relocations, runaways, and kids just up and vanishing. In some cases, the whole family is gone without a trace."

"So you're saying you think students with Talent are being targeted?"

"I'm saying that there are eight hundred kids across four grades in this school. You'd expect seventy-five or eighty of them to have a bit of talent, right?"

She had a point. A good ten percent of all people have some latent magical power. Those are the people who might never use it for anything, might not even know they have it, but they've got a really green thumb, or a really lucky streak that lasts for years, or maybe they just know who's going to call before the phone rings. Those people could develop some power with the right catalyst and the right training, but most of them live out their lives never knowing it.

So yeah, with the number of kids in the school, eighty or so kids should have at least some Talent. "Sure, something like that," I agreed.

"I know of three. And they're all major Talents."

"Three?" I looked at her, and I'm sure she could read doubt all across my features because that number was way off, even by my most conservative estimates. There should have been a lot more people with some ability, and realistically, there should have been *fewer* major Talents, as she described them.

Those major Talents—people like me, and apparently Beth and her whole family, the people with significant power, are really rare. It's even more rare to find someone with power and an environment that believes in it and nurtures it. Even most people with a lot of natural Talent don't ever do anything with it.

And to do anything significant with it took years of training. Most humans die before they master any part of spell casting. Maybe Beth couldn't see latent ability in people as well as she thought she could. Some witches could sense Talent in others better than others.

She let out a sigh that said she knew she wasn't convincing me, then said, "I cast a spell during the pep rally this morning. Three students lit up to my Second Sight like beacons. As did you, Coach Rocco, and Coach Balomb."

"Those are the only coaches that you found?" Now I knew her spell was bullshit. Since half the football coaches were demons, if she couldn't see them, then she was way off base.

"I wasn't looking for demons. I cast the spell specifically to find Talented or magic-touched humans. Or at least mostly humans."

I wasn't sure if she meant me or Coach Werewolf with that and decided not to ask. "Okay, that explains why the rest of the football coaches didn't light you up, but are you sure the spell reached the entire gym? Maybe you missed them."

"I cast it on the doors. Anyone using any type of magic who passed through was dusted with magic that would show up in my Second Sight. It had no effect on normal humans or other-dimensional beings. And I cast it at lunch, so everyone who came through the doors of the gym all afternoon was dusted. I didn't miss anyone. I didn't cast it wrong. I didn't fuck up the spell. I know what I'm doing, and I'm right. There are no Talents left in this school."

If she was right, then I was pretty sure I knew what was going on. "We've got a problem."

"No shit, Sherlock." Now I saw why Holmes didn't like that phrase. It was really fucking irritating when it got turned back on you.

She sat on the top of a desk and stared at me. "Well?"

"Well, what?" I asked, looking at her and trying to figure out how she managed to sit on the desk like that. If I tried that shit, I'd be flat on my ass in a heartbeat.

"Well, what's the problem?"

"Oh, yeah, that. Sorry. Yeah, there's a problem. If the whole football team is hyped up on magical super-juice, and the school only has three kids left with any magical ability, where do you think the demons are getting the mojo?"

Her eyes went wide and the color drained from her face. "Oh, no."

"Oh, yeah."

"You mean...?"

"Yeah," I said with a sigh. "I hate to tell you this, but it's looking very much like your brother and the other missing students were killed for their magical energy, and that energy was pumped into the football team like some kind of mystical steroids."

CHAPTER TWELVE

"**W**hat, that thing? No, there's nothing special about it. Other than fond memories, of course," Luke said when I showed him the sword.

"What kind of memories?" I asked.

"Oh, you know, the normal thing. I remember the look on the face of its previous owner when I ripped his heart out through his chest, the feel of his blood splashing across my face, that sort of thing." He waved a hand in the air like he was talking about the weather, and I was reminded once again just how bizarre my life had become.

I was sitting in my boyfriend's living room with Dracula and descendants of Dr. Watson, John Henry, and Abraham Van Helsing plotting to hunt down and fight a demon before he opened the gates of Hell, with my guardian angel, who, by the way, borrowed her name from a *Buffy the Vampire Slayer* villain, watching over the proceedings. This was not something that I expected when I graduated from the police academy.

"Who was the previous owner, Luke?" Watson asked.

"An SS lieutenant, I believe, or perhaps a colonel. They do all blur together after a certain number, you know. It was in France, I believe...yes, Northern France in about 1943. It would have to be late 1942 or 1943 because I was following Quincy through Europe cleaning up some of his messes and trying to keep attention off the two of us. Yes, it was early 1943, there was still snow on the ground.

"I don't remember the name of the town, but it wasn't a large town. Just one of those typical French towns in the middle of the countryside with a collection of homes, shops, and the occasional farm. The Nazis had taken over some time before, and the population was fairly well quelled. The colonel—I remember now, he was a colonel—had taken over the biggest home in town. It sat atop a hill which once was in the middle of a quaint little forest, but the Germans had cut all the trees down and set up a few small barracks buildings surrounding the mansion. I suppose the colonel wasn't feeling all that secure in his position. It turns out that was a good idea.

"Quincy was in a very bad place, emotionally. His love, Anna, had been murdered by a Nazi less than six months before, and the severing of his bond with her drove him to savagery the likes of which I haven't seen...well, since my own losses drove me to certain unpleasant excesses some many years ago." Luke paused, and you could hear a pin drop.

I had certainly never heard him mention his life before becoming Dracula, back when he was Vlad Tepes, ruler of Wallachia. I'd read some of the stories before meeting him, and after I learned that not only was he real, he was in my city, I consumed every piece of Dracula and vampire lore I could. And there's a lot, not all of it good. Some guy even wrote a book about a vampire accountant, if you can believe that crap. But I never mentioned any of that to Luke. It seemed rude, somehow, like I was trying to pry into something that was none of my business. But here he was, talking about it, despite the obvious cost to himself.

He took a deep breath, seeming to push away memories that still pained him over about six centuries and continued. "Regardless, I was following Quincy's trail of Nazi corpses through Europe when I came upon him in France. He was in the living room of the mansion, surrounded by dead soldiers, battling the colonel. He was obviously tired because the colonel was actually doing him harm. Quincy was staggering, bleeding from several cuts along his arms and legs. Both his and the Nazi's guns lay on the ground out of reach, and it looked as though their battle would quickly become one of attrition, where whoever could withstand the most punishment would be the survivor. While I had faith in Quincy's abilities, I did not think it wise to leave anything to chance given his current mental state."

"You thought he was out of his head enough to let the Nazi kill him?" I asked.

Luke gave me a long look. "Anna was the first woman he ever shared his blood, his essence with. Her death would have devastated him had it happened under normal circumstances. When she was murdered in front of him, he went completely insane. His rampage was terrifying to watch, and I am not a man who is unaccustomed to the sight of carnage." I looked into his

587

cold eyes and remembered that this was the man they dubbed "The Impaler" because of his ferocity in battle and his treatment of captured foes. Carnage was his milieu, so if whatever Quincy was doing scared him, then it was seriously awful.

He continued. "I stepped into the room behind the colonel and pulled out his heart. I drank my fill of his blood from the still-beating reservoir, then dropped it at Quincy's feet. I still remember the words I said to him that day as I dropped the drained heart at his feet. 'Eat it,' I said. 'If you're going to behave like a beast, you may as well go the whole way.' Then I plucked the sword from the dead man's hands as a trophy, turned on my heel, and walked out. I didn't see Quincy again for nearly seven years, until he met up with us in America near the beginning of 1950."

He clapped his hands, breaking the spell he'd held us all in with his words. "And that's the story of how I came to possess that sword. It is also all I know about the blade. I have never sensed anything supernatural about it in all the time it has been in my possession, although I can tell you from the manufacture that it was made around the time of my mortal life."

"What was that, the early fifteenth century?" I asked, more to confirm than anything.

"Yes," Luke said. "I was born around 1430. Records in that time were a little sparse, and I was ill-equipped to write down the date myself."

"Fair enough. So the sword was in France in the 1940s, and it originates from some time in the fifteenth century, that's all we know?" I asked the group.

"And it resonates to those with the ability to sense magical items, and Orobas wants to get his hands on it," Jo added.

"Then all we care about is that the demon doesn't have it, right?" Gabby asked. "Good deal. Demon doesn't have it. What's next?"

"It is important to understand why our adversary is interested in the weapon, Gabriella," Watson said.

"But she's right, isn't she?" I asked. "It's nice to know the provenance of the weapon, but if none of us have any magical ability, then all we care about is that we kept it out of the hands of the guy who wants to destroy the world, right? Or did you graduate from Hogwarts when I wasn't looking?"

Watson held up his hands in mock surrender. "Fine, fine, Detective. Far be it from me to want to know as much information as possible about the tools we have on hand before rushing into a fight. I'm sure that the American method of rushing in guns blazing will sort everything out just fine."

"Worked okay in Yorktown," I said, leaving the word "prick" unsaid, but heavily implied. I turned to Luke. "What's the plan? What's our next step?"

"I suppose it isn't any different than it was before we found the sword. We find Orobas, and we put a stop to his plans. Along the way, we should probably clear Quincy's name and think about finding a way to send Orobas back to Hell."

"All admirable goals, Luke, but do you have an actual plan to accomplish any of them?" Watson asked.

"Well, I could sit around the apartment staring at a sword, or I could start punching all the members of the local supernatural community. While diametrically opposed, I think that both methods would meet with a similar lack of success." Luke didn't look offended at Watson's snottiness. I guess when you've been around for a few centuries, a snotty Englishman isn't a big deal.

"There's always Option C," Jo said from her computer. All eyes turned to her as she stood up and grabbed a jacket from the back of her chair. She slipped on the leather jacket, then reached under the table and picked up a big maul with a long handle and hefted it over her shoulder. "I just got an email from Sparkles. He found Mort."

"Why was he looking for Mort? I mean, wasn't he just going back to the bar after we left Luke's place?" I looked over at Watson, who shrugged.

"That's what he said he was doing, but what's to say he wasn't lying? He's a demon. Who knows what he had in mind?" he replied.

"I can't argue with that," I said. "But that doesn't answer the question. Why was Sparkles looking for Mort? And am I ever going to meet this Sparkles person?" Who the hell even answers to a nickname like Sparkles? Was this an out-of-work stripper moonlighting for the Shadow Council?

"Probably not," Jo said. "And I had Sparkles put a trace on Mort's phone when he was with you two. He seemed pretty motivated to find Orobas, and he has connections that none of us have, so I figured if we all kept in contact, and I had a way to track Mort, then all our bases were covered."

"Seems good," I said. I grabbed my jacket and car keys. "What's with the hammer?"

"It's a family heirloom," Jo replied. "Besides, I don't like shooting people."

"You should really give it a try," Gabby chimed in, strapping a pair of nickel-plated Colt 1911 pistols to her hips. "It's a lot of fun. Especially arterial spray. That's my fave."

I sighed, then looked at Watson and Luke. "You two coming?"

Luke gestured to the window. "Still daylight. I think I shall continue my long-standing tradition of not bursting into flames for a little longer, for all the good it does me." I stared at Luke, and saw, not for the first time in the past few days, a level of melancholy and loneliness haunting his eyes. This was a man that was accustomed to people dying around him, often at his hands, but losing Renfield was different somehow. There was something cracked inside Luke, and it would take a long time to heal, if it ever did.

"I suppose I may as well," Watson said. He walked to the end of the sofa and picked up a bowler hat, trench coat, and a cane topped with a wolf's head.

"What the hell are you supposed to be? A parody of an urban fantasy novel cover? Do you come with your own smoke machine and creepy soundtrack?" I managed not to laugh at Watson, but only just.

"I think we'll find that my cane serves multiple purposes, and the coat is a type of tightly-woven fabric that is similar to Kevlar, but more puncture-resistant and is completely flame retardant." He huffed. He walked past me to the door of the apartment and held it open. "Shall we?"

"That depends. Jo, where are we going?" I asked.

"I have an address on Brookshire Boulevard. It's someplace called Coyote Joe's?" She looked at me with an eyebrow up.

"I know where it is, but I don't know why in the hell Mort would be there, unless he's looking for cheap beer and loud music," I said.

"So you can get us there? Good," Watson said.

"I can get us there, but why in the world is a demon in a biker suit in the city's largest country music bar?"

"Wet t-shirt contest?" Gabby asked.

"He's a fan of terrible music?" Watson offered.

"He wants to drown his sorrows over his daughter's death and he's already drank all the booze in his own bar?" Jo suggested.

"I don't know, but something tells me that the answer is going to be even stranger than any of those ideas," I said as we trooped out into the afternoon light to hunt down a demon in a giant country bar.

CHAPTER THIRTEEN

"Nothing about this seems like a good idea to me," Beth said to my back.

"You just described most of my life, particularly any of the parts of it I spent in Rio," I whispered. "Now shut up. I'd really rather not get caught here. I think it would end up on my permanent record."

"Oh, you're a regular comedian, Harker," she muttered.

"Laughter is not typically the response I look to elicit in women," I replied, and immediately thought of Becks. That was a mistake. My chest got tight, and my focus on the task at hand was completely gone for a moment as I sent feelers down the invisible connection tying me back to Rebecca, hundreds of miles away in North Carolina working to clear my name and find out how high in Homeland Security our problem went.

I couldn't see through her eyes, or even contact her with coherent thoughts, the physical distance was just too great. But I could feel her, and as my consciousness brushed hers, I felt a whirl of feelings pass through me, not all of them mine. Fear, anger, stress, worry, love, more anger tied really closely to that love, and pain both physical and emotional. All that coursed through me in half a second as my steps faltered and I went to one knee.

"Are you okay, Harker?" Beth's voice brought me back to the present, to Lockton, Ohio, and to the task at hand. Said task was breaking into the main office to steal Coach Durham Balomb's personnel file so we could go to his house and try to deal with Lockton High's demon infestation once and for all.

I shook my head to clear it, then nodded to Beth. "I'm fine. Just a little wave of psychic impression. Let's go."

"Are you sure you can do this?" she asked, pointing to the door to the main office.

"It's a door. With a standard cylinder lock. I've been magicking these things open since before you were born," I replied. I didn't mention that I'd been magicking them open since before her parents were born, too. So far, Beth Kirkland hadn't asked any questions about my origin, and I wasn't looking to talk about it right now.

People tend to look at you strangely when they find out that the "Uncle Luke" you mention from time to time is actually Dracula, Lord of the Vampires, Vlad the Impaler, source of dozens of movies good and godawful, and arguably the most famous monster in history. Needless to say, I'd whammied my fair share of locks all over the world in the century and change I'd been around, so I wasn't really worried about popping open the door to a high school principal's office in the middle of nowhere Ohio.

I walked down the hall, sticking to the shadows and avoiding the few security cameras running on a Friday night. I stepped up to the door and put my hand on the lock. I focused my will on the tumblers inside, whispered "*Sesame*," and turned the knob. The door clicked open, and Beth and I slipped inside.

"Sesame?" she asked.

"What?" I said. "It's just something to focus my will on the doorknob. I could have said 'cheeseburger,' as long as I believed it would work."

"You didn't have to cast a ritual, or beseech the Goddess for help, or ask the blessings of the Four Winds, or anything?"

"Neither do you," I said. "Magic doesn't really work like that. It doesn't come from some divine place. At least, not the magic I do. It's energy, and if you know how manipulate that energy, then you can do it. Simple as that."

"So you're not a believer?"

"Darlin', I've seen so much shit in my life, I believe in just about everything. But I don't mix my magic and my religion. Except when I need to send some demonic douchebag back to Hell. Which is what we need to do here, so point me to where the employee records are kept and let's go show Coach Balomb the way to go home."

"In that room next to Principal Nettles' office." She pointed, and I walked over and put the whammy on that lock, too. We stepped into the file room and started looking through cabinets. It only took a few seconds to find the right drawer, and Beth pulled out her cell phone as I grabbed the right folder.

"I don't think this is the time to take a selfie," I said as I saw her open the camera app on her phone.

"No, but I thought I'd take a picture of his address so we can put the file back and maybe still have an element of surprise."

"That's fine, but you don't really think our little expedition is going to be discovered in the time it takes us to drive from the school to the coach's house, do you?"

"We're going after him tonight?" She looked at me like I was crazy. I probably am, but I didn't think it had anything to do with Coach Balomb.

"No time like the present, right? Why wouldn't we?"

"I don't know, I thought maybe we'd take time to research him, find a weakness, get some help, that kind of thing."

I snorted. "Nah, that kind of planning works great if you're Giles or Willow, but I'm way more of a kick down the door and beat the shit out of everything in the room kind of guy." I handed her the folder. "Now let's go. You're navigating."

———

I hate it when demons invade the suburbs. It fucks with my sense of the universe. Demons belong in cities, in abandoned sewers, nasty-ass empty factories, or even creepy old houses tucked away in old neighborhoods. Demons don't belong in ranch houses with two-car garages. But that's where Coach Balomb lived. Not even at the end of a cul-de-sac, right in the middle of the damn street like he was some kind of insurance adjuster or something like that.

"What do you know about the coach?" I asked as I pulled my pickup onto a side street two blocks past the address on the file and turned off the lights.

"I don't know much," Beth replied. "He started here last year as an assistant coach and economics teacher. When Coach Pate had a heart attack last June, they promoted Coach Balomb to Head Coach, and he brought in some old friends from the last school where he taught. I don't know where, just that it's somewhere down south, apparently."

"I think he's from a little further south than anybody suspects. Sounds like he engineered the old coach's heart attack and has brought in his buddies from the Pits to serve him here in Lockton."

"Yeah, that's what I figured," Beth agreed.

"But why?" I asked. "Lockton isn't big enough to be a real target, and there's no magical ley lines that run through the place, nothing special about this town whatsoever."

"Just a town willing to sell its soul for a winning football team and a bunch of missing Talented kids." Beth opened her door, and I slapped my hand over the dome light to hide its glow.

"*Eclipso*," I whispered, and a small cloud of absolute darkness enveloped the bulb. I took my hand off the light and got out of the truck.

"Now you're just showing off," she said, closing the door and walking around the front of the truck to join me. "What's the plan?"

"Well, we can either knock on the door and try to bullshit our way inside, then try to fight our way out..."

"Which sounds like a recipe for certain death."

"Or we can blast through the front of the house and the back door at the same time, kill anything we encounter, and hope the element of surprise can buy us enough time to take out Balomb before he gets his shit together enough to fight back."

"Do you have any plans that don't involve our almost certain death in an exceptionally bloody fashion?"

"Not really, no."

"Goddess only knows how you've lived this long."

"If you only knew," I quipped.

Beth sighed. "Let's go with the two-pronged attack, then. I certainly don't trust you to be able to bluff your way through the door, so this way we at least have the potential to take a few of those assholes with us when we go."

"That's what I love in a sidekick, Kirkland—positive thinking. You take the back; I'll take the front."

"How will I know when to go?"

"You'll see the signal."

"What's the signal?"

"I'll figure it out when I send it. But you'll know it. I promise." She shook her head at me and peeled off toward the back of the house.

I walked up the sidewalk to the front of the coach's house and checked the ammunition in my Glock. The front door looked pretty easy to fortify, with a small porch that glowed like Christmas in my Sight. That wasn't going to work as an entrance. I scanned the front of the house and spotted a picture window with no magical enhancements on it.

"Bingo," I muttered. "This oughta serve as a pretty good signal." I pulled in my will, focusing my magical energy over my left hand, then drew my pistol. I put three rounds through the big window and flung a fireball through the shattered glass. It exploded with a massive *BOOM*, and I sprinted across the lawn to leap through the hole in the wall where a window used to be.

I heard a muffled *crump* from the back of the house, followed by a string of small explosions like firecrackers. Sounded like Kirkland blew in the back door, then flung a fistful of those mini-fireballs into the house. Between us, we had the place burning pretty good, which might not have been our best move as the humans surrounded by denizens of Hell. They were a lot more resistant to fire than we were, but I had enough protections woven around me to keep me alive for a couple minutes at least.

Which might be more time than I had, given the fact that I had four demons staring at me from the living room and the door to what looked like the kitchen. None of them wore their human suits, but when wearing their natural forms, they didn't look that far removed from people. Just a little taller, way skinnier, with red skin, yellow eyes, and porcupine spikes instead of hair. Oh yeah, and preternaturally long arms, double-jointed knees, and three-inch curved talons on the ends of each of their six fingers.

So maybe they didn't really look anything like people, except for being bipedal and having roughly human faces, only more angular and sporting curved fangs. So they were nasty little bastards, but these were definitely low-level demons. The ones staring back at me now weren't even as strong as the one I'd banished a couple nights before, so I was only a little bit convinced that I was about to die.

They were way more confident in their ability to kill me than I was because they all charged me at once. I flung up a shield of force with my left hand, effectively blocking the three coming at me from the den. The one rushing me from the kitchen required a different approach, since I still held my gun in that hand. So I shot him. In the face. Four times. He dropped, but not fast enough to actually stop moving, so his momentum drove him right into me, which drove me hard into the other three with my shield, sending me and all four demons tumbling ass over teakettle to the floor.

I dropped my pistol, but held my shield, and wriggled out from under the dead demon that sprawled across my legs. The other three writhed on the ground, scratching, clawing, and biting at each other trying to get to their feet.

"*Electro!*" I shouted, reaching my hand in the air and pointing my index finger toward the ceiling light. Electricity flickered from the light fixture to gather around my fist, and I flung a ball of lightning at the squirming mass of demon dickheads on the floor. I've smelled a lot of nasty shit in my life, but nothing quite so foul as fried demon on old shag carpet. I'm not sure if it was the sulfurous stench of demon flesh or the horrific stink of polyester fibers, but that was the grossest thing I've ever smelled.

Beth came into the front room, covered in soot and demon blood. She leaned against the door into the den and looked at me. "Maybe next time we can try *not* to burn the house down before we run into it?"

"Maybe next time we don't have a next time?" I asked, then looked around. "Did you put the fire out?"

"Yeah. I called to it and channeled it into the ground outside. Scorched some grass and turned the dirt to glass, but at least we aren't going to die."

"You won't die from the fire, witchy-witch, but you will most certainly die tonight." I didn't even turn around. I didn't have to. Whenever somebody shows up and makes a pithy comment at what I really wanted to be the end of a fight, it's usually something bigger and badder than whatever I just fought. So I knew Coach Balomb had decided to join the fight, and shit was about to get real.

CHAPTER FOURTEEN

I t all made sense to me when I pulled into the empty parking lot. Mort was a demon, and country music bars are a special kind of Hell, so it only made sense that he wanted to be there. His motorcycle was parked in the portico by the front door, and the door hung from broken hinges. We were in the right place.

I parked right behind Mort's bike and killed the engine. The four of us got out and made a quick check of our weapons. I ejected the magazine from my Sig and replaced it with bullets dipped in holy water and blessed by a Catholic priest who did things for Harker like bless bullets. Apparently in his line of work, it's a good idea to have people around for stuff like that. Life was so much less complicated when all I had to do was solve murders by humans.

The noise coming from inside told me that someone objected to Mort's presence and was doing something about it, with extreme prejudice. The sound of shattering glass and splintering wood rang through the parking lot. I drew my sidearm and waved the others in around me.

"Okay," I said, "when we get in there, let me take the lead. Mort's familiar with me, so I might be able to talk him down a little, and I am still a cop, so that gives me some authority with whoever else is in there. Watson, you go around and see if there's a back or side door. I don't want any of these guys getting away—"

"Is this because of my leg? Because I assure you, I can hold up my end of a fight." He scowled at me, and I looked down at his leg.

"Shit, sorry, I forgot. Is it better for you to come in the front with me, so you don't have to walk as far?"

The scowl changed to confusion as he tried to process what I was asking. "No, I simply meant that I am capable of handling a frontal assault, that my leg will not prove a liability in the fight."

"Oh," I said. "Sorry, didn't think about that. No, I just need somebody to cover the door, and you're the most lightly armed, so I wanted to put you out of the line of direct fire. But if you—"

"No, that's fine. Thank you, Detective."

"Thank me if we all get out of this alive. Jo, you and Gabby are with me. I'll lead, and you two fan out...god*dammit*." I swore as I heard loud reports from inside and noticed that Gabby was nowhere in our little huddle. "Fuck it, let's go!" I ran into the building where Gabby was laying down a pretty serious field of fire with her two .45 semiautomatics. That's a big bullet, and she was a decent shot, so everything she hit was on its ass seconds later.

The problem was that everything she shot was a demon, and bullets aren't very effective against a lot of Hellspawn. So while Gabby was knocking them down, they were getting right back up again. A few of them stayed down after headshots, so a change in tactics was obviously required.

"Headshots, Gabby!" I shouted. She nodded, then holstered one pistol and switched to a two-handed grip to give herself better control for the difficult task of shooting a moving target in the face before said target kills you. Nothing's ever as easy as it looks on *NCIS*.

I scanned the room for Mort, but all I saw was a shit-ton of demons. Red demons, black demons, demons still in human form, whatever you wanted, apparently they were all redneck day drinkers because this bar was full of them. I heard the scrabble of claws above me and looked up just in time to see a little green bastard with talons on all four limbs and a long tail with a scorpion spike on the end of it drop to the ground right in front of me.

"Duck and roll!" I heard from behind me, and I did just as I was told, diving to my right into an awkward roll that would probably result in some bruises in the morning. If I kept this shit up, I was definitely going back to *krav maga* class. I spun back to the demon just in time to get splashed with black blood and little bits of demon skull as Jo swung that nine-pound hammer like she was Babe Ruth. The demon's head disintegrated into the world's nastiest oatmeal, and she reached out a hand.

"Good reflexes," she said.

"I date Harker," I replied. "Fireballs are a thing that happens in my life," I said by way of explanation. There was a brief moment when nothing was immediately charging us, so I took the opportunity to shout for our quarry.

"MORT!" I yelled. "Cut this shit out and come talk to me!"

"Not until he tells me where to find that murdering son of a sulfur-sucking pitworm!" A voice from the center of a writhing cluster of demonic bodies on the floor bellowed back.

I looked at the others and nodded. "Let's get him out of there." Gabby, Jo, and I walked toward a pile of a dozen demons all struggling and scrambling to get a grip on a piece of Mort's new body and rip it off. It looked like a pileup on the football field, only with more claws and fangs, and about ten percent fewer tattoos.

We got to within a few feet of the squirming mass of demons and raised our weapons. "Get off the interloper, assholes," I said over the barrel of my pistol.

A seven-foot demon with stubby little horns and a tail that looked like the one you get in the naughty devil costumes at Halloween got to his feet and glared down at me. "And what if we don't want to, human?"

"I don't waste much time on what a demon does or doesn't want, fucktard," I said, then I shot him. In the groin. He dropped to his knees, making him a much more reasonably sized foe, and I stepped to the left. Jo took one long stride forward and came around with her great-great-grandfather's hammer again. The rectangular head of the hammer caught the demon right on the hinge of its jaw and knocked its head clean off.

The pile of demons froze, and the room fell silent as the *thump, thump, thump* of the head bouncing along the bar's hardwood floors reached everyone's ears. The body made a wet *thwap* sound as it fell over, and the entire mass of a dozen or more demons separated and came to its feet almost in unison. I took a step back as the three of us stared down at least twelve or fifteen monsters straight out of humanity's worst nightmares.

"Ummm, Mort?" I said. "A little help here?"

Mort's voice, when it came to me from the floor, was weak and thready. "I'm not sure how much help I shall be, Detective. I seem to have more than one dislocated limb."

"Well, shit," I said. I looked at the nearest demon, a skinny little monster with four arms and three-inch claws on the end of four fingers on each hand. He grinned up at me and showed off a pair of fangs that dripped with green ichor. I grinned right back and put two .40 rounds from my Sig into his forehead.

"Who's next?" I looked around at the assembled demons and heard Gabby draw and cock one of her pistols. "We probably can't send you all back to Hell, but which one wants to go first?"

"I would suggest that you believe the human," Mort said as he staggered to his feet. I looked past the mob in front of me to see how he was doing, and he was in surprisingly good shape for a guy who was under a pile of demons less than a minute before.

"You okay, Mort?" I asked.

"I have certainly seen better days, but my need for a new meat-suit is not immediate. I do appreciate your concern, but your coming here was mostly unwarranted. I was merely allowing these boys to vent some of their frustrations before moving on to the real reason for my visit."

"Which is?" Jo asked. She stepped forward to stand at my left elbow, her hammer slung across both shoulders and her hands draped over the handle.

"I need information, and I am of the opinion that Terry has it."

"Who's Terry?" Gabby asked, stepping up on the other side of me.

"I'm Terry," said an Asian man in an expensive suit seated at one of the tables near the stage. I hadn't noticed him before on account of he wasn't immediately trying to eat my spleen, but he certainly had my attention now. He stood up and buttoned his jacket, his long fingers delicate as they handled the sleek fabric. "Ter'i'math," he said, extending a hand to Gabby, then me, then Jo.

We each shook hands with him. I was surprised to feel the strength in his grip, given his slight frame. He was built more like a fencer than a monster, with neat, close-cropped hair, no facial hair, and dark brown eyes. He stepped back to stand between us and Mort.

"What can I do for you, Mort? It's been far too long since I've seen you in my establishment. Would you like a drink?"

"No thank you, Terry. I'm here on business."

"And from the looks of my staff, it might be unpleasant business indeed." He gestured at the gathered demons, most of whom were bleeding from split lips, had eyes swelling shut, and generally looked like they'd been through a war. At least one of the bigger ones was missing an ear, and a solid half dozen of them were not getting up from the floor.

"Sorry about that," Mort said. His tone made it clear that he wasn't the least bit sorry about anything. "I told them I was here to see you, and they said you weren't here. I explained to them that I could see you sitting right there, and I was not leaving until we concluded our business, and things may have become heated from that point." Mort looked a tiny bit chagrined. "I did hope that you would make things easy and simply provide me with the information I desire."

"Which is?" Terry asked.

"The whereabouts of Orobas." If Terry had any reaction to Mort's desire, he didn't show it.

"And why do you need to find Orobas?" Terry asked. I held my breath for the answer. My Sig was still in my hand, and I flexed my fingers on the butt of the gun.

"To kill him. He murdered someone I care about, or his minion did, and since the minion is dead, my vengeance must be visited upon Orobas, and anyone who shelters him." I didn't miss the thinly veiled threat in Mort's words, and neither did Terry. But his only response was slightly raised eyebrows and a mild smile.

"I'm afraid I can't give you that information, Mort. Orobas works for me occasionally, and it would be poor form to just hand him over freely. It also would hinder my operations here."

"What operations are those?" I asked. Terry's gaze swung to me, and we locked eyes. I'd stared down junkies, murderers, gangbangers, vampires, and demons, but something in Terry was just *different*. It was like a whole universe floated behind his eyes, a depth of knowledge and power very different from anything I'd ever gazed upon before.

"And what the hell *are* you?" I asked in a whisper.

"I am an Agent of Chaos," he replied, addressing the last question.

"A what?" Jo asked.

"I care not for good or evil, as those are purely mortal terms, and subjective ones at that. After all, you cannot think that the Morningstar considers himself evil, can you? He certainly has all the characteristics of a hero. A failed relationship with his father, a long trip from home, a valiant failed effort to return home in spectacular fashion, extended torment far from the home he loves, then the inevitable attempt to return home again. Sounds just like a movie, doesn't it? It just needs more Jedi to make a franchise."

"So you don't buy into the whole good and evil thing, I get it. But what is this whole Agent of Chaos thing?" Gabby asked, her eyes flicking from Terry to the demons surrounding us, then back again. She had that look on her face that said she really wanted to get back to shooting things, and I really didn't want to deal with that at the moment.

"I work to upend the status quo, regardless of what it is. If there is peace, I work for war. If there is war, I work for peace. Stasis is death, and boring besides. I am change, I am randomness, I am..."

"You are droning on, Terry," Mort interrupted. I couldn't hide the chuckle, just like Terry couldn't hide the scowl that crossed his face for the briefest of seconds before flashing away.

"My apologies, Mort. As I was saying, I can't give you Orobas's whereabouts so you can kill him because he is useful to me alive. Have a nice day." He turned to walk back to his table, apparently done with us.

He stopped short at the sight of a slim man in a trench coat sitting at his table sipping a beer. "Sorry about the drink, friend. Proselytizing makes me thirsty," Watson said as he stood up. "But you can have your chair." He waved to the seat with a little bow.

"You come into my place of business uninvited and drink my beer? You are a brazen one, human. Tell me, how would you like to learn to walk with *two* metal limbs?" Terry's hands were glowing with power, and I could hear the fury in his voice even if his back was to me.

I raised my pistol and pointed it at the back of his head. Gabby did the same. "That would be a mistake, friend. Two rounds in the back of your head might not kill you, but it would fuck up that snazzy haircut you're sporting," I said as I pulled back the hammer on my Sig.

Terry raised his hands and turned back to me. The purple glow around his hands was matched by one coming from his eyes, and the anger on his face was unmistakable. I had pissed off an Agent of Chaos in his living room. I used to think being around Harker made my life more dangerous. Now I was seeing the kind of trouble I could get into when he was gone.

CHAPTER FIFTEEN

I didn't turn around. I didn't need to. After enough decades, and enough fights, it just wasn't necessary anymore. "Coach Balomb, I presume?" I asked, still looking at the remains of the electrocuted demons on the living room floor. If this place was a rental, nobody was getting a security deposit back after tonight.

"And you are Harold Quinn, or should I just call you Quincy Harker? Would you prefer Reaper? I hear that's something you've answered to in the past."

Now I turned around. I was incognito, or at least I was supposed to be. So how did this fuckwad of a life-sucking demon in Dipshit, Ohio, know who I was? I looked him up and down. He wasn't anyone I'd fought before, at least not in his natural form.

Human suits were apparently optional at Casa Balomb because this assclown wasn't doing anything to hide his demonic nature, either. He stood a little over six feet tall, with six-inch curved horns protruding from his gleaming crimson skull. His face was shaped more like a human than the other demons, but his lower jaw stuck out, and a pair of wicked tusks protruded up and rested against his cheeks.

His torso was covered in black and red scales, making a shimmering suit of armor that I was glad I wouldn't have to try to stick a sword through, but which certainly made my pistol useless. He wore jeans, but no shoes, and his feet had the cloven hooves of the upper-level demonic horde. He wasn't an

Archduke or anything like that, I would have felt the power in him then, but he wasn't going to go down to a lightning bolt, either.

"You have me at a disadvantage, then, demon. You know who I really am, but I have no idea of your name." I kept it cool, drawing in my will so I would have enough power at the ready to react to whatever he threw at me.

"You may call me Balomik. I am Ruler of the Second Circle, Master of Lust and Tempter of Mortals." He threw his arms open wide and black bat wings sprouted from his back, filling the room and knocking over a chair.

"Really?" I asked, folding my arms over my chest. "Does Asmodeus know about this? I doubt he'd take the demotion kindly."

Balomik looked startled, like I'd called him out on something huge. Which I had. Kings of Hell don't take lightly to lower-rung demons laying claim to their territory, and Asmodeus was a particularly jealous dude. Probably had something to do with being the *actual* King of the Second Circle and the Master of Lust. Kinda goes hand-in-hand with jealousy.

"I mean, if you think he wouldn't mind, we can call him up. I'm sure if you're really the boss, you wouldn't have any trouble controlling a wimpy little piece of shit like Asmodeus." I whipped out my pocketknife and sliced open my thumb, then used the blood to draw a hasty, but slightly incomplete, circle around myself. Then I called up my will and started the ritual to summon a demon.

Balomik's eyes went wide before the third word of Latin passed my lips, and he charged me. I sidestepped his bull-rush, then pressed my thumb to the floor as he crossed the line of my circle. I poured my will into the ring of my blood, snapping the containment spell into being and trapping the demon inside.

"You bastard!" Balomik shrieked as his head crashed into the magical barrier. "Set me free this instant or I will tear your soul to shreds!"

"I think that might be a bad idea for me, Bally. I'd probably be in way better shape if I just kept you trapped in this circle until Beth here calls the local Catholic priest and he jumps on his hotline to the Vatican and we get a fuckton of exorcists down here. How long do you think it will take them to get here? Six hours? Maybe four if they've got a helicopter nearby. And I bet they *always* have a helicopter nearby. You know The Church, they always have the coolest toys."

"What do you want, Harker?"

"What's the most valuable thing in the world, Bally? I want information."

"Nothing's free, Harker. I'll tell you anything you want to know, but I'm going to want my freedom in exchange."

"Not a problem," I said, ignoring the bulging eyes on my current partner.

"What the hell are you saying, Harker?" Beth yelled. "There is no way I'm letting you set this demon loose! He killed my brother, and he's going back to Hell for it."

"We don't know that," I said.

"Oh, no, she's right," Balomik interjected. "I killed her brother. Freddy Kirkland, right? He was good. A lot of power in that little warlock. Tasty morsel. I skimmed a little cream off the top before I distilled his essence into the 'supplements' we gave the football team. Yummy."

"Yeah, what's that all about?" I asked. "I get killing Talents, and I even understand sucking the magic from their souls and selling it, or using it to power up your meat-suits, or whatever. But making the high school football team better? That seems a little altruistic for your kind."

"Let's not be speciesist, Quincy. I can call you Quincy, can't I? After all, we're buds now, right?"

"I don't give a shit what you call me, assclown. Just answer all my questions and I'll think about not telling Asmodeus that you've been claiming his crown."

"Fine," he grumped. I was afraid for a minute that he was going to sulk and I wouldn't get anything else out of him. But he went on. "Jazzing up the football team wasn't my idea. I was just going to kill the Talents, bottle their essence, and sell it on the black market. I know a guy in Cincinnati that moves a lot of that type of product."

"But..." I prodded.

"But when I called up Jerry over there—" He pointed to one of the charred demons lying on the floor. "His name is Jeraxil, by the way. In case you care about the names of the men and women you sent fleeing back to Hell in unspeakable agony."

"I don't." I didn't. Really. Couldn't possibly give less fucks about the well-being of any of the demons I've banished, battered, mutilated, or actually destroyed over the years. I feel more remorse about killing a black widow in Luke's garage. The spider at least isn't malevolent; it's just hanging around spinning webs in the wrong places. Demons are universally bad mother-fuckers at heart, and every one of them would rather fuck you over than look at you.

"I didn't expect you to," Bally continued. "So Jerry comes up with the idea of using a winning football team to rouse school spirit and get people distracted from the missing kids. He's a Demi-lord of Deception, really good at that kind of thing. So I went with it, and we started giving the team 'nutri-tional supplements.' All the kids that took them turned into super-athletes almost overnight. And suddenly nobody was paying attention to a bunch of missing nerds and malcontents."

"My brother wasn't a malcontent!" Beth snarled.

"No, that one was a huge nerd. Right down to his Deadpool boxers, sweetie. But he had a ton of magical energy. He singlehandedly won us that game against Martin Luther King Jr. High."

"What's the end game?" I asked.

"Don't have one, really," Bally said with a shrug. I gave him a sharp look, and he raised his hands in protest. "I'm a *demon*, you dipshit. I saw a chance to fuck with some humans, and I took it. One day I was in Hell, working like a dog, then this portal opens up and it's all blue skies and buckeyes, so I stepped through. And here I am. Look, all I know is I'm not in Hell poking some cheating husband in the balls with a pitchfork, and I don't plan to go back. So let me out of here and I'll vanish into the wilds of America. I hear Nebraska is nice this time of year."

Whatever. This asshole was never going to get near a cornfield if I had anything to say about it, and I did. While it's not a good idea to lie to monsters as a general rule, you could bend the fuck out of that rule if you planned on killing or banishing the monster in the immediate future. And since I really hoped I wouldn't run into Bally after I died, all I needed to do was get him off this plane of existence to take care of him.

"So you just wandered into town with a plan to kill off all the Talented humans?"

"Not exactly. I wandered into town and decided to kill *all* the humans. But Jerry got here before I did, and he spotted all the Talents in town. When me and the rest of the boys showed up, Jerry came up with the plan."

"And you just did what Jerry said without caring who was in charge?" That didn't fit with the hierarchy-obsessed demons I'd known in the past.

"I didn't care who was the boss then and don't care now. Jerry and me got along good, and he let me be the human with the whistle. He got to make his nasty little plans, and I got to eat humans. Where I come from, we call that a win-win."

Time for the million-dollar question. "Okay, asshat. One more bit of information, and you can get out of that circle. Who sent you here?"

"No idea." I stared at him, not believing a word of it. "Look, somebody opened a door out of Hell, and I took a fucking stroll, alright? I don't know why, and I don't know who. And frankly, I don't give a fuck."

"So all this shit has nothing to do with what's been going on in Charlotte? Or Orobas?" On the one hand, it meant that not every demon in the world was looking for me. On the other hand, it meant that somebody was just randomly setting demons loose on Earth. The bad in that scenario far outweighed the good.

"Not everything revolves around you, Quincy my boy," the smug prick said with a grin.

"No, sometimes things are all about other people. And this is all about my baby brother, you fucking asshole." Beth's voice came from right behind my left elbow, and I turned to her just in time to watch her throw a fistful of something white at Bally.

Salt. *Fuck.* Nothing disrupts magic like salt. This was gonna hurt.

My mouth fell open as the magical barrier I had trapped the demon in flashed into view for a second, then popped like a soap bubble. I turned back when I felt something scrabbling at my jacket and stepped back as Beth reached under my arm and yanked my pistol free.

"What the fuck are you doing?" I asked, my head swiveling from a suddenly free demon to an enraged English teacher.

"What you obviously don't have the balls to do. I'm killing this son of a bitch." She raised my Glock in a two-handed grip and squeezed off six rounds at Balomik. The shots rang out, making my ears ring in the enclosed space, and three holes appeared in the demon's chest.

But that's all. Just three little holes, roughly nine millimeters in diameter. No blood, no falling down, and certainly no dead demon on the floor. Balomik looked down at his chest, then looked back at Beth and grinned.

"Ouch," he said, then took two steps forward and plunged his hand into the woman's chest. Her eyes went wide as the demon turned his hand sideways, then yanked it back out, taking three ribs, a huge chunk of flesh, and Beth Kirkland's heart with it. The demon looked me in the eye, brought the still-beating heart to its mouth, and bit a chunk out of the muscle, letting Beth's lifeblood pour down his chin and drip onto the floor.

"Delicious," the demon said with a smile as Beth collapsed to the floor, dead before she even started to fall. "I love it when the meat is fresh."

"*In the name of—*" My incantation was cut off short as Balomik backhanded me into a china cabinet. Dishes and silverware clattered to the floor around me as I slid down in a heap of shattered glass and stoneware.

Balomik stood over me, munching on the dead teacher's heart like he was eating an apple. I shook my head to clear the stars from my vision and tried to rise, only to find a cloven hoof planted square in the center of my chest.

"Stay," the demon said. "Let me be very clear, Quincy Harker. I know you planned to double-cross me and send me back to the Pits. But I left something out of my little origin story. When I first got to Lockton, I got a message. It showed up on my doorstep one day. Just a plain white envelope with a typed letter inside. The letter said, 'No one touches the Reaper.' I don't know who sent it, but they had enough juice to let me out of Hell and keep tabs on me through my best magical disguises.

"So you get to live, Quincy Harker. But so do I. And I don't just get to live in Hell, I get to live right here on Earth. You can chase me, and you can maybe even catch me. But you can't chase me and hunt down your old pal Orobas, who I hear has something big planned *in Atlanta* in a couple weeks. So you make the call, Reaper. Let a low-level demon loose on Middle America, or let Orobas do whatever he wants in the biggest city in the Southeast. Take your time. Think it over."

I didn't miss the clue. Orobas was in Atlanta, or he would be soon. I looked up at the demon, weighing my options. I had time. He was going to terrorize Middle America for a while, but I'd eventually chase him down. After all, I'm Quincy Harker, it's what I do.

I nodded at him. "You've got a deal, dickhead. You get away, today. But I'll find you again. And when that happens, it'll be your heart served for dinner." I didn't know who in the world would eat a demon's heart, but it was still a good line.

Balomik smiled down at me. "I look forward to our next meeting, Quincy Harker." Then he pulled his cloven foot off my chest and snapped a kick upward into my chin, slamming my head into the remains of the wooden cabinet I was tangled in. My vision went all starry, and the last thing I heard before I passed out was the clip-clop of hooves on the front sidewalk and the taunting laugh of a very self-satisfied demon.

CHAPTER SIXTEEN

S o there I was, in the middle of a country bar, staring down an Agent of Chaos, whatever that really was, with a gun pointed at his head to keep him from de-limbing my newfound partner in the magical Super Friends.

Some days I really hate my life.

Terry, the neatly groomed aforementioned Agent of Chaos, stared at me for an interminable moment, then broke out into a laugh. I had a lot of ideas in my head about the way I was going to die, most of them involving alternately a junkie in a liquor store holdup or a nursing home out of my mind with dementia, but none of them ever included a magical Asian man in an expensive suit laughing in my face as he killed me.

"You are one hilarious human," Terry said.

"I'm glad I amuse you," I said, working to keep my gun steady. Holding a gun on somebody looks really easy in the movies, but after the first minute, keeping your arms extended with a couple of pounds of plastic, metal, and ammunition in your hands is exhausting.

The purple glow around his hands winked out and Terry glanced over his shoulder at Watson. "You should thank your friend, Dr. Watson. She just saved your life."

"So you're not going to kill Watson," I said. "That's good. I don't know how to kill Chaos Agents, or whatever you call yourself, but if you'd made meat out of my lawyer, I would have been honor-bound to try."

"Well, good," Terry replied. "That saves all of us disappointment and annoyance. You would have been disappointed because I can't be killed, and I would have been annoyed because getting blood out of hardwoods is annoying."

I looked over at the splattered brains of the demon I'd shot in the face earlier. "Sorry about that, then."

"Well, we all have our off days, Detective. Now would you all please leave so I can clean my club before we have to open?"

"No," Mort said. "I'm not leaving without Oro's location. I'm sorry, Terry, but he has to pay for what he did to me."

"And I'm sorry, Mort, but Orobas is too useful to me. He sows chaos in his wake like a little demonic Johnny Appleseed, and that's very valuable to me. Unless..." Terry's face took on a thoughtful expression. "No, you wouldn't do that. Not even for revenge."

"Do what?" Mort asked. "I'm willing to do almost anything."

"But only almost," Terry said.

"Well, even demons have our limits. What did you have in mind?" Mort asked.

"Take Orobas's place."

"What?"

"Become my new agent. Work for Chaos. Sow discord, foment revolution, spread disinformation, convince terrible candidates to run for high elected office, that kind of thing." Terry walked back over to his table and took a sip from his drink. The same one Watson had been drinking from a few minutes before. I guess if you can't die to a bullet in the brain, germs aren't exactly a concern either. He smiled at Mort. "Come on, Mortivoid. It'll be fun. It'll at least be interesting."

"What would the Morningstar have to say about that?" Mort asked. "I'm intrigued, but Lucifer still scares the shit out of me."

"As well he should," Terry said. "But we have an arrangement. As long as you don't start rescuing kittens from trees, Lucifer is fine with his people working for me. After all, you lot are the original unruly children, aren't you?"

Mort fell silent for a moment, seeming to consider the idea before finally nodding. "You're not wrong, Terry. We did sort of invent the rebellious teenager stereotype. Fine, give me Oro's location, and as soon as I have things sorted with that bastard to my satisfaction, I'll add sower of chaos to my list of duties and accomplishments."

Terry stepped closer to Mort and held his hand out, pressing it to his borrowed forehead. "Mortivoid, demon of the Pit, do you so solemnly swear to sow discord where there is none, bring war to the peaceful, peace to the contentious, and become the true random element in every situation?"

"Fuck you, I do what I want," Mort replied, and instead of a refusal, that seemed to be the acceptance of the pledge to chaos because the demon's body was bathed in that same purple light, only this time it strobed with random intensity and time, pulsing crazily as it washed over Mort, eventually spilling out his eyes, nose, and ears like chaos was simply pouring out of him.

"Your term of employment begins once you have extracted your revenge from Orobas. Until then, you are still wholly Lucifer's man. Once you come into my employ, however, the Dawnbringer shall have to share dominion over your wretched soul," Terry said. The purple lightshow went dark, and I blinked to get the afterimage out of my vision. I felt like I'd been to a Prince concert, without the amazing guitar solos.

Mort looked at his new boss and said, "Okay, now that's done. Where's the bastard that killed my daughter?"

"Oh, that," Terry said. "Oro is at the airport. He's flying out of here in an hour. Said something about Charlotte losing its luster." Mort didn't say a word, just turned and hauled ass out of the bar. Seconds later, I heard his motorcycle roar to life.

I sighed. "Great, now we get to chase a demon and probably a bunch of hellspawn Homeland Security agents through airport security. I'm totally going to end up on a no-fly list after this."

On the way to the door, I called Captain Herr to fill him in on what was up. "Captain, I've got a lead on—"

He cut me off. "Bad news, Flynn."

"What?"

"You need to come in to the station."

"Captain, I've got a hot lead on the asshole that's behind—"

"Did I stutter, Detective?" He cut me off again.

"No sir, but...sir, what's going on?"

"I will discuss this with you *back at the station, where you are coming right now. I will expect you to wrap up that arrest and be back here within the hour.* Is that understood, Detective?" I got it. There was someone there with him, and if I showed my face at the station, I was screwed. He was probably under orders from someone to take my badge and gun. But I had an hour, maybe two if he could stall, before they put out an APB for me and considered me a fugitive.

"Yes, sir. I understand. I'm all the way down in Pineville near the mall, and you know what 485 is like in the afternoon, so it might be more like an hour and a half or two hours before I get there."

"Fine, two hours," he said. "But if you aren't here by shift change, Detective, it'll be your ass." He hung up, and I walked faster.

"What was that all about?" Jo asked.

"Somebody's pressuring my captain to get me off the case, or arrest me, or suspend me, or something. I have two hours before I'm out of any kind of official juice. Good thing the airport's just a couple minutes from here because I'm now on a serious clock."

———

I pulled into the airport and glanced over at Jo, who was staring at her cell. "Any idea where we're going?"

"Just got a text from Sparkles. Looks like Buprof used his Homeland credentials to request special clearance for a flight from Charlotte to Atlanta on a private jet. The hangar is over by the aviation museum."

"I got it," I said, turning right and heading that way. "How are we going to know when we find the right place?"

"I think the sight of burning automobiles may be a sign that demons are trying to cover their tracks," Watson said from the back seat.

I looked around and saw pillars of smoke off to the left. "Nobody likes a smartass, Watson," I said, turning the car in the direction of the smoke. We pulled up in front of Mona Lisa Air, a small charter jet company. A small Lear Jet was pulling out of the hangar as I parked the car and jumped out.

"Watson, go to the office and tell the tower there's a terrorist on that plane and he's going to fly it into the White House!" I sprinted in the direction of the plane, but the whine of a bullet and the flat crack of a revolver sent me diving behind the nearest car. Watson peeled out toward the tower in my car, and I heard a couple of bullets smack into the pavement behind him as he went.

"Hello, Detective," Buprof's voice rang out across the tarmac. "You should have run with your boyfriend. Now you're going to die, just like he will when I catch up to him."

"I'm not dead yet, you hellspawn son of a bitch!" I yelled back at him. I looked over at my car, where Gabby and Jo were hiding behind the engine block. Jo's hammer wasn't going to do much good at a distance, but I had high hopes for Gabby's marksmanship. She crawled on the ground along the side of the car to the back, then took up a position by the back wheel on her belly, giving her a decent vantage point to light up Buprof. All I had to do was get him to poke his head up.

So I stood up, hoping my battered Kevlar vest still had plenty of stopping power, and that Buprof wasn't going to try to manage a headshot from fifty yards. He popped up from behind a toolbox in the hangar, and sure enough, the bastard squeezed off three rounds, all of them *spang*-ing off the car in front of me. He was trying for body shots, good. I could probably live through one of those.

Gabby opened up on Buprof the second he was visible, but all her shots either went wide or ricocheted off the toolbox. So much for counting on the sniper skills of a psychopath. Out of the corner of my eye, I saw Jo running in a crouch from her car toward the hangar, weaving from car to fuel truck to a random prop plane to a black SUV near the hangar doors.

I stuck my head out from the front bumper and let loose a few more random shots at the last place I saw Buprof. There was no return fire, just a high-pitched whine of a jet engine spinning up. *Fuck.*

"The plane just started up!" I yelled to Gabby.

"What do you want me to do about that?" she asked.

"I don't know, shoot something!" I poked my head back up above the hood, only to be met with a hail of bullets. I dove for cover, then peeked around a tire to see if I could spot where he was shooting from.

"He's at your ten o'clock," Gabby said from my shoulder. "And moving left. He's trying to get enough of an angle on us to shoot around the car."

"We should make sure that doesn't happen," I said. "Any ideas?"

"I thought you said I was a psycho."

"I did. Still think you're nuts. But right now, you're the psycho that's been in more shootouts than me."

"Good point. Okay, when I give the signal, run like hell away from the car."

"Which direction?" I asked.

"It won't matter." Gabby smiled at me, and I felt strangely like I just had a bonding moment with Charles Manson. She laid down on the asphalt and slid under the car for a few seconds, then scooted back out, trailing a small plastic battery holder with two wires running from it. She pulled a battery out of her pocket and pressed one end of it into the holder, making very sure not to let the other end touch the other contact and complete the circuit.

"Gabby, are you going to blow up this car?" I asked.

"I sure hope so," she said. "Now shut up and let me listen." She didn't have to listen for long. I popped up into Buprof's view, then dropped straight down again. He fired half a dozen shots at where my head was, but I was long gone.

"Run!" Gabby said, then slammed the battery home. A loud beep came from under the car, and we sprinted away from the vehicle, trying to use the car to shield us from Buprof's view. That part didn't work for shit because he opened up on us before I took my second step.

Gabby's bomb, however, worked just fine. We each covered about twenty yards before a loud *WHOMP* came from under the car, and it flew several feet into the air before crashing to the ground engulfed in flames. The burning wreckage gave us a few seconds of distraction to find cover, and I even had a couple seconds to look for Buprof and put a few ounces of lead in his general direction. Nothing hit the asshole, of course, but I reminded him that I was there.

Until the plane pulled out of the hangar and made all of us completely irrelevant. The sleek little private jet rolled onto the tarmac, and priorities shifted in a big way. The door to the plane was still open, and I caught glimpses of motion inside, then Mort's body came flying out to crash onto the asphalt. He rolled over two or three times, then came to his knees, beating at the pavement with his fists.

"OROBAS!" Mort screamed, and the pain and fury in his voice was terrible to behold.

"Sorry to shoot and run, Flynn, but dear old dad and I have somewhere much more interesting to be," Buprof shouted. He darted out from behind the sedan he was hiding behind and hauled ass toward the accelerating aircraft. He made it to within about ten yards of the plane before something whirled out at him from his right, hit him around the knees, and he went down like a sack of really ugly potatoes.

Jo ran to the downed Deputy Director's side, and brass knuckles flashed in the sun as she knocked him unconscious. Gabby and I ran over to her, our pistols trained on the fallen Cambion. There was no point; he was out cold. I holstered my weapon and looked over at Jo, who had retrieved her hammer and stood over Buprof with a little smile on her face.

"Fond memories?" I asked.

Jo looked up at me and a shadow flickered over her face. "Not really. Okay, not at all. I hate demons, and all demonspawn. It's a long story." I decided it was definitely one I wanted to hear, but this wasn't the time.

We turned and watched as the plane taxied onto the runway and took off, with Orobas and our best lead to the investigation locked safely aboard. I heard a car pull up behind us and turned to see Watson stepping out of my car.

"I couldn't stop the plane, I'm sorry." He sounded about as beaten down as I felt.

"You tried. We couldn't stop him, either. But we got a consolation prize." I pointed down at the unconscious demonspawn. "Maybe he can tell us where the plane was going."

"Oh, I can tell you that," Watson said. "I couldn't stop it from taking off, but I got the flight manifest and the owner of record from the airport. The plane belongs to one Reginald Barton, a tech billionaire and art speculator from Atlanta. It's headed home."

"So Orobas is headed to Atlanta?" I asked.

"It certainly appears so," Watson concurred.

"Well done, old chap!" I said in my worst British accent. He actually winced.

"Please don't ever call me that again," Watson said, but there was a little smile on his face that belied his grumpy tone.

"So we're going to Atlanta to stop Orobas once and for all?" Gabby said. "Good deal. I love Atlanta. Great food, good shopping, plenty of nasty things to shoot. It's my kind of town."

I looked at her. "Have you ever considered therapy? Like, lots of it?"

"Nah. I'm crazy, but it's a really fun crazy. Kinda like Harley Quinn, without the abusive relationship. So when do we leave? I'm ready to head to the ATL and kick some demon ass!"

A groggy Buprof chuckled from the ground at our feet. "Foolish bitch, Daddy dearest will eat your soul for breakfast, then he will take dominion over this worthless plane of existence!"

"Oops, sorry about that," Jo said, standing above Buprof at his ribcage.

"Sorry about what, you worthless piece of human waste."

"This," Jo said, then dropped her hammer squarely on the half-demon's crotch. He doubled over and rolled around on the pavement in agony, spewing out a steady stream of profanity as Watson zip-tied his wrists together and dumped him into the trunk of my car.

"Now what?" Jo asked. "It's a good four hours to Atlanta, and we can't leave until it gets dark. So what do we do until then?"

"We take Director Buprof back to the condos and let Mort and Luke take turns ripping off limps. Sound like a plan?" I looked at the others.

"At least a decent way to waste a couple hours," Gabby said, then hopped into the back seat.

We gathered up Mort and drove off into the welcome sunset, with a half-demon in the trunk and a loose idea of a destination in mind. This was going to be the strangest road trip in history.

EPILOGUE

"**H**arker, you sure know how to make a goddamn mess." The voice was low, gravelly, and familiar. Way too familiar. And nothing like what I imagined either Rebecca Romijn or Heidi Klum sounded like, so I guess my very pleasant dream of pillow fights and back rubs was over.

I didn't open my eyes. My head felt like someone had pried the top off, dropped a grenade inside, and slammed the lid shut again. "Hello, Adam. What are you doing here?"

"Fetching you. It's time to come in."

"Is the heat off already? It's only been a few days."

"Nah, you're still radioactive as hell. But Luke needs you more than you need to lay low. It's time to roll out and end this shit. And for that, they need their big guns."

Adam wasn't kidding when he referred to himself as one of the big guns. He was honestly one of the biggest dudes I'd ever seen, and was as strong as a bull elephant besides. "Sounds good. The boss got away, but he told me where Orobas was headed. Balomik has his own shit to answer for, but that's going to have to wait for another day."

"Shit to answer for? Like the pretty woman with her heart ripped out lying on the scorched carpet surrounded by demon carcasses?"

"Well, when you put it like that..." I said. Adam looked around, and I heard the sirens. "Fuck. We gotta go." I struggled to my feet, not helped by the mountain of ugly china and dishwater scattered around me. I kept sliding on plates and Adam finally had to pick me up and deposit me on my feet beside him.

The giant bent over, then straightened up and handed me my pistol. Apparently I'd dropped it when I got my ass beat by the demon. "Yeah, wouldn't do to have you involved in *two* mysterious murders and destroyed crime scenes, would it?"

"You're a regular laugh riot, Adam."

"Thanks, I've been working on new material." Part of the problem in dealing with someone who isn't exactly human is that you never know when they're joking or not. Some of the wiring is just off enough that their sense of humor doesn't exactly match the norm.

"You got a car?" I asked. My pickup was parked a few blocks away, and walking even that far with my swimming head and the police presence that was about to be swarming this place was right out.

"Yeah."

"Good. The demon told me before he knocked me out that Orobas is in Atlanta, or he will be soon."

"That fits with what I've got. Luke called me a couple hours ago to come get you. They lost Orobas at the airport, but he's on a charter to Atlanta right now. They're already on their way down there."

"Sounds good. Let's roll." We picked our way through the wreckage of the house out to a massive Hummer idling by the street.

"This thing's your ride?" I asked. "Could you maybe have gone for the inconspicuous option?"

"Harker, you might have missed the fact that I'm over seven feet tall and am carrying more muscle mass than the Bengals' offensive line. Inconspicuous is not a word that is often associated with me."

"Good point. I suppose you're driving?"

"You're damn skippy I'm driving. I've ridden with you before, Harker. I'm not in a hurry to take my life in my hands again."

"That's something I've always meant to ask you. Can you die?"

"Haven't found anything that can kill me yet. Bullets won't do it, old age won't do it, knives won't do it. And as a bunch of peasants learned to their despair a long damn time ago, fire and pitchforks sure as hell won't do it. Now let's go meet up with the rest of the crew and kill this fucking demon."

"Sounds good, pal." I followed the giant out to the Hummer and me and Frankenstein's monster rode off to Atlanta on a demon hunt.

PART IV
HEAVEN CAN WAIT

CHAPTER ONE

"Get out, I have to go find a parking spot." Adam's gravelly voice shook me from my doze as he pulled into the packed parking lot in Little Five Points. I looked out the window, erasing the fog from my brain as I processed that we had made it to Atlanta intact.

"Where the hell do you think you're going to find a place to put this thing in Little Five in the middle of the afternoon?" I asked, rubbing sleep from my eyes. The parking lot had a few spaces, but they looked tight for normal cars, much less Adam's Hummer.

"I know a guy. I'll meet you inside in ten minutes. They've got a big table. I told Jack to save us seats." I never heard him make a call. I must have been out cold. But that made sense. We'd been driving all night, leaving Lockton, Ohio, a little before midnight. With stops for gas and bathrooms, and one longer break at a truck stop where I showered off the worst of the blood and smoke covering me from my fight with a band of demons masquerading as high school football coaches, it took the better part of twelve hours to get to the middle of Atlanta.

I made it almost to Knoxville before I crashed hard, the last remaining bits of energy, excitement, and abject horror from the night's festivities running out of me about an hour after sunup. I finally gave in to my exhaustion, leaned the seat back, and slept for a few hours. I wasn't too worried about Adam falling asleep at the wheel, since I'd never known him to sleep. I'd never asked, it seemed rude somehow, but I honestly didn't know if the big man *could* sleep. There were a lot of things I didn't really know about Adam, despite having known him for as long as I could remember.

Adam had been a fixture in my life since my childhood, attending a few family functions now and then with Luke. My uncle often referred to Adam as my "cousin," but it didn't take me too long to realize that he was no more my cousin than Luke was my "uncle."

But when your parents are Jonathan Harker and Mina Murray, you don't question the vagaries of your family tree. You just say hi to whatever strange "uncle" or "cousin" might be visiting and get on about your business.

So, I commenced to getting on about my business. I restored the passenger seat to its upright and locked position, opened the door, and slid down from the giant vehicle onto the damp asphalt. It was a cool, drizzly afternoon, and Atlanta's artsy district seemed to be just waking up. The bookstore and drug store both looked almost deserted from where I stood, but if there's going to be one place in Little Five Points that will always be hopping, it's The Vortex.

The Vortex is a local landmark, the kind of place that a city's residents talk about with pride no matter if they've ever darkened the doors or not. Starting out in the 90s, the bar and burger joint boasts good food, cold beer, funky-ass wait staff, and serious attitude. In other words, it was my kind of joint. I walked through the giant skull façade over the front door and stepped into the dimly-lit joint. Music blared, rock and roll posters covered every surface, and the smells coming from the kitchen reminded me that Adam doesn't eat, and doesn't let anybody else eat in his car, so the food options on our trip had been limited to whatever I could shovel into my face while he was refueling his battle wagon.

A tiny hostess with more tattoos than I had teeth stood by the door. She wore a laughing skull t-shirt, a pair of cut-off jeans, and black Chuck Taylor high-tops. A silver ring winked at me from one eyebrow, and she looked me up and down, appraising the new arrival, before finally speaking.

"You must be the guy they're waiting on," she said after a few seconds. "Where's your friend?"

"Parking the car," I replied. "And what do you mean I must be the guy?"

"Your friends are over there." She jerked a thumb over one shoulder to a long table where Detective Rebecca Gail Flynn, Gabby Van Helsing, and a bunch of people I'd never met face-to-face sat around a laptop. "They told me to be on the lookout for a giant and a dude that looked like a mass murderer. You're nowhere close to being a giant, but I wouldn't be surprised if you left a pretty high body count in your wake." She gave me a grin and reached under the hostess stand for a couple menus and some rolled silverware.

"Follow me." She turned and walked toward the table.

I did, thinking she was way more accurate than she wanted to know. There was a trail of bodies behind me a mile long and twice as wide, and I felt pretty sure that trail was going to get nothing but longer before I was through with Atlanta.

You gonna stare at that screen or you gonna get up and give me a hug? I asked across the mental link I shared with Flynn. I saw her straighten up in her chair, then stand up like a shot and turn around, her head whipping side to side, tossing brown curls around her face as she looked for me.

I stood ten feet away, drinking in the sight of her. It had only been a few weeks since we were last together, but it felt like ten years. The bond we shared was more than just partners, or boyfriend/girlfriend, or whatever we were. When I shared my blood with her to save her life a year ago, she got inside my head. Literally. Distance weakened the connection, so when I was in Ohio and she was in North Carolina, it felt like a part of myself was missing. A part that just came rushing back all at once when our eyes met.

She was gorgeous, there was no question about that. This woman, who I had looked out for since she was a little girl, had grown into a beauty. And that beautiful woman took three steps across the restaurant floor, wrapped her arms around my neck, and kissed me like I haven't been kissed in a very long time. I kissed her back with everything I had and wrapped my hands around her trim waist. I felt her suck in a breath, and I pulled back.

Her dark brown eyes squinted in pain, and her mocha skin was suddenly a little pale.

"What's wrong?" I asked, then I remembered. Her side. That fucking demon back in Charlotte stabbed her while I was inside dealing with Smith. "Shit, I'm sorry. Are you okay?"

"I'm good, I'm good." She smiled up at me. "No, seriously, I'm good. You just pulled me in when you kissed me and my side pressed up against... what the hell is that, anyway?" She pointed at my side with a little grin.

I looked down at the offending hardware, a short gladius I had hanging from my belt. I'd picked it up from a stash of weapons in Adam's car when a couple of bikers got a little more interested in the Hummer at a gas station than I was comfortable with, then forgot to take it off.

"Sorry, I must have poked you with my giant rigid sword," I said with a lopsided grin.

"In your dreams, Romeo," Flynn said, slapping me on the chest. "It's good to see you again, Harker."

"Good to be seen, Detective." We were both using that formal tone that lovers use when they're teasing each other in front of people. It's really cute to the lovers, but often less so to the spectators.

"Oh for God's sake, do you two need a moment? I'm sure it won't be the first time the lavatories in this place have been used for purposes God never intended, but you're putting the rest of us off our lunch," a skinny British guy at the end of the table protested.

"Shut up, Jack, you're just mad nobody's ever greeted you with that much enthusiasm," said the woman next to him. She was an athletic woman in a leather jacket with an easy grin and black hair pulled back into a tight ponytail.

I walked over to the table and pulled out one of the empty chairs. I looked around the table and gave a little wave. "So… I'm Quincy Harker. I guess you all know that. Who is everybody? Everybody that I haven't either fought beside or against, that is. I assume you're Jack Watson?" I said to the British guy.

"What gave it away? My dashing good looks, the obvious intellectual superiority to everyone in the room—"

"The fact that you're the only guy at the table he didn't grow up with?" the mystery woman said. She leaned over the table and extended a hand. "Ignore Jack, we all do. I'm Jo Henry. I hit things."

"With a big damn hammer," Gabriella Van Helsing added. My first meeting with Gabby wasn't the most festive occasion I'd ever experienced, but we settled into a tentative truce by the time that case finished up. I hadn't known Luke recruited her into the Shadow Council until I found out she was in Charlotte while I was on the run. I still wasn't sure how I felt about her. Our last meeting had left me thinking she might be a little more insane than my normal partners.

"Good to meet you, Jo. And Jack. And good to see you again, Gabriella," I said. "I assume Luke is stashed somewhere lightproof?"

"I am indeed safely ensconced in a room at the Westin downtown. While blacking out the windows was an unusual request, I doubt it was the strangest thing the hotel has been asked to do for a guest." Luke's voice came from the speakers on the laptop. Video conferencing and ubiquitous Wi-Fi made it a lot easier to keep a vampire in the loop in the modern era.

Luke peered around me. "Where is Adam?"

"Looking for parking," I replied. "Kind of an Olympic sport in Atlanta."

"It wasn't really a problem," Adam's rumbling voice came from behind me. I looked up, a little surprised that someone that damn big could move that quietly.

"Good to see you, Adam," Luke said with a nod. "I believe you know Mr. Watson, and this is Gabby Van Helsing." Luke waved his hands around the screen, and Adam nodded to the new players in turn. Apparently, he knew the Brit, but I knew he spent a lot of time in Europe.

Adam stretched out a hand to Gabriella. "I knew your grandfather," he said. "He was a good man."

Gabby looked confused. "Is there anyone who didn't know Grandpa Abe? Because I'm starting to think I'm the only one on this team with a normal human lifespan."

"I'm one hundred percent human, Gabs, no need to worry about that," Jo said, standing up. She shook hands with Adam. "Joanna Henry. Call me Jo."

"I've heard of your great-grandfather, but we never met. He was reputed to be a man of great character. As was yours, Mr. Watson," he said to Jack.

"Thank you, Mr.... I'm sorry, I don't believe I caught your last name?" Watson said.

Adam looked at me, and I shrugged. If the folks around the table hadn't figured it out yet, it wasn't on me to tell tales. He turned his gaze to Luke, who, likewise, gave him no help. "Franks is the name I have used most often in this country recently. That will suffice, I believe."

Watson knit his brow, and I could see Flynn's shoulders shaking as she stifled laughter. She knew exactly what was going on, of course, thanks to our restored mental connection. Jo leaned over and whispered something into Watson's ear, and his head whipped around and up to look back at Adam.

"You're...you're really...*really?*"

"He says while he sits eating wings and Skyping with friggin' Dracula," I said, waving a waitress over. "Adam, grab a seat. I'm gonna get some lunch and maybe a few beers and we can get this party started. Can I get a Laughing Skull and a dozen wings, crispy, with the hottest sauce you've got on the side?" The waitress walked off, and I turned to the table.

"Okay, what's the deal?" I asked. I guess it was mostly directed at Luke, but it was Becks everyone looked to for the answer.

"Alright, I'll start. Orobas is here in Atlanta. Some bajillionaire named Reginald Barton flew him down here on a private jet. We don't know what he's up to, or how he's tied to Barton, but Orobas with a bankroll can't be good. What was going on in Kentucky?" She looked at me with a little grin. She knew damn well I hate Kentucky thanks to some bourbon-induced bad decisions in the 90s.

"Ohio, but close," I replied. "There were demons, and the one in charge knew about Orobas, but from what he said, it sounded like Oro wasn't the lead dog in the team. So, we need to figure out who's pulling the strings and what their endgame is."

"According to Sparkles, Barton is a collector of antiquities, with a specific taste for artifacts thought to have some mystical properties," Jo said, looking up from her phone.

"Sparkles texts now?" I asked.

"I think he does whatever he wants with anything connected to the internet," she replied with a nod.

"Yeah, probably so," I agreed.

"Who is this mysterious Sparkles, and am I ever going to meet him?" Flynn asked.

"Almost certainly not," Luke said, then smoothly changed the subject. "Well, it seems that Barton's taste for magical items explains his interest in this." He picked up a sword and held it up in view of the camera.

"Since when did you get all Ren Faire on us, Luke?" I asked.

"As it appears this sword was what Orobas wanted from the wreckage of my home. I felt that leaving it in the car would be ill-advised," Luke replied.

"I thought Smith was trying to open a portal to Hell to bring all his buddies across and invade the world?" I asked. "I mean, I'm just the dude that shot him in the face, but that's sure what it looked like he was doing from where I was standing."

"That may well have been Agent Smith's goal, but once you thwarted that attempt, it seems that Orobas turned his attention to acquiring this weapon."

"Why?" I asked. "I mean, swords are great if you need to cut off an arm or make a hole in somebody, but I haven't found one that can open a doorway to Hell."

"That doesn't mean there's not one out there, just that we have yet to encounter it," Adam chimed in.

"Aren't you just a ray of fucking sunshine?" I grumbled.

"I am typically considered somewhat dry and sardonic, so no, I would assume that I am not, in fact, a ray of sunshine," Adam replied. I looked over at him, but his face betrayed nothing. I'd worked with Adam for decades, and I could never tell if he was fucking with me or not. Either he had the greatest sense of humor in the world, or absolutely none.

I gave my head a shake and went on. "Okay, so we have the sword, and we know who's partnered up with Orobas down here. How do we plan to fuck up his plans and save the world?" I asked.

"This week," Flynn added.

I looked at her, questioning.

"You left out a bit. It's supposed to be 'how do we save the world *this week?*'"

Luke's face blurred on the laptop, and suddenly we had a split image, with

Luke on half the screen and a unicorn head on the other. The unicorn's mouth started to move as we all stared at the computer.

"Well, you might want to start by killing the demons that are currently climbing the Ferris Wheel outside Centennial Park," the unicorn said.

"Goddammit, Sparkles," I said. "Why can't you just say hello like a normal person?"

CHAPTER TWO

I threw an American Express Black Card at the waitress and told her I'd be back for it later. Then we hauled ass out of the restaurant. Flynn and I sprinted down the sidewalk after Adam toward a small hidden parking lot where he'd stashed the Hummer while the others jumped into what looked an awful lot like Flynn's unmarked police car.

"Did you just give two people you barely know and a psychotic the keys to your cop car?" I asked after I got into the passenger seat and clicked my seat belt on.

"Yeah, kinda," Flynn replied. "I'm not a hundred percent sure it's going to be my cop car when I get back to Charlotte, so I only kinda give a shit. Besides, Jo's an excellent driver."

"Gabby is driving," Adam said, looking in the rearview mirror.

"Goddammit," Becks replied. I couldn't help but laugh.

I pulled out my phone and fired up a Skype link to Sparkles. "What do we know, pal?" I asked.

Sparkles popped up on my phone screen and the computer screen built into the dash. "Hang on, let me loop the other car in." The unicorn head vanished, then reappeared with a smaller inset image of Gabby, Watson, and Jo.

"Someday I'm going to learn how you do that shit," Jo said.

"I don't think you will, Jo, but you're welcome to try," said the unicorn.

"Give us the skinny, horn-boy," I said.

"What do you want to know, Harker? There are demons climbing the outside of the Ferris Wheel and eating people. Here, watch the video."

The image on the screen switched from a unicorn head to a live security cam feed. Sure enough, there were demons on the Ferris Wheel. I was pretty sure that shit wasn't included in the price of admission. A pair of the nasty bastards, mid-level Torment Demons from the looks of them, had the wheel stopped and were calmly climbing the center chords, then walking out onto the supports, ripping the door off its hinges, and swinging in. Once inside, the demons vanished from the camera shot, but after a few seconds, a head flew out the door.

"Oh, that's nasty," I said.

"They're discarding the bits they can't eat," Adam said. "No meat or muscle on a skull, except the jaw. Nothing worth consuming, unless you're a big fan of tongue."

I gave him a sharp look, but he just shrugged. "I don't eat anything, Harker. You don't have to worry about me turning cannibal on you."

If that was supposed to reassure me, it didn't work. The video switched back to Sparkles and the occupants of the other car.

"Okay," I said. "The good news is that Torment Demons are fairly run-of-the-mill bad guys. They're big, strong, and very hard to hurt, but they don't have any magic. They have to get their hands on you to do any harm. They're not any faster than normal humans, but they do have seriously sharp claws, teeth than can chew through chain, and very tough skin. Normal blades probably won't do anything. We'll need magic, blessed weapons, or something crazy sharp to make an impression. But if there are only two of them, we should be in pretty good shape. I've dealt with two on my own before. It sucked, and I almost died, but I did it."

"Yeah… about that," Sparkles said.

"What about it, bud?" I asked.

"There's a half a dozen Reavers running around on the ground."

"Fuck," I said.

"What's a Reaver?" Flynn asked.

"Yeah, clue us in, Harker," Jo agreed. "We don't all hunt demons that often."

"Reavers are nasty little bastards," I said. "They're like overgrown imps, only instead of being mischievous, they're just fucking mean. They're about five feet tall, skinny little fuckers, with extra-long arms, razor-sharp talons on the ends of their fingers, and elongated jaws with a shit ton of pointy little teeth. All Reavers do is eat, fight, and fuck, and you don't really want to be part of any of the three. I know I don't. A pair of hungry Reavers can strip an elephant to bone in five minutes, and they're always hungry."

"So how do we kill them?" Gabby asked.

"Reavers go down easier," I replied. "That's about the only good news. They can be hurt with normal weapons. They heal fast, but not so fast that you can't take them out of a fight. The only way to kill one is to behead it, and even then, you probably need someone to consecrate the body to make sure it's really dead."

"And even that doesn't really kill it, does it?" Becks asked from the back seat.

I turned to look at her, and she went on. "That just sends it back to Hell, right?"

"Most of the time, yes. There are weapons that can actually kill a demon, but not many, and I sure as shit don't have one. But sending it back to Hell is good enough for our purposes because that makes them stop killing people, and that's about all we can ask for on short notice. So, when we get there, I want to put you, Jo, Gabby, and Watson on the Reavers, working in pairs back-to-back. These fuckers are *fast*, so you need somebody to watch your six. Adam and I will work on taking out the Torment Demons."

"How exactly do you plan to do that without blessed weapons? You just going to throw fireballs at them and hope they don't kill you too quickly?"

"Nah, I'm going to shoot them off the Ferris Wheel with a high-powered rifle and ask friggin' Frankenstein to rip them limb from limb. Once they're torn apart, I'll figure out a way to kill them."

"You know I don't like being called that. My father's name was Dr. Frankenstein. My name is Adam."

"I know, pal, but it's the twenty-first century in America, and that's what everybody knows you as over here. Sorry, but it's just a lot faster this way."

Becks just sat in the back seat muttering about the level of surreal in her life since she'd met me. If she only knew what was coming, she would have known everything until then had just been a warmup.

Adam didn't bother trying to find a parking space this time; he just ran his Hummer up onto the sidewalk and pulled up close to the Ferris Wheel. That also happened to put him right on top of a Reaver demon, which I'm sure was no accident. I stepped on an arm as I got out of the truck and almost busted my ass, but I managed to catch myself.

A cop ran over to us, sidearm out and a wild look in his eyes. "You can't be here! This is dangerous, you people have to—"

I held up my Homeland Security badge. "We'll take it from here, officer. This is a National Security matter. Please tell your men to focus on setting up a perimeter and getting the wounded to safety. We'll handle the terrorists." My badge wasn't worth the metal it was stamped out of since my consultant status with Homeland was revoked a few seconds after I shot my Supervisory Agent in the face, but this beat cop didn't know that. All he saw was somebody who wasn't shit-scared, had a badge, and was giving orders.

He nodded and grabbed his radio, relaying my message to the rest of the locals.

"Terrorists?" Flynn asked, sliding out of the back seat to stand beside me.

"Yep. These guys will be a lot more likely to accept any mundane explanation, no matter how stupid, than they will a supernatural one. In their world, demons are something in comic books and movies, but terrorists are hiding behind every trash can."

Flynn nodded. "If they only knew that the real threat from illegal aliens came from other dimensions instead of other continents."

Just then the others ran up behind us, Watson coming to a limping stop behind the two women. "You alright, Jack?" I asked.

"The leg makes it a little difficult in a sprint, friend. I walk fine, but running is right out except in most extreme cases." He pulled up his pants leg a little to show me a steel rod where his leg used to be.

"Shit, man, I'm sorry, I didn't know. Maybe you should—" I started, but he held up a hand to stop me.

"Oh sod off, mate. I can do anything except run and the high hurdles. Now what's the plan?" He drew a small pistol from under his jacket and chambered a round. I noticed Gabby had strapped on her guns as well, and Jo carried a gigantic friggin' hammer. I looked at her, then at the hammer.

"I don't like guns. And anything a bullet can stop, a damn nine-pound hammer can stop, too. Plus, one head is silvered, and the other head is cold iron, so it's good against most things. And in a pinch, I can do this." She gave the end of the handle a twist and a yank, and it came off into a wooden stake.

"Nice. You four are on Reaver duty. Adam and I will work on the... fuck, let's go." I gave up on the instructions as the body of a fifty-something woman slammed into the bricks a dozen paces from where we were standing. I looked up to see a Torment Demon holding a teen boy out of a gondola by his hoodie. The fabric started to rip, and even from a couple hundred feet away, I watched the demon's smile get wider and wider and the boy struggled to grab hold of something to save himself.

"Adam, can you try to catch him?" I asked. "I don't know what that kind of impact will do..."

"It won't matter, Quincy," Adam said, his deep voice quiet. "Even if I caught him, the impact with my arms would shatter his bones. And probably tear my arms off, which would render me useless for a time."

"For a time?" Flynn started to ask, then her mouth closed with a *click*. "My life is so fucking weird. Come on, y'all. Let's go kill some demons." With the wave of an arm, her team moved off into the park, hunting Reavers and helping the cops get the civilians out of the way.

The kid was dead. I had to let that one go. It sucked, and it pissed me off, but that's all I could let it do. I walked around to the back of the Hummer and opened the tailgate. I popped open a compartment in the floor and pulled out a Remington 700 rifle with a scope and bipod. I picked up a pair of three-round magazines from a slot labeled "Holy Water" and slapped one into the rifle.

Walking around the front of the Hummer, I flipped down the bipod and found I couldn't get the angle right to steady the gun on the hood of the truck. I was too tall to shoot up at that kind of angle. So, I put the bipod up and steadied my elbows on the hood, sighting through the scope until the view was full of demon chest. No point in trying to get fancy, I just needed to hit the bastard and make him fall. No headshots here, not that I had too much faith in my ability to make one.

I let out my breath and squeezed the trigger. The big rifle bucked, and I saw the bullet spark off the metal frame of the gondola. The demon spun around, looking for me, and my second shot didn't miss. Quite. I was a little low, but hitting the nasty bastard in the knee had the desired effect. The demon's leg went out from under it, and he tumbled to the ground, slamming into the bricks with a sickening *thwap*. The worst part about that sound was that I knew it wasn't enough. The demon would be out of the fight for maybe a full minute, but unless we banished it, it would heal, even from that fall, in not near enough time.

"My turn," Adam said, running toward the downed demon while I swung the rifle around to find the next target. This one was smarter, of course, because he knew I was coming. He had a woman acting as a human shield, and there was no way I was sniper enough to shoot the demon without killing the woman.

"Fuck," I muttered, trying to think of another option.

"Leave us alone, Reaper!" the demon shouted. "This is our city, and before long it will be our world!"

"Fuck you, asshole!" I yelled back, because I'm witty like that.

"What are you going to do, shoot me? You can't hit me unless you're willing to kill this human, too. And then what? You going to raise this sweet little girl she's got up here?"

Fuck me, she's got her kid with her. "Why don't you come on down here and show me just how much this is your city, dickweed?" I yelled up at the demon.

"After I'm done with the bitch, maybe I will!" It shouted, then pulled back from the door into the gondola. I cursed whoever decided that Ferris Wheels should advance from the old bench seats into having big people-cages because I had no shot at the demon.

But I guess I didn't need to since I saw a dark form swing over from the main body of the wheel onto the spoke where the carriage swung. Adam hadn't stopped to fight the first demon after all; he'd apparently just scrambled up the Ferris Wheel like a really ugly Spider-Man and was now on top of the cage carrying the demon, mother, and child. He swung into the gondola, and the tinted windows blocked my view. The thing rocked wildly, and I wondered how anybody managed to stay inside through all that. Then someone didn't.

Two someones, actually. Two giant forms tumbled out the door and plummeted to the brick below, turning over and over and scrabbling at each other the whole way down. Adam and the demon landed with a mighty *THUD*, and I sprinted over to see what was left of them.

Not much left of the demon, as Adam managed to land on top. He rolled over, sprawled on his back looking up at me.

"Ouch."

"You're not dead? I think that fall might have even killed Luke," I said, absolutely baffled by how he was able to speak.

"I don't know how I'm alive, Quincy, and I don't know that I can be killed. But I know we need to banish these things before they reconstitute themselves. And I know that both my legs are very severely broken, so could you please carry me somewhere that I will not be lying in demon entrails? They smell horrible."

He wasn't lying. The scattered demon guts gave off a wretched odor, like three-day-old gamer funk mixed with rotted asshole. I leaned over and hoisted Adam over my shoulders in a fireman's carry, then deposited him into the grass a couple dozen feet away.

"Before you begin the ritual of banishment, could you take a moment to set the bones in my arms and legs? They will heal quickly, and I would prefer that everything line up correctly when they do."

I looked at the twisted mass of bones that were Adam's extremities, and an involuntary shudder ran through me. Any human would have died instantly, and even if they didn't, the pain from those injuries would have put them into shock. But Adam wasn't even as close to human as I was, so he just sat there stoically as I set his arms and legs.

"Lay there, and don't move," I said. "I'll deal with these fuckers, then we'll…

son of a *bitch*!" I cut myself off as I looked over and saw the first demon getting to his feet. He was *not* supposed to heal that fast. Bastard was messing with my timetable.

Oh well, stuck fighting an unkillable demon with my backup sidelined by injury. Story of my stupid life.

CHAPTER THREE

The Torment Demon wasn't anywhere near full strength yet, and I could only hope that was going to be enough to let me trap it and banish it before it killed anymore people. Notably me. The rifle was still up at the Hummer, so all I had on me was my Glock and the short sword I'd strapped to my waist hours before. This was about to suck.

The demon hadn't turned his attention to me yet, mostly because it was currently regrowing an arm, but I figured I didn't have a lot of time. I drew my sword and dashed in behind the big bastard, slashing down to hamstring him. Which was a great idea, except that my gladius was in no way conse-crated, or blessed, or holy, or magical. So, it hit the demon's skin and bounced off, sending vibrations up my arm and making my fingers tingle with the impact.

That got the demon's attention. Just what I always wanted—the undivided attention of a pissed off, invulnerable, seven-foot tall monster with a mouth full of razor-sharp fangs and claws that could rip me from nuts to nose in half a second. It spun around and backhanded me with its one good arm, sending me sprawling to the ground a good four feet from where I started. I rolled to my feet and drew in my will, coalescing energy into a glowing sphere three inches in diameter above my outstretched hand.

I flung the ball of purple light at the demon and smacked it right in the chest. It had part of the desired effect, smacking into the creature and leaving a burned mark on its chest, but not the rest of it, which was to knock it down or maybe make it give a shit about the damage in some way. No, it just grinned at me and stalked forward, not even bothering to charge me.

I fired energy ball after energy ball at the creature, backing up at about the same pace that it was moving forward, but it was a losing proposition. I was running out of energy at about the same rate the demon was healing, and that was going to put me staring down a fully-healed Torment Demon sooner rather than later.

"Adam, a little help!" I shouted over my shoulder.

"Busy right now, Quincy," came the reply. I spared a glance and saw he wasn't joking. He was standing toe to toe with the other demon, trading punches that would have caved in the skull on a normal man. Every once in a while, he darted forward to pull the demon's leg out from under it, but the beast was quick to spring back up. I turned my attention back to the problem at hand, racking my brain for anything I could come up with on destroying tormentors. Nothing came to me, so I just kept flinging fireballs at the demon until I backpedaled off the sidewalk and tripped over a discarded bicycle.

I flopped down on my ass atop somebody's mountain bike and looked up at a grinning Torment Demon. There are a lot of things I don't mind looking up to: mountains, stars, even a full moon, but a happy demon is never something I want to see looming over me.

Fortunately, the demon's smile faded abruptly as a gleaming blade sliced through its neck. The head toppled to the ground, and both segments of the dead thing dissolved in a cloud of sulfur, sent back to Hell where it belonged.

I stared up at a much more welcome sight, a blonde woman resplendent in silver chain mail with wings and a shiny gold-rimmed helmet. "Hi Glory," I said. "I was really hoping you'd show up."

My guardian angel just shook her head at me. "You know that's not supposed to be how this works, right? You aren't supposed to just randomly jump into lethal situations counting on me to save you. I'm supposed to be here for the unplanned things that could kill you."

"In my defense, I didn't plan on demons attacking a Ferris Wheel today," I countered.

"You're a dick, Q. A real dick." Glory turned and unfurled her wings, flying across the grass and finishing off the demon Adam was ripping apart. Then she took out the last of the Reavers, and we all gathered back at the Hummer.

"Did you just call me a dick?" I asked the angel.

"If the shoe fits," Adam muttered.

"Screw you, golem," I said, an old crack that never failed to get under his skin. He hated being called a golem more than Luke hated being asked if he sparkled. I turned my attention back to Glory. "Did you call me a dick? I didn't think angels could curse."

"Swearing isn't a sin, Q. Lying is a sin, but since you really are a dick, I get to say that as much as I want."

"She's not wrong about that part, is she, pal?" Watson asked with a grin. I just glared at him, and he took a step back. I didn't dislike the Brit, but I didn't want him getting the opinion that since we were on the same side, that we were friends or anything like that.

I glanced around the park at the carnage the demons wrought. There were bodies and body parts scattered across the whole area beneath the Ferris Wheel, and a veritable army of cop cars and ambulances were lined up just outside the perimeter the first cops had established.

I pulled out my cell phone. "Sparkles," I said to the blank device. "Can you do something about the curious locals?"

"Already on it," said the unicorn that popped up on my screen. "The officer in charge just had a video conference with the head of the local FBI office, who had never met, about the 'terrorist incident' in the park today. And all the video shot by those news vans will find itself mysteriously erased."

"Thanks, man. Any live feeds get out?" I asked.

"I'm almost insulted that you felt you had to ask. But no, you're good. But you've only got maybe two minutes before the crowd grows past the size I can manage. After that, you're gonna be all over YouTube."

"Got it," I said. I slipped the phone into my pocket and looked around. "Let's get out of here, kids."

"Just a second," Flynn said. "Glory, who called these bastards? And what did they want?"

"I would assume that Orobas summoned them," the angel replied. "But I have no idea why."

"Is nobody else going to maybe remark on the fact that we are standing in the middle of a park in Georgia chatting with an angel like we're talking about the weather?" Jo asked. I noticed that while her jacket was torn and there was blood running down one arm, the head of her hammer was streaked with gore and what looked like little flecks of Reaver skull. She had obviously given as good as she'd gotten.

I took a second then to give her, and the others, a once-over. Flynn was untouched, but I wasn't surprised by that. She'd been through enough shit with me to know when it's best to fight from a distance. Watson was similarly unscathed, but Gabby. Well, Gabby looked like she'd taken time off from shooting a Manson family biopic to remake *American Psycho*. She was covered in blood from her knees to the top of her head, and gore streaked her arms like she'd been kneading bread made with blood and entrails.

"What the fuck happened to you?" I asked. "I thought you had guns."

"I did," she said with a grin. Her white teeth shining through a mask of blood across her face was truly unnerving. "But then I had to get up close and personal with a couple of the Reavers. It didn't go well for them." She drew a pair of foot-long daggers from somewhere behind her back and twirled them around, all the while keeping that godawful grin plastered across her face.

"Has anybody ever told you about the message of our Lord and Savior Hannibal frickin' Lecter?" Flynn asked, taking a big step sideways to create some separation with Gabby.

"Don't worry, Detective. I still mostly like you," Gabby said, putting her knives away.

I shook my head, trying to focus on the questions at hand more than the mental wellness, or lack thereof, of my partners. "Okay, let's focus for just a minute, people. It makes sense that Orobas called these bastards, but why? Was there something here worth going after? Have there been any other incidents around the city? Why right here, right now?"

"I'll go ask the constables," Watson said, and walked off to the nearest pair of cops.

"I don't know of anything spiritually or mystically significant about this park," Jo said. "But I'll jump online and see what I can grab real quick." She walked over to a park bench and sat, pulling a tablet out of her jacket pocket and tapping away.

"She kept her iPad from getting busted while fighting demons? Maybe she does have super-powers," I said.

"Glory, can you make a quick lap around the city and make sure this was the only demon summoning on the calendar for this afternoon? I'd hate to think we missed an important engagement," Flynn asked.

"I can do that." Glory gave me a stern look. "Try not to do anything suicidal in the next hour." Then she vanished.

I looked at Gabby, standing there covered in gore like an extra in a community theatre *Titus Andronicus*. "Why don't you go run through the fountain or something?"

"It's cold," she grumbled.

"Unless you're planning on walking back to the hotel, which probably won't let you in looking like Carrie, you should at least rinse off," I replied. She scowled at me, then handed her gun belt to Flynn and stomped off toward the Olympic Ring-shaped fountain.

Becks watched her go, then looked at me. "Sometimes I think you're one hundred percent batshit crazy, Harker. Then I spend time around some of your friends."

"She raises a valid point, Quincy," Adam said. "I believe I shall also go rinse off the worst of the gore before I have to drive to the hotel. I do not relish getting blood out of my upholstery. Again." He gave me a sharp look before following Gabby to the fountain.

"Sorry!" I called after him. "Demons," I explained to Flynn. We stood there, alone for the first time since I'd joined them, and of course, things got awkward.

"Umm," I started, not really sure what I wanted to follow that brilliant opener with. "Did you get the... box I left for you with Glory?"

"I did." Her voice was cold, and she didn't look at me.

"And?" I asked. I could outwait her. I was over a hundred years old. I had the long game down.

"And I'm not going to respond."

"Why not? Are you not interested? Because I thought we..." I could feel a lot of things bouncing through our link, but they were all jumbled up. At the root of it all, I could feel interest, along with fear, anger, worry, and a host of less fun things.

"Oh, we definitely did. But if we're going to take that kind of step, and I'm not saying we should, but if we are, I sure as hell am not going to be proposed to by a proxy, even if she is an angel. Let's get through this whole end of the world thing, make sure neither one of us comes down with a bad case of the deads, and then talk about maybe going on a date.

"Harker, I'm nowhere near ready to get married. Two years ago, I thought you were just a conman fleecing people out of cash by spinning horror stories, and now I'm fighting demons in a park with Frankenstein, and I've got Dracula on speed dial.

"My life has gone from zero to a monster movie in eighteen months, and I don't even know if I'm still going to have a *job* when I get back to Charlotte, much less know if I want to marry you. And *then* there's the whole thing where I get old and you don't, and I've seen *Highlander*, and I know how well that turns out, so... we've got a lot of shit to figure out before I put that ring on my finger."

I looked down into her brown eyes and saw the emotion welling up, right behind the tears that threatened to spill down her caramel-colored cheeks. I gave her a little smile, sending emotion across our link to make sure she understood that I meant what I said. "You're right, Becks. I was scared when I sent that ring with Glory, and it was dumb to put you in that position. I'll slow down a little. But make no mistake about one thing, Rebecca Gail Flynn

—I love you, and I will tear down the Gates of Heaven itself to make sure we are never separated again."

She smiled up at me, then threw her arms around my neck and kissed me, jamming her lips to mine with a ferocity that reminded me I was with a warrior woman. She pulled back and looked me in the eye. "Nicely said. Sometimes I forget that you weren't raised by wolves, but that was actually poetic."

"Live long enough and you read a lot. Even poetry. I'm partial to Billy Collins, myself," I said.

"I hate to interrupt your little *tete-a-tete*, but I think I know why the demons attacked here," Jo said, walking up with her iPad in hand.

"What's up?" I asked.

"There was a some kind of strange disturbance up at Stone Mountain about an hour ago, just about the time the demons hit the first gondola. Lots of flashing lights in the sky were reported, and the rangers that went to check it out are now being called in as missing, their vehicles abandoned."

"Shit," I said. "There was something there, and Orobas went after it."

"And got it, from what these reports sound like," Jo agreed. She handed me the tablet, and I read a string of messages from Sparkles. Everything was just like she said—rangers missing, lights over the mountain, and a big hole in the ground at the summit. Whatever was there, it was gone now.

"Fucking hell," I grumbled. "Alright, we still have to check it out, just to see if we can pick up any clue as to what was there. Jo, you and the others go circle back to Luke and see if Sparkles has found out anything about Barton. Flynn and I will ride up to Stone Mountain with Adam and poke around. We still have our Homeland credentials, even if we're fired."

"*So* fired," Flynn agreed.

"Adam!" I yelled. "Get your big ass over here! We gotta go hunt demons in the woods."

"Again?" he called back. "Must be Tuesday."

CHAPTER FOUR

W e took the back road up to the top of Stone Mountain and pulled off to the side behind half a dozen cop cars and one lost-looking UPS driver. Adam and Flynn followed me as I badged us past the uniformed cop on crowd control duty, and we started to look around for any traces of Orobas or anything magical.

"I guess that's what we came here for," Flynn said, pointing at a smoking crater in the rock some ten feet in diameter.

"And that's why she's the detective, ladies and gentlemen," I replied. We walked over to the hole, which looked just like any other big hole in a big rock. There was smoke, there was rock blasted to pebbles, and there was one really shaken college kid in khakis and a polo shirt talking to a cop. The kid was tall and so terrified his man-bun was shaking as I walked over to eavesdrop.

"I dunno, dude," the kid was saying as I walked up. "It's like I said, man, one minute he was a normal dude, and the next he was a friggin' monster. He was like ten feet tall, with six arms and gigantic teeth. Scared the shit out of me, so I hid, man."

More like seven feet tall with two arms and a shitload of attitude most likely, but I didn't need to correct the kid. He'd just survived his first demon encounter; he could see as many arms as he wanted. "So you didn't see anything after the dude turned into a monster?" I asked.

The kid looked at me like I was his best friend just for even thinking that I believed him, but the cop he was talking to was way less enthused. He was the kind of guy who looked like he broke a sweat just walking up from his car, and he certainly didn't need any interlopers in his case. He was in his fifties with a belly that stuck out so far I wonder if he just took it for granted that he still had feet and a scowl on his red face that looked permanent.

"And who the hell do you think you are, mister? And how the hell did you get past Gerald?"

"Quincy Harker, Homeland Security," I said, flashing my badge. He wasn't as inclined to just automatically yield the floor as his younger buddy down by the crime scene tape line, so I passed over my wallet when he held out his pudgy little hand.

He squinted at the picture, then at me, then passed it back over. "Who're they?"

"They're with me," I said.

"I didn't ask who they were with, smartass, I asked who they were. You want to stay on my crime scene, son, you better—"

I stepped forward and picked him up by the front of his shirt. I lifted him up about two inches off the ground so we could look eye to eye. "Look here, Deputy Fuckwit. This shit is so far out of your jurisdiction it might not have even come from the same galaxy. You're so far in over your head you can't even see the sun, and you don't even know it yet. There are things out there that your little pea brain can't handle. That's what I'm here for. I handle the shit you only see in your nightmares, and that's what shit we're dealing with here. Now unless you can come up with some normal criminal that can carve a ten-foot hole in solid fucking granite in a matter of seconds, you need to get out of my way and let me do my job. You got me?"

He nodded, silently, and I put him down. I gave him a steady look and said, "Now fuck off out of here while the adults deal with the bad things." He hustled back down the hill toward his car, and I turned my attention to the kid.

"Don't kill me, man," the kid said, shrinking back a little closer to the edge of the hole than was probably safe. I reached out and grabbed his shirt, too, but only to pull him back before he fell in the crater and smashed his skull in. "I'm not gonna kill you, kid. I just want to know what you saw."

"Like I said, man. There was a dude, then he was a monster. He made some kind of weird light show with his hands, and then the ground blew up. A chunk of rock whizzed by my head, and I screamed a little. That's when it came at me. But I fought it off." He puffed up at that last bit, proud of himself for standing up to the monster. Too bad it was a load of shit.

"You fought it off?" Flynn asked, incredulous.

"Yeah, man. It came after me, but I judo-chopped it right in the nose, and it flew off out of here, man."

"Is that why you pissed yourself?" I asked. "Because you were so damn proud of the way you judo-chopped a demon? A demon that would have ripped off your arm and beaten you to a bloody pulp with it had you even so much as looked crosswise at it."

His long face fell, and I felt like I just nut-shotted Shaggy from the Scooby-Doo cartoons. "It's okay, kid," I said. "You can tell all the girls that you fought the thing off. I just need to know what it got out of the hole."

"The hole?" the kid asked, and I revised my opinion on the harmlessness of marijuana. This kid had definitely smoked his last brain cell.

"Yes, dumbass, the hole! The great big fucking hole in the rock that you almost fell into ten seconds ago!" This time I yelled. It had been a long couple of weeks. I think I was allowed a little yelling.

"Oh, yeah. Sorry, man. I didn't see what it took out of the hole. I was kinda hiding."

I took a deep breath because the more deep breaths I took, the less likely I was to throw this idiot kid off the mountain. "*Kinda* hiding?"

"Okay, I was totally hiding. In there." He pointed over to the snack bar beside the sky tram stop at the top of the mountain. "I pulled the drink machine out from the wall, and I hid behind it. Sorry, dude."

I looked at my feet, then up to Heaven, then back at the kid. Just as I opened my mouth to say something truly vicious, Flynn stepped in. She doesn't always play the peacemaker, but she's a hell of a lot better at it than I am, so I let her do the talking.

"Hey... Dave," she said, reading the kid's nametag. "Why don't you and I go into the office and look at the security camera footage. Maybe there's something useful there." She pointed up at a small camera mounted to an overhang on the roof of the tram stop. It pointed in the general direction of the hole.

That's why you're the detective, I thought to her.

Shut your pie-hole is what came back to me across our mental link, but I felt a little smile behind it.

"Yeah," Dave said. "I think there's a monitor in the electrical closet."

"I'll go with Dave, and we can take a look at the footage," Flynn said.

"We'll stay out here and in the crater, see if we can pick up any... forensic evidence." I went with that lame excuse to poke around the crater because saying "I'll open up my Second Sight and see what's going on in the metaphysical spectrum" always sounds so pretentious. And had the potential to get me put in a padded room.

Flynn and Dave headed off into the little snack shack, and I turned to Adam. "Watch my back for a minute."

"Story of my life, Quincy," he said, but I knew he'd cover me if there was anything dangerous in the mundane world while I was focused on the Otherworld. I didn't need to wonder long. The instant I opened my Sight, I found plenty of trace all over the mountaintop. There had definitely been a demon close by, and Stone Mountain wasn't going to be considered sanctified ground anytime soon, but there was also nothing useful. I saw where Orobas changed, because his taint on the rock got stronger, and I could see the trail he left going down into the crater. The crater itself literally glowed with dark purple magical residue, both from demon taint, which usually has a reddish tinge to it, and the destructive magic used to dig the crater.

I got closer to the edge of the crater, which really wasn't much more than a big hole about ten feet across and maybe five feet deep in the center. I scrambled down into it, kicking over the occasional rock to make sure I didn't miss any mystical trace that I could follow back to Oro, but the big bastard had covered his tracks pretty well. No blood, no hair, nothing I could really use in hunting him down in a city as sprawling and jammed with different energies as Atlanta.

There was a rectangular depression in the very bottom of the crater, so I got down on my hands and knees to examine it more closely. The stone was shaped here, not naturally formed or blasted away, so whatever had been down here had been here for a long time, and hidden by something powerful enough to make the very stones of the earth bend to its will.

The hole left by whatever it was measured about a foot-and-a-half by two feet and was about eight inches deep. I couldn't tell anything else about it, except there was a hint of pale blue energy glowing faintly in my Sight. Whatever was there, it was long gone, and it had enough power to tint the soul of the mountain.

I dropped my Sight and poked around the dirt a little, looking for actual physical clues, but there was nothing. The only hope I had was that Orobas left a fiber or something behind, but there was very little chance of that leading me to him, no matter how many episodes of *CSI* I watched. I clambered back out of the hole just as Flynn came back.

"No Dave?" I asked.

"He had to go call his boss. Something about a demon attack being a very good reason for shutting down the snack bar for the rest of the day," Flynn replied.

"Makes sense. Anything on the video?" Adam asked.

"Just a big damn demon hauling a box out of the ground. But he made that crater with a spell, Harker."

"Yeah?" I had kinda figured that much.

"Can you do that? I mean, look, I know you wizard types have a lot of juice, but that's a big damn hole."

"I don't know if I have that much power or not, Becks. Oro isn't just a Reaver or a Torment Demon like we fought this afternoon. He's a legitimate big deal in the Armies of Hell, and we've been lucky all the times we've dealt with him before not to have a lot higher body count." I remembered the last casualty of Orobas's plan to remake Charlotte into his own private Hell-condo. Renfield was more than just my uncle's butler; he was a friend, and I watched him die. It wasn't the first time that happened to me, and it wouldn't be the last, but that didn't make it any easier.

"I guess I didn't realize just how powerful he was," Flynn said, her face a little drawn.

"Would it have mattered?" Adam said. I looked up at him, but there was no sarcasm there, just acceptance of our place in the world. We stood between the bad things and the helpless, and sometimes the waves of shitty washed one of us away.

Flynn looked at him, then at me. Then she shrugged her shoulders, let out a sigh, and said, "No, it wouldn't. I picked up a badge to stop bad things from hurting good people, and this is just more of the same, only on a bigger scale."

"Ain't that the truth," I agreed. "Now let's get back into town and find this demonic fuckwit before he annexes all of Georgia into the Fifth Circle of Hell."

"If you think we're not already in Hell, Harker, then you've never driven through rush hour on I-285," Flynn said, walking off down the hill to the truck.

CHAPTER FIVE

uke hadn't just rented a few rooms at the Westin Peachtree downtown. In his typical European royalty fashion, he'd rented the entire top floor. I walked into the room he and his band of merry people had converted into their war room, and I had to say, I was impressed. All the furniture was gone, and heavy blackout fabric masked all the windows. That left enough space in the center of the floor for a conference table with a bunch of decent desk chairs, no doubt carted in from the surrounding rooms.

The rest of the crew was already there, and Sparkles' face was up on the wall-mounted TV. I'll admit, even when you're as old as I am, there's something a little unnerving about walking into a room and seeing a giant unicorn staring at you from the television. I walked over to one end of the table and gave Luke a hug. He stiffened because we aren't usually the hugging type, but it had been a strange couple of weeks.

"How you doing, Luke?" I asked, pulling back. I kept my voice low. The room wasn't big enough to lose any of our words, but at least folks could pretend to let us have a moment.

"I have had better months, Quincy. My house was destroyed, my manservant slain, and now I am forced to reside in a hotel and dine upon supplies garnered from a local blood bank. It is altogether a barely tenable situation, and I sincerely desire to resolve this unpleasantness and return home as soon as possible."

"Yeah, I'm right there with you. Let's get these goofballs in line and save the world." I started to turn, but Luke put a hand on my arm. I turned back to him. "Yeah?"

"Did he suffer, Quincy?" Luke's voice was thick with emotion, and the look on his face would put the lie to all those years of people calling him "monster." This was not the King of the Vampires, the Impaler, the source of so many nightmares and horrific stories across the centuries. This was just a man who'd lost one of the very few people in the world he thought of as a friend, and he wanted some reassurance.

I remembered the scene. I remembered Smith grinning at me as I tried without success to break through his protective circles. I remembered the dazed look in Renfield's eyes as he came out of his drug-induced stupor. I remembered the knife in Smith's hand, then flashing down and burying itself in Ren's chest. I remembered the blood, the gore as Smith cut open my friend's chest in front of me and pulled out his heart, as if to prove to me that Renfield was really dead. I saw all of that in an instant while Luke stared back at me.

"No," I said. "It was quick. He didn't suffer." Neither did Smith, much to my chagrin. I shot him in the head, and he dropped like a stone. I wanted him to suffer, wanted him to feel a shred of the pain he inflicted on me, on Luke, on the families of the other men and women he murdered. But I didn't take him alive, or even torture him. I just dropped him in his tracks. I thought that was the end, but it turned out to be just the beginning.

I turned from Luke to look at the rest of the team. Adam and Becks had taken seats on one side of the table with Watson, Jo, and Gabby on the other. The foot of the table had no chair, presumably so we could all see and hear Sparkles. I took the empty seat next to Flynn, and Luke sat at the head of the table. I wanted to make some joke about carving the turkey, but between a couple of demon fights in one afternoon, plus reliving Renfield's last moments with Luke, my sense of humor was seriously lacking.

"What do we know?" I asked.

"We know the demons in the park were a distraction, that whatever Orobas was after, it was hidden at Stone Mountain," Watson said.

"Yeah, under ten feet of rock," Flynn added. "Solid rock, too. Orobas used a spell to blast the rock away and get to what he was after. That smacks of serious magic to me."

"You're not wrong," I said. "And not only was there some serious magic being thrown around up there, whatever was hidden there was pretty serious all on its own."

"What makes you say that?" Jo asked. I looked over at her, but there was no challenge in her eyes, only curiosity. I still wasn't sure where I stood with all these people, but she didn't look like she wanted to get into a pissing match. Which was good. I didn't know what exactly was going on in Atlanta, but it sure felt like we were going to be on a tight schedule.

"The magical blast had the force of several sticks of dynamite. For whatever was in the hole to survive that, it wasn't just a run of the mill magic wand," I replied.

"Is that even a thing, or are you just using magic wand as like an example," Gabby asked from her seat to my left. She leaned back, feet on the table and a beer in her hand.

I decided to make an example of my own. I stood up, using some of my enhanced speed to go faster than normal, and grabbed one of Gabby's feet. I pulled up, dumping her on her ass against the wall. "Pay attention, Gabby," I growled at her. "This isn't fucking playtime. Orobas is the real fucking deal, and we don't have any idea what he's up to yet. If we fuck this up, all of Atlanta could go up in smoke, so sit up straight, shut your mouth, and focus." I never raised my voice, but I didn't have to. Everybody could see where my head was.

"I don't think that's quite correct, Harker," Sparkles' voice came from the screen.

I sat down and turned to face him. "You know it's pretty hard to take you seriously when you're wearing that face."

The unicorn face frowned, which is even stranger than you would expect it to be, and the image on the screen shifted to a round-faced young man with short curly hair and freckles. "Is this better, asshole?" he asked.

"Much," I replied. "You want to introduce yourself to the nice people, or should I?"

"I got this," Sparkles said. "My real name is Dennis Bolton."

I heard Flynn gasp from beside me. Good to know she'd been listening when I told her about the first set of Orobas's sacrifices I encountered.

Dennis turned to look at her. "You've heard of me? Probably from your asshat boyfriend there. Well, it's all true. He got me killed. Well, mostly killed, but there was enough of me left to magically transfer my soul into the internet."

Flynn sat there, gaping. Jo leaned forward and said what I figure everyone else was thinking. "What the fuck?"

Dennis laughed. "Yeah, exactly. What. The. Fuck? So there I was, deader than shit on stage at the theatre, when Harker casts a binding spell to trap my soul."

"He stuck you back in your body?" Gabby asked.

Dennis laughed again. "Yah, not exactly. Orobas has a bad tendency to leave big holes in bodies when he's finished with them, so there wasn't enough of my body to hold the soul in. So Harker put me in the next best place. At least that's what he thought at the time."

"Where was that?" Flynn asked. I didn't answer. To be honest, it was a little embarrassing. I couldn't think of anything better at the time, but looking back on it, it wasn't my most shining magical moment.

"Come on, Quincy, spill it. Where did you put your fine horned friend?" Watson asked, and I could almost hear the ration of shit he was preparing to give me.

"I put him in my cell phone," I said.

"What?" "How the...?" "Where?" I let the explosion of questions go on for a few seconds until I raised my hand for quiet.

"I had a new phone with a big hard drive. I cast a binding spell to tie Dennis' soul to the phone, hoping it had enough memory to hold all of him."

"But he missed one small detail," Dennis added.

"I forgot that the phone was tied to the internet. So as soon as I put Dennis into the phone..."

"I left," the face on the screen said. "I got pulled into the phone, then dove right back out along the nation's most powerful wireless network, and suddenly I could hear *everything* now."

"I think that's two different commercials," Jo said.

"I'm allowed," Dennis replied.

"Fair enough," Jo said with a nod. "So then what?"

"Well," Dennis said. "I kinda surfed on the web for a little while, figuring out how to reconstitute myself, at least my consciousness, figured out how to interact with Harker via text message, then later on Skype, then FaceTime and other video chat apps. But I stay away from Chatroulette. That's some fucked up shit right there."

"So now you're alive on the internet?" Gabby asked.

"Let's not get out of hand with the whole 'alive' thing," Dennis said. "But I'm conscious at least."

"And very useful," I said.

"Don't patronize, Harker. I know I'm a badass cyber-ninja. You don't have to tell me." Dennis glared at me from the wall.

I held up both hands in surrender. "Okay, Bruce Lee, what do you have for us?"

"I think I know what Orobas is up to. At least what his eventual plan is. And I *think* I have an idea how he plans to do it, but it doesn't make a whole lot of sense."

"He's a demon, dude," Gabby said, leaning back in her chair again. She started to move her feet toward the table, but Jo reached out and smacked her knee. She gave me a guilty glance and sat up straight. "They don't make sense."

"That's where you are incorrect, Gabriella," Luke said. "There are certain aspects of a demon's personality that will always bleed through, no matter what type of disguise or subterfuge they attempt."

"So what is he up to?" I asked, looking at the screen.

"He wants to open a doorway to Hell," Sparkles said.

"We stopped that plan, bud," I replied.

"No, you stopped one version of that plan," my disembodied friend countered.

"What do you mean?" Flynn asked. "Harker killed Smith and disrupted the spell. They missed the date for the ritual. We should be good until the spring, at least."

"If I'm right, Orobas isn't planning a ritual. He's just planning to rip the fabric of the universe apart with brute force," Sparkles said.

You could have heard a pin drop on the carpet as everyone sat there trying to digest that little bombshell. After almost a full minute of silence, Watson looked at me, face pale and a little bead of sweat on his forehead and asked, "Can he do that?"

I thought about it for a second. Frankly, I'd been thinking about it ever since Dennis made his proclamation, but I didn't like the conclusion I kept coming to. "Yeah," I said. "Yeah, I think he probably can. It would take the release of an incredible amount of magical energy, and it would have to be concentrated in one spot, but I think it could be done."

"How?" Jo asked. "I mean, I know I'm the least magically inclined of anyone here, probably, but that just doesn't make any sense to me." There were nods and murmurs of agreement from around the table as everyone tried to wrap their heads around the concept.

"Okay." I stood up and held up my hands for quiet. "I'll try to explain it as best I can. Think of Earth, Heaven, and Hell not so much as up, down, and center, but more like just adjacent dimensions. There are a few more, as I understand it, but I don't have the ability or interest in trans-dimensional travel, so I haven't spent a lot of time studying it."

I started to pace, trying to put my thoughts into coherent sentences. Luke caught my eye and gave me a nod, so I just took a deep breath and pushed on. "The dimensions all touch each other, pretty much at all points, like a weird Venn diagram. When someone summons a demon or an angel, or an angel travels to Earth, they basically use their magic to open a tiny hole between the dimensions, called a Gate. These Gates take a shitload of energy to open, and even more energy to hold open."

"That's why you always use a ritual for summoning, because you have to focus your energy more than with most of the magical shit you do?" Gabby asked. She was leaning forward on her elbows now, her pose of calculated indifference completely forgotten.

"Yeah, exactly. I also try to tap into a ley line if I can, kind of a network of magical energy that crisscrosses the world. Whenever I can draw from a line, it's less of my own energy I have to use. So, I can create manageable Gates for a limited time with just my own energy. If I have a group of people working together, lending me their energy, then I can open a bigger Gate, and for a longer time."

"That's what Smith was doing back in Charlotte," Flynn said, making the jump.

"Again, there's a reason you're the detective, Becks," I agreed. "Smith was doing exactly that. The only difference was that the people lending their energy to his ritual weren't willing participants, and he was using every drop of their life force so he didn't have to use any of his own."

"The bastard," Luke muttered. I didn't acknowledge him with words, just gave him a short nod.

"So, what is he saying about making a rip in the dimensional fabric?" Watson asked.

"A Gate is a managed portal between two places, and it takes a lot of power to keep it open for longer than a few seconds. The dimensions are always shifting, and the natural order of things is to keep them tangential but separate. So, a permanent Gate between Heaven and Earth, for example, would take such a constant stream of power as to be almost impossible to maintain," I said.

"So what's the problem?" Gabby asked. "If you can't keep it open, then we just kill anything that comes through, and when it closes, no problem, right?"

"I wish," Sparkles said. "That's true about a managed Gate between two places. But that's not what I think Orobas is trying to do."

"Oh fuck me sideways," I said as the full enormity of what he was saying hit me.

"Yup, you got it." Sparkles gave me a wry grin. "That's exactly what I'm thinking."

"Would you care to let us mere mortals in on the secret?" Watson asked, then glanced at Luke and Adam. "Mortals and et cetera, of course."

"He's not trying to just open a doorway between Earth and Hell anymore," I said. "He wants to blow open a hole in the fabric of every dimension that touches ours. A rip in the fabric of reality that wouldn't be a link between two specific places, but a hole that would stay open forever between Earth and every other realm of existence."

"But wouldn't that mean..." Flynn's voice trailed off as she tried to process it.

"Yeah," I said. "Not only could Orobas and all his demonic buddies take over the Earth, they could storm Heaven, too."

CHAPTER SIX

"Two questions," Flynn said, standing up and waving everybody silent. She was looking at Sparkles' image on the screen, but also around the table at me, Luke, and the rest of the team. "First, how does one go about tearing a hole between dimensions? And second, how do we stop him?"

"I think the idea is to destroy a bunch of magical artifacts at one time, releasing all their stored energy into one focused blast," Dennis said.

"That fits with what we've heard about the Barton character that rescued Orobas from Charlotte," Watson said. "He has a reputation as an avid collector of occult objects and magical instruments."

"That also explains why they were digging around Luke's place," Jo added. "There's something magical about the sword, we just don't know what it is. They wanted to add it to their mystical bonfire."

"More like mystical pipe bomb," Gabby said. "I like a good explosion as much as the next girl—"

"More," Flynn piped in. "For the record, Gabs, most 'next girls' don't actually like blowing things up."

"Their loss," Gabby said, then went on. "But even setting aside my love for things that go boom, blasting open a hole between Heaven and Hell sounds like a terrible idea. Most of the stuff in Hell is there because it doesn't deserve Heaven, right?"

"Or because they were there once and tried to take it over," Adam's rumbling voice chimed in.

"Even worse, there wouldn't be a direct link from Hell to Heaven," I said. "They'd have to pass through our dimension to get upstairs."

"And I'm guessing that most demons aren't the type to just casually pass through, leaving things unmolested," Watson said.

"Yeah, not so much," I agreed.

"So back to Question Number Two—how do we stop it?" Flynn spoke over the rest of us, and we settled down.

All eyes turned to the screen, and Dennis shifted his image back to the unicorn. "Sorry, kids, I have no fucking idea."

"Neither do I," Luke admitted with a rueful shake of his head. "Despite magic being the force that keeps me alive and sentient, I have very little experience with its actual performance."

"Well, I suppose that's my department," I said. "But I have no clue, either. I've never even heard of a ritual with this kind of power, much less any kind of counterspell or way to undo it."

"So what do we do? Just run like hell and hope that the demons leave something left of the world to live in?" Jo said. "Fuck that. There's got to be a way. There's *always* a way, if we just fight hard enough."

"Your namesake would be proud," Luke said, and I saw just the slightest blush on Jo's dark skin.

"She's right," I said. "There's got to be a way to stop, or worst case, reverse what Orobas is trying to do. I'll get to work researching the most powerful spells and artifacts I can find to see about coming up with a reversal or blocking spell."

"I'll help," Watson said. "I'm good with research. Got to put that posh Cambridge education to use, right?"

"Nightfall is still a few hours away, so I will assist the two of you until such a time as any of my contacts in the city will be available, then Adam and I will go have a few quiet meetings."

"I know a few people in town, too. I'll take Flynn with me to poke around the more interesting parts of Atlanta. Maybe we can dig up some dirt on our Mr. Barton," Gabby added.

"That leaves you and me digging through the interwebs again, buddy," Jo said to Sparkles.

"It's what I live for," he said with a whinny.

———

Six hours later, I drove back to the hotel with a disappointed Watson in the passenger's seat of my rental car, a stack of spellbooks in the trunk, a huge box of takeout from Fox Brothers' Barbecue in the backseat making me hungry, and bad attitude.

I carried the books up the elevator, and Watson handled the food. We walked into the "war room" to see Jo buried in her laptop and Becks sitting with her head down on the table, fast asleep. Jo made a shushing motion to me as the door opened, but Flynn sat up and rubbed her eyes, looking at me sleepily.

"Anything?" she asked, her voice thick with sleep.

"No," I said. "Looks like you had about the same luck."

"Yeah, Gabby punched a lot of people, but nobody could give us shit on Barton. It's like the dude is a ghost."

"A ghost with a hell of a bankroll," Sparkles said from the TV. He was wearing his Dennis face this time, and I reflected for just an instant on the cost of associating with me. Sure, maybe he would have ended up trapped in the internet like a modern-day Tron without my influence, but it's pretty damned unlikely. Anna, Flynn's dad, Dennis, now Renfield—I was starting to have the death of a lot of good people on my conscience. I looked around the room as I set my spellbooks down on the counter and wondered if any of these folks were going to get added to the list before we were done here.

"Penny for 'em," Flynn said.

"Huh?"

"You were a million miles away. What's up?"

I looked around the room. Sparkles and Watson were exchanging status reports, but Jo was looking right at us. *Not a lot getting past that one.* "Nothing," I lied. I could see in Flynn's face that she knew I was lying, and it didn't sit well with her. Hard to lie to someone who can see inside your head. But right at that moment, I didn't care. I couldn't stand in the middle of our war room, such as it was, and express my doubts that we'd be able to do this job, or get everybody out alive if we could. That wouldn't help anyone. I kept a tight rein on my emotions and my thoughts, sending a quick promise across our mental link to explain later, when we were alone.

"Nah, it's cool," I continued the lie. "I was just thinking about this one spell I heard a rumor about. It diverts energy from one place to another. Maybe we could use it to spread out the magical energy released from Orobas's plan to a bunch of places, so it couldn't open a permanent rift."

"But wouldn't that open a lot of small, temporary, rifts? That might be just as bad," Jo said. "Opening a dozen gateways to Hell all over the world, even for a little while until they closed on their own, seems like a recipe for a demonic invasion."

"And without having a team on the ground everywhere we diverted the energy to, who knows what kind of shitshow we'd be in for," I agreed. "Yeah, that's *no bueno*."

"Well, let's eat, then we can get back to it after dinner," Watson said, setting containers of food out on the table.

"Did somebody say food?" Gabby asked as she came in. She was in a tattered t-shirt, jeans, and no shoes, with a towel wrapped around her head.

I looked at her with one eyebrow raised.

"Had to shower," she said. "My clothes got a little blood on them."

"Some of the people we talked with weren't very cooperative," Flynn agreed.

"Funny, you're not covered in blood," I said. "Or did you already wash off the evidence?"

"No, I managed to stay out of the splash zone," she replied. "But trust me, interrogations with Little Miss Sunshine here are messier than a Blue Man Group show."

"Adam and Luke already head out?" I asked.

"Yeah, they're off looking for seedy underworld connections to cajole, bribe, or intimidate," Jo said.

"I wanted to go, but they said I would intimidate their contacts," Gabby whined. "Imagine that—Frankenstein's monster meets Dracula, and *I'm* the scary one?"

"I think that says something about your negotiation methods, Gabriella," Watson said, looking at the containers of food with a skeptical eye. "Is there anything in this assortment of, dare I call it, food that isn't fried?"

"The barbecue isn't fried, but the pickle are," I said, pulling a paper plate out of the box and piling it high with pulled pork, macaroni and cheese, and fried pickles. "I thought about getting Frito pie, but that would have taken way too long to explain to Captain Cambridge here." It was a statement of geographical prejudice that only Flynn smiled at my culinary humor.

"What's next?" Flynn asked as we all sat down to eat. Sparkles had vanished from the TV screen, not enjoying watching people eat.

"Oh yeah, that reminds me." I pulled a map of Atlanta out of my back pocket and tossed it into the middle of the table. "After we eat, I'm going to need everybody but Becks to clear out of here for an hour or so. I have a ritual that may let us locate the other major magical artifacts in the area, but I need quiet to perform it."

"So you're going to perform a 'ritual' with your girlfriend for about an hour that requires the conference table?" Gabby asked with a smirk. "You know, one of the bedrooms on the floor might be more comfortable for that."

"Blow me, Gabs. It's a geolocation spell, so I have to spread the map out.

I'll use Rebecca as an anchor while I send my astral form out into the city, using the map as a guide. That should let me locate any hot spots of mystical energy a lot faster than driving all over town. Flynn will be my tether back to my body in case I get lost or run into anything with bad intentions. Any happy fun time will have to wait until Orobas is dealt with."

"Not that it's any of your business," Flynn added. Gabby put up her hands in mock surrender, but the little upturn at the corner of her mouth never vanished.

We plowed through healthy servings of barbecue and fried pseudo-vegetables in silence for a few minutes, then cleared the table. Jo, Gabby, and Watson retired to a nearby room with a stack of arcane books to scour for world-rending spells while I dug four big white pillar candles and a box of Morton's salt out of another bag Watson brought up with the food.

I spread the map out onto the table and held the corners down with the candles. I poured a circle of salt around the table, making sure there were no breaks in it, then had Flynn step over the line and sit at the foot of the table.

"You're going to be my anchor. All you have to do is keep our link open, and every once in a while, just throw a thought my way."

"Kinda like psychic radar? I just ping you every so often to make sure you can find your way back to me?"

"Exactly like that," I agreed. I sat in the chair at the head of the table and looked behind me to make sure the line of salt was still intact.

"What's the circle for?" Becks asked.

"It's just a little precaution," I replied. "I don't think anything is looking for me, and what I'm doing is unlikely to set off any defenses that local magicians have put on their stash of toys, but just in case, I want a little extra security around my physical form while I'm off dancing in the astral plane."

"Makes sense. But what if I need to bring the circle down for some reason?"

"Obviously, I hope you won't, but if something gets in here with us, and you need to bolt, just scrub the line of salt with your foot. Because we'll be linked when I invoke the circle, your essence will be tied to it as well as mine, and you can take it down just like I can. Sound good?"

"As good as anything."

"Okay, then. Let's go on a magical scavenger hunt."

CHAPTER SEVEN

I put my hands on the table, touching the map, and sent a tendril of my consciousness out to Flynn, strengthening the link that was always there, bolstering it with a mental image of steel cables wrapped around each other into a thick, sturdy rope of metal wire, tying us together.

Whoa, I "heard" in my head. *That's way tighter than we're usually linked.*

Yeah, I sent back. *Because I'm leaving my physical body, I needed to beef up the psychic tether so I'll have something to follow if I get lost or need to jump back in a hurry. You good? I'm about to start the spell.*

I'm good.

I closed my eyes and poured a little bit of my essence into the circle, invoking it. The rest of the hotel room fell away as a shimmering barrier of magical energy snapped into place around me, the conference table, and Becks. My circles are a little different from the old-school ones that people used in the days before electricity, indoor plumbing, and hotels. My "circle" was shaped more like a dome, a semi-circle of magical energy with a flat bottom under our feet. It took me about ten years to figure out how to shape the energy to flow in a dome over my head with a flat disk under me, but it became a necessary evil once the floor beneath me was pretty much guaranteed to have conduit and wires running through it. That kind of breach makes a typical circle, which is more like a sphere, very vulnerable, and is why a lot of practitioners only work outside nowadays. If you can get far enough into the woods, you know that the bottom part of your circle is only going through dirt and roots, and it's still intact beneath your feet.

That doesn't work for me. The demons I hunt are most often in buildings. Or in people who are in buildings. And after the first time an imp rode a water pipe through my circle and knocked the shit out of me, I learned that the old ways weren't very good anymore. But now my circle was secure from attacks from below and above, so I could start my ritual.

There wasn't a spell for what I was trying to do, so I was making it up as I went along. The story of my life. I focused my consciousness inward, concentrating on the core of *me*, those things that defined my very Quincy Harkerness. Not my height, weight, hair color, or clothes. More my sense of being, my smart-ass personality, my slightly off-kilter moral compass, my friendships, my desires, my love for Rebecca, my regrets about Dennis and Anna… all the things that over a century of life built up to make me into the man I am. I took that essence of myself and separated it from my physical form, stepped outside myself, and with a slight tearing sensation, I was free.

I looked to my right, and there I sat. My hair needed a trim, I could use a shave, and I was a little too skinny. My jacket needed desperately to go to the cleaners, and my Doc Martens had seen better days. But my jeans were mostly clean, and my black button-down shirt still held a vestige of a crease here and there where it once saw the bottom of an iron. The bags under my eyes told the real story, though.

This was a man who needed about a week's worth of sleep, a month's worth of good meals, and if the beginnings of a spider web of broken blood vessels on my nose was any indication, a serious decrease in the alcohol intake.

I look like hell, I thought.

You've seen better days, Flynn agreed.

Why didn't anybody tell me?

I thought we'd save the world first, and if we didn't all die in the process, I'd bring up the idea of a vacation.

Makes sense.

Now go find us some magical trinkets so we can finish up the world-saving and move on the sunny beaches and umbrella drinks.

Yes, ma'am.

I turned to the map, spread out over the conference table. It was a lifeless thing, but I knew how to change that. This was sympathetic magic, where I wanted to use the map as a representation of the real city to show me the location of items. I focused myself on the map and poured energy into it, strengthening its representational link to Atlanta. As I did, I concentrated on the mystical ebb and flow of the area, the pulse of magic that breathes in the heart of everywhere people live.

The map started to glow in my Sight, a spider web of ley lines criss-crossing the surface as the natural pathways of magical energy materialized. Wherever they crossed, the light flared a little brighter, and where enough lines converged, a node appeared, a hub of magical focus where the power was closer to the surface, easier to access for practitioners and the mundane alike. Nodes began to flare into my view all over Atlanta: one in Centennial Park, one at the Fox Theatre, one right down the street at the Marriott Marquis hotel of all places. A smaller one at the Margaret Mitchell house, one at The Vortex, no surprise there. There were even a couple of churches built on nodes, a fact that would amuse the local witches and likely horrify some of the pastors.

I focused past the nodes to the less natural hot spots. Some places popped into view that were instantly recognizable to me. The Masquerade nightclub was a long-standing meeting place for supernatural types, so I disregarded that one. Anything near Little Five Points was going to be too popular with local weirdos and wannabes to house any artifacts of real use, but three places twinkled in my view. Sitting far from any ley lines, nodes, or known locations of magical practitioners, there was a house in Buckhead that shone like a beacon to my astral self. There was also a hot spot in Grant Park near Zoo Atlanta, and one more right on top of the CDC.

Great, do I want to go into the house of likely a powerful magician, go argue with a wild animal, or play with the plague? I'll start with the magician. Looks like I'm off to see a wizard.

I concentrated on the image of the house in Buckhead, focused my mental imagery on the map, the surrounding streets, fixed an image in my head of tree-lined avenues and ridiculously large homes, and stepped into the map.

I closed my eyes tight as I dove forward, half-expecting to run face-first into the walls of my own circle and get slammed back into my body and knocked silly with magical backlash, but the spell worked exactly how I wanted it to, and when I opened my eyes I was "standing" on a sidewalk in front of a two-story house on a tree-lined street in north Atlanta.

Well, that went better than expected. I reached out along my mental link to Flynn and felt her respond with a little tug. Good, my anchor line was holding. *So far, looks like everything's coming up Harker.*

I walked to the front door and stepped right through it into a grand foyer. The floors were marble, and a huge staircase curved up in front of me, banister gleaming in the light from a crystal chandelier above me. I was a little confused at the ease of my entry. This house was warded to high heaven, but only against physical threats. There was nothing in place to keep out spirits or astral projections, which seemed off to me. Why ward against one type of threat, but not the other?

"Probably because I am not afraid of ghosts or spirits," came a voice from my right. I turned to see a man standing there with a pair of long curved daggers in his hands. He was a big man, easily six-three and about two-fifty, and nothing about him looked soft. He wore his brown hair short, and he was dressed for bed, in a pair of pajama pants with no shirt and bare feet. He held the knives like he knew how to use them, and they glowed like a pair of miniature suns in my Sight. I knew right away that those blades could cut me to ribbons, even in my incorporeal state.

I knew that was too easy.

"Yes, you should have," the man replied.

I cocked my head sideways. *You can hear me?*

"Of course I can hear you. You are in my home, my domain. I am the master here, and I can do whatever I choose. I can hear the spirits, I can see ghosts, and I can send you back to the afterlife!"

I'm not a ghost! I'm an astral projection. I realized a little belatedly that admitting I was essentially a psychic cat burglar might not be any more endearing than being a ghost. My host apparently decided the same thing, since he charged me with those glowing knives aimed straight at my chest.

CHAPTER EIGHT

I felt for the tether to Flynn, looking to use it as a quick escape, but it was gone. I had no connection to the outside world, nothing tying me to my body, and no good way to get out of this house before its owner skewered me with his glowing spirit blades.

I dodged left to avoid his first charge, my mind racing as I tried to come up with a plan. I couldn't fight him because I didn't have any mass or form. But he could hurt me with his magical blades. At least they certainly looked like they would hurt, and he was waving them around like they would hurt, so I figured it best not to take the chance.

He swiped at me with one hand, but I kept dancing back. I'd never fought anyone while incorporeal before, so I was at a disadvantage. Worse for me, my opponent moved like it wasn't his first ghost battle. I danced around the foyer until I got to the front door, then dove forward to get outside and start making my way back downtown to the hotel the best I could.

Except I couldn't get through the door. I smacked into the wood just like I was solid, crossing my eyes and sending stars shooting through my vision. *What the fuck?*

"By the way, revenant, my domicile is built as a spirit trap. Think of it as a roach motel for the supernatural—ghosts check in, but they don't check out." He laughed, an ugly thing that bubbled up from some dark place, and I started to wonder about his intentions in turning his home into a beacon of mystical energy, then setting a trap for anyone who decided to take a peek. This was not a dude who just stumbled onto an artifact. This guy knew what he was holding and how to use it.

And he wanted to use them on me, as evidenced by him charging me again. I was hamstrung without my connection to Becks, trapped in this house with a pissed off ghost hunter, but I was the furthest thing from helpless. As I leapt over his charge, I started to remember all the things I knew about astral projection and defending myself while spirit walking.

I couldn't kick his ass, but I could still touch magic. Hell, I pretty much *was* magic at that point. I sprinted up the stairs, and when he followed, I vaulted the railing down to the first floor to create some separation. He spun around and sprinted down the stairs after me, but I had the seconds I needed.

I drew in my will and muttered *"momentum torporos."* I released the spell, and a ball of flickering blue-white energy shot toward the man. He intercepted the spell with one of his knives, slicing it out of midair.

I followed up with a bolt of pure energy, this one much more solid and red in color. He blocked the onslaught with his other blade, seeming to absorb it into himself.

"Is that all you've got, spirit!" He laughed, a big grin splitting his grim face. "That won't be enough to keep me from draining what remains of your life force!" He charged me again, twirling his blades around his hands like the star of a badly dubbed kung fu movie. I spun to the right and conjured a gleaming blade of pure power, a soul blade capable of carving this bastard to ribbons, even in my spirit form. I slashed at his hamstring, but there was no hamstring there. He stopped on a dime, gathered his legs under himself, and leapt backward over my head, landing about two feet in front of me.

He grinned at me as I stared at him, mouth hanging open, and thrust both daggers for my exposed midsection. "Die, you dead bastard!"

I didn't bother to point out to him just how odd that sounded. I was too busy knocking his blades aside and shoving one hand into his chest up to the wrist. I might be incorporeal, but that didn't mean I couldn't affect things in the material world. When my spirit hand closed around his heart, his eyes went wide with pain and shock.

My astral form was made of energy, so I couldn't really squeeze his heart until blood poured out of his eyeballs like I wanted to. But since I was currently made of energy, I *could* disrupt the normal rhythm of his heartbeat, leaving him feeling like someone was playing bongos inside his chest. It didn't look very pleasant, judging by how pale he went, and by how quickly he dropped both knives and clutched his chest.

I withdrew my hand and took a step back. "Can we talk like civilized people now, or am I going to have to do something rude to your bladder?

You'd be amazed what organs are susceptible to low-grade electrical impulses."

He rubbed his chest and stepped farther back from me. He made no move to pick up his magical blades, so I didn't see a need to pursue him. "You speak?"

"Yeah, I speak. My girlfriend tells me I speak was too much, and my shrink says I don't ever really say anything, so the jury's still out on that bit. But I speak. For now, though, I'll let you have the floor. Who the fuck are you, pal, and how did you learn to use those pig-stickers?"

"You don't know who I am?" He looked confused, but at least he stopped darting glances at the knives on the floor like he was going to dive for them and start after me again any second.

"I have no fucking clue who you are, dude. All I know is there's some kind of serious magical mojo in this house, I'm guessing those knives, and that this place is built like a motherfucker of a ghost trap."

"So you're not here to punish me for neglecting my duty?"

"I'm not into that, man. I'm sure there are plenty of ladies in the ATL who'll cater to whatever fetish you're into. Or dudes. Whatever, it's none of my business. But no, that's not why I'm here. I'm here for the knives. Well, really to keep somebody else from getting the knives."

"Who would want my Spirit Blades?"

"Do you really call them that? A little pompous, don't you think?"

"What else would you call them? They're blades that can send ghosts to their final rest. They've been called The Spirit Blades of Callanwolde as long as I can remember. They are passed down to the firstborn of every generation for safekeeping, so when I came of age, my father bestowed them upon me and dubbed me the newest Knight of Callanwolde. It is our duty to defend the city against mystical threats and cleanse haunted locales of restless spirits."

"You talk like a guidebook entry," I said. "Who told you that bullshit?"

He looked offended. I guess I couldn't blame him, but I only have so much patience for people who try to stab me. It's a miracle I'm as chill around Gabby as I am, given the circumstances of our first meeting.

"That was the charge laid upon me when I came of age, to take up the mantle of the Callanwolde defenders and keep the civilians safe from vengeful spirits and evil specters. I have not fulfilled my obligations of late and am willing to accept whatever judgement the keepers of the spirit realm wish to lay upon me." Wow, this guy *really* took himself seriously.

"Look, I'm going to give you the benefit of the doubt because it sounds like somebody has fed you a line of crap, and it was probably somebody you trusted, like a parent or something. So, it's not really your fault you're an idiot, it was obviously drilled into you from a very early age. But let me make something clear—you are not Ghost Avenger Batman, I am not an evil spirit, and there is somebody very big and very bad coming for those knives, and if he gets them, you will be fucked beyond belief. And not in a good way."

He didn't look convinced, but I didn't have a chance to use my "pretty please" voice because just then the front door exploded inward, and a pair of demons stepped into the foyer.

"Fucking great," I muttered. "Party crashers." I turned to the superhero wannabe. "Run!"

He did. Except instead of running away like any sane person would when a pair of seven-foot dudes with crimson skin, goat legs, horns, yellow eyes, and fangs crash through their front door, Captain Stupid ran forward, scooped up his knives, and charged the demons.

It went almost as badly as I expected it to go. I got the hell out of his way, pushing off from the floor and sailing halfway up the staircase before turning to watch the carnage. The demons either couldn't see me or rightly didn't consider me a threat because they focused their attention on Sir Callanwolde, or whatever his name was.

He was fast, I had to give him that. That was about all he had going for him against a couple of heavily-muscled monsters that made Hulk Hogan look like Bill Gates. His initial charge took the demons off guard, and he actually scored a hit on the left-hand demon, carving a deep groove in its chest with his knife. The monster howled and lashed out with a wild looping punch that Callanwolde ducked effortlessly, then darted in to stab the demon under the armpit. It screeched in pain and dropped to one knee, rolling away from the crazy human with the glowing knives.

I had a moment of hope for the guy when it looked like he was holding his own and getting some good licks in. Then the second demon stepped in, and it all went to shit. While Callanwolde was focused on the first beastie, its partner clubbed him across the back of the neck with both fists. I heard the *crack* of bone all the way across the room, and the formerly courageous defender of Atlanta fell in a heap to the marble floor of his foyer.

I fired off a blast of pure power at the demon as it raised a foot to crush the downed man's skull. I caught it right on the side of the head, with all the effect of a fruit fly on a semi-truck. I think it might have noticed, but my energy was depleted from the fight, and some more powerful demons have certain types of magical resistance. Looks like I found one of the ones resistant to psychic blasts. Just my luck.

The demon's foot came down on the dark-haired man's skull, and the sound was like a melon dropped from a great height, a wet cracking sound followed by the *splat* of his brains squirting across the gleaming floor.

The second demon reached down and hauled the first one to its feet, then picked up the knives and tucked them into its belt. It looked up at me and smiled. "Normally I'd kill you for that cheap shot, Harker, but Orobas has something special planned for you. It's okay, though. He promised me I get to flay you for a century or two after you die, so we've both got that to look forward to."

The other demon grinned up at me, then said, "But don't worry. You won't have to wait long. Orobas is going to turn this shitheap dimension into a brand new Hell soon enough, then we can play with what's left of your tattered, pitiful soul. Bye for now." They turned and walked through the shattered door out into the night, unfurling their wings and leaping to the sky as soon as they were clear of the building.

I hurried after them, but they were out of sight before I cleared the front steps. *Becks, are you there?* I felt our connection as strong as ever, restored when the homeowner/magician died and his jamming spell was abruptly snuffed out.

Yeah, where the hell have you been?

Long story. Have somebody head over to this address with a body bag and a spatula. I'm coming back to you. I lost this one, but we've still got to try and keep the other artifacts out of Orobas's hands.

CHAPTER NINE

I blinked quickly, adjusting my vision to the physical spectrum and physical eyes. Flynn sat at the side of the table, her sidearm out and her chair positioned where she could see me and the door without moving.

"You're taking this whole bodyguard thing pretty literally, Detective," I said.

"You have a way of making people want to kill you, Harker," Becks replied with a sideways grin. "Even people who like you. So, I thought it might be a good idea to stay armed while I was watching over you."

"And here I expected to wake up with pictures of dicks drawn all over my face."

She grinned at me. "Who says you didn't?"

I laughed as I got up from my seat to go piss, then grabbed at the table for support as my rubbery legs almost gave out. Flynn stood up like a shot and got my arm over her shoulders, providing a stable base.

"Shit, sorry about that," I said. "I forget how draining astral travel can be."

"Not to mention astral demon-fighting," Flynn replied. I'd filled her in on the scrap at the magician's house on my way back.

"Yeah, that's not the best, either," I agreed. "I'm good now, just needed a second." I straightened up, but kept my arm around her, more for internal stability than physical this time.

"Look, Rebecca..." I started, but she put a finger to my lips.

"I know," she said, cutting me off. She looked up into my eyes, her brown pools deep with emotion. "We've got a lot of shit to sort out when this is over. But the key part of that is *when this is over*. We can't figure out what we're doing until we know there's going to be a world to do it in. So, let's put all kinds of talk about the future on the shelf until we kick Orobas's ass back to Hell and make sure we *have* a future. Then you can tell me how much you adore me, and we can talk about this ring." She pulled on a chain around her neck, and the diamond engagement ring I bought for her came into my view.

I looked at her, feeling a familiar jumble of emotions through our psychic link. She loved me, just like I loved her, and when we were this close, there was no chance of hiding that. But she was also scared. Scared of what it might mean to be with me, scared of the world I lived in, scared of losing me, and of losing herself in me.

I knew those feelings all too well because they rattled around in my head all the time. I felt all those things and more. I felt the fear of the inevitable pain of losing her, the pain of a man who's lived more than a century looking like he's thirty and knows that he has to watch his loved ones grow old and die while he just stays stuck in the same place forever.

We stood there, and the moment stretched out as we looked in each other's eyes, a lot of unspoken communication passing back and forth through our link without words. Just feelings flowing back and forth as I enjoyed the feeling of her in my arms.

But biology eventually won out. "I gotta piss," I said, breaking contact and heading the hotel room's surprisingly large bathroom. I looked in the mirror after washing my hands and decided she was right—I looked like refried shit.

"You're right, babe, I look like ten miles of bad road," I said, walking out into the war room. "As soon as we kill this motherfucker, we're going somewhere with white sand and umbrella drinks."

I cut off as I saw we weren't as alone as I thought. Watson, Gabby, and Jo sat around the table with Flynn. The map was rolled up at one end of the table, and Watson sat behind an open book with a grim look on his face.

"I'm guessing you don't look like you just ate a lemon raw just because I piss too loud," I said.

"No, and I wish I were only concerned with your bathroom habits," the slightly prissy British man said. It was a little hard to reconcile this slender man with a perfectly groomed beard and a limp with my memories of his portly ancestor. John Watson was a man with a ready smile and a peppermint in his pocket for the neighborhood children, his "Baker Street Irregulars" that served as his lookouts, his intelligence network, and his errand boys. I remembered him as an older man, but there was always steel beneath his love for fine Scotch and good meals. This new Watson hadn't shown me anything like that, but he acquitted himself well against the Reavers, and Becks trusted him, so he must not be a complete douche.

"Well, spill it, Doc," I said, pulling out a chair and leaning back with my arms across my chest. "What did you find out that's worse than knowing that Orobas plans to use a metric fuckton of magical artifacts to tear open a gaping doorway between Earth and Hell?"

"We found out what it takes to cast the spell in the first place," Watson said. His voice was somber without a hint of the pompous attitude he'd displayed ever since I first met him. I took a closer look at the man, taking in the dark look in his eyes, the pallor of his skin. He was shit-scared.

I took a deep breath. "What does it take, other than a metric fuckton of powerful magical artifacts?"

"Life," Watson said.

I let out the breath I was holding in almost a laugh. "Well, yeah! We knew that. I mean, shit, Watson, it took the combined life force of half a dozen people just to try and open the Gate Orobas wanted to open in Charlotte. I figured somebody would have to die to make this hole in the universe."

"Not somebody, Harker. A lot of somebodies," Jo said.

I looked at her. She looked just as rattled as Watson. "Am I missing something?" I asked. "How many people are we talking about?"

"The book doesn't say," Watson said, sliding a huge leather-bound tome across the table to me. "But it seems to indicate that the loss of life would be somewhere near double the population of Paris at the time the book was written."

I took a second to look at him, thinking about the French city I knew. "When was the book written?" I asked.

"The original text dates to the thirteenth century, give or take a few decades," he replied.

I shook my head. "I'm sorry, I'm not that old. Part of me really hates to ask, but how many people are we talking about?"

Watson just looked at me. It was Jo who answered. "It looks like the spell requires the energy of about a hundred thousand souls to fuel it."

"Holy fuck," I said.

"Yeah, pretty much." Gabby spoke for the first time. Even she looked rattled by the potential loss of life, and she was pretty much a psychopath.

"Where the fuck are they going to find that many people? And how are they going to harness that many souls at one time?" I asked.

"They're going after the Georgia Dome," Flynn said.

I turned to see her on her laptop. "What?" I asked.

"The Falcons have a playoff game tomorrow night, and there's a country concert at Philips Arena at the same time. Between those two events, you've got well over a hundred thousand people concentrated in a couple of blocks."

I stood up and slid the book back over to Watson. "Give me that map," I said to Jo, who handed me the rolled-up paper. I spread the map out, concentrating on the area around the Georgia World Congress Center and the Georgia Dome, just a few blocks from the building we were in. I poured a tendril of energy back into the map, reactivating the sympathetic spell I'd cast earlier, and opened my Sight. The lines of power flared into life all over the representation of Atlanta, with brighter points glimmering at the intersections.

"Looks like I remembered right," I said, pointing to the map.

"Remembered what?" Watson asked. "I can't see anything."

"Oh yeah, sorry," I shifted the spell slightly so that the lines showed up in the normal spectrum, and the others gasped.

"What is that?" Jo pointed at the lines and glowing dots.

"Those are ley lines," I said, giving them the condensed explanation of lines and nodes and how they moved magical energy around the world. "And that," I added, pointing to a spot near the Ferris Wheel attacks we'd foiled just the day before, "is a big-ass node right in the middle of the park."

"Just a block or two from the arena and the football stadium," Flynn said.

"Yep," I nodded. I released the spell, and the glow faded from the map. I sat down and looked around the table. "Orobas is going to try to open the rift in the middle of the park, probably under the Olympic Fountain. The summoning yesterday was probably just a test run to see how strong the node is and how active the lines in that part of town are."

"If the size of the monsters summoned is any indication, they are both strong and active," Watson said.

"Pretty much," I agreed.

"So he's going to destroy Philips Arena and the Georgia Dome to open a doorway to Hell in the middle of downtown Atlanta," Flynn said.

"And this time when we use the words Hell and Atlanta in the same sentence, we're not talking about changing planes at the airport," Gabby said.

We all sat silent for a long moment before Gabby spoke again. "Well, if nobody else is going to ask the hundred-thousand-dollar question, I will. What are we going to do about it?"

I looked around the table at a whole bunch of eyes staring back at me. Sometimes it really sucks being the oldest guy in the room. It means that everybody looks to you for answers, no matter how unqualified you might be. And this was a situation where I was starting to feel uniquely unqualified.

"I'll be honest with you, kids," I said. "I have no fucking idea."

Nobody spoke for several minutes after I admitted to having no clue how to stop the oncoming apocalypse. Finally, Watson pushed his chair away from the table and walked over to the small wet bar against one wall of the room. He poured himself a highball glass half full of amber liquid, then poured another one and brought it to me without a word.

"Sorry, ladies," he said. "I have no idea what you drink, but having seen Mr. Harker's home liquor stores when we were in Charlotte last week, I know him to be a man who appreciates a good whiskey. And barring the presence of that, this American swill shall have to do."

I nodded my thanks, ignoring for the moment that fact that he had been in my apartment more recently than I had.

Watson rolled up the map, pushed the books of magical history to the side, and leaned forward, his elbows on the polished wood of the conference table. His glass cradled between his hands, he looked across at me. "It seems to me we will have to deal with a three-pronged attack from our adversary. Orobas will be at or near the ley line node to cast the spell. Then there will be someone—"

"Or something," Gabby interjected.

"Thank you, Gabriella," Watson replied. "There will be a force of some sort at the football stadium, and another at the concert hall. We will need to eliminate all three forces in relatively short order to avoid giving away our foreknowledge of events and losing the element of surprise. Does that sound roughly accurate?"

Once he started talked tactics, I revised my opinion of Watson in an instant. "Where did you serve?" I asked.

He started a little. "Afghanistan. Why?"

"You don't talk like that unless you've been somewhere facing a determined and inventive opposition force."

"What they lacked in resources, they made up for in knowledge of the area, improvisational ability, and dedication to their cause. I lost a lot of good men thanks to IEDs over there."

"I'm sorry," I said. "I don't know exactly what that's like, but I've seen a few wars, and they don't get better as we get more efficient at killing each other, just bloodier."

"True words," Watson said with a little nod. "Now, back to the problem, or problems, at hand. We have an opposing force that will be entrenched in three positions, surrounded by civilians, and with weapons of nearly unimaginable power. And we need to dispatch all of them simultaneously without arousing undue suspicion from the local populace or constabulary."

"Just another day at the office," Jo said. "We do more impossible shit before nine a.m. than most people do in their entire lives."

CHAPTER TEN

"Nothing here," Watson said into his Bluetooth headset. He scanned the crowd below him through the scope pressed to his cheek. He wondered, not for the first time, why exactly Adam carried a hunting rifle with a scope in a hidden compartment in the back of his Hummer, but it seemed better not to ask. And it certainly came in handy in their current endeavor.

"Concourse looks clear, too," Jo replied.

"I've got nothing except a couple dozen horny stagehands back here," Gabby said from her position backstage.

"There's nothing on the cameras," Sparkles added.

"Hells," Watson muttered. "Do we have any idea when this massacre is supposed to take place?"

"Harker thought around nine p.m. made the most sense. The concert will be in full swing, and the game will still be early enough that even if the Falcons are getting killed, most folks won't want to leave yet," Jo replied.

"I'll never understand you Americans. Leaving a match before the last goal is scored. You call yourself fans?" Watson said. "Gabby, have you seen anything at all out of the ordinary?"

"Have you ever been backstage at a concert, Jack? Everybody back here looks out of the ordinary. I can't tell if I'm at a tattoo convention or a meetup for middle-aged men with beer guts and ponytails. Wait a second, there's something... never mind."

"What is it?" Watson asked.

"There was a dude who was way too young and pretty to be backstage, but then he picked up a guitar. He must be with the band. What are you seeing?"

Watson took his eye from the scope and gave the crowd a broad once-over. He knelt on the catwalk high above the scoreboard and peered over the thousands of t-shirt-clad people beneath him. "I see an outlandish number of John Deere hats, quite an obscene amount of flannel, and absolutely no one wearing pants that aren't at least a size too small. And that's just the women."

"Welcome to a pop country concert, Watson," Jo said, chuckling a little into her headset. "Wait a second, that's not right…"

"What is it?" Watson and Gabby asked simultaneously.

"There's a service door open," Jo replied. "I'm going to go check it out." She said nothing for a couple of tense moments, then came back on the line. "There's a stairwell going down behind this door. I'm going to head down and take a look."

"Wait for us," Watson said. "I can be to you in just a couple of minutes."

"Yeah, me too," Gabby added. "Don't think you're going to get to go kill stuff without me there."

"Okay, first, have you ever considered therapy? Like, a lot of it. And second, fine, I'll wait. I'm beside the restrooms at Section 114."

"On my way," Gabby said.

"There in a moment," Watson added. He made one more pass over the crowd through the rifle's high-powered scope; saw nothing more than excessive consumption of overpriced and watery beer, poor fashion decisions, and even more poorly thought-our hairstyles; and put the gun back in the soft case Adam supplied. He walked down the catwalk, tucked the gun and case behind a large breaker panel, and descended a short ladder to the spotlight booth. A befuddled stagehand looked up from his phone as Watson stepped into the small space.

"What are you doing up there, man? You're not supposed to be here…" The young man looked from Watson to his headset hanging on the safety rail several feet away. Watson pointed to his chest at "MAINTENANCE" embroidered there over the name "Steve" in script.

"There was a circuit breaker needed replaced. Lights flickering in the bathroom in one of the skyboxes. Sent me up here to take care of it. I been up there for like an hour messing with it." Watson's southern accent wasn't great, but it looked like it was going to be good enough to get past one bored stagehand.

"Oh, alright," the spotlight operator said. "Well, you better get down, then. My call light's blinking, so I guess the show's about to start." He picked up his headset, clicked a button on his belt pack, and said, "Spot 3 on headset."

Watson gave the man a little wave and slipped past him to the metal ladder that took him to the steady concrete of the last row of the upper level. He wasn't as fast on a ladder anymore—only having one foot that felt the rungs made him proceed with caution—but he managed.

Three minutes later, he joined Gabby and Jo beside the concession stand.

"You leave Adam's gun up in the rafters?" Gabby asked.

"Had to," he replied. "Couldn't exactly go carrying a hunting rifle through the concourse with twenty thousand people around, could I?"

"You obviously don't know the country music audience," Jo said. "That's the door." She pointed to a door across the wide expanse of tile and glass with "AUTHORIZED PERSONNEL ONLY" on it in big letters. The white letters on a red sign left absolutely zero doubt as to who they were directed at.

"You think our quarry might be down those stairs?" Watson asked.

"That's the best option I've found," Jo said.

"I think she's probably right," Sparkles said over their earpieces. "Those stairs lead down into the maintenance tunnels, and the only better place to plant a bomb for maximum carnage is underneath the stage."

"I checked there," Gabby said. "Nothing out of the ordinary." The others stared at her. "What?" she protested. "I made friends with one of the stagehands."

"Is he still alive?" Jo asked.

"Of course! I don't go around indiscriminately killing... Oh screw it, I can't even say that with a straight face. But yes, this one is alive." Gabby grinned, then continued. "Unconscious and tied up inside a wardrobe case that isn't slated to get opened until their next show in Baltimore, but alive."

"Why do I even ask?" Jo rolled her eyes. "Let's get down there and see if we can find this bomb."

"What makes you so sure it's a bomb?" Gabby asked.

"How else would you kill everyone in this arena?" Jo fired back.

"Acid in the sprinkler system would be a good start. Incendiary devices scattered throughout the seating area, then bar the doors. Wouldn't be as efficient, but could lead to more mayhem. I could also just release a couple dozen demons, or a couple of machine gun teams, although I think Jack would have seen those from the catwalk. A biological agent in the beer could take out a good half the crowd, and if we used a contact poison on the doors and seat arms, we could make sure we got everyone that way..."

"You're truly disturbed, did you know that?" Jo looked at her teammate with a look of mild horror on her face. "Do you sit around dreaming up ways to kill thousands of people in one shot?"

"Nah, but it's something to pass the time on the toilet. I got tired of Angry

Birds. Let's go." Gabby walked across the crowded concourse, opened the door, and started down the stairs. A security guard spotted her and started in that direction, but Watson intercepted him.

"I got her, man," he said, pointing to his jacket. "She's a... new friend, if you get my drift." He put a lascivious waggle into his eyebrows. The guard laughed and slapped Watson on the back, then walked off.

Watson followed Gabby down the stairs, drawing his Glock as he did so. Jo slid into the stairwell last, shrugging out of her long duster and dropping it to the floor, then pulling her hammer from the ring on her belt.

"No more Wyatt Earp cosplay?" Gabby said with a smirk.

"You try carrying around a three-foot hammer and see what your wardrobe looks like," Jo grumbled.

"I'm good with my leather jacket," Gabby replied. "It hides the girls perfectly."

"The girls?" Jo asked. "I don't think that jacket does much to minimize your boobs."

Gabby reached under her arms and drew a pair of pistols from well-concealed shoulder holsters. "Yeah, but if people are looking at my boobs, they aren't looking at the girls." She turned the nickel-plated Colt 1911 pistols so they glinted in the light of the stairwell. "This is Thelma," she said, holding up the gun in her right hand. "And this is Louise." She gestured with the left-hand gun. "My new girls. I had a friend deliver them to the hotel this afternoon."

"You have a friend who runs a firearm delivery service?" Watson asked.

"You don't?" Gabby replied. "Let's go shoot something. I want to try these ladies out."

The trio descended the stairs into the basement of the building, then spread out in three directions as they entered the larger area below ground. The basement was a huge area directly under the basketball floor, with huge concrete pilings holding up the rest of the building and a network of pipes and electrical conduits snaking overhead.

"Dennis, can you hear me?" Watson whispered into his earpiece. There was no reply from the disembodied computer wizard. Watson pulled out his cell phone and saw NO SERVICE at the top of the screen. Swearing under his breath, he slid the phone back into his pocket.

He looked across the room at Jo, then over at Gabby, then focused his attention on the middle section of the room. He moved across the room, dodging behind pieces of equipment and pallets of program books and plastic beer cups in a crouch, a position made more difficult by the fit of his prosthetic. After all these years, Watson moved with barely a limp, but some positions were very painful to walk in, and stooping down to make a smaller silhouette was one that made his stump rub painfully and the straps bind in uncomfortable ways. He stopped, pressing his back to a pillar, and massaged his thigh. Not for the first time, he cursed the IED that took his leg below the knee and the lives of two of his squad mates.

Momentary pity party over, he took a deep breath and stepped around the concrete support. His eyes caught a flash of red up ahead and at his two o'clock, and he moved in that direction. He slid from shadow to shadow, ducking behind pillars to conceal his progress. Moving slowly cost him time, but he reached the pulsing red LED barely a minute later nonetheless.

"Fucking hell," he whispered, looking at a block of C4 the size of a loaf of bread sitting on the floor next to the central support pillar. Glancing around, Watson estimated them to be almost exactly at center court, where an explosion would take out most of the floor seats and weaken the entire structure considerably. The amount of explosive material staring at him would certainly bring down a good chunk of the floor above them, but it wasn't enough to destroy the building.

The device was an ugly thing, nothing like the elegant bombs on the television shows. There was no convenient countdown timer on the front of the device. Watson had no idea what was supposed to trigger the explosion, just that he had to stop it.

"This would be a lovely time to have studied munitions," he muttered to himself. "My uncanny skills at interpreting contract clauses are somewhat less than useful here."

"I've got something." Jo's whisper cut through the still air. Watson looked in her direction, then started running her way as he heard a muffled *oof* from his right. He looked back at the bomb, hoping that he could devise a way to stop it by the time he got back. Or he could just get killed by whatever Jo was fighting. That would save him a lot of headache.

Jo was trading kicks and hammer blows with a pair of six-foot demons. They were all teeth and claws, with no real strategy. Jo dodged, jabbing with her hammer and using the handle to block more than swinging it the traditional way.

Gabby stepped out from behind a pillar and fired off four quick shots into the backs of the demons. They went down in a heap, and Jo smashed their skulls to gravy with her hammer. Watson turned back to the bomb, ringing ears now adding to his distraction.

"What did you... oh, shit," Jo said as she came over to Watson's side.

"Oh shit, indeed," the Brit said as he knelt in front of the device, looking in vain for something as simple as an OFF switch.

"Do you know how to disarm that thing?" Jo asked.

"No bloody clue," Watson admitted.

"Then get out of the way and go find the other charges," Gabby said, putting a hand on his shoulder.

Watson looked up at her. "You know how to disarm a bomb?"

"I'm not just a pretty face, Jacky-boy. I spent a year doing underwater demolitions while I was looking for a sea serpent in the Gulf of Mexico."

"There are sea serpents in the Gulf of Mexico?" Jo asked.

"Not anymore" was Gabby's simple reply. She holstered her pistols, took Watson's spot in front of the device, and pulled a small multi-tool from her belt. "There are probably four more devices just like this, set to go off about thirty seconds after this one blows. That would pretty much guarantee the whole building comes down. There might be some perimeter bombs for the first responders, but I doubt it. Orobas wants to maximize death toll, not instill maximum long-term fear in the population." Watson looked down at the woman with new eyes. The wise-cracking Harley Quinn-inspired psychotic was gone, and in her place was a smart, capable woman who was an expert in her craft. The wild-eyed grin she usually wore plastered across her face was nowhere to be seen, replaced by a wry smirk.

"Yeah, I'm like an onion, Jackie-boy. I've got layers. Now go find those other bombs while I figure out whether it's the red wire or the blue wire."

Watson nodded to Jo, and they split up. Jack headed off to one side of the arena's underbelly, his pistol in one hand. It took only a few moments to locate the other devices, and by the time he returned to Gabby's side, she had removed the detonator and separated it from the plastic explosive.

Jo walked up just as Watson did. "I found two more bombs," she said.

"As did I," Jack replied.

"Okay," Gabby said, showing them the electronics in her hand. "Now, we'll split up and take them all out faster. All you need to do is cut the—" Her words died in her throat in a strangled gasp as she clutched her neck.

"What's wrong?" Jo asked as Gabby dropped to her knees.

Jack looked past the stricken woman to see a slight man holding his arm out toward Gabby, his hand in a choking motion. He drew his pistol, but a blur of black crashed into him, and he tumbled to the floor under a ball of hair and teeth. Jack let the gun fly, concentrating on the monster atop him.

He used his momentum to carry himself and his assailant over in a tumble, shoving against the thing's body to create some separation. Jack let out a yell as razor-sharp teeth clamped down on his arm, and their skid across the floor came to bone-jarring halt against a massive concrete support pillar. Watson stared at the thing chewing on his arm and saw it was some type of dog, or wolf, or wolf-demon. Whatever it was, it had his left arm in its mouth and was worrying it like a chew toy.

Jack swung around until he could get his right hand near the thing's head and started punching. He quickly abandoned that idea when he found the skull as hard as the concrete he was writhing on. Claws ripped at his chest and belly, and Jack was very glad he had kept his wool coat on when they descended into the basement; otherwise the creature would have disemboweled him. Blood ran freely from the creature's mouth, and blood and spit splattered Watson's face.

He finally contorted himself around enough to reach his pocketknife and flipped the small Gerber knife open. Jack jammed the knife into the dog-thing's eye, then withdrew the short blade and did it again. He repeated the process several times, feeling the jaws clamp down ever tighter on his forearm with every stroke, until finally, with one last great thrust, he heard a soft *crunch* as he pierced the beast's brainpan and drove the knife into its brain up to his fist.

The beast opened its maw wide in one final yelp of pain, and Jack drew his arm back. He heard an echo of the dog's yelp behind him, then another, louder *crunch*, followed by a muttered, "Take that, you low-rent Vader motherfucker" in Jo's voice.

"Is everyone alright back there?" he called.

"Yeah, we're good. Whatever you did to the dog hurt the magician, too, so he couldn't hold us anymore. Then I bashed his head in. You okay?" Jo asked.

"Been better. Been worse. How's Gabriella?"

"I'm fine," came a hoarse croak. "As long as that fucker's dead. I'm going to take the rest of the bombs. Jo's coming with to cover me. Quicker that way. We'll meet you at the stairs."

"Aces," Jack replied.

Watson gritted his teeth and looked at his arm. It wasn't completely ruined, but it would be useless for several weeks, if not months. The major veins seemed intact, and he could move all his fingers independently, if not with any strength. He slithered out of his coat and used the dark wool to wipe off as much blood as he could. Then he cut away the sleeve of his shirt at the shoulder and fashioned a crude bandage from his shirt sleeve and strips cut from his coat. By the time he was finished with his field dressing and made it back to the stairs, the women were waiting for him.

Gabby held five electronic devices in her hands, and Jo carried her hammer loose. "Wanna help?" Jo asked, hefting the hammer.

"No, be my guest," Watson replied.

"Fair enough." With a nod to Gabby, Jo hoisted the hammer. The dark-haired woman set the electronics on the ground, and Jo smashed them to tiny pieces. After a few quick hammer blows, the detonators were blissfully inert.

"What did you do with the plastic explosive?" Jack asked.

"I left it there," Jo said. "With no detonator, it's completely harmless, and we can send a bomb disposal unit in here if we manage to save the world tonight."

"And if we don't, nobody will care," Gabby added, the mad gleam returning to her eye. "Now let's go to the park and see if Harker found something else to shoot. You and Jo killed the bad guys this time, so I *really* want to shoot somebody." She spun around and took the stairs two at a time heading out into the night.

"Sometimes I wonder how much of that is an act..." Jo mused.

"Then you decide that if you knew the answer, it would terrify you?" Watson said.

"Yeah, exactly. How's the arm?"

"Well, I fear I will have to postpone my piano recital, but I think with work and good whiskey, I will manage to make a full recovery."

"Assuming we save the world in the next two hours," Jo said.

Jack nodded. "Because if we don't do that, I fear I shall have much more to worry about than an injured arm." He turned and followed Gabby up the stairs to the next impossible task.

CHAPTER ELEVEN

Luke stepped onto the concourse at the Georgia Dome, wincing at the roar of the crowd as the Falcons' starting lineup took the field. "I can't believe I allowed myself to be talked into this," he muttered.

"Let's face it, Luke, you're a sucker for anything that kid asks you to do. You always have been." Adam's voice rumbled across into Luke's ear from the Bluetooth headset he wore.

"It's not so much the activity that I loathe as it is the disguise," the ancient vampire replied. "You do understand that I have the ability to cloud men's minds and make myself invisible to their perceptions, correct?"

"I remember," Adam said. "I also know that clouding seventy-five thousand minds at once is probably a stretch, even for the Lord of the Undead."

"You know I hate that name."

"I do," Adam admitted. "But not as much as you hate your disguise."

Luke looked down at himself and had to admit that his old friend was correct. He was currently decked out in blue jeans, sneakers, a Matt Ryan jersey purchased from the team store, and a black Falcons baseball cap. "I feel as though the only thing missing from this ludicrous ensemble is a giant foam finger," he muttered.

"You should have said something," Adam replied. "We could have gotten you one of those, too." Adam stepped up beside Luke, a giant cup of beer looking tiny in his massive hand. Adam wore his usual brown pants but added a bright red Falcons hoodie to his wardrobe. With the hood up to conceal his scars, he just looked like a very large fan walking around the concessions area.

"Where should we begin?" Luke asked. "I have only a limited familiarity with explosives. My methods of dispatching enemies are typically much more... immediate."

"I think we might need to look at a different idea than explosives," Sparkles said in Luke's ear. "I don't know how much C4 it would take to bring down an entire football stadium, but it's going to be much harder to kill all these people that way. The building is just way too spread out."

"That makes sense," Adam said, adjusting the Bluetooth device in his own ear. "Even if you collapse a whole end zone, you might leave half the people alive. So, what's the other idea? How do we kill a stadium full of people in one shot?"

"A small nuclear device would almost certainly do the job," Luke said, and both Adam and Sparkles fell silent as the truth of his words sunk in.

"Fuck me, Luke," Sparkles said. "I don't even have a body anymore, and I just got a chill down my spine."

"Am I incorrect, Dennis?" Luke asked.

"No, no," Sparkles said. "You're right, it's just... shit, a nuke?"

"It makes sense," Adam said. "It's about the only thing that could take down an entire stadium without having a plane to deliver the payload. And it's not like Orobas is going to give a shit about what happens with the fallout since he's trying to destroy the Earth anyway."

"It also explains why Quincy sent the two of us here to handle this site and sent the three humans to handle the arena," Luke said.

"Because you can bring down an arena with traditional explosives, and you guys wouldn't be harmed by any leaking radiation," Sparkles agreed. "Well, goddamn, boys, what do you want to do?"

Luke let out a deep breath, more for effect than any need. "Well, we were sent here to find and disable an explosive device. I suppose now it's more critical than ever that we do so."

"Agreed," Adam said. "Now where do you suppose one hides a nuclear bomb in a football stadium?"

"That's not something I've ever considered, Adam. As I mentioned, large-scale slaughter hasn't been my forte for quite some time," Luke replied.

"I have the plans called up," Dennis said over their link. "There is an access tunnel underneath the stadium that circles the field. I'd start down there."

"And how are we supposed to find this thing, Dennis?" Adam asked. "Do we just go around the underbelly of the stadium whistling and calling out 'here bomb, here bomb'?"

"I thought we'd be a little more scientific than that, but not too much," came the reply. "Let's start by looking for anything or anyone out of the ordinary. People that don't look like they belong at a football game. Or in this dimension."

"Oh, so look for people like us?" Adam asked.

"Pretty much," Dennis agreed.

The big man nodded and stepped over to a nearby service entrance. Finding it locked, he wrapped his huge hand around the knob and squeezed. The squeal of metal crushing in his grip was almost drowned out by the roar of the crowd as the opening kickoff spiraled into the air, but not quite. One particularly alert security guard walked over to the pair with one hand on his pistol and the other on his radio.

"What are you doing over here?" the rotund guard asked, his moustache quivering.

Luke turned to him and waved a hand in front of the man's face. "These are not the droids you are looking for."

The man's eyes glazed over in a blink. "These are not the droids I am looking for."

"Go on about your business."

"I will go on about my business." The guard turned around and walked off.

Adam looked down at Luke. "Did you really just Jedi mind trick that guard?"

"Whatever works, my giant friend. Whatever works."

The two descended the narrow stairwell into the bowels of the stadium, concrete pressing in on all sides. Luke opened his senses wide, listening for anything out of the ordinary, but the din of the crowd above and the bustle of an active stadium below were simply too much for him to sort anything out.

Adam pushed open the door into a wide curved hallway, big enough to drive team buses into. Several television trucks were parked in a loading area ahead of them with cables snaking across the floor to various ports and panels. People in headsets and baseball caps hustled to and fro, all at an almost-run.

"I think it's safe to say we're not going to find anything in all this chaos," Adam said, keeping his voice low.

"As loathe as I am to insert myself into that fray, my friend, I have to disagree. Were I to plant a bomb under a venue such as this, the place where the most people would be rushing by is exactly where I would do so."

"Because it would have the highest death toll?" Adam asked.

"No," Luke disagreed. "If we are indeed looking for a nuclear device, it will kill everyone in the building regardless. No, I would hide something here for the simple fact that the more people rushing through an area, the less likely it is that a disguised package would be noticed. As long as it isn't bright red with

'BOMB' on the outside in giant letters, a box could sit here for hours, and everyone would just assume that someone else put it there."

"That actually makes a lot of sense," Adam said.

"It's the same method I used to smuggle coffins on freighters," Luke said. "Just put one more box in a crowd of boxes and busy people, and no one ever noticed."

"And here I thought it was some kind of magic."

"Simply my near-mythic understanding of human nature, my oversized friend. Nothing more."

"Well, I suppose if you live through enough centuries, you're bound to pick up a thing or two. So, let's go check things out." The two stepped out of the stairwell and walked over to the nearest TV truck, striding across the concrete like they owned the place. Luke peeled off to the right and circled around the first truck while Adam turned left and walked to the back of the second. They met behind the trucks, and each shook their head.

"There's nothing lying around. Nothing bigger than a Cheetos bag, anyway," Adam said.

"I cannot smell any plastic explosive or dynamite," Luke added.

"You can smell explosives? What are you, a TSA dog?" Adam asked.

"I have been around enough war zones to know that explosives all have a distinct odor that cannot be effectively masked," Luke replied.

"I'm not picking anything up on any of the infrared scans or... wait... what the ever-loving fuck is *that*? You guys gotta move. I think I found what you're looking for, and it is most certainly *not* a nuke," Dennis said over their headsets.

"Where are we going?" Adam asked, already in motion toward the front of the trucks. He stripped off his hoodie as he went, getting rid of the too-small garment so his arms could move more freely. A man stepped out of the truck into his path, but Adam just swept the two-hundred-pound man aside as if he were a fly.

The man stared up from the ground as the scarred giant stepped over him. "I thought wrestling was in here tomorrow..."

"The thing you're after is about halfway around the walkway from where you are," Dennis said. "Go to the right and haul ass. If it's putting off anywhere near the light that it is heat, you won't be able to miss it." Luke and Adam did as they were told, sprinting down the corridor to confront whatever awaited.

Luke quickly outpaced his bulkier friend, pouring on his enhanced speed and moving far past any human pace. He rounded a bend in the hall and came up short, almost toppling over in his haste to stop. "Dennis..." Luke said into his Bluetooth.

"Yeah, Luke, did you find the thing?"

"Oh, I found it… I'm just not sure what you think I can do about it."

"What do you mean? You've got to kill it. Or destroy it, or something."

"I can't even get near it, Dennis. Remember? I'm invulnerable to many things. Garlic is a myth. I care nothing about running water. I don't stop to count grains of rice or salt. I am no more affected by holy water or religious iconography than a human, and driving a stake through my heart will only render me unconscious, not turn me to dust. But there are two things I cannot, under any circumstances, come into contact with. One of those is sunlight. The other is, if you'll recall…"

"Fire," Dennis finished the sentence.

"Yes, Dennis. Fire. Now given that knowledge, what in all the hells am I supposed to do with *that*?"

The "that" in question was a six-foot walking bonfire. A fire elemental. And it was walking straight toward Luke. Luke did something he hadn't done in a fight in literally centuries. He started backing away.

"Luke, what are you doing?" Dennis said over the comm. "I've hacked the security cameras, so I can see you. Don't back up, charge that thing!"

"I can't, Dennis. I'm hundreds of years old. I am the very definition of 'highly flammable.' If I get near that thing, I will burst into flames."

"If you don't do something, the whole place will burst into flames! That red pipe over your head, the one that makes a right turn into the room beside you?"

"Yes?" Luke said.

"That's the main gas line for the building! It branches out from that room to every skybox kitchen and every concession stand in the stadium. If the flame guy gets to that pipe, it could shoot fireballs out of every gas port in the place. The whole joint would go up in flames!"

"That doesn't sound good." Adam's rumbling voice came from both Luke's headset and his right ear as the giant man came to a halt right beside the vampire. "Dennis, can you tell from the video exactly what this thing is?"

"Not exactly, but I think it's a fire elemental. It's made entirely of flame, so there's not really anything to punch."

"That makes things a little more complicated," Adam said.

"And also simpler," Luke added.

The big man turned to him, a puzzled look on his scarred face. Luke continued. "If it's an elemental, then something summoned it. If I can find that something, or someone, and dispatch it, then the elemental should return to its own plane."

"Should?" Adam said.

"Nothing is definite, my large friend. Nothing except the fact that I cannot go near the creature, so I must render my assistance in another fashion." With that, Luke dashed off past the elemental, farther into the bowels of the stadium.

"I suppose that leaves me to wrestle the man made of fire," Adam said with a sigh.

"Bring back memories?" Dennis asked.

"Yes, and not good ones," Adam replied. His mind flashed back to a crowd of angry villagers, pitchforks, the supposed death of his "father," Victor, and a pretty blonde girl who died at the hands of a monster who didn't know his own strength. Adam had spent decades working to atone for that one accidental murder, and it seemed that now, after all these years, the fire had finally caught up with him.

He rolled his shoulders, turned his head side to side, and cracked his knuckles. "Any suggestions would be welcome right about now," he said.

"Sorry, big guy," came the voice in his ear. "I've got nothing. I'm working to hack the sprinkler system and at least douse him a little bit, but so far no good."

Dennis's words sparked something in Adam, a flicker of inspiration that the heat and situation fanned into a plan. He looked around the immediate area, and finding nothing that fit the bill, grabbed a golf cart and tossed it into the path of the oncoming elemental. The man of fire barely slowed, just flowing around the obstruction like it wasn't even there. Adam then grabbed a cart full of metal cylinders with soda company labels on them and shoved the cart at the monster.

The metal tubes exploded upon contact with the fire-beast, dousing the elemental in a spray of de-carbonated soda syrup. The monster shrank upon contact with the liquid, but slowed its approach only for a few seconds. Adam dashed a dozen yards back up the tunnel and smashed the glass cover of a nearby fire box. He pulled the fire extinguisher from the wall and marched into the path of the elemental, extinguisher in hand and a faint hope for survival in his heart. Whatever happened next, it was going to hurt.

L uke sprinted along the tunnel, looking for anyone who looked deep in concentration and testing every doorknob he passed. He finally found an unlocked electrical room and ducked inside. This was as likely a place as any to hold a summoner, and he needed to find and dispatch this magician before Adam was burned to a crisp. Luke wasn't sure exactly how much flame his friend could endure before succumbing to the damage, but he was in no rush to find out.

His normally placid features split into a wide smile as he came upon a slender woman seated inside a protective circle, head bowed. She was obviously the summoner, and just as obviously vulnerable. Her magical circle would keep out any energy or mystical attacks, but it wouldn't stop Luke from simply stepping across the line and snapping her scrawny neck. He opened his mouth to warn the woman that this moment was going to be her last when something large and heavy crashed into him from the side.

Luke slammed into a breaker panel, his head smacking painfully into the metal cover. He turned to see his attacker and found himself face to face with a demon. This was a Reaver demon, one of the smaller creatures Quincy and his friends had faced the day before, but it was still a vicious close quarters opponent. Its overlong arms and wicked claws shredded Luke's overcoat but were unable to reach his flesh.

Luke smashed his right elbow down into the demon's grinning face, pulping its nose and eye socket, but it didn't release its grip. Luke wriggled his other arm free and rained fists down upon the demon's skull, to no avail. After almost a full minute of struggling in the monster's grip, Luke pushed off the wall with his left arm, ripped the cover off the breaker panel with his right, then reached into the electrical box, gripping one of the hot lugs with his left hand.

High-voltage electricity rocketed along every nerve ending, passing through his body into the demon. Luke's body went rigid; the demon's body began to convulse. As more and more power flowed through him, Luke noticed the unmistakable stench of burning hair—his own. Finally, the demon shook itself off Luke, who managed to pull his hand out of the panel and break the connection. He collapsed to one knee and looked over at the demon. Or rather, he looked as the scorched concrete where the demon last fell. There was no demon there, just the reek of sulfur and burned flesh.

Luke knew all too well that the burned flesh was his own, but there wasn't time to worry about that now. He took three long strides across the floor, stepped on the edge of the magician's magical circle, and kicked her under the chin. Even in his weakened state, Luke's power was more than strong enough to topple the woman backward, her head smacking into the concrete floor with the sound of a cantaloupe dropped from a great height.

Luke looked at the unconscious woman, then down at his smoldering flesh, and a small smile flitted across his features. "Dennis, did the elemental disappear when I rendered the spellcaster unconscious?"

"It did, Luke. I don't see anything else on the security cameras. I think you got the only one. And the arena team took out their bomb, so all that's left is to find Orobas and send that fucker back to Hell where he belongs."

"I concur. Please let Adam know that I will be with him momentarily. I feel a slight hunger that I must indulge before rejoining him." Luke clicked off his headset and put it in his pocket without waiting for an answer. He smiled down at the unconscious magician. "And you, my dear, can rest easy in the knowledge that your death will not be in vain. You may not have accomplished your initial goal, but healing me before I rend your employer limb from limb is a fate not without its merits."

He started toward the woman, fangs extended and a smile on his face that would have chilled the blood of anyone near enough to see it. "Just a little snack, and then we'll return to our regularly scheduled program of saving the world."

CHAPTER TWELVE

Centennial Olympic Park looked like the set of a horror movie when I walked up to the site of Orobas's planned ritual. I don't mean that there were dead bodies lying around and people covered in fake blood and effects makeup; I mean that it looked like someone was shooting a movie right in the middle of the Olympic Fountain. There was a crane with huge lights hanging from it, a team of gophers running around with clipboards and headsets, and a crowd of curious onlookers standing behind portable metal barricades.

I chuckled a little at the sheer balls of it all. Oro hadn't just found a way to hide his ritual from the authorities and people who might want to stop him, he'd found a disguise that would get him extra souls to destroy just off the bystanders and hopefuls looking for half a second of screen time. It would have been an incredibly elegant solution, except that I planned to spoil the whole damn party.

I walked up to the barricade with Flynn on my left side and a step behind to clear my hands in case I needed to fling a spell in that direction on short notice. I threw one leg over the barricade, and a minion rushed over to intercept me.

"Excuse me, sir," the minion said. She looked human, a short woman in a Walking Dead Crew t-shirt, jeans, hiking boots, and a Madea's Your Mama baseball cap with a long curly brown ponytail pulled through the back. She wore a radio on her belt and carried a clipboard, the uniform of production assistants the world over. "You can't come onto the set. We're going to start shooting in just a couple—"

I didn't slow down, just kept walking like she hadn't even spoken. I held up my Homeland Security badge and said, "Get the people out of here. A biological agent has been released in the Georgia Dome, and we need this area evacuated as quickly as possible." I pitched my voice loud enough that the nearest civilians also heard me. I saw out of the corner of my eye the nearest people turn to their neighbors and start to chatter. Good, I needed to sow a lot of confusion and more than a little panic if my sketch of a plan was going to work.

The PA got a confused look on her face, and she reached for her radio. "I need to check on that. But until I do, could you please step behind the barricade?"

"No, I can't," I said. "Detective, will you see that these people begin the evacuation quickly and efficiently?"

Becks' face flashed dark, and a hint of red appeared at the tips of her ears. She was pissed that I stuck her on crowd control, but I was not letting her go toe-to-toe with Orobas. That guy beat the shit out of me the first time we met; I was not about to let him get his hands on Flynn.

You're going to have some explaining to do about this bullshit when we get out of here, I "heard" across our mental link.

Deal, I replied. *Now let's focus on that whole "getting out of here" part.* I turned my attention back to the little PA who was frantically trying to convince me to stop marching onto the "set."

"Look, kid. I'm not stopping. And you're not going to wrestle me to the ground and sit on me, so why don't you go talk to my partner back there and start getting these people, and yourself, to safety?"

She looked at me like I was completely insane. It wasn't even close to the first time I'd gotten that look from a woman, so I knew it well. "Sir, I can't *leave.* That would be highly unprofessional, and I might never work in this town again."

I didn't bother telling her that if she didn't get as far away from this park as humanly possible, and in the next few minutes, she probably wasn't ever going to work again anywhere. I just shook my head. "Fine, lady. Do what you gotta do. But I'm going to go put a stop to this shitshow before anyone gets hurt or killed." *Preferably before I get hurt or killed.* I kept that thought to myself, though.

I shouldered past the woman and heard her radioing for security behind me. It only took a few more seconds for me to break through the next security barricade and see what Orobas had going on. It was an elaborate ritual, apparently, because there was a huge double circle drawn on the brick plaza at the park's fountain. There were people lying on their backs dressed in white robes at the cardinal points of the circle and a grinning Orobas in the center. The circle glowed with so much magical energy that its purple light was visible even without opening my Sight. Even the mundanes could see this thing, although they doubtless thought it was just a little bit of movie magic.

"Hello, Harker," the demon called to me. "I'm so glad you could make it to our little film shoot." He smiled even bigger, showing more teeth than I felt comfortable seeing, much less having aimed at me. His double circle was, at least, drawn in chalk, not blood, and the people positioned around his circle were alive, for the moment, but the Enochian scribblings in the space between the circles told a story of demons, dimensions, and doorways that I really didn't want to see come to pass.

"Hi, Oro. I think there are some folks in town that would like to have a word or two with you. Why don't you step out of that circle, and I'll see if Luke is free to say hi?"

"I'm just fine in here, thanks. But please pass along my condolences to your uncle. I know how fond he gets of his lackeys."

"And what about Mort? I think he's got a couple things he wants to say to you, too," I said, stepping close to the mystical barrier. The double circle was reinforced against both magical and physical attacks. If I was going to have any shot of stopping Orobas from completing his ritual, I had to get that circle down. I reached out to test the barrier, but drew my hand back before I actually touched the circle. The tingle in my fingertips told me all I needed to know—Oro's boundaries were strong, and I was not getting through to him easily.

I looked around, trying to find something to disrupt his circle, and my eyes landed on the people at the compass points of the circle. Each of them held an item on their chest, and all of them looked ancient. One held a book, another a dagger, then a helmet, and a folded bundle of fabric. At Oro's feet was another book, and this one was bigger and more ornate than the one held by his minion.

"What's with the toys, Oro?" I asked. "Planning a magical garage sale after your apocalypse?"

"You know full well what I intend to do with these artifacts, Quincy. It would have been much simpler with the sword of St. Joan, but she always was a contrary bitch, even in life."

"The sword of..." It took me a second, but I realized Orobas was talking about the blade we dug out of the rubble of Luke's house. Apparently, it was more than just a souvenir Luke took off a dead Nazi, but the sword worn by

Joan of Arc, supposedly a gift to her from God himself when she took up arms as a man to go into battle.

I reached over my shoulder with my right hand and drew the sword. "You mean this old thing? I just grabbed it on my way out the door thinking if you wanted it, it must be important. Might even have a way to fuck up your little tea party here. So, what's the deal, Oro? Is this little pigsticker important?"

I answered my own question as I slowly extended the sword, point-first, toward Orobas in his circle. I expected nothing more than to get my arm halfway out and bump the blade into his magical barrier. But that's not what happened. Not even close. As the tip of the sword made contact with the circle, it collapsed. The glowing purple sphere blinked out of existence with an audible *pop*, and I saw Oro jerk within his inner circle as the power used to create it rushed back into him causing a painful magical backlash. I took two steps forward and jabbed the sword into the inner barricade, and it popped like a soap bubble, too, rocking Oro almost flat onto his back.

With his circle down and the mother of all backlash headaches, Oro looked up at me. "You will not thwart my plans again, Quincy Harker. I *will* open the Gates of Hell upon this miserable world, and I *will* storm Heaven itself, proving once and for all that it is Orobas, not that pitiful twat Morningstar, that is the true King of Hell. Mere moments from now, the power of a hundred thousand souls will flow into me, and I will be unstoppable!"

"Oh, are those the souls at the concert?" Jo asked, walking up beside me with her hammer in her hand. "They're a little drunk, and you'd have to be to listen to that godawful excuse for music, but they're fine. We defused your bombs. Because we're cool like that."

"Or did you mean the souls at the football game?" Luke asked, kicking over the metal barricade behind me. "Because they're all safe as well. We disposed of your little firebug, and now it's your turn."

Orobas stood, glaring at me and my friends. Then he raised his arms, and a half dozen demons flew in to stand beside him. Looks like I wasn't the only one who brought backup. These weren't anything special, just run-of-the-mill demonic soldiers. They each were basically human in size and shape, except for the crimson skin, bat wings, the hooves where feet should be, the barbed penises (shut up, they were impossible to miss), and the curved black horns.

"Is that all you've got, Harker? A monster, a bloodsucker, a half-vampire illusionist, and a few humans? I obviously brought far too many demons along." He snapped his fingers, and the demons charged us.

Or at least the demons tried to charge us. They took the first step, but then a blur of motion appeared from my left, and the demons suddenly fell to the ground, every one of them missing a head. I looked to my right, and standing there covered in gore with a pyramid of demon skulls at its feet was an eight-foot demon with obsidian skin, a four-foot curved blade, and a double row of teeth smiling at me from an elongated mouth that reminded me of an alligator with a bad attitude.

"You killed my daughter, you son of a pit imp." The voice that came out of the demon was something I've heard in my nightmares ever since. It was a low, rumbling, viscous sound, like boiling tar covering searing flesh. That voice held within it centuries of screams and millennia of torture, and every word came out of that double-razored mouth with a smile.

"Mort?" I asked, almost under my breath. I'd never seen Mort's true form since he was a passenger demon and preferred to possess others. Now that I saw his real body, and particularly his red, pupilless eyes, I understood why. Nothing he could ever possess would give me cause to almost piss myself just by having it turn its gaze on me.

But that's exactly what it did. It looked at me, and that awful voice spoke again. "Hello, Harker. Please do not interfere. This putrescent cock-boil is mine, and I will have his soul for breakfast."

"You can do what you like with his soul, Mortivoid," Luke said, stepping up beside me. "But I get to take a piece out of his flesh."

"Are you threatening me, Vlad?" Mort asked, reverting to Luke's birth name.

"Not at all," Luke replied. "Simply proposing an alliance. We kill him together, then you may have him for any length of time after that such as you desire."

"I may have something to say about that," Oro chimed in. All heads swiveled back to the demon, who stood in the center of his shattered circle with his hands pointed to the sky.

"Attack!" he screamed, and from the skies above Atlanta, it started to rain demons of all shapes and sizes.

I looked at my team, gathered around me looking terrified but determined. "Get as many humans to safety as you can, then start sending these bastards back to Hell!" They jumped into action, some drawing weapons and some moving toward the PA and the civilians clustered around her.

Orobas took advantage of my momentary distraction to leap from his circle and swat me to the ground, knocking the sword from my grip and cracking my head on the ground. I looked up at the monster, and not for the first time, thought, *I fucking hate demons.*

CHAPTER THIRTEEN

I t was raining demons over Atlanta; I was flat on my ass in front of the monster responsible for the death of Renfield, Christy, and countless others; and Count Dracula was about to get into a pissing contest with a hitchhiker demon about who got to kill the bad guy first. And I dropped my sword and was pretty sure I had a slight concussion. My day was quickly approaching Defcon Fucked.

Orobas was distracted from his desire to rip my head off and shit down my neck by Luke crashing into him from the side and sending him ass over teakettle across the brick pavers around the Olympic Fountain. Mort followed a split second behind, his sword blurring through the air like a Cuisinart with more teeth. I almost felt bad for Orobas, until I remembered that he wanted to blow open the doors of Hell and relocate a couple million demons into my dimension.

Fuck, the demons. I looked up and saw a solid dozen Reavers scurrying across the park after any civilians who lingered outside the metal barricade protecting the "film set" of Oro's ritual. There were at least as many Torment Demons stalking the fleeing humans, and one twelve-foot demon of a kind I'd never encountered before. It was an ugly bastard, to be sure, with four legs, a spiked tail, and half a dozen arms. It looked like the uglier brother of a Kali statue mated with a tarantula, without any of the charm of that kind of pairing.

"Adam, go for the Torment Demons," I yelled. "Becks, Gabby, take out the Reavers. Watson, you and Jo cover the civilians." The four humans Oro used in his ritual were just red splotches on the ground, the first victims of the demons, but there were still plenty of people that needed help.

"What are you doing, Harker?" Flynn called back to me.

"I'm doing what I do, Becks," I shouted. "Sending the big nasty back to Hell." I took a deep breath, picked up my fallen magic sword, and charged the four-legged giant with a wordless bellow. *It's a good thing I'm a fast healer because this might hurt.*

The thing looked at me, its inhuman face splitting into a grin as I ran at it. It reached down with one clawed hand, but I'm a little quicker than the average bear, so I ducked under and opened a long gash in its forearm. The wound glowed with a blue-white light, and a smell like roasted assholes engulfed me. The demon jerked its hand back, and it reared up on its back pair of legs to strike at me again, this time much more seriously.

I guess it still thought I was human, though, because instead of trying to run or dodge, I did what no human should ever do when confronted with a demon—I leapt right at the thing. I vaulted into the air, my sword flashing down in an overhead strike worthy of its own Mortal Kombat move, and split the demon's head right down the middle.

My momentum crashed me into the thing's now-bleeding face, and we tumbled to the ground in a heap of blood, demon brain, and godawful funk. I've smelled some truly unholy things, and seen things no human should ever see, but when I stood up, one foot firmly planted in the skull of a dead demon, my stomach did barrel rolls at the stench.

But it was dead. With one shot I had killed the biggest damn demon I'd ever seen. And not just "sent it back to Hell" killed it, but "turning to slush on the ground" killed it. This thing was forever-dead, the kind of dead that's really hard to manage with extra-planar beings. I looked at the sword in my hand with a new appreciation. It didn't look any different, just a plain blade, about three feet long, with a glided cross guard and a leather-wrapped hilt.

"Good sword," I said, then turned to see who needed a hand. Adam was the nearest, and also the one in the deepest shit as three torment demons were pummeling the shit out of him. I figured he was probably fine as long as they didn't literally rip him limb from limb, but I still took a running start and chopped two of the demons down before they even turned to look at me. The third one got a single swipe at me with its claws, but I cut that hand off before I spun the sword around and opened the nasty fucker from his nuts to his nose. Demon guts spilled out onto the ground, and I whirled around in a lethal spin, taking the monster's head.

"Nice sword," Adam said, giving me a nod.

"Yeah," I said. "If I'd known it was a demon-slayer, I would have been carrying this thing for the last seventy years instead of letting it hang on the wall in Luke's study."

"But where's the challenge in that, right?" Adam asked, and for just a piece of a second, I thought I saw a smile flit across his face.

"I could use a few less challenges, old pal," I replied. "Now let's get rid of the rest of these bastards and see if Luke needs a hand."

"You take the last three Torment Demons," Adam said. "I'll go back up Flynn and the others."

As much as I wanted to be the knight charging to Becks' rescue, he was right. The Reavers were nasty little shits, but they could be killed with mundane weapons, or even Adam's bare hands. I had the only weapons we could really use against the Torment Demons, my magic and this shiny new toothpick in my hand. I nodded and set out to clear the plaza of demons while Frankenstein's monster rushed off to save my girlfriend.

My new weapon proved to be way more than Oro's army of dickheads could handle, and just minutes later, I joined Flynn, Gabby, Watson, Adam, and Jo as we converged on the scrap still taking place in the middle of the fountain where Orobas's circle used to be. His spellground was totally wrecked with ritual elements scattered all across the brick. Becks was covered in blood, but she assured me none of it was hers, and the team looked largely uninjured, with the exception of a growing shiner on Jo's left eye and blood dripping from Watson's knuckles.

Orobas had all he could handle with Luke and Mort both taking chunks out of his ass almost at will. Luke went high, and Oro threw up his arms to block the Vampire Lord from literally ripping his head off, and that left his gut open for Mort to slash across his belly with his sword. Then Oro doubled over to protect his midsection, but that left the back of his head exposed for Luke to rain down elbows on his exposed head that would make Royce Gracie proud.

"They're just playing with him," Jo said.

"This isn't a game," I replied. "They're going to torture him until he knows just what kind of pain they can inflict, then they're going to hurt him some more. Maybe sometime right before sunrise they'll kill him. But only if they get tired enough."

I stepped forward to end the scrap and put Orobas out of all our misery, but stopped at the sight of a man stepping into the far side of the fountain. He was a big man, at least six-and-a-half-feet tall, and thickly muscled, with close-cropped brown hair and a dark brown beard. He wore a tailored suit and shoes that looked more expensive than my car, although that set the bar pretty low.

I walked around the torture scene in the center of the fountain to meet the man. "Reginald Barton, I presume?"

"You do, indeed, Mr. Harker. You presume a great deal," the man said with a terse nod. He gestured to the destroyed ritual and demon bodies littering the landscape. "You presume to interfere with my plans yet again. You presume to massacre my minions, disrupt my ceremonies, and generally stick your nose in where it doesn't belong again and again. I begin to tire of your interference."

"Well I guess it's a good thing you're here, then. This way you can ask me nicely not to fuck up your plans to destroy the world, and I can tell you to your face to kiss my lily-white ass. Now, do you want to get back in your car and go back to playing Aleister Crowley in your McMansion on the hill, or would you rather I beat your ass a little first?" I sheathed my sword and summoned a trickle of energy from the nearby ley lines. Power flooded into me, and I channeled it into glowing balls of crimson energy floating above my readied fists.

"You think to threaten me, human?" Barton asked, an incredulous look passing over his face. "You must truly be the stupidest mortal this hunk of rock and celestial shit has ever produced." He raised his hands to the sky. "Look upon my true form, mortal, and kneel before your Lord and Master!"

White light poured from Barton's body, growing in intensity until it was painful even through my closed lids. My concentration shattered; my energy globes vanished with a crackling *pop*. I turned away and covered my face with my hands, only looking back when the light finally faded. Through the multi-colored spots in my vision, I saw a tall figure, nearly seven feet in height, clothed head to toe in white robes, with a nimbus of light surrounding its head and giant wings of purest white peeking out over its shoulders.

Fuck me, it's a goddamn angel.

CHAPTER FOURTEEN

The angel formerly known as Reginald Barton sneered at me. "Now do you understand the heights of my superiority, mortal? I am not just an incredibly wealthy human. I am of the seraphim, placed in dominion over this world by God Himself, destined to rule over all of the inferior beings such as yourself."

I couldn't help it. I tried, I really tried not to be an asshole to the angel, but I couldn't stop myself. Not even Flynn in my head warning me to shut the fuck up could keep my mouth shut. "If you're so goddamn superior, show me your dick, you neutered assclown." Then I took two long steps forward and punched the angel right in the face.

I liked the angel a lot better when he was looking up at me from his now-soaked ass in the middle of the gorefest that was the Olympic Fountain. His robes looked a lot less impressive covered in water and demon blood, too. I knew the second I did it that it was a mistake, but it didn't matter. This celestial cocksucker was responsible for all the pain Orobas, and by extension Smith, had wrought, including Renfield, Christy, Dennis, and God Himself only knew how many others. If that didn't call for a good right cross, I didn't know what did.

Barton glared up at me from the ground, then quicker than my eye could follow, he stood before me again, this time clad in gleaming white armor. "You dare to lay hands on one of The Host, you sniveling worm?"

"I've been called a lot of things, pal, but sniveling has never been one of them."

"You have interfered with my plans for the last time, Quincy Harker," he said, reaching out and wrapping a hand around my throat. He didn't even seem to strain as he lifted me off my feet. I gasped in his grip, kicking my feet in futility.

"Don't bother to struggle. It will only make this hurt more." The angel grinned up at me, and spots started to dance around in my peripheral vision.

Then a shot rang out, and the angel dropped me to the ground. I slammed into the bricks in a heap, rolling to the right to create some space between me and the pissed-off celestial. The angel stood with a hand pressed to its back, a look of shock spreading across its face. Flynn stood about fifteen feet away, her service weapon in a standard grip leveled right at the angel.

"Don't move, asshole. I might not be Homeland Security anymore, but I will still put a dozen rounds in your ass if you touch Harker again." From the look on her face, I believed her.

The angel smiled, and my heart sank. He turned to Flynn, waved a hand, and she flew back into Adam, knocking him into Watson and making a huge pile of bowled-over Shadow Council scatter like tenpins. "Do not presume to assault your betters, mortal. Now all of you lay there and let the grownups talk."

He turned his attention back to me, which was marginally better than trying to kill my girlfriend, I guess. "All I wanted to do was open a little bitty doorway to Hell and take over Heaven. Is that so much to ask?"

"I don't give a shit what you do with Heaven and Hell, but when you use Earth as a landing zone, that's when I get a little grumpy. So why here? Why not just go straight from Hell to Heaven?" I thought if I could get him talking, I could maybe come up with an idea for how to beat up a celestial being before he got bored with monologuing and just crushed me like a gnat.

"Because what better way to get the attention of the Father than by destroying His favorite children?"

"Huh?" I was honestly confused. Of course, it's always been tough to keep track of who was God's chosen people at any given time.

"Man, you idiot. If I threaten the very existence of humanity, then God will *have* to take notice again," the angel replied. There was definitely some shit going on that was above my mystical pay grade, but I didn't care. All I cared about was keeping this fucker's attention while Mort and Luke crept up on him from behind.

"You mean God isn't paying attention to Earth anymore, and you want to... make Him?" I asked. My cavalry was almost within striking distance. I just needed a couple more seconds.

"I mean that no one has seen the Father since the end of the war on

699

Heaven, you idiotic mortal! God, Lucifer, Michael, and the rest of the Archangels—they're all gone! They've been gone for millennia, and no one can find them. So if I kill enough of you fucking overgrown gorillas and let Orobas relocate a few million demons to right outside the Gates, He'll have to come back and take care of things again! I'm tired of cleaning up your fucking wars, and disease, and poverty, and... fucking filth! How are you all so *dirty*? It's truly disgusting. And stop that." He waved a hand behind him, and Luke and Mort flew back, bowling over Adam, who had just made it to his feet. It was like slapstick comedy, only way more terrifying.

The angel stepped over to me, holding out his hand. A blade of pure white light materialized out of thin air, and he raised it high over his head. I reached over my shoulder and drew my own sword, barely getting it up in time to block his decapitating stroke.

Barton stepped back, shock written all over his face. I was pretty surprised, too, since I was staring up at him from behind a blade suddenly wrapped in flame. There was heat coming off the sword, but none of it hurt me. The hilt didn't get warm, the flames didn't scorch my eyebrows off, nothing like that. It just lined the edge of the blade in a bright red-yellow inferno. Sometimes I love magic.

"Where did you get that?" the angel gasped.

"Oh, this old thing?" I replied. "I took it off a Nazi in France a long time ago. Your pal Oro seemed to think it might be important. Looks like he was right."

"Important?" The angel's face was incredulous. "Oh, you ignorant ape. That is the sword of the Archangel, the blade that Michael wielded in the war with Lucifer. That sword is far too powerful and sacred to be sullied with your touch."

"Well, then you'd better back the fuck up, pal, because otherwise I'm gonna do a lot more than touch you with it. I'm gonna stick it so far up your ass fire shoots out your ears." I scrambled to my feet, sword in front of me.

Barton grinned. I hate it when the bad guys smile. It usually means that my life is going to get a lot more complicated. The grinning angel raised his blade of Heavenly light over his head and ran at me, raining blows down upon my head and shoulders. I parried the best I could, but I started to wear out in seconds. Swords are heavy, and angels are *fast*. I put all my power into one big block and shoved him back, then conjured a circular shield of force around my left forearm. Now I could deflect with my shield and strike back with my own sword.

I went after him, my own sword ready for battle, but quickly realized that fighting with a sword and shield is a lot harder than it looks in the movies. I got my feet tangled up in each other trying to move, swing, and defend all at the same time, and with a flick of his sword and a quick kick to my left knee, Barton toppled me to the ground, my sword again skittering across the ground. If I couldn't hold onto it any better than that, maybe the angel was right and I didn't deserve to wield the thing.

I looked up at the angel. He smiled down at me, a grim, tight smile that held no real mirth. "It's time for this to end, Harker. You have fought valiantly and well, for a human, but I marched across the plains of paradise to throw back Lucifer's horde. You could never stand against me in battle." He raised his blade over his head and brought it down to cleave my skull and end me once and for all.

I'm sorry. I love you, I thought to Flynn as the blade rushed down at my face. I closed my eyes, hoping that if there was someone upstairs taking notes, that my good deeds finally outweighed my sins.

Then there was a ringing crash, and the blade struck brick inches from my cheek. I opened my eyes, and there was a blade hovering six inches from my nose, but it wasn't the white-lined blade that Barton tried to kill me with. This was a sword outlined in brilliant blue light and held by decidedly feminine hand.

"Stop this, Barachiel. Your insanity ends now." I knew that voice, but not the tone. I followed the arm holding the blue-lit blade all the way up to the face of Glory, my guardian angel. She had been peculiarly absent through most of this endeavor, particularly to show up now, right before I was going to get my head split open. Of course, I guess that is what guardian angels do.

"You?!?" Barton, now Barachiel I guess, gasped. "Get away from here, cherub. You have your orders. You are not to interfere in my plans. You cannot disobey me. I outrank you."

"You do, and you are right. I cannot disobey an order or a duty. It is not possible. But I was also ordered to protect this man, and those orders were given long before you embarked on this mad attempt to recall the Father and the Archangels."

I rolled out from under Glory's sword and stepped behind her, stooping to pick up my sword as I went. I was no kind of match for Barachiel in a fair fight, but if I got lucky, maybe I could find a way to cheat.

"That's a loophole, cherub, and you know it. Now get out of my way and let me destroy this mortal," Barachiel said, raising his sword.

"I cannot," Glory replied, her face grim. "He is my charge, and I am his guardian. That is my role, to protect his line. I have done so for millennia and will not stop now just because it inconveniences you."

Millennia? Who the fuck are you, Harker? Flynn asked in my head.

Fucked if I know, apparently, I thought back. I leaned forward and whispered to Glory, "Can you take this guy?"

She didn't bother to lower her voice. "Not a chance. But I will defend you from all threats, or surrender myself in the attempt." With that, she raised her sword and charged Barachiel.

She made a better go of it than I did, but not very much. She immediately spread her wings and took to the air, but Barachiel responded in kind. They danced an aerial duet of blades and flame for almost a minute before Barachiel parried a thrust and responded with a long slice across Glory's belly. She doubled over, and the seraph's blade flashed across her back in a looping slash.

There was an explosion of white lights, and Glory crashed to the ground, crushing bricks to red powder and leaving a foot-deep crater with her impact. Barachiel floated down above her, his sword held high in his right hand, and in his left, dripping with glowing golden blood, he held Glory's wings. He stood over her, wings held high in one hand. While he spoke, the beautiful white feathered wings turned to ash and drifted off onto the wind. When the last of the wings had disintegrated, Barachiel opened his hand and let Glory's holy essence blow away into nothingness.

"Now you are not even a cherub. You aren't fit to soar across the heavens. You shall never again pass through the Gates. You are worse than a mortal. At least they live out their pitiful little powerless lives with the hope of getting into Heaven. But you? No, Glory. You will die here and your essence will be scattered across the ethereal plane. You are nothing, and to nothing you shall return."

"You talk too fucking much," I said, shoving my flaming sword through Barachiel's back. A foot and a half of fiery sword emerged from his chest, and he let out a howl like nothing I've heard even in my worst nightmare. Red-orange flame spread from his chest to engulf his entire form, from head to feet, and he erupted in a brilliant flash of purest white light.

I sprawled to the bricks, knocked loopy from the force of the explosion. I dimly noted that every bruise, scrape, cut, or torn muscle was instantly healed by the outpouring of divine energy. I raised myself up to my elbows, looked around the plaza at my friends and the bodies of dead demons, and managed to croak out, "Does that mean we won?"

Then I passed out.

EPILOGUE

The sun rose on Atlanta again, something none of us could have guaranteed mere hours before, and we gathered in the war room for one last debrief before heading off to our various homes, or what remained of them in Luke's case.

Glory sat at the table with us, her face pale. She was dressed in a spare t-shirt of Flynn's, and it turned out she and Gabby were close enough in size for Glory to borrow pants and other clothes. She hadn't said much since the battle ended, and I was a little worried. Glory was usually pretty quick to let me know what was going on, usually in the snarkiest way possible.

"So is he dead?" Jo asked, grabbing a cruller from the middle of the table. Adam, being the most considerate among us even though he didn't eat or require caffeine, had made a coffee and donut run while the rest of the team showered and searched for unbloodied clothes.

"He is," Glory replied. "His essence will return to the fabric of Heaven, from which we all were formed."

"I don't know what all that means, but I'm good with it," Gabby said. An almost-solid line of powdered sugar rimmed her mouth, making her look somehow even more psychotic than usual.

"What about Orobas?" Adam asked. "He was the one that started this whole mess, after all."

"Well, sort of," I said. "It turns out, even Oro was a little bit of patsy in Barton... I mean Barachiel's plan."

"But is he a dead patsy?" Adam persisted.

"Not exactly," Luke said with a slight smile.

"What does that mean?" Watson asked.

"It means that Mort kept him alive and is taking him back to Charlotte to play with him some more," Luke replied.

"Isn't that a little dangerous?" Watson asked.

"More than a little. We did our best to make sure that he can do no harm, removing his appendages and cauterizing the stumps. Then Mort put him in a casket and is ferrying the torso back to his bar, where he plans a lengthy process of torment for the demon that dared harm his family. I have been invited to assist whenever I so desire." Luke smiled, and I got a little chill.

I'd been in the room in France when Luke had what he referred to as "an unpleasant conversation" with a Nazi spy. Every once in a while I still woke up with those images haunting my dreams. And that guy hadn't hurt anyone Luke actually knew personally. I didn't want to be in Oro's shoes. Not that he needed them anymore.

"What about the Chaos thing?" I asked.

"What Chaos thing?" Luke replied.

"Isn't Mort supposed to take Oro's place as an Agent of Chaos?"

"Yes," Luke said. "Once Orobas dies. That is another reason Mort is keeping Orobas alive." He gave me a smile. "He isn't breaking his word, or even amending his deal. He is simply shifting the timetable."

"Lesson number twelve," I said. "Don't make deals with demons."

Flynn leaned over to Glory. "What about you?"

Glory looked at her. "What about me?" Her voice was flat, lifeless, like someone had ripped away her very essence. Which he had.

"What are you going to do?"

"I don't know what I can do. Without my wings, I am merely a human. And the only one who can restore my wings is the Father Himself. And Barachiel was telling the truth—no one has seen Him since the Great War."

"Well, how do we find him?" I asked.

"How do you find God?" Glory asked. "You might be the last one of all of my charges I expected to ask that question." A little smile crept across her face as she started the long climb back out of the dark places inside herself. As an angel, Glory had never seen those dark places before. We were going to have to watch her as she got used to being human. Hopefully we could make it very temporary.

"Yeah," I said. "I guess it's high time I got a little religion."

"There are two theories on how to bring the Father back to his throne—"

"Is it really a throne?" Gabby asked. I glared at her, and she shrugged.

"Yes, it really is a throne," Glory said. "As you may imagine, the Father is somewhat old-fashioned. In fact, I believe He may be the very meaning of the word. Many feel as Barachiel did, that if humanity is placed in enough jeopardy, God will return to rescue His creation. But so far, despite the human race's best efforts, you have not managed to create enough carnage to get His attention."

"What's the other theory?" Jo asked.

"That if all the Archangels, including Lucifer Morningstar, were brought into one place and called for Him at once, that their collective voice would be enough to call Him."

"Well, okay then. We just need to hunt down some Archangels and get them to ring up old Dad on the phone and get Him to come home, and bring you a set of new wings while He's at it," I said.

"Too bad all the Archangels fled at the same time the Father did," Glory protested. "But..."

"Yes?" Watson prodded.

"You have Michael's sword." She pointed to it leaning in a corner of the room. "That implement is a part of his very being. With that, we may be able to call and bind Michael to one place."

"Okay, that's one," I said. "How many Archangels are there?"

"Seven," Glory said, "plus Lucifer, who was an Archangel before he was cast down."

"So we just need to find their favorite sword, or teddy bear, or whatever, call the Archangels, and by the way, *Satan*, into one place without starting another interdimensional war, then convince them to send God a telegram saying you need your wings back," I said.

"Pretty much," Glory said. She stood up and pushed her chair back from the table. "Thank you for the thought, but it's impossible. I should just get used to being human." She started walking to the door.

I cut her off, putting my hands on her shoulders. "Come on, G," I said. "Look around the room. Impossible is kinda our thing."

"But it will be incredibly dangerous, and quite likely deadly, to handle some of these artifacts. Not to mention the Archangels themselves."

Flynn stood up and moved next to me. "Yeah, dangerous, possibly suicidal? Sounds like every Tuesday. Glory, you saved us all out there. Not just Harker, but the rest of us, too. We had no chance at stopping that bastard until you showed up. We owe you for that. The human race owes you for that."

"And more than that, you're our friend," I said, "and we take care of our own."

"Damn straight," Jo said, standing.

"Absolutely." Watson rose from the table.

"I don't feel the need to stand to add my affirmative response," Adam said, still seated.

"Oh, come on, Frankenstein," Gabby said, tugging on the big man's arm. "We're having a Spartacus moment. And, of course, I'm in. It sounds like the kind of gig where I get to shoot stuff. A lot of stuff."

Adam rose and looked down at Gabby. "I do not like being referred to as Frankenstein. My father's name was Frankenstein."

"Nobody likes a grump, Franky," Gabby said with a smirk.

"So it looks like everybody's with you, G," I said, motioning around the table at the group, every one of them on their feet and looking at us. "Now let's go hunt down some angels and find God."

I looked around the room at my friends, my former guardian angel, and my... what was she now?

"So..." I said, turning to Flynn. "About that ring around your neck..."

She looked at me, that smartass smile on her face, the one that made me realize this was the woman for me in the first place. "What about it?"

"Can I have it back?" I kept my face completely calm and composed, despite the fact that my stomach was roiling.

Becks' face fell, but without a word, she reached around behind her head, unfastened the clasp of her necklace, and handed me the engagement ring I left for her with Glory. Flynn had made it very clear that a proposal via proxy was neither accepted, nor acceptable.

I took both her hands in mine and dropped to one knee. "Rebecca Gail Flynn, I am not a perfect man. A lot of times, I'm not even a good man. And I am so much too old for you that it's not even funny. I don't know where this next quest will take us, but I know this—I want you by my side for it. For this, and for everything that follows. Rebecca... Becks... will you marry me?"

She looked down at me, a pair of tears rolling down her cheeks, a smile that lit up even the darkest corners of my soul on her face, and nodded. "Yes."

I stood up and kissed her thoroughly, then pulled back to look her in the eye. "Then let's go storm the Gates of Heaven."

To Be Continued in Quincy Harker Year Three - DAMNATION

DAMNATION

PART I
CALLING ALL ANGELS

CHAPTER ONE

Jo shook her head to clear the cobwebs, spat a mouthful of blood onto the stained canvas, and made a "come at me" gesture to her opponent.

The other woman obliged, taking two quick steps forward and throwing a low kick in a feint before stepping into a roundhouse designed to catch Jo on the side of the head and end the bout in decisive fashion. And it would have done exactly that, if it had connected.

But there was no head there to kick because Jo dropped to her hands and swept her opponent's legs out from under her. The blonde woman went down flat on her back, and Jo was on her in a flash. Less than ten seconds later, she had her opponent trapped in a fully extended arm bar, and she felt the slap of a glove on her shin as the other woman tapped out.

Jo rolled to her feet, both hands raised in triumph. She took a quick victory lap around the ring—really an eight-foot high cage made of chain link and steel posts wrapped in thick padding. The referee motioned both women to the center of the ring and raised Jo's fist over his head, announcing her victory to the crowd.

Jo turned to her opponent and held out her hand. The other woman leaned in, they shook, and then leaned in for a brief hug.

"I almost had you," the woman said.

"Horseshoes and hand grenades, like my grandma always said," Jo replied. They both laughed, any animosity left lying on the ring with more than one new bloodstain. Jo stepped out of the cage first, high-fiving the crowd on the way back to her locker room with her corner man.

The athletic black woman stripped off her gloves as soon as she was through the door, tossing them into the general vicinity of a basket on the floor. "Holy crap, she kicked like a mule!" Jo said as she sat on a bench and rubbed her inner thigh. "My quads are all kinds of knotted up."

"She landed some pretty good ones," Jake, her corner man, said. Jake picked up her gloves and the shoes she kicked off and shoved them in a big duffel. "You gonna shower before you leave?"

"God yes," Jo said. "I don't want to bleed all over the car on the way home. You keep Shelton the heck out of here while I get the funk washed off?"

"Yeah, no problem. He'll probably run right over to Marla's locker room anyway, to offer her a shoulder to cry on."

"Or whatever," Jo said, her mouth twisting into a grimace at the thought of the sleazy promoter going after the younger woman while she was down from losing the bout. "You wanna stick your head in over there, see if she wants to go get some breakfast?"

"Yeah, I can do that. IHOP or Waffle House?"

Jo laughed. "Let's go big-time tonight. We'll take the winner's purse and spring for Denny's."

Jake chuckled as he made for the door. "I'll be back in a sec. Try not to break anybody for five minutes."

"Okay, but no promises if you run late." Jo leaned back on the bench, her arms folded over her face. She replayed the bout in her mind, going over all three rounds looking for things she could have done better, things she missed, or places she could have ended the match sooner. This one almost went to time, and that put the fight in the hands of the judges. Jo was pretty sure she'd outpunched her opponent, but she'd rather have control of the decision herself.

She opened her eyes and stared up at the bare fluorescent tubes hanging on thin chain from the water-stained ceiling. This wasn't the worst place she'd ever thrown a punch, but fighting the underground scene wasn't anything like the clean, brightly lit gyms she trained in most of the time.

This whole world was new to her—fighting for money in unsanctioned bouts, advertised through word of mouth, ducking the cops and anything that even looked like an athletic commission. But the money was pretty good, which was more than she could say for any other assignment she'd ever had for the Shadow Council. And so far, everyone she'd fought had been one hundred percent human, another improvement over her last scrap, which featured at least three different types of demon trying to open the Gates of Hell into downtown Atlanta.

The door to her dressing room opened after just a couple minutes, and Jo sat up. Jake shouldn't have been back so quickly, but there he was. And he wasn't alone. Right behind him was a fuming Marla Jonas, a scowl on her face and fire in her eyes.

Marla stalked over to her and stood right in front of Jo. "What?" she demanded.

"What do you mean, what?" Jo asked, working to keep her tone mild. She didn't like strangers in her personal space, and this woman was definitely there.

"Your guy said you needed to talk to me. Said it was urgent. Shel was about to tell me about the big fight he's putting me in next month."

Jo looked past the angry fighter at Jake, who shrugged. "Sorry, Jo. It's all I could think of."

Jo sighed, then stood up. She started toward the shower. "Go get her stuff, Jake. We'll be in the shower. The dressing room key is in the side pocket of my bag. Keep Shelton *out* of here when you come back." Jake nodded, then turned to go.

"Wait a minute, what the fuck is going on here? I'm not showering with you. I'm not into that. I mean, it's cool if you are, whatever, but it's not my thing."

"Get over here," Jo said. "I'm not into you, either. But Shelton obviously is, and the next thing he was going to say was how he *wants* to put you in that big fight, but since you lost tonight, he couldn't really do it, so he'd need some kind of...convincing to give you that kind of opportunity." Jo peeled off her top and shorts and turned on the water, adjusting the knobs to get the water as hot as she could stand it. She stood under the spray, letting the heat relax her sore arms and shoulders, wincing now and then as the water pounded on a particularly tender spot.

"Oh, bullshit," Marla called from outside the shower. "Shelton knows better than to try that shit with me."

"Yeah?" Jo said. "You're that special? So special he wouldn't try the same crap he's tried on every single chick that's thrown a punch in his cage? Dang, girl, you must be really amazing. Oh wait, you're not. 'Cause I just tapped you out. Just like I tapped out the last five women I stepped in the cage with. And Shelton's tried that crap on me three times in the past six weeks. So if you really do think you're so special that little weasel won't try to con you into blowing him for a bigger payday, go on back to your locker room and have a great night. But if you think you're probably just like everybody else scrapping on this circuit, then come grab a shower, and we can all go to Denny's and get something to eat."

Jo squirted a healthy amount of the body wash she liked into her scrunchie and started to lather up. It didn't matter if the other woman joined her for a shower or not. Just taking her out of Shelton's line of sight for a few minutes meant she was probably fine. He still had four more fights on the card to run and payouts to handle to fighters, security, and referees. That was before he dealt with paying out the guys running the betting on the fights, the payoffs to the cops who patrolled this neighborhood, and the janitor and principal of the high school where they were holding their unlicensed mixed martial arts event.

The sound of water turning on from a nearby station was Jo's only notice that Marla had entered the shower. "Why do you give a shit?"

It was always either a thank you or that same question. Which one Jo got told her a lot about the woman asking. The broken ones asked why she cared. They didn't understand that some people just wanted to do good in the world, just wanted to make it a little bit better place to live.

"Because we've got to look out for each other," she said.

"All us fighters?"

"All us *people*," Jo corrected. "We stopped being fighters the second the ref raised one of our hands. Now we're just people again. And people gotta look out for people. It's what keeps us from being...I don't know what."

"What world you live in, girl?" Marla asked. "Ain't nobody gonna look out for you but you."

"I've got Jake," Jo said. "And now, I've got you."

"Me? Why you think I'm gonna look out for you?"

"Because you owe me one," Jo said with a grin. She reached over and turned off the water. "Help yourself to the body wash, but I didn't bring any shampoo with me." She pointed to the tight cornrows running the length of her scalp with a smile. Jo wrapped one towel around her head and another around her body, then walked out into the locker room.

Jake stood there, his back to the shower and arms folded across his chest. Another duffel sat on the bench beside Jo's, with Marla's blue silk ring robe lying across it. "I got all her stuff, but Shelly says you both gotta go see him for payout. Said he couldn't give it to anybody but the fighter."

Jo read from the set of his shoulders that there was more to it. She pulled on a pair of fresh panties and a sports bra, then slipped into a pair of loose sweatpants. "He said he wouldn't give my money to a Mexican, didn't he?"

"He said the only way I was getting any cash out of him was to do his lawn." Jake shook his head. "That fucking piece of trash is a disgrace to illegal fights. He should be running cock fights in the backwoods of Alabama, not the biggest underground fight club in Arizona."

"He shouldn't be running anything, but you get more with money than with honor these days," Jo said.

"Hey, did your corner man get back with my bag?" Marla called from the shower.

"Yeah, what do you need?" Jo called back.

"Can you bring me my shampoo?"

"No problem." Jo grabbed a bottle of Head & Shoulders from the bag and carried it into the shower. "Holy crap, girl, did I do that?" she said, pointing to a softball-sized bruise on Marla's upper ribcage.

"Oh, that...um, no, that wasn't you. That was from...sparring a couple days ago."

Jo looked in her eyes, but the other woman wouldn't meet her gaze. She held out the shampoo bottle, then let out a sigh. "I've got some Tiger Balm in my bag. I'll leave it out for you. You should maybe find a new sparring partner. Looks like that one doesn't know how to pull her punches."

Jo walked out of the shower and finished dressing. She pulled out her phone and sent a text to a contact that only said "Sparkles." "Need you to find out everything there is about a fighter named Marla Jonas."

"Problem?" the reply came instantly.

"Not for me. She's got a couple bruises that don't look like they came from fighting legit opponents."

"You're not fighting legitimately," Sparkles replied.

"Yeah, but this looks like somebody hit her in the ribs with a baseball bat."

"Shit. You think husband?"

"Maybe boyfriend. Either way, I think he needs to be persuaded not to do it again."

"I'll get back to you in a flash. Don't do anything stupid until I find out the details."

"Would I ever do anything stupid?" Jo typed back.

"Between you, Harker, and Gabby, if I still had a body, you'd give me a stroke," Sparkles replied.

Jo pulled on a tattered Randy Savage t-shirt and sat down to slip into socks and shoes. "I think we might have a situation," she whispered to Jake's back.

"Hammer time?" he asked.

"You know I hate it when you say that."

"Why do you think I do it?" His shoulders shook with quiet laughter. "What's the problem?"

"I think somebody's hitting Marla outside of the ring."

"You gonna stop it?" It was only nominally a question.

"I can't just let it go," she said.

"I guess you can't, can you?"

"Never have, never will."

Their muted conversation was cut short when Marla stepped out of the shower. "Wow, he actually keeps his back turned while you dress?" She gestured at Jake.

"I told him I'm not that modest, but he insists."

"I've got three daughters, girl. I've seen everything you got, but everybody deserves the respect to not have people staring at them while they're naked," Jake said, his face locked straight ahead.

"Well, thank you, Jake. I appreciate it," Marla said. She quickly slipped into a pair of shorts and a sweatshirt, then slipped some sneakers on and hefted her bag to her shoulder.

"Come on, then. Let's go get paid and head over to someplace that will fill us full of bacon grease and runny eggs," Jo said, motioning for the other two to follow as she headed out the door to argue with Shelton about her cut of the betting and get some much-needed dinner.

CHAPTER TWO

The sun was just peeking over the horizon when Jo walked through the door of her three-bedroom house. She dropped her duffel bag on the sofa and walked into the kitchen, giving a rueful smile to the white-haired woman leaning on the stove with a scowl on her face. Cassandra Harrison was a slender woman in her seventies, but she still stood ramrod straight, the steel in her spine no different from the spikes Jo's legendary great-grandfather had driven into the railroad ties so many years before.

"Good morning, Mama," Jo said, reaching into the refrigerator for a carton of orange juice. She didn't bother with a glass, just turned the carton up, and took a long swig. She put the OJ back in the fridge and closed the door.

"You want to yell at me now or wait until I've had some sleep?" she asked her mother.

"I don't want to yell at you at all, baby, but you been out all night. A mother worries, you know."

"I know, Mama. I know." Jo pulled out a battered ladder-back wooden chair and sat down at the table in what most houses would call a breakfast nook. At the Harrison household, they just called it the kitchen table. It was the centerpiece of the house, no matter how far from the middle of the structure it sat. The family ate as many meals together around that wooden oval as possible, but lately Jo's work with the Shadow Council had kept her away from too many dinners and breakfasts, and her freelance editing had her eating far too many lunches at her desk while answering emails or proofreading manuscripts.

"I'm sorry I was out all night. It was around three when I got done at the gym, and then I wanted to get a bite to eat with the girl I fought tonight," Jo said, leaning her head back and working it side to side to stretch out the knots building in her muscles. Another hot shower might be in order before she finally saw her bed.

"You beat this girl up, then you went out to dinner with her? I don't understand that, Joanna. I really don't."

"It wasn't anything personal, Mama. We didn't fight because we hate each other; we fought for money. Oh, by the way, here, put this in the kitty." She reached into the pocket of her hoodie and tossed a roll of bills to her mother. Shelton was a pervert and a shady fight promoter, but he kept his word about payout. Jo got a guaranteed two hundred per fight, five hundred if she won, plus twenty percent of the house cut of any bets on her fights, and five percent of the door. Tonight that all added up to a little under a thousand dollars. Not bad for a night that she didn't even bleed. Much.

"I don't need your money, child. You my daughter, I'm gonna take care of you," her mother said. But Jo noticed that the money disappeared into a pocket on the front of the flowered apron she wore over her clothes.

"I know, Mama, but I can pull my own weight around here. I'm not living on the streets."

"And you never will be, as long as I've got anything to say about it," Cassandra replied.

Jo let it pass. No point in arguing with her this late. Or early, depending on whether or not you'd slept yet. "How was Ginny?" Jo asked.

"Oh, she's fine," Cassandra said. "Missed having her mama around this past couple months. When you gonna be done with all this nonsense, anyhow?"

"I don't know," Jo said. "I've been winning, and that means I get to fight more, but I still haven't been there late enough in the show to meet the man I'm there to find."

"What's this man done, anyhow, that you got to stay up all night getting your face messed up to find him? Is he a bad man? Is this dangerous, baby?"

"Well, I am working in an illegal club fighting inside a steel cage where there are no rules except to make your opponent tap out or knock them unconscious. But other than that, I don't think it's that dangerous." After her last trip to Atlanta with Quincy Harker and the rest of the Shadow Council, Jo's bar for "dangerous" was significantly higher than it used to be. After all, once you defuse a bomb under a basketball arena and fight off a demonic invasion, getting decked in a fight just isn't quite as scary anymore.

"You don't have to be smart, Joanna. I worry is all." Her mother's voice was quiet, and Jo knew she'd hurt the other woman's feelings.

"I know, Mama. I'm sorry. I like that you worry about me." She stood up and hugged her mother, giving the shorter woman a kiss on the top of her head. "Now I'm going to grab a quick shower and get some sleep. I've got a self-help book to work on today before I go back tonight." Jo made her living most weeks as a freelance copy editor, and fighting in a cage at night meant that her clients weren't getting the attention they deserved. She had to spend at least a little time on her "day job" or she wouldn't have any clients left to ignore.

"You gonna stay up to kiss Ginny goodbye?" Her mother didn't put anything extra into her tone: the recrimination was all there without any help.

Jo nodded as she turned to walk to the bathroom. "I'll stay up 'til she gets on the bus, then I'm crashing for a few hours." She pulled her hoodie over her head as she walked down the hall to the bathroom. She opened the door to the "master" bedroom, more a name than anything designating extra size in the compact little home. She stripped and slipped on a robe before padding back down two doors to the bathroom.

She turned the water on until steam poured from the shower, then stepped under the near-scalding spray. The heat immediately started to soak into her abused shoulders and arms, making her eyelids heavy. She snapped awake as the door to the bathroom opened, but she relaxed as she made out the form of her ten-year-old daughter Ginny through the gauzy shower curtain.

"Morning, Mama," the little girl said as she sat on the toilet.

"Good morning, Ginny-girl." Jo forced her voice into a chipper, high-pitched thing that Shelton and the girls at the gym would never recognize.

"Did you win?" Ginny asked, flushing the toilet.

"Yes, I did," Jo said, raising her arms over her head and letting the water beat down along her ribcage. She felt the knots slowly ease on her sides, soothing the tense muscles that Marla had pounded earlier.

"Did you hurt the other lady?"

"Not very much, sweetie. I put her in an arm bar and she tapped out. She was a smart lady, and she knew she was beat." Jo saw no point in hiding what she did from her daughter. It was a lot easier to explain to her that she was doing MMA at night than trying to make up some lie about why she came home with split lips and bruises all the time. Plus, doing what Ronda Rousey did on TV got Jo some "cool mommy" points, and Ginny was fast approaching the age where those would be in short supply.

"That's good. You shouldn't hurt people," Ginny said with the conviction of a child who knows everything in the world is black and white.

Jo smiled at her daughter's voice. "That's right, sweetie. You shouldn't hurt people. Now you go get ready for school and let Mommy get some clothes on."

"Okay," Ginny said. Jo watched through the curtain as the door opened, then closed after the girl. She pulled the shower curtain aside and looked at herself in the mirror. *Looking a little rough, Joanna. Gotta stop pulling these all-nighters for no pay. Might be time to hit up Luke about Council members drawing a salary. Or at least get a group insurance plan. God knows I go through enough painkillers working for those fools.*

She got out of the shower and toweled off, slipping into clean underwear and sweatpants with a tattered Arizona Cardinals t-shirt. She walked barefoot down the hall to the table, then took a seat next to Ginny.

"What are you doing in school this week, honey?" Jo asked.

"Fractions in math, and in drama we're doing a scene from *Alice in Wonderland*. I'm the Mad Hatter." Ginny grinned up at her mother, a little dribble of milk running down her chin. "Ms. Holman says I'm the maddest hatter she's ever seen."

"I bet you are, baby. I bet you are," Jo said.

"Will you be home tonight, Mommy? I can show you my part." The girl's enthusiasm jabbed a dagger into Jo's gut and twisted.

"I can't, sweetie. I have to work again."

Disappointment flashed across the girl's face, but it fell away as Cassandra sat down at the table with half a grapefruit and two pieces of toast on a plate. "I'll be here, honey-bear. We can make a video on my phone and your mama can see it when she gets home."

Jo shot her mother a grateful look, then stood at the sound of a car pulling up outside. "There's Katie's mom," she said to Ginny. "Get your backpack and lunch."

The girl did as she was told, then kissed her mother and grandmother, and dashed out into the sunny morning. Jo locked the door behind her, then sat down at the table across from her mother.

"Thank you for that," Jo said.

"I know what you're doing is important, honey..."

"I know, but she's important, too. It's just...what I'm doing, with the Council? It could literally change the world. The stuff we did in Atlanta saved lives, maybe everybody's lives. It's...surreal, you know?"

"Oh honey, I know. Your daddy wasn't even in the Council when we got married. That damn Luke came to him just a few weeks after our first anniversary. If I'd known who he was, I never would have invited that fool into my home." Cassandra took a sip of her coffee, then smiled at Jo. "You know that ain't true, neither. Your daddy never would tell me any of the stuff he got up to with Luke and those people, but sometimes he would come home all battered and beaten, but smiling. He had that same smile you got on your face right now, thinking about what y'all did in Atlanta. I knew that he was helping people, just like you are. And I know that my way of helping those people is to let you go do what you do."

The women sat at the table for another few minutes, then Jo stood up. "I've got to go get some sleep, Mama. Will you make sure I'm awake by two? If I get up then, I'll have time to get some work done before I have to go to the club tonight."

"You fighting two nights in a row?"

"Yeah," Jo said. "I'm moving up the card. Maybe tonight is the night I finally get to meet him."

"I hope so, honey. But you never did explain it to me. What in the world is the Archangel Michael doing beating up people in an illegal fight club in Phoenix?"

"I have no idea, Mama. I don't even know if he knows who he is. But that's why I'm there—to find him, to make him remember his duty, and get him back in Heaven where he belongs."

"And what you gonna do if he don't want to go?" Cassandra asked.

Joanna grinned at her mother, then cracked her knuckles. "Well, Mama. I'm a fighter. If he don't want to do what's got to be done, I reckon I'm gonna have to kick an angel's ass."

CHAPTER THREE

I might have spoken too soon about kicking anybody's ass, much less Michael's, Jo thought as she shook her head to clear the cobwebs. It was the beginning of the third round, and she was pretty sure she was behind on points. Not that things were very scientific in Shelton's club—if the match went to time, he decided who won. And that, more often than not, had as much to do with where the money was laying than with number of punches thrown.

Her opponent was a thick-bodied woman who looked like the poster child for the 1980 Soviet women's shot put team. She had boulders for shoulders and biceps the size of Jo's thighs. And her fists felt like blocks of cement crashing into Jo's upraised forearms.

A kick slammed into Jo's thigh, and she took a step back, anticipating the other woman's next move. She was right, the blonde behemoth shot in, trying for a single-leg takedown, but Jo met her with a stiff left that landed behind her ear and rocked the big woman for the first time in their match. Jo followed up with a flurry of strikes, raining punches to the sides of the other woman's head. She knew a knockout wasn't coming, but if she could create just enough frustration to make to giantess drop her guard, she might have a chance.

In a flash, the opening she was looking for appeared. After a stinging left to the other woman's ear, Jo saw her guard slip for just a fraction of a second. But it was enough. She darted forward and jammed her flat belly up against the woman's shoulder, sliding her right arm around her opponent's head and

722

neck, then cinching the front choke tight before the big woman could block the hold.

I've got you now...oh shit! Jo smacked hard into the cage with her back as the larger woman picked her up and bull-rushed her across the octagon. Her spine met the support beam with a jarring crash, but she kept the choke applied as though her life depended on it. Which, judging by how pissed off the woman struggling in her grip seemed, it just might be.

"Off!" Jo grunted as she was slammed into the cage again, this time on the opposite side of the ring. There might have been slightly less force in this charge than the one before, but if so, Jo couldn't tell.

Jo hung on doggedly as her opponent picked her up again, using her body as a battering ram against the steel. Jo's head snapped back against the beam, and she saw stars. The beam was padded, but there was still steel under there. Jo held on, though, knowing the only way she was winning this fight was by choking out her opponent. The bigger woman straightened up, taking Jo off her feet once again, and charged across the ring. She stumbled before she made it all the way to the other side and fell forward. Jo locked her feet around the other woman's waist, adding pressure to the choke. She squeezed, feeling the veins pop out in her forehead from the effort, then finally felt the welcome tap on her shoulder.

The referee called for the bell, and Jo released the hold. The exhausted women slumped to the ground, Jo rolling to her feet as the referee walked over to check on both combatants.

"You okay?" he asked.

"Yeah," Jo panted. "I'm good."

"What about you?" he asked her opponent.

"I'm okay," the larger woman gasped. Both women scrambled to their feet and stood by the referee awaiting his announcement. He raised Jo's hand in victory, and she turned to her opponent, hand out.

"I'm Jo," she said.

"Gladys," the other woman said, taking her hand. "Good fight." Without another word, she turned and walked out of the cage, leaving Jo to celebrate for a moment before the ref cleared her out. Jake walked her back to the dressing room, slapping her on the shoulder and hugging her the whole way.

They burst into the empty room, smiles plastered on their faces. Jo peeled off her clothes as Jake resolutely faced the wall. "You know you don't have to do that, right?" she said over her shoulder. "I'm a fighter, just like everybody else you work with. You don't have to not look at me."

"You ain't like everybody else I work with, Jo," he corrected. "You're a lady, and I was raised to respect that. Besides, if my Daniella found out I was looking at some beautiful naked woman, she'd choke me out a lot faster than you tapped that Russian chick."

Jo laughed as she headed to the shower. "You didn't think I could beat her, did you?" She fiddled with the water until steam billowed around her.

"No," Jake said. His honesty didn't surprise Jo. It was one of the reasons she had hired him. That and his reputation as one of the best corner men on the scene. It was only a falling out with his last client that left him available when she started fighting three months ago.

"I didn't either. Probably wouldn't have, if she hadn't dropped her guard finally." Three months. A long three months of getting her ass kicked almost every night. Even the fights she won left their marks on her skin, and she wasn't sure what left deeper bruises on her soul: losing, or what she sometimes had to do to win. But she was close, she could feel it. Maybe tonight, maybe tomorrow, but she was going to end up close enough to Michael to put his sword in his hand, and hopefully that would wake the Archangel from his slumber and get him back to Heaven where he belonged.

"I'm sorry, Shel. You can't go in right now. She's taking her shower." Jo heard Jake say from the locker room.

"Jake, baby, you know the deal. It's my club, and I go where I want, when I want." This wasn't the first time Shelton had tried to walk in while Jo or other female fighters were showering or dressing. It was the main reason she liked having Jake around outside of his corner man duties. She didn't mind fighting for Shelton, didn't even mind him getting the lion's cut of the betting take on her work, but letting him see her naked wasn't one of the perks he got out of the deal. Besides, she didn't trust the little sleaze not to hide a tiny video camera in the locker room and broadcast "naked fight girls" on the internet for extra cash.

An enchanted stone in the bottom of her duffel bag took care of that, thanks to Harker and his magical mojo. Any video recording within a ten-yard radius of the stone turned to static.

"I know that's your rule, Shel. And you know my rule: you want to look at naked women, go to the strip club. You want to talk to my fighter, you wait until she's dressed. I'll send her to your office when she's cleaned up."

Jo wished she could see the look on Shelton's face as the implacable Jake stood in front of him, arms crossed and feet planted. Shel wouldn't toss Jake. He was too good a corner man, and too many of his fighters would walk with him. And Jake wouldn't budge on his morals for Shelton, no matter how much the promoter argued, threatened, or cajoled.

Jo turned off the water and dried off, then wrapped a towel around herself and stepped out into the locker room. "You need me, Shel?"

The promoter looked up, hope blossoming on his face, then wilting like a daisy in the July sun when he saw her completely covered by the huge towel she carried in every night. "Yeah, come to my office when you're dressed. I'll settle up with you and talk about Saturday night. You're off tomorrow to rest up. You're headlining Saturday with Mitchell."

Finally. Mitchell Carson was the name Michael fought under, and apparently lived under these days. Fighting right before him on Saturday would put them in close contact, and hopefully give her a chance to get the Archangel's sword back to its owner and get her back to her normal life where nobody tried to knock her unconscious on a daily basis.

"Sweet," she said, trying to keep the excitement out of her voice. "I'll come to your office in a few minutes. Just let me throw some clothes on and get my gear together."

"Okay," Shelton said, then turned to go. He stopped at the door. "Good fight tonight. I thought she was going to kick your ass." He walked out into the hall, the metal locker room door slamming behind him.

Jo dropped the towel and started to pull her clothes on. "Yeah. You, me, and everybody else in the world," she said, pulling on her jeans and sitting down to lace up her boots. "You can turn around now, Jake."

He did, then sat next to her. "How bad you hurt?"

"I've got a couple of bruises from last night that didn't get any better for the pounding, and I'll probably have a shiner in the morning, but I don't think she did any real damage."

"Good thing," Jake said. "I've seen some of the people Gladys has fought. She's a killer."

"I guess I'm faster, or luckier, than they were."

"Yeah, one of those," Jake said. His voice was low, like he was thinking about something.

"What's bugging you, Jakey?"

"Something doesn't smell right."

"What do you mean?"

"Look, don't take this the wrong way. You're a good fighter. You've got natural instincts, and have obviously had some training. And you've come further in no time than anybody I've ever seen. But there's no way you should have been able to beat Gladys tonight. Most of the girls you've fought are just that—girls. They've been at this maybe six months, maybe a year. They haven't been hit in the face a lot. You've taken some licks, and it lets you compete with people at your level."

"Yeah, that all makes sense," Jo said. She knew enough to let Jake get to his point in his own time. He didn't often say a lot, but Jo had learned to value the man's opinions when he gave them.

"But Gladys has been around for years. She had a couple of UFC and Strikeforce tryouts, and got close to fighting in the big time more than once. But something always fell apart at the last minute. Either there was a drug thing, or a visa thing, or something sketchy. So she ended up back here."

Realization dawned on Jo, and she nodded. "You think she threw the fight." She wasn't offended—everything Jake said made perfect sense. She should have been more banged up after going three rounds with a musclebound monster like Gladys. And an experienced fighter like that should never drop her guard and get caught in a submission so easily.

"Yeah, I do. I'm sorry, Jo—"

"Don't be," Jo interrupted. "You're right. But who? And why?"

"I got no idea, girl. But I know one thing. You be careful dealing with Shelton. He's more than just a pervert running a fight club. He's connected to some bad people, and I've seen some bad things go on in some of his clubs before."

"Like what?" Jo asked, but Jake just shook his head.

"Nah, I ain't telling no tales. That's a good way for somebody who don't bring in no fans and don't get no bets laid on the table to find himself sitting outside looking in real fast."

Jo nodded. "I can respect that. I guess there's nothing for it but to go get my money from Shel and see what he's got planned for Saturday night. My luck he'll have me fighting a grizzly bear."

"Some of the women I've seen come through this place, I think a grizzly bear would be an easier scrap."

CHAPTER FOUR

I should have just fought the damn grizzly, Jo thought as she stared across the ring at her opponent. She was not looking forward to five rounds against the woman they called La Machina, or The Machine. She fought under a mask, like the Mexican *luchadores*, and because Shel thought it added drama to the matches, he allowed it. But the black mask covering her face was a layer of protection from strikes and cuts and made life a lot harder on her opponents.

Not that Rochelle, as La Machina was known outside the octagon, needed any advantage. She was a tall, solidly built woman with a strong background in Muy Thai and boxing. Her combination of strikes and kicks made her a tough opponent for anyone, and her grappling ability made her even more dangerous.

Jo moved around the ring, circling her opponent with a wary eye. She knew Rochelle was quicker than her size led most people to expect, and her long legs made for some vicious head kicks to the unsuspecting. Rochelle strode in with her hands up, confidence oozing in her every step and blood in her eyes, but just before the women closed on each other, Jake flung open the door of the cage and stuck his head in.

"Raid coming, ladies. Time to book!" Both women turned to see him gesturing frantically for them to come to him. Jo followed without hesitation, Rochelle snapping into action a half-second later. They fled the cage just as the sound of splintering wood told the truth of Jake's words—someone had screwed up. The cops had joined the party.

Guess I'm not getting paid even the loser's purse tonight. Jo ran behind Jake, then stopped cold. "My bag!"

Jake turned to her. "Girl, forget your shoes and underwear. We gotta go!"

"I can't leave my bag," Jo insisted. She couldn't tell Jake that her hammer, her great-grandfather's legendary hammer, was in the bag. That would lead to all sorts of explanations about why she was carrying a nine-pound hammer in her gym bag.

Jo spun to the right and dashed off down a deserted hallway, away from the shouting and the stampeding footsteps behind her, toward the locker room where her stuff was stashed. She flung open the door and skidded to a halt, her bare feet slipping on the tile.

"Shit, sorry, man," she said to the back of the man in the room. The naked man in the room. The tall, blond, very chiseled man in the room. The man with two long scars on his back making a "V" along the lines of his heavily muscled torso. *Well, I guess that's what they mean when they say "heavenly body." Da-yum, with extra yum.* Jo got her first good look at Mitchell, the current persona of the Archangel Michael, and decided it was pretty angelic indeed.

The man turned, his blue eyes piercing, and a curl of that impossible blond hair falling just perfectly across one of them to make him even more irresistible. *Eyes up top, Joanna. Eyes up—oh my goodness.*

"I told Shel I didn't want a girl before the fight," the beautiful man said, a little smile playing across his chiseled jaw. "Come back after I beat this mook, and we can play."

"Wait, what?" *Oh no, he didn't. Oh yes, he did.* "I'm not one of Shel's girls. I'm a fighter. And you want to get some pants on and get the hell out of here with me, right now."

His smile grew. "I wouldn't mind leaving with you, sweetheart, but I've got a fight in a few minutes. As soon as the girls are done with the warm-up act, I'll take out tonight's jamoke and we can go get better acquainted."

Great. Not only is he beautiful, and an angel, but he's a chauvinist douche, too. "I'm still not here for that," Jo said. "I'm here for that." She pointed at her bag, which she picked up and slung over one shoulder. "We take turns in the locker room, remember? I was dressing here before you got in tonight. Now it's time to go. You need to come with me. Right now. The cops are raiding the place, and I don't think you want to take that pretty face to jail, no matter how good a fighter you are."

The grin fell from his face like a boulder. "You're not wrong there, toots. Let's skedaddle."

Toots? What is this guy, eighty? More like eight million, Jo mentally corrected. *I guess he's allowed to be a walking anachronism.* She turned to the door, then back to Mitchell. "You should probably put on some clothes before we run out into the alley."

He jumped into a pair of jeans and slipped on a pair of shoes, then followed her out of the locker room. Jake stood at the end of the hall, peering down a long corridor to the gym where the fights were held. "Come on, girl. We got to roll."

"I'm coming, Jakey. I'm coming." She made good on her promise, running to her corner man and looking up at him. "Which way?"

He pointed back toward the gym. "Looks like all the po-po are down that way, so if we go this way, we should be okay." He jerked a thumb behind him. "He coming with?" Jake gave a nod to Mitchell, who ran up just then.

"Yeah, he's with us. Let's go." She started off at a brisk walk in the direction Jake indicated, keeping an ear out for shouts of police behind them. Hearing nothing, they took a left turn at the first hallway, heading in the general direction of the parking lot where their cars awaited them. They stopped short at a pair of chained fire doors, looking at each other as if for new ideas.

"I guess we look for another way out," Jake said.

"I doubt you'll find anything," came a new voice from behind them. They turned to see a lone police officer standing in the hallway about ten yards from them. He was almost completely in shadow, but looked...off somehow, like his muscles and joints didn't fit together quite right, or like he wasn't used to walking in this form.

"Get behind me, Jake," Jo said, pulling open the zipper from her bag and dropping to one knee to reach inside.

"What's wrong, Jo-Jo? Nervous? Scared about what happens to pretty girls in jail?" the "cop" asked.

"Might be more scared of what happens when people dress up like police," Jo said. She stood up, a nine-pound rectangular maul head in one hand and a twelve-inch handle in the other.

"Looks like Grandpappy's hammer needs a little repair work," the man said, stepping closer. He made no move to draw a weapon, but his posture was full of menace. Jo drew in a sharp breath as the man's eyes began to glow crimson in the gloom of the darkened hallway. Jake took a step back, muttering *"Dios mio"* under his breath.

"No, Jacob," the "man" corrected, bat-like wings stretching out from his shoulders to fill the width of the hallway. "Not God. Never God. That lazy fuck hasn't cared about you worthless meat sacks for millennia, no sense praying to him now. You'd be better off throwing up a tweet to Superman. You've got a better chance of getting an answer."

He turned his attention back to Jo. "Now, where was I? Oh yes, I was going to rip your guts out and paint the ceiling with your blood." He stretched out his arms, and Jo watched in horror as his fingers lengthened and narrowed, coming to razor-sharp points.

Jo pressed a button on the handle in her hand and flicked her wrist. The titanium handle extended to two-and-a-half feet, and she jammed the maul head onto it. The handle and head snapped together with a twist of her wrist and the click of a pair of heavy-duty magnets. She swung the assembled hammer in a lazy circle in front of her.

"Come get some, monster. It's been a couple weeks since I splattered demon brains all over something," Jo said with a grimace.

Jake gaped at her, then turned and started jerking at the chain on the doors. The demon just laughed and stepped closer, swiping his hands through the air with a terrible *snick-whoosh* sound as he flicked his claws together.

Mitchell stepped in front of Jo, shielding her with his body. "Get back, whatever-the-fuck-you-are. Leave this girl alone."

Girl? Oh, I am definitely gonna have to have a talk with this dude if we survive this. Jo pushed past the man and gave him a dark look. The demon leapt at her, but Jo was ready. Weeks in the cage had her reflexes honed to a razor's edge, so she easily side-stepped the creature's charge and brought the hammer around to smash into the back of its knee.

The monster went down with an ear-splitting shriek, and Jo slammed the hammer down at its head. The demon was fast, though, and sprang to its feet and lashed out at her with its talons. Jo ducked under the first slash and brought the hammer up to block the second, kicking out at the thing's midsection with her right foot.

Pain raced up her leg as her toes crashed into the demon's chitinous exterior. The dim light revealed more of the monster in all its unnatural glory. It looked like a two-legged insect of some sort, with a glistening exoskeleton and razor-sharp mandibles protruding from what passed for a face.

"What the fuck is that thing?" Mitchell asked, his voice hushed with fear.

"It looks like the world's ugliest ant," Jake said.

"It's a demon," Jo replied. "And right now, it's a demon that wants to kill us all, so could we please have a little less chit-chat and a little more kicking demon behind?" She swung the hammer in wide figure-eights in front of her, slowly forcing the demon back but doing no damage. The beast appeared content to bide its time, waiting for a hole in Jo's defenses.

So she manufactured one. On the next spin of her hammer, she wobbled just a little, just enough to give a tiny opening. The monster took the bait, charging forward with claws darting in for the woman's throat. Jo spun to the left and put everything she had into a massive swing at the back of the creature's head.

The silvered side of the hammer smacked into the demon's skull with a sound like an egg hitting the kitchen floor. The hammer buried itself up to the haft in the creature's brainpan, and the force of Jo's swing carried it and the weapon around to smack into a wall of lockers with a resounding *clang*. Yellow-grey brain matter and blood splattered along the wall and coated Jo, Mitchell, and Jake with a healthy splattering of demon goo.

Jo planted her foot in the monster's back, grimacing at the feel of the slimy carapace under her bare foot, and yanked her hammer out of the crushed skull. The weapon came loose with a wet sucking sound, and Jo staggered back, almost slipping but pinwheeling her arms to catch her balance at the last moment. *That's all I need, to land flat on my ass in demon guts in the middle of a deserted high school that I'm already trespassing in.*

The trio stood in the darkened hallway staring at each other for a long moment before Jake finally broke the silence. "That was damn gross, Jo-Jo. What the hell was that thing?"

"If I had to hazard a guess, I'd say it was a demon."

"You say that like it ain't the first time you've seen this kind of thing," he continued. Mitchell just stared at her like she was from another planet.

"I wish it was, Jakey, I wish it was," Jo said. "But we still need to be somewhere else, and pretty soon. I can't hear anything from the other end of the building, but that doesn't mean all the cops are gone."

"Well, you can't get in a car with all that goop all over you, and I know I can't go home looking like this," Jake said. "My Daniella is an understanding woman, but if I start dripping demon-snot all over her rugs, I better look for someplace else to sleep at night."

"Yeah, let's go find a bathroom, get cleaned up as best we can, and get out of here," Jo agreed. She turned to Mitchell. "You okay, big guy? You haven't said a word since that thing came at us."

He looked at her, a haunted expression on his face. "I knew that thing. I knew it was a demon, and I knew it the second it opened its mouth."

"Okay..." Jo said.

"How did I know that?" Mitchell asked. "I've never seen a demon before. I don't know anything about demons. Shit, lady, I don't even go to church!"

Jo sighed. "We're gonna need to go ahead and deal with this, aren't we? Okay, let's get the worst of the muck wiped off and get somewhere better lit. With coffee."

"How about someplace with whiskey?" Jake asked. "I got a feeling we're gonna need something stronger than coffee."

"Whiskey it is. But first, a bathroom. I think I've got demon brains between my toes, and I really need to pee."

CHAPTER FIVE

"So, Mitch, what else do you know?" Jo asked. The three of them were seated around her small kitchen table, with the warm yellow glow of the bulb overhead holding most thoughts of demons and monsters at bay for the moment. The steady *drip-drip* of the coffee maker in the background and shuffle of Cassandra's slippers on the worn linoleum were the only sounds in the house.

Mitch looked at Jo over folded hands. "I don't know what I know. And I don't know how I know it." The big man looked confused, with a healthy dash of frightened. "Why was there a demon in the schoolhouse, and what did it want with us?"

"I think that's probably more of a 'you' than an 'us,' pal," Jo said, accepting the mug her mother brought to the table. Jo took a long sip from the "World's Greatest Grandma" mug and let out a sigh. Cassandra knew how she took her coffee—two heaping spoonfuls of sugar with a dash of Kahlua for good measure.

"Why do you think the thing was after me?" Mitch asked. "It seemed like it wanted to kill you pretty bad, too."

"Yeah, but I was just a bonus," Jo said. She looked over at her mother, who gave her a little nod. "Mitchell, I think there are some things you might not understand about yourself, and it might be better if I showed you rather than tried to tell you."

Jake and Mitch exchanged perplexed looks and shrugs as Jo got up from the table. She walked to the small living room, got down on her hands and knees, and reached under the sofa. She fished around under the couch for a moment, then pulled her arm back with a cloth-wrapped bundle in hand. She stood and walked back to the table, unwrapping her prize as she did.

Jo laid the sword on the table, hilt toward Mitch. "Do you recognize this?" she asked.

"It's a sword," Mitch replied.

"That's right, but is there anything familiar about the sword?"

"No, I've never seen it before in my life."

"I don't think that's correct," Jo said. "Why don't you pick it up and take a closer look?"

Mitchell shrugged and reached out his hand for the weapon. The second his fingers wrapped around the hilt, the blade of the sword burst into flames, and a sound like choirs of angels rang through the minds of everyone in the room.

Jo felt like a grenade of sunlight had gone off in her chest, and light and goodness and *right* filled her almost to overflowing. Then, in an instant, the flames winked out, the light vanished, and Mitchell toppled out of his chair with an unceremonious *thump*.

"Holy shit!" Jo said, springing to her feet and hurrying to where Mitch lay curled up in a ball on the floor. "Mitch, are you okay? What happened? I mean, I know what happened, but what happened to you?"

Mitch shook his head, then snapped to full awareness and shoved Jo back. "Get away from me! What the fuck did you do to me? Jesus fucking Christ, what was that?"

Jo sat back on her heels, stunned, but Cassandra leaned over and slapped Mitch right across the face. "You keep a civil tongue in your mouth when you speak the Lord's name in my house, son."

Mitch rolled to his feet, glaring at the seemingly frail older woman, but she didn't flinch. After a few seconds of silent confrontation, Mitch turned, righted his chair, and sat. "My apologies, ma'am. I'll try to contain myself."

"I appreciate that," Cassandra said, a tight smile playing across her lips. "Now," she looked around the table, "why don't you tell us what happened, and what you *thought* was gonna happen, sweetheart, because they are obviously two very different things."

Jo nodded. "You're not wrong there, Mama. I expected something to happen when Mitch touched the sword, but I didn't expect it to knock him on his butt, and I sure didn't expect to almost burn down my kitchen."

"Sorry about that," Mitch said.

"Not your fault," Jo replied. "There's no real good way to say this, so I'll just throw it out there. You're an angel. You're actually kinda *the* angel.

You're the Archangel Michael, the warrior of Heaven, and this is your sword."

"Huh?" Mitch looked at Jo like she had grown a second head.

"Jo-Jo, did that girl crack you across the face one time too many last night?" Jake asked.

"I don't know, Jake. Did we get attacked by a giant bug-demon in the halls of a high school tonight?" Jo shot back.

"Good point. Stranger things on heaven and earth and all that, I guess," Jake said.

Cassandra raised an eyebrow. "*Hamlet?*"

"Hey, I read!" Jake protested. "Plus, it was in that movie with Ethan Hawke and Bill Murray."

"Anyway," Jo said. "There's a whole thing going on where a bunch of the archangels are kinda on vacation and neglecting their duty, and a friend of mine really needs their help. So, me and a bunch of other friends are hunting them down, and we're supposed to be able to use their implements to wake them up and get them back to acting like angels."

"Implements?" Mitch asked.

"Apparently each of the archangels has an iconic item associated with them. Michael's is his sword. It's the flaming blade he wielded in the War on Heaven when Lucifer was cast out and the rebellion of the angels was put down. We thought that when you touched it, you'd remember who you are, and that would be all we needed to do. But apparently that's not how it works. At least not with you."

"How has it worked with the other angels you've found?" Jake asked.

Jo didn't answer right away, just took a long sip of her coffee and wished for much more liquor in the drink. "Well, that's the thing..."

"I'm the first one you've found," Mitch supplied.

"Yup," Jo agreed.

"Why me?"

"Well, we already had the sword, so we were halfway there. And when the spell led us to Phoenix, it made sense to start with you, since I already live here. So, I started looking for warriors, and that led me to this undefeated fighter kicking tail all over the underground fight scene."

"But how do you know I'm really your guy?" Mitch asked.

"Remember the whole sword bursting into flames thing?" Jo asked with a smile.

"But maybe that's just some kind of switch or trigger that I couldn't see," Mitch said.

"Jake, pick up the sword," Jo said.

"Why do I got to pick up the fiery angel sword?" Jake protested.

"Because you don't know where the mystery switch is, so if it's there, you're as likely to hit it as Mitch."

"That makes sense, I guess," he said, reaching for the hilt. He picked up the sword. Nothing happened. He stood up and waved it around a little. Nothing happened. He slashed through the air, and Cassandra ducked.

"Sorry," Jake said, sitting back down. He turned to Mitch and held out the sword. "You wanna try again?"

"Not really, but I guess I—" His words abruptly cut off as he touched the hilt and a line of flame erupted around the blade. Mitch jerked his hand back, and the sword tumbled to the kitchen floor. The flames winked out as soon as he broke contact, but the blade clattered on the tile with a loud *clang*. "Oh, shit!" he exclaimed.

"Mommy? Gramma?" a small voice called from the back of the house. "Who's out there?"

"Now you've done it." Cassandra glared at Mitch as she stood. "She'll never get back to sleep if there are new people to meet." The older Harrison woman hustled to the hallway and disappeared, making reassuring noises as she went.

Jo looked at the men. "My daughter, Ginny. She's ten."

"Her dad?" Mitch asked.

"Your business?" Jo shot back. "Sorry," she said, raising her hands to Mitch. "I'm sorry. He died four years ago. Stroke. I just get defensive, you know. Black woman, single mom, living with her mother, that whole thing. But we were the perfect suburban couple. Two incomes, minivan, the whole thing. Then Darren...got hurt at work and was on life support for two weeks. Even with insurance, the part we had to pay was back-breaking. So I moved in with Mama so I'd have some help with Gin."

"I'm sorry," Mitch said. "For asking, and for what happened. It's none of my business. You don't owe me anything."

I certainly don't owe you the truth, Jo thought. *So if you'll buy the stroke story, that's the story you'll get.* Angel or not, Mitch didn't need to know the real story of her husband's death, and the demon that killed him. That was Council business, and her business.

Cassandra came back to the table, a small smile on her face. "I promised her you'd read to her tonight before bed if she stayed in her room and tried to go back to sleep." She handed Jo a battered copy of *Darwen Arkwright and the Peregrine Pact.*

"She loves these books," Jo said. She turned to Mitch. "So, do you believe us now?"

"Believe that there's something about that sword? Yeah. Believe that I'm an archangel? Not by a long shot." He held up a hand to Jo. "I know, you think this is some kind of proof. Well, maybe it is. But maybe there's something else. But something is going on with this sword, and there was a demon in the high school last night, so if this thing helps us kill them, then I guess I'd better learn how to swing it." He picked the sword up from the floor, and it burst into flames right on cue. Mitch held on to the blade this time, standing up and taking an experimental swing through the air.

His jaw was tight, and the crinkling around his eyes told of the strain he was under. After a minute, he set the blade carefully on the table. The flames winked out the second he let go. Cassandra reached out with a fingertip to push the blade aside, but there wasn't even a hint of burn or scarring on the table's surface.

"Good boy," she said. "You'da been in for a world of hurt if you'd messed up my table. And I don't care if you an angel or not, I'da whooped your butt good."

Mitch chuckled. "I believe it." He turned to Jo. "What's next? For now, I'll go along with something being all...messed up." He nodded to Cassandra as he censored his language. She gave him a sly smile. "But I don't know what to do about it."

"Neither do I, but I know where to start looking. We need to go back to the school tonight and see what we can find. I'll touch base with some of my sources today and meet you over there tonight around eleven."

"Let's meet at my gym instead," Jake said. "That way we park and only take one car on our felony field trip."

"Good idea," Jo agreed. The three exchanged cell phone numbers, then Jo said, "We'll meet you at your place at eleven and drive over to the school. We find out where the demons are coming from and what they're after, and then maybe we can find some more clues to waking Michael up."

"You make it sound like he's taking a nap in my head," Mitch said.

"That's probably pretty close," Jo said. "I have a couple ideas I want to run past some folks, then we can go demon-hunting."

"You gonna bring that big hammer?" Jake asked. "Or do you have something better?"

"I like my hammer," Jo said. "And it did alright last night, didn't it?"

"Can't argue with that," Mitch said. "But why a hammer?"

"It's a family tradition," Cassandra said. "People in this family been swingin' a nine-pound hammer at the bad things for a long, long time."

"Well, let's hope we don't have to fight anything tomorrow night," Jake said.

"Optimism," Jo said with a smile. "I'd forgotten what that looked like. It's kinda cute. Now get out of my kitchen. I'm going to go cuddle up with my little girl before I turn around and it's her senior prom. I'll see y'all tomorrow night."

Jake and Mitch walked to the door. Mitch stopped, his hand on the knob, and turned back to Jo. "This is pretty weird, right? I mean, how crazy is this whole thing?"

Jo laughed, a bright, sincere, melodic thing that brightened the room. "Mitch, you think this is weird, remind me to tell you about my last trip to Georgia."

CHAPTER SIX

J o sat on the floor of her den, laptop on the coffee table in front of her with half a dozen browser tabs open, four leather-bound books arranged carefully in a leaning tower of research on the carpet to her left, and a giant sports bottle full of Mountain Dew sitting on the end table behind her to the right. Her mother sat in a rocking chair in the corner of the room, occasionally looking up from the scarf she was knitting to cluck at Jo and her "organization."

Jo glared at the smiling unicorn head on the screen. Sparkles was resplendent with his rainbow mane and glittering diamond teeth, but he was ultimately useless. "I'm sorry, Jo," the horse-headed tech genius said. "There's nothing on the net anywhere that would explain Michael's memory loss. Everything I can find that would destroy a celestial being's memory would destroy the angel's mind as well, and you said he's not crazy." If it was on the net, Sparkles would find it. Even before he got turned into pure energy and had his soul transferred into the internet, Dennis Bolton was an amazing programmer and hacker. Since becoming a latter-day Tron, there was nothing connected to the internet that he couldn't access, hack, or take over.

"Well, I don't think I actually said he wasn't *crazy*, I just said his brain seemed to be in working order. Could it have anything to do with his fighting? Like maybe post-concussion syndrome or something?"

"I thought about that, but I checked in with Glory, and she says it's pretty much impossible for an angel to get a concussion. Since they're pure energy, when they manifest, it's not like they have real bodies," Sparkles replied.

"If you think that, you've never seen him without a shirt on," Jo muttered under her breath.

"What's that? Oh, you're a giant horndog? That's what I thought you said," Bolton teased.

Jo heard her mother chuckle in the corner and shook her head. "I'm sitting in the floor of my den in sweatpants with my hair up talking to an imaginary man who chooses to present as a unicorn instead of going out and actually *meeting* a human being. Yeah, I'm the tail-chaser."

Cassandra chuckled from her chair, and Jo turned to her. "You stay out of it, Mother," Jo said. Her face grew serious as she turned back to the screen. "So there's nothing?"

"There's not a whole lot of information out there on angels hiding their light under the proverbial bushel," Bolton replied. "Pretty much everything I've found has a lot more to do with Michael swinging that giant flaming toothpick of his around than it does with his mental state. I think you might be dealing with the first recorded case of angelic amnesia in history."

"Yay," Jo replied, leaning back against the couch. "So what next?"

"Are you asking me?" Sparkles asked.

"Well, yeah."

"Oh," he said. "I was kinda hoping you were talking to your mother again. Because I have absolutely no idea."

"What about Harker?" Jo asked.

"He knows less about angels than you do," Bolton said. "His studies have all been on the other end of the celestial spectrum, as it were. So, no help coming from that quarter. Are there any friends of your dad that could help?"

Jo turned to her mother. "Ma, do you know anything about that?"

"Hmmm?" Cassandra looked up from her knitting.

"Oh, don't even try to play me, old woman," Jo said, her voice warm. "I know you've heard every word we've said for the past thirty minutes."

"Well, I reckon that's true enough," the older woman agreed.

"So, did Daddy have any friends that might be useful?" Jo asked.

"I don't think so, honey. Most everybody he worked with on the Council was either Luke, Harker, or more interested in shooting monsters than learning about the good creatures out there. There was one man, though...what was his name?" She thought for a moment, then held up a finger as it came to her. "That's it! Robert Blinn. He teaches religion and philosophy at Gateway."

"The community college?" Jo asked.

"That's the one. He said he liked teaching at a smaller school. But he was a sharp one. Did a lot of research into angels. He always said if you're going to understand demons, you needed to know where they came from."

"That makes sense," Jo said. "Dennis, you got a number—"

"Way ahead of you, sunshine," the disembodied unicorn head replied. "I sent it to your phone already. According to his class schedule, he's got office hours tomorrow from ten to noon, and he's in class today until like six p.m."

"Do I want to know how you got that little tidbit?" Jo asked.

"I hacked the college's computer system," Bolton said.

"So, no, I don't want to know," Jo said, shaking her head. "You are so going to get me thrown in jail."

"Nah, it's fine. I left just enough footprints in their system to make them think the Russians did it."

"Great," Jo said. "When I get sent to Gitmo, just make sure Luke can get a night flight into Cuba to save me."

"Oh relax," Dennis said, tossing his mane. "It was on his public Facebook page. I didn't even have to pretend to be a student to friend him."

Jo's reply was on the tip of her tongue when her cell rang. She picked up the phone and looked at the screen, but didn't recognize the number. She swiped her finger across the screen and held the phone to her ear. "Hello?"

"Jo?" The voice on the other end was soft, tentative, like the speaker was afraid they'd dialed a wrong number, or maybe afraid they hadn't.

"This is she," Jo replied. "Can I help you?" She kept her tone light, but motioned to Sparkles then pointed to the phone. The horse head nodded, then vanished, a map of Phoenix popping up on the screen with a large circle blinking around the city. As the call went on and Dennis was able to trace the call through more towers, the circle grew smaller and smaller until finally it was a blinking dot immunizing the caller's location.

"I'm sorry, it's nothing. Never mind..." Jo had a brief moment of recognition. That voice...

"Marla?" Jo asked.

"Yeah," the woman's voice was quiet, as though she was afraid of being overheard. "I'm sorry, I shouldn't have called you. But I found your number from when we went out to breakfast the other night, and..."

"Do you need someplace safe to be?" Jo asked.

Cassandra's head snapped up, and she mouthed, "Is that her?"

Jo nodded. Cassandra nodded back, and that settled that. Now Jo just needed to talk the frightened woman into coming to her house.

After long seconds, Marla said, "Yes." Her voice was heavy with resignation and regret, like it took serious effort to agree.

"Do you have a car? Or can you get here if I text you the address?"

"No," the other woman said. "Our car's broke down, and if I take an Uber or something..." Her words trailed off.

"It'll be too easy to track it," Jo supplied.

LET ME HANDLE THAT. The words appeared on Jo's computer screen. *NOBODY TRACES ME UNLESS I LET THEM.*

Jo smiled. "I've got a guy that can send someone. Nobody will be able to follow. I promise."

"I don't know," Marla said. "Brian's pretty good about finding stuff out."

"Not as good as my guy is at hiding stuff. Trust me. Now where are you? I'll have a car there in fifteen minutes."

───────

I t was nearly an hour later when Jo heard a car door slam in her driveway. She was up like a shot, moving toward the front door and pulling it open before Marla even had a chance to knock. The blonde woman had a giant bruise on her cheek and a haunted look in her eye. She ducked inside, looking around like she expected pursuit any second, then stopped a few feet into the small but neat living room.

"Um...thanks," she began, then stopped awkwardly.

"Don't mention it," Jo said, reaching out to take the duffel from the woman's hand. "This all you brought?"

"I don't have much."

I bet you don't. Bet that jerk doesn't let you have *much, no matter how much money you bring in.* "Well, we don't have a guest room, but the couch is comfy, there's plenty of food, and—"

"And you can stay as long as you like," Cassandra said, coming around the corner from the kitchen carrying a plate piled high with sandwiches. "But it's almost lunchtime." To Joanna, "Why don't you set the table while our guest washes her hands? It's the second door on the right, honey." Cassandra waved her hand down the hall, and Marla nodded at her.

After she was gone, her mother turned to Jo. "That one needs your help."

"That's what I'm doing, Mama."

"I know, baby. But be careful. A man that lays hands on a woman is worse than a dog."

"That's alright, Mama. I know how to take care of a rabid dog." Jo's voice was cold, the set of her jaw as hard as the hammer she frequently carried. The women bustled in the kitchen and dining nook, setting out three plates for a light lunch of sandwiches and fruit.

Marla came back from the bathroom and clapped her hands together. "What can I do to help? I might be a freeloader, but I can at least set a table." Her eyes were bright and her shoulders back, once more exuding some of the confidence Jo saw in the cage a few nights before.

The table was set in short order, and the women tucked into their meal. They ate in a companionable silence for a few minutes before Cassandra looked at Marla and spoke. "So Marla, what do you do besides fight? Jo tells me you're pretty good, but I don't expect nobody much is making the rent beating people up in cages for nasty men like that Shelton."

"You're not wrong there," Marla agreed. "But I don't have another job right now. I worked in a hospital for a while, but they cut back on their maintenance staff and let me go."

"What were you doing there?" Jo asked.

"General facilities stuff. You know, change lightbulbs, fix toilets, fix doorknobs, that kind of thing. I've been trying to get on with an apartment complex as a super or site manager job, because a lot of times those come with a place to stay, and then..." Her voice trailed off, and she looked down at her plate.

"Then you could get away from the son of a bitch who gave you that shiner?" Cassandra asked.

"Mother!" Jo exclaimed.

Marla just laughed. "It's fine. She's right. He is a son of a bitch. I would have left him months ago, but I didn't have any place to go. We used to work together, and then we started seeing each other. Then, when I lost my job, he let me move in, and we got serious for a while, but he started getting real jealous, and then..."

"Then he started using you for a punching bag," Cassandra finished for her.

"Pretty much," Marla said.

"But you're a fighter," Jo said. "Why not fight back?"

"'Cause he's a fighter, too, and he's been fighting longer than me, and he's bigger—"

"And stronger, and faster." Jo nodded. "It doesn't matter how tough Ronda Rousey is, she ain't never taking down Brock Lesnar."

"Yeah. He's no Brock, but I ain't no Ronda, neither. So I'm broke, unemployed, and beat up," Marla said.

"But now you're here, sweetheart," Cassandra said, reaching out to pat the other woman's hand. "And that asshole won't find you here. And if he does, he'll have to deal with me."

"Mother, language," Jo said, but her tone was mild. She looked at the steel in her mother's jaw and knew she'd defend this new charge against all threats if need be. Jo nodded slightly, planning to go out that evening and do a little defending of her very own. Pre-emptive defending, if you will.

CHAPTER SEVEN

"Y ou know this isn't really what the Council does, don't you?" The cultured British voice coming across her car's Bluetooth speaker was mild, but there was a hint of disapproval apparent. Or maybe he was just British. Jo could never tell if the condescension was real or a by-product of the accent.

"I know, Jack, but if our job is to protect innocents, this certainly falls under that umbrella." Jo backed her car out into the street and turned the headlights on, piercing the darkness between the pools of streetlight.

"Our mandate is to protect innocents from *demons* and supernatural beings, love. Not jealous boyfriends with heavy fists and substance abuse issues."

"Not all demons are summoned," Jo said. "And not every hell has lakes of fire."

"I know that all too well," the voice of Jack Watson, great-grandson of the legendary doctor and detective sidekick, replied. "But what exactly are you planning, Joanna?"

"Are you sure you want to know? Wouldn't want to mess up your plausible deniability." She grinned into the darkness, her face illuminated by the amber lights of the dash and the flickering white of oncoming headlights. Jo put on her blinker and slowed as she exited off I-17 and turned left back under the highway, headed toward the Prosperity Park neighborhood.

"I think being two thousand miles away gives me an excuse for not stopping you. Besides, if you end up in jail, I'll need to fabricate a plan for your extrication, and having all the information will give me what I need to make that happen." Jack sounded tired, Jo thought. Of course, New York made her tired just thinking about it, much less being there hunting angels. The Londoner was probably fighting subways as often as he was fighting demons or magical impediments to his search.

"I really just want to talk to the guy," Jo said. "I want to let him know that it's not cool to hit people, and he really shouldn't be using his girlfriend for a punching bag."

"You can appreciate the irony in that statement, given your current nocturnal employment, can't you?"

"Piss off, Watson. Don't you have back episodes of *Sherlock* to catch up on?"

"Not since I realized Moffat was involved," Jack replied. "I hated what that prat did to *Doctor Who*."

"God forbid I get into a conversation on *Doctor Who* with a Brit," Jo said with a laugh. She turned left down a side street where "Prosperity" was certainly nothing more than a name, any decent jobs or concept of home maintenance having left these run-down houses years ago.

"That seems somehow racist, or at the very least, nationalist, Joanna," Jack said, chuckling. "How goes the battle on your other front? You know, the one the Council actually assigned?"

Jo sighed. "I found him. But he doesn't know I found him. Or rather, he doesn't know who he is."

"Well, just—"

"I gave him the sword. It burst into holy fire and everything."

"What happened then?"

"He dropped it. Scared the crap out of the dude. He has no idea he's an angel, and I have no idea how to unlock that part of him. And there are demons in Phoenix, chasing us both. Because of course there are. I think I'm here." She saw the rusted-out Pontiac Fiero sitting in front of the small tract home, painted black with Bondo highlights. Sparkles had given her the make and model of Marla's boyfriend's car, and her address. Looked like Captain Butthead was home.

"Good luck," Jack said. "Try not to get arrested."

"If I do, I know exactly who to call."

"Yes," he agreed. "Someone else." He laughed and disconnected the call.

"Jerk," Jo muttered at the phone. She turned right at the next street and parked her car. Jo got out and slipped on her black biker jacket. It wasn't cold, but the thick leather provided a little padding in case things did get heated with her target.

She stepped onto the sidewalk, and a young white man immediately stood up from the steps of a nearby house. "Hey baby, you looking for me?" he catcalled.

Jo ignored him, walking without turning around. She heard footsteps get closer as the man, more a boy than anything, jogged up to her.

"Hey baby, I'm talking to you," the kid repeated.

Jo ignored him again, not speeding up, not slowing down. She just kept her eyes front, kept walking. She didn't know how many of his friends might be watching, and she didn't need to cause a ruckus before she got to Marla's place.

Then he grabbed her elbow. Jo stopped, and the man pulled her arm to turn her back to him. He was tall, maybe twenty years old, with a cursive neck tattoo and acne spilling across his narrow features. His red hair was close-cropped, barely peeking out from under the brim of a San Jose Sharks cap.

"Bitch, I'm talking to you!" he snarled at her.

"You must not be because I don't see any bitch here," Jo said. She looked the boy right in the eye, refusing to show fear. She'd stared down demons—one little suburban shithead wasn't going to scare her. As long as it wasn't half a dozen suburban shitheads, she was probably okay.

"Now why don't you go back to your porch and sit there like a good dog until your master gets home because I don't feel like playing tonight." Jo's words were soft, her voice even, but the look on her face was hard.

"I see a bitch, alright. I see one big stuck-up black bitch walking through my 'hood all alone. I reckon you goin' to meet a trick, ho?" He pushed up on her, walking her backward by pressing his chest against her. Jo steered herself away from the chain link fence behind her, then spun to the right. She put on hand on the boy's left shoulder and stepped on the back of his left knee, pushing him forward. He staggered forward into a parked Toyota, catching himself on the front fender of the car with his hands.

"Oh, you done done it now, bitch. I was just gonna fuck with you a little bit. Now I'm gonna fuck you up." He pulled a butterfly knife from his back pocket and flipped it open.

"What is this, 1987?" Jo asked. She shook her head at the boy, then stepped forward and kicked him between the legs. The toe of her hiking boot impacted his testicles, and the force of her kick stood the young man up on his tiptoes. He dropped to his knees as Jo pulled her foot back, then she put her hands on the side of his head and rammed her knee into his face. His nose broke with a wet *crack*, and blood poured out, covering his mouth and chin.

Jo took a step back, then leveled her would-be attacker with a snap kick to his temple that spun him around and slammed his face into the Toyota's tire before he bounced face-first to the sidewalk. He lay there motionless as Jo turned to see if he had any friends looking to join the fight.

Nobody approached, or even seemed to have taken notice of the fight. Jo left him lying on the concrete, blood seeping from his broken nose to pool under the car tire by his head. She turned and walked back to the address Sparkles had given her, taking note of the flickering light in the front room. Marla's boy-thing must be watching television.

Jo stepped up on the porch and knocked on the door.

"Fuck off!" came from inside, accompanied by the muffled sounds of gunfire and explosions.

Jo knocked again, louder and longer this time.

"I said, fuck off!" The sound of the TV got louder as the man inside turned the volume up to drown out her knocking.

Jo shook her head, then knocked again. She wasn't against kicking the door in on principle, but getting shot as a burglar was not part of the evening's plans.

"Goddammit, what does a man have to do—Well, hello there, what can I do for you?" The man almost tripped over himself changing gears as he answered the door and saw an attractive woman standing on his porch.

Jo could definitely see the attraction for Marla. Brian Krill was a good-looking man of about thirty. Tall, blond, with a strong jaw and patrician nose, he definitely had the body of a man who spent a lot of time in the gym. And Jo could see most of that body in front of her, since he answered the door in nothing but a pair of boxer briefs and a black tank top. His heavily muscled arms ended in a pair of thick hands with scarred up knuckles that spoke of many fights survived and many punches thrown.

"Are you Brian?" Jo asked.

"Who wants to know, pretty lady?" He pasted on a smile that made the hair on Jo's arms stand up, and not in a good way.

"I'm a friend of Marla's. I'm here to pick up a few of her things." The smile fell from his face like a stone.

"Is she with you? Where is she? I need to talk to her." He seemed nervous, like he was afraid of something. He peered around Joanna, looking up and down the street. Jo felt good about her decision to park a couple of blocks away. At least he wouldn't see her car and show up at her house when nobody was home but Ginny and Cassandra.

"She's not with me. I'm just here to pick up the rest of her things and to tell you she won't be coming back. Now where are her clothes?" She stepped forward, trying to get into the house, but Brian blocked her path.

"She doesn't have anything here. Everything in this house is mine. You tell that bitch that I don't want her back. No, tell you what, I'll tell her myself. Where is she?" His face got redder with every sentence, and Jo started to see the veins bulging on the side of his neck.

Jo stepped back onto the porch, but Brian grabbed her arm. "No, come on in." He pulled her into the living room and kicked the door shut behind her. "Who are you? Are you the bitch that told her to leave me? Is this all your fault? Are you a dyke? Is that it? You want to fuck my girl, so you stole her from me? That makes sense, you ni—"

Jo slapped him across the face. "Stop right there. You don't call me that word. Nobody calls me that word. As a matter of fact, you don't call me anything. You don't think about me. You don't think about me, and you don't think about Marla, either. She's out of your life, and she doesn't ever have to put up with your mouth or your abuse ever again. Now get out of my way. I'm leaving."

"The fuck you say, you dyke cunt. I'll beat you so black and blue my girl won't even look at you when I'm done." Brian threw a punch, a big, lazy right that had about as much chance of connecting as John Belushi running a marathon.

Jo ducked under the punch and stuck out three quick left jabs, tagging the larger man right in the mouth and nose with her fist. She drew back a bloody hand, her knuckle laid open on his front teeth. Brian staggered back, then lowered his head and charged her. He caught Jo right around the middle and slammed her into a far wall. Her back cracked the drywall, and she felt dust fall into her hair as his shoulder drove the air from her.

Jo lashed out, nailing Brian with three sharp elbow strikes to the back of the neck. He quickly retreated, then kicked at her head. Jo dropped down and wrapped her hands around his other ankle. She stood up sharply, pulling Brian down to flop on his back with a *whoof!* She held his ankle, then stepped forward to drive her heel into his lower abdomen. He covered up the best he could with his hands, but Jo had the advantage of position and holding his leg.

She stomped his stomach and chest mercilessly, hearing at least two ribs crack under her foot. After six or seven vicious stomps, she let his foot drop and knelt on the floor beside his head. Brian curled up in a fetal position on his side as Jo said to him in a low voice, "You will not come after Marla. You will forget you ever knew her. If I ever hear of you laying a finger on her again, I will be back. And that night I won't go so easy on you."

Then she drove her fist into the side of his skull, sandwiching his head between her strike and the floor. His eyes rolled back in his head, and Brian passed out cold. Jo thought for about half a second about the permanent brain injury she may have caused, then chalked it up to just desserts and stood up.

She looked around the living room, saw a framed photo of Marla and a smiling older woman on the mantle. Jo took the picture, slipped it into her jacket pocket, and walked out the door, whistling into the night.

She got back to her car and pressed the speed dial for Sparkles. "One monster down, at least one to go. Anything new?"

Dennis's human face appeared on her phone's screen, his unicorn head uncharacteristically absent. "Jo, you need to get home. Now. There's a police escort waiting for you at the on-ramp to the 17. There's been an attack at your place. Get home now."

CHAPTER EIGHT

J
o burst through her front door, then drew up short as the burly police officer took hold of her arms and steered her to the kitchen table. "You don't need to go in there," he said, motioning with his head to the hallway. "Just come here and sit down. Let's talk for a minute, and we'll tell you what we know."

"Who's hurt? Where's Ginny? Where's Mama? What about Marla? Who was here? What happened?" The words tumbled from her pell-mell, almost on top of each other in her panic. She looked up, noticed that she knew the cop, and her shoulders released a fraction of the tension there.

Randall Currence was a beat cop who patrolled the neighborhood. His partner this year was another rookie; Jo thought she remembered his name was Freddy or something like that. Randall got a lot of rookies to be their first partner out of the Academy. He'd been on the Phoenix PD for almost twenty years, and he was a calming influence in a tense situation. Freddy was nowhere to be seen tonight. *Maybe got sent home for puking at a crime scene. Again.* Jo thought.

His good looks and easy smile made the women trust him, and his broad shoulders and strong jaw made the men respect him. Randall was a big man, over six foot and a bit over two hundred pounds, but his uniform shirt had no bulge in the middle, and he moved like a man much younger than the thirty-nine years he'd only admit to if pushed.

Jo looked in his face. His normally sparkling blue eyes were somber. She took a deep breath. "Randall, I need you to tell me what happened here."

751

Her eyes scanned the living room from the seat where she's eaten just a few hours earlier. One of Ginny's socks peeked out from under the sofa, the pink one with blue trolls that she couldn't find when she did laundry on Saturday. Cassandra had left her sewing needles sticking in the arm of the rocker/recliner again, just waiting for Jo to put her hand down there all unsuspecting.

Those little Norman Rockwell snapshots felt so incongruous with the red and blue flashing lights strobing across the wall, the coppery scent of blood laying over a deeper, harsher smell of pain and death coming from somewhere. The smiling snapshots hanging on the refrigerator door with magnets cast in sharp relief by the snap of crime scene photographer flashes.

Joanna turned her attention back to Randall, to the policeman sitting in front of her. She tuned in halfway through his sentence. "...we don't know everything yet, Jo. It seems there was a home invasion. There was a young woman here..."

Jo shook off her shock and stupor enough to reply. "That's Marla, we met at work."

"Work?" Randall knew Jo usually made her living as a freelance editor, working from home.

"I've been picking up some side gigs here and there. I met Marla at one of those. She was having boyfriend problems, so I let her crash here."

"What do you know about her boyfriend? Is he the type to hold a grudge?" Randall pulled a small cop's notepad from the chest pocket of his uniform and flipped it open.

"It wasn't the boyfriend," Jo said with a shake of her head.

"How do you know?"

"Because I was just at his place beating the crap out of him and letting him know he wasn't ever to contact Marla again. Whoever broke into my place did it while I was there, so it wasn't him." Her words were flat, lifeless, like she was recounting something that happened to someone else, not something she'd done. That's how it felt, like her life was happening to someone else, like it wasn't real. It had felt like this the first time she saw a monster, the night she learned there were more wicked things in the world than even the stories could explain. The night she lost Darren. She shook her head, trying to focus on the policeman—Randall—staring at her.

"You know you just confessed to assault, right?" Randall asked, his brows knit.

"I also know you'll never find a jury without at least two women on it, and no woman will ever convict me for kicking that abusive jerk's behind. Now what happened here? Where is my mother? Where is Ginny?"

Randall didn't answer for a long moment. When he looked up at Jo again, his eyes told a deeper story. "We don't know. They aren't here."

"Then whose blood is splattered all over my...oh no." Jo stood, knocking Randall's hands aside as he tried to push her gently back into the chair. Jo walked past him, following the trail of blood down the hall. It arced along the walls like the start of a demented Jackson Pollack painting, the splatter going high then low as it traced the path of a fight. A fight that one player was destined to lose, and badly.

Jo stopped at the doorway to her bedroom, where the trail of blood on the walls ended and ran down to become a pool on the floor. Too much blood to soak into the carpet, it stood in a puddle running from under the door out into the hall.

"Randall, is my daughter in there?" Jo reached out, but couldn't bring herself to touch the door.

"We haven't seen any sign of Ginny. We don't know where she is, but she's not in there."

Jo pushed the door open. The lake of blood ran from just past the doorway all the way to her bed, where it seeped into the carpet and ran under the furniture out of sight. There was a void of lighter blood, an amorphous outline where a body had lain. Jo saw a few strands of blonde hair stuck in the blood, along with chips of bone, and other organic bits that marked the spot where Marla had died.

"Where is she?" Jo asked. She didn't turn around. She didn't need to, she could feel Randall right behind her.

"She's in the ambulance. They're going to take her to the morgue where the ME can do a more thorough exam."

"Who did this? Did anyone see anything?"

"We're canvassing neighbors now, but so far we've come up empty. Do you have any idea who would do something like this?"

Jo did, but she couldn't tell the police about it. Not only would that put her mother and daughter in more danger, but it would almost certainly get Randall killed, along with anyone else who tried to bring the demon into custody.

Her phone buzzed in her pocket. Jo ignored it, but it buzzed again.

"You should get that," Randall said. "It might be important." Jo knew that was code for "it might be ransom," but she hoped it wasn't. She didn't want the police to know anything about all this, but it seemed a little late for that now.

Jo pulled her phone out and looked at the screen. She had one new text message. She opened the text and saw an image of her mother's face.

Cassandra had a bruise on her cheek and a split lip, but a defiant look on her face. Below her image was a caption that said *Midnight. School. Bring the Sword. Bring the Angel.*

Jo swiped a finger across the screen to delete the image, then looked up at Randall. "Nothing. It's just a client. Can I see Marla?"

Randall gave her a long look, but nodded. He led her from the house to the ambulance. Jo climbed in and unzipped the body bag. Marla's faced was battered, bloodied, and several bones in her jaw and cheeks were obviously broken. It was obvious to Jo that she didn't go down easily.

"I'm so sorry, sweetie," Jo said in a whisper. "I am so, so sorry. I was out trying to protect you, and you give your life protecting my family? Oh, you were a real fighter, girl, and I am so sorry for this." She looked to the heavens, then said, "Lord, please protect this child of yours and see her to your side, Amen."

A little part of her felt like a hypocrite, praying after everything she found out recently—that God had left Heaven centuries ago and his angels were all scattered across Earth completely ignorant of their true nature. But another part of her felt comforted in the prayer, like somebody heard her and would look after Marla in the next life. Jo wiped her eyes, then zipped the bag closed and stepped out of the ambulance.

"What's the plan, Jo?" Randall asked as he walked up to her. "I know that look. There's something going on more than you're telling me, and I want in on it. I owe you."

"You don't owe me nothing, Randall. I was just doing my job."

"Doing *my* job, more like it," the cop replied. He was talking about an incident a year before when Jo had put down a necromancer with a zombie fetish. The necromancer had raised a bunch of people all across the city, including a cousin of Randall's, and he got way more involved in the supernatural scene than he ever wanted to before she was laid to rest again.

"Either way, I can't have you involved in this," Jo said.

"Does it have anything to do with that text you got? Because you know the feds will subpoena your phone and read all your texts."

"I know they will, but I hope this will all be settled before they can find a judge, get the data from the phone company, and figure out what anything means. Until then, I need you to cover for me." Jo started back toward her car.

Randall followed close behind. "Cover for you? With who? What am I covering for?"

"This is some more of that stuff you don't like to know about," Jo said.

"Yeah, but if I'm going to lose my job, I think I'd better know what's going on," Randall said to her back.

Jo stopped. She turned back to Randall, who spread his hands in front of him. She sighed. "There's a lot more going on here than your job, Randall. There's a lot more going on than my mom and kid, not that I care much about that right now. But this is not anything you want to be involved in. Trust me."

"I can't, Jo. It doesn't matter how much I don't want to be involved, I *am* involved. I got involved the second you told me you were beating up this dead woman's boyfriend while somebody was at your house turning her insides into her outsides. You can't unring that bell. There's a dead woman here, and you're the alibi for our best suspect. That makes you our best suspect. Add to that the fact that your mother and daughter are missing, and you're not freaking out over that, and I am not letting you out of my sight."

Jo hung her head. "Fine. Then get in the car." She opened the driver's door and slid in behind the wheel. A pair of plainclothes police waved and started heading in her direction. She gave Randall a sharp look, and he opened the passenger door and got in.

"This is so gonna cost me my job," he said, clicking on his seat belt.

"Well, look at it this way, Randall. At least now you'll be able to get in all that deep-sea fishing you've been missing."

"We live in Phoenix, Jo. We're like three hundred miles from the ocean."

"Good thing you've got plenty of time to make the trip, then." She jammed the car in reverse and backed out of her driveway, narrowly missing the front of the ambulance as it turned around and headed to the hospital. Jo noted soberly that it wasn't running any lights or siren. It didn't need to, there was no need to hurry.

The same couldn't be said for them. With three hours until midnight, she had to wrangle an angel and devise a plan to get her mother and daughter back safely. And try to keep a nosy cop alive. And maybe kill a demon or three. *Well girl, nobody said this superhero life would be easy.*

CHAPTER NINE

"Why are we at a gym? You need to get a little workout in before we go find your daughter?" Randall asked as Jo put the car in park.

"I'm supposed to meet some people here," Jo said as she opened the door and slid out of the car. She walked to the side door of the squat cinderblock building. A large mural depicting champions of boxing and MMA from Muhammad Ali and Joe Frazier to Royce Gracie and Anderson Silva ranged across the wall, with graffiti-styled lettering two feet high proclaiming it "Dempsey's Gym & Fight Club—the best place nobody talks about."

Jo reached out to knock on the door, but her hand froze as she saw the twisted hunk of metal where the doorknob used to be. She reached under her jacket and unclipped the hammer head from her belt, then drew the handle from the other side, snapped the expandable titanium handle to its full length, and twisted it into place with a *click*.

"Nice toy," Randall said, drawing his sidearm and flashlight.

"I don't like to shoot things," Jo replied.

"I don't either," the stocky cop replied. "But some things really need to get shot."

Jo pulled the door open, and the pair entered the building. Randall played his flashlight around the room for a few seconds, then reached over and flipped on the light switch. Fluorescent tubes flickered to life through the cavernous room, illuminating heavy bags, speed bags, and weight benches arrayed around a central elevated boxing ring. A rough wooden desk sat in one corner of the room in a makeshift "office" consisting of the desk, two chairs, and one battered four-drawer file cabinet with a dead fern on top of it.

Along the back wall was a row of lockers with low wooden benches in front of them and a door marked "SHOWERS" nestled into the far corner. The room was empty, but signs of a struggle were everywhere. Weight benches lay scattered like pieces of a demented Erector Set, a dumbbell rack was overturned in front of a shattered mirror, and the water cooler lay gurgling on its side, its contents pouring out onto the floor.

"Looks like somebody put up a hell of a fight. Who were you supposed to be meeting here?" Randall asked, moving farther into the room.

"My corner man, Jake. He runs this place."

"He a fighter?"

"Not anymore. Says he used to fight some back in the day, but not for years."

"Yeah, looks like he remembered how to throw a punch," the cop said. Randall stepped close to the ring, then holstered his gun. "Jo?" he called.

"Yeah?"

"Your Jake a Hispanic guy?"

"Yeah, he's Latino." Jo stepped forward, then brought her hand to her mouth. "Oh no, Jake." She started forward but froze as Randall raised a hand to her.

"No," he said, all cop. "This is now a crime scene. And you can't be here. Hell, I shouldn't be here either, and I'm probably going to end up an ex-cop before this whole mess is said and done. But there's obviously something going on here that's more than I know, and I'm guessing you have to sort it out on your own."

Jo looked at him, then looked back into the ring, where she could just make out Jake's still form laying spread-eagled on the mat. She could tell even from a distance that his body had the stillness of death about him, and that was before the coppery scent of blood registered above the ever-present gym smell of leather and sweat.

"Give me a minute before you call it in," Jo said, moving toward the ring. "Please?"

Randall looked at her, then nodded. "Seriously, though. One minute."

Jo nodded, swallowing past the lump in her throat. She walked up the cinderblocks that served as de facto ring steps and ducked through the ropes. She pulled out her cell phone and started shooting video as she walked around the body.

"Dennis, video coming your way," she said quietly.

"Got it," the disembodied hacker replied. "That writing looks Enochian."

"I don't know anything about that, but have you seen this kind of...ritual before?" Jo asked.

"Yeah, I have. Unfortunately, I was a part of one. This is a summoning." Jo closed her eyes, but the image before her was seared into her mind's eye.

Jake was staked to the mat, spread-eagled like some demented Da Vinci sketch. He was stripped naked, but it was hard to tell because his body looked almost like it was wearing a red suit, it was covered in so much blood. His hands and feet were nailed to the mat with long spikes, and his body had been split down the middle, the skin peeled back in the center. His organs were set aside in neat piles around the circle, and words in some strange script were scrawled all around the canvas mat in blood and bodily fluids. The dead man's eyes were clenched shut, but his open mouth told the tale of the terrible suffering he had endured.

"Summoning?" Jo asked.

"Yeah, someone has called a demon and used your buddy as the portal. Judging by the amount of blood, it wasn't a very large demon. That's the good news."

"The bad news is that it's still a demon, and it's here."

"And in the company of someone with the knowledge and power to call it forth," Dennis agreed.

"There was already one demon here," Jo said. "We ran into it last night. I sent it home with my hammer."

"Good girl, but that one obviously wasn't the boss."

"How do you know?" Jo asked.

"You aren't dead," Dennis replied. "A boss demon, something like an Archduke, or even a Duke of Hell, would have just ripped your head off and sucked out your soul like eating a crawdad."

"That's an image that will spoil jambalaya for me forever," Jo said. "But yeah, I took that one out pretty easily."

"You're out of your weight class, Jo," Dennis said. "I'll put in a call to Luke. He can get a flight out of Charlotte and be there in four hours, tops. With a little luck, we can have this all settled by sunrise."

"That would be great, if I had that long," Jo replied. "But I have a midnight deadline or this monster kills my mother and my little girl. So you can put Luke on a light-tight private plane if you like, but I can't wait around for the cavalry. I have to take the fight to the monsters, and to do that, I need to wake up an archangel. Any ideas?"

"Yeah, but you aren't going to like it," came the voice from her phone.

"Is it any worse than having a demon murder my whole family?"

"Probably not, but it might be a close second," Dennis said.

A sinking feeling came over Jo as she realized what he was going to suggest. "Oh, come on. There has got to be someone else."

"I've been scouring the web, Dark and light, the whole time we've been on the phone. Phoenix isn't exactly a hot-spot of magical activity, you know. That's probably why Michael hid out there in the first place."

"I know there aren't many high-level practitioners, but this guy? Come on, there's not *anybody* else in the city who can help?" Jo wracked her brain through every Shadow Council contact, every seedy supernatural creature, and every undead or half-alive magic wielder she had ever come into contact with. Every road led back to the same place.

"Fine, call Dr. Evil and tell him I'm coming," she said with a sigh. She turned back to Randall. "You coming with me, or are you going to stay here and try to cover up my mess again?"

"I'm with you," the cop said. "Who's Dr. Evil? Is that his nickname or something?"

"Or something," Jo said, shaking her head as she turned toward the door. *This is gonna suck so bad. Why couldn't I just fight another demon?*

CHAPTER TEN

Jo pulled up in front of Dr. Evil's Magical Emporium and Internet Cafe thirty minutes later. Despite the late hour, the front of the shop was brightly lit, and she had to park at the far end of the lot, jockeying for space between a cavalcade of Prius hybrids and Tesla electric cars. One battered pick truck stood out like a sore thumb, the exact opposite of the normal automotive distribution of Arizona.

"What the hell is this place?" Randall asked as they got out of the car. He gaped at the garish display of color-chasing LED signs screeching words like "GAMING" and "FREE WI-FI" into the desert night. "And doesn't the owner know we have ordinances on signage in this town?"

"I don't think he cares," Jo said, and I'm pretty sure he's located on the correct side of that for a reason." She jerked a thumb at the Phoenix City Limits sign that sat just at the edge of the Emporium parking lot. "As to what this place is, I like to call it heaven for nerds. Also the lair of one of the most powerful magicians in the Southwest, and the one most likely to help me with a case, provided the right incentive."

"Incentive? Are you going to bribe somebody?" Randall asked.

"Oh God, I wish," Jo said. By now she stood at the door, waiting for him. The entrance to the store was covered in window decals proclaiming the store a dueling center for Magic: the Gathering, Yo-Gi-Oh, Cardfight Vanguard, Bushiroad, Pokémon, and half a dozen other games with brightly colored stylized lettering.

The two stepped into the room, and Jo's ears were assailed with shouts of joy and fury as energetic gamers cajoled, cawed, and cackled at their vanquished opponents. A twelve-year-old white kid with faded green hair and freckles slumped in his chair, vanquished by a laughing Asian boy with a Justin Bieber haircut and a smattering of acne across his cheeks. Two overweight men with goatees and black t-shirts pored over a scattering of cards on a table, each pointing to one or another and making suggestions or snide comments while a wide-eyed college kid looked on, apparently soaking in the knowledge of older gamers. A trio of high school girls sat around a board game with a husky African-American man reading from a rulebook.

Everywhere Jo turned, people were playing one game or another, laughing, joking, and generally enjoying themselves. Until they noticed her companion. As soon as they took in Randall's uniform, a hush fell over the room.

Jo looked at the man. "You must be a real killer at parties."

"My wife always wonders why I never get invited," he said with an easy smile. "You wanna let them know I'm not here looking for illegal Adderall and an ounce of weed, or should I let them sweat?"

"Let's scare 'em a little. A little healthy fear of incarceration will do the youth of the world some good." She turned to the room. "I'm looking for Doctor E. Where is he?"

The green-haired boy pointed behind her. "He's in the Gundam Room."

Randall looked at her. "Do I even want to know what a Gundam Room is?"

Jo laughed at her friend's discomfort. "You're gonna get your nerd card revoked, Randall. A Gundam is a scale model of a Japanese battle mech from a cartoon. Don't you know anything?"

Randall just looked around the room, his eyes wide at the multitude of nerddoms on display. "Apparently not."

"Follow me. Let's go see Dr. Evil." Joanna turned around and walked through dozens of folding tables and matches of various collectible card games toward a small doorway. Through the door, she saw a desk with a big man in a lime-green dress shirt seated behind three brightly colored boxes. She stopped at the door and knocked. "Doc? Got a minute?"

The big man looked up from the boxes and motioned to the teenager sitting across from him. "Take these up front to David. Tell him to give you ten percent off whichever one you decide on. Fifteen percent if you buy all three." The kid nodded, scooped up the model boxes, and headed for the door.

Jo stepped in with Randall and closed the door behind her. "Good sale?" she asked.

"Not bad. Two fifty if he buys them all, about ninety for each one if he buys them separately," Dr. Evil replied.

"Does that math work?" Jo asked. She sat in one of the metal chairs across from the desk. Randall leaned against the door frame.

"Eh, rounding," the big man replied. "Now, what can I do for you, Joanna? I'm sure you aren't here just to help me maximize profits on model sales."

"I need your help," Jo said. Her voice was tight, clipped, and it was pretty obvious from the set of her shoulders that those were the last words she ever wanted to come from her lips.

Dr. Evil leaned forward, a grin splitting his face as he rubbed his hands together. "Absolutely, Jo. What can I do for you? You interested in getting back into the game? I'd be happy to sponsor The Iron Maiden in any tournaments you wanted to play. I'll get you cards, sleeves, supplies, teammates, anything you want. Hoodies, t-shirts...you name it, I'll have it made."

"Not that kind of help. The other kind. Magic."

"That's what I was talking about. Magic. I didn't think you were going to step down into Yu-Gi-Oh after playing in the big...oh." His face fell, and he leaned back in his chair. "You mean the real stuff."

"What else would she mean?" Randall asked. "What is this Iron Maiden stuff?"

"There's a card game called Magic: the Gathering," Jo began.

"Yeah, I saw signs and stuff out front. Looks interesting."

"Don't," Jo said with a sharp wave of her hand. "It's more addictive than crack, and at least as expensive. Anyway, I used to play. A lot. And I was good. Really good."

"One of the best," Dr. Evil agreed. He wore a solemn look, like he mourned something lost. "She was one of the best I'd ever seen. Until she quit. The world lost a great Magic player when you retired, Joanna."

"I grew up, Leon," Jo replied. "Sometimes we have to do things like that."

"I disagree. Growing older is mandatory; growing up is optional." Dr. Evil shook his head.

"Anyway," Jo went on. "I played a lot of Magic, and Leon...excuse me, Dr. Evil always wanted me to play on his team."

"I wanted you to anchor my team," Leon added. "I wanted to build the whole team around you. A different kind of Magic team. Not just a bunch of nerdy misfits, but a team with something dramatically different."

"A girl," Jo said.

"Women are dramatically underrepresented on professional teams and at competitive events, and you could have helped change that. But you quit." Leon's forehead wrinkled. "But I understand. You got married, had a kid, then..."

"Yeah, then," Jo said, her tone making it clear she didn't want to discuss "then." "But now I'm here, about magic, and not the card game. There's trouble, and I need your help."

"The demon?" the big man asked.

"You know about the demon?" Randall's eyes went wide. "Did you—"

"No," Leon waved a hand sharply. "I don't mess with the dark stuff. I don't even let the dabblers run their LARPs out of here."

Randall looked from Leon to Jo. "I don't..."

"Live Action Role Play," Jo supplied. "It's the stuff that even nerds think is nerdy. Look, Leon, I need your help. This demon, he's bad news. I don't know what he's up to, but he's after somebody I know. He...killed a friend of mine tonight, and he took my mom and..." Her words trailed off. Jo took a deep breath and squared her shoulders. "He's got my kid, Leon. He took Ginny, and I have to take my friend to him or he'll hurt her."

Leon looked at her for a long minute. "Ginny? I never even knew her name, Jo. Of course I'll help. What do you need? What's so special about your friend here?"

Jo looked confused for a second, then let out a sharp laugh. "Oh no, it's not Randall. He's just a cop. He's helping. The friend I have to take...well, he's an angel."

Dr. Evil's head snapped up. "What? What do you mean, an angel?"

"I mean an angel like wings, Heaven, harps, all that crap. You know, an angel. A big one."

The big man's eyes widened. "Is he here?"

"No, I have to go find him next. We were supposed to meet up tonight, but things have changed since we made our plans. So I'm going to him, then I have to convince him that he's really an angel and has to help me rescue my little girl."

"So he's asleep?" Leon asked.

"He doesn't know what he is, if that's what you mean by asleep," Jo agreed.

"Do angels sleep?" Randall asked. "I mean, the normal way."

"I have no idea, and I don't care right now. All I care about is getting Mitch to grab hold of that sword in my trunk and take the fight to this demon so I can get my mama and baby girl back home safe. Now, what do you have that can bring this angel to his senses, Leon?" Jo asked.

Leon leaned back in his chair, the metal protesting at the abuse. He clasped his hands on his expansive chest and looked up at the ceiling as though the answer was written in the fluorescent fixture. After almost a full minute, he looked at Joanna and Randall. "I don't know, but I have a couple of ideas. Can you go get him and bring him back here? I need to make a few preparations, and I'll have to clear out space in the back room. It's been a while since I did any major rituals. I've got some overstock in the middle of my circle."

Jo nodded. "Yeah, I can do that. We'll go get Mitch and bring him back here. But Leon, we have to hurry. I've got to meet this demon at midnight or he'll hurt Ginny."

"It's ten now, so don't screw around. Where does your guy live?" Leon asked.

"I'm not sure, but I can find him," Jo said. She stood up and turned to Randall. "Let's go."

"I need him," Dr. Evil said, pulling himself to his feet. He was even bigger standing, almost six-and-a-half feet tall, with his neon green shirt glaring in the hideous fluorescent light. "There's a lot of crap to move in the back."

"Fine," Jo said. "I'll be back as soon as I can." She opened the door and headed to the front of the store, pulling out her cell phone as she went. She swiped her finger across the screen and typed in her security code. "Dennis, I need you."

"What's up?" the unicorn head on her screen asked.

"I need you to trace Mitch's cell phone for me."

"Do you have the number?" the unicorn asked.

"Yeah, it's in my contacts."

"I've got him. But Jo?" The unicorn head was gone, replaced by Dennis's human face.

"Yeah, what's wrong?"

"He's moving."

"Okay, I guess he's headed over to the gym early. I can meet him there before he gets in and finds—"

"He's not going to the gym. He's driving east, toward the airport. I just checked the flights. He's booked on a redeye to New York leaving in ninety minutes."

"Son of a gun," Jo muttered. She jerked open her car door and slid behind the wheel. She stuck the phone in a cradle and activated the Bluetooth, then jammed the car in reverse and squealed out of the parking lot. "Get me on him, Dennis. We've got to catch that angel before he gets the heck out of Dodge."

———

M itch was standing in the clear Plexiglas shelter marked with a blue "Z" when Jo pulled her red Kia Soul to a stop in front of him. The undercover angel's head snapped up and his eyes went wide as she walked around the front of the car, opened the passenger door, and gestured to him.

"Get in," she said. A thin blonde girl in sweatpants with pink headphones pressed to her ears looked up and pulled her headphones down around her neck. "Put the 'phones back on, Princess. This is grown-up business."

The girl opened her mouth to speak, but Jo held up one finger at her. "Didn't anybody ever tell you not to mess with a pissed-off black woman when she's fussin' at her man? Now sit your lily-white behind down and stay out of my business." The girl's eyes widened, but she put her headphones on and sat down. She pulled a cell phone out of her pocket and started typing furiously on the screen.

Jo looked back at Mitch. "Now get your butt in the car before Princess Barbie's tweet goes viral and I end up starring in the remake of *Diary of a Mad Black Woman*."

Mitch took the green duffel bag off his shoulder and let it drop to the ground by his feet. "I'm not going with you, Jo. I don't know how you did that trick with the sword, and I don't know what you want out of me, but I'm no angel, and I'm not going to go fight no monster."

"You are, and you are," Jo said. "I don't have time to play games with you, Mitch. You are the Archangel Michael, you are going with me to deal with this demon, and you are getting in my car right now."

"Is there a problem, sir?" Jo turned to see the airport shuttle idling behind her car with the door open. The blonde girl stepped up into the bus and leaned down to the driver's ear. He nodded, then said, "You folks take care of your personal business at home. I've got runs to make. You getting on or not?"

Mitch picked up his bag and stepped forward, but Jo put a hand on his chest. "He's got my daughter, Mitch. He came into my house, murdered Marla, and kidnapped my mother and my baby girl. I need you to help me get them back. I can't do it without you." Her voice was low, her words urgent. She looked up into the big man's blue eyes, saw his resistance start to waver.

"Please, Mitch. You're the only one that can help me." Her voice cracked, and she hated herself a little bit for it, but she couldn't hold everything inside. Not this time.

Mitch stepped back, then waved to the bus driver. "Go ahead. I'll catch the next one."

"Your funeral, dude. You gotta look out for the crazy ones." The driver closed the door and pulled around Jo's car, belching black diesel smoke all over the two of them.

Mitch looked down at Jo. "You fucking with me?"

"I don't do that," Jo said. "And watch your mouth."

"Did somebody really take your mother and kid?"

"Yeah. Slaughtered Marla in my living room. She must have put up some kind of a fight. Tore down a couple bookshelves and wrecked my TV. But apparently that wasn't a clear enough message. Got Jake, too. Left him lying in the middle of the gym in a pool of his own blood."

"Shit," Mitch said. He glanced at Jo, who frowned at him. "Sorry, slipped out. What are we going to do?"

"I've got a guy working on that right now. We need to go meet up with him, then get to the school by midnight or they'll hurt Mama and Ginny."

"Do you know how many there are?" Mitch asked.

"I don't know anything," Jo said. "I know where to be and when to be there. I don't know what we're going up against, or how many. I don't care. They've got my baby, and I'm going to get her back." She stood there, fists clenched and jaw set, looking up at Mitch.

"And I'm going to help you," Mitch said. He put a hand on her shoulder. "But we need to get as much information as we can. We can't just go in there half-cocked. We need to do some surveillance, get the lay of the land before we go charging in there guns blazing."

"Sword," Jo corrected.

"Huh?"

"We're going in there sword blazing, not guns blazing. Now where did you learn all that military talk? I thought you were just a dumb jock."

"I've been some places," Mitch said. "Seen some things."

"Yeah," Jo agreed. "More than you even remember. Now get in the car. We've got to go save my baby girl."

CHAPTER ELEVEN

The parking lot was empty when they pulled back into Dr. Evil's game shop twenty minutes later. Jo opened the door, and Mitch turned to her. "This is the place? Your guy works here?"

"Something like that. Now come on. We've got to be at the school in an hour, and I don't know how long whatever Leon is planning will take."

Jo got a long duffel bag out of her trunk, and they walked into the deserted game shop. Half the overhead lights were off, and the green-haired boy was sitting at a long table playing something on a handheld game. He looked up when Mitch closed the door behind them.

"Go ahead and lock the deadbolt," the kid said. "I'll take you back to the Doc."

"You really call him that?" Jo asked.

The kid shot her a crooked grin. "Depends on whether I want to yank his chain or not. But yeah, sometimes I call him Doc. He says there used to be a chick that called him that, and we're the only two people who could ever get away with it. That you?"

Jo smiled, memories of a simpler life playing across her mind as they followed the kid through the darkened store. "Guilty as charged. I'm Jo."

"Spencer," the kid replied.

"You involved in the other business?" Jo asked.

"I'm learning. Leon thinks I've got some talent, so he's been teaching me a few things."

"Be careful. There's some bad things in the world."

"That's why I want to learn magic. I want to stop the bad things from hurting people. That's what you do, right? That's why you're here?" The kid stopped in front of a door with two deadbolts.

"Yeah, that's why I'm here. And sometimes it's what I do," Jo said. She reached out for the knob, then looked at the kid. "But you think hard before you go down this road, kid. There are doors that can't be closed again and things that can't be unseen. Once you start messing with the ugly stuff in the world, it has a bad habit of messing with you right back. That's why we're here. Something nasty has my mother and my daughter, and we've got to fight it to get them back and keep this thing from hurting anybody else."

Spencer looked up at her, his round face pale in the dim light. "I've already seen plenty of ugly. This isn't the best neighborhood, you know. And I live two blocks from here."

Jo knew the area. There were flop houses, whorehouses, and at least one meth lab within a quarter mile. Leon set up his shop there not just because the rent was cheap, but in hopes that he could give the kids in that part of town a safe place to go. It never hurt to have a wizard hanging out in a tough neighborhood, either.

She nodded to the kid. "Okay, just be careful."

He looked at her, then opened the door for her. "You too."

Jo and Mitch stepped through the door into the shop's storeroom, and Spencer closed and locked the door behind them. Mitch spun around, but Jo put a hand on his arm.

"It's okay. The deadbolts will open from either side, but if something mean and stupid gets loose, it gives the kid at least a chance of getting away." She pointed to the door, and there were indeed latches to throw the deadbolts on both sides. Mitch relaxed, then turned back to the room. His eyes grew wide as he took in the room.

What was probably a normal warehouse room less than an hour before now looked like something out of a bad horror movie. A large circle was drawn in the floor with a five-pointed star touching the circle with all the points. Strange symbols Jo recognized and wards in various ancient languages ringed the perimeter, Celtic runes alternating with Enochian script and hand-scrawled Latin. White pillar candles burned at each point of the star. Incense burned in several holders around the room, filling the air with the mixed scents of sandalwood, vanilla, lavender, and clove. A smudge stick lay smoldering in the upper segment of the circle, its smoke wafting up behind of Leon, who was seated in the center with his legs crossed and his hands extended, palm out.

The big man wore loose black pants that looked like they were homespun cotton, with a formless grey shirt on top. It looked like nothing more than a pair of cheap sweat pants, or maybe long-sleeved hospital scrubs, with blobs of colored wax and other odd stains dotting the shirt and pants. He was barefoot, and bareheaded, sweat beading on his expansive forehead, but there was a tranquility about him that made Jo smile. If she had to guess, she would say that he was happier than he'd been in quite some time.

She knew, from long conversations years ago, that he wanted nothing more than to do good in the world, but had stepped away from actively practicing magic when his son was born. He didn't want to attract the wrong kind of attention to his family, a concern that Jo felt all too acutely just then.

Leon looked up at her and smiled. "You're back. Good. Everything is in place, we can begin."

"It better all be in place," panted Randall from a folding chair in the corner of the room. "I can't even count how many boxes of crap I had to move. You'd think stock in a toy store would be easy, but no, that crap is heavy!"

Jo laughed. "Let me guess, Leon had to work on his very important preparations, so you did all the heavy lifting?"

"Girl, you ain't wrong," Randall said, wiping a bead of sweat from his chin. "I can't even pronounce most of the crap I moved, but I know I don't ever want to lay hands on it again!" He waved a hand at boxes of anime action figures, collectible card games, and stacks and stacks of Gundam models.

"What are we doing here, Jo? I thought we were going to get your daughter," Mitch said.

"Mitch, this is Leon. I hope he can wake you up." Jo gestured to the man seated in the circle, who nodded.

"Hello, Mitch. I would get up, but let's face it, I'm a big old man, and it's not easy to get up from the floor at my age. Now come sit down across from me in the circle, and we'll see what we can see. Jo, did you bring the sword?"

"Right here," she said, pulling the duffel from her shoulder. She set the bag on the floor, unzipped it, and drew out the sword. It was a plain weapon, nothing outwardly special about it. But she'd watched it burst into flames when Mitch touched it, and she'd seen demons tear through ruins to get it. She knew the unadorned weapon was actually one of the most holy objects on Earth, in the right hands.

She held it out to Mitch, who stepped back, his hands up. "No thank you," he said. "I remember the headache that thing gave me last night."

"You're going to have to touch it, Mitch. This whole thing hinges on you taking up the sword," Jo said. She stepped forward, hilt extended to the fighter, but Mitch just kept backing up.

"You guys do your hocus-pocus, then we'll talk about me putting my hands back on that thing," Mitch said.

Jo took a deep breath and turned to Leon. "It's okay," he said. "Give me the sword."

She handed him the sword, and Leon looked up at Mitch. "Sit." All hints of the jovial game shop owner were gone. His voice had steel behind it, and Mitch stepped into the circle and sat down in the center, his knees almost touching Leon's.

Leon laid the blade across his lap and stretched out his hands, palms up. "Put your hands on mine."

Mitch did as instructed.

Leon closed his eyes and began to mutter under his breath. Jo took a step back, making sure that her toes were nowhere near the edge of the circle, and closed her eyes as a bright flash of blue filled the room. When she opened her eyes and blinked away the dazzle-spots, a dome of blue-white energy crackled over the circle, completely enclosing Leon and Mitch. She could see the big man's mouth moving, but no sound penetrated the protective barrier of the circle.

Randall stepped to her side. "What the ever-loving shit is going on here?"

"You didn't buy any of it until right now, did you?" Jo asked.

"Not really," the stunned cop admitted. "I mean, I hoped you weren't crazy because I like you. I really hoped you weren't stupid *and* crazy because after what I saw at your house and your friend's gym, that was probably going to get me killed. But never in a million years did I think you were just telling me the truth. Like, the real truth. I figured you weren't lying because I've been a cop long enough to know when somebody's just lying to my face, but I thought you were probably..."

"Crazy or stupid?" Jo finished for him.

"Or both," he agreed.

"Yeah, a lot of times I think I probably am both, for ever getting mixed up in this mess."

"Then why?" Randall asked.

"Why what?"

"Why get mixed up in this stuff? It's not safe, and it can't pay much."

Jo laughed quietly. "Try nothing at all. This is a volunteer position, my friend."

"So why do it?"

Jo looked at him. "Why are you a cop? I know that ain't for the money."

Randall didn't hesitate for a second. "People need help. I can help. I'm supposed to do that." He nodded at her. "Okay. I get it."

"Yep," she said. "It's the exact same thing. There are bad people in the world. We have people like you to take care of that. There are bad things in this world, too. Things that might not have started in this world and might not be the kind of things that police can deal with. For those things, for the monsters in the closet, the creatures under the bed, the things that go bump in the night? For those things, you have me. Me and people like me. The Shadow Council. We fight against the dark, so the people we love can live in the light."

Randall nodded. "I get it. Kinda. I'm still trying to process the whole 'magic is real' thing. But I get why you mess with it."

"Because somebody's got to," Jo said. Just then, the light surrounding the circle winked out, and Leon looked up at them.

"I'm sorry," he said. "I can't reach him. I mean, there's something blocking him off from the divine part of himself, and I can't break through it. I'm just not strong enough, or don't know the right spells, or something. I don't even know what I don't know." The big man heaved himself to one knee, then stood as he spoke. His voice was tight with frustration, his forehead furrowed. "I don't get it, Joanna. I looked at him for mystical influences, and there was nothing. I dove into his consciousness looking for tampering, and there was nothing. It's like whatever makes him...I don't even know how to explain it, but the angel part of him is just missing. I'm sorry. I can't help you."

He kicked over one of the candles, and it flickered out, spilling wax on the floor. "Spencer!" he bellowed. "Come on back here and help clean up." Leon turned back to Jo and handed her the sword. "I could feel the power in this weapon. It *wants* to come to life. It wants to fight. Maybe that will be enough."

"It'll have to be," Jo said. She took the sword from him and turned to Mitch. "Let's go. We've got less than an hour before we have to meet up with whoever has my baby."

Mitch stood up, flowing to his feet in an easy motion. Even without the sword burning in his hand, he looked dangerous. "Okay," he said. "Let's do this."

Jo looked at him, her eyebrows raised. "You're not going to argue with me?"

"They've got your kid, right?"

"Yeah."

"Then we'll get her back. I was a dick before. I'm sorry. I won't let a little kid get hurt just because I don't want to play magic angel or whatever. I'll help."

"Me too," Randall said. "Besides, if I stay here, I have to help put all this crap back where it was." They all laughed but turned somber as they walked to the door.

Joanna put her hand on the door and turned back to Leon, who was gathering up candles and blowing them out. "Thank you, Doc."

"You're welcome," he said. "And don't call me Doc," he said with a smile.

She gave him a little smile back and stepped out into the dark store. "Come on boys, let's go fight a monster."

CHAPTER TWELVE

J o stepped out of her Kia and walked around to the back of the car. Randall and Mitch joined her as she lifted the door and pulled out her hammer and a long brown leather duster. She clipped a ring to her belt and threaded the handle through it, then slipped on the heavy coat.

"Are we in a blacksploitation remake of *Tombstone*, Jo?" Randall asked.

"No, and I'm too short to be Pam Grier," she replied. "This thing is heavy, hot as hell, and makes me look stupid, but the leather is thick and tough enough to stop a knife or claw, and I wish I'd had it last night when we ran into that thing in the hall."

She reached in and picked up the sword wrapped in a blue tarp. She held the bundle out to Mitch.

He stepped back, holding up both hands. "I'm not touching that thing, Jo."

"You're probably going to have to," she said. "It might be the only thing that can kill whatever is waiting for us in there."

Mitch shook his head and held up the shotgun Randall had given him. "Anything I can't kill with a twelve-gauge is something I shouldn't be trying to kill in the first place."

"I'll take it," Randall said, holding out his hand.

"Do you know how to use a sword, Randall?" Jo asked.

"I've seen *Braveheart* twice and every *Lord of the Rings* movie. That oughta count for something, right? Besides, I have my Sig for backup if I can't remember which end to put in the bad guys."

Jo shook her head and handed him the sword. He stripped the tarp off the blade and tested the weight, then slashed at the air a few times, getting the feel of the weapon.

"Let's go," Jo said. She closed the hatchback and passed a flashlight to Mitch. "I need both hands free," she said, gesturing with the hammer.

Randall pulled a flashlight from his belt and clicked it on. He led the way, with Jo behind him and Mitch bringing up the rear as they walked across the deserted parking lot. There was only one car on the premises besides Jo's little Kia, and it was parked on the opposite side of the building, pulled all the way up the sidewalk right to the door. Randall led the trio toward the back of the school, traversing a basketball court and an expansive lawn before coming to a closed double door.

Jo reached out and tried the handle, finding it unlocked. She looked at her companions. "You think they unlocked all the doors, or did they plan on us coming in this way?"

"This is the only door on this side of the building, so they probably parked where they did on purpose, assuming we'd use the door farthest from their car. So yeah, I guess they planned on us coming this way," Randall said.

"Should we look for another way in?" Jo asked.

"Why bother?" Mitch asked. The others turned to him. "You said these guys have your daughter and your mom, right?"

Jo nodded.

"Then it doesn't matter where we come in. All they have to do is sit in one place with the hostages, and we'll go to them. They know where we'll be, and they know roughly when we'll be there because you've only got about twenty minutes to get there before your midnight deadline now. Makes way more tactical sense for them to just let us in and wait for us."

"So that's we do, huh? We just do exactly what they want and go in there?" Randall asked.

"Yep," Jo said. "We go in there, kick some ass, and walk out with my daughter and my mother. Any questions?"

"Yeah," Randall said. "What are we waiting for?" He pulled open the door and stepped through, his flashlight cutting a narrow blue-white beam through the darkened hall. Jo followed, with Mitch again bringing up the rear. They walked down the long hallway, then turned right at the first intersection, heading toward the gym.

"He's probably got Mama and Ginny in one of the locker rooms. Randall, why don't you go see if you can find them while me and Mitch look for the demon?"

"We should stick together," Randall said. The others looked at him as if

774

demanding a reason. "Oh come on, haven't you two ever seen a horror movie? You split up, and the one who goes off by himself dies. Especially if it's the black dude. Just in case you missed it, this doesn't rub off." He held up the back of his hand and rubbed the skin with a finger. His dark brown skin didn't change.

"So the black dude is not going off by himself in this movie," Randall said.

"One problem with that whole thing, Randall," Jo said. "I'm black, too."

"Doesn't matter. You're the hero. They won't kill you first. This isn't some M. Night Shamalamadingdong movie, just going for the cheap plot twist. This is real life, and I ain't getting killed tonight."

"Okay, we stay together. Then we need to go this way," Jo said, pointing down the hall. The men followed her lead, and they began to see a sliver of light under the double doors at the end of the hall.

"Is that the gym?" Randall asked.

"Yeah," Mitch said. "Keep an eye out up here. There are two locker rooms. If anybody's going to jump us, that's where they'll be."

They crossed to the far side of the hall to avoid passing directly in front of the locker room doors, but no one leapt out at them. Moments later, they stood at the entrance to the gym. Jo shifted her hammer to her left hand, reached out with her right, and yanked the door open.

They gym was lit by about a third of the overhead lights, casting deep shadows around the walls but illuminating the empty cage in the center of the basketball court. Jo's eyes scanned the room until she found her mother and daughter sitting on the one extended section of bleachers. Both Harrison women had their hands tied behind them and silver duct tape over their mouths, but even at a distance, Jo could see a fierce determination in their eyes. They may have been captured, but their spirits were unbowed.

Shelton stepped into the light, his hands clasped in front of him and a broad smile on his face. "Joanna, thank you so much for coming. I am thrilled that you could make our little soiree, and so pleased that you brought guests. I know Mitchell, of course, but who is your little blue friend?"

"Phoenix PD," Randall announced in a booming voice. "Get on your knees and put your hands on your head." He holstered his flashlight and drew his pistol, leveling the weapon at Shelton.

"Shel?" Jo said, bewildered. "You're part of this?"

"Part of this?" Shelton repeated. "Oh sweetie, I'm not part of this at all. I *am* this. This is all my operation. The whole fight club has been a plan to get my hands on your divine little friend here." He gestured to Mitch.

Mitch glared at the promoter and pointed the shotgun at him. "I think the officer gave you an order, Shel. I think you should do what he said."

"I think you should shut up when your betters are speaking, angel," Shel snapped, waving a hand at the group. A wave of force struck them, carrying away the shotgun and Randall's pistol. Jo held onto her hammer, drawing a raised eyebrow from Shelton. "Really? That's interesting."

Shelton walked forward, his eyes glowing red in the gloom. His appearance began to change as he approached, growing larger, his clothes vanishing as he grew to six, then seven feet tall. Black bat wings extended from his shoulders, and his skin took on a deep crimson tone. A long, spiked tail waved sinuously behind him, and his heavily muscled arms ended in black inch-long claws.

He shook his head, long black braids flowing down his back. "Ah, that's better. You have no idea how cramped my wings get after being folded up in that stupid human suit. But this is better, isn't it? No need for subterfuge, no need to hide anything. Just good, old-fashioned, honest murder."

Jo stepped forward, swinging her hammer in a looping blow. Shel raised an arm and wrapped his hand around the head of the weapon, enclosing it in his huge fist. Smoke billowed from his fingers, and he snatched his hand back. "Ouch! That hurt, Jo. What did you do, have this thing blessed?"

"First thing I did when I got home from Atlanta. I went to church, prayed about what I'd seen, and asked Father Timothy to bless my hammer. He was a little confused, but he did it."

"Well, that hurt, and that means I'm going to have to kill you, too. I was just going to kill the angel and let you go, but now...well, everybody into the cage!"

"Screw you, demon," Jo said, raising the hammer again. "I'm not getting into that cage again, especially with you."

Demon-Shel smiled at her. "Of course you are. Or I'll kill your family."

Jo took a menacing step forward, but stopped at the demon's upraised hand. "You don't want me to prove it, do you?" he asked. Shel pointed his hand at the opposite bleachers, and his eyes glowed red. Seconds later, a tendril of smoke curled up from behind the bleachers. The fire broke free and climbed the stacked wall of closed wooden seats, engulfing the entire wall in flame. Shel waved his hand, and the fire vanished, leaving soot and cinders behind.

"I don't have to be near them to kill them, Jo. I just have to want to make it happen. Now get your ass in the cage, or I will cook them from the inside out!" He bellowed the last, and Jo saw the pair of wicked fangs jutting up from his lower jaw.

Jo glared at him. "If I do this, if I fight you, you let them go?"

"You have my word. If you get into the cage and fight me, your mother and daughter will leave this place unharmed. I will even return your grandfather's hammer to them after I finish gutting you."

Jo recognized this for the generosity the demon thought it was and nodded. "Fine, I'll fight. Come on, Mitch." She started toward the cage, Mitch beside her.

"Well, I'm not going in no cage. And you aren't going to hurt them, asshole." Randall punctuated his words with five shots from the small revolver he held in his hand.

Jo shouted, "Randall, no!" then watched in horror as Shel took all five rounds right to the chest, staggering but not falling down.

The demon looked at Randall, then looked down at the cluster of five small holes in his torso. "Ouch," he said. "That wasn't very nice, Randall. Or very smart." He snarled at the stunned police officer, then took three big strides forward and ripped Randall's throat out with his right hand.

Shel looked at the trachea in his hand, licked the blood pouring from it, then spat on Randall's dying body. "Too many trans fats, Randall. Your cholesterol was awful. Makes the blood too thick, messes with the texture." He dropped the bloody hunk of flesh on the floor, then leaned down and wiped his hand on Randall's pants leg.

Shel straightened up and waved to the cage. "Let's go, children. We have a fight to get to, and your daughter has years of therapy to earn." He walked past Jo and Mitch, straight into the cage. Jo handed her hammer to Mitch and went to kneel at Randall's side. She closed his eyes, folded his hands on his chest, and picked up the sword from where it lay by his body.

Mitch and Jo went into the cage together but split as soon as they entered the octagon, spreading out to attack from two angles. As they readied for a charge, Shel held up his hand.

"Wait for it, my dears. You don't think this is a private event, do you?" He snapped his fingers, and the rest of the lights in the gym flashed to life. Jo blinked from the sudden brightness, bringing one hand up to shield her eyes.

"Welcome, my friends, to the show that never ends," Shel said in a singsong voice. "Tonight we have your inimitable host—me, facing two challengers at once. Please welcome Iron Jo Henry and the Archangel Michael!" Canned applause echoed through the deserted room as Shel twirled in place and pumped his arms over his head.

He sighed and looked at Jo. "Aren't you two even going to *pretend* to be excited? I mean it's not every day you get to battle a demon, is it?"

"You'd be surprised," Jo replied.

"Okay," Shel said. "But how often do you get it streamed live direct to Hell!" He waved his hand around the ring, and Jo looked up. Mounted above the cage were half a dozen GoPro miniature video cameras, no doubt doing exactly what Shel said—streaming the match to whatever and whoever wanted to see it.

"Great, I get to die on live TV, and I forgot to wear makeup," Jo growled.

"Don't worry," Shel said. "When you're dead, I'll paint your face in angel blood. I hear it does wonders for the skin. Now let's ring the bell!"

Shel waved his hand again, and a bell rang from somewhere. He grinned across the ring at Jo and Mitch, then said, "Who wants to die first?"

CHAPTER THIRTEEN

itch and Jo spread out farther, working to make life as difficult for their opponent as possible. Jo tossed the sword in Mitch's direction, but he just scowled at her and shook his head. She hefted her hammer and charged the demon, hoping Mitch would at least take a couple of shots at its head while she distracted it.

She swung, but Shel ducked the blow easily. He came up with a slash at her stomach, his claws flashing out just an inch or two in front of her as she hopped back out of range. She ducked a slash at her face, then rolled to one side as she heard the bark of a gun at close range.

"Ow, dammit!" Shel said, his hand going to the back of his head. He turned around, and Jo saw Mitch standing there, a smoking pistol in his hand.

"Where the hell did you get that?" she asked.

"I swiped it out of Randall's trunk," he replied, squeezing off three more rounds. The bullets smacked into the demon's head and neck, tearing chunks of flesh from his face. Shel didn't go down, though, just waved his hand at Mitch and grinned as the gun flew from his hand over the top of the cage.

Jo took advantage of the momentary distraction and laid a shot on Shel's knee that landed with a sickening *crunch*. The big demon dropped, a howl of pain piercing the night. He spun on one knee, then sprang at Jo, who dove to the left in a frantic attempt to avoid getting ripped to shreds by an angry demon.

"Bitch, I will eat your entrails for that," Shel snarled.

Jo stood and squared her shoulders. "Don't call me that."

"I will call you anything I want, bitch," the demon said, moving forward at a limp. Its right leg dragged, nearly useless, but in a cage barely thirty feet across, Shel didn't have to get far. One good lunge and Jo had to duck under outstretch claws and lash out with her hammer again to keep from being crushed.

The hammer landed a glancing blow on the demon's hip, just enough to spin the monster around and give Jo a little breathing room. Mitch darted in, his gun forgotten, and launched a series of kicks at Shel, alternating between head and knee shots. Nothing significant landed, though, and when the demon planted its good leg and sprang away from Mitch's assault, it caught Jo around the middle and tumbled her to the floor.

Before she could react, Shel was on her. He straddled her middle and wrapped his hands around her neck. Even without using his claws, the demon's hands enveloped her throat. Jo thrashed and struggled the best she could, but the beast was too big, and she couldn't get any leverage to hit it with her hammer.

She lay there, struggling, as the world started to shift to grey, and black dots closed in on her vision. She turned her face to the side, and just before everything went away, she caught one last glimpse of her mother and daughter in the stands, looking on in terror. Ginny's eyes were huge, and Cassandra's face was streaked with tears, but the old woman didn't look away, just like she hadn't looked away when Jo's father died, all those years ago. Jo saw one last loving look in her mother's eyes, then her vision faded to nothing.

Suddenly a shriek like a thousand tormented bats filled the air, and the pressure vanished from Jo's throat. The weight on her chest gone, she rolled to her side and coughed, sucking in huge gasps of sweet, welcome air.

After long seconds of coughing and trying to breathe, Jo looked up and saw Mitch standing over her, flaming sword in his hand. His face was a rictus of pain, and his knuckles were white on the hilt of the sword, but he held it. He held it upright, the flames dancing along the edge of the blade and casting yellow-orange light across the ring.

"Come at me, motherfucker," Mitch said in a low growl.

Shel leaned against the far wall of the cage, a mixture of fear and elation on his face. "It really is you. I didn't know, but now...the sword...I see it. You really are Michael."

"Apparently so," Mitch said.

"I have to leave," Shelton said. "There are people who will be very interested in this news."

"You're not going anywhere, demon. Not even to Hell." Jo levered herself up from the floor with her hammer, then hefted it into both hands as she caught her balance. She looked over to Mitch, who nodded. "Let's finish this."

Mitch and Jo advanced on the demon, who now had a black-rimmed wound in its shoulder to match its pulped knee. Shel waved his clawed hands in front of his body, holding them at bay with his razor-sharp talons. He steered their fight around the perimeter of the octagon, turning slightly to his left with every step, working to position himself with his back to the cage door for a quick exit.

Jo took in his plan in an instant and took a deep breath. "There's no way this doesn't suck," she said, holding her hammer straight out in front of her and letting out a guttural yell. "Aaaahhhh!"

Jo charged the demon, lowering her shoulder into Shel's abdomen and slamming his spine into the cage, right on one of the lightly padded uprights. She knew from experience just how thin the padding was and just how solid the four-inch metal tubing that made up the corners of the homemade ring was.

Shel's head snapped back and impacted the ringpost with a hollow *gong* sound, and Jo heard a rib or two snap under her shoulder. She backed up a few inches, then drove her shoulder into the demon's gut again, letting a grim smile play across her lips at the *whoosh* of air escaping the monster's lungs.

She felt the claws scrabbling across the leather coat on her back, tearing the thick material but unable to get to her flesh. She jammed the hammer into Shel's lower abdomen, pressing the blessed silver-coated head into the demon's body for a little more damage. The beast howled and tried to pull back, but there was nowhere to go. Jo felt the hammer blow of an elbow crash into her spine, and she fell to her knees.

On the ground, she bobbed her head side to side avoiding knee strikes from the demon, then slammed the hammer down onto one of Shel's unprotected feet. A shriek filled the room, and Jo found herself rolling to the side as he thrust her off and dove for the middle of the ring.

Only to run right into a flaming sword held by a pissed-off angel in disguise. Mitch jabbed the blade at the demon's middle, forcing Shel to backpedal and pinwheel his arms to keep balance. Jo stood up and swung her hammer at the demon's head, connecting with a resounding *crack*.

The monster fell to the canvas, unmoving. Jo stayed back, rolling her shoulders and checking for wounds. Her coat was much the worse for wear, but the leather did its job in protecting her from the demon's claws. She looked at Mitch, who stood with the sword in hand, a grimace of pain fixed on his face.

"Still nothing?" she asked.

"I still don't feel like picking up a harp and dancing on clouds, if that's what you mean," he replied, his voice tight.

"That still hurt?" She nodded at the flaming blade.

"Like somebody jabbing needles into my palms," he said with a nod.

"Let's trade." Jo walked over to him and held out a hand. He passed her the sword and took her hammer with a relieved sigh. The flames winked out the instant the sword left his grasp, and the room dimmed considerably. Jo looked up at the bleachers. "Y'all okay up there?"

Her mother and daughter nodded vigorously, and Jo called out, "I'll be up there in just a second. Mama, you cover Ginny's eyes." She looked back at the demon sprawled in the center of the ring.

"I don't know if this will work, or if you have to do it," she said, walking to Shel's lifeless body. "But there is no way I'm leaving this son of a gun in one piece."

"Do you ever just say son of a bitch like a normal person?" Mitch said, stepping up next to her.

"I'm trying to set a good example for my baby," Jo replied. She raised the sword up over her head and brought it down in a sharp chopping motion designed to sever the demon's head from its shoulders.

And it would have, if there had been a demon there when her blow landed. But Shel sprang to his feet in a lightning-fast kip-up, going from flat on his back to standing before the pair in a blink, and he laid Jo out with an uppercut right on the point of her jaw. She fell back like a redwood toppling in a forest, and the sword went flying all the way across the ring. Jo lay on the mat, her head ringing and her vision blurry, as Shel stalked Mitch.

"Now it's just you and me, angel. Just like in the bad old days, when you killed thirty of my brothers in the Battle for the Gates," Shel said, his voice a sibilant rasp.

"I don't remember any of that, but if you want to join them, come get some." Mitch rolled his neck and popped his knuckles, bouncing from one foot to the other as he backed away from the demon.

"You know you're going to die, right? It doesn't matter how divine you are, once I rip that meat suit into half a dozen pieces, your pure little essence will just float away, scattered to the ends of the cosmos. There won't be enough of your soul to put back together. You'll be dead, angel, and I'll be left here laughing and pissing on your corpse."

"That's nasty," Jo said, struggling to her feet. "Don't you know there's a lady present?"

"Show me a lady, bitch," Shel growled at her. He swung a looping back-handed left at her and knocked her ten feet sideways.

"She said, don't call her that," Mitch said. Shel turned and Mitch swung the borrowed hammer like he was Babe Ruth in the bottom of the ninth. The silver blessed hammer head crunched into the demon's face again, and Shel crumpled to the ground like his strings had been cut.

"Nice one," Jo gasped from the floor. "But I don't think he's done." She pointed, and Mitch turned from her to see Shel rising from the mat once more. This time the demon didn't spring up, but rolled over to one knee and stood, a little shaky on its feet.

"What's the matter, big guy?" Mitch asked. "That one hurt?"

"Foolish angel, without access to your divinity, you can't destroy me. But I can destroy you. Without you, there will be no return to the Throne. That means that we get to play on Earth as long as we like." Shel smiled and advanced on Mitch. He kept his arms low and stretched out to the sides, claws extended. Mitch watched the demon's hands but had to dive to the floor when the spiked tail lashed out at his face. Mitch swung the hammer at the demon's ankles, but Shel leapt over it easily.

Shel landed with one foot on the hammer's handle, and kicked Mitch in the face with the other. He reached down and picked Mitch up, holding him high overhead with his left hand. The hammer discarded, Mitch dangled in the demon's grasp, unarmed and defenseless.

"Look upon the face of your slayer, angel. Know that I, Shelaxis, will go down in the annals of our history as the demon that slew the great Archangel Michael." Shel drew back his right hand, claws extended to rip Mitch's heart out.

Just before he struck, a blade suddenly protruded from the demon's chest. Shel looked down, his eyes going wide as he took in the tip of Michael's sword sticking through just above his left nipple. Mitch dropped to the ground, landing on his feet, and reached out to the blade. He wrapped his hand around the blade where it sprang from the demon's chest and shut his eyes against the brilliance as the sword burst into flames. Still inside the demon, the sword burned with a holy fire that consumed Shelaxis from the inside out, and within seconds, the demon was reduced to a pile of ash in the middle of the ring.

The sword clattered to the floor, and Jo and Mitch sagged against the chain link walls of the cage. They looked at one another, exchanged weary smiles, and turned for the door. Jo held the cage door open for Mitch, who picked up the sword as he walked.

"I think this is yours," he said, passing her back the hammer.

"Yep," she said. "You keeping the sword?"

"If I can figure out how to turn these damn flames off," he replied. "Otherwise it's a little conspicuous."

Jo laughed, then looked up at the bleachers. "I'm coming, Mama. It's all over. We can go home now."

EPILOGUE

"What the fuck do you mean, he doesn't know he's an angel?" the voice on the phone growled.

"Language, Harker," Jo replied. "My little girl is in the car."

"Sorry, Jo," the voice said. "Sorry, Ginny. Don't talk like me. Nice people don't talk like me."

"Are you not a nice person, Mr. Harker?" Ginny asked from the back seat of Shel's Lexus. The keys were hanging from the ignition, and Jo knew he wouldn't need it anymore.

"No, Ginny, most of the time I'm not a very nice person. Now please cover your ears while I talk to your mommy. I will probably use some other not very nice words," Harker said over the speakerphone.

Ginny did as she was told, and Jo smiled at her. "I don't know what the deal is, Harker. I put the sword in his hand, and it burst into flames, just like we thought. He used it to kill a demon, so there's definitely some divine something going on here. But he has no idea about who he really is."

"I think you people are batshit crazy," Mitch said from the passenger seat, then winced as Cassandra leaned forward and smacked him on the back of the head. "Ow!"

"My daughter has done told y'all about cussing in front of her little girl. I might not be able to slap Harker right now, but he knows what he's got coming to him the next time I see him," the older woman said.

"Hello, Cassie." Harker's voice was softer now, with a tinge of sadness. "It's been a while."

"Almost thirty years, Quincy. Your uncle doing okay? I heard about his latest Renfield. Please pass along my condolences."

"Thank you, Cassie. I will. Next time your daughter comes back east, why don't you come along and bring that little girl? I know Luke would love to meet her."

"Quincy, as much as I love your uncle, I am not in the habit of taking my granddaughter on cross-country plane rides to visit vampires," Cassandra said with a laugh.

Harker laughed right back. "I can understand that, but I guess you're probably not in the habit of driving around with an angel in your car, either."

"You have a point, you old rascal. Tell Luke we'll get out there sometime this year. I promise." Cassandra leaned back in her seat and put her arm around Ginny. She pulled the girl close and replaced one of the hands covering the girl's ears with her own.

"I'm going to hold you to that, old woman. If you're not here by Christmas, I'll send Adam to play Santa Claus at your house."

"Oh Lord," Cassandra laughed, a rich, deep sound that filled the car. "I know I don't want that big oaf trying to fit down my chimney! Now you finish up with my baby so we can go home."

"Will do," Harker said. When he spoke again, his tone was all business. "Okay, Jo. I don't know what the deal is with your angel, but we need him back here. Put him on a plane tomorrow. I'll get you a credit card number. He'll be able to carry the sword on the flight. I'll take care of TSA."

Jo looked over at Mitch, who nodded at her. "Fine, Harker. But what are you going to do with him when he gets there?"

"Honestly? I have no idea. I suppose I'll put him in a spare bedroom and start working on breaking whatever spell has his memory blocked. It's not going to be pretty, and it's going to take a lot of time. Mind magic is complicated as—heck. It's complicated as heck, and I'm not very good at it to start with. I'm usually more the 'burn it all down and sift through the ashes' kind of magician. But we'll figure it out."

"And you have to have him there for this?" Jo asked. Mitch shot her a grateful smile.

"Yeah, I do," Harker replied. "It's not just for my research and the spell; it's to keep you safe. You got lucky killing Shelaxis. He was a low-level Pit Lord. If the folks downstairs get wind of an amnesiac angel wandering around without anybody watching his back magically, they're going to be on you like dogs on a bone. I can't let that happen."

"He's right," Mitch said. "You almost lost your mom and daughter once because of me. I won't let that happen again. I'll be on that plane in the morning."

"Good deal. I'll email you flight details and where to pick up your new IDs," Harker said, then hung up.

"New IDs?" Mitch asked.

"Yeah, welcome to working with Quincy Harker," Jo said. "He knows a guy. Doesn't matter what the problem is, he knows a guy."

"You live a century or more, sweetheart, you'll know a few of those kind of guys, too." Cassandra said. "Now let's get this precious baby home and in her own bed."

"Good idea," Jo said. She put the car in gear and headed out of the parking lot.

"Joanna?" Cassandra said from where she sat in the back with Ginny's head in her lap.

"Yes, Mama?"

"I'm proud of you tonight. You did good. Grandaddy John would have been proud, too. You carried his hammer like a Henry," Cassandra said. "I hope you don't have to take it up in violence again, but I know if you do, it's in good hands."

"Thank you, Mama," Jo said, then turned the car toward home.

PART II
DEVIL INSIDE

CHAPTER ONE

I called up "Amazing Grace" on my phone, pushed play, and set the sleek black plastic rectangle on a nearby headstone. I stepped to the head of the slightly bulging patch of ground, the sod still trying to take root even after a couple of weeks, and I started to speak.

"Sylvester Thomas Efor, IV. That was his name. That was the name he abandoned when he joined our family. It's part ritual, part homage, and part convenience that makes the name Renfield into as much a title as a moniker. It's a throwback, to be sure. It hearkens back to a time when things were less complicated, a time when it was easier to walk the night unseen, but still a time when some things had to be done in the light of day.

"When a man takes on the mantle of Renfield, we know we will outlive him. We've certainly done it before, more times than we care to dwell on. We know that our connections with the living and with the unenhanced are, by their very nature, fleeting. That doesn't stop us from making those connections, from expanding our family, from caring.

"Ren was one of us. He was family, caregiver, guardian, partner, and brewer of lovely teas. He was brave; he was funny; he was stalwart; he was loyal. It was that loyalty that led him to save my life on more than one occasion, and it was that loyalty that cost him his life in the end.

"We have avenged Renfield, but that doesn't mitigate our loss. We have balanced the scales, but that doesn't fill the hole in our hearts. We have seen the debt paid, but we still miss our friend.

"Sylvester Thomas Efor the fourth, Renfield, we will miss you. May God bless you and keep you close to His bosom, and may you find rest and all the peace you deserve."

I took a flask from my inside jacket pocket and twisted the top off. I poured the clear liquid in a continuous path around the grave, making an unbroken line around the perimeter of Ren's resting place.

"Pater noster,
qui es in caelis,
sanctificetur nomen tuum.
Adveniat regnum tuum.
Fiat voluntas tua,
sicut in caelo et in terra.
Panem nostrum quotidianum da nobis hodie,
et dimitte nobis debita nostra sicut et nos dimittimus debitoribus nostris.
Et ne nos inducas in tentationem, sed libera nos a malo.
Amen."

With a tiny flash of brilliant white light, I poured my will into the blessing, offering protection for Ren's remains and hopefully securing his soul from being dragged out of Heaven and used against us. The grave was empty, just a coffin with a light sprinkling of his ashes within, but even those tenuous bonds can sometimes be enough to conjure a shade. The blessing would hopefully keep that from happening and ensure my friend remained in the paradise he deserved.

"Amen," Rebecca, Glory, and Adam said in unison. Luke didn't say anything, just stood off to one side watching the ceremony.

I knelt on the ground and whispered, "Goodbye, old friend. May you find peace and comfort."

I walked over to where the others stood, heads bowed and voices muffled.

"Don't forget your phone," Detective Rebecca Gayle Flynn reminded me. I nodded my thanks and retrieved it from the headstone, ending the song and slipping the cell into the pocket of my jeans. We certainly weren't the most formal grouping to ever host a funeral, but when you're burying people by moonlight, the dress code gets a little more flexible.

Adam extended his hand as I walked up again. "That was well-spoken, Quincy. If I could die, I would ask that you perform my funeral."

"Well, old buddy, if we ever find anything that can kill you, it'll probably take me out, too, so I think I'm off the hook," I replied.

A grin split his scarred visage and he said, "That's probably true, Harker. That's probably true. Now I must take my leave. There are things I need to see to before I begin my hunt, and none of them are in North Carolina. We will speak soon." The giant man nodded to the women, patted me on the shoulder, and walked over to where Luke stood alone.

"That is a very odd individual," Flynn said.

"Becks, you don't even know the half of it," I agreed.

"I'm good with that," she continued. She looked at the grave and sighed. "What's Luke going to do?"

"Hire a new Renfield, I suppose. This isn't the first time we've had one die suddenly or depart unexpectedly. Luke keeps a file of qualified replacements around, and it's usually at least marginally current."

"I hope so," Glory said. "I'm not looking forward to having to wash Dracula's socks." She grinned when she said it, but I knew that living in the mundane world without her divine powers was really worrying her.

"It's okay, G," I said, trying to be encouraging. "We'll get your wings back. I mean, come on, we just stopped a demon attack in Atlanta and kept the world from coming to an end. How hard could this shit be?"

"How hard could it be to track down the most powerful of the Heavenly Host, awaken them from their Earth-induced slumber, and convince them to find God Himself and put Him back on The Golden Throne? Nah, we should have this taken care of by lunch, no problem. Then this afternoon, we're going to fix global warming and make David Letterman funny again."

"I don't think we need to be asking for miracles, Glory. Letterman hasn't been funny in a looooong time," I said.

"You know what I mean." She folded her arms across her chest and scowled at me.

"Yeah, I know what you mean. But come on, Glory. We do the difficult in no time flat. Impossible takes a little longer."

"Harker, you sound like a Hallmark card."

"I was going for motivational. I saw it on a poster in the CMPD the last time I was arrested."

"Leave the motivational stuff to the ministers. You're built more for the magical killing."

I couldn't argue with her. I try to make it a point not to get into debates with celestial beings, even the ones who have lost their wings. I walked over to Luke, who stood alone after his brief farewell with Adam.

"Quincy," he said without turning around. That kind of thing unnerves normal people, but I've never been accused of normalcy.

"Luke," I said, walking around in front of him and sitting on a headstone. Irreverent, I know, but I've met a lot of dead people, and none of them have ever expressed outrage at the habit. Some of them have tried to kill me, but that's always unrelated to my nonchalance toward monuments.

"What's the plan?" I asked.

"Plan? I don't have a plan, Quincy. I don't have a home, I don't have a manservant, and I most certainly do not have a plan."

"Well, it's not like there's a shortage of things to do. We have a bunch of angels to find, and we need to get you a new place to live, for starters—"

"Are you kicking me out, Quincy?"

I spluttered for a few seconds before I looked at his face, startled into silence at the wry smile there. Even after all these years, I sometimes forget that Luke has a sense of humor. A very, very dry sense of humor. He got me. Again.

"No, just saying that you snore," I said, then turned and walked off. It's really the only way to get the last word in when you're in a battle of wits with someone who's outlived you by centuries. He really has heard it all by this point.

I walked back to my car with a chuckling vampire in tow and slid into the passenger seat. "Nice of them to let you keep your motor pool privileges. I didn't think crossing guards got unmarked cars," I said to Flynn as Luke got in the back seat beside Glory, muttering something about "shotgun." I ignored him.

"They didn't actually bust me down to crossing guard," Becks said. "It turns out that a good word from the Director of the FBI's Atlanta Field Office goes a long way with the Charlotte-Mecklenburg police department. I didn't even get docked vacation days; they just chalked it up to my being on interagency assignment to Homeland Security."

"Pretty sure those days are over," I said as Flynn put the car in gear and pulled us out of the cemetery.

"Oh yeah," she agreed. "The Charlotte office of Homeland is completely shut down, and the few agents who survived the encounter with you at Luke's house and were found to be free of Smith's influence were reassigned."

"What about the ones who weren't free of Smith's, how did you say, *influence?*" Luke asked from the back seat. He had a special loathing in his heart for the deceased Agent Smith, since he was the one who killed Renfield and blew up Luke's house. I shot Smith in the face, but not before he'd done plenty of damage.

"Anyone the agency even thought had close ties to Smith was sent to a secure facility for interrogation and examination," Becks said.

"What aren't you saying?" I asked.

"What do you mean?" she asked, her innocent mien fooling no one.

"You remember that I can literally hear you thinking, right?" I asked.

"You'd be better off trying to lie to your mother about what you did after your senior prom."

"And I can not only hear your heart speed up when you lie, I can smell the stink of deception on you," Luke said, slipping into full-on Dracula creepy mode.

"That's a load of crap," Flynn said. She turned to me for a second. "Not you, him. I know you can hear me thinking, but I thought we could still mask specifics?"

"Is that why all I get is Kelly Clarkson lyrics? We really need to introduce you to Motorhead. You're right, he can't *literally* smell a lie. He can just smell the tiny bit of sweat that something like ninety-five percent of people emit when they tell a lie. Which is basically the same thing."

"Exactly," Luke said, leaning back in the seat. "Speaking of smells…"

"Don't say it," Flynn said. "You are in a cop car, after all. The motor pool tries, but some things don't ever really come out of upholstery."

"Don't change the subject," I said. "Where are the corrupt Homeland agents?"

"I honestly don't know. They were sent somewhere, but I have no idea where. I just know the last thing I heard when I was leaving the building after turning in my badge was somebody talking about putting them on a plane south."

"You think they got sent to Gitmo?" I asked.

"There's also a place down in the swamps somewhere near the Gulf. I don't know if it's in Florida or Louisiana, but apparently, the government has some kind of facility down there with some pretty enhanced interrogation facilities."

"Oh, you mean Fort Pontchartrain?" Luke asked.

I spun around in my seat. "You know about this place?"

"Of course. It's where the United States houses any paranormal creatures it feels the need to contain and study. It's part laboratory, part prison, all ungodly. I quite like the ambiance, personally."

"Yeah, we know your decorating tends toward eighteenth-century European creepy," I said. "So you think that's where they would send these Homeland agents?"

"Almost certainly," Luke said. "But why do you care? I thought you had angels to find."

"He does," said Glory, turning in from the window. "He has a lot of angels to find."

"Yeah, I'd just feel more comfortable if the government had found a more...permanent solution to the corrupted agents. You never know when one will turn out to be possessed."

"Oh, they will certainly discover that at Fort Pontchartrain," Luke said. "The fort has a full complement of wizards and priests. I have used their services several times over the years. They are very competent at handling possession."

"So my vampire uncle is tight with the wizards at the government's secret supernatural prison buried deep in the swamps of Louisiana. This somehow surprises me not at all," I muttered and turned to bang my head against the passenger window. Flynn didn't comment, just drove us home with a little smile on her face.

CHAPTER TWO

The next morning saw me standing in baggage claim C at Charlotte Douglas International Airport at a ridiculous hour of the morning, holding a cardboard sign that had "Mitch" written on it in my barely legible scrawl. I watched another stream of passengers ride the escalator down from the concourse, and my eyes widened as an absolute monster of a human being walked up to me.

"I'm Mitch. You Harker?"

"Yeah, that's me. Shit, Jo didn't tell me she was shipping Andre the friggin' Giant to me. Have you had breakfast? You know, did you eat a stewardess or anything?"

The big man laughed. "You think I'm big, you should see the guy we fought a couple nights ago. Last night? Shit, I dunno. The redeye always makes me all fucked up on my days. Sorry, is my language gonna be a problem? I kinda swear a lot."

I looked up at him, not really believing that somebody just apologized to *me* for swearing, then I remembered where he'd just come from. "Nah, it's fine. Jo's the only one who objects to a little spicy language, and I think that's mostly for her kid's benefit."

"And her mom," Mitch added.

"Oh yeah, you do not want to piss off Cassandra. She will fuck your shit right up. You got any luggage?" I looked at the duffel he carried, which didn't look like it held a lot in the way of clothes.

"Nah, I've got a couple things in here, but I travel pretty light."

"Is the..." I looked around the baggage claim, but everybody looked pretty mundane. I quickly opened my Sight to the supernatural world and saw nothing other than one security guard with a minor protection spell glowing around his neck. Probably a saint's medal or something like that.

"Is the sword in the bag?" I asked.

"Yeah, that's what takes up most of the space. Doesn't exactly fit in just anything, you know? How did you get them to let me go through without security finding it?" the giant asked. It wasn't that he was all that tall. He was about my height, which put him several inches over six foot. And it wasn't just that he was big. I mean, Adam was bigger, sure, but this dude was built like a damn brick wall. His hands looked like he broke rocks with his fists, and his shoulders and arms stretched against the fabric of the black fleece jacket he wore. Blond hair and a square jaw sat on a neck like a tree trunk, and he generally looked like somebody saw the *Captain America* movie and said, "I can do that. Just a little better."

"I know a few people, and the Director of Homeland Security owes me a couple of favors." Government agencies are big on promising favors and less big on paying them back, but when an entire division of the agency turns out to be working for a demon, killing that demon gives you a lot of leverage. Getting a sword through airport security wasn't a big deal. I didn't mention that the sword was magical and the guy carrying it was an Archangel. The government has plenty of ways to gather information. They don't need me telling them every little thing.

"Well, if you don't need to piss, and you don't have any bags, let's get out of here. I'm parked illegally." I turned and walked toward the sliding doors, stepping outside into the melee of airport parking and passenger pickup just as a cop was motioning a tow truck over to my Honda.

"That's me, officer," I called out, holding up my badge wallet. Just because Flynn did the ethical thing and turned in her Homeland Security credentials didn't mean I had to. I didn't let the fact that impersonating a Homeland Security official was a federal offense bother me.

"Goddammit, Harker, get this thing out of here," the cop yelled at me. I recognized him as Smith, or Jones, or some other generic-named cop I'd seen around police headquarters once or twice.

"Will do, Bob," I said, holding up a hand to stop traffic as I opened the driver's door. A horn blared from a Mercedes SUV as a little blonde realtor or soccer mom rolled right up to me before stopping. I drew the Glock 9mm from my hip and leveled it at the woman, whose eyes went wide. Her head whipped from side to side as she looked for an escape, but there were cars stacked up behind her.

I walked around to the driver's window, gun still trained on her. I motioned for her to roll down the window, and she actually did it. I will never understand people. I leaned in the open window, pistol just kinda casually pointing in her general direction.

"That wasn't very nice," I said. "You shouldn't honk your horn at people. It's not polite. There are people who would respond very poorly to such bad manners."

She stared at me and nodded silently.

"I'm not one of those people, so I'm not going to paint the ceiling of your car with what little brains are rattling around in that fucking head of yours. Let's just consider this a friendly reminder to be considerate of others while driving. Sound good?"

She nodded again. She still hadn't said a word, which was probably good. I wouldn't have shot her. Probably. But I might have turned her into a toad.

I walked back to my car, holstered the gun, and got behind the wheel. Mitch sat in the passenger seat looking at me. "That was kinda mean, don't you think?"

"You're the angel, pal. Not me," I said as I put the car in drive and pulled out of the passenger pickup line, heading for the airport exit and downtown.

H alf an hour later, I walked into my apartment with an angel in tow. Another one. There were getting to be entirely too many heavenly bodies living in my building. "You can throw your bag in a corner. You'll be crashing in one of the apartments down the hall."

"You own the floor?" Mitch asked.

"I own the building," I said, going to the fridge. "You want a beer?"

"Dude, it's seven a.m."

"Yeah, you're right." I put the beers back in the fridge and pulled out the orange juice. I poured two healthy glasses of orange juice, carried them over to the bar, and topped them off with a couple shots each of Grey Goose. A few seconds with a stir stick, and I carried the drinks to the sofas. I passed one to Mitch and sat down on the couch across from him. He laughed a little and held up his glass to me.

We sipped our orange juice for a minute, then I asked, "So, you're an Archangel, huh?"

"Apparently so."

"You don't think so?"

"Man, I don't know." He took a big drink of his screwdriver. It's one of the reasons I poured us each a stiff drink. One, because I hate getting up in the morning, and two, because I thought it might loosen our boy up a touch.

"I know that stupid sword starts flaming like a Lady Gaga backup dancer whenever I touch it. I know the demon back in Phoenix sure thought I was special. Other than that, I don't know shit. I poke and prod at my memory, but it only goes back about three years. I remember working construction for a while, fighting at night, then fighting full time, but nothing further back than that."

"Do all your memories involve Phoenix?"

"Yeah. Literally the first thing I can remember is walking out of the desert, sunburned as fuck and hungry as hell, wandering up to a dude with a taco truck, and collapsing before I could even order. I woke up with a Mexican dude splashing water on my face and a crowd looking on. Some chick bought me a burrito and a Coke, some dude gave me twenty bucks, and that's the first memory I have."

"Interesting," I said. I had no idea what it meant, but his memories coincided with the time I started working with Flynn and the former Agent John Smith. "What do you think, Becks?" I asked the woman standing in the doorway of the bedroom.

Rebecca stood there, shoes in one hand and her Sig in the other, glowering at me. "I think I want to know about it when you're bringing strange men into the apartment while I'm in the shower. What if I had walked out here naked?" She wasn't naked now, but she looked good nonetheless. A pair of gray slacks and a burgundy blouse outlined her athletic figure, and her long brown hair was down, hanging past her shoulders.

"Our mornings would have been dramatically improved," I said. She didn't smile, but I felt a pleased little glow down the mental link we shared. I got up and walked over to kiss her, but she put a hand on my chest.

"Not this morning, Harker. You smell like vodka, and I'm going back for my first day on duty after being a murder suspect. I'd rather not show up reeking of cheap booze." She walked over to the couch and held out her hand to Mitch. "Rebecca Flynn. I'm Harker's...girlfriend. I'm also a detective with the Charlotte-Mecklenburg Police Department."

"Girlfriend?" I asked. I'd offered Becks a ring a few months back. She hadn't returned it, but she hadn't put it on her hand yet, either. We loved each other, and had been pretty close to inseparable in the weeks since we got back from Atlanta, but she wasn't sure where she fit with all the other weird moving parts in my life. I wasn't pushing. The last thing I wanted to do with a brilliant, smart, independent, gorgeous woman who could literally read my mind was to push her away.

"For now." She gave me a little half-smile. "As long as you don't bring too many strangers into the apartment. Especially not strangers with arms like those." She leered at Mitch, who blushed a little. "How cute, I embarrassed him! You should introduce him to Gabby. She'd like him. For lunch."

"Gabby?" Mitch asked, kinda like she'd mentioned a new type of venomous snake. She kinda had.

"Gabby is another member of the Council. The group that Jo is a part of with us," I explained. I didn't explain that Gabby was Gabriella Van Helsing, granddaughter of the legendary vampire hunter. That always got awkward, especially once they met Luke and realized exactly who *he* was.

"I'm off," Flynn said, walking over and giving me a kiss on the cheek. "Try not to get into too much trouble." She picked up her keys from the table by the front door and her jacket from the closet and out the door she went. I watched her go with no shame. She was a good-looking woman, and like the song said, I hated to see her go, but I loved to watch her leave.

"That's your girlfriend?" Mitch asked. "I guess you've got more going on than meets the eye."

"Hey!" I exclaimed. "I'll have you know that women on five continents have assured me that I am a very good-looking man."

"There are seven continents."

"I've never tried to get laid in Antarctica, and for some reason I've had shit luck with Australian women. They're immune to my charms for some reason. Now, about that sword…"

CHAPTER THREE

Two days later, I had a sword that would burst into flames on command, a mopey vampire, an overworked cop girlfriend, and two powerless angels hanging around my place. If that sounds like fun to anybody anywhere, they're on better drugs than I am.

Glory, Mitch, and I were in my apartment, clustered around my minuscule table with a laptop and a pile of Bibles and other religious research material. Becks was at work, chasing down mundane criminals for a change, and Luke was in his apartment interviewing potential Renfields. I couldn't speak for Luke or Becks, but me and the Heavenly Bodies were finally making headway in our angel hunt.

"Okay, who do we have on the list?" I asked Glory.

"There's Michael," she said. "We found him."

"For all the good I'm doing anybody," the musclebound grump chimed in.

"Hey," I interjected. "Baby steps, pal. Baby steps. Let's make sure we can find all the Archangels, then we can worry about making sure you all know who you are. Hell, for all we know, you're the only one with amnesia. Maybe the others are just lazy or having fun playing human."

"I doubt that," Glory said. "This whole being human thing sucks. I have to sleep, I have to walk places, I have to use the bathroom! Do you have any idea how disgusting the digestive process is?"

"Yeah, G," I said. "I've been digesting for over a century. I'm pretty well acquainted with the process. Back to the matter at hand..." I waved a hand at the legal pad in front of her.

"Okay, then there's Gabriel, the keeper of the chronicles of Heaven. He's basically God's scribe," Glory said.

"Okay, the Celestial Secretarial Pool. Next," I said.

"Raphael is the healer. Metatron is the voice of God—"

"I know that dude," I said.

"You do?" Glory and Mitch said simultaneously.

"Yeah, he was on *Supernatural*. Didn't the guy who played Booger in *Revenge of the Nerds* play him?"

Glory sighed. "I don't know why I even bother sometimes."

"Me neither," I replied. "Next?"

"Uriel is God's punisher, and no *Daredevil* jokes," Glory said, pointing at me. I motioned like I was zipping my lips. "Sealtiel is the herald of the apocalypse, and Azrael is the angel of death."

"He doesn't sound like anyone I want to spend very much time with, so let's leave him for last," I said.

"Probably a good idea," Glory agreed.

"So how does this whole thing work?" I asked. "Do all of you angels know each other? Is it racist to think that? Or are there like class divisions and the Archangels don't hang out with the guardian angels, and the guardian angels don't go out drinking with the...I don't know, the rescue cats from trees angels or whatever. Is there a hierarchy in Heaven?"

"There is, and it's very rigid," Glory replied. "The Seraphim rule Heaven, and they make all the day-to-day decisions. The lower-level angels, like me, don't consort with the Seraphim unless we're called upon to do something, and we never see the Archangels. Mitch is the first of the Highest Host that I've ever encountered."

"Sorry it's not a more impressive meeting," the Highest muttered.

"Don't worry, man. I'm sure you're plenty impressive...sometimes...when you know who you are and stuff." My attempt at reassurance sounded lame even to me.

"Thanks, I guess," Mitch said, leaving no doubt as to how ineffectual my words were.

"So no, I don't know all the angels. I don't even know how many there are, honestly. It's not like there's a census," Glory said, trying to get us back on something like a track.

A thought struck me, and as usually happens, I didn't bother processing it very much before I just spewed it out. "How do angels get made, anyway?"

Glory looked at me, and I could almost see the wheels turning in her head. "I...I can't talk about that, Harker. I'm sorry, but that's one of the few hard and fast rules about what guardians can and can't do. We never discuss with mortals where angels come from."

"Just tell me one thing," I pleaded. "Does it have anything to do with bells ringing?"

She laughed, and it was good to hear that crystalline bell-tone again. There hadn't been a whole lot of laughing since she got her wings sliced off and became human. But I got her. "No, Harker. Every time a bell rings, an angel does not get their wings. All that happens when a bell rings is that a bell rings."

"Okay, I can be satisfied with that. Is that all the Archangels?" I asked.

"Well..." Glory didn't meet my eyes.

"Glory..." I used my best "dad" voice, which is harder to do when the person you're talking to is both thousands of years old and just a few weeks old at the same time.

"There's another angel that technically may still qualify, but he's a little more difficult to get in touch with, and a *lot* more self-aware than our buddy Mitch here," she said, still not looking at me.

"Come on, out with it, young lady," I said. She laughed at my ridiculous attempt at authority, but quickly sobered.

"Lucifer."

"Wait, what?" I asked. I looked to Mitch, but he just shrugged and stared back at me.

"Lucifer was one of God's favorites, and he was one of the most powerful of the Host. I have no idea what status he retains in the hierarchy, or what kind of power he now possesses. But if we're listing off the most powerful angels, he definitely qualifies."

"Fuck me sideways," I said. "So if we want to get your wings back..."

"Only God can make an angel," Glory said. "I can tell you that much."

"And if want to find God?" Mitch asked.

"The Archangels are the ones with the direct communication," Glory replied.

"But I'm an Archangel, and I don't have any idea how to, I don't know, call God or whatever," he said.

"That's why we have to find the rest of them," I said. "Because hopefully one of you will still have an idea what you are, or at least how to call Dad."

"And if they don't?" Mitch prodded.

"I don't know, man," I admitted. "Maybe it's like box tops. You collect the whole set and you get a prize. I have no fucking idea. I just know there's a bunch of rogue angels trying to take over Heaven and pretty much destroy all of humanity, and we need the Big Guy to get His ass home and take care of business. Barring that, we need all the big brothers to pick up the slack and beat some angelic ass."

"So we're hunting angels," Mitch said.

"We're hunting angels," I confirmed.

"This could get dangerous," he said.

"Danger is my middle name," I quipped.

"You have a lot of middle names, Harker," Glory said. "But none of them are Danger. Now I have to pee again. I'm telling you, this body sucks!" She got up and walked to the bathroom. Mitch and I both watched her walk across the apartment.

"I have to disagree with her," Mitch said. "I think her body's pretty awesome."

"Pig," I replied.

"Like you weren't looking, too."

"I have a girlfriend."

"You're not dead. And that is a woman who can fill out a pair of blue jeans." He wasn't wrong. On either count. I wasn't dead, and Glory was a gorgeous woman.

I still didn't really think of her as a sexual creature, since not only was I in love with Becks, in my head Glory was still an angel, a sexless being who chose a gender at random. She could have just as easily decided to appear to me as a guy. Mitch obviously didn't have those hangups since he was still checking her out.

"Where do we start hunting?" Mitch asked.

"That's where I come in," said a new voice. A unicorn head with a rainbow mane and horn appeared on the laptop screen.

"Do you know how much I hate that avatar, Dennis?" I asked my disembodied hacker friend Dennis, who also answered to Sparkles the Magical Unicorn. Especially when he wanted to annoy me.

"I do, Q. I know exactly how much you hate the charming visage of Sparkles, who wants nothing more than to bring joy to the lives of good girls and boys everywhere, coming down the chimney and turning their abandoned teeth into baskets full of toys and candy."

"That's like three different myths all mixed up into one," I said.

"But you can never say I'm not a complex guy," Sparkles replied.

"What do you have for us, horn-boy?" I asked.

"I don't have any idea about the angels, but I think I found Gabriel's book. If nothing else, the book shop can help us find old Gabe."

"Is that what you did with me, used the sword to home in on my location?" Mitch asked.

"Kinda," I said. "I worked on the assumption that there would be some kind of bond between you and the sword, so I cast a spell to follow the sword to its owner."

"You were able to track me all the way to Phoenix?" he asked.

"I was able to do way more than that. Magical items like the sword of an Archangel warp the fabric of magic around them. Once I took a good look at how the sword bends the magical energy around it, I was able to pick out its unique power signature and locate you within a couple of miles."

"So it's going to be easy to find the others?" he asked.

"Not exactly," I admitted. "The spell was harder than I expected and took a lot more out of me than I thought it would. I was a little drained when we were finished."

"A little drained?" Glory said, coming back into the room and retaking her seat at the table. "He was unconscious for two days and too weak to leave his bed for the rest of a week. Just tracking you down almost killed him, and you were the most powerful of the Host. Finding anyone else would be harder because they won't bend reality around them the way you do."

"What do you mean, bend reality?" Mitch asked.

"You're not from this plane," Glory said. "So you shouldn't be here. That means that everything around you is going to actively fight your influence or bend to your will."

"You make it sound like I'm some kind of infection."

I spoke up. "Hate to tell you, pal, but you kinda are. All that chaos is the world's way of telling you to get your gringo ass home."

"Why aren't the other angels as much of a blight on the world as I am?" The bitterness in his voice crept through the joking tone. I couldn't really blame him. I wouldn't want to be told that the universe was trying to flush me from its system, either. Although I'd certainly entertained the idea on more than one occasion.

"You're the dude," I said. "You're *the* badass boss Archangel, especially after Lucifer was cast out. It was your sword that cut the Morningstar's face, scarred his perfect beauty and showed him that he wasn't invulnerable. That one slice turned the tide of the War on Heaven."

"You know a lot about a war in the sky for a dude who claims to be human."

"I claim to be mostly human," I clarified. "And I know a lot of people. Some of them were there, and they remember you very clearly. You were *the* Archangel. That's why the others aren't as reality-warping. Because they don't have your stroke."

"Yeah, too bad I don't have any of that stroke anymore."

Glory reached across the table and put a hand on top of his. "You'll get it back. That's what we do. We help people."

And here I thought all this time that all I did was chew bubblegum and kick ass. Guess I shouldn't worry about being out of bubblegum. Nowadays I "help people."

Fuck me running, I'm surrounded by celestial hippies.

CHAPTER FOUR

L uke's apartment was dark when I walked in. That wasn't a huge surprise; he kept the place pretty close to pitch black most of the time. Being Lord of the Vampires came with a few perks, one of which was cat-like night vision. I didn't inherit that quality, so I reached out to flip on the lights as I walked into the room.

"Leave it, please," came my uncle's voice from the middle of the living room. I heard the scrape of a match across a box, and a flame burst into life. Luke touched the burning tip to a red pillar candle on an end table, and a soft yellow light spread throughout the room.

I shrugged and walked over to the sitting area and took a spot on the end of the sofa nearest the candle. Luke sat in an armchair, his slick hair and perfect creases at odds with the forced casual appearance of his untucked dress shirt and open collar.

"How were the interviews?" I asked.

"Dreadful." He didn't elaborate for a long time, and I didn't push. I couldn't tell what Luke needed from me right now, if he needed to talk or just needed company, but I knew he didn't need to be left alone to his thoughts. Down that path was a gauntlet of self-doubt and recrimination about why he wasn't awake and able to save Renfield when Smith broke in. We'd all been able to shove our thoughts of Ren's death aside when we went to Atlanta to fight Orobas and keep the world from ending, but now that we were back home, we had a lot of pieces to pick up.

"Brandy?" Luke asked, rising from his chair with the fluid grace that spawned legends of him turning to smoke and vanishing in thin air. He can do none of those things, but he can move with amazing speed and stand perfectly still in a shadow, so to the uneducated eye, he can seem to disappear at will.

"No, thank you, but I'll take a single malt if you have one."

"I do not. The Council had a fondness for scotch, Dr. Watson in particular."

"I don't know if he's really a doctor, or if he's got some kind of lawyer doctor degree. Good to know who drank all my scotch, though. Brandy will be fine, then."

Luke poured me a brandy and poured himself a glass of red wine. We both knew it wasn't exactly red wine, but as long as I never drank from his glass, I didn't need to know exactly what blend of wine, blood, and anticoagulants he kept in his wine cellar.

He handed me my glass and sat back down in his chair. We sipped our drinks in silence for several minutes. I was content to wait. Luke and I have spent a lot of time together in my century and change on this Earth, and we don't have to make small talk. It's one of the things I like about being with him—no bullshit.

"Does the angel know anything?" he asked, breaking the silence.

"Nothing useful. He can turn the sword on, but he has no idea what he is. I had hoped being around Glory would spark him somehow, some kind of jump-start to his memory or something, but nothing yet."

"Do you know anything about the next angel you need to find?"

"We've come up with a list of who they are, and Dennis is searching the web for any anomalies that might correspond to their presence. He said he wouldn't have anything until the morning, so I left him to it. Glory is talking to Mitch about Heaven, trying to jog his memory of people, angels, that he should have known. Besides being boring as balls, I kinda didn't care, so I thought I'd come check on you."

"While I appreciate your concern for my hiring process, I am perfectly fine and completely capable of doing this without any assistance."

"I know that, but it's been a while since you hired a Ren—"

"Don't call him that."

"What? You always call your manservant Renfield. It's been a thing since you met my dad."

"That is over. I am no longer hiring a manservant. I am hiring a live-in personal assistant. I will learn his name, and he will become a valued member of my staff, nothing more." Luke's jaw was tight and his voice clipped. He was working very hard to keep his emotions in check.

"Nothing?" I asked after a few seconds.

"Nothing." He didn't look at me, just stared into the dregs in his wine glass. "I can't anymore, Quincy. I simply can't. I have to remain detached from these...people. I became attached to Sylvester. He was much more than a manservant or a butler. He was..."

"A friend?" I supplied the word.

"Yes. He was a friend."

"Sylvester." I rolled the name around on my tongue. It felt odd, like I was saying something wrong. I'd honestly forgotten Ren's real name until the day before. After a while, I just ignored the fact that he had another name, another life.

"Yes, Sylvester. He had an entire life before coming to me. He had a sister whom he loved very much, and he sent most of his salary to her until her death two years ago. His parents were long deceased when he entered my service, and he never married. His sister died childless, so his generation, his entire family line, ended when he passed."

"I don't know if that's good or bad," I said, thinking about the various family lines that I had running around out there. Both of my brothers died before they had children, James because his wife couldn't conceive, and Orly because he was still mostly a child himself when the influenza took them.

There were aunts and uncles scattered across England, but none that I kept track of after I started traveling with Luke. I realized that I had no idea if I was the last Harker or not. Then I realized that I had no idea if I had any children scattered across Europe and America. The twenties had definitely roared, that was a sure enough thing.

"It certainly makes my life simpler when there is no next of kin," Luke said. "Out of eight men interviewed today, four of them were married and one other had a serious girlfriend. That makes them completely unsuitable for my service."

"Yeah, someone can't exactly keep all your secrets if there's the possibility of pillow talk," I agreed. "I guess that's another reason to keep a level of detachment from your new...assistant." An idea hit me. "Have you interviewed any women?"

"Excuse me?" Luke looked genuinely shocked at the concept.

"Luke, it's the twenty-first century, get with it. You're not hiring someone to wrestle a coffin into the back of a wagon, or drive a carriage, or defend your lair against roving villagers with pitchforks and torches."

"I never have," he replied. "I believe you have me confused with Adam. He was the one chased from his home with pitchforks and torches. Although he assures me that was purely cinematic license."

"My point is that there's nothing in the job description that requires your...assistant be male."

Luke looked at me, a thoughtful expression bouncing around his face. "Perhaps you are correct, Quincy. I shall consider female applicants during my next round of interviews. I shall contact the headhunter tomorrow with new directions."

"I wish you wouldn't call them that," I said.

"Why not? It is, I believe, the acceptable term."

"It is, but just looking around at all the people and things we deal with, it might ring a little too close to true for us." Luke actually smiled a little bit at that, the first time I'd seen that in a week or more.

"What is your plan now, Quincy? You have located an angel, but he does not understand his nature. If all the Host are in such a state, then how will you manage to coerce them into helping you restore Glory's divinity?"

"Yeah," I said, taking a long pull on my drink. "That's a really good question." The truth was, I had no idea. There's only one way angels get made, and that's by the hand of God Himself. With the Big Guy AWOL, the only way to find Him was using the Archangels. If the Archangels had no idea they were angels, then the chances of their homing beacon for the Almighty being turned on were slim to none.

I let out a sigh and leaned back in my chair. "I don't know, Luke. All I can think of right now is that we need to find them all. I guess I'm hoping that if we get them all in the same place, some kind of spontaneous anti-amnesia thing will happen, and everybody will suddenly sprout wings, pick up harps, and fly off to the Pearly Gates, leaving Glory with a nice new pair of wings."

"Somehow that seems more ludicrous than even some of your worst ideas." Luke never has been one to pull punches with me.

"Yeah, I know. But I can't think of anything else to do. I have to get her wings back. I need her, Luke. I need her at full strength, I need her fighting beside me, and I need her to not have lost everything because of me. I need..." I let the words just hang there. My chest was tight, and my breath came in short gasps.

"You need to save one of them." The words were almost a whisper, but I heard them as well as if he'd used a megaphone.

"Yeah," I choked out. "I need to not have another one die, or lose everything about themselves just for being near me. I need to save one of my people. It's all well and good to save some faceless people on a Ferris wheel, or a bunch of people at a concert, but goddammit, once in a while, I need to be able to save *my* people. The folks who put their lives on the line for strangers all the time. The people who took up weapons and stepped forward just because I asked them to, because I said it was important. I need to be able to save them, too. Just this once." Tears rolled down my cheeks as I thought about the people I couldn't save, going all the way back to my younger brothers, who both died in the flu epidemic of 1918. I couldn't do anything for them, I couldn't do anything for Anna, I couldn't do anything for Dennis or Renfield or Rebecca's dad, but goddammit, I was *not* letting Glory lose her divinity on my account.

"Then we shall find the angels, Quincy," Luke said, standing up and taking my glass. I sat silently and watched him walk across the room and refill my drink, turn to me, then return to the bar and pour me a double.

He stood in front of me, glass full of that lovely amber liquid. "Now, have yourself a nice drink, and let's figure out where we start, shall we?"

CHAPTER FIVE

I pulled into the downtown Historic District of Charleston, South Carolina, around two in the afternoon a couple days later. I had the windows down and the breeze rolling across my arm as I hung it out the window of my new car, a deep red Honda Accord. I've never been a "car guy," looking at my vehicles mostly as a mode of transportation and not some expression of my soul or my worth as a human being.

When I got back to North Carolina, I realized that the junker pickup I'd bought when I went to Ohio was still in Ohio and that my old car had been destroyed in the same explosion that blew up Luke's house. Something about a door through the grill. So I took the insurance payout and a little cash I had floating around from being over a century old, and I bought myself a nice little four-year-old car. It had plenty of room, rode the highway well, and had a jack for me to hook up my phone, which meant that I had all the internet music I ever wanted. There are some bonuses to having a friend who's made up of electrons and can travel through the web.

I turned into the small parking lot of the King Charles Hotel and got out, taking a deep breath and cracking my back. I patted myself down to make sure my pistol was secure, pulled on a long-sleeve shirt to mask the gun, and walked into the lobby.

"May I help you, sir?" a young lady behind the desk asked as a bell on the door jingled my arrival. The lobby was well-appointed in what looked like either antiques or decent replicas. Nice chairs with striped upholstery and rounded backs flanked a small table with flyers for ghost tours and upscale restaurants scattered across its surface. A huge gilt mirror dominated one wall, and I smothered a smile at my recollection of Luke's face when I told him where I was staying.

He hated that lobby, most particularly that mirror. New mirrors with their acrylic and glass construction weren't an issue, but he still didn't show up in older mirrors. Something about the way the silver they used to back the mirrors reacted to the magic that sustained him. I didn't understand it, but I knew that wasn't the only reason he didn't accompany me. He was still interviewing new Renfields and beginning the cleanup and reconstruction process on his house. While I hated the reason he had to do it, I was glad he was moving forward with the project. The sooner he wasn't living in the apartment next to me, the better.

I walked over to the front desk and leaned my arms on the dark green granite-topped counter. "Room for Harper, please. I have a reservation."

She tapped on the keyboard for a few seconds, then smiled up at me. "Mr. Harper, I have you down for a king bed corner suite for seven nights. Will you be needing a parking pass?" I nodded, and she passed me a garish yellow slip of paper for my dash, then took my credit card and fake ID. I knew the feeble attempt at masking my identity wouldn't stand up to any serious scrutiny, but I had Sparkles lurking in the internet ready to alert me if anyone queried the name of Orly Harper from Battle Creek, Michigan.

Orly was a traveling consultant working with several major hotels on energy efficiency. He was in Charleston to review the power consumption of their ballroom lighting and make recommendations on how to reduce their overhead through the use of LEDs, occupancy sensors, and daylight harvesting. If that wasn't enough to bore any Curious George chatting me up in a bar, I could go on for hours about Orly's hobby, which made Charleston *such* a fascinating section of his sales territory. Orly loved architecture, particularly French-inspired architecture from the antebellum South.

I know slightly more about antebellum architecture than I do about nuclear submarines, but only slightly. If anybody looked like they really wanted to chat me up about that crap, I was either going to have to develop an acute case of irritable bowel syndrome or kill them.

I retrieved my credit card and Michigan driver's license, signed the slip for the room rate, and pocketed my key. I took a few minutes to take my bags to the room and unpack my crap, then I walked back out to the car and slipped my pistol under the driver's seat. It was still broad daylight, and I was in the middle of downtown. If there was an ambush of pissed-off Homeland Security demons waiting for me, they would have been in the hotel lobby. They wouldn't be walking The Battery, which was where I was eventually headed.

I walked a couple of blocks from the hotel, then took a right on East Bay and headed toward the tip of downtown. I stopped by the big fountain and walked out on the pier at Waterfront Park, sitting for a few minutes on a swing until a family with a pair of toddlers wandered up really looking like they needed a seat. I walked all the way to the end of the pier and leaned out, letting the smell of the water and the slight spray of the salt air lull me into a deep sense of calm. My heart beat in time with the *slap-slap* of the waves against the rocks, and the gulls overhead pierced the peace with an occasional screech.

"Penny for 'em," a soft voice said beside me. I opened my eyes to see a young woman leaning on the rail to my left.

"Just thinking," I said, not wanting to get involved. She was too young for me, and not my type anyway.

"I could see that, silly. What were you thinking *about?*" I looked at her a little more closely this time. Dark hair cascaded down to her bare shoulders, partially obscuring a large tattooed undersea scene that sleeved her right arm in vibrant blues and greens. She wore a tank top and threadbare khaki cargo pants with black Chuck Taylor high tops and a belt studded with pouches and pockets like a utility belt slung low across her hips. She had narrow features, almost pixie-ish, but a little too angular for that. Dark eyes looked up at me, a challenge written in huge letters across the smirk she wore. There was a lot more going on in that face than just dimples, but I wasn't at all sure why she was talking to me, out of all the people closer to her age on the pier.

"My thoughts." This time I didn't bother trying to keep the "piss off" hidden from my tone. I wasn't really thinking about anything, just taking a minute to center myself before I opened my Sight and started scouring the city for an amnesiac angel. Now, as they said on *Firefly,* this girl was starting to seriously damage my calm.

I turned to walk away, and she put a hand on my arm, stopping me. I don't mean that she put a hand on my arm, and I stopped, like most people do when they're being polite. One, I'm rarely polite, and two, that isn't what happened. She *stopped* me. I couldn't break free of her grip, and I couldn't push past her.

I looked at her hand, then back at her face. All smirk was gone now, and the face that looked up at me was cold. "I'm going to need a little more than that," she said.

Well, she was about to get it. I pulled in my will and muttered "*cumu-lonimbus*" under my breath. Just as I clapped one hand on the pier railing behind me, a huge wind blew up, a solid forty-mile-per-hour gust that sent tourists and one hot dog cart tumbling.

It did absolutely nothing to the pixie-ish girl holding onto my arm. She waved a hand, whispered *"disperse"* like she was blowing a kiss, and the wind died down.

"That wasn't very nice," she said, her eyes taking on a deep purple glow. My arm started to tingle through my shirt, a pins and needle sensation running down to my fingertips and back up to my shoulder.

"Let go of me before I have to show you how not nice I can get," I replied.

"I don't think that's going to happen, mister. I don't like strange wizards coming into my city without going through the proper channels. That happens, and people start to think there aren't any rules at all, or that they just don't apply to them. Can't have that, can we?" She raised a fist toward my face, wrapped in that same purple glow.

I decided enough was most certainly enough. There were probably plenty of circumstances in which dancing around the Charleston Harbor with an escapee from a *Sandman* comic would be fun, but I was attached, and I had a job to do. So instead of going into my usual witty repartee, or even growling out a few manly threats, I just picked the girl up by her belt and jumped backward.

I counted on her hanging on to my arm, and that was a good guess. The second my feet left the wood of the pier, her deathtrap on my bicep tightened to almost painful levels. We hit the water with a *splash*, and her strength instantly dropped to what I'd expect from a ninety-pound woman who tops out at maybe five feet in shoes.

We popped up to the surface instantly, and I started treading water. The tide was in, so I had to swim a few yards to stand comfortably, but I dragged my witchy attacker along with me. Her magic disrupted by the salt water, she was just a bedraggled twentysomething girl who tangled up with somebody way out of her league. I held onto her belt despite her beating on my chest and shoulder with ineffective punches.

"If you don't stop that, I'm going to knock you out," I said under my breath. "Then I'll tell everybody you're my niece, you fell over the rail being an idiot teenager, and I'll carry you back to my hotel over my shoulder. Then we'll have a very unpleasant conversation where nobody can see you, and I'll make sure nobody can hear you scream."

She stopped struggling and opened her mouth to yell, but I was anticipating that very thing. "No, Delilah!" I shouted. "Don't panic, I've got you!" I wrapped one arm around her throat, making it look like I was having trouble dragging her to the shore, and tightened my grip on her carotid arteries. A few seconds later, she was out. I released the hold and threw one of her arms over my shoulder, wrapping my arm around her waist and lifting her into a perfect *Weekend at Bernie's* drunk friend carry pose. We got a few odd looks as

I hauled her back to the King Charles, wrestled her into the elevator, and then down the hall to my room.

I dropped her in the center of the king bed and walked back to the door. I traced my finger around the door frame and stepped back. A whispered *"silencio"* insured that we wouldn't be overheard, and a quick *"sonjunctare"* fused the wood of the door to the frame. Nobody was getting in or out of that room without a fire axe or a chainsaw until I wanted them to.

I grabbed a fresh set of clothes and went into the bathroom to change. The last thing I needed was some kid waking up from being choked out while I'm bare-assed naked five feet away. I walked back out rubbing my head with a towel just as she started to stir. I dug through my suitcase for a pair of sweat-pants and a t-shirt and threw them on the bed next to her.

"Here's some dry clothes. You might as well go into the bathroom and dry off," I said as she looked around the room in a panic.

The girl opened her mouth to scream, then closed it with a snap. I nodded. "Yes, I warded the room against sound. So why don't you go get changed and we can sit and talk about this like civilized people?"

She gathered up the clothes and went into the bathroom. A few minutes later, she came back out, rubbing her own head with a towel. "Sorry," I said. "I don't carry any women's underwear around, and anything that would have been lying around my apartment wouldn't fit you anyway. My girlfriend is full-grown."

"Fuck you, sorcerer," she said, sharing with me the accompanying hand gesture to let me know that I was number one in her book.

"You could be a little nicer to the guy who saved your life," I said.

"You're also the only person who's threatened my life today," she shot back.

"Then obviously I'm the first person you've talked to today, given your winning fucking personality."

"I don't have to take this shit," she said. Her eyes glowed purple again, and she raised her right hand.

I stood up from my chair, crossed the ten feet between us in less than half a second, and backhanded her to the ground. Then I reached down and grabbed a handful of dark hair and yanked her back to her feet. This time I picked her up by her throat.

"Let's get this very clear, little girl. I am not a nice person. I am not the guy who takes a bunch of shit and finally gets fed up enough to lash out. I am the guy who takes zero shit, gives zero fucks, and knows every incantation needed to open up a portal to the sixth circle of Hell and throw your scrawny ass through it. So unless you really think you're in my fucking league, I'd suggest you lay off the fireworks before I lose my fucking patience."

If looks could kill, I'd have been killed, reanimated, and killed a couple more times. After about ten seconds, which must have felt like an eternity to the one hanging by her throat in my hand, she let go of the power she'd summoned, and the purple light faded. I tossed her over to the bed, and she bounced clear across it to the floor.

"Sorry," I said. "I actually didn't mean to throw you that far. You seem to have a way with me." I walked back to the one chair in the room and sat down.

The girl got to her knees on the other side of the bed, still looking daggers at me. She stood up and walked over to sit on the end of the bed in front of me, just out of arm's reach.

"Good," I said. "Now who the fuck are you?"

CHAPTER SIX

S he didn't speak for a long time, then she finally took a deep breath and said, "My name is Arianne. I…protect the city."

"Like Batman?" I asked.

"Kinda, except I only worry about mystical threats. There are plenty of ways that people are defended against mundane attacks. The kinds of threats I deal with are a little more…"

"Complicated?" I offered.

"Sure, we can use that one. I deal with complicated threats to my city."

"What made you think I was complicated?" I asked. I ran down a mental checklist in my head. I hadn't cast any spells since leaving Charlotte, hadn't opened up my Sight to the magical world, hadn't done anything out of the ordinary except…*motherfucker*.

I pulled out my phone and set it on the table. I didn't have to press any buttons, I knew the ethereal bastard was snooping. "Okay, Dennis, time to fess up," I said to the phone.

"You know you have to dial those things, right?" Arianna said from her seat on the bed.

I glared at her. "It's complicated," I said, keeping with what was apparently the word of the day.

"You also know they're not waterproof?"

"Mine is. I've learned to protect my tech." I wasn't kidding. Magic is bad enough on delicate equipment, but with the number of times I've been burned, drowned, buried, or defenestrated, I caught on to the need to spend some resources on keeping my gear alive. That way it can keep me alive.

"What spell is that?" the girl asked. For the first time, she looked like she thought I might actually be competent.

I almost hated to burst her bubble. "It's called an Otterbox," I replied, gesturing to the heavy-duty protective case around my phone. "Now quit hiding in there and answer me, Dennis."

"Oh come on, Harker, don't be a dick about this." The digitized image of Dennis "Sparkles" Bolton appeared on the screen. At least he wasn't wearing his unicorn face this time. Instead, he looked like his normal moon-faced ginger self, perennially twenty-two going on fourteen with tight curly hair and about three hairs on his chin. A spattering of freckles dotted his grinning cheeks, and he used the magic of computer imaging to make his green eyes a blazing emerald.

"Why should this be any different, Dennis? I'm a dick about everything. Now why did you sic the Junior Adventurer on me?" The girl on the bed gave me the finger, and I returned the gesture.

"Arianne's good, Harker. I thought she could be useful. Especially since you're flying solo on this one." He wasn't wrong. Luke was back home overseeing the reconstruction of his new house, a process made difficult by his need to schedule construction meetings after sunset. Flynn wasn't exactly in the doghouse with her bosses at the police department, but she was on a pretty short leash nonetheless. The other Shadow Council folks were out chasing angels of their own or trying to pick up the pieces of their mundane lives. That left me on my own.

"I'm tracking down one...person, Dennis. I think I can handle it on my own. You know I've handled cases without backup before, right?"

"Oh, I remember. I think I'm the prime example of how sideways shit can go when you don't have your usual support system behind you." That stung a little, but only because it was true. Dennis was a casualty of me chasing a demonic serial killer and not being fast enough to figure out the murderer's identity. He was sacrificed in a ritual to open a doorway to Hell, and I managed to transfer his consciousness into the internet, only partially on purpose.

"So she's supposed to be Batgirl or something?" I asked.

"That's sexist," Dennis said.

"Go fuck yourself," Arianne said at the same time.

"Is that to me or him?" I asked. "I don't care. Just shut up for a minute while the grownups talk."

"Oh, one hundred percent go fuck yourself," the girl said, standing up from the bed. I put a hand on her chest, just under her throat, and pushed her back down.

"Sit. Stay."

"One *thousand* percent go fuck yourself," she said. She sprang up with her fists clenched at her sides. She was ready to go.

I wasn't. I put my hand on the top of her head this time and pressed down. She fell back to the bed, and I pointed a finger at her. "I said *stay*."

She looked up at me and saw something in my face that made her pause. I was getting pretty irritated, so there might have been a little bit of "I can and will turn you into a toad" written across my forehead.

"What's the plan, Dennis? Do I take her under my wing, or just use her as cannon fodder?" I asked.

"I just thought it might be helpful to have someone who knows the town's players, magically speaking. So I sent Arianne a few simply encoded texts and emails with your picture, saying that a powerful and dangerous wizard was coming to her town, and I thought she might want to know about it."

"So you tell her I'm dangerous, and you expect her to just jump right in and work with me? Yeah, that seems to make sense."

"Okay, it might not have been the best way to go about it, but the end result was good, right? I mean, you guys are together now, and you can figure out how to find Gabriel and his book and then work on getting Glory her wings back, right?"

"Wait, what?" Arianne said. "What is he talking about? Gabriel? A book? Wings? Are you messing around with angels? Because I'm not messing around with angels. Angels are *assholes*."

I thought back to Barachiel, the angel behind all the shit in Atlanta, and couldn't find it in my heart to disagree. "You're not wrong," I said. "A lot of angels are assholes. But there's one who's not, and she needs my help. The only way I can help her is to find a bunch of other angels and get them to go back to Heaven and do their jobs. From what we can figure, one of them might be here in Charleston."

"Which one?"

"Gabriel," I said.

"The Archangel Gabriel?"

"That's the one," Dennis said from the phone.

"Fuck that," the girl said. "I'm out of here, and you need to be out of here, too. You don't just need to be out of this hotel room, you need to be out of my city. I'll give you until nightfall. Then I'm coming back with a bunch of my sisters, and we're going to make sure you're gone. We don't need any trouble with angels around here." She stood up, and I blocked her path to the door.

"Get out of the way."

"Sit down."

"Get out of the way." I hoped eventually she'd realize that the glowy eyes thing wasn't impressing me, but apparently, we hadn't gotten there yet.

"Please sit down, and stop trying to look badass. You're maybe twenty years old, and I've forgotten more spells that you've cast in your whole life." My powers of persuasion being what they are, that went over like a lead balloon. She shoved her hands out at me, and a bolt of pure purple energy shot out toward my face.

I closed my eyes against the glare and tapped my belt buckle. A small *pop* sounded under the crackle and hiss of magical energy, and the purple energy dissipated around me.

"What the fuck was that?" the girl asked.

"It's a dampener," I replied. "A little piece of obsidian set into the buckle of my belt. I invoke the right spell, and the stone sends out what amounts to a magical EMP, knocking out any active spells in a quarter mile and sucking away all the magical mojo for a couple hours."

"But that kills your magic, too!" The girl obviously decided that meant I was going to be old and slow, so she tried to dart past me to the door.

I might be old, but I'm far from slow. I caught her around the waist and flung her back to the bed. "Stop that," I said.

"How did you do that? Your magic should be dead, too."

"It is. That wasn't magic. That was just me being a badass." I gave her my most annoying grin, and she just gave me the finger again. I was really getting tired of seeing this kid's middle finger. I might have to feed it to her before this whole mess was finished.

"So what now, you just gonna tie me up and keep me in your hotel room?"

"Nah, I'm not into that Fifty Shades shit. Plus, I'm seeing somebody. The way I see it, we've got two options. You can either help me, or you can leave me alone. Despite my kinda dead friend's ideas, I'm pretty sure I can find one angel and one book and get them back to Charlotte on my own. So if you want to walk out of here and leave me the hell alone, that's fine."

"Sold," she said, standing up again. I dispelled the binding holding the door closed with the wave of a hand, and she rushed toward it.

I got in her way again. "You can go. I just want to be perfectly clear about one thing: I am not here to fuck with the local witches. I do not *want* to fuck with the local witches. If given the choice, I *will not* fuck with the local witches. But if you get in my way, I will rain hellfire down upon you the likes of which you have never seen."

That got her blood up again, of course. "Who the fuck do you think you are, John Fucking Constantine?"

"Kid, I make John Constantine look like John Lennon. I'm Quincy Fucking Harker, and I've been hunting big nasties since your grandparents were babies. Now I'm only going to be here for a few days, then you can get back to dancing around naked under the full moon and explaining to the mundanes why love potions don't really work."

Her eyes got big, and she took a step back. I guess she'd heard of me. "*You're* Quincy Harker?"

"Yeah, I thought I'd be better looking, too."

She didn't say anything, just ducked her head and bolted past me out the door. I closed it behind her and threw the deadbolt, then walked over to sit at the small table where I had my phone sitting.

"So…that happened," I said.

"Yeah," Dennis' voice came from the speaker.

"Looks like I'm famous."

"Not in a good way."

"Nope, she didn't even offer to sleep with me."

"You're too old for her."

"I'm over a hundred years old, Sparkles. I'm too old for everybody."

"You're not wrong."

"Think I oughta wait around here for her to come back?"

"What makes you think she's coming back? I might not have eyes, but it sure sounded like she hauled all kinds of ass out of there."

"Oh, she did. But she'll be back."

"A lot of people would think that's a misogynist attitude, that the woman can't get along without you."

"Those people would be stupid. I don't have any attitude, just proof."

"What kind of proof?"

"She left her keys on the bed with her clothes."

CHAPTER SEVEN

She didn't come back in the next hour, so I went down the street and got myself an early dinner. I just ducked into a little English-themed pub, had some fish and chips that were good enough to remind me of my childhood, and downed a couple pints of Guinness. The thick stout and the vinegar on my chips were almost enough to make it feel like home, except the place was far too clean, nowhere near smoky enough, and I couldn't smell goat or horse shit anywhere. It's easy to romanticize my upbringing if you never smelled it.

The sun was setting when I walked out of the pub, so I meandered over to King Street and decided to start my investigation on familiar ground. The sign for Trifles & Folly glowed with magic even without my Sight open, so I ducked in the shop, looking around to see who was running things these days.

"Good evening," a trim young man with crisp creases in his pants and nice cufflinks called out to me from behind the counter. "Welcome to Trifles & Folly. Is there anything we can help you find today?"

We were the only two people I could see in the shop, a well-appointed antique shop with a reputation in the occult circles as the place to go to find magical trinkets. The proprietress, Cassidy, was psychokinetic, and she worked with a group of people to take dangerous artifacts off the street and either lock them away somewhere safe or deal with any malevolence surrounding the stuff. I'd met her a few times, but we tried to stay out of each other's way.

I didn't know this guy, though, so I wasn't sure how much I could say to him. "I'm looking for a book," I said.

"Well, we don't do much with rare and antiquated books," he replied. "There are several excellent used bookstores in town, including Harbor Books over on East Bay, and Battery Tales up on St. Phillips."

"This would be a 'special' book. The kind your boss often takes a particular interest in," I said, hoping that if he didn't know the deal, that he at least had enough of a clue to know that Cassidy sometimes dealt in weird stuff and would give her a call.

A shadow crossed his handsome face, and I knew he knew what I was talking about. I also knew he didn't really want to talk about it with someone he didn't know, and that seemed smart to me. I leaned forward. "Hey, look, it's cool. Why don't I leave Cassidy a note?"

He relaxed a little when I used the name, and he slid me a pencil and piece of paper across the counter. I noticed he made it a point not to touch me, and I smiled a little. Working with someone who can pick up psychic impressions off objects would give me an increased personal bubble, too.

C— *In town for a few. Nothing you need to worry about. Council stuff. Next time I'm through, I'll give you a call and we can grab a drink. Regards to S. Harker*

I scribbled my message on the paper, wrote my cell number under it, and passed it back to the young man. "Here you go. Thanks for the tip on the books. I'll give those places a shot."

"For special books, you probably want to start with Harbor Books. Gerry over there has been known to pick up some oddball things from time to time."

"Thanks, um...what was your name again?" I asked.

"Teague," he said. "And you are?"

"Quincy Harker," I replied. "I'm an old acquaintance of the shop and the owners."

His eyes widened just a tiny bit. "I've heard the name."

I smiled at him. "All true, pal. Every word." I turned and stepped back out onto the street.

Full night had fallen, and Charleston was a different world. The bright pastels of Rainbow Row were whitewashed in the moonlight, and the whole town felt more like Victorian London than a modern American city. Even several blocks from the water, I could smell the thick ocean musk and taste the salt hanging heavy in the air.

My boots clomped across the brick sidewalks as I dodged broken stones and ankle-snapping divots. I crossed the street and headed south, turning left onto Market toward East Bay and stopping cold as I saw a shimmering figure walking into the old City Market.

"I really don't want to get involved in this," I muttered. I said it like a mantra as I walked down the street outside the open-air craft market that stood on the site near where so many men, women, and children were sold as property. I kept pace with the ghost, having no desire to leave a wandering spirit at my back, even if it was a harmless specter.

Most of them are. Harmless, that is. It's the rare ghost that can affect the material world more than a little knocking and the occasional moaning in the night. But it's a pretty rare ghost that wanders much more than a few feet from its resting place, and this ghost was moving into its third block since I spotted it, so there was definitely something odd going on.

I opened my Sight and immediately understood what was going on. The ghost itself glowed white and yellow in my vision, a pretty common color for the non-malevolent haunting types. Around its waist was the interesting thing. A band of pulsating crimson energy encircled the ghost like a belt, or a lasso, leading off down through the market. This ghost wasn't just wandering through the streets of Charleston. That happened all the time. This ghost had been summoned and was being compelled to do someone's bidding. Compelled with blood magic and necromancy, two things that ranked only slightly below "demon summoning" on Quincy Harker's List of Things that Get Your Ass Kicked. It looked like I was going to get involved in this mess after all.

I dropped my Sight, snapping my vision back to the mundane world just as I passed the delicious smells of one of Charleston's many seafood restaurants. There was a line to get in the place, and I lost sight of the ghost for a few seconds pushing through the crowd. When I finally emerged on the other side, the glowing image was a block ahead of me, passing out of the end of the market and turning down a narrow passage between two buildings. I hurried after it, only to get to the mouth of the alley and see nothing.

"Shit," I said. I opened my Sight, and the amount of magic around me left me momentarily blind. The entire alley glowed a deep red, almost the color of blood, shot through with streaks of gray, green, and a glaring piss-yellow. There was nothing good being done here, and all that not good was being done an awful lot.

I saw just a hint of white glowing amidst the darker sheen on the bricks and strode down the alley to where the last flicker of the ghost's essence lingered. A dingy metal door with heavy hinges and a thick deadbolt stood there, just the barest hint of magical essence glowing through the crack under the door. I dropped my Sight, and the ugliness of the psychic world around me faded to the normal nasty of an urban back alley with a few random garbage bags, a hint of piss wafting into my nostrils, and the acidic reek of a puddle of vomit by the opposite wall. The gray door in front of me had no identifying marks, but the new lock and well-worn scrape marks in the dirt at my feet told the story of frequent use.

I pressed my ear to the door, but it was too thick for even my enhanced hearing to pick up anything. There was no knob, just a bent piece of metal bolted to the door, so I gripped the makeshift handle and pulled. The door was unlocked and swung open with just a whisper, more evidence that not only was this entrance used a lot, but by someone who took pains to make sure their passing was as quiet and unobserved as possible.

I slipped into the building, all my mundane senses open as wide as I could manage. I kept my Sight closed off except for brief scans because there was so much red and gray pain and death magic coating the walls and floor that I could barely stand the onslaught. I stepped into a narrow corridor running the length of the building, illuminated by one flickering fluorescent tube and glaring green LED glow of the EXIT sign over my head. My boots were nearly silent on the scuffed tile floor, but I kept to the walls and shadows as best I could regardless.

There was a hallway to my right that ran to the front of the building and what looked like a simple wooden door. To my left, the corridor went a dozen yards back into the building and turned a corner, away from the street and, presumably, any prying eyes. I went left, thinking that most things done with ghosts are probably best done as far from public view as possible.

I rounded the corner only to find the hallway ran just ten more feet into a dead end. There was an open door, and a little more light fed in from the next room or passage. I crouched down to make my shadow smaller and walked to the door. I peered through the door into a large room, some kind of warehouse or storeroom. It was a huge open space, easily sixty feet on all sides, completely empty except for the naked man standing in the center of the room in a casting circle, his hands raised to the heavens.

Great, I thought. *Nothing better than fighting a naked wizard in a strange city when you're supposed to be hunting down missing angels. I guess it could be worse. I could be wrestling a nude Sasquatch.*

I drew in some energy from my surroundings, a little unsteady from the corruption coursing through the area, and released a trickle of it into the air around my hands. A bright blue glow filled the room, and the man in the circle stopped mid-incantation to gape at me.

"Who dares interrupt the workings of the Grand Barathan?"

"Is Grand your first name, or is it more of a description? I think you're the only Barathan I've met, so I don't have much of a basis for comparison. Is that a thing now? Should I start calling myself the Grand Harker? I mean, I'm the only one left, so it's not like anyone's going to fight me for the title belt or anything."

My new buddy apparently had nothing in the way of a sense of humor because he waved his arms and a dozen spirits floated up from the floor of the warehouse and floated toward me, every one of them wailing and flailing like bad guys in a haunted house.

I'm usually not very worried about ghosts. With the exception of the random banshee, most things are pretty harmless when they're dead. The exception is malevolent poltergeists, who can sometimes throw things with a lot more aim than they should have for denizens of the ethereal plane. Then there are wraiths—angry spirits summoned by necromancers. Wraiths can't cause physical harm, but they drain your life essence with every touch, kinda like Death in the old *Gauntlet* video game. Except you can't get this essence back by eating a digital turkey leg.

I blinked my Sight in and out just to confirm my worst suspicions about the spirits currently coming for me across the floor of the abandoned warehouse. Yep, every one of them had the sickly yellow-tinted aura of a wraith. So I was all alone staring down a naked necromancer and a dozen ghosts that could suck the life right out of me.

It was looking like a bad night for our hero.

CHAPTER EIGHT

I let loose a bolt of energy from each hand, not even bothering to coalesce it into a spell, just pouring sheer power into the wraiths. I managed to blast four of them back to the Otherworld with my first shot, but that still left eight.

I leapt for the rafters and grabbed a joist, using it to swing over to the other side of the room, buying myself a few extra seconds. Unfortunately, in escaping the ghosts, I put myself a lot closer to the evil necromancer (yes, I know it sounds redundant, but I have met more than one non-evil necromancer). He lobbed a ball of fire at me, which exploded in a textbook circular blast and singed me even with my enhanced reflexes. Obviously, somebody played a little too much *D&D*.

The problem with tossing around fireballs inside buildings is twofold. First, buildings burn, which is generally a bad day for everyone in them, often including the person who threw the spell in the first place. Second, fire sucks a lot of the oxygen out of a room, which is even worse for the people inside than the fire. You can run away from a fireball, but it's a lot harder to run from suffocation. The bad guy's spell not only caught the walls and ceiling insulation on fire, it also made it tough to breathe between the smoke and the lack of oxygen.

I drew my pistol and shot out a couple of the windows up near the ceiling line, letting more air into the room. On the one hand, that move kept me from dying right that second. On the other hand, it gave the fire in the insulation more fuel, and it raced across the desiccated fiberglass, spreading to every corner of the room in seconds.

I looked away from the blazing ceiling to see a pair of wraiths closing on me. I called up my personal reserves of power and shouted *"begone!"* at the top of my lungs. The wraiths vanished, but I staggered as the power flowed out of me in an instant. I ran across the room, firing a couple of rounds at the necromancer in his circle as I passed. They pinged off his magical protections, but it was worth a shot. Some folks forget to ward against physical threats when they believe their surroundings to be secure, and putting a couple of bullets into the wizard would have been an easy way to bring most of my troubles to a quick resolution.

I leapt over a wraith in my path and lowered my shoulder as I approached what looked like a standard office-issue, hollow-core wooden door. I heard a resounding *crack* as I slammed into the door, but it didn't come from the door splintering into a million pieces like I'd really, really hoped it would.

Nope, it came from my collarbone as I hit a steel-reinforced door clad in what only looked like cheap wood. The door held up to my onslaught, but the surrounding wall wasn't reinforced, so the door and jamb went down, with me on top of them. I took out a solid four to six inches of wall on all three sides of the door, and the whole mess fell flat underneath me.

"FUCK!" I shouted, scrambling to my feet and spinning around to see the four wraiths gliding toward me, an inexorable tide of suck preceded by the fire racing across the ceiling at me. The necromancer was nowhere in sight, having yanked down his circle and vanishing while I attempted my escape. I offered up a brief and petty hope that his pants had already burned.

I tried to raise my right hand and summon magic, but my shoulder screamed at me, and I dropped to one knee as the pain hit me like a bullet. From a crouch, I held up my functioning left arm and drew a hasty circle on the floor in front of me with a Sharpie I carry in my back pocket. I bit my thumb and smeared a little blood across the line, invoking the circle and buying me a few seconds. The circle would keep the wraiths out, and it would keep me from burning to death, but it wouldn't do shit to stop me from suffocating, dying of smoke inhalation, or just broiling inside my own skin.

I wracked my brain for an incantation that would banish four wraiths at once, but the pain in my shoulder made it hard to concentrate. Even if I could whip up something of sufficient power to do the job, there were no guarantees that I wouldn't fuck it up in my addled state. There are worse things than miscasting a spell and being trapped inside your own circle with it, but not many.

The four wraiths surrounded my circle, not touching the mystical barrier, just surrounding it. It was like they knew I couldn't hold it forever, and all they had to do was be patient and they'd be able to get their fill of my soul. Their faces were twisted in a rictus of pain and hunger, and they bore no resemblance to the people they'd been. These were no friendly Caspers; these were monsters eager to rip my soul to pieces and feed on the scraps.

I reached out with one hand, cautiously extending my fingertips until I just brushed the surface of the glowing sphere of force surrounding me. Magical circles are kinda like soap bubbles. They have very little surface tension, but if you do it just right, you can actually touch one without destroying it. That's what I did now, I just barely connected my fingertips with the circle's inside edge. A push too hard, and it would pop out of existence, and I'd be wraith food. Not enough contact, and my silly plan wouldn't work.

I pointed my right hand toward the floor and spun my essence out through my fingers until I found what I was looking for. I lit upon a fat conduit carrying electrical wires underneath the building and drew power from it up through the floor, through myself, and poured it into my circle.

The barrier flickered, blinked a little in spots, then strengthened, its power bolstered by the power from the building. I opened the flow of energy a little, channeling more power into the circle. Like bubblegum, the sphere of energy started to expand as more and more juice poured into it. I cranked up the juice, and the circle grew exponentially faster. The wraiths whirled around faster and faster, torn between their desire to get at me and their fear of the power expanding outward.

I kept the flow increasing at a steady pace for several seconds, then cranked the floodgates wide open, drawing as much energy through myself as I could handle, blowing the circle wide open and sending a wave of energy out from myself like a shockwave from a nuclear blast. Except this shockwave was pure magical force, and when the wave hit the wraiths, it slammed into them like a hurricane wind, tearing the spirits to shreds and scattering their essence across the Otherworld.

The wraiths gone, I ran for the front of the building, found a plate glass window, and hurled myself through it. I intentionally used my already-injured shoulder, which ended up with me screaming and rolling around on the sidewalk covered in glass and soot, smoke rising from my hair and clothes.

A pair of boots materialized in front of my eyes, and I looked up the legs attached to them to see Arianne scowling down at me. *Great, from a necromancer to a pissed-off witch. This night really sucks.*

"I knew you were trouble the first time I laid eyes on you," the witch said, waving a hand at the mess behind me as if it were evidence.

Sometimes I can't keep my mouth shut when I really should. This was not the time for old Meat Loaf quotes, but I couldn't stop myself. I smiled up at her and said, "I bet you say that to all the boys."

The last thing I saw was a combat boot coming at my forehead; then everything went black.

CHAPTER NINE

I woke up with a headache, a really sore shoulder, and the smell of smoke lingering in my nose. All in all, I've had worse. I tried to sit up, and immediately, the pain in my shoulder went through the roof, and I moved right into the "worse" category. I fell back to the bed I was on, and that sent another wave of pain rolling through me. I fought desperately to keep my lunch in place as the waves of blinding pain radiated from my shoulder to my skull and back again.

"Fuuuuuuck," I groaned.

"Oh good, you're awake. We didn't want to try healing you until we could at least let you scream a little." I didn't try to sit up this time, but I did manage to turn my head to the side and look at Arianne. She was sitting in a cheap hotel chair, and by my best guess at the chair and the table beside her, we were back at the King Charles. I assumed we were in my room, but they all pretty much look the same, and I couldn't see any of my crap lying around, so maybe not.

"Heal me?" I asked. My voice cracked, and I sounded like a man who had just walked for a week in a desert. Or spent five minutes in a burning building. They sound about the same. "Feel free to start that process any time."

"Okay, but this is going to hurt," came a new voice. I turned my head to the other side and saw a young man with blond curls and a goatee sitting on the bed next to me. He held a pair of very large scissors and wore a serious expression. I didn't like where this was going.

The stranger leaned in, scissors moving toward my throat. I sucked back the agony in my shoulder enough to roll away from him and bring my hands up as I tumbled off the bed and came up to my knees.

"Back off, pal. I don't know what you're planning with the scissors, but nothing I've got going on requires surgery."

A puzzled look flashed across his face, then he relaxed and let out a little laugh. "Don't worry," he said, exactly the kind of thing a psychopath with scissors *would* say. "I have to cut your shirt off to set your clavicle. Otherwise, when we heal it, your shoulder won't work right. I don't think you want to try to raise your arm over your head right now, do you?"

I looked down at my clothes. I had just survived a fire, so it's not like anything I was wearing was really salvageable except for my trusty Doc Martens. My jeans were pretty much okay, except for a little soot and a scuff at the knee, but my shirt and t-shirt were pretty well fucked.

"Fine," I said, standing and moving back over to the guy. "Why don't we at least introduce ourselves first. I'm Quincy Harker."

His eyes widened a little, and he shot a nervous look over at Arianne. "The Reaper?"

I nodded. "I've been called that. Among other things." I didn't bother mentioning that "asshole" was chief among the other things, but he didn't need to know that.

"I'm Marcus. I'm the healer for..." He looked to the girl in the chair.

"My group," Arianne supplied.

"It's cool, doll," I said, throwing in the "doll" just to wind her up a little. Judging by the red tips on her ears, I'd say it worked. "I understand if you don't want me to know what you call your little coven. You don't have to tell me where the Hall of Justice is either."

"Let's get you patched up so we can figure out how we can help you," Marcus said.

"Or if we're just going to throw you out of town," Arianne countered.

I didn't bother responding. There wasn't any point. I just sat down on the bed and turned a little toward Marcus. "Go for it, Doc. Perform your sartorial magic on these poor garments."

He looked a little confused.

"Cut my clothes and fix my shoulder," I translated.

He nodded and got to work. First, he helped me out of the long-sleeve button-down shirt I wore over my gray *Transformers* t-shirt. Then he cut the t-shirt up the sleeve to the neck, and down from the armpit to the bottom hem, and peeled it back.

"This is probably going to hurt," he said. "Do you need something to bite on to keep from screaming?"

"Yeah, we wouldn't want the hotel security to come running, thinking we're killing you," Arianne agreed.

I opened my Sight for a second and saw that my sound-dampening spell from earlier was still in effect. It would last for a couple of days at least. I blinked my vision back to normal and looked at my makeshift doctor. "Nah, we're good," I said. "Nobody outside this room will hear anything that happens inside it as long as my spell is still going."

"Okay," Marcus said, and put one hand on my elbow. He pulled, lifted, pushed, and tweaked my elbow and shoulder for several minutes until I felt everything click back in the right spots with a sickening pulse of sheer blinding agony. Then he put his right hand on my collarbone, holding my elbow and arm stationary with his left, and closed his eyes.

"Blessed Mother, share your light and energy with this man. Mend his hurts and cure his ills so that he may once more sally forth in battle against thine enemies. Make him whole once more, and repair the source of his pain. Bathe him in your cleansing light and make him as new again."

My shoulder screamed and throbbed when Marcus began his invocation, but as he spoke, a deep warmth suffused my arm, radiating out from the palm of his hand, pouring heat into my fractured clavicle to engulf my entire upper body in warm, pulsating energy. I *felt* the bones knit together, and the muscles strengthen, and the ligaments reattach, and even the damage to my lungs from the fire was repaired. A couple of minutes later, and I felt good as new. Better, actually, because for the first time in years, no part of my body was in pain or even uncomfortable.

I turned to look at Marcus, and he smiled at me, then passed out on the bed.

"That happens," Arianne said from behind me. "Healing takes a lot out of the healer. It takes a lot out of the patient, too, even though it doesn't feel like it at the time. I know you feel like a million bucks right now, but don't go chasing down anyone else to scrap with tonight. You'll probably die, and then Marcus would have wasted his efforts."

I stood up and could feel how right she was. I felt fantastic, but it was a very tired fantastic. I got a clean shirt from my dresser, threw it on, and pulled out a pair of sweats. "I'm gonna go get out of these smoke-scented clothes," I said. "If you're still here when I get back, we can talk about why you knocked me out, then healed me."

I walked into the bathroom, took care of some necessary bodily functions, and washed my face, neck, and arms. Then I shucked my Docs, dropped my jeans and boxers onto the floor and contemplated a shower. I decided that I was more likely to pass out and give myself a concussion than actually get clean, so I just did a quick sink bath and slipped on the sweats.

When I stepped back into the hotel room, I was alone. The kid was good, I had to give her that. I never heard the door close, and I was listening. There was a note on the bed, with an address and a time.

Meet me tomorrow. 2 p.m. We both have some explaining to do.

I couldn't argue with that. I ordered a couple of beers from room service, turned on *Law & Order* on the room TV, and was asleep before I finished the first Heineken.

CHAPTER TEN

O f course I walked around the block three times before I entered the restaurant Arianne had directed me to. I made the first lap half an hour before our meeting to see what kind of place I was walking into, checked for back exits and adjoining buildings, then took another pass with my Sight overlaying on top of my normal vision, looking for spells or magical booby traps. It all seemed safe, so I did one more trip around the building five minutes before two in the afternoon just to make sure there were no suspicious vehicles lurking or demonic portals hanging out around the perimeter.

I stepped into The Cannonball Cafe on Meeting Street at precisely one minute after two, just in case the room was set to explode at two on the dot. I'm really not paranoid by nature, but experience has taught me several things. I hate being ambushed, I really hate being blown up, and just because you're paranoid, doesn't mean that someone isn't trying to kill you.

The restaurant was nice, a real white linen tablecloth kind of place. The maître' d looked down his nose at me, which was impressive given the six inches I had on the guy. He stood behind what would be called a hostess stand in a normal restaurant, but probably had some kind of French name in this joint, and sneered at me.

"Mr. Harker, I presume?" I've never understood how somebody manages to be haughty in a Southern accent, but some folks in Charleston seem to have mastered the art.

"How'd you guess?"

"I was instructed to expect a tall Yankee with terrible taste in clothing and a perpetual scowl. You seem to fit that description. Please follow me." He turned and walked away without looking to see if I was behind him. I was, and only partly because I wanted to strangle him. I saw nothing wrong with my choice of black pants and a maroon dress shirt for this meeting. I even put on my good belt.

I followed my snooty guide up three flights of switchback stairs to a rooftop veranda with two tables set up under a white fabric awning. A large black man stood behind a small bar with a martini shaker in his hand and a white apron around his waist. I swallowed every comment that crossed my mind about progressive cities and stereotypes as Pepe le Asshat led me across the roof to a round table set for four. Three people already sat there. Arianna, Marcus, and a white-haired woman with a kind face but steel in her blue eyes, all rose to greet me as I stopped a few feet from the table.

The exposed rooftop lunch spot was not something I considered in my reconnaissance, and I didn't like being so exposed. There were a lot of buildings taller than this one in the surrounding blocks, and a sniper could easily take me out before I could raise any type of shield. Especially with a head shot.

"Have a seat, Mr. Harker. We promise not to try to kill you before you've had dessert. You simply must try the peach cobbler. It's to die for." Arianna motioned to the fourth chair as my lunch companions took their seats.

I stood in front of my chair for a moment, then extended my hand to Marcus. "I never got the chance to thank you for your help last night. I appreciate it. I felt great this morning. I hope it didn't take too much out of you."

He half-stood and shook my hand. "I was a little more draggy than usual, but I'm okay now. That's why Ari called our meeting for so late. She knows what a healing like that takes out of me."

I turned to the other woman. "I don't believe we've had the pleasure. Quincy Harker." I held out my hand. The woman just looked at it.

"I know you, Reaper. I know your uncle, the parasite, as well."

"Never heard him referred to in quite that fashion, but I suppose it's valid enough," I said, pulling my hand back and sitting. "Sorry, I suppose I missed your name."

"I am Tara, High Priestess of the Moon. And you are an interloper in my city."

"I prefer the term tourist, but whatever." The table was set with ice water and an amber beverage I assumed was sweet iced tea. A pretty safe assumption in South Carolina, where the default seemed to be tea so sweet a spoon could stand up in the glass. I sipped on my water.

"When do you plan to leave and take your necromancy with you? We find that type of magic an abomination, and its practitioners are not welcome here," Tara continued.

"I'll leave when I'm done with my business," I replied. "Are we going to order lunch, or was this all just a charade to get me here with the promise of a free meal?"

Arianne ducked her head, a tiny smile making her look even younger. There was some slight resemblance between the razor-cheeked Tara and the goth cherub Arianne, but it was pretty minor. I couldn't tell if they were distant cousins or just spent so much time together they started to look alike.

"I will not break bread with one who sucks the souls of the dead into lifeless husks for his own nefarious purposes." Tara's voice boomed across the rooftop.

"Well, I guess this is why you went for the private dining room, huh?" I asked. I stood up, and Marcus followed suit, his hand drifting around behind his back. "Calm down, Junior. There's nothing you're pulling out from behind your back that I'm afraid of, so don't even try."

His hand slipped back to his side, and he looked a little abashed. I turned my attention back to Tara. "Okay, lady, here's the deal. I'm here on a job, and I'm going to do that job with or without you. I don't know fuck-all about your necromancer problem, just that he tried to fricassee me last night, and that means he's number nine on my shit list with a bullet. So if you didn't call me here to help me hunt him down, then at least do me the professional courtesy of staying the fuck out of my way."

I turned to go and made it halfway across the roof before Tara spoke. "Wait," she said, and her tone was that of a woman who was on the edge of losing the last tiny grasp on her shit.

I stopped, but didn't turn around. "We gonna talk like civilized people over a burger with enough bacon to give bystanders cholesterol problems, or am I going to keep walking?"

"Please, come sit down, Mr. Harker," Arianne said. "I'm sure this is all just a misunderstanding."

I turned around and walked back to the table, but I didn't sit. "There's nothing to misunderstand," I said. "You fuckers have been popping up in my shit since the minute I got here. I was just minding my own business down on the pier when you decided to come down and piss on the ground to mark your territory. I appreciate the save last night, that was really helpful, but this bullshit today? Fuck you. Fuck you, and the broomstick you rode in on. You say you know me? You say you know my uncle? Then you know what we do for people who need it, and you know what we do *to* people who threaten us.

So if you want to dance, let's dance. But if you're not going to help me or fight me, then leave me the fuck alone."

I stood there, the pissed-off rolling outward from me in waves, and me not giving a single fuck. I stood there watching Arianne, Marcus, and their snooty friend exchange meaningful glances for a solid couple of minutes before finally Tara looked up at me and nodded.

"Please sit, Mr. Harker. I apologize for my earlier rudeness. It was uncalled for."

"Apology accepted," I said, pulling my chair out and sitting back down. I was really glad she hadn't called my bluff. I was pretty good physically after last night's singeing, but there was no way I had enough mojo to duel three witches at once, and that's not even taking the waiters into account.

"Now," I said, taking a sip of tea and managing not to wince at the sweetness. "I met a necromancer last night who's doing some nasty shit to ghosts in your famously haunted city. What's up with that?"

Tara looked at Arianne, who made a "go ahead" gesture. "His real name is Lawrence Barathan, he now calls himself The Grand Barathan, as you heard. He is one of our former members who had designs on a greater amount of power and influence in the mundane world than we are comfortable pursuing. We cast him out, but he has continued in his efforts to influence events and gain personal wealth and authority. He seems to be using the spirits of the departed to identify objects of power, and then he works to acquire them, by any means necessary."

I could feel my brow wrinkle. "Isn't this exactly the kind of thing Sorin and his people are here to prevent? Why haven't they stepped in?"

"Cassidy and her group have been occupied with some other, more lethal, events of late. It seems that Lawrence's actions have flown beneath their radar as of yet. He has been very cautious in what type of artifact he pursues, trying to remain beneath Sorin's notice."

"Seems like a good idea. I've dealt with Sorin once or twice. Guy's a legitimate badass. So what is your pal Barry's endgame? What's he trying to do?" I asked.

Arianna leaned forward. "We think he's going to try to destroy the Coven of the Moon."

"I assume that's you guys?" They nodded. "What makes you think he wants to kill you?"

"He told us so," Marcus replied. "When we threw him out of the coven, he threatened to kill the three of us and everyone he saw wearing the symbol of the Moon." He pulled a pendant out from under his shirt, a full moon on a silver chain.

"That seems pretty clear," I said. "So why is he still walking around?"

From the looks on their faces, you'd have thought I suggested reenacting Sherman's march instead of eliminating an obvious threat to their lives.

"What are you talking about, exactly?" Arianna asked.

"Killing the bad witch before he kills all of you was the first thing that came to mind," I said.

"We are not murderers, Mr. Harker," Tara said with a haughty sniff.

"Neither am I," I replied. "But I'm also not going to just sit around and wait for some assclown with a ghost fetish to kill me in my bed. This guy has got some serious chops; I felt them last night. He almost took me out. He might have, if not for Marky Marcus and Arianne showing up when they did. So it's not murder. It's self-defense, just the magical version."

"We do not kill," Marcus said.

"Speak for your—oh, I get it now," I said as realization dawned. I stood up and once again walked toward the rooftop door. This time it wasn't a negotiating tactic; this time I was legitimately done with these fuckers.

"Wait, please!" Arianna called after me.

"Go fuck yourself," I said. "I might be a killer, but I'm not an assassin. You want this jackass dead, you're going to have to do your own dirty work."

"They can't," said the bartender, who was between me and the door for some reason. "It's not in their nature."

"Too bad," I replied. "Now step aside, dickhead."

"I don't think so, Mr. Harker."

"Oh for fuck's sake," I muttered, calling up a tiny bit of power, just enough to shove the man to the side. I gestured at him, releasing the power with a low "sidestep."

Nothing happened. The power struck him in the shoulder and just flowed around him.

"That's not how that's supposed to work," I said.

"Sorry about that," the bartender said, as he reached up to pull his face off, revealing the wizard who scorched me half to death last night standing in front of me. "I'm glad to hear you won't be hunting me down to kill me. Unfortunately, I've already hunted you down, so now I suppose I'll just kill you instead."

Goddammit.

CHAPTER ELEVEN

e looked different with clothes on, and in the daylight, and not surrounded by soul-sucking ghosts, but I was pretty sure this was the same guy who threw a fireball at me last night. Now he was three feet in front of me, dressed like a waiter, his dark skin a sharp contrast to the white tuxedo shirt he wore. A thick, ropey scar ran diagonally the entire length of his face, from his forehead across his nose and mouth, all the way down his cheek. The way it lifted one lip in a perpetual sneer made him look a little menacing, and little like a low-rent Billy Idol impersonator.

"Lemme see if I remember this right, you're the Great Baratheon? Or is that the guy from *Game of Thrones*? I can never keep track of everybody on that show. And to be honest, I just watch it for the boobs."

He snarled and raised a glowing hand. I made a mental note to never make my hands glow again. Ever since *Doctor Strange* hit DVD, every asshole in the world with an ounce of magical ability makes their hands glow for everything. I took the hint and stepped forward, punching him hard in the nose.

"Ow!" he shouted, stepping back. The punch had the desired effect, though, scattering his attention and breaking his spell. Marcus looked like he was still pretty tired, so I didn't want him to have to heal me again. And with my magic still pretty low, punching the snot out of this asshole seemed like my best plan to resolve things quickly, and without bloodshed on my part.

"*Stoneskin!*" he shouted, and his skin turned gargoyle-gray. I checked myself before I punched him again, not wanting to break my fist.

"Really?" I asked. "The best you can come up with is a third-level *D&D*

spell? You're a disgrace to magicians everywhere, and quite possibly infringing on copyright just by saying that shit."

Instead of punching him, I put one hand on his throat and one on his upper thigh and heaved him up into the air. Like so many things in a fight, this was way more difficult against a guy now made of granite. He was heavy as fuck, but I managed to wrestle him up and over my head.

The wizard thrashed around, but I got him to the edge of the roof before losing my grip. I tossed him over and turned back to the witches, who were no damn help whatsoever. At least Arianne had the courtesy to stand up and look like she thought about helping.

"Thanks for nothing, assholes," I said, clapping my hands together and walking over to the table. I sucked back the last of my sweet tea and glared at Tara.

"Now I definitely don't want to work with y'all. You didn't even…" My words trailed off as I noticed how wide her eyes were. "He's back, huh?"

This time all three of them sprang into action. Arianna moved over in front of Marcus and conjured a pair of short swords from pure energy that sprang from her clenched fists. Tara strode across the rooftop to stand toe to toe with Barathan, who was back on the roof and appeared to no longer be made of stone. She threw punches like a Jackie Chan movie, and Barathan dodged like he was the only one who knew how to control The Matrix.

It was fun to watch, but it really made me wish for my pistol. Of course, it was locked in the glove compartment of my car because that's where it was going to do me the absolute least amount of good. I watched them try to fight for a few seconds, then pointed two fingers at Barathan and shouted "*torporus!*"

A green ball of energy flew from my fingertips and struck him right in the chest. He never stopped dodging, but his movements slowed, then slowed some more. Tara landed one punch, then another, then a knee strike, then another punch. She took a sidestep to create some separation, then drew back one leg for what looked like a devastating roundhouse kick.

A kick that sliced through empty air as the necromancer back-flipped out of range. He was slower, but still quick for a normal human. I threw a few blasts of energy at him, just to keep him off-balance, but never came close to hitting him. My slow-down spell wore off after just a few seconds, and he smiled as he drew a pair of curved knives from his belt.

"I will enjoy slicing your souls from your bodies and adding you to my reserves of power. You will help me draw nearer to my ultimate goal," he said.

"Which is?" I asked. I pulled my own pocketknife and clicked it open. It wasn't nearly as impressive as a twelve-inch curved dagger, but it's what I had.

I settled into a fighting stance and stalked forward, moving left while Tara came at him from the right.

"I'll pass on the soliloquy, thanks." He clapped both hands together and set off a blinding light and a minor thunderclap on the roof, the mystical equivalent of a flash-bang. I closed my eyes and clapped my hands over my ears, but the sensory overload to my half-vampire senses still drove me to my knees.

When I could blink my eyes clear of tears, Barathan was gone, and so was Tara. I looked around the roof, and she was nowhere to be found. Arianna was still by the table, shielding Marcus with her body from any threats, but no necromancer and no high priestess.

"Well, fuck," I said. "I guess now we've got a rescue mission on our hands."

CHAPTER TWELVE

"Well, now what?" I asked Arianne.

"What do you mean, now what? Now we go get her back!" Marcus almost shouted.

"Sounds great," I said. "Where are they?"

He at least had the good sense to look chagrined. I turned my gaze to Arianne. "Any ideas, sunshine?"

"Not right offhand, no."

"Well, let's see what we can See." I walked over to a clear spot of roof and sat down cross-legged, my boots under my knees. I closed my eyes and opened my Sight, scanning the surrounding area for any magical hot spots. Trifles & Folly glowed like a fireworks display in the supernatural spectrum, all the artifacts lying around that place making it a beacon in the Otherworld. Farther away, I could see Cassidy's house, the residual magic that suffuses a place when a major Talent lives there making it glow like a gentle nightlight. There were several other shops that had a strong aura of magic around them and a few bright dots moving around downtown as several practitioners walked the streets. Nothing had the reddish-green tint of the necromancer though. I tried looking for Tara's aura, which I assumed would be a lot like Arianne's, only stronger. Nothing. No matter how far I ranged out of downtown, I could find no hint of her.

"Nothing," I reported. "Wherever he took her, he's got her hidden."

"We have to find her!" Marcus looked on the verge of tears.

"Suck it up, buttercup," I growled at him. "I'm dancing as fast as I can here." I pulled out my phone and tapped the home button. "Dennis, you there?"

"I'm everywhere, my cracker," Dennis said over the speaker.

"Dennis," I said, pitching my voice low, "you're as white as I am."

"I'm dead, man. I have transcended race. What do you need?"

"I need you to find someone for me. He goes by the name of Barathan."

"I'm pretty sure Robert was murdered, and that tall blond chick killed Tanis in the woods in season five."

"Everybody's gonna make the same *Game of Thrones* jokes, aren't they? Barathan, not Baratheon."

"Tomato, to-mah-toe. What else can you tell me about this Barathan?"

"He's a black necromancer, and he's kidnapped a witch named Tara."

"Is Willow pissed?"

"Are you just going to make TV references, or are you going to help me find this guy?"

"Pretty sure I can do both. By the way, I think necromancy counts as black magic from the jump, so your description was a little repetitive."

I looked at the phone, more puzzled than usual by Dennis' weird leap of logic, then it hit me. "No, dipshit, he's an African-American necromancer. I thought *that* might narrow the field a little."

"Oh! Why didn't you say that in the first place? Yeah, that might help, especially in South Carolina. I'll poke around and get back to you."

"Fine." I put the phone in my pocket. One bonus about having a friend who's basically a mystical pile of electrons, getting in touch with him doesn't use up my minutes. I turned to the two witches who just stood there staring at me.

"Don't you two have something to cast or something?"

"I'm a healer, man. That's pretty much the only magic I have," Marcus said.

"I've got a couple of ideas, but first I want to see how many of the coven I can pull together in case we need to throw down with this asshole," Arianne said.

"That makes sense," I replied. "I'm going to poke around a couple of the hot spots I saw in my Sight, but I've got a feeling we're going to end up back at the Market late tonight."

"What makes you say that?" Arianne asked.

"It's the first place I saw any activity from this dick," I said. "Plus, there's a lot of magic running around that place, thanks to years and years of people traipsing through there. It's past noon now, so midnight is the next strong time for magic, and the Market should be deserted then. Makes it prime time for nasty magic."

I handed Arianne a card with my cell phone number on it. "Take this and call me if you find anything. Otherwise, let's plan to meet up at my hotel at eleven. That should give us plenty of time to gear up and stop whatever this asshole has planned for your boss-lady," I said. It would also give me a little time to look around the city for Gabriel, my real reason for coming to Charleston in the first place.

The witches both nodded and headed off to do whatever it is witches do in the daytime, while I gave the city another quick scan with my Sight. The guy at Trifles & Folly, Teague, had mentioned a bookstore down on East Bay that might have something useful, so I peered over in that direction. I spotted a small place giving off a faint blue glow a half dozen blocks or so away, so I headed inside and took the stairs down to the street.

Twenty minutes of leisurely walking later, I stood in front of one of the very few businesses in the exclusive section of Charleston known as South of Broad. This part of East Bay was home to the famous Rainbow Row, the pastel houses that faced the waterfront, all with the long porches running perpendicular to the street to catch as much of the ocean breeze as possible when the ridiculous summer heat blanketed the city like a hot, damp towel.

Harbor Books was a converted house, probably worth north of a million bucks on the real estate market, but it certainly didn't seem to do very brisk business. In the ten minutes I watched the entrance, not a soul went in or out, and I only saw one old coot puttering around inside. I walked up the creaky wooden steps and looked at the sign on the door. "Open, mostly" it read, listing hours from noon until seven p.m. on weekdays and Saturdays. "CLOSED SUNDAYS" was written in large letters along the bottom of the page.

It being Tuesday, I turned the knob and stepped inside. I was instantly assailed by the papery dry smell of old books and almost knocked down by the magic in the place. The last time I was anywhere near this many magical tomes, there was a guy summoning demons for kicks who threw me out a window later that night. I hoped history didn't repeat itself. Although in downtown Charleston, there weren't any buildings nearly as tall as the one I went out of in Charlotte, so that was fortunate.

The inside of the shop was a mecca for readers and a nightmare for a fire marshal. I couldn't tell if I was in a bookstore or a documentary on book hoarding. Floor-to-ceiling bookshelves lined every wall, many of them double-stacked with tattered paperbacks from Ludlum, Clancy, Robb, King, Sanderson, Patterson, and the like. One entire shelf was dedicated to used copies of *Twilight*.

Every shelf was full almost to bursting, and hardbacks, encyclopedias, and coffee table books were stacked two and three feet high as endcaps on every aisle. The books were like multicolored literary kudzu, overtaking every inch of available floor space.

Floor lamps and tall windows provided the illumination, so there were some spectacularly shadowed corners, and as I meandered through the stacks, wandering semi-aimlessly and counting on my intuition to lead me to the most interesting texts, I uncovered various pieces of furniture scattered throughout the rooms. I felt like an urban archaeologist, unearthing settees and armchairs unseen for generations, tucked into corners with lamps behind them to provide little reading nooks all around the shop.

I saw fiction, nonfiction, memoir, biography, self-help, romance, thriller, fantasy, science fiction, science science, textbooks, comic books, manga, graphic novels, children's books, Bibles, Torah, Qur'an, and *The Book of Mormon*, both the religious text and the Broadway libretto. What I didn't see was a proprietor, unless you count the overweight and fluffy black and white cat who lounged on a chest-height stack of *Fifty Shades of Grey* paperbacks.

I reached out and scratched the cat behind its ears, and it looked up at me with a sleepy "Mrrrr?" before putting its head back down and starting to purr.

"How dost thou, sweet lord?" asked a voice from behind me.

I turned, my hand drifting to the small of my back where my pistol should have been, but wasn't, cursing myself for leaving it at the hotel. I relaxed when I saw the kind-faced old man who I'd watched through the windows standing there. He smiled at me, a little vacantly but pleasant enough, his head bobbing like a dashboard doll. He was a slight man, stooped with age and wearing a truly bizarre getup. His shoes were mismatched, one brown loafer and one white sneaker. He wore jeans, but they looked like they were patched by a psychotic clown with big fabric swatches of red and yellow sewn over the blue. An untucked dress shirt hung out lower than the pin-striped jacket he wore, and a brown tweed English driving cap sat on his head. His round face was smiling, and his deep-set eyes were rimmed with crows' feet, but his full beard was dark, and the stringy hair that I could see was brown, not gray.

"Hello," I said. "Are you the proprietor?"

He smiled at me and bobbed his head. "I like this place and willingly could waste my time in it."

Okay, not exactly what I was asking, but I guess it's close enough. "Can you help me find something?"

"Wise men never sit and wail their loss," he said, then turned and toddled off back into the stacks.

"Hey, wait," I said to his retreating back.

"Parting is such sweet sorrow!" he called back over his shoulder.

Is he answering me completely in Shakespeare quotes? Even for my life, that's pretty odd. I followed the old man through the winding stacks, past the armchairs, past piles of paperbacks that threatened to topple onto the floor at any moment, past the cat, who raised its head and meowed at me for once again disturbing its rest.

"Nice kitty," I said.

"A harmless necessary cat," the man replied. *Okay, maybe we're getting somewhere. That actually seemed to connect to what I said.*

I decided to push my luck. "Do you have any books of magic?" I asked.

"'Tis true; there's magic in the web of it," he said.

I shook my head. Nope, back to nonsense. I just kept my mouth shut and followed the old man until he stopped at the end of a long row of bookcases. I would almost swear that we had walked farther than was possible in the medium-sized house, but since we wove in and out of rooms, hallways, and stairwells, I wasn't sure.

The strange little man stood, looking up at a bookcase filled with leather-bound volumes. Some of these books looked old, and some looked downright ancient. I opened my Sight, and the entire wall glowed with a rainbow of colors. Red, blue, green, yellow, and white attacked my senses, and I staggered a little.

The little man heard the floor creak under me and turned to me, holding out a hand to catch my arm. When I caught a glimpse of him in my Sight, I saw through his mortal masquerade. Overlaid on top of the five-and-half-foot-tall human with as much curly brown hair coming out of his ears as was on his head was an ethereal image of a being wrapped in light with golden wings on his back. This batshit crazy little old man was exactly who I was looking for. This was the Archangel Gabriel, scribe of God Himself.

When I switched my vision back to the mundane world and took a good look in his eyes, I realized something else about my newfound divine entity. He was one hundred percent. USDA Grade A batshit crazy.

Now I've got a kidnapped witch and an angel with Alzheimer's. Some days I really hate my life.

CHAPTER THIRTEEN

I looked from the shelf, to the disguised angel, and back again. "You've got to be shitting me," I said.

"There are stranger things in heaven and earth, than are dreamt of in your philosophy," he replied, waving an arm at the books.

I let out a sigh. I couldn't read the titles with my Sight active, and I couldn't tell which ones were divine in nature with my normal vision. So I opened my third eye and pulled down all the books that glowed white, golden yellow, or pale blue. Those were usually the aura colors of positive or protective magic, the kind typically associated with the divine. I handed about ten volumes to Gabriel, who bobbled off to the front of the store in his odd little short-legged rocking gait. I took another ten and carried them myself, noting their weight.

"If anybody ever realized how strong the little bastard is, there certainly would have been some questions," I muttered as I followed him. He stopped at a large table and with one sweep of his arm knocked dozens of paperbacks to the floor. I dodged a couple, let a couple more bounce off my shins, and set my load of books down on the table by his.

"Is the information I need in here?" I asked, hoping against hope that I might get a reasonable answer.

"Ignorance is the curse of God; knowledge is the wing wherewith we fly to heaven."

"Of course it is," I said. I looked over the spines of the books and was able to immediately discard four of the two dozen as books I recognized. I set aside eight others that had titles on the spine and pulled up a chair to examine the last half more closely.

The first one was a French summoning text from the seventeenth century. Valuable, certainly, but far from the Word of God. Next was a three-volume set of spell books from the library of someone who called himself Alric the Grand. Judging by his spells, grand was not a word often used to describe him. He had spells for the shrinking of warts, spells for the reduction of passing odorous gas, spells to make himself seem more attractive, and a spell to summon a wood nymph to do his bidding.

Knowing what I do about the sexual proclivities of wood nymphs, I shuddered a little to think about him summoning one for a rent-a-date. There was no way a hornball wizard calling up a mischievous and powerful forest elemental was going to end well for the wizard. No wonder that was the last entry in his spell books.

When I whittled the pile down to three books, I turned to Gabriel. One of the books was from his stack, so I thought it was unlikely that it was his book. If our time with Michael was any indicator, as soon as he touched the book, it would manifest some outward sign, and so would Gabe. At least, I hoped Gabe would be coherent enough to do something.

That left me two books, both looking very old, and both radiating power like a mystical Chernobyl. I pulled the first one to me, and Gabe frowned, shaking his head. "Not to be," he mumbled. "Not to be, not to be, not to be."

I pushed the book away, and he relaxed. I stood and picked up the second book. He didn't look pleased, but he didn't look like I was about to shoot his puppy, either. I turned the book over in my hands, honestly a little nervous about opening the thing. If it worked like the sword, I could read it like a Stephen King novel and it wouldn't do anything in my hands. Of course, there was also the chance that it was the handwritten Word of God and would burn out my brain like an overused lightbulb if I opened it.

The book was big, encyclopedia-sized, and thick. It certainly looked old enough to have been around for hundreds of years, but it looked and felt professionally bound, so I couldn't tell if it was the original book or if it was a replica, or a manifestation, or what. There were some markings on the spine, but they looked like no language I'd ever seen before, and I can, at least, struggle through in most of them.

I opened the book, squinting my eyes to narrow slits in case I got another case of the magical dazzles, but nothing happened. Not, it didn't hurt me, but *nothing*. I just opened the book. It didn't blast me, didn't turn me into a pillar of salt, didn't call down a heavenly choir, just fell open to a spot in the middle. I looked at the pages, then back at my incomprehensible friend.

"Is this it?" I asked.

"But soft, what light through yonder window breaks?" He answered my question not just with a question, but with a completely stupid one to boot. I sighed. "This gig was supposed to be easy, you know. A simple FedEx quest, like the first few things in *A Bard's Tale*. I get a book, find an angel, put the two of you together, and *viola*, instant awesome. Instead I have Captain Incomprehensible and some old book of Enochian rituals..." I trailed off as I heard the word coming out of my own mouth.

Enochian? The language of the angels? I looked down at the book again, and sure enough, it was written in the looping characters of holy magic. "This is your book," I said, looking at Gabe.

He didn't reply, just looked at me. He kinda looked scared, to be honest.

"You have to take it," I told him. I pushed the book toward him. He sank back in his chair.

"A woman's life is in danger," I said. He shook his head and seemed to shrink in on himself.

"Fuck," I said. "I'm sorry." I closed the book, then shoved it into his chest. He put his hands up as the tome touched him, and the second he came into contact with the book, a brilliant yellow-white light shone forth from it like a miniature sun. I jerked back, letting go of the book, and covered my eyes.

Between my fingers and my eyelids, I saw the glow fade. I cracked my eyes open, then opened them wider, and my jaw dropped at the picture in front of me. The little balding crazy man was gone, replaced by a tall, muscular angel with blond curls and seven-foot wings.

"Gabriel?" I asked.

"You were expecting maybe George fucking Burns?" the angel replied, his lip curling up in a sneer as he looked down on me.

"Angels can say fuck?" Yeah, that was the part that surprised me. I mean, Glory swears, but I just assumed it was prolonged exposure to me that did it. Kinda like when you binge-watch *Deadwood* and every third word you say is "cocksucker" for the next week.

"I can say any goddamn thing I want, I'm an *Archangel*, you mewling worm." Gabriel stretched his wings and let out a huge sigh. "Ahhh, that feels good. Do you have any idea how cramped those things get while I'm wrapped in that silly form? Of course you don't. You don't know anything. You're human, why would you?"

I blinked a couple of times to rinse the condescension from my eyes, and said, "I need your help. A woman's life is in danger. Immediate danger. We've gotta go." I reached out to grab his arm, and he jerked back like I had the plague.

"Don't touch me, mortal! What makes you think you can lay hands on one of the Host, you repulsive slug."

"Wow, the Archangel's kind of a dick. Didn't see that one coming," I muttered. I looked up at Gabriel. "Look. I get that you're a little disoriented from being trapped in a crazy dude for a while, but there's a badass necromancer sucking the magic out of ghosts somewhere in the city, and he's got the High Priestess of...oh fuck it, will you just come with me? I need a little divine intervention."

"No."

No explanation, no apologetic refusal, just a flat, disinterested "no." "No?" I repeated.

"Do I stutter? Of course not. I'm perfect. I'm an angel. Listen closely. No," Gabriel said.

"You're perfect?" This guy was starting to piss me off.

"Perfect."

"Flawless in every way?"

"Completely."

"No way to improve upon your form at all?" Oh yeah, this guy was a total douche.

"None whatsoever."

"Where's your dick?" I gave him a nasty grin as he spluttered something about choosing a form and gender being irrelevant and all the things I knew he'd say. All I cared about was that in his bluster he loosened his grip on the book for a second, allowing me to snatch it out of his hands.

The general light in the room dimmed like someone had flipped off a light switch, and Gabriel turned back into a doddering old man, looking from side to side in befuddlement.

I held the book out in front of him. "I need to borrow this for a little while."

"Neither a borrower nor a lender be," he replied, shaking his head. No borrowing was apparently a store policy.

"Then you come with me while I steal it." I grabbed his arm, tucked the book under my arm, the one not near to the masquerading angel, and turned for the door.

He struggled, flailing at me with his arms, raining useless punches onto my arm and shoulders. I held on and kept walking, practically dragging him out of the store. He calmed down when we got out onto the sidewalk, turning this way and that and staring up at the sky with wide eyes.

"How long has it been since you left the shop?" I asked. I knew angels didn't need to eat or sleep, so if Gabriel was running the interior components, so to speak, he might have been in that shop for years.

He just looked at me, confusion written all over his face. "Tomorrow, and tomorrow, and tomorrow, creeps in its petty pace from day to day."

I took his arm and walked with him, heading back to my hotel and our eventual rendezvous with the witches and hopefully not futile rescue attempt. I had no idea what this Barathan was planning, but it's been my experience that whenever somebody wants to harvest the power of a bunch of dead souls, it's never good. Like that time a crazy angel wanted to blow up most of Atlanta to tear open the barriers between Heaven and Hell. Yeah, good times.

CHAPTER FOURTEEN

I got Gabe back to my hotel without much incident, just a slight panic attack on his part when he had to cross the street. I couldn't tell if it came from being trapped as a human for too long or being stuck in a bookstore with no human contact, but it certainly seemed like my amnesiac angel wasn't just prone to speaking in iambic pentameter, but was also a little agoraphobic.

I closed the door to my hotel room and threw the deadbolt, then sealed it with a binding spell again. I was pretty sure it couldn't stop Gabriel in all his Archangelic glory, but I was willing to bet it would give Crazy Gabe a few seconds' pause at least.

"Have a seat, Gabe," I said as I walked toward the small bathroom. "I gotta visit the euphemism real quick." I tossed the book on the bed and turned the corner. I had just enough time to get unzipped when I realized exactly what I'd done. I put everything away and spun around, returning to the bedroom just in time to see Gabriel standing there holding the book. And looking *pissed*.

"I bet you're wondering what you're doing here," I said with a sheepish grin. I didn't really know exactly where on the power scale Archangels landed, but I was willing to bet two things. One, I was about to find out. Two, that it was pretty high.

"I know why I'm here, mortal," Gabriel replied. "You have some stupid quest that you cannot fulfill yourself, and you are here to beseech me for my aid."

Not technically wrong, I thought. Still no need to be a dick about it. "That's partly right. Well, I guess it's completely right, I just have more than one thing I, we, the world, needs your help with."

"No."

"No, what?" I asked.

"No, I will not assist you in whatever idiotic endeavor you think is so important. I assure you, it is not. The world will still be here long after you have shuffled off your minuscule and ineffectual mortal coil, the cities will still thrive, civilizations will still be born and die, and the Father will still sit on the High Throne of Heaven."

"Yeah, that's exactly the problem," I said, folding my arms over my chest. This guy was an asshole, but I needed him to be *our* asshole, at least until we found God and put Him back on that throne.

"What is the problem?"

"God. He's AWOL."

"What? I do not understand your stupid human words."

"Do you understand 'dick'?" I asked, grabbing mine through my jeans. "Because you're being a dick. God is on vacation, missing in action, quit, evacuated the premises. He's not sitting on the High Throne of Goddamn Anywhere, and that's why I'm in this fucking hotel talking to a fucking prick of an angel!"

"The Father is...missing?" he asked, and a lot of the asshole seemed to run out of him with that realization. The golden light that had rolled off him in waves vanished, he seemed to shrink a little within himself until he was barely taller than me, and his wings folded back into his shoulders.

"I don't know if He's missing, or if He's just on vacation," I said. "But according to very good sources, He's not in Heaven and hasn't been for a very long time."

"Balls," he said, then sat down on the bed. "He meant it?" I don't think he was talking to me but decided it might be important anyway.

"What do you mean, He meant it?" I pulled a chair out from under the table and sat with my back pressed against the door. I usually won't do that, but everybody who wanted to kill me in Charleston was going to use magic, not bullets, so I didn't have to worry about anybody going all Wild Bill Hickok on me. I was a little concerned about Gabriel trying to bolt, so I thought by putting myself in front of the door, I'd at least slow him down a little if he decided to leave.

Gabriel opened his book and flipped through pages, running his finger down the page like he was looking for the right passage. He must have found it because his finger stopped moving and he looked up at me. "He told us if we didn't take care of the humans that He'd leave it all in our hands and we could see how we really enjoyed being in charge. I think He was pissed off at Azrael for something again."

I was having a little trouble wrapping my head around the concept of God Almighty getting pissed off at one of his angels, and I'm sure it showed on my face because Gabriel laughed.

"You humans," he said, slapping his knee. Yeah, really. He slapped his knee. I suppose it's worth mentioning that he was dressed this time. In basically normal clothes, if size extra-extra-tall. He wore black slacks, a white button-down shirt, and loafers. Basic banker wear, only without the tie. "You mortals are always so baffled whenever you find one of us behaving in what you consider to be 'human' ways. Haven't you ever considered that perhaps you are behaving like angels?"

I thought about it for a second, then shook my head. "Nope, never considered it. Of course, for the first *century* I was on this planet, I'd never encountered an angel!"

"That you know of," he corrected. I got the sinking feeling that correcting was something this well-read douche of an angel did a lot.

"I'll grant you that," I said. There were plenty of times that I'd encountered a supernatural or divine creature that masked its identity from me. Most notably one asshole demonspawn that hid himself under my nose and murdered a couple of people I cared about.

"Well, we have all the same failings that you have, except for the physical ones, of course. But we are subject to sloth, anger, petty jealousy—all the emotions you feel, we felt them first."

"Especially that jealousy part," I said with a wry look.

"Yes, Lucifer and his followers were jealous of the attention Father lavished upon you mortals. As were we all, if we're to be honest with ourselves. That didn't stop just because we pitched a few rabble-rousers into The Pits. Father never liked that and told us if we didn't start acting like the older brothers He wanted us to be, that He'd give up the throne and leave us to deal with your messes all on our own."

"So you're telling me that the past few thousand years of human history have all sucked because you pissed off Dad and He pulled the metaphysical car over?" Suddenly every bit of bitching I'd ever done about the universe feeling like a ship without anyone at the wheel seemed more real than ever. Definitely one of those days that I hate being right.

"I suppose that's right. I wasn't in Heaven when He left, obviously. But if He's gone, and He's been gone for a long time, then that's the only logical answer."

"Where were you? Why weren't you in Heaven? Isn't that kinda your job, to write down all the shit that happens?" My research had referred to Gabriel as the Herald of Heaven, the Word of God, so I assumed he was kinda like a scribe.

"Not exactly," he said. He gestured to the book. "This is the repository of all the knowledge in the world, yes. I am the Keeper of the Word, yes. But I don't write the book. The book writes the book."

"That sounds very Zen."

"I think it's more Tao than Zen, but it's an easy mistake to make." Now that he was in teacher mode and not intimidating angel mode, he was a lot less of a prick. I was starting to have hope that he'd help us save the priestess and kick the shit out of a necromancer.

Gabriel went on. "Everything that happens in God's Kingdom is recorded in the book. Like I said, I don't write it. I can, however, access all of it."

"*All* of it?" I asked.

"All of it," he confirmed. "All I have to do is think about an event, open the book, and every piece of information ever gathered on Earth, in Heaven, or even in Hell, will be right there at my fingertips."

"Seems like a good book."

"It is one of the most powerful magical items ever created, as are all the Implements. Simply being near the book has completely worn through the mind of the poor human body I created to mask myself. Now he remembers nothing, save Shakespeare. He keeps that to read to me at night."

"I don't understand how he reads to you. He is you."

"It's complicated," the angel said. "Our host forms exist both with and apart from our divine selves at the same time."

"Yep, sounds complicated," I agreed. "So now what? You're an angel again, at least as long as you hang onto that book, and you know we need to get all your brother angels back together and doing your angelic duty so we can find God, literally, and get Him back to work."

"Why?" he asked.

"What do you mean, why?"

"You don't strike me as the altruistic type. So why do you want us to do all this?"

He had me there. I thought the world was running along pretty well without very much divine intervention. But it wasn't about me. "I have a friend..."

"Surprising in and of itself," Gabriel interjected.

"Go fuck yourself. Oh wait, you can't. No dick. Never mind," I shot back. "As I was saying, I have a friend. Her name is Glory. She's more like my guardian angel than just a friend. She lost her wings helping me, and apparently only God can restore her wings."

"That is true; only Father can restore lost divinity. Wait, did you say Glory?"

"Yeah, apparently my guardian angel is a *Buffy* fan."

"*You're* the Reaper?" He looked like he was trying very hard not to laugh. I was getting really tired of that nickname.

"I swear, I didn't come up with it," I said. "What the fuck are you laughing at?"

"Nothing, I'm sorry, it's just...well, I thought you'd be bigger."

"Oh, come the fuck on!" I said. "We're gonna start quoting *Roadhouse* now? I'm fucking six-three!"

"Well, yes, but you're terribly thin. Not very intimidating at all, to be frank. Given your reputation, I honestly expected someone...well, a little more frightening."

"I don't have to be scary," I said. "I just have to get shit done."

"Well, I will grant you that was fairly intimidating. That line, that was quite good. Still...I guess I just expected the Reaper to be...more, somehow."

"I thought you'd been trapped in the body of a nutbar bookseller for eons. How have you even heard of me?"

"Humans," he sniffed. "Still thinking of time as a straight line. Even if it were, it doesn't matter. I have the book. I read it. Don't let this go to your head, but you were foretold. You have important work to do, Mr. Harker."

"More important than restoring God to the Throne of Heaven? Because that's the current project, and it's pretty important to me."

"Fair point," he conceded. "You do realize that it will take all of us to find Father, right?"

"Yeah, all seven Archangels combining their power to locate God. I guess it's like some kind of mystical GPS, or cell phone signal, or something."

"Well, that's essentially true. Except there aren't seven Archangels."

"Sure there are. I got all their names written down somewhere. Even did the research and found out that the one with the Transformer name is really Raguel, not Metatron."

"There are eight."

I pulled out my phone and called up my notes. "Michael, Gabriel, Raguel, Raphael, Uriel, Azrael, Sealtiel. Seven."

"There are eight."

"I just named all seven."

"There *were* eight."

"Angels don't die. Well, okay, they can, but it takes Michael's sword or something…you've gotta be fucking kidding me."

"Nope. He's number eight."

"He totally doesn't count."

"I don't think you get to make that call, Reaper."

"Don't call me that. How the fuck does he still count? Wasn't he fired?"

"Still counts."

"God*dammit!*"

"In a lot of places, that would be considered blasphemy. I'm not the judging type, so I'll let it slide."

"Fucking hell."

"Exactly."

"Lucifer is the eighth Archangel?"

"Well…at one time he was the first."

"If we're getting Glory's wings back, we have to make a deal with the devil?"

"Literally."

"Fuck me."

Then my phone rang, and my day went from shitty to *spectacularly* shitty.

CHAPTER FIFTEEN

"What?" I said into the phone.

"We need you, Harker." The voice on the other end of the phone was almost panicked, but it was still mostly recognizable as Arianne.

"What's going on? It's still full daylight. There's no way anything's going down this early—"

"You ever been wrong before?" The girl cut me off.

"Yeah, once or twice." It's the kind of thing that's bound to happen in a century of wandering the planet. I even made a few fashion misplays in the sixties, but everybody was on so many drugs nobody noticed.

"Well, add this one to the list because Barathan has Tara on the steps of the old Slave Market and is ranting about burying the whole city under the waves to wash away the blood of his ancestors. Now please get your ass down here with whatever magical grenades or rocket launchers or whatever else you've managed to dig up." She hung up before I could respond, and I was left staring at a dead phone.

I turned to Gabriel. "How do you feel about mass murder?" I asked.

"Typically not a fan although I was willing to make an exception for Gomorrah, and for the assholes who destroyed the Library at Alexandria."

"Just Gomorrah?"

"I never cared that much about Sodom. They were all cool, actually. The Gomorrans were rude, so I helped wipe them out. And don't get me started on my Library. I'm still upset about that."

I just shook my head. Sometimes my life is weird even to me, and I'm the one stuck in it. "We need to go stop a psycho witch from sinking Charleston into the sea, apparently. Come on."

"No can do," the angel replied, not moving. Not even making the beginning of an attempt at moving.

"What the fuck, dude?" I asked, already at the door with my Glock in my waistband. "Are you coming or not?"

"Not."

"Is there any reason for this, or do you just feel like being a dick?"

"I can't go out there in my true form. It would cause too much of a stir. People would see me and think that Revelation has begun. It's not time for that yet, so it would not be advisable for me to leave in my current, glorious state."

"So change back into less-awesome Gabe and come on. This asshole will kill this woman, and probably a lot of other people, if we don't stop him."

"I refuse to return to that addlepated form. I have spent many years quoting that Elizabethan hack *ad nauseum*, and I will not do it any longer."

"So you're not going to de-angel?"

"I will remain in my true form, that is correct."

"And you won't go out in public like that?"

"Also correct."

"How do you plan to go to Charlotte with me?"

"I plan to travel mystically. I will meet you there."

I forgot about that whole popping from place to place thing. I always thought Glory went to Heaven, flew over to the right spot on Earth, and came back, but teleportation (or mystical travel) made more sense. "So you're not going to help me?"

"Unless you can move the confrontation to later in the evening, or this room—no."

I was pretty sure I couldn't just raincheck the guy trying to shove the entire city off into the ocean, so I just walked to the door. "Just for the record," I said, stepping out into the hall, "you're a dick." Slamming the door behind me didn't really get me anywhere in the argument, but it sure made me feel better.

I didn't bother with the car. I just sprinted down the street to the Old Slave Market. Sure enough, there was a skinny black dude holding balls of crimson energy standing in front of the building, under the big arch proclaiming it the "Old Slave Mart Museum." He'd invoked a circle in the flashiest way possible —by surrounding himself with a four-foot-high ring of fire. It had the combined effect of keeping people back and, honestly, making him look totally badass. I had to give the guy credit, he knew how to stage a photo op.

Behind him, hanging from the arch with magical bonds, was Tara, Arianne's priestess. She looked mostly unharmed, but royally pissed. I couldn't blame her, honestly. She was hanging by her wrists from magic chains in front of the whole city, looking helpless in the worst place of all —public.

Arianna stood across the cobbled street surrounded by other witches, an island of stillness against the raging tide of humanity flooding up Chalmers Street toward Church Street, trying to put the flaming nutjob behind them as quickly as possible. I skipped the normal pleasantries, just walked right up to the edge of Barathan's flaming circle.

"I think the Iron Throne is missing one asshole. They'd like you to come home as soon as possible," I said.

"I will sink this entire city beneath the waves for the crimes it has committed against my people!" the crazy wizard yelled.

It was a little hard to hear him over the crackling flames in front of me, so I waved a hand and shouted "*QUELL!*" I made a bet that his fire was really just an outer ring of flash, instead of being part of his actual circle, and it paid off as a couple hundred gallons of water condensed out of the air around us and doused the flames.

I stood in the giant cloud of steam with my arms crossed. When I could see Barathan again, I gave him a little smile. "That's better. Now, what were you saying?"

His eyes bugged out, and his face contorted into a grimace as he tried to raise his fire again and ran into my own magic stopping him. "This place is just a monument to hate and racism. This whole city was built on the backs of my people. Now their descendants will pay for what they did!" Spit flew from his mouth as he shouted.

"You do know that none of these people enslaved you, right? Oh, and by the way, you were never a slave. You're a fucking hipster millennial just looking to make a name for yourself. Get a job, fuckwit."

He turned the peculiar shade of purple I've usually associated with eggplants and one particular breed of lycanthropic Fae that I met in Lichtenstein. I've never seen it in a human before.

"Just because I wasn't a slave doesn't mean I don't know what it feels like to be hated. They killed my brother, you bastard!"

Shit. He wasn't just a run-of-the-mill magical asshole looking to get famous. He was a crusading magical asshole with what he thought was a good reason to sink Charleston under the Atlantic. If he killed Tara inside his circle, he might have enough power to do it.

Letting out a primal yell, he dropped his shield just long enough to throw a fireball at my head. He was really good at that throwing fire trick. Good thing I was prepared for him this time.

I murmured *"suffocate"* under my breath and held up my hands, palms out, at the onrushing ball of fiery doom. My magic flew right at the streaking missile and hit it square. All the air vanished from around the sphere, and the flame winked out, just like snuffing a candle. I felt a warm tingle as the magic passed through me, but there was no fire left, not even smoke.

"Nice try, asshole," I said, my mind racing. *Brother? Who killed his brother?* I looked around to Arianne for a little assist, but she and her coven had turned their attention to the fleeing crowd, trying to keep people from trampling each other and healing the folks who fell or twisted ankles.

"I'm sure your brother would have been proud of you, murdering all these people and destroying the city in his honor. That's really the kind of thing that makes somebody feel the loving memory, you know."

"Fuck you!" he shouted back. Obviously, my witty repartee was going to be lost on this one. "You don't know shit about Derek. He wasn't doing nothing, and they shot him down like a dog in the street!"

Something in the back of my head started to tickle, like I'd heard this story before. There was a kid, something about a traffic stop, and the cop thought he had a gun, and it turned out to be a wallet. The cop wasn't prosecuted, and there were a lot of people pissed off about it. Including one brother with a fair chunk of magical talent.

"You're Derek's brother?" Arianne's voice came from my left elbow.

"You probably shouldn't be here right now," I said.

"Don't act like you knew Derek, bitch!" Barathan screamed. "I will burn you to ash right where you stand!"

"I did know Derek. We had Spanish together a couple years in school. He went to West Ashley, right? Graduated three years ago? He wrote in my yearbook."

"Yeah, we both went there. I graduate next year."

Next year? This fucking kid's sixteen? Oh sweet bleeding Jesus. If he has power like this at sixteen, by the time he hits twenty, he really will be able to sink a city. This kid couldn't go to jail; no jail would be able to hold him. I had to think fast, but first I had to make sure he didn't cut Tara's throat and make Chucktown go the way of Atlantis.

"If you ever want to hold a diploma, you need to cut this shit out, Junior," I said. Maybe appealing to his sense of the future would get me somewhere.

"Fuck you, asshole!"

So much for appealing to his future self. "So what's the play, kid? You gonna cut her throat and harness her energy to open the fault line under Charleston Harbor? Crack that bad boy wide open and flatten South Carolina all the way up to Charlotte? Maybe you'd rather summon up a tsunami and just wipe out the whole coastline? That oughta run out of steam somewhere around Wilmington if you're lucky. Shouldn't kill more than a couple million people. That sounds fair, right?"

He started to look a little unsure, so I pressed my advantage. "Oh, you thought you could just, what? Dig a moat around Charleston and push this place into the ocean? You thought that wouldn't wreck anything else? Maybe you shouldn't bother trying to get a diploma. You're obviously too stupid to get out of high school. I'm surprised you've made it this long remembering to look both ways before you cross the street. I guess your big brother really did get a raw deal. It's bad enough he got killed by a cop, but he had to take care of your dumb ass his whole life, too? That really sucks."

The teenaged mage did exactly what teenagers do when you poke them enough—he lost his shit. In this case "his shit" didn't just consist of his temper or his control on his profanity, which if we're being fair, he never really had under wraps in the first place. He also lost his sense of his surroundings, so when he took his first step forward to deliver the ass-kicking I certainly deserved, and just as certainly was *not* going to receive, he broke the plane of his circle, and all his wards dropped with a *POP*.

Normally when I bait someone into dropping their shields, I step forward and knock them out. Sometimes I shoot them in the face. Sometimes I trap them in a circle of my own or send them back to Hell. I didn't do any of that to Barathan. As a matter of fact, I didn't do anything. I didn't have to.

The second his circle fell, all the other bindings and protections he'd woven into it disappeared as well. That left him standing three feet in front of a very pissed-off High Priestess, who dropped to her feet and stepped forward, conjuring a huge green glowing war hammer as she did. She laid that hammer upside Barathan's head, and he dropped to the ground like a marionette with its string cut.

I looked over at Arianne who gave me a thumbs-up. "Great work, Harker!"

"Yeah, great. Except this guy mopped the floor with us just a couple hours ago. Do you ever get the feeling that something was just a little too easy?"

I've really got to learn to keep my mouth shut.

CHAPTER SIXTEEN

1⁶

Barathan was out, but he had one last trick up his sleeve. Just like terrorists rig up secondary charges to go after the first responders to a bomb attack, he had a bomb of his own lurking in the shadows. Well, not really the shadows so much as the slave market. When his circle fell, a second wall of magical fire that had been obscured by his flaming barrier also fell. This magical barricade wasn't holding us out; it was filling the gate to the old slaver's auction house holding something *in*.

Stepping out of the darkened market into the sunlight was one of the biggest damn demons I'd ever seen. It was huge and walked on four legs, then stood up in the middle with two arms and even more badness. It looked like a cross between a lobster, one of H.R. Geiger's Aliens, and a yellow jacket. Pincers the length of my legs protruded from its midsection, and a triple row of teeth populated its mouth. It had a forked tongue and two tails, one with a club-like growth at the end, and the other one ending in a nasty-looking spike dripping green ichor to sizzle on the brick pavers.

"That's not good," I said with my typical talent for understatement.

"Nope," Arianne agreed, walking backward to get away from the thing and keep an eye on it at the same time.

"Oh yeah, that's real bad," Tara said from her spot directly in front of the monster. It swept its left pincer at her, and she managed to duck, but it right arm came across and punched her in the face, splitting her nose and laying her out across the sidewalk.

"Shit," I said, drawing my Glock. I fired eight shots in about six seconds, most of them finding a home in the demon's torso and face, but to no effect. The beastie looked over at me, smiled down from its ten-foot height, and flicked out its forked tongue to lick its lips.

"I picked a bad day to leave my guardian angel at home," I said, dropping to one knee and invoking a quick circle. The magic sprang into existence just fast enough to deflect the two pincers that were coming for me. They dug into the concrete on either side of me, making divots three inches deep and eight inches long in the sidewalk. I was protected, until my magic couldn't hold any more, but I was now stuck, unable to move, unable to cast offensive spells, unable to do anything to stop the giant lobster demon from picking Tara up in one huge claw and lifting her over its head.

The demon threw its head back and unhinged its jaw like a snake. It dangled Tara high in the air by one foot and made to swallow her whole. I dropped my circle and poured every bit of energy I could draw upon into a stream of brilliant blue energy aimed right at the demon's throat. It staggered and dropped the unconscious priestess. She hit the ground with a sickening *crack*, and I wondered briefly if I had done any saving at all, or if I'd just found my Gwen Stacy moment.

I poured power into the demon for a solid minute, drawing more energy from the city around me and adding it to the blast. It wavered, wobbled, and smoked a little, but it never fell. My power slowed from a torrent to a trickle, then all my juice flickered out, and I dropped to my knees in the street.

"Now you die, human," the demon bellowed, rising up on its back two legs to strike a killing blow.

"Not today, motherfucker," I said under my breath, and leapt up like an expanding spring. I pulled my Kershaw knife from my pocket as I vaulted the creature's head and flicked the razor-sharp blade open one-handed. I hooked my left hand in the demon's nostril and pulled myself down to drape over its head. I jabbed my pocketknife into its three-inch eyeball and grinned as it screamed in rage and pain.

It started to writhe, probably trying to throw me off at the same time, but I wrapped my legs around its thick serpentine neck and held on like a champion bull rider. It thrashed and convulsed, but I held on tight and kept jamming that little pocketknife farther and farther into its eyeball. I dug in until I felt resistance, then gave a mighty shove. I felt something crunch beneath the tip of the blade, and my hand sunk in its eyeball up to the elbow.

The demon made one last giant spasm, then went still, topping over like someone had just pulled the plug on it. Which, in a way, I guess I had. I twisted my hand around inside the demon's cranial cavity a couple times for good measure, then pulled my arm out. My fist was covered in greenish-yellow ichor and black demon blood with a sliver of brain stuck between my fingers.

Arianna walked up beside me and looked at my arm. "That might be the most disgusting thing I've ever seen."

"I wish I could say the same," I replied.

"Does it at least make the Top Three?"

"Top Ten for sure. Maybe Top Five if that smell gets any worse...yep, definitely Top Five." The demon's body was rapidly turning to a putrid yellow ooze as its soul returned to Hell and its corporeal form lost consistency. My knife wasn't any kind of blessed object, and I certainly am nowhere near holy enough to destroy a demon without one, so it wasn't dead, just banished.

"Is Tara okay?" I asked. I almost didn't want to know the answer, because I was afraid I knew already.

Arianne surprised me, not for the first time. "She will be. Marcus got to her pretty fast. Is that thing..."

"Gone," I said. "As long as nobody calls it back, it won't bother Charleston again."

"Speaking of people calling up demons..." She jerked her head over to where Barathan lay unconscious and bound across the street.

"I could shoot him," I said. She looked horrified, so I quickly went on. "I'm kidding. I swear. I know a guy. Well, it's actually his girlfriend who will be useful here. She works for a government agency that doesn't exist, if you get what I mean."

"I get it."

"Well, they have facilities where they can handle people like Barathan without them posing any more danger to society."

"Seems kinda shitty, doesn't it? I mean, all he wanted was justice for his brother."

"Don't confuse justice with revenge, Ari," I said. "I should know." Images flashed through my memory, over two hundred faces of men I slaughtered across Europe after the Nazis killed my Anna. They were bad people, they deserved punishment, but not all of them deserved to die, and no one deserved to die the way I killed the men. Except demons. Fuck demons. Kill them however you want.

I looked around at the dissolving demon, the police cars surrounding the block, the unconscious necromancer, and my slime-coated right arm, and sighed. "I think this was my last clean shirt."

"Don't you have an angel to find or something?" Arianne asked.

Oh shit, Gabriel! I turned and started sprinting up the street, hoping to get back to the hotel before he decided to smite someone. Or worse, before he put the book down and Gabe came back out to play.

EPILOGUE

Gabriel was sitting on the bed when I got back to the hotel. The book of Gabe, as I was calling it in my head, leaned against his side, but he was completely absorbed with his task. For my part, I was completely baffled by the scene in front of me. Instead of meditating, or doing kata, or basically doing anything I would expect from a divine being, he had my iPad in his hands and was tapping on the screen at lightning speed.

"You know how to use an iPad?" I asked.

"I do now. Your friend Dennis was very helpful. This internet you mortals have created, it is...quite remarkable. There are things on there that I never even dreamed possible. And the games! Astounding! This one, with the zombies eating the plants...the lawnmowers...the little catapult zombies! I love this game!" He grinned at me like an idiotic eight-year-old proud of finally learning to tie his own shoes.

"As your buddy Gabe would say, there are stranger things on heaven and earth. You ready to go?"

"Go where?"

"Charlotte. I need to introduce you to Michael, again, and maybe you can help him find himself, so to speak."

"No." His attention was fixed firmly on the screen, and he tapped furiously. If Dennis wasn't already dead, I'd kill him for teaching this angelic savant how to play *Plants vs. Zombies*.

"What do you mean, no?"

"I mean I'm not going. I don't wish to accompany you, I do not wish to

870

participate in your quest for Father, and I certainly don't wish to see Michael again, amnesia or no. My brother is, as you mortals put it, a dick."

"I don't doubt it," I said. "But that doesn't matter. I need you to go to North Carolina with me, get Michael back in his right mind, and then help restore Glory's wings."

"No. Now be silent, human. I am trying to beat this final level, and I am down to only two lawnmowers." I assumed that was bad. I never got into video games, except for *Neverwinter Nights*. Most of the fighting games feel too much like your average Tuesday for me, and first-person shooters are way too close to home. Gabriel bent over, pouring all his attention onto the screen, and tapping with lightning speed. I hoped briefly that he wouldn't break the screen, then he sat upright and pumped his fists.

"Yes! Got you, zom-boss! Is this where we high-five?" He turned to me, one hand held up. I slapped palms with him, then leaned in for a bro-hug. But instead of pounding his back as prescribed in the Official Manual of Bro-Hugs, I reached down and picked up the tome leaning against his hip.

As soon as the book broke contact with Gabriel, there was a huge flash of light and a small *pop*. I almost fell over as the big-ass buff angel turned into the skinny little bookseller with tufts of brown hair sticking out from under a porkpie hat and a Mr. Magoo look on his face. The robe he had worn as Gabriel transformed this time into an ill-fitting brown suit with a white dress shirt, round glasses, and a brown vest with a pocket watch chain stretched across his little pot belly. He looked like a cross between the dotty uncle in a British period flick and an absent-minded college literature professor.

"Who goes there?" he asked, looking around with obviously no clue where in the world he was.

"Hi, Gabe," I said. "It's almost time to go on our trip. Are you ready to go see your old friend Michael?"

His face lit up in a huge oblivious grin, and he raised his right hand, finger to the sky. "Lay on, Macduff! And damned be he that first cries 'Hold, enough!'"

PART III
ANGEL DANCE

CHAPTER ONE

T he last time I walked these streets, the water reached up my chest, black fingers of cold digging into my bones, threatening to drag me down into the depths of despair and death. But Lady Death has long refused to take me in her arms, and those September days and nights were different. While so many fell beneath the roiling waters of the Gulf when the levees failed, I remained, like New Orleans herself, waterlogged and battered, but still whole at the core of me.

I waded through years of pain and memories in those days just after Katrina battered the Crescent City. I was able to save some, to aid some, and to lay some to rest when they were thought lost. It was ugly work, but I am particularly well suited for such as that, being a hideous specimen myself. I slogged through the despair of a city, her waters pooling in my boots as I strode through neighborhood and business district searching for survivors.

Even in those darkest hours, I felt the life of the city thrumming under my feet, the lifeblood of New Orleans pulsing in the slow, torpid *thump-thump* of the nearly drowned. No matter how much water God poured down her throat in the torturous hours of the hurricane's onslaught, nothing could choke the spirit of the Louisiana gem.

Now I was back in New Orleans, more than a decade later, not searching for signs of life, but a needle in a haystack. I was looking for a horn in the brassy city of jazz, one instrument in a mecca for musicians, and the tune I needed it to play was more important than any heard since man first set foot outside the Garden of Eden.

There was no water filling the streets of the French Quarter this night, only jazz and the raucous sounds of tourists shouting up to or down from the balconies lining Bourbon Street. My search would begin in earnest with the dawn, but tonight I was at leisure, such as it was for me. Tonight, I walked the shadows, not a hunter, but merely an observer. I have done that often through my decades on this Earth, simply lurking in alleys and hidden corners of the cities, watching humanity rush from start to finish before me.

I am separate from the madding crowd. I do not share their everyday concerns of living and dying. I am not completely certain you can call what I do the first, and despite many attempts, I seem to be incapable of the second. I can, however, watch. So tonight, from a table in the corner of a patio in a less-traveled part of the Quarter, I settled in to watch.

I watched a quintet of bachelorettes weave along a sidewalk, bumping into an emaciated teen who leaned, smoking, against a lamppost. I watched the gangly boy slide the drunkest girl's wallet from her purse and into the pocket of his unseasonable hoodie, then spin around the light pole and stride off down a side street. I watched him slide the cash into his pocket and toss the wallet into a nearby garbage can.

I briefly considered retrieving the wallet and returning it to the woman. It would have been the chivalrous thing to do. Then I looked down at the line of stitches along my right wrist, the jagged suture line where my "father" attached the hand of a pickpocket to the arm of an axe murderer so many years ago, and I remembered how poorly it has gone for me when I have tried to interact with mundane women in the past.

I felt no need to battle through an army of pitchfork- and torch-wielding peasants to finish my task in New Orleans, so I left the wallet where it lay. Perhaps the young woman would consider the inconvenience a life lesson and pay more attention to her surroundings. Perhaps not. Either way, the hooded Artful Dodger was out of my view, and the parade of drunken mortals careening from Hurricanes to Hand Grenades to other frozen concoctions with festively destructive names continued on in its garish parade of beads, breasts, and brightly colored masks.

I motioned a waiter to my table to refresh my pitcher of water, passing him another folded twenty-dollar bill. I ordered no food and only water to drink, but as long as I paid a reasonable rent on the table, I sat as long as I liked. In exchange for being very little trouble and a very consistent tipper, the waiter kept the tables near me free of children or loud parties and left me largely to my own devices.

I watched the sea of human randomness ebb and flow until nearly midnight, then stood. I nodded to the waiter and stepped over the low wrought-iron fence surrounding the patio. My size is often an annoyance, but I will admit that there is a certain directness in being able to just walk over three-foot barriers.

I walked the Quarter, keeping to the side streets and alleys, feeling the pulse of humanity without ever truly immersing myself in it. The heat and the crowd contributed to a miasma about the area, a foggy stink of beer, sweat, and lust that permeated every corner. I stepped in front of another teen before he could slip his hand in a businessman's pocket. I tapped a thug on the shoulder and asked him for directions just as he reached for a knife to cut a purse strap. I stepped into the mouth of an alley at the right moment to startle a would-be mugger. These petty crimes I could deter, and did, through my very size and presence.

It was not enough. It was not fulfilling. I needed more. The crush of so many people, so many desires, so much sound was an unbearable pressure upon me. Perhaps leaving the patio was a mistake. This close to so much that is so overwhelmingly alive, I desperately needed to feel a part of that in myself. I needed release. Violent release.

I found it. I found it in the form of two men too greedy or confident or stupid to evaluate their situation effectively. I found it in a woman too brave or too rushed to stick to the brightly lit streets when walking back to her car, parked just one block too far from the safe spaces of the Crescent City. I found it in her muffled scream as the men converged on her just as she reached her car and thought she was safe.

I stepped into the pool of orange light cast by the streetlamp above my head. The smaller man had a curved knife in his hand, his index finger threaded through a hole in the hilt. A karambit, it was called. He held it correctly, the blade protruding from the bottom of his clenched fist, pressed up against the woman's throat. She was tall, taller than her attacker, with a lovely head of curly brown hair. He was a thickly built man, bald, with tattoos crawling up his neck from the edge of his leather jacket.

His companion hung back, watching the show and laughing. He was big, almost my height, and fat. I expected him to be slow and probably heavily armed. The big ones aren't always stupid, and when they aren't, they can be dangerous. But he was probably stupid. Most of the petty criminals are.

"You should let her go," I said from my place in the light. I wore a hoodie myself because my appearance draws unwanted attention in brightly lit places, but I took the hood down now. I wanted the attention my scarred face would bring, and the type of attention it brings was exactly the type I wanted.

"You should go fuck yourself," the big man said, turning toward me and putting a hand under his jacket. Armed. As I suspected. That added a new dimension to the encounter, but it didn't present as much of a complication for me as it would for many people.

"Not only is that not possible, it is also not polite to suggest," I replied. "You should still let her go."

"Tony, take care of this sumbitch," the small one said. "He's making my pecker wilt with his ugly-ass face." He reached up at the woman to paw her breasts, and she slapped him. He laughed and pressed the knife closer to her neck. "That's a bad idea, honey. You be nice and maybe I won't let Tony have a turn when I'm done."

"Tony most certainly will not be having a turn," I said. "And you are already done." I charged Tony, closing the distance between us in a few long strides. He got his pistol out but did not have time to fire before I bull-rushed him to the ground. I didn't slow, just planted a shoulder in his sternum and lifted my body on impact. He flew back several feet and sprawled flat on his back, where I stepped on him en route to his partner.

The smaller man half turned to me but kept the knife pressed to the girl's throat. "Take another step and I'll cut her throat," he said with a sneer. "You think you're so tough? Let's see what you do against me."

He spun in a tight circle, his foot flashing up to catch me on the side of the jaw. I let the kick turn me around, dropping to one knee as I did. I came around, and up, with my right hand extended. I picked the bald man up by the throat and slammed him down on the hood of a nearby parked car. A car alarm blared into the night, and lights flashed on the BMW. I had apparently picked a good car to abuse.

My adversary stabbed me in the shoulder with his karambit, and I let go of his throat. Tony was recovered enough to come at me then, and I felt a hammer blow to my right kidney. I lashed out with an elbow strike that pulped his nose, then reached over my right shoulder and flipped Tony onto his partner, setting off a fresh cacophony of noise as the impact shattered the windshield of the car and set off the airbag. The air filled with the stench of airbag chemicals and the groaning of two battered thugs.

I looked at the men, neither of whom looked in any hurry to re-enter the fray, then I looked at my left shoulder, a small curved knife protruding from it. I pulled it free with a hiss of pain and stabbed it into the small man's upper thigh.

"You lost this. I wanted to return it," I said, twisting the knife in his leg. He howled in pain, and Tony tried to roll off him. I let the big man drop to the sidewalk, then hit him in the side of the head with a sharp knee strike. His head bounced into the fender of the car, and he collapsed to the ground. The little man was moaning and rolling around the hood of the car clutching his leg. I picked him up by his belt and bounced him on the hood a few times until he passed out. The car alarm gave one last plaintive squawk as I battered it into submission with the body of the mugger, and blissful quiet once again settled over the street, only broken by the woman's sobbing and the distant sounds of Bourbon Street revelry.

"Are you hurt?" I asked the woman.

"N-no," she said.

"Is that your car?" I pointed to one just past the now-defunct BMW that I had defiled with the bodies of Tony and his little friend.

"Y-yeah."

"Do you have someone at home to help take care of you? You shouldn't be alone tonight."

"My sister is there." Good. She was coherent, mostly, and seemed capable enough to drive home.

"Do you want to call the police? These men tried to rape, and possibly kill, you."

"N-no. I just want to go home."

"Then you should do that. Can you get there safely by yourself?" She looked up at me, and the fear in her eyes told me that even if the answer wasn't a resounding "yes," that I would not be the person she asked to escort her to safety.

I didn't mind. She wasn't chasing me from the village with torches and pitchforks, so that was at least a minor improvement. She got in her car and drove off. I leaned down to Tony's friend, nominally the brains of the operation, such as they were, and said to him, "I think you should consider another line of work. This one seems too dangerous for you."

Then I pulled up my hoodie and walked off into the night, the beast within satiated once again. For now.

CHAPTER TWO

Morning in the Quarter is a strange time, stranger even than the late nights. I walked the damp sidewalks, bright sun hammering my eyes through the dark glasses I wore, dodging the shopkeepers with their brilliant green garden hoses, water snakes cascading cleanliness across the face of the city, sending the sad remnants of last night's revelry pouring down the storm drains in a river of spilled beer, puke, and broken strands of beads cast aside like virtue after last call. My tattered work boots left giant wet footprints on the brick steps in front of the Sisters of the Sword Convent, an innocuous unmarked building wedged back in an alley behind a strip club and a high-end steakhouse, the dichotomy of a white linen restaurant sharing airspace with a club where the women wore less than a napkin not lost on me.

I knocked on the thick oaken door, the surface worn smooth with the touch of centuries' worth of supplicants. I waited, then checked my watch for the time. It was early enough for the sisters to still be at lauds, so I waited. Thirty minutes later, I knocked again, and moments later, a novice in jeans and a gray wimple answered the door.

"May I...help you?" She paused as she looked up, then up again, to see my face was normal. She was a slight woman, short in stature by normal standards, and I must have seemed a true giant in her eyes.

I spoke softly, as not to terrify the poor girl. My voice is a low growl at best, a grating roar at its worst, and I had no desire to be responsible for the scarring of one of the novitiate. "I am looking for Sister Evangeline. She is an old friend."

A shadow passed across the child's face, as though she were unsure how to proceed. "Um...Sister Evangeline isn't...here right now. She's..."

"She is hunting?" I asked. Sister Evangeline was a Templar, a historical militant arm of the Church. Modern-day Templars are tasked with defending a specific part of the world from supernatural threats. They are often referred to as Monster Hunters. Evangeline was the Hunter for the Gulf Coast, including New Orleans.

The novice relaxed considerably when she understood that I already knew what Evangeline was and that she would not betray her confidence by speaking freely with me. "Yes, sir. She is hunting. There is a...creature of some sort in the swamps up by Lake Maurepas. She been gone a couple days, oughta be back before long. It never takes Sister Evangeline very long to bag her...um, critter." The young nun blushed a little as she realized she may have said more than was entirely proper to a stranger. I smiled as gently as my mangled features allowed in an attempt to put her somewhat at ease.

"Thank you. I will return in a few days' time. If she returns before I come back, please ask her to call Adam." I handed her a card with my name on it, Adam Franks, and a number.

"I will, Mr. Franks. Have a nice day," she said, stepping back into the convent and closing the door.

I turned from the door and mused for a moment on the subject of names. Adam Franks is not my name, no more than Lucas Card is Vlad's, although it is what we are known by in these times. I have been called many things in my time walking this Earth, but I have had few names. Adam is what my father called me, but that was just another example of his overweening hubris. He did not think himself God, but he certainly aspired to godhood. That is what drove him to create life from a pile of lifeless parts, or to reinstall life into formerly lively parts, to be more precise.

When I was awakened, for I was never born in any true sense of the word, my father's first words were not, as popular culture has decreed, "It's alive!" No, the first utterance to pass from his lips to my ears was "I've done it." I was alive, or aware, for two days before he ever addressed me as "Adam." I have worn many names through the intervening decades, but only two words have ever truly felt like they were my name: "Adam" and "monster."

I stepped back out of the alley into the sun and put up the hood of my sweatshirt. More tourists filled the sidewalks now, and I chose to avoid the stares of the adults and the innocently horrible pointing and screeching of the children.

Without Evangeline and her knowledge of the city's seedy underbelly, I had to take a moment to reconsider my plan of investigation. Somewhere in New Orleans was a horn, a needle in the gilded jazz-infused haystack. This horn was not simply a musical instrument; it was an Implement of the Archangel Sealtiel, the herald of the End Times. I needed to find this horn, and without any magical ability of my own, I needed a guide.

I pulled out my phone and summoned an Uber. A round freckled face appeared on the screen. "You know I can do that for you, and rig it so you don't have to pay, right?"

"I know that, Dennis, but I would prefer to save your interventions for when I actually need them. I am perfectly capable of paying for a taxi service."

"Sure, whatever, bro. Just saying, if you need anything done on the internet, I'm your guy. It's not like those fingers of yours are the nimblest things in the world. Your ride's almost here. Later." Dennis' face vanished into the maze of electrons connecting almost every digital device in the world. When his body was murdered close to a decade ago, Dennis' soul had been cast into a cell phone. The phone had an internet connection, and in a real-life version of *Tron*, Dennis became truly a ghost in the machine, and an invaluable, if temperamental, asset to me and the other members of the Shadow Council.

A black SUV pulled up to the corner, the familiar black and white sticker on the windshield marking it as a car for hire. I opened the door and leaned in. "Are you Matt?"

The man behind the wheel looked me up and down and said, "I am. Are you Adam?"

I slid into the front seat, pushing it as far back as possible. My knees still pressed up against the dash, a situation I was well-acquainted with. "I am Adam. Do you know the address?"

"Not really, but the GPS will get us there," the man said. "It looks like it ain't the best neighborhood. You sure that's where you want to go?"

"An old friend lives there. It was a very different place when he first moved in." I didn't mention that my friend first moved to the neighborhood in question over fifty years ago or that he cared little about the condition of the sidewalk or the dilapidated state of his eaves and shutters. My friend was a blind sorcerer and saw the world only through his Second Sight. He was also one of the most dangerous practitioners of battle magic I had ever known, so I was not at all concerned about a few drug dealers and gangbangers on his block.

The driver was correct, though. The neighborhood had declined precipitously since my last visit. There were several cars on blocks stationed along the street, and a collection of young men sat on the stoop and porch of the house across the street from Oliver's home. They watched my approach with undisguised mistrust, and I saw one step inside the house and return with a sawed-off shotgun as we pulled up to the curb.

"Look, man, no offense, but I don't think I'm gonna wait around for you. If you wanna bail and have your friend meet you someplace else, we can cruise outta here right now, but if you need a pickup out of here later, I ain't taking the fare," the driver said, his head on a swivel as he tried to talk to me and watch the men on the porch at the same time.

I opened the door and got out. "That is fine," I said. "I will make other arrangements for a ride. Thank you." I closed the door and pulled out my phone.

"Dennis?" I spoke into the phone.

"Yeah, Adam?" Dennis appeared again on the screen, this time represented by his favorite avatar, a unicorn with a rainbow mane and blue eyes. I did not pretend to understand this appearance, but he held that it annoyed our friend Quincy Harker, and that was enough for him.

"Please see to it that the driver has a generous tip added to his fare."

"Will do. I've also rerouted three NOPD patrol cars to be within two blocks of the address you're in front of. The guys across the street? They're Gulf Coast Bloods, an offshoot of the LA street gang. They run the coke and weed trade for five of six blocks around you."

"I need neither cocaine nor marijuana, nor do I care about the dealing thereof, so I have no reason to interact with those young men," I replied. I turned and walked up the steps to Oliver's door.

I knocked, and after a few moments, I heard the click of several locks on the other side of the door. A young woman's head appeared in the crack between the door and the jamb, looking up at me. Everyone looks up at me. Sometimes I am gripped by an almost irresistible urge to get down on my knees before I knock on a door, just to see someone look down at my eyes for once. I never have. Perhaps someday, when I am feeling particularly frolicsome.

"Can I help you?" the woman asked.

"Hello," I said. "May I speak with Oliver?"

Her guarded expression shifted in an instant to defensive, with a hint of anger. "No, you may not. But you know that, don't you?"

I was taken aback, literally, as I took an involuntary step back. "I'm sorry, miss. I don't know what you mean? Is Oliver not home? Does he no longer live here? It has been some time since we last spoke, but I heard nothing of him moving." I kept my voice soft, both to keep our words guarded and to not sound monstrous.

She cocked her head to the side and gave me an appraising look. I took the moment to examine her as well. She was young, in her twenties, but with the eyes and set of her jaw that said she had seen many things in her years. She was a solidly built woman, with broad shoulders and thick wrists. She looked like someone who knew what work looked like and was unafraid of it.

"I'm sorry," she said after she looked me up and down again. "My grandfather passed away two weeks ago. If you hadn't talked to him in a while, I guess you might not have known. I'm Eliza, his granddaughter. Is there something I can do for you?"

I sighed and stepped back from the door. "No. Thank you for the kind offer. I am very sorry for your loss. Your grandfather was fine man, a man of strong principles and fierce love for his family."

"Yes, he was," she agreed. "How did you know him? He didn't have many... friends outside the neighborhood."

I smiled at her very polite way of saying that Oliver didn't have many white friends. "That's true, I suppose. When you grow up in the time he did, you are unlikely to be very trusting of...people outside your neighborhood." I took down my hoodie, showing her the full landscape of my scarred face. "We both had some experience with people judging us on the basis of our appearance. That made for a common bond that grew into a strong...mutual respect, if not friendship."

"Are you...Adam?" the young woman asked, her eyes wide.

"I am."

"You should come in. Papa O told me about you. He left something for you if you ever came back again." She pushed the screen door open and stepped back to let me into the house. I went inside, curious to see what Oliver thought was worth my having after his passing.

I followed the young woman into the house through a maze of boxes labeled "Goodwill" and "Keepsakes" and "Terry." Black plastic garbage bags sat piled in the corners of the living room, and I moved a cardboard box full of books onto the floor and sat in the chair she indicated.

"I'm sorry for the mess. You knew Pop, he was a bit of a hoarder," she said, sitting on a couch opposite me. There was just enough room on the couch for her wide frame between a pile of papers and another in a seemingly endless cavalcade of brown boxes.

"He was that," I said with a smile. I didn't know that. I didn't know much about Oliver, really. I have made very few attachments as I have meandered through my long life, avoiding too many connections with people destined to die long before me. I had never been inside Oliver's home before today, always meeting with him either on his porch, where he loved to sit, or at the library to research some threat or another.

"He didn't speak of you often, but he seemed to like you. He said you were a good man, and that was high praise from Pop."

"Thank you," I said. "I had a great deal of respect for him as well. He was a stalwart companion and possessed a very sharp mind."

"I guess you want to see what he left for you," Eliza said, standing. She walked to the mantle and took down a wooden box. She handed it to me, and I turned it over in my hands. I had not seen the box before, nor its contents. I opened it to reveal a silver cross on a long chain, with an unmistakable purple heart-shaped medal affixed to it.

"This is his Purple Heart," I said, giving the girl a questioning look. "He once told me he was wounded in Korea, and that injury probably saved his life."

"That's what he told us, too. He got shot in the leg, ruined his knee, and came home after just a month over there. He never walked right again, but three weeks after he got home, most of his unit was wiped out by mortar fire. He said that's when he learned to never assume anything is all bad or all good, that you have to—"

"Look below the surface of a thing," I finished with her. We shared a smile, and I remembered sitting in rocking chairs on that porch watching the sun set and drinking cheap domestic beer after a bad fight with a nest of vampires, and Oliver telling me that very thing, only about myself.

I stared down at the medal, wondering how often Oliver thought of our adventures together. Eliza cleared her throat, and I lifted my head. She had an expectant look on her face, and I stood. "I will have to be going. I am very sorry for your loss. Thank you for keeping this for me. I appreciate it very much." I turned, then paused. "How did Oliver die? Did he have a heart issue that no one knew about, or some health condition?"

A shadow fell on the young woman's face, quickly wiped away by a flash of anger. "He was killed," she said. "Some of those bastards from across the street, probably."

I made the conscious effort not to clench my fists. I didn't want to damage the medal. "What happened?" I didn't bother with the platitude of whether or not she minded my asking. I didn't care. If those thugs harmed my...friend, there would be hell to pay.

"I don't know, honestly. I came over to visit him a week ago Sunday, like always. I've been bringing him Sunday dinner every week for a while now, since I moved back to New Orleans. I got here with supper, and he was on the floor, dead."

"Shot? Stabbed? Beaten? What made you feel that the men across the street were responsible?" It sometimes surprised me how quickly the old instincts

Vlad and Abraham instilled in me came back to the fore when I needed to investigate something.

"No, there wasn't a mark on him. The coroner didn't find anything, ether. Said it just looked like he decided it was time to go, and he died. I thought that was really strange. But I know those thugs had something to do with it. Look at them, just sitting around on the porch drinking beer and smoking weed all day. You know they sell drugs. And Pop had a couple run-ins with them the past few months, too."

That death didn't sound like gang violence to me, but there was no point in trying to convince Eliza of that. Her mind was made up, and I saw some of Oliver's stubbornness peeking through under her curls. It was prettier on her, but her resolve was no less steely for being sheathed in an attractive wrapping.

"That sounds very odd. I had not seen Oliver in some time, but the man I knew was not the kind to lay down and die. He was the kind to battle the Reaper with every fiber of his being."

"I know, right?" she agreed. At least, I thought it was agreement. I sometimes have difficulty parsing the grammar of young people. "That's how I know it was those Blood bastards. They won't tell me nothing, and I can't get the police to even question them, on account of there not being any evidence of foul play. Hell, the fact that my pop is dead seems pretty damn foul to me."

"I agree that something seems amiss about his death. I shall go speak to the young men across the street. Perhaps they will be more forthcoming with me."

"What makes you think they gonna tell a giant white boy anything? I mean, no offense, but you ain't exactly who they're used to having a conversation with."

I gave her a small nod and my most vicious smile. "I can be very persuasive."

CHAPTER THREE

There were five young men sitting on the porch across from Oliver's house when I stepped out his front door. One of them watched me, his baleful guise tracking my every movement as I walked down the steps and across the street. His hand drifted to the waistband of his pants as he shushed his friends and nodded in my direction.

"Hey, shut that shit off, we got us some company," he said. Another man, late teens or early twenties, reached over and turned off a speaker that was connected to someone's phone playing music.

"I need to speak to you gentlemen for a moment," I said. I stopped at the foot of the steps, still several feet away from the nearest man, but close enough that my presence could not be mistaken for innocuous. They were sitting on steps, which made them taller than me, but only just. I could still easily look them in the eye, except for the man I deemed to be their leader, the one who kept his eye on me my entire trek across the street.

"What you wanna say?" he said, standing up. I took a step back to be able to look at him more comfortably, and he took two steps forward, coming down the steps to my eye level and staring at me, asserting his dominance. Or attempting to do so, at any rate.

"I have some questions about Oliver's death. His granddaughter seems to think you or your men may have contributed in some way to his demise." I kept my tone mild, as mild as possible when your voice sounds like a bass hum through gravel.

"What you trying to say, man? You think we offed the old man?" He pushed forward at me, bumping chests in a display of aggression and dominance.

It often amuses me how humans revert to their gorilla ancestry when threatened or threatening. The bared teeth, the metaphorical chest-thumping, the thrusting themselves against their opponent: it's all very primal. And all completely ineffectual against someone who has no primal instincts, no participation in the collective unconscious.

"I do not," I replied. "But Eliza does. I would like to know which of us is correct. Would you be willing to answer some questions for me?" I have often found that exceeding politeness in a fraught situation can defuse an adversary's anger. That was not the case here.

"I ain't answering shit, man. Now you better fuck off back to whatever white boy tower you climbed down and don't ever let me see you on my street again!" He pulled up the front of his New Orleans Saints t-shirt to show me the pistol wedged into the waistband of his pants.

Growing tired of this charade, I reached down and grabbed the butt of the pistol. "I've always wondered exactly why so many people seem to want to carry a gun there," I said. "It seems very dangerous." I angled the gun to the right, then to the left. "It seems like it would be very simple for someone to make a mistake and shoot themselves in the leg, perhaps severing the femoral artery. If that happens, you'll bleed to death before an ambulance ever arrives. Even if you don't hit an artery, shooting yourself in the leg promises to be both embarrassing and painful, and that's if you manage not to destroy your knee in the process."

I turned the gun slightly to angle the barrel straight down. "And that's without even mentioning perhaps the most nerve-wracking of all possible occurrences when carrying a gun in the front of your pants, the direct downward misfire. I would certainly be concerned for my own genitals if I had a loaded handgun just inches above my private parts."

I pulled the gun from his waistband, and he let out a sigh of relief. I ejected the magazine and tossed it back over my head. I ran the slide to clear the chamber and tossed the gun aside to lie in the grass. Then I reached forward and grabbed the man directly in front of me by his testicles. "I can only surmise by the bulging eyes and the fish-mouthed gasping that you are in significant pain right now. Good. That was my intent. But just imagine how much more it would hurt if I came back here and shot your dick off." I generally dislike resorting to colloquialisms, but it seemed appropriate for the situation.

"Now, let's answer my questions, shall we?" The young man's eyes got huge and he nodded.

"What about your friends?" I asked. "Would you like them to cooperate as well?" He nodded again, then croaked out instructions for everyone there to answer my questions, no bullshitting around allowed.

"Did you or any of your people hurt Oliver?"

"Nah, man, we liked the old dude. He was kind of a dick, but he was a funny dick. We had a deal. We'd sling weed and pussy and make sure nobody fucked with the kids in the 'hood. We didn't bring nothing harder than weed onto the block, and he didn't call the cops on us. He was a cool old dude. I was sorry to see him go."

That was what I had expected. Oliver was no prude, but he did not tolerate fools lightly. He would have brokered a peace with the local thugs, and he would have kept his part of the bargain as long as they did. That meant he either died of natural causes, or someone else killed him. "Did you see anyone go into his house in the days before he died?"

"What I look like, the fucking neighborhood watch?" he asked, and I squeezed his crotch. His legs sagged, putting even more pressure on his testicles. He struggled to get his feet under him and shook his head. "I don't know, man. I don't even know when the old dude died."

"It was Wednesday a couple weeks ago, homes," one of his companions said. Every head turned to him. He was the youngest-looking of the Bloods, only the tiniest hint of a mustache shadowing his upper lip. He wore a red track suit and an Adidas t-shirt, looking like he stepped off a vintage Run-DMC album cover from before he was born.

He looked nervous at the attention, but continued. "I saw this other dude go in there Tuesday night. He was like some middle-aged white dude, maybe forty. Drove a sweet ride, a Maserati, man. He went inside, and I heard some yelling, then some shit lit up in the window like fireworks and shit, and the white dude came out. I didn't see Pops after that."

I tilted my head to one side and looked at the boy. "You called him Pops?"

"We all did. All us that grew up here, anyway. He was Pops. He took care of you, but don't let him catch you fucking around, he'd whoop your ass, then call your mama and *she'd* whoop your ass." The kid sitting next to him on the porch nodded, and they bumped fists.

The man I was holding scowled at the younger boy. "Why you ain't tell nobody that shit, Junior? You know we take care of our own. Pops was our people, man. You can't be letting some cracker motherfucker come up in here messing with our people." I let go of his crotch, and he took a step back to sit on the steps, rubbing his sore groin.

Junior looked at his shoes, not meeting his friend's gaze. "I don't know. I thought if y'all heard me talking about magic fireworks and shit, y'all wouldn't believe me."

"Fool, this New Orleans," another one of the boys on the porch said, laughing. "Everybody know magic real, fool. We all got a granny or aunt doing the root. You don't believe in magic, you ain't been in Nola long."

A general murmur of agreement went through the young men, and I nodded. I certainly was more well-acquainted with magic than even these young men would readily believe. I looked at the young man. "Do you remember anything else about the man you saw? Any details that might help me find him?"

"Nah, man, I was pretty high. I don't remember shit." He bumped fists with one of the other boys, but the one I had released reached up and slapped him.

"I told you about getting high. You don't do that shit. You gone go to college, get the fuck out this 'hood. Tell him, big man." He turned to me.

"He is correct. You should go to college. Your friends here will very likely end up imprisoned or dead before they are thirty years old. If you leave this environment as soon as possible, you are more likely to survive and have children of your own someday." The boys on the porch glared at me, but no one spoke up to contradict me.

"What if I don't wanna go nowhere?" the youth said with a sneer.

"Going to college will still allow you to earn more money with less risk of jail than any career you can find without a degree. I see nothing wrong with recreational marijuana use, but the price typically does not agree with me." I didn't bother to mention that a side effect of my unusual physiology is a complete lack of capacity to become intoxicated. Since I am animated by magical means, my body is merely a vessel for my soul. There is no real connection between me and my body, so mind-altering substances have little to no effect on me. That is the theory Vlad, Abraham, and I crafted, at any rate.

"Whatever, man." He waved me off with the dismissive air of the internally wise teenager.

I shrugged and held out my hand to his friend. "Thank you for your help. I do not think I did any permanent damage to your firearm. I hope I did not do any permanent damage to your person."

He shook my hand. "Yeah, big man, I think both my pistols gonna be okay." He grinned at me and said, "You need a ride back into town? Frodo'll drop you." He jerked a thumb at one of the men on the porch behind him. "Frodo" waved.

"That would be nice," I said. "My Uber driver did not feel safe in this neighborhood."

"Yeah, lot of people think that," the young man said. "I think we got us a public image problem." The crowd on the porch laughed, and Frodo stood up. He walked to a black Escalade parked on the street and got behind the wheel. I walked over and got in on the passenger's side, then gave him the address of my hotel.

"Fancy," he remarked.

"Why do they call you Frodo?" I asked. "You are not particularly short." He wasn't. He wasn't tall, either, at somewhere slightly below six feet tall, but he was not a short man by any rate.

Frodo held up his right hand, and I saw that he was missing his ring finger. "Got it shot off. So now they call me Frodo."

"What did they call you before Frodo?"

"My moms named me Gerald, but that didn't sound real tough. So my street name was Skullfucker, on account of—"

I raised a hand to stop him. "Please, don't share the origin of 'Skullfucker.' I think Frodo is a much better choice."

We rode in silence back to my hotel, but could only get within three blocks. The streets were blocked by emergency vehicles and police cramming the streets of the French Quarter. Frodo pulled over, and I got out of the SUV, looking up into the sky ahead of us.

Whoever killed Oliver apparently heard that I was in town and wasn't thrilled at the news. My hotel was surrounded by firetrucks attempting to save the adjacent buildings as a pillar of black smoke rose to the sky. Onlookers crammed the sidewalks and nearby streets, all necks craning to see the inferno that was my lodging. My hotel was on fire, and I had no doubt that I was the intended target.

CHAPTER FOUR

I ducked into a restaurant with a sandwich board out front announcing "Live Music Every Day!" and requested a table for one. Then I wove through the tables to the bathroom and locked the door.

I took out my phone. "Dennis, are you there?"

His unicorn face popped onto my screen and he said, "I'm everywhere, baby. Except in your hotel room, which is a good thing. Before you ask, no I can't get into the hotel security system, because the hard drives burned up and they didn't back that shit up to the cloud. And yes, all your shit is now toast, so you're going to need to find a Big & Tall Men's store to buy some new underwear."

"And perhaps a t-shirt," I agreed.

"Nah, there's plenty of 'I Support Single Moms' shirts available on Bourbon." His image on the screen changed to a stocky young man with a head full of tight red curls wearing a t-shirt with an image of a woman swinging on a pole. The connection took a moment, but when I made it, I laughed.

"I think my life can be considered more or less complete without ever owning a shirt that promotes that level of misogyny," I said.

"Okay, fine, whatever," Dennis replied, changing his avatar into a giant frowny face. "I've called you an Uber to take you to the nearest tailor that does big and tall work. They have a delivery service, too, so once you get measured and pick out some stuff, they can deliver it to your new hotel. I've already got you a reservation at Harrah's casino, with a new laptop and tablet en route to you."

"Thank you, Dennis. I will pass on the trip to the tailor for now, however. I wish to speak to these firefighters and police officers." I pressed the button on the screen to disconnect the call, but Dennis' face remained.

"Dude. You don't really think you can actually hang up on me, do you? Not gonna happen. Anyway, nobody is going to talk to you until they're sure the whole Quarter isn't going up in flames. Go get some new threads ordered and come back in a couple of hours."

As much as I longed to push my way through the throngs of people and demand answers from those in charge, I recognized the wisdom in his words. Hopefully my sartorial side trip would allow enough time for the onlookers to disperse and give me an opportunity to speak with the arson inspector. A slight delay would also remove much of the cover for the firebug if he was still in the area.

———

Two hours later, I returned with a hefty receipt for a very large selection of clothing that all promised to make me look far more presentable than my normal black pants, boots, and thin sweatshirts. I tend to wear durable clothing in solid dark colors. It hides blood better. It usually is not my blood that stains my clothes. I did choose to wear the new hat I purchased, a jaunty fedora in a dark gray check with a small feather in the hatband. I decided that it made me look somewhat less threatening than my normal appearance.

I approached a man standing near a firetruck in a heavy turnout coat, rubber boots, but without the facemask and fireproof pants of an active firefighter. "Are you the investigator?" I asked.

"Naw," he drawled. "I'm the assistant. The investigator's in there, poking around where she ain't got no business being 'til things cool down a bit. But she's always been hard-headed." The slight smile on his face and the pride in his voice told me that he considered "hard-headed" a compliment.

"Do you have any idea what caused the fire?" I asked.

He turned to me and started a little when his eyes were even with the middle of my chest. He looked up at my face, then took a step back to make conversation easier. I gave him my most reassuring smile, but that never seems to reassure anyone. He took another step back. "I'm sorry, mister...?"

"Franks," I said, reaching into my back pocket for the badge holder there. I flipped open my credentials and passed them to him. "Department of Homeland Security. I'm not official, just curious. My room was in that hotel, and I want to know if the office is going to give me too much crap about getting my laptop replaced." I tried to affect a more casual tone, to use more slang in my speech that he would perceive me as a fellow law enforcement officer.

The badge went much further toward that end than anything, I believe. It was an excellent forgery, one Dennis had created for me by a contact he knew in North Carolina.

The firefighter, or assistant inspector, nodded at the badge and handed it back to me. "You ain't working?"

"No sir, just down here to see the sights," I said. "Might be now, if anything about this looks suspicious."

"Jerry, get over here!" a voice called from inside the wreckage of the building. The assistant turned and moved at a fast walk to the sound. I looked around, then set my hat on the back of a nearby firetruck, picked up a helmet that lay nearby, clapped it on my head, and followed Jerry into the skeletal frame of my burned-out hotel.

A red-haired woman with a spray of freckles that stood out on her pale skin was bent over, cursing at a large chunk of wood. "I can't move this son of a bitch. Can you give me a hand? I need to look at the burn pattern on the bottom side of this beam."

She looked up and scowled at me. "Who the hell is this, Jerry? You know better than to—"

Jerry's head whipped around to me, and he fixed me with an icy glare. "This is Agent Franks. He's a DHS agent on vacation. He was staying here."

"Well, Agent, you gonna stand there like a lump or you gonna help us move this beam?" the woman asked.

I looked at the beam, estimating its weight. I stepped to the broken end and bent my legs. I reached down with both hands and stood, bringing the end of the beam up with me. "Where do you want it?" I asked.

The woman just pointed, her mouth hanging wide open as I hoisted several hundred pounds of charred wood and moved it sideways just far enough for her to get an unimpeded view of the floor. I rolled the beam slightly when I set it down, so she could photograph the side of the beam that was on the bottom.

"There we go," she said, pointing to a silvery residue on the alligator-like burned area of the beam. "That's phosphorous residue. It burns super-hot."

"And water only makes it burn more," I continued.

"That's right," she said. "Very good."

"So this fire was definitely set and was designed to get worse once fire-fighters arrived," I said.

"Or when the sprinklers kicked on, which happened several minutes before the first trucks got here," Jerry said.

"Why?" I asked.

"This wasn't just arson," the redhead replied. "This fire was set to kill someone."

I was pretty sure I knew who was supposed to end up dead. Now I just needed to find out why.

"I'm Anna Hernandez," the redhead said, holding out her hand. "Chief Arson Inspector for the City of New Orleans."

"Pleased to meet you, Inspector…Hernandez," I replied, looking at her pale skin and red hair.

She laughed. "Married name, Agent. My wife is from Chile. Now, what brings you to my fire scene?"

"I just popped by to pick up my luggage, but it seems to have been incinerated," I said.

"You were staying in this hotel?" she asked, pulling out a little notebook.

"Yes, I was."

"How many people were aware of that fact?"

"I suspect the entire hotel staff knew about it, but unless I have been followed, no one else would have been aware of that. I am not here working. I am on vacation." The lie came easily to me. I do not have the many physical tells that humans have when they are lying. My pupils do not dilate; my heart rate does not increase. Lying comes as naturally to me as breathing. This has proven very useful in my work with Quincy Harker, but sometimes provides a moral conundrum when trying to live a better life than I have in the past.

"Do you have any active cases that may cause someone to seek retribution?" Inspector Hernandez asked.

"I sincerely doubt it," I said. "I am not a field agent. I am a backline support evidence technician. I make sure that the chain of custody is followed precisely to aid in achieving a conviction. My work is essential, but not glamorous." Quincy came up with that cover story for me several years ago. His thought was that if he made me utterly boring, no one would want to delve deeper into my fabricated employment. So far, life had proven him quite correct.

Inspector Hernandez's eyes glazed over long before I finished the summary of my mythical job duties. "Yeah, doesn't sound like you were the target. But I doubt that anything in your room would be salvageable. What floor were you on?"

"The sixth. Where did the fire originate?"

"It's hard to tell with the amount of interior damage. There was so much accelerant used that it burned out a big chunk of the center of the building. So we can't tell yet what floor it started on. All we're sure of is that it was above the third, given the amount of damage on the lowest floors."

"Well, if I can be of any assistance, please let me know." I produced a business card and passed it over. It had an authentic Homeland Security logo and a fabricated office number that Dennis monitored. The cell number did correspond to the phone in my pocket, though.

I turned and walked away to retrieve my hatg and return the helmet, pulling out the cell phone and tapping at the screen. Dennis' face appeared, and I pressed the phone to my ear, since my earbuds were now melted slag in what used to be my duffel bag. "What did you find out?" I asked.

"A whole lot of nothing. Like we already knew, the hotel's security footage is literal toast, and the ATM camera across the street mysteriously went on the fritz about two minutes before the first 911 call came in."

"Mysteriously."

"Yeah, like a mysterious hand went in front of the lens, a mysterious spark came out of the hand, and the camera mysteriously didn't work anymore," Dennis said.

"Magic," I said, nodding.

"Yup."

"That sounds reminiscent of what the young boy said he saw at Oliver's the night he died. Bright flashes of light. Perhaps you could—"

"Check traffic cams in the area to see if I can find a black Maserati anywhere near the hotel before the fire? Yeah, that's a good idea. I'll hit you back. The address of your new hotel is in your phone. Your clothes are being delivered in two hours."

"I have another old acquaintance to visit. I will go chat with her, then go to my hotel to see my new threads, as you kids say."

"Okay, one—I'm not a kid. I'm a sentient bundle of super-genius electrons. And two—pretty sure nobody says 'threads' anymore. Not since 1940, anyway."

"What's seven decades between friends?" I asked. I took the phone down from my ear and tapped a query into the device's map function. It popped up the name of my next destination—Marie Laveau's House of Voodoo. It was time to visit my old friend the voodoo priestess.

CHAPTER FIVE

The walls of Marie Laveau's House of Voodoo pressed in on my massive shoulders. Tourist-trap tchotchkes and bundles of decorative beads and herbs hung from spikes on the slatted display wall, and bookshelves dominated one entire side of the store. I ducked to avoid a grinning sugar skull hanging from the ceiling and addressed the young man behind the counter. He was a thin black man with an afro broader than his shoulders, bobbing his head to the reggae music that rumbled through the shop, providing a deep undercurrent to both conversation and commerce. He was reading a tattered *Shadowman* graphic novel, oblivious even to my decidedly stealth-less approach.

"I am here to see Madison," I said, trying to smile to soothe the young man as he jumped at my words. My smile was about as soothing as it normally is, and he slipped off the backless stool he was sitting on to stagger back. He knocked into a display of incense, then whirled around to catch the spinning rack before it spilled all its contents on the ground.

"I'm sorry, who are you?" he asked.

"I am an old friend of Madison's. Please tell her I am here." I handed him one of my cards. Not the one with Homeland Security on it. The one that is just my name, Adam Franks, and my cell number.

"I'm sorry, sir," he started. "We don't have anyone—"

I leaned forward, snarling at the young man. His dark skin turned ashen, and I said, "Do not play with me, child. I am here to see Madison, and you can tell her I am here, or I can injure you and find her myself. I would prefer not to do that, but you have a decision to make."

He backed up against a wall of herbs, incense, dried chicken feet, and other conjuring supplies and spun around to make sure nothing fell to the floor. Since I knew Madison kept the real supplies behind the counter, I didn't blame him for being nervous. I stood, waiting like a silent sentinel, until he turned back to face me.

"Well?" I packed as much threat into one syllable as I knew how, and that is not an inconsiderable amount. The young man gulped and pointed toward the back of the store. I followed his finger with my gaze, and my eyes lit on a narrow passage covered with multi-hued silks, a festoon of colored fabric forming a camouflaged door into Madison's work and stockroom.

"Thank you," I said, nodding at the boy. "You can call her and tell her Adam is coming back. Or I can surprise her, but we both know that is not the best option."

He gave a nod in return and picked up the telephone, pressing an intercom button and saying, "There's a giant on his way back to see you. He says his name is Adam. I'm sorry, I couldn't…okay."

He hung up the phone and almost certainly turned to me, but I was already wending my way through the labyrinthine shop to the faux door made of fabric. I heard his footsteps as he walked to the door and clicked the deadbolt in place, then I heard the slight whisper of cardboard as he flipped the OPEN sign to CLOSED. Good. Madison remembered me, and remembered that trouble often accompanied me. That trouble is frequently named John Abraham Quincy Holmwood Harker, but not this time.

This time my trouble didn't have a name as yet but seemed to have a taste for expensive foreign cars. I've noticed in my time that evil is often concerned with the trappings of wealth, while good often cloaks itself in poverty. I wonder if that is something that started with Jesus of Nazareth, or if it is a trait he adopted as well… I made a mental note to discuss that with Vlad the next time we were together, and perhaps to bring it up with Sister Evangeline as well, but then I shoved that thought to the back of my mind and stepped through the curtain of dazzling peacock silks.

Lady Madison, any surname she once possessed long lost, now merely a secret between herself and various government agencies that cared about such things, sat behind a small round table with a crystal ball nestled in a depression in the center of the table. She was a lovely older black woman, somewhere between seventy and one hundred years old, her wizened face a road map of laughter and tragedy, of love and life and loss and all the moments in between. Brilliant blue eyes shone from the crinkles of her caramel face, a parting gift from some Frenchman generations back.

She once told me that in her family blue eyes meant the child would be a powerful witch or sorcerer and asked me what the color of my eyes meant. I told her it meant that the freshest corpse in the graveyard had hazel eyes.

I looked at the small metal folding chair and smiled. "I think I'll try something different," I said. I folded the chair and leaned it against the wall, then stepped through the open doorway into the shop's tiny storeroom. I picked up four cinderblocks and brought them out in front of Madison. I arranged them into a sturdy, if somewhat firm, seat and settled my massive frame onto them.

"How are you, Adam?" Madison asked. Her voice was like warm honey, smooth and slow, seeming to flow around the room twice before it got to my ears. I had heard that voice boom and crack like a thunderstorm on the ocean, though. I knew full well the power this old woman wielded, and I was not fooled for an instant by her honey-chile sweetness and her disarming old-lady grin. This was one of the most powerful witches in the world, and she did not suffer fools lightly. I tried never to be the fool with her.

"I survive, Madison," I replied. "Despite the best efforts of friend and foe, it seems, I survive."

"You still running with that Harker fool?" she asked, and her brow knit with frustration. "I told you that white boy gonna get you killed one of these days. It don't matter how big or strong you are, if it lives, it can die. And you most definitely alive, boy."

I chuckled at that. Madison knew full well what those words meant to me, and her using them was no coincidence. "I am still working with Quincy on occasion, yes."

"You part of that mess in Atlanta?"

"I was."

"You here in New Orleans on account of some bullshit errand he got you running?"

I had to pause for a moment to consider my answer. I was, in fact, working with Harker to recover the Implements in order to restore the Archangels to Heaven and God to His throne, but I didn't look upon this quest as an "errand." It was best to be clear with Madison, however.

"I am here on his behalf, yes."

"Shit, Adam." She dragged out the curse into multiple syllables, making it sound like *sheeeee-it*. "You know that dumbass cracker magician is fucking around with things he don't understand again, right?"

"This time I fear that we are dealing with forces that none of us understand," I said. "This job involves Archangels."

"Oh, shit, son. You messing with stuff way above your pay grade now. Yours and Harker's and his damn bloodsucking uncle's, too. You Shadow Council jackasses always got to be messing with stuff. Always got to be trying to fix shit that don't need to be fixed. What you trying to do now? Bring back God?" She glared at me across the table, almost daring me to tell her that's exactly what we were doing.

And, of course, that's exactly what we were doing. "Yes," I said. There's no point trying to lie to Madison—she can sense it, even in me.

She leaned back in her chair and folded her arms over her abundant chest. "You are a damn fool, Adam. You might be the most foolish damn fool that has ever lived."

"I'm not going to argue that point, Madison," I said. "I fear at this point in my long life there is too much evidence to support your opinion. My foolishness aside, will you do a scrying for me?"

"I suppose," she said with a sigh. "I might not be done fussing with you yet, though. But you ain't here just for a scrying. I can see something is heavy on your heart today, old friend. What is it?"

Madison has always had a gift for seeing, and not just what is foretold in the cards or what appears in the crystal globe she has resting over the fiber-optic projector set into her table. She can read the body language of any mark at any card table, which led to her being banned from hundreds of casinos across the country. She can read auras from people and objects, and she can read the emotions of even a manufactured man such as myself. I asked her once how she accomplishes such a thing, and she simply replied with, "It's magic, you great big idiot."

"Oliver is dead," I said. There was no need to elaborate. She knew Oliver, in the way that all talented practitioners of magic in an area come across each other at some point in their lives. They were not friends, but I knew of no animosity between them.

"I heard about 'dat. It's a shame, it is. He was a good man and a strong wizard. He did a lot of good in that part of the city. Loved that granddaughter of his, too. You meet her? She's a fine-looking woman."

"I did meet her, and yes, she is a lovely woman," I replied. I have learned long ago that Madison has a hint of the matchmaker about her, and it is better to just let her go on about her hints and innuendos and pretend to miss the clues than it is to make any objections to her interfering in my nonexistent love life.

"But why does that have you worried, *cher*? Oliver had a heart attack, from what I hear. He was an old man, and that happens to old men. He didn't have nothing on you, of course, but you a special case." That was certainly one way of putting it. Madison and I had never gone in-depth as to my origins, but she was not an unintelligent woman, and the scars I bear in particular places make it fairly clear that I am not what anyone would consider "normal."

"He did not have a heart attack," I said. "One of the local youth saw a man in an expensive car go into Oliver's house. There were flashes of light in the windows, in many colors, then the next day Oliver was found dead."

Madison looked troubled, and I knew this was the first she was hearing about this man. "What kind of car? What did the man look like?"

"The boy said it was an expensive sports car, and all he knew about the man was that he was a white man."

"That drew some eyes in that 'hood," Madison said.

"Especially from the gang members who live across the street," I agreed.

"Too many shady white men in the Quarter to pick one out of the crowd, and ain't no parking down here, so I don't know if I'd know him if he walked in the front door."

"Well, if your security camera suddenly stop working, I would take that as cause for alarm," I said. "I believe this man was responsible for the fire at my hotel earlier today, and the security footage was destroyed."

"That makes sense, though, if it was in a fire," Madison said.

"True enough," I agreed. "But the camera on the ATM across the street also failed within a few minutes of the fire."

Madison nodded, her close-cropped white hair framing her skull as she did. "Yeah, that's more than a little bit strange, my friend. I'll keep a look out, and I'll make sure Alexander does the same."

"Please apologize to Alexander for my poor manners earlier. I was perhaps a bit intense when I spoke with him."

"Oh, it's fine. Boy needs to toughen up anyway. He's too much of a delicate damn flower. Now, you done warned me about the bad mojo man. What you want me to see for you?"

"I'm looking for a horn," I said.

"Boy, you in New Orleans," she said with a cackle. "If we didn't invent jazz down here, we damn sure perfected it. You gone need to be a touch more specific with what you asking for."

I leaned forward and lowered my voice. No matter how much Madison trusted her employee, I didn't know the boy and didn't need him knowing my business. "I am looking for the Horn of the Herald. I have to find the Horn of Archangel Sealtiel, so I can call him back to service and return him to Heaven."

Madison looked at me for a long moment, then nodded. "Well, I suppose that's a relief. I was worried it was going to be something difficult, like making the Earth rotate backward. No, all you need to do is find the Implement of one of the most powerful beings in the whole world and coerce an Archangel to return to Heaven after millennia on Earth. What do you plan to do after lunch, go to Disneyland?"

"So you can't do it?" I asked.

"Oh no, son, you not getting out this that easy," she said. "Remember, boy. The difficult we can do immediately; the impossible takes just a little more time. This is going to take a little time, but we'll find your horn. Now put your hands on the crystal. I'm going need a little blood for this."

CHAPTER SIX

Madison knew better than to try and use my blood for her invocation. Not only is it a thick, viscous substance more akin to crude oil than the sanguine stuff of human life, no one is exactly sure what it is made up of. Since my father's death, which was regrettably not at my hand, there has been no one living who knew exactly how he transformed me from my dead component parts to the walking, talking, thinking, and somewhat living creature that I am. His notes were lost in the fire that destroyed his laboratory, and I was somewhat too preoccupied with my pending incineration to rescue them.

No, she drew a small *athame* from beneath the table and pricked her thumb, bringing a small drop of bright crimson to the surface. She smeared the blood onto the crystal and pressed her palms to the stone. The cool orb immediately grew warm and began to glow with a soft amber light as her essence fused with the magic of the stone.

I have spent many years around practitioners of magic, both dark and light, and had many conversations with them about the origin of their ability to manipulate the natural forces of the world and bend the world to their whim. I have received as many answers as I have had questions as to the source of their power, and Madison was no different. She believed firmly that the spirits of her ancestors lent her their power to manipulate the world around her, and that she was merely a vessel for power and information from the spirit realm. It made as much sense as any other explanation I had received, so I merely sat mute with my hands on the still-warming crystal sphere.

"Grandmother Maybelle, hear my plea," Madison said, her voice light and child-like as she called upon one of her favorite ancestors. She once explained to me that her Mamaw Maybelle had been her favorite elderly relative when she was a little girl, that Maybelle always had a mint or a Werther's candy tucked away in an apron pocket and that little Madison would sit on her lap and dig through the old woman's pockets for the sweet, giggling along as her grandmother pretended to be ticklish at the child's quest. She called upon Grandmother Maybelle most often when I asked her for help, but I had also seen her call on the spirits of other relatives, including once her father, a big, bellicose man who she only went to in times of great need and in search of strength and power.

The stone pulsed in a deep, slow rhythm, almost like a heartbeat, and Madison's head lolled forward. Seconds later, her head snapped up, and she fixed me with a sharp gaze. "What you want now, man of dead men?" Her voice was waspish, her words more pointed, and her eyes narrowed as she spoke. "Why you back here looking to drag my grandbaby into your mess with that Harker boy?"

I started at Grandmother Maybelle's tone. She had never spoken to me directly before, choosing to communicate with Madison and let her relay her words to me. Apparently, my work with Quincy Harker and the Shadow Council had attracted attention past the mortal plane.

"Don't look at me like something done bit you on your big dead behind, golem," she ordered. "I done asked you a question, and I expect you to answer it before I start worrying myself with any of yours."

"I am here because Madison has helped me in the past, and I need her assistance once more. I seek—"

"I know what you looking for, boy, and it better to not speak of it while you talking straight to the other side. We got eavesdroppers on both sides of this rock, and I don't want to hear about you bringing any pain down on Maddie's head."

"Nor do I, but I believe that pain may be here regardless," I said. "There have been attacks against practitioners of the arts in New Orleans. That is the other reason I am here—to warn Madison." I paused, then went on. "She is a friend, and I have precious few of those. I would not see her harmed if I can prevent it."

Madison/Maybelle's expression softened, and she nodded at me. "That's good, boy. She my last grandbaby, and as much as I want to see her again, I'm in no hurry for her to cross that river, if you know what I mean."

"Only in theory," I said with a rueful smile.

The laugh that ripped from Madison's mouth was pure and loud, almost startling in its intensity. "You a funny one, golem. Maybe one day you find where that nasty man that made you tucked your soul away and you can be a real boy, just like the puppet in that cartoon."

"What do you mean?" I asked, my mind whirling at the suggestion.

"Oh child," the woman laughed again, throwing her head back. "You done spent all these years trying to find out what you are, but you got no idea what you could be. You need to take a look past the mirror someday. But for now, you can find what you seek just behind the door." Her head sagged forward, and Madison let out a long sigh. She jerked once, then sat up straight, looking around at the room.

"Did she give you anything useful?" she asked, taking her hands off the stone. Grandmother Maybelle was obviously gone, and now it was back to me and Madison in the storeroom of her voodoo shop.

"She certainly gave me things to consider," I said. "I don't know how useful the information will be, but there was a lot to think about in her words."

Madison peered at me, as always seeing more behind my words than I tried to show. "I don't think you're just talking about finding a fancy trumpet in the Quarter, are you?"

"No, I'm not. There are things your grandmother mentioned that have caused me to rethink many of the preconceived notions that I have long held about myself. I shall have to spend some significant time exploring these ideas. After we have you somewhere safe and I have located my absentee angel and his Horn."

"What do you mean, have me somewhere safe? I'm not going anywhere." She said it very matter-of-factly, like I was insane for even considering the idea.

"Madison, there is someone killing magic users in New Orleans. They have already murdered Oliver, and they tried to kill me today. This is not someone without resources or power. I would not wish to see you hurt."

"Neither would I, Adam, love. But I am not leaving this shop. Marie Laveau's is a New Orleans institution and the only place in town some folks can find the things they need to practice their rituals. We can't just shut down."

"I'm not asking you to shut down, just to take a few days off. Leave Alexander here to manage the shop while you get somewhere safe until things calm down."

"You mean until you kill this man hunting down magicians," she corrected. Her disapproval was clear on her face.

"Oliver was a friend," I said. "I don't have many of those. It makes me very protective of the ones I do have."

She stared at me for a moment, then sighed. "It don't matter. I can't leave. Xander can't run the store by himself. I got to look out for him. He's my dead sister's boy, and he's blood, but he don't have the touch. There's nothing to protect him from some of the things I keep in the back room here. He can't sell that stuff—only somebody with power can touch it without getting hurt. I leave him alone here for more time than it takes to go get lunch, and it's liable to mean his life."

I looked at my friend, and there was nothing about her that said I would be able to persuade her to leave this place. "There is nothing I can say to dissuade you from this path, is there?"

"I could ask you the same question, couldn't I, old friend?" She gave me a slight smile, and I nodded.

"That is fair," I said. That settled to no one's satisfaction, I changed the subject. "Your grandmother said something about looking for what I seek behind the door. Does that mean anything to you?"

Madison thought for a moment, then shook her head. "Not a damn thing, Adam. I'm sorry, but you know how ghosts are. Sometimes I swear they like to be obtuse just for the pure hell of it."

I smiled and stood up. "I do, yes. Thank you, Madison. Please try to stay safe in the coming days. This man, or whatever he is, burned down an entire hotel in an attempt to do me harm. I have no doubt that he will be at least as serious in his attempts to eliminate you if he deems you a threat."

She chuckled. "If he don't think I'm a threat, then he's a bigger damn fool than you are," she said. "Oliver was my friend, too. More than that, back in the day." A wistful smile crossed her lips. "I will miss that grouchy old bastard. If that son of a bitch comes for me, he'd better come heavy because I'll set the ghost of Queen Marie her damn self on his sorry ass." She gave a real laugh then. "We'll see how the son of a bitch likes that."

"Take care, Madison. Do not underestimate this man. He is dangerous."

"So am I, Adam son of no man, so am I."

I looked in her eyes, and there was no fear there, just the steely resolve of a woman who has spent a lifetime dealing with powerful forces and still stood to tell the tale. I gave her a nod and left the back room, pushing through the rainbow silks into the main part of the shop.

"She's going to need some water, and you'll need to make sure that shotgun stays loaded," I said to Alexander as I stretched my back, stiff from sitting on the cinderblocks for so long.

"It's always loaded," he said, reaching beneath the counter. His hand came up with a bottle of Aristocrat vodka. "And she don't never drink water. You can let yourself out." He walked past me into the back room, and I wove between the counter and the display to the front door. I flipped the sign back to OPEN and stepped out onto the sidewalk.

Somewhere in New Orleans was a missing angel, a magical trumpet, and a man who wanted to kill me. I needed to find them all, and I had no idea where to look. I turned left out of the shop and headed toward Jackson Square, unsure if I was trying to clear my head or just make myself a more visible target.

CHAPTER SEVEN

The square surrounding the park was crowded in the mid-afternoon sun. Tourists milled about, stopping here and there to listen to buskers or to admire the art hung on the wrought iron fences by the street vendors. One enterprising band of youths combined a pair of young men beating on buckets with drumsticks with a group of four teens dancing and leaping in choreographed chaos, blending capoeira combat dance with breakdancing and hip hop dance moves. I stopped to watch them for a few minutes and dropped a five-dollar bill in a hat before I moved on.

Near the southwest corner of the park, I came upon a young man playing jazz, the sun glinting off the chrome of his trumpet's bell and flickering into my eyes to draw my attention. He played energetic covers of rock songs with a jazz flavor, and behind him, a homeless man shuffled a little flat-footed dance in time to the music. On the ground before him sat an upside-down fedora in front of a chalkboard sign. The sign read, in big pink chalk letters, "TONIGHT - One Night Only - The Alley Club - behind The Famous Door - Thunder Travis Blows Blues – 9 PM"

I stopped cold as my brain processed the words on the sign. Behind The Famous Door. The trumpet gleaming in the sun. It all clicked together in my head in an instant. This was the man I sought. Or at least the instrument I sought. Now I just had to convince him to either accept his true form as an Archangel, or give me the trumpet so I could find Sealtiel with it.

Thunder Travis, as the sign named him, was a large young man, a Clarence Clemons-sized musician, only with a trumpet instead of a saxophone. His dark skin glistened in the sun, and tattoos ran the length of his bulging arms, sweat obscuring the details and dampening the front of his white tank top. His short dreadlocks stuck out from his head at all angles, and a long silver chain with an ankh on it hung from his neck. He wore cargo shorts and sneakers, and generally looked like a college kid out for a good time, only he was here working to make ends meet blowing jazz for tips in the middle of the afternoon.

I pulled out my phone and aimed it at the man playing the trumpet. "Dennis, are you there?"

"I'm always here, big buddy. What can I do ya for?" the unicorn head on my screen asked.

"I need you to access my phone's camera and get me any information you can gather on the man playing the trumpet," I said.

"You get that's not really how facial recognition stuff works, right? I don't just beep a few times like R2-D2 and then spit out this dude's home phone number and address."

"You always tell me how amazing you are, Dennis. I am merely providing you with an opportunity to prove yourself correct."

"Sometimes I think you gave Harker asshole lessons when he was a kid," my electronic unicorn companion muttered.

"Any of his formative years are purely the fault of Abraham and Vlad. I was merely a witness to their corruption of the young Harker. What do you know about this musician?"

"Jesus, dude, gimme at least a minute, will you? Okay, he doesn't come up in a scan of military records from the last ten years, same for any wanted posters, ditto any TV star websites or major search engines. It looks like your dude is just a dude, playing jazz in the park trying to make a living. Sorry."

"Is there anything else you can do to try and find out more about him?" I asked. "Driver's license records, anything like that."

"I'm scanning the Louisiana and Mississippi DMV records now, but there's nothing. Sorry, Adam. I've got nothing. I'll start a deep scan, see what I can see on Facebook and other social media stuff. I mean, it's not like the guy is trying to stay out of sight, maybe he just doesn't drive. I don't know. I'll let you know what I find."

"Thank you," I said, then slipped the phone into my pocket. I sat on a nearby bench and watched the crowd pass by. People of all shapes and sizes walked along the sidewalk in front of me, never looking twice at the huge man in the hooded sweatshirt sitting there watching the world. Men, women, children, all absorbed into their own little worlds, their attention often dominated by the tiny screens they held in their hands.

A man stepped up to the musician, bent down, and dropped a bill in the hat. He sat on another bench for a time watching the musician and his dancing homeless man, a dirty shuffle-stepper scuffing his worn shoes in some semblance of time to the music. The spectator sat in the shade, only his wingtip shoes catching the bright sunlight, the patent leather shining to an almost blinding gloss. He wore an expensive suit, with an Italian tie and a matching pocket square. His watch cost more than everything I wore combined, and likely didn't smell of burning hotel. His hair was immaculate and his face shaved so smooth I wondered if one could use his cheekbones as their own razor.

He was a fiendishly handsome man, and his attention was not locked on the musician, as mine so often was, but skipped across the crowd, the musician, the sidewalk artist making a three-dimensional image on the ground in nothing but chalk, an impermanent masterpiece to be washed away with the next rain. The man's gaze even fell on me once or twice, and he gave me a friendly nod as we locked eyes. I nodded back, acknowledging him, and returned to watching the trumpeter and his dancing hobo.

After thirty minutes or so, the man set his trumpet down on a small folding stand and took a long drink of water from a plastic bottle at his feet. Then he opened the case next to his water bottle, lay the trumpet inside, and slid the case and stand into a small backpack. He transferred the money from his hat to his pocket, then put the hat on his head. He stood, slipped his arms through the loops on the backpack, and picked up his sign. He turned to the man in the suit, gave him a slight bow, then did the same to me.

"Like the sign says, I'll be at The Alley Club tonight at nine. Hope y'all can come join us. Bring a friend. Don't bring too many friends, though. The place isn't that big." He laughed, downed the last of his water, and tossed the bottle into a nearby wastebasket. I watched the young man walk off up the sidewalk, whistling a tune as he went. His dancing homeless man stood around for a moment watching him go, then wandered off back the way I came, toward the restaurants and bars of the Quarter.

I waited until he had almost vanished from view, then stood. I noticed the well-dressed man walking ahead of me, his languid gait belied by the way his head never wavered from his target. He was following the young musician, pursuing the same quarry. I pulled my phone from my pocket and held it to my ear.

"Dennis?"

"Yeah, big guy?"

"Have you found anything on our young Mister Travis?" I asked.

"Who's Mr. Travis?"

"The trumpet player," I replied. "His name is Thunder Travis."

"Do you think you could have told me that any later?" Dennis' voice rose in my ear.

"I'm sorry," I said. "I thought you were amazing."

"I am *amazing*," he retorted. "I'm also incorporeal and trapped in the internet. It's not like I can just hop out of here on a lightning bolt and take a look around."

"But wouldn't that be interesting?"

"Yeah, that would be great," replied my disgruntled disembodied friend.

There are very few times in life that I enjoy tormenting people, but for one reason or another, they always seem to center on either Dennis or Quincy Harker. Perhaps it is the fact that they are so high-strung. It is just a simple matter to wind them up a little more and watch them go around in circles.

"Okay, here we go," Dennis said. "Jermaine 'Thunder' Travis was a standout running back in high school, second-string at LSU, good enough to get a scholarship for all four years, but nowhere near good enough to play in the pros. He graduated LSU six years ago with a degree in music education, worked for three years at a high school in Baton Rouge, then moved back to New Orleans...looks like he came back to take care of a grandfather who was sick. Grandpa was the original Thunder Travis, a popular sideman in New Orleans in the fifties and sixties. He was in the house band at The Famous Door for a little while, played in the Preservation Hall band for a couple of years, then quit playing as he got older. He died about a year ago. Jermaine was his only living heir."

"What happened to Jermaine's parents?"

"Looks like not much record of his dad being involved. He's listed on the birth certificate, but he's lived in Montana since 1999. Dad is remarried, has a couple of newer model kids, looks like he sent a check every month until Jermaine turned eighteen, but no real contact. Mom...whoof, that's a bitch. Mom died six months before Grandpa. Grandma died before Jermaine was born. No other relatives that I can find, no wife, no serious girlfriend according to social media. Looks like he's pretty much a loner."

"Send me the address of his grandfather's house," I said. If he was headed home to sleep before his gig that night, I could take an Uber and beat him there. I didn't know why the man in the expensive suit was following him, but anyone paying that much attention to the bearer of the Horn of the Herald was probably someone I didn't want getting to Jermaine before I did.

"Uber's around the corner," Dennis replied. "And it's paid for. Don't worry, I didn't hack anything. Except Harker's debit card, that is."

"Well, if it's Quincy's money, it's all the better. I believe he still owes me money from an old poker game."

"The one where Hickok got shot?" Dennis asked.

"I'm not that old," I replied, hanging up the phone.

"You know you can't hang up on me!" I heard from my pocket as Dennis worked valiantly to get the last word in.

I got in the Uber, glad once again that Dennis knew to specify an SUV to accommodate my seven-foot height. The driver didn't try to make small talk as he drove, letting me lean my head back and relax after a morning spent surrounded by people. I let the soft faux leather of the seat envelope me as I closed my eyes. I didn't sleep, not even a doze, but I did manage a small moment of meditation, working to center myself after being battered by crowds almost since rising.

The Suburban pulled up to the curb two blocks from Jermaine's house, as instructed, and I got out. I walked down the sidewalk toward the address Dennis listed and stepped into the shadows between two houses across the street. It was a typical city neighborhood with houses crammed as close together as any sense of privacy would allow. Jermaine rode up on a dark red bicycle about ten minutes after I began my surveillance, chaining the bike to the pipe-built railing of his front steps and walking up to enter his house. Jermaine opened the door, and a flash of light exploded from within, hurling him back through the air to slam into a panel van sitting at the curb.

The wooden door was obliterated, nothing more than a smoking hole in the front of the house, and stepping through it was a demon. Not just a little, run-of-the-mill Reaver or even a bigger, badder Torment Demon. No, this was a nine-foot-tall Demon Warrior, a soldier of Hell's armies, complete with a flaming sword and armor so black it seemed to absorb all the light around it, making the entire world feel darker, more gray.

I sighed and stepped forward, looking around for a weapon. The last time I'd gone toe-to-toe with a demon unaided, it hadn't ended well, but it was worse for the demon. Ripping something's head off with your bare hands tends to ruin its day. I just hoped this demon wasn't about to ruin mine.

CHAPTER EIGHT

I ran to Jermaine's side and knelt beside his unconscious form. He lay sprawled on the grass beside the dented van with blood oozing from a small cut on the back of his head. The demon stood at the top of the steps, looking around for its prey, then its glowing red eyes locked on me. The thing was nearly two feet taller than me and broad in the shoulders. It was fully encased in what looked like obsidian plate armor with a flaming black sword in one hand. A horned helmet covered its entire face save a slit for its crimson eyes to glare through, and smoke hissed from a grate where its mouth should be, spewing sulfurous stench across the yard.

"Remove thyself from my field of battle, mortal, and I shall spare thy life."

I stood and faced the demon. "I can't do that, demon. This man is not yours, nor shall he be as long as I live."

The monster laughed, a chilling, hollow sound coming through the armor from the bowels of Hell. "Then he will be mine in mere seconds, human. For that is all the longer you shall live!"

He leapt off the steps and charged me with his sword. I turned, ripped the passenger door off the panel van, and brought my makeshift shield around to intercept the charging demon. We slammed together with a mighty crash, and I managed to shove him back. My reprieve lasted less than a breath as he slashed at me with that terrifying blade. I got the door up into its path, but his fiery sword sliced through the metal like it was butter. I gaped at the two hunks of van clenched in my fists, and for the first time in many decades, thought I might actually die.

I threw the chunk of door in my left hand at the demon's head, and he swatted it away with his sword. That exposed his left side, and I slammed into his knee with the other chunk of door, feeling a grim smile stretch across my face at the satisfying *crunch* that came from the joint. The impact bent his greave on that leg as well, and he was unable to straighten his leg. He spun around, dancing on one foot and the toes of his left leg, and swirled his sword in a deadly arc before him.

"It seems I underestimated you, human," he said, his voice sounding like an earthquake mating with a forest fire, all pain and disaster and wreckage, crackling through his throat.

"I won't give you a second chance to make that mistake, demon," I said, lowering my shoulder and slamming into him with the remnants of my door-shield. The glass shattered all over the back of my head, and the heat from his sword caught my hoodie ablaze, but I had him at a bad angle to strike, and he could do nothing but tumble backward onto the concrete steps of what remained of Jermaine's house.

I fell atop the demon and grabbed his right wrist with mine. Agony shot through my palm as the spikes on his gauntlet pierced all the way through the back of my hand, but I knew to let go was to most likely die. It had been many years since I had battled alone against a foe that could possibly take my life, and I didn't intend to go easily, if at all.

The demon growled in my face, and its rotten-egg breath wrapped around my face in a foul miasma. It thrashed, and kicked, and howled, and still I sat astride it, pressing down with the van door into its chest, trying to punch it somewhere that would do more damage to the monster than to my fist, but its armor thwarted me at every turn. It bucked in one giant convulsion, and I flew off to the side, only connected now by my grip on its wrist and the spikes through my hand. The pain was immense, tearing at my palm and grinding the bones on the metal studs that protruded through the back of my hand. I rolled onto my side and gripped that right arm with my other hand, grabbing above the wrist this time so as not to destroy my other hand.

I wrapped both hands around the creature's forearm, planted both feet in its ribcage, and pulled with all my considerable might. The demon let out an anguished scream and thrashed about on the grass, starting small fires and scarring the sidewalk with its intense heat. I felt its other fist slam into my shin once, twice, again and again, the spikes on that gauntlet ripping deep furrows in my calf and lower leg. I bent forward, relaxing the tension for an instant, then snapped back, giving one huge yank, and with a shriek of pain and rage, and a squeal of rending plate mail, I pulled the demon's arm off at the shoulder.

Black blood spurted from the wound, and every blade of grass that blood touched smoked and died away down to the dirt in an instant. The gouts of demon blood sizzled on the sidewalk and melted part of one of my shoes, burning my toes and sending yet more pain through my battered body. I got to my knees, turned the demon's hand around in my bloodied grip, and plunged the obsidian blade into its wielder's chest. The blade pierced the breastplate with a *crunk*, and the demon let out a howl of rage and pain that shattered every car and house window on the block.

The demon stared up at me, its red eyes growing dim, and as the light winked out, I heard it hiss, "I will remember you." Then its eyes went black, and the demon's body turned to nothing more than black soot and ash. I knelt on the grass, somehow still holding the gleaming black demon sword, and looked over at Jermaine. He was unconscious, probably concussed, and would need medical attention quickly. And that's without even beginning to address the damage I had endured. I fumbled in my pocket and pulled out my phone. The screen was shattered, but as I pressed a button on the side, it lit up in a few places.

"Dennis?" I croaked.

"Holy shit, Adam!" The face on the screen was his human face, and concern was written in every line. "How the hell are you still alive? That was—"

"I know," I managed to gasp out. "We need..." I couldn't speak any more. The pain was too great.

"Hang on buddy, I got people coming to get you. Just hang on, big guy, they'll be there..." Anything else he said was lost as I toppled sideways to the ground and blackness filled my vision.

———

I woke on a hard surface in a bare room. It was as much a cell as a room, except there were no bars on the door. There was no door at all, just an arched entry into the tiny room, so I did not consider myself a prisoner in any way. It is usually better for the structural integrity of the building if my egress is not impeded. The floor was bare concrete, with a drain set in the center. I lay on a metal "bed" for lack of a better word, with a pillow of sorts under my neck. I looked up at the bright white fluorescent light, then at the stark walls, and let out a dry chuckle. I was in one of the cryptid autopsy rooms at Sisters of the Sword.

The Sisters were not just a militant arm of the Church and the home of the Hunter for the Gulf region. If that were not enough for one small collection of nuns, they also were, to a woman, research scientists dedicated to the study and understanding of cryptids, supernatural or paranormal or simply odd beings that defied conventional understanding of science in some way.

I had stood on the other side of one of these stone walls, watching via video feed, as a Sister had autopsied, or attempted to autopsy, a rogue vampire. It did not end well. The problem most humans have with studying the body of a deceased vampire is that such a thing does not exist. Vampires are already dead by definition, so when the magic that animates them is removed, they either crumble to dust, or if they are more recently turned, they explode in a shower of blood and gore.

You can't really autopsy a vampire because it's still alive after death. But you can, with the proper precautions, take tissue samples from an animate vampire to study. Most creatures take exception to being participants in vivisection, however, and vampires are very strong. In the case I witnessed, a pain-mad vampire who already had exhibited no compunction against taking human life, ripped his arms off to get free of his bonds, then chewed through the throat of the Sister attempting to perform the autopsy. It took four of us to put the vampire down, even with no arms. It only took two to dispatch the Sister once she turned. She was much fresher than the original vampire.

Now I found myself in a similar room, the major exception being the lack of door. I sat up and waved to the small video camera mounted in a corner. "Hello. Thank you for tending my wounds. I would like to speak to Sister Evangeline now."

A tall nun in full wimple came into the doorway a few moments later. She was a severe-looking woman, the reputation of nuns as disciplinarians notwithstanding. She did not speak, simply gestured toward the open door.

As I stood, the sheet covering my lower body slipped to the floor, and I realized for the first time that I was nude. "Pardon me," I said, retrieving the drape and fastening it around my waist. "I seem to have lost my clothes. The nun showed neither surprise nor disgust at the patchwork landscape of scars, stitches, and seams that made up my skin, so I merely hiked the sheet up to free my feet and passed through the doorway into the hall.

This passage felt somehow as if it were underground. The muffled sounds of our feet on the stone floor, the slightly musty smell that pervaded the entire area, and the light chill in the air all contributed to a sense of a tunnel or catacomb. It was well-lit with electric light, so there was no gloomy flicker of torchlight or choking smoke to sting my eyes. My feet slapped along the cool slate paving stones until I came to a door ahead of me.

I turned to my escort, who stopped several feet behind me. "I am to enter?" She nodded.

I raised my hand and knocked. A cheery "Come in!" rang out from the other side of the door, and I lifted the handle and pushed on the thick iron-bound wooden door. The hinges swung noiselessly, and the thick oaken door glided open to reveal a library with a vaulted ceiling and a roaring fire in a fireplace.

Two armchairs sat on a round area rug before the fireplace, and a plump smiling nun occupied one of them. "Come in, come in, love. And close the door behind you. We don't want to let Agatha's chill follow you in!" The woman's voice was bright and crisp, like sunlight dancing on water, and I felt something for her that I almost never felt when dealing with mortals, particularly those associated with religion. I trusted her and felt safe in her presence. Something resonated within me, making me feel as if no harm would come to me as long as I was with her. I felt an unfamiliar warmth on the flesh of my chest, and I looked down to see the medal Oliver's granddaughter gave me lying on my bare skin.

The Purple Heart was glowing with a faint white light, just enough for me to see it. I touched the medal, and it was warm. Not the warm of being in contact with living flesh, as I give off very little heat, but a gentle radiance that came from the amulet itself.

"You are Oliver's friend. Adam, I believe he said your name was." I tore my eyes from the necklace and stared at the woman. She stood before her chair, her eyes fixed on mine.

"My name is Mother Eunice. I'm glad to see the child gave you that necklace. I think you're going to need it. Please, sit down. We have quite a lot to talk about."

CHAPTER NINE

"I am happy to join you, but before I do, may I have my pants?" I asked.

Eunice's laughter was a thing to behold. It swelled from within her copious bosom like a geyser, rippling out from her in waves and infusing the entire room with joy. I smiled as she laughed, but I remained standing. I did, after all, want my pants.

"I am sorry, my son," she said after a moment of mirth. "Your clothes were either burned horribly or torn to shreds in your fight with the demon. Then there's the matter of the demon blood eating through much of the fabric, and your own blood soaking the remainder. There really was very little worth saving. We have nothing here to fit a man, much less a man of your size. Your friend Dennis is having some clothes delivered from your hotel. Once those arrive, they will be brought to you."

"You have spoken with Dennis?" I asked.

"Oh yes, my son," she said. She reached over to a table between the two chairs and held up my abused cell phone. "I would hand this to you, but I am aware of the lack of pockets in your current wardrobe." She put the phone back on the table and motioned to the other chair. "Won't you sit by the fire? I find these tunnels to be a little chilly, and it helps my arthritis to stay warm."

I moved to the chair and sat, then asked, "If it is uncomfortable for you down here, why not simply work aboveground?"

She waved an arm around us at the bookshelves. "The books, love. I can't take the books upstairs into the humidity. The Louisiana atmosphere would destroy this old paper in a heartbeat. We are digitizing everything as fast as we can, but it's not a quick job. So as long as the collected knowledge of the Sisters resides here, I stay underground, and every once in a while, I stoke the fires with another copy of this drivel." She gestured to a kindling box near the fireplace, where a stack of popular, and well-worn, romance novels stood. "I do, of course, have to read them all multiple times, just to make sure they're drivel. Wouldn't want to torch a literary masterpiece by mistake."

"Perish the thought," I said, feeling an unaccustomed smile stretch my features. Something about this funny little woman put me very much at ease. I found myself enjoying her company, with her romance novel habit and her arthritis. She was obviously hard at work down here, protecting the accumulated knowledge of her order, but she just as obviously loved her work.

I cleared my throat and drove on toward my initial purpose in New Orleans. "I had hoped to speak with Sister Evangeline," I said. "Her assistance would be welcome in my current endeavor."

"Finding the Horn of the Herald?" Mother Eunice asked. My face must have registered my surprise because she laughed again. "When I spoke with your digital friend," she nodded to my phone, "he told me who you are and what you are doing here. We typically stay far from Council business, but this seems important. Evangeline isn't here, however. She is hunting in the swamps. We have had several bodies appear in recent weeks, and the most recent was a teenage boy who went out frog gigging last weekend. His body was found Wednesday. His legs were not."

"I am sorry to hear that," I said. "Do you think you could help me?"

"Our archives and my knowledge are at your disposal, but Evangeline is the Arm of the Order. She is the only Sister who bears weapons. The rest are all pure researchers."

This took me aback, and I let that show. "I was led to believe that the Sisters of the Sword were a military order."

"We are," Eunice replied. "But we are much more the weapon development side of the military. All our Sisters are trained in the arts of war, and all *can* bear arms if the situation warrants it, but unless the end times are truly upon us, Sister Evangeline is the only armed one among us."

"So, I can use your library, but you won't stand with me against whoever is calling demons in New Orleans," I said.

"Unless His Holiness in Rome orders us to do so, which I doubt even your friend Luke could persuade Him to do."

So she knew about Luke. That almost certainly meant they knew exactly who and what I was and had plans to deal with me if I became unruly. That put a damper on any arguments I had planned, so I switched tactics. "You knew Oliver?" I asked, pointing to the necklace I wore.

A sad smile crossed her face. "I did. We know most of the major practitioners in the city and have traded knowledge with them over the years. Oliver was a good man, and he cared deeply for his friends. He spoke often of you, wishing that you would visit more frequently."

"I wish it, too, now." I found the words to be true. No matter how diligently I worked to avoid human connections, the stolen heart in my chest kept drawing me back to the short-lived candles. It was just like a fire, warm and comforting right up to the second it burns. That is exactly how humans are to me. They are sources of such inspiration and joy, and the source of almost all my pain as well.

"I think whoever called the demon today is the same person that murdered Oliver," I said. I hoped that this information would persuade Eunice to join my hunt for his killer.

"I believe you are almost certainly correct," she said.

"And still you will not aid me?"

"I will lend you every bit of aid that we can. We have healed your wounds, added a number of impressive stitches to the patchwork quilt of your flesh, and I am here to walk you through our library in search of any information you need. But we will not become involved in your quest, either the one for vengeance or for the Horn."

"Not vengeance," I said. "Justice."

"Be careful that you can tell the difference between the two," she replied. "Many men cannot."

"I have known both in my time," I said, remembering the feeling of a delicate throat beneath my fingers. Murdering Victor's bride had been vengeance. There had been no justice in taking her life. She never harmed me, and killing her did not balance accounts between my "father" and me.

"Do you know who this man is that is killing magic users in New Orleans?"

"I do not," she replied.

"Do you know if he is the one who summoned the demon to attack Jermaine?"

"I do not," she repeated. "But it seems likely."

"Where is Jermaine?" I asked.

"He is here. We can keep him here, or you can take him to Evangeline. If this man is as dangerous as we believe, then it may be best if he is not within the city."

"Where is Evangeline?"

"She's up by Baton Rouge in the Atchafalaya Wildlife Refuge. There have been reports of a black gator up there that's gone man-eater. She went up three days ago. We confirmed this morning that she is staying at a cabin in the swamp, hunting the creature."

"I've never heard of a black gator," I admitted.

"I would be surprised if you had. It is not a natural gator," she said. "It's a zombie gator. Some of the priestesses out in the swamp raise them up for security. They're big, strong, and terrifying, but they tend to be very docile as long as their creator maintains tight control over them. That has not happened in this case, and several people were killed by the creature. Evangeline is also looking for the person who raised the alligator. She has expressed a desire to have a conversation with them."

I was not surprised by this. I would be surprised, however, if the voodoo practitioner left the "conversation" unscathed. I had seen the results of Evangeline's conversations before. They often featured brass knuckles, and once or twice, a shotgun.

"I will take Jermaine to stay with Evangeline in the morning," I said.

"Why do you wish to wait? If you leave as soon as your clothes arrive, you could go and get to Evangeline before full dark."

"Jermaine has a show tonight," I said. "I would hate to deprive him of that income, particularly since part of his home was destroyed today."

She smiled at me, a tight, mirthless grin. "And you think that the man you seek may come to this show, giving you an opportunity to kill him."

"Killing a man in a crowded nightclub, even if the man murdered one of my few friends, is not something that I would consider a wise choice." I paused and touched the medal hanging on a chain around my neck. "But I would not speak ill of fate should it place me in an alley with the man who attacked Oliver." I offered up a mirthless smile of my own.

"Well, far be it from us to keep you from your chosen path of destruction, Adam." She stood, and I got the distinct impression that I had disappointed her somehow. I felt a brief pang for that, but it subsided quickly. I have spent over a century disappointing people; it has become almost second nature to me.

"I will go to the club, watch Jermaine's set, and make sure that he is not attacked and that the Horn remains safe. Tomorrow morning, we will set off to find Evangeline, and hopefully she will be able to keep him safe until the threat has been resolved."

"You will not offend me if you use the word killed, Adam," she said with a smile.

"I doubt you have such delicate sensibilities," I said. "But some things are better left unsaid."

Eunice stood and motioned for me to follow her. "Let me escort you to a room where you can change. I believe the delivery man should be here with your clothes by now."

We stepped into the hall and walked down a different corridor than the one I had taken to her library. "Is there anything you can tell me about this medal?" I asked, fingering the heart with the cross affixed to it.

"I don't know very much about it," Eunice admitted. "I blessed the crucifix in the waters of our sanctuary, and I believe Oliver mentioned fashioning some protective spells into the medal, but if it possesses any mystical properties, I am unaware of them. Why? Does it bother you?"

"It doesn't bother me, but when we first met, it glowed and grew warm to the touch, as if letting me know that you meant me no harm."

I saw her nod, but could not see her face, walking behind her in the narrow hallway. "That seems like the type of protection Oliver would have imbued the medallion with. He was very concerned with some of your associations. He felt that many people would attempt to manipulate you, and that you may not always be sophisticated enough to see it, given the isolation you typically prefer."

I closed my eyes against a rising tide of annoyance. Oliver spent decades working to convince me that Vlad was the monster the books made him out to be, and nothing I ever told him would change his mind. I had no doubt that he, or Harker, was the manipulator that Oliver intended to protect me against.

"Well, I don't need a personal good intentions meter, but if it contains any additional protective capabilities, I would be a fool to discard it," I said.

"It may well be the thing that kept you alive this afternoon by dissipating the demon warrior's fire just enough for you to slay it."

"I wouldn't mind if it had dissipated a little of the piercing agony I had in my hands, but I suppose that is too much to ask," I said.

"It is a very small necklace, Adam. It can only do so much." She stopped before an unmarked door and opened it. A room very similar to the autopsy room I awakened in lay before us, but this one had a pair of shopping bags on the bed. I ducked through the doorway and turned back to Eunice.

"Thank you," I said. "I appreciate your help. Were it not for your healing magics, I would undoubtedly be incapacitated, and that could prove ruinous to our quest. I do not wish to seem ungrateful, for I certainly am thankful for your aid."

She smiled, a warm thing that spread across her face like dawn. "Of course, Adam. Some of us are required to walk a darker path while some of us are fortunate enough to stride through the light. Your path is a shadowed one, but you may take some of our light with you on your journey." She reached out and placed a hand on my chest, covering the amulet Oliver left me. I felt the medal grow warm and saw a golden light bleed out through Eunice's fingers.

"Go with God, Adam. May He watch over you always." She turned and walked back down the hall as I stepped inside the room to dress.

"Thank you, Eunice," I whispered as I closed the door. "But He might not want to see all the things I have to do in His name."

CHAPTER TEN

I stepped out into the evening air, the muggy Louisiana heat fading with the moonrise, and pulled the new phone from my pocket. I pressed a button on the side, and Dennis' unicorn face appeared.

"How's it hanging, big guy? Don't answer that. You can get kinda literal at times, and there are some things I really don't want to know."

"I'm fine, Dennis. I don't know what the Sisters did to me in there, but my wounds are mostly healed."

"From what I understand, they prayed a lot, gave you like eight units of blood, and then shocked your heart back to pumping with some ridiculous amount of electricity. I think I'm going to need to make a donation to the convent just to help them pay their power bill next month."

"That is quite a lot of blood," I said.

"Yeah, most people have like twelve units in them, at most. You're bigger than most people, but you were running on empty by the time they got you here. And there was a lot of blunt force trauma going on, and a bunch of shredded tendons. Whatever prayers they sent up, they must have been answered. I didn't think you were going to be moving for days, and I figured it would be at least a week before you could use your hands again," Dennis' face morphed into his human guise, and the concern was evident on his digitized mien.

I looked at my right hand where I had gripped the demon's armor and driven spikes clear through the back of my palm. There were fresh white scars all over it, crisscrossing my skin with more reminders of the punishment I have inflicted upon myself over the years, but I felt no pain. The fingers flexed, the wrist bent, everything worked perfectly. "I suspect there may have been more than simple prayers at work in that convent, Dennis."

"Well, you know the Templars, Adam. They've got all their ancient rituals and spells and shit. At least some of them do. That big goofball in Georgia seems to get by on dumb luck and large-caliber bullets."

"There are worse ways to go through life," I replied. "How far am I from the club where Jermaine is playing tonight?" I wanted to move the subject from my miraculous recovery before we got too far down the rabbit hole of contemplating my existence. That road never takes me anywhere good.

"About six blocks," Dennis replied. "He's already there, holed up in a back room. The ER docs said he didn't have a concussion, so they cleared him to play. I made sure the bills were covered. You know jazz musicians aren't exactly rolling in money."

"I do not approve of theft, Dennis."

"I do not care, Adam. Besides, I stole it from David Duke's offshore bank account. If you can't steal from a former Klansman to pay for a black horn player's hospital visit, who can you steal from?"

I had to admit, the concept did have a certain ironic appeal to it. "I suppose I can let that go this time," I said, calling up a map on my phone and walking toward the blinking lights of the nightclub. "Dennis, I have to ask. What in the world made you decide upon these clothes?" I was dressed in the ensemble provided by the Sisters, which they assured me was sent over by "my associate." I wore a New Orleans Saints black hoodie with "Who Dat?" on the chest in huge letters, a pair of neon green and purple high-top basketball shoes, and a pair of blue jeans with patches of various colors on them. Under my zip-up hoodie was a black t-shirt with a silhouette of a woman swinging on a pole and a caption that read, "I support single moms." The entire chaotic mess was topped with my fedora. The overall effect was, in short, awful.

"Do you like 'em?" Dennis asked. "I just thought about something I'd like to wear after almost dying at the hands of a demonic warlord and super-sized it. I thought the feather in the hat really topped off the outfit nicely. Gives you kind of a rakish vibe, you know?"

His face looked so enthusiastic, so genuinely happy at the spectacularly awful things I wore, that I couldn't bring myself to tell him what I really thought. "They're lovely, Dennis. I couldn't have picked out a better outfit myself."

He looked at me for a brief moment, then doubled over with laughter. "Dude," he exclaimed. "That was great! You looked like somebody had switched your sugar with salt and you just put three spoonfuls in your coffee.

Yeah, I know it's all awful. Except the t-shirt. I thought that was hilarious. It was the first shop I could find with enough crap in your size to get you out of the convent not wrapped in a sheet. You've got plenty of time to get to your hotel and change before you go make sure nobody murders Jermaine. There should be a room key in the pocket of those pants. Here, I'll reroute your map."

I looked at the screen, and a detour appeared, showing my hotel. "Thank goodness," I said. "I was afraid I was going to have to wear these horrible shoes all night."

"Hey, cut me a little slack. Size nineteen shoes aren't easy to come by on short notice, so try not to wreck everything in your room this time. I'm gonna have to raid the Saints' equipment room if you need more clothes. I think New Orleans is now officially out of size 4XL, Tall."

I walked to my hotel and changed, then headed to the club. I was now dressed in a much more subdued pair of black cargo pants, black t-shirt, and black combat boots. I kept the Saints hoodie to make me look more like a tourist than a Delta Force operative and had a pair of oversized brass knuckles in each pocket. I also had Oliver's medal around my neck under my shirt and a long silver dagger in a sheath hidden in the small of my back.

I stepped into the alley beside The Famous Door and pulled a five-dollar bill from my pocket. I handed it to the doorman at the aptly named Alley Club, and he looked up at me.

"Please don't start anything," he said. "I don't want to find out which one of us is the baddest man in the room."

"I have no intention of starting anything," I replied. "I just want to hear Thunder Travis play."

"That's good, man. Thunder's good, dawg. He can blow that horn, man. Here's a ticket for a free drink. On me." He passed me a small orange carnival ticket with the smile of man who has been in many bar fights in his time and has no desire to be in any more. I took the ticket with a nod and ducked into the club.

It was a small room, maybe thirty feet by twenty, with a long bar down one wall and windows lining the opposite. A low stage, perhaps twelve inches high, took up most of one end of the room, with a narrow hallway leading back to what I assumed was a dressing room or green room area. A dozen or so round tables were scattered around the room, and I took a seat at one that allowed me to put my back to the far wall and maintain a clear line of sight to the rest of the room. Once the room grew crowded, it would be more difficult, but as long as the crowd was small, or seated, I could see the stage and the entrance perfectly.

I ordered a whiskey and water from the young waitress and passed her the ticket and two singles when she brought it. She smiled and tucked the cash into her front pocket, then dropped the ticket onto her tray and hurried off to deliver more drinks.

The room began to fill up as nine o'clock drew near, and shortly after the hour, Jermaine stepped on stage. He wore a dark suit, with gleaming white shoes and dark sunglasses, a far cry from the itinerant street musician I'd watched play in the park earlier that day, and a different person altogether from the terrified young man I'd seen after the demon attack. This was a cool cat, a calm, collected musician about to ply his trade in front of room full of adoring fans. Admittedly, the room was only about half full, and the fans were more intoxicated than adoring, but he was still very much a man in control of his destiny. At least as long as I could keep him alive.

"Good evening," he said into the microphone. "My name is Jermaine Travis, but my coaches used to call me Thunder."

Polite applause rippled across the gathered listeners, and I watched one overweight man wearing several dozen strands of colorful Mardi Gras beads lean over to the emaciated woman next to him and whisper something in her ear. I could almost make out "LSU" from his words and assumed he was a football fan.

Jermaine put the trumpet to his lips and started to play. He was, as I saw that afternoon in the park, a good musician, but there was nothing extraordinary about his playing. I detected no magic coming from him other than the magic that all talented musicians bring to their performances. His band was tight, full of obvious professionals, but it was just as obvious that playing gigs in bars was likely the pinnacle of their careers.

The spark that transforms a pleasant night listening to music with good whiskey into a memory, the tiny flame that fans into a life-changing talent, that was nowhere present in these men. They were good, perfectly enjoyable, but there was no hint of the divine in them. This was not my missing Archangel. But judging by the heat growing in the amulet pressed to my chest, *something* supernatural was nearby.

I looked around, shifting my focus from the band on stage to the room around me, and noticed two things. First, the bouncer had left his post at the door to roust a homeless man from hanging around outside the bar's alley window, and second, that the well-dressed man from this afternoon was now sitting right next to me.

I turned to him, looking up and down at the interloper at my table, and he smiled at me. The song ended, and he extended a hand. "Pardon the intrusion, friend, but I saw your table was empty and thought you could maybe spare the seat."

He made no threatening moves, and I had no desire to cause a scene in the crowded bar, so I just nodded at him. I took his hand and said, "You're welcome to join me. I'm Adam."

"Thank you. My name is Martin." He drew his hand back, and I noticed a spot of brown on the French cuff of his shirt, just by the diamond-studded cufflink.

He saw my gaze and pulled his jacket down to cover the spot. "Sorry," he said with a rueful smile. "I had a po' boy for dinner and got a touch of sauce on my sleeve."

I could read the lie, but not the reason, so I let it stand. I cared not a bit about the man's dinner, just his plans for Jermaine. Everything about him made my senses scream, but this was not the time or place. I turned back to the stage as Thunder and his Lightning Bolts began a new tune, but my pocket began to vibrate. I stood, pulling out my phone, and wove through the tables and out the front door.

I tapped the screen and held the phone to my ear. "Hello?"

"Adam?" The voice on the other end was female, and frantic. "Adam, it's Madison. Come quick. Something killed Xander. Right here in my shop, Adam. Something got in here through all my wards and murdered my nephew."

CHAPTER ELEVEN

I got to the back entrance on Marie Laveau's less than five minutes after Madison's call, and there was already a crowd gathering in the tiny courtyard behind the narrow building. A large black man with a shaved head and a pistol on his hip stepped into my path, putting one hand on my chest and the other on the butt of his gun. He was dressed in black tactical pants, black boots, and a black t-shirt. Everything about him screamed former military, particularly the flat glare he gave me as he looked up into my eyes.

"The store is closed, sir. There's been an emergency. You'll have to come back later." He pushed against my chest, but I just kept moving forward.

"Where is Madison? Is she hurt?"

"Sir, I'm going to need—" I swatted him aside, knocking him into another guard and taking them both down. He did everything right, working to control my movements, shift my momentum, all the things he should have done to stop me without causing harm. He just didn't take into account exactly what he was dealing with.

"Adam?" I heard Madison's voice and turned to see her sitting at a round wrought-iron table. A white man in a suit knelt beside her, and he was taking a blood pressure cuff off her arm as I went to her.

"What's wrong, Maddie? Are you okay? Did it hurt you?" I heard the questions tumble over my lips faster than anyone could hope to answer, but I couldn't stop myself. The torrent of words poured forth, and I recognized a rarely-felt emotion in myself: fear. I was afraid for her. Afraid to lost another one of my very few friends to violence. A violence that I may very well have brought into her life.

I knelt beside her and took her hand. It felt even smaller than usual, and I could feel the butterfly wingbeats of her pulse in her wrist. Her heart raced as she looked up into my eyes, too tall to look directly at even on one knee.

"I'm not injured, if that's what you mean. Frederick just wanted to make sure I wasn't having a heart attack." She patted the leg of the man, who now stood slightly behind her. Madison turned back to me. "Whatever got in there, Adam, it tore Xander to pieces. It was...horrible. I've never seen so much blood."

Coming from Madison, and knowing the sanguine nature of some rituals she had performed, that was saying something. "Can I go in?" I asked. "Are the police coming?"

"No." The voice came from behind me, and I turned to see the big security guard standing there. He looked angry, and his gun was in his hand now. It was pointed down at the ground, but it was definitely positioned to raise and fire faster.

"No, I can't go in? Or no, the police aren't coming?" I asked, rising. I probably could have avoided the macho posturing, but I was upset, and feeling guilty, and it brought out my inner masculine idiot.

He stared up at me for long enough to count to twenty, and it felt like none of the other people in the small courtyard breathed. There was a sense of anticipation in the air, like a fuse had been lit and an explosion of violence was imminent. Finally, just before I thought I was going to have to smear this man across the walls like spackle, he let out a deep breath and holstered his pistol.

"No, the police aren't coming. I would prefer if you didn't go in there, but I won't try to stop you."

"Thank you," I said, and I could see the surprise in his eyes. "I think this part of New Orleans has seen enough violence for one night."

"I think there's still a little violence to be meted out, myself," he replied with a tight smile, and I knew he didn't mean to me.

I nodded, and we silently acknowledged each other in that way that men who shed the blood of others regularly have. I turned back to Madison and knelt beside her.

"Was he alone, Maddie? Or were you here?" I asked, keeping my voice soft. The rest of the alley didn't need to know these things.

"He was alone, Adam. I left him here cataloging some herbs and some new books that we got in. Harmless things, not anything with true power of their own. I never let him mess with the real magic. He didn't have no power to protect himself with, so I couldn't let him mess around with anything that might be carrying a curse."

"Do you have security cameras? Do they show anything?" I asked.

Maddie looked up at the big man, who dropped to a knee beside me. "There are cameras. We haven't reviewed the footage yet. It's one of the first things we'll do after we..." He looked at Madison. "Um..."

"He trying to say they got to get Xander's body out the way first," she said. I noticed her accent was heavier than normal, the stress of the night making her slip back into some of the patois she was raised around.

"I have people coming," the security man said.

"I would like to see the scene without any disturbances," I said. "I won't move anything, and I certainly won't touch anything," I said. This last was to Madison. I knew there were very potent magical items around the store, and some of those things could be triggered by contact with human blood, or by being in the presence of death. Her entire store would be on a hair trigger, only needing one misstep to bring about a magical devastation the likes of which had been unseen in the United States since the Great Chicago Fire.

"You can go in," Madison said. "Be real careful by the door, though. There's a big puddle of blood there. I wouldn't want you tracking that all over my store." She tried to smile, but it broke down into a sob. I stood, patted her on the shoulder in a gesture I hoped appeared more supportive and less awkward than it felt, and walked across the courtyard to the back door of the shop.

I motioned the security guard over. "Keep an eye on her. If anything comes at her, do not hesitate, just shoot it. Shoot it and keep shooting it until you are out of bullets. Then run like hell. I will try to be back out here as fast as I can. Do not try to fight this thing, just put as much lead into it as you can and don't let it get to Maddie."

He nodded, and I turned and walked to the back door. Another guard stood there blocking my path, but he stepped aside after a second of alpha male posturing. I let him posture. I had nothing to prove to the assembled crowd, and he and I both knew how much I cared about whether or not he looked tough.

I pushed the red-painted wooden door open with an elbow and stepped inside. The coppery scent of blood twined with the visceral stench of death to curl around my throat and draw my gorge forth. I took a moment just inside the door to adjust to the dim light and the foul miasma of odors coming from the shop, then stepped into the tiny storeroom. I flipped on a light switch beside the door, and blazing cool fluorescent light illuminated the shelves and the bare wooden floor. The storeroom was clean and seemed undisturbed.

Either Alexander was the attacker's target, or it had found its quarry elsewhere in the store.

The passage to the back of the store stood before me, a cascade of discarded Mardi Gras beads fashioned into a curtain over the years by Madison and her predecessors. I pushed my way through the clicking barrier into the small room where Maddie did her readings and scanned the area for anything out of place.

The room was in slight disarray, but far from ransacked. The crystal orb in the center of the table had a huge crack running through the center of it, but it remained intact, except for the new flaw. The box of prognostication implements Madison kept beside the table was overturned, her Tarot cards scattered on the floor, and herbs and runestones tossed across the tabletop. The shelves of books were untouched, and the furniture stood upright. Again, the signs of a casual search.

The front of the store was a different matter, I could see that from the doorway. The curtain door of silks was matted with blood and gore, and as I passed through it, I saw the true savagery that had been unleashed. Alexander was not simply killed, he was *destroyed*. His limbs were torn from his body and cast into the corners of the room, painting the walls and shelves with arterial blood.

His chest and abdomen were ripped open, not by a knife or anything that would leave a clean slice, but by something jagged, something tearing. The front section of his ribcage was ripped from his body and flung at the front door so hard it shattered into pieces no larger than a finger bone. His heart and entrails were removed from his body and placed on the altar to Marie Laveau, his heart's blood smeared over the painting of the Voodoo Queen that sat in an alcove in the store. Alexander's intestines were piled on the altar in a slimy heap, a bastardized offering to the Queen, defiling both her store and her altar.

Worst of all was his head. Whatever had killed Alexander had ripped his head from his body, taking part of the spine and esophagus with it. This gruesome trophy, with eyes wide and mouth fixed in a permanent scream of agony, was given a place of pride atop the cash register, jammed down over the plastic and metal construct hard enough to be immobilized on the makeshift stand.

I reached out and closed his eyes, my one concession to human sentiment. Otherwise, the horrible scene affected me not at all. It was far from the first time I had seen dismembered bodies, some of them at my own hand. This was not my work, though. This was not the work of any human, either. The sheer strength required to pull someone's head from his shoulders is immense, only possible for someone with strength born of the deaths of many men, or the souls of thousands.

I took a deep breath, letting all the scents of the bookstore-turned-abattoir fill my nose. There it was, underneath the blood and the shit and the guts—sulfur. The stench of the Pits confirmed my suspicions. This was the work of a demon. I wondered briefly if this was connected to the attack on me that afternoon, then pushed all thoughts of investigation aside.

More pressing business demanded my attention—Madison's safety. I twisted and turned my way through the narrow shop and emerged into the small cobblestone courtyard.

I walked over to where Madison sat with three security guards around her. The one who traveled with me held and stroked her hand while two others stood over her shoulders, their heads on a swivel.

"Madison, we have to leave," I said, standing over her.

She looked up at me, her eyes red-rimmed. "Where can we go, Adam? I won't be safe anywhere. Whatever hurt Xander got through all my wards, got past my threshold, everything."

That was impressive. Threshold magic is old magic, powerful, and not many magicians today can create it, especially in a public place like a store. But Madison was not like many magicians, and that may be the only thing that would keep her alive.

"You have to leave, and you have to leave now, Maddie. That thing was not after Alexander; it was after you. We should not mince words, so I will not call it a thing. We should just call it for what it is. It is a demon, Maddie. I fought a Knight of Hell this afternoon, and barely survived, and now there is another demon in New Orleans, and it means to kill you. So come with me if you want to live."

CHAPTER TWELVE

It was either my persuasive argument or my uncharacteristic popular culture reference, but Madison agreed to leave the city with me. Her security team, who she referred to as members of her congregation, provided us with a battered passenger van and a pair of armed escorts. We rolled north out of the city in a twenty-five-year-old Ford van with "2nd Antioch Missionary Baptist Church, Metairie, LA" emblazoned on the side in faded white script letters. I drove, Madison rode in the front bench seat behind me, and one of her "congregation members" rode shotgun. Literally, as he carried a pump-action shotgun and a scowl. The other congregant sat on the rear seat facing out the big back window with an AK-47 on the seat beside him and enough ammunition to invade Lichtenstein.

I have been to Lichtenstein many times. It is a lovely country but offers very little in the way of military might. It is quite possible that I could invade the country with an old van and two armed men by my side. Having a witch along with us would just be overkill.

We rode north for several hours, until my passengers were all fast asleep. I remained perfectly alert, as I require very little sleep. I was unable to contact Evangeline or any of her people, but Dennis assured me that he had a lock on her position, and as long as we made it to her camp before sunrise, she would still be there. While speaking with him, I asked that he maintain surveillance on Jermaine while I was gone, just in case our predator went after him in my absence. I had no reason to believe the musician was in danger, but in light of recent events, I felt justified in being overly cautious.

So it was that I pulled an antique church van up in front of what appeared to be an old bootlegger's or smuggler's cabin deep in the swamps of Louisiana in the predawn glow. I stopped the van, and my cargo came awake with a groan. I rolled down my window, and the thick scent of swamp moss and over-still water rankled my nose. The early morning sounds of bullfrogs and owls echoed through the clearing, and I heard a small splash as something dropped into the water nearby.

"Oh sweet Jesus on the cross, Adam, why did you let me fall asleep?" Madison groaned from behind me. She grinned at me and stretched, the bones along her spine crackling with stiffness and age.

"I was not in a position to stop you, Madison," I replied. "Besides, you needed your rest. You had quite the shock last night."

"You can say that again," she replied, her smile vanishing. The two gunmen got out of the van and fanned out in opposite directions, guns held low and heads sweeping from side to side. I thought about calling out to them, but decided to let them test their training and ability against that of a sleeping nun. I have often been accused of having no sense of humor, but I found the concept of Sister Evangeline disarming two militaristic members of a voodoo cult hilarious.

Perhaps I simply have a more well-developed sense of humor than most people.

A series of thuds and a small *crack* came from one side of the shack, and I opened my door and slid out to the ground. "Don't kill them, Evangeline," I called out. "It's Adam. They're with me."

"Shit, *cher*," a rich voice said from behind the shack. "I been out here nine days and ain't been able to kill anything. I was hoping a little voodoo thug blood be what I needed for gatorbait."

A minute later a striking woman came around the corner with one of Madison's security draped across her shoulders. Sister Evangeline dumped the unconscious man on his back in the front yard of the cabin and shot me a grin. I smiled back, unable to help myself. Evangeline was a lovely woman, with skin the color of coffee with two creams, long black curly hair, and almond-shaped violet eyes that told the story of her mixed African, French, Asian, and something indeterminate heritage like a roadmap of the world.

She was a tall woman with broad shoulders. Strongly built, she had little trouble carrying the unconscious man and her ever-present twelve gauge at the same time. She was dressed for the swamp in high mud boots and a tattered t-shirt, her hair pulled back in a long ponytail. She walked over to me and wrapped her arms around my waist, squeezing tightly.

"It's good to see you again, you big idiot," she said into my chest.

I felt a warmth suffuse me at her words, and I returned her hug, albeit much more lightly. I am not known for my approachability, and I am far from what one would consider a "hugger," but Evangeline cared nothing for that, or for anyone's personal space. If she wanted to hug you, you were getting hugged. And at that moment, I was very definitely getting hugged.

After a brief moment, she stepped back and extended her hand to Madison. "Ms. Laveau, I'm Sister Evangeline. I'm the Hunter for this region."

Madison cocked her head to the side and looked Evangeline up and down. "How you know my last name, girl?"

"Like I said, I'm the Hunter for dese parts, ma'am. I make it my business to know everybody in my city." The two women looked at each other for a long time, and I got the distinct feeling that something was passing unsaid between them, but I neither knew nor cared.

"Evie," I said, and Evangeline's head snapped around at my uncharacteristic use of her nickname. "We need your help. There is a demon in New Orleans, and it's after Madison."

"Could you be a tad more specific, *cher*? Is this a new demon, or is this one of the regulars?" Evangeline asked.

I will admit, I was taken aback by the question and had to blink a few times to collect myself. "I'm sorry," I said. "You have regular demons?"

"Well, not in the sense that they customers or something, like I run a bar, but there's some demons that live in the city, yeah. One runs a tattoo parlor out by the airport, but he ain't nowhere near strong enough to make you run out of town, even if he decided to stop tattooing and start harvesting the old-fashioned way. Then there's a couple in the Quarter, but they mostly just pouring beers or playing jazz. One's a hooker at the casino, but she's just a run-of-the-mill succubus. I reckon couldn't none of the local demons make you nervous, much less leave town. I reckon that makes this a new one."

I looked at Evangeline, not quite understanding how to proceed. A Hunter, a Knight Templar, with demons living in her city, and she allows them to remain? She saw the confusion writ large upon my face and laughed.

"Oh good Lord himself, Adam, cut a girl some slack. These demons just want out of Hell. They ain't causing no trouble. Not like whatever got you so riled up. So tell me, what brings the son of Frankenstein and the granddaughter of Marie Laveau out to the swamp to chase down one stupid ol' nun?"

I explained the situation, how I believed a sorcerer or demon murdered Oliver, the attack on me at Jermaine's house, Alexander's dismemberment, and how I brought Madison to her for protection. When I was finished, Evangeline looked up at me, shaking her head.

"Man, Adam, that Quincy Harker, he get you into some of the stupidest things. You must really feel like you owe him something."

I nodded, then said, "It is much more to do with what I owe his uncle, but yes, I do owe Harker and the Shadow Council a debt."

"And I owe one to you, so I reckon this is where you call dat in," she said with a rueful smile.

"I was of the hope that you would help me because it was the right thing to do, not to balance any ledgers between us," I replied.

"Whatever helps you sleep at night, you big ox." But she smiled when she said it, a genuine smile this time, full of the warmth I had come to expect from the salty monster-hunting nun. "I'll keep an eye on the voodoo princess, but you got to help me finish something first. I can't dedicate no time to looking out for her while I still got a man-eating gator in these swamps."

"You want me to hunt an alligator with you?" I asked. I will admit to feeling a slight thrill at the idea. I had never battled an alligator but had always had immense respect for the creatures. Nearly unchanged for eons, the alligator has always been a fascinating creature to me. Their muscled bodies, their armored skin, it all combined to form a brilliant hunting machine. I found myself looking forward to engaging one of these legendary beasts.

"Yeah, and to be honest, I might need you with me," the nun replied. "I found the wreck of an airboat this beastie got hold of yesterday, and it was pretty wrecked. Last I heard, there were three old swamp rats going out lookin' for this bad boy the day before I got here, and by the looks of this boat, they found him. Or he found them, rather. There weren't enough left of any of them boys to Carbon-14 date, and unless you can match dental records to three teeth, we ain't ever gonna be sure if it's them, but I found an airboat tore into half a dozen pieces and painted with blood, and one old Caterpillar boot with a foot and ankle still in it. That's all that was left of them boys. Made me think this critter might be more than I can handle on my own."

That was a sobering thought. Evangeline had been the Hunter for the Gulf Coast region for more than a decade, and I had known her to battle vampires, lycanthropes of all variety, shades, ghouls, more zombies than a season of *The Walking Dead* extras, and at least one banshee. All without batting an eye. If this alligator was giving her pause, it would certainly be a challenge.

"I will be more than happy to assist you, but we need to make sure that Madison will be safe here without our protection," I said.

"She oughta be fine," Evangeline said. "I don't know how you found me, much less how anyone else would get to this place."

"I have some...unusual resources," I replied. She gave me a questioning look, but I did not elaborate. Dennis was a very useful associate, but I felt that his peculiar existence may be objectionable to the Church, and Evangeline was, after all, a nun.

"Well, your resources must be pretty damn unusual indeed," she agreed. "'Cause this place ain't on no maps, or no property records, and my cell phone oughta be untraceable. Evidently not, though."

I did not reply. I merely turned to Madison. "What do you think? Can this shack be defended with only two men?"

Evangeline held up a hand. "Hold up a second before you answer that." She turned to go into the small building and waved for us to follow her.

We did, and once we were inside the shack, many of my doubts about the security of the small patch of swampland faded away. What appeared from the outside to be a one-room shack was, in fact, the top floor of a multi-level reinforced concrete bunker, complete with metal blast shutters to close over the windows, sealable airlock hatches separating the floors, and a front door worthy of a bank vault. On the lowest level was a command center with multiple displays showing views of the entire perimeter from hidden security cameras; an armory with a full complement of guns, blades, and one rocket launcher; and shelves with enough food to last for at least a month.

Madison looked up at me and said, "Somehow I think we'll be just fine."

I turned to Evangeline. "Then we can go hunt your killer alligator, then I can return to New Orleans and hunt a killer demon."

She laughed and said, "Adam, I don't know if you really are immortal, but I swear you keep running with that Harker boy and you damn sure gonna find out. Let's go get us a gator."

CHAPTER THIRTEEN

The brownish green water rippled out from the sides of the airboat as Evangeline steered us into the narrow channel. I glanced behind us to see the reeds already popped back into place and the wake dying to leave no hint of our passing except the silence of the birds and the frogs behind us. Spanish moss hung down from huge live oak trees, masking the snakes that undoubtedly nestled above us, just waiting to drop from the branches onto our unsuspecting heads and necks. Every ripple in the water was a moccasin, every splash another alligator. The mosquitos were the size of small birds, and not for the first time I was very happy that my blood did not flow normally.

We delved into the heart of the swamp for nearly an hour before Evangeline cut the engine and allowed us to drift. "This is where the monster was last seen," she said, standing up from her pilot's seat and hefting her shotgun. "I don't see no sign of it, but I reckon if it heard our boat, it'll take it a minute or two to come looking after us."

I scanned the water for ripples, knowing nothing better to do. I have never been an aquatic creature. My mass makes it difficult for me to float, and I do not disrobe in public for fear of frightening crowds, so trips to the beach have never been my chosen vacation. I can swim if need be, but as I do not require breath for anything other than speech, if I must traverse a body of water, oftentimes I simply walk across the bottom.

A splash from behind and to my left caused me to spin around, bringing my own shotgun to bear on the sound. Evangeline laughed, a deep, throaty sound full of mirth, but no malice.

"It's alright, *cher*," she said, her voice cutting through the muggy air like a knife. "Just chumming the waters, as they say."

I looked at her and saw her with one hand deep in a white five-gallon bucket at her feet. She pulled her hand out, and I saw it held a fistful of entrails. I gave her a questioning look.

"Pig guts, *cher*. How we gonna catch a predator if we ain't got no bait? Unless you want to jump in the water and splash around a little bit?" She grinned and lobbed the mass of innards into the water on the other side of the boat.

"Have you any concern with attracting other predators too numerous to handle?" I asked.

"Nah, baby," she said, an easy smile playing across her lips. "Anything stupid enough to share the water with a black gator gonna get eat up real fast, so we either gonna get some little nasties, which I figure we can handle easy enough, or we gonna get one great big nasty, and that might take more work." She flicked on the flashlight slung under the barrel of her Mossberg and pointed the gun back at the water. The flashlight's beam only penetrated a few inches into the swamp water, the brown and greens of muck and algae too much for the sharp, blue-white light.

We drifted, listening for any sign of the man-eater, following the gentle currents of the swamp for nearly an hour before Evangeline waved a hand at me. I looked where she was pointing and saw nothing but an enormous rock protruding from the surface of the brackish water. I peered around the boulder for any sign of the gator, then started when the boulder itself opened one eye and cast a baleful gaze at us. The head, easily six feet long, rotated around, and the massive creature heaved itself to its feet. At least twelve feet of alligator loomed above the surface of the water, with none of the tail visible.

"Mary, Mother of God," I heard Evangeline whisper behind me.

I turned to her and said, in all sincerity, "I think we're going to need a bigger boat."

"And bigger guns," she replied with a nod.

"And perhaps a tank," I agreed.

The gator slid into the water, moving with surprising speed and silence for such a massive creature. Its tail coursed through the water, and I could see that it was at least as long as the rest of the alligator. We had somewhere in the neighborhood of twenty-five feet of massive, toothy lizard swimming toward us, and two shotguns with which to handle it. I felt uneasy about our chances, and by the look on her face, so did Evangeline.

"Did you know it was this big?" I asked.

"The guide who took me to the wrecked airboat told me it musta been at least twenty feet long based on the bite marks in the hull. I thought he was exaggerating. Ain't never been no gator more than twenty feet long, according to the official records."

"I suppose this little fellow is making unofficial records, then," I said. I thumbed on the flashlight on my own shotgun and aimed the beam at the water. The gator's tail disappeared as it approached, and Evangeline jumped down from the pilot's chair.

"Be careful, he might have dove down to—" Her words were cut off as a huge *THUMP* came from beneath the boat, and the shallow craft rocked hard to one side. The airboat flipped, and Evangeline and I flew out in opposite directions. I held onto my gun but saw hers spin through the air, leaving her defenseless.

I hit the water on my back and sank like a stone. I managed to right myself in the few seconds I had before making contact with the bottom and opened my eyes to find the alligator. The murky water made it very difficult to see anything, but the thrashing mass about eight feet in front of me looked like the most likely spot for my quarry.

I took two steps toward the thrashing gator and raised my shotgun. The chamber was loaded, with five more slugs behind, so I stood on the bottom of the swamp and pressed the gun into my shoulder. I squeezed the trigger, and a cloud of bubbles issued from the barrel of the shotgun as it exploded in my hands. Pieces of the shattered barrel whizzed by my face, and a few fragments of shrapnelized Mossberg lodged in my chest, arms, and legs.

I stared at the ruined weapon as the gator emerged from the cloud of silt and air bubbles that had hidden it from view. I dove to my right as the creature bit down on empty space that I had occupied seconds before, then skidded backward, falling to my rear and then throwing myself flat on my back as the gator spun around unbelievably fast and snapped hundreds of razor-sharp teeth shut right above me.

The monster whirled around again as I scrambled to my feet, this time heading straight for me with its mouth open wide enough to fit half of my torso inside with one gulp. I jammed the gun between those massive teeth as its jaws slammed together, wedging the beast's mouth open. The jagged edges of the destroyed barrel pierced the gator's soft upper palate and its tongue, and the shredded metal stuck fast. The monster jerked its head back, bringing me with it, as I had not let go of the gun. It swam backward, dragging me along and thrashing all the way. Then it spun around, and I was forced to let go of the gun with one hand and reposition myself astride the beast's head.

The alligator swam through the swamp, thrashing and rolling and contorting and twisting to free itself from the thing biting its mouth and the nuisance on its back, but neither I nor my gun would be dislodged.

The monster thrashed, but I held on. It rolled, throwing huge clouds of sand and muck into the water, but I held on. It worried me like a rag doll hanging from a St. Bernard's mouth, but I held on. After almost a full minute of wrestling with this enormous predator, my strength began to flag. My arms felt leaden, my back and legs were battered and ready to give, and my lungs filled with mucky water and algae stirred up from the bottom of the river.

The gator swam forward, shoving me back. I slid along the bottom of the swamp bed, leaving great parallel furrows in the brown water. I clung to the shotgun as though my life depended on it. It likely did depend on it, given the size of the alligator. For the first time in many years, I actually thought I might not survive a fight. Even battling demons with Harker, I always thought that I would eventually prevail. I was much less certain about the outcome of this battle.

I felt the uncertainty morph within me into something different, something I had not felt in decades. I felt a prickle of fear, and a rush of excitement coursed through me. My lips pulled back in a fierce grin, and the muscles in my arms and shoulders grew taut with fresh, exhilarated blood. I shifted my weight and planted my feet, halting the creature's forward progress. It thrashed from side to side, but the shattered barrel was jutting through the alligator's snout at one end, and wedged tight between two teeth at the stock. The creature could neither open nor close its mouth, just flail wildly trying to free itself from the thing that pained it.

I let go of the gun, releasing the huge reptile. It spun around in a flash, and I lunged for its back before it escaped. My fingers gripped the scaly spines at its front shoulders, and I was hauled off my feet as the alligator swam toward the far shore, dragging me with it. I pulled myself up along the creature's back, slowly climbing closer and closer to my goal, fighting the rush of the water as the gator swam at enormous speed. It slammed into the riverbank with its snout, trying to dislodge the gun from between its jaws. When that didn't work, it lurched up out of the water and rolled on the bank, its tremendous weight crushing me into the earth as it lay on its back and writhed from side to side. I held on, though I both felt and heard ribs cracking under the beast's onslaught.

The alligator righted itself, and I pulled myself farther forward, until I finally sat astride the thing's shoulders, with its head and snout in front of me.

I punched downward with one fist, caving in its right eye with a single blow. I slammed my left fist into the other eye, blinding the creature and sending it into another paroxysm of pained thrashing. I leaned forward, pulled my right fist back, and pounded its head and orbital socket again and again until finally I felt the bone crunch beneath my blows.

I unclenched my bloodied and battered fist, made a tight spike from my fingers, and jammed my hand into the alligator's eye socket. My hand met resistance inside the orbital socket, but I leaned forward, wrapping my left arm around the alligator's snout and pressing forward with my entire body weight. I shoved my hand in and in, harder and harder, until finally, with a resounding *crunch*, I shoved my hand through the monster's eye socket into its brain. The beast gave one last mighty shiver, then collapsed, its brain mangled by my fist, dead.

The alligator slumped to the ground, and I rolled off to the side, slamming into the mud and the reeds with a splash. I lay there, staring up at the green canopy, listening as the sounds of life came back to the swamp as our mighty battle, so enormous to me and the gator, was forgotten by the other creatures almost immediately. A smile crept across my face as I lay there cataloging my injuries. I counted three broken fingers; one dislocated pinky; innumerable scratches, scrapes, and cuts; four broken ribs; and what felt like three loose teeth. And one shotgun, dead on the scene.

"Adam!" I heard Evangeline's voice calling for me from somewhere nearby.

I groaned, then when making that much noise proved to not be harmful, I called out, "Here!"

"Where are you?"

"Can you see the gator?"

"Yeah, I see him. He looks dead."

"That's because he's dead," I replied. "I'm lying next to him."

"You two need some alone time?" the nun asked. I frowned for a moment, then understood her question and laughed.

"Ouch. Don't make me laugh," I said.

"It only hurts when you laugh?" Evangeline asked, now standing over me. She was soaked to the skin, but looked otherwise unhurt.

"No, it hurts no matter what I do, but it hurts in extra places when I laugh," I said.

She walked around the gator, inspecting the monster's corpse. "Adam, what in the holy hell happened to your shotgun?"

"I tried to shoot the alligator with it."

"While you was underwater?"

"Yes. It seems that was a poor choice."

"You, my friend, are a master of understatement. But, and I will admit that I'm almost afraid to ask, but I'm going to anyway…how exactly did you kill that gator? It looks like you reached in its eye socket and yanked its brains out."

I lay there for a moment trying to come up with a less barbaric way to phrase it. It didn't exist. "I reached in its eye socket and yanked its brains out."

Evangeline looked down at me for a long few seconds, then said, "I'm gonna go get the boat. You lay there until you feel like you can stand up, then you go wash that arm off. You are not dripping gator brains all over the bottom of my boat."

That sounded like an absolutely fantastic idea.

CHAPTER FOURTEEN

Several hours later, I was in Madison's battered church bus headed back to New Orleans with the sun setting over the swampland all around me. I had spent an entire day with Evangeline, hunting a giant alligator, killing said alligator, and then cleaning alligator brains from under my fingernails. When I left, Madison and her two-man security detail were gearing up for a marathon bridge session with Evangeline, a bottle of whiskey sitting in the center of the table with the cap tossed somewhere into the far corners of the shack. I felt the irony of leaving my friend the voodoo priestess in the care of my friend the nun, but they seemed to be fast friends.

I set my phone on the center console of the van and pressed a button. "Dennis, can you hear me?"

"Yeah, I can hear you, but you're a little muffled. What did you do to your phone this time?"

"I wrestled an alligator. The phone was in my pocket. I am surprised it still works."

"It better work," he said. "That case cost me a hundred bucks."

"You steal all your money from Harker, or corporations you don't like," I pointed out.

"Doesn't mean I want to overpay for stuff," he replied. "What do you need?"

"Do you still have surveillance on Jermaine?"

"Thunderlips?" he asked. "Yeah, I've got him."

"I think he only calls himself 'Thunder,'" I corrected.

"I know, I was...never mind," Dennis sighed. I smiled into the windshield. Frustrating my electronic friend was fast becoming an enjoyable pastime, almost on par with making Quincy wonder if I understood his feeble attempts at humor. Most of the time I did, I just didn't think he was funny. That made it better.

"Okay, I've got eyes on your guy," Dennis said. "He's at the club, cleaning up. He's booked to play starting at ten tonight."

"Is there anyone else there? And have you seen them before?"

"There's a couple of touristy looking guys in khaki cargo pants, looking like soccer dads. There's a young couple making out between bites of crème brûlée, a homeless dude sitting at the end of the bar with his head down, and one guy in an expensive suit sitting alone with his back to a wall. He's not there for the food or the hurricanes, I can tell you that much."

"Why is that?"

"He's got an untouched po' boy in front of him, a glass of water he hasn't touched, and his head is on a swivel. He's trying real hard not to look like he's watching Jermaine, but he picked a table with an unobstructed view of the entire joint."

"Does he look familiar?"

"Yeah, it's the same dude that sat next to you the other night."

"Martin," I said, remembering the man, his graceful movements, and the spot of dark red, almost brown on the cuff of his shirt. "I do not trust that man."

"Me neither, but I don't trust anybody. Call it a side effect of getting murdered by a homicide detective, but my trust level is shot to shit."

"Understandable. My own caution is an outgrowth of being chased from my home by a rampaging horde of villagers with pitchforks and torches," I replied, remembering the smell of smoke pouring into my home, driving me farther up the narrow, winding staircase until I reached the roof of my father's manor house. I could hear the chants of the mob below me, the crackle of the flames and the shattering of windows from the heat as the only home I had known was consumed in the fire that threatened to devour me. I felt the rush of water envelope me as I dove from the roof into the rushing river far below, then the crushing impact as I crashed and bounced into the rocks as the current swept me away.

"Hey, Adam!" Dennis' voice yanked me from my reverie, and I focused once more on the present, and the immediate future.

"Yes, Dennis?"

"You with me, buddy?" There was honest concern in his voice, the usual snark gone.

"Yes, I apologize. I was lost in memory for a moment. Is there anything else happening?"

"Nah, just Thunder straightening up, waiting on the bar customers, and every once in a while going over to the stage to polish his horn. And, man, am I glad that is not a euphemism for something else. Is Madison all squared away? Evangeline has her place so damn locked down I can't even get a satellite image of the place."

"Yes, Madison is safe. But if the camp is blacked out, how did you find it in the first place?"

"I looked for the black hole in my net. There's a blackout zone a half-mile in diameter that I figured was centered on Evangeline's camp, so I pointed you to the middle of it."

I thought for a moment. "What if it had been something else? Something unfriendly?"

"Well...that would have been bad," Dennis admitted. "But it wasn't, so we're good, right? Good deal. Talk to you later, pal!" He disconnected the call before I could point out the errors in his logic. And he was right, it had all worked out, so there was no point in harassing him about it now.

———

I left Madison's church van in the public parking lot that her people designated, then proceeded on foot to the French Quarter. The club was busier by far than Dennis had described, but I still found an empty table with little trouble. I placed my back to a wall, making sure I had clear sightlines to both the stage and the man who introduced himself as "Martin."

He still sat at a table alone, an untouched sandwich and drink before him. I observed a waitress walk over to him, reach for his glass to clear it, and him wave a hand to stop her. A folded bill and she nodded and walked off, shaking her head at his behavior but obviously content to ignore him as long as he continued tipping.

I sat, ordered a drink, and kept watch on the room. Jermaine ducked out from behind the bar as his replacement showed up, then a few minutes later, he stepped onto the small stage, drawing a smattering of applause from the crowd.

"Hey, y'all," he said, leaning down into a microphone before him. "I'd like to thank y'all for coming out tonight. We gonna play some old stuff, some new stuff, and a few originals. I hope you all have a good time. So now, without any further ado, I'm Thunder Travis, and these are my Lightning Bolts!" He pressed the trumpet to his lips and blew out the first few notes of an upbeat jazz number. The band picked up the rhythm, and they were off to the races.

Thunder and the Bolts played the crowd as much as they played their instruments, dropping into slower, cooler jazz when the crowd was thin, pumping things up when the crowd was hopping, and generally keeping everyone in the room dancing, drinking, or at least tapping toes for the next two hours. Everyone but me, that is. Everyone but me and the businessman in the corner, who kept his head on a swivel as if he were waiting for someone in particular to show up.

After a long set, Jermaine leaned into the mic and said, "Thank y'all! We're gonna take a short break, but we'll be back in twenty minutes or so. If we don't give Ellis a break every couple hours, he sobers up, and the last thing you want in a jazz band is a sober drummer!" The crowd laughed along with the drummer, a stout bald white man in his fifties, who waved at the crowd with a big grin on his face.

The band stepped off the low stage and wove through the crowd toward the bar and the restrooms, accepting congratulatory backslaps and hand-shakes as they passed happy drunken revelers. Jermaine paused at the end of the bar to exchange an elaborate handshake and hug with the homeless man I had seen in the park the day before. He'd been sitting on the same stool sipping water through the entire set, eyes closed and swaying in time to the music.

I turned my head to resume surveillance on "Martin," only to find his chair empty and his table cleared. I scanned the room but could not see him through the throng of people. I stood, and my height made it a simple thing to spot the man in the expensive suit near the stage. I saw "Martin" pick up Jermaine's trumpet from the stand on the stage, tuck it under his coat in a horrible attempt to mask the thing, and start for the door.

I moved to intercept and cut off his route in the middle of the crowd. "I don't think that belongs to you," I said, nodding at the oddly misshapen lump beneath his suit coat.

"This is none of your business, freak. Get out of my way before you get hurt." His voice was low and gravelly, with an inhuman growl behind it.

"I've been hurt before," I said. "It all heals. And that doesn't belong to you."

"You are meddling in things beyond your ken, mortal," he hissed, and now it sounded as though his tongue was forked, the sibilance taking over his diction.

"There is at least one misconception in that sentence," I replied, then punched him in the face. He staggered back and crashed into the clumped humanity behind him.

"That's for running out on my sister, you dick!" I bellowed, advancing on the well-dressed man as he struggled to get back to his feet and hold on to the trumpet at the same time. I threw an uppercut that lifted him off his feet and flung him back through another clump of people. I stepped into the punch, swinging from my heels and putting nearly my full strength into the blow. If he were human and merely a trumpet thief, that punch would have decapitated him.

It didn't. He flew back, his arms flying out from his body as he lost consciousness for an instant. The trumpet flew from his hands and landed in the arms of a woman in the crowd, who turned and set it on the bar. The man struggled to his feet, shoving away the hands of people trying to help. His eyes glowed red for a brief second, then he rocked his head from side to side and gave me a nasty grin.

"Martin" glowed with a red and purple aura for a brief moment, then red light blazed from his form. When the dazzle cleared, the well-dressed businessman was gone. Standing in his place was a humanoid form, only larger, nearing my own seven-foot height. His skin was the darkest ebony, with short horns extending from his forehead. His mouth stretched preternaturally wide, almost from ear-to-ear, with fangs extending down past his lower lip. He wore chain mail and carried a curved sword in one hand. A long narrow tail hung down nearly to the floor, until he twitched it up over one shoulder to point the needle-sharp spike on the end of it straight at me.

"That was a mistake, mortal," he said, and his forked tongue flicked out across his fangs.

"Again, you have some misconceptions about me, demon," I replied.

"What would those be?"

"You assume that I didn't mean to expose you for what you truly are. Then you assume that I am mortal." I waded forward against the crush of humanity rushing for the exits and got almost within grappling distance of the demon before throwing my first punch.

He ducked, far too fast for my impeded punch to score a hit, and slashed across my forearm with his tail. The sea of onrushing humanity split apart around us, and I found myself with a clear space to fight. The demon grinned at me and ran his tail spike in front of his face. We locked eyes as the creature licked my blood from its tail and grinned at me.

"Are you ready to die, human? Will you die screaming like the little bitch you are, or can you hold on to some shred of dignity like the old man?" the demon asked. There was no question in my mind that he meant Oliver, and the grin that stretched across its disgusting face said that he expected me to die horribly.

For the second time in as many nights, I found myself fighting a stronger opponent in unfamiliar territory with insufficient weapons. Perhaps Evangeline was right. It seemed I needed to re-evaluate my life choices.

Then the demon charged, and the time for thinking was past.

CHAPTER FIFTEEN

How does one battle a demon in a crowded bar? There are no rulebooks on this type of combat, and no amount of travel to ancient masters of meditation can prepare one for having a mammoth demon warrior attack with flailing sword and razor-sharp tail. Sparring with the world's oldest and most decorated vampire, who also happens to possess centuries of battlefield experience does prove useful, however.

The demon charged straight in, the bullrush of a monster accustomed to being the strongest and most fearsome creature in every battle. In that sense, the terrifying unstoppable force met the horrific immovable object because all I did was plant my feet and throw an elbow at the beast's onrushing forehead.

The point of my elbow crashed into "Martin's" head with a sickening *crunch*, and I spun on my heel at the impact. "Martin" dropped like a stone, falling flat on his face to the hardwood floor. I shook my numb right arm, then pounced on my momentarily downed foe. I drove a knee into his spine, hearing another set of grotesque crunches as I broke at least four ribs. I wrapped my left arm around the demon's throat and pulled upward, bending his body almost to ninety degrees. I drew back my right fist for what I hoped would be a killing blow, then bellowed as hot agony shredded my wrist and hand.

I looked up to see the monster's tail spike protruding through my wrist, my thick blood coursing down my forearm. It withdrew the spike, causing fresh fire to run through me, then it jabbed the spike at my face, forcing me to launch myself sideways off the demon's back. I skittered back on my rear, narrowly avoiding losing an eye to the tail's jabs, and pulled a table in front of one fierce thrust. The tail slammed into the dark wood surface of the table and stuck, allowing me a moment's grace to scramble to my feet.

"Martin" had regained his footing as well, looking considerably the worse for wear. Mere seconds into our battle, and he was clutching his ribs, had blood streaming down his face where my elbow split his forehead to the bone, and had a round table stuck on the end of his tail, effectively negating that weapon.

I was in better shape, but still far from whole. My elbow throbbed from the impact with the demon's skull, and my right hand was essentially useless and was dripping blood all over the floor, making my footing treacherous. Nevertheless, I persisted. I stomped toward the demon, picking up a splintered chair leg as I went. Armed with my makeshift club, I squared off against the monster.

"I will accept your surrender at any point," I growled to the demon. Quincy tells me often that I need to improve my mid-fight banter, but I often find myself clinging to my shreds of humanity by the most tenuous of threads, making conversation difficult.

"I will eat your heart with pralines, monster," the demon hissed back. It dragged the table around in front of itself, planted a foot on the edge, and yanked its tail free. Thus unencumbered, it charged me again, vaulting over the table and covering the twenty feet between us in two leaping strides.

I stepped to the right and swung the chair leg at its knees with my left hand. I heard a resounding *crack*, like small-arms fire, as I connected, and "Martin" went sailing into the far wall. A pulling sensation along my face followed by a line of fire drawn along my cheek told me the tail had scored another hit even before I reached up and drew my fingers away red.

The demon fetched up against the wall in a heap, but righted itself instantly. I looked down at the shattered club in my fist and dropped it. My right arm was almost usable again, my healing sped along by whatever strange magics kept me alive and ambulatory long after my component parts should have decayed.

I felt the pain subside, replaced by a familiar fury. This monster didn't belong here. This monster was too small and puny to challenge me. This *monster* must die! A red haze suffused my vision, and I attacked, lowering my shoulder and charging the demon. I slammed into the monster, pancaking him into the plaster wall, then fire erupted in my neck and abdomen, and I staggered back.

I looked down, and saw the demon's ebon blade protruding from my stomach. I had impaled myself in my fury, not the first time rage and pain had obscured the dangers of my actions. I felt another ripping in my flesh, this time in the junction of my neck and shoulder, and turned my head right to see the tail spike pulling out of my mangled flesh.

The demon stepped forward, driving the sword through the meat of my left shoulder. The tail flashed forward, jabbing through my neck sideways, the point coming out in a pointed parody of the neck bolts Boris Karloff wore in the film depiction of me. My grinning opponent yanked both the sword and spike free at the same moment, and I fell. I collapsed backward, my knees bending in a painful outward splay, and my head impacting the floor with a hollow *thunk* that was certainly a commentary on my empty-headed frontal assault on a demon.

I knew better. I wasn't the wild-eyed monster I once was. I knew how to attack a superior enemy, how to distract the demon, how to feint, how to draw it into fighting me on my terms. But in the moment, when I saw an opportunity to destroy Oliver's killer, I lost my way.

The demon stood over me, a wicked grin splitting its midnight-black countenance. Its eyes flickered red with the fires of the Pits shining from within the monster's darkened, condemned soul, and its smile was the stuff of toothy nightmares.

"Time to die, creature," the demon said with a low chuckle. "I'll eat your spleen, then I'll hunt down that magical bitch you've got tucked away in the swamp somewhere. When I'm finished with her, I'll have all the time in the world to hunt down the Horn of the Herald without interference."

It raised the black sword high overhead, my blood running down to spill off the cross guard, and as the blade started to fall, I whispered one thing.

"I'm sorry, Oliver. I failed you, my friend."

Then the sword flashed down, and as the tip cut though my shirt and touched the medal lying on my chest, a white light shone forth with the force of a supernova, and I was suddenly wrapped in a gold-and-purple cocoon of light and power. The demonic blade shattered against my shield, and I felt the healing light course through me. My wounds were flashed closed, and I felt the power trapped in the amulet knit my shattered bones and stitch torn tendons back together.

New strength flowed through me, and I felt power the likes of which I hadn't known since that storm-filled night of my birth so many years ago. I sat bolt upright, hearing two voices mingled in my ears. One, my father's demented, prideful screeching, "I've done it!" The other, a softer, subtler voice with the slightest lisp and the scent of the Gulf in every word saying, "Live, my friend. Live!"

Victor Frankenstein animated me in a thunderstorm many decades ago, and for that, I will never forgive him. My friend Oliver Rambeoux resurrected me in the middle of a battle on an autumn night in New Orleans, and for that, I will always be grateful. I stood, glaring down at the demon lying sprawled on the floor of the small jazz club, and in his eyes, I saw a most familiar and welcome sight. I saw the thing that had filled most every eye to land upon me for more than a century. I saw it, and for the first time, I welcomed it.

In the demon's eyes, looking up at me as he held the hilt of his broken obsidian blade, I saw fear.

I picked the monster up by his throat and hefted him up over my head. I slammed him into a nearby table, turning it to splinters. I hauled the demon to his feet, then spun him around and slammed him face-first into a wall. I drove his horned head into the surface of the bar, then pounded his ribs with knee strikes until his ribs were ground glass. I shattered the monster's spine with a brutal double-fisted hammer strike that drove him to the ground and left a horn snapped off in the front of the bar.

I rolled his limp form over with an ungentle nudge of my boot, then I hauled the demon up to look me in the eye. Its head lolled on a shattered neck, and it was barely able to speak through its shattered jaw, but I didn't care. I wanted this thing to look me in the eye as I dispatched it.

"Are you ready to return to Hell, demon?" I growled.

"Yes, send me home, fool," it said with a grin. "You can't kill me, so just send me back to the fires where I shall be re-forged into a stronger weapon for my Lord to use against you foolish mortals! Nothing you can do will ever truly hurt me!"

"What about me?" a soft voice said from my left. I looked, and standing in front of the stage was the homeless man from the end of the bar. He held Jermaine's trumpet in his hands, and there was a pale white light surrounding him.

"Can I hurt you, Ezariem, Lieutenant of the Seventh Army, Baronet of the Pits? Can I hurt you, my poor, beaten, broken cousin?" The man's voice was soothing, like the mist after a summer thunderstorm, and the expression on his face was beatific. Tears streamed down his cheeks as he raised the trumpet to his lips, and he began to play.

The melody was soft and low, almost inaudible. I *saw* the magic as it flowed from the Horn, wrapping around the demon in my grasp and gently prying loose my fingers. Blue, white, and golden light surrounded the demon, Ezariem, and he floated in midair, rotating slowly like a glowing top. He spun faster, picking up speed and glowing brighter with every revolution. He spun faster, and as he spun, he began to scream. He screamed in terror, then in agony, then in the silent shrieking of someone undergoing so much torment that their voice is simply shattered. He spun, and screamed, and glowed, and flared brighter, and shrieked higher, and spun faster until, with a silent explosion of multi-hued dust, he vanished.

I turned to the homeless trumpeter, who now stood before me a six-foot-tall woman in white robes with huge golden wings sprouting from her shoulders, and was amazed to find tears still pouring down her face.

"Why are you crying?" I asked, wanting very much to reach out to her, but also terrified of defiling this glorious creature with my touch.

"He was my kin," she said, and the sound of her voice at the same time filled me with peace as I had never felt, and the horrible anguish of loss that I had never escaped.

"I am sorry you had to hurt him," I said. "But I am grateful for the assistance. Sealtiel, I presume?"

"I am Sealtiel," she confirmed. "I am the Herald, and if I am needed, then these must indeed be dark times."

"You are needed. You are *all* needed," I said.

"Then I will come." She turned and walked over to the bar, where Jermaine cowered. "You may come out now, Jermaine. You are safe."

The big man's head poked up from under the bar. He looked around and shook his head at the destruction, then took another look at Sealtiel. "Steve? Is that you?"

"Yes," the angel replied. "You knew me as Homeless Steve, or Stevie Shoes, and you were always kind to me. That is appreciated, Jermaine. I must go, and I must take the Horn of the Herald with me." She motioned to the trumpet she carried, and Jermaine nodded.

"I always thought there was something special about that horn, man. I mean, ma'am. I mean, Your Angelness. What am I supposed to call you?"

"You may call me Steve, if that is easier."

"Thanks. Yeah, Steve, I always knew I wasn't as good on any other horn. There was just something about that one, ya know?"

Sealtiel looked at the trumpet in her hands and smiled. "I do know. But I would not leave you without an instrument." She gestured to the stage, where a new trumpet sat on Jermaine's stand, gleaming in the spotlight from one of the few unsheltered bulbs in the building. "I think you will find it satisfactory."

"Wow, um, thanks!" Jermaine said. He vaulted the bar and almost slipped in a puddle of demon goo.

"That will not do," Sealtiel said. "The people here were kind, unlike many I have encountered." She waved a hand, and the bar was restored to its former state, with no sign of the devastation the demon and I had wreaked upon it. I was beginning to understand why Quincy often traveled with a guardian angel. If nothing else, they were good for cleanup.

The angel stepped over to me, her eyes fixed on the medal around my neck. "Curious," she said, reaching out to touch the Purple Heart. "Do you know what this is?"

"I thought it was just a memento from a friend. I now believe it to be much more."

"Yes, much more indeed." She looked up into my eyes. "Shall we go? I believe my brothers are in need of me." Then she turned and walked out of the bar, her wings fading with each step until she took the form of an ordinary, if very pretty, human woman.

I turned to Jermaine. "Now that the demon is gone, you should be safe. If you need me, just dial 'Adam' in your phone."

He looked confused. "How did you get in my contacts list?"

"I have a friend," I said, and walked out into the street after my angel to meet the sunrise over the Crescent City.

PART IV
RUNNING WITH THE DEVIL

CHAPTER ONE

"This is so not my scene," I said, sipping a Stella Artois and looking around, feeling spectacularly out of place. I've been all over the world and seen all manner of wonders and horrors. I can converse in several languages and have dealt with heads of state, heads of corporations, and heads of dark covens. I've been arrested, celebrated, intoxicated on six continents, and gotten laid on five (never did the deed in Asia, oddly enough). But Purgatory was very much not my scene.

Not the metaphysical dimension between Heaven and Hell, though that may very well be an apt description of my life. No, this Purgatory was Purgatory 124, the Carolinas' longest-running fetish party, held in a converted warehouse set off the beaten path in an industrial park in Charlotte. Part rave, part S&M club, part geek convention dealer room, and part mosh pit, Purgatory was the kind of place where the freak flags flew loud and proud. There were more nipple rings on display than earrings, and the last time I was around that much leather, it was still part of a cow. I stood at the bar, my Doc Martens, long black coat, black dress shirt, and black jeans letting me blend in just a little, but I was pretty sure I stuck out like a sore thumb.

Maybe if you didn't stare so much, you'd fit in more, Detective Rebecca Gail Flynn said through our mental link.

Maybe if you weren't walking around in leather pants and boots straight out of a teenage boy's spank bank, I wouldn't stare. And that's not even mentioning that bustier. Where'd you get that thing, anyway? And why haven't I seen it before?

Don't be crude, Harker. We're on the clock. Flynn danced out of my line of sight, much to my chagrin. She was a good-looking woman in sweats and a burlap sack, but tonight she looked like sex on two legs. I really wanted to get this gig over with, find the missing Archangel Uriel, and get Becks home so I could show my appreciation for her help. And her wardrobe.

"You need another drink, honey?" a short woman with pale skin and brown-and-green hair asked from my elbow. I looked down at her and got a view straight down her open blouse to the leather bra she wore. When I tried to look somewhere a little more modest, I realized that her blouse was see-through and that she was wearing nothing more than the blouse, bra, matching black leather panties, a garter belt, and fishnets. I didn't look at her feet. Frankly, I didn't give a shit what kind of shoes she was wearing, if she wore shoes at all.

"Nah, I'm good," I said, trying very hard to look at her eyes.

"Then how about a spanking? I'm Mistress Amy, and I have a few minutes before my next appointment." She gestured over to a wooden apparatus that looked like a waist-high bench with four leather cuffs. It took me a minute to figure out how everything was supposed to line up, but I eventually realized that she was inviting me to lean over it so she could paddle me.

"You know, another beer sounds great, now that I think about it," I said, draining mine in a long gulp.

Mistress Amy laughed, a gentle, high-pitched giggle that was infectious. I found myself smiling as the bartender put another Stella in my hand. "What are you having, hon?" I asked her.

"Oh, I never drink when I play. I don't want to dull the sensations," she said with a smile. I found myself smiling back. This was not what I expected from a fetish party. "Is this your first time here?"

"Does it show?" I replied with a smile of my own.

"Oh yeah, sweetie. It definitely shows. Plus, the newbies always hang onto the bar like it's a life raft. It's kinda cute."

"Yeah, this is a new one for me. I…a friend invited me, and now I can't find him in the crowd."

"If you think this is crowded, just wait until things really get going. DJ Spider is up next, and she always brings the fun." She pointed to the stage, where a gorgeous woman stood behind a pair of turntables. She was dressed as the superhero Dazzler and must have been over six feet tall in her sparkly platform shoes. She touched a few buttons on the DJ rig, and Rob Zombie's "More Human than Human" blared from the speakers. I bobbed my head to the music and drank my beer, scanning the crowd for anyone who looked like they might be an archangel in disguise. There weren't many candidates in this crowd.

I opened up my Sight, peering at the throng of dancing humanity in the supernatural spectrum. I saw a dozen or so minor charms, probably designed to enhance attractiveness or lower inhibitions. There were several moderately powerful witches peppered through the crowd, and one minor demon who looked around in panic as soon as he felt my Sight on him. He bolted through a side exit and was gone seconds later. I spotted a couple of vampires and what might have been one succubus, but nothing divine.

Well, until Rebecca sidled up next to me, reached out with her slender hand, and wrapped her caramel-colored fingers around the neck of my bottle. I released my grip as she pulled my beer to her lips and turned to her, admiring her graceful neck as she swallowed. She was out of my league on my best day, and we both knew it. I was a moderately good-looking guy of somewhere north of a century old, and she was a beautiful young woman with her whole life ahead of her. I decided not to dwell on that too long and stared at her boobs instead. Much happier topic.

Of course, it being a crowded bar, I wasn't the only one looking. "Can I buy you a drink?" the meathead next to her asked.

"I've got a drink," she said, holding up my beer and waggling it in front of the guy's face. "And a date. But have a good time." She turned her back on the guy and handed me back my beer. I looked at the meathead, and if there was anybody who looked more out of place than me, it was him. He wore a bright red New England Patriots t-shirt, and a Boston Red Sox baseball cap on backwards. He was rocking khaki cargo shorts and flip-flops, the official uniform of the American fraternity douchebro, and I wondered for a second if he just happened to stagger into the wrong bar.

Then he put his hand on Becks' shoulder, and I knew I was going to have to break somebody tonight.

"Hey," he growled. "I was talking to you."

Before I could step around her to deal with the idiot, Becks whirled on him, jabbing three fingers into his throat and one knee into his groin in one smooth motion. As he collapsed, she leaned forward and caught him. "If you ever lay a hand on a woman without her permission again, I'll find out. Then I'll hunt you down and wear those tiny little balls I just crushed for earrings. Do you understand me, asshole?"

Meathead nodded, and Rebecca let go of his shoulder. He dropped almost to his knees but caught himself on a bar stool before he went all the way down. After a few seconds of gasping and wheezing, he straightened up and wove his way through the crowd for the door. I motioned for the bartender to bring us another pair of Stellas and gestured to the stool. Becks shook her head, so I sat. "Nice shot," I said.

"You're a bad influence on me. A couple years ago, I would have just slapped his face. Now I had to restrain myself from putting that idiot in the hospital."

"Then I'd say I'm a good influence. He deserved a lot more than you gave him. Besides, fuck that guy, we've got important angel hunting to do. And you've got more dancing to do."

"You just like looking at my boobs in this top." She was smiling when she said it, so I figured whatever moment of introspection she was in was over.

"Nah," I replied. "I like looking at your boobs no matter what top you're wearing, or even if you're not wearing one. I'm an equal-opportunity ogler."

Becks shook her head and sipped her beer, giving me a smile as she did. "Yeah? Well, what kind of opportunity was Miss Lingerie giving you when I was dancing?" She nodded over to where Mistress Amy was paddling a chubby guy who was strapped into her apparatus. The solid *thwacks* coming from that direction told me she was swinging for the fences, but if the grin on the guy's face was any indication, he was into it.

"She had a cancellation and wanted to know if she could work me in for a spanking. I told her I appreciated the offer, but I passed."

"Good idea. Nobody kicks your ass but me, Harker."

"Oh, if only that were true," I said with a smile.

"Any luck finding our angel?"

"Nothing," I said. "There's some magic running around, but nothing divine. No big surprise there."

We stood at the bar people-watching and drinking for a while, then wandered upstairs where there were a few vendor tables set up. I skipped over the displays of paddles and nipple clamps to check out the jewelry stand manned by a smiling African-American man with long dreads. I picked up a silver ankh on a long black leather thong. "How much?"

"Twenty-five," he said. "I made it myself." I paid the man and slipped the necklace on over my head. I'm not much of a jewelry guy, but having a little bit of bling helped me fit in. Besides, he was nice.

"Your first Purgatory?" he asked.

"Am I wearing a sign?"

"No, but there aren't many men here wearing jeans," he said.

"My ass-less chaps are at the cleaners," I said, tipping my beer to him. We both laughed, and I sidled up behind Becks, who was browsing a display of corsets.

"What do you think of this one?" She held up a garment for my perusal, and I raised an eyebrow.

"I think you'd look great in it," I said, giving her and the corset appraising glances. "But I'm not sure where you'd hide your gun."

"I think if I wear this, I'd just knock people dead with my boobs," she replied with a smile.

"But what a way to go." I grinned back at her. We wandered off from the vendors and leaned over the rail, looking down into the crowd. "Maybe this is a bust. The seeing I cast really made it look like it would be here tonight, though. You ready to bail?"

"I'm good to hang out for a while," Becks said. "This is kinda fun. Like a walk on the wild side, but safe, you know?"

"Okay, then lemme grab us another couple beers." I walked over to the upstairs bar and ordered two Stellas, returning to the rail just as a dark-haired man with a goatee stepped up to the microphone.

"Ladies, gentlemen, and perverts of all persuasions, please welcome to the stage, for a demonstration of whip play, the amazing, the inimitable, the one and only...TORCH!"

Applause erupted as a man of about forty stepped out onto the stage, wearing leather pants, a black leather vest, and a top hat. In his hand, he held a bullwhip, which he spun around his head and cracked to even more thunderous applause. The second the whip cracked, I felt a tingle along all my magical senses that had nothing to do with the beautiful scantily-clad woman on my arm.

I opened up my Sight and looked to the stage, dropping back to the normal spectrum immediately to keep from being blinded. The glow from the stage was bright as the sun. I leaned over to Flynn. "The guy with the whip? That's our angel."

"Ummm, are you sure, Harker? I went to the Purgatory website. That's the guy that runs this show."

"Well, then the founder of Charlotte's largest fetish party is also the Archangel Uriel. That's awkward."

Then the doors burst open, a dozen religious zealots charged in, and things got really awkward.

CHAPTER TWO

They came in dressed all in white, but without the hoods I've come to expect from people wearing white after Labor Day. Close though, since they did wear bandannas covering the lower half of their faces, Western bank robber-style. Where do you even buy a dozen white bandannas? I guess if they're all white, they're hankies. So these religious zealots burst into the room wearing hankies on their faces, and the party went to shit in a hurry.

One of the assclowns reached over to the wall by the door and slapped the light switches, bathing the room in a bright white fluorescent glare that isn't conducive to any kind of sex, kinky or otherwise. If you ever want to throw cold water on a party that involves a lot of black leather and handcuffs, fluorescents and Jesus are a great combo for that, believe me.

Four of the jerks ran straight for the stairs and to the balcony, then began showering the people below with what looked like religious tracts. One fat guy in a white t-shirt with his belly hanging out (it's okay, his belly was almost as white as his shirt, so he was still all the right color), white jeans, white shoes (after Labor Day, no less), and a hankie around his face shoved a tract in my hands. He yelled "Repent!" in my face, getting so close that I could smell the broccoli on his breath.

I did what I usually do when assholes get in my face. Okay, maybe not exactly what I usually do, since I didn't shoot him. But I did punch him right in the nose, screwing up his monochromatic life by putting a splash of red all over his hankie. He dropped to the floor, and I turned around, looking for the angel.

"Son of a *bitch!*" I growled. "Becks, I gotta get down there," I said as I watched my quarry stage dive all two hundred fifty pounds of himself right onto a pair of the invaders. He took them out, but more swarmed him, screaming about patron saints of sin and dragging him toward the front door.

"Easier said than done, Harker," Flynn said from beside me.

I turned and sighed as I saw the entire place erupting in chaos. The dozen dickweasels who came through the front door had been joined by another twenty or so streaming in from the back, and the whole place, balcony included, was turning into a vicious mosh pit. Only with mosh pits, most people don't really want to beat the shit out of everybody else. Not so much the case with these guys. The backdoor assholes swung bats and two-by-fours while the partygoers armed themselves with paddles and whips from the vendor tables. Some of them just wisely hid behind the bars or under the tables, but a solid two or three dozen gleefully joined the fray.

"Back off, fuckwit," I heard Rebecca say, and I turned back to her. A white-clad douchebag held a slab of lumber over his head, looking like he wanted nothing more than to crack her skull.

I stepped forward, snatched the board from his grip, and backhanded him across the face. He spun around and dropped to one knee, but came back up and stepped up to me again, doing that stupid thing where guys bump their chest into you. That's never a good idea against someone who actually wants to fight you, and I really wanted to hit somebody right then. So I gave him a headbutt to the face, hearing a satisfying *crunch* as his nose pulped under the impact of my forehead. Our assailant staggered back, hands pressed to his face, and I kicked him in the jewels. He dropped to his knees, and I slammed my fist into the hinge of his jaw, probably dislocating it, and definitely rendering him unconscious. He slumped to the floor, and I turned back to the balcony rail.

"I gotta go," I said to Becks. "Try not to shoot anybody." Then I vaulted the rail and dropped into the fight on the ground floor.

The last thing I heard before I went over was her saying, "Where the hell do you think I could hide my gun?"

I landed on the back of two scrapping partygoers, driving them to the floor. "Sorry," I said, getting to my feet.

One of them, a big guy with a shaved head and a goatee that reached halfway to his bellybutton, got up and glared at me. I looked up at him, giving him my best "that's a bad idea" glare, and he got the hint. Something cracked across my shoulders, and I went down in an explosion of pain. I rolled over, both to see who I had to kill and to try and avoid getting my head bashed in, and saw an albino asswipe with a baseball bat standing over me grinning. His white clothing hid everything but his blue eyes, and they crinkled at the corners as he smiled down at me.

"I will drive the sin from your soul with pain and justice!" he yelled, raising the bat.

I called up a red-tinged ball of energy and flung it at his chest, slamming him into the air and setting his shirt on fire. I got to my feet, calling up enough power to make myself glow with a crimson aura. I stalked over to the bat-wielding dickhead, enhancing my voice so my words were easily heard even over the Skinny Puppy blaring from the speakers. "I will send you to Hell for all eternity, you cowardly ratfuck bastard. I will shove that bat so far up your ass you get splinters in your retinas. I will use your ears for handgrips while I skullfuck your eye sockets, you miserable bag of excrement. You have three seconds to get the fuck out of this time zone or I will mutilate you so bad even dental records won't help identify your body."

Then I started throwing magic at him. I flung bolt after bolt of bright colorful energy at the jerk as he skittered along his ass trying to get away from me. I tossed yellow, red, blue, green, purple, white, pink—every color I could imagine. The bolts didn't do anything more than singe his ass and cripple his pride, they were more for show than anything else, but my little display had the desired effect. Every motherfucker in the room stopped fighting and focused their undivided attention on me. I hit the Babe Ruth wannabe with one last rainbow-hued energy bolt, which was really just a sleep spell with fireworks wrapped around it, then turned to examine the room and the shocked combatants standing frozen while they gazed at me in shock and awe.

I threw a blast of power at the sound board, and with an explosion of sparks, the music stopped. "Who is responsible for this bullshit?" I bellowed.

Nobody moved. I saw some of the white guys carefully not looking at one guy on the stage, so I knew it was him. "WHO?" I shouted, punctuating my question with a blast of power flung at the stacks of speakers on the sides of the stage. They were harmless sparkler-spells, but nobody needed to know that I was just playing the modern-day equivalent of Gandalf at Bilbo's birthday party. The last thing I needed was some fool of a Took getting in my way.

The guy nobody seemed willing to look at stepped to the center of the stage. "I called this rally. We are here to bring an end to this den of filth in our community. We shall have no truck with the devil, and we wish to see this type of perversion brought to a close immediately." I was fifty feet away from him, and I could see even at that distance that I had the worst kind of opponent on my hands—a true believer.

"Do you have a problem with fun? Or just public fun?" I asked, walking forward both to get closer to the stage and to get a better line of sight on where the guy I'd pegged as the Archangel ended up. I couldn't see him, but that didn't really mean anything. There were a lot of guys with goatees in black leather around.

"I have no problem with fun. I have a problem with perversion!" the man thundered. He had a big voice for a skinny dude, and I hoped he didn't have too much of a bad habit of his mouth writing checks his ass couldn't cash. If he'd gotten away with this kind of shit too often, it was unlikely I was going to be able to talk him into leaving quietly and letting these folks get back to running angle grinders over metal brassieres and using people as swingsets.

"If you have a problem with kink, then don't get kinky. But don't go telling these folks how to live. That's not cool, man." I tried to keep my voice level, but the more I scanned the crowd, the more I didn't see the guy they called Torch anywhere. If this doucherocket got my Archangel disappeared, I was really going to beat his ass.

"I don't care about cool—" he started, but I interrupted.

"I can tell. I mean, your wardrobe alone gives that one away."

His face turned red, bringing a little color to his ensemble at least. He yanked his hankie down and scowled at me. "I will not be mocked. You are just another sinner, and you will be brought to the way of the Lord. By force, if necessary! Lightbringers, show this fool his sin!"

Half a dozen of his white-clad thugs rushed me, and I figured the time for talking was over. This was a lot tougher than most of my fights because I couldn't just kill these idiots. I couldn't shoot them because my gun was sitting useless locked in the glove box of my car, and I couldn't just rip their spines out because they were human. I never thought I'd say it, but sometimes it's just easier fighting demons.

I threw out a quick side kick and caught one guy in the gut. He went down, and I ducked a big looping roundhouse from a giant in white. Where the hell did they find an Andre the Giant lookalike willing to wear all white and beat up freaks on a perfectly good Saturday night? I kicked Andre in the knee, and he did what all giants do when they can't stand up—he fell down.

Two of them grabbed my arms, but they expected a normal human level of resistance. I'm far from normal, and not completely human, so I pulled my arms around in front of myself and slammed the goons together. Then I punched them both in the face, and they collapsed in a heap of bloody noses.

Pro tip—don't wear all white to a fistfight. Red shirt and brown pants are recommended. The stains don't show as bad.

That left two assholes in white standing in front of me. I rushed one of them and bowled him over. Unfortunately, he dragged me down with him, and we hit the floor in a heap. I said a silent thanks to Uncle Luke and his psycho wives for my enhanced immune system because a bar floor on a Saturday night is no safe place for man nor beast. I bounced my opponent's head off the floor a couple times, then turned around, looking for the last asshole.

He was already down, his baseball bat laying on the floor beside him, and my girlfriend, the always-awesome Rebecca Gail Flynn, standing over him in leather pants and a spiked corset. He was unconscious, so he couldn't even enjoy the view, which, trust me, was stunning. "Nice work," I said, getting to my feet.

"Thanks. Looks like your little debate partner flew the coop."

"Not surprising." I looked around. Most of the white-garbed dickheads were gone, and a fair number of the partygoers were streaming out the back door as the first members of the Charlotte-Mecklenburg Police Department came through the front. They had their tasers out, and Flynn made her badge appear from somewhere beneath her corset.

"You seen the angel?" she asked.

"Not since the fight broke out and he decided to stage dive into the fray," I said. I opened up my Sight and scanned the room. "Fuck,"

"What is it? You see him?"

"No, he's gone. But there's demon sludge in the air." I could see the taint a demonic entity left behind, like an oil slick across our plane. Not only was the angel gone, but it looked like a demon took him. Now I had to not only find the Archangel Uriel, I had to rescue him from demons.

CHAPTER THREE

An hour later, I sat on the couch in Luke's apartment with a bag of frozen peas on my Saran-wrapped to my right fist and a tumbler of Maker's Mark in my left hand. Becks sat across from me on the other couch in a pair of my old sweatpants and a ratty old *Hellblazer* t-shirt. Luke puttered around the living room, straightening cushions and generally looking grumpy. The sun would be up in a couple hours, so he was nesting. This was a new thing for my uncle, better known as Count Vlad Dracula, the most famous vampire in history. But ever since the last Renfield died and we saved the world from getting turned into a conduit between Hell and Heaven, Luke had been downright domestic. It was a little creepy.

"Why do you even have frozen peas? You don't eat," I asked, more to get him to sit down than anything else.

It worked. He stepped around the overstuffed armchair and sat next to Rebecca. "I have you in my life, Quincy. That has led to innumerable adventures, no small amount of joy, and an appreciation for first aid that would otherwise be unknown to me. I have a bag of frozen peas in my home for precisely the application you are using them now, to reduce swelling and conform to difficult to bandage body parts. You are prone to injure yourself in new and interesting ways, and I cannot always spare the blood to heal you immediately."

"Not to mention you like to watch me suffer," I grumbled, taking a long sip of my whiskey.

"There is also that," Luke agreed. "Now, tell me again what happened at the club."

He wasn't being a dick, making me repeat shit over and over just out of spite, or trying to catch me embellishing my fighting prowess or anything stupid like that. This had been a part of our post-combat ritual for decades. Luke makes me repeat a story at least three times, and he listens for the new bits each time, the pieces that don't pop out in the first telling. Sometimes pertinent details get glossed over by the front brain, but if you poke at a story long enough, the lizard brain brings them out. That's what Luke was pushing by making me tell the story over and over again—my lizard brain.

I got to the part where I started to scrap with the half-dozen assholes, and Luke stopped me. "What did he call his minions?"

"Lightbringers," I replied. "I said that."

"You said that this time. But not the first time you told the story." And just like that, we had a clue. I looked over at Rebecca.

"On it," she said, grabbing the TV remote. She pointed the remote at the wall-mounted fifty-five-inch LCD "smart TV" and fired up the internet-connected device. "Dennis, you there?"

A giant unicorn head with a rainbow mane popped onto the screen. "Technically, yes and no. I'm always here because there isn't really a 'here' here, if that makes any sense." Dennis Bolton, often called "Sparkles" because of his tendency toward stupid internet avatars, was the disembodied soul of an old friend who was murdered during one of my first fights with the demon Orobas and his minions. I transferred his soul into my cell phone in an attempt to save it, and he hopped out of my phone and into the internet. It was kinda like *Tron* with less glowing Frisbees and more demons.

"Not in any relevant universe," Flynn said. "What do you know about a group of religious zealots called Lightbringers?"

"One second," he said, then the unicorn head spun around, emitting a shower of rainbow-colored sparkles and cartoon stars. "You like my new effect? I've decided to do that anytime I come up with the answer to a question. Do you love it?" Sometimes I think my disembodied thirty-year-old friend is actually the soul of a k-pop fashionista and not an American tech wizard who happened to get murdered by a demonspawn and sent into the Matrix.

"I love it," I said, my voice James Bond martini-dry.

"Perfect!" Sparkles said. "If it annoys Harker, then I love it." These are my friends. My enemies are nicer; they just want to kill me.

Sparkles started talking, and I leaned forward. "Okay, *Lightbringer* is a series of fantasy novels by a guy names Brent Weeks..."

"Nope," I said.

"It's also the name of a sword on George R.R. Martin's *A Song of Ice and Fire*…"

"Is that like *Game of Thrones?*" I asked.

"You have read a book once in your life, right, Harker?" Flynn asked.

"If it's worth a shit, they'll make a TV show," I said. "Regardless, that's not it."

"Okay, this one should be a little closer to home," Sparkles said. "Light-bringers are the militant arm of an ultra-conservative Evangelical Christian Church based in Fort Mill, South Carolina, called the League of Light."

"That's gotta be them," I said. "This douche sounded like a bad street preacher."

"That's pretty much what he is. Their leader is Pastor Rob, who started off as a twenty-something crusader against immoral behavior and condoms in schools. His views are somewhere to the far right of Rush Limbaugh, but he couches his words in so much hip language and flashy lights that his followers have no real idea what they're cheering for. He's made Jesus cool for thousands of people around the country, thanks to his YouTube channel and streaming video of his sermons."

"And now he's crashing BDSM parties?" I asked.

"That's not a new thing," Dennis said. "The scale is bigger than most, but he's led marches outside sex shops and adult video stores, protested movies that he deemed inappropriate for the community, and picketed burlesque shows at comic cons."

"Wow," Flynn said. "This guy needs a hobby."

"Or a girlfriend," I said. "Oh wait, he's a religious leader. He probably has more sex than anyone in this room."

"Given the fact that one of us is undead and another is a disembodied soul, that's not hard to accomplish," Luke chimed in. "Has this League of Light become violent before tonight?"

"There are no records of it," Dennis said. "But there are a lot of emails flying back and forth between members advocating for beating up pornographers and perverts in the lead-up to the 'Raid of Shame,' which is what they're calling their attack on Purgatory."

"Yeah, it's a shame they showed up and all the hot girls in leather pants left," I remarked. "What do we know about this Pastor Rob dude?"

"Just a second, you're getting a visitor. I'll be back." Dennis vanished from the screen in a shower of digital glitter and rainbows just as the buzzer from the condo building's parking garage sounded. I bought the building a while back, and when Luke's house was destroyed a few months ago, I vacated the top floor of the place and moved him into one of the apartments up here. The secure elevator led from the parking garage directly to this floor with no exposure to sunlight, so he could use it even in daytime. I don't know what he would want to do in the parking garage in the daytime, maybe change a tire, but I made it happen.

I looked over to Luke. "You gonna see who it is?"

"Go ahead," he said. "It's for you, anyway."

"How do you figure?"

"There are only a few people who know about the elevator, which is hidden in a room clearly marked 'Authorized Personnel Only.' Out of those people, three of them are in this room, one is a disembodied digital spirit, and the rest are the Shadow Council, all of whom have access codes to use the elevator. Therefore, anyone who knows about the elevator, and the hidden door that disguises it from anyone randomly curious enough to snoop in the mechanical room of an apartment building, but does not have an access code to get up to this floor, must have been told about it by one of those people. Dennis obviously didn't do it since he vanished immediately upon seeing this person. Rebecca has shown no indication that she knows what is happening, no one on the Council would ever give out information about my living quarters without my knowledge, and I didn't tell anyone. That leaves you."

"I hate it when you get all Sherlock on me," I said.

"Well, I did know the man and was not only impressed by the deductive leaps he was able to undertake but was also a student of his methods." Luke leaned back on the sofa and crossed his arms, a slight smile on his lips. He loved being the smartest one in the room, and when you've got as many centuries under your cape as he does, it's a pretty common occurrence. But this time, I had a surprise for him.

Looking back from the video display was a trim African-American woman in her late sixties or early seventies. I certainly wasn't going to ask her exactly how old she was. She had white hair pulled back in a bun and a no-BS look on her face. I pressed the button beside the screen and said, "Glad you could make it. I'll buzz you up. When you come up the elevator, come to Number Four."

"I can do that," Cassandra Harrison replied with a smile. "I'll see you in a few minutes, Quincy."

"Who did you just invite into my home? At less than an hour before sunrise? You know I like my rest, Quincy. This is most unusual." Luke stood beside me at the screen, but the display was blank, Cassandra having already stepped into the elevator downstairs.

"Your new Renfield is here, Uncle. She'll be up in a couple of minutes." I walked to the fridge and dropped another ice cube in my glass, then took a tumbler out of the cabinet and poured an ice water for Cassandra.

Luke stood by the door, staring at me. In over a hundred years of living, I'd almost never seen my "uncle" speechless. But there he was, mouth hanging open like a twelve-year-old who just discovered internet porn. "My new…what?"

"Your new Renfield," I said, setting the ice water on the kitchen counter and walking over to my uncle. I took him by the elbow and walked him over to the armchair. He sat, looking up at me like I'd grown another head.

"Quincy," he said after his words returned. "As I am sure you understand, the search for a new manservant is one that I have undertaken with great diligence, interviewing countless individuals for the post. As of yet, there has not been a suitable applicant, but I have the utmost faith that the right person shall reveal themselves in due time."

"Yeah, whatever. The right person is about to walk through that door in about minute and a half. I've already hired her, so you might as well get used to it." I made sure I was out of arm's reach before I dropped that last bombshell on him.

Good thing, too, since he shot up out of his chair like his ass was springloaded. "You cannot hire someone to be my manservant! The position of Renfield is a time-honored one, immortalized in literature for decades. The role requires the utmost discretion, plus a certain level of intellect and physical ability that not everyone possesses. This is not a role you can advertise on your Craigslist, or wherever it is that you found this woman. And a woman? Be serious, Quincy." He looked at Becks, who just stared at him. I didn't envy my uncle in that moment. Flynn's glares can intimidate even the Lord of the Undead.

"No offense, Rebecca, but a manservant is, by definition, a *man*. There are things that I require that a woman simply cannot do."

"Name one," I challenged.

Luke looked at me, opened his mouth, closed it, opened it again, closed it again, then sighed. "I cannot think of them right at the moment, but I am certain that this will not work. Send this woman on her way." With that, he folded his arms across his chest and turned away from me, doing everything but stomping his feet in his little vampire temper tantrum.

A knock came at the door, and I walked across the room. I opened the door, and there stood Cassandra Harrison, granddaughter to John Henry, the legendary steel-driving man and demon hunter, mother to Jo Harrison, member of the Shadow Council, and the newest Renfield. "Hello, Quincy. A pleasure to see you again. Hello, Lucas." Her voice was warm, but there was iron in it. I got the feeling, just like I did every time I was in Cassie's presence, that no matter what, this woman had her shit under control.

I saw Luke's back stiffen, and he turned. His eyes were wider than I'd ever seen them, and he looked across the room at his new Renfield. "Cassandra? You?"

"Me, Lucas." Her soft tones melted my uncle's resolve, and he blurred across the room.

"Gods above, woman, why didn't you tell me you were coming! It is so good to see you again. How is your granddaughter? What is her name again?"

"Ginny. She's good, she's good. Her mama is bringing her out next week."

Luke looked to Cassie, then to me. "What is going on here? Is Joanna moving here?"

"We all are, Luke," Cassie said. "After what happened out west, Jo wanted me to be somewhere nearer to powerful people so that Ginny and I would have somewhere to go if she ran into more trouble in her work for the Council. So, when Quincy told me about his friend's death, I came here. I'm your new Renfield. Am I good enough, or do you still want a man?" The corner of her mouth turned up, and I could tell she enjoyed making Luke squirm as much as I do.

Luke straightened himself and took a step back. "Well, I suppose you will suffice. After all, you already know all my secrets, so the learning curve will certainly be simpler."

"Suffice?" Cassie raised an eyebrow. "Vampire, you need to get your behind to bed and let me get some work done in this pigsty. Then I'll show you 'suffice.'"

Luke and Cassie both laughed, then Luke did something completely out of character. He hugged the slim woman. "I am glad you're here, Cassandra. Thank you." Then he blurred his way off into his bedroom to sleep through the day, but before he went, I was pretty sure I saw a glint of a red tear in the corner of one eye.

CHAPTER FOUR

Several hours later, I stepped up to the nondescript door on the side of Mort's Tavern. The parking lot looked a lot worse than the last time I was here, with weeds peeking up through cracks in the concrete. I pegged that as a solid metaphor for life in Charlotte these days, and maybe the whole planet, and knocked on the door. The panel in the door slid open, and Doug the Door Demon's eyes came into view.

"Goddammit, it's too early for this shit," he muttered, his raspy voice cutting through the morning air like a buzz saw. The panel slid shut with a metallic clang, and I heard deadbolts unlock from the other side. "It's open!" Doug yelled, his voice muffled.

I pushed the door open and stepped through. "What's wrong, Doug? You don't love me anymore?"

"I hate your fucking guts, Harker, and you know it. You've broken my nose more times than Tiger Woods broke his marriage vows."

"Yeah, and you're uglier than my backswing," I said, walking to the inner door. "Is he in?"

"He hasn't been anywhere else in months. Whatever you fuckers did in Atlanta, the boss didn't like it. The vibe's real different now, Harker. Watch your ass."

I stopped cold. Doug wasn't lying. He really did hate me. "Why are you giving me the heads up? If there's something in there likely to kill me, wouldn't that make you happy?"

"I don't want to see you dead, Harker. I want to see you live an even longer life than you have. Preferably blind from syphilis and with your dick swollen to three times its normal size thanks to the clap, with a couple of bleeding anal warts thrown in for good measure. If you're dead, I don't get a chance to torture you. And that sucks. But as long as you're alive, my dream of ripping off your jawbone and taking a shit straight down your throat lives on."

"You're a fucking prince, Doug." I opened the door, but not before I sent a small bolt of magical energy into Doug's desk chair. Every bolt in the thing fell to the floor, leaving it primed to dump the fat fuck right on his slimy ass the second he sat down. Petty, I know, but that's just the kind of prick I am.

I could see the truth in Doug's words the second I stepped into Mort's. What used to be a paragon of mediocre decorating was now just a shithole. Tables with broken legs stacked up against the far wall, piled with the remains of chairs shattered in brawls that never would have happened with Christy behind the bar. But Christy was dead, another victim of the asshole demon-spawn "John Smith," who served the demon Orobas. He murdered Christy, Mort's bartender and, much to my dismay, daughter, in an attempt to destroy the world. She'd been the enforcer of Mort's Sanctuary status and made one hell of a Bloody Mary. I missed her every time I smelled tomato juice.

There were other signs of Mort's decline in the place. The floors were dirty, spots of last night's blood and puke lingering in the corners. The lights were dim, about half the bulbs burned out, and the smell of old grease and half-rotten food permeated the air. Then there was the new bartender. I could tell from the second I walked in that he was going to be a pain in my ass.

"We're closed," said the musclebound half-dragon without turning around.

"I'm not here to drink," I replied.

That got his attention. He turned around, and his hands dropped below the surface of the bar. I called up a little rivulet of power and sent a tiny bolt of electricity out to zap him on the nose. "Don't do that," I said.

"Do what?"

"Touch the shotgun under the bar. I know it's there, I know it's loaded with silver flechette rounds, and I know that I can cook the scales off your ass before you can squeeze off a shot. So let's pretend we've gone through all the bullshit and you just let me back to see Mort."

"Mort's not here."

"Go back and tell him Quincy Harker is out here." I hoped dropping my name would get a reaction, and I wasn't disappointed. Of course, like so many reactions, it didn't exactly go as I'd planned. The half-dragon spread his wings and came at me over the bar, claw and fangs bared. I drew my Glock and fired off four quick shots, but the bullets didn't even nick his hide. He was on me before I could holster the weapon, and my pistol went clattering across the floor as I went down under four hundred pounds of muscled-up, pissed-off dragon-man.

I didn't have any idea what this guy had against me. I'd never seen him before, and I hadn't fought any dragons since Europe, and those were Scandinavian Ice Dragons. This guy looked like a South American Red, maybe even a Mayan Feathered Dragon, but nothing I'd ever scrapped with. "What's your fucking problem?" I croaked out as I tried to keep his clawed hands off my throat.

"You motherfucker, I'll rip your lungs out," he growled, smoke billowing from his mouth with every syllable.

I turned my head to the side to get a breath of non-scorched air, then headbutted the draco right in the nose. Bad idea. Dracos, or half-dragons, have thick ridges of bone running up their faces right above their noses. This reinforces their skulls against things they might run into while flying and also makes their noses really strong. Instead of breaking his nose, I made myself see stars, and my arms went slack for a second.

That's all the time he needed to wrap his huge hands around my throat and start to dig in with his claws. I kicked and flailed, but even my enhanced strength was useless against a draco's power. I started to see spots around the edges of my vision, and just as the pain started to overwhelm my anger, I pressed my index fingers into his armpits and channeled lightning again. This time a lot more, and a lot closer.

My finger-tasers sent thousands of volts of electricity coursing through the half-dragon, and he jerked and danced like an epileptic at a rave, but didn't let go of my throat. His grip slacked enough for me to suck in one deep breath, then he was back on me, rage filling his eyes and smoke pouring from his mouth. He drew in one deep breath, and I knew what was coming—a face full of dragonflame, hotter than lava and able to burn my skull to a cinder.

As his mouth opened wide, I gasped out one word, hoping it wasn't going to be my last. "*Conglacio!*" It came out more a croak than a command, but it had the force of my entire will behind it, and as the power surged through me, a blast of crippling cold rolled from my mouth, right into the draco's throat. He froze, literally, from the inside out. The magical blast of ice froze the fire in his esophagus and everything around it. His throat, mouth, tongue, lungs, and heart turned to solid ice instantly. His eyes went wide in a second of what must have been incredibly agony, then they went blank as the life fled from them. He dropped onto me, knocking even more wind out of me, dead as a stone. I struggled out from under the corpse of the dragon-sicle and struggled to one knee. I knelt on the disgusting floor, gasping for air, just waiting for the next attack, but nothing came at me. Maybe killing a half-dragon before noon gave me a little bit of badass street cred. Then I looked around the room and realized that the dragon and I were the only ones there. So much for street cred.

"Goddammit, Harker, why'd you have to kill him? Do you have any idea how hard it is to find someone who can mix a decent drink who's willing to tend bar for a bunch of demons?" Mort's voice came from the doorway into his back room.

"Do you have any idea how very few fucks I give? Your little shithead of a barkeep tried to burn my face off!"

"Well, Stewart was a little impetuous."

"And lazy. This place looks like shit. Next time, maybe hire somebody who knows which end of a broom should touch the floor."

"Maybe next time don't get my fucking daughter killed." I looked up at Mort, and the pain on his borrowed face was heartbreaking. Sure, he was a demon, and a hitchhiker at that, jumping from body to body on a whim, but he wasn't what I ever really thought of as a "bad" demon. If he was, I wouldn't be talking to him. Not outside a protective circle, anyway.

"I'm sorry about Christy. I liked her, Mort. She was good people." Well, only half-people, since she was Mort's daughter and, therefore, half-demon, but that didn't seem important at the moment. I stood up, giving Mort a good once-over. He looked like refried shit. The body he inhabited wasn't up to his usual standard, to start with. It wasn't famous, or good-looking, or even funny, like the time he was a cat for a year. He looked like some middle manager, or maybe an accountant. He had brown hair, a scruffy beard that looked like he was dirty instead of looking hip or cool, and he had a little paunch. I mean, whatever, you be you and all that, but the last time I saw Mort, he was riding in the body of an NFL quarterback. Now he looked like a featured extra on *The Office*. I guess losing Christy hit him harder than I thought.

"What do you want, Harker? I'm assuming you didn't come here just to kill my bartender and make my life difficult."

"I need information, Mort. This used to be the kind of place where people heard things. Of course, it also used to be a Sanctuary, but I guess the fact that your bartender tried to fucking kill me puts the lie to that idea, huh?"

"Oh, it's still a Sanctuary, just not for you. My baby girl is dead because of you, Harker, so you don't get any protection. Ever."

"Fucking Hell, Mort, I thought we were good!" I protested. "We fought Orobas together. We beat the fucker and shit all over his plans. Together. Remember Atlanta? Bad traffic, raining corpses from the Ferris Wheel, explosives in the Georgia Dome? Any of that shit ring a bell?"

"Oh, I remember it all. I remember cutting a deal with a Lord of Chaos to serve him once I killed Orobas. So, I never killed him. But it turns out keeping one of your fellow demons prisoner and torturing him on the material plane is kinda a no-no to the legions of Hell. And it turns out the forces of Chaos don't like people who poke loopholes in their contracts. So, I've got a couple million demons back home pissed off at me for torturing Oro, and I've got all the Chaos Lords pissed off at me for not just killing the bastard." The smell of pine trees almost knocked me down when he spoke, and I understood more of what was going on. It takes a *lot* of fucking booze to keep a demon drunk. Their metabolisms burn it off even faster than mine. Even faster than Luke's. But Mort was shitfaced, and obviously had been for a while. That kind of shit plays hell on the mind, even a mystical one.

"And this is my fault…how, exactly?"

"Because you got Christy killed!" Mort blurred out of sight, then reappeared right in front of me, his eyes blazing red. Shit, he was *fast*.

"I had not a goddamn thing to do with that, and you'd know it if you'd crawl out of the fucking gin bottle long enough to think shit through, you lush."

I hated to do it, but there was only one thing to do if I was going to get the information I needed without fighting Mort. I kinda liked the silly hitchhiker demon, I didn't want to chop him into hell-kibble if I could help it, so I drew in my will and placed a hand on each side of Mort's head. I poured magic straight into his skull and whispered, "*Sobrietas.*" Cleansing magic poured out of my hands, and Mort's red eyes cleared in an instant. He spun around, puked violently on the nasty tile, then whirled back around to glare at me.

"You miserable fuck. What did you do that for?" Then he dropped to his knees, wracked by sobs. I sighed, more in sympathy than frustration, and knelt down beside the grief-stricken demon. I wrapped my arms around his shoulders as he poured out his grief in the middle of the bar.

CHAPTER FIVE

Half an hour later, I was seated at a table in Mort's back room with the door locked and warded for silence. More to keep the sounds of Doug the Door Demon eating the dead half-dragon out than to keep anything Mort and I said in. Doug was a messy eater. "You feeling better?" I asked.

"Not really." Mort finally looked at me, the first time since he broke down in the bar that he'd managed that. "She was my baby girl, Harker. You don't know what that's like."

"No, I don't." I kept my answers simple and didn't want to argue with him. Besides, he was right. I've never lost a child, since I've never had any children. In all my conversations with Luke, we don't know if I even *can* have children, or how they would turn out. The magic that Luke's "wives" had with my dear old dad, not to mention Luke's own interactions with my mother, made some fundamental changes in my DNA that gave me long life, magical power, incredible strength, heightened senses, and a resistance to many forms of physical damage. The charm is all mine. But we don't know if I can procreate, and frankly, I've never wanted to.

"It's the worst thing I ever imagined. And I've been to Hell. Like, literal Hell. Lakes of fire and all that shit? Been there, done that, bought the pitchfork. Losing Christy was worse. She was with me for centuries, Harker. I know you're old for a human, but she and I watched the *pyramids* going up. Did I ever tell you those were supposed to just be big squares? I fucked with the engineers. My best gag until I came up with disco."

I let him ramble, figuring he'd either get to the point and give me information about these Lightbringer assholes, or he'd let something slip that I could use. After he waxed poetic about his daughter, who I always thought was only part demon, but the way he was talking today made me think otherwise. Demons. Lying sacks of shit, every one of them.

Finally, he blew his nose one more time and looked over at me. His eyes were red-rimmed, but clear. "Okay, Harker. You've listened to me bitch and moan about my dead daughter for half an hour, and I think you even believed some of what I was saying. So what do you want?" The tone of his voice made it clear that the whole conversation had shifted. We weren't drinking buddies commiserating about a lost buddy; we were now in the business portion of our relationship, and doing business with demons is a place to tread lightly.

"I'm looking for information."

"On who?"

"A bunch of religious kooks called The Lightbringers. They're led by some douchebro who calls himself—"

"Pastor Rob," Mort cut me off, with a look on his face like he'd just bitten into something rotten. "Yeah, I know him. And his band of assholes. What do you want with those twats, Harker? I promise, if you're going to kill them, I'll give you a discount on any information I give you."

"What's your beef with them?" I asked. "Aside from the obvious Christianity thing, of course."

More looked genuinely offended. "What makes you think I have anything against Christianity? I love the Christians! Shit, Harker, belief is currency to my kind, and nobody believes more in demons and Hell than dickhead Sunday morning Christians who fuck their secretaries every Friday before they go out to the strip clubs and pay for hand jobs in the VIP rooms while their wives stay home raising their kids. Those dickheads keep my people in business!"

"Makes sense," I said with a shrug. "So why do you hate Pastor Rob?"

"I just hate hipsters," Mort said. "I like my bad guys to wear fedoras and trench coats, smoke cigarettes, and carry a gat. This kid uses more hair product than I do deodorant and wears skinny jeans. I hate skinny jeans."

I leaned back from the table and folded my arms across my chest. "What aren't you telling me?"

"Do I need a reason to hate somebody? I'm a demon, remember?"

"Yeah, I remember. I remember that you're a hitchhiker demon, and you buy and sell rides within the meat suit of the week. I also remember that I just watched you cry your eyes out over the death of a half-human demonspawn and that I fought side-by-side with you to keep other demons from turning our dimension into a freeway. So you aren't exactly what I would call a 'normal' demon." Sometimes I take a minute to realize that my life includes me using the phrase "normal demon" in a completely sincere fashion, and I regret all of my decisions.

Mort looked around the room as if he were about to say something he didn't want overheard. "Alright, so…yeah, there's something fucked up about that guy. You remember when I was a cat?"

"How could I ever forget? How does that work, anyway? I thought you had to inhabit a willing vessel, or one without a soul. Do cats not have souls?"

"Nah, they've got souls. They just don't give a fuck. Cats will let you come in and hitchhike for a while as long as they have a pretty good idea that you're going to do something fucked up, or at least interesting. They're assholes by nature, so as long as there's potential for chaos, cats are always willing vessels."

Like I said, my life is weird. "So, what does you being a cat have to do with Pastor Rob?"

"There were a bunch of guys coming and going through here last year, all of them bitching about how tough it was to score new souls. They were all blaming this Pastor Rob dude. Word on the street was that he was giving people hope, and lots of it. That kind of thing really fucks with the normal ebb and flow of a city, at least in our line of work. We need a certain baseline level of despair to get enough souls sold to us. It's why we don't do much in Canada. Those fuckers are all too polite and happy. Can't make deals with people like that."

"Except Quebec," I grumbled.

"Yeah, they're great!" Mort agreed. "Fucking miserable people, always happy to sell their souls to shit on their neighbor. Totally my favorite province. But anyway, my customers were having a tough time collecting souls, and that's not good for me. No souls, the guys downstairs get pissy and yank the boys back home to tend the Pits. No demons, no customers in the demon bar. No customers, no new PS5 for Morty."

"You're all heart, Mort," I said. "So what did you do? Go have a come to Satan meeting with Pastor Rob?"

"Nah, that wouldn't do fuck-all. I was a cat, remember? Nah, I decided to do what cats do. I stuck my nose where it didn't belong."

So Mort had been inside the Lightbringers' main facility? This oughta be good. "What happened?" I asked.

"I snuck in there one Thursday night. The Bible-thumpers are crawling all over that joint on Wednesdays, between evening service and choir practice and circle jerk practice and whatever else bullshit they practice. But Thursdays are pretty quiet. So, I waited by the door until the cleaning crew showed up around ten—I'd gotten their schedule from an imp who was fucking the sister of one of the cleaning crew guys. When the janitors went back out to their van to bring in the vacuum cleaner, I slipped inside through the front door. Let me tell you, Harker, this lobby was nicer than a few mansions I've been in. I mean, we're talking marble floors, half a dozen flat screen TVs on the walls, coffee bar by a giant reception desk—the whole place looked more like a plastic surgeon's reception area than a church."

I wondered how many plastic surgeons' offices Mort had been in, then thought about how many men and women would sell their souls for a little extra here, or a little less there, and figured probably a lot.

The demon went on. "I crept around behind the reception desk when the guys emptied the trash cans, and that's when I got my first surprise. Harker, this joint has better security than Fort Knox. There were a dozen monitors set into the front of the desk, and they cycled through what must have been a hundred or more cameras scattered all over the building, including in all the offices and bathrooms. That was my first clue something was off with that place. My second was the guns hidden under the desk."

"Guns?" I asked. "Plural?" It's North Carolina, so one firearm randomly scattered around in a public building was no surprise, but two hidden at the reception desk of a church? That was weird, even for the South.

"Yeah, *guns*." Mort drew out the "s" sound for emphasis. "There was a pistol mounted in a quick-release holster under the desk's surface and a sawed-off shotgun hanging under the desk on clips right behind the pistol. I never met the receptionist, but she was ready for shit to go down."

So maybe kidnapping archangels masquerading as S&M moguls wasn't that far out of character for these guys. I motioned for Mort to continue.

"I poked around the lobby for a while until the guys opened a door to the sanctuary. I gotta tell you, being a cat is cool for having claws and basically being expected to shit in the shoes of people who annoy you, but not being able to reach a doorknob was a pain in the ass. The sanctuary was pretty basic, for your modern-day rock and roll church with a ton of lights and enough sound equipment to run Woodstock without a strain. There were padded movie theatre-style seats, video projectors all over the place, and a clear Lucite podium with Pastor Rob's face emblazoned on it. I swear, Nero didn't have nearly as high an opinion of himself as this little peckerhead does.

"Anyway," Mort continued. "I poked around in the giant monument to ego that was the sanctuary for a while, then wandered backstage. There was a door standing open, and the lights were on, not that I needed much in the way of light, being a cat and all. I slipped through the door and found myself in

Pastor Rob's office. And there, sitting behind his desk in all his skinny jeans-wearing glory, was the man himself. Contrary to what I'd been led to believe, he didn't have a halo, and there weren't dozens of virginal Christian girls throwing themselves at his feet. Or virginal Christian boys, for that matter. Nah, he was just a good-looking dude in his early thirties, sitting at a huge computer watching YouTube videos and making notes.

"Of course, the videos were all of violent rioting in the streets from all over the world and all throughout history, and he was making notes with one hand and holding a big goddamn pistol in the other. I sat on the floor looking up at him as he watched police beat the shit out of protestors in Egypt, soldiers shoot a crowd of civilians in Iraq, a kid in China stand in front of a tank, and a bunch of cops drive tanks through the streets of Missouri. The worse the videos got, the bigger Pastor Rob's grin got. I swear, Harker, I thought at any minute he was going to start jerking himself off, the way he was fondling that .45 pistol. He must have watched that shit for fifteen minutes with me watching him, but when he finally noticed me, he swung that big pistol around and aimed it right between my pointy little ears.

"'I know you're not a cat. So whatever you are, you have about fifteen seconds to get the fuck out of here before I spray kitty brains all over the carpet. And I like this carpet.' He didn't raise his voice, didn't even make any real threatening moves, unless you count pointing a Colt 1911 at my fuzzy little face, he just told me exactly what he was going to do unless I made myself disappear. So I did. I arched my back and hissed at him, just like a normal cat would, but I hauled ass out of there. I'm telling you, Harker. That dude was bad mojo. He pegged me for supernatural the second he laid eyes on me, and I have no doubt he would have splattered me all over the walls of his office if I hadn't run like hell."

I looked at Mort and raised an eyebrow. "I've known you a long time, Mort. What aren't you telling me?"

"What do you mean?"

"You're a pain in the ass, arrogant, braggadocios hitchhiker, and I've never known you to play down your involvement in anything. But you're really just giving me the highlights of this dude. So spill it. What's the rest? Did he do something? Kick you and break your kitty ribs? Have you spayed?"

Mort sighed and didn't meet my eyes for a long time. Finally, he looked up at me and said, "I clawed him."

"What?"

"As I was leaving, I jumped up on his desk and took a swipe at him. I tagged him right on the side of the face with my claws—ripped him a good one. Then I ran like hell before he shot me."

"Okay, so he's got another reason to want to kill you, since you fucked up his pretty face," I said.

"That's just it, Harker. I didn't. I laid into him good. It should have scarred up that face enough to make your pal Adam look gorgeous. But he didn't even bleed. I sat on his desk, paw hanging in midair, and watched the skin knit right back together like I'd never touched it. That's what made me run like hell, not some stupid pistol. I don't know who this Pastor Rob is, Harker, but he ain't human, and he's powerful as fuck."

"And now he has his own personal archangel, unless I can get Uriel back." Now I not only needed to know where Pastor Rob was holding Uriel, I needed to know what he was planning, or shit could get real bad, real fast.

CHAPTER SIX

So after a demon warns me to stay away from the charismatic pastor and his oddball church, what's the first thing I do? Break into their main sanctuary, of course. I suppose "break in" is a pretty strong term for what I did, since it was the middle of the day, but I'm sure nobody would have signed me up for the All-Access Pass I granted myself.

I walked in the front door, just like any random schmuck off the street. A perky blonde sat at the desk, a cute twenty-something with her hair pulled back in a sensible ponytail. I couldn't help thinking about the armaments Mort said were tucked under that desk. The image of a grim-looking shotgun didn't mesh well with the girl I saw. She looked way more like she should be rushing a sorority than anyone who should be slinging lead at bad guys. Or good guys, depending on what side of the lead you're on. But that's when bad guys are effective—when they don't look like bad guys. Somebody walks in wearing a black trench coat in July with dark sunglasses, combat boots, and a flak jacket, and people are going to have their guard up. But when Bible-Thumping Barbie whips out an Uzi in the middle of her prayer meeting, nobody expects that crap.

Except me. I don't trust prayer circles.

I walked up to the desk and leaned on the polished marble surface with my elbows. The receptionist looked up from her command center and chirped, "Hi! Welcome to Lightbringers Ministries! How can I help you?" The level of cheerful she exuded from every pore was somewhere above "high school pep squad" and slightly below "eight-year-old girl watching a sea otter video."

986

I tried to push my face into something more like a smile than something small children ran away from and asked, "Hi there! How are you? I'm looking to speak with Pastor Rob, is he in?"

The plastic smile dropped from her face like a curtain on a bad opera, and she gave me a wary look. "I'm sorry, sir," she said, in a voice indicating she was anything but sorry. "Pastor Rob isn't at this location today. I believe he is visiting some of our church members in the hospital, or he may be doing some volunteer work somewhere in town. He's hard to keep track of." She gave me one of those "I'm just a long-suffering secretary" smiles that let me know she was completely aware of Pastor Rob's whereabouts at all times, had no intention of giving me any information, and would tolerate little to absolutely none of my bullshit. I liked her. Not enough to feel bad for what I was about to do to her, but a little bit.

I summoned up my will, waved my hand in front of her face, and said, "Dormio." My magic pulsed from my palm in a gentle blue orb, floating toward her face like a big glowing dandelion puff, until the necklace around her throat flared with a reddish light, and my spell was sucked into it like it never existed. Well, that wasn't supposed to happen, I thought.

"What the hell are you doing?" Barbie asked, leaning forward and reaching under the desk. Thanks to Mort's little story, I knew she was either pressing an emergency call button, reaching for a pistol, or both. None of those courses of action were good for me.

"Well, shit," I sighed. "Sorry about this." I leaned over the desk, reached out with my right hand, and cupped the back of her skull. I slammed her forehead down onto the desk's wood surface with a serious crack. Barbie slumped to the floor, out like a light and hopefully with no serious brain trauma. Keeping an eye peeled for security or anyone else who may have noticed our little scuffle, I hurried around the desk and shoved Barbie deep under the desktop where a casual observer wouldn't see her. I did a quick check to make sure she was still breathing, then I grabbed the medallion hanging around her neck, intending to yank it off and study it in depth at home later.

"Fuck!" I hissed, snatching my throbbing hand back. I looked at my palm, and the outline of the pendant was seared into the flesh of my hand. "Fuck me," I muttered. "I gotta stop getting burned. That shit hurts." Looking closer at the necklace, I couldn't pick up anything out of the ordinary about it. For all I could see, it was a simple silver cross with a red jewel in the center. Behind the cross was a sun design that matched the Lightbringers logo emblazoned somewhere every twelve inches along the walls of the lobby. I took a picture of the cross with my phone, hoping that Dennis would snoop as much as he usually did and have some info on it when I was done snooping.

Looking up under the desk, I saw that Mort hadn't exaggerated the arsenal under there. I pulled the pistol from its holster and unloaded it, slipping the magazine into my back jeans pocket. The shotgun was a little tougher, but with a serious grunt, I managed to bend the barrel enough to be way more hazardous to anyone trying to shoot it than to any potential targets. Since I thought there was a good chance I'd be the next target, that was good enough for me.

Barbie's computer was password-protected, so I got nothing from there, but the security videos showed the sanctuary as completely empty. I figured if they had Uriel stashed on site, it would be in one of the rooms Mort told me about backstage, so I headed into the main worship center to poke around.

It was everything Mort described, and then some. I paused just inside the entrance and took a good look around, soaking in the smell of millions of dollars as a shrine to God and ego, in distinctly unequal portions. The room was shallow, but wide. At the back of the church, I was still probably less than a hundred feet from the stage. And this was no pulpit, this was a *stage*. Easily fifty feet wide, with a Lady Gaga-level lighting rig hanging over it, the stage was littered with microphones, music stands, instrument stands, and various chairs. A drum kit that would make Keith Moon drool sat on a riser upstage center, with a huge percussion kit off to one side. There was a multi-keyboard rig, a baby grand piano, three Marshall guitar amps, a Fender bass head, and a small set of chairs arranged like a jazz ensemble. Two dozen chairs in rows on one side of the stage made for a choir area, and the whole thing focused on a clear podium made of plastic and gleaming metal, with that same cross etched in the front of its Plexiglas surface, a red gem gleaming in the center like a dormant Eye of Sauron.

"One church to rule them all," I muttered, walking toward the stage. I put one foot on the four steps leading up to the platform, then all hell broke loose.

"Hey!" came the shouted voice from behind me. I turned, and there was Barbie, five feet of fury with a lump on her forehead and a Sig Sauer in her hand. Of course, I didn't search the desk for extra magazines. Who in their right mind would keep extra ammo for the pistol strapped to the underside of their desk? This ignores the fact that most people with guns strapped under their desks aren't in their right mind.

Seconds after Action Figure Barbie burst in with her ponytail and Pepto-pink sweater, the other rear door to the sanctuary flew open and a pair of armed security guards came through, drawing their guns and aiming them in my direction. *Great, now not only do I have a pissed off receptionist with a concus-*

sion and a gun, I have two bargain-basement Barney Fifes with poor trigger discipline.

I drew in my will and flung orbs of pure energy at Barbie and the Renta-Cops, but red light blazed from necklaces around each of their throats, and my magic dissipated like my hope for getting out of there undiscovered.

"Surrender now, and we won't have to use deadly force," Renta-Cop Number One said, but the way his finger twitched around the trigger said all he really wanted to do was to pour hot lead into my ass. Fortunately for me, most people shoot for crap under stress, and I felt pretty good about my ability to avoid getting killed by this guy. I felt less good about none of the three of them catching me with a stray bullet, so I put my hands up.

"Okay, I surrender. I'm really sorry about the whole desk thing. I just really, *really* want to meet Pastor Rob, so I can tell him what a ginormous positive impact his teachings have had on my life. I think I'm almost ready to move up in levels, and I just need to know what it costs to progress." They kept moving forward in a steady, crouched heel-to-toe walk that made me think they'd all received at least some training in tactics. Maybe this wasn't going to be as easy as I thought. Like taking down three armed attackers was ever easy, especially when they had amulets that made my magical attacks useless.

Useless on them, maybe, but not on the things around them. While Barbie and the security dweebs kept their eyes and their guns trained on me, I kept my hands pointing to the heavens. Maybe not straight up, but definitely toward the ceiling. And toward the hundred-foot lighting truss that they walked directly under as they approached the stage.

About two steps before they passed directly under the truss, I let fly with a burst of my will and a shouted *"Abrumpo!"* The chains holding the lighting rig in the air snapped with a loud *TWANG*, and several tons of metal and electronics came crashing to the ground. The guards and receptionist dove for cover, and the metal monstrosity missed them entirely as it sent plastic light parts and aluminum shards whirring through the air to lodge in the backs of seats and the front of the stage. I threw up a quick shielding spell to keep from getting brained by my own brilliant idea and sprinted to the backstage office area.

The darkened hallway seemed deserted, a fact I confirmed by whispering *"lumos"* and summoning an orb of light to float along beside me. From the sanctuary, I heard the sound of guards calling for backup and Barbie using some very un-churchy language as they tried to get over or around my road-block. I peeked in a few doors, but they were your basic offices. Just a few desks, chairs, family pictures, that sort of thing. One held a circle of chairs, a coffeemaker, and a table with an empty Krispy Kreme box, the universal signs of an AA meeting.

I came to the end of the hall and opened a door marked "Pastor Rob." No last name, no title, just "Pastor Rob." I thought about it for a moment, then realized that I'd never heard of Pastor Rob *having* a last name. It was weird, but everything about this whole deal was weird. The door was locked, but a little extra *oomph* and the knob twisted off in my hand. I pushed the door open, not really caring about any alarms I might trip. At least, not any mundane alarms. I did give a quick sweep of the area with my Sight, but nothing showed up. Just your average demon-tainted room in the back of a rock and roll church.

Yeah, more demon taint. This room practically reeked with it, making me think that there was a lot more our buddy Pastor Rob than just thumping the Bible and passing the collection plate. What was conspicuously absent, however, was any hint that Uriel, or anything divine in nature, had been in that office ever, much less in the last twenty-four hours. I scanned the book-cases, flipped through an blank day planner, and generally came up completely empty as far as clues to the location of my missing Archangel or to the long-term plans of a demon building a megachurch in my hometown.

I turned to go and found myself in a position I'd occupied many times before—staring down the barrel of a Sig Sauer .40 pistol held by a uniformed member of the Charlotte-Mecklenburg Police Department. Between dating Detective Rebecca Gail Flynn and working for an official, albeit heinously corrupt, branch of Homeland Security for over a year, I'd forgotten exactly how much I disliked cops pointing guns at me. I mean, let's be honest, I hate anybody pointing a gun at my face, but something about one of the good guys drawing down on me particularly annoys me. I guess it's because we're supposed to be on the same team or something.

"Let me guess," I said. "This isn't about that parking ticket Detective Flynn said she was going to take care of for me."

"Get on the ground!" the cop shouted. When he raised his voice to talk to me, barely ten feet away, I got a good look at just how young he was. *Fuck.* He was barely out of the Academy. He'd probably never even fired that gun off the range. I sighed and got down on my belly, fingers laced behind my head. The last thing I needed was to get shot in the face by an overzealous rookie. I didn't know if it would kill me, but I wasn't in a mood to find out.

"Quincy Harker, you are under arrest for trespassing, breaking and enter-ing, assault with a deadly weapon, and anything else we can think of to throw at you." The voice was familiar, but the last time I'd heard it, it hadn't come from a uniformed officer. I looked up, and my heart sank. Standing in the doorway behind the rookie was Darrell Grizzle, a former detective who I thought got fired after the whole Agent Smith debacle, since he worked closely with the man who turned out to be a half-demon murderer. But there he stood, smirking up at me and holding his sidearm trained on my face.

"You're the reason I got busted back down to patrol, asshole. I know your bitch girlfriend will have you out sooner than I want, but let's see how some of my buddies in the holding cells treat you tonight." I think I would have had better luck if I'd just burst into the office and found a demon. So off to jail, and a pretty guaranteed beating, I went.

CHAPTER SEVEN

I n all my dealings with Detective, now Officer, Grizzle, I never thought he was evil. Lazy, yes. Stupid, maybe. Vindictive, absolutely. So, when he tried the old trick of slamming my head into the roof of the car while trying to "gently" push me into the back seat, I knew how to go completely limp at just the right moment so he didn't "accidentally" crack my skull. He cursed and tried to maneuver my dead weight and keep me from falling to the ground while I pressed down on the arch of his left foot with my left heel, grinding the bones in the top of his foot together.

"So sorry about that, Officer. I lost my balance," I said from the back seat of the squad car as he and the rookie took their spots in the front seat. Squad car back seats smell pretty universally bad, and the advent of methamphetamine just added a stink of rancid cat piss to the miasma of flop sweat, vomit, blood, and shit that roils around in every cop cruiser I've ever been in. And there have been a lot. I'd say I've probably been riding around in police cars in America since within a couple of decades of the invention of the police car.

"Go fuck yourself, Harker," Grizzle growled from the front seat. "We'll get your ass taken care of at the jail."

I leaned back into the stinky seat and tried to recap what I'd learned. It didn't take long since there was practically nothing learned. Pastor Rob was either a demon or possessed by a demon. That wasn't exactly news since Uriel's abduction site fairly dripped with demon taint all over the building, but knowing that the source was Pastor Rob complicated life just a little. He was a public figure with a *lot* of people looking at him all the time. Any demon driving him or just masquerading as him had to be powerful to hold that illusion in place consistently. Perhaps more disturbing was the lack of demonic magic I sensed anywhere else in the church. That meant the trigger-happy security guards and the Rambo Receptionist were completely human, unpossessed, and just batshit crazy. Not to mention highly armed. I had to wonder how many other of Pastor Rob's pals would be packing, and probably heavier artillery than just pistols.

We pulled into the underground parking deck at CMPD Headquarters, and the rookie got out of the passenger seat and hurried to the back door to let me out. I guess he decided that police brutality was passé and he'd just follow the Geneva Convention. I slid out of the car and handed him the cuffs. The kid gaped at me as I walked toward the elevator. "Don't worry about me, kid. I know the way to the booking sergeant's desk."

"Take another step, and I'll blow your goddamn head off, Harker," Grizzle said, and I heard the hammer click back on his Sig Sauer pistol and turned around. He was in a classic Weaver stance with one hand cupped under the other on the butt of the gun. The forty-caliber pistol was center on my head, and I got pissed. I really don't like it when people threaten to kill me, especially when I know they want to.

So, I decided it was time to remind Grizzle who the Alpha dog was, no matter who was wearing the badge. I let my eyes glow red, sending tendrils of magic out to waft through the air around my face. "Go ahead, Darrell. Pull the fucking trigger. See what happens. You remember how life turned out for your pal Smith when he pissed me off, right? Well, I don't like being threatened, and you're *really* starting to piss me off."

I cut my eyes over to the rookie. "Don't touch that goddamn pistol, kid. You've acted like a decent person all night, let's not fuck it up now." I turned my attention back to Grizzle. "Now, Darrell. This can go down one of two ways. You can shoot me, which is just going to piss me off and scare this rookie. Then I'll have to get unpleasant. Or you can holster your weapon, and we can go upstairs, where you book me on charges you know will be dismissed before nightfall, and you can try to have somebody murder me in the holding cell. That's not going to get you anywhere either, but it's the option that doesn't end with your head sitting on your patrol car as a goddamn hood ornament. Now let's go upstairs and get this charade underway."

I turned to walk to the elevator, then turned back. "Unless, of course, you'd like to see if your life expectancy is any better than your buddy Agent Smith's after *he* tried to fuck with me."

I stared at Grizzle for almost a full minute, then he finally holstered his weapon and stomped past me to the elevator. The metal doors slid open, and the three of us stepped in.

We stood for a few seconds in an uncomfortable silence, then the kid drew in his breath to speak. I held up a hand and cut him off. "Don't ask, kid. If you ask, I'll tell you, and there are lot of things in this world that you're better off not knowing. Just trust me on that one."

He stood there contemplating my words long enough for the elevator to rise the two floors to the booking desk, and I stepped out and walked over to my old buddy Sean, the sergeant in charge of booking. Sean had been taking my prints and processing my arrests for well over a decade, and we were friendly, if not friends. And I didn't blame him—it was probably frowned upon to be friends with a guy he arrested all the time. Lucky for me, incarceration was never really my style. Banishment and immolation were more my bailiwick.

"What is it this time, Harker?" Sean said with a sigh. "I thought we were done going around in these circles with you once you and Flynn got cozy."

"I did, too, Sean," I replied. "But your buddy Darrell over there didn't get the memo that I'm one of the good guys now, so here we are again."

"Fair enough," Sean said. Sean Fitzpatrick had been around the block enough times to not even bother sticking his nose into political crap. He was a solid cop—did his job, didn't try to pull anything over on anybody, and was just biding his time until retirement. I remembered Sean as a young tyro twenty-five years ago, chasing the biggest collars and the most dangerous assignments. Then he caught an arrow to the knee in an armed robbery of a sporting goods store, of all ridiculous things, and that put an end to his adventuring days. Now he pushed papers instead of chasing purse-snatchers, and he'd turned into one of the most efficient desk sergeants Charlotte-Mecklenburg PD had on their roster.

Sean walked me through the process, taking my prints (again), taking my mug shots (again), then handing me over to Grizzle to take me back to holding. "Darrell, I know you've got issues with this man, but he needs to come out of that holding cell in the same shape he goes in."

"No worries on that one, Sergeant. He'll still be an asshole when he comes out." Grizzle laughed and led me down the hallway to one of the holding cells. He perp-walked me past three empty cells before stopping in front of the one farthest from the door. His rookie partner opened the door, and four giant men that looked like a cross between brown bears and Hell's Angels stood up. It was feeding time at the zoo, and I was the entree.

"Let me guess," I said. "This is the one in the security cameras' blind spot?"

"Nah, this is the one with the biggest drain in the floor. It'll be easier to wash the blood away when they're done with you." Darrel shoved me through the open cell door. He tried to trip me as I went in, but I stepped over his foot. The shove did put me most of the way into the cell, and I heard the heavy *clang* of a steel door slamming shut behind me.

"Try not to let him make too much noise," Darrell said, his leather shoes slapping across the tile floor as he walked away from the cell. "I'd hate for anybody to hear your ruckus and interrupt you." With a creak of hinges and the thud of another heavy door closing, I was alone with four men who probably weren't interested in a rousing game of gin rummy.

"Hi fellas," I said, backing up to make sure none of them could get behind me. "We don't need to make this unpleasant, do we?"

"Unpleasant is what we do," one of them said, a giant at nearly seven feet tall with a cascading black beard and arms the size of my thighs. His eyes glowed red, and I know that Grizzle's days of consorting with demons hadn't ended when I put a bullet in his boss's head.

"I guess there's no point in me asking if you want to do this the easy way, is there?" I asked. The jolly demonic giant laughed, and I threw a fireball in his face. Then the others came at me, and the shit really hit the fan.

CHAPTER EIGHT

"*Infiernos!*" I shouted, leaping to my left. I flung out my right hand, and a ball of flame the size of a volleyball shot forth, catching Blackbeard right in the face. I didn't expect much reaction and didn't get much. Demons are pretty used to being on fire, after all. But it bought me the moment's distraction that I needed to get my back into a corner and limit the thugs' angle of approach even more.

The demons stopped chuckling and concentrated on their attack. Blackbeard was busy putting out the fire on his face since it turns out no matter how impervious you are to fire, your beard won't be, but that left three demons to come at me. And come at me they did. Two smaller men shed their human forms, literally ripping the fleshy disguises into piles of disgusting skin and clothes, then sprang at me with razor-sharp claws. Reaver demons. I hate Reavers, more even than a character in a Joss Whedon space western. These little buggers had claws the size of steak knives and twice as sharp. The first one went high, and I ducked his slash.

Of course, that put my face right in line from the stabbing strike of the Reaver who went low, but I knew he was coming. It wasn't my first Reaver fight, and I knew that without serious weapons, I was going to be sporting several new orifices before the end of the day. With that in mind, I grabbed the demon's right arm and used those razor-bladed nosepickers to slice off its left hand at the wrist. Blood fountained from the severed limb, but I grabbed my newly created weapon and jabbed a still-twitching demon finger into its owner's left eye. The Reaver shrieked like Lucifer himself was wielding the whip and scuttled backward, flailing around like it couldn't decide whether to hold its perforated eye, or try to stem the bleeding with its remaining hand. Life's tough for the one-handed man with two fatal injuries.

The demon pulled back, but I held onto the severed hand, the claw sliding out of its face with a wet squelching sound. The other Reaver drew back for a downward slash at the back of my neck, and I dove to my right, whipping the severed hand up and toward the remaining Reaver. I missed, and the hand flopped around on the floor of the cell, dripping blood into a pool right by the drain. Nice of Grizzle to comment on the ease of cleanup. At least I wouldn't have tormenting the janitor on my conscience.

Reaver Two came at me again, and I barely pulled in enough energy to thrust power wildly at the little shit before he impaled my spleen on his fingertips. He staggered back, knocking into the third man, who still looked mostly human, except for his obsidian skin and gleaming red horns and teeth. I didn't recognize his type of demon, but since he wasn't currently trying to remove any parts of my body, I put him firmly in the "deal with later" column. Reaver Two recovered way faster than I wanted him to and dove at my knees this time, bowling me over and opening up cuts all over my thighs and calves with his claws. I went down, driving an elbow into his back on my way down. That, at least, stunned the little bastard for a couple of seconds, giving me enough time to suck in a breath, press my hands to the sides of the demon's head, and croak out a strangled "*conglacior*."

A blast of crippling cold flowed from my hands, plunging the Reaver's temperature into the negatives in a heartbeat. Its eyes glazed over, and it let out one last mist of breath before its entire skull froze from the inside out. I pushed myself up to my knees and slammed the demon's head into the concrete floor. It shattered into a million disgusting pieces, and its entire body dissolved into steaming pools of black ichor.

I scrambled around until my back was to a wall again and looked for Blackbeard. He was nowhere to be seen, at least not in that form. Instead, what faced me was the thickly muscled form of a Greater Pit Fighter. "Fuck me," I muttered, my brain scrambling for a way out of this fine mess.

The Pits of Hell are a real thing, at least from what I can find in my research. I've never actually been to Hell, although I'm pretty sure I've been a few places that were in the same zip code. The Pits are more than just lakes of fire where sinners are punished and theoretically absolved of their transgressions. I say theoretically since I've never found record of anyone who has ever expiated their sins and moved on to Heaven.

Never.

No one. In millions of years, no one has ever made it from Hell to Heaven.

That makes it pretty obvious that the Pits are for more than rehabilitation. They're also for the enjoyment of the greater demons, the Dukes, Archdukes, and Lords. Think the Roman Colosseum, only with a lot more lions and a *lot* more bloodshed. New souls that show a predilection for murder and mayhem get tossed into the Pits, where they get matched up against increasingly stronger opponents to fight for the entertainment of the masses. Since they aren't alive, they can't die. Whatever injuries they receive heal, albeit slowly and in the most painful ways possible. Hell, remember.

Well, after a few thousand years of getting their asses kicked, most souls either give in to despair and refuse to fight anymore, at which point they get moved on to other, more horrific punishments, or they get good at kicking ass. If they choose the latter, they move up through the Pits to fight demons instead of just the souls of human assholes. If the souls excel there, they can get turned into demons themselves.

This isn't much better, from what I hear, except that you're the one doing most of the tormenting, and you have the ability to leave Hell once in a while if you get summoned or find a crack in the walls, which happens way more often than I would like. So, what stood in front of me was a damned soul, who was enough of a badass to get promoted out of the Pits after a few thousand years into becoming an actual demon, then he was either strong enough or cunning enough to find a way out of Hell.

Things were not looking good for our hero. The literal only thing I had going for me was that the fourth demon had removed himself from the field of battle, at least as much as one could in a twenty by twenty holding cell. He sat on a bench fastened to the far wall, his hooves feet folded underneath him, just watching the proceedings with what looked like only the mildest of interest. I didn't mind that much. The less interest I could draw from another creature determined to rip my spine out and beat my head in with, the better.

"You burned me, human!" Hulk Hogan Demon bellowed, and even from ten feet away, I could smell the charred death on his tongue. Seriously, what do these guys *eat?*

"Yeah, but your little friends cut me up, so you wanna just call it even and play pinochle?" I don't even know how to play pinochle, but if it would mean I didn't have to fight a demon hand to hand in an enclosed space, I was willing to learn.

Hulk didn't respond, at least not with words. He did raise his huge hands over his head and charge me, so I took that as a hard "no" on the pinochle. I crouched into a little ball and hid behind a curved shield of my magic, letting him punch himself out on my shield as I fed the magic coursing through the building into my defenses. I don't do it often because it's pretty unethical and has the unpleasant side effect of sometimes accidentally killing people, but when I'm in a pinch and really short on power, I can leech energy off whoever is around me. It's kinda like what Luke does to survive, in that I'm actually consuming the life force of the people around me. The difference is that I don't need a bib, and I only replenish my magical stores with it, not any of my physical strength. But since this was a matter of life and death, I figured the rest of the guys in the jail would cut me a little slack. Nah, I didn't even think twice about it. I just reached out and sucked power into my shield so I could survive Hulk's initial onslaught.

HIs fists slammed into shield again and again, then he lifted his arms over his head and bellowed in rage. "I will crush you to paste!"

"Not if you keep taking your eyes off your opponent, asshole," I muttered, and dropped my shield. I might be over a century old and stronger than most things on Earth, but I know my limits. I am never, *ever* going to be able to take out a Pit Fighter in a fair fight. Good thing for me, I don't fight fair.

I sheathed my fists in magical energy and shouted, "*GLADIO!*" Blue-white energy flared from my hands in a pair of two-foot magical short swords. I thrust my energy swords into the demon's legs just above the knee and twisted with all my strength. I felt the tendons sever beneath my summoned blades, and the demon bowed at the waist like a puppet with his strings cut. I let the swords dissipate back into the aether and sprang up from my crouch, laying both of my magically wrapped fists under the demon's jaw in an uppercut that would have made Rocky Balboa proud.

I didn't just swing from my heels, I *launched* myself into that punch, and it showed. The demon's forward fall arrested, he straightened up and flew backward a good three or four feet before he slammed to the concrete floor in a puddle of Reaver blood. His head hit the floor with a sickening *crack*, and his entire body shuddered, then lay still.

I've been in a lot of fights. It's a byproduct of having generally poor impulse control, associating with vampires, animated corpses, and magicians for over a century, and still having the nagging voice of Abraham Van Helsing in the back of my head like a grim Germanic Jiminy Cricket, constantly pointing out injustice and horrors in the world that needed to be corrected. Thanks to all that horrible life experience, I learned a long time ago not to believe an opponent was dead until you'd taken the second bite of his still-beating heart.

Metaphorically. Okay, mostly metaphorically, but there are few things in the world tastier than fresh werewolf heart. So, I walked over to the apparently dead demon, but I wasn't relaxed. I held a ball of glowing magical energy in my right hand and had a shield spell readied with my left. I was totally prepared to pour enough power into the monster's head to turn him into a red smear on the concrete, but I didn't have to. I was still a foot or more away when he dissolved into smoking black sludge, filling the cell with the stench of sulfur, cooked demon blood, and burned hair.

I dropped my shield and my ball of power, backed slowly across the cell, and sat down on the bench. I looked across at the last demon, who just watched me, his gaze completely ignoring the dissolving bodies of his three fellow denizens of Hell. His eyes locked onto mine, and he unfolded his legs and stood up. I didn't get up. One, I didn't want to give him the courtesy, and two, I was fucking tired. Drawing that much power through me left all my nerve endings feeling raw and abused, and casting spells with that much juice behind them gave me a headache. So, I sat there as the demon approached, stepping through the puddles of Reaver and Pit Demon like they weren't even there.

I readied another shielding spell and prepared to summon another blade of magical energy, but there's nothing in the world that could have prepared me for the next words to come out of the demon's mouth.

He stood right in front of me, his black skin glittering in the fluorescent light. He bent his head down to me, and I looked up into his black pupil-less eyes. He smiled, which was made more nerve-wracking than usual by the fact that there was no malice in it. He looked genuinely happy that it was his turn.

He's happy that I killed three demons in five minutes and now he gets his shot at me. I am so fucked, I thought, then did what any sane person would do—I smiled back.

"Hello there, human. Would you like to play a game?"

I know I should've been shit-scared, and I pretty much was, but all I kept thinking about was how this dickhead probably had no idea he'd just dropped a *War Games* reference on me. Yup, one-hundred percent fucked.

CHAPTER NINE

"Ummm...sure?" I said. "As long as the game isn't called 'Eat the Human,' I think I'm good with that."

The demon smiled, one of the most unnerving sights I've ever experienced, and said, "That depends on whether you win or lose, I suppose, doesn't it?"

I couldn't argue with his logic. But I still wanted to know a little more about what, or who, I was dealing with. "What are you called?" I asked. I've learned through painful experience not to ask a demon for its name because it will lie. Names, true names, have power, and demons hate more than anything giving up power to another creature. But the names of many demons are also well-known, which makes it worth trying to figure out who you're dealing with. And since most demons are glory-hungry little pricks, they want you to know who you're dealing with, so you'll be intimidated and fuck up into promising them something you really shouldn't give away. Like your soul.

It's convoluted, but they're basically immortal beings, and assholes at their very core, so they spent a lot of time parsing semantics and coming up with more and better ways to screw with mortals. I was interested not only to see what this particular asshole's plan was, but also who he was.

"My apologies, John Abraham Quincy Holmwood Harker, I see I have you at a disadvantage. I am known as Zepar, commander of fifty legions of Hell's armies, and the greatest lover of women, and men, your pitiful world has ever known." He made a deep, florid bow, almost sweeping the floor with his ebon knuckles.

Fuck. I knew about Zepar. In my line of work, it paid to know all the legit badasses among Hell's ranks, and Zepar certainly qualified. He was over-stating his importance a little, unless he'd managed to seriously rise through the ranks recently, but he was still a serious mother. He was one of the Fallen, not a demon made from the waters of the river Styx, or forged in the fires, or a pitiful human who fought his way out of the Pits. Nope, the guy standing in front of me used to be an angel, picked the wrong side in the War on Heaven, and followed Lucifer down into the flames for it.

"Pleased to meet you, Zepar. You can call me Harker. Or Q, if we both live long enough to get friendly. But I doubt that's the plan, is it?" I stood up and held out my hand anyway. Just because two beings really want to kill each other is no reason to be rude.

The demon shook my hand, an act that took all my willpower not to run screaming from. His glassy black flesh scraped along my skin like the edge of a knife, just to the point of making me fear he was going to rip me open, but not quite. As we shook, I felt the evil coming off him in waves. It felt like a roiling mass of tar, or lava, only ice cold. The sense of *wrongness* that spread across my hand and up my arm was like dipping my whole fist in a vat of acid, the burning sensation pricked in all the way down to my bones.

I didn't scream, and I didn't pull away. I shook his hand and sat back down, resisting the temptation to wipe my hand on my pants. I kept my eyes locked on his, trying to discern something, anything, about his intentions. "So, what's the game, Zepar? If it's not going to be 'Eat the Human,' what other games do you know?"

The demon smiled at me again, and the flesh along my spine crawled like it was trying to make a break for it. "The game is simple. We shall tell riddles. If you cannot guess one of my riddles, I get to kill you without a fight. If you somehow manage to tell a riddle that I cannot decipher, then I will leave this plane, taking all evidence of your disagreement with my compatriots with me."

Riddles. Well, that was different. I'd fought demons, bargained with demons, wrestled one or two, shot a *lot* of them, and done my level best to outwit a few of them. But I'd never had one want to play at riddles before. I took a moment to think about my options, maybe a moment longer than Zepar thought was appropriate, because after less than a minute, he cleared his throat.

"If you would rather duel in some other fashion, I suppose we could move straight into single combat. But I was one of the Host before my Fall, and I have battled alongside Michael himself. Trust me, Quincy Harker, you at least have a chance at besting me in riddles."

He had a point. There was no chance I was going to beat this guy in a fist-fight, and my magic would likely slide right off of him like a watergun shooting an elephant. "Okay. What are the rules?" There are a lot of races that you can enter an agreement with before you know every detail of the rules. Demons are not on that list. Neither are female police detectives, but that didn't stop me.

"I will begin. I will tell you a riddle. If you can figure out the answer, you get to tell me a riddle. We alternate until someone can't answer the riddle, or can't come up with a riddle of their own and surrenders. All riddles must have a legitimate answer, no Mad Hatter's riddles are allowed. You may make one incorrect guess per riddle, but if you guess wrong twice, you lose. If the loser does not agree that the proffered answer is valid, then a new riddle may be provided. This may only be done once. I would suggest that you take care."

I mulled it over as I looked at Zepar's ebon grin. He had something in mind, but I couldn't for the life of me figure out what it was. Oh well, if I didn't like the way it was going, I could always just fight him. At least that way I'd die quickly. "Okay," I said. "I'm in. Hit me with your first riddle."

"What is so delicate that even speaking its name will break it?" Zepar asked, and I knew he was going easy on me to kick things off.

"Silence," I said with a smile. "That's an old one."

"Well done, Harker. Now it is your turn." He walked a few feet away from me and sat cross-legged on the floor, facing me where I still sat on the metal bench. I had no illusions about getting away, even if I could get out of the cell. One of the Fallen was going to be way faster than even my vampire-enhanced speed.

I thought for a moment, then decided to see how far I could bend the rules. "Okay, here's an oldie but a goodie," I said. "What's in my pocket?"

Zepar actually chuckled. "Tricksy hobbit, that's not a riddle. I couldn't possible know, or guess, but I know it isn't The One Ring. Try again. I'll give you a free pass because it was moderately clever, but Tolkien you are not."

"Fair enough. What walks on four legs in the morning, two legs in the afternoon, and three legs in the evening?" Another old standby, but at least this really was a riddle.

Zepar gave me a steady look, as though slightly insulted. "A man. He crawls in childhood, walks on two feet as an adult, and walks with a cane in his old age. Do try to be more original. I taught that riddle to the Greeks."

"Okay, fair enough. I'm not going to trip you up with anything too old or easy. Your turn." I folded my arms across my chest and waited, my mind tumbling over trying to think of another riddle.

"I travel the world 'round, yet I never leave my corner. What am I?"

I had to spend a little time on that one. *What travels, but doesn't move? What corner? A bus? No...a bus driver? No, that's too easy, too. Besides, he gets off the bus. Okay, think less literal. What kinds of things travel? Information travels—* "A stamp!" I exclaim without a second's hesitation.

Not bad, Harker. For the first time all day, I felt Becks in my head. Sharing my blood made a mental connection between us, one that had only grown stronger as our relationship blossomed, but she'd been strangely absent all day.

Where have you been? I asked in my head.

There's something blocking me. I don't feel cut off, but it's hard to communicate. I'm in the building now, so it's easier. I'm trying to get down to spring you, but Grizzle is cock-blocking me at every turn. He's really got a mad-on for you.

He's still working for demons. Don't come down here. This guy will tear you apart.

"Tell Detective Flynn I wish her the best. And tell her goodbye," Zepar said, and I felt a wall slam into place between Becks' consciousness and mine.

"I guess now I know what was keeping her from contacting me," I grumbled.

"Oh, you most certainly do. I can't have you getting an unfair advantage over little old me, can I? I mean, it's bad enough that you get to spend your life above ground, with all the myriad experiences humanity has to offer. Why should you be allowed to cheat in our little contest, as well?"

"I'm not the demon in the room," I replied. "I think I should be the one worried about getting cheated."

"Well, worry later, after I've eaten your kidneys with rice. For now, get on with the game. Unless you choose to forfeit?" His glittering smile was colder than a Frost Giant's breast milk, and I racked my brain trying to come up with a riddle.

I thought and tumbled old jokes and riddles around in my brain, trying to come up with something useful. Finally, a hint of something came to me. "Many have heard my voice, but none have ever seen me. I only speak when spoken to. What am I?"

Zepar actually looked like he was thinking for a few moments before he turned that chilly grin on me and said, "An echo. And that's what you'll be soon, Harker. Just an echo of yourself, floating around in people's memories."

"Nice," I said, smiling at the demon. "You trying to psych me out, since you know you can't beat me?"

Zepar's grin faded as he said, "I suppose it's time to end this, and it seems only fitting that the riddle that brings about your end starts with the one that brought about your beginning—your pitiful God."

"Wow, bringing the big guy into our little conversation? I must really have you rattled."

He didn't reply, just launched right into the riddle. "What is greater than God, and more evil than Satan? The poor have plenty of it, the rich need it not at all, and if you eat it, you will certainly die?"

I had nothing. A complete blank. Not a single idea came to me. I sat on the metal bench for at least a minute, feeling the cold radiating from the demon seeping into the metal and chilling my skin. I got up and paced, but still no ideas came. I drew in a breath, sure that the inspiration was right on the tip of my tongue, but again...nothing.

Then it hit me, and I felt like a complete idiot, in the way that only riddles can. I turned to face the demon. "I've got nothing, buddy."

He smiled big enough to show me both rows of pointed teeth. "You surrender, Harker?"

I returned his smile with the biggest shit-eating grin I could muster. "No, of course not. I told you the answer—nothing. There's nothing greater than God, nothing more evil than Satan. The poor have all the nothing they could ever want, and the rich don't want any more nothing. If you eat nothing, you'll die, and you're going to starve today because there will be no bits of Harker on your menu." I sat back down, grinning as the demon fumed.

"Your turn," he growled, glaring at me. His eyes began to flicker red, but the cold still poured off him in waves.

"No problem," I said. "Here's another old one for you. A hunter leaves his house and walks south for one mile. He encounters a bear, which chases him east for a mile before he finally shoots and kills it. This incredibly strong hunter then drags the bear one mile back to the front door of his cabin. What color is the bear?"

"What?" Zepar looked at me like I'd just grown another head.

"What color is the bear?" I repeated the question.

"How in the world am I supposed to glean that from the information you gave me? Or am I just supposed to guess? Guessing games aren't allowed. This isn't Samson's game, Harker. There has to be a correct answer that can be discerned from the information at hand. Try again."

"No," I said. "All the information you need is in the riddle. You just have to figure out the color of the bear. Or do you surrender?" It was my turn to smile, even though antagonizing demons isn't the smartest pastime I've ever picked up.

He mused on it for a little longer, then stood up and began to pace. Zepar muttered to himself, going through all the random permutations of bear coloring before finally turning back to me and saying, "I have no idea, Harker, what color was the bear?"

"You give up? You concede that I have won the contest?"

"As long as the answer is fair, then yes, you have won. What color is the damnable bear!" I loved watching the steam almost literally come out of his ears, but decided not to torment him too long lest he decide to ignore the rules of his own contest and beat me to death with my leg.

"White," I said. "The house was located on the North Pole, so the bear was a polar bear. It was white."

"Then how do you...the North Pole," he said, and that scary grin came back. "When he ran east, he actually ran in a slight curve, so he was still a mile directly south of the cabin."

"Yep," I said, waving at the gore behind him. "Don't forget to clean up your mess on your way out."

Zepar turned to me, his frozen grin sparkling white in his inky black face. "Don't worry, Harker. I never forget. *Anything.*" With that, he waved a hand and vanished in a cloud of sulfur. I blinked my eyes against the stinking cloud, and when my vision cleared, the cell door stood open, and all evidence of four dead demons was gone.

Harker? I heard Flynn's voice in my head as clear as ever, probably because the demon wasn't around anymore to cause interference.

Here, babe. I outwitted the demon, so we're good. I'll be up in a minute.

Yeah, you will, but not why you think. Captain Herr has Interview 1 set up for you, and he's on his way down right now.

What did I do now?

I think it's about me. And you. Us, I mean.

Shit. The last thing I need while trying to track down a fetishist Archangel was relationship counseling from my girlfriend's boss. Well, the last thing I needed was to play a game of riddles with a goddamn Fallen Angel, but dealing with Captain Herr was a close second. The door at the end of the hall clanged open, and my day went from bad to worse in an instant.

CHAPTER TEN

err walked to the open door of my cell, looked around for the other men who had occupied the cell with me until mere moments ago, and shook his head. "Harker, and am I ever going to hear your name without thinking about how fucked up my life is that I have to deal with you?"

"Probably not, Bennie. How've you been?" I asked, stepping out of the cell into the hallway.

"Worse every day that you're in my life. And don't call me Bennie."

"No problem, Shirley," I replied.

"I really want to shoot you." It wasn't the first time a cop had said those words to me, and I believed pretty strongly that it wouldn't be the last. But I didn't feel like getting shot at that particular moment, so I let Herr's comment slide. He looked me up and down, noting the tattered remnants of my sleeves thanks to the Reavers' claws, but said nothing. He just let out a sigh, then turned and walked up the hall back the way he came.

I followed close behind, more curious than anything. Why did Herr come to get me himself? Did he know there was more corruption in the building than just the dead Agent Smith? Did he know I was innocent, well, kinda innocent? And what did he care about my relationship with Rebecca?

I didn't get any answers, from Herr or through my mental link with Becks, as I followed the captain up two flights of stairs to the interview room. I don't know when they stopped calling them interrogation rooms, but now they're "interview rooms." The furniture is still the same—one chair on the side of the table facing the big two-way mirror, one table bolted to the floor with a thick metal ring through the table's surface to affix a suspect's handcuffs to. There were not more tape recorders, but there were two cameras in the corners of the room, trained on the center of the table and focused right where the suspect's face would be were he or she sitting in the chair. There were usually two chairs on the opposite side of the table, but this time there was just one. A pair of plastic tumblers sat on the table, with a pitcher of water between them.

Herr sat in the chair across from the "perp seat," and I took the suspect's position. It wasn't an unusual one for me—I'd sat in this chair dozens of times over the years. Up until a couple years ago, it was almost always Detective Rebecca Gail Flynn sitting across the table from me, trying to make charges stick when the evidence, and victims, had a bad habit of turning to dust. I'll admit, I made life difficult for Becks before we started working together. But she was pretty much a giant pain in my ass, too, which I figured it was only fair.

"Water, Harker?" Herr asked, pouring himself a cup.

"Sure," I said. I opened my Sight as he poured, but I saw nothing out of the ordinary in the glass. A murmured "*purificent*" and a slight push of my will into the water, and I was mostly certain that there were no poisons or drugs in my drink. I took a sip, letting the cool liquid soothe my parched mouth. Fighting demons always dehydrates me for some reason.

I set my cup down on the table and looked across the scuffed surface at Herr. "What's up, Captain? I know what Grizzle wanted with me, but why are you here?"

He looked around and pulled a remote out of his front pants pocket. He aimed the black rectangular hunk of plastic at the cameras in the corners and pressed a red button on the device. The red lights on the cameras winked out, and Herr put the remote back in his pocket. He turned around to the big mirror and said, "Turn on the lights so Mr. Harker sees there's no one in the room, then get out."

Lights flickered on behind the mirror, throwing the surveillance room into dim light. There was a video camera on a tripod pointed at the glass, and two people in the room. I watched as a trim woman in a police uniform spun the camera to the ceiling and walked out of the room. The balding cop sitting at the lone desk in the room took off a pair of large over-the-ear headphones and followed her into the hall, leaving the light on.

"Now," Herr turned back to me, "you see that there's no surveillance. This isn't being recorded. You're not under arrest, and you're not under investigation for anything. The Lightbringers aren't pressing charges for trespassing or assault, and there's no proof that the lighting rig falling from the ceiling is anything other than a freak accident. It apparently just happened to occur while you were in the room. Because that's what you are, Harker, just a world of coincidence."

"I can't help it, Captain. I just end up in chaotic situations a lot. It's the burden I must bear." I spread my hands to show my innocence.

Herr wasn't buying it. "Yeah, whatever. I don't give a shit about whatever kind of weirdness you had with Smith. He was dirty, and he took some of my guys down with him. Maybe even fucked up some guys that didn't start off working with him, and now I've got some cancerous fucks floating around my division that I've got to root out."

"What does that have to do with me, Captain?" This wasn't going anywhere that I expected. I had no real idea what Herr wanted out of this secret conversation, so I just sat back and waited to see where he was going.

"Let me lay all my shit on the table, Harker. Flynn has a bright future in this department. She's a hell of a detective, and she can go a long way. As long as she doesn't have any kind of stink of corruption on her. The Smith thing is bad, but he snowed a lot of people up and down the food chain from Becca, so it's not going to stick to her too much."

It sunk in then, to Becks as well as me. I heard her in my head just like she was in the room. *That motherfucker. Who does he think—*

I cut her off, which is even harder to do when somebody's in your head than it is in real life. *Hold on, Becks. Let me just hear him out.*

But he—

He hasn't anything yet, I replied. *Besides, he's just your boss. I'm the one you're stuck with in your head, no matter what the day job says.*

She didn't reply, but I felt a surge of warmth come across our mental connection. She withdrew into the background, and I turned my attention back to Captain Herr. "Let me get this straight. You're saying I shouldn't see Detective Flynn outside of a working relationship, or it could have negative ramifications on her career? Is that what you're saying, Captain?" My voice was low and steady, and I locked eyes with the captain. I was pissed, but anyone looking in from the outside wouldn't be able to guess.

Herr got the message loud and clear, though. "I'm not saying that. I'm simply saying—"

"You're saying that being around me is bad for her career. Well, Captain, let me lay this out for you. I know you might not believe in everything that I deal with. But don't kid yourself into thinking that you have any fucking idea how the world works. There is shit out there, shit that I've seen, that would make you rip your own eyeballs out if you ever had to deal with it. I take care of the nasties that you and your people aren't equipped to deal with, and

Detective Flynn is more than just my girlfriend, she's part of my team. I have stood shoulder to shoulder with that woman and fought literal demons, and I know she's got the goods. So not only will I not stop dating Flynn, and I won't stop sleeping with her, I can't afford to cut her from my team. She's too damn good, and the stakes are too damn high. If that fucks her career, I hate it, but if her career is the sacrifice we offer up to save the world—again—then so be it. Now, are we done?"

Herr sighed, pushed back from the table, and stood up. "I suppose we are." He walked to the door, then stopped with his hand on the knob and turned back to me. "Can you do me one favor, though, Harker?"

I stood up and looked him over. His uniform hung loosely on his wiry frame, and there was more gray in his temples than I'd noticed just last year. "If it's something I can do, Captain, I'll give it a shot."

"Don't get her killed." With that, he opened the door and stepped out into the hall, leaving me alone in the interrogation room to wonder if I had any chance of keeping my girlfriend alive.

CHAPTER ELEVEN

I t was full dark by the time I made it out of the police station. I walked down the front steps with my belt in one hand and a brown paper bag containing my personal belongings in the other. Becks and Luke stood at the bottom of the steps in front of Luke's new car, a mammoth 1973 Dodge Monaco in pristine condition. The land yacht gleamed black under the yellow streetlights, its engine rumbling like a tiger's purr.

"Tell me again why you bought the absolutely biggest, most garish vehicle possible?" I asked, opening the passenger door for Becks then sliding into the back seat.

Luke got in the driver's seat and pulled the door closed with a solid *thunk*. "Because, dear nephew, the more I am around you, the more important it seems to surround myself and my belonging with as much reinforced metal as possible."

I didn't have an answer to that. That's one of the problems with hanging out with people who are centuries older than you—they always have the last word. I swear sometimes that Luke spent the entire 1760s just thinking up snappy comebacks. I had to give him credit, though, the big car rode like a dream. I was just nodding off in the spacious back seat when Rebecca spoke.

"What did you think of what Herr had to say?"

I sat up a little straighter in the seat. The simple fact that she'd spoken aloud instead of just communicating through our mental link told me that either she didn't want me hearing her thoughts on the matter, or that she wanted Luke's opinion. I wasn't going to mention that a dude who kept three psychotic vampires tucked away in a Romanian castle as his "wives" might not be the best person to go to for relationship advice.

"I don't know," I answered honestly. She'd know if I was lying anyway, and it's usually just easier to tell the truth. Way less to keep track of that way. "I mean, there are few things that I know. I know your career has already taken a hit from your association with me. No matter how much good you do, you'll always be tarred with the Agent Smith brush, and I'm sorry for that."

"That wasn't your fault—" she started to protest, but I cut her off.

"It wasn't completely my fault, but we both know that part of the reason Smith brought you into his division was because you and I had worked together, and he wanted to use you to keep an eye on me." I took her silence as agreement and went on. "And he as much as said that if you continued to hang around me, you're never getting captain's bars on your collar. I know that's not what you got into policing for," I said, forestalling another protest. "But you and I both know that if you're going to do something, you want to be the best at it. So, knowing that your association with me will hurt your advancement in the department, that's a real drawback."

I took a deep breath and let it out slow, then said what I really wanted to get across. "But here's the deal. I love you. I love you and am a better person with you than I am without you. If I have to move Heaven and Earth for us to be together, then I will. I understand if your career is more important than some old man and his crazy band of magical misfits, but if you decide that I'm what you want, that this life is what you want, then I'm all in."

"As am I, Rebecca," Luke said, reaching across the long bench seat and patting her knee. From me, that kind of gesture would end in me slapped in the face with my own hand for being a patronizing douche. Luke pulled it off. Another bonus to living forever, I guess.

She sat silent for the rest of the drive home, not that it took more than five minutes. We pulled into the underground parking deck for my building, and Luke parked in his reserved spaces. His car took up the room of two modern cars. Becks got out of the car, then stood leaning with her elbows on the hood while Luke and I stood by her. After at least a minute of standing there in silence, she stood up and looked me in the eye. "All I've ever wanted to do was be a cop. To catch the bad guys. Especially after my dad was killed. I want to make sure that no other little girl has to hear that her daddy isn't coming home because a bad person did a bad thing, and he couldn't quite stop it."

I remembered the night her father died. I remembered the rain, the smell of his blood, the way he looked up at me and asked me to take care of his little girl, to make sure she knew he loved her. I remembered when the light fled from his eyes. That same fire that left her father's eyes that night burned in

Rebecca's eyes now. "I lost my father because of a bad *thing*, not a bad person, and if it weren't for you, I never would have known those things existed. So, if Herr wants me to stop seeing you, to stop associating with the man who pulled back the curtain and showed me the real darkness, the real bad guys, the real reason I became a cop...well, if Herr wants me to turn my back on everything I've ever wanted to do, not to mention turn my back on the man I love, then he can kiss my ass."

"Does this mean you're not breaking up with me?"

"Quincy Harker, you are a certifiable asshole," she said, then threw her arms around my neck and kissed me like there was no tomorrow.

After a long kiss that answered all my questions about her sincerity, I pulled back. "If that's how I get treated for being an asshole, I'll have to do it more often," I said with a smile.

"Well, when you figure out how to cram more hours into the day, I'm sure you'll manage," Luke said from the elevator. "Now let's go upstairs. I'm feeling peckish, and I'm either going to the apartment for dinner, or I'm going around the corner to the sushi restaurant." Flynn and I hustled to the elevator. If there was one thing I knew about Uncle Luke, it's that when he mentioned going to the sushi restaurant for dinner, fish was not on his menu.

"This is a bad idea, Quincy," Cassandra said as I sat across from her in Luke's apartment.

"Why?" I asked. "He likes you, he respects you, and there are very few safer places in the world than the headquarters of a shadowy organization filled with monsters, wizards, and large-caliber weapons."

"Luke is not what concerns me. You are not what concerns me, and by now you should know me well enough to understand that I am not a woman who is easily cowed by things that go bump in the night."

"I seem to recall that from a few adventures you had with Jo's father back in the day," I grinned, remembering Cassandra in her youth. She was a fiery woman, and as lethal with a pistol as her husband had been with his hammer. Unfortunately, longevity is not something the human members of the Shadow Council are often blessed with, and I remembered the call when Alex, her husband and Jo's father, was killed by a lycanthrope in Utah. I buried the body myself, after severing his head with a silver blade to make sure there was no chance of him turning.

"That was a long time ago, Quincy. I'm an old woman now."

"Where's the nearest weapon, Cassie?" I asked, a game I played with her many years ago. She didn't answer, just smiled at me and tipped her chin down. I leaned to my left and saw the pistol pointed at me from her lap. "I thought so. What were you worried about, again?"

"Ginny," she said, and I saw true fear in her eyes. "I don't know if I can have my grandbaby growing up around all this. This insanity, it changes a person, makes them hard in ways I don't want her to be. This past year, it's been hard on Jo. A lot of things got more real for her after y'all's trip to Atlanta, you know? Before that, she would fight monsters, and she knew she was in danger, but I don't know if she understood the stakes you all play for. But Atlanta…"

"Atlanta was rough," I agreed. "It brought a lot of things home for a lot of people. But that's why I need you here, Cassie. You know what's at stake. You know how bad things can get if there's nobody to stand up against these things and the people that help them. I need you around *for* Jo. You keep her grounded. You can do the same thing for Luke. Bring Ginny around, let her get to know him. You know how he loves kids."

I could see the memories in her face. The few times Luke and I spent the holidays with Cassie and Alex when Jo was a little girl. I was pretty sure Jo didn't remember any of it, but I knew full well Cassie did. After a moment of smiling reflection, she nodded. "Alright, Quincy, you win. I'll let Ginny play with Luke from time to time, no matter how much the old bat complains. And we'll stay. For a while, at least."

She leaned forward and her eyes became chips of black flint. "But let me tell you one thing, Quincy Harker. Joanna is a grown woman, and she can make her own decisions. God knows she's told me that enough times. But if you let anything bad happen to my grandbaby…well, there ain't enough magic in the world to save you from the Hell I will unleash on your sorry ass."

I held up my hands in surrender. "Not a problem, Cassie. I promise on my life that I will protect that child as though she were my very own." With those words, I felt a tingle run through my hands, and they were surrounded by a white glow for just a second, then it was gone.

"What was that, Quincy?" Cassandra asked.

"I have no idea. I didn't cast anything, at least not intentionally."

"Well, I guess you're Ginny's godfather now, and I expect you to take that seriously. Now if you'll excuse me, I have to go down the hall and see if *Master Luke* is finished with his snack. I don't know if that old fool expects me to tuck him in and read him a bedtime story or what, but we are going to have a conversation on the duties of a personal assistant in the twenty-first century sooner rather than later." She stood up and walked to the door. She stopped, not looking back at me, and said, "Thank you, Quincy. Thank you for looking out for my family."

"Thank you for looking out for mine," I replied, and could almost hear the smile stretch across her face as she opened the door and stepped out into the hall.

CHAPTER TWELVE

Four hours later, I was nearing exhaustion and feeling further and further away from any kind of solution. I stretched out on the floor of my living room, my bare heels breaking the chalk circle I'd spent the last forty-five minutes sitting cross-legged inside. I heard the crackle of my spine stretching and settling as I lay on the hardwood floor feeling every one of my hundred-plus years. "Fuuuuuck," I said as my everything tried to realign itself.

"What's wrong, old man?" Becks asked from the counter by the kitchen, where she sat on a barstool watching me and reading a book on her Kindle.

"Aside from my ass falling asleep, my back killing me, and my left knee locking up, something's wrong with my magic."

"What do you mean?"

"Something's not working right," I explained. "I cast a spell to locate divine magic, which should have pointed me to Uriel's location, or at least narrowed down the part of town that he's being kept in."

"It didn't find him?"

"Well, it's more than that. Not only did it not find Uriel, it didn't find anything."

Flynn set her Kindle on the counter, slid off the barstool, and came over to sit on the couch by my head. "Do you mean you didn't find Uriel, you didn't find any angels, or you didn't find *anything*?"

I sat up, my butt wiping out more of the circle. Annoyed, I stood up and wiped my hands, ass, and feet off with a small towel, then dropped it on the floor by the circle. I sat on the couch facing Flynn and leaned forward, my hands on my knees. "I kinda mean all three. I sensed the angels in the other apartments here and a trace of the divine coming from Glory, but that's it. Nothing else."

"Okay, then maybe you should look somewhere else. Broaden the search. Could be the Lightbringers took Uriel farther afield than you were expecting."

"Farther afield than twenty-five miles from the center of town? I doubt it, Becks. Their center of power is here. They're pretty damned unlikely to skip town. But that's not the only problem."

"It never is," Flynn said with a shake of her head. "What else?"

"There's no divinity. Not even the baseline of minor artifacts that I can usually sense with that kind of locator spell. Even that's missing. It's not just that the Lightbringers have taken Uriel, they've somehow sucked all the divine magic from the entire city."

Flynn looked concerned, but then brightened. "Maybe there just isn't any to find? I mean, there are a lot of churches around here, but Charlotte isn't what I would call a holy city by any stretch."

I laughed. "You're right about that, but it's got a fair number of minor artifacts floating around, not to mention enough things that have proven to be articles of faith to get imbued with divinity from the belief of people nearby over the years."

Becks leaned forward her curiosity obviously piqued. "Yeah, like what? What kind of things can become holy just by people being close to them for a long time?"

"Well, anything that people talismanize, actually. Howard's Rock in Death Valley Stadium had a ton of divine energy just because of decades of football fans pouring their hearts out for their team. The Ben Long fresco in St. Peter's Church downtown was a huge source of divine energy until it got wrecked a few years ago. The JFG Coffee sign off John Belk Freeway has a little bit. It used to have more, but when they took the sign down for years, it leached away. It got put back up, but it's a different city now, so a lot of the faith and connection that people felt to the sign is gone, so it has less power."

"So anything that a lot of people connect to, feel strongly about, has this energy to it?"

"Yeah," I said. "Maybe 'divine' isn't the right word, especially if God really is MIA, but it's as close as I've got with my limited vocabulary. The only thing is, now it's all gone. There's none of this energy anywhere around Charlotte. Usually even if there aren't any major artifacts, the pulpit of every church holds a little bit of magic. But not anymore. Not here. The only source of divinity in the city is in this building."

"What does that mean?"

"I don't know, and my best resources, or at least, *sources* of information, are all kind of insane."

"Yeah, they're nuts, but they're your nuts, Harker. I'm not going anywhere near those jerks." She stood up from the couch and walked toward the bedroom. "Besides, I've got to be at work in two hours. I'm going to go take a shower. Too bad you've got to go talk to angels, you could help me wash my back." I watched her back, among other parts of her, sway with a rhythm both beautiful and dangerous as she walked away. I hated to see her go, but like the song said, I loved to watch her leave.

"I wish I could, darling. I wish I could in ways I can't even express. But I don't think I have a whole lot of choice in the matter."

———

That's how I came to knock on the door of an Archangel's apartment in the early morning hours, and I didn't even bring doughnuts. Sealtiel answered the door, still wearing the guise of a gorgeous human woman that she was using when Adam brought her to my building a couple weeks before. "Good morning, Quincy. How are you today?" She stepped inside and gestured for me to come inside. I did and smelled the most glorious aroma to pass my nostrils in hours.

"Is that fresh coffee?" I asked, more a grunt than a question. Between my run-in with the Lightbringers, my fight with demons in the jail cell, and my fruitless spellcasting, it had been a long time since I'd seen my bed, with or without Flynn in it. I was running on fumes, and the ones coming from the coffee maker on Sealtiel's counter were just what the doctor ordered.

"It is indeed," Sealtiel replied, reaching into the cupboard above the sink and passing me a mug.

"Hey Stevie?" a rough voice came from behind me.

I spun around to see a shirtless Mitchell Carson standing in the doorway of the apartment's one bedroom. Mitch wore a pair of black boxer briefs and a slightly embarrassed expression on his face. But that was all.

"Yes, Mitchell?" Sealtiel, apparently keeping the "Stevie" nickname for now, replied. She didn't look the least bit embarrassed, and I wasn't really sure she even understood the concept.

"Hi, Mitch," I said, giving him a wide grin as I filled my mug.

"Harker." Mitch nodded at me. "Um, Stevie, I was just going to ask if you had any more clean towels, but…"

"Oh, I'm sorry, Mitchell. I was coming out here to get some spares from the closet by the front door, but Quincy came to visit. I think we'll have to postpone our shower while I speak with him. Or, I suppose you could shower alone, but as you explained, that is horribly inefficient when the shower is certainly large enough to accommodate both of us at once."

"Yeah, Mitch, that's really inefficient. Why don't you throw on some pants, and maybe a shirt, and come out to chat? I just need a little information, then when I leave, the two of you can make sure your backs are plenty clean."

Mitch looked everywhere but at me, acting like a teenager swiping his dad's *Playboy* magazines instead of a grown man. Hell, given the fact that he was really the Archangel Michael, he was even older than Luke. But he didn't remember anything before his Mitchell Carson persona was created, so it was almost like dealing with a human. "Ummm…yeah, I'll do that." He turned around, the tips of his ears flaming red enough to act as turn signals, and ducked back into the bedroom to get dressed.

I turned to look at Sealtiel, leaning against the far counter, her arms crossed over her pink t-shirt. She was simply dressed, with her blond hair pulled back in a loose ponytail. Long tanned legs poked out of the cutoff sweatpants she wore, and a mischievous smile flittered around on her face. "You're a naughty angel, aren't you?"

"I can't help it, Harker," she protested. "You know we don't have gender when we're in our true form, and I was Stevie Shoes for so long, I just wanted to remember what human women felt like! And Michael was always such a stick in the mud as an angel, I thought it would be fun to play around with him a little while he's human. Besides, he's so *cute* when he blushes."

"You seduced the Archangel of War, Stevie. I think that's a little more than 'playing around.'" I was not exactly sure how to deal with a flirty angel wearing a human suit, especially not before eight a.m.

"Probably," she admitted. "But I was right. It's a lot of fun sometimes, wearing these human bodies."

"Don't remind me," I grumbled. "I could be upstairs right now conserving some water of my own, but I'm down here trying to find out what's fucked up in my city."

"This time," Sealtiel added.

"Huh?" I grunted. "This is coffee number one, Stevie. If you're being all snarky, I'm not smart enough for it right now."

She grinned, and the whole room lit up. If this was the woman that was supposed to herald the end of days, all she had to do was smile like that, and all of humanity would go willingly. "I just meant that there's always some-thing wrong with your city, so you need to find out what's wrong *this time*."

"God, I wish you were wrong," I said, reaching for the coffee pot. Sealtiel put out her hand and slapped the back of my wrist.

"Mitch hasn't had any yet. Share and share alike, Quincy. I promise, when he's done, I'll make another pot. Now what do you want our help with?"

Mitch came back out of the bedroom wearing a pair of sweats and a Charlotte Hornets t-shirt. Not having to look at his abs certainly made my life a little less self-conscious. Stevie poured a cup of coffee and handed it to me, then waved me over toward the couch while she set to brewing another pot. "I can hear you from here. Go sit with Mitchell and tell us why you're here."

I did as I was told, even unaccustomed as I was to being told where to go and what to do by an Archangel in pajamas. But I went with it because my life is just weird sometimes. I took the armchair, leaving Mitch to sit on the sofa with enough space for Sealtiel to perch there when she joined us. "The divinity is gone," I said, pitching my voice loud enough to be heard in the kitchen.

"I don't know what that means," Mitch said.

I explained the whole thing about divine magic to him, finishing up just as Sealtiel came in and perched on the arm of the couch. "It means that whoever took Uriel is far, far more powerful than Quincy expected, and shit is about to get real," she said, holding out one of the two mugs in her hands. "Now I wish I'd spiked the coffee."

"Me too, sister," I agreed.

"You can't sense *any* divinity? Anywhere in the city?" Sealtiel asked.

"Outside of this building, there's just the faintest glow around some of the oldest churches. St. Peters has a touch, but that could be trace from the Ben Long fresco that hung there for so long. The theatre downtown, Spirit Square, it has a glimmer, but it went from being a church to a theatre."

"And both of those are holy places, just not always to the same people." She nodded. "But you sense nothing from any artifacts, no relics of power, nothing like that?"

"Nothing that would help me pinpoint Uriel's location," I said.

"What about that demon bartender you hang out with sometimes?" Mitch asked. I glanced at him, but there didn't seem to be any condemnation in his question, just trying to help.

"Mort's not answering his phone, and the recording at the bar says they're closed until further notice. If I didn't know better, I'd say that Pastor Rob has him scared shitless and he's laying low until one of us kills the other one. Mort's a good hand in a fight, but unless there's something in it for him, he's probably not jumping in."

"Can't say as I blame him. People that jump into fights around you people tend to find their lives turned upside down," Mitch said, a bitter twist to the corner of his mouth.

"Sorry, pal," I said in a tone that I sincerely hoped showed exactly how not sorry I was. "Once we've convinced the Almighty to get back to doing His job and gotten Glory's wings back, I'm sure you can mind-wipe yourself again and get back to breaking noses inside an overgrown dog kennel. But until then, either lend a hand or shut the fuck up."

He stiffened, and I held up both hands. "Sorry," I said, and I meant it. "That was out of line. I haven't slept in about thirty-six hours, and I don't know how the hell I'm going to find this angel before the demon masquerading as a tele-vangelist tears my city apart."

"It's okay," Mitch said in that gruff way that guys accept the half-assed apologies we give each other. "I was being a dick, too."

"If you two are quite finished," Stevie interjected before our bromance could truly flourish in her den. "Quincy, why don't you go get some rest, then we can reconvene in a few hours and investigate the mysterious black hole of divinity."

"Yeah, that's a good idea," I said with a yawn. "This coffee hasn't even made a dent in my...wait a second, what did you say?" Something was tickling the back of my head, but I couldn't quite pin it down.

"She said go get some sleep," Mitch said.

I waved him off. "No." I turned to Sealtiel. "Repeat exactly what you just said." She did, and the pieces fell into place. "That's it! Stevie, you're a genius. You two go take your shower and meet me in my apartment in forty-five minutes. So don't fuck around with any lengthy back-washing, just do what needs to be done and get some clothes on. I gotta go." I put the mug on the coffee table, then almost knocked it off with my knee as I stood.

"What are you going to do, Harker?" Mitch asked, standing up as if to catch me.

I steadied myself and headed to the door. "I gotta go cast a spell to find what isn't there. Then we're gonna go kick some demon ass and save the world. Again."

CHAPTER THIRTEEN

Ninety minutes later, I stood outside the back door of a nondescript warehouse on the south side of Charlotte with a pair of angels standing behind me, ready to commit burglary for the second time in twenty-four hours. That might have been a record, even for me. I opened my Sight and looked around the building but saw nothing out of the ordinary.

"Is there an alarm?" Mitch asked.

"I have no idea," I replied. "I was looking for magical traps and things I care about. I just assume I'm getting arrested again for this shit, so I wasn't worried about that."

"You're pretty blasé about getting arrested. Were you like this before you were sleeping with a cop?" Mitch asked.

"I was this way before said cop was born," I said. "I've seen the inside of more jail cells than most people have seen states. It doesn't bother me that much anymore. Until they put demons in the holding cell with me. That was a buzzkill." I put my hand on the doorknob, and it turned easily. I pushed the door open and stepped through, motioning for the others to follow.

I took a few steps, then realized I was alone. I turned back to the doorway, where Mitch and Sealtiel stood. "You guys coming?"

"I'm sorry, Quincy, we cannot," Sealtiel, still in her Stevie guise, honey-blonde hair spilling down over her shoulders and concern in her green eyes. "The vacuum of divine magic that you sensed does indeed emanate from this building, and it begins at the threshold. We cannot enter without our divinity being severely compromised."

"That doesn't sound good," I said.

"If we lose too much of our holy magic, we will disappear entirely. I am not sure if we will become ethereal and return to the Heavenly plane, or if we will just cease to exist. Regardless, that is a chance I would rather not take. While this body is new to me, I rather enjoy it." Mitch let a little smirk flicker across his face, and I gave him a lot of credit for not mentioning how much he enjoyed Sealtiel's body.

"Shit," I muttered. "Okay, then you two stay here and make sure I'm not surprised by anything coming in behind me."

"I can still come in," Mitch said, stepping forward. Sealtiel grabbed his belt and jerked him backward before his foot touched the threshold.

"No, Mitchell, you cannot. While you have no recollection of being Michael, the fact remains that you *are* the Archangel Michael, Defender of Heaver, Dispenser of God's Justice, and the wielder of the one sword that we can least afford to be without in the upcoming conflict. So no, you may not go in."

I nodded at the stunned man. "She's right. We can't afford to lose anyone else, and who knows what will happen to that oversized toothpick on your belt if you bring it in here? I've got a pretty good idea, and it's pretty bad news. My gut tells me that we're going to need that sword, and the angel that wields it, a whole lot in the days and weeks to come, so you're benched for this one, pal." I turned to head into the warehouse, my backup just eliminated without ever throwing a punch. I love going into a fight when I don't know the combatants, the territory, or the schedule.

I closed the door on a pair of disappointed angels and ventured into the building on my own. The section I was in looked like a basic warehouse with a couple of rollup doors at the loading dock near the door I came in. There were a couple of pallets of what looked like random office equipment sitting shrink-wrapped on the concrete floor. Oddly arranged fluorescent lights flickered in the ceiling overhead, casting bright light across the huge empty space. I opened my Sight again, and aside from a few smears of demon-taint here and there across the floor, nothing struck me as odd.

Until I looked up. "Fuck," I said, my voice barely more than a whisper. Glowing in my Sight, but invisible to the naked eye, was a huge casting circle hanging over my head. I immediately understood why the lights were arranged in such a weird pattern—to keep them from breaking the boundaries of the circle, easily the largest permanent magic structure I'd ever seen. A fifty-foot diameter circle was scribed into the ceiling, double-walled with Enochian symbols between the walls of the circle. A pentacle with Norse, Enochian, Hebrew, and Aramaic runes and symbols in each corner was nestled inside the circle. This was created for a major working, more major even than the biggest summoning circles I'd ever seen.

"What the fuck?" I asked, my voice barely above a whisper.

"Impressive, isn't it?" came a familiar voice from the end of the warehouse. I dropped my Sight and looked over to where Pastor Rob stood silhouetted in a doorway on the far wall. I recognized him from his website and his YouTube videos, but he somehow looked even more smarmy in person. I couldn't tell from this distance if he was the one who led the raid on Purgatory and kidnapped Uriel, but he certainly didn't seem surprised to see me.

"I gotta give it to you, it is that," I said. "I've seen a lot of assholes gaping wide and spewing their shit across the planes, but this is the biggest, brownest shithole I've ever seen."

His face darkened for an instant, then the perma-smile was back. "I've heard about you, Quincy Harker. I've heard that you're crude. I've also heard that you're very powerful. I have to admit, I'm not impressed so far." He walked toward me, stepping into the well-lit warehouse so I could get my first good look at the man all the fuss was about.

He was good-looking dude, I'll admit. He was tall and trim and moved like his joints were well-oiled. Dark, curly hair was tousled artfully atop his high brow, and his eyebrows were so perfect I wondered if he plucked them. His jaw was chiseled and covered in the type of stubble that you know wasn't grown, it was trimmed down to be perfectly symmetrical. His full lips gave just the slightest feminine cast to his features, and his razor cheekbones made him look more male model than worship leader. He was dressed in a long-sleeved white dress shirt, open at the collar, skinny jeans just frayed enough at the knee to be cool, and dress shoes that cost more than my car. Admittedly, I have crap taste in cars, but those were handmade and Italian or my dad never banged a vampire.

He walked all the way over to me, his sly smile never wavering. He stalked as much as walked, prowling the room like a big cat, all predator eyes and slow swagger. I didn't move. I'd seen his type before, all quiet confidence and sleek smiles until it was time to throw down. Then he'd go for a one-shot kill, probably a blade to the throat or something equally flashy. If he didn't take me down in the opening attack, I had a good chance to making it through the night.

"Nope, not impressed." He paced around me, the heels of his shoes clicking across the floor. I felt his breath on my neck as he got close and breathed deep. "You smell nervous, Harker. What's wrong?" The mocking lilt of his voice was familiar, but I couldn't remember where I'd heard that tone before.

"That's my asshole repellant. I put it on every morning with my deodorant. I guess today's dose has worn off."

He was back in front of me now, out of easy reach but still close enough to close the gap in an eye blink. "You're funny, Harker. Why don't you give up all this and come work for me? We could run this town. Hell, we could probably run this whole country if you play your cards right. You can be my right-hand man, sitting next to the throne, enforcing the law, slinging spells and kicking ass, just like you do now. Only it would pay a lot better."

"I'm not short on cash," I said, keeping my voice low and slow. The longer he talked, the longer I had to figure out his end game, and the better chance I had to piss all over his cornflakes.

"But your girl, she's having some job troubles, right? I could make all that go away. Maybe induce a vacancy in the department, move a few pieces around on the board to put her in a better position…you just tell me what her favorite position is, and I'll make it happen." His smile stretched ear to ear, and I pushed down the swell of rage I felt when he mentioned Becks.

Keep calm, idiot. He's baiting you. I wasn't sure if the words were coming from my head or if Flynn was listening in, but either way, it was the truth. I let out a deep breath, resolved not to let this asshole throw me off my game. Then he pushed the wrong button, and shit went red.

"Or maybe I'll just introduce myself and find out what her favorite position is myself. Tell me, Harker, is she a screamer? She will be."

The words were barely out of his mouth before I was on him. I didn't reach for magic, didn't try to cast any kind of spell, I just shot forward, covering the ten feet between us in less than a second, clutching his throat with my left hand and pulling my right back to pummel his face to powder. I looked in his eyes, which widened with surprise, then narrowed in anger.

"Oh no, Harker," he growled. "That is *not* how this is going to go." He let me push him back into a pallet of copy paper, of all ridiculous things, then he brought his right hand up in a sweep, knocking my grip from his throat like I was a gnat. He grabbed the front of my shirt, pulled me so close that our noses almost touched, then the smug fuck *smiled* at me. "That's not how this is going to go at all." He flexed, no effort apparent in his movements at all, and I found myself airborne.

I crashed to my back on the concrete floor and slid a good six feet before I came to a slow stop. Pastor Rob, whatever he was, stepped forward away from the pallet of paper and glared at me. "We were having such a nice chat, too. Then you had to go and spoil it. Now I have to be unpleasant. I don't like to be unpleasant. I try to get my way through persuasion, through negotiation, through coercion if I must. But now I have to be unpleasant. And that's not fun for anyone. Well, maybe for the boys."

He snapped his fingers, and four hulking brutes came through the door at the back of the warehouse. "Boys," he said with a sweeping gesture to the goons, "teach Mr. Harker here the consequences of being unpleasant to me."

The thugs advanced on me, and Pastor Rob turned and walked back into the room at the back of the building where they came from. I got to my feet, drew my Glock from under my leather jacket, and got ready to get unpleasant.

CHAPTER FOURTEEN

our demons, one Harker. If I kept this up, it was going to turn into its own internet meme. They looked mostly human, except for every damn one of them being over seven feet tall. All these big guys made me long for the days of scrapping in enclosed spaces with Reaver demons. Oh wait, that was yesterday.

"Hey guys, can we talk about this?" I said, walking backward, keeping the thugs in my sight the whole time.

One of the two in the middle just growled, while the far left goon took three rushing steps forward, his arms held low like he wanted to body-slam me.

"Guess not," I said. I raised my pistol and fired four quick shots to this chest. He jerked with the impact and went down to one foot, but didn't drop. No blood came from the three holes in his chest, and he ripped his black t-shirt away, giving me a great view as the flesh closed in a few seconds and pushed the spent bullets out of his chest to *plink* on the floor.

"Well, shit," I said, tossing the gun at his face. He swatted it out of the air, but it gave me the distraction I was looking for. I reached for my magic, but the second I touched it, I felt it flow out of me as though a vacuum was latched onto my soul. My eyes wide, I staggered and released my hold on the energy.

"Looks like the little wizard found the portal," the far right goon said with a chuckle. "Go ahead, wizard. Cast a spell. See who get hurt, us...or you."

I didn't need to investigate that possibility any further. I knew how that shit was going to go. Shrugging out of my leather jacket, I turned and sprinted for the back door. As expected, the demons charged after me, but I wasn't trying to escape. The last thing I wanted was these assholes running around in my city. Even if it did give me backup in the form of Sealtiel and Mitch, I wasn't sure how much help they would be, since they couldn't touch their magic. I wasn't even sure what would happen if Mitch invoked his sword. Would it work? Would it be drained, just like my magic was? Yeah, getting Archangel Michael's sword busted sounded like the very pinnacle of bad ideas.

So I ran. But before I got to the door, I jumped, channeling every episode of *American Ninja Warrior* I'd ever seen, and ran up the wall. I made it a few feet, but when I pushed off the wall into a backflip, my naturally enhanced strength and agility let me flip over the heads of the pursing demons to land in a crouch behind them. I whipped out my pair of matched fighting daggers from the back of my belt and slashed through the hamstrings of the two center demons. Their flesh and tendons parted easily under the silver-edged blades, which I said a silent prayer of thanks for. If these buggers had some kind of protection against harm by unsanctified weapons, I was screwed. Even so, with their ridiculous healing, they would only be out of the fight for a minute at the most.

Desperately needing to end this quick, I leapt on the back of the nearest standing demon and wrapped my arms around his neck. I could feel the laugh rumble through his chest, until he felt me bury the pair of daggers in the sides of his neck. I wrapped my legs around his chest, leaned back, and pulled my hands together, drawing the knives through his neck and severing his head from his shoulders. The blades scraped through his spine, showering me in the wretched stench of black-green demon blood. I jumped off his back turned to the last demon standing, gore dripping from my face and hair.

I let the grin stretch across my face and called up just enough magic to make my eyes glow red. "Okay, motherfucker, you're next."

He wasn't scared. I really wanted him to be scared. "Is that supposed to scare me, wizard? I can make my eyes glow, too." And he did. His eyes blazed orange in his otherwise human face, and when he opened his mouth, a stream of fire shot out, bathing me in red-orange flame.

I dove out of the way, but not before getting thoroughly scorched. I'm sure there are things in the world that smell worse than burnt demon blood, but I've never smelled them. I gagged and rolled on the floor, putting out my burning clothes, and scrambled to my feet, singed but not hurt too badly. I turned to face the dragon-demon, who stood grinning as his two buddies now

drew themselves up to their feet, hamstrings mended and attitudes significantly worsened.

"Well, shit," I muttered, then ran straight at the nearest goon. His human
mask was slipping, letting a little of his gray skin show through as he used
more energy to put himself back together from his injuries. Gray skin meant
he probably wasn't a big-time Pit Lord or anything I really needed to stress
over, except for the part where there were two of them and I couldn't draw on
my magic to bail me out. I got within about eight feet of him and sprang
forward, thrusting out one leg like I expected to do some kind of awesome
kick.

I didn't expect to do any kind of awesome kick. I know me. I'm a badass,
but I'm no Chuck Norris. What I expected to happen was for the demon to
snatch me out of midair and slam me to the hard concrete, knocking me
breathless and ringing my bell pretty solidly. Since I was expecting it, it didn't
knock me as senseless as it normally would, leaving me enough presence of
mind to jam both knives into the demon's forearms, wedging the blades into
the tight space between the arm bones. I pulled the blades apart sideways,
snapping the forearm bones and leaving the monster's right hand dangling by
a few strands of muscle and flesh.

The thug let his human guise drop completely as he let go of me and
shrieked in pain. He clutched his ruined hand to his chest and fell to his
knees, screaming and spraying blood around the warehouse like a firehose. I
stood up and charged the other demon, who looked at the ruins of two of his
compatriots and turned tail. He was bigger than me, stronger than me, and
probably could have taken me out with a little help from his fire-breathing
buddy, had he not been a chickenshit hellspawn pansy. He was stronger, but I
was faster, and I ran him down in seconds, jamming my knives into his back
and opening him up like he had a zipper on either side of his spine. I opened a
big enough hole in his back, then jammed my right-hand knife in his kidney,
freeing up my right hand to reach into his chest and yank his beating heart
out through his ribcage. He collapsed to the floor, his soul already back in the
fires and his body starting to dissolve on the warehouse floor.

I turned to the firebreather, gore-splattered and panting with exertion and
battle rage. "Okay, fuckwit, your turn."

He didn't speak, just opened his mouth and spat a gout of flame as big
around as my leg at me. I called up a shield and sent the power straight into
the floor. I marched toward him, his fire burning hotter with every step.
Whatever vacuum for magic they had working in this joint was taking a
serious toll, and I struggled to hold my shield against the onslaught of fire and
the constant drain on my power, but I pushed on. I got to within a few feet of

the demon and angled my shield to pour the fire right back in his face. I knew it wouldn't cause him any real harm, but it did burn his human suit off, leaving him standing in front of me in his considerable lack of glory. I drew back, then slammed my magical shield forward, knocking him onto his ass and cutting off the stream of fire.

The demon looking up at me from the floor was actually a lot less intimidating in his true form. As a human, he was a buff giant, carved out of muscle and attitude, with glowing red eyes. Once his concentration on that illusion was shattered, he reverted to his true form, which looked more like an evil Danny DeVito than something out of the pages of Revelation. He sat on his butt, glaring up at me, butt-naked with a huge gut spilling out over his junk. His skin was a mottled gray, with tufts of wiry black hair sprinkled over him like patchy grass or mangy fur. His lower jaw jutted out, and a pair of short fangs stuck up. His eyes were still red, but they are narrow, beady things, more pathetic than frightening. All in all, he looked like a cross between a cherub and a fat gargoyle.

"What the fuck are you?" I asked, then shook my head. "Fuck it, I don't care," I growled, then stabbed him right in both beady eyes. I twisted the blades for good measure and felt the heat in the room start to dissipate as his soul fled back to his home plane.

I turned to the crippled demon, still whimpering and trying desperately to regrow the bones in his wrist and hand. "You have two choices, pal. You can flee this plane and go dive back into the fires you crawled out of, or you can find out why they really call me the Reaper. I don't give a single fuck which one you pick, but make a decision, because as the man said in the movie, it's nut-cutting time." I can't help it, I thought *ZombieLand* was brilliant.

He looked at me, looked down at his hand, still hanging by a few threads of meat, and then looked around the room at the scattered remains of his three demon buddies. "Fuck this place, I'm going back to Hell where it's safer," he said, and his eyes went dark. A black mist rose from the demon corpse's eyes to dissipate into the aether, and the body it once occupied began to decompose into really smelly demon sludge, just like his three buddies. Within an hour, there would be nothing left of them but puddles of goop, and within four hours, even that would evaporate, absorbed back into the magical energy of the planes.

I wiped off my blades and tucked them back into the sheaths on the back of my belt, knowing that I'd be dousing them in holy water, then salt water, then holy water again before I buried them in a churchyard when this was all over. Silver is potent magically, but the last thing I needed was a pair of knives hanging around my apartment that had carved up four demons. That kind of taint lingers, no matter how much you cleanse a weapon. Come to think of it, I'd better just have these things consecrated then melted down. I let out a sigh at this realization. Good knives are hard to come by.

I looked around the warehouse with my Sight, but there were no other surprises waiting for me. Not out here, anyway. So I dropped back into normal vision, retrieved and reloaded my Glock, and walked across the deserted warehouse to kick down a door and fight to the death with a demonic evangelist wearing skinny jeans.

CHAPTER FIFTEEN

S o I did just that. I planted a size eleven Doc Marten just to the left of the doorknob and kicked the door in. The cheap hollow-core door splintered and slammed open with a satisfying crunch, and I stepped through into a scene straight out of Hannibal Lecter's wet dreams. Uriel was pinned to the far wall, hanging from spikes driven through his wrists. He was trapped in a circle drawn on the drywall with what looked like blood, and from what I could see, he provided every drop.

The angel seemed trapped in his human form, and it looked like he'd gone ten rounds with Mike Tyson in his prime, then another ten with Ali. His face was pulped, his jaw hanging loose and spilling blood and drool down his chin and chest. His eyes would have been swollen shut from the bruising around them, except his eyelids had been sliced off and stapled to the wall on either side of his head. Judging from the bruising all over his torso, I'd guess at least most of his ribs were broken, and probably both legs. I wasn't close enough to see his fingers and toes, but given the dedication Pastor Rob had shown to his craft, I assumed the nails were gone and all the digits at least dislocated, if not broken.

"That's impressive, Pastor," I said, stepping into the room. "The last time I saw somebody fucked up that sincerely, they were under a doctor's care. Admittedly, the doctor was Josef Mengele, so you've reached a pretty high bar."

"I'm glad you like what I've done with the place, Harker." Pastor Rob turned from a long table set along one of the room's side walls. As he stepped away from it, I could see the surface littered with knives, spikes, cleavers, needles, and other implements of torture, all stained brown with years of bloody work. Pastor Psycho wore long rubber kitchen gloves now, to protect his delicate skin from blood spatter, and a white apron with a picture of Darth Vader on it that said, "Come to the Dark Side. We have cookies." There was a lot more red on the apron than there was visible white, but I did appreciate the irony.

"I didn't say I liked it, I said I was impressed. Not the same thing," I replied, moving into a clear space in the middle of the room. Part of me wanted to keep my back to a wall, but with as flimsy as the door was, I didn't trust the wall to stop anything I was afraid of.

"Oh well, you can't please all of the people all of the time, right? But forgive me, I'm being rude. Have you met my guest, Uriel? I think you know him better as Torch, legendary local pervert, deviant, malcontent, and loudmouth." Rob covered the distance between himself and the battered archangel in two long strides and grabbed a fistful of Torch's curly red hair. He jerked the man's head up, forcing him to look at me with his reddened, blood-soaked eyes. Tracks of tears and blood carved rivulets down his face, dripping through his red goatee and down the front of his scarred and naked body.

"Uriel, say hello to Quincy Harker," Rob said. "He's here to rescue you from the nasty demon that kidnapped you and stole your little toy."

Uriel hung there, silent except for the sound of his labored breathing. A wheeze came from his mouth, but his shattered jaw couldn't form words.

"What's that, Uriel? Cat got your tongue? Oh, no, not a cat, a rat! That's right, you can't say hello to Mr. Harker because I ripped your tongue out and fed it to the rats last night. Silly me, I forget."

"Hhhhuuuuuuuukkkkk oooooooooo," the angel panted, the hatred on his face perfectly clear even without words.

"I think he doesn't like you very much, Robbie-boy. If your guest is so unhappy, why don't you just let me gather up his belongings and take him over to my place. Maybe being around some of his own people will make him a little more pleasant." I stepped toward a table against the other wall, one with a whip lying in the center of it.

"Maybe you shouldn't try to take things that aren't yours, wizard!" Rob snapped, extending a hand in my direction. Force hit me like a hurricane wind, lifting me off my feet and slamming me into the wall above the table. I crashed down, the cheap particleboard snapping under my weight like I was the star attraction at a pro wrestling show. I groaned and rolled over, picking up the whip as I struggled to my feet.

"Well, if you didn't want me to have the whip, I don't think throwing me on top of it was the best plan, pal." I shook my wrist, and the black braided leather unfurled across the floor. The whip was a dark, hungry thing that felt alive in my hand, like a sinister snake just waiting to lash out at something, and not too particular about its target. I raised my hand, snapped my arm forward, and with a flick of my wrist, the tip sliced through the air, breaking the sound barrier with a resounding CRRRRACK. The whip continued toward Rob's face but halted its flight in mid-air just inches from his cheek.

"That's not going to happen, Harker." He stretched out his right arm, palm up, and the whip's handle flew from my grasp to slap into his hand. He twirled his wrist, and almost before I could see him move, another CRACK rang through the room, and my face burst into flame as the braided leather cut a slash the entire length of my cheek.

I took a step back, blood streaming down my jawline to mix with all the other blood spilled on the room's stained floor. I saw his hand twitch this time and ducked, but that was no defense against the whip wrapping around my left ankle. I crashed to my back on the concrete, my head smacking the floor with a dizzying crunch. Pastor Rob just stood there grinning as he pulled me to him, coiling the whip as I skidded along on my ass.

I grabbed at the nearby table, but he yanked me free. I tried to reach my ankle, but he was on me before I could untangle myself. He reversed his grip on the handle and used it like a club, slamming the polished wood across my face two or three times before I collected myself enough to draw power and blast him off me. I blasted raw magic into his chest, and he flew back, slamming into the wall and collapsing into the table of torture tools. He got to his feet while I was still freeing myself from the whip, casting aside broken table chunks and various knives in all directions.

"That wasn't nice, Quincy. Can I call you Quincy?" he said, walking toward me, that predator's swagger again suffusing his every step.

"Can I call you fuckwit?" I shot back, drawing my Glock. I centered the front sight on his chest and squeezed off three quick shots. He was gone before the third pull of the trigger, moving faster than I could hope to see.

"That's not nice, Quincy," Pastor Asshole whispered in my ear before he snatched me up by the back of my collar like a naughty kitten. He held me up, my feet dangling in the air, for several seconds before hurling me to slam into the wall beside Uriel.

I slid to the ground, covered in a slick smear of commingled angel and human blood. "You wanna get your divine on and help a brother out?" I asked the ruined man. He looked down at me, bloody tears leaking from the corners of his lidless eyes. No help coming from that quarter.

I struggled to my feet and looked around for my pistol, then raised my head as Rob cleared his throat. "Looking for this?" he asked, twirling my gun around on his index finger. "Don't worry, you don't need this anymore." He put one hand on the grip, the other on the barrel, and bent the gun until it shattered and sent shards of plastic and metal all over the room.

Then he was on me again, right up in my face, slamming my back to the wall and shoving me up the vertical surface until my face was level with Uriel's. "Should I just hang you here, Quincy? Just leave you suspended by your wrists next to the angel you were trying to save? Crucify you and let your lungs implode like that stupid carpenter you people rave about?"

"Or you could just give me the whip and the angel and crawl back to whatever rock you've been hiding under," I said, gritting my teeth to get the words out.

"Always the funny man, aren't you, Harker? You just always have to have a quip, no matter how fucking bleak the situation. Doesn't that get old after a while?"

"Not yet," I panted, reaching to my belt and drawing the knife there. "But if it does, I'll give you a call." Then I jabbed the knife into his gut. The demon dropped me and stepped back, yanking the knife free from his belly and glaring at me. He snatched the apron off and poked his finger through the hole in his shirt, glaring down at his belly as if it had offended him somehow. He pulled his finger out and held it up to his face. There wasn't a drop of blood on it. I hadn't even drawn blood, much less injured him.

"I *liked* this shirt," he spat, then charged me. He stepped slightly to one side and lifted his knee into my ribcage. I bent at the waist, and he used the same knee to shatter my nose. I stood up straight, and he grabbed me by the jaw, slamming my head against the wall once, twice, three times before I lost count. Drywall dust showered down over my face, mixing with the blood pouring from my nose to make a disgusting paste that coated my mouth and jaw.

"I" *slam* "liked" *slam* "this" *slam* "shirt!" he yelled into my face, then he jerked me free of the wall and tossed my limp body aside like yesterday's dirty underwear, tumbling bonelessly across the floor. The demon turned to me, hellfire blazing in his eyes now, and stalked me like a jungle cat, all lithe muscle and bad intentions.

"There aren't many things I really like, Harker. I like listening to the screams of innocents as they realize there is no hope for them and their pain will never really end. I like the smell of brimstone in the morning; it smells like freedom from tyranny. I like the taste of angel's blood on my face as it sprays from the soon-to-be dead flesh of my enemies. And I like a nice linen shirt, freshly pressed with a perfect crease in the sleeves. Do you understand how hard it is to get a perfect crease in linen? It doesn't want to crease, Harker, and that makes it very difficult. But if there's anything I ever learned from my no-good, shiftless, absentee judgmental cock of a father, it's that anything worth having is worth working hard to get. And now I don't have this very nice linen shirt with the perfect crease. That makes me angry, Harker. When I get angry, people get hurt." He turned his head from side to side. "Oh look, you're the only person in the room. I guess that means this is going to hurt."

He held out his hand, and the whip flew into it. He held it high for a few seconds, and it began to glow with the same crimson light that came from his eyes. "Oh yes, Quincy Harker, this is going to hurt. You know what Uriel's role was in the Host, don't you? He was God's Enforcer. He was in charge of meting out the punishment of the Almighty. And he used this whip to do it. The very same whip that I'm going to use to strip the flesh from your bones, one agonizing strip at a time. Right after I do...this."

Demon Rob spun on his heel and lashed out at Uriel with the whip. The leather lash wrapped around the imprisoned angel's neck three times, and Rob gave the handle a vicious yank. Uriel found some way to force a shriek through his shattered, tongue-less mouth as his wrists pulled from the wall, straight over the fat ends of the spikes still driven into the wall. Rob flicked his wrist, and the bound and bleeding angel skidded right to the demon's feet. Pastor Rob knelt down by Uriel's side and pressed a hand to his chest. For just a hint of a second, so brief I thought I imagined it, I saw regret flicker over the pastor's glowing red eyes, but it vanished in half a heartbeat.

"I'm sorry, brother. I'm not quite finished with you, but the sound of your bleeding and moaning is terribly distracting. And I'm sure you'll agree that Mr. Harker here deserves my undivided attention. So please, Uriel, brother dear, *SHUT UP*." Then he slammed the angel's head into the concrete hard enough that I heard the skull crack from all the way across the room. The demon stood and turned to me. "Now that we won't be disturbed again, let's wrap up our business here so I can get on with killing everyone you've ever met."

He lashed out with the whip, and it shredded my shirt and carved a line of fire into my chest. I didn't even bother trying to be tough—I screamed. I screamed profanities that I haven't uttered in years, and when he whipped me again, I switched into languages I thought I'd forgotten. I tried to call up enough power to give myself a little bit of a shield, but he picked up the pace of his whipping and I couldn't concentrate enough to do anything but yell and curse. Again and again the whip fell, faster than any weapon like that should be capable of, but between the demon's inhuman speed and the whip's inherent magic, all the laws of physics were shattering on my back and chest today. I rolled over and over, seeking some tiny respite from the brutality he unleashed on me, but there was nothing forthcoming. Just more pain, more blood, and more screaming, until finally, when he decided that I'd been sufficiently flayed, he stopped.

I looked up at him from my position on the floor, curled up in a fetal position trying to keep as much of my flesh attached as I could manage. I watched his feet as he strutted over to me, that feline arrogance oozing from his every pore.

"I'm sorry, Quincy, I truly am. I had such high hopes for our relationship. But you see, I just can't tolerate subordinates speaking to me like you did. So, it seems we can't be friends. And that's all I have in this world—friends. My friends live long, fruitful lives full of riches and the finer things in life. Those who think to style themselves my enemies…well, they don't live long enough to style themselves as anything. Just like you won't."

Pastor Rob, the only sign that I'd even tried to fight him a tiny hole in his favorite shirt, knelt down beside me and put his left hand on my forehead. He pressed my skull against the concrete and started to push. I felt pain radiate out from the back of my head like a spiderweb, arcing out and around my head as he inexorably increased the pressure, slowly, steadily mashing my head until I was just seconds away from my head popping like a grape.

The demonic minister leaned down so that his face was just inches from my own, and said, "Goodbye, Quincy Harker. I promise that when I kill every friend you've ever had that I'll make them suffer just for knowing you." Then he smiled, and I knew in the pit of my soul that he meant every word. He drew in a deep breath, and I felt the muscles in his arm tense as he readied himself for the final thrust that would destroy me and, by extension, everyone I'd ever cared about.

Then I heard a muffled *crack*, and the pressure on my head disappeared. I saw boots with trim female legs in them stomp past my field of vision and heard a voice prettier than any chorus of angels. "Okay, you son of a gun, you have two choices…Nah, screw that, you don't get any choices. Time to die."

I rolled over enough to get a decent view of the action as a dark-skinned woman with very good timing slammed a very large hammer into Pastor Rob's chest. Another *crack* rang through the warehouse, and Rob staggered back. I managed to pull myself into a sitting position just as the glorious Rebecca Gail Flynn stepped up to Jo Henry's side, the Sword of the Archangel in her hand.

Becks, you can't bring that in here, I thought. *It'll get destroyed.*

Too late, idiot. I'm already here. And since I'm not an angel, I don't turn on its full power, so it looks like we're okay. Ignoring the other feelings coming across our mental link, mostly relief and concern, Becks turned to Rob and leveled the sword at him. "Go ahead, asshole. Give me an excuse."

"Oh, my dear detective," Demon Rob said with a grin. "You don't need an excuse. Just my being here is all the excuse you should need. But I can read a room. I know when I'm not wanted. After all, I am, as they say, a man of wealth and taste. Discernment is one of my many virtues." With that, the demonic preacher lashed out one last time with Uriel's whip, this time wrapping it around the legs of the dead angel. Then he held up his hand, drew a few symbols in the air in front of the wall, and perfectly round opening appeared in the air. He stepped through the portal between the planes, dragging Uriel's body with him. I looked through the glowing circle briefly and wished I hadn't. That portal led nowhere I'd ever been, but I've seen enough Francis Bacon paintings to recognize it. Pastor Rob had just opened a doorway to Hell and carried a dead Archangel through it.

I looked to Jo and Becks, who had managed to arrive just in time to keep my brains from becoming an omelet on the floor, and then everything that happened in the past few days, together with Rob's last words, all clicked in a horrifying conclusion. *A man of wealth and taste...fuck.* The terrifying realization was just too much, and my body, having sustained a decade's worth of abuse in the past ten minutes, decided that enough was fucking enough, and shut down.

My last thought as I slid into unconsciousness was that we were exceptionally fucked.

EPILOGUE

"**W**ait, *what?!?*" Becks tried to stand, but couldn't move, since I was currently lying with my head in her lap. My heavily bandaged head, which went well with my heavily bandaged everything else. I still hurt like a mother, but after I came to at the scene of my fight with Rob, I managed to summon up enough magic to heal myself a little. Sealtiel threw a little angelic mojo on me, too, once Flynn and Jo got me out of the warehouse. Then we all piled into two cars and hauled ass back to my place.

Now the whole gang, minus Luke, who was still sleeping, was gathered in the apartment we'd converted to a conference/war room. I was stretched out on one sofa with Becks; Jo and Mitch were on the other sofa with Cassie sitting beside them. Sealtiel and Gabriel sat in armchairs at the end of the sofas, and Dennis looked down at us from the LCD TV on the wall.

"So you're saying that Pastor Rob, the leader of the fastest-growing evangelical church in the Carolinas, is actually Lucifer?" the sparkling unicorn head said from the display.

"Unless you know anyone else that's likely to use *Sympathy for the Devil* as an exit line," I said.

"Nah, I got nothing. I also looked up his records, and there's nothing on Pastor Robert Stellam prior to his appearance in Charlotte twelve years ago."

"Stellam…" I mused.

"Star," Gabriel chimed in. He was in his angel mode, so it wasn't the full-on *non sequitur* of his human guise, but I still looked at him askance. "Stellam is Latin for star."

"The morning star," Jo said. "Son of a bitch." She flinched as her mother held out her hand. Jo reached in her pocket and handed Cassie a dollar for the swear jar. I just put a hundred-dollar bill in it every Monday. Saved time.

"He was flaunting it the whole time," I said, struggling to an upright position on the couch. "His name was Star, short for Morningstar. The church was called Lightbringers, another name for Lucifer."

"And he was so damn pretty, no way was he not dangerous," Flynn said.

I looked at her sideways, but Jo reached out and pounded fists with my girlfriend. If I were a lesser man, I'd have felt insecure. Although I guess since I was missing half the flesh on my torso, I probably *was* a lesser man, but I figured Luke could fix that with a few drops of vampire blood when he woke up.

"So, now what?" Jo asked. "I mean, we have three of the Archangels, but you said he killed Uriel. I mean, can that even...can y'all..." Her words trailed off as she looked at Mitch, Gabriel, and Sealtiel in turn.

"I don't know. I still only halfway believe I am what you guys say I am," Mitch said. "But Harker's paying my way, and I get to hit things, so I'm good for now."

"We cannot be truly destroyed," Gabriel said. "Our physical bodies can be destroyed, but our essence will simply return to Heaven and reconstitute."

"Just like demons," I said. The angels whipped their heads around to look at me, and I felt like I *really* needed to explain myself. "I mean, when the demons die, they just go back to Hell to rebuild. Is that what you do?"

"Exactly," Sealtiel said, putting a hand on the arm of a glowering Gabriel. I got the feeling that the arrogant angel didn't like me very much. I didn't mind. The feeling was mutual. Sealtiel went on. "We cannot be destroyed on this plane. We would simply return to Heaven and craft a new vessel for ourselves."

"But what about in Hell?" I asked. The angels looked at me, their eyes wide. "Rob, I mean Lucifer, he dragged Uriel through the portal to Hell with him."

"Was Uriel dead when he went through?" Sealtiel asked, leaning forward in her chair, her blond curls spilling across her shoulders.

"I don't know, but I don't think so," I said. "Rob said something about not being finished with him, then smashed his head into the concrete. Everything gets a little fuzzy after that because of the never-ending agony and all."

"That's a problem," Sealtiel said, leaning back in her chair.

"Indeed, sister," Gabriel agreed, folding his arms across his chest.

"Want to explain things to the humans in the room?" Jo asked.

"And the ones that don't really believe they aren't human?" Mitch added.

Sealtiel got up and started to pace. I've seen enough shit in my life that not many things worry me anymore, but when something has a no-shit Archangel freaked out enough to pace, I worry.

"Lucifer was the strongest of all of us. Even stronger than Michael, not that we mentioned that very often. Michael was a little sensitive," the beautiful angel said as she wore a path in the carpet. "When he was cast out, Father took his implement, the Star of the Morning, and destroyed it. The only way Lucifer could ever return to Heaven was if he somehow got his implement back."

"Or someone else's," I said. "Like Uriel's whip."

"Not quite, but close," Gabriel said, his tone making it clear that he was impressed that a lesser being like me even got that close to understanding something. I mentioned he was a douche, right? "Our implements are attuned to our divinity. As long as we live, no one else can effectively wield the implements to their full power."

"But if one of you dies, really dies..." Cassie said.

"Then any other divine creature can take up the implement and take the deceased angel's place in the Host," Gabriel said.

"Then we're fine," Dennis said. "Lucifer isn't divine. He's the devil. Problem solved!" The rainbow-maned unicorn did backflips on the TV.

"Not so much, Dennis," Becks said.

"What do you mean?" the unicorn looked perplexed.

"There's no real difference between the divine and the demonic," I said. "Lucifer is still an Archangel. He just fell from grace. So, he can use the whip."

"So, now he can get back to Heaven?" Dennis said.

"And without God on the throne, he might actually manage to take over this time," I said.

"Fuck," Dennis whispered, then his head snapped up. "Sorry, Cassandra. I'll put a dollar in Ginny's college fund, I swear." Cassie just nodded. None of us ever asked where Dennis got the money for the virtual swear jar. Some things, it was better not to know.

"So what do we do?" Mitch asked. "I mean, I might not know much about being an angel, but I know that Lucifer getting into Heaven doesn't sound good for anybody."

"We keep doing what we've been doing," I said. "We're going to need the entire Host behind us if we're going to face Lucifer head-on."

"Head on?" Flynn asked, looking at me.

"Yeah, Becks. Head on. We've got to find the rest of the Archangels and fast. Because we're going to have to take the fight to Lucifer, and that means going straight to Hell."

To Be Continued in Quincy Harker Year Four - Salvation

ACKNOWLEDGMENTS

This series and especially this omnibus collection would never exist without my fans and my patrons. Thank you all so much for spending time with me, Harker, and the gang. For more information on my awesome patrons, and to join them, you can go to Patreon.com/johnhartness.

Melissa McArthur has been with Harker from the very beginning, making the books better and struggling to teach me where the commas go.

James Anderson Foster is the voice of Quincy Harker. His audiobook narration has brought these characters to life in ways that I could not even have imagined.

Natania Barron's covers have defined Quincy Harker, and her striking imagery and incredible eye are a gift that I am grateful for. Lynne Hansen's cover to the limited edition is spectacular, and I couldn't have asked for anything better.

But these stories don't exist without you. So thanks for coming on these journeys with us, and we'll see you next time around!

JGH
11/11/19

ABOUT THE AUTHOR

John G. Hartness is a teller of tales, a righter of wrong, defender of ladies' virtues, and some people call him Maurice, for he speaks of the pompatus of love. He is also the award-winning author of the urban fantasy series *The Black Knight Chronicles,* the Bubba the Monster Hunter comedic horror series, the Quincy Harker, Demon Hunter dark fantasy series, and many other projects. He is also a cast member of the role-playing podcast *Authors & Dragons,* where a group of comedy, fantasy, and horror writers play *Dungeons & Dragons.* Very poorly.

In 2016, John teamed up with several other publishing industry professionals to create Falstaff Books, a small press dedicated to publishing the best of genre fiction's "misfit toys." Falstaff Books has since published over 100 titles with authors ranging from first-timers to NY Times bestsellers, with no signs of slowing down any time soon. In February 2019, Falstaff Books launched Con-Tagion, which has very quickly morphed into SAGA – THE Professional Development Conference for Genre Fiction Writers, held in Charlotte, NC every year.

In his copious free time John enjoys long walks on the beach, rescuing kittens from trees and playing *Magic: the Gathering.* John's pronouns are he/him.

Find out more about John online
www.johnhartness.com

Printed in the USA
CPSIA information can be obtained
at www.ICGtesting.com
LVHW042024250124
769625LV00015B/309